Omnibus
of
A Century
of
South African
Short
Stories

Omnibus of A Century of South African Short Stories

Introduced and edited by
Michael Chapman

AD DONKER PUBLISHERS
JOHANNESBURG & CAPE TOWN

Acknowledgements

The publisher and editor acknowledge and thank the writers or estates and/or publishers who have permitted stories to be included in this anthology. (The source is acknowledged at the start of each story. Translators are also acknowledged at the beginning of the relevant story.)

Every effort has been made to contact the copyright holder. Those copyright holders whom we have been unable to contact are requested to contact the publisher, so that the omission can be remedied in the event of a reprint.

Published in 2007 by
AD DONKER PUBLISHERS (PTY) LTD
An imprint of JONATHAN BALL PUBLISHERS (PTY) LTD
PO Box 33977
Jeppestown
2043

ISBN 978-0-86852-233-3

Cover design and reproduction by Russell Starke, Durban
Typesetting and reproduction by Alinea Studio, Cape Town
Printed and bound by Paarl Print, Cape Town

Contents

INTRODUCTION   9
THE AUTHORS   11

The Sun is Thrown into the Sky   27
The Girl who made Stars   30
The Young Man who was Carried off by a Lion   32
Nkulunkulu, the One who Came First   35
How Death Entered the World   36
Maqinase, the Wily One   38
The Bird that Made Milk   41
The Child with a Moon on his Chest   45
The Man who Threw Away his Bread   47

//Kabbo   'A story is like the wind'   49
Pulvermacher (AG de Smidt) Prayer of Titus Tokaan   55
William Charles Scully   Umtagati   56
J Percy FitzPatrick   The Pool   64
Ernest Glanville   Uncle Abe's Big Shoot   71
HW Nevinson   Vae Victis   74
Olive Schreiner   Eighteen–Ninety-Nine   78
Frederick C Cornell   The Drink of the Dead   100
Arthur Shearly Cripps   The Black Death   107
Perceval Gibbon   Like unto Like   112
Sarah Gertrude Millin   Up from Gilgal   115
                           A Sack for Ninepence   123
Pauline Smith   Desolation   129
                           The Schoolmaster   142
                           The Sisters   149
Eugène N Marais   The Grey Pipit   153

RRR Dhlomo	The Death of Masaba	157
	Murder on the Mine Dumps	160
William Plomer	The Child of Queen Victoria	163
	Down on the Farm	192
Herman Charles Bosman	The Music-Maker	208
	Unto Dust	212
	Birth Certificate	216
	Funeral Earth	220
	A Bekkersdal Marathon	224
Frank Brownlee	The Cannibal's Bird	228
HIE Dhlomo	The Barren Woman	230
C Louis Leipoldt	The Tree	238
Peter Abrahams	One of the Three	247
Nadine Gordimer	The Train from Rhodesia	250
	The Bridegroom	255
	A Chip of Glass Ruby	262
	The Credibility Gap	270
	The Termitary	278
	Once Upon a Time	284
Doris Lessing	The Old Chief Mshlanga	289
	Flavours of Exile	299
	Lucy Grange	306
Uys Krige	The Coffin	311
	Death of the Zulu	321
Bertha Goudvis	Thanks to Mrs Parsons	328
Es'kia Mphahlele	Down the Quiet Street	333
	Mrs Plum	339
Dan Jacobson	Stop Thief!	367
	Droit de Seigneur	373
	Fresh Fields	382
Casey Motsisi	Kid Playboy	392
Jack Cope	The Flight	395
	The Little Stint	401
Alan Paton	A Drink in the Passage	415
	The Quarry	421
Alex La Guma	A Matter of Taste	428
James Matthews	The Park	432
Can Themba	Crepuscule	441
	The Suit	448
	The Will to Die	456
Abraham H de Vries	The Girl with the Bra-pistol	460
	Ruins	465

Jan Rabie	Maiden Outing to Rondebosch	471
Karel Schoeman	Seed in a New Earth	477
Dugmore Boetie	Three Cons	483
Chris Barnard	Bush	493
AC Jordan	The Turban	498
Barney Simon	Joburg, Sis!	507
Perseus Adams	A True Gruesome	512
Sheila Roberts	For No Reason	519
	Carlotta's Vinyl Skin	527
Peter Wilhelm	Lion	533
	Pyro Protram	539
	Jazz	546
Bessie Head	The Deep River	553
	Life	559
	The Wind and a Boy	568
Mbulelo Vizikhungo Mzamane	The Party	574
Richard Rive	The Visits	589
Ahmed Essop	The Hajji	595
	Hajji Musa and the Hindu Fire-walker	606
Christopher Hope	The Fall of the British Empire	615
	Learning to Fly	626
PJ Haasbroek	Departure	633
Marguerite Poland	The Wood-ash Stars	637
Ernst Havemann	A Farm at Raraba	641
Gcina Mhlophe	The Toilet	651
Maud Motanyane	Two Minutes	657
Jayapraga Reddy	The Spirit of Two Worlds	663
Njabulo S Ndebele	Death of a Son	668
Ken Barris	The Questioning	676
Zoë Wicomb	Ash on my Sleeve	685
	Another Story	696
Ivan Vladislavić	Journal of a Wall	707
	The WHITES ONLY Bench	722
David Medalie	The Shooting of the Christmas Cows	733
PT Mtuze	The Way to Madam	744
Stephen Gray	The Building-site	748
Bheki Maseko	Mamlambo	758
Joel Matlou	Man against Himself	766
EM Macphail	Annual Migration	775
Hennie Aucamp	The Coat without End	782

Liz Gunner   The Mandela Days   786
                              Cattle Passing   788
Maureen Isaacson   I Could Have Loved Gold   792
                              Holding Back Midnight   797
Deena Padayachee   The Finishing Touch   801
Sindiwe Magona   The Sacrificial Lamb   810
Lekotse's Testimony
   at the TRC
   [retold by Antjie Krog]   The Sheep-herder's Tale   815
Rosemary H Moeketsi   Guilty as Charged   820
Riana Scheepers   Book   826
John Matshikiza   Of Renaissance and Rhino Stew 833
                              The Purple Man in my Bantustan 836
Eben Venter   Tinktinkie   839
Ashraf Jamal   The Beggar-guest   846
Marlene van Niekerk   Labour   852

Introduction

This *Omnibus* makes available the stories from three best-selling anthologies: *A Century of South African Short Stories* (1978), edited by Jean Marquard; the revised edition of the same title (1993), edited by Martin Trump; and, most recently, Michael Chapman's entirely new selection in *The New Century of South African Short Stories* (2004).

The 'Century' brand has endeared itself not only to students and academics, but also to the wider public. The current *Omnibus* is aimed primarily at the wider audience: an audience that supported the original Marquard edition through eight reprints and the Trump revision – necessitated by the untimely death of Jean Marquard in the early 1980s – through two further reprints before both of these editions were replaced by *The New Century*.

What was Marquard's formula of success? In her Introduction she summarised her own astute understanding of the field that, in the 1970s, she inherited. It was not, in fact, so much a field as a patchwork. South African literature had not yet established itself as a coherent area of interest or study. As far as the short story was concerned, anthologies prior to Marquard's *A Century* reflected either the personal tastes, even whimsies, of the editor, or were confined to a particular era, or perpetuated divisions between white writing and black writing.

Despite her experiencing her own constraints – several distinguished practitioners had been served with apartheid banning orders and could not, therefore, be quoted in South Africa – Marquard succeeded in her overarching aim. This was 'to make a selection [covering] a larger area, both chronologically and artistically, than anything similar that has appeared'. For the first time readers of our short stories, at least in English, were able to appreciate both the development of the genre and the considerable diversity of talent that reveals the short story to be arguably South Africa's most resilient and innovative form of literary expression.

What Marquard did not appreciate – we rely on the wisdom of hindsight – is that stories from this part of Africa did not begin at what *A Century*, in 1978, declared to be the beginning: the last decade of the nineteenth century. There was the earlier beginning of an oral past. Colonial life in the nineteenth century certainly focused on colonial preoccupations, including prejudices, and such responses in stories remain part of our complex and contested literary inheritance. But as *The New Century* in 2004 suggested, colonialism was not only about the hunter with his gun; it was also about more variegated interventions of power, control, and even sympathy. Several colonial linguists, missionaries and civil servants for reasons of their own, for example, recorded in writing a rich oral expression which extends our storytelling back to San/Bushman and traditional African tales.

Neither did *A Century*, in 1978, show curiosity across language barriers. Its domain, unproblematically, was English-language writing. Its substantial companion anthology in the same year, ironically, was Abraham H de Vries's *Die Afrikaanse Kortverhaalboek* which, in 2001, entered its eleventh reprint. It was a condition of our division that neither anthology registered acknowledgement of the other anthology. While Martin Trump extended the late Jean Marquard's selection to the early 1990s, *The New Century* included oral tales, translations from other languages of the region, and fresh selections pertinent to the 'post-apartheid' perspectives literally of the new century. The current *Omnibus* seeks to grant the reader the advantage not only of Marquard's original vision, but also of modifications attendant on a changing social and literary climate in both South Africa and the globalising world. What continues to grow in strength is the conviction that, in the short story, this country has an achievement of which to be justifiably proud.

As the current editor, I have adopted a simple chronological arrangement of the material from the mid-nineteenth century, when oral expression began to be committed to the record, to the start of the new millennium. The chronology usually relies on the appearance of individual volumes of stories, but where there is a significant delay between a writer's initially making an impression (say, in magazine publication) and the appearance of a first volume, I have alerted the reader to the time discrepancy. Bosman's 'Oom Schalk' stories, for example, were initially published in little magazines in the mid-1930s; his first volume, *Mafeking Road*, appeared a decade later in 1947. Hence, Bosman's 'The Music-Maker' is listed as 'first publication, 1935', followed by the identification, 'from *Mafeking Road* (1947)'. Such publication detail is given below the title of each story while an alphabetical list of authors by surname and a brief biography of each, cross-referenced by page number to the story or stories written by that author and included in the *Omnibus*, follows this Introduction. Those who wish to pursue a greater understanding of the genre are directed to the substantial Introductions in the 1978 and the 2004 'Century' editions.

As I said, the *Omnibus* is aimed at the wider public. I invite all of you, whether familiar with the 'Century' anthologies or whether turning to our short stories for the first time, to enjoy a good read.

Michael Chapman
University of KwaZulu-Natal
Durban 2007

The Authors

The Oral Past

An oral tradition in South Africa links Stone-Age San/Bushmen to modern times and encompasses a rich variety of chants, prayers, songs, myths and tales in the several indigenous languages of the region: San and Khoi click languages; isiZulu; isiXhosa; seSotho; seTswana, etc. First recorded in writing and translated into English by mid-nineteenth-century linguists, missionaries and colonial civil servants, subsequently rewritten, recast or re-created by numbers of skilful writers, our oral past emerges as deserving appreciation alongside any of the great mythologies of the world.

(See 'The Sun is Thrown into the Sky' p27; 'The Girl who Made Stars' p30; 'The Young Man who was Carried off by a Lion' p32; 'Nkulunkulu, the One who Came First' p35; 'How Death Entered the World' p36; 'Maqinase, the Wily One' p38; 'The Bird that Made Milk' p41; 'The Child with a Moon on his Chest' p45; 'The Man who Threw Away his Bread' p47)

Abrahams, Peter

Abrahams, who grew up in mixed-race Vrededorp, left for England in the 1940s before settling in Jamaica. A prolific novelist whose autobiography *Tell Freedom!* (1940) charted a direction in black South African writing.

(See 'One of the Three' p247)

Adams, Perseus

Adams taught in Cape Town until 1965 when he left South Africa for the Middle East. He established his reputation as a poet.

(See 'A True Gruesome' p512)

Aucamp, Hennie

Aucamp, who lectured in Afrikaans and education in Stellenbosch, has had a long and distinguished career as a leading practitioner of the Afrikaans short story. A selection of his work appears, in English translation, in *House Visits* (1983). (See 'The Coat without End' p782)

Barnard, Chris

An Afrikaans Sestiger (writer of the sixties) Barnard, as part of a new wave of writers, adapted European absurdist and existential themes to South African concerns. (See 'Bush' p493)

Barris, Ken

Barris lectures in linguistics in Cape Town. (See 'The Questioning' p676)

Boetie, Dugmore

Boetie, who spent his early years in Sophiatown, is best known for his rumbustious account of his life as a tramp, gaol-bird, con man, and soldier, in the episodic and posthumously published *Familiarity is the Kingdom of the Lost* (1969). He died in 1966. (See 'Three Cons' p483)

Bosman, Herman Charles

Bosman's brief experience in the 1920s as a schoolteacher in the Groot Marico district inspired his 'Oom Schalk' anecdotal tales, first collected in Mafeking Road (1947). Bosman died in 1951. (See 'The Music-Maker' p208; 'Unto Dust' p212; 'Birth Certificate' p216; 'Funeral Earth' p220; 'A Bekkersdal Marathon' p224)

Brownlee, Frank

Brownlee entered Cape colonial government service in the 1890s as a magistrate and Native Commissioner. (See 'The Cannibal's Bird' p228)

12

Cope, Jack

A farmer and journalist, Cope had a life-time involvement in South African literature as an editor, a translator, novelist and short-story writer. He died in England in 1991.
(See 'The Flight' p395; 'The Little Stint' p401)

Cornell, Frederick C

Cornell arrived from England in 1902 and first as a prospector with a focus on Namaqualand, later as editor of the *Cape Register*, he published stories and reminiscences on colonial life. He died in 1921.
(See 'The Drink of the Dead' p100)

Cripps, Arthur Shearly

Born in England Cripps spent many years of his adult life as a missionary in Mashonaland. He published poetry and novels as well as short stories. He died in 1952.
(See 'The Black Death' (p107)

De Vries, Abraham H

De Vries lives in Cape Town, where he lectured in Afrikaans. His stories, which first appeared in the 1960s and were influenced by 'Sestiger' avant gardism, have continued in a variety of forms to explore Afrikaner life in a continually changing South Africa. His most recent collection appeared in 2003.
(See 'The Girl with the Bra-pistol' p460; 'Ruins' p465)

Dhlomo, HIE

A journalist on Bantu World, a library organiser and in the 1940s assistant editor of the isiZulu newspaper *Ilanga Lase Natal*, Herbert Dhlomo wrote plays, poems, stories and commentary on African modernisation.
(See 'The Barren Woman' (p230)

Dhlomo, RRR

A clerk on the mines and in the 1940s editor of the isiZulu newspaper *Ilanga*

Lase Natal, Rolfes Dhlomo wrote journalistic pieces, novellas and stories of both traditional and urban Zulu life.
(See 'The Death of Masaba' p157; 'Murder on the Mine Dumps' p160)

Essop, Ahmed

Essop, a schoolteacher, has published novels and stories on aspects of Indian life in South Africa.
(See 'The Hajji' p595; 'Hajji Musa and the Hindu Fire-walker' p606)

FitzPatrick, J Percy

Prospector, editor and, as an 'uitlander', active in British colonial politics in Paul Kruger's Boer republic, FitzPatrick is the author of several books including the boys' adventure *Jock of the Bushveld* (1907). He died in 1931.
(See 'The Pool' p64)

Gibbon, Perceval

Born in Wales, Gibbon joined the merchant service and, in 1902 as a journalist, the Johannesburg *Rand Daily Mail*. He published novels and short stories on racial issues. He died in 1926.
(See 'Like Unto Like' p112)

Glanville, Ernest

Glanville was a claimant on the diamond fields, a war correspondent and, in 1907, editor of the Cape Argus. He produced a considerable number of novels and stories on aspects of colonial life. He died in 1925.
(See 'Uncle Abe's Big Shoot' p71)

Gordimer, Nadine

Nobel laureate for literature in 1991 and best known for her novels set in apartheid South Africa, Gordimer is also a short-story writer of long career and consummate talent, her first collection having appeared in the 1950s and her latest collect, *Loot*, in 2000.
(See 'The Train from Rhodesia' p250; 'The Bridegroom' p255; 'A Chip of Glass

Ruby' p262; 'The Credibility Gap' p270; 'The Termitary' p278; 'Once upon a Time' p284)

Goudvis, Bertha

Goudvis, who came from England to South Africa in 1881, lived variously in South Africa, Southern Rhodesia and Moçambique as a hotelier and journalist. She died in 1966.
(See 'Thanks to Mrs Parsons' p328)

Gray, Stephen

A leading commentator on South African literature, a biographer, poet, novelist and writer of short fiction, Gray lives in Johannesburg where, before his retirement, he lectured in English and African literature.
(See 'The Building-site' p748)

Gunner, Liz

Gunner lectured in English and African literature, and is currently a research-academic in Johannesburg.
(See 'The Mandela Days' p786; 'Cattle Passing' p788)

Haasbroek, PJ

An economist, Pieter Jacobus Haasbroek focused Afrikaans fiction on the violence and often the absurdity of the South African political crisis of the 1970s and '80s.
(See 'Departure' p633)

Havemann, Ernst

Havemann worked in African administration in Natal before emigrating, in the 1970s, to Canada as a mining engineer.
(See 'A Farm at Raraba' p841)

Head, Bessie

Head trained as a teacher and worked as a journalist on *The Golden City*

Post before leaving Johannesburg in 1964 for a teaching post in Botswana where she lived, mainly as a writer, until her death in 1986. Her novels and stories focus on clashes of tradition and modernity in African society as well as on trauma of displacement attendant on Head's 'mixed-race' identity.
(See 'The Deep River' p553; 'Life' p559; 'The Wind and a Boy' p568)

Hope, Christopher

Hope worked in copywriting, teaching and journalism before moving to England in 1975. Currently living in France, he has won international acclaim for his several novels.
(See 'The Fall of the British Empire' p615; 'Learning to Fly' p626)

Isaacson, Maureen

Isaacson is a journalist and the book-page editor on the Johannesburg *Sunday Independent*.
(See 'I Could Have Loved Gold' p792; 'Holding Back Midnight' p797)

Jacobson, Dan

Jacobson, who grew up in Kimberley, left South Africa in the 1950s for London where he lectured in English literature. He has won acclaim for his several novels and collections of stories.
(See 'Stop Thief!' p367; 'Droit de Seigneur' p373; 'Fresh Fields' p382)

Jamal, Ashraf

Jamal lectures English in Stellenbosch.
(See 'The Beggar-guest' p846)

Jordan, AC

A leading Xhosa intellectual, Jordan spent most of his working life in exile, as professor of African languages and literature in the United States, where he died in 1968. Author of critical work and a landmark novel in isiXhosa, Jordan recreated Xhosa folktales, published posthumously as *Tales from Southern Africa* (1973).
(See 'The Turban' p498)

//Kabbo

//Kabbo (his name means Dream) was a San/Bushman who was imprisoned in Cape Town for stock theft and, in the 1860s, was released into the custody of the linguist WHI Bleek and his sister-in-law Lucy C Lloyd to whom he related traditional myths, songs and tales as well as his contemporary experiences under colonialism. The oral expression – in click language – was transcribed and translated into English by Bleek and Lloyd, a selection appearing in their authoritative *Specimens of Bushman Folklore* (1911). //Kabbo returned to his home on the arid plains of the north-western Cape where he died in 1874.
(See 'A Story is like the Wind' p49)

Krige, Uys

After serving with South African forces against Hitler, Krige devoted his life to literary interchanges of English, Afrikaans and African-language literature. His own numerous works include plays and stories in both Afrikaans and English. He died in 1987.
(See 'The Coffin' p311; 'Death of the Zulu' p321)

La Guma, Alex

La Guma, who grew up in Cape Town's coloured community, spent his adult life in active opposition to apartheid. After periods of house arrest, he left South Africa in 1966 and died in exile in Cuba in 1985. He published several political novels.
(See 'A Matter of Taste' p428)

Leipoldt, C Louis

Cape-based journalist, medical doctor and pioneer in the field of Afrikaans literature, Leipoldt wrote poems, novels, reminiscences and stories in both English and Afrikaans. Several of his works were published posthumously. He died in 1947.
(See 'The Tree' p238)

Lekotse's Testimony at the TRC [retold by Antjie Krog]

The seSotho testimony of Lekotse, a sheep-herder in the Free State, was included by the Afrikaans poet Antjie Krog in her dramatic narrative of witness and identity, *Country of my Skull* (1998).

(See 'The Sheep-herder's Tale' p815)

Lessing, Doris

Lessing settled in 1925 with her English parents in a farming district in Southern Rhodesia, the locale of her early novel *The Grass is Singing* (1950). Her first stories appeared in South African magazines. Lessing left Africa in 1949 for England where she established her reputation as a leading contemporary writer.

(See 'The Old Chief Mshlanga' p289; 'Flavours of Exile' p299; 'Lucy Grange' p306)

Macphail, EM

Ella Macphail, who grew up in small towns, became involved in publishing in Johannesburg. Her stories appear in *Falling Upstairs* (1982).

(See 'Annual Migration' p775)

Magona, Sindiwe

Magona, who grew up in a Xhosa homestead, trained as a teacher and for many years worked in development at the United Nations. She is one of the more prolific storywriters of the last decade. She returned to South Africa in 2003.

(See 'The Sacrificial Lamb' p810)

Marais, Eugène N

A versatile figure in the development of Afrikaans language and literature – his poetry co-exists with historical, scientific and popular explorations – Marais in *Dwaalstories* (1927) invokes San tradition in his artistic rendering of a free verse style of mystery tale. He died in 1936.

(See 'The Grey Pipit' p153)

Maseko, Bheki

Maseko was a truck driver when, in the late 1970s, his stories were first published in the popular literary magazine *Staffrider*.
(See 'Mamlambo' p758)

Matlou, Joel

Matlou worked as a clerk in a factory in Pretoria when his stories were first published, in the 1970s, in the popular literary magazine *Staffrider*.
(See 'Man against Himself' p766)

Matshikiza, John

Matshikiza, whose parents went into exile, grew up abroad and returned to South Africa in the 1990s. The selection here is drawn from his weekly column in the *Mail & Guardian*.
(See 'Of Renaissance and Rhino Stew' p833; 'The Purple Man in my Bantustan' p836)

Matthews, James

Matthews, who lives in the Cape Town coloured community, was active in anti-apartheid politics in the 1970s and eighties while offering alternative publishing outlets for committed literature. He has published both stories and poems.
(See 'The Park' p432)

Medalie, David

Medalie lectures in English literature in Pretoria.
(See 'The Shooting of the Christmas Cows' p733)

Mhlophe, Gcina

Mhlophe, who lives in Durban, has a prominent TV and stage presence as a performer of traditional African tales.
(See 'The Toilet' p651)

Millin, Sarah Gertrude

At an early age Millin together with her parents came to South Africa from Lithuania. Having spent her childhood in financial hardship on the diamond fields she married a prominent justice of the Supreme Court. A prolific writer of biographies and novels, she is best known for her novel on miscegenation, *God's Step-children* (1924). She died in Johannesburg in 1965.
(See 'Up from Gilgal' p112; 'A Sack for Ninepence' p123)

Moeketsi, Rosemary H

Moeketsi lectures in linguistics and translation studies in Pretoria.
(See 'Guilty as Charged' p820)

Motanyane, Maud

Editor in the 1980s of the 'upwardly mobile' black magazine *Tribute*, Motanyane now lives in France.
(See 'Two Minutes' p657)

Motsisi, Casey

The legendary 'Kid' Motsisi was the satirical columnist on *Drum* magazine in the 1950s. He died in Soweto in 1977.
(See 'Kid Playboy' p392)

Mphahlele, Es'kia

Dismissed as a teacher for his opposition to apartheid 'Bantu Education', Mphahlele worked for *Drum* magazine before leaving South Africa as an exile in 1957. Having taught literature at various African and American universities he was permitted to return to South Africa in 1977 to pursue his academic career as professor of African literature. His distinguished output includes his early autobiography, *Down Second Avenue* (1959).
(See 'Down the Quiet Street' p333; 'Mrs Plum' p339)

Mtuze, PT

Peter Mtuze, who lectures in African languages in Grahamstown, writes his stories originally in isiXhosa.
(See 'The Way to Madam' p744)

Mzamane, Mbulelo Vizikhungo

Currently director of the Centre for African literature at the University of KwaZulu-Natal, Mzamane came to prominence as a writer of stories during the 'Black Consciousness' years of the 1970s. His collection *The Children of the Diaspora and other Stories of Exile* appeared in 1996.
(See 'The Party' p574)

Ndebele, Njabulo S

An influential literary critic whose collection *Fools and Other Stories* appeared in 1983, Ndebele is currently Vice-Chancellor of the University of Cape Town.
(See 'Death of a Son' p668)

Nevinson, HW

Nevinson was a British journalist who reported from an anti-Imperial perspective on the Anglo-Boer War.
(See 'Vae Victis' p74)

Padayachee, Deena

Padayachee practises as a medical doctor near Durban.
(See 'The Finishing Touch' p801)

Paton, Alan

As president of the South African Liberal Party in the 1960s, Paton was an active opponent of the apartheid government. His numerous works of biography, commentary, autobiography and fiction include the renowned *Cry, the Beloved Country* (1948). He died in 1988.
(See 'A Drink in the Passage' p415; 'The Quarry' p421)

Plomer, William

Plomer travelled frequently between England, where he was educated and worked in publishing, and South Africa which inspired many of his works of biography and fiction, including the seminal novel of interracial relationships, *Turbott Wolfe* (1925). Plomer died in 1973.

(See 'The Child of Queen Victoria' p163; 'Down on the Farm' p192)

Poland, Marguerite

Poland's studies in anthropology and African languages inform her several works of fiction, including her award-winning recastings of San/Bushman tales.

(See 'The Wood-ash Stars' p637)

Pulvermacher [AG de Smidt]

De Smidt was an early contributor to the development of the Afrikaans language, his sketches appearing in Cape-Dutch periodicals of the 1890s.

(See 'Prayer of Titus Tokaan' p55)

Rabie, Jan

One of the experimental Sestigers (writers of the sixties) Rabie lived near Cape Town where in his poems, novels, stories and commentary he continued to seek a non-sectarian, non-racist conception of Afrikaans literature and life in a multiracial South Africa. He died in 2001.

(See 'Maiden Outing to Rondebosch' p471)

Reddy, Jayapraga

Reddy lived in Durban where, during the 1980s, she wrote radio plays and stories on life in the South African Indian community. A paraplegic, Reddy died at a relatively early age.

(See 'The Spirit of Two Worlds' p663)

Rive, Richard

Rive lectured in English literature in Cape Town, the locale of many of his stories of the Cape coloured community of District Six. He was murdered in his home in 1989.

(See 'The Visits' p589)

Roberts, Sheila

Roberts grew up in Potchefstroom, where her father was based in the military, and since 1977 she has lectured in creative writing in the United States. She has published several novels and collections of stories.

(See 'For No Reason' p519; 'Carlotta's Vinyl Skin' p527)

Scheepers, Riana

Scheepers has taught language and literature at universities and schools around Cape Town.

(See 'Book' p826)

Schoeman, Karel

Schoeman, who before his retirement was a librarian at a research library in Cape Town, continues to add to his literary output over four decades of biographies, novels and short stories.

(See 'Seed in a New Earth' p477)

Schreiner, Olive

Born to a German missionary and his English wife, Schreiner spent her young adulthood in the 1860s as a governess on isolated farms in the Karoo, the setting of her famous novel *The Story of an African Farm* (1883). Influenced in England by the literary and social issues of the day, Schreiner in her polemical essays is critical of British imperial ambitions in southern Africa while her novels, stories and commentary reveal her involvement in the cause of women's emancipation. She died in the Cape in 1920.

(See 'Eighteen-Ninety-Nine' p78)

Scully, William Charles

Scully came from Ireland in 1867 to the Cape colony where, before entering the civil service to become a magistrate, he was a prospector and big-game hunter. He published numerous stories, novels and reminiscences of colonial life. He died in 1943.

(See 'Umtagati' p56)

Simon, Barney

Simon was active in anti-apartheid and experimental theatre production in Johannesburg. He died in 1995.

(See 'Joburg, Sis!' p507)

Smith, Pauline

The daughter of an English medical doctor, Smith accompanied her father on his rounds in the Little Karoo, the setting of her tales of rural Afrikaans life, which were written from memory in England where Smith spent her adult years. She died in 1959.

(See 'Desolation' p129; 'The Schoolmaster' p142; 'The Sisters' p149)

Themba, Can

Educated in English literature at Fort Hare, Themba was a leading writer and journalist on *Drum* magazine in the 1950s. Epitomising the free spirit of Sophiatown in its defiance of segregationist laws, Themba went into exile in Swaziland where he died in 1963. His stories and journalism have been published in collected editions.

(See 'Crepuscule' p441; 'The Suit' p448; 'The Will to Die' p456)

Van Niekerk, Marlene

A lecturer in Afrikaans and Nederlands in Stellenbosch, Van Niekerk's novels have been greeted with acclaim.

(See 'Labour' p852)

Venter, Eben

An award-winning Afrikaans writer, Venter returned from Australia to the Karoo where he lives as a writer.

(See 'Tinktinkie' p839)

Vladislavić, Ivan

Vladislavic lives in Johannesburg where he studied literature and is a freelance editor. His award-winning novels and stories reflect the several absurdities of contemporary South African urban life.
(See 'Journal of a Wall' p707; 'The WHITES ONLY Bench' p722)

Wicomb, Zoë

Wicomb grew up in the coloured community in the Cape, and lives in Scotland where she lectures in literature.
(See 'Ash on my Sleeve' p685; 'Another Story' p696)

Wilhelm, Peter

Wilhelm currently lives in Cape Town, where he works as an economics editor. His novels and collections of short stories, which span three decades, have received considerable recognition.
(See 'Lion' p533; 'Pyro Protram' p539; 'Jazz' p546)

SAN/BUSHMAN TRADITION

The Sun is Thrown into the Sky

Translated from the click language by Bleek and Lloyd; reworked by Elana Bregin
From: WHI Bleek and LC Lloyd's *Specimens of Bushman Folklore* (1911)

The First Bushmen, the men of the Early Race – [!Kwi-an told her son //Kabbo] – were those who first inhabited the earth. Their children were the ones who worked with the Sun. The people who came later say that it was those children who made the Sun ascend, for their mothers had told them that they should throw the Sun-person up into the sky, so that he might warm the earth for them; so that they might sit in the Sun and feel its warmth. Until that time, the Sun was a man who lived on earth. In the beginning, he gave forth brightness only in the space around his own dwelling. The rest of the country remained very cloudy, as it looks now when the Sun is behind thick clouds. The sky was dark and black. The shining came from one of the Sun's armpits, as he lay asleep with his arm lifted up. When he put down his arm, darkness fell everywhere; when he lifted his arm up again, it was as if day had come. In the day, the Sun's light used to be white, but at night, it was red, like a fire.

The children of the Early Race gently approached the Sun-armpit to lift him up while he lay sleeping. Their mothers had spoken to them and told them to do this. An old woman was the one who had instructed them. She herself had no young male children, so she spoke to the children's mothers. For she saw that these were clever children, who would understand nicely what to do when they went to that old man, Sun-armpit. The old woman spoke to the children through their mothers, telling them to tell their children that they should throw the Sun-armpit up into the sky, so that the Bushman rice might become dry for them. So that while the Sun moved along across the whole sky, it would make all places bright. This is what the mothers said:

'O children! You must wait till the Sun-armpit lies down to sleep. Then, you must gently approach him while he lies asleep. Take hold of him all together, and lift him up so that you can throw him into the sky.'

This is what the old woman had told the mothers to say to their children.

The children came and the children went away again. The old woman said: 'You must sit down and wait. You must look to see whether the Sun's eyes are still open or whether he sleeps. You must go and sit down and wait for him to fall asleep.'

And so the children sat down and waited, as they had been told to do. The

Sun lay down; he lifted up his elbow. His armpit shone upon the ground as he lay sleeping. The children took hold of him and threw hint up into the sky the way they had been instructed to do. The old woman had said:

'O children going yonder! You must talk to the Sun when you throw him up. You must tell him that he must altogether become the Sun, so that he can go forward as the proper Sun – the Sun which is hot, which stays hot in the sky as he moves along high above us; so that as his heat shines down, the Bushman rice can become dry.'

This was the old woman's message to the children, the old woman whose head was white. And so, when the time was right, the children arose and stealthily approached the Sun. They all took hold of him together and lifted him up while he was still hot and threw him up into the sky.

'O Sun!' they said to him, 'you must stand firmly there, you must go along in the sky and remain there while you are still hot.'

Then the children returned to their mothers. One of them said: 'I and my younger brothers and their friends and their friends' brothers all took hold of him. I told them: "You must grasp him firmly – grasp the old man firmly, and throw him up."'

Another youth spoke and said: 'O my grandmother! We threw the Sun up, we told him that he should properly become the Sun, which is hot, for we are cold. We said: "O my grandfather Sun-armpit! Remain in your place in the sky. Become the sun that is hot, so that the Bushman rice may dry for us. Make the whole earth light, give heat, so that the whole earth may become warm in the summer. Shine properly, taking away the darkness; you must come, so that the darkness will go away."'

And so it is thus. The Sun comes, and the darkness goes away; the Sun sets, the darkness returns and the Moon conies out. The day breaks, the Sun comes out again and the darkness goes away as the Sun moves across the sky. At night, the Moon comes out to brighten the darkness; the darkness departs. The Moon shines, making bright the darkness as it goes along. The Moon sets; the Sun follows it, driving away the darkness. The Sun takes away the Moon. As the Moon stands in the sky, the Sun pierces it with the Sun's knife, and the Moon decays away because of what the Sun does with its stabbing rays. Therefore, the Moon pleads with the Sun, saying: 'O Sun! Leave for my children at least the backbone!'

And so the Sun does this. It promises to leave the Moon's backbone for the Moon's children. And so the Moon goes painfully away. Painfully, he returns home, moving along the sky. The Sun desists from cutting him further. For the sake of the Moon's children, he leaves the Moon's backbone behind. Because of this, the Moon again goes on to become another Moon, which is whole again. He lives again, even though it seemed as if he had died. He becomes a new Moon. He again puts on a stomach; he becomes large. He becomes a

Moon which is whole again. He goes along at night, for he is the Moon which goes by night. He feels that he is a shoe, therefore he walks in the night. For once, the Mantis, inconvenienced by darkness, took off one of his shoes and threw it into the sky, ordering it to become the Moon.

The Sun is here and all the earth is bright. The Sun is here, and the people walk about while the place is light. They perceive the bushes, they see the other people, and the meat which they are eating, and the springbok. They hunt the springbok in summer, and also the ostrich, while the Sun shines down on them. They shoot the springbok, they steal up on the gemsbok and the kudu, while the Sun makes the whole place bright for them. They also visit each other, while the Sun shines upon the path. They travel in summer, hunt in summer, spy the springbok in summer; they go round to head off the springbok and lie down in a little house of bushes, while the springbok come.

Since that time when the Sun was thrown up into the sky, it became round and never was a man afterwards.

The Girl who Made Stars*

Translated from the click language by Bleek and Lloyd; reworked by Elana Bregin
From: WHI Bleek and LC Lloyd's *Specimens of Bushman Folklore* (1911)

My mother was the one – [said //Kabbo] – who told me about the girl who made stars out of wood ashes. This girl arose from where she was lying in her little hut. She put her hands into the wood ashes of the fire and threw them up into the sky. She said to the wood ashes: 'These wood ashes which are here must become the Milky Way. They must lie white along the sky, so that the stars may stand outside of the Milky Way – the Milky Way which used to be wood ashes. The wood ashes must fully become the Milky Way and go around the sky with the stars, lying across the sky while the stars sail along.'

And so it is this way. When the Milky Way stands low upon the earth, it turns across the front of the sky, waiting for the Stars to turn back. The Stars wait for the Sun, until they feel that he has turned back; for he travels on his own path. Then the Stars also turn back and go to fetch the daybreak, so that they may sink nicely to their rest, while the Milky Way goes to rest with them.

The Stars sail along upon their footprints, which they follow across the sky. They know that they are the Stars which are meant to descend. The Milky Way continues to lie along the sky as it travels back to its place, to the place where the girl threw up the wood ashes. It travelled the sky while lying along it. It went around the sky while lying along it, waiting for the stars to turn around as they passed over the sky. The sky lies still. It is the Stars which move, sailing along as they feel that they are meant to do. The Stars begin to set, following their footprints as they sail along. They become white when the Sun comes out. After the Sun sets, they stand all around in the sky and turning, follow the Sun. When the darkness comes out, the Stars wax red, whereas before they had been white. They stand brightly around, sailing along in the night. Then, the people can walk by night, while the ground is made light, while the Stars shine a little.

Darkness is upon the ground. The Milky Way gently glows. It glows because it still feels that it is wood ashes. It obeys the girl who said that the Milky Way should give a little light for the people, so that they might return home by night, even in the middle of the night. For the earth would not have had any light had not the Milky Way been there, the Milky Way and the Stars. The girl thought that she would throw up *!huin* roots into the air, in order that the

30

!huin roots should become Stars, the red, old roots making red stars and the white, young roots making white stars. But first, the girl gently threw up wood ashes into the sky, so that she might presently throw up the *!huin* roots to become the Stars.

The girl was angry with her mother, because her mother had not given her enough roots so that she might eat abundantly; for she could not go out of her hut to seek food for herself. So she was hungry while she lay in the hut. The mothers were the ones who went out. They were the ones who sought for food. They were bringing home *!huin* to eat. The girl lay in her little hut which her mother had made for her. Her stick stood there in the hut; because she was not yet a woman, she did not yet dig out food with the other women. She had to stay in the hut and wait for her mother to bring her food, which she ate lying down in the little hut which her mother had built for her. Her mother had closed her into the tiny hut because she was about to become a woman. During this time, she could not go far from her hut or walk about freely. She could not eat the game killed by the young men. She could only eat the game of her father, who was an old man. For if she ate the young men's game, their hands would become cool. Their arrows would become cool. The arrow head would become cold. The arrow head would feel that the bow was cold, while the bow would feel that the young man's hands were cold. The girl feared to eat the young men's game lest, while eating, she put her saliva into the springbok meat. This saliva would then go into the bow of the hunter, and the inside of the bow would become cool. Therefore, the game hunted by her father was the only game from which she could eat. For her father's hands had been properly worked by her, to take the coldness of her saliva away from them. During the time that she was waiting to become a woman, she must not look at the springbok, lest they should become wild. If she went out of her hut, she had to keep her eyes upon the ground, and not go far. When presently she became a 'big girl', then she would be allowed to leave the small hut, to walk around like the other women and look about again.

But this girl was disobedient. Because she was hungry she arose and went out of her hut and threw up wood ashes to become the stars, so that her father and the other hunters would have light to return home by. This girl is said to have been one of the people of the Early Race (*!xwe-lna-ssho-!ke*) and the 'first' girl, and to have acted wrongly She was finally shot by her husband.

★See Marguerite Poland's 'The Wood-ash Stars' [ed.]

The Young Man who was Carried off by a Lion

Translated from the click language by Bleek and Lloyd; reworked by Elana Bregin
From: WHI Bleek and LC Lloyd's *Specimens of Bushman Folklore* (1911)

A young man of the Early Race – [said Díä!kwain] – while out hunting one day, ascended a hill to look for game. While he sat there, he became sleepy. He felt the need to lie down, for he was very sleepy. What could be wrong with him today? He had not felt such sleepiness before.

He lay down and closed his eyes. While he slept, a lion came. It was on its way to a water pit. The oppressive noonday heat had made it very thirsty. The lion saw the man lying there asleep, and it took him up in its jaws.

The man awoke in fright and found himself being carried away by the lion. He kept very still, knowing that if he moved, the lion would bite him and kill him. He waited to see what the lion intended to do, for it appeared to think that he was dead.

The lion carried him to a zwart-storm tree and carefully placed him in its branches. It still needed to drink, for its thirst was very great. It decided first to go to the water, and then come back and eat him.

It pressed the man's head between the branches of the zwart-storm tree, and turned to go to the water pit. The man moved his head, just a little. The lion caught the movement; it looked back suspiciously – why had the man's head moved? The lion was sure that it had fixed the man's head firmly between the branches. But it had apparently not been firmly enough, for the man fell over. The lion came back and once more pressed the man's head between the branches of the zwart-storm tree, this time very thoroughly. It licked the tears from the man's eyes. For the man was weeping. The man felt a sharp stick piercing the hollow at the back of his head. But he dared not stir, for he saw that the lion suspected that he was alive. Finally, since the man did not move again, the lion concluded that it had pressed him firmly enough into the tree. It went on a few steps, then looked back towards the man. The man kept still, pressing his eyelids together, looking through his eyelashes to see what the lion was doing.

The lion went away. It ascended the hill and began to descend it on the other side. The man gently turned his head to follow its movements. He saw the lion raise its head, peering at him over the top of the hill, wanting to make sure that he was not just feigning death. When it saw that he was still lying as it had left him, the lion ran off quickly to the water, intending to slake its thirst and then return so that it might eat this man. For it was very hungry.

The man watched the lion disappear. It seemed as if this time, it had gone for good. Just to be sure, the man continued to lie still for a time, in case the lion again came back to check on him. For he knew that the lion was cunning. It might deceive him into thinking it had really gone away, only to return to catch him the moment he stirred. A long time passed. Still the man waited; finally, when there was still no sign of the lion returning, he concluded that it had really gone away.

He remained cautious, however. He did not leap up and flee immediately, but got up carefully, and sprang away to a different spot. His intention was to confuse the lion, so that it would find it more difficult to locate his trail from this new place. Then, instead of heading straight for home, the man ran off in a zigzag direction, hoping by this means to throw the lion off his trail. For he knew that if the lion detected his footsteps, it would follow him and seek him out where he lived.

Finally, he emerged at the top of the hill near his home. He called out to his people, telling them that he had been 'lifted up', he had been 'lifted up' by a lion. He instructed them to bring out many hartebeest-skins, and roll him up in them, for he had been 'lifted up' in the middle of the day, while the sun stood high. He knew that the lion, when it came back and found him missing, would resolve to seek him and track him down. For that reason, he wanted the people to roll him up in hartebeest-skins, so that the lion would not be able to scent him and get to him. Everyone knew that the lion does not forget its prey. Once it has killed, it will never leave its prey uneaten.

So the people rolled the young man up in mats and hartebeest-skins. They covered him over with sheltering bushes from around the homestead, so that the lion, when it came seeking him, would not be able to find him. For this young man was their hearts' young man. They loved him, and they did not wish the lion to eat him.

The people went out to seek a special edible root; they dug it out and brought it home at noon and baked it. An old man was one of those out gathering wood for his wife so that she could make a fire to roast the root. He was the one who saw the lion as it came over the top of the hill, exactly where the young man had walked, following the young man's trail. He shouted to the others, 'Look – look at the hill! There at the top where the young man came over – see what's there.'

The young man's mother said, 'You must not allow the lion to come near the houses. You must shoot it dead before it comes here.'

The people quickly slung on their quivers and went to meet the lion. But when they shot at this lion with their poisonous arrows, it would not die.

Another old woman spoke, she said, 'You must give the lion a child, so that it will go away from us.'

But the lion said that it did not want a child. It wanted the person 'whose eyes' tears' it had licked; he was the one that it wanted.

Other people said to those who had shot at the lion: 'How was it that when you shot at the lion you could not manage to kill it?'

Another old man said: 'Can't you see? This lion must be a sorcerer. It will not die when we shoot at it, it insists upon having the man whom it carried off.'

The people threw children to the lion; but the lion ignored them, still seeking the young man. The people continued to shoot at it. But their arrows had no effect. They said, 'Bring us spears, we have to kill the lion.' They stabbed it with spears, hoping to stab it to death, but their spears, too, had no effect. The lion continued to seek the young man, saying that it wanted the young man whose tears it had licked. He was the one it wanted. It tore things apart, breaking the people's houses to pieces, seeking the young man out.

And the people said, 'Can you not see that the lion will not eat the children we have given to it?'

And the people said, 'Can you not see that it must be a sorcerer?'

And the people said, 'You must give a girl to the lion, we'll see if the lion will eat her and then go away.'

But the lion did not want the girl either. It only wanted the man whom it had carried off.

And the people didn't know what else to do. They had been shooting at the lion since morning, and it would not die. It had refused the children whom they gave it, it had refused the young girl. It wanted only the man whom it had carried off.

So finally the people said, 'Tell the young man's mother that, although she loves the young man, she must bring him out. She must give the young man to the lion, even if he is the child of her heart. For she can see that the sun is about to set, and that the lion is still threatening us, it will not leave us, it insists on having the young man.'

The young man's mother wept and said, 'You may give my child to the lion. But you must not allow it to eat my child and live. You must kill it while it is upon my child, so that it dies as my child dies.'

So the people took the young man out of the hartebeest-skins in which they had wrapped him, and they gave the young man to the lion. And the lion bit the young man and killed him. And while the lion was biting the young man to death, the people shot at it and stabbed it.

The lion spoke: 'Now I will die,' it said to the people, 'for I have finally found the man I have been seeking.'

And so it died, lying dead with the young man that it had killed.

AFRICAN TRADITIONS

Nkulunkulu, the One Who Came First

Translated from isiZulu by Henry Callaway
From: NN Canonici's *Izinganekwane* (1993)

The ancients say that Nkulunkulu, the One Who Came First, is God, because they say he was the first to appear; they say he is the people's reed, from which the people were broken off. The ancients say that God exists; he made the first people, the ancients of olden times. Those ancients died but there remained other people generated by them – their children. From them we heard that there were ancient people of olden times who knew about the breaking off of the world from the reed. However, even they did not know God; they had not seen him with their own eyes, but they had heard that God existed and had appeared when people broke off from the reed bed. It was God who generated the people of old, and they generated others. It is our ancestors who have told us the stories about God and about the old days. Today's people pray to the ancestral spirits; they praise their ancestors so that they may come and save them.

How Death Entered the World

Translated from isiZulu by NN Canonici; reworked by Elana Bregin
From: NN Canonici's *Izinganekwane* (1993)

Long long ago, people did not die. They lived for years and years and years without dying. The One Who Created Everything looked out and saw that it was good. It was good that people should not die. It was good that people should live until they were bent over, without ever dying. He called Chameleon to him. Slowly, Chameleon came and stood in front of the Creator.

The Creator said to Chameleon: 'Chameleon, I am sending you on an errand; I am sending you to the people. You must go to them and tell them that I say that they are not to die. Do you understand?'

'Yes, Lord, I understand,' said Chameleon trembling. Its eyes looked first forward then backwards. Finally, Chameleon turned. Its leg shook and went forward; it put it down. It lifted another leg; this too shook as Chameleon put it forward. There is Chameleon, moving now, constantly lifting its shaking legs, with its eyes looking forward and then backwards.

After walking for a long time, Chameleon saw some wild berries. Its eyes saw the berries. Its mouth started watering. It said: 'I'll get to the people, it does not matter when. There is no reason to rush. Let me branch off here for a little while. For I am hungry, and I have no food. The Creator won't see me.'

And so Chameleon made for the berries. It shifted itself, forgetting that it was on an errand. The Creator saw it, however, and was angry. He called Lizard, which came swiftly. The Creator spoke to Lizard, saying: 'Lizard, take off at full speed and go to the people. Tell them immediately that I say they must die. I sent Chameleon, but it is wasting time with wild berries on the way.'

Lizard set off, shaking its tail as it ran. Dust blew up behind it. It did not even try to pluck food on the way. It passed Chameleon still busy with the berries. It hurtled by at great speed and disappeared. When Chameleon saw Lizard it was struck by fear. It remembered that it had a message to deliver. It stopped eating the berries. Shaking, it followed Lizard.

Lizard arrived among the people and said: 'Listen, all of you, listen to the message I bring from the Creator. All of you listen.'

The people listened in silence, setting aside their tasks. All wanted to hear the Creator's message carried by Lizard. 'Listen all of you. The Creator says, people must die!'

Then Lizard turned and went back home. The people stood there talking about Lizard's words. They were still talking when Chameleon appeared, breathing heavily. It kept shaking as it slowly approached them.

The people saw it and said: 'Look at Chameleon! It looks as if it wants to speak.'

Chameleon spoke: 'Listen all of you. Listen to the message coming from the Creator. All of you listen.'

The people said: 'Chameleon also says it carries a message from the Creator. Let's hear what it says.'

The people listened carefully to what Chameleon had to say. Chameleon went on: 'Listen all of you. The Creator decrees that people should not die.'

The people said: 'Away with you! Why are you telling us this? Where were you wasting your time just now? We have already received Lizard's message.'

Chameleon was upset; it turned back and slowly went off again.

Today there is still a proverb which goes: 'We have heard the lizard's message', meaning, we are holding onto what we already know. This is how it originated.

Maqinase, the Wily One

Translated from isiZulu by NN Canonici; reworked by Elana Bregin
From: NN Canonici's *Izinganekwane* (1993)

Children:	Grandmother, please tell us a story.
Grandmother:	Are you asking for a tale now? Don't you know that you'll grow horns if you are told a story in the daytime?
Children:	Yes grandmother, we beg for a story now. We won't grow horns.
Grandmother:	All right, I'll tell you one. If you grow horns it's your business. Don't come crying to me. Have you finished your jobs around the house?
Children:	Yes, we have finished them. We ask for a tale now.
Grandmother:	All right, my grandchildren. However, before I tell you a story, you'd better repeat after me:

Horn Horn, don't grow here (On the head)
It's as hard as a rock here (Head)
It is soft here (Ground)

Children:	(Repeat line by line)
Grandmother:	*Kwesukesukela* … Once upon a time …
Children:	*Cosi, sampheka ngogozwana!* We cook her in a small pot! [i. e. We have got her in a tight corner. Now that she has pronounced the initial formula *'kwesukesukela'*, she must go on with the story.]

There once was a mother pig with five children. One of the children was very fond of wandering about on his own. This child was truly pig-headed. His name, Maqinase (the Wily One), fitted him perfectly. The mother pig did not like her children to go out of her sight. Maqinase, however, was restless. When all the other pigs were sitting at home, he would suddenly disappear. He would go off on his own and return whenever he felt like it. His mother kept scolding him sternly, but it did not make any difference to Maqinase.

One day it was very hot. Maqinase's mother was overcome by the heat and fell asleep. Maqinase realised that his mother was asleep. He looked at his brothers and sisters and saw that they too were asleep, overcome by the heat.

He smiled to himself. He got up and tiptoed away, so as not to awaken the sleeping ones. He went to the door and opened it slowly, without making any noise. He told himself: 'When they wake up I will be gone!'

As soon as he was out of sight of the house, Maqinase started walking straight ahead, moving quickly, as if showing off. The way he walked drew attention to him. There he is, over there!

On the way he met a donkey. Donkey said to him: 'Where are you heading for, Maqinase?'

Without even stopping, Maqinase answered: 'Leave me alone! Do I look like a person who should be addressed by one with ears as big as yours?'

Donkey was upset to hear Maqinase answer in such a way. He said: 'What an arrogant child you are! Why do you insult me when I addressed you nicely?'

'It must be the hot sun that gives rise to such strange happenings,' answered Maqinase still walking fast ahead. 'Do I insult you when I tell you the truth? Have you ever noticed how long your ears are? Do not bother me, when the sun is so hot!' And on he went.

As he walked further, he came across a tortoise. Tortoise said: 'Where are you heading for, Maqinase? You are walking so fast!'

Still walking, Maqinase answered, 'Am I having hallucinations today?' He raised his little nose and said: 'Do you drag your feet so as to delay on the road and ask me such stupid questions?'

Tortoise was hurt and answered back: 'Oh, Maqinase, why answer me with bad manners when I asked you politely? What an arrogant child you are!'

'I am used to being called arrogant by now,' Maqinase shot back. 'That fool over there with long ears also called me that. You leave me alone; mind your own business.'

And Maqinase was off, leaving Tortoise open-mouthed in astonishment.

Maqinase then met a frog. Frog said: 'My goodness, look at Mr Wily in person! Where are you going with such a swinging gait?'

Maqinase was upset by this and answered: 'Today must be my unlucky day. First the donkey, then the tortoise and now you, all asking me questions. Why do you gurgle at me as if too tired to breathe, wasting my time by asking me where I am going? Furthermore, are you so well acquainted with me as to address me as Mr Wily?'

Said Frog: 'Yes, indeed, Maqinase, you are really arrogant. Let those who have eyes see what you are!'

'Let them first see that enormous mouth of yours and leave me alone!' answered Maqinase, walking on ahead.

After passing Frog, he left the main road and crept through a fence. He said to himself: 'Better turn off the road lest others see me. These fields look really beautiful. I shall easily fill my stomach today. Let those who sleep eat their sleep!'

However, Maqinase had been seen as he came into the field. The farmer called his dog: 'There is Maqinase, he is back. Get him!' He had hardly finished speaking when the big dog made straight for Maqinase.

Maqinase was heard crying: 'We ho … ho … ho …! We … ho … ho … ho …!'

The dog was not silent either; it kept barking: 'Heyi heyi heyi! Heyi heyi heyi!'

When Maqinase went through the fence again, it tore his skin. He took to his heels, still crying. Seeing Frog he called: 'Frog, frog, please rescue me!'

But Frog answered: 'Sorry, I am still fixing my mouth!'

Maqinase went on at top speed with the dog at his tail, often nipping him with its teeth. He saw Tortoise and shouted: 'Tortoise, tortoise, please rescue me!'

Tortoise answered: 'How can I rescue you, I who can only drag my feet?'

Maqinase went on, always running. He saw Donkey and said: 'Donkey, donkey, please rescue me!'

Donkey answered: 'Sorry, I have no time, I am still fixing my ears.''

The dog bit him one last time, then turned back and went home.

'Where have you been?' asked Maqinase's mother.

'Nowhere in particular,' Maqinase answered.

His mother was angry at that: 'Nowhere in particular, and you are squeaking and panting?'

Maqinase denied it: 'I was just running around on my own, amusing myself, since you were all asleep.'

'And why was that dog chasing you?' his mother asked.

'No, it wasn't chasing me, it was just accompanying me.'

Said his mother: 'So, you think you are clever do you? Remember that no clever person can lick his own back.'

It is finished.

The Bird that Made Milk

Translated from isiXhosa by G McCall Theal; reworked by Elana Bregin
From: George McCall Theal's *Kaffir Folklore* (1882)

It is said that there was once a great town in a certain place which had many people living in it. They lived only upon grain. One year there was a great famine.

Now in that town there was a poor man, by the name of Masilo, and his wife. One day, they went to dig in their garden, and they continued digging the whole day long. In the evening, when the digging gangs returned home, they returned with them. Then there came a bird which stood upon the house which was beside the garden, and it began to whistle and said: 'Masilo's cultivated ground, mix together.'

The ground did as the bird said. After that was done, the bird went away.

In the morning, when Masilo and his wife went to the garden, they were confused and said, 'Is this really the place where we were digging yesterday?'

They saw by the people who were working on either side of them that it was indeed the place. The people began to laugh at them, and mocked them, saying, 'It is because you are so lazy that your ground remains undug.'

Masilo and his wife continued to dig again that day, and in the evening they again went home with the others.

Then the bird came and did the same thing as before.

When Masilo and his wife went back the next morning, they once more found their ground altogether untouched. Then they believed that they were bewitched by some of the others. They continued digging that day again. But in the evening, when the digging gangs returned, Masilo said to his wife, 'Go home; I will stay behind to watch and find the thing which undoes our work.'

Then he went and laid himself down by the head of the garden, under the same house on which the bird always perched. While he was thinking his thoughts, the bird came. It was a very beautiful bird. Masilo was busy looking at it and admiring it, when it began to speak.

It said, 'Masilo's cultivated ground, mix together.'

Then Masilo caught the bird and said, 'Ah, it is you who eats the work of our hands!'

He took out his knife from its sheath and was going to cut off the bird's

41

head, when the bird said, 'Please don't kill me! I will make some milk for you to drink.'

Masilo answered, 'You must bring back the work of my hands first.'

The bird said, 'Masilo's cultivated ground, appear,' and it appeared.

Then Masilo said, 'Make the milk now,' and, behold, the bird immediately made thick milk, which Masilo began to drink. When he was satisfied, he took the bird home. As he approached his house, he put the bird in his bag.

After entering his house, Masilo said to his wife, 'Wash all the largest beer pots which are in the house.'

But his wife was angry on account of her hunger and she answered, 'What have you got to put into such large pots?'

Masilo said to her, 'Just listen to me and do as I command you, then you will see.'

When his wife was ready with the pots, Masilo took his bird out of his bag, and said, 'Make milk for my children to drink.'

Then the bird filled all the beer pots with milk.

They commenced drinking, and when they were finished, Masilo warned his children, saying, 'Beware that you do not tell anybody of this bird, not even one of your companions.'

The children swore to him that they would not tell anybody.

Masilo and his family then lived upon the milk of this bird. The people were surprised when they saw him and his family. They said, 'Why are the people at Masilo's house so fat? He is poor, but now that his garden has appeared he and his children are so fat!'

They tried to watch and see what Masilo was eating, but they could never find out at all.

One morning, Masilo and his wife went to work as usual in their garden. Around the middle of the day, the children of that town met together to play. They met just in front of Masilo's house. While they were playing, the others said to Masilo's children, 'Why are you so fat while we remain so thin?'

Masilo's children answered, 'Are we then fat? We thought we were thin just as you are.'

They would not tell the others the cause of their good nourishment. The others continued to press them, saying, 'We won't tell anybody.'

Then the children of Masilo said, 'There is a bird in our father's house which makes milk.'

The others said, 'Please show us the bird.'

Masilo's children went into the house and took the bird out of the secret place where their father had placed it. They ordered it as their father did to make milk, and it made milk, which their companions drank, for they were very hungry.

After drinking the children said, 'Let it dance for us,' and they set it free from the place where it was tied.

The bird began to dance in the house, but one of the children said, 'This place is too confined for it.' So they took it outside the house. While they were laughing and enjoying themselves, the bird flew away, leaving them in great dismay.

Masilo's children said, 'Our father will kill us this day; we must go after the bird.'

So they followed it and continued going after it the whole day long. For when they were at a distance, the bird would sit still for a long while, but when they approached, it would fly away.

When the digging gangs returned from digging late that afternoon, the people of the town cried for their children, for they did not know what had become of them. When Masilo went into the house and could not find his bird, he knew where the children were; but he did not tell any of the other parents. He was very sorry about the bird, for he knew that he had lost his source of food.

When evening set in, the children wanted to return to their homes, but there came a rain storm with heavy thunder, and they were very much afraid. Among them was a brave boy, named Mosemanyanamatong, who encouraged them and said, 'Do not be afraid. I can command a house to build itself.'

The children said, 'Please command it.'

Mosemanyanamatong said, 'House appear!' and it appeared, and also wood for a fire. Then the children entered the house and made a large fire and began to roast some wild roots, which they dug out of the ground.

While they were roasting the roots and making merry, there came a big cannibal, and they heard his voice saying, 'Mosemanyanamatong, give me some of the wild roots you have.'

The children were afraid; the brave boy said to the girls and the other boys, 'Give me some of yours.' They gave him some, and he threw the roots outside.

While the cannibal was still eating, the children stole out of the house and fled. The cannibal finished eating the roots and then pursued them. When he approached, the children scattered more roots upon the ground, and while the cannibal was picking them up and eating, they again fled.

At length, they came among mountains, where trees were growing. The girls were already very tired, so they all climbed up into a tall tree. The cannibal came there and tried to cut the tree down with his long sharp finger-nail.

Then the brave boy said to the girls, 'While I am singing, you must continue saying, "Tree be strong, Tree be strong!"'

Mosemanyanamatong sang this song:

It is foolish,
It is foolish to be a traveller,
And to go on a journey
With the blood of girls upon one!
While we were roasting wild roots
A great darkness fell upon us.
It was not darkness,
It was awful gloom!

While he was singing, there came a great bird which hovered over them, and said, 'Hold fast to me.'

The children held fast to the bird and it flew away with them, and took them to their own town.

It was midnight when it arrived there, and it sat down at the gate of Mosemanyanamatong's mother's house.

In the morning, when that woman came out of her house, she took ashes and cast them upon the bird, for she said, 'This bird knows where our children are.'

At midday, the bird sent word to the chief, saying, 'Command all your people to spread mats on all the paths.'

The chief commanded them to do so. Then the bird brought all the children out, and the people were greatly delighted.

The Child with a Moon on his Chest

Translated from seSotho by SM Guma; reworked by Elana Bregin
From: SM Guma's *The Form, Content and Technique of Oral Traditional Literature
in Southern Sotho* (1980)

It is said it was a great chief, Bulane. He had two wives. Now one of them did
not have any children, while the other one had them. This chief had a moon
on his chest. One of these women was very much loved by Bulane; it is the
one who had children. He ill-treated the one who was without children.

After a short while, the childless woman conceived. A few months passed
and it was time for her to be confined. The woman who had children came
and helped her. She gave birth to a child who had a moon on his chest.
Now the midwife took it, and threw it behind the pots in the cupboard. A
mouse quickly took it, and went into its hole with it. The baby's mother was
unconscious. The midwife quickly went outside. She found a puppy in a
hen's nest, and quickly returned with it and put it next to the child's mother.
Then she shook her. 'Wake up and see; you have given birth to a dog.' And
this childless woman was disappointed when she found she had given birth
to a dog.

Then this midwife quickly went outside to Bulane and said, 'Your wife has
given birth to a dog.' Bulane was greatly disappointed. He said, 'Go and take
that dog and throw it away.' They took it and threw it away. And the poor
little woman came out of her hut disappointed.

A few days passed and Bulane's (senior) wife came to that hut. She found
the mouse having taken out the child with a moon on his chest and playing
with it. She was shocked and said, 'I thought that child had died!'

Then she quickly went out and said to her husband, Bulane, 'You can see,
my lord, I am really ill. Divining bones say before I can get well, you must burn
down your wife's hut, this one who has just given birth to a dog. Bulane
answered his wife and said, 'It is well that it should be burnt down,' because he
loved her very much. Now this woman thought that if the hut were burnt by
the fire, the child would die, the mouse would also be burnt by the fire,
and she would no longer see this child with a moon on his chest, because she
wanted to destroy it.

The mouse overheard the secret of the senior wife and the chief, and
quickly left the hut with the child with a moon on his chest, and went into a
donga with it. The chief went out the next day and burnt that hut. The *mofuma-*

45

hadi was convinced she had destroyed the child and the mouse, and would not see them again.

A few days passed and the *mofumahadi* went to get cow-dung from the cattle kraal. She found the child with a moon on his chest sitting under a cow. She was shocked and said, 'What can I do to kill him?' When she left the cattle kraal, she moaned aloud and said she was very sick. The chief asked her, 'What are you suffering from? What can I do that you should be well again?'

She said, 'Divining bones say you should pull down your cattle kraal. It is only then that I shall get well.'

The mouse overheard the secret of the chief and the senior wife. It went out with the child and took him to a house of traders, *bahwebi*. When the cattle kraal was pulled down, the child with a moon on his chest was not there. The mouse parted with him there, and went to its home. One day certain people went to exchange goods, *bapatsa*. Now a certain man from Bulane's village also went there to buy. He found this young man, who had something shining on his chest. He returned home and told Bulane about the handsome young man he had seen with a moon on his chest. Bulane left there and then to go and see him. On arrival, he asked him, 'Whose child are you? How did you come here?'

The young man with a moon on his chest explained to him and said, 'My mother gave birth to me, and my father's wife threw me into a cupboard, *mohaolwana*. Then the mouse received me, went with me into its hole and there looked after me. My father's wife took a dog, and said my mother had given birth to it.' Bulane started examining him closely, *qamakisisa*, and remembered that his senior wife had said the other wife had given birth to a dog. Now the child with a moon on his chest told him how he had gone to the cattle kraal, until the mouse fled with him, and took him to the house of traders.

Then his father opened his chest, in order to see whether he was really the child with a moon on his chest. He found that it was the child with a moon on his chest. He took him and went home with him. He hid him in his hut. He called a big *pitso*, and invited all his people to it. Cattle were slaughtered and numerous pots of beer brewed. He said they should spread mats on the ground from where he had hidden the child with a moon on his chest. Then he took him out and brought him to this great *pitso*. He showed him to the people and explained how his senior wife had treated him (Bulane) in a treacherous way. Then the mother of the child with a moon on his chest was made to take off her rags and was dressed in beautiful clothes. And the child with a moon on his chest was made a chief by his father. As for the woman who had children without a moon on the chest, it was said she is a wicked person, *molotsana*. She was given her belongings, *thepa*, and it was said she must leave and return to her original home.

The Man who Threw Away his Bread

Translated from isiZulu by Henry Callaway; reworked by Elana Bregin
From: H Callaway's *Nursery Tales, Traditions and Histories of the Zulus* (1868)

This is the tale of a man who was going on a journey carrying his bread with him. He set out, having already eaten at home; and not knowing how to provide sufficient bread for himself, he took a large quantity. He thought he would eat it all. He ate, until he could eat no more. He could not tell what to do with the rest of the bread. He did not say to himself: 'Let me carry it; perhaps in front there is hunger, and I shall want food; perhaps I may meet a man who is hungry.' There were no such thoughts. But through being satisfied, the thought of taking care of the bread became lost; he did not wish to carry it, because he was then full; he saw one thing only that would enable him to go easily. He threw the bread on the lower side of the path, and so went on no longer burdened. He did not return by that path for many days. Mice took the bread, and ate it all up.

It came to pass when the land died, it being killed by famine, as he was going by that way, going and digging up roots (for there was no corn left; roots only were now eaten), the path made him remember the bread. He saw it still there; a year was as it were a day of yesterday. He was at once summoned by the place by merely seeing it, and said, 'This is the very place where I threw away my bread.' He arrived at the place; he saw where the bread had fallen; he said, 'It fell yonder.' He ran to find it. But he did not find it. He began to look earnestly in the long grass, for it was very thick; he searched, feeling with his hands in the thick grass until some time had elapsed. He rose up, and thought, saying: '*Hau!* What happened after I threw away the bread? For I say, I do not yet forget the place where I threw it. No, surely; there is no other; it is this very place.' He stooped down and searched. For whilst he is thus seeking he has gained strength, and is now strong through his efforts. 'Though I am hungry, my hunger will end; I may find my bread.' At length he was confused, he went up again to the path, he found the place where he first began to stand, and he said, 'I passed over all this place before I threw it away.' For where he threw it away, there was an ant heap; he saw that, and said, 'Ah, when I was here, I did thus!' He said this, imitating with his arm; the arm goes in the direction in which he threw the bread. And now he runs quickly, following the direction of the arm. He came to the place, and at once felt about; he did not find the bread. He went back again, and said: '*Hau!* What has become of it? Since I threw it exactly here; for no man saw me, I being quite alone.' He ran. At length the time for digging roots had passed; he went home without anything; he had dug no roots. He now became faint again, because he had not found the bread.

And that man is still living, yonder by the sea. The man told the tale when the country was at peace, and the famine at an end. It was a cause of laughter that conduct of his, to all who heard it, and they said: 'So-and-so, sure enough famine makes a man dark-eyed. Did you ever see bread, which was thrown away one year, found in another, still good to eat?'

He said: 'Sirs, famine does not make a man wise. I thought I was seeking wisely, and should find it. But famine takes away wisdom. And for my part, through my hunger, I believed – in truth – that I should find it; for I was alone, there being no man with me. But in fact that was the means of increasing my want, until I was nearly dead.'

//KABBO

'A story is like the wind'

Translated from the click language by Bleek and Lloyd; reworked by Elana Bregin
First recorded c1866
From: WHI Bleek and Lucy C Lloyd's *Specimens of Bushman Folklore* (1911)

CAPTURE AND JOURNEY TO CAPE TOWN

[*On being accused by a white farmer of having stolen a sheep*] [ed.]

My wife was there, I was there, my son was there; my son's wife was there, carrying a little child on her back; my daughter was there, also carrying a little child; and my daughter's husband was there. We were like this in number. Therefore, the Kafirs [African policemen] took us when we were like this, while we were not numerous; the Kafirs took us while we were not numerous.

I was eating a springbok when the Kafir took me; he bound my arms. My son and I, together with my daughter's husband, were put into the wagon while the wagon stood still. We went away, bound, to the magistrate. We who were in the wagon ran along swiftly upon the road while our wives walked along upon their feet. We ran, leaving them; we altogether ran, leaving them behind.

We went to talk with the magistrate; we remained there with him. The Kafirs took us away to the gaol at night. We had to put our legs into the stocks; another white man laid a piece of wood upon our legs. We slept, stretched out in the stocks. The day broke, while our legs were in the stocks. Early, we took our legs out of the stocks to eat meat; then we again put our legs into the stocks; we sat, while our legs were in the stocks. We lay down, we slept, while our legs were inside the stocks. We arose, we smoked, while our legs were inside the stocks. The people boiled sheep's flesh, while our legs were in the stocks.

The magistrate came to take our legs out of the stocks, because he wished that we might sit comfortably while we ate; for it was his sheep that we were eating.

The Korannas came to join us. They also came to put their legs into the stocks; they slept while their legs were in the stocks. They were put into another gaol's house. While we were eating the magistrate's sheep, the Korannas also ate it with us. We all ate it together, we and the Korannas.

We left that place and went to Victoria. On the way, we ate sheep. Our wives ate their sheep on the way too, as they came with us to Victoria. We came to Victoria to roll stones, as we worked on the road. We lifted stones with our chests. We rolled great stones. We carried earth with a big handbarrow that needed many Bushmen to lift it. We loaded the wagon with earth and we pushed it. Other people – Bushmen people – walked along with us. We were pushing the wagon's wheels; we were pushing. We poured the earth down and we pushed it back. We again loaded it, we and the Korannas. Other Korannas were carrying the handbarrow. Bushmen were with the Korannas; they were also carrying earth upon the handbarrow.

We again had our arms bound to the wagon chain; we walked along to Beaufort, fastened to the wagon, under the hot sun. Our arms were set free on the road. We got tobacco from the magistrate; we smoked it in a pipe of sheep's bones as we went along. We came into Beaufort gaol. The rain fell upon us while we were there. Early the next morning, our arms were made fast and we were bound again. We splashed into the water; we splashed, passing through the water in the riverbed. We walked upon the road. We walked, following behind the wagon until, still bound, we came to the Breakwater [prison]. On the way there, we ate sheep again. We came to work at the Breakwater.

Intended Return Home

[*After being entrusted by the Cape governor to the 'guardianship' of the linguists Bleek and Lloyd who, having learnt the oral click-language of //Kabbo and other San prisoners, created a written script and then translated the stories told to them into English. //Kabbo, who in the records of Cape authority remained a Bushman convict, had no hope of attaining the hunting gun on his return home.*] [ed.]

You know that I sit waiting for the moon to turn back for me, so that I may return to my place; so that I may listen to all the people's stories when I visit them – the Flat [plain] Bushmen's stories from their own place and other places too. These are the stories which they tell while the sun grows warm. I want to return to my place so that I may sit in the warm sun listening to the stories which come from a distance. Then, I shall get hold of a story from yonder, because the stories float out from a distance, while the sun is a little warm. I feel that I must visit there, so that I can talk with my fellow men. For I do work here at women's household work. My fellow men are those who listen to stories which float along from afar; they listen to stories from other places. But I am here; I do not obtain stories because I do not visit, I do not hear the stories which float along. I feel that the people of another place are here; they do not possess my stories. They do not talk my language. They visit their like, for they are 'work's people'; they are those who work to keep the houses in order. They work at food, so that the food may grow for them, so that they may get food which is good, which is new food.

The Flat Bushmen go to each other's huts and sit smoking in front of them. They obtain stories there, because they are used to visiting each other; for they are 'smoking's people'. As for me, I am waiting for the moon to turn back for me, so that I may set my feet forward on the path. I only await the moon; then, I will tell my Master that this is the time when I should be sitting among my fellow men, those who walking meet their like. I ought to visit; I ought to talk with my fellow men; for I work here together with women; I do not talk with them, for they merely send me to work.

I must first sit a little, cooling my arms so that the fatigue may go out of them. I must merely sit and listen, watching for a story that I want to hear, waiting for it to float into my ear. Those are the people's stories to which I will listen with all my ears, while I sit silent. I must wait, listening behind me along the road, where my name floats; my three names (Jantje, /Uhi-ddoro and //Kabbo, meaning 'Dream') float behind me along the road to my place. I will go and sit down there and, listening, I will turn my ears backwards to where my feet's heels have stepped, and wait for a story to travel to me along the road. For a story is like the wind. It is wont to float along to another place. In this way, our names pass through to the people of that place, even though they do not perceive our bodies going along. For our names are those which, floating, reach a different place.

The mountains lie between the two roads. A man's name passes behind the backs of the mountains, those names with which he returns. The road curves around his place, and the people who dwell at another place hear him coming. Their ears go, listening, to meet the returning man's names. The people know all his names. He will examine the place he returns to. For the trees of that place will seem to be handsome, because they have grown tall while the man of the place was not there to see them and walk among them. For he, //Kabbo, came to live at a different place; his place it is not. For it was this way with him that people brought him to another place, so that he should first come to work there for a little while. He thinks of his own place, and longs to return there.

He only awaits the return of the moon. He waits for the moon to go around, so that he may return home, so that he may examine the water pits, those at which he drank. He will work, putting the old hut in order, gathering his children together, so that they may work, putting the water in order for him; for he went away, leaving the place, while strangers were those who walked there. Their place it is not; for it was //Kabbo's father's father's place. And when //Kabbo's father's father died, //Kabbo's father was the one who possessed it. And when //Kabbo's father died, //Kabbo's elder brother was the one who possessed it; then //Kabbo's elder brother died, and //Kabbo possessed the place. //Kabbo married when he was grown up, bringing !Kuobba-an to the place, because he felt that he was alone there; thereafter, he

51

grew old with his wife at this place, the place that is called //gubo, or Bitter-pits. His children's children now were married. They fed themselves without help, they talked with understanding. //Kabbo's children placed huts there for themselves. They made their huts nicely; my hut stood alone in the middle, while my children dwelt on either side.

Because my elder brother's child Betje married first and my own children married afterwards, their cousin's child grew up first. She married, leaving me; she who had come to me from afar. It was I who brought her up and fed her. Her father was not the one who fed her. For her father died, leaving her. I was the one who went and fetched her when her mother also had just died; I brought her to my home. I had not seen her father die or her mother die, I only heard the story. And then I went to fetch Betje to come and live with us. For at that time, I was still a young man, and I was fleet in running. So I thought that she would get plenty of food, which I would be able to give her. She would eat with my own child, who was still an only child. And they would both grow well, going out to play near the hut, because they were both eating the game I shot for them. For I was young and fresh for running; I could catch things by running after them.

I used to run and catch a hare. I brought it to my home in my bag while the sun was hot. I had not seen any springbok, but I saw a hare. First, I used to shoot my arrows to send up a bustard. I would put it into the bag and bring it home. My wife would come to pluck it at home. She boiled it in the pot so that we might drink the soup. The next day, I would hunt the hare. I would be peeping about in the shade of the bushes and I would flush it out by shooting arrows, so that the children might eat. I would make it spring up from its form where it was lying and run away so that I could chase it. For the springbok were all gone away. For that reason, I was shooting hares. By chasing them, I would force them to run about in the noonday sun until they died from the heat, until they were 'burnt dead' by the sun. For I remembered that the hare does not drink; it eats dry bushes and does not drink, putting its own water upon the dry bushes which it crunches. Therefore, it remains thirsty where it dwells. It sits in the summer heat and does not drink, because it does not understand water pans, so it does not go to the water to drink. It waits, sitting in the sun.

Therefore, I chase it in the sun, so that the burning sun may kill it for me; so that I may eat it, dead from the sun. For it was I who chased it, while it ran along in fear of me. In fear it lay down to die in the sun, because it saw me following it and it ran about in the sun until it became dry. It did not stop to walk, so that it could look behind it. It ran about when it was tired; it was obliged to run about even at the point of death. Therefore, it went to lie down to die, because fatigue had killed it while it ran about in the heat; for this was the summer sun, which was very hot. The ground was very hot and burned its feet.

I would go and pick it up as it lay dead. I laid it in the arrows' bag. Then, I would look for another hare. This too would spring up running into the sun; being afraid, it would run through the sun while I ran following it. I would have to keep going until the sun could kill it by burning it. Then I would go and pick it up when it lay dead. Sitting on the ground, I would break its four legs and put it in the bag. It seemed that another hare might dwell in its vicinity. And so I would go to search around the neighbourhood of the hare's form. For the first hare had seemed to be married. Seeking around, I must now look for the female hare, so that I might also chase that. When I had unloosened and laid down the bag, I would chase it with my body, running very fast. If I felt myself becoming thirsty, I would know that I could go and drink at home. For the children would have fetched water for me. My wife used to send them to the water, knowing that I had walked about in the sun when the sun was very hot. I did this because the children needed meat, because I was worried that too much *gambro* would kill my children.

After the rain fell, I would look around for a pair of ostriches which like to seek the water along the Har Rivier. Going carefully around them, I must descend into the Har Rivier and, stooping low, steal up to them inside the riverbed. I must lie on my stomach in the riverbed; so that I may shoot my arrows at them. For the western ostriches, seeking water, come back to drink the new water after the rain has fallen.

And so I must sit waiting for the Sundays to pass that I remain here, on which I continue to teach you. I will not wait again for another moon; for this moon is the one about which I told you. Therefore, I desire that it should do as I have said and return for me. For I have sat waiting for the promised boots, that I must put on to walk in, which are strong for the road. For the sun will go along above me, burning strongly. And the earth will become hot, while I am still only halfway. I must go together with the warm sun, while the ground is hot. For a little road it is not; it is a great road and it is long. I should reach my place when the trees are dry. For I shall walk there, letting the flowers become dry while I still follow the path.

Then, autumn will quickly be upon us there, when I am sitting at my own place. For I shall not go to any other places; I must remain at my own place, the name of which I have told my Master; he knows it — he knows, because he has put it down. And my name is plain beside it. It is there at my place that I will sit waiting for the gun; he will send the gun to me there, in a cart which, running, will bring the gun to me. He must know that I have not forgotten; he must send the gun so that my body may remain quiet, and not hungry, as it was when I was with him; so that I may shoot to feed myself. For starvation was the reason that I was caught and bound. It was on account of starvation's food that I was caught when, starving, I turned back from following the sheep. Therefore I have lived with my Master, in order that I might get a gun from him, that I might possess it. So that I might shoot and feed myself, and not eat my neighbours' food; with a gun I would be able to eat my own game.

A gun is that which takes care of an old man; a gun is that with which we kill the springbok which go through the cold wind. We go to eat in the cold wind. Satisfied with food, we lie down in our huts in the cold wind. The gun is strong against the wind. It satisfies a man with food in the very middle of the cold.

PULVERMACHER [AG DE SMIDT]

Prayer of Titus Tokaan

Translated from Dutch / Afrikaans by Sharon Meyering
First published c1893

Hallelujah! ... Lord; you have behaved very well recently. Look at the grass! ... Look at the calendula! ... Look at the plentiful water in the ditch! ... Look at the cattle! ... They all want to burst out of their skin with happiness. Look how they run, kicking their back legs high in the air; just like young girls dancing energetically.

People are looking at their corn, their oxen, their potatoes, their sheep, their beans, their pumpkin, their peas. Everything is in abundance, and their children are pot-bellied from the fat of the earth. Yes, everyone, except for Jeremiah, his children are not!

We want to acknowledge, Lord, that you carried out your plans well, and that you did your best this year; yet Lord, you did not keep your word with Jeremiah. Jeremiah, he has behaved well recently. He gave up swearing, and has avoided women, every week he puts his three pence in the church plate, and he hasn't given you any trouble in a long time. And look what you did, Lord? ... You sent your lightning and struck dead all Jeremiah's milk goats. Jeremiah, Lord, he doesn't feel good about these things. When he was in trouble, you let his best lead ox die! It was not at all nice to reprimand him in such a fatherly manner, and for his ungodliness you let his small Lukas die quietly in the soap pot. Now, that was also unmannerly; and look now? ... There, the vultures are eating all his milk goats. Now just imagine, Lord, that Jeremiah was in your place: What would he do? Would he let your children and your goats die? ... But Lord we must continue under your rules and above all else we must forgive all mistakes. Hallelujah!

WILLIAM CHARLES SCULLY

Umtagati

From: *Kafir Stories* (1895)

'The great witch-doctor has come, and all
Sit trembling with cold and fear
As they list to the words from his lips that fall, –
The words all shrink to hear.
Lo! Look at the seer as he whirls and leaps
The awestruck circle within,
Where each one shudders, and silence keeps
As he thinks of the untold sin.

'On his head is a cap of dark brown hair, –
The skin of a bear-baboon,
And the tigers' teeth on his throat, else bare,
Jangle a horrible tune;
The serpents' skins and the jackals' tails,
Hang full around his hips,
And a living snake from his girdle trails,
And around each bare limb slips.'

The Witch-Doctor

I

The motive and controlling factors of great issues are not always recognised by those most interested, neither does honour nor yet reward always fall to those who best deserve or earn them. In proof of the foregoing propositions the following narrative is adduced.

Teddy's full name was Edmund Mortimer Morton. He was a Government official holding the appointment of clerk to the Resident Magistrate of Mount Loch, which district, as everybody knows, is situated in the territory of Bantuland East, and just on the border of Pondoland.

Vooda was a native Police Constable attached to the Mount Loch establishment.

Teddy's age was twenty-six, but he looked several years younger. He was a pleasant-looking little chap, about five feet four inches in height, slightly built, with blue eyes, yellow hair and an incipient moustache upon which he bestowed a great deal of attention. His hobby was popular chemistry. This he indulged in, greatly to the entertainment of his friends and the detriment of his hands, which were generally discoloured in a manner that defied soap. He lived in a little hut just outside the village. This hut consisted of one room, and was shaped like a round pagoda. It had a pointed roof and projecting eaves made of Tambookie grass. The walls were of sod-work, plastered over and whitewashed. Here Teddy dwelt – taking his meals elsewhere – and experimented in parlour-magic to his heart's content.

Vooda was a constable. He was a short, stout man, with a deep, although not wide knowledge of human nature; not wide only for lack of experience. He had dwelt all his life amongst the natives surrounding Mount Loch, and he could read them like so many books of Standard I. He could, moreover, tell by looking at a witness in court, whether that witness were speaking truth or lying, and the magistrate recognised and utilised this faculty. Vooda and Teddy were great friends, Vooda taking a lively and intelligent interest in Teddy's experiments.

Everyone knows that in the early part of 1894, Pondoland, the last independent native State south of Natal, was annexed to Cape Colony. Much to the general surprise, the annexation was effected peacefully, but for some months afterwards the greatest care had to be exercised in dealing with the Pondos. The people generally were glad of the change from the harsh, arbitrary, and irresponsible rule of the native chiefs to the settled and equitable conditions of civilised government; but the chiefs gave trouble. They naturally would not, without struggling and agitating, submit to the loss of power and prestige which they sustained, and they bitterly resented being no longer permitted to 'eat up' those who annoyed them. Now, the instincts of clannishness and loyalty are so strong amongst the Kaffirs, that even against what they well know to be their own vital interests, they will follow the most cruel and rapacious tyrant, so long as he is their hereditary tribal chieftain, into rebellion.

Now, the Kwesa clan of Pondos dwelt just on the boundary of Mount Loch, and within thirty miles of the Magistracy. The head of this clan, a chief named Sololo, had not objected to the annexation, and was consequently looked upon as well-affected towards the Government. But within a few months after the annexation, a serious difficulty arose between the authorities and this man. One of his followers quarrelled with another, and after the time-honoured local custom, assuaged his feelings by means of a spear-thrust, which had a fatal result. The murdered man was one whom Sololo disliked, whereas, on the other hand, the murderer was one whom the chief delighted to honour. Consequently, when the magistrate demanded the surrender of the culprit for the purpose of dealing with him according to law, Sololo refused delivery, and couched his refusal in an extremely insolent and rebellious message.

Cajolements, remonstrances, and threats were of no avail; Sololo remained obstinate. His tone, however, somewhat changed; he sent polite, but evasive and unsatisfactory replies to all messages on the subject. The Chief Magistrate was at his wits' end. Of course the law had to be vindicated, but were an armed force to be sent against Sololo, the odds were ten to one that within twenty-four hours signal fires would be blazing on every hill, and the war-cry sounding from one end of Pondoland to the other. The Chief Magistrate's native name was 'Indabeni', which means 'The one of counsel'. He was a man of vast experience in respect of the natives, and moreover, he did not belong to that highly moral, but sometimes inconvenient class of officials who are known as 'the hide-bound'; that is to say, his ideas ranged beyond the length of the longest piece of red tape in his office, and he knew for a certainty that things existed which could not conveniently be wrapped up in foolscap paper. He was, moreover, one who trusted much to the effect of his own considerable personal influence, and he believed in utilising the talents of such of his subordinates as possessed faculties similar to his own in this respect.

Indabeni had taken Vooda's measure accurately. He knew the Constable to have a persuasive tongue, to be honest, loyal, and discreet, and, above all, to possess that nameless and almost indescribable quality of imparting trustfulness in those with whom he came in contact.

One afternoon a telegram marked 'confidential' came from Indabeni to the Resident Magistrate of Mount Loch. The purport of the message was that Vooda should go to Sololo and talk quietly to him, endeavouring by means of persuasion to effect a compliance with the reasonable demands of Government. Teddy, being in the fullest confidence of his Chief, was present when instructions were accordingly given to Vooda, who was directed to start early next morning for the kraal of the Chief of the Kwesas, in Pondoland.

When the offices were closed for the day, Teddy went home to his hut, and it was noticed by one who met him on the road that his manner was very pre-occupied, and his walk unusually slow. Shortly afterwards he was seen to stroll over to the police camp, and go straight to Vooda's hut.

At eight o'clock that evening Vooda visited Teddy's dwelling, and a long and serious conversation ensued. This was varied by a series of experiments of a nature so striking that even Vooda was startled. At about ten o'clock a stranger passing noticed strange flashes lighting up the back of the hut behind the reed fence. Shortly before eleven Vooda returned to camp, carrying a small satchel which contained a packet of lycopodium powder, a piece of potassium about as large as a walnut, and a number of whitish lumps about an inch in diameter, such as are known amongst practitioners of parlour magic variously as 'serpents' eggs' or 'Pharaoh's serpents'.

II

At daylight next morning Vooda left the police camp, but it was late in the afternoon when he reached the kraal of Sololo. He found a number of strangers there, including Shasha, the 'inyanga', or war-doctor. The men, all of whom were armed, were sitting on the ground in a half-circle. Before them stood a number of large earthen pots of beer. Vooda, being an old friend of the Chief, was invited to sit down and drink, so, after removing the saddle from his horse, he joined the party. He soon saw, however, that his presence had imported an element of restraint. He was careful as yet not to allude to the business upon which he had come. Later on others began to arrive, some carrying guns, some spears, and some assegais. It was plain that an important discussion was on hand, and that Vooda's presence was unwelcome. The beer was not in sufficient quantities to cause intoxication, but nevertheless all were somewhat mellow when the sun went down.

Shortly afterwards, Sololo asked the visitor point blank 'where he was thinking of'. This was an unusual thing to do under the circumstances, such a question to a visitor being held amongst natives to be discourteous and sug- gestive of inhospitality.

Vooda replied to the effect that he had an important matter to discuss with the Chief, and asked Sololo to grant him a private interview.

Now Sololo, having had experience of Vooda's persuasive tongue and knack of casuistry, did not wish to argue the point – knowing, as he did full well, the object of Vooda's visit – and at once made up his mind that he would not see the glib-tongued constable alone.

'Son of my father,' he said, 'what you have to say, let it be said before these my councillors and friends.'

Vooda saw there was no chance of a private discussion, and determined therefore to play his game boldly and in public. The dusk of evening was just setting in, and some women had kindled a bright fire.

'My Chief,' he said, 'I come with the words of Indabeni, who has chosen me because he knows I am your younger brother' [figurative].

'Indabeni is a great man,' said Sololo; 'he has eyes all round his head. His words are good to hear – speak them, son of my father.'

'Indabeni's heart is heavy, my Chief, because you, the leopard, are placing yourself in the path of the buffalo, which is the Government. Men have told Indabeni that you refuse to deliver to the Magistrate one who has done wrong.'

'The leopard may stand on one side and tear the flank of the buffalo as he passes. He may then hide in the caves of the rocks where the buffalo cannot follow,' said Sololo, sententiously.

'The buffalo may call the wolves to his aid to drive the leopard from his cave,' rejoined Vooda, developing the allegory further; 'but why will you not give up the wrong-doer to the Magistrate?'

'Why must I give up my friend to be choked with a rope?' said Sololo, excitedly. 'He has not slain a white man, but one of my own people. Government must leave him to be punished according to the law of the native. If one of my tribe slays a white man, I will deliver up the slayer.'

'But you know what the Government is, my Chief – it is over all of us. Even Indabeni himself has to do as it tells him.'

'Indabeni is not a Pondo, neither am I Indabeni,' said Sololo, appealing, with a look, to the audience.

'Yebo, Yebo, Ewe – E-hea,' shouted all the men.

'I did not ask Government for its laws,' continued the Chief. 'U-Sessellodes [the native attempt at pronouncing the name of Mr Cecil Rhodes, Premier of the Cape Colony] came here and said in a loud voice that we all belonged to him. We were surprised, and could not think or speak. Besides, who listens to the bleating of a goat when an angry bull bellows? Now we have thought and spoken together, and we can also fight. I will never give up my friend to be choked with a rope.'

'E-hea,' shouted the audience.

'My Chief,' said Vooda, 'your words are like milk flowing from a great black cow ten days after she has calved, but there is one thing you have not seen, but which I have seen and trembled at.'

'What is this thing that frightens a man who is the father of children?'

'The magic (umtagati) of U-Sessellodes, which he has taught to Indabeni – the terrible magic wherewith he overthrew Lo Bengula and the Matabele.'

'We, also, have our magic,' said Sololo, glancing at Shasha, the war-doctor.

Shasha came forward in a half-crouching attitude, and approached Vooda, who appeared to be very much impressed. The war-doctor's appearance was startling enough. He was an elderly man of hideous aspect. On his head he wore a high cap of baboon skin. Slung around his neck, waist, elbows, wrists, knees, and ankles were all sorts of extraordinary things – cowrie and tortoise-shells, teeth and claws of various beasts of prey, strips of skin from all kinds of animals, inflated gall bladders, bones, and pieces of wood. In his hand he carried a bag made by cutting the skin of a wild cat around the neck, and then tearing it off the body as one skins an eel. Out of this he drew a long, living, green snake (inushwa, the boomslang), which he hung over his shoulder, where it began to coil about, darting out its forked tongue. As Shasha advanced quivering towards Vooda in short, abrupt, springs, all the things hanging about him clashed and rattled together. He bent down and beat the ground with the palms of his hands and the soles of his feet, making the while a low rumbling in his throat, the apple of which worked up and down. His eyes glared and his nostrils dilated. The snake hissed, and wound itself round his neck and limbs. The whole audience appeared to be struck with superstitious dread.

Shasha suddenly drew himself straight up, and chanted in a sing-song voice, rattling his charms at every period:

'I am the ruler of the baboons and the master of the owls. I talk to the wild cat in the bush. I call Tikoloshe (a water spirit) out of the river in the night-time and ask him questions. I make sickness do my bidding on men and cattle. I drive it away when I like. I can bring blight to the crops, and stop the milk of cows. I can, by my magic medicines, find out the wicked ones who do these things. I alone can look upon Icanti (a fabulous serpent) and not die. I know the mountain where Impandulu (the Lightning Bird) builds its nest. I can make men invulnerable in battle with my medicines, and I can cause the enemies of my Chief to run like a bushbuck pursued by dogs.'

The speech ended, Shasha again bowed down, quivering and contorting, beat the ground with his hands and the soles of his feet, and then sprang aside into the darkness.

Sololo looked at Vooda as though he would say, 'What do you think of that: is he not a most terribly potent war-doctor?' All the other men looked extremely terrified.

Dead silence reigned for a few moments, and then Vooda spoke:

'O Chief, the magic of your war-doctor is indeed dreadful to behold, but, believe me, the magic of U-Sessellodes and Indabeni is stronger, and I can prove it.'

This caused a murmur of incredulity and indignation. The magic paraphernalia of the war-doctor rattled ominously in the gloom.

'U-Sessellodes,' continued Vooda, ' has found the Lightning Bird sitting upon its nest, and plucked its feathers; he has discovered how to make water burn, and he has robbed the cave of Icanti of its eggs, which he can strew over the land to hatch in the sun, and produce snakes that will kill all who see them. These secrets he has taught to Indabeni, and Indabeni has taught them to me so that I might warn you, and having warned, prove the truth of my words.'

At this a loud 'ho, ho,' accompanied by a rattling noise, was heard from the war-doctor. Sololo laughed sarcastically. Several of the audience did the same. Then Sololo said:

'Are we children, to believe these things?'

'My Chief,' said Vooda, impressively, 'you are not a child, neither is Indabeni; as you know — nor is the potent war-doctor, nor are any of these great men (madoda makulu) that I see around me. For that matter, neither am I a child. I have said that I can prove my words, and I say so again.'

'Prove them, then,' said Sololo.

'Three things will I do to show the magic of U-Sessellodes, which he has taught to Indabeni — I will show you a feather of the Lightning Bird, I will make water burn like dry wood, and I will produce some of the eggs of Icanti and make them, when touched with fire, hatch into young serpents before your eyes.'

There was not a breath of wind. Vooda seized a small firebrand, and stepped a few yards away from the fire. He held the firebrand in his left hand, and put his right into one of the pockets of his tunic. This pocket contained a quantity of loose lycopodium powder. He filled his hand with this, waved it over his head several times, and then projected the handful of powder high into the air with a sweeping throw. Then he slowly lifted the firebrand, and as the cloud of powder descended, it ignited with a silent, blinding flash. A loud 'Mawo' from the spectators greeted the success of the experiment.

The war-doctor gave a harsh laugh and shouted that there was no magic in the business, and that the Lightning Bird's plumage was still intact so far as Vooda was concerned; he, the war-doctor, knew how the thing was done, and would presently explain. Sololo and the others murmured amongst themselves.

'Now,' said Vooda, 'I will make water burn with a bright flame like dry wood.'

'You have, no doubt, brought the water with you in a bottle,' said Shasha, the war-doctor, with a sneer in his voice. He was evidently thinking of paraffin.

'No, O most potent controller of baboons,' said Vooda, 'I will, on the contrary, ask you to get me some water for the purpose, in a vessel of your own choice.'

Shasha went to one of the huts and returned with a small earthen pot full of water, which he placed on the ground near the fire.

Vooda took the lump of potassium which he had cut into the form of a large conical bullet, from his pocket, and advanced to where the chief was sitting. He beckoned to the war-doctor to approach, and then said:

'This, O Chief, and O Discourser-with-the-wild-cat, is a new and wonderful kind of lead which U-Sessellodes has dug out of a hole in the ground far deeper than any other hole that was ever made. You will observe that my knife is sharp, and therefore I cut the lead easily. You may see how the metal shines when newly cut. Now, if a bullet such as this be shot into a river, the water blazes up and consumes the land.'

'Give it to me that I may examine it,' said Shasha.

Vooda handed a small paring of the potassium to the war-doctor, saying: 'Be very careful, O You-whom-the-owls-obey-in-the-dark, because it is dangerous stuff.'

Shasha did exactly what Vooda anticipated – he looked carefully at the shred of metal, and lifted it to his mouth, meaning to test it with his teeth. When, however, the potassium touched the saliva, it blazed up, and the unhappy war-doctor spat it out with a fearful yell. His lips and tongue were severely burnt. Sololo and the men, who had seen the flame issuing from Shasha's mouth, were terror-stricken.

Vooda now cut the lump of potassium into several pieces, and these he dropped into the pot of water. The lumps began to flame brilliantly, dancing on the top of the water and gyrating across and around. All the spectators were horribly frightened, and shrank back, their eye-balls starting, and their lips wide apart.

'Now,' said Vooda, who felt that he had practically won the game, 'I will produce the eggs of Icanti, the terrible serpent, and make them hatch out live snakes. Were I to do this without having other greater magic ready wherewith to overcome them, the snakes would kill us all. The only magic stronger than that of Icanti is the magic of the Lightning Bird, so I will drop a feather plucked by U-Sessellodes from the tail of Impandulu upon the snakes as they come out of the eggs, and that will cause them to turn into dust.'

Vooda took five large Pharaoh's serpent-eggs out of his pocket and placed them on a flat stone about a yard from the fire. He then asked Shasha to approach, warning him to be very careful, as the serpents might be dangerous. After the experience with the potassium, such a warning to Shasha was quite a work of supererogation. He came forward with hesitating steps, and stood behind Vooda, watching.

Vooda had a small quantity of lycopodium powder in his left hand. With his right he seized a flaming firebrand, and with this he touched each of the eggs in turn. At once five horrible-looking snakes began uncoiling, blue flame surrounding the spot at which each emerged from its egg. Vooda then shouted loudly, calling on the name of Impandulu, and making mystic passes over the coiling horror with his firebrand. Stretching forth his left hand, he liberated a small cloud of lycopodium powder, which ignited with a brilliant flash. At this, all the spectators leaped to their feet, wildly yelling, and, with the exception of Sololo, who stood still – although the picture of terror – disappeared into the surrounding darkness. For some seconds after the sound of the last footfall had died away, the rattle of Shasha's charms, as he fled, could be heard.

Vooda approached Sololo:

'My Chief, what word am I to carry to Indabeni?'

'Tell Indabeni that the wrong-doer will be given up to the Magistrate to choke with a rope. Yet you need not tell him, because the man will be in the Magistrate's hand before your voice can reach Indabeni's ear.'

And so he was.

Thus was a war averted, and yet neither Vooda nor Teddy Morton ever received any reward for their distinguished services.

J PERCY FITZPATRICK

The Pool

From: *The Outspan: Tales of South Africa* (1897)

Everyone remembers the rush to De Kaap some years ago. How everyone said that everyone else would make fortunes in half no time, and the country would be saved! Well, my brother Jim and I thought we would like to make fortunes too; so we packed our boxes, donned flannel shirts, felt hats and moleskin trousers, with a revolver each carelessly slung at our sides, and started. We intended to dig for about a year or so, and then sell out and live on the interest of our money − £30 000 each would do. It was all cut and dried. I often almost wished it wasn't so certain, as now one hadn't a chance of coming back suddenly and surprising the loved ones at home with the news of a grand fortune.

Full of excitement (certainties notwithstanding) we went down to Kent's Forwarding Store, and met there Mr Harding, whose waggons were loaded for the gold-fields. This was our chance, and we took it.

On November 10, 1883, we crossed Little Sunday's River and outspanned at the foot of Knight's Cutting. The day was close and sultry, and Harding thought it best to lie by until the cool of the evening before attempting the hill. It wasn't much of a cool evening we got after all; except that we had not the scorching rays of the sun beating down upon us, it was no cooler at 10 p.m. than at midday. We were outspanned above the cutting, and the oppressive heat of the day and the sultriness of the evening seemed to have told on our party, and we were all squatted about on the long soft grass, smoking or thinking. Besides my brother and myself there were two young Scotchmen (just out from home) and a little Frenchman. He was a general favourite on account of his inexhaustible good−nature and unflagging high spirits.

We were, as I have said, stretched out on the grass smoking in silence, watching the puffs and rings of smoke melt quietly away, so still was the air. How long we had lain thus I don't know, but I was the first to break the silence by exclaiming:

'What a grand night for a bathe!'

There was no reply to this for some seconds, and then Jim gave an apathetic grunt in courteous recognition of the fact that I had spoken. I subsided again, and there was another long silence − evidently no one wanted to talk; but I had become restless and fidgety under the heat and stillness, and presently I returned to the charge.

'Who's for a bathe?' I asked.

Someone grunted out something about 'no place'.

'Oh yes, there is,' said I, glad of even so much encouragement; and then, turning to Harding, I said:

'I hear the water in the kloof. There is a place, isn't there?'

'Yes,' he answered slowly, 'there is one place, but you wouldn't care to dip there ... It's the Murderer's Pool.'

'The what?' we asked in a breath.

'The Murderer's Pool,' he repeated with such slow seriousness that we at once became interested – the name sent an odd tingle through one. I was already all attention, and during the pause that followed the others closed around and settled themselves to hear the yarn. When he had tantalised us enough with his provoking slowness, Harding began:

'About this time last year – By-the-by, what is the date?' he asked, breaking off.

'The tenth!' exclaimed two or three together.

'By Jove! It's the very day. Yes, that's queer. This very day last year I was out-spanned on this spot, as we are now. I had a lady and gentleman with me as passengers that trip. They were pleasant, accommodating people, and gave us no trouble at all; they used to spend all their time botanising and sketching. On this afternoon Mrs Allan went down to the ravine below to sketch some peculiar bit of rock scenery. I think all ladies sketch when they travel, some more and some less. But Mrs Allan could sketch and paint really well, and often went off alone short distances while her husband stayed to chat with me. She had been gone about twenty minutes when we were startled by a most awful piercing shriek – another, another, and another – and then all was still again. Before the first had died away Allan and I were running at full speed towards where we judged the shrieks to have come from. Fortunately we were right. Down there, a bit to the right, we came upon a fair-sized pool, on the surface of which Mrs Allan was still floating. In a few seconds we had her out and were trying restoratives; and on detecting signs of returning life we carried her up to the waggons. When she became conscious she started up with oh! such a look of horror and fright. I'll never forget it! Seeing her husband, however, and holding his hand, she became calm again, and told us all about it.

'It seems she had been sitting by the side of the stream sketching the pool and the great perpendicular cliff rising out of it. The sunlight was playing on the water, silvering every ripple, and bringing out every detail of the rocks and foliage above. Feathery mosses festooned from cliff to cliff; maidenhair ferns clustered in every nook and crevice; the drops on every leaf and tendril glistened in the setting sun like a thousand diamonds. That's what she told us.

'She sat a few minutes before beginning, watching the varying shades and hues, when, glancing idly into the water, she saw deep, deep down, a sight that horrified her.

'On the rocks at the bottom of the pool lay the body of a gigantic Kaffir, his throat cut from ear to ear, and the white teeth gleaming and grinning at her.

'Instinctively she screamed and ran, and in trying to pass along the narrow ledge she slipped and fell into the water. Had her clothes not buoyed her up she would have been drowned, as when the cold water closed round her it seemed like the clasp of death, and she lost consciousness.'

'Well, what about the nigger?' I asked, for Harding had stopped with the air of one whose tale was told.

'Oh, he was dead right enough – throat cut and assegai through the heart. A fight, I expect.'

'What did you do?' I asked.

'Raked him out and planted him up here somewhere. Let's see – yes, that's the place' – indicating the pile of stones my brother was sitting on.

Jim got up hurriedly; perhaps, as he said, he wanted to look at the place. Yet there was a general laugh at him.

'Did you think he had you, Jim?' I asked innocently.

'Don't you gas, old chap! How about the bathe you were so bent on?'

Merciful heavens! The words fell like a bucket of ice-water on me. I made a ghastly attempt at a laugh, but it was a failure – an utter failure – and of course brought all the others down on me at once.

'The nigger seems to have taken all the bathe out of you, old man,' said one.

'Not at all!' I answered loftily. 'It would take more than that to frighten me.'

Now, why on earth didn't I hold my tongue and let the remark pass? I must needs make an ass of myself by bravado, and now I was in for it. There was a perfect chorus of, 'Go it, old man!' 'Now, isn't that real pluck?' 'Six to four on the nigger!' 'I pet fife pound you not swim agross and dife two times.' This last came from the little French demon, and, being applauded by the company, I took up the bet. The fact is I was nettled by the chaff, and in the heat of the moment did what I regretted a minute later.

As I rose to get my towel I said with cutting sarcasm:

'I don't care about the bet, but I'll just show you that *everyone* isn't afraid of his own shadow; though,' I added forgetfully, 'it's rather an unreasonable time to bathe.'

Here Frenchy struck a stage attitude, and said innocently:

'Ah! vat a night foor ze bade!'

The shout of laughter that greeted this sally was more than enough to decide me, and I went off in search of a towel.

Harding, I could see, did not like the idea, and tried to persuade me to give it up; but that was out of the question.

'Mind,' said he, 'I'm no believer in ghosts; yet,' he added, with rather a forced laugh, 'this is the anniversary, and you know it's uncanny.'

I quite agreed with him, but dared not say so, and I pretended to laugh it off. I was ready in a few moments, and then a rather happy idea, as I thought, struck me, and I called out:

'Who's coming to see that I win my bet?'

'Oh, we know we can trust you, old chap!' said Jim with exaggerated politeness. 'It'd be a pity, you know, to outnumber the ghost.'

'Very well; it's all the same to me. Good-bye! Two dives and a swim across — is that it?'

'Yes, and look out for the nigger!'

'Mind you fish him up!'

'Watch his teeth, Jack!'

'Feel for his throat, you know!'

This latter exclamation came from Jim; it was yelled out as I disappeared down the slope. Jim had not forgotten the incident of the grave, evidently.

I had a half-moon to go by, and a ghostly sort of light it shed. Everything seemed more shadowy and fantastic than usual. Besides this, I had not gone a hundred yards from the waggons before every sound was stilled; not the faintest whisper stirred the air. The crunching of my heavy boots on the gravel was echoed across the creek, and every step grated on my nerves and went like a sword-stab through me.

However, I walked along briskly until the descent became more steep and I was obliged to go more carefully. Down I went, step by step, lower and lower, till I felt the light grow dimmer and dimmer, and then quite suddenly I stepped into gloom and darkness.

This startled me. The suddenness of the change made me shiver a bit and fancy it was cold; but it couldn't have been that, for a moment later the chill had gone and the air was close and sultry. It must have been something else. Still I went down, down, down, along the winding path, and the further I went the more intense seemed the stillness and the deeper the gloom.

Once I stood still to listen; there was not a stir or sound save the trickling of the water below. My heart began to beat rather fast, and my breath seemed heavy. What was it? Surely, I thought, it is not fright? I tried to whistle now as I strode along, but the death-like silence mocked me and choked the breath in my throat.

At last I reached the stream. The path ran along the side of the water among the rocks and ferns. I looked for the pool, but could not see a sign of it. Still I followed the path until it wound along a very narrow ledge of rock.

I was so engrossed picking my steps along there that, when I had got round and saw the pool lying black and silent at my feet, I fairly staggered back with the shock. There was no mistaking the place. The pool was surrounded by high rocks; on the opposite side they ran up quite perpendicularly to a good height. Nowhere, except the ledge at my feet, would a man have been able to get out of the water alone. The black surface of the water was as smooth as glass; not a ripple or bubble or straw broke its awful monotony.

It fascinated me; but it was a ghostly spot. I don't know how long I stood there watching it. It seemed hours. A sickening feeling had crept over me, and I *knew I was afraid*.

I looked all round, but there was nothing to break the horrid spell. Behind me there was a face of rock twenty feet high with ferns and creepers falling from every crevice. But it looked black, too. I turned silently again towards the water, almost hoping to see something there; but there was still the same unbroken surface, the same oppressive deadly silence as before. What was the use of delaying? It had to be done; so I might as well face it at once. I own I was frightened. I would have lost the bet with pleasure, but to stand the laughter, chaff, and jeers of the others! No! that I could never do. My mind was made up to it, so I threw off my clothes quickly and came up to the water's edge. I walked out on the one low ledge and looked down. I was trembling then, I know.

I tried to think it was cold, but I *knew* it was not that. I stooped low down to search the very depths of the pool, but I could see nothing; all was uniformly dark. And yet – good God! what was that? Right down at the bottom lay a long black object. With starting eyes I looked again. It was only a rock. I drew back a pace and sat down. The perspiration was in beads on my forehead. I shook in every limb; sick and faint, my breath went and came in the merest whispers. So I sat for a minute or two with my head resting on my hands, and then the thought struck me, 'What if the others are watching me above?'

I jumped up to make a running plunge of it, but, somehow, the run slackened into a walk, and the walk ended in a pause near the ledge, and there I stood to have another look into the dark, still pool.

Suddenly there was a rustling behind me. I jumped round, tingling, quivering all over, and a pebble rolled at my feet from the rocks above. I called out in a shaky voice, 'Now then, you chaps! none of that: I can see you.' But really I could see nothing, and the echo of my voice had such a weird, awful sound that I began to lose my head altogether. There was no use now pretending that I was not frightened, for I was. My nerves were completely unstrung, my head was splitting, and my legs could hardly bear me. I preferred to face any ridicule rather than endure this for another minute, and I commenced dressing. Then I pictured to myself Jim's grinning face, Frenchy's pantomime of the whole affair, Harding's quiet smile, and the chaff and laughter of them all, and I paused. A sudden rush, a plunge and souse, and I was in. Breathless and gasping I struck out, only twenty yards across; madly I swam. The cold water made my flesh creep. On and on, faster and faster; would I never reach it? At last I touched the rocks and turned to come back. Then all their chaff recurred to me. Every stroke seemed to hiss the words at me, 'Feel for his throat! Feel for his throat!' I fancied the dead nigger was on me, and every moment expected to feel his hand on my shoulder. On I sped, faster and faster, mad with the dread of being entangled by the legs and pulled down – I swam for life. When I scrambled on the ledge I felt I was *saved!* Then all at once I began to feel my body tingling with a most exhilarating sense of relief after an absurd fright, a sense of power restored, of self-respect and triumph and an insane desire to laugh. I did laugh, but the sepulchral echoes of my hilarious cackle rather chilled me, and I began to dress.

Then for the first time occurred to me the conditions of the bet: 'Two dives and a swim across.' Now, this would have been quite natural in ordinary pools – a plunge, a scramble on the opposite bank, another plunge, and back. But here, with the precipitous face of rock opposite, it meant *two* swims across and *two dives* from the same spot. But I did not mind; in fact, I was enjoying it now, and I thought with a glow of pride how I would rub it into Jim about fishing up his darned old nigger with the cut throat.

I walked to the edge smiling.

'Yes, my boy,' I murmured, 'I'll fish you up if you're there, or a fistful of gravel for Jim and Frenchy – little devil! It'll be change for his fiver;' and I chuckled at my joke.

I drew a long breath and dropped quietly into the water, head first; down, down, down – gently, softly. A couple of easy strokes and I glided along the bottom. Then something touched me. God in heaven! how it all burst on me at once! I felt four rigid fingers laid on my shoulder and drawn down my chest, the finger-nails scratching me. Instantly I made a grasp with both hands; my left fastened on the neck of a human body, and my right, just above, closed, and the *fingers met* through the ragged flesh of a gashed throat.

I tried to scream – the water choked me. I let go and swam on, and then up. I shot out of the water waist high, gasping and glaring wildly, and then soused under again. As I again came up I dashed the water from my eyes. I saw the surface of the pool break, and a head rose slowly. Kind Heaven! *there were two!* Slowly the two bodies rose across the black margin where the shadow ceased, full in the moonlit portion of the pool – cold, clear and horrible in their ghastly nakedness. And as they rose the murderous wounds appeared. The dank hair hung over their foreheads; the glazed and sightless eyeballs were fixed with the vacant stare of death on *me*. One bore a terrible gash from temple to eye, and lower down the bluish red slit of an assegai on the left breast.

On the other was one wound only; but how awful! The throat was cut from ear to ear; the bluish lips of the great gash hung wide apart where my hand had torn them. I could even see the severed windpipe. The head was thrown slightly back, but the eyes glared down at me with an awful stony glare, while through the parted lips the teeth gleamed and grinned cold and bright as they caught the light of the moon. One glance – half an instant – showed me all this, and then, as the figures rose waist-high, I saw one arm rigid at right angles to the body from the elbow, and the stiff hand that had clawed me. For one instant they poised, balancing; then bowing slowly over, they came down on the top of me.

Then indeed my brain seemed to go. I struggled under them. I fought and shrieked; but I suppose the bubbles came up in silence. The dead stiff hand was laid on my head and pressed me down – down, down! Then the hand of death slipped, and I was free. Once I kicked them as I struggled to the surface, and gasping, frantic, mad, made for the bank. On, on, on! O God! would I never reach it? One more effort, a wrench, and I was out. Never a pause now. One bound, and I had passed the ledge; then up and up, past the cliffs, over the rocks, cut and bleeding, on I dashed as fast as mortal man ever raced. Up, up the stony path, till, with torn feet and shaking in every limb, I reached the waggon. There was an exclamation, a pause, and then a perfect yell of laughter. The laugh saved me; the heartless cruelty of it did what nothing else could have done – it roused my temper; but for that, I believe I should have gone mad.

Harding alone came forward anxiously towards me.

'What's the matter?' he asked. 'For God's sake, what is it?'

The laugh had sobered me, and I answered quietly that it was nothing much – just a thing I would like him to see down at the pool. There were a score of questions in anxious and half-apologetic tones, for they soon realised that something was wrong; but I answered nothing, and so they followed me in silence, and there, on the oily, unbroken surface of the silent pool, floated in grim relief the two bodies. We pulled them out and found the corpses lashed together. At the end of the rope was an empty loop, the stone out of which I must in my struggle have dislodged. Close to the nigger we laid them, with another pile of stones to mark the spot; but who they were and where they came from none of us ever knew for certain.

The week before this two lucky diggers had passed through Newcastle from the fields, going home. Four years have now passed, letters have come, friends have inquired, but there is no news of them, and I think, poor chaps! they must have 'gone home' by another route.

ERNEST GLANVILLE

Uncle Abe's Big Shoot

From: *Tales from the Veld …* (1897)

I had ridden out one day to the outpost, where a troop of young cattle were running, when the horse rode into a covey of red-wing partridges, a brace of which I accounted for by a right and left. Picking up the birds, and feeling rather proud of the shot, I continued on to Uncle Pike's to crow over the matter.

The old man was seated outside the door 'braiding' a thong of forslag or whip-lash.

'Hitch the reins over the pole. Ef the shed was ready I'd ask yer to stable the hoss, but there's a powerful heap o' work yet to finish it off nice an' ship-shape – me being one o' those who like to see a job well done. None o' yer rough and ready sheds for me, with a hole in the roof after the fust rain. A plump brace o' birds – you got 'em up by the Round Kopje.'

'Yes, Uncle; a right and left from the saddle. Good shooting, eh!'

'Fair to middling, sonny – fair to middling – but with a handful o' shot an' a light gun what can yer expect but to hit. Now, ef you'd bagged 'em with one ball outer an ole muzzle-loader, why I'd up an' admit it was praisable.'

'Why Uncle, where's the man who would knock over two birds with a ball? It couldn't be done.'

'Is that so? Well, now yer s'prise me.'

'You're not going to tell me you have seen that done!'

'Something better. That's small potatoes.'

He rose up, went indoors, and returned with an ancient single muzzle-loader, the stock bound round with snake skin. 'Jes yer handle that wepin.'

I handled it, and returned it without a word. It was ill-balanced, and came up awkwardly to the shoulder.

'That wepin saved my life.'

'In the war?'

'In the big drought. You remember the time. The country was that dry, you could hear the grass crackle like tinder when the wind moved, an' every breath stirred up columes of sand which went cavorting over the veld round and round, their tops bending over to each other an' the bottoms stirring up every-thing movable, and the whole length of the funells dotted about with snakes, an' lizards, an' bits of wood. Why, I see one o' em whip up a dead sheep, an' shed the wool off o' the carcase as it went twisting round an' round.'

'And the gun?'

'The gun was on the wall over my bed. Don't you mind the gun. Well, it was that dry the pumpkins withered up where they lay on the hard ground – an' one day there was nought in the larder, not so much as a smell. There was no breakfast for ole Abe Pike, nor dinner nor yet tea, an' the next morning 'twas the same story o' emptiness. I took down the old gun from the wall an' cleaned her up. There was one full charge o' powder in the horn, an' one bullet in the bag. All that morning I considered whether 'twould be wiser to divide that charge inter three, or to pour the whole lot of it in 't once. When dinner-time came an' there was no dinner, I solumnly poured the whole bang of it inter the barrel, an' listened to the music of the black grains as they rattled on their way down to their last dooty. I cut a good thick wad from a buck-hide and rammed it down, "Plunk, plenk, plank, plonk, ploonk," until the rod jumped clean out o' the muzzle. Then I polished up that lone bullet, wrapped him round in a piece o' oil rag, an' sent him down gently. "Squish, squish, squash, squoosh." I put the cap on the nipple, an' sent him home with the pressure o' the hammer. Then I took a look over the country to 'cide on a plan o' campaign. What I wanted was a big ram with meat on him ter last for a month, if 'twas made inter biltong. There was one down by the hoek, but it warnt full grown. He was nearest, but there was one I'd seen over yonder off by the river, beyond the kloof, an' I reckoned 'twas worthwhile going a couple o' mile extra to get him.'

'You were sure of him?'

'He was as good as dead when I shouldered the gun an' stepped off out on that wilderness o' burnt land. The wind came like a breath from a furnace, an' the hair on my head split an' curled up under the heat. Whenever I came across a rock with a breadth of shade I sot there to cool off, panting like a fowl, an' also to cool off the gun for fear 'twould explode. By reason o' this resting the dark came down when I reached the ridge above the river, an' I jest camped where it found me, after digging up some *insange* root to chew. The fast had been with me for two days, an' the gnawing pain inside was terrible, so that I kept awake looking up at the stars an' listening to the plovers.'

'It must have been lonesome!'

''Twas not the lonesomeness so much as the emptiness that troubled me. Before the morning came, lighting up the valley, I was going down to the river on the last hunt. 'Twas do or die that trip – an' it seemed to me I could see the gleam o' my bones away down there through the mist that hung over the sick river. I made straight for the river, knowing there was a comfort an' fellowship in the water which would draw game there, an' the big black ram, too, 'fore he marched off inter the thick o' the kloof for his sleep. By-and-by, as I went down among the rocks an' trees, I pitched head first – ker smash – in a sudden fit o' dizziness, but the shock did me good. It rattled up my brain – an' instead o' jest plunging ahead I went slow – slow an' soft as a cat on the trail – pushing aside a branch here, shoving away a dry twig there, an' glaring around with hungry eyes. I spotted him!'

'The ram?'

'Aye, the ram. The very buck I'd had in my mind when I loaded the old gun. He stood away off the other side o' the river, moving his ears, but still as a rock, and black as the bowl of this pipe, except where the white showed along his side. He seemed to be looking straight at me – an' I sank by inches to the ground with my legs all o' a shake. Then, on my falling, he stepped down to the water, and stood there admiring hisself – his sharp horns an' fine legs – an' on my belly, all empty as 'twas, I crawled, an' crawled, an' crawled. There was a bush this side the river, an' I got it in line. At last I reached it, the sweat pouring off me, an' slowly I rose up. The water was dripping from his muzzle as he threw his head up, an' he turned to spring back, when, half-kneeling, I fired, an' the next moment the old gun kicked me flat as a pancake.'

'And you missed him?'

'Never! I got him. I said I would, an' I did, I got him, an' a 9 pound barbel.'

'Uncle Abe!'

'I say a 9 pound barbel, tho' he might a been 8½ pound, an' a brace of pheasants.'

'Uncle Abe!'

'I zed so – an' a hare an', an',' he went on quickly, 'a porkipine.'

'Uncle Abe! '

'Well – what are you Abeing me for?'

'You got all those with one shot. Never!'

'I was there – you weren't. 'Tis easy accounted for. When I pulled the trigger the fish leapt from the water in the line, and the bullet passed through him inter the buck. I tole you the gun kicked. Well, it flew out o' my hands, an' hit the hare square on the nose. To recover myself, I threw up my hands, an' caught hold o' the two pheasants jest startled outer the bush.'

'And the porcupine?'

'I sot down on the porkipine, an' if you'd like to 'xamine my pants you'll find where his quills went in. I was mighty sore, an' I could ha' spared him well from the bag. But 'twas a wonderful good shot. You're not going?'

'Yes, I am. I'm afraid to stay with you.'

'Well, so long! I cut this yere forslag from the skin o' that same buck.'

'Let me see – it's nine years to the big drought.'

'That's it.'

'That skin has kept well.'

'Oh, yes; 'twas a mighty tough skin.'

'Not so tough as your yarn, Uncle. So long!'

HW NEVINSON

Vae Victis

From: *Between the Acts* (1904)

It was one of the happiest evenings in our lives, for after a year's campaigning we were ordered home. The orders had reached us in Pretoria, and a terrible journey we had made of it so far – riding our starved horses through stinging hail and blue lightning over the high veldt to Johannesburg; stuck up there for days and nights because the train would not start for fear of De Wet; then crawling slowly down the line, feeling at every bridge lest it should plunge us into death; camping out all night by Viljoen's Drift, with nothing to eat but the plunder of an old Scotch-woman's store of onions and tinned milk; brought up sharp next day by a patrol, who told us the train in front had been wrecked and we must wait, just in the centre of nothingness, till the sappers had cleared the line. Then at last we had crept into Kroonstad and jolted on through another night and day to Bloemfontein. There our troubles had ended, and we four had secured a carriage in a corridor train that was thought sure to get through to the Cape. We had shelves to let down as beds, and a smug little conductor in uniform to be tipped. It would still take us two days and nights to reach Cape Town, but what did it matter? The line was clear, and we were going home. So the war correspondent, 'You'll have to marry me now', the artist threw the baggage about for joy, the invalided 'Death-or-Glory Boy' smoked our cigarettes to show he had no nasty pride, and I kept ringing for the conductor. His pasty face, form, his expectant servility, delight; for they were the assurance that civilisation was not far off.

As we kept on telling each other, we were 'fair fed up' with campaigning life. 'No more corrugated iron!' 'No more barbed wire!' 'No more horse and water!' 'No more cantering Colonials!' 'No more Loyalists on the make!' we cried in turn.

'Never again shall I sleep in a puddle with a family of enteric germs using my mouth as a shelter from the cold!' 'Never again will my mare chew a horse's tail for hunger, while another devours her mane!' 'Never again shall I lie rubbing my nose in the sand, afraid to wipe it for fear of the bullets!' 'Never again shall I ask a lord to dinner and give him half a teaspoonful of sugar for a treat!'

'Think of whisky and soda, bucketsful, with ice!' 'Think of several meals a day on board!' 'Think of getting into a bed with sheets!' 'Think of seeing a woman again!'

'Well, I saw some at Durban about six months ago, after the siege, and they seemed to me irrelevant, as the girl said of reading.'

'Poor old boy! How you must have suffered in that siege! You didn't think Mrs What-was-her-name irrelevant on the ship coming out!'

'You mean that woman with the scent-bottles? Yes, I remember. I used to break one wherever I sat down.'

'Yes, and poor old Price worshipped her down to the heels of her open-work stockings. Good thing for him he got shot, after all.'

'Only hope there's a lot like her on the ship going back. None of your long-range women for me!'

'No, not like those Boer girls at Pretoria, stuck over with the Transvaal colours like Christmas trees.'

'Curse them all! How superbly they detest us!'

'I can't for the life of me see why – the women, I mean.'

It does seem against nature, doesn't it? You'd think we ought to be a pleasant change after those hairy Boers. Never mind, we'll have it all our own way at home.'

'Won't we do ourselves proud! Buck too, buck like Hades!'

We all laughed again, and the correspondent began driving his joy into the artist's head with the butt end of his revolver.

'Safe to take off your putties and breeches tonight,' said the 'Death-or-Glory Boy', as I climbed up to my shelf above his bed, and wrapped myself round with a plaid and a kaross of jackal skins. Outside it was freezing hard, and I watched the waning moon moving up from the bare horizon of the veldt among the unknown African stars. The world seemed full of glorious light, for I was going home, and thought only of the welcome that awaited me. Taking some letters stained and worn from my pocket, I read them through till I came to one which I could read without the light. So, drawing the green shade across the lamp, I pulled the end of the plaid well over my head, and fell softly down and lower down into the bottomless sleep, while the train went rumbling on the immense plateau towards the sea and home.

It must have been some hours later that the engine drew up suddenly at a wayside station, and the shriek of the brake against the wheels called me up from the depth of sleep. Into it I should have fallen again, listening to the unequalled silence of a train that has stopped, had not a girlish voice suddenly cried out at the opposite window, 'Where is de Boer prisoner? Where is de wounded Boer?'

She spoke in that distinct and childlike staccato with which most Boer women speak English. At the same time I heard fingers tapping at the window-pane. Then came the tread of the flabby conductor along the corridor.

'There ain't no bloomin' Boer here,' he began, 'so you can just clear.'

'What's that?' shouted the correspondent, throwing off his rug. 'There is a Boer here! There's that wounded prisoner on that shelf!'

'So there is. I quite forgot,' said the conductor, entering at once into the joke. 'Be quick round by the door, my girl, and you can have a look.'

Too sleepy to think, I listened dreamily, and next moment I felt the girl enter the carriage, bringing the frosty air in her clothes. Then I felt her fingers quickly – but, oh, so gently disentangle the dark plaid over my head and draw it down. Turning round, I looked at her. She had put her feet on the berth below, and in the dim light was peering into my face quite close. The ordinary type of Dutch girlhood, broad of feature and strong of bone, her mass of straw-coloured hair not to be hidden even under the enormous construction of her sun-bonnet, a marvel of washing and starch. But at the moment I only saw the wide grey eyes so near to mine.

In them lived the passion of unsure and uncertain hope that dare not trust its joy; the passion of pity, and of an affection too entire for reserves. It was a look with which at the resurrection a lover's soul, careless of its proper grave, might watch for the beloved's body as it formed again from dust. It endured but for one of those crowded seconds which last indefinitely, and then one by one I saw them die – the affection first, the pity next, and last of all the hope, so much the last that it seemed to have grown old with lingering. Then indifference came, and hatred, and the cold darkness which is not living despair, but only the death of hope. The fingers still clung to my plaid, but one by one they moved, so that they might not touch my neck.

'I'm very sorry, but there's no Boer here,' I said.

'Oh, damn! Oh, damn!' she cried in her quick staccato, slid down to the carriage floor, and was gone. Along the corridor I heard her voice: 'Where is de Boer prisoner? Where is de wounded Boer?'

The engine whistled. 'Come, clear off,' shouted the flabby conductor, 'or I'll have to heave you out.'

'Oh, hell!' said the gentle little voice from a distance, and the train moved on.

We all laughed. 'That's a good joke,' said the correspondent. 'I say, old man, she took you for one of your hairy Boers. Oh, damn! Oh, hell!'

He imitated the girl's voice exactly, and we laughed again.

'That's the language they catch from the cultured Colonial.'

'Not a bad-looking girl either. I wish she was coming on the ship.'

'Oh, we'll do better than that. Chuck me a cigarette, somebody. I can't sleep a curse.'

I let down my window and looked back along the line. The little station was already far away, but on the platform I could see the figure of the girl in the great white sun-bonnet, standing immovable. Then the solitary porter turned out the single station lamp, and she disappeared. The waning moon was now far up the sky. Not a house or sign of a farm was anywhere to he seen. All around us stretched the desolate veldt, and a few low kopjes of barren rock rose far in front. They were the beginning of the great Karoo desert, and I remembered again that I was going home.

OLIVE SCHREINER

Eighteen–Ninety–Nine

Written *c*1906

From: *Stories, Dreams and Allegories* (1923)

'Thou fool, that which thou sowest is not quickened unless it die.'

I

It was a warm night: the stars shone down through the thick soft air of the
Northern Transvaal into the dark earth, where a little daub-and-wattle house
of two rooms lay among the long, grassy slopes.

A light shone through the small window of the house, though it was past
midnight. Presently the upper half of the door opened and then the lower, and
the tall figure of a woman stepped out into the darkness. She closed the door
behind her and walked towards the back of the house where a large round hut
stood; beside it lay a pile of stumps and branches quite visible when once the
eyes grew accustomed to the darkness. The woman stooped and broke off
twigs till she had her apron full, and then returned slowly, and went into the
house.

The room to which she returned was a small, bare room, with brown earth-
en walls and a mud floor; a naked deal table stood in the centre, and a few dark
wooden chairs, home-made, with seats of undressed leather, stood round the
walls. In the corner opposite the door was an open fireplace, and on the
earthen hearth stood an iron three-foot, on which stood a large black kettle,
under which coals were smouldering, though the night was hot and close.
Against the wall on the left side of the room hung a gun-rack with three guns
upon it, and below it a large hunting-watch hung from two nails by its silver
chain.

In the corner by the fireplace was a little table with a coffee-pot upon it
and a dish containing cups and saucers covered with water, and above it were
a few shelves with crockery and a large Bible; but the dim light of the tallow
candle which burnt on the table, with its wick of twisted rag, hardly made
the corners visible. Beside the table sat a young woman, her head resting on
her folded arms, the light of the tallow candle falling full on her head of pale
flaxen hair, a little tumbled, and drawn behind into a large knot. The arms
crossed on the table, from which the cotton sleeves had fallen back, were the
full, rounded arms of one very young.

The older woman, who had just entered, walked to the fireplace, and kneeling down before it took from her apron the twigs and sticks she had gathered

and heaped them under the kettle till a blaze sprang up which illumined the whole room. Then she rose up and sat down on a chair before the fire, but facing the table, with her hands crossed on her brown apron.

She was a woman of fifty, spare and broad-shouldered, with black hair, already slightly streaked with grey; from below high, arched eyebrows, and a high forehead, full dark eyes looked keenly, and a sharply cut aquiline nose gave strength to the face; but the mouth below was somewhat sensitive, and not over-full. She crossed and recrossed her knotted hands on her brown apron.

The woman at the table moaned and moved her head from side to side. 'What time is it?' she asked.

The older woman crossed the room to where the hunting-watch hung on the wall.

It showed a quarter-past one, she said, and went back to her seat before the fire, and sat watching the figure beside the table, the firelight bathing her strong upright form and sharp aquiline profile.

Nearly fifty years before her parents had left the Cape Colony, and had set out on the long trek northward, and she, a young child, had been brought with them. She had no remembrance of the colonial home. Her first dim memories were of travelling in an ox-wagon; of dark nights when a fire was lighted in the open air, and people sat round it on the ground, and some faces seemed to stand out more than others in her memory which she thought must be those of her father and mother and of an old grandmother; she could remember lying awake in the back of the wagon while it was moving on, and the stars were shining down on her; and she had a vague memory of great wide plains with buck on them, which she thought must have been in the Free State. But the first thing which sprang out sharp and clear from the past was a day when she and another child, a little boy cousin of her own age, were playing among the bushes on the bank of a stream; she remembered how, suddenly, as they looked through the bushes, they saw black men leap out, and mount the ox-wagon outspanned under the trees; she remembered how they shouted and dragged people along, and stabbed them; she remembered how the blood gushed, and how they, the two young children among the bushes, lay flat on their stomachs and did not move or breathe, with that strange self-preserving instinct found in the young of animals or men who grow up in the open.

She remembered how black smoke came out at the back of the wagon and then red tongues of flame through the top; and even that some of the branches of the tree under which the wagon stood caught fire. She remembered later, when the black men had gone, and it was dark, that they were very hungry, and crept out to where the wagon had stood, and that they looked about on the ground for any scraps of food they might pick up, and that when they could not find any they cried. She remembered nothing clearly after that till some men with large beards and large hats rode up on horseback: it might have been next day or the day after. She remembered how they jumped off their horses and took them up in their arms, and how they cried; but that they, the children, did not cry, they only asked for food. She remembered how one man took a bit of thick, cold roaster-cake out of his pocket, and gave it to her, and how nice it tasted. And she remembered that the men took them up before them on their horses, and that one man tied her close to him with a large red handkerchief.

In the years that came she learnt to know that that which she remembered so clearly was the great and terrible day when, at Weenen, and in the country round, hundreds of women and children and youths and old men fell before the Zulus, and the assegais of Dingaan's braves drank blood.

She learnt that on that day all of her house and name, from the grand-mother to the baby in arms, fell, and that she only and the boy cousin, who had hidden with her among the bushes, were left of all her kin in that north-ern world. She learnt, too, that the man who tied her to him with the red handkerchief took them back to his wagon, and that he and his wife adopted them, and brought them up among their own children.

She remembered, though less clearly than the day of the fire, how a few years later they trekked away from Natal, and went through great mountain ranges, ranges in and near which lay those places the world was to know later as Laings Nek, and Amajuba, and Ingogo; Elandslaagte, Nicholson Nek, and Spion Kop. She remembered how at last after many wanderings they settled down near the Witwaters Rand where game was plentiful and wild beasts were dangerous, but there were no natives, and they were far from the English rule.

There the two children grew up among the children of those who had adopted them, and were kindly treated by them as though they were their own; it yet was but natural that these two of the same name and blood should grow up with a peculiar tenderness for each other. And so it came to pass that when they were both eighteen years old they asked consent of the old people, who gave it gladly, that they should marry. For a time the young couple lived on in the house with the old, but after three years they gathered together all their few goods and in their wagon, with their guns and ammunition and a few sheep and cattle, they moved away northwards to found their own home.

For a time they travelled here and travelled there, but at last they settled on a spot where game was plentiful and the soil good, and there among the low undulating slopes, near the bank of a dry sloot, the young man built at last, with his own hands, a little house of two rooms.

On the long slope across the sloot before the house, he ploughed a piece of land and enclosed it, and he built kraals for his stock and so struck root in the land and wandered no more. Those were brave, glad, free days to the young couple. They lived largely on the game which the gun brought down, antelope and wildebeest that wandered even past the doors at night; and now and again a lion was killed: one no farther than the door of the round hut behind the house where the meat and the milk were stored, and two were killed at the kraals. Sometimes, too, traders came with their wagons and in exchange for skins and fine horns sold sugar and coffee and print and tan-cord, and such things as the little household had need of. The lands yielded richly to them, in maize, and pumpkins, and sweet-cane, and melons; and they had nothing to wish for. Then in time three little sons were born to them, who grew as strong and vigorous in the free life of the open veld as the young lions in the long grass and scrub near the river four miles away. Those were joyous, free years for the man and woman, in which disease, and carking care, and anxiety played no part.

Then came a day when their eldest son was ten years old, and the father went out a-hunting with his Kaffir servants: in the evening they brought him home with a wound eight inches long in his side where a lioness had torn him; they brought back her skin also, as he had shot her at last in the hand-to-throat struggle. He lingered for three days and then died. His wife buried him on the low slope to the left of the house; she and her Kaffir servants alone made the grave and put him in it, for there were no white men near. Then she and her sons lived on there; a new root driven deep into the soil and binding them to it through the grave on the hill-side. She hung her husband's large hunting-watch up on the wall, and put three of his guns over it on the rack, and the gun he had in his hand when he met his death she took down and polished up every day; but one gun she always kept loaded at the head of her bed in the inner room. She counted the stock every night and saw that the Kaffirs ploughed the lands, and she saw to the planting and watering of them herself.

Often as the years passed men of the countryside, and even from far off, heard of the young handsome widow who lived alone with her children and saw to her own stock and lands; and they came a-courting. But many of them were afraid to say anything when once they had come, and those who had spoken to her, when once she had answered them, never came again. About this time too the countryside began to fill in; and people came and settled as near as eight and ten miles away; and as people increased the game began to vanish, and with the game the lions, so that the one her husband killed was almost the last ever seen there. But there was still game enough for food, and when her eldest son was twelve years old, and she gave him his father's small-est gun to go out hunting with, he returned home almost every day with meat enough for the household tied behind his saddle. And as time passed she came also to be known through the countryside as a 'wise woman'. People came to her to ask advice about their illnesses, or to ask her to dress old wounds that would not heal; and when they questioned her whether she thought the rains would be early, or the game plentiful that year, she was nearly always right. So they called her a 'wise woman' because neither she nor they knew any word in that up-country speech of theirs for the thing called 'genius'. So all things went well till the eldest son was eighteen, and the dark beard was beginning to sprout on his face, and his mother began to think that soon there might be a daughter in the house; for on Saturday evenings, when his work was done, he put on his best clothes and rode off to the next farm eight miles away, where was a young daughter. His mother always saw that he had a freshly ironed shirt waiting for him on his bed, when he came home from the kraals on Saturday nights, and she made plans as to how they would build on two rooms for the new daughter. At this time he was training young horses to have them ready to sell when the traders came round: he was a fine rider and it was always his work. One afternoon he mounted a young horse before the door and it bucked and threw him. He had often fallen before, but this time his neck was broken. He lay dead with his head two feet from his mother's doorstep. They took up his tall, strong body and the next day the neighbours came from the next farm and they buried him beside his father, on the hill-side, and another root was struck into the soil. Then the three who were left in the little farm-house lived and worked on as before, for a year and more.

Then a small native war broke out, and the young burghers of the district were called out to help. The second son was very young, but he was the best shot in the district, so he went away with the others. Three months after the men came back, but among the few who did not return was her son. On a hot sunny afternoon, walking through a mealie field which they thought was deserted and where the dried yellow stalks stood thick, an assegai thrown from an unseen hand found him, and he fell there. His comrades took him and buried him under a large thorn tree, and scraped the earth smooth over him, that his grave might not be found by others. So he was not laid on the rise to the left of the house with his kindred, but his mother's heart went often to that thorn tree in the far north.

And now again there were only two in the little mud-house; as there had been years before when the young man and wife first settled there. She and her young lad were always together night and day, and did all that they did together, as though they were mother and daughter. He was a fair lad, tall and gentle as his father had been before him, not huge and dark as his two elder brothers; but he seemed to ripen towards manhood early. When he was only sixteen the thick white down was already gathering heavy on his upper lip; his mother watched him narrowly, and had many thoughts in her heart. One evening as they sat twisting wicks for the candles together, she said to him, 'You will be eighteen on your next birthday, my son, that was your father's age when he married me.' He said, 'Yes,' and they spoke no more then. But later in the evening when they sat before the door she said to him: 'We are very lonely here. I often long to hear the feet of a little child about the house, and to see one with your father's blood in it play before the door as you and your brothers played. Have you ever thought that you are the last of your father's name and blood left here in the north; that if you died there would

82

be none left?' He said he had thought of it. Then she told him she thought it would be well if he went away, to the part of the country where the people lived who had brought her up: several of the sons and daughters who had grown up with her had now grown-up children. He might go down and from among them seek out a young girl whom he liked and who liked him; and if he found her, bring her back as a wife. The lad thought very well of his mother's plan. And when three months were passed, and the ploughing season was over, he rode away one day, on the best black horse they had, his Kaffir boy riding behind him on another, and his mother stood at the gable watching them ride away. For three months she heard nothing of him, for trains were not in those days, and letters came rarely and by chance, and neither he nor she could read or write. One afternoon she stood at the gable end as she always stood when her work was done, looking out along the road that came over the rise, and she saw a large tent-wagon coming along it, and her son walking beside it. She walked to meet it. When she had greeted her son and climbed into the wagon she found there a girl of fifteen with pale flaxen hair and large blue eyes whom he had brought home as his wife. Her father had given her the wagon and oxen as her wedding portion. The older woman's heart wrapt itself about the girl as though she had been the daughter she had dreamed to bear of her own body, and had never borne.

The three lived joyfully at the little house as though they were one person. The young wife had been accustomed to live in a larger house, and down south, where they had things they had not here. She had been to school, and learned to read and write, and she could even talk a little English; but she longed for none of the things which she had had; the little brown house was home enough for her.

After a year a child came, but, whether it were that the mother was too young, it only opened its eyes for an hour on the world and closed them again. The young mother wept bitterly, but her husband folded his arms about her, and the mother comforted both. 'You are young, my children, but we shall yet hear the sound of children's voices in the house,' she said; and after a little while the young mother was well again and things went on peacefully as before in the little home.

But in the land things were not going on peacefully. That was the time that the flag to escape from which the people had left their old homes in the Colony, and had again left Natal when it followed them there, and had chosen to face the spear of the savage, and the conflict with wild beasts, and death by hunger and thirst in the wilderness rather than live under, had by force and fraud unfurled itself over them again. For the moment a great sullen silence brooded over the land. The people, slow of thought, slow of speech, determined in action, and unforgetting, sat still and waited. It was like the silence that rests over the land before an up-country thunderstorm breaks.

Then words came, 'They have not even given us the free government they promised' – then acts – the people rose. Even in that remote countryside the men began to mount their horses, and with their guns ride away to help. In the little mud-house the young wife wept much when he said that he too was going. But when his mother helped him pack his saddle-bags she helped too; and on the day when the men from the next farm went, he rode away also with his gun by his side.

No direct news of the one they had sent away came to the waiting women at the farmhouse; then came fleet reports of the victories of Ingogo and Amajuba. Then came an afternoon after he had been gone two months. They had both been to the gable end to look out at the road, as they did continually amid their work, and they had just come in to drink their afternoon coffee when the Kaffir maid ran in to say she saw someone coming along the road who looked like her master. The women ran out. It was the white horse on which he had ridden away, but they almost doubted if it were he. He rode bending on his saddle, with his chin on his breast and his arm hanging at his side. At first they thought he had been wounded, but when they had helped him from his horse and brought him into the house they found it was only a deadly fever which was upon him. He had crept home to them by small stages. Hardly had he any spirit left to tell them of Ingogo, Laings Nek, and Amajuba. For fourteen days he grew worse and on the fifteenth day he died. And the two women buried him where the rest of his kin lay on the hillside.

And so it came to pass that on that warm starlight night the two women were alone in the little mud-house with the stillness of the veld about them; even their Kaffir servants asleep in their huts beyond the kraals; and the very sheep lying silent in the starlight. They two were alone in the little house, but they knew that before morning they would not be alone, they were awaiting the coming of the dead man's child.

The young woman with her head on the table groaned. 'If only my husband were here still,' she wailed. The old woman rose and stood beside her, passing her hard, work-worn hand gently over her shoulder as if she were a little child. At last she induced her to go and lie down in the inner room. When she had grown quieter and seemed to have fallen into a light sleep the old woman came to the front room again. It was almost two o'clock and the fire had burned low under the large kettle. She scraped the coals together and went out of the front door to fetch more wood, and closed the door behind her. The night air struck cool and fresh upon her face after the close air of the house, the stars seemed to be growing lighter as the night advanced, they shot down their light as from a million polished steel points. She walked to the back of the house where, beyond the round hut that served as a store-room, the wood-pile lay. She bent down gathering sticks and chips till her apron was full, then slowly she raised herself and stood still. She looked upwards. It was a wonderful night. The white band of the Milky Way crossed the sky overhead, and from every side stars threw down their light, sharp as barbed spears, from the velvety blue-black of the sky. The woman raised her hand to her forehead as if pushing the hair farther off it, and stood motionless, looking up. After a long time she dropped her hand and began walking slowly towards the house. Yet once or twice on the way she paused and stood looking up. When she went into the house the woman in the inner room was again moving and moaning. She laid the sticks down before the fire and went into the next room. She bent down over the bed where the younger woman lay, and put her hand upon her. 'My daughter,' she said slowly, 'be comforted. A wonderful thing has happened to me. As I stood out in the starlight it was as though a voice came down to me and spoke. The child which will be born of you tonight will be a man-child and he will live to do great things for his land and for his people.'

Before morning there was the sound of a little wail in the mud-house: and the child who was to do great things for his land and for his people was born.

II

Six years passed; and all was as it had been at the little house among the slopes. Only a new piece of land had been ploughed up and added to the land before the house, so that the ploughed land now almost reached to the ridge.

The young mother had grown stouter, and lost her pink and white; she had become a working-woman, but she still had the large knot of flaxen hair behind her head and the large wondering eyes. She had many suitors in those six years, but she sent them all away. She said the old woman looked after the farm as well as any man might, and her son would be grown up by and by. The grandmother's hair was a little more streaked with grey, but it was as thick as ever, and her shoulders as upright; only some of her front teeth had fallen out, which made her lips close more softly.

The great change was that wherever the women went there was the flaxen-haired child to walk beside them holding on to their skirts or clasping their hands.

The neighbours said they were ruining the child: they let his hair grow long, like a girl's, because it curled; and they never let him wear velschoens like other children but always shop boots; and his mother sat up at night to iron his pinafores as if the next day were always a Sunday.

But the women cared nothing for what was said; to them he was not as any other child. He asked them strange questions they could not answer, and he never troubled them by wishing to go and play with the little Kaffirs as other children trouble. When neighbours came over and brought their children with them he ran away and hid in the sloot to play by himself till they were gone. No, he was not like other children!

When the women went to lie down on hot days after dinner sometimes, he would say that he did not want to sleep; but he would not run about and make a noise like other children – he would go and sit outside in the shade of the house, on the front doorstep, quite still, with his little hands resting on his knees, and stare far away at the ploughed lands on the slope, or the shadows nearer; the women would open the bedroom window, and peep out to look at him as he sat there.

The child loved his mother and followed her about to the milk house, and to the kraals; but he loved his grandmother best.

She told him stories.

When she went to the lands to see how the Kaffirs were ploughing he would run at her side holding her dress; when they had gone a short way he would tug gently at it and say, 'Grandmother, tell me things!'

And long before day broke, when it was yet quite dark, he would often creep from the bed where he slept with his mother into his grandmother's bed in the corner; he would put his arms round her neck and stroke her face till she woke, and then whisper softly, 'Tell me stories!' and she would tell them to him in a low voice not to wake the mother, till the cock crowed and it was time to get up and light the candle and the fire.

But what he liked best of all were the hot, still summer nights, when the women put their chairs before the door because it was too warm to go to sleep; and he would sit on the stoof at his grandmother's feet and lean his head against her knees, and she would tell him on and on of the things he liked to hear; and he would watch the stars as they slowly set along the ridge, or the moonlight, casting bright-edged shadows from the gable as she talked. Often after the mother had got sleepy and gone in to bed the two sat there together.

The stories she told him were always true stories of the things she had seen or of things she had heard. Sometimes they were stories of her own childhood: of the day when she and his grandfather hid among the bushes, and saw the wagon burnt; sometimes they were of the long trek from Natal to the Transvaal; sometimes of the things which happened to her and his grandfather when first they came to that spot among the ridges, of how there was no house there nor lands, only two bare grassy slopes when they outspanned their wagon there the first night; she told of a lion she once found when she opened the door in the morning, sitting, with paws crossed, upon the threshold, and how the grandfather jumped out of bed and re-opened the door two inches, and shot it through the opening; the skin was kept in the round storehouse still, very old and mangy.

Sometimes she told him of the two uncles who were dead, and of his own father, and of all they had been and done. But sometimes she told him of things much farther off: of the old Colony where she had been born, but which she could not remember, and of the things which happened there in the old days. She told him of how the British had taken the Cape over, and of how the

English had hanged their men at the 'Slachters Nek' for resisting the English Government, and of how the friends and relations had been made to stand round to see them hanged whether they would or no, and of how the scaffold broke down as they were being hanged, and the people looking on cried aloud, 'It is the finger of God! They are saved!' but how the British hanged them up again. She told him of the great trek in which her parents had taken part to escape from under the British flag; of the great battles with Moselikatse; and of the murder of Retief and his men by Dingaan, and of Dingaan's Day. She told him how the British Government followed them into Natal, and of how they trekked north and east to escape from it again; and she told him of the later things, of the fight at Laings Nek, and Ingogo, and Amajuba, where his father had been. Always she told the same story in exactly the same words over and over again, till the child knew them all by heart, and would ask for this and then that.

The story he loved best, and asked for more often than all the others, made his grandmother wonder, because it did not seem to her the story a child would best like; it was not a story of lion-hunting, or wars, or adventures. Continually when she asked what she should tell him, he said, 'About the mountains!'

It was the story of how the Boer women in Natal when the English Commissioner came to annex their country, collected to meet him and pointing toward the Drakens Berg Mountains said, 'We go across those mountains to freedom or to death!'

More than once, when she was telling him the story, she saw him stretch out his little arm and raise his hand, as though he were speaking.

One evening as he and his mother were coming home from the milking kraals, and it was getting dark, and he was very tired, having romped about shouting among the young calves and kids all the evening, he held her hand tightly.

'Mother,' he said suddenly, 'when I am grown up, I am going to Natal.' 'Why, my child?' she asked him; 'there are none of our family living there now.'

He waited a little, then said, very slowly, 'I am going to go and try to get our land back!'

His mother started; if there were one thing she was more firmly resolved on in her own mind than any other it was that he should never go to the wars. She began to talk quickly of the old white cow who had kicked the pail over as she was milked, and when she got to the house she did not even mention to the grandmother what had happened; it seemed better to forget.

One night in the rainy season when it was damp and chilly they sat round the large fireplace in the front room.

Outside the rain was pouring in torrents and you could hear the water rushing in the great dry sloot before the door. His grandmother, to amuse him, had sprung some dried mealies in the great black pot and sprinkled them with sugar, and now he sat on the stoof at her feet with a large lump of the sticky sweetmeat in his hand, watching the fire. His grandmother from above him was watching it also, and his mother in her elbow-chair on the other side of the fire had her eyes half closed and was nodding already with the warmth of the room and her long day's work. The child sat so quiet, the hand with the lump of sweetmeat resting on his knee, that his grandmother thought he had gone to sleep too. Suddenly he said without looking up, 'Grandmother?'

'Yes.'

He waited rather a long time, then said slowly, 'Grandmother, did God make the English too?'

She also waited for a while, then she said, 'Yes, my child; He made all things.'

They were silent again, and there was no sound but of the rain falling and the fire cracking and the sloot rushing outside. Then he threw his head backwards on to his grandmother's knee and looking up into her face, said, 'But, grandmother, why did He make them?'

Then she too was silent for a long time. 'My child,' at last she said, 'we cannot judge the ways of the Almighty. He does that which seems good in His own eyes.'

The child sat up and looked back at the fire. Slowly he tapped his knee with the lump of sweetmeat once or twice; then he began to munch it; and soon the mother started wide awake and said it was time for all to go to bed.

The next morning his grandmother sat on the front doorstep cutting beans in an iron basin; he sat beside her on the step pretending to cut too, with a short, broken knife. Presently he left off and rested his hands on his knees, looking away at the hedge beyond, with his small forehead knit tight between the eyes.

'Grandmother,' he said suddenly, in a small, almost shrill voice, 'do the English want *all* the lands of *all* the people?'

The handle of his grandmother's knife as she cut clinked against the iron side of the basin. 'All they can get,' she said.

After a while he made a little movement almost like a sigh, and took up his little knife again and went on cutting.

Some time after that, when a trader came by, his grandmother bought him a spelling-book and a slate and pencils, and his mother began to teach him to read and write. When she had taught him for a year he knew all she did. Sometimes when she was setting him a copy and left a letter out in a word, he would quietly take the pencil when she set it down and put the letter in, not with any idea of correcting her, but simply because it must be there.

Often at night when the child had gone to bed early, tired out with his long day's play, and the two women were left in the front room with the tallow candle burning on the table between them, then they talked of his future.

Ever since he had been born everything they had earned had been put away in the wagon chest under the grandmother's bed. When the traders with their wagons came round the women bought nothing except a few groceries and clothes for the child; even before they bought a yard of cotton print for a new apron they talked long and solemnly as to whether the old one might not be made to do by repatching; and they mixed much more dry pumpkin and corn with their coffee than before he was born. It was to earn more money that the large new piece of land had been added to the lands before the house.

They were going to have him educated. First he was to be taught all they could at home, then to be sent away to a great school in the old Colony, and then he was to go over the sea to Europe and come back an advocate or a doctor or a parson. The grandmother had made a long journey to the next town, to find out from the minister just how much it would cost to do it all.

In the evenings when they sat talking it over the mother generally inclined to his becoming a parson. She never told the grandmother why, but the real reason was because parsons do not go to the wars. The grandmother generally favoured his becoming an advocate, because he might become a judge. Sometimes they sat discussing these matters till the candle almost burnt out.

'Perhaps, one day,' the mother would at last say, 'he may yet become President!'

Then the grandmother would slowly refold her hands across her apron and say softly, 'Who knows? – who knows?'

Often they would get the box out from under the bed (looking carefully across to the corner to see he was fast asleep) and would count out all the money, though each knew to a farthing how much was there; then they would make it into little heaps, so much for this, so much for that, and then they would count on their fingers how many good seasons it would take to make the rest, and how old he would be.

When he was eight and had learnt all his mother could teach him, they sent him to school every day on an adjoining farm six miles off, where the people had a schoolmaster. Every day he rode over on the great white horse his father went to the wars with; his mother was afraid to let him ride alone at first, but his grandmother said he must learn to do everything alone. At four o'clock when he came back one or other of the women was always looking out to see the little figure on the tall horse coming over the ridge.

When he was eleven they gave him his father's smallest gun; and one day not long after he came back with his first small buck. His mother had the skin dressed and bound with red, and she laid it as a mat under the table, and even the horns she did not throw away, and saved them in the round house, because it was his first.

When he was fourteen the schoolmaster said he could teach him no more;

that he ought to go to some larger school where they taught Latin and other difficult things; they had not yet money enough and he was not quite old enough to go to the old Colony, so they sent him first to the High-veld, where his mother's relations lived and where there were good schools, where they taught the difficult things; he could live with his mother's relations and come back once a year for the holidays.

They were great times when he came.

His mother made him koekies and sasarties and nice things every day; and he used to sit on the stoof at her feet and let her play with his hair like when he was quite small. With his grandmother he talked. He tried to explain to her all he was learning, and he read the English newspapers to her (she could neither read in English nor Dutch), translating them. Most of all she liked his atlas. They would sometimes sit over it for half an hour in the evening tracing the different lands and talking of them. On the warm nights he used still to sit outside on the stoof at her feet with his head against her knee, and they used to discuss things that were happening in other lands and in South Africa; and sometimes they sat there quite still together.

It was now he who had the most stories to tell; he had seen Krugersdorp, and Johannesburg, and Pretoria; he knew the world; he was at Krugersdorp when Dr Jameson made his raid. Sometimes he sat for an hour, telling her of things, and she sat quietly listening.

When he was seventeen, nearly eighteen, there was money enough in the box to pay for his going to the Colony and then to Europe; and he came home to spend a few months with them before he went.

He was very handsome now; not tall, and very slight, but with fair hair that curled close to his head, and white hands like a town's man. All the girls in the countryside were in love with him. They all wished he would come and see them. But he seldom rode from home except to go to the next farm where he had been at school. There lived little Aletta, who was the daughter of the woman his uncle had loved before he went to the Kaffir war and got killed. She was only fifteen years old, but they had always been great friends. She netted him a purse of green silk. He said he would take it with him to Europe, and would show it her when he came back and was an advocate; and he gave her a book with her name written in it, which she was to show to him.

These were the days when the land was full of talk; it was said the English were landing troops in South Africa, and wanted to have war. Often the neighbours from the nearest farms would come to talk about it (there were more farms now, the country was filling in, and the nearest railway station was only a day's journey off), and they discussed matters. Some said they thought there would be war; others again laughed, and said it would be only Jameson and his white flag again. But the grandmother shook her head, and if they asked her,

'Why,' she said, 'it will not be the war of a week, nor of a month; if it comes it will be the war of years,' but she would say nothing more.

Yet sometimes when she and her grandson were walking along together in the lands she would talk.

Once she said: 'It is as if a great heavy cloud hung just above my head, as though I wished to press it back with my hands and could not. It will be a great war – a great war. Perhaps the English government will take the land for a time, but they will not keep it. The gold they have fought for will divide them, till they slay one another over it.'

Another day she said: 'This land will be a great land one day with one people from the sea to the north – but we shall not live to see it.'

He said to her: 'But how can that be when we are all of different races?'

She said: 'The land will make us one. Were not our fathers of more than one race?'

Another day, when she and he were sitting by the table after dinner, she pointed to a sheet of exercise paper, on which he had been working out a problem and which was covered with algebraical symbols, and said, 'In fifteen years' time the Government of England will not have one piece of land in all South Africa as large as that sheet of paper.'

One night when the milking had been late and she and he were walking down together from the kraals in the starlight she said to him: 'If this war comes let no man go to it lightly, thinking he will surely return home, nor let him go expecting victory on the next day. It will come at last, but not at first.

'Sometimes,' she said, 'I wake at night and it is as though the whole house were filled with smoke – and I have to get up and go outside to breathe. It is as though I saw my whole land blackened and desolate. But when I look up it is as though a voice cried out to me, "Have no fear!"'

They were getting his things ready for him to go away after Christmas. His mother was making him shirts and his grandmother was having a kaross of jackals' skins made that he might take it with him to Europe where it was so cold. But his mother noticed that whenever the grandmother was in the room with him and he was not looking at her, her eyes were always curiously fixed on him as though they were questioning something. The hair was growing white and a little thin over her temples now, but her eyes were as bright as ever, and she could do a day's work with any man.

One day when the youth was at the kraals helping the Kaffir boys to mend a wall, and the mother was kneading bread in the front room, and the grandmother washing up the breakfast things, the son of the Field-Cornet came riding over from his father's farm, which was about twelve miles off. He stopped at the kraal and Jan and he stood talking for some time, then they walked down to the farmhouse, the Kaffir boy leading the horse behind them.

Jan stopped at the round store, but the Field-Cornet's son went to the front door. The grandmother asked him in, and handed him some coffee, and the mother, her hands still in the dough, asked him how things were going at his father's farm, and if his mother's young turkeys had come out well, and she asked if he had met Jan at the kraals. He answered the questions slowly, and sipped his coffee. Then he put the cup down on the table; and said suddenly in the same measured voice, staring at the wall in front of him, that war had broken out, and his father had sent him round to call out all fighting burghers.

The mother took her hands out of the dough and stood upright beside the trough as though paralysed. Then she cried in a high, hard voice, unlike her own, 'Yes, but Jan cannot go! He is hardly eighteen! He's got to go and be educated in other lands! You can't take the only son of a widow! '

'Aunt,' said the young man slowly, 'no one will make him go.'

The grandmother stood resting the knuckles of both hands on the table, her eyes fixed on the young man. 'He shall decide himself,' she said.

The mother wiped her hands from the dough and rushed past them and out at the door; the grandmother followed slowly.

They found him in the shade at the back of the house, sitting on a stump; he was cleaning the belt of his new Mauser which lay across his knees.

'Jan,' his mother cried, grasping his shoulder, 'you are not going away? You can't go! You must stay. You can go by Delagoa Bay if there is fighting on the other side! There is plenty of money!'

He looked softly up into her face with his blue eyes. 'We have all to be at the Field-Cornet's at nine o'clock tomorrow morning,' he said. She wept aloud and argued.

His grandmother turned slowly without speaking, and went back into the house. When she had given the Field-Cornet's son another cup of coffee, and shaken hands with him, she went into the bedroom and opened the box in which her grandson's clothes were kept, to see which things he should take with him. After a time the mother came back too. He had kissed her and talked to her until she too had at last said it was right he should go.

All day they were busy. His mother baked him biscuits to take in his bag, and his grandmother made a belt of two strips of leather; she sewed them together herself and put a few sovereigns between the stitchings. She said some of his comrades might need the money if he did not.

The next morning early he was ready. There were two saddle-bags tied to his saddle and before it was strapped the kaross his grandmother had made; she said it would be useful when he had to sleep on damp ground. When he had greeted them, he rode away towards the rise: and the women stood at the gable of the house to watch him.

When he had gone a little way he turned in his saddle, and they could see he was smiling; he took off his hat and waved it in the air; the early morning sunshine made his hair as yellow as the tassels that hang from the head of ripening mealies. His mother covered her face with the sides of her kappie and wept aloud; but the grandmother shaded her eyes with both her hands and stood watching him till the figure passed out of sight over the ridge; and when it was gone and the mother returned to the house crying, she still stood watching the line against the sky.

The two women were very quiet during the next days, they worked hard, and seldom spoke. After eight days there came a long letter from him (there was now a post once a week from the station to the Field-Cornet's). He said he was well and in very good spirits. He had been to Krugersdorp, and Johannesburg, and Pretoria; all the family living there were well and sent greetings. He had joined a corps that was leaving for the front the next day. He sent also a long message to Aletta, asking them to tell her he was sorry to go away without saying goodbye; and he told his mother how good the biscuits and biltong were she had put into his saddle-bag; and he sent her a piece of 'vierkleur' ribbon in the letter, to wear on her breast.

The women talked a great deal for a day or two after this letter came. Eight days after there was a short note from him, written in pencil in the train on his way to the front. He said all was going well, and if he did not write soon they were not to be anxious; he would write as often as he could.

For some days the women discussed the note too.

Then came two weeks without a letter, the two women became very silent. Every day they sent the Kaffir boy over to the Field-Cornet's, even on the days when there was no post, to hear if there was any news.

Many reports were flying about the countryside. Some said that an English armoured train had been taken on the western border; that there had been fighting at Albertina, and in Natal. But nothing seemed quite certain.

Another week passed ... Then the two women became very quiet.

The grandmother, when she saw her daughter-in-law left the food untouched on her plate, said there was no need to be anxious; men at the front could not always find paper and pencils to write with and might be far from any post office. Yet night after night she herself would rise from her bed saying she felt the house close, and go and walk up and down outside.

Then one day suddenly all their servants left them except one Kaffir and his wife, whom they had had for years, and the servants from the farms about went also, which was a sign there had been news of much fighting; for the Kaffirs hear things long before the white man knows them.

Three days after, as the women were clearing off the breakfast things, the youngest son of the Field-Cornet, who was only fifteen and had not gone to the war with the others, rode up. He hitched his horse to the post, and came towards the door. The mother stepped forward to meet him and shook hands in the doorway.

'I suppose you have come for the carrot seed I promised your mother? I was not able to send it, as our servants ran away,' she said, as she shook his hand. 'There isn't a letter from Jan, is there?' The lad said no, there was no letter from him, and shook hands with the grandmother. He stood by the table instead of sitting down.

The mother turned to the fireplace to get coals to put under the coffee to rewarm it; but the grandmother stood leaning forward with her eyes fixed on him from across the table. He felt uneasily in his breast pocket.

'Is there no news?' the mother said without looking round, as she bent over the fire.

'Yes, there is news, Aunt.'

She rose quickly and turned towards him, putting down the brazier on the table. He took a letter out of his breast pocket. 'Aunt, my father said I must bring this to you. It came inside one to him and they asked him to send one of us over with it.'

The mother took the letter; she held it, examining the address.

'It looks to me like the writing of Sister Annie's Paul,' she said. 'Perhaps there is news of Jan in it' – she turned to them with a half-nervous smile – 'they were always such friends.'

'All is as God wills, Aunt,' the young man said, looking down fixedly at the top of his riding-whip.

But the grandmother leaned forward motionless, watching her daughter-in-law as she opened the letter.

She began to read to herself, her lips moving slowly as she deciphered it word by word.

Then a piercing cry rang through the roof of the little mud-farmhouse. 'He is dead! My boy is dead!'

She flung the letter on the table and ran out at the front door.

Far out across the quiet ploughed lands and over the veld to where the kraals lay the cry rang. The Kaffir woman who sat outside her hut beyond the kraals nursing her baby heard it and came down with her child across her hip to see what was the matter. At the side of the round house she stood motion-less and open-mouthed, watching the woman, who paced up and down behind the house with her apron thrown over her head and her hands folded above it, crying aloud.

In the front room the grandmother, who had not spoken since he came, took up the letter and put it in the lad's hands. 'Read,' she whispered. And slowly the lad spelled it out.

'My Dear Aunt,

'I hope this letter finds you well. The Commandant has asked me to write it.

'We had a great fight four days ago, and Jan is dead. The Commandant says I must tell you how it happened. Aunt, there were five of us first in a position on that koppie, but two got killed, and then there were only three of us – Jan, and I, and Uncle Peter's Frikkie. Aunt, the khakies were coming on all round just like locusts, and the bullets were coming just like hail. It was bare on that side of the koppie where we were, but we had plenty of cartridges. We three took up a position where there were some small stones and we fought, Aunt; we had to. One bullet took off the top of my ear, and Jan got two bullets, one through the flesh in the left leg and one through his arm, but he could still fire his gun. Then we three meant to go to the top of the koppie, but a bullet took Jan right through his chest. We knew he couldn't go any farther. The khakies were right at the foot of the koppie just coming up. He told us to lay him down, Aunt. We said we would stay by him, but he said we must go. I put my jacket under his head and Frikkie put his over his feet. We threw his gun far away from him that they might see how it was with him. He said he hadn't much pain, Aunt. He was full of blood from his arm, but there wasn't much from his chest, only a little out of the corners of his mouth. He said we must make haste or the khakies would catch us; he said he wasn't afraid to be left there.

'Aunt, when we got to the top, it was all full of khakies like the sea on the other side, all among the koppies and on our koppie too. We were surrounded, Aunt; the last I saw of Frikkie he was sitting on a stone with the blood running down his face, but he got under a rock and hid there; some of our men found him next morning and brought him to camp. Aunt, there was a khakie's horse standing just below where I was, with no one on it. I jumped on and rode. The bullets went this way and the bullets went that, but I rode! Aunt, the khakies were sometimes as near me as that tentpole, only the Grace of God saved me. It was dark in the night when I got back to where our people were, because I had to go round all the koppies to get away from the khakies.

'Aunt, the next day we went to look for him. We found him where we left him; but he was turned over on to his face; they had taken all his things, his belt and his watch, and the pugaree from his hat, even his boots. The little green silk purse he used to carry we found on the ground by him, but nothing in it. I will send it back to you whenever I get an opportunity.

'Aunt, when we turned him over on his back there were four bayonet stabs in his body. The doctor says it was only the first three while he was alive; the last one was through his heart and killed him at once.

'We gave him Christian burial, Aunt; we took him to the camp.

'The Commandant was there, and all of the family who are with the

Commando were there, and they all said they hoped God would comfort you ...'

The old woman leaned forward and grasped the boy's arm. 'Read it over again,' she said, 'from where they found him.' He turned back and re-read slowly. She gazed at the page as though she were reading also. Then, suddenly, she slipped out at the front door.

At the back of the house she found her daughter-in-law still walking up and down, and the Kaffir woman with a red handkerchief bound round her head and the child sitting across her hip, sucking from her long, pendulous breast, looking on.

The old woman walked up to her daughter-in-law and grasped her firmly by the arm.

'He's dead! You know, my boy's dead!' she cried, drawing the apron down with her right hand and disclosing her swollen and bleared face. 'Oh, his beautiful hair – Oh, his beautiful hair!'

The old woman held her arm tighter with both hands; the younger opened her half-closed eyes, and looked into the keen, clear eyes fixed on hers, and stood arrested.

The old woman drew her face closer to hers. 'You ... do ... not ... know ... what ... has ... happened!' she spoke slowly, her tongue striking her front gum, the jaw moving stiffly, as though partly paralysed. She loosed her left hand and held up the curved work-worn fingers before her daughter-in-law's face. 'Was it not told me ... the night he was born ... here ... at this spot ... that he would do great things ... great things ... for his land and his people?' She bent forward till her lips almost touched the other's. 'Three ... bullet ... wounds ... and four ... bayonet ... stabs!' She raised her left hand high in the air. 'Three ... bullet ... wounds ... and four ... bayonet ... stabs! ... Is it given to many to die so for their land and their people!'

The younger woman gazed into her eyes, her own growing larger and larger. She let the old woman lead her by the arm in silence into the house.

The Field-Cornet's son was gone, feeling there was nothing more to be done; and the Kaffir woman went back with her baby to her hut beyond the kraals. All day the house was very silent. The Kaffir woman wondered that no smoke rose from the farmhouse chimney, and that she was not called to churn, or wash the pots. At three o'clock she went down to the house. As she passed the grated window of the round out-house she saw the buckets of milk still standing unsifted on the floor as they had been set down at breakfast time, and under the great soap-pot beside the wood pile the fire had died out. She went round to the front of the house and saw the door and window shutters still closed, as though her mistresses were still sleeping. So she rebuilt the fire under the soap-pot and went back to her hut.

It was four o'clock when the grandmother came out from the dark inner room where she and her daughter-in-law had been lying down; she opened the top of the front door, and lit the fire with twigs, and set the large black kettle over it. When it boiled she made coffee, and poured out two cups and set them on the table with a plate of biscuits, and then called her daughter-in-law from the inner room.

The two women sat down one on each side of the table, with their coffee cups before them, and the biscuits between them, but for a time they said nothing, but sat silent, looking out through the open door at the shadow of the house and the afternoon sunshine beyond it. At last the older woman motioned that the younger should drink her coffee. She took a little, and then folding her arms on the table rested her head on them, and sat motionless as if asleep.

The older woman broke up a biscuit into her own cup, and stirred it round and round; and then, without tasting, sat gazing out into the afternoon's sunshine till it grew cold beside her.

It was five, and the heat was quickly dying; the glorious golden colouring of the later afternoon was creeping over everything when she rose from her chair. She moved to the door and took from behind it two large white calico bags hanging there, and from nails on the wall she took down two large brown cotton kappies. She walked round the table and laid her hand gently on her daughter-in-law's arm. The younger woman raised her head slowly and looked up into her mother-in-law's face; and then, suddenly, she knew that her mother-in-law was an old, old, woman. The little shrivelled face that looked down at her was hardly larger than a child's, the eyelids were half closed and the lips worked at the corners and the bones cut out through the skin in the temples.

'I am going out to sow – the ground will be getting too dry tomorrow; will you come with me?' she said gently.

The younger woman made a movement with her hand, as though she said 'What is the use?' and redropped her hand on the table.

'It may go on for long, our burghers must have food,' the old woman said gently.

The younger woman looked into her face, then she rose slowly and taking one of the brown kappies from her hand, put it on, and hung one of the bags over her left arm; the old woman did the same and together they passed out of the door. As the older woman stepped down the younger caught her and saved her from falling.

'Take my arm, mother,' she said.

But the old woman drew her shoulders up. 'I only stumbled a little!' she said quickly. 'That step has been always too high'; but before she reached the plank over the sloot the shoulders had drooped again, and the neck fallen forward.

The mould in the lands was black and soft; it lay in long ridges, as it had been ploughed up a week before, but the last night's rain had softened it and made it moist and ready for putting in the seed.

The bags which the women carried on their arms were full of the seed of pumpkins and mealies. They began to walk up the lands, keeping parallel with the low hedge of dried bushes that ran up along the side of the sloot almost up to the top of the ridge. At every few paces they stopped and bent down to press into the earth, now one and then the other kind of seed from their bags. Slowly they walked up and down till they reached the top of the land almost on the horizon line; and then they turned, and walked down, sowing as they went. When they had reached the bottom of the land before the farmhouse it was almost sunset, and their bags were nearly empty; but they turned to go up once more. The light of the setting sun cast long, gaunt shadows from their figures across the ploughed land, over the low hedge and the sloot, into the bare veld beyond; shadows that grew longer and longer as they passed slowly on pressing in the seeds ... The seeds! ... that were to lie in the dank, dark, earth, and rot there, seemingly, to die, till their outer covering had split and fallen from them ... and then, when the rains had fallen, and the sun had shone, to come up above the earth again, and high in the clear air to lift their feathery plumes and hang out their pointed leaves and silken tassels! To cover the ground with a mantle of green and gold through which sunlight quivered, over which the insects hung by thousands, carrying yellow pollen on their legs and wings and making the air alive with their hum and stir, while grain and fruit ripened surely ... for the next season's harvest!

When the sun had set, the two women with their empty bags turned and walked silently home in the dark to the farmhouse.

NINETEEN HUNDRED AND ONE

Near one of the camps in the Northern Transvaal are the graves of two women. The older one died first, on the twenty-third of the month, from hunger and want; the younger woman tended her with ceaseless care and devotion till the end. A week later when the British Superintendent came round to inspect the tents, she was found lying on her blanket on the mud-floor dead, with the rations of bread and meat she had got four days before untouched on a box beside her. Whether she died of disease, or from inability to eat the food, no one could say. Some who had seen her said she hardly seemed to care to live after the old woman died; they buried them side by side.

There is no stone and no name upon either grave to say who lies there ... our unknown ... our unnamed ... our forgotten dead.

IN THE YEAR NINETEEN HUNDRED AND FOUR

If you look for the little farmhouse among the ridges you will not find it there today.

The English soldiers burnt it down. You can only see where the farmhouse once stood, because the stramonia and weeds grow high and very strong there; and where the ploughed lands were you can only tell, because the veld never grows quite the same on land that has once been ploughed. Only a brown patch among the long grass on the ridge shows where the kraals and huts once were.

In a country house in the north of England the owner has upon his wall an old flint-lock gun. He takes it down to show his friends. It is a small thing he picked up in the war in South Africa, he says. It must be at least eighty years old and is very valuable. He shows how curiously it is constructed; he says it must have been kept in such perfect repair by continual polishing for the steel shines as if it were silver. He does not tell that he took it from the wall of the little mud house before he burnt it down.

It was the grandfather's gun, which the women had kept polished on the wall.

In a London drawing-room the descendant of a long line of titled fore-fathers entertains her guests. It is a fair room, and all that money can buy to make life soft and beautiful is there.

On the carpet stands a little dark wooden stoof. When one of her guests notices it, she says it is a small curiosity which her son brought home to her from South Africa when he was out in the war there; and how good it was of him to think of her when he was away in the back country. And when they ask what it is, she says it is a thing Boer women have as a foot-stool and to keep their feet warm; and she shows the hole at the side where they put the coals in, and the little holes at the top where the heat comes out.

And the other woman puts her foot out and rests it on the stoof just to try how it feels, and drawls 'How f-u-n-n-y!'

It is grandmother's stoof, that the child used to sit on.

The wagon chest was found and broken open just before the thatch caught fire, by three private soldiers, and they divided the money between them; one spent his share in drink, another had his stolen from him, but the third sent his home to England to a girl in the East End of London. With part of it she bought a gold brooch and ear-rings, and the rest she saved to buy a silk wedding-dress when he came home.

A syndicate of Jews in Johannesburg and London have bought the farm. They purchased it from the English Government, because they think to find gold on it. They have purchased it and paid for it ... but they do not possess it.

Only the men who lie in their quiet graves upon the hill-side, who lived on it, and loved it, possess it; and the piles of stones above them, from among the long waving grasses, keep watch over the land.

FREDERICK C CORNELL

The Drink of the Dead

A legend of Bushmanland

From: *A Rip van Winkle of the Kalahari* … (1915)

This tale was told me over a camp-fire in lonely Bushmanland.

A wild and desolate land it is, but little known except to the occasional nomad 'trek–boer', who in the seasons when rain has made it possible wanders from water-hole to water-hole with his scanty flocks and herds; or to the mounted trooper on his long and lonely patrol; or the even more infrequent prospector in his search for the mineral wealth that abounds in the district, but which scarcity of water and cost of transport have so far rendered use-less. A land with a character all its own – of wide stretches of low grey bush, intermingled with the vivid-green patches of luxuriant 'melkbosch', giving deceptive promise of non-existent moisture; of level plains, gay with bril-liant flowers, from which long humped ranges of granite rise in serried lines.

A common necessity had drawn two of us white men to a distant and iso-lated water-hole, which to our dismay we had found dry and empty. Neither of us knew of other water within twelve hours' trek, our beasts were tired, and it was a great relief when Karelse, my Hottentot driver, declared he knew of good water only about four hours away. I wondered I had never heard of it before, but Karelse, who knew every inch of the country, was confident that though he had never been to the spot we should find plenty of water there; and, sure enough, nightfall brought us to the place, and there was water in abundance. Here we shared coffee and biltong, and afterwards sat smoking and yarning by the cheerful blaze of the dry fire-bush.

The night was wild and stormy, and a cold wind blew in sharp gusts round the fantastic pile of rocks that rose abruptly from the small deep pool of black-looking water, sending the sparks swirling upwards and causing the flames to leap fiercely, whilst the flicker of the fire shone on the glittering 'baviaan-spel' of the rocks, and the black shadows danced to the whistle of the wind.

Overhead the sky seemed charged with rain – the heavy, hurrying clouds lowered and trailed and seemed as though at any moment they might launch a deluge upon the parched and yearning veldt; but the promise was ever an empty one, for not a drop fell, and the rain-charged phalanxes sped onward and ever onward, to shed their precious burthen upon distant and more favoured fields …

Jason I had met before. Like myself he was a prospector, and had known many lands. He was a reserved, reliable man, who possessed a habit of silence rare amongst men of our fraternity. Our talk had been of Brazil, where we had both spent many years of our youth, and almost unconsciously we had fallen into Portuguese – a language we both spoke fluently.

It was then that the Other Man appeared. Suddenly, silently, and alone he stepped from among the flickering shadows of the rocks, so abruptly as to cause both Jason and I to start up with an exclamation. By the uncertain light of the fire he appeared to be an elderly man of medium size, swarthy, weather-beaten, and bearded to the eyes. He strode to the fire, extended a limp, cold hand to Jason and I in turn with an almost inaudible greeting, and crouched down by the dying blaze, his dark eyes bent upon the glowing embers. Naturally expecting him to be Dutch, both Jason and I had greeted him in the usual manner by giving our own names in self-introduction. He had made no reply; but though our hearth was but a camp-fire in a wild country, we felt that whoever he was he was in a measure our guest, and therefore we made no immediate attempt to find out who or what he was. Still he did not speak. He put aside our proffered coffee, gently but without a word, and sat glowering and gazing into the fire.

At last Jason spoke to him direct – first in Dutch, and, getting no reply, in English.

'Come far?' he queried.

There was no sign that the man had heard.

Jason looked at me with a lift of the eyebrow. Then I tried.

'Farming?' I asked.

No answer.

'Trading?'

Still no answer.

'Man's dumb!' grunted Jason.

But he was muttering now. Gradually his words became clearer, and to our amazement he was speaking Portuguese!

'*Pesquisadores – pesquisadores,*' he murmured, '*como nos outras dos tempos antigos.*' (Prospectors – searchers of wealth, like we others of the olden days.) '… Searching for that which is not yours, but mine, mine by every right …But you will never find it – or if you do your bones will lie beside those others beneath the black water, where the dead drink …!'

His mutterings became again inarticulate. I looked at Jason. He sat staring open-mouthed at our strange visitor. For my own part I confess I was puzzled and somewhat startled. Jason's eyes left the stranger abruptly, and met my own, and mutually and silently our lips framed the word – 'Mad!' Yes, surely he must be mad, this strange man who spoke of the 'ancient days' in a tongue rarely heard in this part of Africa; but what was he doing here – here, alone, in this desolate spot, full fifty miles from human habitation.

And as we looked at each other in doubt and hesitation the stranger began again to speak, first in broken, disconnected sentences. But gradually the strange, far-away tone – like that of a man talking in his sleep – became clearer and more connected, and soon Jason and I were gazing at him as though spellbound, and drinking in every word of the queer archaic-sounding Portuguese in which he told his weird story – fragment, delirium, wanderings of a madman, call it what you will.

'...There were Bushmen then – wild dwarf men who shot with poisoned arrows, and had seen no white man before ...

'Alvaro Nunes had still five charges for his arquebus, and I as many for my hand petronel ...When they heard the thunder of the powder they cast aside their weapons and crawled to us on their knees, taking us for gods ... And bearing in mind all that the shipwrecked Castilian we had found at Cabo Tormentoso had told us of the mine of precious stones, we hastened to propitiate them in every way ...The gauds we had brought – gay beads, bright kerchiefs, and the like – with these we won our way to their goodwill. They hunted for us; of buck and of wild game they brought us abundance; but though months passed we were no nearer that which we sought – the mine of bright stones such as the Spanisher had shown us and the whereabouts of which these strange, black, dwarfish people alone knew. Never could we master their strange tongue – like to the creaking and rustling of dry bones upon a gibbet more than the speech of humans – and time and patience alone showed us a way. Their man of magic held great power over them. He was of another race, of our own stature, and with a yellow skin. He had another tongue than these dwarf men of the bush, and this Alvaro and I learnt when his suspicion of us gave way and he found that we wished not to alienate the tribe from his authority ...For the Spanisher had said: "Their magician, because of his black magic, he alone hath the secret of the mine of stones like unto those of Golconda." ...Little did we fear his magic – we who feared nothing in heaven or earth or in the waters beneath – Alvaro and I, old freebooters of the Spanish Main; but they others – Luiz Fonseca, José Albuquerque, and Antonio Mendez – brave men, but ignorant shipmen, they were fearful of the witch-doctor and his black art.

'Then when N'buqu, the witch, had heard all of the wonders of our land across the great water, he would fain plot to come with us and see all these wondrous things of which we spake. And cunningly Alvaro led him on day by day until he was all impatient to leave this tribe of dwarfs, who were not even his own kinsmen. Then when all was ripe he told him that with us there were no wild lands full of buck for those who cared to shoot them, that our wealth was in red gold and shining stones! And at long last he showed the stone taken from the Spanisher at the Cape of Storms ...

'At night when the moon was full N'buqu took us to the black water-pit lying deep and dark at the foot of the rocky hill. Ten fathoms deep was it and full to the brim with icy water. Many times had we drank from it, for though all around the land lay parched in the torrid heat the black water-pit was always full to the brim ...

'But what magic was this? Here was no water, but a yawning shaft gaped black and dismal where the pool had been. The shipmen shrank back in dismay. "Here is magic!" they muttered fearfully, crossing themselves. N'buqu laughed. He also had learnt something of our tongue, and understood. "No magic is here," said he; "'tis but a spring from yonder hill that fills this pool, and it needs but to turn the stream aside and the water will all drain away. Later I will show!"

'From a fire-stick he had brought he lit a torch of dry wood. By its glare we saw that a hide ladder dangled from an overhanging rock into the deep pit. Down it N'buqu led the way, followed by us all in turn − the shipmen with many muttered prayers and misgivings ... Slimy and dank was the fearsome place, but the bottom was firm and rocky, and from it there branched a cavern wide enough for us all to walk abreast. Gently it led upward ... and then we stood in a broader cavern, where the light from the torch in every direction flashed back from a myriad dazzling points: ceiling, walls, every rock protuberance, even the very floor gleamed and scintillated till the whole place blazed as though on fire. N'buqu thrust the torch into Alvaro's hand. "Look!" he cried, and smote with a spear he carried at the wall of the cavern. At the light blow a handful of the flashing points fell to the floor. We picked them up. They were the "bright stones" of the Spanisher − they were diamonds! Here was wealth beyond conception − wealth beside which the fabled Golconda would be as nought, wealth untold for us all. But on the floor among the flashing gems there lay many white bones − the bones of dead men ... Wealth, vast wealth for us all, and yet we quarrelled there as to the division of the stones, and as to how we were to get them away. "Get all we can at once and flee this very night!" urged the shipmen. "And die of thirst in the desert places!" said Alvaro − for it was the season of drought! "Stay only until we can fill our water-skins," they counselled. But Alvaro and myself − we were wiser. N'buqu − his must be the plan. He knew the best paths back to the Cape of Tempests, he knew the water-holes; we must be guided by his counsel. And we forced them to listen. Yes, he had a plan. Three nights hence we must flee. He would have water ready in skins. Meanwhile each night he would divert the water, and we must descend and collect the stones so that we should have enough for all. At night the tribe believed that the spirits of the dead came to the black water to drink, and always avoided the spot … And by the light of the flickering torch we broke down showers of the glittering stones from the soft blue rock in which they were embedded till our pouches were full and the torch had burned out. Then we stumbled and groped our way over slime and bones till we came to the shaft, and one by one we climbed up and out into the fair white moonlight …

'Fools! fools! The shipmen quarrelled over the stones the first day. Alvaro lent them dice and they gambled with each other for their new-found wealth. And as Alvaro wished, they quarrelled; and Albuquerque and Fonseca drew steel upon each other, and there in the sunshine stabbed each other to death. "The more for us," said Alvaro, and we divided the stones they fought for.

'That night we four went again to the black water. Once more we loaded our pouches and climbed out one by one. I the first, for I was faint with the air of the cavern. Then came N'buqu. But Alvaro came not, nor Mendez the shipman. Impatiently I shook the ladder: it was near dawn. Then at length came Alvaro. He was ghastly in the moonlight. And at the top he began to pull up the ladder he had climbed by. "But Mendez?" I muttered. He answered not, but still hauled the hide rope. Then I seized him by the shoulder and looked in his face. There was blood upon him. "He struck me from behind," he said; "my vest of mail saved me; he is dead. The more for us!" I liked not Alvaro's face, and looked to my dagger lest tomorrow he should say, "The more for me …"

That third night Alvaro and I for the last time descended the black shaft. Well watched we each the other. He had both dagger and arquebus, and I my hand petronel and dagger too. N'buqu came not down with us, feigning that he must prepare all things that we might flee as soon as we had loaded our pouches for the last time … There he left us in the black shaft – my life-long comrade and I; and by reason of the lust of wealth that came upon me and because of the fear of that which I saw in Alvaro's eye I struck him unawares as he knelt for the last gem. Deep behind the neck my dagger drank his blood. His vest of mail did not save him from me! … And turning to flee hastily with all the stones, I found the ladder drawn up and N'buqu laughing at me from above.

'"Ho! ho! white man, white wizard!" he called. "Ye who would show me the wondrous things of thine own land. How fares it with ye now? Surely thou hast enough of the bright stones now – thy dead comrade's share and all he had taken; thou hast them all! Handle them, gaze on them, eat of them, drink of them; for of a surety naught else will there be for thee to eat and drink! Ho! ho! surely the black man's magic is vain against the wisdom of the white!" … And thus he taunted me, whilst vainly I strove by means of my dagger to cut footholds in the slimy walls of the shaft and thus climb to freedom. But the holes crumbled as soon as my weight bore on them, and after falling again and again I desisted in despair … And ever the yellow fiend above taunted me, and it was abundantly clear that he had but feigned to fall in with our scheme the more fully to encompass our destruction … Dawn found me raving in terror of my coming fate – alone with the bodies of the friend whom I had slain and the shipman who had been by him slain. Terror had helped to parch my tongue with thirst, and both shaft and cavern, though moist, were drained too dry to afford one mouthful of the precious fluid. Yet though longing for water I knew well that when N'buqu should choose again to direct the stream I should drown like any rat. The day passed. I heard the frightened mutterings of the dwarf men as they crowded round the mouth of the shaft seeking the black water that had vanished; but at my first hoarse shout they fled, yelling in alarm. Day turned to night, and I had become as one dead. The ghosts of dead Alvaro and Mendez and a thousand others crowded round me, gibing, and mouthing, and seeking too for the black water. Again day, and again night came and went. Still the water I longed for and yet feared came not. I suffered the tortures of the damned, and fain would I have scattered my throbbing brains with that last charge of my hand petronel; but ever as I raised it dead Alvaro caught my hand in an icy grip and I could not die …

'Then again I heard N'buqu, and with him certain men of the dwarfs he ruled. And in their whistling, creaking tongue I heard him hold forth: "Lo! ye who doubted me, thus do I show my power. These other white gods that came from afar, ye thought them stronger than I, yet have I caused their utter destruction. But because of the little faith ye had in me, and as a sign of my power and displeasure, have I also caused the spirits that dwell in the black pool to take away the water that is life to ye all!"

'Then I heard them moaning and begging for the water, and the voice of the witch-doctor ordering them to lie flat on their faces and look not up whilst he forced the spirits to bring back that which they had taken. Then he called to me in my own tongue loudly: "Ho! thou white god! eat thou thy fill of the bright stones; of water thou shalt soon drink plenty!" And I knew that he would soon move that rock whereby the water could be diverted back to the pit. But even as he gibed at me, leaning over the brink, dead Alvaro's ice-cold hand guided my petronel till it covered the black fiend's body, and the iron ball struck full and true below his throat. Down at my feet hurtled the body, and at the report I could hear the dwarfs shriek and fly away from the spot in fear.

'Not dead, but dying was he, for his magic was naught against the weapons of the white man. Yet magic had he, and as he died so did he curse me and cast over me a spell of terror: "Thou shalt guard well thy bright stones, oh, slayer of thy friend!" he shrieked. "Water shalt thou have, and yet shall never quench thine awful thirst; hunger shall consume thee and thou shalt not eat; thou shalt long for death, yet shalt thou not die!" And cursing thus he died; and his ghost joined the band of weird watchers in the cavern of bright stones …

'And the tribe of dwarfs one by one died of thirst, for it was a year of fearful heat, and they knew of no other water. Day by day they came shrieking and praying to the spirits of the black shaft to give them back the water. Day by day they flung living men into the pit as sacrifice to join the spirits below, till all, all were dead. Yet could I not die! ...

'Over their bleached bones the black water again runs. Below, guarded by the dread watchers, lie the bright stones. Seek not the spot, ye white men who speak the old tongue, lest ye too watch for ever; for the place is accursed! ...

The strange narration ended as it began, not abruptly, but in indistinct mutterings.

Half-fascinated, Jason and I had followed every word of the strange archaic Portuguese. The rhythmic sentences seemed to have had an almost hypnotic effect upon us, for neither of us afterwards remembered how and when we fell asleep.

I was awakened by Karelse shaking me. It was just break of day. I felt heavy, sleepy, and confused, and for a moment remembered nothing. 'Coffee, *baas*,' said the Hottentot; and as I sipped it I remembered. I looked round. Jason was sleeping like a log. Our strange visitor had gone. 'Where is the other *baas*?' I inquired of Karelse. He stared at me, and then looked over at Jason. 'No, no,' I said impatiently, 'the old *baas* that came in the night?' Karelse's face was a study. He had evidently seen no one, though the boy's fire had been not twenty yards from our own. Had I dreamt the whole thing? I strode over and roused Jason. He woke with a startled exclamation. His first words assured me the old man had been there. 'Damn that mad chap,' he said. 'His horrible old yarn made me dream badly. Where is he?' Karelse stared from one to the other, his yellow face a queer ashen grey. He was plainly frightened. 'Come,' said I to Jason, 'let us go and have a sluice: there is water in plenty.' I led the way to the pool. It had been too dark for us to see it properly when we had arrived the evening before. We bent over the dark, clear water. Sheer and black the pit went down, and it was plainly of great depth. And from the brink the granite kopje rose abruptly. Jason and I looked at each other, then at Karelse.

'Karelse,' I asked, 'have you ever been here before?'

'No, *baas*', he faltered; 'there is always plenty of good water here, they say, but the place has a bad name and no one comes here. They say it is haunted.'

'What do they call the place?' I asked.

'Dood Drenk,' he said – 'the Drink of the Dead!'

ARTHUR SHEARLEY CRIPPS

The Black Death

From: *Cinderella in the South: South African Tales* (1918)

This is a story of a voyage home. The boat was one of the finest on the line and we were not overcrowded. We had wonderful weather that trip, brilliant sunshine relieved by a fresh little breeze that kept its place, doing its duty without taking too much upon itself, or making itself obnoxious. In the third-class we were quiet on the whole, and what is called well-behaved, though neither with millennial serenity nor millennial sobriety.

A red-cheeked gentleman took a red-cheeked married lady and her child under his vigilant protection. Two or three Rhodesians and Joburgers enriched the bar with faithful fondness. Cards and sweeps on the run of the boat and the selling of sweep-tickets – these all stimulated the circulation of savings. Hues of language vied with hues of sunset not seldom of an eventide.

Life was not so very thrilling on that voyage, the treading of 'border-land dim 'twixt vice and virtue' is apt to be rather a dull business.

There was no such incident as that which stirred us on another voyage – the taking of a carving knife to the purser by a drunkard. On the other hand there was no unusual battle-noise of spiritual combat such as may have quickened the pulses of one or two of the boats the year of the English Mission.

We were middling, and dull at that, on the *Sluys Castle*, till we reached Madeira. Then the description I have given of our voyage ceases to apply. The two or three days after that were exciting enough to one or two passengers at any rate.

James Carraway had come down from Kimberley, he told me. He was a spare, slight man, with a red moustache. He sought me occasionally of an eventide, and confided to me views of life in general, and of some of his fellow-passengers in particular. I remember one night especially, when the Southern Cross was in full view and the water about the keel splotched with phosphorescence. Carraway had a big grievance that night. He commented acridly on a coloured woman that I had espied on board. She was not very easily visible herself, but one or two faintly coloured children played often about the deck, and she herself might now and then be seen nursing a baby. I had seen her on a bench sometimes when I had gone to the library to change a book. I had seen her more rarely in the sunshine on deck, nursing the aforesaid baby.

'One man's brought a Kaffir wife on board,' growled Carraway.

I said, 'I thought she might be a nurse.'

'No, she's his wife,' contended Carraway. 'It's cheek of him bringing her on board with the third-class passengers.'

I said, 'Which is her husband?'

'He's been pointed out to me,' he said. 'The other white men seem rather to avoid him. I don't know what your opinion on this point may be,' he said. 'I consider that a man who marries a Kaffir sinks to her status.'

I said nothing. He did not like my silence much, I gathered. He was not so very cordial afterwards. He was a man with many grievances – Carraway.

When we were drawing close to Madeira, two nights before, on the Sunday – Carraway touched the subject again.

The parson had preached incidentally on the advisability of being white – white all round. I thought he played to his gallery a bit, in what he said.

'An excellent sermon,' said Carraway. 'Did you hear how he got at that josser with the Kaffir wife? That parson's a white man.'

I said nothing.

'What God hath divided let no man unite,' said Carraway, improving the occasion. 'I don't uphold Kaffirs. The white man must always be top dog,' etc., etc.

Carraway grew greasily fluent on rather well-worn lines. I smoked my pipe and made no comment. By-and-by he tired of his monologue.

He gave me no further confidences till the night after we left Madeira. Then he came to me suddenly about eleven o'clock as I stood on the well-deck, smoking a pipe before turning in.

'Come and have a walk,' he said, in a breathless sort of way.

We climbed some steps and paced the upper deck towards the wheel-house. There were few electric lights burning now. After a turn or two he drew up under one of them, and looked round to see whether anyone listened.

'Don't give me away for God's sake,' he said. He held up a hand towards the light pathetically.

'It's showing,' he said. 'God knows why. God knows what I've done to bring it.'

I said nothing, but looked at him and considered him carefully. He certainly did not seem to be drunk.

Then I examined the hand he gave me.

'I don't see anything particular,' I said. 'What's wrong?'

'Good Lord! The nails.'

But the nails looked to me pink and healthy.

'Tell me,' I said, 'what you think's wrong.'

Yet he could not tell me that night. He tried to tell me. He was just like a little boy in most awful trepidation, trying to confess some big transgression. He gasped and spluttered, but he never got it out that night. I couldn't make head nor tail of what he said. After he was gone to bed it is true I put two and two together and guessed something. But I was fairly puzzled at the time.

'You're a bit upset tonight,' I said. 'You're not quite yourself, it's the sea I suppose, or something. Come to bed and get a good night.' His teeth chattered as he came down the ladder. I got him down to his cabin.

'Thanks!' he said. 'Good-night! I may come all right in the morning. Anyhow I'll have a bath and try.'

He said it so naively that I could not help laughing.

'Yes, have a sea-water bath, a jolly good idea,' I said. 'You'll have to be up early. There's only one and there's a run on it before breakfast. Good night!'

I saw him again in the morning outside the bath-room. He came out in his pink-and-white pyjamas; the pink was aggressive and fought with the tint of his moustache. He looked very blue and wretched.

'Well,' I asked, 'Have you slept it off whatever it was?'

'No,' he said, 'let me tell you about it.' He began to gasp and splutter.

Just then another postulant came up, making for the bath-room door.

'Afterwards!' I said, 'After breakfast.' And I vanished into the bath-room. It was probably Carraway, I thought, that had left a little collection of soaps in that bath-room. He had brought a bucket of fresh water with him apparently to give them a fair trial. There was yellow soap, a pumice stone, and carbolic soap, and scented soap. 'I'll keep them for him,' I thought. 'Somebody may jump them if I leave them here. I wonder why in the world he's so distrait.' I had my suspicions as to the reason, and I laughed softly to myself.

After breakfast he invited me back to the bath-room; there was no run on it then.

'It's quiet,' he said. Then after many gasps and splutters he enlightened me. His nails were turning colour, he told me.

'Anyone would think I had Kaffir blood in me,' he said.

Also his skin was giving him grave cause for solicitude. I did not resist the temptation to take him rather seriously. I administered philosophic consolation. I reminded him of Dumas and other serviceable coloured people. I rather enjoyed his misery; poetic justice seemed to me to need some satisfaction. He, the negrophobe, who was so ultra-keen on drawing the line was now enjoying imaginative experiences on the far side of it.

'It seems then,' I remarked, 'that you are now a person of colour.'

He nearly fainted. He did not swear. He seemed to have lost all his old truculence. He began to whimper like a child.

'After all, I never shared your prejudices,' I said. 'Cheer up, old man, I won't drop you like a hot potato even if you have a touch of the tar brush.'

He cried as if his heart would break. I saw I had gone too far. It was like dancing on a trodden worm.

'Carraway,' I said, 'it's a pure delusion. Your nails are all right, and so's your skin. You're dreaming, man. You've got nerves or indigestion, or something. It's something inside you that's wrong. There's nothing outside for anyone to see.'

His eyes gleamed. He shook my hand feebly. Then he held up his own hand to the light.

'It's there,' he said wearily, after a while. 'You want to be kind, but you can't make black white. That's what I've always said. It's the Will of God, and there's nothing to gain by fighting it. Black will be black, and white will be white till crack of doom.'

I told him sternly that I was going to fetch the doctor to him. He sprang at me and gripped my arm.

'I trusted you,' he said. 'I needn't have told you. You promised.'

So I had like a simpleton.

'Only give me two days,' he said, 'then I'll go to the doctor myself, if nothing works in all that time.'

So I said I would respect my promise loyally for those two days.

'I only told *you*,' he said, 'because my head was splitting with keeping it in. It's awful to me. I thought you were a negrophil and wouldn't think so much of it as other fellows. But for God's sake don't give me away to them. There's lots of things to try yet. By the way, ask that parson to pray for one afflicted and distressed in mind, body, and estate.'

He did try many sorts of things, poor fellow. He was in and out of that bath-room a good share of both days. He also tried drugs and patent medicines. I saw his cabin littered with them. He would sneak into meals those two days when people had almost finished, and gobble his food furtively.

I caught him once or twice smoking his pipe in the bath-room or the bath-room passage. He would not venture amid the crowd on deck. Only when many of the passengers were in bed would he come up with me, and take my arm and walk up and down. That was on the Wednesday night.

Wednesday night came, then Thursday morning. Thursday forenoon was long, and Thursday afternoon longer.

At last the sun was low, and I began to count the hours to the time when I might consult the doctor.

I secured an interview with Carraway in the bath-room soon after sunset. 'Any better?' I asked for about the twentieth time.

He shook his head dejectedly.

'All right. We must go to the doctor to-morrow morning. But, O Carraway, do go to him to-night, don't be afraid. It's only imagination. Do go.'

'I'll see,' he said in a dazed, dreary sort of way, 'I'll see, but I want to play the last card I have in my hand before I go. It's a trump card perhaps.'

'On my honour,' I said, 'you're tormenting yourself for nothing. You're as white as ever you were.'

Then I said 'Good-night.' I stopped for a moment outside the door, and heard him begin splashing and scrubbing. The thing was getting on my own nerves.

I went off up on deck, and smoked hard, then I read, and wrote letters, and smoked again, and went to bed very late. I had steered clear of the bath-room and all Carraway's haunts so far as I could. Yes, and I had gone over to the second class, and I had asked the parson to do as he wanted. I had asked him the day before. Now I asked him over again.

The steward handed me a letter when he brought me my coffee in the morning. I opened it and read:

'Dear Sir,
'Perhaps my negrophoby is wrong. Anyhow, it's real to me. I had and have it, and see no way to get rid of it properly here on earth. Now God has touched me, me the negrophobe, and coloured me. And to me the thing seems very hard to bear. Therefore I am trying the sea to-night.

'In the bath-room there never seemed to be enough water. I want to try a bath with plenty of water. But I am afraid it may be with me as it would have been with Macbeth or Lady Macbeth. Those red hands of murder could not be washed white by the ocean, they could only "the multitudinous seas incarnadine, making the green one red". What if I cannot be decolorised by any sea? What if my flesh only pollutes the sea, when I plunge, and makes all black? God help me!!! You are a negrophil and don't half understand.

'Yours truly,
'J Carraway.'

I questioned the steward. He had found the letter in my place at table.

Sure enough there was a third-class passenger missing. I suppose Carraway had slipped off quietly in the moonlight to try his desperate experiment. It was a cruel business – his monomania.

If I had broken my promise and called the doctor earlier, could he have been cured? Or would he have lingered in an asylum – shuddering over the fictitious glooming of his nails and skin, shaking in a long ague of negrophoby.

Anyhow, I'm sorry I didn't do more for him, didn't walk him round the deck the last night at least, and try my best to cheer him. Yes, I blame myself badly for not doing that.

May God who allowed his delusion pardon that last manoeuvre of his! I do not think Carraway had any clear wish to take his own life.

I can imagine the scene so convincingly – Carraway pausing, hesitating, then plunging into the moon-blanched water from the dizzy height above, eager to find which the multitudinous seas would do – would they change his imagined colour, or would they suddenly darken, matching in their tints his own discoloration?

PERCEVAL GIBBON

Like Unto Like

From: *The Vrouw Grobelaar's Leading Cases* (1918)

For the most part the Vrouw Grobelaar's nephews and nieces were punctually obedient. Doubtless this was policy; for the old lady founded her authority on a generous complement of this world's goods. However, man is as the grass of the field (as she would constantly aver); and it fell that Frikkie Viljoen, otherwise a lad of promise, became enamoured of a girl of lower caste than the Grobelaars and Viljoens, and this, mark you, with a serious eye to marriage. Even this, after a proper and orthodox reluctance on the part of his elders and betters, might have been condoned; for the Viljoens had multiplied exceedingly in the land, and the older sons were not yet married. But, as though to aggravate the business, Frikkie took a sort of glory in it, and openly belauded his lowly sweetheart.

'Mark you,' said the Vrouw Grobelaar with tremendous solemnity, 'this choice is your own. Take care you do not find a Leah in your Rachel.'

Frikkie replied openly that he was sure enough about the girl.

The Vrouw Grobelaar shook a doubtful head. 'Her grandfather was a *bijwohner*,' she said. 'Pas op! or she will one day go back to her own people and shame you.'

The misguided Frikkie saw fit to laugh at this.

'Oh, you may laugh! You may laugh, and laugh, until your time comes for weeping. I tell you, she will one day return to her own people, *bijwohners* and rascals all of them, as Stoffel Mostert's wife did.'

The old lady paused, and Frikkie defiantly demanded further particulars.

'Yes,' continued the Vrouw Grobelaar, 'I remember all the disgrace and shame of it to this day, and how poor Stoffel went about with his head bowed and looked no one in the face.

'He had a farm under the Hangklip, and a very nice farm it was, with two wells and a big dam right up above the lands, so that he had no need for a windmill to carry his water. If he had stuck to the farm Stoffel might have been a rich man; and perhaps, when he was old enough to be listened to, the Burghers might have made him a feldkornet.

'But no! He must needs cast his eyes about him till they fell on one Katrina Ruiter, the daughter, so please you, of a dirty *takhaar bijwohner* on his own farm.

He went mad about the girl, and thought her quite different from all other girls, though she had a troop of untidy sisters like herself galloping wild about the place. I will own she was a well-grown slip of a lass, tall and straight, and all that; but she had a winding, bending way with her that struck me like something shameless. For the rest, she had a lot of coal-black hair that bunched round her face like the frame round a picture; but there was something in the colour of her skin and the shaping of her lips and nostrils that made me say to myself, "Ah, somewhere and somewhen your people have been meddling with the Kafirs."

'Black? No, of course she wasn't black. Nor yet yellow; but I tell you, the black blood showed through her white skin so clearly that I wonder Stoffel Mostert did not see it and drive her from his door with a sjambok.

'But the man was clean mad, and, spite of all we could do – spite of his uncle, the Predikant; spite of the ugly dirty family of the girl herself – he rode her to the dorp and married her there; for the Predikant, godly man, would not turn a hand in the business.

'Now, just how they lived together I cannot tell you for sure; for you may be very certain I drank no coffee in the house of the *bijwohner's* daughter. But, by all hearings, they bore with one another very well; and I have even been told that Stoffel was much given to caressing the woman, and she would make out to love him very much indeed.

'Perhaps she really did? What nonsense! How can a *bijwohner's* baggage love a well-to-do Burgher? You are talking foolishness. But anyhow, if there was any trouble between them, they kept it to themselves for close upon a year.

'Then (this is how it has been told to me) one night Stoffel woke up in the dark, and his wife was not beside him.

'"Is it morning already?" he said, and looked through the window. But the stars were high and bright, and he saw it was scarcely midnight.

'He lay for a while, and then got up and drew on his clothes – doing everything slowly, hoping she would return. But when he was done she was not yet come, and he went out in the dark to the kitchen, and there he found the outer door unlocked and heard the dog whining in the yard.

'He took his gun from the beam where it hung and went forth. The dog barked and sprang to him, and together they went out to the veld, seeking Katrina Ruiter.

'The dog seemed to know what was wanted, and led Stoffel straight out towards the Kaffir stad by the Blesbok Spruit. They did not go fast, and on the way Stoffel knelt down and prayed to God, and drew the cartridges from the gun. Then they went on.

'When they got to the spruit they could see there was a big fire in the stad and hear the Kaffirs crying out and beating the drums. The dog ran straight to the edge of the water, and then turned and whined, for there was no more scent. But Stoffel walked straight in, over his knees and up to his waist, and climbed the bank to the wall of the stad.

'Inside, the Kaffirs were dancing. Some were tricked out with ornaments and skins and feathers; some were mother-naked and painted all over their bodies. And there was one, a gaunt figure of horror, with his face streaked to the likeness of a skull, and bones hanging clattering all about him. They capered and danced round the fire like devils in hell, and behind them the men with the drums kept up their noise and seemed to drive the dancers to madness.

'And suddenly the figures round the fire gave way, save the one with the painted face and the bones; for from the shadow of a hut at the back of the fire came another, who rushed into the light and swayed wildly to the barbarous music. The newcomer was naked as a babe new born; wild as a beast of the field; lithe as a serpent; and crazy to savageness with the fire and the drums.

'Madly she danced, bending forwards and backwards, casting her bare arms above her, while the horror who danced with her writhed and screamed like a soul in pain.

'Stoffel, behind the wall, stood stunned and bound – for here he saw his wife. He thought nothing, said nothing; but without an effort his hand ran a cartridge into the gun, and levelled it across the wall. He fired, and the lissom body dropped limp across the fire.'

Frikkie Viljoen rose in great wrath.

'This is how you talk of my sweetheart, is it?' he cried. 'Well, I will hear no more of your lies.' And he forthwith walked out of the house.

'Look at that!' said the Vrouw Grobelaar. 'I never said a word about his sweetheart.'

SARAH GERTRUDE MILLIN

Up from Gilgal

First published, 1924

It was night, and there was dancing on the ship sailing from Cape Town to Southampton. The wooden bar that divided the first class from the second class was away, and passengers from both classes were dancing together, and on rows of deck chairs reclined the people who were not dancing.

In the second row of deck chairs on the first-class side sat Mrs Elder with three other women. The four of them sat there every night, watching. They would have liked, very much, to dance too: they danced at home, for they could at least depend on their poor grumbling old husbands to dance with them. But now they were travelling, for one reason or another, without their husbands, and they were of no interest to any other men. So they listened to the bad music, and commented on the dancers, and felt how melancholy it was to be getting old, and remembered with yearning and humility and gratitude their husbands, who, they could see now, were the only human beings on whom they could depend – through the power of habit and pity and an ancient loyalty – for everything.

Mrs Elder had not dreamt it would be like this. She came from a Transvaal town which had a white population of five thousand, and her husband was the magistrate, and, of course, a man of great importance. The Elders lived at the Residency, the best house in the town; and if any influential person came there he had dinner with then – even the administrator of a province or the Prime Minister of the Union. And then Mrs Elder distributed the school prizes and ran the various committees. It would have been strange indeed if, at a dance, she had lacked partners.

Besides, she was not really so unattractive. It was true her skin was burnt and dried and wrinkled by the African sun, and there was a piece of flesh joining her neck to her chin which grew taut when she turned her head, and she was a little too stout. But she was not so old as one would have expected an Englishwoman to be who looked like that: she was thirty-seven; and she had big candid grey eyes, a straight, short nose, and richly brown hair. It wasn't, after all, a serious misfortune for a man to dance with her.

Yet here she had sat night after night, throughout the voyage, and it had never even entered any man's head that she could want to dance, that she was *entitled* to dance. She had sat with these three other women whose husbands had been left at home, and they were looked on – if they were looked on at all – just as four middle-aged women to whom one sometimes said a word or two, and there was an end of it.

She should not have linked herself with these women. She saw it now. They were women of forty-eight or fifty, and when she joined their group she became automatically one of them: she partook of their quality of dereliction, she was no more than the fourth side of a shut-in square.

No one even asked her to play deck tennis. She did not expect it of the jolly young ones. But the elderly bald men, whose white flannels opened at the pleats and were strained about their large waists – why did they not invite her to join them in a mixed doubles? What right had they to be so indecently convinced of their invincible maleness?

She played bridge every afternoon with her friends; and often they gossiped; and in the nights they sat here and commented on the dancers, and noticed who the people were who strolled away after the dances with their partners to make a little love, because, if their husbands or wives were on board, that was really the only chance they had.

And there was a pain in her heart when she thought that this voyage to England was the great event of her life – even although it had come about only because her mother was so seriously ill in England. For her husband's salary was not so grand as his magisterial position – there were three children – they had never been able to save enough to go on such a voyage together.

Out of sheer loneliness she wrote to her husband every day. She told him what a glorious holiday she was having – except, of course, for her anxiety about her mother, and her longing for him and the children. Her husband was greatly moved by her letters. He had not known she loved him as deeply as all that. 'And who do you think is on board?' she asked in her very first letter. 'Charles Devenish. In the first class. Naturally, I haven't spoken to him.'

No, she hadn't spoken to him. But then neither had he spoken to her. He was dancing now with quite a young girl.

★ ★ ★

Mrs Elder had first met Charles Devenish fifteen years ago. At that time her husband was magistrate of a little town called Gilgal, the centre of a diamond-digging district. Since then they had been transferred five times; and, although they were now higher in the service, they possessed hardly a household article that did not show the marks of all this moving about, and their children were in lower classes than they should have been, and they were still very poor.

They had been as happy in Gilgal as anywhere. It was a hot, dry, yellow, sandy, treeless, iron-roofed, ugly little town near a river which was often dry in the winter, for then no rains fell in the Transvaal. It had been called Gilgal because the first diggers had encamped near twelve large stones and, thinking of the dry river they had just crossed to get there, a man had laughingly asked if these were not the stones of the Jordan, and this not the Gilgal of God's command.

Gilgal, however, had not grown beyond one street. In that street were two hotels where men came to drink, the bank, the chemist's shop, several general stores, the school, and the magistrate's court. Yet the Elders were young in those days, all life seemed young, there was a sort of little society, and they were important in it.

To this society Charles Devenish was an event. He had come to Gilgal no one knew why, and he never did the prospecting of which he vaguely spoke. But people did not ask many questions in Gilgal, and he was thirty, he had manner and an accent, and his clothes were good.

The ladies invited him to afternoon tea and tennis, and he made love to several of them.

They told one another, in a competitive spirit, about this love he made, and they exaggerated his advances and their withdrawings — as if it were quite easy for a Gilgal woman to find personable admirers; as if they all knew what it was to keep a man's passion at bay. It was at this time it became customary for the Gilgal people to wear evening clothes at one another's dinner parties. For, without any warning at all, Mr Devenish had arrived at his first dinner in Gilgal — dressed.

And so things went on for nearly two months. And then one day a sum of money came for him through the bank, and immediately everyone understood the sort of prospecting Mr Devenish did, and why he was in Gilgal. He was in Gilgal just because he happened to be in Gilgal, and because he did not much care where he was so long as he could get what he wanted.

And that was, it seemed, a very large quantity of drink. As soon as his money came Charles Devenish went to the bar of the Empire Hotel and drank with and against everybody. He arrived at the bar early in the morning, and he stayed there all day, and all next day, and the whole week through, and as long as he had any cash, and as long after that as the barman would let him. It was as if he had had just enough control over himself to await the coming of this money.

Then, for a while, he disappeared.

When he showed himself again he still had his manner and his accent, but people looked at him now with different eyes. They forgave him his lapse — for every one in those digging districts knew of men who had drinking periods and then, for months afterwards, stayed sober — only they no longer acknowledged his superiority over them. And when the ladies asked him to their houses they did it as if they were being kind.

Even Mrs Elder, who often, without any sense of disloyalty to her husband, wondered if the love of a good woman couldn't reform him, was kind in that way. But he looked at her with careless, indifferent, unashamed eyes that, in some unaccountable way, transferred the consciousness of any misdemeanour from him to her; and sometimes he came to her as to the other people who had forgiven him, and sometimes he did not. It didn't seem, really, as though he wanted all this forgiveness, or the love, just romantically unhallowed, of a magistrate's wife.

And then, one day, another thing happened. Mr Devenish was due at Mrs Elder's for tea, and he went for a walk with her cook instead. There was no secrecy about it. Down the only street of the town they strolled, and he was a little more deferential towards her than, in these days, towards her mistress. He was carrying a parcel for her too. The day's meat, the people said.

It was an insult to all Gilgal, yet most of the ladies could only laugh to hide their chagrin. The doctor's wife, however (who was like that), declared that to bring the doctrine of true knighthood to its foundations, why should not a gentleman assist a housemaid with her pail, or a washerwoman with her bundle, or Mrs Elder's cook with her parcel of meat? Was chivalry, and ladies first, and all that sort of thing, only a matter of class? For her part, she said, she was prepared to receive Mr Devenish as if nothing had happened.

But Mrs Elder was not. For she wasn't, like the doctor's wife, fifty, she was twenty-two, and she was unhappy because he had touched her feelings more than a little, and it was, finally, to her he had forgotten or neglected to come, and with her cook he had walked instead.

She wanted to dismiss the cook. But Mr Elder wouldn't allow it. 'What should she have done?' he demanded. 'Refused to let him carry her meat?'

'Yes,' said Mrs Elder, her throat tight and sore.

'Oh, nonsense,' commented Mr Elder. 'Do you expect a Gilgal poor white to know more than an English gentleman? If you want to kick anyone out, let it be Devenish.'

But no one was henceforth given the opportunity to kick Mr Devenish out, for he spent too much time with the Elders' cook. The doctor's wife suggested that he found her, perhaps, more amusing than Gilgal society; but she could not really believe it. And when she saw him one day walking with the cook under the thorny mimosa trees just outside Gilgal, the mimosa whose scent was so clean and wistful in the hot, still air – like a longing never to be fulfilled – then even she could no longer laugh.

All Gilgal dropped Mr Devenish, and Mr Elder allowed his wife to dismiss the cook.

★ ★ ★

And now there came another phase in the Gilgal career of Mr Devenish. The hotel proprietor said he could not keep Mr Devenish in his hotel unless he paid for his accommodation. Mr Devenish explained that he was expecting money again next month. The hotel proprietor, however, asked him why he had not given him any of the money he had received last month. Mr Devenish answered pleasantly that he, the hotel proprietor, had had all of it. 'But, as to that, there's money owing in the bar too,' said the hotel proprietor. And he looked very disagreeable.

Mr Devenish stared at him a moment.

'I'm arranging to leave your hotel today,' he said in a manner that implied he had found the hotel not very satisfactory.

So now he bought himself a tent and cooked his own food. He bought things at one of the stores, and would have managed quite well if the storekeeper had not, like the proprietor of the Empire Hotel, talked so much about accounts. Why, asked the storekeeper, in due course, had he not been paid out of the new money that had come to Mr Devenish and all gone into the bar of the Royal Hotel?

Mr Devenish said he was not in the habit of bandying words with his tradesmen.

He spoke in these days, to the people he casually met, of leaving Gilgal. And yet he did not leave. For, just about this time, an awkward thing happened. No money came for him to the bank.

This was really a terrible period. He was no longer getting credit anywhere. For a while he did a little borrowing from the diggers who had drunk with him in the bars. Then he exchanged his watch for groceries. Occasionally he had a meal at the home of Mrs Elder's ex-cook. There were a lot of poor-white children about who made a disrespectful noise when he came.

Presently he sold his tent.

One morning an elderly prospector, who made Gilgal the headquarters of his unsuccessful expeditions, found him sitting, dazed, on the bench under the verandah of the Royal Hotel.

The bar was not yet open. The prospector looked carefully at Mr Devenish.

'You come home with me,' he said.

'Home' was a room made of corrugated iron with a window that was a single pane of glass. A dirty mattress lay on the floor, with several old blankets tumbled about on it. There were also a few pieces of crockery on a box turned upside down to make a table; a fork, a knife and a spoon; a smaller box with groceries in it; a chair, a saucepan, a kettle, and a paraffin stove.

'We'll have breakfast,' said the prospector.

He opened a tin of sardines, and made some coffee. The eyes of Mr Devenish grew more bloodshot.

'I'm expecting some money any day now,' he murmured.

'That's all right,' said the prospector. 'You can stay here till it comes.'

It did come, and then they both went to the bar and drank. For, the prospector, too, had not arrived at his present pass through excessive praying. And, in future, whenever money came, they disposed of it together in the bar of the Royal Hotel. For, as Mr Devenish had never stayed at the Royal Hotel, and had consequently never had any discussions about accounts there, he preferred it to the Empire Hotel. Only when there was no money was Mr Devenish ever again something like the Mr Devenish who had once been so pleasantly received by the ladies of Gilgal.

He had not, of course, visited their houses for many months, but they were now able to speak to him when they met him. They were able to speak because it no longer mattered whether they spoke or not. Mrs Elder alone could not bring herself to do so – because of those romantic feelings of hers he had once touched and then shamed.

But this stage, too, passed. Perhaps, before he came to Gilgal, he had lived with people who had done for him what they could, and so that was why he had arrived there no worse than he was. Now, however, he lived with the old prospector, and they went downhill together. Mr Devenish was not even clean in these days. His wardrobe consisted of what he wore, and he wore it a long time. His very manner was only a mirage of his old manner. All he kept intact was his accent.

One day the prospector found some asbestos. He naturally sold his claims for too little – other men afterwards made tens of thousands of pounds out of that asbestos field, but he was not dissatisfied. He added another room of corrugated iron to the first, took a half-caste woman, bought some fowls, and was very happy. He said Mr Devenish could remain with him, and Mr Devenish did so. Mrs Elder's cook married the driver of a transport-wagon.

★ ★ ★

Mr Devenish was not greatly affected by the coming of the Great War. Eighteen months of it passed without agitating him. Then, so it was reported, he got a letter to say that two of his brothers had been killed. A week later he was gone from Gilgal. No one was very interested in his going, not even the doctor's wife (the Elders had left Gilgal by that time) or the prospector. The prospector had given up drink and was deeply domesticated now, and, in his heart, he was relieved about the departure of Mr Devenish, because, in a two-roomed house, and with a new yellow baby, it was more comfortable without him.

So he went, unsped, and was forgotten …

Until, one day, towards the end of the war, Mrs Elder saw something about a Captain Charles Devenish, MC, in a newspaper.

'Captain!' said Mrs Elder, and thought of the days when he had come to

Gilgal and the days when he had left. 'MC! Impossible! It must be another man.'

But it was not another man. The war had resurrected Charles Devenish.

And here it was ten years after the war, it was over twelve years since he had left Gilgal, and what, thought Mrs Elder passionately, as she sat there on the deck chairs of the left-behind and cast-aside watching him dance with that young girl, what had happened to them both during that time? Nothing to her, a virtuous woman, except decay and degeneration – at least, so it seemed, now, here on the ship. But to him, who had snuffled in the slime, soaring life.

She had not felt like this when she had met him on board the first day. She had walked past him with the old contempt of Gilgal; with the contempt of the magistrate's wife for her cook's lover, for the drunkard who had lived with a man who lived with a coloured woman. And he had walked past her – he still did – as if he had no memory of her.

But could that be, she now asked herself, agonised, could he truly have forgotten her? Had she become unrecognisable in twelve years? Was her essential being gone with her youth so that a man might look at her and see not a trace of it left?

Her mind returned to the beginning of the voyage when she had looked forward to having an exciting – even a possible romantic – voyage. How often had she not heard from women of their exciting and romantic voyages! Every one went a little mad on ships, they said. There was no time or space or past or future or success or failure on ships, they said. Things just happened. They happened wildly to anybody.

It seemed, however, that they did not happen always. The days had passed and no adventures had come to Mrs Elder. What did she, a middle-aged woman going to see a sick mother, a virtuous woman with a husband and children, want of romantic adventures? What, indeed? she asked herself bitterly, sitting here, because of her loneliness, with these three women who also sat with one another because of their loneliness.

'Yes, a man of forty-five or fifty and a woman of forty-five or fifty are very different things,' said one of the three as she watched Charles Devenish dancing with his pretty girl. 'Would that man come to me for a dance – and I'm no older than he is? Of course not! Why should he? He can get any of the young girls to dance with him. Only too happy – a popular man like that!'

Mrs Elder opened her mouth to speak of Gilgal. But there was a rancour and a sadness in her heart that would not let her. It was as if she could not betray a something in herself. She remembered how he had once touched her feelings. She wished with a longing that pressed against the walls of her being like an instrument of the Inquisition, that he would come to her now and lift her out of the cast-aside and left-behind. For she could see now: without the small-town dignity her husband gave her, without his affection and support, that was all she was: in her own right, nobody wanted her.

But this man, she had known him in his degradation, she had felt herself infected by his shame – had she no meaning even for him?

The dance ended, and he passed her, chatting with his partner. He found her a seat, and went to fetch her some refreshment.

Mrs Elder had not thought of doing it, but she did it: she followed him hastily through a door. She touched him on the arm.

'Don't you remember me, Mr Devenish?' she said. 'Mrs Elder, of Gilgal.'

'Why, Mrs Elder, why, of course,' he said, as if at a revelation. 'Of Gilgal. And how is Johanna?'

Johanna was the name of Mrs Elder's cook of fifteen years ago.

She wanted to remind him passionately that they had long since been moved up from Gilgal, and how should she know anything of Johanna? But she could not.

He smiled at her – a still sort of smile.

She faced him in a profound silence.

She understood. The magistrate's wife, and the magistrate's wife's cook – he meant that they were equally behind him. What he wanted her to understand, in the bravado of his hatred of the past, was that she and Johanna and Gilgal and himself in Gilgal, were all linked together in his mind as part of an old shabbiness he had outlived and now chose to ignore.

'May I get you something to drink?' he asked her, too politely, and still smiling.

She hated him so, she would have liked the ship to go down with both of them, with all the happy young people, and the elderly cheerful people, and the three women with whom she sat and sat watching the dancing of others.

Her heart ached with the sorrow of being outside things. 'Will you?' she said, and self-contented, returned his smile.

SARAH GERTRUDE MILLIN

A Sack for Ninepence

First published, 1928
From: *Two Bucks without Hair* (1957)

1

The tall native, with his dirty shirt and trousers, the colour of mud, with his greenish-brown coat and dusty peppercorn hair and bare feet, stood in the dock, and his eyes were concentrated on the interpreter. The interpreter was translating to him the judge's concluding remarks to the jury:

'... On the other hand, gentlemen, you must bear in mind, as the learned counsel for the defence has pointed out, that when a native says he will kill a man, he is not necessarily threatening to take his life. He may only mean that he will hurt him. The expression, "You shall not see the sun tomorrow" is another such exclamation of rage which may have no real significance. Moreover, it must be remembered that the principal testimony against the prisoner is that of his wife, Masangape, who has lost her child, and who has been badly treated by him. The matter of the stone has not been satisfactorily explained, yet there is no evidence that the prisoner placed it where it was found, nor did anyone see the burning of the hut. The child is dead. The man who wore the sack is dead. All the inhabitants of the hut are dead. Only Masangape, the wife, is here to tell the story of that day and night. It is for you to say whether you believe Masangape, and whether in the light of the other evidence I have outlined to you, you think the prisoner committed this crime. If you find the evidence insufficient to establish his guilt beyond reasonable doubt, it is your duty to find him not guilty. Consider your verdict ...'

Pepetwayo listened to the interpreter, but he could discover no meaning in the judge's words. The jurymen scrambled to their feet. The judge gathered together his red robes and stood up, and, as he did so, the people in court – mostly natives – rose. The policeman touched the prisoner's arm. The prisoner gave a start, looked round with rolling eyes and, on the policeman's word, began hurriedly to descend the steps that led from the dock to the cells below.

He was still thinking about the sack.

2

This was the story of the sack:

Pepetwayo had married his wife when she was a widow with a year-old child. And it was now seven years since their marriage, and this child she had borne by another man was still the only child in their hut. Pepetwayo spoke to her about it often, and sometimes he beat her. He consulted a witch-doctor and he fought men who made jokes, but the days passed and the days passed and forever he had to father only this child of the dead man.

He grew to hate the child with a terrible deep hatred. He could not bear to see the small white teeth crunching the bread for which he had to break his back hauling up stones on the Transvaal diamond diggings. In summer Gule ran naked, but this winter he had been bought a thick cotton singlet, and Pepetwayo could not rest his eyes on it without wanting to tear it from the boy's back. He could not keep his voice from scolding him or his hands from striking him. He said to Masangape in their speech: 'Send Gule away, or there will be great trouble.'

She decided finally to bestow Gule on some friends in a neighbouring hut. It was, like all the other huts, a circular construction of rags and reeds and mud, a dozen feet in diameter, with no opening for entrance or exit but a flap of sacking. It stood, surrounded by a reed fence, on the side of a low, stony hill, a little apart from the rest of the location where Masangape lived with her husband. In the whole of that location there was no tree or flower or blade of grass. There was no well for water. Little girls, with tin cans on their heads, walked three miles to fetch the muddy water of the Vaal River. Only on the top of the hill there grew, near the half-hearted and abandoned beginnings of a stone wall, a few prickly pears, and, when the sun went down in a flare of scarlet scribbled with fire, these bold and fleshy weeds leaned against the sky in black relief, and the huts themselves clung together like the hives of gigantic wasps.

In this hut there were already five people maintained on the sixteen shillings a week earned by the head of the household. But no native ever questions the right of a fellow-tribesman to share with him, and Gule was accepted without bargain or comment.

Yet only for a few days was there peace in Pepetwayo's home. It happened that he returned from his work on the diggings and Masangape was not there. Where she was he knew, of course. But he particularly resented her absence this evening because he was happy, because he wanted her to exult with him over a bargain. He had bought a grain-sack from the shop for ninepence when everyone knew that the price of one so large as this was always a shilling. But he had said to the store-keeper: 'Look, Baas, how poor I am, and how the weather is cold. I want this sack to wear on my body to keep the wind out. But it is Monday today and I have just this ninepence, and why shall such a great person as the Baas wait till next Saturday for only a little threepence? Let the Baas give me the sack for ninepence.'

And, actually, the Baas had done it, and Pepetwayo loved the sack as if it were a trophy in a game he had won.

124

Now he wanted his wife to open the sides for him and cut a hole for his head so that he might wear it against the cold. He could work better with his hands than she could – he had in his day sewn together the skins of jackals with sinew to make those great rugs which are called karosses – but it simply was his desire that she should do this thing for him.

And the hut was empty. There was no fat-soaked mealie-meal cooking in the tripod pot. His belly was fainting against his backbone, for he had eaten nothing all day except, at twelve o'clock, a piece of bread. There was no one to share his triumph about the sack.

He flung it down in a corner of the hut, and rushed over to the neighbours who housed Gule.

There his wife sat chattering with other women. There his wife's child ran about playing with other children. The air was leaping with gaiety. The terrific smell of a sheep's head and trotters cooking in a tripod pot attacked his nostrils …

He thought of his quiet hut, of his unused pot, of the absence of small, rotund, black bodies and rushing noises and high laughter in his yard, of his bargain of a sack lying rumpled, unhailed, in a corner, and he ran up to his wife and jerked her up by the shoulder and shouted awful words at her and dragged her home.

He beat her when they got home, and would not eat, and would not let her make in the hut the smoky fire of dung and sticks with which they kept themselves warm in the winter nights. And throughout the black hours, wearing still the clothes they used by day, they lay side by side on the goatskins which separated them from the naked earth, covered with two cotton blankets, bitter, hostile, and yet drawn together by the cold.

In the morning Pepetwayo went to work as usual, a white scurf of frost in his face and hands. And when he was gone, his wife packed her belongings into the sack she found lying in the corner and left him, to go and live in the hut that sheltered also her child.

3

Pepetwayo was hungry and tired and cold all day long. And for this he blamed his wife and her child. If his wife had not neglected him the night before to go to see her child, he would have had something in his belly, he thought, he would have slept in the night, he would have been able to wear the sack today against the whipping wind. He could not forget the animation in the other people's yard.

In the evening he walked towards the location, picking up here and there as he went along a stick for the fire. But again, as he reached home, no smoke rose to greet him, and he saw soon enough that Masangape was gone, and her belongings. He stood in the hut looking at he knew not what, and suddenly he remembered his sack. Where was his sack? Had she had the effrontery to take his sack, to steal his sack for which only the day before he had paid ninepence … not a shilling, as was usual, but – a bargain, a diplomatic achievement – ninepence?

Once more he ran along to the other hut. This time there were no visitors in the yard, only the inhabitants of the hut were present, and his wife was sitting, silent, in their midst. She was frightened. She could not live with her husband any more, and she did not know what he would now do to her.

But he entered in among them shouting the word 'sack'.

'Give me my sack. What have you done with my sack?'

He pulled his wife up by the stuff of her dress between her shoulders. 'You –'

His eyes fell on the child.

'He shall not see the sun tomorrow!' he cried. 'There will not be cause for you to leave me again. Where is my sack?'

His wife looked at him dumbly.

He let her go, for his eyes had seen something. There was a man barely visible in the smoke-filled hut and he was wearing a baggy garment over his shoulders. Pepetwayo sprang at the man, and they struggled towards the yard. He could see now, in the last light of the day, that the man was the brother of Gule's protector, and that here was his very sack.

He attempted to pull it from the man as they fought. 'You shall not,' he panted, '– none of you – see the sun tomorrow.'

The sack was torn. His own clothes were torn. People flung themselves forward and separated them. He threatened to kill his wife if she did not come back with him. She walked beside him, weeping.

And, as on the night before they lay down together on the ground in the small, dark hut.

But this time, in the middle of the night, Pepetwayo got up, and began fumbling about the hut.

His wife lay still, listening to his movements. Then she felt that – something – was happening. Terror filled her.

'Pepetwayo! What are you doing?'

'Nothing,' he said, in a voice unexpectedly peaceable.

She heard the rattle of matches as in the dark he put his hand on the box. Now he went outside. She sat up.

'Pepetwayo! Where are you going? Pepetwayo!'

He came back to the hut.

'Lie still. I will be here again in a minute.'

She began to moan.

'Are you mad?' he said. 'Be quiet. I am not going to leave you for long. Wait for me. Don't make this noise. If I do not find you here when I come in I will kill you.'

She drew the blankets over her head, and lay waiting and shivering. He was gone for minutes – for an hour.

When he returned he put his arms round her.

'I am happy again. Let us sleep,' he said.

4

In the morning the hut that contained Gule and the man who had worn Pepetwayo's sack and four other people was found burnt down, and everyone in it was dead. A stone was lying against the flap that was the only opening to the hut, and the inhabitants had thus been fastened in while the old sacks and reeds of which the hut was made burnt round them and over them.

Masangape was led, screaming, to the police-station to tell her story. Pepetwayo was arrested. 'I know nothing,' he said. The police did not question him, and when, towards the end of the six months that intervened before his trial, his young counsel came to talk with him he maintained firmly: 'I know nothing.'

At the trial he was not put in the box. And when he gathered dimly that the defending advocate was explaining to the jury how ridiculous it was that a man should kill six people for the sake of an empty sack, he nodded his head slightly. Yes, that was wise talk. 'I need not inform you, gentlemen,' the advocate continued, 'how often native huts are burnt down, or how often sleeping natives are suffocated because the fire made for warmth has not been removed …'

The judge addressed the jury. Pepetwayo was led back to his cell. The jury went away to deliberate.

They returned presently. The prisoner was once more prodded up the steps to the dock. The judge, who had retired, resumed his seat on the bench. The people in court duly stood up and sat down.

The registrar addressed the foreman of the jury.

'Have you considered your verdict?'

'We have.'

'Are you all agreed?'

'We are.'

'What is your verdict?'

'Not guilty.'

The judge addressed Pepetwayo. He put the facts as he saw them before the jury, though it was reasonably clear to him that Pepetwayo had committed the crime. However, they had apparently considered the evidence insufficient.

He sat up and looked at Pepetwayo from under his heavy brow. 'The jury have found you not guilty. You may go.'

'You may go,' the interpreter translated.

The policeman tapped his shoulder.

'You may go.'

Pepetwayo looked from one to the other. What had happened? Was he free? He could not believe it.

'Hurry up,' said the policeman.

The native did not move.

The policeman pushed him. The man began to scramble down as if an hypnotic influence were directing him.

Outside the court other natives surrounded Pepetwayo, giving him tobacco to chew, and cigarettes.

He was free. He was a hero. The justice of the white man was a miracle.

He blew out a mouthful of smoke, and in a voice hushed by six months of waiting in gaol, he began to tell his worshipful audience about this sack, worth a shilling, which he had bought for ninepence, and which had been given by his wife to the brother of the man who had sheltered Gule.

PAULINE SMITH

Desolation

From: *The Little Karoo* (1925)

Alie van Staden was close on seventy-two years old when she went with her son, Stephan, and her motherless little grandson, Stephan's Koos, to Mijnheer Bezedenhout's farm of Koelkuil in the Verlatenheid. She was a short squarely-built woman, slow in thought and slow in movement, with dark brown eyes set deep in a long, somewhat heavy and expressionless face. In her youth her eyes had been beautiful, but there was none who now remembered her youth and in old age she looked out upon the world with a patient endurance which had in it something of the strength and something of the melancholy of the labouring ox.

All her life, save for six months in her girlhood, Alie had lived in the Verlatenheid – that dreary stretch of the Great Karoo which lies immediately to the north of the Zwartkops Mountains and takes its name from the desolation which nature displays here in the grey volcanic harshness of its kopjes and the scanty vegetation of its veld. This grey and desolate region was her world. Here, as the child of poor whites and as the mother of poor whites she had drifted for seventy years from farm to farm in the shiftless, thriftless labour of her class. Here in a bitter poverty she had married her man, borne her children, and accepted dumbly whatever ills her God had inflicted upon her. With her God she had no communion save in the patient uncomplaining fulfilment of His will as the daily circumstances of her life revealed it to her. Prayer was never wrung from her. That cry of 'Our Father! Our Father!' which comes so naturally to the heart and from the lips of her race never came from hers. Sorrow had been her portion, but this was life as she conceived it, and tearless she had borne it. And now of all her sons Stephan alone was left to her, and already Stephan was suffering from that disease of the chest which had killed first his father and then his three brothers, Koos, Hendrick and Piet.

In her son, the bijwoner Stephan van Staden, there was none of old Alie's quiet endurance of life. The bijwoner could not without protest accept the ills which his God so persistently visited upon him. He was a weak and obstinate man who saw in his God a power actively engaged in direct opposition to himself, and at each fresh blow dealt him by his God he lifted up his voice and cried aloud his injury. At Koelkuil his voice was often thus raised, for here his

129

illness rapidly increased, and here he found in his new master a harsh man made harsher by a drought which had brought him close to ruin.

The drought was in fact the worst that any middle-aged man of the Verlatenheid remembered. When Stephan went as bijwoner to Koelkuil the farm had had no rain for over two years and through all his eighteen months of service with Mijnheer only three light showers fell. Day after day men rose to a cloudless sky and hot shimmering air, or to a dry and burning wind that scorched and withered as it blew. Slowly, steadily, the grey earth became greyer, the bare kopjes barer, the veld itself empty of familiar life. The herds of spring-buck seeking water at the dried-up fountains grew smaller and smaller. The field mice, the tortoises, the meer-kats – all the humbler creatures of the veld – died out of ken. The starving jackal played havoc among the starving sheep. The new-born lamb was killed to save the starving ewe. The cattle, the sheep, the ostriches and the donkeys were drawn in their extremity closer to the abodes of men in their vain search for food. Their lowing and bleating drifted mournfully across the stricken land as slowly, steadily, their famished bodies were gathered into the receiving earth and turned again to the dust from which they had sprung.

In the strain of these months there was constant friction between Stephan van Staden and his master. Nothing done by the one was right in the eyes of the other. Stephan, ill and irritable, was loud in his criticism of Mijnheer. Mijnheer, a ruined man, was unjust in the demands he made of his bijwoner. They came at last to an active open warfare into which all on the farm save old Alie were drawn. From their conflict she alone remained quietly aloof. Sitting on the high stone step in front of the bijwoner's house, gazing in melancholy across the Verlatenheid, she would listen in silence to the arguments of both master and man alike. Stephan's vehemence made him indifferent to her silence. Mijnheer resented and feared it. He read in it judgement of himself, and who was this Alie, the poor white, that she should judge him? Why did she never speak that he might answer? Of what did she think as she sat there, immovable as God, on the high stone step in front of the door? He did not know, and would never know, but he came in the end to hate this old woman, so strong, it seemed to him, in her silence, so powerful in her patience. And when, in a spell of bitter cold, the bijwoner suddenly died, he thought with relief that now old Alie must go.

It was in the early winter of the fourth year of the drought that Stephan van Staden died, and on the day that he was buried Mijnheer, standing by the graveside, told Alie van Staden that his bijwoner's house would be needed at once for the man who was coming in her son's place. He was, he said, but naturally sorry for herself and the child, but doubtless they had relatives to whom they might go, and she must see for herself that it was impossible for him, a man well-nigh ruined by the drought, to do anything whatever to help her. She must know, also, that her son's illness had made him a poor bijwoner and added much to his losses among his sheep. In fact the more he thought of it the more convinced he was that no other farmer in the Verlatenheid would have borne with Stephan so long as he, Godlieb Bezedenhout, had done. And on this note of righteousness he ended.

To all that Mijnheer had to say Alie listened, as always, in silence. What, indeed, was there for her to answer? Mijnheer spoke of relatives to whom she might turn for help for herself and Stephan's child but in fact she had none. She was the last of her generation as Stephan had been the last of his. The poor white is poor also in physique, and of all her consumptive stock only Stephan's Koos remained. Stephan's wife had died when her son was born, and her people had long since drifted out of sight, she could not say where. The child, therefore, had none but herself to stand between him and destitution. All that was to be done for him she herself must do. All that was to be planned for him she herself must plan.

Slowly, while her master spoke, these thoughts passed through her mind. But by no word did she betray them or the desolation of her heart. When he ceased she parted from him with a quiet 'Good-day' and went back to the bijwoner's house with Stephan's Koos.

For her six-year-old grandson Alie had a deep but inarticulate tenderness. All the little warmth that life still held for her came to her through Stephan's Koos. It was she who had saved him when Anna died. It was she who had stood between him and the fury of his father when Stephan, in his illness, turned against his own son. All that Stephan's son had known of love had come to him through her, yet for that love she had found no words and to it she could give no expression beyond a rare and awkward gesture, too harsh or too restrained to be called a caress. Yet the boy – a slim small child with eyes as dark as her own, and long thin fingers like the claws of a bird – was conscious of no shortcomings in his grandmother. His father had always been strange to him, and death had but added another mystery to the many which had surrounded him in life. But with his grandmother nothing was strange or mysterious. With his grandmother he knew where he was going, he knew what he was doing. She was his tower of strength, his shadow of a great rock in a dry and thirsty land. By her side he was safe. Wherever she went, whatever she did, by her side he was safe …

When they reached the house Alie sat down, as was her custom, upon the high stone step in front of the door, and the boy, pressing close to her side to deepen his sense of security there, sat down beside her. For a time they were silent, the child content, his grandmother brooding on the past. She was a woman of little imagination. Her mind, moving slowly among familiar things, was heavy always with the melancholy of the Verlatenheid, and from it she had but one escape – to the village of Hermansdorp where once as a girl she had lived with her mother's cousin, Tan' Betje, and worked with her at mattress-making at one of the stores. Beyond this her thoughts never ventured. And it was to Hermansdorp that her thoughts travelled slowly now with their dawning hope.

Before them, as they sat on the step, there stretched for mile after mile the grey and barren veld, the wild and broken kopjes of the Verlatenheid. But it was not these that old Alie saw. Her vision travelled slowly, painfully through the years to the long low line of hills to the north, in a fold of which lay the village, with near it, in the shade of a clump of thorn-trees, a dam where men and women journeying to the dorp for Sacrament, outspanned their carts and wagons. She saw again the white-washed church, and the graveyard, with its tall dark cypress-trees among the whitewashed tombs, where she and Tan' Betje had walked together on Sunday afternoons spelling out the names of those who lay buried there. She saw again the long wide straight Kerk Straat, with its running furrows of clear water and its double row of pear-trees in blossom. Behind the pear-trees were whitewashed dwelling-houses set back in gardens or green lands, and stores with *stoeps* built out on to the street under the trees. At the head of the street, across it, stood the square whitewashed gaol – and she remembered how, when first she had seen it, not knowing it to be the gaol, there had come into her mind that saying of our Lord: 'In my Father's house are many mansions' – so big and gracious had this building seemed to her.

Tan' Betje's little house, she remembered, had been up a narrow lane. Three rooms it had had, with green wooden shutters, and a pear-tree in the yard. Under the pear-tree they had sat together cleaning the coir for mattresses – dipping it first into buckets of hot water, then teasing it and spreading it out in the sun to dry. For the poor they had made mattresses of mealie-leaves, stripping the dried leaves into shreds with a fork and packing them into sacks … It had been pleasant in the yard, and Tan' Betje's talk pleasant to hear. And in the little house there had always been food. She could not remember a day when there had not been food. Good food. Tan' Betje had been kind to her, and at the store too they had been kind. Her master's son had himself come several times to speak to her when she went for the coir. The old master would be dead now, perhaps. But the young master would be there. And he would remember. He would give her work …

As if following her thoughts her fingers, stiff with labour and old age, fell awkwardly into the once familiar movements of teasing the coir in the sunlit yard. The boy, wearied at last of her long silence, pressed closer to her side. She looked down upon him sombrely and drew his thin, claw-like hand into hers. Slowly, halting often in her speech, she began to talk to him of Hermansdorp where together they would go. And into the child's sense of security there came a new sense of romance and adventure, deepening his confidence in the wisdom and rightness of all that his grandmother said and did.

132

That night, while her grandson slept, old Alie bundled together their few possessions. Mijnheer had given her three days in which to make her plans and preparations, but she needed in her poverty less time than that for these. Stephan had come to Koelkuil a poor man and he had died a poorer, and in the meagre plenishing of the bijwoner's house there was little that could not be piled on to the rough unpainted cart by which, eighteen months earlier, they had journeyed to the farm. At dawn she roused the boy and with his help loaded the cart and inspanned the two donkeys. The donkeys were poor and starved, as were also the pitiful handful of sheep and goats which were all that remained of Stephan's flock. These, when all was ready, Koos drove out of the kraal towards her. And slowly, as the sun rose, they set off.

As they left the farm — the boy on foot herding the little flock, his grandmother perched high on the cart peering out upon the world from the depths of her black calico sunbonnet — there was little to mark their exodus as differing from any other that one might meet at any time in the Verlatenheid. The poor white here, though he belongs to the soil, has no roots in the soil. He is by nature a wanderer, with none of that conservative love of place which makes to many men one spot on earth beloved above all others. Yet the range of his wanderings is limited, and the Verlatenheid man remains as a rule in the Verlatenheid, dwelling in no part of it long, and coming, it may be, again and again for short spells at a time to the farms which lie, for no clear reason, within the narrow course he sets himself.

For old Alie there was no longer any such course by which she might steer the rough unpainted cart across the wide stretches of the Verlatenheid. The graves of her sons were now the only claims she held there, and to the vision of old age these graves were become but dwindling mounds of earth in a grey and desolate veld which treasured no memories. The bitter freedom of the poor and the bereft was hers. But it was without bitterness that she accepted it and, uncomplaining, took the road to Hermansdorp.

Throughout the first day it was in the Verlatenheid, with frequent outspans, that they journeyed. And here, from sun-up to sun-down they met no human being and saw in the distance only one whitewashed and deserted farmhouse, bare and treeless in the drought-stricken veld. Every *kuil* or water-hole they passed was dry, and near every *kuil* were the skeletons of donkeys and sheep which had come there but to perish of their thirst. Of living things they saw only, now and then, a couple of *koorhan* rising suddenly in flight, or a lizard basking lazily in the sun. And once, bright as a jewel in that desert of sand and stone, they came upon a small green bush poisonous to sheep and cattle alike.

On the following day they struck the Malgas-Hermansdorp road and, turning north, left the Verlatenheid behind them. The country ahead of them now was flat as a calm grey sea, its veld unbroken by any kopje until the long low line of the Hermansdorp hills was reached. Yet in the shimmering heat of noon

133

this sea became a strange fantastic world that slipped into being, vanished, and slipped into being again as they gazed upon it. Around them now were ridges of hills where no hills could be, banks of trees where no trees grew, and water that was not water lying in sheets and lakes out of which rose strange dark islands and cliffs. For these phenomena old Alie had neither explanation nor name. They were indeed less clear to her than they were to the boy. But to him their very mystery brought an added sense of his own personal security. Whatever amazing and inexplicable things the distance, like the future, might hold, here, on the Hermansdorp road with his grandmother in the cart by his side, he was safe.

Yet already, as his grandmother well knew, their margin of safety on the Hermansdorp road was narrowing. Though on that second day they reached a water-hole in which, surrounded by deep slime, there still remained a small pool at which she could water her flock and her donkeys, by nightfall three of her sheep had died by the roadside and she knew that she must lose more. The veld here, though less bare than that of the Verlatenheid, yielded no grazing for them, and the longer the journey the less could she save. Yet in their weakness she dare not press them, and their progress was broken now by more and more frequent outspans which meant no food as well as no water for her donkeys and sheep, no food as well as no coffee for herself and Koos. The water in the water-cask which hung below the cart must be dealt out sparingly if it were to carry them to the end of their journey, and there had been little to pack into the tin canister of food when they set out. This she explained to Koos when, after lighting a fire of dried-up bushes, she put on no kettle to boil for coffee. The boy accepted her ruling as she herself accepted the ruling of God. All, he felt, would be right when they reached Hermansdorp.

It was on the morning of the third day that they came within sight of the township, lying, as old Alie remembered it, in a fold of the hills. In the cold bright winter air its whitewashed buildings stood out clearly against their dark background, and the boy forgot for a moment his increasing hunger and burst into eager questioning. His grandmother answered him slowly, patiently, her thoughts on the dam outside the village where she would water her donkeys and sheep.

This day, however, was the hardest and most tedious of their journey. Many hours passed before they reached the dam and in these hours more of the sheep died and the going of the donkeys became a painful somnambulistic crawl. To ease their burden of her weight old Alie left her seat in the cart and walked by the side of the patient suffering beasts, calling them quietly by name. From time to time they turned towards her seeking with their tongues such moisture as her clothes might hold. And always when they did so she would speak to them quietly, as if speaking to children, of the Hermansdorp dam.

The dam lay about three miles to the south of the township, and for over fifty years men journeying to the village for market or the Sacrament had watered their flocks and spans here, and made it their last outspan on entering the dorp, their first upon leaving it. It had been, too, the general picnic place of the village, and all old Alie's memories of it were stirring and gay. But as at last they neared it in the fading light of that winter afternoon there crept into her heart a sombre foreboding. The thorn-trees around it were not, as she had remembered them, laden with the scented golden balls of spring, for this was winter, and in winter they must be bare. But she knew before she reached them that they were bare not because winter had made them so but because drought had killed them. And she needed no telling, though a small dark girl broke away from an inspanned wagon, standing solitary beneath the trees, to cry the news aloud, that the dam was dry.

In the bitter wind of winter drought, which all day long had blown across the veld, these barren trees, this empty sunbaked hollow gaping to the indifferent heavens, this eager child triumphant with disaster, brought desolation to old Alie as it had never been brought to her in the familiar world of the Verlatenheid. Yet she gave no sign that her strength of mind and of body were well-nigh spent, but, wheeling the donkeys off the road, began patiently to outspan. As she did so there came towards her from the wagon a tall dark man smoking a pipe, and a cheerful round-faced woman carrying a child in her arms.

These strangers gave her greeting, and the man, beginning at once to help her, fell into easy friendly talk. It was true, he said, that there was no water in the dam, and never before had any man seen it so. If Mevrouw needed water and food for her donkeys and sheep there was none to be had until one reached the coffee-house in Hermansdorp. But it was clear that Mevrouw could take her sheep and donkeys no farther now. Let her rest then at the fire he had made for his wife, and which they were just leaving, and he would see what he could do for her.

Old Alie thanked him, and asked his name. He was, he said, Jan Nortje, bijwoner to Mijnheer Ludovic Westhuisen of Leeukuil, and this was Marta his wife. He had been to the dorp on business for his master and was now on his way back to the farm. Had Mevrouw come from far, and had she far to go? It looked to him as if she had made a hard journey.

From Koelkuil in the Verlatenheid, answered old Alie, where but three days ago she had buried her son, the father of her little Koos here. And to Hermansdorp they were now going.

Then surely, said Jan Nortje, Mevrouw had journeyed in sorrow. But let her go now and sit with his wife by the fire and drink coffee and he would see to her donkeys and sheep.

With the numbed docility of utter weariness Alie obeyed him and, holding Koos by the hand, followed Marta to the fire. Here, handing the baby over to the child who had first run out to greet them, Jan Nortje's wife busied herself about her guests, putting coffee and food before them. She was a plump motherly young woman, many years her husband's junior, and in her pleasant soothing voice there was a persuasive kindliness which made old Alie think of her mother's cousin Tan' Betje. Just in the same gentle and pitying way had Tan' Betje mourned over the sorrows of others. Was it but three days ago, asked Jan Nortje's wife, that Ouma had buried her son? Our Father! And this was his only child? And an orphan? Then surely the hand of the Lord had been heavy upon her! But upon whom was His hand not heavy in this bitter time of drought? Throughout all the land was ruin and desolation such as no man living remembered. Turn where one would there was sorrow. Men that had been rich were now poor, and those that had been poor were now starving, taking their children like sheep to be fed at the orphan-house in Hermansdorp. It was to the orphan-house that they had been that day with gifts from Mijnheer and Mevrouw at Leeukuil. The pastor had asked that all who could do so should send food and clothing to the orphan-house for those in need, and several times now Mijnheer had sent Jan Nortje in with the wagon. Was it perhaps to the orphan-house that Ouma was taking the child?

To the orphan-house? repeated old Alie vaguely. No, it was not to the orphan-house she was going. It was to Canter's store. To work there at mattress-making.

Was Ouma then a mattress-maker? asked Jan Nortje's wife in wonder. And where was this Canter's store?

At the head of the Kerk Straat, answered old Alie. Close by the gaol.

Was Ouma sure?

Sure? asked old Alie sombrely. How could she be but sure? Had she not worked there with her mother's cousin Tan' Betje?

In her answers, as in her silence, there was that quiet aloofness which had so baffled Mijnheer Bezedenhout, and Jan Nortje's wife said no more. There was no such store as Canter's in the Kerk Straat, nor had there ever been within her memory. But who was she that she should disturb the faith of old age? In Hermansdorp Ouma must surely have friends, or why should she go there? And they would see how it was with her … She turned, smiling, to the boy. His little eager face was pinched with hunger and cold, but his eyes were bright, his spirit still adventurous, his safety still assured. For him, she knew, Canter's store was where his grandmother said it was – at the head of the Kerk Straat, close to the gaol. And who was she that she should disturb the faith of childhood?

She had turned to more practical matters and was packing some food into a canister for Ouma and the boy when Jan Nortje rejoined them. He had, he said, reloaded Mevrouw's cart so that its weight should be more evenly balanced, and he had done what he could for her sheep, but it was doubtful if more than four of them could reach the dorp. As things were Mevrouw had better spend the night here and set off again at dawn. He wished much that he could have done more for her, but doubtless in Hermansdorp she had friends who would help her. And now, as it was already late, he himself must be moving …

When Jan Nortje and his wife had left them and the sound of their wagon wheels had died away into the swiftly gathering darkness old Alie settled down with the boy before the fire. Warmed and comforted he soon fell asleep, but for her there was no sleep, no escape from her weariness, no relief to her melancholy. Throughout the long night pain crept through her body with the quiet, gentle insistence of a slowly rising tide. By no effort of will and no physical means within her power could she stem it. In her discomfort her mind fell into a confusion of thought for the future and memory of the past. It was now Tan' Betje's voice that she heard, speaking of work to do for Canter's store. It was now Jan Nortje's wife who spoke, telling of the orphan-house in Hermansdorp. Out of the darkness beyond the firelight the orphan-house and the store took shape in her thoughts, vanished and took shape again as the mirages in the veld had done in the heat of the previous noon. When dawn came it was in weariness of body and with mind unrested that she roused herself to the labours of a new day and set off for the coffee-house.

The coffee-house in Hermansdorp, one of the oldest houses in the village, was a long, gabled, yellow-washed building at the lower end of the Kerk Straat. Its yard stood open to the street, and here, as in the market-square, carts and wagons were outspanned by those who came to the dorp for the quarterly Sacrament or the weekly market. In good seasons Andries Geldenhuis and his wife did brisk trade with their coffee and cakes, but in this time of drought there were few with money to spend, and those who outspanned at the coffee-house now were those who had been driven in distress from their lands to seek help from their church, or relief from the government. Among these, when she reached the village at noon, old Alie with her grandson, her rough, unpainted cart, her exhausted donkeys and famished sheep, took her place almost unnoticed. Only with Andries himself did she have speech. And to him, when her sheep and donkeys had been watered and fed, she said briefly that she had business at the head of the Kerk Straat: that tomorrow she would be selling her sheep and her donkeys at the morning market and that after the sale she would pay him what was due.

In spring, when the pear-trees which lined it were in blossom against the dark background of the enfolding hills, the wide straight Kerk Straat in Hermansdorp had an enchanting beauty, and it was in spring that, as a young girl, old Alie had first seen it. Today, like the thorn-trees at the dam, the trees were bare, and the furrows at their roots all waterless. In the open roadway the dust lay deep in ruts, and here, as in the veld, the wind which raised the dust in stinging blinding clouds had the bitter cold of winter drought. Against the wind and the flying dust old Alie's progress was slow. There was, it seemed to her now, no part of her body which was not in pain. As she leant on his shoulder for a moment her hand felt hot to Koos through his jacket and shirt. She spoke little, but the boy who had never seen the Kerk Straat in spring and to whom the bare trees, the stir of life, the shops, the houses, the very dust brought an enchantment of their own, was unconscious of her silence. This was not perhaps the Hermansdorp his grandmother had described – but that, as yet, he had hardly realised. Here was romance. Here was adventure. And here still, at his grandmother's side, was safety.

They came presently to a high, long, whitewashed wall and here his grandmother halted. Over the top of the wall the boy could see row upon row of straight slender trees, all a dull rusty brown – cypress-trees killed by the drought. Between the trees, out of his sight, were the whitewashed tombs among which in her youth old Alie had wandered. But what had been a garden to her then was now a wilderness in the drought and she turned heavily away.

Beyond the graveyard came the church and the parsonage, and dwelling-houses set back in deep gardens or built close on the street with *stoeps* slightly raised above the side-walk. Fifty years had brought little change to these, but at the upper end of the street where the business of the dorp was carried on, only the old whitewashed gaol was as she remembered it. And here, when at last they reached the grey stone buildings which now surrounded the gaol, she searched for Canter's store in vain. That it still existed she could not bring herself to doubt. And as the signs above the doorways meant nothing to her – for without Tan' Betje's help she could not spell them out – she entered the building which stood, as far as she could judge, where Canter's once had stood and asked to see the master.

A young man was appealed to and came forward pleasantly to ask what he could do for her. She said again that she wished to see the master, and was told that he himself was the master.

Was his name Canter? she asked. And was answered that it was Isaacs.

Was not this then Canter's store?

The young man repeated that it was Isaacs's. There was, he said, no Canter's store in Hermansdorp nor any family of that name, though there might well have been before his time. But what was it that she had wished to buy at Canter's store? No doubt, whatever it was, he himself, Isaacs, would be able to supply it.

Old Alie answered that she had not come to buy but to seek for work. Many years ago she had worked here, at Canter's store, at mattress-making, and it was such work she sought now. Could Mijnheer perhaps employ her?

That, said the young man, was impossible. Mattresses were sent to him ready-made from wholesale stores in Cape Town, and no stores in Hermansdorp now made their own. But was she sure that there was nothing he could sell her? Prints? ... Calicoes? A warm shawl, let down in price because of the drought? A coat for the boy?

There was nothing. Aloof, patient, giving no sign of the blow that had fallen upon her, old Alie waited for the young man to cease, then bade him a quiet good-day and left the store.

Out in the wind-swept street she paused, and the boy, conscious for the first time of some hesitation in her movements, looked up at her anxiously. In the store he had heard nothing of the young man's talk with his grandmother, for his mind had been held by the strange and wonderful things displayed around him there. But now suddenly, in his grandmother's hesitation, came his first hint of insecurity, and with it romance died out of the long bare Kerk Straat in which they stood forlorn. Quickly his hand slipped again into hers. She looked down upon him vaguely, strangely, and saying no word moved heavily down the street.

Against the wind, on their way to the store, their progress had been slow, but it was slower than ever now. What now must she do for the child? Where now must she turn for work? Andries Geldenhuis had said that in the morning market donkeys were sold for a shilling and less, for who in this drought could afford to feed donkeys? And sheep, he had said, in such poor condition as hers, could bring her but little more. When these and the cart were sold she would have money perhaps for a few days' shelter and food at the coffee-house – but afterwards? ...

She could not see what was to come afterwards ... Yet the boy must have food. At Tan' Betje's little house there had always been food. Good food. If she could find Tan' Betje's house now there might still be people there who remembered her – Betje Ferreira, the mattress-maker. And they, perhaps, might help her ...

In their slow progress they had come now to the opening of a lane which ran from the Kerk Straat to the upper street, and it was up such a lane that Tan' Betje had lived. Right at the head of the lane the house had stood ... and to the head of the lane she would go.

To the head of the lane they went in silence – and came not to the whitewashed green-shuttered house of Betje Ferreira, the mattress-maker, but to a plain double-storeyed building in a bare wide playground. Here boys and girls together, some Koos's age, some older and some younger, were playing at ball. In a corner of the playground, against a sunny wall, sat a young girl of twenty, sewing. From time to time the children appealed to her in their play, or were joined by her in their laughter. In the cookhouse, close to the main building, the midday meal was being prepared, and from the house itself came the clatter of plates being set out on a long trestle table by a coloured girl who sang at her work.

Slowly, as she halted with Koos in front of the fence, these sights and sounds impressed themselves upon old Alie's mind. The talk of Jan Nortje's wife came back to her. This, then, was the orphan-house. This, then, was where the children of the poor were taken to be fed ... At first her mind grasped nothing but this ... Then slowly she began to reason. If she could not find work how could she feed Koos? And where was she to find work in a place where mattresses were no longer made? How was she now to plan for the child? He, too, like these others, must have food. And here, for the asking – had not Jan Nortje's wife said it? – was food.

For herself old Alie had at that moment no thought. What she herself would do if she left the boy here, and where she herself would turn for food were questions which simply did not arise in her mind. Nor, in her ignorance of the ways of the world, did it occur to her that certain formalities might have to precede a child's acceptance at the orphan-house. With no note from the pastor, no order from any of those who supported the orphan-house, but with Koos's hand held close in her own, she pushed open the gate and entered the yard.

From the seat against the wall the young girl came forward quickly to greet her. Had Mevrouw come to leave the child with them? she asked. The pity then was that Juffrouw Volkwijn was not here to receive him. Only she herself, Justine de Jager, was here – in charge for the day. But if it was all in order that the child was to come to them, would Mevrouw leave him and come again herself in the evening to see Juffrouw Volkwijn? Would it suit Mevrouw to do so?

She spoke at a rush, giving no pause for answer. That old Alie had come with the necessary note of admission she never doubted and did not stop to question. Her eager nature had little time for formality of any kind. Let Koos – Koos was his name? Koos van Staden? – let Koos take his place as the children lined up for the midday meal – the bell was just about to ring – and let Mevrouw come again in the evening ...

As she spoke the bell rang. Instantly the children ceased their play and formed into line, the girls in one row, the boys in another. Taking him quickly but not unkindly by the shoulder Justine pushed Koos into place at the end of the row of boys. At a sharp word of command from her the girls filed into the house, the boys followed. At the doorway Koos lagged, looking back in bewilderment and appeal to his grandmother. Again Justine seized him by the shoulder and pushed him into the room before her. The door closed, but through the open windows old Alie could hear the tramp of feet on the bare carpetless floor: then silence: then the raising of sweet clear shrill voices in the children's grace – 'Thanks to our Father now we give' ... She turned and made her way with slow heavy steps to the gate.

140

It was long past the dinner hour when old Alie at last reached the coffee-house and crossed the yard to her outspanned cart. As she passed them two women seated near a wagon gave her greeting. She made no answer. The women exchanged glances. Who was she then, this old woman who was too proud to return their greeting? For a moment or two they watched her curiously, resenting, as Mijnheer Bezedenhout had resented, her aloofness – then fell again to their talk.

Unaware of their glances as she had been of their greeting old Alie sat down on her low folding-stool. The pain which had racked her limbs throughout the previous night and throughout the morning had given way now to a numbness which made it difficult for her to control her movements, and she sat awkwardly on the stool, seeking such support as she could get from the wheel at her back. Her hands lay idle on her lap, and from the depths of her black calico sunbonnet her dark eyes looked out upon a world that was growing each moment more strange and unreal to her. It was not the coffee-house yard that she saw. It was the Verlatenheid: it was the orphan-house: it was Canter's store: it was Tan' Betje's little house with the pear-tree in the yard. But always, whatever it was, it was Koos's face turned towards her in bewilderment and appeal – adding sorrow to her sorrow … The young girl, Justine, ought not to have parted them so, closing the door between them. But surely she had meant no harm. And presently, when it came towards evening, she, Alie, would go back to the orphan-house and explain to him that she must leave him there until she found work … Just a little while she would leave him, and then, when she had found work, she would come for him again and they would go together to Tan' Betje's little house. Up some other lane it must be, but she would find it. A little house with green shutters and a pear-tree in the yard … buckets under the pear-tree … and coir spread out in the sun …

Once again the bent fingers began to play in her lap – teasing the coir as once long ago she had teased it: dipping it into the bucket at her side: shaking it: teasing it: spreading it out in the sun to dry …

One of the women seated by the wagon, chancing to look up, saw this strange play, watched it for a moment, then rose and ran towards the cart. She shook old Alie's shoulder gently and spoke to her.

'Ouma, are you ill? Are you ill then, Ouma?'

Old Alie did not hear. A little while longer she played with the coir – teasing it, plucking it – then at last her fingers grew still.

PAULINE SMITH

The Schoolmaster

From: *The Little Karoo* (1925)

Because of a weakness of the chest which my grandmother thought that she alone could cure, I went often, as a young girl, to my grandparents' farm of Nooitgedacht in the Ghamka valley. At Nooitgedacht, where my grandparents lived together for more than forty years, my grandmother had always young people about her – young boys and girls, and little children who clung to her skirts or were tossed up into the air and caught again by my grandfather. There was not one of their children or their grandchildren that did not love Grandfather and Grandmother Delport, and when Aunt Betje died it seemed but right to us all that her orphans, little Neeltje and Frikkie and Hans, Koos and Martinus and Piet, should come to Nooitgedacht to live. My grandmother was then about sixty years old. She was a big stout woman, but as is sometimes the way with women who are stout, she moved very easily and lightly upon her feet. I had seen once a ship come sailing into Zandtbaai harbour, and grandmother walking, in her full wide skirts with Aunt Betje's children bobbing like little boats around her, would make me often think of it. This big, wise, and gentle woman, with love in her heart for all the world, saw in everything that befell us the will of the Lord. And when, three weeks after Aunt Betje's children had come to us, there came one night, from God knows where, a stranger asking for shelter out of the storm, my grandmother knew that the Lord had sent him.

The stranger, who, when my grandmother brought him into the living-room, gave the name of Jan Boetje, was a small dark man with a little pointed beard that looked as if it did not yet belong to him. His cheeks were thin and white, and so also were his hands. He seldom raised his eyes except when he spoke, and when he did so it was as if I saw before me the Widow of Nain's son, risen from the dead, out of my grandmother's Bible. Yes, as if from the dead did Jan Boetje come to us that night, and yet it was food that I thought of at once. And quickly I ran and made coffee and put it before him.

When Jan Boetje had eaten and drunk, my grandparents knew all that they were ever to know about him. He was a Hollander, and had but lately come to South Africa. He had neither relative nor friend in the colony. And he was on his way up-country on foot to the goldfields.

For a little while after Jan Boetje spoke of the goldfields my grandmother sat in silence. But presently she said:

'Mijnheer! I that am old have never yet seen a happy man that went digging for gold, or a man that was happy when he had found it. Surely it is sin and sorrow that drives men to it, and sin and sorrow that comes to them from it. Look now! Stay with us here on the farm, teaching school to my grandchildren, the orphans of my daughter Lijsbeth, and it may be that so you will find peace.'

Jan Boetje answered her: 'If Mevrouw is right, and sin and sorrow have driven me to her country for gold, am I a man to be trusted with her grandchildren?'

My grandmother cried, in her soft clear voice that was so full of love and pity: 'Is there a sin that cannot be forgiven? And a sorrow that cannot be shared?'

Jan Boetje answered: 'My sorrow I cannot share. And my sin I myself can never forgive.'

And again my grandmother said: 'Mijnheer! What lies in a man's heart is known only to God and himself. Do now as seems right to you, but surely if you will stay with us I will trust my grandchildren to you and know that the Lord has sent you.'

For a long, long time, as it seemed to me, Jan Boetje sat before us and said no word. I could not breathe, and yet it was as if all the world must hear my breathing. Aunt Betje's children were long ago in bed, and only my grandparents and I sat there beside him. Long, long we waited. And when at last Jan Boetje said: 'I will stay', it was as if he had heard how I cried to the Lord to help him.

So it was that Jan Boetje stayed with us on the farm and taught school to Aunt Betje's children. His schoolroom was the old wagon-house (grandfather had long ago built a new one), and here my grandmother and I put a table and stools for Jan Boetje and his scholars. The wagon-house had no window, and to get light Jan Boetje and the children sat close to the open half-door. From the door one looked out to the orange grove, where all my grandmother's children and many of her grandchildren also had been christened. Beyond and above the orange-trees rose the peaks of the great Zwartkops mountains, so black in summer, and so white when snow lay upon them in winter. Through the mountains, far to the head of the valley, ran the Ghamka pass by which men travelled up-country when they went looking for gold. The Ghamka River came down through this pass and watered all the farms in the valley. Coming down from the mountains to Nooitgedacht men crossed it by the Rooikranz drift.

Inside the wagon-house my grandfather stored his great brandy casks and his tobacco, his pumpkins and his mealies, his ploughs and his spades, his whips and his harness, and all such things as are needed at times about a farm. From the beams of the loft also there hung the great hides that he used for his harness and his *veldschoen*. Jan Boetje's schoolroom smelt always of tobacco and brandy and hides, and when the mud floor, close by the door, was freshly smeared with *mist* it smelt of bullock's blood and cow dung as well.

We had, when Jan Boetje came to us, no books on the farm but our Bibles and such old lesson books as my aunts and uncles had thought not good enough to take away with them when they married. Aunt Betje's children had the Bible for their reading-book, and one of my grandfather's hides for a blackboard. On this hide, with blue clay from the river bed, Jan Boetje taught the little ones their letters and the bigger ones their sums. Geography also he taught them, but it was such a geography as had never before been taught in the Platkops district. Yes, surely the world could never be so wonderful and strange as Jan Boetje made it to us (for I also went to his geography class) in my grandmother's wagon-house. And always when he spoke of the cities and the wonders that he had seen I would think how bitter must be the sorrow, and how great the sin, that had driven him from them to us. And when, as it sometimes happened, he would ask me afterwards: 'What shall we take for our reading lesson, Engela?' I would choose the fourteenth chapter of Chronicles or the eighth chapter of Kings.

Jan Boetje asked me one day: 'What makes you choose the Prayer in the Temple, Engela?'

And I, that did not know how close to love had come my pity, answered him: 'Because, Mijnheer, King Solomon who cries, "Hear thou in heaven thy dwelling-place, and when thou hearest forgive," prays also for the stranger from a far country.'

From that day Jan Boetje, who was kind and gentle with his scholars, was kind and gentle also with me. Many times now I found his eyes resting upon me, and when sometimes he came and sat quietly by my side as I sewed there would come a wild beating at my heart that was joy and pain together. Except to his scholars he had spoken to no one on the farm unless he first were spoken to. But now he spoke also to me, and when I went out in the veld with little Neeltje and her brothers, looking for all such things as are so wonderful to a child, Jan Boetje would come with us. And it was now that I taught Jan Boetje which berries he might eat and which would surely kill him, which leaves and bushes would cure a man of many sicknesses, and which roots and bulbs would quench his thirst. Many such simple things I taught him in the veld, and many, many times afterwards I thanked God that I had done so. Yes, all that my love was ever to do for Jan Boetje was but to guide him so in the wilderness.

When Jan Boetje had been with us six months and more, it came to be little Neeltje's birthday. My grandmother had made it a holiday for the children, and Jan Boetje and I were to go with them, in a stump-cart drawn by two mules, up into a little ravine that lay beyond the Rooikranz drift. It was such a clear still day as often happens in our Ghamka valley in June month, and as we drove Neeltje and her brothers sang together in high sweet voices that made me think of the angels of God. Because of the weakness of my chest I myself could never sing, and yet that day, with Jan Boetje sitting quietly by my side, it was as if my heart were so full of song that he must surely hear it. Yes, I that am now so old, so old, was never again to feel such joy as swept through my soul and body then.

When we had driven about fifteen minutes from the farm we came to the Rooikranz drift. There had been but little rain and snow in the mountains that winter, and in the wide bed of the river there was then but one small stream. The banks of the river here are steep, and on the far side are the great red rocks that give the drift its name. Here the wild bees make their honey, and the white wild geese have their home. And that day how beautiful in the still clear air were the great red rocks against the blue sky, and how beautiful against the rocks were the white wings of the wild geese.

When we had crossed the little stream Jan Boetje stopped the cart and Neeltje and her brothers climbed out of it and ran across the river bed shouting and clapping their hands to send the wild geese flying out from the rocks above them. Only I was left with Jan Boetje, and now when he whipped up the mules they would not move. Jan Boetje stood up in the cart and slashed at them, and they backed towards the stream. Jan Boetje jumped from the cart, and with the stick end of his whip struck the mules over the eyes, and his face, that had grown so dear to me, was suddenly strange and terrible to see. I cried to him: 'Jan Boetje! Jan Boetje!' but the weakness of my chest was upon me and I could make no sound. I rose in the cart to climb out of it, and as I rose Jan Boetje had a knife in his hand and dug it into the eyes of the mules to blind them. Sharp above the laughter of the children and the cries of the wild geese there came a terrible scream, and I fell from the cart on to the soft grey sand of the river bed. When I rose again the mules were far down the stream, with the cart bumping and splintering behind them, and Jan Boetje after them. And so quickly had his madness come upon him that still the children laughed and clapped their hands, and still the wild geese flew among the great red rocks above us.

God knows how it was that I gathered the children together and, sending the bigger boys in haste back to the farm, came on myself with Neeltje and the little ones. My grandfather rode out to meet us. I told him what I could, but it was little that I could say, and he rode on down the river. When we came to the farm the children ran up to the house to my grandmother, but I myself went alone to the wagon-house. I opened the door and closed it after me again, and crept in the dark to Jan Boetje's chair. Long, long I sat there, with my head on my arms on his table, and it was as if in all the world there was nothing but a sorrow that must break my heart, and a darkness that smelt of tobacco and brandy and hides. Long, long I sat, and when at last my grandmother found me, 'My little Engela,' she said. 'The light of my heart! My treasure!'

The mules that Jan Boetje had blinded were found and shot by my grandfather, and for long the splinters of the cart lay scattered down the bed of the river. Jan Boetje himself my grandfather could not find, though he sent men through all the valley looking for him. And after many days it was thought that Jan Boetje had gone up-country through the pass at night. I was now for a time so ill that my father came down from his farm in Beaufort district to see me. He would have taken me back with him but in my weakness I cried to grandmother to keep me. And my father, to whom everything that my grandmother did was right, once again left me to her.

My father had not been many days gone when old Franz Langermann came to my grandparents with news of Jan Boetje. Franz Langermann lived at the toll-house at the entrance to the pass through the mountains, and here Jan Boetje had come to him asking if he would sell him an old hand-cart that stood by the toll-gate. The hand-cart was a heavy clumsy one that the road-men repairing the road through the pass had left behind them. Franz Langermann had asked Jan Boetje what he would do with such a cart? And Jan Boetje had answered: 'I that have killed mules must now work like a mule if I would live.' And he had said to Franz Langermann: 'Go to the farm of Nooitgedacht and say to Mevrouw Delport that all that is in the little tin box in my room is now hers in payment of the mules. But there is enough also to pay for the hand-cart if Mevrouw will but give you what is just.'

My grandmother asked Franz Langermann: 'But what is it then that Jan Boetje can do with a hand-cart?'

And Franz Langermann answered: 'Look now, Mevrouw! Through the country dragging the hand-cart like a mule he will go, gathering such things as he can find and afterwards selling them again that he may live. Look! Already out of a strap that I gave him Jan Boetje has made for himself his harness.'

My grandmother went to Jan Boetje's room and found the box as Franz Langermann had said. There was money in it enough to pay for the mules and the hand-cart, but there was nothing else. My grandmother took the box out to Franz Langermann and said:

'Take now the box as it is, and let Mijnheer give you himself what is just, but surely I will not take payment for the mules. Is it not seven months now that Jan Boetje has taught school to my grandchildren? God help Jan Boetje, and may he go in peace.'

But Franz Langermann would not take the box. 'Look now, Mevrouw,' he said, 'I swore to Jan Boetje that only for the hand-cart would I take the money, and all the rest would I leave.'

My grandmother put the box back in Jan Boetje's room, and gave to Franz Langermann instead such things as a man takes on a journey – biltong, and rusks and meal, and a little kidskin full of dried fruits. As much as Franz Langermann could carry she gave him. But I, that would have given Jan Boetje all the world, in all the world had nothing that I might give. Only when Franz Langermann had left the house and crossed the yard did I run after him with my little Bible and cry:

'Franz Langermann! Franz Langermann! Say to Jan Boetje to come again to Nooitgedacht! Say to him that so long as I live I will wait!'

Yes, I said that. God knows what meaning my message had for me, or what meaning it ever had for Jan Boetje, but it was as if I must die if I could not send it.

That night my grandmother came, late in the night, to the room where I lay awake. She drew me into her arms and held me there, and out of the darkness I cried:

'Grandmother! Grandmother! Is love then such sorrow?'

And still I can hear the low clear voice that answered so strangely: 'A joy and a sorrow – a help and a hindrance – love comes at the last to be but what one makes it.'

It was the next day that my grandmother asked me to teach school for her in Jan Boetje's place. At first, because always the weakness of my chest had kept me timid, I did not think she could mean it. But she did mean it. And suddenly I knew that for Jan Boetje's sake I had strength to do it. And I called the children together and went down to the wagon-house and taught them.

All through the spring and summer months that year, getting books from the pastor in Platkops dorp to help me, I taught school for my grandmother. And because it was easy for me to love little children and to be patient with them, and because it was for Jan Boetje's sake that I did it, I came at last to forget the weakness of my chest and to make a good teacher. And day after day as I sat in his chair in the wagon-house I would think of Jan Boetje dragging his hand-cart across the veld. And day after day I would thank God that I had taught him which berries he might eat, and which bulbs would quench his thirst. Yes, in such poor and simple things as this had my love to find its comfort.

That year winter came early in the Ghamka valley, and there came a day in May month when the first fall of snow brought the river down in flood from the mountains. My grandfather took the children down to the drift to see it. I did not go, but sat working alone with my books in the wagon-house. And always on that day when I looked up through the open half-door, and saw, far above the orange grove, the peaks of the Zwartkops mountains so pure and white against the blue sky, there came a strange sad happiness about my heart, and it was as if I knew that Jan Boetje had at last found peace and were on his way to tell me so. Long, long I thought of him that day in the wagon-house, and when there came a heavy tramping of feet and a murmur of voices across the yard I paid no heed. And presently the voices died down, and my grandmother stood alone before me, with her eyes full of tears and in her hand a little damp and swollen book that I knew for the Bible I had sent to Jan Boetje ... Down in the drift they had found his body – his harness still across his chest, the pole of his cart still in his hand.

That night I went alone to the room where Jan Boetje lay and drew back the sheet that covered him.

Across his chest, where the strap of his harness had rubbed it, the skin was hard and rough as leather. I knelt down by his side, and pressed my head against his breast. And through my heart there ran in farewell such foolish, tender words as my grandmother used to me – 'My joy and my sorrow ... The light of my heart, and my treasure.'

PAULINE SMITH

The Sisters

From: *The Little Karoo* (1925)

Marta was the eldest of my father's children, and she was sixteen years old when our mother died and our father lost the last of his water cases to old Jan Redlinghuis of Bitterwater. It was the water cases that killed my mother. Many, many times she had cried to my father to give in to old Jan Redlinghuis whose water rights had been fixed by law long before my father built his water furrow from the Ghamka river. But my father could not rest. If he could but get a fair share of the river water for his furrow, he would say, his farm of Zeekoegatt would be as rich as the farm of Bitterwater and we should then have a town-house in Platkops dorp and my mother should wear a black cashmere dress all the days of her life. My father could not see that my mother did not care about the black cashmere dress or the town-house in Platkops dorp. My mother was a very gentle woman with a disease of the heart, and all she cared about was to have peace in the house and her children happy around her. And for so long as my father was at law about his water rights there could be no peace on all the farm of Zeekoegatt. With each new water case came more bitterness and sorrow to us all. Even between my parents at last came bitterness and sorrow. And in bitterness and sorrow my mother died.

In his last water case my father lost more money than ever before, and to save the farm he bonded some of the lands to old Jan Redlinghuis himself. My father was surely mad when he did this, but he did it. And from that day Jan Redlinghuis pressed him, pressed him, pressed him, till my father did not know which way to turn. And then, when my father's back was up against the wall and he thought he must sell the last of his lands to pay his bond, Jan Redlinghuis came to him and said:

'I will take your daughter, Marta Magdalena, instead.'

Three days Jan Redlinghuis gave my father, and in three days, if Marta did not promise to marry him, the lands of Zeekoegatt must be sold. Marta told me this late that same night. She said to me:

'Sukey, my father has asked me to marry old Jan Redlinghuis. I am going to do it.'

And she said again: 'Sukey, my darling, listen now! If I marry old Jan

Redlinghuis he will let the water into my father's furrow, and the lands of Zeekoegatt will be saved. I am going to do it, and God will help me.'

I cried to her: 'Marta! Old Jan Redlinghuis is a sinful man, going at times a little mad in his head. God must help you before you marry him. Afterwards it will be too late.'

And Marta said: 'Sukey, if I do right, right will come of it, and it is right for me to save the lands for my father. Think now, Sukey my darling! There is not one of us that is without sin in the world, and old Jan Redlinghuis is not always mad. Who am I to judge Jan Redlinghuis? And can I then let my father be driven like a poor white to Platkops dorp?' And she drew me down on to the pillow beside her, and took me into her arms, and I cried there until far into the night.

The next day I went alone across the river to old Jan Redlinghuis's farm. No one knew that I went, or what it was in my heart to do. When I came to the house Jan Redlinghuis was out on the stoep smoking his pipe.

I said to him: 'Jan Redlinghuis, I have come to offer myself.'

Jan Redlinghuis took his pipe out of his mouth and looked at me. I said again: 'I have come to ask you to marry me instead of my sister Marta.'

Old Jan Redlinghuis said to me: 'And why have you come to do this thing, Sukey de Jager?'

I told him: 'Because it is said that you are a sinful man, Jan Redlinghuis, going at times a little mad in your head, and my sister Marta is too good for you.'

For a little while old Jan Redlinghuis looked at me, sitting there with his pipe in his hand, thinking the Lord knows what. And presently he said: 'All the same, Sukey de Jager, it is your sister Marta that I will marry and no one else. If not, I will take the lands of Zeekoegatt as is my right, and I will make your father bankrupt. Do now as you like about it.'

And he put his pipe in his mouth, and not one other word would he say.

I went back to my father's house with my heart heavy like lead. And all that night I cried to God: 'Do now what you will with me, but save our Marta.' Yes, I tried to make a bargain with the Lord so that Marta might be saved. And I said also: 'If He does not save our Marta I will know that there is no God.'

In three weeks Marta married old Jan Redlinghuis and went to live with him across the river. On Marta's wedding day I put my father's Bible before him and said: 'Pa, pray if you like, but I shall not pray with you. There is no God or surely He would have saved our Marta. But if there is a God as surely will He burn our souls in Hell for selling Marta to old Jan Redlinghuis'.

From that time I could do what I would with my father, and my heart was bitter to all the world but my sister Marta. When my father said to me: 'Is it not wonderful, Sukey, what we have done with the water that old Jan Redlinghuis lets pass to my furrow?'

150

I answered him: 'What is now wonderful? It is blood that we lead on our lands to water them. Did not my mother die for it? And was it not for this that we sold my sister Marta to old Jan Redlinghuis?'

Yes, I said that. It was as if my heart must break to see my father water his lands while old Jan Redlinghuis held my sister Marta up to shame before all Platkops.

I went across the river to my sister Marta as often as I could, but not once after he married her did old Jan Redlinghuis let Marta come back to my father's house.

'Look now, Sukey de Jager,' he would say to me, 'your father has sold me his daughter for his lands. Let him now look to his lands and leave me his daughter.' And that was all he would say about it.

Marta had said that old Jan Redlinghuis was not always mad, but from the day that he married her his madness was to cry to all the world to look at the wife that Burgert de Jager had sold to him.

'Look,' he would say, 'how she sits in her new tent-cart – the wife that Burgert de Jager sold to me.' And he would point to the Zeekoegatt lands and say: 'See now, how green they are, the lands that Burgert de Jager sold me his daughter to save.'

Yes, even before strangers would he say these things, stopping his cart in the road to say them, with Marta sitting by his side. My father said to me: 'Is it not wonderful, Sukey, to see how Marta rides through the country in her new tent-cart?'

I said to him: 'What is now wonderful? It is to her grave that she rides in the new tent-cart, and presently you will see it.'

And I said to him also: 'It took you many years to kill my mother, but believe me it will not take as many months for old Jan Redlinghuis to kill my sister Marta.' Yes, God forgive me, but I said that to my father. All my pity was for my sister Marta, and I had none to give my father.

And all this time Marta spoke no word against old Jan Redlinghuis. She had no illness that one might name, but every day she grew a little weaker, and every day Jan Redlinghuis inspanned the new tent-cart and drove her round the country. This madness came at last so strong upon him that he must drive from sunup to sundown crying to all whom he met: 'Look now at the wife that Burgert de Jager sold to me!'

So it went, day after day, day after day, till at last there came a day when Marta was too weak to climb into the cart and they carried her from where she fell into the house. Jan Redlinghuis sent for me across the river.

When I came to the house old Jan Redlinghuis was standing on the stoep with his gun. He said to me: 'See here, Sukey de Jager! Which of us now had the greatest sin – your father who sold me his daughter Marta, or I who bought her? Marta who let herself be sold, or you who offered to save her?'

And he took up his gun and left the stoep and would not wait for an answer.

Marta lay where they had put her on old Jan Redlinghuis's great wooden bed, and only twice did she speak. Once she said: 'He was not always mad, Sukey my darling, and who am I that I should judge him?'

And again she said: 'See how it is, my darling! In a little while I shall be with our mother. So it is that God has helped me.'

At sundown Marta died and when they ran to tell Jan Redlinghuis they could not find him. All that night they looked for him, and the next day also. We buried Marta in my mother's grave at Zeekoegatt … And still they could not find Jan Redlinghuis. Six days they looked for him, and at last they found his body in the mountains. God knows what madness had driven old Jan Redlinghuis to the mountains when his wife lay dying, but there it was they found him, and at Bitterwater he was buried.

That night my father came to me and said: 'It is true what you said to me, Sukey. It is blood that I have led on my lands to water them, and this night will I close the furrow that I built from the Ghamka river. God forgive me, I will do it.'

It was in my heart to say to him: 'The blood is already so deep in the lands that nothing we can do will now wash it out.' But I did not say this. I do not know how it was, but there came before me the still, sad face of my sister Marta, and it was as if she herself answered for me.

'Do now as it seems right to you,' I said to my father. 'Who am I that I should judge you?'

EUGÈNE N MARAIS

The Grey Pipit

Translated from the Afrikaans by Annie Gagiano
From: *Dwaalstories* (1927)

The small girl Nampti, the grey bird, was so tiny that the tame baby goats would push her over as they played.

The grandmother was so old that she scarcely remembered to gather wood every day. Nampti had to set the fire, cook food, and guard the goats. And the others in the yard treated these two badly. When there was meat, they got nothing, and the young girls would mock the granny for not walking upright and for being lame in one leg. They called her the old Wolf.

And on the plain Nampti found the small nest of a grey bird, and she led the goats past it and she sang to the mother:

> *Gampta, my little grey sister!*
> *All I have in the world*
> *Besides my old grandmother.*
> *As you sing up there in the sky*
> *You can see all the wondrous things below:*
> *Where the small hare hides*
> *And the steenbok has his hiding place.*
> *And the maidens cannot touch you,*
> *For you're stronger than everyone,*
> *Even though you're weaker than I,*
> *Even the mountain lion who frightens us*
> *When he roars at night*
> *Cannot touch you.*
> *I will guard you, my sister,*
> *Until all your little ones are grown.*

And the small grey bird sang over her head:

> *My grey sister Nampti I see you!*
> *I shall tell you something important:*
> *Last night when the female Ostrich*
> *Took shelter with her chicks,*

The mountain lion, who scares you,
Set off the poison trap in the fountain gorge,
And he lies dead in the big ghwarrie bush.
The one who inserts a hair of his beard under their skin
Becomes a lion, as long as the female Ostrich grazes
In the wide veld with her chicks.

And she rolled up her small grey kaross over one arm and she ran quickly to the fountain gorge; and in the ghwarrie bush she saw the dead mountain lion who had for so long terrorised the yard. And she pulled out the longest hair of his beard and inserted it under the skin of her arm.

And the mother bird sang above her head in the sky: 'Nampti, my little grey sister! Now she is stronger than everyone; and outshines all the girls who mock her granny.'

And that evening, when she arrived at home with the goats, her granny said: 'Why are the eyes shining in the dark like that?' And Nampti laughed.

And when the moon rose, she stood up from her sleeping mat and went outside. And when she entered the yard, the dogs howled, and the goats started bleating behind their shelters. And she saw that her shadow was the shadow of a mountain lion. And softly she walked towards the shelter of the headman, Okiep. They were sitting by the fire, roasting meat, and around them were many calabashes with milk. And Nampti blew through the branches of the shelter, and all of them jumped up and ran into the straw house slamming the door, and she heard the women screaming inside. And she took the fattest pieces of meat and the biggest calabash of milk, and she carried these to her granny. And as they were eating, the old woman, who was blind in the dark, said: 'Why does my little one lick with the tongue to drink her milk? A person doesn't drink like that.' And Nampti laughed out loud.

And every night when the female Ostrich was in the mountain Nampti went out, and she brought all the best food in the yard back to their shelter.

And by day the young women would say: 'Why is the little grey bird getting so fat and good-looking and big? Where does the crook-backed old Wolf get the food to give to her?'

And Nampti would only laugh.

And when she grew up, all the young fellows said: 'There is no girl in our yard who can touch Nampti!'

And young Okiep, the son of the headman, brought ten goats to her granny to ask to marry Nampti. And Nampti said: 'As long as you'll guard my Grey Sister while her nest lies in the grass, you may have me.' And he promised.

And this was the biggest wedding that they had ever had in their yard.

When the food had been shared out, Nampti brought a fat reed-buck from her shelter. And young Okiep said: 'What kind of wife have I taken? Where does a maiden get the power to catch buck at night?'

And Nampti only laughed; but the bridegroom felt his heart shiver. And when Nampti walked in the veld that day, the grey bird sang above her head:

Nampti, my Grey Sister, never take a drink at night;
and if she wakes up, she must pull the skin blanket
over her head.

And that night when Nampti was sleeping in the new straw house, she woke up, and she got up to take a drink from the large calabash on the food platform. And young Okiep saw her, and he hid trembling under the bedding.

And when day dawned, he went to consult with the elders and the councillors and he said: 'In the night her eyes glow like green fire, and when she drinks water she licks it with her tongue.'

And the councillors said: 'This is something deeply wrong. Tonight we shall stand guard outside and peep through the smoke-hole, and if it is as you say we'll rid our yard of this monster.'

And Nampti, listening behind the shelter, heard what they were saying.

And as soon as the grass was dry, she went to the veld and she called: 'Oh, my Grey Sister, the heart of your little sister is sore. You have helped me and now your advice has led me to disaster!'

And the tears ran down her face.

And the grey bird sang above her head: 'Where is the danger? Is it not the task of the husband to rub *buchu* on his bride's arms?' And Nampti laughed as she returned to the yard.

And when night fell, she said: 'My husband, is it not the custom that the husband should rub *buchu* on his wife's arms? Why then is this custom not maintained in our home?'

And young Okiep took the ground *buchu* from the veld bag and he rubbed her arms, and it began to get dark, and behind the shelter lurked the councillors.

And young Okiep said: 'Why do my Nampti's eyes glow green in the dark?' And Nampti laughed. And he said again: 'Why are my Nampti's nails growing longer and curved?' And Nampti laughed.

And his voice trembled and she said: 'Rub the *buchu*; let us keep the custom.'

And his heart weakened; and he said: 'There's a thorn here in my Nampti's arm.'

And Nampti said: 'Is it not the task of the man to extract it?' And he rubbed with the *buchu* and felt her arm turning into the forepaw of a lion, and heard her voice deepening. And he extracted the beard-hair and then called to the elders: 'It's a lion! Help me, my Dad, or I am done for!'

155

And in they ran with knives and lights, and when the inside of the straw house was lit up, they saw Nampti sitting in the centre, and young Okiep rubbing her arms with *buchu*. And they said: 'Where is the lion?'

And young Okiep blushed and he said: 'I was scared in the dark. I was dreaming.' And they greeted Nampti courteously.

And she always remained the foremost woman of the entire yard.

RRR DHLOMO

The Death of Masaba

First published, 1929

From: *Selected Stories* (1991)

'Fellows, what do you think of this business of Masaba?'

'Yes, just tell us what happened.'

'Men, the boy is dying. I heard from Stimela, the boss-boy of the lashers, that Masaba fainted twice in the mine today. Stimela he ran to tell Boss Tom, who did not even want to listen to him, but only said: "Get away, there are lots of boys in the compound.'''

'But what made Masaba faint in the mine?'

'Well … I saw that there was a mistake in his ticket. It was not stamped *ten days' light underground work.*'

The others they laughed when they heard the word 'mistake'.

'Clear out,' they cried, 'there is no *mistake* there! We old boys know well that if Masaba had been a white man there would have been no *mistake*. Didn't Boss Tom say "there are lots of Kaffirs in the compound"? "If one dies," meaning Masaba, "the Government will bring more." He said that after Stimela had told him, "Masaba is fainting, he cannot lash."'

The others were silent; each was busy with his own thoughts.

This affair was worrying their hearts a great deal. These men – they were five, sitting round a glowing bucket fire – had left their kraals for the mines, forced to do so by hunger and want. They left their homes knowing of the terrible accidents that occur below the surface of the mines. Their only hope was that the always-wise white people would be true to them and treat them well: safeguard them from underground dangers, and work them as people with equal feelings though their skins were black.

The working place where they were stationed was deep down on the 18th level. The heat on that level was terrible; so intense that unacclimatised boys were liable to get heatstroke. Behind them a yawning, dreary shaft threatened their lives; while in front a naked, creaking rock rose sheer above them. From its grim, muddy face trickled drops of dirty, poisonous water.

Under these disabilities, with death everywhere beckoning, Boss Tom made them lash as though the Furies were after them. Here their half-naked bodies were bent unceasingly over the shovels. Even old lashing hands were seen staggering under the heat, and through the pangs of hunger. As these were their daily lot in life, they did not mind it at all, for they had infinite trust in their masters.

But today, when they saw Masaba, the victim of callous indifference, yes Masaba, their young fellow countryman, who was not even supposed to be placed on the lashing gang, their hearts were filled with blood. The first incident happened when they were shovelling madly. Masaba suddenly dropped down ... and fainted.

Boss Boy Stimela ran and told Boss Tom: 'Nkosi, the boy Masaba has fainted. He can't lash.'

Boss Tom was greatly surprised when he heard that a 'Kaffir' could not do the job for which he was solely created, the handling of the shovel. He said to Steamer: 'What! Masaba can't lash? A bloody Kaffir ... can't lash?'

'I know, sir,' replied Steamer, 'that Masaba faints as soon as he stoops to lash. I think he's not used to it yet.'

'Oh, kick him, Steamer.'

Steamer was, however, one of those fast-dwindling Boss Boys who, instead of 'waking up' Masaba with a kick, according to orders, went to him and said, 'Try and lash, boy. The Boss will hit you, say you're loafing.'

Poor Masaba went and threw himself at his master's feet.

'Nkosi, I am not used to lashing yet. I get so tired, sir, and my head aches so. My eyes get clouded and misty when I stoop to lash, sir. I beg you, sir, my good Boss, my father, give me another job until I'm used to this job of lashing. I will work well, sir. I will do anything for you, Boss. But lashing kills me, Boss, please.'

And he burst into tears, while his fellow workers muttered ominously under their breath.

It is difficult for a boy and his Boss to come to quick understanding down there. Because in the mine their language is different from ours. There their speech is made up of all those naked and revolting phrases that would shame the Prince of Darkness. Still muttering amongst themselves, they said, 'Masaba, isn't your ticket stamped?'

'I don't know,' sobbed Masaba. 'This is my first time to work in the mine. I began work yesterday.'

'Hey, what's up there?' bawled Boss Tom, drawing nearer. 'If I get you talking again, Masaba, there'll be hell for you.'

'He is dying, sir,' cried Stimela in a strained voice.

It was then that Boss Tom uttered words seemingly innocent in his thoughts, but to natives' minds full of damning meanings. This thoughtless ganger who did not know the working of a native's mind said: 'There are lots of Kaffirs in the compound!'

The boys having digested these words bent once more over their shovels. A piercing cry stopped their labours. For, with a heartrending cry, Masaba fell

158

with a sickening thud, knocking his head against a jagged piece of rock on the stope. Without delay he was carried to the surface and from there was hurried to the hospital. When his fellow countrymen heard that Masaba was seriously ill, they brooded.

'Lord Jesus, please save Masaba for his poor mother's sake. She will be left alone in this world.'

The next day, as they were changing from their wet clothes, a mine police boy entered their room: 'Er ... er ... Madoda, the manager said I should come to tell you that Masaba is dead.'

When an inquiry was held over the death of Masaba, it was found that Boss Tom was guilty. For he had caused a new boy to lash before putting him first on light undergound work, as was the rule with new boys. Through his carelessness and indifference he had caused the death of Masaba.

'I say, fellows, if Masaba had died accidentally, it would not have mattered. But I hold that he was murdered. For his ticket was stamped: *Not to be employed on lashing.*'

'*Hau*, didn't you hear that Boss said to Stimela, "There are many Kaffirs in the compound"? Ho! Ho! You don't know the white people!'

And they went out to dig Masaba's grave.

RRR DHLOMO

Murder on the Mine Dumps

First published, 1930

From: *Selected Stories* (1991)

Those who slept in room thirteen seemed worried and anxious as though something was at the back of their minds. Their eyes were fixed on the compound gate; they kept looking at it and now and then uttered profane oaths.

What worried them at that gate was the presence of the compound manager. He was standing there waiting for the shift to come off, before he went to his own house. These people knew this; he did this every day. Tonight, however, their hearts were very bad. It was the night of their meeting on the mine dump.

Presently the shift was declared off and the compound manager went home. Just as he turned round the corner of the compound, these men left room thirteen one by one. The first made as if he were going to the Jew stores to buy; the second walked slowly in the direction of the dump with his carbide lamp, as though to clean it with sand. The third went on picking bits of dry wood for the good purpose of making a fire in the room.

When eight o'clock struck they had all assembled on the dump. They then followed one another down a deep, dark, narrow tunnel which became wide and gloomy at the bottom, though it was wet and somewhat muddy. They sat down in a semi-circle.

'Men,' began their leader, 'we have come here this night for two things. The first thing is this: the dump on which we now are is our hiding place. It is full of small holes which would help us when we were in trouble with the police. They would not follow us here, even in the day. We can stay here for many months even without passes. We can also put all our stolen things here. No one would think of looking for them here. We can here form all our plans for sending to hell our exploiters.

'Remember, men, that this dump was piled here by our blood. You hear that, fools? By our blood! Keep that in your minds so that on the great day you will know that you are fighting for your rights as all civilised men have had to fight.'

'We hear you well, Sipepo.'

Sipepo glared at them and then spat angrily on the ground. They listened silently. Fear did not allow them to speak. They were mine workers these boys.

160

But from some foolish meetings which they had attended they had been impressed by the idea that they should rise as one man and make the white people feel the pinch, too, as they felt it. They now hated white people.

So every evening they made it their African duty to meet on the mine dump and talk of what they would do to 'down the rich people who exploited them'. They had appointed Sipepo as their leader because it was he who went to those meetings and knew what was meant by 'exploitation' and 'revolutions'.

In these meetings Sipepo was always impressed by the words: 'Passive resistance', 'Down with tools', or 'to hell with our exploiters – the capitalists!'

So he had formed this gang for his own purposes.

'Now open your ears,' began Sipepo. 'There is a great thing I want you to see tonight. You know that in these past days our compound manager nearly sacked me for going to the meetings on Sunday? You know, too, that the induna knows that we have joined the meetings in town and that we also want to spread the spirit of burning passes here in the compound on the day of Dingane. Who tells these people all these things? Eh, you don't know. I know and I'll make you know tonight, true – follow me!'

They followed him along a narrow, muddy tunnel, their hearts beating with fear and wonder.

'Blow out your candles!'

They did so.

'We are now out of our hole,' said Sipepo. 'Do you see that small white spot there which looks like water?'

'We see it, Sipepo,' they said in answer.

Sipepo, their leader, laughed a funny, bad laugh. Into his eyes came a wild light.

'You have not seen it. You are about to see it well. Sit down here. Yes, speak as much as you like, policemen never come up here.'

They sat down, their lungs lifted, as the Zulu tongue expressed it.

Sipepo eyed them strangely for five minutes and then said: 'You, July, go straight to that spot and stand on it.'

July, a tall, broadchested Msutu, rose and stood. His brow became a little wet, and his big chest began to move quicker. He tried to smile but the smile died foolishly on his face, for it was he who had told the compound manager that they went to town meetings on Sundays and came back with evil talks about burning passes and refusing to work. This had led to some of the boys losing their work and to others being given blows down in the mine.

Foolishly, July had also divulged to the induna their secret meeting place on the mine dumps. But he had done this under the influence of skokiaan. He was not to blame for that, was he? All these thoughts and others ran swiftly across his mind as he stood trembling before the members of the gang.

There was nothing strange in being told to go and stand on a certain spot upon the dump and yet there was something fearful in the way Sipepo spoke and in the way he looked at him with his blood-shot eyes.

'He is afraid, the Msutu,' said Sipepo quietly. 'What is the use of your fear, July? You are going to stand on that spot to-night — you hear? To-night and now! Go and stand there, do you hear what I say — this dog!'

As July obeyed he thought of his mother, and what she said when he left his father's kraal for the mines:

'July, my child,' she had said, with tears in her eyes, 'where are you going? To Johannesburg? You are my only child. You leave me for the mines — Your death, where you'll come back a man of nothing: full of sickness — ho!'

He had laughed then at his mother's tears. And now? He went slowly towards the patch of mud and stood on it.

'Now,' Sipepo's voice had changed. It was hard and cold like the hissing of a puff adder. 'Look at that bloody Msutu well,' he said.

The others were now greatly excited. They felt that something bad was going to take place. They felt this by looking at Sipepo's face.

Now they looked at July, and their lungs again rose and stood close to their mouths.

'Do you see him?' asked Sipepo laughing.

'Hau, we see him, Sipepo. But he seems to be sinking down. What is it, Sipepo? Isimangaliso Impela.'

'Look at him! Look at him!'

Again they looked at July; and heard his pitiful cry. For July was slipping down the slimy hole. Desperately he tried to jump over to a firmer place, but his feet stuck fast in the mud. When he stretched out his hands to clutch seemingly strong ground, it caved in. Something seemed to be dragging him down …

Down, down, down, down he sank!

He lifted up his voice and shrieked in terror and bitterness of heart. 'Help me, my fellowmen!' he choked. 'Help me, my kind and good brothers. Help me, please, I am dying!'

Now he was waist deep in the slimes.

Impulsively one of the weak-hearted of the gang rose to his feet, only to be struck on the face by Sipepo's cycle chain. 'Sit down, dog!'

Bleeding and frightened the man fell down beside his trembling fellows.

'Save me, my own brother!' wept the poor Msutu. 'Help me … help me …'

But the slimy mud covered him entirely and he choked to death before the eyes of the gang.

Sipepo laughed and drew strongly on his dagga-filled pipe.

'Now you have seen him die who told all our secrets to the white people. A dog of dogs … Suka!'

And he spat on the ground.

162

WILLIAM PLOMER

The Child of Queen Victoria

From: *The Child of Queen Victoria and other Stories* (1933)

Coelum non animum ...

1

A Ford car, rattling its way up a rough road in Lembuland in the most brilliant sunshine, carried two very different people – a hard-bitten colonial of Scotch descent, a trader, MacGavin by name, nearer thirty than forty, with a sour red face, and a young Englishman called Frant who had just left school. It was really very awkward. They did not know what to say to each other. MacGavin thought his passenger was despising him simply for being what he was, and Frant, feeling foolish and useless in contrast with this sunburnt, capable man, made a painful effort to be hearty, and looked inquiringly at the country. The road wound in and out, climbing through grassy hills, with patches of virgin forest here and there, especially in the hollows. There were outcrops of rock, and small tilled fields of red earth, and any number of beehive-shaped huts perched here and there in twos and threes. And there were always natives in sight, with herds of bony cattle and ragged goats. It did not need a specially acute eye to see that the landscape, though picturesque, was overcrowded, and that the whites, coveting the lowlands for sugar-cane, had gradually squeezed the natives up into these heights which were poor in soil, coarse in pasturage, and too full of ups and downs to afford space for any proper attempts at cultivation. Frant looked at the natives, naturally, with some curiosity. He wondered what they were like when you got to know them, and then he wondered if he couldn't say something suitable to MacGavin about them. At last he said:

'It seems a pity the natives haven't got a higher standard of living, then there would be so much more money to be made out of them.'

MacGavin looked at him with the savage expression sometimes to be seen on the faces of the ignorant when confronted with what seems to them a new and difficult and rather mad idea.

'The black bastards!' he exclaimed. 'There's bloody little to be made out of *them*, as you'll pretty soon find out.'

And he violently changed gear. As the car began to strain its way up a steep hill, Frant, vibrating by his side, was glad that the noise of the engine destroyed what would have been a painful silence.

Sons of the 'new poor', young wasters, retrenched civil servants or Indian

163

Army officers, and other mostly misguided wretches, they went to settle overseas – one even heard of suicides, because not everybody is tough enough to stand an absolute change of environment, or frightful isolation in some magnificent landscape. And Frant, lured by advertisements, driven by enterprise, encouraged by supposedly responsible persons, went out like them, only fresh from a public school.

His incipient relationship with MacGavin was not made easier by the practical basis on which it rested, for Frant came to him neither as a partner, nor as a servant, nor as a guest, nor had he paid one penny by way of premium. A committee in London had picked out MacGavin's name as that of a person who had declared himself willing to give a young Englishman free board and lodging and two or three years' training in the art of trading with the Lembus in exchange for nothing but that young stranger's 'services'. MacGavin was in some ways a practical man, and the chance of obtaining a responsible white servant who need be paid no wages seemed to him a good one. Frant had been brought up to be eager to oblige. And that was how they started.

Frant was young – so young that, bumping adventurously along into the heart of Lembuland, he could not help thinking of his former school-fellows and of how they would have envied him if they could have seen him at that moment. A fatal eagerness possessed him. He was flying in the face of the world, as the young are apt to do, with the finest of ambitions. For some of us when young it does not seem so important that we should be successful in a worldly sense and at once enjoy money and comfort, so that we should try and become our true selves. We want to blossom out and fulfil our real natures. The process is complex, and is obviously conditioned by our approaches to the work we mean to do or have to do in life, by the way our heredity and upbringing make us react to our environment, and especially by our relations with other people. In the long run this affair of becoming a grown-up person, a real person (for that is what it amounts to) is, for most of us, an affair of the heart. We hear a great deal about sex nowadays; it is possible to overestimate its importance, because there are always people who pay it little attention or who apparently manage, like Sir Isaac Newton, to get along, without giving it a thought. But Frant came of a susceptible family. He arrived in Lembuland with a pretty appetite for life, and little knew what he was letting himself in for.

2

The trading station at Madumbi occupied the top of a slope a little back from the road, or track rather, and consisted of two main buildings, the store and the house, about fifty yards apart, and a number of ramshackle outhouses. In front, there had been some attempt at a garden – not much of an attempt, for cows and chickens always roamed about in it, and it was now and then invaded by monkeys. At the back, there was some rough grazing land and a patch of forest that went with the place. The buildings themselves were made of corrugated iron, painted khaki and lined with deal boards, looking out, curiously hideous, on the land which sloped away from them on all sides with streams, and clumps of trees, and grassy spaces like a well-planned park. But Mr and Mrs MacGavin, in settling at Madumbi, had been little influenced by the scenery.

The store itself was lighted only by two small windows and the open door, and as you came in from the strong sunlight it was at first difficult to get your bearings. The place was so crowded with goods that it looked like a cave crowded with all sorts of plunder. Your head bumping against a suspended trek-chain or storm-lantern, you looked up and saw that the ceiling was almost entirely hidden in festoons of kettles and baskets, hanks of Berlin wool, enormous bouquets of handkerchiefs of all sizes and colours, bunches of tunics and trousers interspersed with camisoles, frying-pans, wreaths of artificial forget-me-nots, hatchets and matchets, necklaces and ploughshares. As for the shelves, they were entirely crammed with different kinds of goods, for the production of which a hundred factories had smoked and roared in four continents. All kinds of shoddy clothing and showy piece-goods, brittle ironmongery and chinaware, the most worthless patent medicines, the gaudiest cheap jewellery, the coarsest groceries, bibles, needles, pipes, celluloid collars, soup tureens, hair-oil, notebooks, biscuits and lace curtains rose in tiers and patterns on every side. Certain shelves were full of refuse left over from the war – grey cotton socks made in Chicago for American recruits who had never enlisted, khaki tunics and breeches, puttees, Balaclava helmets and so forth, all ugly and serviceable, made and carried by machinery to contribute to a scene of universal murder, produced in too great quantities, by contract instead of by necessity or impulse, and at last deposited here, so that a profit might be made out of the pleasure these things, by their novelty, gave to the blacks. The whole world seemed to have conspired to make a profit on this lonely Lembu hilltop.

Two doors at the back of the store itself gave access to two other rooms. One was large, and was used for storing reserves of bulky goods – sacks of salt, sugar and grain; ironware; boxes of sweets and soap; besides a profusion of bunches of Swazi tobacco leaves, at least two feet long, their fragrance preserved by an occasional sprinkling with water. It was the custom to give away a leaf or two of tobacco to each adult shopper, and to the young a handful of the cheapest sweets, their virulent pinks and greens and acid chemical flavours promising a quick decay to strong white teeth. The other and smaller room was used as an office, and contained a table, a chair, a safe, and a great accumulation of MacGavin's papers. The window, which received the afternoon sun, would not open, and was always buzzing with flies and hornets in various stages of fatigue. A flea-bitten dog was usually asleep on a pile of unpaid bills in the corner, while the ink, from standing so much in the sun, was always evaporating, so that when one had occasion to write one had to use a pencil.

But all that was only the background. The space before the counter was often thronged with Lembus of all ages and both sexes. The noise was overpowering. They would all be talking at once, some laughing, some arguing, some gossiping, some bargaining, while all the time a peculiarly strident gramophone was playing records of Caruso and Clara Butt. Sometimes an old black woman, nearly blind and nearly naked, her last peppercorns of hair grizzled to a pepper-and-salt colour, and her dry old dugs so long that she could comfortably tuck the ends of them into her belt, might be seen listening to it, with her head on one side, for the first time, uttering occasional exclamations of incredulity (*'Abantu! Inkosi yami! Maye babo!'*) and slapping her scrawny thighs, as she demanded whether the voice was the voice of a spirit.

In another part of the room the only vacant space on the wall was occupied by a pier-glass, before which a group of very fat girls were fond of comparing their charms, to the accompaniment of shrieks of delight. Their main wish was to observe the reflection of their bottoms, partly out of pure curiosity and partly with a view to interesting the men present. Standing among the older customers there were always some children, patiently awaiting their turn to be served with threepennyworths of this and that. Some brought eggs or wild fruit to trade, which they carried in small bowl-shaped baskets on their heads. One might have a fowl under her arm, and a little boy of seven would perhaps bring an enormous scarlet lily, complete with leaves and root.

To say that all this was strange to Frant would be an understatement. It was a new world. Into this exotic atmosphere he was plunged; this was where he had to work; this was what he had to learn. What is called adaptability is little more than freshness and keenness and readiness to learn, and Frant, who had been brought up to obey, made himself completely and at first willingly subservient to MacGavin's instructions. He didn't like MacGavin, and it was plain that he never would do so, but it was also plain that MacGavin knew his business, and Frant's presence at Madumbi was, in theory, a business matter. So he rose early and retired late, working hours that no trade union would approve at a job that needed endless patience and good humour, with diligence and imagination as well. He struggled with a strange language, did accounts, avoided cheating or being cheated (he had been brought up to be honest) and toiled morning, noon and night, without haste, without rest, never for a moment questioning what he conceived to be his duty. And MacGavin, finding that he had to do with an honest and docile and responsible person, confided to his wife that the plan was succeeding beyond his hopes. Very soon, he felt, he would be able to leave Frant in entire charge of the proceedings, while he himself attended to other money-making operations out of doors. Mrs MacGavin was pleased too, because she found she was less often required to help in the store, and could spend more time in the house. Though God knows the store was the pleasanter building of the two.

On his very first afternoon Frant had been given tea on the veranda of the house, in order to afford Mrs MacGavin an early chance of sizing him up, but after that his tea was always sent over to the store. Apart from that he had meals in the house, and he slept in it, and spent part of his Sunday leisure in it as well. There were only four rooms. Frant's own room, nine feet by seven, was oppressively hot, was never properly cleaned, and had a disagreeable smell. The living-room, not large in itself, was so crammed with furniture that one person could with difficulty turn round in it, whereas three people were supposed to eat and sleep and rest in it, quite in addition to the fact that, the house lacking either hall or passage, it had to serve as both. Thus the pattern on the linoleum was in places quite worn away, and behind the front door was a rack bulging with hats, coats and mackintoshes, which gave off a greenish odour of stale sweat, cheap rubber and mildew. The middle of the room was occupied by a large table covered with a khaki mohair table-cloth with bobbles round the edges, and in the middle of that stood a large oil-lamp with a shade of crinkly pink paper. A sideboard held a load of worthless ornaments, and on the walls faded wedding-groups in bamboo Oxford frames alternated with dusty paper fans, cuckoo clocks and fretwork brackets supporting electro-plated vases containing dusty everlasting flowers in process of perishing from dry-rot. With difficulty it was possible to make one's way to a small bookcase which stood beneath a reproduction of a problem picture, showing a woman in evening dress in the fashion of 1907 kneeling on the floor before a man in a dinner-jacket, the whole suffused in a red glow from a very hot-looking fire in the background, and called 'The Confession'. Among the books were several by Marie Corelli, a brochure on the diseases of cattle, and a girlish album of Mrs MacGavin's, in which her friends had written or attempted to draw personal tributes and pleasantries. Had this album been a little more vulgar, it might have been almost a curiosity, but the commonness of colonial schoolgirls in the second decade of this century has scarcely even a period interest. It must be admitted, however, that one contributor had written the following very appropriate wisecrack:

Roses are red and violets blue,
Pickles are sour and so are you.

'Fond of reading?' MacGavin, in an expansive moment, once asked Frant. 'No time myself.'

'Yes and no,' said Frant, who was trying to make up for his education and had a copy of *The Brothers Karamazov* in his bedroom. 'It depends.'

167

On the table in that front room there was nearly always a fly-haunted still-life consisting of a teapot and some dirty cups, for Mrs MacGavin drank very strong tea seven times daily, a habit which no doubt accounted partly for the state of her complexion. But all day long and most evenings the double doors on to the veranda were open, and there was the view. As the trading station was on the top of a hill and partly surrounded with groves of mimosa trees, the outlook was very fine. Beyond the trees, it could be seen that every depression in the landscape had its rivulet and patch of forest, and that in every sheltered and elevated place there was a kraal of beehive-shaped huts with small fields of grain and roots; cattle were grazing here and there; and in the distance rose range upon range of blue mountains. At first sight it seemed, like so many African landscapes, a happy mixture of the pastoral and the magnificent, but those who lived under its influence came to feel gradually a mingled sense of uneasiness and sorrow, so that what at first seemed grand became indifferent or menacing, what at first seemed peaceful was felt to be brooding, and stillness and quietness seemed to be an accumulation of repressed and troubled forces, like the thunderclouds that often hung over the horizon of an afternoon. Those sunny hills seemed to be possessed by a spirit that nursed a grievance.

3

Frant's approach to the natives was complicated by his character and education, which in some ways helped and in some ways hindered him. As a polite person, he treated them with a good-humoured consideration which they were quite unused to receiving from the whites, but then the whites in Lembuland are an unusually discouraging lot – the way they behave to one another is proof of that. A natural quick sympathy and warmth in his character immediately attracted the natives, who are uncannily quick at character, but at the same time they found a certain reserve in him. It was not that he stood on his dignity with them, but simply that he was a little too conscientious. There were certain vague ideas about the white man's prestige and so on which made him rather careful in his behaviour. He imagined that if he let himself go at all he might in some way damage MacGavin's standing and do harm to the trade, and of course MacGavin, in teaching him the trade, was careful to try and instil various principles about treating the natives firmly. And to MacGavin's credit it may be added that he insisted on the natives being treated as fairly as possible, though this was a matter of business rather than principle with him. And after all, there was no need to tell Frant to be fair – it was clear that though a trifle priggish, he was no swindler. This priggishness of his was easy to account for. It was partly in his nature, but also he had been brought up with certain rigid English ideas about being a gentleman, playing the game, and all that sort of thing, and until now he had had no reason to doubt that they were right. The effect of being abruptly transferred to a completely new environment; of being cut off from those familiar companions and surroundings which had enabled his principles to be taken for granted; and of associating with Mr and Mrs MacGavin, was not to make him doubt those principles but to convince him that they were right. And to be all by oneself and to think oneself right is really rather fatal, especially if one naturally tends to be both straightforward and severe. Already he would receive some of the opinions of MacGavin and his wife in a silence that was even stronger in its effect than the quiet and smiling 'Oh, I'm afraid I can't quite agree with you' which he often had to use in conversation with them.

'He always thinks he's right,' MacGavin remarked to his wife, 'but it doesn't matter about that. What's more important is that the niggers like him. There's a slight improvement in the takings this month, and I shouldn't be surprised if it's partly due to him. He does what he's told for the most part, and I shouldn't be surprised if he turns out a good salesman when he knows the lingo a bit better.'

The Lembu language presents no great difficulties, and it is surprising what good use one can make of a language as soon as one has a small working vocabulary and a few colloquial turns of phrase. Frant enjoyed speaking it, because it is one of those Bantu languages which, to be spoken well, have to be spoken with gusto, and it can be both sonorous and elegant. His progress in the language naturally made his work more easy and pleasant, but it had other effects – it drew him closer into sympathy with the Lembus, and showed him how little they liked the whites. In fact, he began to realise that the remains of the white man's prestige, in Lembuland at least, rested mainly on fear – fear of the white man's money, his mechanical genius and his ruthless and largely joyless energy – and not on love or respect. And since he himself had very little money, no mechanical genius and a certain joyful vitality, he felt that there must be something rather 'un-white' about himself. This discovery acted directly upon his pride – it made him resolve to treat the natives with as much kindness and dignity as were consonant with his odd position (the ruling race behind the counter!), as if to show that there were still white men who knew how to behave humanely. This made him think himself better than MacGavin and the few other whites with whom he came in touch, and shut him up in a small cell of his own (as it were) closely barred with high principles.

He did not pretend to himself that the Lembus were paragons of virtue. The very fact that as customers in a shop they had a certain right to order the shopkeepers about, added to the fact that these shopkeepers were nominally their 'superiors', was a temptation to some of the natives to be tiresome, cheeky or even insolent, and that was one reason why a great deal of persevering good temper was needed in dealing with them. By the time they had convinced themselves that Frant was both patient and cheerful he had already begun to get a good name amongst them. They were used to MacGavin, whom they thought of as a beast, but a just beast, and finding Frant just without being a beast, and youthful and personable as well, they undoubtedly began to come to Madumbi in greater numbers.

At first he had been much struck by the extreme suspiciousness and diffidence of the customers. They never entered the place with that air of cheerful confidence which, in the dreams of good shopkeepers, is found on every customer's face. On the contrary, they always seemed to come in expecting the worst. Many an old, wild woman, skirted in skins, smeared with fat and ochre, hung with charms, a bladder or an antelope's horn suspended at her neck, her hair dressed high and stuck with bone ornaments, a snuff-box at her waist, perhaps having about her too a couple of pounds, every penny of which she meant to spend, would pause in the doorway with a roving eye and an expression of extreme disillusionment and contempt, as though she found herself there unwillingly and by chance. After some time she would perhaps help herself to a cupful of water from a tank that stood at the door, and would then sit down in the shade and take a lot of snuff with immense deliberation, the expression on her face seeming to say, 'Well, here I am, and I don't give a damn for anybody. I haven't lived all these years for nothing. Experience has taught me to expect the worst of every situation and every person, particularly if he or she happens to be white. If I condescend to do any shopping here, I mean to see everything, and to have exactly what I want or nothing at all. Don't think you can swindle me, because you can't. However, I shall proceed on the assumption that you mean to try, that all your goods are damaged, that you're a cunning profiteer, and that you think I'm a fool.' And when at last she deigned to enter the store, she would proceed accordingly.

But it was not only old women who were so much on their guard. Many and many a customer would show the same symptoms of a deep and cynical mistrust, walking in as if they were threading their way among mantraps all carefully set for them. Even children would show plainly how they had been forewarned, repeating innocently the last parental injunctions, and carefully counting their change from sixpence. And all this was not due to MacGavin but to the reputation which the white overlords of Lembuland had managed, in the course of two or three decades, to build up for themselves.

If for Frant this unpleasant relationship between the two races was one of his earliest and most enduring impressions, even stronger was that of the immediate physical presence of the Lembus. So many more or less naked bodies of men and women, coloured a warm brown, smooth-skinned and mostly graceful, with white teeth, straight backs and easy manners, do not leave one, when one is young and susceptible and unfamiliar with them, exactly indifferent.

'Don't worry about the stink,' MacGavin had said. 'You'll get used to it.'

Stink? The whites always say that the blacks have a bad smell. Well, there at

Madumbi was a confined space usually tightly packed with natives, but although the weather was hot and the air sometimes scarcely moving, it could not have been said that the smell was much more than strange, though to Frant it was heady, like the very smell of life itself, and excited him with a promise of joys not yet tasted. The wholesome smell of an out-of-door race cannot in any case seem unpleasant, except to diseased nerves, and the lightly clad or unclad bodies of the Lembus are continually exposed to sun, air and water, while they are almost as vegetarian as their flocks and herds. If some of the old women were a little inclined to accumulate several layers of ochre and fat all over them by way of skin treatment, they were quite amusing enough in their manners and conversation, and had quite enough natural style, to make up for it. At Madumbi there was a far more oppressive smell than that of the natives, and that was the combined aroma of the dressing that stiffened the calicoes of Osaka and Manchester into a dishonest stoutness, and, to speak figuratively, of the sand in the sugar.

4

In places like Madumbi, time seems more of a thief and enemy than in crowded cities or even in circles where the months are frittered away in useless leisure. In that part of Lembuland the changing of the seasons is less marked than in the highlands, and at Madumbi life was a packed routine; work began at half-past five or six in the morning; fatigue often precluded thought; and the tired eyes, turning towards clock or calendar, would close in sleep. Sometimes all sense of chronological sequence was lost; sometimes it seemed almost as if time were going backwards; and now and again Frant would realise with a shock how many weeks or months had slipped by since this or that trifling break in his existence. But he was not discontented, for he was interested in his work, not so much for its own sake as for the close contact with some of the realities of human nature into which it brought him.

There were certain things which he could never sell without a smile. Now and then a young Lembu would come in and say rather furtively, 'Amafuta wemvubu akona na?' That is to say, 'Have you got any hippopotamus fat?' Whereupon Frant used to go to the small showcase in which the medicines were kept, and produce a small bottle with a label bearing a Lembu inscription, and underneath, in very small letters, PEDERSEN'S GENUINE HIPPO FAT. This commodity looked like ordinary lard, probably was ordinary lard, was put up by a Norwegian chemist in Dunnsport, and sold for a shilling a bottle. It was used for a love philtre, and helped the manufacturer to maintain his son at a theological seminary in Oslo. But other 'lines' were more lucrative than hippo fat. Love philtres, after all, were usually only required by the young and romantically inclined, whereas PEDERSEN'S BLUE WONDERS, as another Lembu inscription testified, were indispensable to both young and old.

Certainly they were always in demand. Pills as large as peas and the colour of gun-metal, they were not merely an infallible, but a powerful aphrodisiac. When MacGavin happened to be asked for either of these medicines, he would never sell them without a clumsy pleasantry, a habit which had resulted in a falling-off of the sales of the hippo fat, for the younger natives, though their morals, according to some standards, were not above reproach, had their finer feelings. However, his misplaced humour did not much affect the demand for Blue Wonders, which were usually bought by customers of a coarser fibre. Mrs MacGavin herself came to lend a hand in the store when business was brisk, and it would sometimes happen that she would be called upon to serve a customer with these things, which she would do with the grimmest face in the world — her expression might well have suggested a subject for an allegorical picture, 'Avarice overcoming Chastity'. But still, out of all the hotchpotch that the store contained, there was one kind of goods which she would neither buy nor sell. The male natives of those parts were in the habit of using a peculiar kind of *cache-sexe* made of the leaves of the wild banana. At Madumbi these were made, in assorted sizes, by an old vagabond of a native who sold them to MacGavin at wholesale prices. When he came to the store it was always at some odd time, when there was nobody else about, either on a very hot afternoon or just after the store had been locked up, or at dawn, or when the moon was rising. If he saw MacGavin, the business was soon settled. If he encountered Mrs MacGavin, he would wave his bundle of unmentionables right under her nose, saluting her with his free hand and uttering all sorts of highflown and wholly ironical compliments before crying the virtues of his wares. Nothing annoyed her more, as he very well knew. She always told him rudely to wait for her husband. If it was Frant he chanced to find, he would say with real politeness, '*Sa' ubona, umtwana ka Kwini Victoli!*' Greetings, child of Queen Victoria! This became shortened later to 'Child of the Queen' and at last simply to 'Child'. The very first time he had seen Frant he had said, 'Ah, I can see you're a real Englishman from *over there*,' and since England suggested Queen Victoria to him more than anything else it was not hard to account for the complimentary title. The old man, to whom Frant always gave an extra-large leaf or two of tobacco, was also fond of saying that the *amaBhunu*, the Boers, were 'no good', which was partly his real opinion and meant partly as a piece of indirect flattery, though as Frant had not had anything to do with any Dutch people it was not particularly effectual.

'How can you allow that dirty old swine to call you "child!"' exclaimed MacGavin.

'Why, he's old enough to be my grandfather!' Frant retorted.

Frant's point of view seemed so fantastic to MacGavin that he laughed a short, harsh laugh.

'My advice is, don't stand any cheek from any nigger,' he said.

'He isn't cheeky to *me*,' said Frant. 'Only friendly.'

And with an irritable grunt from MacGavin the conversation was closed. It seemed extraordinary how full of prejudice the trader was. He was fond of generalisations about the natives which were not even remotely true, such as that they were incapable of gratitude (as if they had such a lot to be grateful for!) and he seemed to have a fixed idea that every black is determined to try and score off every white, under any conditions whatsoever. And when, as occasionally happened, a native addressed him politely in English, it made him so furious that he was no longer master of himself – it seemed to him a suggested assumption of equality between the races!

The MacGavins were amazed at Frant's continued progress, and if they welcomed his popularity with the natives as being good for trade, they resented a little that a stranger and a rooinek should be able to beat them at their own game. As to what went on in his mind, they knew and cared nothing. They neither knew nor cared that neither work nor fatigue could prevent him from feeling at times an overwhelming loneliness and an intolerable hunger for experiences which his youth, the climate and the glorious suggestiveness of his surroundings did everything to sharpen, while its satisfaction was firmly forbidden by circumstances – or so it seemed to Frant. Already esteemed by the natives, he valued their good opinion of him too much to take chances with it, and in the background of his thoughts, in spite of the MacGavins, or perhaps because of them, there still presided that tyrannical spectre, the 'white man's prestige'. What it is to be an ex-prefect of an English public school!

5

It was bound to happen that sooner or later his attention would become centred in some individual out of the hundreds he had to do with in the course of a week. One drowsy afternoon, when he was alone behind the counter and there was nobody in the store but a couple of gossips and a child, a young woman came in rather shyly and stood near the door, hesitating to speak. He couldn't see her very well because of the bright sunshine behind her, but he asked her what she wanted and she made a small purchase.

'Do you remember me?' she asked suddenly in a very quiet voice, looking at him gravely while she spoke.

He was surprised. He didn't remember ever having seen her before, but not wishing to offend her, he said in a slightly ironical tone of voice:

'Oh, when I've once seen people, *just once*, I never forget them.'

'Well!' she exclaimed, and uttered a little peal of laughter, partly because she was surprised at his ready answer and amused at his white man's accent; partly because, as a Lembu, she could appreciate irony; and partly because it made her happy that he should talk to her. But as soon as she had uttered that little laugh she grew shamefaced and cast down her eyes with the incomparable grace of a young woman with whom modesty is natural, and not a mere device of coquetry. There was more sadness than usual in her expression, because she had at once understood that he did not remember her, and no woman likes to be forgotten by any young man. She had moved now, and the diffused radiance reflected from the sunburnt hilltop outside shone full upon her through the open door. Her hair was dressed in a cylinder on the crown of her head, stained with red ochre, and stuck with a long bone pin at the broad end of which was a minute incised design; she wore no ornament but a flat necklace of very small blue beads and a few thin bangles and anklets of silver and copper wire. She was dressed in a single piece of dark red stuff which was supported by her pointed young breasts and fastened under the arms – it fell in straight, classical folds almost to her feet, and at the sides it did not quite join but revealed a little her soft flanks. From bearing weights on her head from early childhood she carried herself very erect; she was slender, and an awareness of her graceful nubility gave every movement the value of nature perfectly controlled by art. The fineness of her appearance may have been due to some remote Arab strain in her blood, for though unmistakably negroid, her features were in no sense exaggerated. Her nose, for example, though the nostrils were broad, was very slightly aquiline; her skin was unusually light in tone; and the modelling of her cheeks and temples could only be described as delicate. Her mouth was good-humoured, her eyes were lustrous, and though one side of her face was marked with a long scar, this only drew closer attention to its beauty.

'You don't come here very often, do you?' said Frant, leaning on the counter, partly because he did not want their conversation to be overheard by anybody else, and partly because he felt somehow weak in the legs. He was in the grip of an unaccustomed shyness, he felt unsure of himself, and so excited that his heart was beating very quickly.

'No,' she said, avoiding his eyes. 'I don't live very near.'

'Where do you live?'

'Down there – down in the valley,' she said, extending an exquisite arm and looking out through the open doorway with a vague and dreamy air. He noticed the light colour of the insides of her hands. 'Near the river,' she said.

'That's not very far away,' he said.

'You've been there, then?' she said. 'You know the place?'

'No, but I don't think it's very far.'

'The hill is long and steep,' she said

Frant suddenly remembered two lines of verse –

Does the road wind uphill all the way?
Yes, to the very end.

174

'I don't know your name,' he said.

She looked at him quickly and uttered an exclamation of surprise. 'What's the matter?' he said.

'Why do you want to know my name?' she asked anxiously, for the use of names is important in witchcraft.

'I'm just asking. I just want to know it.'

'My name is Seraphina,' she said, with a mixture of modesty and seductiveness.

'What?'

'Seraphina.'

'How on earth did you get a name like that? It's not a Lembu name! You're not a Christian, are you?'

She laughed, as though the idea of her being a Christian was absolutely ridiculous — which indeed it was.

'No!' she said. 'A missionary gave it to me when I was a child. He made magic water on my head and said that Christ wanted me to be called Seraphina.'

This time Frant laughed.

'Christ chose well,' he said. 'But none of your family are Christians, are they?'

'No, it just happened like that.'

He laughed again.

'You don't know my name,' he said.

'Yes, I do,' she said, and pronounced it 'Front', and they both laughed. Just then some noisy customers arrived, and he had to leave her. Suddenly bold, he said:

'Goodbye, go in peace. Please come again. I like talking with you.'

He couldn't possibly have dared to speak so directly of his feelings in English, but somehow in Lembu it was easier. Besides, he was stirred as he had never been stirred before.

'Goodbye', she said, smiling. 'Stay in peace.'

She turned to go, and looked like some virgin in an archaic frieze saying farewell to the world. As for Frant, his hands were trembling, and there was a wild gladness in his heart.

6

His tortures now began in earnest. His dreams and waking thoughts were haunted by the image of the black girl, tantalising and yet infinitely remote. As his desire for her increased, so did its fulfilment seem to recede. He knew little or nothing of her; he knew little enough of her language and nothing at all of her situation in life. He had been so busy learning to make a profit out of the natives that he had had little chance of learning much about their customs, the way they lived and thought. Supposing, he said to himself, for the sake of argument, this girl were to become my mistress? First of all, is it possible? I am certain that to some extent she reciprocates my feelings, but to what extent? What would she expect of me? What would her family think of her? How would the affair be possible in any case? How am I to communicate with her? And then the MacGavins – presumably his success in his trading depends to some extent on the fact that he is not one of these white men who get mixed up with the natives; and if I were to become the lover of Seraphina, should I not damage his livelihood, besides ruining my own? Whatever happened, everybody would know about it, of course. And how could we live together? Are we to meet furtively in the forest? And have I the right to take this black girl? How can I pretend to myself that I love her? Is it not simply that I want to sleep with her, to touch, kiss, embrace and caress her? He found no answers to his questions, but the very fact that he could ask them was significant. His loneliness and his difficulties had taught him one of the very things that his education had been evolved to prevent – the habit of introspection. He was being Hamletised by circumstances.

Of the numerous forms of anguish which Providence has designed for her creatures few can be more intense than the state of mind and body of a man who is young, sensual by nature and sexually repressed; and who, instead of yielding to the voluptuous provocations of his surroundings, tries to exorcise them with the public-school spirit. When he might well have acted with bold-ness, he found himself filled with doubts, scruples and equivocations, in addi-tion to the ordinary fears of a lover. And he had nobody to turn to, there was nobody who would say to him what so much needed to be said, 'Well, go ahead and have the woman. You will have your pleasure and she will have hers, and you will both be a bit the wiser and possibly the happier for the experi-ence. You will treat her with consideration, because it is your nature to be con-siderate. You are in no danger of "going native", because you aren't the sort of person who goes native. And as for worrying about the MacGavins, do you imagine they worry at all about you, or are likely to do so as long as you rake in the bawbees for them? Be a man! *Carpe diem*, etc.' Lacking such an adviser, Frant continued to torment himself.

Each day he got up with Seraphina in his thoughts. Day followed day, and Seraphina did not appear. Round the trading station, meanwhile, Africa unrolled her splendours and her cruelties. The seasons did not assert themselves overmuch. One waited for the rains to stop, or one suddenly noticed buds among thorns. One was aware, all too aware, of the spring, the season of trou-ble, when more people die, in all countries, than at any other time of the year. The sap was troubled, and the heart with it. All the mimosa trees at Madumbi broke into pollenous clouds of blossom, creaming in a light wind against the cobalt morning sky. Glossy toucans with scarlet bills nested in them, swooping among the boughs, and uttering the most touching mating-cries. Fireflies went through their luminous rites under a coral-tree; crested hoopoes, the colour of cinnamon, pursued their fitful flight across the clear green of dawn; on long, sultry afternoons a group of turkey-bustards, as grave as senators, would plod grumbling across some grassy plateau, looking carefully for the snakes which they could kill at a blow; raindrops pattered down on leaves as large as tables, magenta-veined; and on dry, tranquil afternoons, when the days were still short and some solitary voice was singing far away, an aromatic smell of burning sweet-grass sometimes drifted through the air, the clear light, and the music, and the odour all playing together on the nerves, and inducing an emotion inexpressibly painful and delicious.

When he was free, Frant could not bear to stay near the house: but in roaming about, which became his habit, he was none the less a prisoner. Fettered by scruples and afflicted with a kind of moral impotence, he wandered in a lovely world from which he was barred almost as effectually as if he were literally in a steel cage on wheels. His troubled eyes turned to the natural scenes around him but found no rest in them, and his repression might just have gone on increasing in morbidity had not a number of unexpected things happened.

Now the arrival of Frant at Madumbi had put a check on certain of MacGavin's habits. At one time, when the Scotchman was alone in the store, in the afternoons for instance, when the weather was hot or wet and business slack, or when his wife was busy in the house, he had not been disinclined for a little amusement at the expense of some of the coarser Lembu girls who came to deal with him. Joking with them in order to try and convert their apprehensive titters into abandoned fits of giggling, he had sometimes gone so far as to pinch their breasts and slap their behinds in order to win their confidence. The bolder ones had quickly taken advantage of his susceptibilities in order to try and get something for nothing, and pointing to this or that, had copied the horse-leech's daughters and cried, 'Give, give!' When MacGavin so far overcame his sense of commercial fitness as to give them a string of beads or a damaged Jew's harp, they immediately asked for more, determined to lose nothing for the want of asking. He would then refuse, but they would not go away, leaning on the counter and repeating their requests over and over again in a whining voice until he began to fear that his wife might come in. Whereupon he would suddenly fly into a raging temper. Purple in the face and trembling with anger, he would hammer on the counter with his fists and utter violent threats and abuse, and if that did not frighten the young women away he would hustle them out. One or two in particular loved to provoke him to the utmost, and then fly screaming with laughter down the road, their large naked breasts wobbling and flapping and tears running out of their eyes. But he had grown tired of these scenes, and even before Frant's arrival had abstained from inducing them. With the arrival of Frant he determined to behave himself, at least in Frant's presence, as he wanted the young man to concentrate on business and not begin his stay by getting obsessed with black women. But now that he had found Frant what he could have called 'steady', he was about to revert to his old habits, and it cannot be said that his wife, that freckled virago, with her ever-increasing indigestion and her less and less amiable moods, acted exactly as a strong deterrent.

But the first time Frant saw MacGavin behaving familiarly with a gross fat girl it gave him a shock — not because he was prudish by nature, but because it was something he was not used to, and the discovery that MacGavin did not always practise what he preached seemed likely to modify his own behaviour. The thought immediately occurred to him that MacGavin might abuse the modesty of Seraphina, and the idea that the trader's bloodshot and slightly protuberant eye might focus itself upon her natural elegance produced in him a most violent reaction. He said nothing. After MacGavin's wench had departed he came up to Frant and said:

'You'll excuse my saying so, Frant, but don't you feel you want a woman sometimes?'

The effect of this remark upon the young man was extraordinary.

'I do,' he answered at once in a quiet voice, 'but not a black one.'

And he launched into a flood of abuse! He said that he would rather do anything than touch a black woman; he said that they were dirty, that they stank, that they were not better than animals; he said that the blacks and whites were in his opinion races apart, and that on no account should they mix in any way; he said that white men ought to be respected by black ones, and that that could only be possible if they treated them as inferiors, absolute inferiors. He grew white with passion and the heat of his denunciation. His words almost choked him.

MacGavin was astonished beyond measure. He did not know whether to take it all as an attack on himself, or whether Frant had not gone a little out of his mind.

'Well, you do surprise me,' he said, in what was meant to be a sarcastic tone of voice. 'You've always given me the impression of being a bit too fond of the niggers, and treating them a bit too much as if they were really human beings.'

'I get a bit sick of the sight of them at times,' said Frant in a much quieter voice, not in the least meaning and indeed hardly knowing what he said. Then he turned away, and the incident was closed, except that MacGavin confided to his wife that he thought Frant was getting a bit restless, and perhaps needed a change or a holiday.

'He can surely wait till Christmas,' she said in an aggrieved whisper, for the walls of the house were thin. 'We could take him away with us then for a couple of days. But if you ask me, he's unsociable and disagreeable by nature.'

178

'Don't forget that the takings showed another increase last month,' said MacGavin.

'That's just why I don't want him to go away now,' she said.

It was a brilliant moonlight night, as quiet as the grave, and in his little room Frant was asking himself what on earth could have made him say a whole lot of things he did not mean, what on earth had made him lose control of himself. He felt he had come to the end of everything, that he could not bear this impossible kind of life any longer, and would have to go away. His head was hot, he could not sleep, and he rolled uneasily on his bed. Suddenly, somewhere in a tree, a galago began to scream. Its screams filled the naked air and the heavy silence, the African silence; scream after scream, like prophecies of endless and unthinkable supernatural horrors, uttered by a furred and furtive little creature, hidden large-eyed among moon-drenched branches. Frant got up from his bed and drew back the curtains on a world chalk-white like the face of a clown or pierrot, silent and heartless, and with a sense of terror, of madness almost, let them fall back again.

And the next day Seraphina appeared.

7

There she stood, balancing on her head a light bundle tied with grass. Her arms hung by her side, and when she turned her head authority and resignation, patience and sensibility were in the movement.

Nowhere but here did ever meet
Sweetness so sad, sadness so sweet.

Before the coming of the white man the Lembus lived under a system of strict discipline and formality, which did not, however, fail to allow various channels for the various passions of the Lembu heart. It was a system which recognised that some of life's best rewards are best appreciated by those who have not been able to win them too easily. In those days they were all warriors under a mad military autocrat, who believed that too easy an access to heterosexual pleasures might impair the morale and efficiency of his regiments; he trammelled them with a hundred taboos and would not allow them to marry young, while adultery was punished by pushing the guilty parties over separate cliffs of no small height. As for the girls and women, they had a most clearly prescribed course of life, and each stage in their development was made to conform to strict rules. The later relaxation of tribal ethics, for which the white man offered little substitute but calico drawers and hymns A and M, rapidly weakened the fibre of the race. But it still happened that there were members of it who managed to live lives not wholly devoid of order and dignity, there were still families 'of the old school' who from the force of heredity or a kind of good breeding managed to do homage to the ghosts of the beliefs of their forefathers. And such a family was Seraphina's. Both its ancient pride and its present obscurity had gone to the making of her features, and its vigour and vitality as well.

They were alone together in the space before the counter.

'Greeting, Seraphina.'

'Greeting, my white-man.'

Frant could hardly speak, he was so agitated. His heart seemed to fill the whole of his breast with its leaping, and he could scarcely recognise the sound of his own voice as he asked:

'Why have you been so long returning?'

'Do I know?' she said. 'Perhaps I was afraid.'

She had reason to be afraid – of gossip, of her family, of herself, of Frant, of consequences. With an unhurried movement she took down the bundle from her head and laid it on the floor without bending her knees. Then she untied the grass ropes that held it together and began to open it.

'A snakeskin!' said Frant.

It was a broad snakeskin, and crackled stiffly as it was unrolled. She put her foot on the tail to hold it down while Frant unrolled it. Fully opened, it was at least fifteen feet long, and a great part of it was quite two feet in width. It was the skin of a python, and there were two large rents in the middle of the back as if a spear had killed it. It was not often that the natives traded such things.

'How much are you asking for it?' said Frant in a caressing voice most unsuitable for a commercial transaction.

'I am not selling it,' said Seraphina without looking at him. 'I am giving it.'

'Giving it! To me?'

'To you.'

'I thank you very much indeed,' he said. In Lembu the same word means to thank and to praise.

There was a pause, then he said:

'Where did it come from? Who killed it?'

'I was hoeing in a maize-field near the river, and it disturbed me. Besides, two of the children were with me. So I killed it.'

'You killed it! What with?'

'With my hoe.'

When he had got over his astonishment he said, his face shining with admiration:

'But you mustn't give it to me. I must give you some money for it.'

'I don't want money,' she said, and looked at him with troubled, almost angry eyes.

'I thank you very much,' he said again, with the humility and the pride of

180

a lover, and hardly knowing what he was doing he caught hold of her and kissed her on the mouth.

She uttered a cry of surprise and sprang away from him. She simply did not understand him, and was afraid. Natives do not make love as we do. She laughed, just a trifle hysterically.

'What are you doing?' she said.

'What's the matter?' said Frant, approaching again. 'I won't hurt you.'

'How do I know?' she said.

And he would have answered 'Because I love you' (which would have been so hard to say in English and was so easy in Lembu) had they not just at that moment been interrupted.

'Come again soon,' Frant said hurriedly. 'I want to see you.'

And he stooped down and rolled up his snakeskin. When he had finished she was gone.

In the evening he nailed up the skin on the walls of his bedroom. It was so long that it took up the whole of two sides. And very late, before putting out the light, he lay in bed looking at it. Like a banner it hung there to celebrate the intensity of his happiness; it hung like a trophy – the skin of the dragon of his misery, killed by Seraphina as she hoed her father's field of maize.

The next day at noon Mrs MacGavin said:

'Oh, Mr Frant, that skin in your room – it gave me such a nasty turn when I went in there this morning!'

'Isn't it a beauty? You don't mind my putting it up, I suppose?'

'Oh, I don't mind,' she said, 'though I couldn't bear to have such a thing over my bed. If there's one thing I can't stand it's snakes, alive or dead.'

It was nearly Christmas time and the MacGavins told Frant they thought a holiday would do him good, and that they would take him with them to the nearest town. The trading station would be closed for three days, and would be quite safe in the care of the servants. They were extremely surprised when he refused – not because he wanted to help to guard their property, but because the nearest town, of which he had had a few glimpses, did not attract him, and because he had other plans in mind. He felt no inclination to attend the gymkhana or the dance at which, in an atmosphere of false bonhomie and commonplace revelry, the white inhabitants tried annually to forget for a time all about the white man's burden. The MacGavins thought him almost mad for refusing.

'Whatever will you do with yourself?' they said.

'I shall be quite happy,' he said.

They felt that something was amiss.

'What, are you "going native" or something?' cried MacGavin. 'You need a change, you know.'

He always did his work well, and on account of his natural air of independence they both respected and feared him a little. They gave up trying to argue with him and murmured to each other instead. Then on Christmas Eve the Ford car, newly washed, went rattling away, leaving behind it a cloud of blue smoke and a stink, both of which soon vanished. After the MacGavins had gone Frant felt greatly relieved. It was such a blessing to be free to see and hear what was going on round him instead of being haunted by those harsh stupid voices, that sour red face and that pasty drab one, which had already got on his nerves. Unlike most white men alone in native territories, he had neither a gun nor alcohol in his possession. He did not feel the want of them. For the first time in his life he was to spend Christmas by himself. There would be no exchange of presents; no heavy meals; no forced gaiety; no stuck-up relations. His time, for once, was his own.

8

On Christmas morning he stood on the veranda and stretched his arms, filled with a delicious sense of anticipation. Then he felt in his pocket for a cigarette, and failing to find one took a key and went to fetch a packet from the store. The atmosphere in that building, so closely shuttered at holiday times, was more than oppressive. It was a brilliant morning, and the heat of the sun on the corrugated-iron roof made the interior like an oven. He found some cigarettes, and paused a moment in the doorway to look round at the place where his days were spent. He shuddered slightly, then went out, locking the door behind him. Enjoying his cigarette, and the sun, and the shade, and the peacefulness of not having to look at *those* faces, of not having to listen to *those* voices, he took a path which led through a deserted garden, on the site of the first settlement at Madumbi, towards the forest. In the old garden the foundations of the earlier house remained, but the whole place was now a tangle of vegetation. The hardier growths had survived, and some still withstood the wildings that struggled to oust them. Thickets of ragged junipers and berberis made a forbidding fence which few ever sought to penetrate, and indeed the natives thought the place haunted. Snake apples, those cruel trees, with every bud a barb, and every fruit an ugly bulb filled with dry and poisonous powder, extended their angry foliage over crumbling brickwork. Rankly growing mimosas split with their coarse-grained roots what had once been a path, and month by month in the summer raised their smooth bark and feathery foliage perceptibly higher into the air. A solitary yucca, survivor of several, had produced a single spire thickly hung with white bells, which the mountain wind shook together as if they were made of paper. Tendrils of Christ-thorn put out here and there a few sticky scarlet flowers, and passion flowers hung in unexpected places, in the grass or high up among the junipers, together with the oval, dented granadillas into which they too would change.

182

Leaving the garden, Frant followed the path to the forest. Then, forcing his way through the undergrowth, parting lianas and monkey-ropes, breaking cobwebs so thick that their breaking was audible, being scratched by thorns, sinking up to the ankles in leaf-mould, he reached a glade he had been to before in times of unhappiness. In the middle of the glade there was a shallow stream of very clear water gliding over sand, and it was sheltered by the vast indigenous trees from the heat of the day.

Here, as he had done before, he threw himself on the breast of earth, surrendering himself to the trees, the water and the quietness. He lay on his back and looked up through half-closed eyes at the topmost branches, watching the fall of a leaf, hearing the call of a bird, the lapse of water, and the thin cries of insects. Under his hand lay a skeleton leaf, over his head a few epiphytic orchids lolled their greenish mouths open over the ancient, rotting bough that gave them life, and at times the wind brought a hint of the perfume of a hidden syringa or laurustinus. A clump of clivia lilies were blooming in a deep shadow — they were living and dying in secret, without argument, and untroubled by eyes and voices. A humming-bird appeared from nowhere, and poising itself on the wing before every open flower, whirred there like a moth, gleamed like a jewel, darting its thin curved beak, as sharp as a needle, into each for honey. Nature is inevitable — this stone lies on that one, because it must; fronds uncurl from the hairy trunk of a tree-fern; each new growth and decay seems spontaneous and impersonal; there is a kind of harmony of conflict, and it may have been some sense of that harmony that brought Frant to a decision he might, had he not been so solitary, have taken long before. He was roused. He would act boldly. He would give up caution, discretion, doubt, hesitation, he would forget all about the MacGavins, the trade, the future, he would break through the bars of his prison. He would go that very day down into the valley and visit the home of Seraphina. He would behave with candour, he would be open in his dealings. He had proved in commerce that he was 'a white man'; he would now be bold, and prove it in love.

Such was his resolution, but the enterprise was not entirely successful. He set out early in the afternoon, carrying a camera, and a stick in case he should meet snakes. He walked as fast as if he were in a more temperate climate, and felt the heat. The first part of the journey took him across an undulating plateau, through country much like that immediately round Madumbi. But after about an hour he came to the top of a hill which marked the end of an escarpment ('The hill is long and steep,' Seraphina had said) and he began to follow a downward path winding among rocks and thorn trees. This brought him out on to a platform or small tableland and before him lay suddenly open an immense view. Directly below lay the valley of the Umgazi river, where Seraphina lived, and he sat down under a bean tree to rest and to gaze at the scene.

Somebody was coming up the hill. It was a young man. He was a typical Lembu, naked except for a fur codpiece and some bead ornaments, upright, slender and vigorous. He came striding along, singing joyfully as he went, glistening with oil and sweat, his movements full of natural pride. He was holding a tiny shield, a stick and a knobkerrie in one hand, and in the other a large black cotton Brummagem umbrella, to shelter himself from the sun. When he saw Frant he looked surprised and then saluted him with a large and cheerful gesture. Frant knew him by sight and responded cordially.

'What are you doing here?' said the young man. 'Are you out on holiday?'

'Yes,' said Frant. 'I am just out on holiday.'

'Why aren't you riding?'

'I have no horse.'

'But white men don't walk!'

'I like walking.'

The native expressed surprise.

'Is that a camera?' he said.

'Yes, it's a camera.'

'Will you take my picture?'

'All right. Go and stand over there. But you must close your umbrella.'

'What, must I close my umbrella?'

So Frant stood under the bean tree with his feet among the open pods and little black-and-scarlet beans that had fallen from it, and took a photograph of the native, who stood smiling and glistening in the sun.

'Do you know me?' said the young man.

'Yes,' said Frant.

'Do you know Seraphina?'

Frant was startled.

'Yes,' he said, unable to conceal his surprise.

'She is my sister.'

'What! You're her brother?'

'Yes.'

'Fancy that!'

'Seraphina likes you,' said her brother. But, thought Frant, is he really her brother? The natives used such terms somewhat loosely. Was this perhaps a rival trying to warn him off? He put the thought out of his mind, for the native was so friendly. 'Seraphina likes you,' he said. But in Lembu the same word means to like and to love, so perhaps he meant 'Seraphina loves you'.

'I like Seraphina,' said Frant.

'It is not good', said the native, 'when a white man likes a black girl.'

There was no condemnation in his tone, no threat, no high moral purpose. He smiled as he spoke what he no doubt regarded as a self-obvious truism.

'Why?' said Frant.

'Do I know? It is so.'

Frant wanted to say 'Would you be angry if your sister married a white man?' But he had no wish to suggest any such thing. And it seemed too crude to say 'Would you be angry if your sister slept with a white man?' So he said:

'We are all people.'

'Yes, we are all people, but we are different.'

'I like natives,' said Frant.

'I know you do. But you live in Lembuland, and there are no white people near here for you to like.'

This was really unanswerable.

'There are Mr MacGavin and his wife,' said Frant.

Seraphina's brother (if he was Seraphina's brother) laughed. 'Nobody likes them!' he said.

'What is your name?' said Frant.

'Me? Umlilwana.'

'And where do you live?'

'Down there,' said Umlilwana, pointing to the valley.

The river Umgazi, which seemed to consist mostly of a broad bed of stones, with only a small stream of water in the middle, curved in a gigantic S-shaped bend just below where they stood. And on some slightly raised ground in one of the curves of the S were a group of grass domes, which were huts, and a cattle kraal made of thorn trees and brushwood, and a few patches of maize and millet and sweet potatoes. And that was the home of Seraphina. It looked the most peaceful place in the world.

'Will you take me there?' said Frant.

'Take you there! What would you do there?'

'I want to see your home. I want to see Seraphina.'

'Seraphina is not there.'

'Not there! Where is she?'

'She has gone on a journey to the mountains for several days with our mother and father to see our cousins. There's nobody down there but an old woman and some children.'

'Oh,' said Frant, and was silent a moment. 'I am sorry,' he said then. 'I wanted to see Seraphina.'

And suddenly everything seemed utterly remote. The view was like a view in a dream. Seraphina (*could* that be her name?) seemed only an idea and her cousins like characters in a myth. And even the friendly smiling Umlilwana seemed utterly strange and unapproachable.

'Yes, I am sorry,' Frant repeated in a dull voice. 'But I should like some day to visit your home and take photographs of Seraphina – and of all your family.'

Umlilwana was a little suspicious of this, but he said Frant would be welcome.

'Will you do something for me?' said Frant. 'Will you come and tell me when Seraphina returns? Tell Seraphina I want to see her. Tell her I want to see her again.'

'All right,' said Umlilwana in English and with great affability. It was about all the English he knew.

'Umlilwana, you are my friend.'

'All right, will you give me some cigarettes?'

Frant smiled, and gave him all he had. Umlilwana was loud in thanks.

Some children could be seen playing near Seraphina's kraal. They looked as small as ants. The distant mountains looked infinitely blue and remote, with the shadows of a few light clouds patterning their peaks. There was nothing to do but to return to Madumbi.

9

Frant returned to Madumbi. So, a couple of days later, did the MacGavins, both with a touch of righteous indignation at Frant's oddness in not having gone with them, and Mrs MacGavin with more than a touch of dyspepsia. Life then resumed its usual course. But things were not quite the same. First of all, Frant was in a far more cheerful frame of mind. Not only had he begun to act with some initiative, not only had he seen Seraphina's home and made friends with her brother, but he had told somebody of his love for her. As soon as she returned he meant to bring matters to a head, even though he and she were 'different'. And if her continued absence was a great trial to his patience, he got up every morning in hopes of a visit and news from Umlilwana in the course of the day. But day followed day, and Umlilwana did not appear. Frant played with the idea of sending him a message, but as it would have to be a verbal one, he thought it more prudent not to do so. And when he once ventured to inquire about Umlilwana, and to ask if he were really Seraphina's brother, the people he spoke to said they had never heard of either of them. And at night he lay naked and sweating on his bed, tortured continually with the image of Seraphina, remembering her gestures, her 'sadness so sweet', and the touch of her flesh.

'Frant should have gone away with us,' MacGavin remarked to his wife. 'He's quite liverish now at times.'

'This weather's enough to make anybody liverish,' said she. 'I always did say that January was the worst month of the year. It's bilious weather. But it's not his liver, if you ask me, it's his nerves.'

January was certainly a bad month at Madumbi, and that year it was more trying than ever. There had been no rain for weeks, and things were beginning to look parched. The heat was dry and intense. And then, day after day, clouds would collect in the morning and accumulate in the afternoon, thunder was occasionally heard and once even a few drops of rain fell in the dust, as if a few devils had spat from a great height. Every morning seemed to promise a thunderstorm, and one began to imagine how the earth would smell after rain, and how cool the air would be, and how the flying ants would come out in the twilight, but every evening the clouds dispersed and left a hot moon to glare down on the veld, or the glittering arrogance of the stars. And every morning Frant said to himself, 'Umlilwana will come, or Seraphina herself,' but every evening he found himself alone again, exhausted and restless. Even the natives, in their anxiety about their crops, were beginning to get on one another's nerves. The air seemed charged with electricity, it seemed to brace one's very muscles against a shock which was not forthcoming, and to leave them at once taut and tired. Even MacGavin took to glancing often at the sky, at the great cumulus clouds that hung in it all the afternoon, and he would say, 'It'll be serious if something doesn't happen soon.'

It was like waiting for an earthquake, a revolution, the day of judgement almost. There was an awful mixture of certainty that something was going to happen, and of uncertainty as to when it would happen. 'We only want a storm to clear the air,' Mrs MacGavin repeated every day until Frant almost felt that he could murder her. The sweat ran down inside his shirt, his overheated blood inflamed his overstrained imagination, he found it more and more difficult to sleep and eat. Trade grew slack, because few could endure to climb up the slopes to Madumbi, and when the store was empty it was far less tolerable than when it was full. The morning sun beat down on the corrugated iron and the interior grew so hot that it failed to cool down during the night. Strange stories came in – that some grass had caught fire simply from the heat of the sun shining through an empty bottle, and several huts had been burnt in consequence; that a young crocodile had come right up one of the little tributaries of the Umgazi and had been found less than a mile from Madumbi itself, an occurrence never before known; and that a native woman had been arrested for killing a newborn baby with six fingers on one hand, in the belief that this deformity was keeping the rain away. Where was Umlilwana? Where was Seraphina? 'I will wait till next Sunday,' said Frant to himself, 'and if neither of them has come by then I shall go down to the kraal itself on the pretext of wanting to take photographs.' But he did not have to wait till Sunday, for the weather broke.

The worst day of all was the fourteenth of the month.

'Well, this is the worst we've had yet,' said Mrs MacGavin at supper time.

'You've said that for the last four days,' observed her husband.

All the doors and windows were wide open. The sky was completely overcast and nothing was stirring but the moths and other insects which flew in from the garden and bumped against the paper lampshade, or against the glass which covered 'The Confession', or fell into the soup, the powder from their wings mingling with the film of grease which already covered that liquid. The rays of lamplight lay on the creepers of the veranda itself and on the path, but beyond them was utter silence and hot, heavy darkness.

'Hark! Was that thunder?' said Mrs MacGavin.

'You always say that at supper time,' remarked her husband.

'It *was* thunder,' she said, her head on one side, as she pushed a stray wisp of hair out of her eye.

Yes, it *was* thunder. They all heard it. Low, continuous thunder.

'That's up in the mountains,' said MacGavin. 'It's a bad sign if it begins up there. If there is a storm, it'll probably miss us altogether ... Ah, did you see the lightning? Yes, that's where it is. I bet it's pouring up there already. And I don't like a dry storm. It's much more dangerous. More likely to strike the trees.'

Frant's heart was beating loud and fast as if in anticipation of some personal, not a meteorological event. He walked alone to the bottom of the garden, and stood there watching the play of lightning in the distance, but it did not seem much more than on previous nights. He came in and tried to read a paper, lighted several cigarettes in succession, throwing one or two away half-smoked, paced up and down in the garden, glancing up at the darkness, and then retired to his room where he lay on his bed without undressing. His hands were clenched, the nails dug into the palms, and he was conscious of little but the beating of his heart. He couldn't hear the MacGavins talking anywhere, or any natives, and had lost all sense of the time. He put out his light, and like a convict without a crime, in a prison that was not locked, for a sentence of indeterminate duration, he just lay there sweating.

At last he got up and went to the window. The moon was out again. It was almost full, and stood high in the sky, flooding the landscape with light. To the south, vast banks of cloud were ranged above the forest, and among them, now and then, a worm of lightning played, followed by a distant roll of thunder. Not a leaf seemed to be stirring, when he noticed that a light breeze was rising and feathering the tops of the distant trees. Very soon the tops of the mimosas near the house bowed, lightly swaying towards the moon, and a tremor ran through the grass as if an invisible hand had stroked it. The wind rose, the clouds towered and toppled upwards, the moon was caught in a web of flying mist, the thunder grew louder, and the flashes of lightning more frequent. A greenish light seemed to emanate from the moon, and as the sky grew more heavily loaded, the forest, by contrast, appeared more ethereal, the heavy boscage and the trunks of the huge indigenous trees appearing in great detail, all dry and luminous and lurid, the foliage beginning to churn and writhe slowly on the topmost boughs. The tenseness of the atmosphere, the expectancy of nature, and the way in which the whole landscape, the very buildings and their shadows, seemed to take part in the great symphony of the impending storm, combined to produce an effect so dramatic as to seem almost supernatural.

The rolling of the thunder was now continuous. All the mountain country was overhung with incessant play of sheet-lightning, as if a curtain of fire, continually agitated by unseen forces, hung over half the world. The wind began to howl round the house, leaves and twigs to fly from the trees, a pile of timber was blown over, and the moon was half hidden in a swirl of clouds. Chains and forks of lightning, steely-blue and sulphurous red, larger and brighter and more frequent than Frant had ever seen, lighted everything with a continuous, shaken glare. Thunder pealed almost overhead, phalanxes of cloud advanced like avenging armies, the house shook, the windows rattled, and he put his hand to his burning and throbbing head. His pulses raced, sweat poured down his face and body, and he felt as if his veins would burst. Suddenly he caught sight of a white horse, which had broken loose from heaven knows where, and was careering madly, its mane and tail flying, its halter trailing, along the slope of the nearest hill. It seemed a creature of fire as it tossed its head, swerved at sudden obstacles, and galloped up to the ridge. There for a moment it stood, quivering with fear and exertion in the quivering glare of the lightning, and then, made splendid by freedom, disappeared from view.

'I can't stay in the house an instant longer!' Frant said aloud to himself, and taking up an electric torch, he stepped out into the garden. A strong refreshing breeze was blowing, but not a drop of rain had fallen. 'It looks as though MacGavin was right – the storm seems to have missed us altogether ...' He wondered what on earth he had brought the torch for, since the lightning was quivering incessantly, like a network of luminous nerves.

'Is that you, Frant?'

It was MacGavin calling from the house.

'Yes. I can't sleep. I'm going for a walk. It's much fresher out now.'

'A walk. At this time! Don't go far. It's risky. And if it should come on to rain ...'

'I'll be all right, thanks. Good night.'

He disappeared from view, and instinctively found himself taking the path he had taken on Christmas Day. He was frightened of the night, of losing his way, of the storm. He had at first no thought of going far, but when he paused to try and calculate how far he had already come he was almost as afraid to turn back as to go on, so he went on. He had got an idea that he must get to the bean tree, and he kept telling himself that it was not really very far. The wind was behind him now, and its freshness gave him energy. The glare and racket of the storm grew no less – it now seemed to be everywhere except immediately overhead. He hurried on, stumbling now and again, for the path was in places rough and narrow. He saw lights once or twice but did not meet a soul. And back at Madumbi MacGavin had grown anxious about him.

Before he came to the escarpment there was a loud detonation just overhead, and it began to rain. He had come too far now to turn back, so he hurried on, vaguely imagining that he would ask for shelter at Seraphina's. Near the top of the hill he realised that the worst of the weather was in front of him. The lightning revealed a thick grey veil of rain beyond the valley, and he could hear a tremendous steady downpour in the distance. The nearer he got to the top the louder the tumult grew, and he thought, 'the river must be a lot fuller by now than when I last saw it.' He was going downhill at last, but not so fast as he wanted, for it was raining pretty hard now and the paths were getting slippery. A feeling of terror seized him. He felt that he would never get down to the valley, that the storm would beat him, that it was no good thinking of turning back.

There was no doubt as to what he could hear now. The river must be in flood. And he suddenly thought, would the kraal be safe? Hardly … He was running now, to reach the bean tree. He was soaked to the skin, and his feet kept slipping. He missed the way twice and found it again, and then, waiting for the lightning to show him where he was, he found he was only a few yards from the tree.

And just at that moment, exactly as before, he saw a man coming towards him. Only this time the man was running. And this time it was not Umlilwana he saw. And this time he was terrified.

The man didn't see Frant until he almost ran into him, and he was too frightened.

'*Au!*' cried a familiar voice. '*Umtwana ka Kwini!* Child of the Queen! What are you doing here? Where are you going? Child! My child! Have you *seen*? Look, look!'

He dragged Frant over the slippery rocks to the very edge of the table-land.

'Look!' he cried.

A prolonged flash of lightning lit up the whole valley with a tremulous, pale violet glare like the light of some hellish arc-lamp, and in a few seconds Frant had understood. Gone was the S-shaped bend, gone were the grassy domes, kraal and little fields! There was nothing where they had been but a gigantic swirl of greyish water, in which trunks of trees could be seen travelling, spinning and half raising themselves above the surface like animate things.

'Seraphina!' cried Frant. 'Do you know Seraphina?'

He had caught hold of the little old man, who was shivering with fear and cold and seemed the only reality left in the world.

'Seraphina'!' cried Frant. 'Do you know her? Did she come back? Was she at home?'

'She was at home for two weeks, *umtwana*,' said the old man, shaking like a leaf. 'The cattle are drowned!' he cried in the voice of Job and of Lear. 'The houses, the people – all are drowned!'

190

'Drowned?' cried Frant, shining his torch full in the old man's face. 'Why? Why are they drowned?'

'The water came like a wall, my child,' said the old man, and the torchlight made the raindrops running down his face look as if it was covered with tears. He was shivering violently from top to toe, and his old tunic clung to his skin.

'Umlilwana,' said Frant. 'Was Umlilwana her brother?'

'Umlilwana?' said the old man. 'Umlilwana wasn't her brother! She was going to marry Umlilwana.'

In the lightning glare he saw Frant's face.

'All is finished!' he cried, putting out a black and bony claw, as if to defend himself from some unknown danger. In Lembu the same word means to be finished or to be destroyed. 'Are you bewitched?'

Yes, all was finished, all was destroyed. Already the rolling of the thunder was increasing in volume, but the roar of the flood seemed to grow louder, and the rain was coming down like whips of ice and steel. It was like the coming of the deluge itself. It was like the end of the world.

Something in Frant urged him to leave the old man and run down the hill and plunge into those maddened waters and lose himself, but something stronger told him that he must return to Madumbi, to the store, to the MacGavins, to the making of a livelihood, to the fashioning of a way of life, to a roll of undeveloped negatives, and to a python skin nailed to a wall like a banner, with two large holes in it cut by a girl with a hoe.

'I must go back!' he said to the old man, and gripped his shoulder for an instant. Then he made off in the direction of Madumbi, flashing the torch on the path. The old man called after him to take care, but he was at once out of earshot in the downpour. After he had stumbled a short way one spasmodic sob escaped from him, and he began to run.

WILLIAM PLOMER

Down on the Farm

From: *The Child of Queen Victoria and other Stories* (1933)

In the middle of that superb landscape there is a patch of low-lying ground which is thickly covered for a few days in the spring with yellow flowers. They spring from the bulb so quickly that nobody notices them until they are out, when the wind, already warmer, carries their fragrance towards one or other of the two farmhouses. For right through the middle of the flowers runs the fence which divides the two farms, Adventure and Brakfontein, lying in a broad valley shaped like an amphitheatre. And although this is away up in the mountains, thousands of feet above sea-level, and not very far from 'bleak Tarka's dens and Stormberg's rugged fells', the surrounding heights afford a certain amount of shelter. In some places the country is well grassed, in others it is more like the Karoo, and covered with stunted shrubs and heaths. In winter it is all bleached and bone-dry, standing water freezes at night, and there are one or two heavy falls of snow. In summer there are sometimes great storms, but for the most part the climate is pleasant enough, the days never excessively hot and the nights always cool.

The farm called Adventure is less pretentious than the other – a farmhouse, some stone outbuildings, an iron windmill and a dam of water, an orchard and garden with overgrown quince hedges, the whole surrounded by great sweeps of open veld and backed by precipitous rocks. A few fields of wheat and alfalfa (maize will not ripen at this height) and a row or two of Lombardy poplars and firs, with straggling flocks of sheep, combine to vary the landscape. The place belongs to a man called Stevens, who is not at present on speaking terms with his cousin Kimball at the other farm. Stevens is a man of thirty-five, rather taller than the average. He has a slouching way of walking which makes him look lazier than he really is. He has a slow way of talking, and in one of his large red hands, which look ungainly because his coat sleeves are always too short, he usually carries a small leather whip, more from habit than as a symbol of authority, though he is such a simple man that the habit no doubt originated in the wish to seem a person of importance at least on his own ground. As for his face, with its short, insignificant nose, large ears and small clear eyes, it is healthy and innocent and even has a certain shrewdness, though you have only to compare it with the face of its owner's little son to see that it is a baby face, and will always remain so, only it is at present rather more tanned and anxious than that of the child, by reason of a good many more years' waiting for rain. Stevens's way of talking is simple in the extreme, and his vocabulary is as limited as his thoughts. He likes especially to use a few proverbial expressions, which he applies, at what seems to him a suitable turn in the conversation, with all the air of having said something really witty and original. For instance, when somebody proposes an alternative, or corrects a misapprehension, he will say, 'Ah, that's a horse of a different colour!' On facing a dilemma he will say, 'It's six of one and half a dozen of the other.' And on failing to receive a letter, 'Well, no news is good news.'

Mrs Stevens is even more unassuming than her husband. A small, untidy woman of indeterminate age, her life is entirely centred in her husband, her children and her home. What if her hair is wispy and escapes continually from its fastenings? What if her few clothes are useful rather than beautiful? Her temper is mild and she is not much troubled by vain ambitions. Certainly she would be glad of more money with less work and more variety in her life, but if she possessed it, she would find nothing more worthy to devote it to than her home and family. She makes efforts, in the intervals of making jam and washing the baby, towards the adornment of her house. Somewhere she has picked up a kind of handiwork, which she calls appliqué-work, and she sees to it that no surface shall go unadorned. Thus all the linen, every curtain and every towel, bears some conventional pattern in appliqué-work – which means cutting up an old pair of knickers, a duster, or a pair of dyed pyjamas into the shapes of stylised poppies and tulips and sewing rows of these shapes onto some plain surface. For her husband she feels an admiration that tends to increase with time, the admiration women almost invariably feel for any man in whom they can recognise a real ability of any kind. Not that Stevens is in any way a talented man, but he has reached a kind of maturity and seems able to maintain in his own life and in the lives of those about him a balance and harmony which cannot easily be shaken.

His cousin Kimball, on the adjoining farm, is his only near neighbour. Kimball is richer and works harder than Stevens, who has never liked him. It is true that for a long time Kimball's manner, and his wife's, was superficially amiable. He seemed to do as much as could reasonably be expected of a relation and neighbour, and any suspicion of patronage in his manner might have been put down to the fact that he was older and richer. But the attitude of the Kimballs was not really satisfactory. Setting up to be kind, they were mainly patronising, and much freer with advice than with practical help; also, they allowed themselves, as relations, liberties they would never have dared to take merely as neighbours and acquaintances. Under a mask of affability they were actually contemptuous. When anything went wrong with Stevens's affairs, Kimball's manner was positively sickening, for nothing ever went wrong with *him* – droughts always found him provided with reserves of water, floods were carefully conducted down previously prepared channels, hailstorms arrived too late to do any damage, and he always managed to sell his wool just at the top of the market. 'Poor old Tom,' he would say to Stevens, 'you *are* having a run of bad luck.' And from his kindly, bantering tone it was obvious that he was not ungratified by Stevens's misfortunes and regarded him as a poor fool for encountering them at all. Besides, he always contrived that Stevens should be more or less indebted to him, and this, he felt, gave him an additional right to be rude. Something in his very appearance seemed, when they were together, to be a kind of reproach to Stevens. 'Look at me,' it seemed to say, 'I am a little older and uglier than you, but tougher and more active; where you are shrewd, I am deeply calculating; I prefer justice to mercy, and I know what I want!' Mrs Kimball's appearance contrasted in much the same way with that of Mrs Stevens. Her hair was bright red instead of colourless; she frowned and complained shrilly when things went wrong, instead of smiling and grumbling quietly; and said she simply couldn't understand the want of success that occasionally attended Mrs Stevens's domestic undertakings.

A transient envy passed over the naturally amiable natures of the Stevenses when they saw the Kimballs achieving some success or other merely by means of better materials and facilities, and perhaps this accounted for their occasional fits of fecklessness and irresponsibility. There was nothing furtive about their emotions, and they made little attempt to conceal the envy, resentment, and even dislike which were mingled with their tolerance of and civility to the Kimballs. 'It's all very well for you to lecture me,' Stevens would say to his cousin 'but we haven't all got your advantages. Do be reasonable.' But Kimball's reasonableness was too often the smugness of the self-made man, and forgetting how fortune and his own lack of sensibility had helped him, he would incite Stevens to imitate him and even boast of his successes. It was for a long time plain that, unless the parties concerned had always been fairly busy, they would soon have been at loggerheads.

Once a week Stevens went to town. Whereas Kimball had a car and could easily make the double journey in a morning, Stevens had to go by cart and devote the whole day to it. He did not mind this, because he was naturally leisurely, and although he and his wife sometimes talked of the day when they would be able to afford a car, they didn't greatly care whether they ever had one or not. Besides, when Kimball returned from the town, nobody came out to meet him; he drove the car straight into its garage and was as often as not back in the house before anybody had even heard him returning. But Stevens, while the buggy creaked over the veld towards the farm, on some radiant after-noon when the shadows were beginning to lengthen over the silent, golden plains, was visible for ten minutes before his arrival, and was sure of a welcome. His wife would come out with one of the children to meet him, and would stand on a patch of grass outside the house, the light prairie wind blowing her hair and her dress about, the child waving both its hands, and the chickens also assembling in the hope that they were going to be fed. And then Willem, the Coloured servant, would step quietly forward and take charge of the horses, perhaps without saying a word. By no means the least important elements in Stevens's pleasure at coming home was the presence of Willem, the knowledge that he would certainly be there to unharness the horses and put the cart away and carry the parcels into the house. And although it sometimes happened that scarcely a single word would be exchanged between master and man, there was a deep understanding and even affection between them, which slightly puzzled Mrs Stevens but which she regarded with respect. It made her husband more mysterious and so more attractive to her than he would have been without it.

Willem was not exactly what is called a Cape Coloured Person; still, he was a person, he was Coloured, and he came from the Cape. Mrs Stevens used to say she had no doubt that Plaatje had Chinese blood, but Stevens smiled and said it was Hottentot. It seemed evident that Bantu and European (Portuguese perhaps) had combined with something Oriental Malay or Chinese, to produce this strong but lightly built man with large dark eyes set in a smooth honey-coloured face with high cheekbones. His movements were feline, his voice was high and soft, and his temperament sad. He was married to a large taciturn Xhosa woman who dressed in stiff blue drill with a small waist and very full skirt down to her feet, a fine creature, but surly, perhaps because she was nearly always pregnant. Her confinements were short and sharp, and a day before or after each event she could be seen striding alone to or from the horizon carrying on her head an enormous basket of the washing she did for both the Stevenses and the Kimballs. This heroic-looking woman had the name of Zenobia.

Every evening, during the lambing season, Stevens used, before going to bed at about ten o'clock, to take a storm-lantern and make the round of the three stone sheep-sheds near the house, which were filled at that time with lambing ewes. Perhaps some obstinate ewe and her lamb would have to be brought together, she would be propped up on her hindquarters, unwilling and struggling, and milk squirted from her udder into the mouth of the puzzled lamb, which was either apathetic or so frantic with hunger as to devote all its attention to trying to draw milk from Stevens's finger. All this was a strain on his temper, but it had its consolations. The floor might be thick with dung and the air saturated with ammoniac vapours, but the freshness and grandeur of the southern night, the lamplit interior behind him, the immense silence and space on all sides, the darkness sprinkled with stars or the brilliant moonlight, the sighing of the night wind, the distant bark of a dog or sombre echo of a dirge from the kraals – all these things combined to comfort and content his inarticulate spirit. But in spite of the pastoral simplicity of the scene, the whole atmosphere of deep natural instincts being fulfilled, with only a rough stone wall between them and the vast uncertainty of the outside world, the grace of animal intimacies in the semi-darkness, the sight of a sleeping lamb, than which there is nothing more touching – in spite of all this, Stevens never felt entirely satisfied unless, as sometimes happened, a sudden shadow, a footstep on the straw, or the striking of a match indicated that Willem had appeared, as if from nowhere, to give him a hand. He never expected Willem to work at night, never even encouraged him to do so, but on these evenings when, for twenty minutes or half an hour, they both concerned themselves in the heart of silence, with the flock that afforded them a living, Stevens went to bed feeling tired, trusted, loved, and slept soundly.

In the mornings he rose early, for there was always something waiting to be done. When the lambs were a few weeks old they had to have their tails docked, and this was always done in the early morning. Merino sheep, being bred for wool, have come in the course of time to carry a great bulk of it, and a woolly tail would expose them, in summer, to the risk of getting flyblown. Stevens used to stand at the entrance to a stone kraal, holding a sharp knife in his hand, while the lambs were caught by natives and brought to him one by one. He found the suitable joint with his left forefinger and thumb, and severed it in one moment. The male lambs, with some very few exceptions, had not only to lose their tails but also their sex. Two more mutilations followed. Since overbreeding often tends to produce in sheep an extra fold in the skin of the eyelid, so that blindness or ophthalmia are likely to result, or at least the blindness caused by an overgrowth of wool about the eyes, such dangers had to be averted by another piece of rough and ready surgery. The extra eyelid was simply snipped off with a pair of shears, and although it always bled freely, in a few days the wound was bound to knit, the contraction of the skin opening the eye to a proper extent. Finally, small pieces were usually clipped out of each ear for purposes of identification. Thus it often happened that a lamb would be turned out into the dust and heat and jostling of the day, without tail or testicles, its eyes blinded by its own blood, and its six wounds all undressed. And Stevens, watching the bleating flock crowding out of the kraal, felt the same sort of satisfaction as a gardener feels when he looks at a tree that he has just finished pruning, or a sculptor in scraping imperfections from an imagined outline. But he never lost sight of the fact that sheep are living creatures, and that, like all living creatures, they are able to display either a pitiable weakness or a surprising savagery.

One day he was crossing the lands on some task or other when he noticed a large crow rising from a field with something in its beak. He marked the place where the bird had risen, and as he was not in a hurry went to see what it had been doing. He found a lamb a few weeks old lying on its right side and bleeding from an empty eye-socket. Its sides were quite flat and were still heaving with its last few breaths. Its small tongue already hung in the dust. It was plain that the lamb had strayed, starved, and lain down from exhaustion, and that the carrion-crow had profited by its weakness to tug out its eye. Stevens turned it over gently to see if he could judge how much life was left to it, but it was plainly in the last stages of existence. The right side had been for some time flattened against the earth, and nightly dews and natural moisture had reduced it to an unpleasant condition, so that the flies and other insects had already taken advantage of it. The right eye was also missing. The lamb collapsed and died in Stevens's hands.

One morning when he was with Willem and two natives in a kraal where they were sorting a small flock of rams into two divisions he was abruptly reminded that the sheep is not such a mild animal as it is supposed to be. Willem and one of the natives were engaged in catching each sheep in turn by one of the hind legs, and then holding it firmly by the curved horns while Stevens examined its wool on the shoulders, flanks and back, looked it over with an appraising eye, and decided whether it was to stay or be urged through a gate, kept by the other native, into the next kraal. They had nearly finished the job. Stevens made occasional remarks to Willem about the sheep, and the natives exchanged a joke or two. By the time there were only half a dozen sheep left there was quite a scuffle as each had to be caught. One in particular, an upstanding young ram with proud movements, was both wild and strong, and seizing what it thought was a suitable moment, attempted, with head lowered, to rush the gate, caught the native there unawares, and threw him violently off his balance. In falling, he caught his head on a projecting stone in the wall, and almost before anybody had time to realise what had happened, was half sitting, half lying by the gate, and all without uttering a sound. The other native was about to laugh and make some bantering remark, when he broke instead into an exclamation of concern. The three men hurried forward, but the man was already dead. His skull had been split open, and he had been killed instantaneously.

And all this happened before breakfast, before the routine of the day had even begun. A young man with a wife and child, helping to sort out some sheep, had suddenly left a widow and an orphan, and it was clear that a skull could be cracked almost as easily as a joke. A string of living rubies ran down on to that dark hand which would never again grip a ram by the horns, guide a plough, caress a woman or carry a child. The body and the traces of blood were removed, the lamentations of the widow rose shrilly in the distance, the ram, ranging among the rocks, tore up the sweet mountain-grass with its teeth, and the mystery remained. At happy and tranquil moments, when the early morning sun warms some remote valley and the breakfast smoke rises straight upwards in a slow and gauzy arabesque, it becomes suddenly possible to imagine God, an Old Testament God, saying, 'Take note, there is no barrier between you and Me.' The 'act of God' which they saw together that morning was just one more of the innumerable experiences that Stevens and Willem had in common, and without the exchange of a single comment the bond between them was strengthened by one more thread – in the presence of sudden death they were joint survivors …

Hardly was the lambing season over than it was succeeded, in early summer, by the shearing. A large sorting-table was set up in the cart-house, which had been cleared for the occasion and carefully swept. The building was windowless, but there was enough light, for the whole of one end was occupied by a pair of tall wooden gates, now left wide open. Work began at five in the morning and went on all day, the shearers working in the open doorway, just out of the sun. There were five of them, and as they were paid for each sheep they sheared, there was a lively competition among them. All expert workmen, they sheared off the heavy fleeces in the shortest possible time. After releasing the sheep they would cleverly pick up each fleece in a compact bundle from the floor, and then, raising their arms above their heads, hurl it out with a swing flat upon the sorting-table. It was a godlike movement, and might have put one in mind of Zeus scattering a silver cloud over the heavens. Stevens and Willem sorted and rolled the fleeces, and packed them in bales which, when full, were deftly sewn up by a boy who did this same work every year. The wool was agreeable to the touch, fine and dense, the long staples crimped and gleaming with rich natural oils, so that the workers' hands and arms glistened. For long intervals the shearers, stripped to the waist and stooping over their task, would work in a silence broken only by the sound of the shears, but sometimes they sang a chorus or burst out laughing over some inscrutable Bantu joke, ever and again first one and then another coming up to the table to scatter proudly the fruits of his effort, while out of doors behind and beyond them the mountains wore their early verdure and the veld sparkled in summer splendour.

The rhythm of this pastoral, primitive life was broken by storms and droughts and small disasters. Sometimes, for a day or more at a time, a wind blew steadily from the Karoo, bringing with it heavy clouds charged with crimson dust which crowded on through the sky until at last the mountains withdrew in a blood-coloured fog. After such a dust-storm, rain would follow, the lightning leaping from cliff to crag and sewing sound to fury with giant stitches of livid light. Or a vast hailstorm, miles wide, would come drumming its way along the mountain ranges, the roar of ice on ironstone audible long before its arrival above the amphitheatre of Adventure. Sometimes such a storm would miss the valley and the nearest peaks could be heard ringing with it, and the rocks could be seen thrashed with falling veils of steely bullets, and smoking with the rebound of the hurrying volleys; sometimes the storm would fall on Adventure itself, stripping the trees and making such a din on the iron roofs that Stevens's little boy would run and hide his head in the bed-clothes or creep under the sofa.

Very occasionally there was a visitation of locusts, and then the child was in the seventh heaven of delight. One morning his father caught him up and perching him on his shoulder pointed out what seemed to be a mist pouring and spreading over some low hills in the distance. Within half an hour the whole sky was darkened by an immense swarm of locusts, flying, leaping along the ground, swarming over every green thing. A stray hen at the door went almost mad with excitement, longing to eat these succulent angels and not knowing where to begin; no sooner did she begin on one than she rushed to attack others, clucking with frantic excitement at such an *embarras de richesses*. The swarm was such a rapidly moving one that it did little damage, and such damage as was done was quickly restored by the eager growths of the season, which was spring.

Stevens was familiar with the whole place as one is with a lover; he got to know both its contours and its spirit, and never tired of either. Parts of the mountain behind the house were so wild and hard of access that they were scarcely ever entered except in quest of missing sheep. Sheer rock-faces, ten-anted by bats, birds, and rock-rabbits, and tufted with small shrubs and tree-heaths, rose one above the other to bar the way to lost pastures and hidden uplands. Often the face of such a cliff, or *krans* as it was called locally, contained a low cave or two, and once, hurrying to shelter from a storm, he noticed strange markings on the walls of one of these caves, and looking closer, dis-covered a whole series of Bushman drawings, partially rubbed out by time and by sheep crowding against it. It was still possible to make out an elaborate hunting scene, in which naked figures with bows and arrows were running with grace and agility after ostriches and various kinds of antelopes; besides some sort of festival, where numbers of fat women were clapping their hands while the men-folk were dancing with long sticks and knobkerries. The colours were red and yellow ochre, and black, and the drawing was free and lively. Looking out from the cave on superb mountain views with misty blue lowlands faint in the distance, Stevens remembered that the Bushmen had been hunted up and up into these craggy fastnesses, being shot at sight as if they were no more than baboons, until the advancing invader had, by reducing and finally extinguishing the race altogether, succeeded at once in obtaining pos-session of wide acres and in securing his flocks and herds against theft.

On the very afternoon that Stevens took shelter in the cave, an extraordi-nary thing happened. His cousin Kimball was driving back to his farm from the town, when the storm, which was a severe one, and which had been gath-ering for a day or two, suddenly broke overhead. It was what is called a 'dry' storm, that is to say, there was a great deal of thunder and lightning and very little rain. And Kimball happened to be driving a Cape-cart, because his car was being repaired. He had with him a native servant, and had just reached the highest and narrowest part of the road, which, for a hundred yards or so, was in that place actually composed of solid rock. With some presentiment of danger he urged the horses forward, but it was already too late, and the cart was struck by lightning. The hood was buckled; the native was killed instantaneously; Kimball was dazed and momentarily blinded; and the horses bolted. Down the rough mountain road they rushed, the wheels bounding over the stones and ruts, the corpse at the back jogging from side to side, and Kimball, who by a miracle had never relaxed his hold on the reins, straining every nerve to guide and restrain them. Half an hour later he was safely back at his farm, trembling all over from exhaustion and shock, the smell of singed hair and scorched flesh in his nostrils, his horses in a lather, and his whole being agog with the news of his escape. If, when a white and a native are together and are struck by lightning, they are not both killed, then it is the white who gets off most lightly or even unscathed, as in this case. God helps those who help themselves …

During the following winter, which was a severe one, there were several heavy falls of snow. One day, for example, Stevens was entirely occupied in mending the roof of a sheep-shed which had been torn off bodily in a blizzard the night before, so that in the morning the sheep were discovered standing huddled together with snow on their backs. Not that the sun came out then, or that the storm stopped to make things easier. On the contrary, if the bitter black wind had lost some of its fury, it gained in steadiness, and brought with it continually, in a strangely darkened world, swirling drifts of snow. And Stevens, wrapped up to the ears, gloved and gaitered, his face burning, spent the day carrying beams of wood or sheets of corrugated iron edgeways against the wind, using by turns a saw, a chisel, a screw-brace, a hammer, to anchor his new roof with iron wires to the massive walls that supported it, and finally laying large stones on the top to prevent the accident recurring. And over the fire in the evening, which had set in early, he thought with satisfaction of the stupid, woollen sheep, so vulnerable, but now by his labour made snug against the elements.

The snow continued, off and on, for several days. It was already late in the season for such weather to be in the least likely, and as it happened to coincide with the arrival of the first lambs, many anxious hours had to be spent to ensure the safety and comfort of a new generation of wool-bearers. In one field, sheltered a little by an angle of the mountain, some tufted herbage protruded from the driven snow, and there some thirty ewes, lambing or about to lamb, were taken for the day. A strange scene it was, the sky and mountains looming sombrely through the now more scantily falling flakes, and the dark figures of Stevens and Plaatje moving among the grey sheep, a scene almost colourless, but for a little blood on the snow.

Along rock-edge and roof-edge the icicles had lengthened into rows of crystal stalactites, and as the wind and the thermometer tended to fall, they now began to drip. On the following day the thaw set in. A brilliant sun, and a warm one, burst upon a cloudless, silent, sugary world, so that in a few hours the air was full of varying sounds of water, running, dropping, gurgling and splashing. By noon there was little snow left except in shady places. At night, and indeed every succeeding night, there was a sharp frost. Under a sky in which the very stars seemed to crackle and gleam like ice the breathless earth was quickly rendered brittle, and in the mornings one stepped out into a vast clear landscape that gave one the sensation of being in a glass case of infinite dimensions, under whose flawless canopy everything sparkled and shone with newness and freshness and hope. Sounds travelled infinitely far, tinkling and ringing; every step seemed to be taken on broken glass; while the breath of living creatures rose up comfortably warm and misty in an air too rarefied to last.

Even a week after the snowstorm, a few patches of snow, in spite of the African sun, still lay about in odd places; one came across them in the afternoon, in stray hollows under the mountain, or behind some sunward rock, the shadows upon them intensely blue; while if one took up a handful of snow one found that the repeated frosts had reduced it to a strange consistency like that of innumerable glass beads. Even the mud had dried, and a little dust was beginning to rise from the roads, so that there was little to remind one of recent events. Things being in this state, Stevens happened to wake very early one Sunday morning. The sun had not yet risen, and once more there had been a frost, but he decided to go out and enjoy the opening day, for he could not go to sleep again, and the household rose late on Sundays. After dressing, he opened a drawer to find himself a handkerchief and happened to notice lying there a small silver brandy-flask, which he thought he might just as well slip into his pocket against the cold. Considering how rarely he used it, it was a lucky chance that prompted him to do so on this particular occasion. He had meant to walk, but as soon as he got out of the house changed his mind and went and saddled one of the horses. It was with a feeling of extreme exhilaration that he cantered away from the homestead, the fresh air stinging his ears, the horse snorting at the cold, and the whole sky, not yet starless, warming to its matutinal rose. To be raised above the earth and to move rhythmically through freshness and silence was in itself delightful, and he rode with natural ease, so between him and his mount was that tacit sympathy without which riding is nothing. – 'How well I ride you, and how well you carry me!' He decided to take a road which led through the remotest part of the farm and likewise through the remotest part of Kimball's adjoining farm to a kraal where some shepherds lived with their families, a kraal called Klipplaats, built among the ruins of an old farmhouse surrounded with poplars and straggling peach trees, where he wished to inquire about some building-stone. The exercise soon made him warm, and approaching the boundary he slowed down to a walk, and lighted a cigarette. Some smoke blew into his eye, which was already inclined to water from the cold, and he rubbed it. It was just at this moment, when the sun had caught the western heights, that he thought he heard a sound like a groan. In that lonely place at such a time it not only surprised but alarmed him, and he looked anxiously round to see where the sound could have come from, but seeing nothing supposed he had imagined it, and was about to ride uneasily on when he heard it again. He hurriedly dismounted, and tying his horse up to the fence, prepared to solve the mystery.

'Hullo!' he cried aloud, but the echo of his voice rang bell-like up the kloofs, and there was no answer. It was then that he caught sight of what seemed at first to be a bundle of old clothes, lying under the lee of a large rock. It proved to be a human being, a woman in a dark blue dress, which had about it something familiar. 'Asleep?' he thought, 'asleep here, at this time? Is it possible? Who is it?' It was Zenobia, the wife of Willem. Her eyes were closed, and she groaned again. He spoke to her, but she made no answer. He, of course, wanted to find out what was wrong with her and how long she had been there, and was just wondering what to do when he noticed the ashes of a small brushwood fire by her side. They were quite cold. Then when he also saw that she had been very sick, he suddenly understood why she was here. There had been a beer-drink the previous night at Klipplaats and she had been too drunk to get home. It was only lately that he had heard of two men getting frozen to death in similar circumstances, and he looked anxiously at her again. Heaven alone knew how long she had been there. Her hands and face were swollen and purple with cold, her lips were cracked, and he could not find her pulse. As was often the case with her, she was far gone in the family way – surely she was risking two lives? He now remembered the brandy-flask, and tried to force her to drink, but it was evident that she was in too much pain to be even conscious of his presence; her teeth were firmly set together, and her lips twitched spasmodically, while a greenish foam appeared upon them. For a moment he thought she might be in her death agony, but determined to take no more chances and waste no more time, he forced her jaws apart and held the mouth of the bottle between her teeth so that she was obliged to swallow some of the brandy. This he repeated three times, between her groans, but the only result was that she opened her eyes for an instant, showing only the whites, which were discoloured. He tried to make her sit up, he tried to chafe her wrists into some sort of warmth, but it seemed useless. Then with a sudden movement she rolled over with her face on the earth and uttered an almost inhuman shriek. His blood ran cold as a fearful suspicion came into his mind, a suspicion which, when he saw her suddenly clutch at her belly, ripened into a certainty. These were labour pains!

The mild sun rose higher on this remarkable scene; the horse awaited its rider; the rocks re-echoed the cries of the unfortunate Zenobia, who, from being half-frozen, was now forced by agony into a profuse sweat; and Stevens, with his coat off, and his mind running on Caesarean sections and such matters, prepared, without experience or equipment, to act as doctor and midwife combined.

It is hardly an exaggeration to say that Stevens sweated almost as much as his patient, and that had he not been so busy he too might have been sick. What is important is that Zenobia's delivery was at last successful, and that the moment came when Stevens actually held in his hands a tiny, slippery, wizened caricature of Willem, and heard it utter its first unearthly cry, so small and weird that it seemed a protest and an entreaty to be returned to pre-natal security. He had no water to wash it with, and could only make it presentable to its mother by using a piece of his shirt, which he took off for the purpose and tore in pieces. He wrapped the infant with infinite care in his coat, and put it in the arms of Zenobia, telling her to hold it till he could get help. He kept reminding himself how lucky it was that this was not by any means a first confinement, that Zenobia was a strong woman, and that there seemed some faint chance of both her and her offspring surviving. He was able to make her understand that all would soon be well ('one way or another,' he said to himself) but that she must remain as she was for a short time. Having said which, he turned to his horse, and left Zenobia moaning and the infant faintly wailing.

Imagine the astonishment of Willem, rubbing his sleepy Sabbath eyes in the sun at the door of his hut, and preparing to see to the milking, when his master, stripped to the waist, approached him at a gallop out of nowhere, and told him the news! And the further astonishment of Mrs Stevens, brought out by the sound of frantic hoofs, and still in her nightgown, with a border of pansies appliqué! In an incredibly short time these three drove off in the buggy to the succour of the unfortunate woman, leaving the cows to call for their calves and wonder why they were not being milked.

Breakfast was late that morning, but the conversation was animated. 'You ought to be a doctor, Tom,' said Mrs Stevens, 'instead of a farmer.' And she looked at her husband's large red hands and thought of the wonders they had performed. Later in the day Zenobia was so much better that she asked to see Stevens in order to thank him. He found her very weak, but holding at her breast the absurd little baby, towards which he felt almost paternal. To her gratitude Willem joined his, and even called his new child 'Stevens' after his master, who had now risen to the status of a hero. Mrs Kimball, however, thought that Mrs Stevens had lowered herself by driving to minister to Zenobia, and Kimball told Stevens he was inclined to spoil his servants, whereupon a distinct coldness ensued between the two families.

For a long time Zenobia had acted as laundress for both the Kimballs and the Stevenses, but she suddenly decided that the work was too much for her, in view of her increasing family, and asked that in future she might wash only for the Stevenses. Actually, she had taken a great dislike to Mrs Kimball. She now proposed that her young half-sister, Rita, who was living with her, should take her place on the other farm, an arrangement to which Mrs Kimball reluctantly agreed. It happened that Rita was in many ways the exact opposite of Zenobia. Zenobia was rather stately and sombre but Rita was something of a minx. Her body was thin and supple, her eyes were roguish, and she loved to strut about with her hands on her hips in order to make her short skirt swing from side to side and to call attention to her somewhat boyish posterior. She promised, or rather threatened, to be too much of a success with the opposite sex, and for some time both Stevens and Willem had been inclined to shake their heads when they saw what a demoralising effect she had on the other servants. After Rita had made her first excursion to wash for the Kimballs, they had cause to shake their heads, for it was also her last. Not that she was an inefficient washer girl – far from it – but what actually happened was this. Mrs Kimball decided that she would go along in the middle of the morning and see how Rita was progressing at the stream. It was the most brilliant spring morning, and even Mrs Kimball could not help noticing how green the grass was, how loudly the birds were chirping, and how frisky the lambs were. However, it was not only the lambs that were frisky, as she very soon discovered when she came upon the secluded spot where the washing was done, and found that, among the suds and chemises, Rita had invited a handsome young wagoner to help her to appreciate the beauties of the season. Her choice did credit to her taste, for the young man, who had lately arrived from Kaffraria, was already the idol of every feminine heart among the natives of the environs. And now it was a case of love among the linen! Instead of tactfully withdrawing and later checking the clean linen by the list in the usual way (which must surely be the procedure recommended by books of etiquette in a situation of this kind) Mrs Kimball rushed in where angels would have been too delicate to tread, and seizing a scrubbing-board, proceeded to belabour the amorous pair, uttering meanwhile the most frightful threats and imprecations. The unlucky Rita fled, bruised and howling, to her sister for protection, while the wagoner was instantly dismissed by Kimball, who was nothing if not a puritan, and who tried, with only moderate success, both to cheat the man out of his wages and to do him physical violence. Zenobia was not easily roused, but when she was roused it was to some purpose, and it seemed to her a shocking injustice that Rita should have been knocked about just because she had seen fit to improve the shining hour with a little innocent fun. She at once made a fierce scene for the benefit of her husband, Willem, and persuaded that usually meek man to go and complain in his turn to their master Stevens. And the immediate result of this was a very decided difference of opinion, and, indeed, some exceedingly plain speaking between Stevens and his wife on the one hand and Kimball and his on the other. They parted now on really bad terms and, although the two farmhouses were within sight of each other, held no communication for weeks …

When they were brought together again, it was by the arrival of two letters. Both of these letters were written by an old lady, a Mrs Didgett, a frail and elderly relation of both families, who addressed one letter to each of them. To Mrs Stevens she wrote saying that she would like to come and stay with her for a month or two; to Mrs Kimball she wrote telling of her intention. As soon as the Kimballs heard that the old woman was coming, they were ready to move heaven and earth to get her to go and stay with them, for she had money. But Mrs Didgett was not so blind that she could not see through their cupidity, and in any case her will had already been secretly made in favour of the Stevenses, whom she had always preferred. The Kimballs now, with an extraordinary lack of pride, hastened to be nicer than they had ever been before to their cousins, and the foot-path that led from Brakfontein to Adventure was soon quite worn with their comings and goings.

Mrs Didgett came to stay at Adventure, and stay she did. She was a very old woman and very absent-minded, and would sometimes come to meals in her petticoat, having completely forgotten to put on her skirt. She often mistook the afternoon for the morning, and had a morbid fear that while she was in the country Sunday might slip by without her noticing. She was very garrulous, and had repeated her memories so often that some of them had become a perfect farrago. She was especially fond of talking about local celebrities of an earlier generation. Although she had never known any of them well, she liked people to think that she had, and tried to achieve this result by saying something to the discredit of the celebrities in question, and looking very knowing, as if she had had inside information.

'Olive Schreiner!' she would exclaim shrilly. 'I knew Olive quite well when my father took us to the diamond fields. Headstrong, asthmatic, ambitious! She never wrote any of those books, you know … And confessed as much!'

Kruger was half-Coloured, Rhodes had a secret vice, and so on …

When Mrs Didgett fell suddenly ill, the Kimballs at once tried to get her moved to Brakfontein, where, they said, it would be much easier to look after her, but the doctor said she was not to be moved on any account, and was likely to die within a few days. The assiduity with which Mrs Kimball insisted on dancing attendance on the death-bed was positively indecent, particularly as Mrs Didgett took a very long time to do her dying.

One morning at eleven o'clock Mrs Kimball appeared on the veranda and called loudly for Willem. She told him to hurry off and call his master as quickly as possible, for Mrs Didgett was much worse. Unfortunately Stevens was at least two miles away, up in the mountain, where he had gone to mend a fence, and it was no little trouble for Willem to reach him – indeed, as the Coloured man himself expressed it later, 'I sprang from rock to rock like a goat, sweating like a pig, and panting like a dog, but did that prevent the old woman from dying?' It did not prevent her, for she died before Stevens could reach the house. Late that afternoon it was Stevens who appeared on the veranda to call Willem. He was holding a small parcel in his hand.

'I want you to do this for me,' he said. 'Get a spade and bury these somewhere – anywhere – in the garden. Fairly deep. I don't know what else to do with them.'

'Yes, *baas*,' said Willem, in a mild but rather puzzled and questioning voice, so that Stevens felt he ought to explain.

'As a matter of fact,' he said, unaccountably serious and shamefaced, 'it's the old missus's false teeth. She didn't die in them.'

Willem took the parcel rather gingerly and went and dug a hole under a poplar tree in the garden, carefully burying the teeth in it. So instinctive and spontaneous was his trust in his master that it was not until he was finally patting the earth with the flat of his spade that he began to be troubled by the possible consequences of his action. Might not the spirit of the deceased seek vengeance on behalf of these exiled molars? Would not bad luck come upon his master, himself, or the garden, or upon all three? These questions made him uneasy, but he did not care to discuss them with anybody. And just because he kept the matter to himself it lay on his conscience, got mixed up with his dreams, and made him more silent than usual during the several days' absence of both Stevenses and Kimballs on account of Mrs Didgett's funeral. He looked forward impatiently to his master's return, and when Stevens came back, took the very first chance of broaching the matter.

'*Baas*,' he said, 'I wonder if it was wise to bury those teeth apart from the body?'

Many people would have laughed at this question, but Stevens remained quite serious, though there was certainly a twinkle in his eye.

'As she did not choose to die in them,' he said, 'it is clear that her spirit wanted to discard them. There's no need to trouble yourself.'

And he immediately went on to talk of more practical affairs, as though the matter had been settled once and for all. Thus a heavy load was taken off Willem's mind.

A day or two later, the terms of Mrs Didgett's will became known. She was found to have left everything unconditionally to the Stevenses. At this, the annoyance of the Kimballs knew no bounds, and once more the two families ceased to be on speaking terms …

And now it is spring again, and those yellow flowers are all out, just as they are every year at about this time. Stevens is walking through them, quietly tapping his leg with the old riding-crop which he carries in his hand. He stands still a moment, and a yellow light from the flowers is dimly reflected on his boots. He looks a little fatter, as he raises his head and gazes across the boundary fence towards Brakfontein. He smiles to himself, because he knows that the Kimballs will soon try to get on good terms with him again, for after all, he is now a man of property, and deserves the respect due to such a person ... He turns round, and is pleased to see Willem coming towards him. He has prudently refrained from increasing Willem's wages. He gives him ten shillings a week and half a bag of maize flour, and since he is absolutely satisfied with him, why should he give him any more? 'I couldn't do without him,' he said to his wife, 'and I'm not going to run any risk of spoiling him. I don't want to *show* him that he's just everything to me.'

'*Everything*, Tom?' she said.

'Well,' he answered, 'you know what I mean.'

HERMAN CHARLES BOSMAN

The Music-Maker

First published, 1935
From: *Mafeking Road* (1947)

Of course, I know about history – Oom Schalk Lourens said – it's the stuff children learn in school. Only the other day, at Thys Lemmer's post office, Thys's little son Stoffel started reading out of his history book about a man called Vasco da Gama, who visited the Cape. At once Dirk Snyman started telling young Stoffel about the time when he himself visited the Cape, but young Stoffel didn't take much notice of him. So Dirk Snyman said that that showed you.

Anyway, Dirk Snyman said that what he wanted to tell young Stoffel was that the last time he went down to the Cape a kafir came and sat down right next to him in a tram. What was more, Dirk Snyman said, was that people seemed to think nothing of it.

Yes, it's a queer thing about wanting to get into history.

Take the case of Manie Kruger, for instance.

Manie Kruger was one of the best farmers in the Marico. He knew just how much peach-brandy to pour out for the tax-collector to make sure that he would nod dreamily at everything Manie said. And at a time of drought Manie Kruger could run to the Government for help much quicker than any man I ever knew.

Then one day Manie Kruger read an article in the Kerkbode about a musician who said that he knew more about music than Napoleon did. After that – having first read another article to find out who Napoleon was – Manie Kruger was a changed man. He could talk of nothing but his place in history and of his musical career.

Of course, everybody knew that no man in the Marico could be counted in the same class with Manie Kruger when it came to playing the concertina.

No Bushveld dance was complete without Manie Kruger's concertina. When he played a vastrap you couldn't keep your feet still. But after he had decided to become the sort of musician that gets into history books, it was strange the way that Manie Kruger altered. For one thing, he said he would never again play at a dance. We all felt sad about that. It was not easy to think of the Bushveld dances of the future. There would be the peach-brandy in the

208

kitchen; in the voorkamer the feet of the dancers would go through the steps of the schottische and the polka and the waltz and the mazurka, but on the riempies bench in the corner where the musicians sat, there would be no Manie Kruger. And they would play 'Die Vaal Hare en die Blou Oge' and 'Vat Jou Goed en Trek, Ferreira', but it would be another's fingers that swept over the concertina keys. And when, with the dancing and the peach-brandy, the young men called out 'Dagbreek toe' it would not be Manie Kruger's head that bowed down to the applause.

It was sad to think about all this.

For so long, at the Bushveld dances, Manie Kruger had been the chief musician.

And of all those who mourned this change that had come over Manie, we could see that there was no one more grieved than Letta Steyn.

And Manie said such queer things at times. Once he said that what he had to do to get into history was to die of consumption in the arms of a princess, like another musician he had read about. Only it was hard to get consumption in the Marico, because the climate was so healthy.

Although Manie stopped playing his concertina at dances, he played a great deal in another way. He started giving what he called recitals. I went to several of them. They were very impressive.

At the first recital I went to, I found that the front part of Manie's voorkamer was taken up by rows of benches and chairs that he had borrowed from those of his neighbours who didn't mind having to eat their meals on candle-boxes and upturned buckets. At the far end of the voorkamer a wide green curtain was hung on a piece of string. When I came in the place was full. I managed to squeeze in on a bench between Jan Terblanche and a young woman in a blue kappie. Jan Terblanche had been trying to hold this young woman's hand.

Manie Kruger was sitting behind the green curtain. He was already there when I came in. I knew it was Manie by his veldskoens, which were sticking out from underneath the curtain. Letta Steyn sat in front of me. Now and again, when she turned round, I saw that there was a flush on her face and a look of dark excitement in her eyes.

At last everything was ready, and Joel, the farm kafir to whom Manie had given this job, slowly drew the green curtain aside. A few of the younger men called out 'Middag, ou Manie,' and Jan Terblanche asked if it wasn't very close and suffocating, sitting there like that behind that piece of green curtain.

Then he started to play.

And we all knew that it was the most wonderful concertina music we had ever listened to. It was Manie Kruger at his best. He had practised a long time for that recital; his fingers flew over the keys; the notes of the concertina swept into our hearts; the music of Manie Kruger lifted us right out of that voor-kamer into a strange and rich and dazzling world.

It was fine.

The applause right through was terrific. At the end of each piece the kafir closed the curtains in front of Manie, and we sat waiting for a few minutes until the curtains were drawn aside again. But after that first time there was no more laughter about this procedure. The recital lasted for about an hour and a half, and the applause at the end was even greater than at the start. And during those ninety minutes Manie left his seat only once. That was when there was some trouble with the curtain and he got up to kick the kafir.

At the end of the recital Manie did not come forward and shake hands with us, as we had expected. Instead, he slipped through behind the green curtain into the kitchen, and sent word that we could come and see him round the back. At first we thought this a bit queer, but Letta Steyn said it was all right. She explained that in other countries the great musicians and stage performers all received their admirers at the back. Jan Terblanche said that if these actors used their kitchens for entertaining their visitors in, he wondered where they did their cooking.

Nevertheless, most of us went round to the kitchen, and we had a good time congratulating Manie Kruger and shaking hands with him; and Manie spoke much of his musical future, and of the triumphs that would come to him in the great cities of the world, when he would stand before the curtain and bow to the applause.

Manie gave a number of other recitals after that. They were all equally fine. Only, as he had to practise all day, he couldn't pay much attention to his farm-ing. The result was that his farm went to pieces and he got into debt. The court messengers came and attached half his cattle while he was busy practising for his fourth recital. And he was practising for his seventh recital when they took away his ox-wagon and mule-cart.

Eventually, when Manie Kruger's musical career reached that stage when they took away his plough and the last of his oxen, he sold up what remained of his possessions and left the Bushveld, on his way to those great cities that he had so often talked about. It was very grand, the send-off that the Marico gave him. The predikant and the Volksraad member both made speeches about how proud the Transvaal was of her great son. Then Manie replied. Instead of thank-ing his audience, however, he started abusing us left and right, calling us a mob of hooligans and soulless Philistines, and saying how much he despised us.

Naturally, we were very much surprised at this outburst, as we had always been kind to Manie Kruger and had encouraged him all we could. But Letta Steyn explained that Manie didn't really mean the things he said. She said it was just that every great artist was expected to talk in that way about the place he came from.

210

So we knew it was all right, and the more offensive the things were that Manie said about us, the louder we shouted 'Hoor, hoor vir Manie.' There was a particularly enthusiastic round of applause when he said that we knew as much about art as a boomslang. His language was hotter than anything I had ever heard – except once. And that was when De Wet said what he thought of Cronje's surrender to the English at Paardeberg. We could feel that Manie's speech was the real thing. We cheered ourselves hoarse, that day.

And so Manie Kruger went. We received one letter to say that he had reached Pretoria. But after that we heard no more from him.

Yet always, when Letta Steyn spoke of Manie, it was as a child speaks of a dream, half wistfully, and always, with the voice of a wistful child, she would tell me how one day, one day he would return. And often, when it was dusk, I would see her sitting on the stoep, gazing out across the veld into the evening, down the dusty road that led between the thorn-trees and beyond the Dwarsberg, waiting for the lover who would come to her no more.

It was a long time before I again saw Manie Kruger. And then it was in Pretoria. I had gone there to interview the Volksraad member about an election promise. It was quite by accident that I saw Manie. And he was playing the concertina – playing as well as ever, I thought. I went away quickly. But what affected me very strangely was just that one glimpse I had of the green curtain of the bar in front of which Manie Kruger played.

HERMAN CHARLES BOSMAN

Unto Dust

First published, 1949

From: *Unto Dust and other Stories* (1963; 2002)

I have noticed that when a young man or woman dies, people get the feeling that there is something beautiful and touching in the event, and that it is different from the death of an old person. In the thought, say, of a girl of twenty sinking into an untimely grave, there is a sweet wistfulness that makes people talk all kinds of romantic words. She died, they say, young, she that was so full of life and so fair. She was a flower that withered before it bloomed, and it all seems so fitting and beautiful that there is a good deal of resentment, at the funeral, over the crude questions that a couple of men in plain clothes from the landdrost's office are asking about the cattle-dip.

But when you have grown old, nobody is very much interested in the manner of your dying. Nobody except you yourself, that is. And I think that your past life has got a lot to do with the way you feel when you get near the end of your days. I remember how, when he was lying on his death-bed, Andries Wessels kept on telling us that it was because of the blameless path he had trodden from his earliest years that he could compose himself in peace to lay down his burdens. And I certainly never saw a man breathe his last more tranquilly, seeing that right up to the end he kept on murmuring to us how happy he was, with heavenly hosts and invisible choirs of angels all around him.

Just before he died, he told us that the angels had even become visible. They were medium-sized angels, he said, and they had cloven hoofs and carried forks. It was obvious tht Andries Wessels's ideas were getting a bit confused by then, but all the same I never saw a man die in a more hallowed sort of calm.

Once, during the malaria season in the Eastern Transvaal, it seemed to me, when I was in a high fever and like to die, that the whole world was a big burial-ground. I thought it was the earth itself that was a graveyard, and not just those little fenced-in bits of land dotted with tombstones, in the shade of a Western Province oak tree or by the side of a Transvaal koppie. This was a nightmare that worried me a great deal, and so I was very glad, when I recovered from the fever, to think that we Boers had properly marked-out places on our farms for white people to be laid to rest in, in a civilised Christian way, instead of having to be buried just anyhow, along with a dead wild-cat, maybe, or a Bushman with a clay-pot and things.

When I mentioned this to my friend, Stoffel Oosthuizen, who was in the Low Country with me at the time, he agreed with me wholeheartedly. There were people who talked in a high-flown way of death as the great leveller, he said, and those high-flown people also declared that everyone was made kin by death. He would still like to see those things proved, Stoffel Oosthuizen said. After all, that was one of the reasons why the Boers trekked away into the Transvaal and the Free State, he said, because the British Government wanted to give the vote to any Cape Coloured person walking about with a *kroes* head and big cracks in his feet.

The first time he heard that sort of talk about death coming to all of us alike, and making all of us equal, Stoffel Oosthuizen's suspicions were aroused. It sounded like out of a speech made by one of those liberal Cape politicians, he explained.

I found something very comforting in Stoffel Oosthuizen's words.

Then, to illustrate his contention, Stoffel Oosthuizen told me a story of an incident that took place in a bygone Transvaal Kafir War. I don't know whether he told the story incorrectly, or whether it was just that kind of strory, but, by the time he had finished, all my uncertainties had, I discovered, come back to me.

'You can go and look at Hans Welman's tombstone any time you are at Nietverdiend,' Stoffel Oosthuizen said. 'The slab of red sandstone is weathered by now, of course, seeing how long ago it all happened. But the inscription is still legible. I was with Hans Welman on that morning when he fell. Our commando had been ambushed by the kafirs and was retreating. I could do nothing for Hans Welman. Once, when I looked round, I saw a tall kafir bending over him and plunging an assegai into him. Shortly afterwards I saw a kafir stripping the clothes off Hans Welman. A yellow kafir dog was yelping excitedly around his black master. Although I was in grave danger myself, with several dozen kafirs making straight for me on foot through the bush, the fury I felt a the sight of what that tall kafir was doing made me hazard a last shot. I pressed the trigger. My luck was in. I saw the kafir fall forward beside the naked body of Hans Welman. Then I set spurs to my horse and galloped off at full speed, with the foremost of my pursuers already almost upon me. The last I saw was that yellow dog bounding up to his master – whom I had wounded mortally, as we were to discover later.

'As you know, that kafir war dragged on for a long time. There were few pitched battles. Mainly, what took place were bush skirmishes, like the one in which Hans Welman lost his life.

'After about six months, quiet of a sort was restored to the Marico and Zoutpansberg districts. Then the day came when I went out, in company of a handful of other burghers, to fetch the remains of Hans Welman, at his widow's request, for burial in the little cemetery plot on the farm. We took a coffin with us on a Cape-cart.

'We located the scene of the skirmish without difficulty. Indeed, Hans Welman had been killed not very far from his own farm, which had been temporarily abandoned, together with the other farms in that part, during the time that the trouble with the kafirs had lasted. We drove up to the spot where I remembered having seen Hans Welman lying dead on the ground, with the tall kafir next to him. From a distance I again saw that yellow dog. He slipped away into the bush at our approach. I could not help feeling that there was something rather stirring about the beast's fidelity, even though it was bestowed on a dead kafir.

'We were now confronted with a queer situation. We found that what was left of Hans and the kafir consisted of little more than pieces of sun-dried flesh and the dismembered fragments of bleached skeletons. The sun and wild animals and birds of prey had done their work. There was a heap of human bones, and here and there leathery strips of blackened flesh. But we could not tell which was the white man and which the kafir. To make it still more confusing, a lot of bones were missing altogether, having no doubt been dragged away by wild animals into their lairs in the bush. Another thing was that Hans Welman and that kafir had been just about the same size.'

Stoffel Oosthuizen paused in his narrative, and I let my imagination dwell for a moment on that situation. And I realised just how those Boers must have felt about it: about the thought of bringing the remains of a Transvaal burgher home to his widow for Christian burial, and perhaps having a lot of kafir bones mixed up with the burgher – lying with him in the same tomb on which the mauve petals from the oleander overhead would fall.

'I remember one of our party saying that that was the worst of these kafir wars,' Stoffel Oosthuizen continued. 'If it had been a war against the English, and part of a dead Englishman had got lifted into that coffin by mistake, it wouldn't have mattered so much,' he said.

There seemed to me in this story to be something as strange as the African veld. Stoffel said that the little party of Boers spent almost a whole afternoon with the remains in order to try to get the white man sorted out from the kafir. By the evening they had laid all they could find of what seemed like Hans Welman's bones in the coffin in the Cape-cart. The rest of the bones and flesh they buried on the spot.

Stoffel Oosthuizen added that, no mattter what the difference in the colour of their skin had been, it was impossible to say that the kafir's bones were less white than Hans Welman's. Nor was it possible to say that the kafir's sun-dried flesh was any blacker than the white man's. Alive, you couldn't go wrong in distinguishing between a white man and a kafir. Dead, you had great difficulty in telling them apart.

'Naturally we burghers felt very bitter about the whole affair,' Stoffel Oosthuizen said, 'and our resentment was something that we couldn't explain, quite. Afterwards, several other men who were there that day told me that they had the same feelings of suppressed anger that I had. They wanted somebody – just once – to make a remark such as "in death they were not divided". Then you would have seen an outburst all right. Nobody did anything like that, however. We all knew better. Two days later a funeral service was conducted in the little cemetery on the Welman farm, and shortly afterwards the sandstone memorial was erected that you can still see there.'

That was the story Stoffel Oosthuizen told me after I had recovered from the fever. It was a story that, as I have said, had in it features as strange as the African veld. But it brought me no peace in my broodings after that attack of malaria. Especially when Stoffel Oosthuizen spoke of how he had occasion, one clear night when the stars shone, to pass that quiet graveyard on the Welman farm. Something leapt up from the mound beside the sandstone slab. It gave him quite a turn, Stoffel Oosthuizen said, for the third time – and in that way – to come across that yellow kafir dog.

HERMAN CHARLES BOSMAN

Birth Certificate

First published, 1950

From: *Idle Talk: Voorkamer Stories 1* (1999)

It was when At Naudé told us what he had read in the newspaper about a man who had thought all his life that he was White, and had then discovered that he was Coloured, that the story of Flippus Biljon was called to mind. I mean, we all knew the story of Flippus Biljon. But because it was still early afternoon we did not immediately make mention of Flippus. Instead, we discussed, at considerable length, other instances that were within our knowledge of people who had grown up as one sort of person and had discovered in later life that they were in actual fact quite a different sort of person.

Many of these stories that we recalled in Jurie Steyn's voorkamer as the shadows of the thorn-trees lengthened were based only on hearsay. It was the kind of story that you had heard, as a child, at your grandmother's knee. But your grandmother would never admit, of course, that she had heard that story at *her* grandmother's knee. Oh, no. She could remember very clearly how it all happened, just like it was yesterday. And she could tell you the name of the farm. And the name of the landdrost who was summoned to take note of the extraordinary occurrence, when it had to do with a more unusual sort of changeling, that is. And she would recall the solemn manner in which the landdrost took off his hat when he said that there were many things that were beyond human understanding.

Similarly now, in the voorkamer, when we recalled stories of white children that had been carried off by a Bushman or a baboon or a werewolf, even, and had been brought up in the wilds and without any proper religious instruction, then we also did not think it necessary to explain where we had first heard those stories. We spoke as though we had been actually present at some stage of the affair – more usually at the last scene, where the child, now grown to manhood and needing trousers and a pair of braces and a hat, gets restored to his parents and the magistrate after studying the birth certificate says that there are things in this world that baffle the human mind.

And while the shadows under the thorn-trees grew longer the stories we told in Jurie Steyn's voorkamer grew, if not longer, then, at least, taller.

'But this isn't the point of what I have been trying to explain,' At Naudé interrupted a story of Gysbert van Tonder's that was getting a bit confused in parts, through Gysbert van Tonder not being quite clear as to what a werewolf was. 'When I read that bit in the newspaper I started wondering how must a man *feel*, after he has grown up with adopted parents and he discovers, quite late in life, through seeing his birth certificate for the first time, that he isn't White, after all. That is what I am trying to get at. Supposing Gysbert were to find out suddenly −'

At Naudé pulled himself up short. Maybe there were one or two things about a werewolf that Gysbert van Tonder wasn't too sure about, and he would allow himself to be corrected by Oupa Bekker on such points. But there were certain things he wouldn't stand for.

'All right,' At Naudé said hastily, 'I don't mean Gysbert van Tonder, specially. What I am trying to get at is, how would any one of us feel? How would any White man feel, if he has passed as White all his life, and he sees for the first time, from his birth certificate, that his grandfather was Coloured? I mean, how would he *feel*? Think of that awful moment when he looks in the palm of his hands and he sees …'

'He can have that awful moment,' Gysbert van Tonder said. 'I've looked at the palm of my hand. It's a White man's palm. And my fingernails have also got proper half-moons.'

At Naudé said he had never doubted that. No, there was no need for Gysbert van Tonder to come any closer and show him. He could see quite well enough just from where he was sitting. After Chris Welman had pulled Gysbert van Tonder back on to the rusbank by his jacket, counselling him not to do anything foolish, since At Naudé did not mean *him*, Oupa Bekker started talking about a White child in Schweizer-Reneke that had been stolen out of its cradle by a family of baboons.

'I haven't seen that cradle myself,' Oupa Bekker acknowledged, modestly. 'But I met many people who have. After the child had been stolen, neighbours from as far as the Orange River came to look at that cradle. And when they looked at it they admired the particular way that Heilart Nortjé − that was the child's father − had set about making his household furniture, with glued klinkpenne in the joints, and all. But the real interest about the cradle was that it was empty, proving that the child had been stolen by baboons. I remember how one neighbour, who was not on very good terms with Heilart Nortjé, went about the district saying that it could only have *been* baboons.

'But it was many years before Heilart Nortjé and his wife saw their child again. By *saw*, I mean getting near enough to be able to talk to him and ask him how he was getting on. For he was always too quick, from the way the baboons had brought him up. At intervals Heilart Nortjé and his wife would see the tribe of baboons sitting on a rant, and their son, young Heilart, would be in the company of the baboons. And once, through his field-glasses, Heilart had been able to observe his son for quite a few moments. His son was then engaged in picking up a stone and laying hold of a scorpion that was underneath it. The speed with which his son pulled off the scorpion's sting and proceeded to eat up the rest of the scorpion whole filled the father's heart of Heilart Nortjé with a deep sense of pride.

'I remember how Heilart talked about it. "Real intelligence," Heilart announced with his chest stuck out. "A real baboon couldn't have done it quicker or better. I called my wife, but she was a bit too late. All she could see was him looking as pleased as anything and scratching himself. And my wife and I held hands and we smiled at each other and we asked each other, where does he get it all from?"'

'But then there were times again when that tribe of baboons would leave the Schweizer-Reineke area and go deep into the Kalahari, and Heilart Nortjé and his wife would know nothing about what was happening to their son, except through reports from farmers near whose homesteads the baboons had passed. Those farmers had a lot to say about what happened to some of their sheep, not to talk of their mealies and watermelons. And Heilart would be very bitter about those farmers. Begrudging his son a few prickly-pears, he said.

'And it wasn't as though he hadn't made every effort to get his son back, Heilart said, so that he could go to catechism classes, since he was almost of age to be confirmed. He had set all sorts of traps for his son, Heilart said, and he had also thought of shooting the baboons, so that it would be easier, after that, to get his son back. But there was always the danger, firing into a pack like that, of shooting his own son.'

'The neighbour that I have spoken of before,' Oupa Bekker continued, 'who was not very well disposed towards Heilart Nortjé, said that the real reason Heilart didn't shoot was because he didn't always know – actually *know* – which was his son and which was one of the more flat-headed kees-baboons.'

It seemed that this was going to be a very long story. Several of us started getting restive … So Johnny Coen asked Oupa Bekker, in a polite sort of way, to tell us how it all ended.

'Well, Heilart Nortjé caught his son, afterwards,' Oupa Bekker said. 'But I am not sure if Heilart was altogether pleased about it. His son was so hard to tame. And then the way he caught him. It was with the simplest sort of baboon trap of all … Yes, *that* one. A calabash with a hole in it just big enough for you to put you hand in, empty, but that you can't get your hand out of again when you're clutching a fistful of mealies that was put at the bottom of the calabash. Heilart Nortjé never got over that, really. He felt it was a very shameful thing that had happened to him. The thought that his son, in whom he had taken so much pride, should have allowed himself to be caught in the simplest form of monkey-trap.'

When Oupa Bekker paused, Jurie Steyn said that it was indeed a sad story, and it was no doubt, perfectly true. There was just a certain tone in Jurie Steyn's voice that made Oupa Bekker continue.

'True in every particular,' Oupa Bekker declared, nodding his head a good number of times. 'The landdrost came over to see about it, too. They sent for the landdrost so that he could make a report about it. I was there, that afternoon, in Heilart Nortje's voorkamer, when the landdrost came. And there were a good number of other people, also. And Heilart Nortje's son, half-tamed in some ways but still baboon-wild in others, was there also. The landdrost studied the birth certificate very carefully. Then the landdrost said that what he had just been present at surpassed ordinary human understanding. And the landdrost took off his hat in a very solemn fashion.

'We all felt very embarrassed when Heilart Nortje's son grabbed the hat out of the landdrost's hand and started biting pieces out of the crown.'

When Oupa Bekker said those words it seemed to us like the end of a story. Consequently, we were disappointed when At Naudé started making further mention of that piece of news he had read in the daily paper. So there was nothing else for it but that we had to talk about Flippus Biljon. For Flippus Biljon's case was just the opposite of the case of the man that At Naude's newspaper wrote about.

Because he had been adopted by a Coloured family, Flippus Biljon had always regarded himself as a Coloured man. And then one day, quite by accident, Flippus Biljon saw his birth certificate. And from that birth certificate it was clear that Flippus Biljon was as White as you or I. You can imagine how Flippus Biljon must have felt about it. Especially after he had gone to see the magistrate at Bekkersdal, and the magistrate, after studying the birth certificate, confirmed the fact that Flippus Biljon was a White man.

'Thank you, baas,' Flippus Biljon said. 'Thank you very much, my basie.'

HERMAN CHARLES BOSMAN

Funeral Earth

First published, 1950

From: *Unto Dust and other Stories* (1963; 2002)

We had a difficult task, that time (Oom Schalk Lourens said), teaching Sijefu's tribe of Mtosas to become civilised. But they did not show any appreciation. Even after we had set fire to their huts in a long row round the slopes of Abjaterskop, so that you could see the smoke almost as far as Nietverdiend, the Mtosas remained just about as unenlightened as ever. They would retreat into the mountains, where it was almost impossible for our commando to follow them on horseback. They remained hidden in the thick bush.

'I can sense these kaffirs all around us,' Veldkornet Andries Joubert said to our seksie of about a dozen burghers when we had come to a halt in a clearing amid the tall withaaks. 'I have been in so many kaffir wars that I can almost *smell* when there are kaffirs lying in wait for us with assegais. And yet all day long you never see a single Mtosa that you can put a lead bullet through.'

He also said that if this war went on much longer we would forget altogether how to handle a gun. And what would we do then, when we again had to fight England?

Young Fanie Louw, who liked saying funny things, threw back his head and pretended to be sniffing the air with discrimination. 'I can smell a whole row of assegais with broad blades and short handles,' Fanie Louw said. 'The stabbing assegai has got more of a selon's rose sort of smell about it than a throwing spear. The selon's rose that you come across in graveyards.'

The veldkornet did not think Fanie Louw's remark very funny, however. And he said we all knew that this was the first time Fanie Louw had ever been on commando. He also said that if a crowd of Mtosas were to leap out of the bush on to us suddenly, then you wouldn't be able to smell Fanie Louw for dust. The veldkornet also said another thing that was even better.

Our group of burghers laughed heartily. Maybe Veldkornet Joubert could not think out a lot of nonsense to say just on the spur of the moment, in the way that Fanie Louw could, but give our veldkornet a chance to reflect, first, and he would come out with the kind of remark that you just had to admire.

Indeed, from the very next thing Veldkornet Joubert said, you could see how deep was his insight. And he did not have to think much, either, then.

'Let us get out of here as quick as hell, men,' he said, speaking very distinctly. 'Perhaps the kaffirs are hiding out in the open turf-lands, where there are no trees. And none of this long tamboekie grass, either.'

When we emerged from that stretch of bush we were glad to discover that our veldkornet had been right, like always.

For another group of Transvaal burghers had hit on the same strategy.

'We were in the middle of the bush,' their leader, Combrinck, said to us, after we had exchanged greetings. 'A very thick part of the bush, with withaaks standing up like skeletons. And we suddenly thought the Mtosas might have gone into hiding out here in the open.'

You could see that Veldkornet Joubert was pleased to think that he had, on his own, worked out the same tactics as Combrinck, who was known as a skilful kaffir-fighter. All the same, it seemed as though this was going to be a long war.

It was then that, again speaking out of his turn, Fanie Louw said that all we needed now was for the kommandant himself to arrive there in the middle of the turf-lands with the main body of burghers. 'Maybe we should even go back to Pretoria to see if the Mtosas aren't perhaps hiding in the Volksraad,' he said. 'Passing laws and things. You know how cheeky a Mtosa is.'

'It can't be worse than some of the laws that the Volksraad is already passing now,' Combrinck said, gruffly. From that we could see that why he had not himself been appointed kommandant was because he had voted against the president in the last elections.

By that time the sun was sitting not more than about two Cape feet above a tall koppie on the horizon. Accordingly, we started looking about for a place to camp. It was muddy in the turf-lands, and there was no firewood there, but we all said that we did not mind. We would not pamper ourselves by going to sleep in the thick bush, we told one another. It was wartime, and we were on commando, and the mud of the turf-lands was good enough for *us*, we said.

It was then that an unusual thing happened.

For we suddenly did see Mtosas. We saw them from a long way off. They came out of the bush and marched right out into the open. They made no attempt to hide. We saw in amazement that they were coming straight in our direction, advancing in single file. And we observed, even from that distance, that they were unarmed. Instead of assegais and shields they carried burdens on their heads. And almost in that same moment we realised, from the heavy look of those burdens, that the carriers must be women.

For that reason we took our guns in our hands and stood waiting. Since it was women, we were naturally prepared for the lowest form of treachery.

As the column drew nearer we saw that at the head of it was Ndambe, an old native whom we knew well. For years he had been Sijefu's chief counsellor. Ndambe held up his hand. The line of women halted. Ndambe spoke. He declared that we white men were kings among kings and elephants among elephants. He also said that we were rinkhals snakes more poisonous and generally disgusting than any rinkhals snake in the country.

We knew, of course, that Ndambe was only paying us compliments in his ignorant Mtosa fashion. And so we naturally felt highly gratified. I can still remember the way Jurie Bekker nudged me in the ribs and said, 'Did you hear that?'

When Ndambe went on, however, to say that we were filthier than the spittle of a green tree toad, several burghers grew restive. They felt that there was perhaps such a thing as carrying these tribal courtesies a bit too far.

It was then that Veldkornet Joubert, slipping his finger inside the trigger guard of his gun, requested Ndambe to come to the point. By the expression on our veldkornet's face, you could see that he had had enough of compliments for one day.

They had come to offer peace, Ndambe told us then.

What the women carried on their heads were presents.

At a sign from Ndambe the column knelt in the mud of the turf-land. They brought lion and zebra skins and elephant tusks, and beads and brass bangles and, on a long grass mat, the whole haunch of a red Afrikaner ox, hide and hoof and all. And several pigs cut in half. And clay pots filled to the brim with white beer, and also – and this we prized most – witchdoctor medicines that protected you against goël spirits at night and the evil eye.

Ndambe gave another signal. A woman with a clay pot on her head rose up from the kneeling column and advanced towards us. We saw then that what she had in the pot was black earth. It was wet and almost like turf-soil. We couldn't understand what they wanted to bring us that for. As though we didn't have enough of it, right there where we were standing, and sticking to our veldskoens, and all. And yet Ndambe acted as though that was the most precious part of the peace offerings that his chief, Sijefu, had sent us.

It was when Ndambe spoke again that we saw how ignorant he and his chief and the whole Mtosa tribe were, really.

He took a handful of soil out of the pot and pressed it together between his fingers. Then he told us how honoured the Mtosa tribe was because we were waging war against them. In the past they had only had flat-faced Mshangaans with spiked knobkerries to fight against, he said, but now it was different. Our veldkornet took half a step forward, then, in case Ndambe was going to start flattering us again. So Ndambe said, simply, that the Mtosas would be glad if we came and made war against them later on, when the harvests had been gathered in. But in the meantime the tribe did not wish to continue fighting.

It was the time for sowing.

Ndambe let the soil run through his fingers, to show us how good it was. He also invited us to taste it. We declined.

We accepted the presents and peace was made. And I can still remember how Veldkornet Joubert shook his head and said, 'Can you beat the Mtosas for ignorance?'

And I can still remember what Jurie Bekker said, also. That was when something made him examine the haunch of beef more closely, and he found his own brand mark on it.

It was not long afterwards that the war came against England.

By the end of the second year of the war the Boer forces were in a very bad way. But we would not make peace. Veldkornet Joubert was now promoted to kommandant. Combrinck fell in the battle before Dalmanutha. Jurie Bekker was still with us. And so was Fanie Louw. And it was strange how attached we had grown to Fanie Louw during the years of hardship that we went through together in the field. But up to the end we had to admit that, while we had got used to his jokes, and we knew there was no harm in them, we would have preferred it that he should stop making them.

He did stop, and forever, in a skirmish near a blockhouse. We buried him in the shade of a thorn-tree. We got ready to fill in his grave, after which the kommandant would say a few words and we would bare our heads and sing a psalm. As you know, it was customary at a funeral for each mourner to take up a handful of earth and fling it in the grave.

When Kommandant Joubert stooped down and picked up his handful of earth, a strange thing happened. And I remembered that other war, against the Mtosas. And we knew – although we would not say it – what was now that longing in the hearts of each of us. For Kommandant Joubert did not straightway drop the soil into Fanie Louw's grave. Instead, he kneaded the damp ground between his fingers. It was as though he had forgotten that it was funeral earth. He seemed to be thinking not of death, then, but of life.

We patterned after him, picking up handfuls of soil and pressing it together. We felt the deep loam in it, and saw how springy it was, and we let it trickle through our fingers. And we could remember only that it was the time for sowing.

I understood then how, in an earlier war, the Mtosas had felt, they who were also farmers.

HERMAN CHARLES BOSMAN

A Bekkersdal Marathon

First published, 1950

From: *Idle Talk: Voorkamer Stories 1* (1999)

At Naudé, who had a wireless set, came into Jurie Steyn's voorkamer, where we were sitting waiting for the Government lorry from Bekkersdal, and gave us the latest news. He said that the newest thing in Europe was that young people there were going in for non-stop dancing. It was called marathon dancing, At Naudé told us, and those young people were trying to break the record for who could remain on their feet longest, dancing.

We listened for a while to what At Naudé had to say, and then we suddenly remembered a marathon event that had taken place in the little dorp of Bekkersdal – almost in our midst, you could say. What was more, there were quite a number of us sitting in Jurie Steyn's post office who had actually taken part in that non-stop affair, and without knowing that we were breaking records, and without expecting any sort of a prize for it, either.

We discussed that affair at considerable length and from all angles, and we were still talking about it when the lorry came. And we agreed that it had been in several respects an unusual occurrence. We also agreed that it was questionable whether we could have carried off things so successfully that day if it had not been for Billy Robertse.

You see, our organist at Bekkersdal was Billy Robertse. He had once been a sailor and had come to the bushveld some years before, travelling on foot. His belongings, fastened in a red handkerchief, were slung over his shoulder on a stick. Billy Robertse was journeying in that fashion for the sake of his health. He suffered from an unfortunate complaint for which he had at regular intervals to drink something out of a black bottle that he always carried handy in his jacket-pocket.

Billy Robertse would even keep that bottle beside him in the organist's gallery in case of a sudden attack. And if the hymn the predikant gave out had many verses, you could be sure that about half-way through, Billy Robertse would bring the bottle up to his mouth, leaning sideways towards what was in it. And he would put several extra twirls into the second part of the hymn.

When he first applied for the position of organist in the Bekkersdal church, Billy Robertse told the meeting of deacons that he had learnt to play the organ in a cathedral in northern Europe. Several deacons felt, then, that they could not favour his application. They said that the cathedral sounded too papist, the way Billy Robertse described it, with a dome 300 ft high and with marble apostles. But is was lucky for Billy Robertse that he was able to mention, at the following combined meeting of elders and deacons, that he had also played the piano in a South American dance hall, of which the manager had been a Presbyterian. He asked the meeting to overlook his unfortunate past, saying that he had had a hard life, and anybody could make mistakes. In any case, he had never cared much for the Romish atmosphere of the cathedral, he said, and had been happier in the dance hall.

In the end, Billy Robertse got the appointment. But in his sermons for several Sundays after that the predikant, Dominee Welthagen, had spoken very strongly against the evils of dance halls. He described those places of awful sin in such burning words that at least one young man went to see Billy Robertse, privately, with a view to taking lessons in playing the piano.

But Billy Robertse was a good musician. And he took a deep interest in his work. And he said that when he sat down on the organist's stool behind the pulpit, and his fingers were flying over the keyboards, and he was pulling out the stops, and his feet were pressing down the notes that sent the deep bass tones through the pipes – then he felt that he could play all day, he said.

I don't suppose he guessed that he would one day be put to the test, however.

It all happened through Dominee Welthagen one Sunday morning going into a trance in the pulpit. And we did not realise that he was in a trance. It was an illness that overtook him in a strange and sudden fashion.

At each service the predikant, after reading a passage from the Bible, would lean forward with his hand on the pulpit rail and give out the number of the hymn we had to sing. For years his manner of conducting the service had been exactly the same. He would say, for instance: 'We will now sing Psalm 82, verses 1 to 4.' Then he would allow his head to sink forward onto his chest and he would remain rigid, as though in prayer, until the last notes of the hymn died away in the church.

Now, on that particular morning, just after he had announced the number of the psalm, without mentioning what verses, Dominee Welthagen again took a firm grip on the pulpit rail and allowed his head to sink forward onto his breast. We did not realise that he had fallen into a trance of a peculiar character that kept his body standing upright while his mind was a blank. We learnt that only later.

In the meantime, while the organ was playing over the opening bars, we began to realise that Dominee Welthagen had not indicated how many verses we had to sing. But he would discover his mistake, we thought, after we had been singing for a few minutes.

All the same, one or two of the younger members of the congregation did titter, slightly, when they took up their hymnbooks. For Dominee Welthagen had given out Psalm 119. And everybody knows that Psalm 119 has 176 verses.

This was a church service that will never be forgotten in Bekkersdal.

We sang the first verse and then the second and then the third. When we got to about the sixth verse and the minister still gave no sign that it would be the last, we assumed that he wished us to sing the first eight verses. For, if you open your hymnbook, you'll see that Psalm 119 is divided into sets of eight verses, each ending with the word 'Pouse'.

We ended the last notes of verse eight with more than an ordinary number of turns and twirls, confident that at any moment Dominee Welthagen would raise his head and let us know that we could sing 'Amen'.

It was when the organ started up very slowly and solemnly with the music for verse nine that a real feeling of disquiet overcame the congregation. But, of course, we gave no sign of what went on in our minds. We held Dominee Welthagen in too much veneration.

Nevertheless, I would rather not say too much about our feelings, when verse followed verse and Pouse succeeded Pouse, and still Dominee Welthagen made no sign that we had sung long enough, or that there was anything unusual in what he was demanding of us.

After they had recovered from their first surprise, the members of the church council conducted themselves in a most exemplary manner. Elders and deacons tiptoed up and down the aisles, whispering words of reassurance to such members of the congregation, men as well as women, who gave signs of wanting to panic.

At one stage it looked as though we were going to have trouble from the organist. That was when Billy Robertse, at the end of the 34th verse, held up his black bottle and signalled quietly to the elders to indicate that his medicine was finished. At the end of the 35th verse he made signals of a less quiet character, and again at the end of the 36th verse. That was when Elder Landsman tiptoed out of the church and went round to the Konsistorie, where the Nagmaal wine was kept. When Elder Landsman came back into the church he had a long black bottle half hidden under his *manel*. He took the bottle up to the organist's gallery, still walking on tiptoe.

At verse 61 there was almost a breakdown. That was when a message came from the back of the organ, where Koster Claassen and the assistant verger, whose task it was to turn the handle that kept the organ supplied with wind, were in a state near to exhaustion. So it was Deacon Cronje's turn to go tiptoeing out of the church. Deacon Cronje was head warder at the local gaol. When he came back it was with three burly Native convicts in striped jerseys, who also went through the church on tiptoe. They arrived just in time to take over the handle from Koster Claassen and the assistant verger.

At verse 98 the organist again started making signals about his medicine. Once more Elder Landsman went round to the Konsistorie. This time he was accompanied by another elder and a deacon, and they stayed away somewhat longer than the time when Elder Landsman had gone on his own. On their return the deacon bumped into a small hymnbook table at the back of the church. Perhaps it was because the deacon was a fat, red-faced man, and not used to tiptoeing.

At verse 124 the organist signalled again, and the same three members of the church council filed out to the Konsistorie, the deacon walking in front this time.

It was about then that the pastor of the Full Gospel Apostolic Faith Church, about whom Dominee Welthagen had in the past used almost as strong language as about the Pope, came up to the front gate of the church to see what was afoot. He lived near our church and, having heard the same hymn-tune being played over and over for about eight hours, he was a very amazed man. Then he saw the door of the Konsistorie open, and two elders and a deacon coming out, walking on tiptoe – they having apparently forgotten that they were not in church then. When the pastor saw one of the elders hiding a black bottle under his *manel*, a look of understanding came over his features. The pastor walked off, shaking his head.

At verse 152 the organist signalled again. This time Elder Landsman and the other elder went out alone. The deacon stayed behind in the deacon's bench, apparently in deep thought. The organist signalled again, for the last time, at verse 169. So you can imagine how many visits the two elders made to the Konsistorie altogether.

The last verse came, and the last line of the last verse. This time it had to be 'Amen'. Nothing could stop it. I would rather not describe the state that the congregation was in. And by then the three Native convicts, red stripes and all, were, in the Bakhatla tongue, threatening mutiny. 'Aa-m-e-e-n' came from what sounded like less than a score of voices, hoarse with singing.

The organ music ceased.

Maybe it was the sudden silence that at last brought Dominee Welthagen out of his long trance. He raised his head and looked slowly about him. His gaze travelled over his congregation, and then, looking at the windows, he saw that it was night. We understood right away what was going on in Dominee Welthagen's mind. He thought he had just come into the pulpit, and that this was the beginning of the evening service. We realised that, during all the time we had been singing, the predikant had been in a state of unconsciousness.

Once again Dominee Welthagen took a firm grip on the pulpit rail. His head again started drooping forward onto his breast. But before he went into a trance for the second time, he gave the hymn for the evening service.

'We will,' Dominee Welthagen announced, 'sing Psalm 119.'

FRANK BROWNLEE

The Cannibal's Bird
From: *Lion and Jackal* … (1938)

The girls of a certain village went one day to fetch red clay for colouring their clothing and bodies.

The day being warm, the suggestion of one of the girls that they should bathe in a pool in the neighbouring river was readily agreed to.

The girls sported for a while in the water, then dressed themselves and made for home, each carrying her lumps of red clay. When they had gone some distance a girl who was daughter of the chief of their village, found that she had left one of her ornaments at the pool where she and her companions had bathed. She asked one girl, then another, and another to accompany her back to the pool, but each refused; so the chief's daughter had to return alone.

As she approached the water a cannibal sprang out from the reeds, caught her, and put her in his bag. The girl was very frightened and lay still in the bag. The cannibal carried her off and took her to a village. When he got there the people asked what he had in his bag. He said it was a bird, and if he were given meat he would make his bird sing. These people gave him meat and he caused the girl to sing. So the cannibal went from village to village, and on being given meat he caused the girl, who he always said was a bird, to sing.

Meantime the chief missed his daughter, and the girls who had gone with her to fetch red clay, being questioned, said that the daughter of the chief, having reached womanhood, had, as custom required, 'gone into seclusion'.

With this explanation the chief was satisfied, and in celebration of his daughter's coming of age killed a fat ox. The ox was cut up, and the meat apportioned among people who had gathered at the chief's kraal.

The boys, not being permitted to eat with the men, took their portion of meat to the bush, where they lit a fire and began to grill it. As the meat was grilling, the cannibal, who had the girl in his bag, came up. The boys asked what he had in his bag. As before, he said he had a bird in his bag and if he were given meat he would make the bird sing.

The boys gave the cannibal some meat, and when the girl sang, one of the boys who was the son of the chief, thought he recognised the voice as that of his sister, but being afraid to ask the cannibal to let him see what was in the bag, he advised him to go to the place of the chief where, he said, there was plenty of meat.

The cannibal went to the chief's village, and when he got there, without asking for meat he made his bird sing. The chief was very anxious to see the bird but the cannibal would not open his bag. The chief offered him an ox, then two oxen, if he would open his bag, but the cannibal refused.

Then one of the councillors, speaking to the chief in whispers, arranged a plan. The cannibal was asked to go and fetch water on the promise that on his return he would be given plenty of meat. The cannibal said he would fetch water if everyone promised not to touch his bag till his return. The people agreed to this.

The cannibal was given a leaky pot with which to fetch the water. While he was away the chief opened the bag and released the girl. He did not at first recognise her as his daughter, the other girls having told him that she was in the hut of seclusion, but when he found out who she was and how he had been deceived by the other girls, he gave orders that they be killed. After that he put scorpions and snakes in the bag.

When the cannibal came back with water, he complained of the leaky pot and said it had taken him a long time to patch up the cracks with clay. He was given plenty of meat and when he had eaten it he picked up his bag and went on his way.

When he got to his home he bade his wife make a fire and call his friends to a feast he would make ready for them.

Expecting a great feast, his friends came in numbers. When the bag was opened and only snakes and scorpions were found in it, the other cannibals were so angry that they killed their host and ate him.

HIE DHLOMO

The Barren Woman

Written *c*1940

From: *Collected Works* (1985)

[handwritten annotation: Mamkazi after being barren for four years finally concieves, however, her daughter gets smothered by blanket & dies. she exchange the twin baby]

The Bantu love of children is well known. This love is partly natural, just like that of other human beings. It is partly the result of a social system in which lobola, the demands and difficulties of labour, and a man's prestige and status in society all put a premium on the size of the family. Because of lobola girls are considered as valuable as boys. Perhaps more. Whatever may be said about the evils of the system today, in tribal society lobola enhanced the status of a woman and gave her protection and a high niche in a society where men held autocratic powers, and great value was placed on boys as potential military power.

Barrenness in women was a stigma and disgrace. Even today most Bantu people spend large sums of money and endure many hardships to fight it.

In the past African women were also reputed for their remarkable powers of surviving antenatal, actual labour and postnatal troubles. Just as warriors regarded death as a matter of course, women took giving birth in their daily stride, as it were – not as an exceptional event requiring special preparation and associated with anxiety.

Of the two modern social evils reported from time to time, child stealing (although unknown in Bantu communities) is more in line with the tribal tradition of love for children, and the abandonment of unwanted babies, foreign to it. But neither child stealing nor adoption as we know it was practised in tribal society. That is why barrenness was such a tragedy.

The story of Mamkazi Zondi is interesting because it involves most of the elements above. It is simple, has no dramatic climax, and no element of surprise. She lived in the remote but thriving and, therefore, well-populated village of Manzini. As in many other rural areas part of the population was tribal and 'heathen', and part 'Christian' – meaning anyone who wore European clothes, sent their children to school, lived in square houses no matter how humble and dilapidated, or did not conform to tribal patterns one way or another.

Mamkazi belonged to the 'Christian' group, had been married for three years, and would have been happy and her story not worth telling but for one curse.

230

She was barren.

She and her husband had gone to great trouble and wasted a fortune trying to get a baby. European doctors and African herbalists and witchdoctors had been consulted without success.

The couple were unhappy. Temba Zondi, her husband, loved her and was kind and devoted to her. Except on three or four occasions when they had had exceptionally violent quarrels, he never blamed her for her defect. However, the curse hung over their house and life. She was reminded about it frequently and in many ways. When her husband silently stared at her or took more than usual interest in a neighbour's or visitor's child, it hurt her deeply for she felt he was chiding and blaming her bitterly, if silently. Garrulous or unfeeling and spiteful neighbours gossiped about it. Innocent visitors and old, distant acquaintances who meant no harm hurt her when they asked if she had no child yet.

Of all her friends and neighbours, the best and most intimate was Ntombi Mate. But Mamkazi did not know whether to regard Ntombi as a blessing or a curse, a solace to her soul or a thorn in her flesh.

Unlike most 'Christian' women of her age in the village, who could only read and write (the younger generation were more progressive), Ntombi was considered 'educated'. She had passed Standard Six, had travelled to several big towns, and had worked for some time in a large mission hospital where she acquired a rudimentary knowledge of midwifery. Although she had not been out of Manzini village for years, was married and had a big family, she still retained her reputation and status. She was the unofficial, unqualified, but useful district midwife of the place. Whether she thought and believed it was professionally necessary or she was too lazy (and had grown fat) and too snobbish (was she not above others?), she insisted that those who needed her help must come to her 'clinic', which was a large hut with four beds. She never answered calls to homes, no matter what happened. Homes were far away and had no comforts, the way was rough, and calls came at inconvenient hours of the day and night. Well known and never without work, she was yet never inundated with cases because most women were strong and healthy enough to give birth successfully in their homes, and the others did not care about clinics and hospitals except in cases where there were complications.

The snag in the deep and warm friendship of Mamkazi and Ntombi was that whenever the latter referred to her work, Mamkazi was reminded of her plight. Otherwise each woman could do almost anything for the other. And Ntombi had done all to help her friend.

During the fourth year of her marriage, Mamkazi conceived. The fact lifted her to the seventh heaven of ecstasy, pride and expectation. But there were times when she was slain by doubts, fears and worse. Doubts and fears about miscarriage, stillbirth, and other accidents. Worse? Possibly. There was the sad case of the Kozas where the coming of a child after five years of barren marriage completely wrecked their home because of the allegation – supported by some and denied by others, and not open to proof or disproof in that backward society – that Koza's wife had been unfaithful and the child was illegitimate.

Mamkazi's fears were unfounded. Zondi was intoxicated with joy, and treated her with poignant tenderness and devotion. Doctors and hospitals were very far away. But urged by their own gratitude and caution and Ntombi's strong advice, Mamkazi paid four visits to the nearest town to consult a doctor. When the time came she, of course, placed herself under the care of her friend who was determined to display to the utmost her knowledge and experience on this occasion.

The baby came without trouble. It was a girl. Mamkazi was so fit that she could have returned home the next day and gone about her business. Two other women were in the clinic at that time. The same night they, too, had children, one a girl, and the other twins – a boy and a girl. The twins were not identical – but at the time this struck no one, not even Ntombi, as being significant.

The following night Mamkazi's heaven changed into hell. Zondi had almost been overpowered with joy and pride, and had found it difficult to leave the clinic even for a few moments or to return home in the night. Ntombi and Mamkazi had congratulated one another a dozen times. Many friends had come and stood amazed at the 'miracle'. Ntombi had openly given special attention to her friend. Expensive and lovely things had been bought for the baby. Everything was in striking contrast to the two other poor women, one of whom was a 'Christian' and the other – the mother of the twins – a tribal person.

Ntombi insisted on cleanliness and on what other 'modern' professional rules and methods she knew. One of these was not to cover heavily with blankets the new arrivals (and other sick persons), as fond mothers and relatives were inclined to do.

In the still hours of the second night, Mamkazi, who could hardly sleep for joy, woke up to find that her precious child had been smothered to death! It was impossible! A thousand-to-one-chance accident! And of all people, this to happen to her! No. God would not let it happen!

'O God, Almighty Father! It cannot be! Give life to my child! Restore it back to me! How can God be so cruel, mock with such evil! After years in hell, to lift me into heaven for a moment, only to plunge me back into deeper hell! Hear, Holiest Father, hear. I kiss and beg at Thy feet!'

Thus she prayed silently and insanely. But the ways of God are unfathomable. The child was dead. Demented, she had no power to cry out aloud or rave. After trying gently but excitedly to stir and suckle the baby into life, some demoniacal spirit descended upon her, making her cool and determined, and propelling her to some devilish scheme. There is no God! Why stand in the way of the Devil, then! In a flash, the evil plan was born and executed. Mechanically, rapidly, and with mad courage and precision, she undressed her dead baby, exchanged it with the scantily attired twin girl whom she dressed as her child, wrapped up the twin boy and the dead child heavily in a blanket as she had found them and retired to her bed in a state of nervous and insane anxiety.

'I have done it! Who will find out! Who dare accuse me! Three of us have girls — and how can they tell? I have the right to the living baby! It is mine! She does not need it. She has many other children. Come close to me, my dear one. Live and thrive! There is life in you, and your life is my life, hope and light. Let us sleep in peace.'

A raving maniac, she could not sleep, but managed to lie still.

As if by some evil spell, she had carried out her plan without disturbance. Hardly an hour later, a piercing cry rent the clinic. Soon there was bedlam. The mother of the twins had awakened and made the tragic discovery. Her lamentations were broadcast far and wide. The clinic was soon filled by the agitated Ntombi, members of her family and people who lived close by. The rare 'accident' left everyone dumbfounded and mentally paralysed. The mother of the twins could not be consoled.

The next day the whole village knew about the strange happenings. The husbands of the three women had rushed to the clinic early to stand by and comfort their wives. So did others. The tragedy was discussed excitedly, if in whispers.

After some time, the excitement and sense of grief subsided, and life in the village and in the families directly concerned took its normal course. No one had the least suspicion about foul play. The women of the village were amazed and impressed that Ntombi's constant and seemingly unnecessary and irritating warning about wrapping children in heavy blankets — advice she gave purely on 'hygienic' and snobbish grounds — had been justified so tragically. The old tribal superstition that giving birth to twins is bad luck was revived for a time. It helped seal the matter as 'natural' and in accordance with hoary tradition and sacrosanct custom.

The three women's agitation, sallowness and wild behaviour were considered natural and excusable under the circumstances. This was especially true of Mamkazi who received special and universal sympathy as her rare blessing coincided with such a misfortune. Of the three women, she was the most pitied and 'understood' for whatever strange behaviour and attitude she adopted. Her husband and friends repeatedly congratulated and consoled her with the words, 'Thank God, it did not happen to you!'

The excitement subsided and life in the village and in the families concerned took a normal course. No one had the least suspicion of foul play. Not so! Nature is 'scientific', omniscient and deeply jealous and revengeful when her course and ends are disturbed.

One person was keenly suspicious about the whole episode. It was Ntombi. Instinctively and intuitively the truth was revealed to her through a glass darkly. However, as a rational human being and a realist, she held her peace. But there was conflict, not peace, within her. She had carefully taken notice of Mamkazi's unnatural behaviour and agitation on the fateful day and after. More experienced, observant and trained than others, including the three mothers, she could tell the difference between newborn babes – in weight, behaviour, and even in physical features that would be imperceptible to others. Besides, she was the only person who had seen and handled all three girls. She was sure that there was something wrong. But was it possible? How could mediocre-minded and nervous Mamkazi have conceived and executed without help and discovery such a foul act?

What was she to do! The knowledge that, in bigger and more accessible centres, the thing would have led to an embarrassing, and even incriminating investigation, added to her uneasiness and inner conflict. It might be a sin in the eyes of God, also.

Thus, while the rest of the village had forgotten about the occurrence, two women – Mamkazi and Ntombi – remained restless, unhappy and guarded.

Time heals, makes us forget and helps solve problems. Pleasant but deceitful philosophy! Time festers old wounds, opens patched-up scars, complicates and increases problems, and makes us remember and grow afraid at every turn. Time plagues, derides, incapacitates.

Far from achieving happiness and triumph, Mamkazi found that she had set herself a problem that became more complicated as time went on. If someone spoke of Jabu Buthelezi, the mother of the twins, her child or her family, she became apprehensive. If she herself met one of the family, it was worse.

The passage of years had wrought many changes in Manzini village. The population had increased rapidly. With the opening up of new roads and the introduction of a bus service, there was more progress. A European district surgeon now visited the village on certain days of the week. He had a trained nurse assisting him. Ntombi's 'clinic' was a thing of the past. There was a fine, large new school, and the local store had been expanded and the goods improved in quantity and quality. There was no need for children and adults to trudge many weary miles to the distant school or the better store. Some tribal families – among them the Buthelezis – had become 'Christians'.

Mamkazi was reminded of her act at every turn.

'Ma! I met Zidumo Buthelezi and his mother at the store,' her daughter Simangele would report innocently and excitedly. 'His mother said "I love you as much as my boy. You look like one another." She kissed me and gave me sweets.'

Returning from a beer-drinking party her husband would blabber, 'And there was Buthelezi who said that he would be disappointed if our little Simangele did not marry into his family when she grew up. He is crazy about the child, just like the others. Ha! Ha!'

On such occasions she would weep, burst out into a violent temper or behave in some inexplicable manner. And remarks and incidents of this kind came every day.

She had quarrelled with her husband when she tried arbitrarily to restrict the movements of the little girl; when she said the child must be sent to the distant not the local school; when she suggested that they should go and live in another district. Zondi could not understand all this, and they became increasingly unhappy.

Mamkazi and Ntombi were hardly on speaking terms now for the latter had tried to discover the truth by subtle and friendly hints at first, but, at last, had bluntly demanded to know the truth.

'We are the best of friends. You can rely on me. We are growing old and must not die with certain secrets. Let me know the truth if only to ease my conscience. You can trust me not to tell. It would serve no purpose,' Ntombi had implored.

'Inquisitive spy! Blackmailing informer! Nagging cheat! It would wreck you as completely as myself! Of course, you dare not tell! It was your clinic. You are more educated! You should have known, and it was your responsibility. I can also blackmail you! The police and the people would believe it was done with your connivance. In fact, that it was your evil idea and scheme. For how else could a convalescent, ignorant, grieved woman like me have succeeded in carrying out the thing without your help and knowledge! Know then that your suspicions are true. I "switched" the two girls! I did! Simangele is her twin child! But she is forever mine! Mine, you hear! Go and tell! I hate you! Get out of my sight!'

Mamkazi aged rapidly. She cut herself off from society almost completely. Old villagers talked about it but, unsuspecting, gave the wrong reason for the change. Newcomers and the young did not care. Her husband drank heavily and more frequently. From being one of the most loving and happy couples, they became one of the most unhappy in the village. She had done all this for her husband's and her own triumph and happiness. Instead, she had wrecked both. Retreat was impossible. She clung to her tragic secret and followed her deadly course as if for life.

* * *

235

It is summer. The grass is green. Birds sing. Wild flowers gently sway every-where. Near a humming stream rest two shy young lovers, Simangele Zondi and Zidumo Buthelezi. They are nineteen years of age, good-looking and in the full bloom of health. It is college vacation time. Although they grew up together, they have had little time to see each other in the past three years for they have been attending different and distant colleges.

'In youth when we were always together, we did not care whether we were together or not. Now that we crave always to be together we cannot always be together,' said Zidumo.

'Always speaking as if you were a full-grown man. I like to stay young,' laughed Simangele.

'I am a man. You will always be young.'

But you were right. And mother would be raving mad to know that I have been seen with you, let alone that I am in love with you!'

'I cannot understand it. It has always been so, I am told, since we were tots. But I never noticed it. Did you?'

'I knew it. Perhaps some silly old family feud.'

'Possibly. But I doubt it, for my people love you and have nothing against your people. They seem just as puzzled. There is one solution. As soon as I complete my degree studies next year, I will elope with and marry you!'

At this, they laughed and kissed.

★ ★ ★

Tormented and vigilant, Mamkazi had heard of their meeting and of their being in love. The climax followed rapidly.

Zondi's largest room was soon crowded with distressed, puzzled and expec-tant people. The audience had been carefully selected. They had been hurriedly and secretly summoned at the persistent and intolerable ravings of Mamkazi who appeared to be near death and wanted to say something.

There was Ntombi and her husband; Buthelezi, his wife and Zidumo; the priest and his assistant; the Zondis.

Aware of impending tragedy, the priest had prayed for peace and guidance. But Mamkazi could not wait or be controlled. She groaned and raved in her bed. Supported, she sat up and spoke. There was mingled supreme triumph and utter despair, joy and bitterness, sanity and madness in her words and visage. She wept and laughed, defied and implored.

'Silence! Who dares! Ha! Ha! Listen to me. They shall not, cannot, marry. Yes, you two! The Buthelezis shall not have my daughter. Foiled? Indeed, you are! Ha! She is mine and I will have my way. Mine, I tell you, forever mine! O God, O Evil, the daughter you gave me! What? Yes, I stole her from you – your girl twin. Your child lives forever mine! How can brother and sister be married? Can't you leave her – me – alone! Ask her – ask my nagging, evil friend, there – the midwife. She knows! She will …'

Mamkazi collapsed. Jabu Buthelezi wept aloud and sank on the floor. There was amazement, incredulity and confusion.

But the priest was equal to the situation. He called for and restored some measure of order, sent his assistant to call for the doctor at once, asked for God's help in a sentence, and finally commanded Ntombi to speak and explain. Trembling and old, she wept and stammered.

'It is true. It happened long ago in my clinic …,' she began.

C LOUIS LEIPOLDT

The Tree

Translated from the Afrikaans by Philip John
Written *c*1940

Time and again the missionary was vexed by his converts. It was all good and well. They were lovely, soft-hearted people who regularly attended catechism classes and who earnestly allowed themselves to be placed under censure. In general he had nothing to remark against their conduct. Only this *one* problem vexed him a little too much.

In the forest stood a big tree, the trunk branchless for the first fifty feet, and from there gigantic branches spread, forming a canopy over the small grass-covered spot where the tree grew. It was, according to the heathens in the area, a holy tree. In it were evil spirits, idols, the personification of everything evil, cruel and inhuman, as well as of everything that was simply good and inclined to love. The malicious and the loving spirits lived between trunk and bark, emerging in the dusk of late afternoon with the setting sun and the green forest pigeons on their way to their sleeping places.

The missionary naturally didn't believe any of it. That heathens could believe it, that he could well understand. They were not yet enlightened, he thought, and in his pride he forgot that the light of his own little candle flickered as that of a firefly shimmering against the strong glittering blaze of age-old tradition, fed by the experience of innumerable repetitions of the spirit of being. But for him his surroundings were heathenish. What he couldn't understand and comprehend was simply not worth understanding and comprehending.

For his converts, it was different. They, at least, should know better. They, at least, could see that apart from the sole grace-giving creed that they had to repeat in the catechism class, there was nothing else that could bring solace and relief, salvation and deliverance. This he always emphasised in his two-hour-long sermons in the small church which they had built for him and his doctrine. With unsurpassable emphasis he showed that his faith, and nothing else, was the one, true faith. In this manner he converted many.

Even so, amongst the converts were some who apparently still believed in the nonsense about that old tree. Now and then, when he went for a promenade in the forest and reached that place, he could see that fruit and flowers had been placed next to the tree. Even more disgusting, sometimes there were figurines, cut out of soft wood or made of similarly soft clay, placed in worshiping rows around the tree. When he encountered such outrageous things, he always kicked them away, in the most public and demonstrative manner. Usually there was no one to witness the public but vicarious punishment, but every now and then he saw a loincloth hiding in the depth of the virgin forest, and then he was particularly satisfied.

'At least they can see that I am not scared of it,' said the missionary, half aloud, and he walked home pleased. Duty accomplished affords one the right to feel contented.

But despite his reprimands and vicarious punishment, the disobedience of his converts persisted. Sometimes he tried to reason with the enslaved heathens – with his converts naturally he didn't want to, because a Christian should believe without needing the support of reason.

'It is ridiculous,' he said, 'it is completely ridiculous that you should fear that old rotten tree.'

It was a figurative exaggeration of which he was very aware because the tree was definitely not rotten, but rather sturdy and healthy. He spoke thus to express his contempt.

'Yes, Master,' said the heathens, because they were always polite and friendly and never gave offence, even when he ridiculed their faith. The kind of people who don't respect themselves.

'A dead tree' – once again an exaggeration, a manner of speaking – 'which is worth nothing and can do nothing for you. Shame.'

'Yes, Master,' the heathens said once again, and added: '*Him* has the angry spirits, Master; *him* hurts when you don't appease him.'

'Ridiculous,' said the missionary, half passionately. 'A tree can hardly hurt you if you stay out of it. What is the matter with you people?'

'We appease him, Master,' said the heathens. 'Those clay figurines, we make sacrifices for him, so that he doesn't hurt us.'

It is a strange lot that can be so superstitious, the missionary thought, and once again forgot that he spoke in a similar superstitious manner in the catechism class. I have to put an end to it.

That evening he said to his servant, 'Abdoer, sharpen the axe well. Tomorrow I am going to cut down your ... your tree.' He had wanted to say, damn tree, because he was very angry, but a missionary must be an example, so he restrained himself.

The next morning, after the church service – where he had told the converts about the wonderful ship that contained all the animals of the earth, together with their food – he arrived home cheerful and invigorated. Abdoer had his midday meal ready and the missionary thoroughly enjoyed the curry and bananas. Then he read a psalm for Abdoer and his own edification and took up his axe. First he had wanted to take Abdoer along, but he possessed enough humanity not to do it. Thus, he walked alone down to the forest.

It was a beautiful afternoon because he had waited until the rainshower was over. The whole forest was glimmering with the last rays of the setting sun. Big butterflies, a glory of pitch black and bright red, fluttered over the fragrant geranium flowers. In the branches the cicadas were in tumult, and high above the green doves cooed a harmonious choral which reverberated softly in the expanse of the forest. The shiny leaves of the fan palms were still wet from the rain, and he smelt waves of the strong fragrance of jasmine. Here, at the tree, it was peaceful and quiet except for the droning of the cicadas and the song of the doves, both muted by the thick forest wall which surrounded him. It was nearly dark here with the greenish-brown darkness of the virgin forest, where shadows appeared purple and lost rays of light, falling from above through the great canopy of leaves, rested like small flecks of silver on the carpet of grass. Dark and quiet it was, and the thick tree trunk stood like a beige giant against the background of dusky green.

The missionary removed his jacket and rolled up his sleeves. The tree trunk was thick, and he would have to work, work hard, to cut through it. Even then the tree would not topple. The creepers and surrounding tree branches would support it solidly. Only months later, after rain had fallen on it and ferns had grown on it, after small beetles had eaten off the bark, and the fungus which grows so abundantly in the virgin forest and consumes everything had destroyed the inside of the trunk, would it tumble, piecemeal, like an old king who has been dethroned and sinks decrepitly into his grave. The quiet and the attractiveness of the place made an impression on the mood of the missionary. He let go of his little axe and sat down on the grass, even though it was still wet.

Strange, wasn't it? That the people continued to honour this old tree. Naturally, nothing of it was true – all the sayings and superstitions about the evil spirits and the good spirits living between the bark and the wood. It would surely be ridiculous to give to this the slightest credence. Especially for some-one who was a Christian and opposed to idolatry.

And still? Transmitted tradition, sustained by the experience of circles of lives – should one disregard this? Should one withhold respect from that which everyone else honours, or should honour, if they are human, a thinking human being standing in a normal relation to his surroundings?

No, it would be ridiculous to agree even to this. What then would be the point of everything that he had to tell his converts in the catechism class? About his own faith? About his own experience and the life he had lived?

The thought gave the missionary new courage, new strength. He stood up and didn't even notice that he had sat on the wet grass. With determination he held the little axe in his right hand and walked to the tree.

But the tree trunk was very big and he could see that he would not be able to chop through it in one afternoon. To chop halfway through, especially if there were no one to see him chopping, wouldn't mean much. His objective was to destroy the idol, just as the Iconoclasts had destroyed idols in Catholic churches in the Middle Ages, as an example to and as edification of their fellows. It is true, they destroyed many works of art, but about that they hadn't thought or concerned themselves. Just as little as the missionary would concern himself with the tree.

The tree was a masterpiece, a magnificent artwork of nature. Hundreds of years of slow growth were needed to let him rise up so high, so impressively beautiful. The dampness of thousands of days through years that were constantly summer had invigorated him and brought his roots a store of life provisioned by the decomposition of thousands of lives in his vicinity. A complicated system of transmutation worked in his tissue, diligently, patiently, through thousands of days, until the colourless metal was changed into the sparkling green of leaves and the unseen gases into solid wood and bark. Against this the best chemical workshop thought out by people was like a heap of children's toys. A miracle was the tree, something in front of which humans should kneel, humbly, in the silent amazement which, in reality, is sister to worship.

The missionary thought nothing about this aspect of the issue. To him the tree was an ordinary forest tree which vexed him because it was a stumbling block to his converts.

He took his axe and started chopping at the tree trunk.

And he continued chopping until there was a deep gash in the side of the tree trunk. The wood was hard and durable and the axe wasn't too sharp. After half an hour's work he was tired.

'Enough for one day,' he said. 'Tomorrow I come again.'

Then he walked home.

And nothing happened.

★ ★ ★

That evening, lying on his bed, the missionary could not sleep. Usually it wasn't difficult for him to fall asleep. Usually, his head barely touched the pillow and he was asleep because he was healthy and not weakened by the fever. He swallowed his quinine pills regularly and his conscience had never bothered him.

But *this* evening he was restless, awake as never before. There was something – what, he couldn't make out – which prevented him from falling asleep. He could hear his heart beating and, much more unpleasantly, he was conscious of the fact that he had to breathe. Quite natural, in fact. Everyone has to

241

breathe, but it is such an ordinary process that no one is conscious of it, and if you do become conscious of it, you experience it as a personal insult. Such a thing you would never forget.

It wasn't long before the missionary became conscious of something else. His breathing wasn't regular anymore, it was fitful, with long intervals accompanied by a nauseous feeling in the upper part of his chest. Breathing in was close to how it always was, but breathing out was more difficult, and low down in his throat it sounded as if there were a little whistle which whistled irregularly. A thin, sickly sound was produced by the whistle, just like the small sugarbirds in the geraniums when they were looking for small insects in the flowers. Definitely not pleasant – on the contrary, highly unpleasant and uncomfortable. The missionary had never before experienced anything like this and it didn't please him one bit.

I believe I am going to experience an asthma attack, he thought. I don't know what the correct treatment is. Maybe a few quinine pills … Then he stood up and swallowed half a dozen pills. It made his head buzz, but it didn't alter the noise made by the whistle. The whole night the missionary turned from the one side of his bed to the other without finding relief. The old general who had been victorious at Waterloo had the habit of immediately rising after he had turned once in his bed. 'Tossing time is rising time,' the old Duke had said, and he had always practised what he said.

Thus the missionary also rose. He lit his lamp and tried to read under the mosquito net. But he could barely read anything, because the whistle in his throat drew his attention away from his reading matter. At the crack of dawn he called his servant.

'Make coffee,' he said, and his voice was hoarse because he had difficulty in breathing.

Abdoer made the coffee and stared at his master.

'Why do you look at me like that, Abdoer?' the missionary asked.

'Master had …' said Abdoer, embarrassed, because he was a convert and would be confirmed soon, if he managed to recite the creed fluently.

'I had done what?' the missionary asked curiously.

'They all get it who … malign the tree,' Abdoer answered. 'It is the spirit under the bark, Master, which gives it …'

'Insanity,' said the missionary, more and more irate. 'All clear insanity – pure hogwash. How many times do I have to repeat it to you, Abdoer, the stories are all fairy tales? Shame. And you call yourself a Christian.' Abdoer left the room shamefaced with an empty cup and the missionary took up his medical book and read up about asthma. His reading consoled him, because asthma was an affliction which didn't last long and which usually only happens at night. The causes – well, he was a fool not to have thought about it.

'It is the wetness of the grass. I am glad that I didn't get rheumatism in addition,' the missionary said to himself. 'I will now take a little bit of lobelia tincture and potassium bromide, and in a few hours it will all be over.'

But the remedies that he used – and in the course of the day he tried everything that the medical book suggested – didn't help. He couldn't conduct the service and in the catechism class he was so hoarse that he could barely utter a word. But what he found worse and even more unpleasant was the manner in which the catechism class, from Abdoer to the youngest, looked at him and whispered amongst themselves. Their interest was extremely unpleasant, but he didn't want to give attention to it. Even so, their interest wasn't only because of curiosity. His catechism class held the white man in extremely high regard. He was higher, more reasonable, more knowledgeable than they. He could read two, three languages, and could talk with experienced priests about what transpires in the hereafter. Not an ordinary man. Someone, on the contrary, who stood high above them, and who deserved a measure of deference and respect.

But all of them knew about the hoarseness and that strange noise coming from their master's throat with every breath. They knew where it came from. It was the punishment of the tree.

And the only remedy against it was to placate the tree spirits.

But they were too scared to give their master this advice.

That night the missionary had an even more restless and uncomfortable time. He thought nothing about the chopping down of the tree. His thoughts were concentrated solely on his own physical condition. The whistle now went berserk and he had to get up repeatedly, because it was as if he couldn't breathe and suffocated when he lay his head on the pillow. Even the few drops of chloroform on his handkerchief – the last, and most dangerous remedy, according to the medical book – brought no relief. How he survived the night, no one knows. But when Abdoer came in with the coffee the missionary was a broken man who had just about given up all hope of recovery. Asthma is a terrible illness, especially when it continues for days.

With a barely audible voice the missionary whispered: 'What do you do when – when it whistles like this in your throats?'

Abdoer turned his eyes to the other side of the room because he was too embarrassed to meet the gaze of the missionary.

'We – we make sacrifices to the spirits of the tree, Master,' he eventually said. And he first had to swallow hard before he could utter the words.

'Shame,' the missionary whispered. 'And you are Christians … I will stay home today and the class will have to wait until tomorrow.'

The missionary spent the whole day reading his Bible and his medical book, and made diligent use of the armoury of a servant of the gospel.

But the whistle continued blowing and by midday he went out for a short walk.

Involuntarily he walked in the direction of the tree, and shortly arrived at the tree. Here everything was quiet, but he could see that there was a heap of flowers around the tree, and a whole row of figurines. It was the work of his converts, who had made vicarious sacrifices for him, to placate the spirits of the tree. Seeing it vexed him immensely. The flowers he kicked away and the figurines he simply stood upon. The last one which he destroyed in this manner was a passable representation of his own figure, with hat and walking stick. The sole of his shoe pressed the head askew, so that the face carried a satiric expression. But he didn't even notice this, because what grabbed his attention was that the cut in the tree trunk where he had worked with the axe was almost completely filled up with hardened sap.

'You wait,' he said, between his teeth, 'you I will still cut down. It is all complete insanity.'

Back in his house, he could barely breathe. The whistle had now multiplied into dozens of smaller whistles squeaking everywhere in his chest, and the noise which they kicked up in unison when he had to breathe in, was unbearable. He wildly swallowed a handful of quinine pills, but it made him nauseous and for a few minutes he thought he was dying.

'As well,' he said, 'because I cannot bear it anymore. A torment like this – it is unbearable.'

But still he had to bear it, because he couldn't lie down. He couldn't even sit, because as soon as he bowed his head forward it was as if he were being throttled and he wanted to choke. Now and then he became light-headed, and it brought a measure of relief, but as soon as he regained his composure, the suffering was as severe as before.

In the middle of the night he got up and went to Abdoer's hut. But he didn't reach the hut. Abdoer was next to the door outside his room, on his knees on the ground and it was clear that he had kept vigil the whole night. Because Master was not just an ordinary person, and such a person deserved a measure of deference and respect.

'Abdoer,' the missionary whispered. 'What are you doing here?'

'O Master,' the servant replied, 'the tree spirit acts like this ... Master, we all know ... the axe ... what Master has done ...'

'Yes, Abdoer. I wanted to chop down the tree, chop it up ...'

'We know, Master. But the spirits ... they will not allow ... and Master is ... not one of us ... The illness ...'

'Will it kill me, Abdoer?' asked the missionary, because he had thought: Well, the people know more about the local illnesses than I do ... and one can only ask.

'No ...' said Abdoer, and the missionary was astonished to hear something sad in the sound of Abdoer's voice ... 'Never ... it doesn't kill. But it ... more than kills. Syma ... she bothered the spirits ...'

With a shudder the missionary understood what Abdoer referred to. Syma was a middle-aged woman, but seemed very old. And she had the mind of a baby … a lunatic, whose cough and unnatural behaviour were familiar to all in the camp.

'Syma was Goeniang's wife when Goeniang died of smallpox, Master,' said Abdoer, 'and in her sorrow she cursed the tree. The same evening she began to whistle, and four days later, she was … Syma, like she is today, Master.'

'Couldn't she … couldn't she,' the missionary whispered, and he was too ashamed to ask the question, but Abdoer knew what he wanted to know.

'It was too late, Master,' he said. 'After the third day the spirits do not want to be merciful … That is why I am here now, Master … please Master …' And with hands shaking he handed the missionary a basket full of fruit and flowers and a little cooked rice. And on top of the fruit was a clay figurine with a hat and a walking stick in his hand – a figurine which, in a small comic form, represented the missionary.

'What must I do?' asked the missionary, and he could nearly not utter the words because of the loud squeaking of the whistles in his chest.

'Master must go to the tree … with the axe,' replied Abdoer. 'I will go with Master. We make a big fire … burn the axe … come on, Master. And Master places the fruit … where we always put it, and puts the figurine on top … to … to …'

'Yes … to?' asked the missionary, and his whisper was barely audible, because he was close to choking.

'To remain and to pray, Master,' said Abdoer, and he didn't want to look at his master.

'And what happens then?' the missionary asked again, and took the figurine and studied it.

'Master just becomes healthy again,' said Abdoer enthusiastically. 'It happens a lot … I myself saw … And then Master can … again become Christian … just like us in the catechism class.'

The missionary stood motionless for a moment. Then he took the basket and said curtly, or rather he whispered, because he couldn't speak: 'Come Abdoer … you know the way in the dark.'

In the indigo above, the stars sparkled in their multitudes and in the virgin forest thousands of fireflies lit up the trees. The small monkeys groaned monotonously and innumerable frogs sang in a choir, a roaring harmony, which went up and down as if the singers had moved closer and then further away. The night was deliciously cool with a little damp of the morning dew and with the smell of the earth everywhere. On the tree shone spots of green light where big candle bugs were clamped like lanterns against the mast of a ship.

'Here, Master,' Abdoer whispered, 'Master, not too close … the figurine here ... and the fruit there. And now Master has to – please, Master ... now Master has to pray.'

It was a nightmare for the missionary and he couldn't gather his thoughts because in everything there was one thought, one concept that coloured everything. He wanted to be rid of the terrible constriction in his chest, the terrible burden of a death that constantly threatened, but didn't want to come. His pride and his faith were both broken ... relief and deliverance: that is what he wanted.

'Deliver me ... deliver me from this illness,' he managed to say ... 'I ... I regret that I ... that I disturbed the tree.'

The words were barely uttered than the missionary found that his breathing was easier. Yes truly, he could draw his breath in without hearing the whistle. But he was tired, tired and sleepy, and before he could prevent it he tumbled over, right next to the tree. Abdoer picked him up, carried him home and lay him down on his bed.

Late in the afternoon of the next day the missionary awoke. He was still tired and weak, and with a shudder of indignation he thought back to the events of the previous night.

Then he stood up, went to his table, and immediately began to write. The letter ended: 'Because I can no longer serve as example, I herewith tender my resignation.'

Now he farms and Abdoer is his first foreman. On the tree there is a scar. In the lounge of the farmer's house stands a small shrivelled clay figurine.

'My remedy against asthma,' says the former missionary, now free from asthma attacks.

PETER ABRAHAMS

One of the Three

From: *Dark Testament* (1942)

The three of us had always stuck together after we had met. Tommy, Johnny and myself. We had been in the same class and had gone through school together. These two, Tommy and Johnny, were the only fast friends I had throughout those years at school.

Tommy was not very ambitious. He just wanted to overcome the dreaded thing: Poverty. All he wanted of life was a chance to earn enough money, so that his mother would stop having to carry big bundles of washing on her grey head. He loved her very much. He was an only son, and both his mother and father lived only for him. They used to say their day was past, and now they wanted to see the day of their son. So part of his one ambition was to get them out of the one room that was too small and stuffy for the three of them, and to make the old people rest from their labours. The other part of his ambition, completing it, was to have a fairly secure job, with enough money to marry a good-looking Coloured girl; to have enough to eat in their home, go to shows and dances as often as they could, and live as comfortably as possible. He used to say that he wanted, at any rate, a good run out of life. He worked very hard. His aim was to obtain a teacher's certificate. Both Johnny and I criticised him for his narrow ambition, but secretly we envied him. But that did not worry Tommy. He laughingly told us that he would love to do bigger and greater things, but that his life had been starved too long, and that he just had not the strength to go on starving for something that he might never achieve. He was always reminding us that this was South Africa, and that everything worthwhile here was reserved for Europeans only.

Both Johnny and I wished that we could adopt the same attitude. We knew it was the safest; then at least there would be some sort of certainty about things. But we could not look at the future as Tommy did.

Tommy was in love with a girl who worked on the Hill. She was simple and beautiful. He was happy with her. He enjoyed talking about simple nothings with her. She could not discuss any of the things that were so important to the three of us. Books meant nothing to her, if they were not of the *Peg's Paper* variety. The only music she knew was the music to which she danced. To Tommy serious books and music, and, above all, the discussion of these, were very important. She knew nothing about these things. She just tried to sink her identity in Tommy's.

Johnny and I could not understand it. The girl was sweet and simple, and we loved her as a little sister. This may sound highbrow, but it is not. Even Tommy admitted that he could not turn to her for serious companionship. But he said it was impossible to find the type of girl who would suit him in this country, with conditions as they were, so he was making the best of a bad job. And he was happy with the girl.

Johnny and I tried to do the same, but we failed completely. Johnny was very different from Tommy. The three of us were so utterly different from one another that we sometimes wondered what kept us together.

Johnny was very jovial and noisy. Always doing the wrong thing. Always playing pranks on somebody. Always getting into trouble, out of which Tommy and I had to help him. To those who did not know him he appeared an entirely superficial person with no sense of values whatever. But deep down he was very sensitive. His devil-may-care attitude was a mask which hid the true Johnny.

His mother had died of starvation. He had been at school, and he knew about it only when it was too late. She had starved to keep him at school, and he had not known. For a long time afterwards he was alone and quiet. Even Tommy and I could not get to him. He had built a wall round himself. His strongest weapon of defence was mockery. But after a while the three of us were together again. To us he was the same Johnny, only very unhappy. To everyone else he had changed. He had taken up a queer mocking attitude to everything. They all said that his brilliant brain was useless. Johnny did not shrink from hurting people, and he had a brilliantly biting tongue and brain with which to do it. But for all the old and poor he had a motherly tenderness. Very few people understood him. Most condemned him.

My life was pretty much the same. Poverty, want of a woman's companionship, and the other things which the non-European South African of education knows so well. There were the three of us. Tommy, Johnny and myself.

When we had finished our schooling we broke up, and each went his own way. Tommy tried to persuade us to teach. He said: 'What's the use of passing anything if you are not going to make money out of it?' But Johnny said he wanted to see the world. He did not know for sure what he wanted out of the world, but he would find out. I said I was going to wander about the country and learn to know my people, and try to earn my living as a writer. They were both worried because of my poor physical condition, but I was insistent.

So we agreed to keep in touch with one another, and broke up. Johnny was going to a coastal town, where he would try to get away in a boat; I was going inland among the natives; Tommy was going to take up a teacher's post after the holidays.

For three years I wandered about. Now and then I received a letter from Tommy, when he saw something of mine in the African papers, and traced my whereabouts through that. Then one day he wrote to me to tell me that Johnny was coming back, and that I must be there for the reunion. Somehow I managed to scrape my fare together and went back.

I arrived a day before Johnny was expected, and I spent it with Tommy. He was married to the girl with whom he had been in love. They were not happy. There were continual fights in the house. I asked him about his mother. She had died. His father had gone off, and there was no trace of him. Tommy had changed. His quiet acceptance of things had hurt him more than he had expected. He could not live the superficial life of the average Coloured teacher. He wanted to break away and do something worthwhile for his people. He had read revolutionary literature, and wanted to do something about conditions, but he was terribly afraid of losing his job. Afraid of insecurity. So he chafed against his chains, but could not break them.

The next day we went to the station to meet Johnny.

The fine sensitive Johnny was no more. There were only glimpses of him. They appeared only when we spoke of old times. Life had beaten Johnny. All the fire and force had gone out of him. His fine brown eyes, that used to sparkle with defiance when things were black, were dull and lifeless. He had come home, he said, to try and see himself as he used to be …

For a few months he drifted about. Tommy and I did everything we could to bring the old life back, but we failed. Then one night Johnny took lysol …

One out of the three had gone.

Things were black with Tommy. He was afraid of insecurity, but the keeping up of appearances was getting him down. And always when we were together Johnny came and weighed heavily upon us. Tommy and I agreed not to see each other again. We both felt it would be better that way. Fighting ourselves was bad enough; if we had to fight Johnny too it might be too much for us.

It is one of the saddest things I remember.

NADINE GORDIMER

The Train from Rhodesia

First published, 1947
From: *The Soft Voice of the Serpent* (1953)

The train came out of the red horizon and bore down towards them over the single straight track.

The stationmaster came out of his little brick station with its pointed chalet roof, feeling the creases in his serge uniform in his legs as well. A stir of pre-paredness rippled through the squatting native vendors waiting in the dust; the face of a carved wooden animal, eternally surprised, stuck out of a sack. The stationmaster's barefoot children wandered over. From the grey mud huts with the untidy heads that stood within a decorated mud wall, chickens, and dogs with their skin stretched like parchment over their bones, followed the pic-canins down to the track. The flushed and perspiring west cast a reflection, faint, without heat, upon the station, upon the tin shed marked 'Goods', upon the walled kraal, upon the grey tin house of the stationmaster and upon the sand, that lapped all around, from sky to sky, cast little rhythmical cups of shadow, so that the sand became the sea, and closed over the children's black feet softly and without imprint.

The stationmaster's wife sat behind the mesh of her veranda. Above her head the hunk of a sheep's carcass moved slightly, dangling in a current of air.

They waited.

The train called out, along the sky; but there was no answer; and the cry hung on: I'm coming … I'm coming …

The engine flared out now, big, whisking a dwindling body behind it; the track flared out to let it in.

Creaking, jerking, jostling, gasping, the train filled the station.

Here, let me see that one – the young woman curved her body farther out of the corridor window. Missus? smiled the old man, looking at the creatures he held in his hand. From a piece of string on his grey finger hung a tiny woven basket; he lifted it, questioning. No, no, she urged, leaning down towards him, across the height of the train towards the man in the piece of old rug; that one, that one, her hand commanded. It was a lion, carved out of soft dry wood that looked like spongecake; heraldic, black and white, with impressionistic detail burnt in. The old man held it up to her still smiling, not from the heart, but at the customer. Between its vandyke teeth, in the mouth opened in an endless roar too terrible to be heard, it had a black tongue. Look, said the young husband, if you don't mind! And round the neck of the thing, a piece of fur (rat? rabbit? meerkat?); a real mane, majestic, telling you somehow that the artist had delight in the lion.

All up and down the length of the train in the dust the artists sprang, walking bent, like performing animals, the better to exhibit the fantasy held towards the faces on the train. Buck, startled and stiff, staring with round black and white eyes. More lions, standing erect, grappling with strange, thin, elongated warriors who clutched spears and showed no fear in their slits of eyes. How much, they asked from the train, how much?

Give me penny, said the little ones with nothing to sell. The dogs went and sat, quite still, under the dining car, where the train breathed out the smell of meat cooking with onion.

A man passed beneath the arch of reaching arms meeting grey-black and white in the exchange of money for the staring wooden eyes, the stiff wooden legs sticking up in the air; went along under the voices and the bargaining, interrogating the wheels. Past the dogs; glancing up at the dining car where he could stare at the faces, behind glass, drinking beer, two by two, on either side of a uniform railway vase with its pale dead flower. Right to the end, to the guard's van, where the stationmaster's children had just collected their mother's two loaves of bread; to the engine itself, where the stationmaster and the driver stood talking against the steaming complaint of the resting beast.

The man called out to them, something loud and joking. They turned to laugh, in a twirl of steam. The two children careered over the sand, clutching the bread, and burst through the iron gate and up the path through the garden in which nothing grew.

Passengers drew themselves in at the corridor windows and turned into compartments to fetch money, to call someone to look. Those sitting inside looked up: suddenly different, caged faces, boxed in, cut off after the contact of outside. There was an orange a piccanin would like ... What about that chocolate? It wasn't very nice ...

A girl had collected a handful of the hard kind, that no one liked, out of the chocolate box, and was throwing them to the dogs, over at the dining car. But the hens darted in and swallowed the chocolates, incredibly quick and accurate, before they had even dropped in the dust, and the dogs, a little bewildered, looked up with their brown eyes, not expecting anything.

– No, leave it, said the young woman, don't take it ...

Too expensive, too much, she shook her head and raised her voice to the old man, giving up the lion. He held it high where she had handed it to him. No, she said, shaking her head. Three-and-six? insisted her husband, loudly.

Yes baas! laughed the old man. *Three-and-six?* – the young man was incredulous. Oh leave it – she said. The young man stopped. Don't you want it? he said, keeping his face closed to the old man. No, never mind, she said, leave it. The old native kept his head on one side, looking at them sideways, holding the lion. Three-and-six, he murmured, as old people repeat things to themselves.

The young woman drew her head in. She went into the coupé and sat down. Out of the window, on the other side, there was nothing; sand and bush; a thorn tree. Back through the open doorway, past the figure of her husband in the corridor, there was the station, the voices, wooden animals waving, running feet. Her eye followed the funny little valance of scrolled wood that outlined the chalet roof of the station; she thought of the lion and smiled. That bit of fur round the neck. But the wooden buck, the hippos, the elephants, the baskets that already bulked out of their brown paper under the seat and on the luggage rack! How will they look at home? Where will you put them? What will they mean away from the places you found them? Away from the unreality of the last few weeks? The young man outside. But he is not part of the unreality; he is for good now. Odd ...somewhere there was an idea that he, that living with him, was part of the holiday, the strange places.

Outside, a bell rang. The stationmaster was leaning against the end of the train, green flag rolled in readiness. A few men who had got down to stretch their legs sprang onto the train, clinging to the observation platforms, or perhaps merely standing on the iron step, holding the rail; but on the train, safe from the one dusty platform, the one tin house, the empty sand.

There was a grunt. The train jerked. Through the glass the beerdrinkers looked out, as if they could not see beyond it. Behind the flyscreen, the stationmaster's wife sat facing back at them beneath the darkening hunk of meat.

There was a shout. The flag drooped out. Joints not yet co-ordinated, the segmented body of the train heaved and bumped back against itself. It began to move; slowly the scrolled chalet moved past it, the yells of the natives, running alongside, jetted up into the air, fell back at different levels. Staring wooden faces waved drunkenly, there, then gone, questioning for the last time at the windows. Here, one-and-six, baas! – As one automatically opens a hand to catch a thrown ball, a man fumbled wildly down his pocket, brought up the shilling and sixpence and threw them out; the old native, gasping, his skinny toes splaying the sand, flung the lion.

The piccanins were waving, the dogs stood, tails uncertain, watching the train go: past the mud huts, where a woman turned to look up from the smoke of the fire, her hand pausing on her hip.

The stationmaster went slowly in under the chalet.

The old native stood, breath blowing out the skin between his ribs, feet

252

tense, balanced in the sand, smiling and shaking his head. In his opened palm, held in the attitude of receiving, was the retrieved shilling and sixpence.

The blind end of the train was being pulled helplessly out of the station.

The young man swung in from the corridor, breathless. He was shaking his head with laughter and triumph. Here! he said. And waggled the lion at her. One-and-six!

What? she said.

He laughed. I was arguing with him for fun, bargaining – when the train had pulled out already, he came tearing after ...One-and-six, baas! So there's your lion.

She was holding it away from her, the head with the open jaws, the pointed teeth, the black tongue, the wonderful ruff of fur facing her. She was looking at it with an expression of not seeing, of seeing something different. Her face was drawn up, wryly, like the face of a discomforted child. Her mouth lifted nervously at the corner. Very slowly, cautious, she lifted her finger and touched the mane, where it was joined to the wood.

But how could you, she said. He was shocked by the dismay of her face.

Good Lord, he said, what's the matter?

If you wanted the thing, she said, her voice rising and breaking with the shrill impotence of anger, why didn't you buy it in the first place? If you wanted it, why didn't you pay for it? Why didn't you take it decently, when he offered it? Why did you have to wait for him to run after the train with it, and give him one-and-six? One-and-six!

She was pushing it at him, trying to force him to take the lion. He stood astonished, his hands hanging at his sides.

But you wanted it! You liked it so much?

– It's a beautiful piece of work, she said fiercely, as if to protect it from him.

You liked it so much! You said yourself it was too expensive –

Oh you – she said, hopeless and furious. You ... She threw the lion onto the seat.

He stood looking at her.

She sat down again in the corner and, her face slumped in her hands, stared out of the window. Everything was turning round inside her. One-and-six. One-and-six. One-and-six for the wood and the carving and the sinews of the legs and the switch of the tail. The mouth open like that and the teeth. The black tongue, rolling, like a wave. The mane round the neck. To give one-and-six for that. The heat of shame mounted through her legs and body and sounded in her ears like the sound of sand pouring. Pouring, pouring. She sat there, sick. A weariness, a tastelessness, the discovery of a void made her hands slacken their grip, atrophy emptily, as if the hour was not worth their grasp. She was feeling like this again. She had thought it was something to do with singleness, with being alone and belonging too much to oneself.

She sat there not wanting to move or speak, or to look at anything even; so that the mood should be associated with nothing, no object, word or sight that might recur and so recall the feeling again … Smuts blew in grittily, settled on her hands. Her back remained at exactly the same angle, turned against the young man sitting with his hands drooping between his sprawled legs, and the lion, fallen on its side in the corner.

The train had cast the station like a skin. It called out to the sky, I'm coming, I'm coming; and again, there was no answer.

Theme — Poverty and wealth.

Plot —
- A white couple on train back from honeymoon.
- Impoverished people at station trying to sell crafts.
- However, she finds craft (lion) expensive.
- Later, as the train is leaving, the husband buys it in cheaper price
- Woman is angry coz she realizes that lion is beautifully carved. the poor people were rich in culture. Therefore, it was wrong to pay a cheaper price.

NADINE GORDIMER

The Bridegroom

From: *Friday's Footprint* (1960)

He came into his road camp that afternoon for the last time. It was neater than any house would ever be; the sand raked smooth in the clearing, the water drums under the tarpaulin, the flaps of his tent closed against the heat. Thirty yards away a black woman knelt, pounding mealies, and two or three children, grey with Kalahari dust, played with a skinny dog. Their shrillness was no more than a bird's piping in the great spaces in which the camp was lost.

Inside his tent, something of the chill of the night before always remained, stale but cool, like the air of a church. There was his iron bed with its clean pillowcase and big kaross. There was his table, his folding chair with the red canvas seat, and the chest in which his clothes were put away. Standing on the chest was the alarm clock that woke him at five every morning and the photograph of the seventeen-year-old girl from Francistown whom he was going to marry. They had been there a long time, the girl and the alarm clock; in the morning when he opened his eyes, in the afternoon when he came off the job. But now this was the last time. He was leaving for Francistown in the Roads Department ten-tonner, in the morning; when he came back, the next week, he would be married and he would have with him the girl, and the caravan which the department provided for married men. He had his eye on her as he sat down on the bed and took off his boots; the smiling girl was like one of those faces cut out of a magazine. He began to shed his working overalls, a rind of khaki stiff with dust that held his shape as he discarded it, and he called, easily and softly, '*Ou Piet, ek wag.*' But the bony black man with his eyebrows raised like a clown's, in effort, and his bare feet shuffling under the weight, was already at the tent with a tin bath in which hot water made a twanging tune as it slopped from side to side.

When he had washed and put on a clean khaki shirt and a pair of worn grey trousers, and streaked back his hair with sweet-smelling pomade, he stepped out of his tent just as the lid of the horizon closed on the bloody eye of the sun. It was winter and the sun set shortly after five; the grey sand turned a fading pink, the low thorn scrub gave out spreading stains of lilac shadow that presently all ran together; then the surface of the desert showed pocked and pored, for a minute or two, like the surface of the moon through a telescope, while the sky remained light over the darkened earth and the clean crystal pebble of the evening star shone. The camp fires – his own and the black men's, over there – changed from near-invisible flickers of liquid colour to brilliant focuses of leaping tongues of light; it was dark. Every evening he sat like this through the short ceremony of the closing of the day, slowly filling his pipe, slowly easing his back round to the fire, yawning off the stiffness of his labour. Suddenly he gave a smothered giggle, to himself, of excitement. Her existence became real to him; he saw the face of the photograph, posed against a caravan door. He got up and began to pace about the camp, alert to promise. He kicked a log farther into the fire, he called an order to Piet, he walked up towards the tent and then changed his mind and strolled away again. In their own encampment at the edge of his, the road gang had taken up the exchange of laughing, talking, yelling and arguing that never failed them when their work was done. Black arms gestured under a thick foam of white soap, there was a gasp and splutter as a head broke the cold force of a bucketful of water, the gleaming bellies of iron cooking-pots were carried here and there in the talkative preparation of food. He did not understand much of what they were saying – he knew just enough Tswana to give them his orders, with help from Piet and one or two others who understood his own tongue, Afrikaans – but the sound of their voices belonged to this time of evening. One or other of the babies who always cried was keeping up a thin, ignored wail; the naked children were playing the chasing game that made the dog bark. He came back and sat down again at the fire, to finish his pipe.

After a certain interval (it was exact, though it was not timed by a watch but by long habit that had established the appropriate lapse of time between his bath, his pipe, and his food) he called out, in Afrikaans, 'Have you forgotten my dinner, man?'

From across the patch of distorted darkness where the light of the two fires did not meet but flung wobbling shapes and opaque, overlapping radiances, came the hoarse, protesting laugh that was, better than the tribute to a new joke, the pleasure in constancy to an old one.

Then a few minutes later, 'Piet! I suppose you've burned everything, eh?'

'Baas?'

'Where's the food, man?'

In his own time the black man appeared with the folding table and an oil-lamp. He went back and forth between the dark and light, bringing pots and dishes and food, and nagging with deep satisfaction, in a mixture of English and Afrikaans. 'You want *koeksisters*, so I make *koeksisters*. You ask me this morning. So I got to make the oil nice and hot, I got to get everything ready ... It's a little bit slow. Yes, I know. But I can't get everything quick-quick. You hurry tonight, you don't want wait, then it's better you have *koeksisters* on Saturday, then I'm got time in the afternoon, I do it nice … Yes, I think next time it's better …'

Piet was a good cook. 'I've taught my boy how to make everything,' the young man always told people, back in Francistown. 'He can even make *koek-sisters*,' he had told the girl's mother, in one of those silences of the woman's disapproval it was so difficult to fill. He had had a hard time, trying to overcome the prejudice of the girl's parents against the sort of life he could offer her. He had managed to convince them that the life was not impossible, and they had given their consent to the marriage, but they still felt the life was unsuitable, and his desire to please and reassure them had made him anxious to see it with their eyes and forestall, by changes, their objections. The girl was a farm girl and would not pine for town life, but at the same time he could not deny to her parents that living on a farm with her family around her, and neighbours only 30 or 40 miles away would be very different from living 220 miles from a town or village, alone with him in a road camp, 'surrounded by a gang of kaffirs all day', as her mother had said. He himself simply did not think at all about what the girl would do while he was out on the road; and as for the girl, until it was over, nothing could exist for her but the wedding, with her two little sisters in pink walking behind her, and her dress that she didn't recognise herself in being made at the dressmaker's, and the cake that was going to have a tiny china bride and groom in evening dress on the top.

He looked at the scored table and the rim of the open jam tin and the salt-cellar with a piece of brown paper tied neatly over the broken top, and said to Piet, 'You must do everything nice when the missus comes.'

'Baas?'

They looked at each other and it was not really necessary to say anything. 'You must make the table properly and do everything clean.'

'Always I make everything clean. Why you say now I must make clean —'

The young man bent his head over his food, dismissing him.

While he ate, his mind went automatically over the changes that would have to be made for the girl. He was not used to visualising situations, but to dealing with what existed. It was like a lesson learned by rote; he knew the totality of what was needed, but if he found himself confronted by one of the component details, he foundered: he did not recognise it or know how to deal with it. The boys must keep out of the way. That was the main thing. Piet would have to come to the caravan quite a lot, to cook and clean. The boys — specially the boys who were responsible for the maintenance of the lorries and roadmaking equipment — were always coming with questions, what to do about this and that. They'd mess things up, otherwise. He spat out a piece of gristle he could not swallow, his mind went to something else. The women over there — they could do the washing for the girl. They were such a raw bunch of kaffirs, would they ever be able to do anything right? Twenty boys and about five of their women – you couldn't hide them under a thorn bush. They just mustn't hang around, that's all. They must just understand that they mustn't hang around. He looked keenly through the shadow-puppets of the half-dark on the margin of his fire's light; the voices, companionably quieter, now, intermittent over food, the echoing 'chut!' of wood being chopped, the thin film of a baby's wail through which all these sounded – they were on their own side. Yet he felt an odd, rankling suspicion.

His thoughts shuttled, as he ate, in a slow and painstaking way that he had never experienced before in his life – he was worrying. He sucked on a tooth; Piet, Piet, that kaffir talks such a hell of a lot. How's Piet going to stop talking, talking every time he comes near. If he talks to her. Man, it's sure he'll talk to her. He thought, in actual words, what he would say to Piet about this; the words were like those unsayable things people write on walls for others to see in private moments, but that are never spoken in their mouths.

Piet brought coffee and *koeksisters* and the young man did not look at him.

But the *koeksisters* were delicious, crisp, sticky and sweet, and as he felt the familiar substance and taste on his tongue, alternating with the hot bite of the coffee, he at once became occupied with the pure happiness of eating, as a child is fully occupied with a bag of sweets. *Koeksisters* never failed to give him this innocent, total pleasure. When first he had taken the job of overseer to the road gang, he had had strange, restless hours at night and on Sundays. It seemed that he was hungry. He ate but never felt satisfied. He walked about all the time, like a hungry creature. One Sunday he actually set out to walk (the Roads Department was very strict about the use of the ten-tonner for private purposes) the fourteen miles across the sand to the cattle-dipping post where the government cattle-officer and his wife, Afrikaners like himself and the only other white people between the road camp and Francistown, lived in their corrugated-iron house. By a coincidence, they had decided to drive over and see him, that day, and they met him a little less than half-way, when he was already slowed and dazed by heat. But shortly after that Piet had taken over the cooking of his meals and the care of his person, and Piet had even learned to make *koeksisters*, according to instructions given to the young man by the cattle-officer's wife. The *koeksisters*, a childhood treat that he could indulge in whenever he liked, seemed to mark his settling down; the solitary camp became a personal way of life with its own special arrangements and indulgences.

'*Ou Piet! Kêrel!* What did you do to the *koeksisters*, hey?' he called out joyously.

A shout came that meant 'Right away.' The black man appeared, drying his hands on a rag, with the diffident, kidding manner of someone who knows he has excelled himself.

'Whatsa matter with the *koeksisters*, man?'

Piet shrugged. 'You must tell me. I don't know what's matter.'

'Here, bring me some more, man.' The young man shoved the empty plate at him, with a grin. And as the other went off, laughing, the young man called, 'You must always make them like that, see?'

He liked to drink at celebrations, at weddings or Christmas, but he wasn't a man who drank his brandy every day. He would have two brandies on a Saturday afternoon, when the week's work was over, and for the rest of the time the bottle that he brought from Francistown when he went to collect stores lay in the chest in his tent. But on this last night he got up from the fire on impulse and went over to the tent to fetch the bottle (one thing he didn't do, he didn't expect a kaffir to handle his drink for him; it was too much of a temptation to put in their way). He brought a glass with him, too, one of a set of six made of tinted, imitation cut-glass, and he poured himself a tot and stretched out his legs where he could feel the warmth of the fire through the soles of his boots. The nights were not cold, until the wind came up at two or three in the morning, but there was a clarifying chill to the air; now and then a figure came over from the black men's camp to put another log on the fire whose flames had dropped and become blue. The young man felt inside himself a similar low incandescence; he poured himself another brandy. The long yelping of the jackals prowled the sky without, like the wind about a house; there was no house, but the sounds beyond the light his fire tremblingly inflated into the dark — that jumble of meaningless voices, crying babies, coughs and hawking — had built walls to enclose and a roof to shelter. He was exposed, turning naked to space on the sphere of the world, but he was not aware of it.

The lilt of various kinds of small music began and died in the dark; threads of notes, blown and plucked, that disappeared under the voices. Presently a huge man whose thick black body had strained apart every seam in his ragged pants and shirt loped silently into the light and dropped just within it, not too near the fire. His feet, intimately crossed, were cracked and weathered like driftwood. He held to his mouth a one-stringed instrument shaped like a lyre, made out of a half-moon of bent wood with a ribbon of dried palm-leaf tied from tip to tip. His big lips rested gently on the strip and, while he blew, his one hand, by controlling the vibration of the palm-leaf, made of his breath a small, faint, perfect music. It was caught by the very limits of the capacity of the human ear; it was almost out of range. The first music men ever heard, when they began to stand upright among the rushes at the river, might have been like it. When it died away it was difficult to notice at what point it really had gone.

'Play that other one,' said the young man, in Tswana. Only the smoke from his pipe moved.

The pink-palmed hands settled down round the instrument. The thick,

259

tender lips were wet once. The faint desolate voice spoke again, so lonely a music that it came to the player and listener as if they heard it inside themselves. This time the player took a short stick in his other hand, and, while he blew, scratched it back and forth inside the curve of the lyre, where the notches cut there produced a dry, shaking, slithering sound like the far-off movement of dancers' feet. There were two or three figures with more substance than the shadows, where the firelight merged with the darkness. They came and squatted. One of them had half a paraffin tin with a wooden neck and other attachments of gut and wire. When the lyre-player paused, lowering his piece of stick and leaf slowly, in ebb, from his mouth, and wiping his lips on the back of his hand, the other began to play. It was a thrumming, repetitive, banjo-tune. The young man's boot patted the sand in time to it and he took it up with handclaps once or twice. A thin, yellowish man in an old hat pushed his way to the front past sarcastic remarks and twittings and sat on his haunches with a little clay bowl between his feet. Over its mouth there was a keyboard of metal tongues. After some exchange, he played it and the others sang low and nasally, bringing a few more strollers to the fire. The music came to an end, pleasantly, and started up again, like a breath drawn. In one of the intervals the young man said, 'Let's have a look at that contraption of yours, isn't it a new one?' and the man to whom he signalled did not understand what was being said to him but handed over his paraffin-tin mandolin with pride and also with amusement at his own handiwork.

The young man turned it over, twanged it once, grinning and shaking his head. Two bits of string and an old jam tin and they'll make a whole band, man. He'd heard them playing some crazy-looking things. The circle of faces watched him with pleasure; they laughed and lazily remarked to each other; it was a funny-looking thing, all right, but it worked. The owner took it back and played it, clowning a little. The audience laughed and joked appreciatively; they were sitting close in to the fire now, painted by it. 'Next week,' the young man raised his voice gaily, 'next week when I come back, I bring radio with me, plenty real music. All the big white bands play over it –' Someone who had once worked in Johannesburg said 'Satchmo', and the others took it up, understanding that this was the word for what the white man was going to bring from town. Satchmo. Satch-mo. They tried it out, politely. 'Music, just like at a big white dance in town. Next week.' A friendly, appreciative silence fell, with them all resting back in the warmth of the fire and looking at him indulgently. A strange thing happened to him. He felt hot, over first his neck, then his ears and his face. It didn't matter, of course; by next week they would have forgotten. They wouldn't expect it. He shut down his mind on a picture of them, hanging round the caravan to listen, and him coming out on the steps to tell them –

He thought for a moment that he would give them the rest of the bottle of brandy. Hell, no, man, it was mad. If they got the taste for the stuff, they'd be pinching it all the time. He'd give Piet some sugar and yeast and things from the stores, for them to make beer with tomorrow when he was gone. He put his hands deep in his pockets and stretched out to the fire with his head sunk on his chest. The lyre-player picked up his flimsy piece of wood again, and slowly what the young man was feeling inside himself seemed to find a voice; up into the night beyond the fire it went, uncoiling from his breast and bringing ease. As if it had been made audible out of infinity and could be returned to infinity at any point, the lonely voice of the lyre went on and on. Nobody spoke, the barriers of tongues fell with silence. The whole dirty tide of worry and planning had gone out of the young man. The small, high moon, outshone by a spiky spread of cold stars, repeated the shape of the lyre. He sat for he was not aware how long, just as he had for so many other nights, with the stars at his head and the fire at his feet.

But at last the music stopped and time began again. There was tonight; there was tomorrow, when he was going to drive to Francistown. He stood up; the company fragmented. The lyre-player blew his nose into his fingers. Dusty feet took their accustomed weight. They went off to their tents and he went off to his. Faint plangencies followed them. The young man gave a loud, ugly, animal yawn, the sort of unashamed personal noise a man can make when he lives alone. He walked very slowly across the sand; it was dark but he knew the way more surely than with his eyes. 'Piet! Hey!' he bawled as he reached his tent. 'You get up early tomorrow, eh? And I don't want to hear the lorry won't start. You get it going and then you call me. D'you hear?'

He was lighting the oil-lamp that Piet had left ready on the chest and as it came up softly it brought the whole interior of the tent with it; the chest, the bed, the clock, and the coy smiling face of the seventeen-year-old girl. He sat down on the bed, sliding his palms through the silky fur of the kaross. He drew a breath and held it for a moment, looking round purposefully. And then he picked up the photograph, folded the cardboard support back flat to the frame, and put it in the chest with all his other things, ready for the journey.

NADINE GORDIMER

A Chip of Glass Ruby

From: *Not for Publication* (1965)

When the duplicating machine was brought into the house, Bamjee said, 'Isn't it enough that you've got the Indians' troubles on your back?' Mrs Bamjee said, with a smile that showed the gap of a missing tooth but was confident all the same. 'What's the difference, Yusuf? We've all got the same troubles.'

'Don't tell me that. We don't have to carry passes; let the natives protest against passes on their own, there are millions of them. Let them go ahead with it.'

The nine Bamjee and Pahad children were present at this exchange as they were always; in the small house that held them all there was no room for privacy for the discussion of matters they were too young to hear, and so they had never been too young to hear anything. Only their sister and half-sister, Girlie, was missing; she was the eldest, and married. The children looked expectantly, unalarmed and interested, at Bamjee, who had neither left the dining-room nor settled down again to the task of rolling his own cigarettes which had been interrupted by the arrival of the duplicator. He looked at the thing that had come hidden in a wash-basket and conveyed in a black man's taxi, and the children turned on it too, their black eyes surrounded by thick lashes like those still, open flowers with hairy tentacles that close on whatever touches them.

'A fine thing to have on the dining-room table,' was all he said at last. They smelled the machine among them; a smell of cold black grease. He went out, heavily on tiptoe, in his troubled way.

'It's going to go nicely on the sideboard!' Mrs Bamjee was busy making a place by removing the two pink glass vases filled with plastic carnations and the hand-painted velvet runner with the picture of the Taj Mahal.

After supper she began to run off leaflets on the machine. The family lived in the dining-room – the three other rooms in the house were full of beds – and they were all there. The older children shared a bottle of ink while they did their homework, and the two little ones pushed a couple of empty milk bottles in and out the chair legs. The three-year-old fell asleep and was carted away by one of the girls. They all drifted off to bed eventually; Bamjee himself went before the older children – he was a fruit and vegetable hawker and was up at half-past four every morning to get to the market by five. 'Not long now,' said Mrs Bamjee. The older children looked up and smiled at him. He turned his back on her. She still wore the traditional clothing of a Moslem woman, and her body, which was scraggy and unimportant as a dress on a peg when it was not host to a child, was wrapped in the trailing rags of a cheap sari, and her thin black plait was greased. When she was a girl, in the Transvaal town where they lived still, her mother fixed a chip of glass ruby in her nostril; but she had abandoned that adornment as too old-style, even for her, long ago.

She was up until long after midnight, turning out leaflets. She did it as if she might have been pounding chillies.

Bamjee did not have to ask what the leaflets were. He had read the papers. All the past week Africans had been destroying their passes and then presenting themselves for arrest. Their leaders were jailed on charges of incitement, campaign offices were raided – someone must be helping the few minor leaders who were left to keep the campaign going without offices or equipment. What was it the leaflets would say – 'Don't go to work tomorrow', 'Day of Protest', 'Burn Your Pass for Freedom'? He didn't want to see.

He was used to coming home and finding his wife sitting at the dining-room table deep in discussion with strangers or people whose names were familiar by repute. Some were prominent Indians, like the lawyer, Dr Abdul Mohammed Khan, or the big businessman, Mr Moonsamy Patel, and he was flattered, in a suspicious way, to meet them in his house. As he came home from work next day he met Dr Khan coming out of the house, and Dr Khan – a highly educated man – said to him, 'A wonderful woman.' But Bamjee had never caught his wife out in any presumption; she behaved properly, as any Moslem woman should, and once her business with such gentlemen was over would never, for instance, have sat down to eat with them. He found her now back in the kitchen, setting about the preparation of dinner and carrying on a conversation on several different wave lengths with the children. 'It's really a shame if you're tired of lentils, Jimmy, because that's what you're getting – Amina, hurry up, get a pot of water going – don't worry, I'll mend that in a minute, just bring the yellow cotton, and there's a needle in the cigarette box on the sideboard.'

'Was that Dr Khan leaving?' said Bamjee.

'Yes, there's going to be a stay-at-home on Monday. Desai's ill, and he's got to get the word around by himself. Bob Jali was up all last night printing leaflets, but he's gone to have a tooth out.' She had always treated Bamjee as if it were only a mannerism that made him appear uninterested in politics, the way some woman will persist in interpreting her husband's bad temper as an endearing gruffness hiding boundless goodwill, and she talked to him of these things just as she passed on to him neighbours' or family gossip.

'What for do you want to get mixed up with these killings and stonings and I don't know what? Congress should keep out of it. Isn't it enough with the Group Areas?'

She laughed. 'Now, Yusuf, you know you don't believe that. Look how you said the same thing when the Group Areas started in Natal. You said we should begin to worry when we get moved out of our own houses here in the Transvaal. And then your own mother lost her house in Noorddorp, and there you are; you saw that nobody's safe. Oh, Girlie was here this afternoon, she says Ismail's brother's engaged – that's nice, isn't it? His mother will be pleased; she was worried.'

'Why was she worried?' asked Jimmy, who was fifteen, and old enough to patronise his mother.

'Well, she wanted to see him settled. There's a party on Sunday week at Ismail's place – you'd better give me your suit to give to the cleaners tomorrow, Yusuf.'

One of the girls presented herself at once. 'I'll have nothing to wear, Ma.'

Mrs Bamjee scratched her sallow face. 'Perhaps Girlie will lend you her pink, eh? Run over to Girlie's place now and say I say will she lend it to you.'

The sound of commonplaces often does service as security, and Bamjee, going to sit in the armchair with the shiny armrests that was wedged between the dining-room table and the sideboard, lapsed into an unthinking doze that, like all times of dreamlike ordinariness during those weeks, was filled with uneasy jerks and starts back into reality. The next morning, as soon as he got to market, he heard that Dr Khan had been arrested. But that night Mrs Bamjee sat up making a new dress for her daughter; the sight disarmed Bamjee, reassured him again, against his will, so that the resentment he had been making ready all day faded into a morose and accusing silence. Heaven knew, of course, who came and went in the house during the day. Twice in that week of riots, raids, and arrests, he found black women in the house when he came home; plain ordinary native women in doeks, drinking tea. This was not a thing other Indian women would have in their homes, he thought bitterly; but then his wife was not like other people, in a way he could not put his finger on, except to say what it was not: not scandalous, not punishable, not rebellious. It was, like the attraction that had led him to marry her, Pahad's widow with five children, something he could not see clearly.

When the Special Branch knocked steadily on the door in the small hours of Thursday morning, he did not wake up, for his return to consciousness was always set in his mind to half-past four, and that was more than an hour away. Mrs Bamjee got up herself, struggled into Jimmy's raincoat, which was hanging over a chair, and went to the front door. The clock on the wall – a wedding present when she married Pahad – showed three o'clock when she snapped on the light, and she knew at once who it was on the other side of the door. Although she was not surprised, her hands shook like a very old person's as she undid the locks and the complicated catch on the wire burglar-proofing. And then she opened the door and they were there – two coloured policemen in plain clothes. 'Zanip Bamjee?'

'Yes.'

As they talked, Bamjee woke up in the sudden terror of having overslept. Then he became conscious of men's voices. He heaved himself out of bed in the dark and went to the window, which, like the front door, was covered with a heavy mesh of thick wire against intruders from the dingy lane it looked upon. Bewildered, he appeared in the dining-room, where the policemen were searching through a soapbox of papers beside the duplicating machine. 'Yusuf, it's for me,' Mrs Bamjee said.

At once, the snap of a trap, realisation came. He stood there in an old shirt before the two policemen, and the woman was going off to prison because of the natives. 'There you are!' he shouted standing away from her. 'That's what you've got for it. Didn't I tell you? Didn't I? That's the end of it now. That's the finish. That's what it's come to.' She listened with her head at the slightest tilt to one side, as if to ward off a blow, or in compassion.

Jimmy, Pahad's son, appeared at the door with a suitcase; two or three of the girls were behind him. 'Here, Ma, you take my green jersey.' 'I've found your clean blouse.' Bamjee had to keep moving out of their way as they helped their mother to make ready. It was like the preparation for one of the family festivals his wife made such a fuss over; wherever he put himself, they bumped into him. Even the two policemen mumbled, 'Excuse me,' and pushed past into the rest of the house to continue their search. They took with them a tome that Nehru had written in prison; it had been bought from a persevering travelling salesman and kept, for years, on the mantelpiece. 'Oh, don't take that, please,' Mrs Bamjee said suddenly, clinging to the arm of the man who had picked it up.

The man held it away from her.

'What does it matter, Ma?'

It was true that no one in the house had ever read it; but she said, 'It's for my children.'

'Ma, leave it.' Jimmy, who was squat and plump, looked like a merchant advising a client against a roll of silk she had set her heart on. She went into the bedroom and got dressed. When she came out in her old yellow sari with a brown coat over it, the faces of the children were behind her like faces on the platform at a railway station. They kissed her goodbye. The policemen did not hurry her, but she seemed to be in a hurry just the same.

'What am I going to do?' Bamjee accused them all.

The policemen looked away patiently.

'It'll be all right. Girlie will help. The big children can manage. And Yusuf –' The children crowded in around her; two of the younger ones had awakened and appeared, asking shrill questions.

'Come on', said the policemen.

'I want to speak to my husband.' She broke away and came back to him, and the movement of her sari hid them from the rest of the room for a moment. His face hardened in suspicious anticipation against the request to give some message to the next fool who would take up her pamphleteering until he, too, was arrested. 'On Sunday,' she said. 'Take them on Sunday.' He did not know what she was talking about. 'The engagement party,' she whispered, low and urgent. 'They shouldn't miss it. Ismail will be offended.'

They listened to the car drive away. Jimmy bolted and barred the front door, and then at once opened it again; he put on the raincoat that his mother had taken off. 'Going to tell Girlie,' he said. The children went back to bed. Their father did not say a word to any of them; their talk, the crying of the younger ones and the argumentative voices of the older, went on in the bedrooms. He found himself alone; he felt the night all around him. And then he happened to meet the clock face and saw with a terrible sense of unfamiliarity that this was not the secret night but an hour he should have recognised: the time he always got up. He pulled on his trousers and his dirty white hawker's coat and wound his grey muffler up to the stubble on his chin and went to work.

The duplicating machine was gone from the sideboard. The policemen had taken it with them, along with the pamphlets and the conference reports and the stack of old newspapers that had collected on top of the wardrobe in the bedroom – not the thick dailies of the white men, but the thin, impermanent-looking papers that spoke up, sometimes interrupted by suppression or lack of money, for the rest. It was all gone. When he had married her and moved in with her and her five children, into what had been the Pahad and became the Bamjee house, he had not recognised the humble, harmless, and apparently useless routine tasks – the minutes of meetings being written up on the dining-room table at night, the government blue books that were read while the latest baby was suckled, the employment of the fingers of the older children in the fashioning of crinkle-paper Congress rosettes – as activity intended to move mountains. For years and years he had not noticed it, and now it was gone.

The house was quiet. The children kept to their lairs, crowded on the beds with the doors shut. He sat and looked at the sideboard, where the plastic carnations and the mat with the picture of the Taj Mahal were in place. For the first few weeks he never spoke of her. There was the feeling, in the house, that he had wept and raged at her, that boulders of reproach had thundered down upon her absence, and yet he had said not one word. He had not been to inquire where she was; Jimmy and Girlie had gone to Mohammed Ebrahim, the lawyer, and when he found out that their mother had been taken – when she was arrested, at least – to a prison in the next town, they had stood about outside the big prison door for hours while they waited to be told where she had been moved from there. At last they had discovered that she was fifty miles away in Pretoria. Jimmy asked Bamjee for five shillings to help Girlie pay the train fare to Pretoria, once she had been interviewed by the police and had been given a permit to visit her mother; he put three two-shilling pieces on the table for Jimmy to pick up, and the boy, looking at him keenly, did not know whether the extra shilling meant anything, or whether it was merely that Bamjee had no change.

It was only when relations and neighbours came to the house that Bamjee would suddenly begin to talk. He had never been so expansive in his life as he was in the company of these visitors, many of them come on a polite call rather in the nature of a visit of condolence. 'Ah, yes, yes, you can see how I am – you see what has been done to me. Nine children, and I am on the cart all day. I get home at seven or eight. What are you to do? What can people like us do?'

'Poor Mrs Bamjee. Such a kind lady.'

'Well, you see for yourself. They walk in here in the middle of the night and leave a houseful of children. I'm out on the cart all day, I've got a living to earn.' Standing about in his shirt sleeves, he became quite animated; he would call for the girls to bring fruit drinks for the visitors. When they were gone, it was as if he, who was orthodox if not devout and never drank liquor, had been drunk and abruptly sobered up; he looked dazed and could not have gone over in his mind what he had been saying. And as he cooled, the lump of resentment and wrongedness stopped his throat again.

Bamjee found one of the little boys the centre of a self-important group of championing brothers and sisters in the dining-room one evening. 'They've been cruel to Ahmed.'

'What has he done?' said the father.

'Nothing! Nothing!' The little girl stood twisting her handkerchief excitedly.

An older one, thin as her mother, took over, silencing the others with a gesture of her skinny hand. 'They did it at school today. They made an example of him.'

'What is an example?' said Bamjee impatiently.

'The teacher made him come up and stand in front of the whole class, and he told them, "You see this boy? His mother's in jail because she likes the natives so much. She wants the Indians to be the same as natives."'

'It's terrible,' he said. His hands fell to his sides. 'Did she ever think of this?'

'That's why Ma's *there*,' said Jimmy, putting aside his comic and emptying out his schoolbooks upon the table. 'That's all the kids need to know. Ma's there because things like this happen. Petersen's a coloured teacher, and it's his black blood that's brought him trouble all his life, I suppose. He hates anyone who says everybody's the same, because that takes away from him his bit of whiteness that's all he's got. What d'you expect? It's nothing to make too much fuss about.'

'Of course, you are fifteen and you know everything,' Bamjee mumbled at him.

'I don't say that. But I know Ma, anyway.' The boy laughed.

There was a hunger strike among the political prisoners, and Bamjee could not bring himself to ask Girlie if her mother was starving herself too. He would not ask; and yet he saw in the young woman's face the gradual weakening of her mother. When the strike had gone on for nearly a week one of the elder children burst into tears at the table and could not eat. Bamjee pushed his own plate away in rage.

Sometimes he spoke out loud to himself while he was driving the vegetable lorry. 'What for?' Again and again: 'What for?' She was not a modern woman who cut her hair and wore short skirts. He had married a good plain Moslem woman who bore children and stamped her own chillies. He had a sudden vision of her at the duplicating machine, that night just before she was taken away, and he felt himself maddened, baffled, and hopeless. He had become the ghost of a victim, hanging about the scene of a crime whose motive he could not understand and had not had time to learn.

The hunger strike at the prison went into the second week. Alone in the rattling cab of his lorry, he said things that he heard as if spoken by someone else, and his heart burned in fierce agreement with them. 'For a crowd of natives who'll smash our shops and kill us in our houses when their time comes.' 'She will starve herself to death there.' 'She will die there.' 'Devils who will burn and kill us.' He fell into bed each night like a stone, and dragged himself up in the mornings as a beast of burden is beaten to its feet.

One of these mornings, Girlie appeared very early, while he was wolfing bread and strong tea – alternate sensations of dry solidity and stinging heat – at the kitchen table. Her real name was Fatima, of course, but she had adopted the silly modern name along with the clothes of the young factory girls among whom she worked. She was expecting her first baby in a week or two, and her small face, her cut and curled hair, and the sooty arches drawn over her eyebrows did not seem to belong to her thrust-out body under a clean smock. She wore mauve lipstick and was smiling her cocky little white girl's smile, foolish and bold, not like an Indian girl's at all.

'What's the matter?' he said.

She smiled again. 'Don't you know? I told Bobby he must get me up in time this morning. I wanted to be sure I wouldn't miss you today.'

'I don't know what you're talking about.'

She came over and put her arm up around his unwilling neck and kissed the grey bristles at the side of his mouth. 'Many happy returns! Don't you know it's your birthday?'

'No,' he said. 'I didn't know, didn't think –' He broke the pause by swiftly picking up the bread and giving his attention desperately to eating and drinking. His mouth was busy, but his eyes looked at her, intensely black. She said nothing, but stood there with him. She would not speak, and at last he said, swallowing a piece of bread that tore at his throat as it went down, 'I don't remember these things.'

The girl nodded, the Woolworth baubles in her ears swinging. 'That's the first thing she told me when I saw her yesterday – don't forget it's Bajie's birthday tomorrow.'

He shrugged over it. 'It means a lot to children. But that's how she is. Whether it's one of the old cousins or the neighbour's grandmother, she always knows when the birthday is. What importance is my birthday, while she's sitting there in a prison? I don't understand how she can do the things she does when her mind is always full of woman's nonsense at the same time – that's what I don't understand with her.'

'Oh, but don't you see?' the girl said. 'It's because she doesn't want anybody to be left out. It's because she always remembers; remembers everything – people without somewhere to live, hungry kids, boys who can't get educated – remembers all the time. That's how Ma is.'

'Nobody else is like that.' It was half a complaint.

'No, nobody else,' said his stepdaughter.

She sat herself down at the table, resting her belly. He put his head in his hands. 'I'm getting old' – but he was overcome by something much more curious, by an answer. He knew why he had desired her, the ugly widow with five children; he knew what way it was in which she was not like the others; it was there, like the fact of the belly that lay between him and her daughter.

NADINE GORDIMER

The Credibility Gap

From: *Livingstone's Companions* (1972)

'You go.'

'No, it'll be for you.'

The timid ring of the front doorbell or the two-syllable call of the telephone produced the same moment of obstinacy: everyone appeared to be going on with what he was doing. The young brother continued to hammer away somewhere. The elder, if it so happened that he was in the house, absolved himself because he now had his own flat with his own front door and telephone. A house guest – there was usually someone who had nowhere else to live – didn't feel it was his or her place to get up. The mother knew it wouldn't be for her. It was for the daughter, inevitably, since she was in one of the expanding periods of life when one moves through and with the zest and restlessness of the shoal. But often there were reasons why she did not want to respond without an intermediary: the complex social pattern meant that she was supposed to be out when she was in, or in when she was out.

You go. It'll be for you.

The schoolboy Rob took no notice, anyway. The cats were disturbed by anyone leaving a room or entering; they lifted back their heads from bodies relaxed to tiger-skin flatness before the fire, and opened their eyes. Pattie's casual, large-footed friends trod into flowered saucers scummed with disdained milk that stood about all over the place. Cats and saucers were the mother's – old-maidish possessions that could be allowed a woman who, if she had no husband by now, had among other things the contrary testimony of children grown and half-grown who were half-bother and -sister. Pattie never thought of her mother when she was alone with friends her own age, but sometimes when she and the friends and her mother were drinking beer and arguing in the living room at home she would have an impulse the converse of that of the parent to show off its child. 'Don't tease her about her cats. It's her passion for cats that got her out of solitary confinement when she was in jug. Honestly. She was supposed to be in solitary for leading a hunger strike among the political prisoners, but the chief wardress was as dotty about cats as she is, and they were such buddies discussing their dear little kitties, the old girl used to let her out secretly to sit in the prison yard. It's true.'

Yes, there once had been a ring at the door in the dark early hours of the morning that was for Mrs Doris Aucamp. Years ago, when the children really were still children, and there still were real political opposition movements in South Africa. The two elder children – Andrew and Pattie – at least, remembered something of that time; someone had moved into the house to take care of them, and they had been set up on the Johannesburg City Hall steps one Saturday among the families of other political prisoners, wearing placards round their necks: WE WANT OUR MUMMY BACK. Most of the friends drinking beer in the living-room and discussing the authoritarianism of the university system or the authenticity of the sense-experience known as getting stoned had heard about the massacre of Sharpeville – if from no other source, then from references to it that came up in overseas magazines; one of the boys, studying abroad, had even discovered that in New York there was a commemorative rally at Carnegie Hall on the anniversary of 'Sharpeville Day', held by South Africans in exile. It was with quite a momentary thrill of admiring curiosity that they realised that this woman – somebody's mother – had actually served a prison sentence for what she believed (of course, what they all believed) about the idiocy of the colour bar. It both added to and detracted from the aura of those among them who now and then were moved to defy minor-sounding laws against marching the streets or assembling for protest: so these 'activists' were not the discoverers that danger, in some times and places, is the only form of freedom? They had only dug up, afresh, to offend the docile snouts of the population, what the major punishments of those minor-sounding transgressions had forced people to bury, and forget where.

This woman wasn't bad, either, in spite of her age, not bad at all. There was at least one of the young men who wouldn't have minded indulging a kind of romantic lust in response to that mature sexuality, confidently lived with for a lifetime, vested in her blunt, nicotine-tanned hands as she stirred her tea and the turn towards the table of those rather big breasts, sloping away from each other a bit like an African woman's bubs – she was a short, broad woman with nice, nine-pin calves, too wide in the hip ever to wear trousers. Mrs Doris Aucamp caught the look and was smiling at him, not taking it up but not offended – kindly amused: of course, as well as having been a jailbird, she was also a writer. He hadn't read her; but it was a well-known name.

* * *

I'll go – it's for me.

There were times when Pattie leapt up because she had the instinct that some irreparable usurpation would take place if anyone other than herself were to open the door upon the face she expected, or respond with a voice other than hers to the summons of the telephone. A word of criticism of one of her friends roused a fierce solidarity. 'Oh Kip's not what you think at all. People get it all wrong. People just don't understand. He wouldn't trust anyone else. You have to be one of us.'

Her mother slapped down a cat who was trying to filch off a plate. 'Of course. Every set of friends has private dependencies that make it hang together. Why do I put up with Scoresby? Why do any of his pals?' The man she spoke of was a long-time friend, long-time alcoholic.

Rob was finely paring the wart on the inner side of his third finger, right hand. He looked up a moment, saw that man, who sometimes played chess with him, lying as he had once found him in a lumpy pool of pink vomit in the bathroom. He turned the blade towards his finger once more; everyone told him it was dangerous to cut warts, but he was getting rid of his by persistently slicing them away, right down to the healthy flesh, without squeamishness.

'It's not that so much. I mean, you think it's peculiar because I bring someone home and don't know his surname – even if we don't know each other personally, *we know –*'

'But you don't really think it's a matter of age? There're people under thirty you couldn't trust as far as I could throw this greedy, shameless cat – mmh?'

'No – I'm sorry – in some ways you just can't –'

Her mother nodded her head as if in sympathy for some disability. 'You know what Lévi-Strauss says? Something, something "… as man moves forward he takes with him all positions he's occupied in the past and all those he'll occupy in the future." Wait, I'll get it.' They heard her running upstairs; padding down more slowly, probably leafing through the book on the way. She stood behind her daughter, silently following the passage over the girl's shoulder. *As he moves forward within his environment, Man takes with him all the positions that he has occupied in the past, and all those that he will occupy in the future. He is everywhere at the same time, a crowd which, in the act of moving forward, yet recapitulates at every instant every step that it has ever taken in the past.*

The girl put the book down; the two of them looked into each other, but it became purely a moment of physical comprehension: Pattie saw that the skin of her mother's forehead would never have the shine of tautness again, the mother saw that little scars of adolescent turmoil had left their imperfections on the slightly sulky jawline that attracted men.

★ ★ ★

No – it's all right, I'll go. I'm expecting a friend.

Some of the girls feared themselves pregnant, one or two had had abortions, and there were even beginning to be a few contemporaries who got

272

married and furnished flats. Pattie knew that if she became pregnant, her mother could deal with the situation; on the other hand, if she got married and bought furniture, well, that was all right, too.

'Isn't there anything else?'

Her mother was putting flea powder on the cats: Liz and Burton, Snorer, and the mother cat of all three, Puss. Snorer's name was really Schnorrer, dubbed for his greedy persistence at table by the Jewish professor who – the girl understood, looking back at things she hadn't known how to interpret then – had been her mother's lover for a time. Dolly, the black servant, had heard the name as Snorer; and so it had become that, just as the professor was now become a family friend, like Scoresby, only less troublesome.

'No. You meet them years later and they tell you their son is married, their daughter's engaged. All smiles, big surprise.'

'Except you. You count yourself outside.' The girl had trudged the summer through in a pair of Greek sandals whose soles had worn away completely beneath each big toe. She was examining with respect these alien, honest, workmanlike extremities of herself, thickened, ingrained with city dirt round the broken nails, assertive as the mechanic's black-ringed fingernails that can never be scrubbed to deny their toil. After a pause: 'People say that story you wrote was about me.'

Which story?'

'The one about the donkey.'

'It wasn't about you, it was about me.'

'But I saved up for a donkey?'

'Never. It was something I told you about myself.'

★ ★ ★

You go.

No, you.

Rob did not know that Snorer was not the cat's name any more than he knew that Julius, the professor, had not always been an old family friend. He didn't answer the phone because he was not yet interested in girls, and his boy friends used the kitchen door, coming tramping in past Dolly without knocking. Dolly's man repaired bicycles on the pavement outside the local hardware shop, and she treated the boys like the potential good customers they were, sycophantically addressing them as 'My baasie', 'Master' Johnny or Dick, although her employer didn't allow her to corrupt the young people of the house in this way into thinking themselves little white lordlings. '"Master" my eye! Really, Dolly! You should be putting them across your knee and warming their behinds. Nothing's ever going to change for the blacks, here, until people like you understand that nobody's born "master", never mind white kids in short pants.' But Dolly was unresponsive, for another reason. She resented having been given, with equal forthrightness, an ultimatum about closing her backyard trade in beer.

When the children of the house were small the front door had opened often upon black faces. The children had sat on the knees and laughed at the jokes of black men and women who were their mother's friends and political associates. Pattie remembered some of them quite well; where was so-and-so now, she would sometimes remark; what happened to so-and-so? But all were in exile or prison. She had tentatively, through her own student set, a different sort of association. The political movements were dead, the university was closed to black students, but there were Africans, usually musicians, with whom was shared the free-for-all of jazz, the suspension from reality in the smoke of the weed – white hangers-on, black hangers-on, there: it depended whose world you decided it was. She even went once or twice on a jaunt to one of the black states over the border, and there met Africans who were not creatures of the night but students, like herself.

If I fall for a black one, how would we manage?'

'You must leave the country.' Before the mother or anyone else could answer, Rob had spoken.

He put down the coloured supplement on vintage cars he was studying. His gaze was hidden under lowered lids, but his head was slightly inclined to the polarity of his mother as she sat, a cigarette comfortably between her stained first and third fingers, her square-jawed, sunburned face looking on with a turned-down neutral smile. They were waiting for her to speak, but she said nothing. At last she put out her hand and passed it again and again through the boy's hair, firmly, as the cats loved to be raked along the fur of their backs.

'There's a nice, God-fearing guardian of the white race growing up.' Andrew had dropped in to pick up his allowance; he addressed the room after his younger brother had left it.

Mrs Doris Aucamp remained serenely in her silence; as her Professor Julius had once remarked, she could turn bullets to water. She irritated her elder son by giving him the brief, head-tilted, warm glance, old childish balm for sibling fears of favoured dispensation granted the last-born.

'Sorry, no dice, my little brother doesn't think we should do it.' Pattie was amused. 'Poor kid.'

'A man once gave me up because I didn't know the boiling point of water.' But the elder son didn't accept his mother's diversion of subject; in his turn, did not appear to hear.

'Fahrenheit or centigrade?' A Peace Corps girl from Uganda, in the house for the time being, was eager to show herself to be on the family wavelength.

'Neither. I'm sure that was it. Couldn't get over it. Thought he'd found a real intellectual to appreciate him, and then discovers she doesn't even know a thing like that.'

'Black or white?' Pattie asked.

There was laughter. 'Oh he was white, *very* white.'

When the two of them were alone together, the daughter returned to the subject. She did not know, for sure, of anyone since Julius. 'When you were young? The man with the boiling water?'

'Oh no, only a few years ago.'

The girl was looking for a number in the telephone directory. She covered her silence by saying kindly, politely, 'What is the boiling point of water, anyway? I've forgotten.'

'Oh I found out quickly enough. Two-hundred-and-twelve Fahrenheit.' Mrs Doris Aucamp had the smoker's laugh that turns to coughing.

The number Pattie tried was busy. Resting on the receiver fingers wearing as many rings as a Renaissance pope, she said of her little brother, 'It's just that he wants God-to-keep-his-hand-over-us.'

'Of course.' The expression was a family one, derived from a grand-mother who mistook superstition for piety.

'Poor little devil.' The girl spoke dreamily.

* * *

You go. Go on. It'll never be for me.

When their mother was out, no one – certainly not Dolly – would answer the bell for Pattie. One afternoon it was a student friend standing there, come to tell her one of their friends had been killed. He and some others had been climbing with the girl the day before on a Sunday picnic, and she had slipped and fallen before their eyes. They picked her up fifteen minutes later at the bottom of a waterfall, her neck broken.

Mrs Doris Aucamp was waylaid by Dolly as she got out of the car in the garage. She thought for a moment Dolly had been drinking again, but it was not drink that widened her nostrils with drama but the instinct of all servants to enter swiftly into those fearful emotions that they can share with employers, because there, down among death and disaster, there are no privileges or exemptions to be claimed by anyone.

'The friend with the big eyes. The one that always laugh – that Kathy. She's die. It's true.' A big shuddering sigh took the black woman by the throat.

In the doorway of the living room the mother stood before her daughter and the young man, two faces for which there was no expression to meet the fact of death. They merely looked ashamed. There were tins of beer and cigarettes about. Their eyes were upon her, waiting.

She must have a face for this, of course.

But she stood, with the cats winding themselves about her calves. She said, 'Oh *no*?' People said that in books they had all read or films they'd seen. Then she saw the untidy hair and rosy nose of her daughter, alive, and, hand over her open mouth a moment, emotion came for what hadn't happened just as if it had: it could have been this one, mine. There was no face to meet that at the door.

The three of them sat drinking beer, breaking the awkward silences by repeating small certainties left by the girl who had died. 'She was here for supper last week. Didn't she forget a raincoat?'

'It's behind the door in my room. I noticed it this morning. It smells of her –'

'She always looked just like that when she was asleep. Honestly, it was just the same. Limp. Soft.' The young man himself looked afraid; sleeping with her, making love to her, then, he had been holding death in his arms.

He was a witty young man whose instincts were always to puncture the hot air of a distrusted solemnity. As the talk drifted away from the dead girl, tugged back to her, away again, he dashed off one of his wry mimicries of someone, and they found themselves laughing a little, slightly drunk by now, anyway. There was a closeness between them, a complicity of generations.

It had grown dark. Mrs Doris Aucamp got up to pull the curtains and wandered off upstairs by way of the kitchen, telling Dolly there would be an extra mouth at dinner. And then she met her younger son; he was repairing Dolly's radio. 'I wish my darned sister would leave my things alone. I look all over the house for my small pliers, and where are they? Lying around in the mess in her room, of course.'

'Well, don't make a fuss now. You see, darling, Kathy –'

'I heard about it.'

'It isn't the time. She's upset.'

There were shiny patches on his thin, dirty fingers where the warts had been pared away. The patches were watermarked, like moiré, in a design of whorls unique to him out of all the millions of human beings in the world. He was carefully, exasperatedly scraping the insulation tape from wire. He lifted his face and the preoccupation fell away. He said, 'She wasn't crying at all. She and Davy were yapping in there, quite ordinary. And then when one of her girl friends phoned she started to make herself cry over the phone, she put it on.' His face was without malice, clear, open, waiting.

His mother said, 'I wanted to cry – for a moment.'

He asked, 'Did you believe in it?'

'What?'

He gave a little jerk to his shoulder. '*It* … I mean, you didn't see that girl lying dead.'

276

'Davy did.' She searched his eyes to see if the explanation was one. He said nothing.

She said, hesitantly, 'Davy says she was the same as when she was asleep. It didn't seem she was dead.'

He nodded his head: *you see* – in the manner of one who accepts that no one will have an explanation for him.

This time she did not put out her hand to touch him. She wandered back into the dark hall of the house, her bent head making a double chin; the followers of those African prophets who claimed bullets could be turned to water had, after all, fallen everywhere on battlefields, from the Cape to Madagascar.

NADINE GORDIMER

The Termitary

From: *A Soldier's Embrace* (1980)

When you live in a small town far from the world you read about in municipal library books, the advent of repairmen in the house is a festival. Daily life
is gaily broken open, improvisation takes over. The living room masquerades as
a bedroom while the smell of paint in the bedroom makes it uninhabitable.
The secret backs of confident objects (matchwood draped with cobwebs
thickened by dust) are given away when furniture is piled to the centre of the
room. Meals are picnics at which table manners are suspended because the first
principle of deportment drummed into children by their mother – sitting
down at table – is missing: there is nowhere to sit. People are excused eccen-
tricities of dress because no one can find anything in its place.

A doctor is also a kind of repairman. When he is expected the sheets
are changed and the dog chased off the patient's bed. If a child is sick, she
doesn't have to go to school, she is on holiday, with presents into the bargain –
a whole roll of comics tied with newsagent's string, and crayons or card
games. The mother is alone in the house, except for the patient out of earshot
in the sickroom; the other children are at school. Her husband is away at
work. She takes off her apron, combs her hair and puts on a bit of lipstick to
make herself decent for the doctor, setting ready a tea-tray for two in the
quiet privacy of the deserted living room as for a secret morning visit from
the lover she does not have. After she and the doctor, who smells intoxicat-
ing, coldly sweet because he has just come from the operating theatre, have
stood together looking down at the patient and making jolly remarks, he is
glad to accept a cup of tea in his busy morning round and their voices are a
murmur and an occasional rise of laughter from behind the closed living-
room door.

Plumber, painter, doctor; with their arrival something has happened where
nothing ever happens; at home: a house with a bungalow face made of two
bow-window eyes on either side of a front-door mouth, in a street in a gold-
mining town of twenty-five thousand people in South Africa in the 1930s.

Once the upright Steinway piano stood alone on the few remaining boards
of a room from which the floor had been ripped. I burst in to look at the time
on the chiming clock that should have been standing on the mantelpiece and

instead flew through the air, and found myself jolted down into a subterranean smell of an earth I'd never smelled before, the earth buried by our house. I was nine years old and the drop broke no bones; the shock excited me, the thought of that hollow, earth-breaking dark always beneath our Axminster thrilled me; the importance I gained in my mother's accounts of how I might so easily have injured myself added to the sense of occasion usual in the family when there were workmen in.

This time it was not the painters, Mr Strydom and his boys, over whom my mother raised a quarrel every few years. *I'm not like any other woman. I haven't got a husband like other women's. The state this house is in. You'd see the place fall to pieces before you'd lift a finger. Too mean to pay for a lick of paint, and then when you do you expect it to last ten years. I haven't got a home like other women.* Workmen were treated as the house guests we never had; my mother's friends were neighbours, my father had none, and she wouldn't give house-room to a spare bed, anyway, because she didn't want his relatives coming. Mr Strydom was served sweet strong tea to his taste many times a day, while my mother stood by to chat and I followed his skills with the brush, particularly fascinated when he was doing something he called, in his Afrikaner's English, 'pulling the line'. This was the free-hand deftness with which he could make a narrow black stripe dividing the lower half of our passage, painted dark against dirty fingerprints, from the cream upper half. *Yust a sec while I first pull the line, ay.*

Then he would drain his cup so completely that the tea leaves swirled up and stuck to the sides. This workmanlike thirst, for me, was a foreign custom, sign of the difference between being Afrikaans and English, as we were, just as I accepted that it must be in accordance with their custom that the black 'boys' drank their tea from jam tins in the yard. But Mr Strydom, like the doctor, like deaf dapper Mr Waite the electrician, who had drinking bouts because he had been through something called Ypres, and Mr Hartman who sang to himself in a sad soprano while he tuned the Steinway upright my mother had brought from her own mother's house, was a recurrent event. The state the house was in, this time, was one without precedent; the men who were in were not repairmen. They had been sent for to exterminate what we called white ants — termites who were eating our house away under our feet. A million jaws were devouring steadily night and day the timber that supported our unchanging routines: one day (if my mother hadn't done something about it you may be sure no one else would) that heavy Steinway in its real rosewood case would have crashed through the floorboards.

For years my mother had efficiently kicked apart the finely-granulated earth, forming cones perfect as the shape taken by sand that has trickled through an egg tinier, that was piled in our garden by ordinary black ants. My father never did a hand's turn; she herself poured a tar-smelling disinfectant down the ant-holes and emptied into them kettles of boiling water that made the ground break out in a sweat of gleaming, struggling, pin-head creatures in paroxysm. Yet (it was another event) on certain summer evenings after rain we would rush out into the garden to be in the tropical snowfall of millions of transparent wings from what we called flying ants, who appeared from nowhere. We watched while frogs bold with greed hopped onto the veranda to fill their pouched throats with these apparently harmless insects, and our cat ate steadily but with more self-control, spitting out with a shake of her whiskers any fragment of wing she might have taken up by mistake. We did not know that when these creatures shed their four delicate dragon-fly wings (some seemed to struggle like people getting out of coats) and became drab terrestrials, and some idiotically lifted their hindquarters in the air as if they were reacting to injury, they were enacting a nuptial ceremony that, one summer night or another, had ended in one out of these millions being fertilised and making her way under our house to become queen of a whole colony generated and given birth to by herself. Somewhere under our house she was in an endless parturition that would go on until she was found and killed.

The men had been sent for to search out the queen. No evil-smelling poisons, no opening-up of the tunnels more skilfully constructed than the London Underground, the Paris Metro or the New York subway I'd read about, no fumigation such as might do for cockroaches or moles or woodborer beetles, could eradicate termites. No matter how many thousands were killed by my mother, as, in the course of the excavations that tore up the floorboards of her house, the brittle passages made of grains of earth cemented by a secretion carried in the termites' own bodies were broken, and the inhabitants poured out in a pus of white moving droplets with yellow heads – no matter how many she cast into death agony with her Flit spray, the termitary would at once be repopulated so long as the queen remained, alive, hidden in that inner chamber where her subjects who were also her progeny had walled her in and guarded and tended her.

The three exterminators were one white and two black. All had the red earth of underground clinging to their clothes and skin and hair; their eyes were bloodshot; the nails of their hands, black or white, were outlined in red, their ears rimmed. The long hairs in the nostrils of the white man were coated with red as a bee's legs are yellow with pollen. These men themselves appeared to have been dug up, raw from that clinging earth entombed beneath buildings. Bloodied by their life-long medieval quest, they were ready to take it up once more: the search for a queen. They were said to be very good; my mother was sceptical as she was about the powers of water diviners with bent twigs or people who got the dead to spell out messages by moving a glass to letters of the alphabet. But what else could she do? My father left it all to her, she had the responsibility.

She didn't like the look of these men. They were so filthy with earth; hands like exposed roots reaching for the tea she brought. She served even the white man with a tin mug.

It was she who insisted they leave a few boards intact under the piano; she knew better than to trust them to move it without damage to the rosewood case. They didn't speak while children watched them at work. The only sound was the pick stopped by the density of the earth under our living room, and the gasp of the black man who wielded the pick, pulling it free and hurling it back into the earth again. Held off by silence, we children would not go away. We stolidly spent all our free time in witness. Yet in spite of our vigilance, when it happened, when they found her, at last − the queen − we were not there.

My mother was mixing a cake and we had been attracted away to her by that substance of her alchemy that was not the beaten eggs and butter and sugar that went into it; even the lightest stroke of a quick forefinger into the bowl conveyed a coating of fragrant creamy sweetness to the mouth which already had foreknowledge of its utter satisfaction through the scent of vanilla that came not only from the bowl, but from her clothes, her hair, her very skin. Suddenly my mother's dog lifted his twitching lip back over his long teeth and began to bounce towards and back away from the screen door as he did when any stranger approached her. We looked up; the three men had come to the back steps. The white gestured his ochre hand brusquely at one of the blacks, who tramped forward with a child's cardboard shoebox offered. The lid was on and there were rough air holes punched in it here and there, just as in the boxes where we had kept silkworms until my mother thought they smelled too musty and threw them away. The white man gestured again; he and my mother for a moment held their hands the same way, his covered with earth, hers with flour. The black man took off the lid.

And there she was, the queen. The smallest child swallowed as if about to retch and ran away to the far side of the kitchen. The rest of us crowded nearer, but my mother made us make way, she wasn't going to be fobbed off with any-thing but complete satisfaction for her husband's money. We all gazed at an obese, helpless white creature, five inches long, with the tiny, shiny-visored head of an ant at one end. The body was a sort of dropsical sac attached to this head; it had no legs that could be seen, neither could it propel itself by peri-staltic action, like a slug or worm. The queen. The queen whose domain, we had seen for ourselves in the galleries and passages that had been uncovered beneath our house, was as big as ours.

The white man spoke. 'That's 'er, missus.'

'You're sure you've got the queen?'

'We got it. That's it.' He gave a professional snigger at ignorance.

Was she alive? − But again the silence of the red-eyed, red-earthed men kept us back; they wouldn't let us daringly put out a finger to touch that body that seemed blown up in sections, like certain party balloons, and that had at once the suggestion of tactile attraction and repugnance – if a finger were to be stroked testingly along that perhaps faintly downy body, sweet and creamy stuff might he expected to ooze from it. And in fact, when I found a book in the library called *The Soul of the White Ant*, by Eugène Marais, an Afrikaner like the white man who had found the queen's secret chamber, I read that the children-subjects at certain times draw nourishment from a queen's great body by stroking it so that she exudes her own rich maternal elixir.

'Ughh. Why's she so fat?' The smallest child had come close enough to force himself to look again.

'S'es full of ecks,' the white man said. 'They lays about a million ecks a day.'

'Is it dead?'

But the man only laughed, now that his job was done, and like the showman's helper at the conclusion of an act, the black man knew to clap the lid back on the shoebox. There was no way for us to tell; the queen cannot move, she is blind; whether she is underground, the tyrannical prisoner of her subjects who would not have been born and cannot live without her, or whether she is captured and borne away in a shoebox, she is helpless to evade the consequences of her power.

My mother paid the men out of her housekeeping allowance (but she would have to speak to our father about that) and they nailed back the living-room floorboards and went away, taking the cardboard box with them. My mother had heard that the whole thing was a hoax; these men went from house to house, made the terrible mess they'd left hers in, and produced the same queen time and again, carrying it around with them.

Yet the termites left our house. We never had to have those particular workmen in again. The Axminster carpet was laid once more, the furniture put back in its place, and I had to do the daily half-hour practice on the Steinway that I had been freed of for a week. I read in the book from the library that when the queen dies or is taken away all the termites leave their posts and desert the termitary; some find their way to other communities, thousands die. The termitary with its fungus-gardens for food, its tunnels for conveying water from as much as forty feet underground, its elaborate defence and communications system, is abandoned.

We lived on, above the ruin. The children grew up and left the town; coming back from the war after 1945 and later from visits to Europe and America and the Far East, it bored them to hear the same old stories, to be asked: 'D'you remember Mr Hartman who used to come in to tune the piano? He was asking after you the other day – poor thing, he's crippled with arthritis.' 'D'you remember old Strydom, "pulling the line" … how you kids used to laugh, I was quite ashamed …' 'D'you remember the time the white ant men were in, and you nearly broke your leg?' Were these events the sum of my mother's life?

Why should I remember? I, who — shuddering to look back at those five rooms behind the bow-window eyes and the front-door mouth — have oceans, continents, snowed-in capitals, islands where turtles swim, cathedrals, theatres, palace gardens where people kiss and tramps drink wine — all these to remember. My father grew senile and she put him in a home for his last years. She stayed on, although she said she didn't want to; the house was a burden to her, she had carried the whole responsibility for him, for all of us, all her life. Now she is dead and although I suppose someone else lives in her house, the secret passages, the inner chamber in which she was our queen and our prisoner are sealed up, empty.

NADINE GORDIMER

Once upon a Time

From: *Jump and other Stories* (1991)

Someone has written to ask me to contribute to an anthology of stories for children. I reply that I don't write children's stories; and he writes back that at a recent congress/book fair/seminar a certain novelist said every writer ought to write at least one story for children. I think of sending a postcard saying I don't accept that I 'ought' to write anything.

And then last night I woke up – or rather was wakened without knowing what had roused me.

A voice in the echo chamber of the subconscious?

A sound.

A creaking of the kind made by the weight carried by one foot after another along a wooden floor. I listened. I felt the apertures of my ears distend with concentration.

Again: the creaking. I was waiting for it; waiting to hear if it indicated that feet were moving from room to room, coming up the passage – to my door. I have no burglar bars, no gun under the pillow, but I have the same fears as people who do take these precautions, and my windowpanes are thin as rime, could shatter like a wineglass. A woman was murdered (how do they put it) in broad daylight in a house two blocks away, last year, and the fierce dogs who guarded an old widower and his collection of antique clocks were strangled before he was knifed by a casual labourer he had dismissed without pay.

I was staring at the door, making it out in my mind rather than seeing it, in the dark. I lay quite still – a victim already – but the arrhythmia of my heart was fleeing, knocking this way and that against its body-cage. How finely tuned the senses are, just out of rest, sleep! I could never listen intently as that in the distractions of the day; I was reading every faintest sound, identifying and classifying its possible threat.

But I learned that I was to be neither threatened nor spared. There was no human weight pressing on the boards, the creaking was a buckling, an epicentre of stress, I was in it. The house that surrounds me while I sleep is built on undermined ground; far beneath my bed, the floor, the house's foundations, the stopes and passages of gold mines have hollowed the rock, and when some face trembles, detaches and falls, three thousand feet below, the whole house shifts slightly, bringing uneasy strain to the balance and counter-balance of brick, cement, wood and glass that hold it as a structure around me. The misbeats of my heart tailed off like the last muffled flourishes on one of the wooden xylophones made by the Chopi and Tsonga migrant miners who might have been down there, under me in the earth at that moment. The stope where the fall was could have been disused, dripping water from its ruptured veins; or men might now be interred there in the most profound of tombs.

I couldn't find a position in which my mind would let go of my body – release me to sleep again. So I began to tell myself a story; a bedtime story.

★ ★ ★

In a house, in a suburb, in a city, there were a man and his wife who loved each other very much and were living happily ever after. They had a little boy, and they loved him very much. They had a cat and a dog that the little boy loved very much. They had a car and a caravan trailer for holidays, and a swimming pool that was fenced so that the little boy and his playmates would not fall in and drown. They had a housemaid who was absolutely trustworthy and an itinerant gardener who was highly recommended by the neighbours. For when they began to live happily ever after they were warned, by that wise old witch, the husband's mother, not to take on anyone off the street. They were inscribed in a medical benefit society, their pet dog was licensed, they were insured against fire, flood damage and theft, and subscribed to the local Neighbourhood Watch, which supplied them with a plaque for their gates lettered YOU HAVE BEEN WARNED over the silhouette of a would-be intruder. He was masked; it could not be said if he was black or white, and therefore proved the property owner was no racist.

It was not possible to insure the house, the swimming pool or the car against riot damage. There were riots, but these were outside the city, where people of another colour were quartered. These people were not allowed into the suburb except as reliable housemaids and gardeners, so there was nothing to fear, the husband told the wife. Yet she was afraid that some day such people might come up the street and tear off the plaque YOU HAVE BEEN WARNED and open the gates and stream in ... Nonsense, my dear, said the husband, there are police and soldiers and tear gas and guns to keep them away. But to please her – for he loved her very much and buses were being burned, cars stoned, and schoolchildren shot by the police in those quarters out of sight and hearing of the suburb – he had electronically-controlled gates fitted. Anyone who pulled off the sign YOU HAVE BEEN WARNED and tried to open the gates would have to announce his intentions by pressing a button and speaking into a receiver relayed to the house. The little boy was fascinated by the device and used it as a walkie-talkie in cops-and-robbers play with his small friends.

The riots were suppressed, but there were many burglaries in the suburb and somebody's trusted housemaid was tied up and shut in a cupboard by thieves while she was in charge of her employers' house. The trusted housemaid of the man and wife and little boy was so upset by this misfortune befalling a friend left, as she herself often was, with responsibility for the possessions of the man and his wife and the little boy that she implored her employers to have burglar bars attached to the doors and windows of the house, and an alarm system installed. The wife said, She is right, let us take heed of her advice. So from every window and door in the house where they were living happily ever after they now saw the trees and sky through bars, and when the little boy's pet cat tried to climb in by the fanlight to keep him company in his little bed at night, as it customarily had done, it set off the alarm keening through the house.

The alarm was often answered — it seemed — by other burglar alarms, in other houses, that had been triggered by pet cats or nibbling mice. The alarms called to one another across the gardens in shrills and bleats and wails that everyone soon became accustomed to, so that the din roused the inhabitants of the suburb no more than the croak of frogs and musical grating of cicadas' legs. Under cover of the electronic harpies' discourse intruders sawed the iron bars and broke into homes, taking away hi-fi equipment, television sets, cassette players, cameras and radios, jewellery and clothing, and sometimes were hungry enough to devour everything in the refrigerator or paused audaciously to drink the whisky in the cabinets or patio bars. Insurance companies paid no compensation for single malt, a loss made keener by the property owner's knowledge that the thieves wouldn't even have been able to appreciate what it was they were drinking.

Then the time came when many of the people who were not trusted housemaids and gardeners hung about the suburb because they were unemployed. Some importuned for a job: weeding or painting a roof; anything, baas, madam. But the man and his wife remembered the warning about taking on anyone off the street. Some drank liquor and fouled the street with discarded bottles. Some begged, waiting for the man or his wife to drive the car out of the electronically-operated gates. They sat about with their feet in the gutters, under the jacaranda trees that made a green tunnel of the street — for it was a beautiful suburb, spoilt only by their presence — and sometimes they fell asleep lying right before the gates in the midday sun. The wife could never see anyone go hungry. She sent the trusted housemaid out with bread and tea, but the trusted housemaid said these were loafers and tsotsis, who would come and tie her up and shut her in a cupboard. The husband said, She's right. Take heed of her advice. You only encourage them with your bread and tea. They are looking for their chance … And he brought the little boy's tricycle from the garden into the house every night, because if the house was surely secure, once locked and with the alarm set, someone might still be able to climb over the wall or the electronically-closed gates into the garden.

You are right, said the wife, then the wall should be higher. And the wise old witch, the husband's mother, paid for the extra bricks as her Christmas present to her son and his wife – the little boy got a Space Man outfit and a book of fairy tales.

But every week there were more reports of intrusion: in broad daylight and the dead of night, in the early hours of the morning, and even in the lovely summer twilight – a certain family was at dinner while the bedrooms were being ransacked upstairs. The man and his wife, talking of the latest armed robbery in the suburb, were distracted by the sight of the little boy's pet cat effortlessly arriving over the seven-foot wall, descending first with a rapid bracing of extended forepaws down on the sheer vertical surface, and then a graceful launch, landing with swishing tail within the property. The whitewashed wall was marked with the cat's comings and goings; and on the street side of the wall there were larger red-earth smudges that could have been made by the kind of broken running shoes, seen on the feet of unemployed loiterers, that had no innocent destination.

When the man and wife and little boy took the pet dog for its walk round the neighbourhood streets they no longer paused to admire this show of roses or that perfect lawn; these were hidden behind an array of different varieties of security fences, walls and devices. The man, wife, little boy and dog passed a remarkable choice: there was the low-cost option of pieces of broken glass embedded in cement along the top of walls, there were iron grilles ending in lance-points, there were attempts at reconciling the aesthetics of prison architecture with the Spanish Villa style (spikes painted pink) and with the plaster urns of neoclassical facades (twelve-inch pikes finned like zigzags of lightning and painted pure white). Some walls had a small board affixed, giving the name and telephone number of the firm responsible for the installation of the devices. While the little boy and the pet dog raced ahead, the husband and wife found themselves comparing the possible effectiveness of each style against its appearance; and after several weeks when they paused before this barricade or that without needing to speak, both came out with the conclusion that only one was worth considering. It was the ugliest but the most honest in its suggestion of the pure concentration-camp style, no frills, all evident efficacy. Placed the length of walls, it consisted of a continuous coil of stiff and shining metal serrated into jagged blades, so that there would be no way of climbing over it and no way through its tunnel without getting entangled in its fangs. There would be no way out, only a struggle getting bloodier and bloodier, a deeper and sharper hooking and tearing of flesh. The wife shuddered to look at it. You're right, said the husband, anyone would think twice … And they took heed of the advice on a small board fixed to the wall: Consult DRAGON'S TEETH The People For Total Security.

Next day a gang of workmen came and stretched the razor-bladed coils all round the walls of the house where the husband and wife and little boy and pet dog and cat were living happily ever after. The sunlight flashed and slashed off the serrations, the cornice of razor thorns encircled the home, shining. The husband said, Never mind. It will weather. The wife said, You're wrong. They guarantee it's rust-proof. And she waited until the little boy had run off to play before she said, I hope the cat will take heed … The husband said, Don't worry, my dear, cats always look before they leap. And it was true that from that day on the cat slept in the little boy's bed and kept to the garden, never risking a try at breaching security.

One evening, the mother read the little boy to sleep with a fairy story from the book the wise old witch had given him at Christmas. Next day he pretended to be the prince who braves the terrible thicket of thorns to enter the palace and kiss the Sleeping Beauty back to life: he dragged a ladder to the wall, the shining coiled tunnel was just wide enough for his little body to creep in, and with the first fixing of its razor-teeth in his knees and hands and head he screamed and struggled deeper into its tangle. The trusted housemaid and the itinerant gardener, whose 'day' it was, came running, the first to see and to scream with him, and the itinerant gardener tore his hands trying to get at the little boy. Then the man and his wife burst wildly into the garden and for some reason (the cat, probably) the alarm set up wailing against the screams while the bleeding mass of the little boy was hacked out of the security coil with saws, wire-cutters, choppers, and they carried it – the man, the wife, the hysterical trusted housemaid and the weeping gardener – into the house.

DORIS LESSING

The Old Chief Mshlanga

From: *This Was the Old Chief's Country* (1951)

They were good, the years of ranging the bush over her father's farm which, like every white farm, was largely unused, broken only occasionally by small patches of cultivation. In between, nothing but trees, the long sparse grass, thorn and cactus and gully, grass and outcrop and thorn. And a jutting piece of rock which had been thrust up from the warm soil of Africa unimaginable eras of time ago, washed into hollows and whorls by sun and wind that had travelled so many thousands of miles of space and bush, would hold the weight of a small girl whose eyes were sightless for anything but a pale willowed river, a pale gleaming castle – a small girl singing: 'Out flew the web and floated wide, the mirror cracked from side to side ...'

Pushing her way through the green aisles of the mealie stalks, the leaves arching like cathedrals veined with sunlight far overhead, with the packed red earth underfoot, a fine lace of red-starred witchweed would summon up a black bent figure croaking premonitions: the Northern witch, bred of cold Northern forests, would stand before her among the mealie fields, and it was the mealie fields that faded and fled, leaving her among the gnarled roots of an oak, snow falling thick and soft and white, the woodcutter's fire glowing red welcome through crowding tree trunks.

A white child, opening its eyes curiously on a sun-suffused landscape, a gaunt and violent landscape, might be supposed to accept it as her own, to take the msasa trees and the thorn trees as familiars, to feel her blood running free and responsive to the swing of the seasons.

This child could not see a msasa tree, or the thorn, for what they were. Her books held tales of alien fairies, her rivers ran slow and peaceful, and she knew the shape of the leaves of an ash or an oak, the names of the little creatures that lived in English streams, when the words 'the veld' meant strangeness, though she could remember nothing else.

Because of this, for many years, it was the veld that seemed unreal; the sun was a foreign sun, and the wind spoke a strange language.

The black people on the farm were as remote as the trees and the rocks. They were an amorphous black mass, mingling and thinning and massing like tadpoles, faceless, who existed merely to serve, to say 'Yes, Baas,' take their money and go. They changed season by season, moving from one farm to the next, according to their outlandish needs, which one did not have to understand, coming from perhaps hundreds of miles north or east, passing on after a few months – where? Perhaps even as far away as the fabled gold-mines of Johannesburg, where the pay was so much better than the few shillings a month and the double handful of mealie meal twice a day which they earned in that part of Africa.

The child was taught to take them for granted: the servants in the house would come running a hundred yards to pick up a book if she dropped it. She was called 'Nkosikaas' – Chieftainess, even by the black children her own age.

Later, when the farm grew too small to hold her curiosity, she carried a gun in the crook of her arm and wandered miles a day, from vlei to vlei, from kopje to kopje, accompanied by two dogs: the dogs and the gun were an armour against fear. Because of them she never felt fear.

If a native came into sight along the kaffir paths half a mile away, the dogs would flush him up a tree as if he were a bird. If he expostulated (in his uncouth language which was by itself ridiculous) that was cheek. If one was in a good mood, it could be a matter for laughter. Otherwise one passed on, hardly glancing at the angry native in the tree.

On the rare occasions when white children met together they could amuse themselves by hailing a passing native in order to make a buffoon of him; they could set the dogs on him and watch him run; they could tease a small black child as if he were a puppy – save that they would not throw stones and sticks at a dog without a sense of guilt.

Later still, certain questions presented themselves in the child's mind; and because the answers were not easy to accept, they were silenced by an even greater arrogance of manner.

It was even impossible to think of the black people who worked about the house as friends, for if she talked to one of them, her mother would come running anxiously: 'Come away; you mustn't talk to natives.'

It was this instilled consciousness of danger, of something unpleasant, that made it easy to laugh out loud, crudely, if a servant made a mistake in his English or if he failed to understand an order – there is a certain kind of laughter that is fear, afraid of itself.

One evening, when I was about fourteen, I was walking down the side of a mealie field that had been newly ploughed, so that the great red clods showed fresh and tumbling to the vlei beyond, like a choppy red sea; it was that hushed and listening hour, when the birds send long sad calls from tree to tree, and all the colours of earth and sky and leaf are deep and golden. I had my rifle in the curve of my arm, and the dogs were at my heels.

In front of me, perhaps a couple of hundred yards away, a group of three natives came into sight around the side of a big antheap. I whistled the dogs close in to my skirts and let the gun swing in my hand, and advanced, waiting for them to move aside, off the path, in respect for my passing. But they came on steadily, and the dogs looked up at me for the command to chase. I was angry. It was 'cheek' for a native not to stand off a path, the moment he caught sight of you.

In front walked an old man, stooping his weight onto a stick, his hair grizzled white, a dark red blanket slung over his shoulders like a cloak. Behind him came two young men, carrying bundles of pots, assegais, hatchets.

The group was not a usual one. They were not natives seeking work. These had an air of dignity, of quietly following their own purpose. It was the dignity that checked my tongue. I walked quietly on, talking softly to the growling dogs, till I was ten paces away. Then the old man stopped, drawing his blanket close.

'Morning, Nkosikaas,' he said, using the customary greeting for any time of the day.

'Good morning,' I said. 'Where are you going?' My voice was a little truculent.

The old man spoke in his own language, then one of the young men stepped forward politely and said in careful English: 'My Chief travels to see his brothers beyond the river.'

A Chief! I thought, understanding the pride that made the old man stand before me like an equal – more than an equal, for he showed courtesy, and I showed none.

The old man spoke again, wearing dignity like an inherited garment, still standing ten paces off, flanked by his entourage, not looking at me (that would have been rude) but directing his eyes somewhere over my head at the trees.

'You are the little Nkosikaas from the farm of Baas Jordan?'

'That's right,' I said.

'Perhaps your father does not remember,' said the interpreter for the old man, 'but there was an affair with some goats. I remember seeing you when you were ...' The young man held his hand at knee level and smiled.

We all smiled.

'What is your name?' I asked.

'This is Chief Mshlanga,' said the young man.

'I will tell my father that I met you,' I said.

The old man said: 'My greetings to your father, little Nkosikaas.'

'Good morning,' I said politely, finding the politeness difficult, from lack of use.

'Morning, little Nkosikaas,' said the old man, and stood aside to let me pass.

I went by, my gun hanging awkwardly, the dogs sniffing and growling, cheated of their favourite game of chasing natives like animals.

Not long afterwards I read in an old explorer's book the phrase: 'Chief

Mshlanga's country'. It went like this: 'Our destination was Chief Mshlanga's country, to the north of the river; and it was our desire to ask his permission to prospect for gold in his territory.'

The phrase 'ask his permission' was so extraordinary to a white child, brought up to consider all natives as things to use, that it revived those questions, which could not be suppressed: they fermented slowly in my mind.

On another occasion one of those old prospectors who still move over Africa looking for neglected reefs, with their hammers and tents, and pans for sifting gold from crushed rock, came to the farm and, in talking of the old days, used that phrase again: 'This was the Old Chief's country,' he said. 'It stretched from those mountains over there way back to the river, hundreds of miles of country.' That was his name for our district: 'The Old Chief's Country'; he did not use our name for it — a new phrase which held no implication of usurped ownership.

As I read more books about the time when this part of Africa was opened up, not much more than fifty years before, I found Old Chief Mshlanga had been a famous man, known to all the explorers and prospectors. But then he had been young; or maybe it was his father or uncle they spoke of — I never found out.

During that year I met him several times in the part of the farm that was traversed by natives moving over the country. I learned that the path up the side of the big red field where the birds sang was the recognised highway for migrants. Perhaps I even haunted it in the hope of meeting him: being greeted by him, the exchange of courtesies, seemed to answer the questions that troubled me.

Soon I carried a gun in a different spirit; I used it for shooting food and not to give me confidence. And now the dogs learned better manners. When I saw a native approaching, we offered and took greetings; and slowly that other landscape in my mind faded, and my feet struck directly on the African soil, and I saw the shapes of tree and hill clearly, and the black people moved back, as it were, out of my life: it was as if I stood aside to watch a slow intimate dance of landscape and men, a very old dance, whose steps I could not learn.

But I thought: this is my heritage, too; I was bred here; it is my country as well as the black man's country; and there is plenty of room for all of us, without elbowing each other off the pavements and roads.

It seemed it was only necessary to let free that respect I felt when I was talking with old Chief Mshlanga, to let both black and white people meet gently, with tolerance for each other's differences: it seemed quite easy.

Then, one day, something new happened. Working in our house as servants were always three natives: cook, houseboy, garden boy. They used to change as the farm natives changed; staying for a few months, then moving on to a new job, or back home to their kraals. They were thought of as 'good' or 'bad' natives; which meant: how did they behave as servants? Were they lazy, efficient, obedient, or disrespectful? If the family felt good-humoured, the phrase was: 'What can you expect from raw black savages?' If we were angry, we said: 'These damned niggers, we would be much better off without them.'

One day, a white policeman was on his rounds of the district, and he said laughingly: 'Did you know you have an important man in your kitchen?'

'What!' exclaimed my mother sharply. 'What do you mean?'

'A Chief's son.' The policeman seemed amused. 'He'll boss the tribe when the old man dies.'

'He'd better not put on a Chief's son act with me,' said my mother.

When the policeman left, we looked with different eyes at our cook: he was a good worker, but he drank too much at weekends – that was how we knew him.

He was a tall youth, with very black skin, like black polished metal, his tightly-growing black hair parted white man's fashion at one side, with a metal comb from the store stuck into it; very polite, very distant, very quick to obey an order. Now it had been pointed out, we said: 'Of course, you can see. Blood always tells.'

My mother became strict with him now she knew about his birth and prospects. Sometimes, when she lost her temper, she would say: 'You aren't the Chief yet, you know.' And he would answer her very quietly, his eyes on the ground: 'Yes, Nkosikaas.'

One afternoon he asked for a whole day off, instead of the customary half-day, to go home next Sunday.

'How can you go home in one day?'

'It will take me half an hour on my bicycle,' he explained.

I watched the direction he took; and the next day I went off to look for this kraal; I understood he must be Chief Mshlanga's successor: there was no other kraal near enough our farm.

Beyond our boundaries on that side the country was new to me. I followed unfamiliar paths past kopjes that till now had been part of the jagged horizon, hazed with distance. This was government land, which had never been cultivated by white men; at first I could not understand why it was that it appeared, in merely crossing the boundary, I had entered a completely fresh type of landscape. It was a wide green valley, where a small river sparkled, and vivid water-birds darted over the rushes. The grass was thick and soft to my calves, the trees stood tall and shapely.

I was used to our farm, whose hundreds of acres of harsh eroded soil bore trees that had been cut for the mine furnaces and had grown thin and twisted, where the cattle had dragged the grass flat, leaving innumerable criss-crossing trails that deepened each season into gullies, under the force of the rains.

This country had been left untouched, save for prospectors whose picks had struck a few sparks from the surface of the rocks as they wandered by; and for migrant natives whose passing had left, perhaps, a charred patch on the trunk of a tree where their evening fire had nestled.

It was very silent: a hot morning with pigeons cooing throatily, the midday shadows lying dense and thick with clear yellow spaces of sunlight between and in all that wide green parklike valley, not a human soul but myself.

I was listening to the quick regular tapping of a woodpecker when slowly a chill feeling seemed to grow up from the small of my back to my shoulders, in a constricting spasm like a shudder, and at the roots of my hair a tingling sensation began and ran down over the surface of my flesh, leaving me gooseflesh and cold, though I was damp with sweat. Fever? I thought; then uneasily, turned to look over my shoulder; and realised suddenly that this was fear. It was extraordinary, even humiliating. It was a new fear. For all the years I had walked by myself over this country I had never known a moment's uneasiness; in the beginning because I had been supported by a gun and the dogs, then because I had learnt an easy friendliness for the natives I might encounter.

I had read of this feeling, how the bigness and silence of Africa, under the ancient sun, grows dense and takes shape in the mind, till even the birds seem to call menacingly, and a deadly spirit comes out of the trees and the rocks. You move warily, as if your very passing disturbs something old and evil, something dark and big and angry that might suddenly rear and strike from behind. You look at groves of entwined trees, and picture the animals that might be lurking there; you look at the river running slowly, dropping from level to level through the vlei, spreading into pools where at night the buck come to drink, and the crocodiles rise and drag them by their soft noses into underwater caves. Fear possessed me. I found I was turning round and round, because of that shapeless menace behind me that might reach out and take me; I kept glancing at the files of kopjes which, seen from a different angle, seemed to change with every step so that even known landmarks, like a big mountain that has sentinelled my world since I first became conscious of it, showed an unfamiliar sunlit valley among its foothills. I did not know where I was. I was lost. Panic seized me. I found I was spinning round and round, staring anxiously at this tree and that, peering up at the sun which appeared to have moved into an eastern slant, shedding the sad yellow light of sunset. Hours must have passed! I looked at my watch and found that this state of meaningless terror had lasted perhaps ten minutes.

The point was that it was meaningless. I was not ten miles from home: I had only to take my way back along the valley to find myself at the fence: away among the foothills of the kopjes gleamed the roof of a neighbour's house, and a couple of hours' walking would reach it. This was the sort of fear that contracts the flesh of a dog at night and sets him howling at the full moon. It had nothing to do with what I thought or felt: and I was more disturbed by the fact that I could become its victim than of the physical sensation itself: I walked steadily on, quietened, in a divided mind, watching my own pricking nerves and apprehensive glances from side to side with a disgusted amusement. Deliberately I set myself to think of this village I was seeking, and what I should do when I entered it – if I could find it, which was doubtful, since I was walking aimlessly and it might be anywhere in the hundreds of thousands of acres of bush that stretched about me. With my mind on that village, I realised that a new sensation was added to the fear: loneliness. Now such a terror of isolation invaded me that I could hardly walk; and if it were not that I came over the crest of a small rise and saw a village below me, I should have turned and gone home. It was a cluster of thatched huts in a clearing among trees. There were neat patches of mealies and pumpkins and millet, and cattle grazed under some trees at a distance. Fowls scratched among the huts, dogs lay sleeping on the grass, and goats friezed a kopje that jutted up beyond a tributary of the river lying like an enclosing arm round the village.

As I came close I saw the huts were lovingly decorated with patterns of yellow and red and ochre mud on the walls; and the thatch was tied in place with plaits of straw.

This was not at all like our farm compound, a dirty and neglected place, a temporary home for migrants who had no roots in it.

And now I did not know what to do next. I called a small black boy, who was sitting on a log playing a stringed gourd, quite naked except for the strings of blue beads round his neck, and said: 'Tell the Chief I am here.' The child stuck his thumb in his mouth and stared shyly back at me.

For minutes I shifted my feet on the edge of what seemed a deserted village, till at last the child scuttled off, and then some women came. They were draped in bright cloths, with brass glinting in their ears and on their arms. They also stared, silently; then turned to chatter among themselves.

I said again: 'Can I see Chief Mshlanga?' I saw they caught the name; they did not understand what I wanted. I did not understand myself.

At last I walked through them and came past the huts and saw a clearing under a big shady tree, where a dozen old men sat cross-legged on the ground, talking. Chief Mshlanga was leaning back against the tree, holding a gourd in his hand, from which he had been drinking. When he saw me, not a muscle of his face moved, and I could see he was not pleased: perhaps he was afflicted with my own shyness, due to being unable to find the right forms of courtesy for the occasion. To meet me, on our own farm, was one thing; but I should not have come here. What had I expected? I could not join them socially: the thing was unheard of. Bad enough that I, a white girl, should be walking the veld alone as a white man might: and in this part of the bush where only government officials had the right to move.

Again I stood, smiling foolishly, while behind me stood the groups of brightly clad, chattering women, their faces alert with curiosity and interest, and in front of me sat the old men, with old lined faces, their eyes guarded, aloof. It was a village of ancients and children and women. Even the two young men who kneeled beside the Chief were not those I had seen with him previously: the young men were all away working on the white men's farms and mines, and the Chief must depend on relatives who were temporarily on holiday for his attendants.

'The small white Nkosikaas is far from home,' remarked the old man at last.

'Yes,' I agreed, 'it is far.' I wanted to say: ' I have come to pay you a friendly visit, Chief Mshlanga.' I could not say it. I might now be feeling an urgent helpless desire to get to know these men and women as people, to be accepted by them as a friend, but the truth was I had set out in a spirit of curiosity: I had wanted to see the village that our cook, the reserved and obedient young man who got drunk on Sundays, would one day rule over.

'The child of Nkosi Jordan is welcome,' said Chief Mshlanga.

'Thank you,' I said, and could think of nothing more to say. There was a silence, while the flies rose and began to buzz around my head; and the wind shook a little in the thick green tree that spread its branches over the old men.

'Good morning,' I said at last. 'I have to return now to my home.'

'Morning, little Nkosikaas,' said Chief Mshlanga.

I walked away from the indifferent village, over the rise past the staring amber-eyed goats, down through the tall stately trees into the great rich green valley where the river meandered and the pigeons cooed tales of plenty and the woodpecker tapped softly.

The fear had gone; the loneliness had set into stiff-necked stoicism; there was now a queer hostility in the landscape, a cold, hard, sullen indomitability that walked with me, as strong as a wall, as intangible as smoke; it seemed to say to me: you walk here as a destroyer. I went slowly homewards, with an empty heart: I had learned that if one cannot call a country to heel like a dog, neither can one dismiss the past with a smile in an easy gush of feeling, saying: I could not help it, I am also a victim.

I only saw Chief Mshlanga once again.

One night my father's big red land was trampled down by small sharp hoofs, and it was discovered that the culprits were goats from Chief Mshlanga's kraal. This had happened once before, years ago.

My father confiscated all the goats. Then he sent a message to the old Chief that if he wanted them he would have to pay for the damage.

He arrived at our house at the time of sunset one evening, looking very old and bent now, walking stiffly under his regally draped blanket, leaning on a big stick. My father sat himself down in his big chair below the steps of the house; the old man squatted carefully on the ground before him, flanked by his two young men.

The palaver was long and painful, because of the bad English of the young man who interpreted, and because my father could not speak dialect, but only kitchen kaffir.

From my father's point of view, at least two hundred pounds worth of damage had been done to the crop. He knew he could not get the money from the old man. He felt he was entitled to keep the goats. As for the old Chief, he kept repeating angrily: 'Twenty goats! My people cannot lose twenty goats! We are not rich, like the Nkosi Jordan, to lose twenty goats at once.'

My father did not think of himself as rich, but rather as very poor. He spoke quickly and angrily in return, saying that the damage done meant a great deal to him, and that he was entitled to the goats.

At last it grew so heated that the cook, the Chief's son, was called from the kitchen to be interpreter, and now my father spoke fluently in English, and our cook translated rapidly so that the old man could understand how very angry my father was. The young man spoke without emotion, in a mechanical way, his eyes lowered, but showing how he felt his position by a hostile uncomfortable set of the shoulders.

It was now in the late sunset, the sky a welter of colours, the birds singing their last songs, and the cattle, lowing peacefully, moving past us towards their sheds for the night. It was the hour when Africa is most beautiful; and here was this pathetic, ugly scene, doing no one any good.

At last my father stated finally: 'I'm not going to argue about it. I am keeping the goats.'

The old Chief flashed back in his own language: 'That means that my people will go hungry when the dry season comes.'

'Go to the police, then,' said my father, and looked triumphant. There was, of course, no more to be said.

The old man sat silent, his head bent, his hands dangling helplessly over his withered knees. Then he rose, the young men helping him, and he stood facing my father. He spoke once again, very stiffly; and turned away and went home to his village.

'What did he say?' asked my father of the young man, who laughed uncomfortably and would not meet his eyes.

'What did he say?' insisted my father.

Our cook stood straight and silent, his brows knotted together. Then he spoke. 'My father says: All this land, this land you call yours, is his land and belongs to our people.'

Having made this statement, he walked off into the bush after his father, and we did not see him again.

Our next cook was a migrant from Nyasaland, with no expectations of greatness.

Next time the policeman came on his rounds he was told this story. He remarked: 'That kraal has no right to be there; it should have been moved long ago. I don't know why no one has done anything about it. I'll have a chat to the Native Commissioner next week. I'm going over for tennis on Sunday, anyway.'

Some time later we heard that Chief Mshlanga and his people had been moved two hundred miles east, to a proper native reserve; the government land was going to be opened up for white settlement soon.

I went to see the village again, about a year afterwards. There was nothing there. Mounds of red mud, where the huts had been, had long swathes of rotting thatch over them, veined with the red galleries of the white ants. The pumpkin vines rioted everywhere, over the bushes, up the lower branches of trees so that the great golden balls rolled underfoot and dangled overhead: it was a festival of pumpkins. The bushes were crowding up, the new grass sprang vivid green.

The settler lucky enough to be allotted the lush warm valley (if he chose to cultivate this particular section) would find, suddenly, in the middle of a mealie field, the plants were growing fifteen feet tall, the weight of the cobs dragging at the stalks, and wonder what unsuspected vein of richness he had struck.

DORIS LESSING

Flavours of Exile

From: *The Habit of Loving* (1957)

At the foot of the hill, near the well, was the vegetable garden, an acre fenced off from the Big Field where the earth was so rich that mealies grew there, year after year, ten feet tall. Nursed from that fabulous soil, carrots, lettuces, beets, tasting as I have never found vegetables taste since, loaded our table and the tables of our neighbours. Sometimes, if the garden boy was late with the supply for lunch, I would run down the steep pebbly path through the trees at the back of the hill and along the red dust of the wagon road until I could see the windlass under its shed of thatch. There I stopped. The smell of manure, of sun on foliage, of evaporating water, rose to my head; two steps farther, and I could look down into the vegetable garden enclosed within its tall pale of reeds – rich chocolate earth studded emerald green, frothed with the white of cauliflowers, jewelled with the purple globes of eggplant and the scarlet wealth of tomatoes. Around the fence grew lemons, pawpaws, bananas – shapes of gold and yellow in their patterns of green.

In another five minutes I would be dragging from the earth carrots ten inches long, so succulent they snapped between two fingers. I ate my allowance of these before the cook could boil them and drown them in the white flour sauce without which – and unless they were served in the large china vegetable dishes brought from that old house in London – they were not carrots to my mother.

For her, that garden represented a defeat.

When the family first came to the farm, she built vegetable beds on the kopje near the house. She had in her mind, perhaps, a vision of the farmhouse surrounded by outbuildings and gardens like a hen sheltering its chicks.

The kopje was all stone. As soon as the grass was cleared off its crown where the house stood, the fierce rain beat the soil away. Those first vegetable beds were thin sifted earth walled by pebbles. The water was brought up from the well in the water-cart.

'Water is gold,' grumbled my father, eating peas which, he reckoned, must cost a shilling a mouthful. 'Water is gold!' he came to shout at last, as my mother toiled and bent over those reluctant beds. But she got more pleasure from them than she ever did from the exhaustless plenty of the garden under the hill.

At last, the spaces in the bush where the old beds had been were seeded by wild or vagrant plants, and we children played there. Someone must have thrown away gooseberries, for soon the low-spreading bushes covered the earth. We used to creep under them, William MacGregor and I, lie flat on our backs, and look through the leaves at the brilliant sky, reaching around us for the tiny sharp-sweet yellow fruits in their jackets of papery white. The smell of the leaves was spicy. It intoxicated us. We would laugh and shout, then quarrel; and William, to make up, shelled a double handful of the fruit and poured it into my skirt, and we ate together, pressing the biggest berries on each other. When we could eat no more, we filled baskets and took them to the kitchen to be made into that rich jam, which, if allowed to burn just the right amount on the pan, is the best jam in the world — clear sweet amber, with lumps of sticky sharpness in it, as if the stings of bees were preserved in honey.

But my mother did not like it. 'Cape gooseberries!' she said bitterly. 'They aren't gooseberries at all. Oh, if I could let you taste a pie made of real English gooseberries.'

In due course, the marvels of civilisation made this possible; she found a tin of gooseberries in the Greek store at the station and made us a pie.

My parents and William's ate the pie with a truly religious emotion.

It was this experience with the gooseberries that made me cautious when it came to Brussels sprouts. Year after year my mother yearned for Brussels sprouts, whose name came to represent to me something exotic and forever unattainable. When at last she managed to grow half a dozen spikes of this plant in one cold winter that offered us sufficient frost, she of course sent a note to the MacGregors, so that they might share the treat. They came from Glasgow, they came from Home, and they could share the language of nostalgia. At the table the four grownups ate the bitter little cabbages and agreed that the soil of Africa was unable to grow food that had any taste at all. I said scornfully that I couldn't see what all the fuss was about. But William, three years older than myself, passed his plate up and said he found them delicious. It was like a betrayal; and afterward I demanded how he could like such flavourless stuff. He smiled at me and said it cost us nothing to pretend, did it?

That smile, so gentle, a little whimsical, was a lesson to me; and I remembered it when it came to the affair of the cherries. She found a tin of cherries at the store, we ate them with cream; and while she sighed over memories of barrows loaded with cherries in the streets of London, I sighed with her, ate fervently, and was careful not to meet her eyes.

And when she said: 'The pomegranates will be fruiting soon,' I offered to run down and see how they progressed. I returned from the examination saying: 'It won't be long now, really it won't — perhaps next year.'

The truth was, my emotion over the pomegranates was not entirely due to the beautiful lesson in courtesy given me by William. Brussels sprouts, cherries, English gooseberries — they were my mother's; they recurred in her talk as often as 'a real London peasouper', or 'chestnuts by the fire', or 'cherry blossom at Kew'. I no longer grudged these to her; I listened and was careful not to show that my thoughts were on my own inheritance of veld and sun. But pomegranates were an exotic for my mother; and therefore more easily shared with her. She had been in Persia, where, one understood, pomegranate juice ran in rivers. The wife of a minor official, she had lived in a vast stone house cooled by water trickling down a thousand stone channels from the mountains; she had lived among roses and jasmine, walnut trees and pomegranates. But, unfortunately, for too short a time.

Why not pomegranates here, in Africa? Why not?

The four trees had been planted at the same time as the first vegetable beds; and almost at once two of them died. A third lingered on for a couple of seasons and then succumbed to the white ants. The fourth stood lonely among the Cape gooseberry bushes, bore no fruit, and at last was forgotten.

Then one day my mother was showing Mrs MacGregor her chickens; and as they returned through tangles of grass and weed, their skirts lifted high in both hands, my mother exclaimed: 'Why, I do believe the pomegranate is fruiting at last. Look, look, it is!' She called to us, the children, and we went running, and stood around a small thorny tree, and looked at a rusty-red fruit the size of a child's fist.

'It's ripe,' said my mother, and pulled it off.

Inside the house we were each given a dozen small seeds on saucers. They were bitter, but we did not like to ask for sugar. Mrs MacGregor said gently: 'It's wonderful. How you must miss all that!'

'The roses!' said my mother. 'And sacks of walnuts … and we used to drink pomegranate juice with the melted snow water … nothing here tastes like that. The soil is no good.'

I looked at William, sitting opposite to me. He turned his head and smiled. I fell in love.

He was then fifteen, home for the holidays. He was a silent boy, thoughtful; and the quietness in his deep grey eyes seemed to me like a promise of warmth and understanding I had never known. There was a tightness in my chest, because it hurt to be shut out from the world of simple kindness he lived in. I sat there, opposite to him, and said to myself that I had known him all my life and yet until this moment had never understood what he was. I looked at those extraordinarily clear eyes, that were like water over grey pebbles; I gazed and gazed, until he gave me a slow, direct look that showed he knew I had been staring. It was like a warning, as if a door had been shut.

After the MacGregors had gone, I went through the bushes to the pomegranate tree. It was about my height, a tough, obstinate-looking thing; and there was a round yellow ball the size of a walnut hanging from a twig.

I looked at the ugly little tree and thought, Pomegranates! Breasts like pomegranates and a belly like a heap of wheat! The golden pomegranates of the sun, I thought ... pomegranates like the red of blood.

I was in a fever, more than a little mad. The space of thick grass and gooseberry bushes between the trees was haunted by William; and his deep, calm, grey eyes looked at me across the pomegranate tree.

Next day I sat under the tree. It gave no shade, but the acrid sunlight was barred and splotched under it. There was hard, cracked, red earth beneath a covering of silvery dead grass. Under the grass I saw grains of red and half a hard brown shell. It seemed that a fruit had ripened and burst without our knowing – yes, everywhere in the soft old grass lay the tiny crimson seeds. I tasted one; warm sweet juice flooded my tongue. I gathered them up and ate them until my mouth was full of dry seeds. I spat them out and thought that a score of pomegranate trees would grow from that mouthful.

As I watched, tiny black ants came scurrying along the roots of the grass, scrambling over the fissures in the earth, to snatch away the seeds. I lay on my elbow and watched. A dozen of them were levering at a still unbroken seed. Suddenly the frail tissue split as they bumped it over a splinter, and they were caught in a sticky red ooze.

The ants would carry these seeds for hundreds of yards; there would be an orchard of pomegranates. William MacGregor would come visiting with his parents and find me among the pomegranate trees; I could hear the sound of his grave voice mingled with the tinkle of camel bells and the splashing of falling water.

I went to the tree every day and lay under it, watching the single yellow fruit ripening on its twig. There would come a moment when it must burst and scatter crimson seeds; I must be there when it did; it seemed as if my whole life was concentrated and ripening with that single fruit.

It was very hot under the tree. My head ached. My flesh was painful with the sun. Yet there I sat all day, watching the tiny ants at their work, letting them run over my legs, waiting for the pomegranate fruit to ripen. It swelled slowly; it seemed set on reaching perfection, for when it was the size that the other had been picked, it was still a bronzing yellow, and the rind was soft. It was going to be a big fruit, the size of both my fists.

Then something terrifying happened. One day I saw that the twig it hung from was splitting off the branch. The wizened, dry little tree could not sustain the weight of the fruit it had produced. I went to the house, brought down bandages from the medicine chest, and strapped the twig firm and tight to the branch, in such a way that the weight was supported. Then I wet the bandage, tenderly, and thought of William, William, William. I wet the bandage daily, and thought of him.

What I thought of William had become a world, stronger than anything around me. Yet, since I was mad, so weak, it vanished at a touch. Once, for instance, I saw him, driving with his father on the wagon along the road to the station. I remember I was ashamed that that marvellous feverish world should depend on a half-grown boy in dusty khaki, gripping a piece of grass between his teeth as he stared ahead of him. It came to this – that in order to preserve the dream, I must not see William. And it seemed he felt something of the sort himself, for in all those weeks he never came near me, whereas once he used to come every day. And yet I was convinced it must happen that William and the moment when the pomegranate split open would coincide.

I imagined it in a thousand ways, as the fruit continued to grow. Now, it was a clear bronze yellow with faint rust-coloured streaks. The rind was thin, so soft that the swelling seeds within were shaping it. The fruit looked lumpy and veined, like a nursing breast. The small crown where the stem fastened on it, which had been the sheath of the flower, was still green. It began to harden and turn back into iron-grey thorns.

Soon, soon, it would be ripe. Very swiftly, the skin lost its smooth thinness. It took on a tough, pored look, like the skin of an old weatherbeaten country-man. It was a ruddy scarlet now, and hot to the touch. A small crack appeared, which in a day had widened so that the packed red seeds within were visible, almost bursting out. I did not dare leave the tree. I was there from six in the morning until the sun went down. I even crept down with the candle at night, although I argued it could not burst at night, not in the cool of the night; it must be the final unbearable thrust of the hot sun that would break it.

For three days nothing happened. The crack remained the same. Ants swarmed up the trunk, along the branches, and into the fruit. The scar oozed red juice in which black ants swam and struggled. At any moment it might happen. And William did not come. I was sure he would; I watched the empty road helplessly, waiting for him to come striding along, a piece of grass between his teeth, to me and the pomegranate tree. Yet he did not. In one night, the crack split another half inch. I saw a red seed push itself out of the crack and fall. Instantly it was borne off by the ants into the grass.

I went up to the house and asked my mother when the MacGregors were coming to tea.

'I don't know, dear. Why?'

'Because. I just thought ...'

She looked at me. Her eyes were critical. In one moment, she would say the name 'William'. I struck first. To have William and the moment together, I must pay fee to the family gods. 'There's a pomegranate nearly ripe, and you know how interested Mrs MacGregor is ...'

She looked sharply at me. 'Pick it, and we'll make a drink of it.'

'Oh, no, it's not quite ready. Not altogether ...'

'Silly child,' she said at last. She went to the telephone and said: 'Mrs MacGregor, this daughter of mine, she's got it into her head – you know how children are.'

I did not care. At four that afternoon I was waiting by the pomegranate tree. Their car came thrusting up the steep road to the crown of the hill. There was Mr MacGregor in his khaki, Mrs MacGregor in her best afternoon dress – and William. The adults shook hands, kissed. William did not turn round and look at me. It was not possible, it was monstrous, that the force of my dream should not have had the power to touch him at all, that he knew nothing of what he must do.

Then he slowly turned his head and looked down the slope to where I stood. He did not smile. It seemed he had not seen me, for his eyes travelled past me, and back to the grownups. He stood to one side while they exchanged their news and greetings; and then all four laughed, and turned to look at me and my tree. It seemed for a moment they were all coming.

At once, however, they went into the house, William trailing after them, frowning.

In a moment he would have gone in; the space in front of the old house would be empty. I called 'William!' I had not known I would call. My voice sounded small in the wide afternoon sunlight.

He went on as if he had not heard. Then he stopped, seemed to think, and came down the hill toward me while I anxiously examined his face. The low tangle of the gooseberry bushes was around his legs, and he swore sharply.

'Look at the pomegranate,' I said. He came to a halt beside the tree, and looked. I was searching those clear grey eyes now for a trace of that indulgence they had shown my mother over the Brussels sprouts, over that first unripe pomegranate. Now all I wanted was indulgence; I abandoned everything else.

'It's full of ants,' he said at last.

'Only a little, only where it's cracked.'

He stood, frowning, chewing at his piece of grass. His lips were full and thin-skinned; and I could see the blood, dull and dark around the pale groove where the grass stem pressed.

'Now,' I thought wildly, 'now – crack now.'

There was not a sound. The sun came pouring down, hot and yellow, drawing up the smell of the grasses. There was, too, a faint sour smell from the fermenting juice of the pomegranate.

'It's bad,' said William, in that uncomfortable, angry voice. 'And what's that bit of dirty rag for?'

'It was breaking, the twig was breaking off – I tied it up.'

'Mad,' he remarked, aside, to the afternoon. 'Quite mad.' He was looking about him in the grass. He reached down and picked up a stick.

'No,' I cried out, as he hit at the tree. The pomegranate flew into the air and exploded in a scatter of crimson seeds, fermenting juice, and black ants.

The cracked empty skin, with its white, clean-looking inner skin faintly stained with juice, lay in two fragments at my feet.

He was poking sulkily with the stick at the little scarlet seeds that lay everywhere on the earth.

Then he did look at me. Those clear eyes were grave again, thoughtful, and judging. They held that warning I had seen in them before.

'That's your pomegranate,' he said at last.

'Yes,' I said.

He smiled, 'We'd better go up, if we want any tea.'

We went together up the hill to the house, and as we entered the room where the grownups sat over the teacups, I spoke quickly, before he could. In a bright, careless voice I said: 'It was bad, after all; the ants had got at it. It should have been picked before.'

DORIS LESSING

Lucy Grange

From: *The Habit of Loving* (1957)

The farm was fifty miles from the nearest town, in a maize-growing district. The mealie lands began at a stone's throw from the front door of the farm-house. At the back were several acres of energetic and colourful domestic growth: chicken runs, vegetables, pumpkins. Even on the veranda there were sacks of grain and bundles of hoes. The life of the farm, her husband's life, washed around the house, leaving old scraps of iron on the front step where the children played wagon-and-driver, or a bottle of medicine for a sick animal on her dressing table among the bottles of Elizabeth Arden.

One walked straight from the veranda of this gaunt, iron-roofed, brick bar-racks of a house into a wide drawing room that was shaded in green and orange Liberty linens.

'Stylish?' said the farmers' wives when they came on formal calls, asking the question of themselves while they discussed with Lucy Grange the price of butter and servants' aprons and their husbands discussed the farm with George Grange. They never 'dropped over' to see Lucy Grange; they never rang her up with invitations to 'spend the day'. They would finger the books on child psychology, politics, art; gaze guiltily at the pictures on her walls, which they felt they ought to be able to recognise; and say: 'I can see you are a great reader, Mrs Grange.'

There were years of discussing her among themselves before their voices held the good-natured amusement of acceptance: 'I found Lucy in the vege-table patch wearing gloves full of cold cream.' 'Lucy has ordered another dress pattern from town.' And later still, with self-consciously straightened shoulders, eyes directly primly before them, discreet non-committal voices: 'Lucy is very attractive to men.'

One can imagine her, when they left at the end of those mercifully short visits, standing on the veranda and smiling bitterly after the satisfactory solid women with their straight tailored dresses, made by the Dutch-woman at the store at seven-and-six a time, buttoned loosely across their well-used breasts; with their untidy hair permanent-waved every six months in town; with their femininity which was asserted once and for all by a clumsy scrawl of red across the mouth. One can imagine her clenching her fists and saying fiercely to the mealie fields that rippled greenly all around her, cream-topped like the sea: 'I won't. I simply won't. He needn't imagine that I will!'

'Do you like my new dress, George?'

'You're the best-looking woman in the district, Lucy.' So it seemed, on the face of it, that he didn't expect, or even want, that she should …

Meanwhile she continued to order cookbooks from town, to make new recipes of pumpkin and green mealies and chicken, to put skin food on her face at night; she constructed attractive nursery furniture out of packing cases enamelled white – the farm wasn't doing too well; and discussed with George how little Betty's cough was probably psychological.

'I'm sure you're right, my dear.'

Then the rich, overcontrolled voice: 'Yes, darling. No, my sweetheart. Yes, of course, I'll play bricks with you, but you must have your lunch first.' Then it broke, hard and shrill: '*Don't* make all that noise, darling. I can't stand it. Go on, go and play in the garden and leave me in peace.'

Sometimes, storms of tears. Afterward: 'Really, George, didn't your mother ever tell you that all women cry sometimes? It's as good as a tonic. Or a holiday.' And a lot of high laughter and gay explanations at which George hastened to guffaw. He liked her gay. She usually was. For instance, she was a good mimic. She would 'take off', deliberately trying to relieve his mind of farm worries, the visiting policemen, who toured the district once a month to see if the natives were behaving themselves, or the government agricultural officials.

'Do you want to see my husband?'

That was what they had come for, but they seldom pressed the point. They sat far longer than they had intended, drinking tea, talking about themselves. They would go away and say at the bar in the village: 'Mrs Grange is a smart woman, isn't she?'

And Lucy would be acting, for George's benefit, how a khaki-clad, sun-raw youth had bent into her room, looking around him with comical surprise; had taken a cup of tea, thanking her three times; had knocked over an ashtray, stayed for lunch and afternoon tea, and left saying with awkward gallantry: 'It's a real treat to meet a lady like you who is interested in things.'

'You shouldn't be so hard on us poor colonials, Lucy.'

Finally one can imagine how one day, when the houseboy came to her in the chicken runs to say that there was a *baas* waiting to see her at the house, it was no sweating policeman, thirsty after fifteen dusty miles on a motorcycle, to whom she must be gracious.

He was a city man, of perhaps forty or forty-five, dressed in city clothes. At first glance she felt a shudder of repulsion. It was a coarse face, and sensual; and he looked like a patient vulture as the keen, heavy-lidded eyes travelled up and down her body.

'Are you looking for my husband, perhaps? He's in the cowsheds this morning.'

'No, I don't think I am. I was.'

She laughed. It was as if he had started playing a record she had not heard for a long time, and which started her feet tapping. It was years since she had played this game. 'I'll get you some tea,' she said hurriedly and left him in her pretty drawing room.

Collecting the cups, her hands were clumsy. Why, Lucy! she said to herself, archly. She came back, very serious and responsible, to find him standing in front of the picture that filled half the wall at one end of the room. 'I should have thought you had sunflowers enough here,' he said, in his heavy, overemphasised voice, which made her listen for meanings behind his words. And when he turned away from the wall and came to sit down, leaning forward, examining her, she suppressed an impulse to apologise for the picture: Van Gogh *is* obvious, but he's rather effective, she might have said; and she felt that the whole room was that: effective but obvious. But she was pleasantly conscious of how she looked: graceful and cool in her green linen dress, with her corn-coloured hair knotted demurely on her neck. She lifted wide, serious eyes to his face and asked, 'Milk? Sugar?' and knew that the corners of her mouth were tight with self-consciousness.

When he left, three hours later, he turned her hand over and lightly kissed the palm. She looked down at the greasy dark head, the red folded neck, and stood rigid, thinking of the raw, creased necks of vultures.

Then he straightened up and said with simple kindliness, 'You must be lonely here, my dear;' and she was astounded to find her eyes full of tears.

'One does what one can to make a show of it.' She kept her lids lowered and her voice light. Inside she was weeping with gratitude. Embarrassed, she said quickly, 'You know, you haven't said what you came for.'

'I sell insurance. And besides, I've heard people talk of you.'

She imagined the talk and smiled stiffly. 'You don't seem to take your work very seriously.'

'If I may, I'll come back another time and try again?'

She did not reply. He said, 'My dear, I'll tell you a secret: one of the reasons I chose this district was because of you. Surely there aren't so many people in this country one can really talk to that we can afford not to take each other seriously?'

He touched her cheek with his hand, smiled, and went.

She heard the last thing he had said like a parody of the things she often said and felt a violent revulsion.

She went to her bedroom, where she found herself in front of the mirror. Her hands went to her cheeks and she drew in her breath with the shock. 'Why, Lucy, whatever is the matter with you?' Her eyes were dancing, her mouth smiled irresistibly. Yet she heard the archness of her 'Why, Lucy,' and thought: I'm going to pieces. I must have gone to pieces without knowing it.

Later she found herself singing in the pantry as she made a cake, stopped herself; made herself look at the insurance salesman's face against her closed eyelids; and instinctively wiped the palms of her hands against her skirt.

He came three days later. Again, in the first shock of seeing him stand at the door, smiling familiarly, she thought, It's the face of an old animal. He probably chose this kind of work because of the opportunities it gives him.

He talked of London, where he had lately been on leave; about the art galleries and the theatres.

She could not help warming, because of her hunger for this kind of talk. She could not help an apologetic note in her voice, because she knew that after so many years in this exile she must seem provincial. She liked him because he associated himself with her abdication from her standards by saying: 'Yes, yes, my dear, in a country like this we all learn to accept the second-rate.'

While he talked his eyes were roving. He was listening. Outside the window the turkeys were scraping in the dust and gobbling. In the next room the houseboy was moving; then there was silence because he had gone to get his midday meal. The children had had their lunch and gone off to the garden with the nurse.

No, she said to herself. No, no, no.

'Does your husband come back for lunch?'

'He takes it on the lands at this time of the year, he's so busy.'

He came over and sat beside her. 'Well, shall we console each other?' She was crying in his arms. She could feel their impatient and irritable tightening.

In the bedroom she kept her eyes shut. His hand travelled up and down her back. 'What's the matter, little one? What's the matter?'

His voice was a sedative. She could have fallen asleep and lain there for a week inside the anonymous, comforting arms. But he was looking at his watch over her shoulder. 'We'd better get dressed, hadn't we?'

'Of course.'

She sat naked in the bed, covering herself with her arms, looking at his white hairy body in loathing, and then at the creased red neck. She became extremely gay; and in the living room they sat side by side on the big sofa, being ironical. Then he put his arm around her, and she curled up inside it and cried again. She clung to him and felt him going away from her; and in a few minutes he stood up, saying, 'Wouldn't do for your old man to come in and find us like this, would it?' Even while she was hating him for the 'old man', she put her arms around him and said, 'You'll come back soon.'

'I couldn't keep away.' The voice purred caressingly over her head, and she said: 'You know, I'm very lonely.'

'Darling, I'll come as soon as I can. I've a living to make, you know.'

She let her arms drop, and smiled, and watched him drive away down the rutted red-rust farm road, between the rippling sea-coloured mealies.

She knew he would come again, and next time she would not cry; she would stand again like this, watching him go, hating him, thinking of how he had said: In this country we learn to accept the second-rate. And he would come again and again and again; and she would stand here, watching him go and hating him.

UYS KRIGE

The Coffin

From: *The Dream and the Desert* (1953)

In the early hours of the morning on which his first great-grandchild was born, Great Oupa Lourens was the first to be up. And when later he heard of my safe and happy entry into life, he tiptoed through the house and stooping to get his large frame through the kitchen door, came out under the bright, still stars.

In the wagon-house he took his whip from its hook, swung it over his shoulder and strode out on to the veld. There, amongst the dark hills about a mile from the homestead, he let fly at the sleeping world around him.

The long lash curled and writhed, tearing apart the deep, early morning stillness as if the peace of the fields were something fragile and brittle. With his feet planted wide apart and his tall figure – supple in spite of his sixty years – slightly bent, Great Oupa stood on the ridge, outlined against the starry sky. With powerful arms – on which the muscles stretched taut as wires – he plied the whipstock: a mobile pitch-black shape against the immobility of everything around him and the faint, grey light now touching the hilltops.

Now the lash would coil round the long stock like a nest of snakes. Then it would rustle like a scythe. And when Great Oupa laid about him with greater gusto, the whip would crack continuously, the echoes rippling away down the dark kloof.

A dim light was stealing over the veld. Through the gaps among the sombre clouds, massed over the horizon, the day, bronze and scarlet, was breaking. Then the light came so quickly, it was as if the whip had split the clouds, letting in the new life and investing that spacious world with another dawn.

A last lazy flick of the *voorslag* and a cluster of dewdrops on a tuft of grass splintered into sparks.

With his boots wet from the dew, Great Oupa Lourens stood in the *voorkamer*, gazing pensively up at the framed family tree that occupied a place of honour on the wall. An old Dutch tramp who had arrived on the farm one morning with a little bundle and a black case full of paint and brushes on his back, had painted the tree with great care according to the details provided him by Great Oupa. No one could have said to what species the family tree belonged, but there was no doubt about it ... it was the Lourens tree, gnarled and old, with its roots deep in an unknown fruitful soil, and with spreading branches and many fresh shoots, reaching to the heights.

And now Francina would have to take down that picture and paint in – as meticulously as the old pedlar – the new green bough ... Why, for a whole year he, Great Oupa, had paid for special drawing lessons for Francina in the village and he hadn't sent her to that old English spinster to gather pumpkins ...

It was in the *voorkamer* that the old Coloured woman, Ai Rosie, who had helped Great Ouma bring me into the world, came upon her master. A few years older than he, she had looked after him when he was a baby, often carrying him on her back about the house or outside on the wide, sloping *werf*.

'Why on earth is Oubaas looking at a dead painted old tree,' she broke into his reverie, 'when there's a fat bouncing baby shouting to be looked at in that room over there?'

'You're right, Ai Rosie!' Great Oupa said gaily. 'But how strange to think you are only a branch of the tree, yet you feel as old and as strong as one of its deepest roots ...'

Somewhat ill at ease, he stood in front of the bed where Mother and I were lying. He bent over me, looked at me with a frown, and gave Mother's pale forehead a slight caress with his large, rough hand.

'Anna, child, it's a fine strong son!' was his only remark. 'We are proud of you.'

In the kitchen he drank three cups of coffee and finished off a plate of rusks; then walked slowly towards the sheep-kraal where he slaughtered six sheep, hanging the skins in a row to dry among the cobwebs in a far corner of the wagon-house. One for the new Petrus Lafras Lourens who this morning for the first time had opened his eyes to God's fair world; the second for Ai Rosie and her family; the third for his Coloured labourers who were dipping sheep at Kleinplaas; another for the Dominee who would later come and baptise the child; number five for the first visitor to set foot on the farm. And the last sheep for his neighbour, pig-headed old Kobus van Graan, with whom he was always at loggerheads – for two long years the two families hadn't spoken a Christian word to one another and all because of a cursed patch of grazing land; once the Van Graans, by planting an open garden right on the boundary between the two farms, had even enticed some of his cattle beyond the disputed piece of grazing land into the garden and then whisked the cattle off to have them impounded in the village miles away; but that was an old story, he did not want to think about it any more ...

About noon that day Great Ouma was at last free to fetch the apples she needed for the midday meal from the loft. The door at the top of the stone staircase stood ajar, and a greyish-blue mistiness lingered about the loft. Broad tobacco leaves – a ripe gold and deep brown – hung in rows from the roof; and in the dim corners there was a reddish glow where apples lay in heaps.

Great Oupa's coffin stood in its customary place in the middle; but the small bags of dried fruit, tea and sugar, and the tinned food that were usually stored inside the coffin, now surrounded it in disorder, either dumped on one side or clumsily stacked one on top of the other. On a tin of sardines, at the head of the coffin, lay Great Oupa's pipe. Puzzled, Great Ouma walked towards the coffin, and stopped beside it. There, stretched out on his back, lay Great Oupa, fast asleep.

Nonplussed, Great Ouma stood gazing down at her sleeping husband. When she had been a young girl people had said, 'Young Lafras has got a screw loose …' or, 'Sure as eggs that *pokkel* of a Piet Lourens hasn't got all his little pigs in his sty …' But during all the years of their happy marriage it had been precisely his sudden whims or 'inspirations' – something spontaneous and boyish in his character – that had given her some of the happiest hours of her life. He looked contented lying there … Then her lips tightened and her small, square chin set in its usual firm lines. What nonsense was this, lying in his coffin in broad daylight! Bending over, she shook him by the arm.

Without stirring, Great Oupa gazed up at her with a happy, calm expression on his face. Then, with his voice a little drowsy from the sleep, he explained:

'I was standing here, thinking … My bed I know only too well, I have long since got used to it. My parents slept in it, I was born in it, you and I have slept in it these many years. And I must die in it. But what of my bed later on? The coffin in which I shall have to lie so much longer – until this teak wood and I, my very bones, are dust and ashes? So I climbed in just to see what it feels like. I lit my pipe, lay looking at the cobwebs up there' – he had picked up his pipe and was pointing at the cobwebs – 'and with the pleasant smell from the tobacco leaves and the apples, my thoughts started drifting …' And Great Oupa made several slow gestures with the pipe as if to indicate just how smooth and elegant had been the drift of his thoughts.

'But, old Santa' – he now sat upright in his coffin – 'what about those mutton chops of yours? You know it is my favourite dish … And I am so hungry my insides are shouting for food!'

Laughing happily, they went arm-in-arm down the broad staircase.

In those days the farmers whose farms, like that of Great Oupa, were a long way from Swellendam, went very seldom into the village. Death, like a hailstorm in the wheat, rinderpest among the cattle, blue tongue among the sheep, could come at any moment. So everyone had his coffin ready in the loft.

Great Oupa's coffin must have cost quite a sum. It had stood there, a glossy brown, among half a dozen black coffins in the undertaker's shop at Swellendam. Great Oupa did not hesitate for a moment. 'This is it, my cot!' and he drummed with his knuckles against the coffin lid. He had it put on his wagon and then drove to the house of his friend, Jan Steyn, where he, his host and three or four of their cronies had a long 'session' on the Drostdy stoep, swilling old Cape wine until the shadows crowded around them so they couldn't see the glasses in their hands.

I often saw the coffin up there in the loft. I remember distinctly when I first came upon it. I had crept into the loft to steal some dried fruit; and suddenly I saw it – slim but solidly built, dark but with a gleam to it in that half-light among the red and green tins, white boxes, warmly glowing apples and the pendant tobacco leaves with their warm tones. Without knowing it I had removed my cap; and I remained standing there, unable to take my eyes off the coffin. But it wasn't long before I got busy on the dried fruit. The next time I saw the coffin, the lid was off and Great Ouma was again using it as a larder for her tea, sugar and tinned foods.

When Great Oupa with Francina, his favourite grandchild, seated on the *wakis* beside him, drove off from Bontebokskloof on his thousand-mile trek to the Transvaal to visit relations he hadn't seen for years and also to do some business there, the coffin, filled to the brim with provisions, stood jammed amongst a clutter of other bulky articles at the back of the covered wagon.

Great Oupa cracked his whip, bellowed to the oxen, for the last time Francina waved her spotted bonnet – her head, tilted back, fair as ripe corn in the sun – and soon the groaning, creaking wagon had dropped behind the ridge.

Nine months later they returned from their long trip – without the coffin. When Oom Lewies of Tant Sarie had died there in the wilderness of the Bushveld of the poison from the lion's claws, Great Oupa had ceded his 'teak bed' to him. Why, he asked, should he worry about so small a thing as death? He was as strong as an ox and felt stronger every day.

But when communion came round again, he took the precaution of making a fresh choice from a number of brand-new 'black sheep' in the undertaker's shop at Swellendam.

In those parts it was the custom among the farmers to give their coffins in loan to one another. For instance, if there was a sudden death with no coffin handy and the village was too far away for a wagon or cart and horse to get there in time, well, then you just had to help your neighbour to a 'last haven'.

I remember Great Oupa's coffin making at least three changes up there in the loft. First Koos Badenhorst was carried in Great Oupa's coffin to the Badenhorst churchyard near the old homestead at Soetwater. In its substitute provided by the Badenhorsts, 'Squint-eye' Frans de Vries, of Ouplaas, found his last resting-place. And a year later, if I remember correctly, it was old 'Barrel-belly' Hans Boshoff, of Heuningrant, who went to his grave in Great Oupa's 'cot'.

Once again I was spending the long summer vacation on the old farm. The second afternoon after my arrival the old dispute between the two families was again nagging at Great Oupa's mind. Beside the kraal gate he discussed it with his eldest son, Oom Piet.

'What a contrary fellow Neef Kobus is!' he was saying. 'Just like a sheep that won't go into the kraal gate! Everything I could do to make an end of this eternal squabbling I have done – but nothing helps! I even suggested that he take three-quarters of that piece of grazing land. He can do what he likes with it, plough and sow there, even put a fence round it. I hear some of our farmers have no more use for beacons. They're beginning to use barbed wire now, strange idea – then we'll call it our Wire of Peace! Only we must retain that small strip next to the stream so that we can have some of the water. They get most of it, in any case, higher up.'

The long summer days passed quickly. Great Oupa, I soon discovered, had developed a new habit. During the day one would suddenly miss him, find him neither in the wheatfields nor at the dam.

One afternoon I was walking along the riverbed, about two miles from the homestead. There, in a desolate kloof against the mountain, I was startled by a weird protracted sound from somewhere nearby. It stopped, then began again. It was like a long drawn-out groan; that of an animal, I thought, in great pain. I had come to a dead stop, listening. Then I walked forward mechanically and, forcing my way through some undergrowth, came upon Great Oupa sitting on a grassy bank. He was bending over with his hands clenching his knees. On his contorted face there was an expression I shall never forget; and while he clenched and unclenched his hands, fierce groans broke from his lips.

A cold hand seemed to touch my heart. Then Great Oupa noticed me where I stood, bewildered and speechless, beside a shrub.

At once the agonised expression had disappeared, the face was normal again, the gaze calm and the eyes had the first little spark of a smile. He beckoned to me. I sat down beside him. Within a few minutes he was as amusing as ever, telling me about the good old days when he and his three brothers were small boys; how they practically lived down here in the river-bed; how with enormous guns that today would kick grownup people clean out of their boots, they had hunted wild animals, yes, even leopards, all on their own, there, in this same tangled kloof.

But I had a strong feeling something was wrong and I could hear my heart throbbing. Beads of sweat, I noticed, stood on Great Oupa's forehead; and now and again his fingers would tremble slightly.

We walked through the veld. Great Oupa was still talking animatedly; and as he talked, he would flick off the head of a veld flower with his horse-whip, something I had never seen him do before.

At table that evening he was as humorous as ever. But I did not sleep much that night.

The feeling of fear and horror, the cruel assault on my young mind and imagination that I had experienced that afternoon in the kloof, was repeated with shattering immediacy when a few months later I learned in one of my Latin lessons that the word 'cancer' meant 'crab'.

When with the passing of time the disease struck deeper roots into that big, strong body and Great Oupa was often so exhausted that he no longer felt capable of repairing to his old sanctuary, the veld, he and Great Ouma changed their bedroom – moving to the old part of the house where the walls were several feet thick. It would be cooler there in summer, Great Oupa said. And as far as winter was concerned, it was the only room in the house with a decent fireplace …

Nobody knew what actually was happening behind those thick walls. Only as time went by Great Ouma's face became more wrinkled and her back more bent; as if in her efforts to draw on all her resources of love, patience and an obstinate resistance, her small body was gradually shrinking.

Always after one of those terrible attacks, Great Oupa would be at his gayest. Then there was no coping with his high spirits, his debonair sense of humour. A group of us would sit round the dining-room table or in the warm, late afternoon sun on the stoep, listening spellbound to everything he said. No one would interrupt him. Only one person would be speaking, Great Oupa.

At times his humour would have a light touch – subtle, playful, ironical. But his irony was directed mostly against himself; and where it touched on the failings of his fellowmen, it never hurt.

On other occasions his mood was warm and human, full of understanding – gentle as sunlight on green hills after rain. Sometimes, however, it became boisterous, extravagant. Then his laughter would come in great gusts of bawdy humour; he would be so forthright, so exuberantly coarse that many of us, especially the older ones, would have tears running down our cheeks and Great Ouma, if she were present, would lift up her hands as if to ward off a blow, and then quietly but very effectively put an end to all this 'godlessness'. It was then I always felt his humour was vital and earthy; and it had something physical like sea-water streaming over you on a hot summer's day and making your whole body tingle with coolness.

'Laughter is a glorious, sacred thing,' Great Oupa once said, 'a gift from God … In this old life of ours that can be so hard and bitter, laughter is often our only defence against life. And also our only defence against death, enabling us to look it straight in the face and even, sometimes, play the fool with it …

'Laughter is of us humans, the land, the earth; and the nearer you get to the earth, the nearer you get to heaven.'

In her lean-to against the hill old Mieta was found dead one morning. More than a hundred years old, she had been one of the slaves of Great Oupa's grandfather down at the Cape many, many years ago, and had served the

Lourens family faithfully all her long life. She had had, even in her old age, a vivid personality and a great fund of humour; and with her store of Malay folk-lore, her Boer remedies for every ailment and her endless picturesque anecdotes from the past, she had been Great Oupa's favourite among his Coloured servants. Quite often I would see him standing in front of her shack talking to her where she sat with her back propped up against the mud wall, turning her wizened old face now up at him and then at the sun; and not infrequently during our long talks on the stoep he would embellish some tale he had heard, I knew, from Mieta.

Now Great Oupa again stood in front of old Mieta's lean-to, but this time he seemed angry – rebuking her grandson, Adoons, who until a few minutes ago had been busy nailing together some planks for a coffin for his grandmother.

'Shame on you, Adoons!' he exclaimed. 'Surely your old Granny deserves something better than that? To think of that awful contraption being her crib for all eternity! Go and fetch my coffin from the loft!'

So the small, shrivelled body was laid out in the large, heavy coffin with its glistening copper fittings. Carefully Adoons filled up the large gap at Mieta's feet with two of her own blankets, 'just to balance poor old Oumatjie ...'

The burial service was conducted by Great Oupa himself.

He sat in the driver's seat with beside him his brother, Nicolaas, 'Crazy Nick' or 'Nick the Noodle', as he was called in the neighbourhood. In the middle of the open wagon stood the beautiful dark-brown coffin, the sun striking sparks from its handles. Slowly the wagon rolled over the *werf*. A little ahead, sexton for the occasion, Adoons paced with slow, measured tread – elegant and dignified, conscious of his importance in this last solemn rite, the tails of the morning coat Great Oupa had given him some years ago almost trailing, in spite of the large tuck at the back, in the dust.

The procession swung away from the *werf* to follow the road where a thick aloe hedge shut it off on both sides from the wheatfields.

'Lafras, man, charge Adoons! Get him!' Oom Nicolaas shouted.

I do not know what it was – the fine day, the vitality Great Oupa suddenly felt surging within him in his long pause between two attacks, or perhaps Oom Nic's suggestion – but the next moment the great whip-thong curled through the air. Three loud cracks and the mules had jerked into action, the wagon lurching forward and gravel flying in all directions.

Adoons's first great oath was swept away on the wind. With coat tails spread out almost horizontally, he ran down the road as if the devil and all his impis were jabbing him in the heels.

The first mule was almost on top of Adoons, when he swerved off the road, dashed through a large opening in the hedge and went racing over the open veld. Great Oupa swung the wagon through the opening and started chasing

Adoons over the uneven stubble land, the coffin bouncing up and down on the wagon.

Against the still, golden surface of the freshly mown fields, Adoons was a pitch-black charging form with whirling arms and long coat tails flapping in the wind. After some distance of clattering progress Great Oupa came to his senses, halting the wagon. On top of a small rise, about a hundred yards off, stood Adoons, breathless but full of righteous indignation.

Great Oupa beckoned Adoons with the whip to come and resume his office in the ceremony. Against the ridge above the *drif* he conducted the service, together the three of them sang 'Rest, My Soul, Thy God is King', each dropped a handful of red earth upon the coffin, Adoons filled up the open grave with a spade Oom Nic had placed in the wagon for the purpose, and Great Oupa, seeing a couple of hawks circling high above his head, marched off to fetch his gun and fix those blasted pests that were always gobbling up Great Ouma's eggs.

Death was slow in coming to Great Oupa.

On an afternoon when the last sheaves of the loveliest harvest Great Oupa had ever seen, were being gathered into his sheds, Great Ouma died suddenly of a heart attack. And Great Oupa had to bear his cross in solitude until Francina resigned her teaching post at Swellendam to come and keep house at Bontebokskloof.

Shortly after Great Ouma's death, Great Oupa wrote Oom Kobus a long, friendly letter – but there was no answer.

It was then, in the first few months after her death, that I noticed how deeply the folds and wrinkles had bitten into Great Oupa's face. Above the broad arched forehead the hair had become whiter, scarcer. Great Oupa's long coat now hung loose around his body, he looked thinner and his collars were too wide for him. Under his chin the skin hung slack; and once, when I was sitting next to him on the stoep, I thought of the peculiar neck of the mountain tortoise that I had come upon near the kraal the day before, and that I had finally coaxed into pushing its head out of its shell.

It was at the beginning of the Great Drought that Great Oupa came to hear of the sudden death overnight of his old neighbour and 'bosom enemy', Kobus van Graan; and that the *oubaas* had made no provision for himself and was now lying cold and without a coffin in his large four-poster at Blouklip.

One of Oom Kobus's Coloured servants had told Adoons about it down at the *spruit*. The old quarrel about the grazing land had recently flared up again. Lourenses and Van Graans no longer greeted one another, not even in front of the church door. Great Oupa told his grandson, Mattheus, to get his new coffin from the loft, put it on the wagon and take it to Blouklip.

'When I let Kobus van Graan know the other day he should pay us a visit so that we could clear up this matter once and for all,' Great Oupa said quietly, 'he did not even answer my letter. But he told Neef Jan Louw he would never set foot in my house again. Now he'll be my house's guest till Judgment Day …'

The Great Drought had scorched the earth a grey-black when Great Oupa eventually came to die. Spent, with his face bonier than ever, he lay in his large, wide bed as if for the first time he was utterly abandoned and helpless – and with at times such a calm expression on his face he seemed already dead.

At his bedside Francina wept without restraint and in a bunched group near the farther window the menfolk whispered together; for the eldest among them, Oom Piet, had only just discovered that the coffin in the loft would be too small for his father.

Berend, Kobus van Graan's youngest son, careless bungler that he was, had brought a coffin that in no way conformed to Great Oupa's stature. And to get to Swellendam today or tomorrow, or even this week, was quite out of the question. Where before there had been a wide sheet of water in the pan, the earth now was as cracked as a dead leaf; the few remaining horses had just enough strength to plod from one patch of shadow to the other in their vain search for food; and in the parched riverbed the skulls and bones of oxen lay bleaching in the flat, white glare of the sun.

Of their neighbours, the three De Villiers were short men, and all the other men of medium height … Nowhere in the neighbourhood would they find a coffin to fit Great Oupa's six feet three inches.

Great Oupa, whose ear was so acute he could hear from the front stoep the call of a *tarentaal* against the ridge, slowly opened his eyes and turned his head in the direction of his children.

'Francina, don't cry any more, my child. Life is much too precious for you to mourn over someone's death. Life goes on. It's only death that comes to a dead-end like the cave I showed you one day in the mountain up there.' And lifting his hand, he pointed through the window beside his bed at the distant Langeberge. 'Be glad that we've had such pleasant times together. And for your heartache, the days that lie ahead will be good doctors.

'And Petrus, Mattheus, Johannes, Jacobus, Christoffel, Arnoldus' – it was the first time I heard him solemnly calling his sons by their full, sonorous names and not merely Piet, Tewis, Jan, Koos, Chris and Nols – 'you have your hands full enough just keeping your families alive until the drought breaks for you to be worrying your heads about such a trifle as a coffin that's too small. Do you think I don't know it's too small? I measured it myself the week before last. Funny, that even in death Kobus van Graan should have caught me out …

'Look, Piet, get Adoons. He is a good carpenter. Those deal planks at the back of the wagon-shed, let him knock them together and give them a good lick of varnish. It'll be dry by tomorrow. And don't break your necks because

I won't be put away in a teak coffin. Sailors used to wrap some of our ancestors in a piece of sail and drop them into the sea …

'Piet, you are the eldest. This eternal quarrel with the Van Graans must stop now for good and all. With our everlasting bickering, old Kobus and I were thorns enough in the side of our good Lord. Give Berend and the others the grazing land or what remains of it, and *basta!* Then if I meet Kobus van Graan on the other side, he'll probably greet me …'

A little laugh and Great Oupa turned his head to the window, gazing at the mountains for some time. Then he closed his eyes.

He never spoke again.

On a windstill afternoon full of scorching sunlight, grey bone-dry old Mother Earth took back her son in a plain deal coffin without a single fitting.

On the night after the funeral Great Oupa's twentieth great-grandchild was born.

UYS KRIGE

Death of the Zulu

From: *The Dream and the Desert* (1953)

It was about two hours after our capture. We were marching from Figtree towards Tobruk port. It was midsummer, the sun well up, but, thank God, not too hot yet – though I knew by the brittle cobalt look of the sky that it would not be long before the heat would become unbearable, beating down upon that bone-dry earth in shimmering, scorching waves … We weren't doing anything, not even thinking, just trudging along, dragging our heavy feet through the sand, raising the dust in yellowish-grey clouds in the dips and in little lingering puffs round our boots on the straight.

I appeared to have two minds: the one stunned, the other perfectly conscious, taking in coolly and dispassionately our surroundings. Only one sight was clear-cut, vivid: that silent mob of men streaming towards Tobruk. And only one sound audible: the click or scrunch of desert boots when we struck a rock vein or a loose surface of grit across our path.

Those boots, that everlasting dragging, clogged tramp, tramp tramp … Like a drum … Like the slow, dull, monotonous beat of a drum. And with a single monotonous refrain: out of nothing, through nothing, towards nothing … Out of nothing: the thunderous vacuum of the battle. Through nothing: this strange, unreal scene, as if flickering in a film. Towards nothing: the huge inconceivable emptiness of our life of captivity and exile to come …

It would be more accurate to say I seemed to have, not two minds, but three, the third listening to a monologue by the conscious mind. 'Yes, before it often seemed to you,' it was saying, 'that you were living only in the past or the future, never in the present. The present was always escaping you, slipping like sand through your fingers. Now you have your present, my boy, and a fine present it is too! Very present, very real … And you can't barricade yourself against it by drawing on your memories. They've been washed out. Nor can you throw up a rampart against it with hopes, plans for the future. For your future, too, has gone down the drain. There is no past. There is no future. There's only the present …'

There were bodies lying beside the road, some singly, some in batches. Dead or wounded, I didn't look, I wasn't interested. My eyes slid over them as if they were so many pieces of old motor junk scattered about a disused yard somewhere. 'They're dead and they've a wife like you ...' I heard a faint voice whisper somewhere far off. 'They're dead and they've a mother like you ...' The voice was taking shape, getting stronger. 'They're dead and they've a child like you ...' The voice, now, was quite loud. It was my unconscious mind awaking; and the monologue had become a dialogue.

'I don't care a damn ...' I heard the calm mind say, but it was fast losing its imperturbability. 'Let them all go to hell ... Let them all go straight to hell! I don't care a damn!'

Below the escarpment the track we were following made a curve. I was on the left-hand side of the curve when I heard a shout. Mechanically I looked up. To the right, in the curve's bulge, about fifty metres away, a German officer was standing over someone stretched out on the ground. He shouted again, beckoned with his arm. Though there must have been at least a dozen men in our group, numbly, apathetically, I thought: 'It's me he wants, he's looking straight at me, I can see the blue of his eyes ...'

Automatically I stepped off the track. There were two other South Africans beside me also walking towards the German. I did not know who they were, I had never seen them before. They must have been beside me – or just behind me – during that long, weary trek from Figtree, but I hadn't noticed them. It was only now as, one on each side of me, they too moved forward towards the officer and the figure at his feet, that their presence began impinging upon my consciousness. And though I was to spend at least a quarter of an hour in their company I cannot, to this day, recollect a single feature or physical characteristic of either of them.

The next minute I was standing beside the man lying on the ground. It was one of our native soldiers, and I could tell by his build and features that he was a Zulu. As a Government official in Natal for some years, I had got to know this Bantu race, their language and customs well. A shell must have burst near him. His left arm was off at the elbow. A large splinter must have snapped it off as one snaps crisply and cleanly between one's fingers a dried mealie stalk. His shirt, I noticed, was full of little craters, stiff with caked blood.

Then I saw his eyes. They were a luminous jet black, stricken with pain; yet they seemed, somehow, detached. Although the man was looking straight at me he appeared unaware of my presence.

'*Kiyini umfana* (What is it, young Zulu?)' I asked, bending over him and hearing my voice go trailing over the sand with a gruff undertone as if this were yet another imbecility for which I wasn't in the least responsible and I resented being implicated in it; as if what that droning voice really wanted to say was: 'I'm out of it, do you hear? Out of it ... Leave me alone! Why drag me back? Why –'

Hearing his own language, the young Zulu raised his head slightly. His eyes seemed brighter, but their expression had changed; it was no longer remote, had become intimate. Then his head fell back, his eyes, however, never leaving my face. '*Hau … umlungu …*' he groaned. '*Kuhi … Insimbi ing-shayili …* (O … white man … It is not a good thing … The iron has hit me …).'

Suddenly I realised I was normal again, with my mind no longer split into segments, but an integrated whole with perfectly logical perceptions and reactions.

I had come erect, was looking around. The German officer had gone. About four hundred metres away I saw him, driving away in his truck. I turned to the Zulu again. He was in a half-sitting position with one of the two men who had stepped out of our lines with me, crouched down behind him, holding him up.

'How do you feel, *umfana*?' I asked going down on my right knee. A hard glitter came into his eyes, then he said slowly, clearly: '*Umlungu, ngidubule …* (White man, shoot me …).' There was no doubting it, he was pleading with me — apparently unaware that I, like him, was now a prisoner no longer carrying a weapon and therefore as powerless as he against his fate.

'Don't talk like that, *umfana*,' I said peremptorily, more to get a grip on myself than to rebuke him. 'You've only lost an arm. Many men have lost an arm, and they're walking about now, laughing, with their heads in the sun.'

'*Ca … ca …* (No … no …),' he muttered, almost angrily.

'Yes, yes …' I continued, speaking fast. 'We'll get a doctor for you and we'll take you to the hospital' — we, we, who the hell's we, I thought, we're nothing, less than nothing — 'and they'll be good to you there, soon you'll be a whole man again and it won't be many moons before you'll be going about your work, watching the pumpkins fill out, the maize swell in the cob, and the cattle grow fat in the fields back in Zululand …'

I do not know what made me say this. I knew it wasn't true. My own words, with a hollow false sound, echoed back on my ears.

'*Ca, umlungu … Ngidubule! Ngidubule!* (No, white man … Shoot me! Shoot me!).' How strong his voice is, I thought, out of all proportion to his strength.

'Soon,' I repeated, 'you'll be a whole man again.'

'No, no, white man …' He was shaking his head in exactly the way I had so often seen old Zulu indunas shake their heads, when in tribal councils they would, by their whole expression and attitude, gently but firmly convey to the European that the sum of all his knowledge was as nothing compared with their ancient African wisdom. '*Ngipelile …* (I am finished …).'

A little desert car drew up twenty metres away. A tall, thin German officer with sharp features jumped out and was beside us in a few quick darting steps. Another German officer, short and squat, had followed him — and the next moment the tall officer was bending over the native, feeling his chest beneath the blood-stiffened shirt. Noticing his stars and the snake of Aesculapius in his badge, I felt at once greatly relieved.

I looked at the Zulu's arm again. Most of the stump's end was caked over with dry, hardened blood. It still bled, but very little, only a trickle oozing through the shattered flesh.

'*Ngidubule!*' His voice was no longer supplicating but had a fierce, ringing quality as if raised in protest that this was no extravagant demand but a fitting and just claim upon me. My gaze travelled over his magnificent body. The broad torso bulged beneath the army shirt. The thighs, curving into sight under the dirty bloodstained shorts, were of a classic symmetry, the calves and legs as harmoniously proportionate.

Then the thought struck me that the Zulus, physically, are one of the most beautiful races in the world; that Zulu males have an extraordinary pride in their physique; that they consider any deformity of the body – and particularly disfigurement – as something unnatural, even monstrous; and that formerly they killed all children unfortunate enough to be born cripples. Naturally this young Zulu, descended from generations of warriors, wanted to die now, clamoured for death; for this cracked useless body, this stump of an arm, were they not a shame and a disgrace, a crying offence against both man and the gods?

My eyes slipped over his chest again, met his. I knew they had never left my face even though the German doctor was still bending over him examining him, feeling tentatively for his wounds. Now, quite simply, as if he had read my thought and was confident that his wish would be granted, he said slowly: '*Ngidubule, umlungu* …'

'No, you speak foolish things.'

'*Ngidubule!*' The short spell of calm had broken, the voice was again urgent. Did it contain a note of reproach?

'*Ngidubule, umlungu, ngidubule!*' Yes, it was reproachful. God, would that eternal cry of '*Ngidubule* …' never stop?

The doctor had pulled out his hand, turned and was looking at me. 'What does he say?' he asked me in German.

'It is his request that we shoot him …' I answered, realising at once that I was giving a stiff literal German translation not of what the Zulu had said but of what his headman would have said in slow solemn tone to the other assembled members of the tribe were they here now, squatting in a half circle round the dying man, deliberating his case.

Whether the Zulu finally understood that I could not, would not do it, or whether he recognised the German doctor as his enemy who, according to his subconscious reasoning, would be less averse to such an action, I do not know; but as soon as he had heard this new, foreign voice intruding upon our dialogue, he was no longer looking at me but at the German.

Leaning up against the South African supporting him from behind, he had had until now his right hand on the ground. But now, in a great effort, his lips twitching in pain – there were foam flecks on them, spotted with blood – he brought his hand to his shirt front and slowly, gropingly, uncovered his chest. Next, straining himself forward, he said in a deep resonant voice to the German captain: '*Wena aungidubue!* (You shoot me!).' Strange, but at that moment it sounded almost like a command.

'He wants you to shoot him …' I told the doctor. Standing stiffly beside me, the German made no reply.

'What chance has he of living?' I asked.

'None,' came the incisive answer. 'He must have been wounded yesterday afternoon, has lain here all night. He's lost so much blood, he can't have much more to lose. Had he been a European he would have been dead long ago …' His voice was as jerky as his movements. Though speaking German, we had instinctively moved a few paces away as if afraid the wounded man would understand.

'And he still speaks,' the voice staccatoed on, 'with all that shrapnel inside him! He'll probably die when we move him. Then again, he's so strong he might live for hours.'

I turned to the native. 'The doctor says you are badly hurt, but that you have great strength and must not worry. We're going to carry you to that truck, take you to the hospital.'

'No, no … I am finished … Shoot me … I cannot live any more. The pain is too deep … *umlungu* …' He was groaning again, his voice getting weaker, and for the first time he closed his eyes for longer than a second. His hand, too, had fallen back on the ground, black against the pale yellow earth.

The doctor touched me on the arm. 'Perhaps it would be the easiest way out,' he said, and motioned to the young lieutenant standing a few paces away. An order from the captain, and the lieutenant had pulled out his pistol and handed it to me. I stood there, as if petrified, with the pistol in my right hand.

'*Umlungu … umlungu …*' were the only two words now uttered by the Zulu lying at my feet with closed eyes and quivering lips. He kept on muttering them, his voice never rising above a whisper. Yet the repeated '*umlungu … umlungu …*' seemed to contain a note of awe, almost of reverence – not, I felt, because I was an officer and he a private, but because at the moment I must have appeared to his bewildered mind, half crazed with pain, the great benefactor bearing in my hands the supreme gift of peace and the healing oblivion of death.

I looked from the pistol to the captain, from the captain back to the pistol, then at the Zulu. He, in the meanwhile, had opened his eyes.

'*Ngidubule!*' his voice rang in my ears, as strong as ever.

I shook my head. 'No,' I said to the captain handing him the pistol, 'I do not shoot my friends.'

It was at least two seconds before I realised I had addressed the German in Zulu.

The Zulu's gaze had followed the motion of the pistol; he now stared at the captain. The German stood, irresolute, as if embarrassed by the pistol. He seemed to be debating a point. Then turning to me, he said:

'My business is to preserve life not to destroy it.'

'And not to lessen pain?'

'Yes, to lessen pain.' He was speaking much more slowly; the bark had gone out of his voice. 'But that would be contrary to Red Cross regulations. I'm not even allowed to carry firearms …' This typical German respect for rules and regulations, I thought, how incongruous!

The next moment the captain had handed the pistol back to its owner. 'Herr Oberleutnant Muller,' he rapped out in military tone: 'Shoot this man!'

Then I noticed the Zulu's hand come creeping up his chest again and I forgot everything, watching it, fascinated. It was a broad compact hand with a fair-sized wart on the index finger and at that moment it seemed to pulse with life, to be one of the most living things I had ever seen. The big strong fingers felt for the edge of the shirt-front where the V-opening ended, closed over it in a firm grip, there was the quick, sharp rip of khaki drill tearing, and the shirt fell apart, revealing the entire chest. The right side had hardly been touched but the left, until now concealed by the shirt, was a mass of torn flesh.

I looked away. The lieutenant had stepped forward, was standing a few paces from the Zulu. He had a set look on his face, holding the weapon stiffly in front of him, pointing it at the dying man.

The Zulu's hand was buried deep in the sand, gripping the earth, supporting his body. To me, at that moment, it seemed that in a last superhuman effort he wanted to lift himself, rise and with both feet planted firmly on the ground, meet his death face to face. He had squared his shoulders, throwing them back and was straining his chest out and up, as if to present a better target to the enemy, or to thrust it against the very muzzle of the pistol.

Now his eyes were ablaze as if all the fierce passionate life that remained to him were concentrated in their jet-black depths.

'*Ngidubule! Ngidubule!*' broke from his dry, cracked lips in a crescendo, like a shout of joy, a triumphant roar; and I was reminded of the Zulu battle cry I had so often heard, sonorous and barbaric, bursting from a thousand throats when the war dance reaches its frenzied, crashing climax.

'*Ngidubule! Ngidubule!*'

Yes, he was roaring at his body, roaring at his pain, roaring at death. Rooted to the spot, I stood looking down at him. I wanted to tear myself away. I couldn't.

Carefully, methodically, the lieutenant took aim along the pistol barrel.

I felt a hand clutch my shoulder. For a second it lay there lax. Then it tightened over my collarbone. I half turned. It was the captain. Slowly he turned me completely round. He took a step forward. I followed. I was waiting, I felt, for yet another *'Ngidubule!'* rather than the pistol's report; and when a snail-shell (one of those countless bone-white shells scattered like tiny skulls about the desert) popped under my feet, I shuddered.

We were about five metres away when the pistol cracked. It did not go off again.

I have a very hazy recollection of what happened after that.

I remember the German captain saying, *'Auf Wiedersehen'*; the two officers driving off in the small car; and that for a long time I sat on a flat stone beside the road.

Legs, many legs, milled past, kept slipping in and out of my vision. But they made no impression on me; in a dull, disconnected way I was more interested in the little wisps of sand that kept spiralling, circling about my boots and then settling in a thin, pale yellow dust on the broad square toecaps.

How long I sat there, staring at my boots, I don't know. Someone shouted in Afrikaans: 'Come along, Du Toit! Come along!' and when I found myself again, I was once more among that crowd of prisoners tramping slowly, wearily towards Tobruk.

BERTHA GOUDVIS

Thanks to Mrs Parsons

From: *The Mistress of Mooiplaas and other Stories* (1956)

It all began with the shooting of the little pigs. Mrs Parsons, the storekeeper's wife, believed in pig breeding as a side line. Not in a large way, of course, for she had not the time. She helped Parsons in the store, for he wasn't much of a salesman, and the women usually waited about until she could attend to them. Her sister looked after the house and the cooking, so she was able to do a little maternity work as well. You must know that in her maiden days Mrs Parsons had trained at Queen Charlotte's Hospital, and the women of our little dorp, which is nearly forty miles from a railway station, had infinite faith in her.

When the government eventually appointed a district surgeon he found that there was no call for his services when the stork flew. Dr Drysdale was hardworking and capable, but the jolly little woman who looked so well after her charges was an established favourite. She was very good natured, always ready, as she put it, to do a hand's turn for anybody, but when it came to her professional work the fixed fee had to be paid. On this point she was firm.

With all these duties Mrs Parsons found time to raise a few pigs, and the pigsty was kept in admirable order. She loved to display a newly arrived litter to a favoured customer. 'Come and see my darlings,' she would say, and take you across the yard to the pigsty, where the sow wallowed amongst her pink podgy offspring. I went with her only once, for I thought the sight an ugly one, and when she told me one day of the loss of a whole litter through the voracious appetite of the unnatural mother I refused to look upon that particular sow again, a decision which caused Mrs Parsons to regard me as the victim of a foolish squeamishness. It was her custom to sell the pigs when they were quite small, but for some reason or another she kept one lot till they were old enough to be troublesome to the neighbours, and one day they contrived to wriggle through the fence and find their way to Simon van Rooyen's sweet potato patch, where they did much damage.

Simon was furious and he was only deterred from a violent attack on the despoilers by the pleadings of his wife, who was much attached to Mrs Parsons and feared to lose her friendship. Simon spoke to Parsons and warned him as to what would happen if the pigs trespassed again. Parsons promised his wife that he would render the fence impassable without further delay, but there came a heavy mail that morning and, as he kept the post office in his shop, he was busy and forgot all about the pigs. But the pigs had not forgotten the sweetness of that potato patch, and when Van Rooyen found them in his garden that afternoon he saw red. Before his wife could intervene he fetched his gun and killed the lot. Then he made his natives pick up the carcasses and toss them over the fence of Parsons's garden.

The brutality of this last procedure capped his iniquity in the eyes of Mrs Parsons. When her own servants called her to view the bleeding corpses she broke down and cried. Then she said hard things about Simon van Rooyen. Half the village sided with her, but the other half sympathised with the owner of the ruined garden.

Although Mrs Parsons was a Cockney by birth, you would have suspected an Irish strain if you had heard her lament the little pigs. They were the dearest and most innocent of pets that she had reared from birth, and how anyone could have had the heart to butcher them in cold blood was more than she could ever understand.

She brought an action against Van Rooyen, and the case was tried by Mr Curtis, who was Acting Magistrate during Mr Fellowes's absence on holiday. He was a bachelor of some sardonic humour, who said afterwards that he had found it hard to maintain the dignity of the Bench during Mrs Parsons's impassioned declaration of the innocent lovableness of her slaughtered piglets.

But is was with the utmost gravity that he delivered judgment. He said that the pig's first trespass had been forgiven and their owner duly warned. When their offence was repeated the defendant was justified in taking action. The decision must, therefore, be one of justifiable homicide.

Mrs Parsons burst into tears. Afterwards she transferred some of her anger to the man who had delivered this heartless judgment, saying that he seemed to be actually enjoying himself, but what could one expect of a stony-hearted bachelor who had never reared chick or child. If Mr Fellowes had been on the Bench she knew the result would have been a different one. But while she railed against the magistrate her anger with the Van Rooyens showed no signs of abatement. She vowed that she would have no more truck with them and Anna could look elsewhere for a midwife when her next baby was due.

This was a cruel blow to Anna for she was already expecting her third infant and was convinced that no one could deliver her with the skill of Mrs Parsons, who had brought her two previous babes into the world. Although she was such a busy woman the little midwife usually found time to visit mothers-to-be before their time came, and her bright looks and cheerful rallying were as good as a tonic, or so they said.

She fretted the more because Mrs Parsons met her one morning returning from the opposition store where Simon had transferred his custom and cut her dead.

'I wanted to stop her and tell her that I begged you not to shoot the pigs,' Anna wept to her husband, 'but she never gave me the chance. She didn't even look at little Julie who was with me, and she used to be so fond of her.'

'She was fonder of her pigs,' growled Van Rooyen. He tried to comfort his wife by telling her that she could engage Dr Drysdale for her confinement and also Mrs Steenkamp who had had ten children of her own and should, therefore, know as much about maternity cases as Mrs Parsons.

The months passed quickly, and now the time drew near not only for Anna's confinement but for a vastly more important event in the eyes of the villagers. This was the annual gymkhana and sports meeting, which owed its origin to the sporting proclivities of Dr Drysdale, Jan Vermaak the stock inspector, and Donelly who recruited native labour for the Rand mines.

The programme was so varied and attractive that the attendance increased yearly. Nearly all the neigbouring farmers came in with their families, and even visitors from Meyersdorp would drive over for the meeting and the dance in the schoolroom which wound up the festivities. For days beforehand we would watch the skies for weather signals, but so far the gods had not disappointed and this year was no exception. A sky deeply blue, drifting clouds to mask the sun when it burned too fiercely, a faint cool breeze: the day was perfect.

Early in the morning carts and wagons began to arrive and line up on either side of the racecourse. Women and children who had not met since the last Nachtmaal in Meyersdorp talked and laughed together, while the men inspected the horseflesh. Derby runners were never scanned more closely than the entries for the day's events. No bookmaker would think it worth his while to attend our gymkhanas, but there were many private bets.

The doctor's grey horse, Charlie, was mostly fancied for the big event, a hurdle race with a purse of £25, but many thought that Jan Vermaak's Swartbooi stood a better chance. There were other entries but the experts foretold that the race would be between these two. After some pony races and sports competitions the bell rang for the big event. The spectators hastened to find places on carts and wagons and you could feel the excitement that possessed the crowd.

Bester's roan mare, Maanlicht, with Tom Bester up, led at the start, but she was soon overtaken by Charlie and Swartbooi. Both owners were riding and as they approached the last hurdle there was much shouting. 'Come on Doc.' 'Jan will do it.' 'No, the Doctor!' They leaped the hurdle almost simultaneously, and then a cry of horror rang out, for Charlie had stumbled and thrown his rider.

Jan dismounted as soon as he could and many others ran forward, but before they reached him the doctor was on his feet. 'I am all right, only a broken arm,' he shouted.

He directed their operations, and his arm was soon in a sling. Vermaak offered to drive him to the doctor in Meyersdorp and they set off almost immediately. Drysdale said to Simon van Rooyen before he left: 'Tell your wife not to worry. I'll be all right long before she will want me.'

That night there was a great gathering in the schoolroom. A surprising number of dress suits were to be seen and the ladies looked so elegant that many ventured the opinion that you could not see finer dresses in a Johannesburg ballroom. The hall was gay with bunting and paper streamers; the platform banked with hydrangeas and the blue agapanthus lilies, which grew so plentifully in the spruit beyond. A pianist and a violinist had come from Meyersdorp to supply the music.

Mrs Parsons looked the happiest of all in her new black evening frock with a cluster of red flowers that vied with the flush of exitement on her cheeks. She was a noticeable figure. Her black eyes were shining and her hair had been brushed and brilliantined to a jet-like glisten. Her feet could hardly keep still while the musicians tuned up. She squeezed my arm as she went by with her partner. 'Oh, isn't it wonderful?' she whispered. 'To think that we're going to have real music to dance to.'

I knew how passionately she loved dancing. Whenever she could find an opportunity she would promote a 'social' in the schoolroom, and of all who danced to the strains of Prinsloo's concertina none were more energetic than Mrs Parsons. Her vital little body swayed to music with the rhythm of a born dancer. Given the training and opportunity in her younger days she might have been the leader of a London *corps de ballet*.

The dancing began and I went with Mrs Fellowes, the magistrate's wife, into the marquee to have a look at the supper tables. We were there only a few minutes before a flap lifted and Simon van Rooyen came towards us. He looked as if he were dazed, and I would have suspected a too long sojourn in the hotel bar if I had not known him to be a temperate man.

'My wife's been taken bad,' he said.

'But I thought ...,' began Mrs Fellowes. Then she stopped.

'Yes. Not for another three weeks but she started to worry when she heard about the doctor. Now she's took bad and she's crying for Mrs Parsons.'

Mrs Fellowes looked at me and I looked at Mrs Fellowes. We knew the story of the feud and there was Mrs Parsons just beginning to enjoy the dance she had worked for and looked forward to for such a long time.

'Can't you get someone else?' asked the magistrate's wife. 'It may be only a false alarm.'

Simon shook his head. 'No, it isn't a false alarm. She knows. I've left Mrs

Steenkamp with her but she doesn't want her. She says she knows she's going to die if she can't have Mrs Parsons.'

'Then you will have to ask her.'

'I can't. She wouldn't listen to me.' There was anguish in his eyes. Simon was very fond of Anna.

'I'll bring her here,' said Mrs Fellowes. The dance was over; we could hear the clapping. Mrs Fellowes returned followed by a tight-lipped little woman.

'What is this I hear about Anna?' asked Mrs Parsons.

Simon told her and continued, for despair lent him courage: 'She says she won't have Mrs Steenkamp now the doctor's gone and that she doesn't care if she has to die. She sits there rocking herself and crying for you.'

'That Steenkamp woman is nothing but an old fool. I suppose I'll have to go.'

She fetched her cloak and came back to us.

'Come,' she said to Van Rooyen, 'we must go first to the house to get my things.'

We knew that the little black bag would soon be on its way to Anna.

The next day the village heard that another sturdy boy had been added to the population, and all was well with the mother.

When Dr Drysdale came back he took the news as a good joke against himself, but Mrs Parsons was not quite happy about it.

'Queer that he shouldn't be able to take his first confinement case here,' she remarked. 'But goodness knows it wasn't my fault.'

A fortnight later I was in the shop when Simon van Rooyen came in and asked to speak to Mrs Parsons. He began to urge something in a low voice but she obstinately shook her head.

'No, not this time,' came her penetrating accents, 'I always stand up for what's due to me as a rule, but this case is different. I'll not have the doctor thinking I wanted to pinch his fee.'

Simon went on urging but she proved obdurate saying as she walked back to the counter where I stood: 'No, not a penny. I mean it.'

He went towards the door shamefaced and unhappy. Coals of fire are such uncomfortable wear.

Suddenly her hard look vanished, and a laugh broke over her face. 'Simon,' she called out. He paused in the doorway. 'You can send me a couple of pigs, if you like.'

And he did.

ES'KIA MPHAHLELE

Down the Quiet Street

First published, 1956

From: *The Unbroken Song: Selected Writing* (1981)

Nadia Street was reputed to be the quietest street in Newclare. Not that it is any different from other streets. It has its own dirty water, its own flies, its own horse manure, its own pot-bellied children with traces of urine down the legs. The hawker's trolley still slogs along in Nadia Street, and the cloppity-clop from the hoofs of the over-fed mare is still part of the street.

Its rows of houses are no different, either. The roofs slant forward as if they were waiting for the next gale to rock them out of their complacency and complete the work it has already started. Braziers still line the rocky pavement, their columns of smoke curling up and settling on everything around. And stray chickens can be seen pecking at the children's stools with mute relish. Nadia Street has its lean, barking mongrels and its share of police beer raids.

Yet the street still clings to the reputation of being the quietest. Things always went on in the *next* street.

Then something happened. When it did, some of the residents shook their heads dolefully and looked at one another as if they sensed a hundred years' plague round the corner.

Old Lebona down the street laughed and laughed until people feared that his chronic bronchitis was going to strangle him. 'Look at it down the street or up the street,' he said, 'it's the same. People will always do the unexpected. Is it any wonder God's curse remains on the black nnen?' Then he laughed again.

'You'll see,' said Keledi, rubbing her breast with her forearm to ease the itching caused by the milk She always said that, to arouse her listeners' curiosity. But she hardly ever showed them what they would see.

Manyeu, the widow, said to her audience, 'It reminds me of what happened once at Winburg, the Boer town down in the Free State.' She looked wistfully ahead of her. The other women looked at her and the new belly that pushed out from under the clean floral apron.

1 remember clearly because I was pregnant, expecting – who was it now? Yes, I was expecting Lusi, my fourth. The one you sent to the butcher yesterday, Kotu.'

Some people said that it happened when Constable Tefo first came to patrol Nadia Street on Sunday afternoons. But others said the 'Russians' – that clan of violent Basotho men – were threatening war. Of course, after it had happened Nadia Street went back to what its residents insisted on calling a quiet life.

If Constable Tefo ever thought that he could remain untouched by Nadia Street gossip, he was mistaken. The fact that he found it necessary to make up his mind about it indicated that he feared the possibility of being entangled in the people's private lives.

He was tall and rather good-looking. There was nothing officious about him, nothing police-looking except for the uniform. He was in many ways one of the rarest of the collection from the glass cage at Headquarters. His bosses suspected him. He looked to them too human to be a good protector of the law. Yes, that's all he was to the people, that's what his bosses had hired him for.

The news spread that Tefo was in love. 'I've seen the woman come here at the end of every month. He always kisses her. The other day I thought he was kissing her too long.' That was Manyeu's verdict.

It did not seem to occur to anyone that the woman who was seen kissing Tefo might be his wife. Perhaps it was just as well, because it so happened that he did not have a wife. At forty he was still unmarried.

Manyeu was struck almost silly when Constable Tefo entered her house to buy *maheu*, the sour mealie-meal drink.

'You'll see,' said Keledi, who rubbed her breast up and down to relieve the burning itch of the milk.

Still Tefo remained at his post, almost like a mountain: at once defiant, reassuring, and menacing. He would not allow himself to be ruffled by the subtle suggestions he heard, the meaningful twitch of the face he saw, the burning gaze he felt behind him as he moved about on his beat.

One day Keledi passed him with a can of beer, holding it behind her apron. She chatted with him for a while and they both laughed. It was like that often; mice playing hide-and-seek in the mane of the lion.

'How's business?' Tefo asked Sung Li's wife one Sunday on the stoep of their shop.

'Velly bad'

'Why?'

'Times is bad.'

'Hm.'

'Velly beezee, you?'

'Yes, no rest, till we get over there, at Croesus Cemetery.'

She laughed, thinking it very funny that a policeman should think of death. She told him so.

'How's China?'

'I'm not from China, he, he, he. I'm born here, he he, he. Funnee.' And she

334

showed rusty rotten teeth when she laughed, the top front teeth over-taking the receding lower row, not cooperating in the least to present a good-looking jaw.

Tefo laughed loud to think that he had always thought of the Sung Li's as people from China, which from what he had been told in his childhood conjured up weird pictures of man-eating people.

When he laughed, Constable Tefo's stomach moved up and down while he held his belt in front and his shoulders fluttered about like the wings of a bird that is not meant to fly long distances.

When her husband within called her, Madam Sung Li turned to go. Tefo watched her shuffling her small feet, slippers almost screaming with the pain of being dragged like that. From behind, the edge of the dress clung alternately to the woollen black stockings she had on. The bundle of hair at the back of her head looked as if all the woman's fibre were knotted up in it, and that if it were undone Madam Sung Li might fall to pieces. Her body bent forward like a tree in the wind. Tefo observed to himself that there was no wind.

One Sunday afternoon Tefo entered Sung Li's shop to buy a bottle of lemonade. The heat was intense. The roofs of the houses seemed to strain under the merciless pounding of the sun. All available windows and doors were ajar and, owing to the general lack of verandahs and the total absence of trees, the residents puffed and sighed and groaned and stripped off some of their garments.

Madam Sung Li leaned over the counter, her elbows planted on the top surface, her arms folded. She might have been the statue of some Oriental god in that position but for a lazy afternoon fly that tried to settle on her face. She had to throw her head about to keep the pestilent insect at bay.

Constable Tefo breathed hard after every gulp as he stood looking out through the shop window, facing Nadia Street.

One thing he had got used to was the countless funeral processions that trailed on week after week. They had to pass Newclare on the way to the cemetery. Short ones, long ones, hired double-deckers, cars, lorries; poor insignificant ones, rich snobbish ones. All black and inevitable.

The processions usually took the street next to Nadia. But so many people were dying that some units were beginning to spill over into Nadia.

Tefo went out to the stoep to have a little diversion; anything to get his mind off the heat. He was looking at one short procession as it turned into Nadia when a thought crossed his mind, like the shadow of a cloud that passes under the sun.

Seleke's cousin came staggering onto the stoep. His clothes looked as if he had once crossed many rivers and drained at least one. He was always referred to as Seleke's cousin, and nobody ever cared to know his name.

Seleke lived in the next street. She was the tough sort with a lashing tongue. But even she could not whip her cousin out of his perennial stupor.

Keledi's comment was: 'You'll see, one day he'll hunt mice for food. The cats won't like it.' And she rubbed her breast. But Seleke's cousin absorbed it all without the twitch of a hair.

'Ho, chief!' Seleke's cousin hailed the constable, wobbling about like a puppet on the stage. 'Watching coffins, eh? Too many people dying, eh? Yes, too many. Poor devils.'

Tefo nodded. A lorry drove up the street, and pulled up on the side, almost opposite the Chinaman's shop.

'Dead men don't shout,' said Seleke's cousin.

'You're drunk. Why don't you go home and sleep?'

'Me drunk? Yes, yes, I'm drunk. But don't you talk to me like these pig-headed people around here. Their pink tongues wag too much. Why don't they leave me alone? There's no one in this bloody location who can read English like I do!'

'I'm sure there isn't.' Tefo smiled tolerantly.

'I like you, chief. You're going to be a great man one of these days. Now, you're looking at these people going to bury their dead. One of these days those coffins will tell their story. I don't know why they can't leave me alone. Why can't they let me be, the lousy lot?'

A small funeral party turned into Nadia Street on a horse-drawn trolley cart. There were three women and four men on the cart, excluding the driver. A man who looked like their religious leader sang lustily, his voice quivering above the others.

The leader had on a frayed, fading purple surplice and an off-white cassock. He looked rather too young for such a mighty responsibility as trying to direct departed souls to heaven, Tefo thought. The constable also thought how many young men were being fired with religious feelings these days …

The trolley stopped in front of a house almost opposite Sung Li's. Tefo looked on. The group alighted and the four men lifted the coffin down.

Tefo noticed that the leader was trembling. By some miracle his hymn book stayed in the trembling hand. He wiped his forehead so many times that the constable thought the leader had a fever and could not lift the coffin further. They obviously wanted to enter the yard just behind them. He went to the spot and offered to help.

The leader's eyes were wide and they reflected a host of emotions Tefo could not understand. And then he made a surprising gesture to stop Tefo from touching the coffin. In a second he nodded his head several times, muttering something that made Tefo understand that his help would be appreciated. Whereupon the constable picked up the handle on his side, and the quartet took the corpse into the house. Soon Tefo was back on the Chinaman's stoep.

It must have been about fifteen minutes later when he heard voices bursting out in song as the party came out of the house with the coffin. Again, Tefo noticed the leader was sweating and trembling. The coffin was put on the ground, outside the gate. The others in the party continued to sing lustily, the men's voices beating down the courageous sopranos.

Tefo sensed that they wanted to hoist it onto the lorry. Something told him he should not go and help. One of these religious sects with queer rules, he thought.

At the gate the leader of the funeral party bent forward and, with a jerky movement, he caught hold of the handle and tilted the coffin, shouting to the other men at the same time to hold the handles on their side. Tefo turned sharply to look.

A strange sound came from the box. To break the downward tilt the other men had jerked the coffin up. But a cracking sound came from the bottom; a sound of cracking wood. They were going to hoist the coffin higher, when it happened.

A miniature avalanche of bottles came down to the ground. A man jumped into the lorry, reversed it a little and drove off. The trolley cart ground its way down Nadia Street. Tefo's eyes swallowed the whole scene. He descended from the stoep as if in a trance, and walked slowly to the spot. It was a scene of liquor bottles tumbling and tinkling and bumping into one another, some breaking and others rolling down the street in a playful manner, like children who have been let out of the classroom at playtime. There was hissing and shouting among the funeral party.

'You frightened goat!'

'Messing up the whole business!'

'I knew this would happen!'

'You'll pay for this!'

'You should have stayed home, you clumsy pumpkin!'

'We're ruined this time!'

They had all disappeared by the time it had registered on Tefo's mind that an arrest must be made. More than that: a wild mob of people was scrambling for the bottles. In a moment they also had disappeared with the bottles, the corpus delicti! A number of people gathered round the policeman.

The lousy crowd, he thought, glad that a policeman had failed to arrest! They nudged one another, and others indulged in mock pity. Manyeu came forward. 'I want the box for fire, sir constable.' He indicated impatiently with the hand that she might have it. It did not escape Keledi's attention, and she said to her neighbour, rubbing her breast that was full of milk: 'You'll see. Wait.'

'Ho, chief! Trouble here?' Seleke's cousin elbowed his way to the centre of the crowd. He had been told what had happened.

'Funerals, funerals, funerals is my backside! Too bad I'm late for the party!

Hard luck to you, chief. Now listen, I trust these corpses like the lice on my shirt. But you're going to be a great man one day. Trust my word for that. I bet the lice on my body.'

Later that afternoon Constable Tefo sat in Manyeu's room, drinking *maheu*. Keledi, rubbing her breast, was sitting on the floor with two other women. Manyeu sat on a low bench, her new belly pushing out under her floral apron like a promising melon.

Somewhat detached from the women's continuous babble, Tefo was thinking about funerals and corpses and bottles of liquor. He wondered about funeral processions in general. He remembered what Seleke's cousin had said the other day on the Chinaman's stoep. Was it an unwitting remark?

Just then another procession passed down the street. Tefo stood up abruptly and went to stand at the door. If only the gods could tell him what was in that brown glossy coffin, he thought. He went back to his bench, a figure of despair.

Keledi's prophetic 'You'll see' took on a serious meaning when Tefo one day married Manyeu after her sixth had arrived. Nadia Street gasped. But then recovered quickly from the surprise, considering the reputation it had of being the quietest street in Newclare.

It added to Kaledi's social stature to be able to say after the event: 'You see!' while she vigorously rubbed her breasts that itched from the milk.

ES'KIA MPHAHLELE

Mrs Plum

[handwritten annotations: — story is set in 1960's "Apartheid". Mrs Plum is told in the first person by Karabo, a young black south african woman...]

First published, 1967

From: *The Unbroken Song: Selected Writing* (1981)

I

My madam's name was Mrs Plum. She loved dogs and Africans and said that everyone must follow the law even if it hurt. These were three big things in Madam's life.

I came to work for Mrs Plum in Greenside, not very far from the centre of Johannesburg, after leaving two white families. The first white people I worked for as a cook and laundry woman were a man and his wife in Parktown North. They drank too much and always forgot to pay me. After five months I said to myself No. I am going to leave these drunks. So that was it. That day I was as angry as a red–hot iron when it meets water. The second house I cooked and washed for had five children who were badly brought up. This was in Belgravia. Many times they called me You Black Girl and I kept quiet. Because their mother heard them and said nothing. Also I was only new from Phokeng my home, far away near Rustenburg, I wanted to learn and know the white people before I knew how far to go with the others I would work for afterwards. The thing that drove me mad and made me pack and go was a man who came to visit them often. They said he was a cousin or something like that. He came to the kitchen many times and tried to make me laugh. He patted me on the buttocks. I told the master. The man did it again and I asked the madam that very day to give me my money and let me go.

These were the first nine months after I had left Phokeng to work in Johannesburg. There were many of us girls and young women from Phokeng, from Zeerust, from Shuping, from Kosten, and many other places who came to work in the cities. So the suburbs were full of blackness. Most of us had already passed Standard Six and so we learned more English where we worked. None of us likes to work for white farmers, because we know too much about them on the farms near our homes. They do not pay well and they are cruel people.

At Easter time so many of us went home for a long weekend to see our people and to eat chicken and sour milk and *morogo* — wild spinach. We also took home sugar and condensed milk and tea and coffee and sweets and custard powder and tinned foods.

339

It was a home-girl of mine, Chimane, who called me to take a job in Mrs Plum's house, just next door to where she worked. This is the third year now. I have been quite happy with Mrs Plum and her daughter Kate. By this I mean that my place as a servant in Greenside is not as bad as that of many others. Chimane too does not complain much. We are paid six pounds a month with free food and free servant's room. No one can ever say that they are well paid, so we go on complaining somehow. Whenever we meet on Thursday afternoons, which is time-off for all of us black women in the suburbs, we talk and talk and talk: about our people at home and their letters; about their illnesses; about bad crops; about a sister who wanted a school uniform and books and school fees; about some of our madams and masters who are good, or stingy with money or food, or stupid or full of nonsense, or who kill themselves and each other, or who are dirty – and so many things I cannot count them all.

Thursday afternoons we go to town to look at the shops, to attend a women's club, to see our boy-friends, to go to bioscope some of us. We turn up smart, to show others the clothes we bought from the black men who sell soft goods to servants in the suburbs. We take a number of things and they come round every month for a bit of money until we finish paying. Then we dress the way of many white madams and girls. I think we look really smart. Sometimes we catch the eyes of a white woman looking at us and we laugh and laugh and laugh until we nearly drop on the ground because we feel good inside ourselves.

II

What did the girl next door call you? Mrs Plum asked me the first day I came to her. Jane, I replied. Was there not an African name? I said yes, Karabo. All right, Madam said. We'll call you Karabo, she said. She spoke as if she knew a name is a big thing. I knew so many whites who did not care what they called black people as long as it was all right for their tongue. This pleased me, I mean Mrs Plum's use of *Karabo*; because the only time I heard the name was when I was at home or when my friends spoke to me. Then she showed me what to do: meals, meal times, washing, and where all the things were that I was going to use.

My daughter will be here in the evening, Madam said. She is at school. When the daughter came, she added, she would tell me some of the things she wanted me to do for her every day.

Chimane, my friend next door, had told me about the daughter Kate, how wild she seemed to be, and about Mr Plum who had killed himself with a gun in a house down the street. They had left the house and come to this one.

Madam is a tall woman. Not slender, not fat. She moves slowly, and speaks slowly. Her face looks very wise, her forehead seems to tell me she has a strong liver: she is not afraid of anything. Her eyes are always swollen at the lower eyelids like a white person who has not slept for many many nights or like a large frog. Perhaps it is because she smokes too much, like wet wood that will not know whether to go up in flames or stop burning. She looks me straight in the eyes when she talks to me, and I know she does this with other people too. At first this made me fear her, now I am used to her. She is not a lazy woman, and she does many things outside, in the city and in the suburbs.

This was the first thing her daughter Kate told me when she came and we met. Don't mind mother, Kate told me. She said, She is sometimes mad with people for very small things. She will soon be all right and speak nicely to you again.

Kate, I like her very much, and she likes me too. She tells me many things a white woman does not tell a black servant. I mean things about what she likes and does not like, what her mother does or does not do, all these. At first I was unhappy and wanted to stop her, but now I do not mind.

Kate looks very much like her mother in the face. I think her shoulders will be just as round and strong-looking. She moves faster than Madam. I asked her why she was still at school when she was so big. She laughed. Then she tried to tell me that the school where she was was for big people, who had finished with lower school. She was learning big things about cooking and food. She can explain better, me I cannot. She came home on weekends.

Since I came to work for Mrs Plum Kate has been teaching me plenty of cooking. I first learned from her and Madam the word *recipes*. When Kate was at the big school, Madam taught me how to read cookery books. I went on very slowly at first, slower than an ox-wagon. Now I know more. When Kate came home, she found I had read the recipe she left me. So we just cooked straightaway. Kate thinks I am fit to cook in a hotel. Madam thinks so too. Never never! I thought. Cooking in a hotel is like feeding oxen. No one can say thank you to you. After a few months I could cook the Sunday lunch and later I could cook specials for Madam's or Kate's guests.

Madam did not only teach me cooking. She taught me how to look after guests. She praised me when I did very very well; not like the white people I had worked for before. I do not know what runs crooked in the heads of other people. Madam also had classes in the evenings for servants to teach them how to read and write. She and two other women in Greenside taught in a church hall.

As I say, Kate tells me plenty of things about Madam. She says to me she says, My mother goes to meetings many times. I ask her I say, What for? She says to me she says, For your people. I ask her I say, My people are in Phokeng far away. They have got mouths, I say. Why does she want to say something for them? Does she know what my mother and what my father want to say? They can speak when they want to. Kate raises her shoulders and drops them and says, How can I tell you Karabo? I don't say your people – your family only. I mean all the black people in this country. I say Oh! What do the black people want to say? Again she raises her shoulders and drops them, taking a deep breath.

I ask her I say, With whom is she in the meeting?

She says, With other people who think like her.

I ask her I say, Do you say there are people in the world who think the same things?

She nods her head.

I ask, What things?

So that a few of your people should one day be among those who rule this country, get more money for what they do for the white man, and – what did Kate say again? Yes, that Madam and those who think like her also wanted my people who have been to school to choose those who must speak for them in the – I think she said it looks like a *Kgotla* at home who rule the villages.

I say to Kate I say, Oh I see now. I say, Tell me Kate why is Madam always writing on the machine, all the time everyday nearly?

She replies she says, Oh my mother is writing books.

I ask, You mean a book like those? – pointing at the books on the shelves.

Yes, Kate says.

And she told me how Madam wrote books and other things for news-papers and she wrote for the newspapers and magazines to say things for the black people who should be treated well, be paid more money, for the black people who can read and write many things to choose those who want to speak for them.

Kate also told me she said, My mother and other women who think like her put on black belts over their shoulders when they are sad and they want to show the white government they do not like the things being done by whites to blacks. My mother and the others go and stand where the people in government are going to enter or go out of a building.

I ask her I say, Does the government and the white people listen and stop their sins? She says No. But my mother is in another group of white people.

I ask, Do the people of the government give the women tea and cakes? Kate says, Karabo! How stupid; oh!

I say to her I say, Among my people if someone comes and stands in front of my house I tell him to come in and I give him food. You white people are wonderful. But they keep standing there and the government people do not give them anything.

She replies, You mean strange. How many times have I taught you not to say *wonderful* when you mean *strange!* Well, Kate says with a short heart and looking cross and she shouts, Well they do not stand there the whole day to ask for tea and cakes stupid. Oh dear!

Always when Madam finished to read her newspapers she gave them to me to read to help me speak and write better English. When I had read she asked me to tell her some of the things in it. In this way, I did better and better and my mind was opening and opening and I was learning and learning many things about the black people inside and outside the towns which I did not know in the least. When I found words that were too difficult or I did not understand some of the things I asked Madam. She always told me, You see this, you see that, eh? with a heart that can carry on a long way. Yes, Madam writes many letters to the papers. She is always sore about the way the white police beat up black people; about the way black people who work for whites are made to sit at the Zoo Lake with their hearts hanging, because the white people say our people are making noise on Sunday afternoon when they want to rest in their houses and gardens; about many ugly things that happen when some white people meet black man on the pavement or street. So Madam writes to the papers to let others know, to ask the government to be kind to us.

In the first year Mrs Plum wanted me to eat at table with her. It was very hard, one because I was not used to eating at table with a fork and knife, two because I heard of no other kitchen worker who was handled like this. I was afraid. Afraid of everybody, of Madam's guests if they found me doing this. Madam said I must not be silly. I must show that African servants can also eat at table. Number three, I could not eat some of the things I loved very much: mealie-meal porridge with sour milk or *morogo*, stamped mealies mixed with butter beans; sour porridge for breakfast and other things. Also, except for morning porridge, our food is nice when you eat with the hand. So nice that it does not stop in the mouth or the throat to greet anyone before it passes smoothly down.

We often had lunch together with Chimane next door and our garden boy – Ha! I must remember never to say boy again when I talk about a man. This makes me think of a day during the first few weeks in Mrs Plum's house. I was talking about Dick her garden man and I said 'garden boy'. And she says to me she says, Stop talking about a 'boy', Karabo. Now listen here, she says, You Africans must learn to speak properly about each other. And she says, White people won't talk kindly about you if you look down upon each other.

I say to her I say Madam, I learned the word from the white people I worked for, and all the kitchen maids say 'boy'.

She replies she says to me, Those are white people who know nothing, just low-class whites. I say to her I say I thought white people know everything.

She said, You'll learn my girl and you must start in this house, hear? She left me there thinking, my mind mixed up.

I learned. I grew up.

III

If any woman or girl does not know the Black Crow Club in Bree Street, she does not know anything. I think nearly everything takes place inside and outside that house. It is just where the dirty part of the City begins, with factories and the market. After the market is the place where Indians and Coloured people live. It is also at the Black Crow that the buses turn round and go back to the black townships. Noise, noise, noise all the time. There are women who sell hot sweet potatoes and fruit and monkey nuts and boiled eggs in the winter, boiled mealies and the other things in the summer, all these on the pavements. The streets are always full of potato and fruit skins and monkey nut shells. There is always a strong smell of roast pork. I think it is because of Piel's cold storage down Bree Street.

Madam said she knew the black people who work in the Black Crow. She was happy that I was spending my afternoon on Thursdays in such a club. You will learn sewing, knitting, she said, and other things that you like. Do you like to dance? I told her I said, Yes, I want to learn. She paid the two shillings fee for me each month.

We waited on the first floor, we the ones who were learning sewing; waiting for the teacher. We talked and laughed about madams and masters, and their children and their dogs and birds and whispered about our boy-friends.

Sies! My Madam you do not know – *mojuta oa'nete* – a real miser …

Jo – jo – jo! you should see our new dog. A big thing like this. People! Big in a foolish way …

What! Me, I take a master's bitch by the leg, me, and throw it away so that it keeps howling, *tjwe – tjwe! ngo – wu ngo – wu!* I don't play about with them, me …

Shame, poor thing! God sees you, true …!

They wanted me to take their dog out for a walk every afternoon and I told them I said It is not my work in other houses the garden man does it. I just said to myself I said they can go to the chickens. Let them bite their elbow before I take out a dog, I am not so mad yet …

Hei! It is not like the child of my white people who keeps a big white rat and you know what? He puts it on his bed when he goes to school. And let the blankets just begin to smell of urine and all the nonsense and they tell me to wash them. *Hei*, people! …

Did you hear about Rebone, people? Her Madam put her out, because her master was always tapping her buttocks with his fingers. And yesterday the madam saw the master press Rebone against himself …

Jo – jo – jo! people …!

Dirty white man!

No, not dirty. The madam smells too old for him.

Hei! Go and wash your mouth with soap, this girl's mouth is dirty …

344

Jo, Rebone, daughter of the people! We must help her to find a job before she thinks of going back home.

The teacher came. A woman with strong legs, a strong face, and kind eyes. She had short hair and dressed in a simple but lovely floral frock. She stood well on her legs and hips. She had a black mark between the two top front teeth. She smiled as if we were her children. Our group began with games, and then Lilian Ngoyi took us for sewing. After this she gave a brief talk to all of us from the different classes.

I can never forget the things this woman said and how she put them to us. She told us that the time has passed for black girls and women in the suburbs to be satisfied with working, sending money to our people and going to see them once a year. We were to learn, she said, that the world would never be safe for black people until they were in the government with the power to make laws. The power should be given by the Africans who were more than the whites.

We asked her questions and she answered them with wisdom. I shall put some of them down in my own words as I remember them.

Shall we take the place of the white people in the government?

Some yes. But we shall be more than they as we are more in the country. But also the people of all colours will come together and there are good white men we can choose and there are Africans some white people will choose to be in the government.

There are good madams and masters and bad ones. Should we take the good ones for friends?

A master and a servant can never be friends. Never, so put that out of your head, will you! You are not even sure if the ones you say are good are not like that because they cannot breathe or live without the work of your hands. As long as you need their money, face them with respect. But you must know that many sad things are happening in our country and you, all of you, must always be learning, adding to what you already know, and obey us when we ask you to help us.

At other times Lilian Ngoyi told us she said, Remember your poor people at home and the way in which the whites are moving them from place to place like sheep and cattle. And at other times again she told us she said, Remember that a hand cannot wash itself, it needs another to do it.

I always thought of Madam when Lilian Ngoyi spoke. I asked myself, What would she say if she knew that I was listening to such words. Words Like: A white man is looked after by his black nanny and his mother when he is a baby. When he grows up the white government looks after him, sends him to school, makes it impossible for him to suffer from the great hunger, keeps a job ready and open for him as soon as he wants to leave school. Now Lilian Ngoyi asked she said, How many white people can be born in a white hospital, grow up in white streets, be clothed in lovely cotton, lie on white cushions; how many whites can live all their lives in a fenced place away from people of other colours and then, as men and women learn quickly the correct ways of thinking, learn quickly to ask questions in their minds, big questions that will throw over all the nice things of a white man's life? How many? Very very few! For those whites who have not begun to ask, it is too late. For those who have begun and are joining us with both feet in our house, we can only say Welcome!

I was learning. I was growing up. Every time I thought of Madam, she became more and more like a dark forest which one fears to enter, and which one will never know. But there were several times when I thought, This woman is easy to understand, she is like all other white women.

What else are they teaching you at the Black Crow, Karabo?

I tell her I say, nothing, Madam. I ask her I say, Why does Madam ask?

You are changing.

What does Madam mean?

Well, you are changing.

But we are always changing Madam.

And she left me standing in the kitchen. This was a few days after I had told her that I did not want to read more than one white paper a day. The only magazines I wanted to read, I said to her, were those from overseas, if she had them. I told her that white papers had pictures of white people most of the time. They talked mostly about white people and their gardens, dogs, weddings and parties. I asked her if she could buy me a Sunday paper that spoke about my people. Madam bought it for me. I did not think she would do it.

There were mornings when, after hanging the white people's washing on the line Chimane and I stole a little time to stand at the fence and talk. We always stood where we could be hidden by our rooms.

Hei, Karabo, you know what? That was Chimane.

No – what? Before you start, tell me, has Timi come back to you?

Ach, I do not care. He is still angry. But boys are fools they always come back dragging themselves on their empty bellies. *Hei*, you know what?

Yes?

The Thursday past I saw Moruti K.K. I laughed until I dropped on the ground. He is standing in front of the Black Crow. I believe his big stomach was crying from hunger. Now he has a small dog in his armpit, and is standing before a woman selling boiled eggs and – *hei* home-girl! – tripe and intestines are boiling in a pot – oh, – the smell! you could fill a hungry belly with it, the way it was good. I think Moruti K.K. is waiting for the woman to buy a boiled egg. I do not know what the woman was still doing. I am standing nearby. The dog keeps wriggling and pushing out its nose, looking at the boiling tripe. Moruti keeps patting it with his free hand, not so? Again

346

the dogs wants to spill out of Moruti's hand and it gives a few sounds through the nose. *Hei* man, home-girl! One two three the dog spills out to catch some of the good meat! It misses falling into the hot gravy in which the tripe is swimming I do not know how. Moruti K.K. tries to chase it. It has tumbled on to the woman's eggs and potatoes and all are in the dust. She stands up and goes after K.K. She is shouting to him to pay, not so? Where am I at that time? I am nearly dead with laughter the tears are coming down so far.

I was myself holding tight on the fence so as not to fall through laughing. I help my stomach to keep back a pain in the side.

I ask her I say, Did Moruti K.K. come back to pay for the wasted food?

Yes, he paid.

The dog?

He caught it. That is a good African dog. A dog must look for its own food when it is not time for meals. Not these stupid spoiled angels the whites keep giving tea and biscuits.

Hmm.

Dick our garden man joined us, as he often did. When the story was repeated to him the man nearly rolled on the ground laughing. He asks who is Reverend K.K.?

I say he is the owner of the Black Crow.

Oh!

We reminded each other, Chimane and I, of the round minister. He would come into the club, look at us with a smooth smile on his smooth round face. He would look at each one of us, with that smile on all the time, as if he had forgotten that it was there. Perhaps he had, because as he looked at us, almost stripping us naked with his watery shining eyes – funny – he could have been a farmer looking at his ripe corn, thinking many things.

K.K. often spoke without shame about what he called ripe girls –*matjit-jana* – with good firm breasts. He said such girls were pure without any non-sense in their heads and bodies. Everybody talked a great deal about him and what they thought he must be doing in his office whenever he called in so-and-so.

The Reverend K.K. did not belong to any church. He baptised, married, and buried people for a fee, who had no church to do such things for them. They said he had been driven out of the Presbyterian Church. He had formed his own, but it did not go far. Then he later came and opened the Black Crow. He knew just how far to go with Lilian Ngoyi. She said although she used his club to teach us things that would help us in life, she could not go on if he was doing any wicked things with the girls in his office. Moruti K.K. feared her, and kept his place.

IV

When I began to tell my story I thought I was going to tell you mostly about Mrs Plum's two dogs. But I have been talking about people. I think Dick is right when he says, What is a dog! And there are so many dogs, cats and parrots in Greenside and other places that Mrs Plum's dogs do not look special. But there was something special in the dog business in Madam's house. The way in which she loved them, maybe.

Monty is a tiny animal with long hair and small black eyes and a face nearly like that of an old woman. The other, Malan, is a bit bigger, with brown and white colours. It has small hair and looks naked by the side of the friend. They sleep in two separate baskets which stay in Madam's bedroom. They are to be washed often and brushed and sprayed and they sleep on pink linen. Monty has a pink ribbon which stays on his neck most of the time. They both carry a cover on their backs. They make me fed up when I see them in their baskets, looking fat, and as if they knew all that was going on everywhere.

It was Dick's work to look after Monty and Malan, to feed them, and to do everything for them. He did this together with garden work and cleaning of the house. He came at the beginning of this year. He just came, as if from nowhere, and Madam gave him the job as she had chased away two before him, she told me. In both those cases, she said that they could not look after Monty and Malan.

Dick had a long heart, even although he told me and Chimane that European dogs were stupid, spoiled. He said, One day those white people will put ear-rings and toe-rings and bangles on their dogs. That would be the day he would leave Mrs Plum. For, he said, he was sure that she would want him to polish the rings and bangles with Brasso.

Although he had a long heart, Madam was still not sure of him. She often went to the dogs after a meal or after a cleaning and said to them, Did Dick give you food sweethearts? Or, Did Dick wash you sweethearts? Let me see. And I could see that Dick was blowing up like a balloon with anger. These things called white people! he said to me. Talking to dogs!

I say to him I say, People talk to oxen at home, do I not say so?

Yes, he says, but at home do you not know that a man speaks to an ox because he wants to make it pull the plough or the wagon or to stop or to stand still for a person to inspan it. No one simply goes to an ox looking at him with eyes far apart and speaks to it. Let me ask you, do you ever see a person where we come from take a cow and press it to his stomach or his cheek? Tell me!

And I say to Dick I say, We were talking about an ox, not a cow.

He laughed with his broad mouth until tears came out of his eyes. At a certain point I laughed aloud too.

One day when you have time, Dick says to me, he says, you should look into Madam's bedroom when she has put a notice outside her door. Dick, what are you saying? I ask.

I do not talk, me. I know deep inside me.

Dick was about our age, I and Chimane. So we always said *moshiman'o* when we spoke about his tricks. Because he was not too big to be a boy to us. He also said to us *Hei, lona ban yana kelona* – Hey you girls, you! His large mouth always seemed to be making ready to laugh. I think Madam did not like this. Many times she would say, What is there to make you laugh here? Or in the garden she would say, This is a flower and when it wants water that is not funny! Or again, If you did more work and stopped trying to water my plants with your smile you would be more useful. Even when Dick did not mean to smile. What Madam did not get tired of saying was, If I left you to look after my dogs without anyone to look after you at the same time you would drown the poor things.

Dick smiled at Mrs Plum. Dick hurt Mrs Plum's dogs? Then cows can fly. He was really – really afraid of white people, Dick. I think he tried very hard not to feel afraid. For he was always showing me and Chimane in private how Mrs Plum walked, and spoke. He took two bowls and pressed them to his chest, speaking softly to them as Madam speaks to Monty and Malan. Or he sat at Madam's table and acted the way she sits when writing. Now and again he looked back over his shoulder, pulled his face long like a horse's making as if he were looking over his glasses while telling me something to do. Then he would sit on one of the armchairs, cross his legs and act the way Madam drank her tea; he held the cup he was thinking about between his thumb and the pointing finger, only letting their nails meet. And he laughed after every act. He did these things, of course, when Madam was not home. And where was I at such times? Almost flat on my stomach, laughing.

But oh how Dick trembled when Mrs Plum scolded him! He did his house-cleaning very well. Whatever mistake he made, it was mostly with the dogs; their linen, their food. One white man came into the house one after-noon to tell Madam that Dick had been very careless when taking the dogs out for a walk. His own dog was waiting on Madam's stoep. He repeated that he had been driving down our street; and Dick had let loose Monty and Malan to cross the street. The white man made plenty of noise about this and I think wanted to let Madam know how useful he had been. He kept on saying, Just one inch, just one inch. It was lucky I put on my brakes quick enough ... But your boy kept on smiling – Why? Strange. My boy would only do it twice and only twice and then ...! His pass. The man moved his hand like one writing, to mean he would sign his servant's pass for him to go and never come back. When he left, the white man said, Come on Rusty, the boy is waiting to clean you. Dogs with names, men without, I thought.

Madam climbed on top of Dick for this, as we say.

Once one of the dogs, I don't know which – Malan or Monty – took my stocking – brand new, you hear – and tore it with its teeth and paws. When I told Madam about it, my anger as high as my throat, she gave me money to buy another pair. It happened again. This time she said she was not going to give me money because I must also keep my stockings where the two gentlemen would not reach them. Mrs Plum did not want us ever to say *Voetsek* when we wanted the dogs to go away. Me I said this when they came sniffing at my legs or fingers. I hate it.

In my third year in Mrs Plum's house, many things happened, most of them all bad for her. There was trouble with Kate; Chimane had big trouble; my heart was twisted by two loves; and Monty and Malan became real dogs for a few days.

Madam had a number of suppers and parties. She invited Africans to some of them. Kate told me the reasons for some of the parties. Like her mother's books when finished, a visitor from across the seas and so on. I did not like the black people who came here to drink and eat. They spoke such difficult English like people who were full of all the books in the world. They looked at me as if I were right down there whom they thought little of – me a black person like them.

One day I heard Kate speak to her mother. She says I don't know why you ask so many Africans to the house. A few will do at a time. She said something about the government which I could not hear well. Madam replies she say to her, You know some of them do not meet white people often, so far away in their dark houses. And she says to Kate that they do not come because they want her as a friend but they just want a drink for nothing.

I simply felt that I could not be the servant of white people and of blacks at the same time. At my home or in my room I could serve them without a feeling of shame. And now, if they were only coming to drink!

But one of the black men and his sister always came to the kitchen to talk to me. I must have looked unfriendly the first time, for Kate talked to me about it afterwards as she was in the kitchen when they came. I know that at that time I was not easy at all. I was ashamed and I felt that a white person's house was not the place for me to look happy in front of other black people while the white man looked on.

Another time it was easier. The man was alone. I shall never forget that night, as long as I live. He spoke kind words and I felt my heart grow big inside me. It caused me to tremble. There were several other visits. I knew that I loved him, I could never know what he really thought of me, I mean as a woman and he as a man. But I loved him, and I still think of him with a sore heart. Slowly I came to know the pain of it. Because he was a doctor and so full of knowledge and English I could not reach him. So I knew he could not stoop down to see me as someone who wanted him to love me.

Kate turned very wild. Mrs. Plum was very much worried. Suddenly it looked as if she were a new person, with new ways and new everything. I do not know what was wrong or right. She began to play the big gramophone aloud, as if the music were for the whole of Greenside. The music was wild and she twisted her waist all the time, with her mouth half-open. She did the same things in her room. She left the big school and every Saturday night now she went out. When I looked at her face, there was something deep and wild there on it, and when I thought she looked young she looked old, and when I thought she looked old she was young. We were both 22 years of age. I think that I could see the reason why her mother was so worried, why she was suffering.

Worse was to come.

They were now openly screaming at each other. They began in the sitting-room and went upstairs together, speaking fast hot biting words, some of which I did not grasp. One day Madam comes to me and says, You know Kate loves an African, you know the doctor who comes to supper here often. She says he loves her too and they will leave the country and marry outside. Tell me, Karabo, what do your people think of this kind of thing between a white woman and a black man? It *cannot* be right, is it?

I reply and I say to her. We have never seen it happen before where I come from.

That's right, Karabo, it is just madness.

Madam left. She looked like a hunted person.

These white women, I say to myself, I say these white women, why do not they love their own men and leave us to love ours!

From that minute I knew that I would never want to speak to Kate. She appeared to me as a thief, as a fox that falls upon a flock of sheep at night. I hated her. To make it worse, he would never be allowed to come to the house again.

Whenever she was home there was silence between us. I no longer wanted to know anything about what she was doing, where or how.

I lay awake for hours on my bed. Lying like that, I seemed to feel parts of my body beat and throb inside me, the way I have seen big machines doing, pounding and pounding and pushing and pulling and pouring some water into one hole which came out at another end. I stretched myself so many times so as to feel tired and sleepy.

When I did sleep, my dreams were full of painful things.

One evening I made up my mind, after putting it off many times. I told my boyfriend that I did not want him any longer. He looked hurt, and that hurt me too. He left.

The thought of the African doctor was still with me and it pained me to know that I should never see him again; unless I met him in the street on a Thursday afternoon. But he had a car. Even if I did meet him by luck, how could I make him see that I loved him? Ach, I do not believe he would even stop to think what kind of woman I am. Part of that winter was a time of longing and burning for me. I say part because there are always things to keep servants busy whose white people go to the sea for the winter.

To tell the truth, winter was the time for servants; not nannies, because they went with their madams so as to look after the children. Those like me stayed behind to look after the house and dogs. In winter so many families went away that the dogs remained the masters and madams. You could see them walk like white people in the streets. Silent but with plenty of power. And when you saw them you knew that they were full of more nonsense and fancies in the house.

There was so little work to do.

One week word was whispered round that a home-boy of ours was going to hold a party in his room on Saturday. I think we all took it for a joke. How could the man be so bold and stupid? The police were always driving about at night looking for black people; and if the whites next door heard the party noise – *oho!* But still, we were full of joy and wanted to go. As for Dick, he opened his big mouth and nearly fainted when he heard of it and that I was really going.

During the day on the big Saturday Kate came.

She seemed a little less wild. But I was not ready to talk to her. I was surprised to hear myself answer her when she said to me, Mother says you do not like a marriage between a white girl and a black man, Karabo.

Then she was silent.

She says, But I want to help him, Karabo.

I ask her, I say, You want to help him to do what?

To go higher and higher, to the top.

I knew I wanted to say so much that was boiling in my chest. I could not say it. I thought of Lilian Ngoyi at the Black Crow, what she said to us. But I was mixed up in my head and in my blood.

You still agree with my mother?

All I could say was I said to your mother I had never seen a black man and a white woman marrying, you hear me? What I think about it is my business.

I remembered that I wanted to iron my party dress and so I left her. My mind was full of the party again and I was glad because Kate and the doctor would not worry my peace that day. And the next day the sun would shine for all of us, Kate or no Kate, doctor or no doctor.

The house where our home-boy worked was hidden from the main road by a number of trees. But although we asked a number of questions and counted many fingers of bad luck until we had no more hands or fingers, we put on our best pay-while-you-wear dresses and suits and clothes bought from boys who had stolen them, and went to our home-boy's party. We whispered all the way while we climbed up to the house.

Someone who knew told us that the white people next door were away for the winter. Oh, so that is the thing! we said.

We poured into the garden through the back and stood in front of his room laughing quietly. He came from the big house behind us, and were we not struck dumb when he told us to go into the white people's house! Was he mad? We walked in with slow footsteps that seemed to be sniffing at the floor, not sure of anything. Soon we were standing and sitting all over the nice warm cushions and the heaters were on. Our home-boy turned the lights low. I counted fifteen people inside. We saw how we loved one another's evening dress. The boys were smart too.

Our home-boy's girl-friend Naomi was busy in the kitchen preparing food. He took out glasses and cold drinks – fruit juice, tomato juice, ginger beers, and so many other kinds of soft drink. It was just too nice. The tarts, the biscuits, the snacks, the cakes, *woo*, that was a party, I tell you. I think I ate more ginger cake than I had ever done in my life. Naomi had baked some of the things. Our home-boy came to me and said I do not want the police to come here and have reason to arrest us, so I am not serving hot drinks, not even beer. There is no law that we cannot have parties, is there? So we can feel free. Our use of this house is the master's business. If I had asked him he would have thought me mad.

I say to him I say, You have a strong liver to do such a thing.

He laughed.

He played pennywhistle music on gramophone records – Miriam Makeba, Dorothy Masuka and other African singers and players. We danced and the party became more and more noisy and more happy. *Hai*, those girls Miriam and Dorothy, they can sing, I tell you! We ate more and laughed more and told more stories. In the middle of the party, our home-boy called us to listen to what he was going to say. Then he told us how he and a friend of his in Orlando collected money to bet on a horse for the July Handicap in Durban. They did this each year but lost. Now they had won two hundred pounds. We all clapped hands and cheered. Two hundred pounds *woo!*

You should go and sit at home and just eat time, I say to him. He laughs and says, You have no understanding not one little bit.

To all of us he says, Now my brothers and sisters enjoy yourselves. At home I should slaughter a goat for us to feast and thank our ancestors. But this is town life and we must thank them with tea and cake and all those sweet things. I know some people think I must be so bold that I could be midwife to a lion that is giving birth, but enjoy yourselves and have no fear.

Madam came back looking strong and fresh.

The very week she arrived the police had begun again to search servants' rooms. They were looking for what they called loafers and men without passes who they said were living with friends in the suburbs against the law. Our dog's meat boys became scarce because of the police. A boy who had a girl-friend in the kitchens, as we say, always told his friends that he was coming for dog's meat when he meant he was visiting his girl. This was because we gave our boy-friends part of the meat the white people bought for the dogs and us.

One night a white and a black policeman entered Mrs Plum's yard. They said they had come to search. She says, no they cannot. They say, Yes, they must do it. She answers No. They forced their way to the back, to Dick's room and mine. Mrs Plum took the hose that was running in the front garden and quickly went round to the back. I cut across the floor to see what she was going to say to the men. They were talking to Dick, using dirty words. Mrs Plum did not wait, she just pointed the hose at the two policemen. This seemed to surprise them. They turned round and she pointed it into their faces. Without their seeing me I went to the tap at the corner of the house and opened it more. I could see Dick, like me, was trying to keep down his laughter. They shouted and tried to wave the water away, but she kept the hose pointing at them, now moving it up and down. They turned and ran through the back gate, swearing the while.

That fixes them, Mrs Plum said.

The next day the morning paper reported it.

They arrived in the afternoon – the two policemen – with another. They pointed out Mrs Plum and she was led to the police station. They took her away to answer for stopping the police while they were doing their work.

She came back and said she had paid bail.

At the magistrate's court, Madam was told that she had done a bad thing. She would have to pay a fine or else go to prison for fourteen days. She said she would go to jail to show that she felt she was not in the wrong.

Kate came and tried to tell her that she was doing something silly going to jail for a small thing like that. She tells Madam she says this is not even a thing to take to the high court. Pay the money. What is £5?

Madam went to jail.

She looked very sad when she came out. I thought of what Lilian Ngoyi often said to us: You must be ready to go to jail for the things you believe are true and for which you are taken by the police. What did Mrs Plum really believe about me, Chimane, Dick and all the other black people? I asked myself. I did not know. But from all those things she was writing for the papers and all those meetings she was going to where white people talked about black people and the way they are treated by the government, from what those white women with black bands over their shoulders were doing standing where a white government man was going to pass, I said to myself I said, This woman, *hai*, I do not know she seems to think very much of us black people. But why was she so sad?

Kate came back home to stay after this. She still played the big gramophone loud-loud-loud and twisted her body at her waist until I thought it was going to break. Then I saw a young white man come often to see her. I watched them through the opening near the hinges of the door between the kitchen and the sitting-room where they sat. I saw them kiss each other for a long long time. I saw him lift up Kate's dress and her white-white legs begin to tremble, and – oh I am afraid to say more, my heart was beating hard. She called him Jim. I thought it was funny because white people in the shops call black men Jim.

Kate had begun to play with Jim when I met a boy who loved me and I loved. He was much stronger than the one I sent away and I loved him more, much more. The face of the doctor came to my mind often, but it did not hurt me so any more. I stopped looking at Kate and her Jim through openings. We spoke to each other, Kate and I, almost as freely as before but not quite. She and her mother were friends again.

Hallo, Karabo, I heard Chimane call me one morning as I was starching my apron. I answered. I went to the line to hang it. I saw she was standing at the fence, so I knew she had something to tell me. I went to her.

Hallo!

Hallo, Chimane!

O kae?

Ke teng. Wena?

At that moment a woman came out through the back door of the house where Chimane was working.

I have not seen that one before, I say, pointing with my head.

Chimane looked back. Oh, that one. *Hei*, daughter-of-the-people, *Hei*, you have not seen miracles. You know this is Madam's mother-in-law as you see her there. Did I never tell you about her?

No, never.

White people, nonsense. You know what? That poor woman is here now for two days. She has to cook for herself and I cook for the family.

On the same stove?

Yes, She comes after me when I have finished.

She has her own food to cook?

Yes, Karabo. White people have no heart, no sense.

What will eat them up if they share their food?

Ask me, just ask me. God! She clapped her hands to show that only God knew, and it was His business, not ours.

Chimane asks me she says, Have you heard from home?

I tell her I say, Oh daughter-of-the-people, more and more deaths. Something is finishing the people at home. My mother has written. She says they are all right, my father too and my sisters, except for the people who have died. Malebo, the one who lived alone in the house I showed you last year, a white house, he is gone. The teacher Sedimo. He was very thin and looked sick all the time. He taught my sisters not me. His mother-in-law you remember I told you died last year – no, the year before. Mother says also there is a woman she does not think I remember because I last saw her when I was a small girl, she passed away in Zeerust, she was my mother's greatest friend when they were girls. She would have gone to her burial if it was not because she has swollen feet.

How are the feet?

She says they are still giving her trouble. I ask Chimane, How are your people at Nokaneng? They have not written?

She shook her head.

I could see from her eyes that her mind was on another thing and not her people at that moment.

Wait for me Chimane eh, forgive me, I have scones in the oven, eh! I will just take them out and come back, eh!

When I came back to her Chimane was wiping her eyes. They were wet.

Karabo, you know what?

E – e. I shook my head.

I am heavy with child.

Hau!

There was a moment of silence.

Who is it, Chimane?

Timi. He came back only to give me this.

But he loves you. What does he say, have you told him?

I told him yesterday. We met in town.

I remembered I had not seen her at the Black Crow.

Are you sure, Chimane? You have missed a month?

She nodded her head.

Timi himself – he did not use the thing?

I only saw after he finished, that he had not.

Why? What does he say?

He tells me he says I should not worry, I can be his wife.

Timi is a good boy, Chimane. How many of these boys with town ways who know too much will even say, Yes it is my child?

Hai, Karabo, you are telling me other things now. Do you not see that I have not worked long enough for my people? If I marry now who will look after them when I am the only child?

Hm. I hear your words. It is true. I tried to think of something soothing to say.

356

Then I say, You can talk it over with Timi. You can go home and when the child is born you look after it for three months and when you are married you come to town to work and can put your money together to help the old people while they are looking after the child.

What shall we be eating all the time I am at home? It is not like those days gone past when we had land and our mother could go to the fields until the child was ready to arrive.

The light goes out in my mind and I cannot think of the right answer. How many times have I feared the same thing! Luck and the mercy of the gods that is all I live by. That is all we live by — all of us.

Listen, Karabo. I must be going to make tea for Madam. It will soon strike half-past ten.

I went back to the house. As Madam was not in yet, I threw myself on the divan in the sitting-room. Malan came sniffing at my legs. I put my foot under its fat belly and shoved it up and away from me so that it cried *tjunk — tjunk — tjunk* as it went out. I say to it I say, Go and tell your brother what I have done to you and tell him to try it and see what I will do. Tell your grandmother when she comes home too.

When I lifted my eyes he was standing in the kitchen door, Dick. He says to me he says *Hau!* now you have also begun to speak to dogs!

I did not reply. I just looked at him, his mouth ever stretched out like the mouth of a bag, and I passed to my room.

I sat on my bed and looked at my face in the mirror. Since the morning I had been feeling as if a black cloud were hanging over me, pressing on my head and shoulders. I do not know how long I sat there. Then I smelled Madam. What was it? Where was she? After a few moments I knew what it was. My perfume and scent. I used the same cosmetics as Mrs Plum's. I should have been used to it by now. But this morning — why did I smell Mrs Plum like this? Then, without knowing why, I asked myself I said, Why have I been using the same cosmetics as Madam? I wanted to throw them all out. I stopped. And then I took all the things and threw them into the dustbin. I was going to buy other kinds on Thursday; finished!

I could not sit down. I went out and into the white people's house. I walked through and the smell of the house made me sick and seemed to fill up my throat. I went to the bathroom without knowing why. It was full of the smell of Madam. Dick was cleaning the bath. I stood at the door and looked at him cleaning the dirt out of the bath, dirt from Madam's body. *Sies!* I said aloud. To myself I said, Why cannot people wash the dirt of their own bodies out of the bath? Before Dick knew I was near I went out. Ach, I said again to myself, why should I think about it now when I have been doing their washing for so long and cleaned the bath many times when Dick was ill. I had held worse things from her body times without number ...

I went out and stood midway between the house and my room, looking into the next yard. The three-legged grey cat next door came to the fence and our eyes met. I do not know how long we stood like that looking at each other. I was thinking, Why don't you go and look at your grandmother like that? when it turned away and mewed hopping on the three legs. Just like someone who feels pity for you.

In my room I looked into the mirror on the chest of drawers. I thought, Is this Karabo this?

Thursday came, and the afternoon off. At the Black Crow I did not see Chimane. I wondered about her. In the evening I found a note under my door. It told me if Chimane was not back that evening I should know that she was at 660 3rd Avenue, Alexandra Township. I was not to tell the white people.

I asked Dick if he could not go to Alexandra with me after I had washed the dishes. At first he was unwilling. But I said to him I said, Chimane will not believe that you refused to come with me when she sees me alone. He agreed.

On the bus Dick told me much about his younger sister whom he was helping with money to stay at school until she finished; so that she could become a nurse and a midwife. He was very fond of her, as far as I could find out. He said he prayed always that he should not lose his job, as he had done many times before, after staying a few weeks only at each job; because of this he had to borrow monies from people to pay his sister's school fees, to buy her clothes and books. He spoke of her as if she were his sweetheart. She was clever at school, pretty (she was this in the photo Dick had shown me before). She was in Orlando Township. She looked after his old people, although she was only thirteen years of age. He said to me he said, Today I still owe many people because I keep losing my job. You must try to stay with Mrs Plum, I said.

I cannot say that I had all my mind on what Dick was telling me. I was thinking of Chimane: what could she be doing? Why that note?

We found her in bed. In that terrible township where night and day are full of knives and bicycle chains and guns and the barking of hungry dogs and of people in trouble. I held my heart in my hands. She was in pain and her face, even in the candle-light, was grey. She turned her eyes at me. A fat woman was sitting in a chair. One arm rested on the other and held her chin in its palm. She had hardly opened the door for us after we had shouted our names when she was on her bench again as if there were nothing else to do.

She snorted, as if to let us know that she was going to speak. She said, There is your friend. There she is my own-own niece who comes from the womb of my own sister, my sister who was made to spit out my mother's breast to give way for me. Why does she go and do such an evil thing. *Ao!* you young girls of today you do not know children die so fast these days that you have to thank God for sowing a seed in your womb to grow into a child. If she had let the child be born I should have looked after it or my sister would have been so happy to hold a grandchild on her lap, but what does it help? She has allowed a worm to cut the roots, I don't know.

Then I saw that Chimane's aunt was crying. Not once did she mention her niece by her name, so sore her heart must have been. Chimane only moaned.

Her aunt continued to talk, as if she was never going to stop for breath, until her voice seemed to move behind me, not one of the things I was thinking: trying to remember signs, however small, that could tell me more about this moment in a dim little room in a cruel township without street lights, near Chimane. Then I remembered the three-legged cat, its grey-green eyes, its *miau*. What was this shadow that seemed to walk about us but was not coming right in front of us?

I thanked the gods when Chimane came to work at the end of the week. She still looked weak, but that shadow was no longer there. I wondered Chimane had never told me about her aunt before. Even now I did not ask her.

I told her I told her white people that she was ill and had been fetched to Nokaneng by a brother. They would never try to find out. They seldom did, these people. Give them any lie, and it will do. For they seldom believe you whatever you say. And how can a black person work for white people and be afraid to tell them lies. They are always asking the questions, you are always the one to give the answers.

Chimane told me all about it. She had gone to a woman who did these things. Her way was to hold a sharp needle, cover the point with the finger, and guide it into the womb. She then fumbled in the womb until she found the egg and then pierced it. She gave you something to ease the bleeding. But the pain, spirits of our forefathers!

Mrs Plum and Kate were talking about dogs one evening at dinner. Every time I brought something to table I tried to catch their words. Kate seemed to find it funny, because she laughed aloud. There was a word I could not hear well which began with *sem-*: whatever it was, it was to be for dogs. This I understood by putting a few words together. Mrs Plum said it was something that was common in the big cities of America, like New York. It was also something Mrs Plum wanted and Kate laughed at the thought. Then later I was to hear that Monty and Malan could be sure of a nice burial.

Chimane's voice came up to me in my room the next morning, across the fence. When I come out she tells me she says, *Hei*, child-of-my-father, here is something to tickle your ears. You know what? What? I say. She says, These white people can do things that make the gods angry. More godless people I have not seen. The madam of our house says the people of Greenside want to buy ground where they can bury their dogs. I heard them talk about it in the sitting-room when I was giving them coffee last night. *Hei*, people, let our forefathers come and save us!

Yes, I say, I also heard the madam of our house talk about it with her daughter. I just heard it in pieces. By my mother one day these dogs will sit at table and use knife and fork. These things are to be treated like people now, like children who are never going to grow up.

Chimane sighed and she says *Hela batho*, why do they not give me some of that money they will spend on the ground and on gravestones to buy stockings! I have nothing to put on, by my mother.

Over her shoulder I saw the cat with three legs. I pointed with my head. When Chimane looked back and saw it she said, *Hm*, even *they* live like kings. The mother-in-law found it on a chair and the madam said the woman should not drive it away. And there was no other chair, so the woman went to her room.

Hela!

I was going to leave when I remembered what I wanted to tell Chimane. It was that five of us had collected £1 each to lend her so that she could pay the woman of Alexandra for having done that thing for her. When Chimane's time came to receive money we collected each month and which we took in turns, she would pay us back. We were ten women and each gave £2 at a time. So one waited ten months to receive £20. Chimane thanked us for helping her.

I went to wake up Mrs Plum as she had asked me. She was sleeping late this morning. I was going to knock at the door when I heard strange noises in the bedroom. What is the matter with Mrs Plum? I asked myself. Should I call her, in case she is ill? No, the noises were not those of a sick person. They were happy noises but like those a person makes in a dream, the voice full of sleep. I bent a little to peep through the keyhole. What is this? I kept asking myself. Mrs Plum! Malan! What is she doing this one? Her arm was round Malan's belly and pressing its back against her stomach at the navel, Mrs Plum's body in a nightdress moving in jerks like someone in fits … her leg rising and falling … Malan silent like a thing to be owned without any choice it can make to belong to another.

The gods save me! I heard myself saying, the words sounded like wind rushing out of my mouth. So this is what Dick said I would find out for myself!

No one could say where it all started; who talked about it first; whether the police wanted to make a reason for taking people without passes and people living with servants and working in town or not working at all. But the story rushed through Johannesburg that servants were going to poison the white people's dogs. Because they were too much work for us: that was the reason. We heard that letters were sent to the newspapers by white people asking the police to watch over the dogs to stop any wicked things. Some said that we the servants were not really bad, we were being made to think of doing these things by evil people in town and in the locations. Others said the police should watch out lest we poison madams and masters because black people did not know right from wrong when they were angry. We were still children at heart, others said. Mrs Plum said that she had also written to the papers.

Then it was the police came down on the suburbs like locusts on a corn-field. There were lines and lines of men who were arrested hour by hour in the day. They liked this very much, the police. Everybody they took, everybody who was working was asked, Where's the poison eh? Where did you hide it? Who told you to poison the dogs eh? If you tell us we'll leave you to go free, you hear? and so many other things.

Dick kept saying, It is wrong this thing they want to do to kill poor dogs. What have these things of God done to be killed for? Is it the dogs that make us carry passes? Is it dogs that make the laws that give us pain? People are just mad, they do not know what they want, stupid! But when a white police-man spoke to him, Dick trembled and lost his tongue and the things he thought. He just shook his head. A few moments after they had gone through his pockets he still held his arms stretched out, like the man of straw who frightens away birds in a field. Only when I hissed and gave him a sign did he drop his arms. He rushed to a corner of the garden to go on with his work.

Mrs Plum had put Monty and Malan in the sitting-room, next to her. She looked very much worried. She called me. She asked me she said, Karabo, you think Dick is a boy we can trust? I did not know how to answer. I did not know whom she was talking about when she said we. Then I said, I do not know, Madam. You know! she said. I looked at her. I said I do not know what Madam thinks. She said she did not think anything, that was why she asked. I nearly laughed because she was telling a lie this time and not I.

At another time I should have been angry if she lied to me, perhaps. She and I often told each other lies, as Kate and I also did. Like when she came back from jail, after that day when she turned a hose-pipe on two policemen. She said life had been good in jail. And yet I could see she was ashamed to have been there. Not like our black people who are always being put in jail and only look at it as the white man's evil game. Lilian Ngoyi often told us this, and Mrs Plum showed me how true those words are. I am sure that we have kept to each other by lying to each other.

There was something in Mrs Plum's face as she was speaking which made me fear her and pity her at the same time. I had seen her when she had come from prison; I had seen her when she was shouting at Kate and the girl left the house; now there was this thing about dog poisoning. But never had I seen her face like this before. The eyes, the nostrils, the lips, the teeth seemed to be full of hate, tired, fixed on doing something bad; and yet there was something on that face that told me she wanted me on her side.

Dick is all right, Madam, I found myself saying. She took Malan and Monty in her arms and pressed them to herself, running her hands over their heads. They looked so safe, like a child in a mother's arm.

Mrs Plum said, All right you may go. She said, Do not tell anybody what I have asked about Dick eh?

When I told Dick about it, he seemed worried.

It is nothing, I told him.

I had been thinking before that I did not stand with those who wanted to poison the dogs, Dick said. But the police have come out. I do not care what happens to the dumb things now.

I asked him I said, Would you poison them if you were told by someone to do it?

No. But I do not care, he replied.

The police came again and again. They were having a good holiday, every-one could see that. A day later Mrs Plum told Dick to go because she would not need his work any more.

Dick was almost crying when he left. Is Madam so unsure of me? he asked. I never thought a white person could fear me! And he left.

Chimane shouted from the other yard. She said, *Hei ngoana'rona*, the boers are fire-hot eh!

Mrs Plum said she would hire a man after the trouble was over.

A letter came from my parents in Phokeng. In it they told me my uncle had passed away. He was my mother's brother. The letter also told me of other deaths. They said I would not remember some, I was sure to know the others. There were also names of sick people.

I went to Mrs Plum to ask her if I could go home. She asks she says, When did he die? I answer I say, It is three days, Madam. She says, So that they have buried him? I reply, Yes Madam. Why do you want to go home then? Because my uncle loved me very much, Madam. But what are you going to do there? To take my tears and words of grief to his grave and to my old aunt, Madam. No, you cannot go, Karabo. You are working for me you know? Yes, Madam. I, and not your people pay you. I must go, Madam, that is how we do it among my people, Madam. She paused. She walked into the kitchen and came out again. If you want to go, Karabo, you must lose the money for the days you will be away. Lose my pay, Madam? Yes, Karabo.

The next day I went to Mrs Plum and told her I was leaving for Phokeng and was not coming back to her. Could she give me a letter to say that I worked for her. She did, with her lips shut tight. I could feel that something between us was burning like raw chillies. The letter simply said that I had worked for Mrs Plum for three years. Nothing more. The memory of Dick being sent away was still an open sore in my heart.

The night before the day I left, Chimane came to see me in my room. She had her own story to tell me. Timi, her boy-friend, had left her – for good. Why? Because I killed his baby. Had he not agreed that you should do it? No. Did he show he was worried when you told him you were heavy? He was worried, like me as you saw me, Karabo. Now he says if I kill one I shall eat all his children up when we are married. You think he means what he says? Yes, Karabo. He says his parents would have been very happy to know that the woman he was going to marry can make his seed grow.

Chimane was crying, softly.

I tried to speak to her, to tell her that if Timi left her just like that, he had not wanted to marry her in the first place. But I could not, no, I could not. All I could say was, Do not cry, my sister, do not cry. I gave her my handkerchief.

Kate came back the morning I was leaving, from somewhere very far, I cannot remember where. Her mother took no notice of what Kate said asking her to keep me, and I was not interested either.

One hour later I was on the Railway bus to Phokeng. During the early part of the journey I did not feel anything about the Greenside house I had worked in. I was not really myself, my thoughts dancing between Mrs Plum, my uncle, my parents, and Phokeng, my home. I slept and woke up many times during the bus ride. Right through the ride I seemed to see, sometimes in sleep, sometimes between sleep and waking, a red car passing our bus, then running behind us. Each time I looked out it was not there.

Dreams came and passed. He tells me he says, You have killed my seed, I wanted my mother to know you are a woman in whom my seed can grow ... Before you make the police take you to jail make sure that it is for something big you should go to jail for, otherwise you will come out with a heart and mind that will bleed inside you and poison you ...

The bus stopped for a short while, which made me wake up.

The Black Crow, the club women ... *Hei*, listen! I lie to the madam of our house and I say I had a telegram from my mother telling me she is very very sick. I show her a telegram my sister sent me as if mother were writing. So I went home for a nice weekend ...

The laughter of the women woke me up, just in time for me to stop a line of saliva coming out over my lower lip. The bus was making plenty of dust now as it was running over part of the road they were digging up. I was sure the red car was just behind us, but it was not there when I woke.

Any one of you here who wants to be baptised or has a relative without a church who needs to be can come and see me in the office ... A round man with a fat tummy and sharp hungry eyes, a smile that goes a long, long way ...

The bus was going uphill, heavily and noisily.

I kick a white man's dog, me, or throw it there if it has not been told the black people's law ... This is Mister Monty and this is Mister Malan. Now get up you lazy boys and meet Mister Kate. Hold out your hands and say hallo to him … Karabo, bring two glasses there … Wait a bit – What will you chew boys while Mister Kate and I have a drink? Nothing? Sure?

We were now going nicely on a straight tarred road and the trees rushed back. Mister Kate. What nonsense, I thought.

Look Karabo, Madam's dogs are dead. What? Poison. I killed them. She drove me out of a job did she not? For nothing. Now I want her to feel she drove me out for something. I came back when you were in your room and took the things and poisoned them … And you know what? She has buried them in clean pink sheets in the garden. *Ao*, clean clean good sheets. I am going to dig them out and take one, do you want the other one? Yes, give me the other one I will send it to my mother … *Hei*, Karabo, see here they come. Monty and Malan. The bloody fools, they do not want to stay in their hole. Go back you silly fools. Oh you do not want to move eh? Come here, now I am going to throw you in the big pool. No, Dick! No Dick! No, no! Dick! They cannot speak, do not kill things that cannot speak. Madam can speak for them, she always does. No! Dick …!

I woke up with a jump after I had screamed Dick's name, almost hitting the window. My forehead was full of sweat. The red car also shot out of my sleep and was gone. I remembered a friend of ours who told us how she and the garden man had saved two white sheets in which their white master had buried their two dogs. They went to throw the dogs in a dam.

When I told my parents my story Father says to me he says, So long as you are in good health my child, it is good. The worker dies, work does not. There is always work. I know when I was a boy a strong sound body and a good mind were the biggest things in life. Work was always there, and the lazy man could never say there was no work. But today people see work as something bigger than everything else, bigger than health, because of money.

I reply I say, Those days are gone Papa. I must go back to the city after resting a little to look for work. I must look after you. Today people are too poor to be able to help you.

I knew when I left Greenside that I was going to return to Johannesburg to work. Money was little, but life was full and it was better than sitting in Phokeng and watching the sun rise and set. So I told Chimane to keep her eyes and ears open for a job.

I had been at Phokeng for one week when a red car arrived. Somebody was sitting in front with the driver, a white woman. At once I knew it to be that of Mrs Plum. The man sitting beside her was showing her the way, for he pointed towards our house in front of which I was sitting. My heart missed a few beats. Both came out of the car. The white woman said 'Thank you' to the man after he had spoken a few words to me.

I did not know what to do and how to look at her as she spoke to me. So

I looked at the piece of cloth I was sewing pictures on. There was a tired but soft smile on her face. Then I remembered that she might want to sit. I went inside to fetch a low bench for her. When I remembered it afterwards, the thought came to me that there are things I never think white people can want to do at our homes when they visit for the first time: like sitting, drinking water or entering the house. This is how I thought when the white priest came to see us. One year at Easter Kate drove me home as she was going to the north. In the same way I was at a loss what to do for a few minutes.

Then Mrs Plum says, I have come to ask you to come back to me, Karabo. Would you like to?

I say I do not know, I must think about it first.

She says, Can you think about it today? I can sleep at the town hotel and come back tomorrow morning, and if you want to you can return with me.

I wanted her to say she was sorry to have sent me away, I did not know how to make her say it because I know white people find it too much for them to say Sorry to a black person. As she was not saying it, I thought of two things to make it hard for her to get me back and maybe even lose me in the end.

I say, You must ask my father first, I do not know, should I call him?

Mrs Plum says, Yes.

I fetched both Father and Mother. They greeted her while I brought benches. Then I told them what she wanted.

Father asks Mother and Mother asks Father. Father asks me. I say if they agree, I will think about it and tell her the next day.

Father says, It goes by what you feel my child.

I tell Mrs Plum I say, If you want me to think about it I must know if you will want to put my wages up from £6 because it is too little. She asks me, How much will you want?

Up by £4.

She looked down for a few moments.

And then I want two weeks at Easter and not just the weekend. I thought if she really wanted me she would want to pay for it. This would also show how sorry she was to lose me.

Mrs Plum says, I can give you one week. You see you already have something like a rest when I am in Durban in the winter.

I tell her I say, I shall think about it.

She left.

The next day she found me packed and ready to return with her. She was very much pleased and looked kinder than I had ever known her. And me, I felt sure of myself, more than I had ever done.

Mrs Plum says to me, You will not find Monty and Malan.

Oh?

Yes, they were stolen the day after you left. The police have not found them yet. I think they are dead myself.

I thought of Dick … my dream. Could he? And she … did this woman come to ask me to return because she had lost two animals she loved?

Mrs Plum says to me she says, You know, I like your people, Karabo, the Africans.

And Dick and me? I wondered.

DAN JACOBSON

Stop Thief!

From: *A Long Way from London* (1958)

A black-browed angry-looking man he was, and the games he played with his children were always angry games; he was chasing them, he was growling at them, he was snapping his teeth at them, while they shrieked with delight and fear, going pale and tense with fear, but coming back for more, and hanging on to his hands when he declared that he had had enough. There was a boy and a girl, both dark-haired and thin, the boy a little older than his sister and protective towards her with servants and strangers, with everyone but his father: he did not dare to protect her when his father sprang at her from behind a bush, and carried her shrieking, upside down, to his lair that was, he told them, littered with the bones of other children that he had already eaten.

The mother sat aside from these games – she sat at the tea table at the head of the small sweep of lawn towards the swimming bath, beyond which were the trees where her husband and children played, or she lay in the sun on the side of the swimming bath, with a towel about her head, and it was only rarely that she called to them or warned them of their father's stealthy, mock approaches. She sun-bathed or she read in the sun; they were all sun-tanned in that family, from spending so much time at their swimming bath, and from their annual six-weeks' holiday at the Cape, where they lived the life simple in a seaside cottage with only one servant. The big house in Johannesburg seemed to have innumerable servants, all black men in gleaming white jackets and aprons and little white caps like those of an Indian political movement, but in fact only another sign of their servitude, and these black men kept the house like a house on show: the house shone, unmarked by the pressures, the stains and splashes, the disorder of living. Not that the children were the least bit tidy – they dropped things about them as they went, and left the toys and the sticks and the items of clothing lying where they had been dropped, but the servants followed picking up things and putting them in drawers, as though that was all that they had been born for, this dance of attendance on the two nervous, dark-haired children. And the mother, who had been poorly brought up, loved it in the children that they had, so without question or wonder, the insolence of wealth. Once when he had hardly been more than a baby she had asked the boy: 'Would you like to be a little black boy?'

The child had been puzzled that his mother should have asked this. 'No,' he said, frowning, bringing his dark eyebrows together, and looking up in puzzled distaste.

'Why not?'

The puzzlement had left the boy's face, and there had been only distaste as he replied, 'They have nasty clothes.' And for this he had been given a kiss, which he accepted demurely. The children accepted their mother's affection as a matter of course; it was for their father's mock-anger that they lived. The mother knew this and did not resent it: she believed that the insolence she loved in them had come from their father, and for her her husband's violence was profoundly confused with his wealth.

But sometimes, watching the children at their perilous play with their father, even the mother would be afraid. She would lift her eyes from her book, or unwrap the towel which had been muffling the sun's rays to a yellow blur on her eyes, and her heart would sink with fear to see them run and stand breathing behind some tree while their father prowled on tiptoe towards them. So frail they seemed, with their bony elbows poking out from their short-sleeved blouses, and their knees large and round below the dress or khaki shorts that each wore. And he seemed so determined, so muscular in the casual cloth-ing he wore in the evenings, after he had come from work, so large above the children. But she accepted his violence and his strength, and she never protest-ed against the games. She would sometimes watch them play, but her eyes would go back to the book, or she would again carefully wrap the towel about her eyes and her ears, and sink back into her drowse. She seemed sunken under her husband, under his wealth, under his strength; they had come down upon her as the sun did where she lay at the side of the swimming bath, and she questioned them no more than she could have questioned the sun. She had submitted to them.

The father laughed, showing his white teeth, when the children ran yelling from him. In the shadows of the trees they waited for him to come again. He moved slowly towards them, and a lift of his arm made them scamper. He was king of his castle – and castle enough the house was too, in its several acres of ground, and its trees that cut it off from sight of the road.

Then one night the burglar came to their house. It was not for nothing that their house, like every other house in Johannesburg, had every window barred with steel burglar-proofing, that every door had a double lock, that two large dogs were let loose in the grounds at night. It was not for nothing that the father had a revolver in his wardrobe, always loaded and on a high shelf out of reach from the children. For the burglars in Johannesburg can be an ugly lot – gangsters, marauders, hard black men who seem to have nothing to lose, who carry with them knives and knuckledusters and guns.

But this one was not one of these. This one was a boy, a fool, a beginner, come by himself to the wrong house, barked at by the dogs where he stood in the darkness of a corner of the garage between the large painted mudguard of a car and a workbench behind him. He did not even reach for one of the chisels on the bench behind him, but stood squeezing the fingers of one hand in the grasp of the other, as though by that alone he might be able to stop the shivering which shook his shoulders in quick, awful spasms.

But the house did not know what he was and what he might do. The whole house was wild with lights and shouts and the banging of doors. Men, women, they had tumbled out pell-mell from the rooms in which they slept; one of the servants had been roused by the barking of dogs and had seen the burglar slipping into the garage. The house had all been in darkness, and still, so still that not even the trees had moved under the brilliance of the stars in the early morning sky, when the shouts of the servant had first come calamitously upon it. Wild, hoarse, archaic, the shouts had sounded, like the shouts a dreamer might dream he is making, in his deep terror of the darkness around him. Then there had been the other shouts, the house in uproar.

And the father in his pyjamas and dressing gown, with the revolver thrust unsteadily before him, was advancing across the back yard. The servants fell in behind him, even the one who had been guarding the window of the garage. 'Get to the window, you fool!' the father shouted. 'Guard the window!' Unwillingly, one or two went to the window, while the father came closer to the garage door.

He did not know what might be behind the door; he found that he could not push the garage door open, for fear the burglar might spring at him. He was a stranger to himself, roused out of bed by hoarse shouts, hurried downstairs by danger, chilled by the early morning air: to him it seemed that he had never before seen the place he was in; never before felt the lock under his hand; and when he looked back, the house, with the light falling on the paved yard from the open kitchen door, was the house of a stranger, not his at all. The servants were simply people, a throng, some carrying improvised clubs in their hands, all half-dressed, none of them known.

He could not push the door open. The dread of opening himself to whatever might be there was too great. The servants pushed a little closer; and he felt his fear growing tighter and closer within him. They pressed so closely upon him his fear had no room to move, and when he did at last lift up the revolver it was in desperation to drive away the people, who were constricting his fear and pressing it upon him. He lifted the revolver and shouted. 'Leave me!' He tilted it towards the stars and fired. The clamour of the shot was more loud and gross in his ears than he could have imagined, and with it there sprang from the muzzle a gout of flame, vivid in the darkness. When the servants shrank back he felt a momentary sense of release and relaxation, as though he had done the thing for which he had been dragged out of bed, and could be left now to go in peace. Then he felt the door behind him budge.

He leaped away from the door so violently that he stumbled and fell, and he was on his knees with the revolver scratching uselessly against the paving when the burglar came out of the garage. The servants too had staggered back when their master had leaped towards them, so the burglar stood alone in the doorway, with his hands still squeezed together, but lifted now to his chest, like someone beseeching mercy. From where he sprawled on the ground the master could only gasp: 'Catch him. Get round him!' And one or two of the men-servants came forward. They hesitated, and then they saw the spasms shaking the burglar, so they came to him and took him roughly, pinioning him. Their master was struggling to his feet.

'Bring him into the kitchen,' he said. There was a sigh from the group of servants, and a babble, then eagerly they began jostling the burglar towards the kitchen, and he went unresistingly.

To the father the kitchen too looked harsh and strange, a place of urgency, and there seemed to be too many people in it: all the servants, and his wife, and the two children, and the burglar, and the servants' friends, those who had been sleeping illegally but without harmful intent in the rooms in the back yard. These shrank back now, as if only now realising that the events of the night might have consequences for themselves too, and not only for the burglar they had helped to catch.

'You've phoned the police?' the father asked.

'Yes,' the mother said. 'The flying squad's coming.'

The father sat down at the kitchen table, blowing his cheeks out with exhaustion, feeling the tension beginning to ebb from the pit of his stomach. He could not look at the burglar. The mother too, for different reasons, avoided looking at the burglar, but the two children, in their neat white pyjama suits, had eyes for nothing else. They knew all about burglars: they had grown up in Johannesburg, and they knew why the steel bars lay across their bedroom windows, and why they were not allowed outside the house after nightfall, and why the dogs roamed loose at night. But this was the first burglar they had seen. Even the revolver loose in their father's hand could not draw their eyes from the burglar.

He stood in the middle of the kitchen, and his dark eyes were dazed, unsee-ing. He was a young African – he looked no more than seventeen – an under-sized, townbred seventeen years of age. He was wearing a soiled grey sports coat and a pair of ragged trousers that reached only about half-way down his shins, and when the spasms came he shook from his shoes upwards, even his strained brown ankles shaking, his knees, his loins, his shoulders, his head, all shaking. Then the fit would pass and he would simply stand, supported on each side by the household servants.

He seemed to see nothing, to look at nothing, to hear nothing: there seemed to be within him a secret war between his will and the spasms of shaking that came upon him, like a fit. The colour of his face was terrible: he was grey, an ash-grey, a grey like that of the first thinning of the darkness after a rain-sodden night. Sometimes when every other part of his body was free of the spasm, his mouth would still be shaking; his lips were closed, but they shook, as if there were a turbulence in his mouth that he had to void. Then that too would pass.

The little boy at last looked away from the burglar to his father, and saw him sitting weakly in the chair, exhausted. The hand that held the revolver lay laxly on the kitchen table, and from it there rose a faint acrid scent, but the gun looked in his hand like a toy. The father could not move and he could not speak, he sat collapsed, until even the servants looked curiously at him, as the little boy had done, from the burglar to him, and then back to the burglar again. They murmured a little, uncertainly; the two who were holding the burglar loosened their grip on him and shuffled their feet. They waited for direction from their master, but no direction came. The little boy waited for action from his father, but no action came. The son was the first to see that his father could make no action, could give no word.

So he gave the word himself. In a voice that was barely recognisable as his own, his face with its little point of a nose contorted, he screamed in rage and disappointment: 'Hit the burglar! Hit the burglar!' He danced on his bare feet, waving his small fists in the air. 'Why don't you hit the burglar? You must hit the burglar.' He danced like a little demon in his light pyjamas. 'Hit!' he screamed. 'Hit!' His little sister joined in because she heard her brother shouting, and she added her high yell to his: 'Hit the burglar!'

'Get the children out of here!' the father shouted. The children had raised their voices for a moment only, but it had seemed endless, their little voices shrilling for blood. 'What are they doing here?' the father shouted in a fury at the mother, pulling himself up at last. 'Get them out of here!' But he made no move to help the mother, though he saw that she could not manage both dancing, capering children. And when the little boy saw that his father did not move towards him, again he screamed, 'Hit the burglar!'

'Jerry,' the mother gasped to one of the servants, 'help me. Don't stand there!' She was grappling at arm's length with the flailing hands of the little girl.

The dark body of the servant bent over the boy. Then he sprang back waving his hand. The boy had bitten him. So he too being near-distraught with excitement and this last unexpected little assault, reached out and hit the little boy across the back of the head. The boy staggered; he fell down and lay on the sparkling kitchen floor. But it was only for a moment. He came up growling, with hands lifted, curled inwards, and fell upon the burglar. It took two servants to prise him off, and when he was finally carried away over the black powerful shoulder of the one, he had left two deep scratches on the face of the burglar, both from the forehead down, broken by the shelf of bone over the eyes, and continued down the cheeks. The burglar had made no effort to defend himself, knowing what would happen to him if he did anything to hurt the child.

Then the police came and took the burglar away. By that time the children were safe and quiet in the nursery; and later the mother too fell asleep after taking a sedative.

But the servant who had hit the boy was dismissed the very next day, by the mother, who could not bear it that a servant should have struck a child of hers. Least of all the son to whom she now submitted, the son who after the night the burglar had come to the house was not afraid to protect his sister, when her father fell upon her in their games in the garden, and who fought, when he himself was picked up and carried away, as an adult might fight, with his fists and his feet and his knees, to hurt. His will was stronger than his father's, and soon they were facing each other like two men, and the wild games and the shrieking among the trees grew rarer. For the father was afraid of the games he sometimes still had to play with his son, and there was none among them who did not know it, neither the son, nor the daughter, nor the mother, nor the father from whose hands in one night the violence in the family had passed.

DAN JACOBSON

Droit de Seigneur

From: *Beggar My Neighbour* (1964)

In Johannesburg the university grounds mark the division between the slums of Braamfontein and the expensive homes of Parktown. Braamfontein, I understand, is being rehabilitated now, and expensive blocks of offices are being built where the little slumlike houses once stood. But when I was a student at the university there was no talk of rehabilitating Braamfontein. The streets were narrow, filthy and potholed, and ran between fractured terraces of single-storeyed houses with walls the colour of ox-blood; on the tiny stoeps of the houses old men and women smoked, dozed, spat or simply stared forward with a total immobility of gaze; on every corner ragged children screamed and played. So one went deeper into Braamfontein, until at last one came to the railway shunting yards. The shunting yards ran the full length of the lowest reaches of Braamfontein, and the university ran the length of the other side, so that the area was sharply bounded: a teeming, decrepit slum, on whose streets the soot from the railway yards, mixed with dust from the mine dumps, continually fell. And among all the tumbledown houses, and the fences that yawned open into evil-smelling backyards, and the windows of the Greek shops stuffed with sweets and comic-books and loaves of bread, only one building rose above the height of a single storey, only one building was fronted with bold yellow facebrick, only one building had a neon sign, and that was the Goldreef Hotel.

Though Mr Gellin, the proprietor of the hotel, saw to it that our rooms were kept clean and that there was hot water for the bathrooms, I never thought that he regarded the hotel as anything but the penance he had to do – under the liquor licensing laws – for the money he made from the public bar on the ground floor. Certainly the food entitled one to draw this conclusion; and so too did Mr Gellin's air of immense patience and forbearance when you complained to him that you needed a new light bulb, or that the linen had not been changed for longer than the statutory period. There must have been twenty or thirty guests in the hotel, most of them semi-permanent and most of them either students from the university or railwaymen from the shunting yards. Generally the guests took little part in the vigorous Braamfontein life around them; and when they drank they did it in the privacy of their rooms, and not amid the dangers and noise of the public bar downstairs.

The bar was always busy, but on Friday nights in particular the jukebox would blast out its tunes across the street, and the motor bikes would roar outside even louder than the trains on the other side of the fence, and the young blades of Braamfontein would shout, sing, dance, fight, and chase passing Africans in the street – all to the ultimate enrichment of Mr Gellin. They resented Mr Gellin fiercely, of course; and they often gave tongue to their resentment. But though he was no longer at all a young man, he was still burly, and he had his own kind of courage; he employed a tough barman too, and he usually managed to keep some kind of order within the building, no matter what went on just outside it.

I had no idea that somewhere under his canary-yellow jersey and polka-dotted bow-tie Mr Gellin nourished the ambitions of a true hotelier until there arrived at the hotel Count Jezviecks and Count Petorowiacz. They arrived together and they shared a room: two gentlemen, one of whom was tall and the other of whom was short, and both of whom wore strange dark clothing the like of which I wasn't to see again until I arrived in England. Their overcoats were black and tubular; their shirts were dark blue with stiff white collars; their umbrellas were black and rolled to a degree of slenderness hitherto inconceivable in Braamfontein – where umbrellas were hardly fashionable anyway; their hats were of a largeness and blackness that appeared not less than ambassadorial. Count Jezviecks was the shorter of the two, but he had the bigger head. His face was one of wide surfaces and large features, all coursed with wrinkles, and with fine red and blue veins. Even the whites of his eyes were netted with veins. He never turned his head without turning his body too, and once he had made that effort it seemed natural that he should stare fixedly at whatever it was that had attracted his attention. Count Petorowiacz, on the other hand, never stared at anything. He was tall, and much younger than his companion; he had a tiny head at the end of a long neck, and he would crane his neck forward, bring lower his little face, in order to stare – but at the last moment he would veer away from the hips, and the upper part of his body would follow, the head last of all, like that of some slender, ungainly animal wary of the food before it.

These were the two counts who came to live with us in the Goldreef Hotel. I do not know what particular convulsion of war, revolution, counter-revolution, liberation or re-liberation, had brought them there from Europe; nor do I know how they earned their livings; nor where they went, so carefully dressed, every morning. They did not speak to any of their fellow-guests in the hotel. In the mornings they went off, wearing their dark suits, carrying their tightly rolled umbrellas, picking their way between the potholes and the blown papers on the pavement, past the Greek shop on the corner and the

374

revivalist tent pitched on a vacant plot of sand further up; and when in the evening the rays of the sun slanted down the street and the cries of the children were at their loudest, they returned. As far as I knew they never went out at night. They received many letters, with foreign stamps and continental handwriting on the envelopes; and they were the objects of much speculation on the part of their fellow-guests – students and railwaymen alike.

They became this especially after it became clear how very much Mr Gellin was favouring them. He gave them a table to themselves, though the rest of us had to sit four and six at a table. He put them in the room on the top floor furthest from the public bar. He presented them with bottles of A1 Sauce, Heinz Tomato Ketchup, Sharwood's Mango Chutney, and other rarer condiments and preserves, so that their table was soon laden with jars, though ours stood bare. And Mr Gellin talked to the counts, smiled at the counts, stood over the counts when they ate; sometimes when they were at table Mr Gellin would produce a new bottle of jam or pickles from behind his back, like a conjuror. 'Something to tempt your appetite, gentlemen,' he would say, with a smirk on his large flat countenance. 'It is imported, and it says on the label – look – that it is eaten by the nobility of Scotland.'

These advances were never rewarded by any signs of gratitude from the two counts. On the contrary: a less ambitious hotelier than Mr Gellin would have withdrawn from their table in despair, the counts made their aversion to him and his friendliness so plain. When Mr Gellin approached them in the dining room, Count Petorowiacz would begin to sway over his plate, his head drooping lower and lower; Count Jezviecks either ignored Mr Gellin entirely, or turned his thick body in his chair and tilted his head a little, so that the back of his short neck disappeared entirely, and in utter silence stared from his bloodshot eyes at Mr Gellin for a long time, before turning again and directing his attention at the plate before him. Mr Gellin would smile, a comment on the weather, and receive no reply whatsoever. Yet from these encounters Mr Gellin came away talking cheerfully about the 'nobility' who were 'gracing' our 'poor hotel'.

Now white South Africans are democrats among themselves – that is, where their fellow-whites are concerned – and the guests did not take kindly to the special treatment which the counts were receiving. And being white South African democrats, they said so too. The one who said it most loudly was Fred Turner. This was hardly surprising, because Fred Turner said everything more loudly than anyone else in the hotel. 'They may have been counts where they come from, but they're just two Joe Soaps to me,' was Fred Turner's favourite expression about the nobility who were gracing our poor hotel; and he delivered this opinion frequently, showing his large white teeth in a kind of a grin. Fred Turner, poor chap, had a secret woe. He had married a quiet and a beautiful woman, and he had felt at a disadvantage ever since.

I think everyone in the hotel thought it strange that Mrs Turner had been able to do no more with her beauty than capture Fred Turner – railwayman, noisy bloke, and passionate follower of dog-racing. But to none of us, I am sure, did it seem more strange than to Fred Turner himself. He was always making jokes about what his mother-in-law was going to do to him; but one only had to see the roll of his protuberant blue eyes towards his wife when he made these jokes to realise that it wasn't his mother-in-law of whom he was afraid. Mrs Turner would smile at these jokes, but she would not condescend to meet the surreptitious stare from her husband which followed them; she seemed unconscious of how his gaze would fall from her face to her neck, and then to his own broad red hands. The whole hotel admiringly watched Mrs Turner's entrances and exits from the dining room; and the men frequently embarrassed Fred Turner by congratulating him on his wife, as if he were newly married, and by asking him heartily what he had that they didn't have. 'A mother-in-law,' was Fred Turner's reply to this question. 'That's all I've got out of it.' And he would give a queer, strangled laugh, showing his teeth, locking his hands together, looking with his prominent eyes to the door to see if his wife were coming in.

But one evening, when we were sitting around a table in the dining room, Fred Turner asked about the counts the same question that had so often been asked of himself. 'What,' Fred Turner asked Mr Gellin, 'have those two blokes got that I haven't got?'

Mr Gellin had been going out of the dining room, but Turner's hand was on his arm, and Turner's head was jerking towards the two counts. Of them Mr Gellin was always anxious to talk, so he pulled up a chair, and sat down with us. He did not deny that he was according privileges to the two counts which none of us shared. With a fervour that surprised me, that silenced Fred Turner, and that roused Mrs Turner's interest, he took the opportunity to explain himself. 'Do you know who they are?' he asked Turner.

'Joe Soapovitch and his brother, Hairoil,' Turner replied promptly.

Mr Gellin ignored this answer. 'They are European nobility. Polish nobility. They aren't people you meet any day in any street in a town like this.' Mr Gellin kept his voice low, but he spoke quickly and earnestly, and occasionally moved one hand in a small circular gesture above the table, as if trying to make his words come even faster. 'I'm from Poland, so I know what I'm talking about. I was a small boy when I left, but I can remember a little. And what I don't remember, my parents told me, and their parents told them. You must understand that there is a history behind those two. And what a history, a terrible history! Those men – and their parents, and *their* parents – were lords, they were like gods in the country where they came from. There was no one to say yes or no to them. I'm telling you the truth now. People trembled when such men came riding out, people would even fall on their faces in front of them, in the mud, not looking up. People would shout, "The count is coming," and the women would run into their huts with the children, and the men would stand in front with their hands like this — like this — hoping that perhaps the count would smile today, or just ride past without looking. And the count would come with all the people from his house, the stewards and the men who looked after the horses and the dogs. Such dogs!'

Mr Gellin shook his head at the memory of the dogs. 'A lord, a count, like those two, they were a matter of life and death for us. For the peasants also, but especially for the Jews. And if the count didn't like the Jews, then the Jews suffered, they learned that the lord didn't like his Jews, I can tell you that.'

Mrs Turner asked, 'And is it like that in modern times?'

'Modern times? Modern times they're here; I'm talking of when I was a little boy in Poland, many years ago. It wasn't so modern in the country in Poland then. And I'm talking of my father's time, and my grandfather's time. They're not so long ago: a man has a child, and the child grows up, and he has a child, and there's a memory of all that has gone before. And what we remember is men who were like kings — kings without parliaments, without laws, kings to themselves. Frightening! Frightening men!'

Mrs Turner's lips, painted a dark red, opened a little wider. 'I think it's terribly exciting,' she said.

'For you,' Mr Gellin said, turning towards her, speaking more quickly and even more passionately than before, 'for you it's exciting, and you were born in South Africa, and know nothing. So you can imagine what it is for me, when I have a memory of such things, to have them here, in a place like this, and to have to look after them. Of course I look after them well, I see that they are comfortable, that they have everything good. What else should I do? In a place like this, in Braamfontein, I have two counts!' Mr Gellin held up his forefinger and second finger extended. 'Did I think of such a thing when I came here? Did I imagine that one day there would be two counts living in my own hotel? I can go anywhere, the Carlton, the Langham, any grand place in the town, and I can shake my head and say yes, very fine, very grand, but Gellin has *not less than two* counts in the Goldreef Hotel.'

'I didn't know that they were like that,' Mrs Turner said. Several times, while Mr Gellin had been talking of them, she had glanced from his face across the room to the two men who were the subject of the conversation; but now she stared directly at them. Her eyes were deep and black, and in them there was the glint that comes off coal when a piece is struck through cleanly by a blow. 'That's how men should be,' she said.

Her husband lifted his head at the note in her voice. 'Don't make me laugh.'

'It's true,' Mrs Turner insisted, looking not at him, but still towards the counts. 'You have to admire people who have lived like that.'

'Why?'

Mr Gellin interceded. 'Admire – I don't say that. But some kind of memory, of course, you must have.'

'Admire,' Mrs Turner repeated. 'I admire them. There must be something different about people like that, you can say what you like. They've got something behind them. We've got nothing behind us, we're just what we are, and that's all we'll ever be. I've thought about it sometimes,' Mrs Turner said, in her flat South African voice, that was a disappointment every time she spoke. 'We're always just starting off; but they started off hundreds of years ago, didn't they?'

'What? Those two?' Turner asked incredulously. He also turned to stare at them. Just at that moment, Count Petorowiacz looked up. Fred Turner immediately dropped his gaze; but Mrs Turner did not. For a moment her glance met the count's, before he, in his wavering indeterminate way, had sent his head elsewhere. But an instant later, his head was veering again towards her. 'What's so different about them?' Fred Turner demanded. 'I just don't see it. Why are they so special?'

'It would be worth something to find out,' Mrs Turner said.

'Stop staring like that!' Turner hissed out suddenly. 'You're making a fool of yourself.'

'I don't think so,' his wife replied coolly.

'Well I do.'

'Do you?' Only then did Mrs Turner look at her husband. 'What do you know about it?'

'I know that you're staring like a schoolgirl!'

Mrs Turner smiled: her teeth were regular, and showed up whiter for the darkness of her complexion. 'Nobody thinks I'm a schoolgirl, Fred.'

'That makes it all the worse.'

'Perhaps it does, Fred.'

Just then Mr Gellin was called away to the bar. 'You will excuse me,' he said; and he hurried off. But apparently he was too late; soon after he had gone we heard the familiar sound of the voice of a patron raised in anger in the bar, and a little later the equally familiar sound of breaking glass. As we usually did on such occasions, the residents of the hotel sat on in the dining room, until a prolonged silence told us that it was now safe for us to cross the public foyer, and go upstairs to our rooms. All the time I was with them the Turners did not exchange a single word with one another. Though Fred Turner shifted in his chair, and smiled at me, and opened his lips to speak, he let them close over his teeth again in silence. Count Petorowiacz's head was going up and down over his plate like something suspended on a thread; and Mrs Turner's direct, unequivocal gaze was waiting for it, each time.

If an outsider had heard Mr Gellin's talk of the nobility who were gracing our poor hotel he might have thought immediately that it was Mrs Turner who was being referred to in this way. Her eyes and her brows were dark, her lips were full, her black hair was coiled in a great weight behind her straight neck; her complexion was smooth, and of a perfect, uncommon colouring – she was pale, and yet there was a kind of darkness suffused within her pallor, as if her skin contained the shadow of her hair, eyes and brows. She was tall, and walked upright, and she carried her head like someone who had been trained in the kind of court that no longer exists in Europe and has never existed in South Africa.

The inscrutability of a beautiful woman like Mrs Turner is no mystery: it arises from the simple fact that one cannot see beyond her beauty, it is so rare, the eye is so filled with it. I know that even on that harrowing afternoon when Fred Turner came home earlier than had been expected, and found his wife in their room with Count Petorowiacz I did not know what Mrs Turner was thinking or feeling. To look at her was to see only how close to the surface of her cheeks the darkness within them had moved, and how sluggish was the hair that had escaped from the clasp behind her neck and hung to her shoulders. And to see these things was to be baffled by them.

What – if anything – she and the count had been doing in the room I don't know. She was fully clothed when I saw her, and the disarrangement of the count's clothing was probably due to the manhandling he was receiving from Fred Turner. I was brought into the passage by the loud shout from Turner; my room was next to the Turners', and thus I was the first on the scene, but it was not long before everyone else in the hotel seemed to be there too. We came as close as we could and we stared as hard as we could at everything we saw. In the Turners' bedroom we had glimpses of the hotel wardrobe, the hotel twin beds and the hotel washbasin, and we looked at these as though they were as new to us as Fred Turner's yellow malarial colour, or the count's pallor. Even the count's lips were pale, and his Adam's apple moved all the way up and down his long neck, like something seeking escape. The rest of him seemed to have given up hope of escape: with closed eyes he leaned against the wall at the end of the corridor, trapped in a corner, while Fred Turner yelled, shouted, stamped his feet and eventually struck him lightly across the cheek. I had never seen Count Petorowiacz stand so still – but for his Adam's apple – as he had done before the blow, but when Turner's hand fell on his cheek he jerked convulsively and opened his eyes. His eye was dark, blunt, lifeless, like the head of a match, in the paleness of his face. He writhed convulsively for a moment, and then stood still again.

'Why don't you hit back?' Fred Turner shouted. 'Why do you just stand there? I'll knock your bloody head off, you – you – rotten – who do you think you are?' But he was nonplussed, and swung around to face us. 'I found them together,' he said. 'As if I'm not here. As if I don't count. Well I do count!' Suddenly he screamed, 'Count! I'll count you – you –'

We all gave way as Count Petorowiacz made a desperate lunge, under Turner's uplifted arm. But the count was not striking back; he was merely trying to get away — unsuccessfully, for Turner grabbed him by the back of the neck, and immediately the other sank to his knees, surrendering altogether.

'Why don't you fight?' Turner muttered, desperately and absurdly at a loss, as he shook himself free.

The count got to his feet. For a moment there was no sound, but for the breathing of the two men. Then Mrs Turner's voice came calmly through the door. 'That's enough, Fred. Come inside.'

'You shut up!' Turner shouted.

'Don't talk to me like that, Fred.'

And poor Turner seemed grateful that just then he should have seen Count Jezviecks's thick figure pushing through the little throng of onlookers. 'Aah! There's the other one,' Turner shouted, starting forward.

'Please!' Count Jezviecks lifted his hand. It was the first English word I had heard from him in the several months he had been in the hotel, though I had heard him talking Polish to his companion. It was in Polish that he said his next words — something that sounded abrupt and angry. He put his hand on the other's arm, and began to lead him away.

'No you don't!' But Turner halted, and then burst through us, going down the passage towards Mr Gellin, who had just appeared. 'Your friends! I found him with my wife. The two of them, they're just the same.' The onlookers were now scattered down the passage, some near Gellin and Turner, others at the head of the passage, near the two counts, in front of the Turners' open door. 'I'll kill them both,' Turner shouted at Mr Gellin. 'I'll show them who they are. They can't do as they like.'

Mrs Turner appeared at her door, and we all gave way for her, though she did not come any further forward. Even the two counts, who were standing close together, stepped back a pace or two. Mrs Turner called, 'Come on, Fred. Nothing has happened. You can see what he's like. You're just making a scene.'

'And what were you making inside there? Christ! A man comes home from work, and what does he find —? Jesus Christ!' Turner grabbed at Mr Gellin's jacket. 'Listen, I warn you, if those blokes aren't out of this hotel by tonight, I'm leaving. But before I leave, so help me, I'll go into their room and smash everything there. They won't fight, so they'll see how I'll treat them. But you'll suffer too. So you better choose. Now.'

Mr Gellin surprised us all by choosing, without hesitation. He walked up the passage to the two counts. 'Gentlemen, you will go,' he said. 'You will go immediately. I will forfeit what you owe me for rent. I do not want you in my hotel any longer. The management,' Mr Gellin added with dignity, bringing himself upright and quoting the words that appeared on the bottom of the bills he presented to us at the end of each month, 'reserves the right of admission at all times.' Then Mr Gellin stepped aside. The counts took a pace down the passage.

But Mr Gellin spoke again, from a little behind them. And they halted. 'There's only one reason why I'm sorry to see you go,' he said loudly. 'Do you think I don't know what you've been thinking of me? Do you think I couldn't see how you looked at me – how you didn't look at me, as if your eyes shouldn't fall on such an object as me? And that's why I'm sorry to see you go – exactly. Do you think it's for love that I gave you a table for yourselves, and a fine room, the best room in the hotel? Do you think,' Mr Gellin said, and he was shouting now, 'I don't know what this hotel is? And that's why it was my pleasure to have you in it, for exactly what it is, this hotel in Braamfontein – *not* for what you could do to make it grand, but for what the hotel could do to make you bitter and humble. Do you think I don't remember? Do you think I have ever forgotten what you people were?'

'Jew!' Count Jezviecks said, turning.

'That's right,' Mr Gellin said, from where he stood.

This was a much older quarrel than Fred Turner's. But Turner was glad to use it. 'You don't say a word, chum. You've got your orders. So march. Or I'll smash your face in for you.'

It was painful to watch the two counts making their way down the narrow passage, Count Jezviecks supporting Count Petorowiacz, and everyone standing quite still to see them go, even the Zulu in khaki shorts who polished the floors, and was standing back from the rest of us.

'Fred,' Mrs Turner called, when the two men had gone around the corner of the passage. 'Come.' Fred Turner went to her, all his ferocity gone, his broad shoulders slack. She pulled him gently through the door. Then she closed it on us.

Mr Gellin was the first to move. 'Please,' he said, 'I think we should all go back quietly to our places. We've had enough excitement for one day. And this isn't a part of the building where I expect excitement.' He smiled, and we dispersed, without talking of what we had seen. It was not for several hours that anyone mentioned what had happened.

Mrs Turner appeared for supper in the dining room that same evening. She seemed calm; and the only sign that anything was amiss was that her husband was not with her. He did not come in for meals for two days; on the third day he came in, rolling his eyes and pressing his hands together, and making desperate jokes about how angry his mother-in-law had been with him.

By that time, of course, the counts had left: a taxi had called for them the night of the argument; and never again was Mr Gellin's poor hotel graced with the presence of nobility.

DAN JACOBSON

Fresh Fields

From: *Beggar My Neighbour* (1964)

When I was a student there was one living South African writer whom I, like most of my friends with literary inclinations or ambitions, greatly admired. That writer was Frederick Traill, poet, essayist, and novelist. To us it seemed that Traill, almost alone in the twentieth century, had shown that it was possible for a man to make poetry out of the forlorn, undramatic landscapes of our country; out of its ragged dorps; out of its brash little cities that pushed their buildings towards a sky too high above them; out of its multitudes of people who shared with one another no prides and no hopes. And because Traill had done it, we felt that with luck, with devotion, we might manage to do the same. Like Traill, we might be able to give a voice to what had previously been dumb, dignity to what previously had been without association or depth; in our less elevated moods, we could hope simply that like Traill we would be able to have our books published in London, and have them discussed in the literary reviews.

Traill was for us, therefore, not only a poet, he was a portent or a promise. It was taken for granted among us that Traill should live in England, whence all our books came; his exile, indeed, was part of the exhortatory significance of his career. And in England, too, Traill had remained aloof from the political and artistic furores of his time. He had issued no polemics; he had not voiced his opinions of Britain's foreign policies; he had lived in obscurity throughout the war. The little that we knew of him in South Africa was that he lived in the country, well away from London, that he had always shunned publicity, and that he was known to few people.

All of this, I found out when I first came to England a few years after the war, was true. Everybody had heard of him; nobody knew where he lived; many people thought he was dead, for it was a very long time since he had published his last volume of verse. For me the revelation of that first visit to England can be described by saying that in England I saw, wherever I looked, the word made flesh – made brick, too; made colour; made light; made trunk and leaf. But in the midst of this sudden solidification or enfleshment of almost everything I had ever read, Traill remained no more than a name to me. All around me was the country that others had described and celebrated; the one man who had uttered the words for my own distant country remained unknown. Whatever gossip I could pick up about him, I treasured eagerly; but there was very little of it. I heard that he was married; that he was childless; that his wife was ailing. And that was about all. Eventually, when I met a director of the firm which had published Traill's books — Parkman was the man's name, Arnold Parkman — I blurted out to him the admiration I felt for Traill, and my sense of frustration that there seemed no chance of meeting him. The publisher replied, 'You should write to him. I'm sure he'll be pleased to hear from you.' He must have seen that I was taken aback by the simplicity of the suggestion, because he added, 'Frederick's really a very friendly man, you know. I wish he wrote more, that's all.'

'So do I,' I said.

But I made no promise to write to Traill. Like many people of my generation (I suspect) I wished to lead some kind of 'literary life' without in any way appearing to do so. The thought of writing, as an aspirant author, to a great name — and Traill's name was a great one to me — made me feel embarrassed, pushful, and, worst of all, unfashionable. That kind of thing, I felt, might have been all very well twenty or thirty years before; but in post-war, comfort-clutching, cigarette-grabbing, shabby, soiled Britain — no, it just wouldn't do. All the same, when the publisher told me that Traill lived in South Devon, and gave me the name of the village in which he lived, I made a careful note of it. I felt I had a proprietary interest in South Devon; my girlfriend's parents lived there, and I had visited them, and had travelled about a little in the area.

I didn't remember seeing the name of the village, Colne, on any map or signboard; but when I next visited my future in-laws, I took out a large-scale map and found the village on it without any difficulty. And one fine day (the day was really fine: in mid-summer, cloudless and hot) I set out on a cross-country bus-trip to Colne. The trip promised to be a long one, involving two or three changes, and I did not know what I would do when I got there; I did not even know the name of the house in which Traill lived. But I set out on the trip as though it was something I had always intended to do, and without any doubt that I should succeed in seeing him.

Colne was pleasant without being picturesque. It had a stubby little church with a tower, hidden behind trees, it had a village store and a white-washed pub with a bench and table in front of it, it had a police station, a village hall and a war memorial. The road did not run straight through the village, but turned, spread itself between the pub and the store, and then swung upwards again, towards Dartmoor. For miles the road had been climbing, and from Colne one looked back and saw fields, hedges and woodlands tilted against one another, or sweeping smoothly over the curves of hills, or lying in sunken valleys. Above them all, on the far side of Colne, was the bald, high brow of the moor, its nakedness made more emphatic by the rich, close signs of cultivation evident everywhere else. Below Colne, the land had been measured and measured again, parcelled into little lots, divided a hundredfold by the hedges which met at corners, ran at angles from one another, lost themselves in the woodlands, emerged at angles beyond. But for the purplish shade of the moor, there was greenness everywhere – so many shades of green, from the palest yellow-green of the stubble where the first fields had been cut, to the darkness of the hedges, which you would have thought to be black, had they not been green also.

Most of the houses in Colne seemed to advertise Devonshire Cream Teas, but I went to the pub where I was offered a plate of biscuits with some cheese. I took the food and a lager, and went outside to eat my meal in the sun. The little open space in front of the pub was almost at the edge of the village, not its centre, and I looked out directly on a hedge, the road, a field, an open barn. There were few people about. I saw the village store being closed for the lunch-hour; some workmen who had been bending over a tractor in the barn nearby went into the public bar; a moustached old man with a military bearing and a hard red skin went into the saloon bar. Several carloads of tourists passed along the main road, on their way to the moor; several other cars came in the other direction, from the moor, with bunches of heather stuck into their radiator grilles. Three packed coaches went up in a convoy: I had heard the complaint of their engines, in the quiet of the afternoon, from miles away.

And then I saw Frederick Traill walking towards me. Though he had rarely been photographed, I knew it was him immediately. He was tall, he was bent, bald, and old. I felt a pang to see how old he was; the photographs, my own image of him, had prepared me to meet a younger man. He walked by me, with a glance down at the table, through his small steel-rimmed glasses. I was sure that I was betraying some kind of confusion; I was embarrassed by the crumbs on the table. But he walked on without a second glance, and I turned to see him go into the pub, bending his head at the door. His tweed jacket was peaked over the back of his neck; it hung loosely, wide over his hips.

I finished my food in a hurry, I did not want to be caught with it still in my hands when he came out. But I need not have worried, or hurried. The minutes passed; the workmen came out and went back to their tractor; a car carrying two men and two women stopped a few yards from me, and they all went noisily into the bar. I could have followed them, but I sat where I was: I felt that I would rather approach Traill where no curious or affable barman could overhear us, no stranger could stare. As I sat there I rehearsed how I was going to introduce myself to him; what I was going to say to him. Vainly, foolishly, I even permitted myself the fantasy that he might have heard of me, might have read something I had written, though I had so far published only a couple of stories in the most obscure and ill-printed of little magazines.

In fact, when I approached him as he came out of the pub, he shook his head almost as soon as I opened my mouth. 'Mr Traill?' I had said, and he stood there, shaking his head, looking at me and over me at the same time, his glasses low on his small nose.

'You aren't Frederick Traill?' I felt foolish, and small – literally small, because he was much taller than I, and had the advantage of the step as well.

Still he shook his head. But he said, 'Yes, I am Frederick Traill.'

I was relieved to hear him speak, and not only because he had acknowledged his identity. He kept his mouth half-closed as he spoke, but his accent was unmistakable: it was my own. 'I thought you must be,' I said. 'I recognised you from your photographs.'

He looked suspiciously at me; then moved forward, as if to come down the step. I took a pace back. 'I hoped I might see you,' I said. 'I heard from Arnold Parkman that you lived in Colne. I'm staying near High Coombe for a few weeks. I'm from South Africa originally.'

I caught a glance from his small, pale blue eyes. 'You are? What part of South Africa?'

'Lyndhurst.'

For the first time he smiled faintly. 'I know Lyndhurst. I used to visit an uncle of mine there, when I was a boy.'

'You wrote *Open Mine* about it.'

'Yes, I did,' he said, without much apparent interest in what he was saying; without surprise that I should have known the poem. He stepped down and began walking away; I hung behind, at a loss. I might have let him go, without another word, if I hadn't thought to myself, *That man there is Frederick Traill.* I saw his bald head, and beyond it the Devon countryside; and I felt that if I let him go the encounter would seem no more than a childish dream of my own.

How I was to wish later that I had let him go! But I did not. I called out, 'Mr Traill.'

He stopped and turned to me. 'Yes.'

'I wanted to talk to you,' I said. 'Your work meant so much to me, when I was in South Africa. And – and to lots of people I knew. I'd be so glad if I could – if you would let me –'

'I don't give interviews,' he said bluntly.

The oddity of the remark did not strike me at the time: how many people could there have been who had made the pilgrimage to Colne in order to interview him for the press? 'I don't belong to any newspaper,' I replied.

'No?'

'No, it's just that I've read your work.'

He seemed to consider for a moment what I had said, and then asked hesitatingly, 'What did you want to ask me about?'

'Everything.'

Again he smiled faintly, as if from a distance. 'Well, as long as you don't expect me to answer everything …' The gesture of his shoulders was an invitation to me to join him, which I eagerly did. Together, we walked up through the village; then we turned from the main road and went up a stony little lane. There were a couple of small houses on the lane, but we passed these, and came to a wooden gate, set at the right angle between a brick wall on one side and a stone wall on the other. The stone wall ran on with the lane, until trees hid it from sight. 'This is the back-entrance to the house,' Traill explained, as he led me through the gate, and closed it behind us. 'The lane goes right round to the front. Then he said, 'My vegetable-garden; I spend a lot of time on it.' The vegetable-garden was big and obviously kept up with great care. The house itself was an old rambling double-storeyed cottage with a slate roof and walls half-clad with slate. The house leaned, it bulged, it opened out unexpectedly at doors and little windows; it straightened itself at a chimney that ran all the way down one wall. We walked around the house, past a walled flower-garden; in front of the house there was a meadow, as green and sunken as any pond, with a gravelled drive running to one side of it. The entrance to the drive was hidden behind a bank of trees. Beyond those trees, at a distance of many miles, the single pale curve of a hill filled the horizon.

It was a lovely, ripe, worked-over place. We sat down in deck-chairs on a little lawn in front of the house, and talked casually, for a little while, about the weather and the view. But eventually the conversation turned to Traill's work. I told him of the admiration I felt for it; I told him something of what I and my friends had felt his career to be for us; I said how sorry I was that he had not written anything for so long. And while I talked I kept looking at him, taking in, for memory's sake, his long, slack figure, with his legs crossed at the ankles and his hands clasped behind his head; his bespectacled, small-featured face, with its clusters of wrinkles at the sides of his mouth and eyes. His head was almost entirely bald, and his scalp was faintly freckled. I could see that he was pleased by what I was saying, but I felt that he was saddened by it too, and eventually I fell silent, though there was much which I hadn't yet said to him and though I was disappointed that I had not drawn him out to speak more.

But he said nothing about his work; instead he asked me about mine. He asked me what I had done, where I had published; he questioned me about themes and settings. He had read nothing of my work, but his questions were all kindly, and he spoke to me as I had hardly dared to hope he would: as a professional speaking to an apprentice to the same trade or craft. His voice was deep; his manner of speech was lazy; still he spoke through a half-closed mouth. I was all the more surprised, therefore, when, without changing his position or opening his mouth wider, yet speaking with great vehemence, he said suddenly, 'Go home!'

For a moment I thought he was simply dismissing me, and I got up, confused and taken aback. Again he said, 'Go home!' and added a moment later, with one hand waving me back into my chair. 'Don't do what I did! Go home!'

I sat down again, and stared at him. 'Can't you understand what I mean?' he said, in response to that stare. 'You'll do nothing if you stay here. It's your only chance, I tell you. Go home. Get out of this place.'

He leaned forward and said bitterly, 'I don't want to tell you how many years it is since I've published anything. And that's why I tell you to go back to South Africa. I know, I know,' he said, waving off an interruption with one hand, though I had not spoken, 'I know you'll tell me that South Africa's provincial, and dull – except for the politics, and who wants that kind of excitement? – and there's nobody to talk to. And here there's everything – books, and people, and everything you've ever read about. Elm trees,' he said sardonically, and pointed to the trees at the bottom of the meadow – 'and meadows,' he added, 'and villages like Colne. It's wonderful, you can't imagine anything better. You can't imagine ever tearing yourself away from it. But can't you see that as you live in it, year after year, all the time your own country is getting further and further away from you? And then what do you do?' He slumped back in his chair and put his hands behind his head again. 'I can tell you,' he said. 'You sit here, looking at the elm trees and the meadow. You work in the garden; you go for a drink at lunch-time; you go to the market-town once a week, and sit in the cinema there. They've got three, you know, in Mardle, three cinemas! And you try to work; and there's nothing there for you to work on, because you've left it all behind.'

We were both silent, though I could see that he had not yet finished what he had to say. And soon he did go on. 'I tell you,' he said, 'when I came here I had my store with me, and I began unpacking it, and the more I unpacked the more there seemed to be. I felt free and happy, ready to work for a lifetime. All around me was this – all this – just what I had hankered for, out there in the veld. Until one day I found that there was no more work for me to do, the store was finished. And then what was I to do? Where was I? What did I have left? Nothing – nothing that I felt was really my own. So now I'm dumb. Dumb, that's all.'

This time he had finished, and still there was nothing I could say. At last, not so much because I was curious and wished to draw him out, but simply because I felt sorry for him, I asked, 'Why didn't you go home? You could have, all these years.'

He looked at me oddly. Then he said, 'My wife isn't well. She hasn't been well for many years. I suppose you could call her bed-ridden, though it's a word she hates to hear.'

'I am sorry.'

He said nothing to this; and shortly afterwards I got up from my chair; I had to be going back to the village, to catch my bus.

'You must be off?' Traill asked.

'Yes, I'm afraid so. It really has been a privilege meeting you, Mr Traill. And I do appreciate the way you've given your time to me.'

'Oh – time! I've got lots of time.'

He saw me off as far as the back gate; right at the end, as we said goodbye and shook hands, he seemed reluctant to let me go. 'All this you understand,' he said, 'is my wife's.' He did not gesture, but I knew him to be referring to the house and the grounds. He stood with his eyes half-closed, and the sunlight glinted off the top of his head. 'She loves this place. So do I really. It was quite impossible for me to leave. How could I?' Then he grasped my hand again, and said firmly, 'Go home, while you can. Don't make the mistake I made. Go home!'

He turned and went through the gate; I stood for a moment in the shadowed lane, with the sunlight streaming above me and falling in bright patches on the grass of the bank on the other side. There was no sound but that of his footsteps, beyond the stone wall. I did not like to think of what he was going back to; of what he lived with. Yet the place was beautiful.

The place was beautiful, England was beautiful: rich, various, ancient, crowded, elaborate. But I was much dispirited, as I rode away from Colne in the bus that evening. The warnings and the advice Traill had given to me echoed all the fears I had felt about coming to England, even before Traill had spoken to me of his life. And that life, and the work it had produced, we had conceived to be our models! Give up England, or give up writing, Traill had seemed to say to me; and I wanted to do neither.

I was much surprised, and flattered, when I received a letter from Frederick Traill a few weeks later. It had been addressed to me at one of the magazines which I had mentioned to Traill as having published a story of mine. In the letter Traill asked me to send on to him, if I would, something of my work, published or unpublished, as he would really be most interested to see it. The day on which I received the letter I made up a parcel of carbon copies of stories and other pieces, most of which had been going from magazine to magazine for months, and posted the parcel to him, with a letter in which I thanked him for the interest he was showing in my work, and again for his kindness to me when we had met.

I began waiting for a reply almost immediately. One week passed, a second, a third. Two months after I had sent the manuscripts away I was still waiting for a reply. Four months later, when I thought about it at all, my impatience had given way to a sense of injury which I tried to convince myself was unwarranted. Six months later I was horrified to read a long narrative poem by Traill which was unmistakably a reworking of one of the unpublished stories I had sent him.

Traill's poem was published in one of the leading literary monthlies. Delighted to see Traill's name on the cover, I had bought a copy of the magazine at a tube-station. I read the poem sitting on one of the benches on the platform. The train for which I had been waiting came in and went out, and still I sat there – hotly, shamefully embarrassed, as though I had been the one who had committed the offence. I had no doubt that the offence was gross; but I did not in the least know what I could do about it. How could I write to him, the man whom I had so much admired and had wanted to emulate, accusing him of having stolen my plot, my character, my setting? And there was no doubt that he had done so, none at all; there could be no question here of 'unconscious reminiscence'. As I sat on that station bench I cursed myself for my curiosity in going to see Traill; I damned myself for ever wanting to have anything to do with writers or writing. And within the general flush of shame I felt resentment and anger, too. The crook! The phoney! With his cottage in the country and his bald head and his sick wife and his advice. His advice! I went home and drafted twenty letters to Traill, but I tore them all up. Shame was stronger than anger. I just couldn't say to him what he had done, let alone tell him what I felt about it.

Not only could I not write to Traill; I could not tell anyone else about it either. The sense of shame I felt held me back; and so too did my feeling that no one would believe me. It enraged me to think that Traill had relied on the strength of his position as against mine, and on the very shamefulness of what he had done, to secure my silence. I couldn't smile at what had happened (after all, it had happened to me!) nor, though I tried, could I find much comfort in the lofty thought that it was better to be cribbed from than to crib.

When in the 'Forthcoming Features' panel in the same magazine I saw shortly afterwards an announcement of another long poem by Frederick Traill, I went back to my pile of manuscripts and chose one among them as the most likely for Traill to have stolen from this time. I was not wrong. The poem appeared – a long poem in dialogue. Again, it had my characters, my setting, even a scrap or two of my dialogue. I felt strangely proud of having made the correct guess, when I read the poem; and then I knew that it hadn't been a guess at all: I had chosen correctly because I knew Traill's work so intimately.

Mockingly, winkingly, the idea suddenly presented itself to me of writing a story with the deliberate intention of suiting it to Traill's purposes, and of sending it on to him, challenging him to make the same use of it as he had made of the others. The idea came as if it were no more than a joke; but that night, all night, I was working on the joke. And the next evening I had finished the story. Like the others, it was set in South Africa. I typed it out the day after, and before I could get cold feet I put it in an envelope and posted it off to Traill, together with a note saying that I was pleased to see that my stories had stimulated him into writing once again, and I hoped he would find the story I was sending him equally profitable. It was a sly little note, really, all innuendo, like the submission to him of the story itself, but I didn't feel ashamed of it. To tell the truth, now that I had approached Traill, even in this way, I felt a lessening of shame about the whole series of events; for the first time I began to think of them as comical, looked at in a certain aspect.

Then I prepared to wait for Traill's response, which I fully expected to read, in due course, in the pages of one of the literary magazines. What I did not expect was that I should answer a ring on the door one afternoon, shortly after I had come back from the school at which I was then teaching, and find Traill waiting shyly for me on the porch. He was wearing a fawn raincoat and a hat with its brim turned down at the front and the back; he looked ill-at-ease and more rustic, in Swiss Cottage, than I had remembered him as being in Devon. 'I hoped I'd find you in,' he said awkwardly. 'How are you?'

I stared at him. In my imagination he had become a monster of hypocrisy and unscrupulousness; but he stood before me simply as a rather slow and soft-spoken old man, with a small, tired, bespectacled face. 'Won't you come in?' I asked; and then, while he hesitated, I remembered what my room looked like. 'Actually,' I said, 'I was just on my way down to have a cup of tea somewhere. Won't you join me?'

'With pleasure.'

We went to a tearoom which has since disappeared; it is now a bamboo-decorated coffee-bar. But then it was still sombre, Edwardian and mahogany-coloured. The panelled walls and the massive chairs and tables were agleam with polish; the waitresses wore long black multi-buttoned dresses and little green caps on their heads; an open fire burned in a grate. The food, inevitably, was execrable. Traill was hungry, as it turned out, and had to eat a meat pie which was a little paler outside, and a little darker inside, than the sauce in which it lay. I just had tea. While he ate Traill told me that he very rarely came up to London; it was difficult to leave his wife as they had to get a woman to live in the house while he was away; in any case he did not much care for London. But he had had to come up to attend to various business matters, and he had thought that it would be a good opportunity to look me up.

Was he going to make his confession now? As I waited, I was wondering how I was going to respond to it? Coldly? Angrily? Or pityingly? But Traill gave me no opportunity to adopt any predetermined attitude. He said in a firm, guiltless voice. 'Those stories of yours, they're pretty ghostly, derivative stuff, aren't they? The last one you sent me is by no means the worst, in that way. And you do know,' he went on, 'who they're derived from, don't you?'

His blue eyes were severe in expression, and they stared directly at me. 'It gave me a strange feeling, at first, to meet my own ghosts like that,' he said. 'It was very disturbing; I didn't like it. When I read the stories I felt … how can I describe it to you? … that was where I'd been, yes; there was where I

390

had come from. But none of it was clear, none of it was right, those ghosts had never really lived. And then the more I read the clearer it became to me what the ghosts were trying to say. I understood them. I knew them,' he said, 'even if you didn't.'

'So you took them —' I interrupted.

'Yes,' he admitted calmly. 'And surely you can see that I made a better job of them than you did. My poems are better poems than your stories are stories, if you see what I mean.'

'But even if that's true —!'

'You mean, I still had no right to take your ideas? I thought that's what you'd say. And I sympathise with you, believe me. I'd sympathise even more if you hadn't told me what you did about my work, and what it meant to you. And if I hadn't been able to see it for myself, in the work. Your ideas? Your ideas?' he repeated with scorn; and then, as if collecting himself, 'All the same, I'm most grateful to you. Those manuscripts of yours have stimulated me, in all sorts of ways, they've set me going again. I'm tremendously grateful.'

He fell silent abruptly, leaving me struggling for breath, for relief, for release. When I finally brought out my reply it surprised me almost as much as it did Traill. 'Then you can have the lot,' I said. 'And you're welcome to them. I don't want any of them. I don't want to be like you. I don't want to go home.' Suddenly I discarded a burden I had been carrying for too long, and all sorts of scruples, hesitations and anxieties fell away with it. 'I'll take my chance right here, where I am. It's my only hope. If I don't strike out now, I'm sunk. And if I am to be sunk,' I said, 'I'd rather it happened now, than when I'm at your age. You can have what you've already got, and you can have all the stuff that's still in my room. It's all yours, if you want it. Take it, take the lot.'

'I will,' Traill said simply, after a long silence.

So we parted amicably enough, outside the house in which I boarded, Traill with his arms full of the files I had thrust enthusiastically upon him. 'Good luck,' I said; I had difficulty in restraining myself from clapping him on the back. There went my youth, I thought, looking at the bundle in Traill's arms; but I felt younger and more hopeful than I had for many months, than I had since coming to England.

I still feel that I did the right thing. The only trouble is that Traill has just published a new and very successful volume of poems; whereas I still live on hope, just on hope.

CASEY MOTSISI

Kid Playboy

First published, 1959

From: *Casey & Co: Selected Writings* (1983)

Every time a hick job comes around in the office I get saddled with it. Now the editor pushes this folded white card at me and says to find out what I can get out of this here invite. I walk out of the office and read the card once more. According to the gold-lettered words a certain Kid Mabothobotho stays out Dube is getting hitched to an Alexandra cherrie.

On Saturday the wedding will take place at the cherrie's place in Alex. I decide I'd rather wait for it to come around to Dube on Sunday because I'm somewhat scared of hopping off to Alex especially on weekends on account the bright boys over there have turned the place into a gunsmoke and knife-happy township.

On Sunday I haul out my top hat and tails to make ready to go to Dube. I expect it to be one of those high society shindigs, as you know how hoity-toity these Dubeheimers can get when they want to. I get a good look at myself in my landlord's son's wardrobe mirror as I put on the tie he lent me, and I see that my eyes are unusually clear – sure sign among the boozing fraternity that I've been keeping shebeen queens, especially Aunt Peggy, waiting.

I get to Dube and don't have any difficulty spotting the place where this wedding is taking place on account of the half-a-dozen beribboned convertible cars parked in front of the house. A guy who meets me at the door looks scornfully at my not-too-well-pressed trousers, whereupon he gives me the VIP treatment. Only he reckons the 'I' in VIP stands for 'Inconsequential'. He tells me to go and sit in the tent at the back of the house. I tell him who I am, whereupon he smiles and ushers me into the room.

This girl this guy's getting married to is so beautiful that I can't take my eyes off her for a pretty long time. After a while I manage to pull my eyes away from her to look at the groom. Cripes! It's none other than Kid Playboy. I feel the blood revolting in my veins. This is the same Kid Playboy who took away from me some time back the only girl I ever loved. He promised this girl of mine everything in the world and crowned the long list of promises by telling her that he would build a fire under the ocean just so's she can swim in winter.

And like all starry-eyed girls, this girl of mine went and believed every word he told her. Maybe if she hadn't been so gullible she would still have been alive today. As it turns out, Kid Playboy gives her the bird after stringing her for a month on account another foolish cherrie falls for his sweet talk. So what does she do, but commit suicide!

Kid Playboy's eyes meet mine and I pull out my tongue at him. He turns coal black and his Adam's apple starts moving up and down like someone who's seen a ghost. The guy looks real scared, and I am just beginning to hate myself for having scared the boy by sticking out my tongue at him when I realise that it's not me who's the cause of his sudden jitters. There's a girl who's sitting a few feet behind me who is proving to be the why for Kid's jaded nerves.

I turn around and look at this girl to see what it is about her that can cause so much panic in a satanic soul. But all I can see is that she's an ordinary homely girl, and the small sleeping child she's holding in her arms is the sweetest thing I ever did see.

I'm still busily occupied at looking at this fear-instilling girl and hoping that she's not a ghost, when a voice that sounds like a constipated ostrich's booms, 'Ladees and gentlemen, all those who have presents for the bridal couple may now see the "mabalane" (the MC of the wedding)''. The 'mabalane' stands up, breaks into a toothless grin, bows and sits down again.

I thought they had invited us to a wedding, now they want to fleece presents out of us! But seeing as the announcer man said 'ladies and gentlemen', I reckon he has left me out on account nobody ever accused me of being a gentleman, let alone a lady. So I happily ignore him.

A few folk get away from their eats and drinks with parcels of varying sizes beneath their armpits. They stand in line before the 'mabalane', who jots down the name and address of each and everyone who dumps a parcel on the table. Some guys who had decided beforehand that it would be much better to save the few pennies they have for paying their rent instead of buying presents for Kid Playboy and his spouse – and perhaps a few others who have a needle against him, like yours truly – suddenly discover that the room is too hot and march out.

After some time the last name and address is written down, and I can see the 'mabalane' hinting at the groom's people for his payment for services duly rendered – a nip of hooch. But he doesn't get the hooch. Instead, the girl with the baby, who had so disorganised Kid Playboy a short while ago, stands up and walks to the 'mabalane'. She dumps the child, who is now awake and bawling his young head off, on the table and says, 'Here's my present to the bride and groom. My name is Maisie.' She gives a Mapetla address somewhere in Site and Service. She winds up by saying Kid Playboy's the pop of the child.

All of a sudden, there's a bang of a hullabaloo going on. Kid Playboy is making a hurried exit out of the house, and the bride is tearing at her bridal dress and hurling all sorts of names at Kid Playboy and his family, including the late ones. After every burst of unprintable words she keeps chorusing that she's got a lawyer that's going to show them what makes the grass green.

Up to today nobody ever hears a word about Kid Playboy. But Mr Rumour goes around the townships telling all and sundry that Kid Playboy is in his hometown somewhere in the Tanganyika Territory, although the folks from there pronounce it 'Tananika Torrotoro'.

I reckon the next time the editor tells me to go and cover a 'wedding', I'm gonna take an advance on my salary and hightail it to Aunt Peggy's joint and cover a bottle of hooch with Kid Playboy's ex-bride on my lap, as she now frequents this place ever since her lawyer proved not to be as hot as she had thought him to be.

JACK COPE

The Flight

From: *The Tame Ox and other Stories* (1960)

'Don't touch me, don't touch me. You'll regret it.'

He took her by the jaw with one hand and his fingers pressed into the soft flesh of her cheek and throat. Seeing her so close under the light, he turned paler. The wild bitter fury, the unquenched hate in her look gave him a start of physical fear.

'Are you mad?' he said in his old private voice. And then in the voice and manner which had slowly taken possession of him he began to shout in her face. His colour came back. He was the public man, the estate agent and country auctioneer, forceful, brash.

'What can you do, threatening me?'

'Leave me alone,' she said, and she repeated in a way that chilled him: 'You will regret it, when you are sober.'

'What have I to regret, what more, tell me that. Hell … you! When are you going to admit the child you are carrying is not mine?'

She shook off his hand and panting for breath in a way that sounded like a succession of little sighs she said, looking him in the eyes: 'Danie, before my Holy Maker I have never dishonoured you, all the time you have left me here alone – never. Ah, but what you have done to me …'

'Take that back. It's a lie!'

'I will not take back one word, and I have not …'

He struck her in the face and she stumbled against the table. She turned and he struck her again, shouting in her face.

'Ah, ah,' she panted. She went through to the bedroom. While he poured himself a drink he heard her moving about. Going out on the stoep he was aware at first of the feeling of total darkness and isolation and he listened to the trickle of rain in the downpipes. A fine winter rain but the night was luminous with a moon somewhere behind the clouds, and after a minute he could make out the big bulk of trees standing quite motionless and dripping. The town was two miles off and the nearest house was the forest station beyond the road on the hilltop, a long way even by the footpath. From the bedroom window a soft light shone across the garden and on the white trunk of a tree. Her shadow moved across the light once, twice. A sharp uneasiness came back to him again, remembering her expression, the terrifying concentration that told him as nothing else could the utter truth in her heart. She, small and alone, had the unbearable power to make him afraid.

He heard her footstep on the threshold and she came out on to the stoep. She had put on a raincoat and on one arm was their two-and-a-half-year-old Grieta wrapped in a blanket and a black shawl. In her free hand she carried a small suitcase.

'So!' he put down his glass on the stoep wall.

'Goodbye, you will never see me again if I can help it.'

'So you want to shame me.'

She merely fixed on him her dark large eyes.

'You are running away, you are a coward, Johanna.'

'I am no coward.' She shuddered and her lips trembled so violently that he suddenly laughed.

'Go on – go on then! And where are you heading?'

'I should tell you.'

'All right – you will be back in half an hour. There's nothing out there but the darkness and the forest. And between here and the town no one at all, only the bush Kaffirs and the Kaffirs in the cutters' camp. A nice lot. How will you get past them?'

She went down the steps terribly afraid he would stop her. Her one thought was to get past him and she dared not say anything in case his mood changed and he came down after her. Grieta was asleep with her head resting on her shoulder.

She walked quickly and came out of the open gate on the road. It was all quiet and muffled under the fine cold drizzle; no sound save the drip from the trees, a rustle going like a whisper through the leaves and the faint hum of the overhead telephone wires. In her anxiety to get free from the house she had broken into a run, pausing in moments to listen for her husband's footsteps, and then hurrying on. She did not notice the weight of Grieta or of the case. Being six months with her second baby she did not have her old strength and was easily tired. He had called her mad. Perhaps she was mad. She did not feel things as she used to – she was not fine and balanced and sensitive to all things at once as a girl was and her mind swung about clumsily like a heavy weather-vane. At one moment she was full of a raging self-pity. And then fear took her, fear of all sorts of unknown things, fear for Grieta and herself and the unborn baby, nightmares of fear. And another mood that shut out all other feelings was remorse, bitter regret for the past, for her failings, her love of Danie that she could not keep alive.

They were building two houses on speculation down the road from her entrance and she could smell the wet pine timber and cement. Nobody would be there, not even a watchman. She stood in the road, thinking. Towards the town was the cutters' camp. She was frightened of the hard fierce men living there, black men who were part of the night, wandering the road in twos and threes. The twin thoughts of night on the endless veld and of its possessor the black man were, in her generations, deep blood-anxiety. Sometimes looking at the dark window-panes when her husband was away for the country auctions she would see gleaming eyes in a black face. It might be her own face in the glass or a wild fancy, but it made her heart stop.

Then she thought if her husband followed her in the car he would over-take her on the road to the town. That decided her. She turned the other way thinking to spend the night at the forest station. Geldenhuys, the sub-forester, was an uncouth man, often drunk, but his wife would take in any soul, out of pity. They had twelve children.

She had to keep on the alert for the forest road, a mere gap in the dark wall of trees, and once she went back a little way, thinking she had passed it by. But she found it and heard the water gurgling under the cross-culvert. It was from now on a mere track through the wood and plantations, two paths beaten by truck tyres and grown between with grass and a weed that gave up a strong wild scent when trodden on. Above was the faint ribbon of the sky, and some-times she passed clearings dotted with pale stumps and timber piles.

Now her whole mind swung on the thought of reaching the Geldenhuys cottage. She was not afraid or anxious, but over her limbs and muscles and joints was settling a lead blanket of weariness. She thought how far she had come and how much farther she had to go. She must be half-way – no, not nearly that. The weight of Grieta was drawing fiery bands of fatigue under her shoulder-blades and she set down the case more frequently to change the child from one arm to the other. If only she could sling her on her back like a black woman. But that was a custom of theirs and she would not be seen doing it. Who would see her, there, at dead of night? All the while the road was climb-ing but dipped here and there into a gully and the water of a stream talked to her quietly among the stones. The rain was slowly soaking the shawl and blan-ket round Grieta – how the child slept! Heart against heart, and the little one fearing nothing.

She stopped to change Grieta again. The forest was thick and close on all sides and the tree tops almost touching above. So dark she could hardly see anything, arranging the folds of the blanket. The child woke and began whim-pering.

'Shhh darling, Mammie is holding you,' she crooned. She rocked the big bundle and her heart was low; she wanted to sit on the ground and cry. Could she ever get to the cottage? And what if she had taken a wrong turning of the service track. It wound here and there and she could not remember if there were forks or crossings.

At last the child fell asleep again. She settled its weight on her hip and bent to pick up the case. Away off in the darkness she heard the sound of plucked strings. She listened acutely for it to be repeated, and it came on the night like an echo – five or six falling notes ending on a low distinct beat. The hair seemed to rise on the back of her neck and a feeling of numb cold entered her hands and around her lips. The notes came again, varied, soft and faint guitar notes always ending on the same beat – toom – toom! From the first moment she knew what it was beyond doubt – the way a black man played a guitar keeping pace with his steps and perhaps his thoughts. What dark thoughts? He walked through the night playing, it was his private music played to himself, his private night. A man playing music might not be dangerous, yet how could one trust? It was his way of proclaiming himself, his contempt of everything, his possession of the darkness. Toom – toom, the low note repeating.

She wanted to turn and run, but which way? The sound of the guitar came out of the night as if it were a ripple on the forest's slow steady breath. It was everywhere, now a clear note and now an echo among the dripping trees. She stood so deathly still that Grieta woke again and began talking in a sleepy, milk-warm voice.

'Why is it so dark? Where are we, Mammie?'

'Sshh, my baby-lamb. Go to sleep again. We are going to visit Oom Frik and them.'

'Why are you whispering, Mammie?'

'Sshh, lamb.' They both listened to the guitar.

'Who is that playing, is it Oom Frik?'

The mother kissed her. 'It might be. Are you quite warm, my love?'

'I'm so warm! But your face is wet. Mammie, are you crying? Look! There's a light.'

There was a flare of a match being lit off to the left and for a moment it shone like a spark at the end of a long tunnel. It went out. The guitar had stopped and now she heard voices, liquid voices of the black people, and one laughed. They were ahead of her and coming down the track. If she ran now she could escape them; tired as she was she could run for home.

But she did not move. Her heart and stomach were going in painful flutters and the ground heaved dizzily.

She let the case slip to the ground and sank down on it, folding Grieta in both her arms. 'Lord save me, Lord save this child of mine.' She felt firmer and her head cleared and she was busy for a minute making Grieta comfortable on her lap. It was no use running. She had no strength and nowhere to go. Not back to her husband.

The men's footsteps were quite plain to hear now. She could see nothing but imagined them, one on each wheel-track swinging easily along and at home in the forest and the darkness. The night was theirs and she was in their hands. The guitar started again and Grieta, who had caught her terror, gripped her, crying.

The guitar stopped. They came up cautiously, there were two men looking huge looming shapes in their greatcoats, and one struck a match.

'Hai! Hai!' he said intensely, 'It's a white *nooi* and a child.'

The other who was taller almost by a head, laughed in a strange, almost childlike manner as if such an event was beyond his experience.

'Where is the *nooi* going?' the smaller man asked. She had seen by the flare of his match a glistening savage face, the skin roughly pitted and eyes almost lost between high cheekbones and a bony brow. And yet the voice was milk; it could hardly be the same man.

The mother tried to answer but no sound came from her. Grieta said: 'We are going to Oom Frik.'

'Ha!' they both murmured together.

'It is a long way,' the first man said. 'We will take you.'

'No,' the mother said, 'I will go by myself. I was only resting, I will go now.'

She stood up although her knees trembled. Her supreme moment, she knew, had come. She picked up the case and with all the authority and firmness left in her she said: 'Now leave me.'

'Give me the case,' the smaller man said.

She relaxed her fingers and let it fall. 'Take it and leave me. Leave me and my child. Let me go, will you.'

He took the case and handed it to his companion. She began walking. Grieta clung to her, quiet and tense and her eyes round like a little bushbaby. The men followed. She knew they were behind her and she did not know how long she could go without screaming. No one would hear, and a scream might rouse them. They whispered to each other. She went on and on, she could not stop now. Grieta's head sank against her breast and she fell asleep. It was a miracle, she thought, that the child could sleep. 'Lord save her. Lord save us,' she repeated under her breath. The track dipped fairly steeply to cross a gully and there was an opening in the trees to the right, the sky lifting and full of suffused moonlight. The weight of the child made a burning stripe over her shoulders and it was impossible, going downhill, to keep her knees and ankles from wobbling. She turned her shoe on a loose stone and stumbled but still kept Grieta in her arms. In a moment the black man caught up with her. 'Give me the child, *nooi*,' he said. He took the sleeping baby in her bundle, opened one side of his greatcoat and made a big pouch for her. She disappeared into the coat. He had an acrid smell of wood-smoke and tobacco and sweat. The child went on sleeping in the warm shelter against the smell and the movement of his iron-hard body.

He went ahead and the mother followed, and behind them came the taller man carrying the bag. The guitar was slung by a string on the leader's back and it was a silent procession until he began to sing. She did not understand the words but the song was sad and gentle. It had the melancholy of the guitar music yet it was more complicated, falling in slow rhythms. The man behind added his deeper voice in a natural harmonic and the two seemed to share a feeling between them that shut out and excluded her utterly. Still she was carried along between them and her limbs were like machines and the dead weight of fatigue slipped off her. In her heart was a small flame of gladness and a sense of safety. Grieta was safe. In the strong bitter-smelling folds of the man's coat she was secure. She could not have come all this way without them, she would have fallen and lain there and maybe miscarried. How terrified she had been.

At the forest station a dog barked at them, a small white dog that darted among their legs and almost choked in the fierceness of its alarm. The taller man went on the stoep and banged at the door. 'Baas, baas, baas Frik!'

They banged again and called. Suddenly the door was wrenched open and a tall white man stood on the threshold with a rifle in one hand and carrying a storm lantern, 'Ja?'

He was in a crumpled shirt and khaki trousers and locks of unkempt grey hair strayed down to his beard.

'Baas, we found the *nooi* in the forest and we brought her to you.'

He looked at them in turn, holding up the light. 'Mevrou, what is the meaning of this, Mevrou?' he said, astounded.

'Let me rest,' she said. She took Grieta from the man. 'Thank you,' she said.

'Now clear off,' the forester shouted. 'Ag, you vagabonds, don't let me catch you in these forests.'

'Baas Frik, what have we done, then?'

'Don't ask me, but you are up to no good. That I know.'

They grinned and touched their hats and together they faded back into the darkness. The forester went in to drag his wife from her bed and the mother could hear her sleepy voice somewhere inside the dim, close-smelling house. With all those children sleeping two and three in a bed she knew there would be no place for her, but she sat on a box on the stoep too tired to care. The rain had stopped and somewhere down in the forest the guitar began its endless little private tune coming always to the deep beat, toom – toom! It did not disturb her. Grieta was sleeping and the bundle in which she was wrapped had the smoky acrid smell of the man. Listening and half drowsing she felt mysteriously safe.

JACK COPE

The Little Stint

First published, 1972
From: *Selected Stories* (1986)

Kiep brought me a horse from the stables and I stood on the old stone mounting-block to climb up more easily, not being much of a rider. Kiep held the horse's head while I got my boots into the stirrups. Embarrassing to be shown up as a greenhorn in the saddle – even in this age when the horse-memory is being drained out of our blood – but there was no audience other than Kiep and the boy. The housekeeper remained in the storeroom and the owner, my old school friend, Johan van Zyl, and his family were away on holiday at the coast. The boy's name was also Kiep. What they were to each other I did not discover – father and son I heard, though I could see no trace of a likeness and the boy, only thirteen or so, was already the taller by half a head.

Kiep was my guide and the boy came along to carry the gun and the specimen case. The two of them were on foot while I rode. Kiep went on at a rapid stride, rather a lope, and I followed spurring the horse to a brisk walk, sometimes breaking into a jog-trot. The boy lagged further and further behind until I lost sight of him in the undulations of low scrub and bush. Turning back, I could no longer make out the big grey house in the early-morning murk.

We had come some distance into the desolate plain when the sky flooded with light; levels of oystershell clouds far off towards the Atlantic shore, and I could see the birds lift off in flight. Lonely unpeopled land it was, called *ruens*, wastelands where the wild animals and birds had space to themselves. Van Zyl's ground covered thousands of hectares, much of it good farmland, but here to the south empty, unused, falling to wide stretches of marshland, vleis and shallow lakes.

Late August, the winter rains were over and the country starting to dry out, although water still lay in the hollows crossed by our track. My horse ploshed through up to the fetlocks, shoving aside rushes and fluit-reeds high as my shoulder. The best part of the morning had gone before we reached the eastern edge of the marshlands. Monotonous tough scrub gave way to a strip of driftsand, the white dunes pushing up out of a covering of sparse grass and yellow daisy-like dideltas. The driftsands sloped to the fringe of the marshes marked by a tall dark-green line of sedge, reeds, bullrushes out of which came a continual yacketting of birds. Smells of drying earth, rotting vegetation, waterlilies; the air close and hot.

Kiep chose a slightly raised tongue of ground topped by stunted bushes and green coarse grass and indicated that here the horse would be left – the rest of the way was on foot.

'Will the boy find us?' I asked.

'He will find us, baas.'

'I asked you before, why call me "baas"?'

'He will find us ...'

Kiep showed little change of expression except for a rare quick smile or splutter of laughter when I was able to break through to him. He spoke a kind of clipped Afrikaans, missing out words as if talking with a stumble. From his short stature and deep dark eyes he looked to me of Bushman origin and he all but confirmed this surmise by saying offhand that his grandmother came 'from the Great River' (the Orange). When I followed this with a question as to how he got the name 'Kiep' he answered without interest – 'My name is Willem, they call me Kiep.'

'And the boy?'

'He too they call Kiep.'

'Who is he really?'

Though I could see his face fill with some intense emotion, he merely shrugged and went on tying a knee-halter to keep the horse from wandering. At that moment the boy came in view, trudging in a tired slovenly way and swinging the shotgun. He lowered the specimen case from his shoulder and leant the shotgun against the saddle in the shade of a bush. I noticed a dirt smear on the gun and found both barrels were plugged at the muzzle with clay. The boy had most likely dropped the gun, muzzle foremost, into the soft ground. Fire it in that state and I might have it blow up in my face.

'D'you want to kill me?'

'No, baas,' darting surly green eyes at me.

'That's the way to do it.'

'I never meant to, my baas.'

'And don't call me "baas".'

'Is baas then Englishman?'

'Oh, forget it!'

Kiep knew the marshlands well, or at least this part of the territory, and he knew what I wanted. In single file we threaded the tall growth, starting up birds that whirled off squawking and honking. At the inner edge of the reeds we came on a wide flat sandbank, a kind of beach, left by the receding water which still stretched off into the distance, dotted with small islands and fringed again by a dark-green line of vegetation. Fully a mile away to the south flamingoes, hundreds, maybe thousands of them, made a pinkish smear across the water. On one of the islands a flock of pelicans sunned themselves. Spoonbills, stilts, duck and coots and moorhens … Without raising my fieldglasses I could count and identify any number of the larger waterfowl, waders, even a few seagulls, and a fish eagle on the wing. This marvellous profusion of birds undisturbed in their wild scene owed its being to Van Zyl and his family for generations. They allowed no shooting or trapping and above all they kept quiet about it.

The boy handed me the shotgun, which I had cleaned out, and without thinking I slung it over my arm.

'Any of the small sand-runners come back yet?' I asked Kiep.

'They begin, not so many.'

'The different kinds?'

'Many kinds. Some more, some less. They are here. Every day come more.'

The boy was hacking up a reed with a sharp bowie-knife, not to make anything, such as a flute; he simply chopped and whittled away, scattering the scraps. Mindless destruction. I had noticed him slash with the knife at the soft stems of papyrus as we pushed along the path opened by Kiep. A strong, well-built piece of young humanity, I thought, who should be at school and not running half wild here in the *ruens*.

'Look there, my baas —' Kiep checked himself and changed his word to 'sieur', the local survival from *monsieur*, old-style humble address only a little less servile than baas. I was not out to embarrass him and passed it over, but the boy grinned and turned his back to hide his amusement. Old habits don't die — the old people die first.

Handing the gun back to the boy I got my fieldglasses into focus, following Kiep's direction. There they were! Little pale-buff waders drifting on their stick legs above the sand, this way and that way as if blown by the wind. Then suddenly they rose in close flight up and out of my field of vision. Very beautiful. A species of sandpiper, but too far off to identify for sure.

'What name do you call them?'

'Strandlopertjies,' he said.

'All the small sand-runners?'

'They call them all the same name. Many kinds. But I know them, sieur — they have their own ways, calls too. One claw, the tail feathers — that marks them. I know the difference.'

'That means you have handled them?'

Still with his eyes closely narrowed, looking into the distance, he nodded slightly in his remote way.

'Where did you learn this?'

'Saldanha, Velddrif — I work for people there. Foreign people. They put bands on the birds' legs. I catch them in nets, traps. They did not shoot.'

'Ah, but that's for a different purpose. You think it wrong to shoot the birds?'

He said nothing to this and yet was taut, shifting his weight very slightly from foot to foot so the ooze came up between his toes. I slipped the field-glasses back in their case and hung them with the camera across my shoulder. It looked as if things were going to be a little tricky when I had to use the gun and I wondered if this was something in Kiep or an inhibition built up by the strict rule of the Van Zyl family.

I started along the soft treacherous sand of the beach and Kiep followed. He soon overtook me and went on ahead; he could sense where the underlayer of the bank was firm and able to hold our weight. I wanted him to select a place and build a small one-man observation shelter. His choice of a site was at the head of an inlet flanked by wide sandbanks and dotted with strange rock out-crops forming islands.

In about two hours the shelter was built, cleverly tied together with rope plaited from papyrus and so well concealed it could not be distinguished even at close range in the unending wall of water-plants. The boy worked gamely at this task and his sharp bowie-knife turned out to be as useful here as it was otherwise destructive. The birds, save for the habitually shy species, took little notice of us and went on with their fishing and paddling, sudden flights and whickering noises.

The sun was at about four; Kiep had finished packing in a useful platform of rushes, and we started back so as not to be caught by the dark. Rounding the headland we put up a flight of little waders while a few duck took off from close inshore, beating the water in lines of glistening splashes. The small birds flew in close accord, drifted, turned and dived, chittering to each other, and once in the air did not seem to fear us. Had I wished to take any as specimens, a single barrel of dust-shot fired into them as they blew past would have brought down five or six with ease. As if reading my thought, the boy offered me the shotgun.

'Does the baas want to shoot?'

I shook my head. 'No, I don't need the gun.' I glanced at Kiep who had come to a halt and stood looking out across the water, eyes shaded by the brim of his old felt hat. The two of them, shut inside their secret thoughts, gave me a twinge of unease.

While Kiep freed the horse from its knee-halter and saddled up I put to him my plan — I would have to camp here for at least two or three days at a time. The distance was too great to come down to the marshlands each day. Tomorrow I meant to load the horse with my camping equipment and a few supplies. When I had pitched my tent he could return with the horse and the boy. Later they could bring the inflatable dinghy.

'I will stay on alone. I want to be in that lookout before daylight. You need not be here all of the time, Kiep.'

'I will stay,' he said quietly.

'My tent is small, it was not made for more than one.'

He glanced swiftly up at me as if startled that I should consider his sharing the tent. Then without a word he handed me the reins and waited at the horse's head till I was in the saddle. The boy shouldered the shotgun correctly as I had instructed him. The metal specimen case was left safely hung in the low branches of a bush. I was against leaving the gun behind even if there was small risk of anyone passing by and taking it. The cartridge-belt I buckled around my own waist with its dozen or so charges of No. 4, No. 6 and dust-shot, the last for bagging without damage the lighter bird specimens. The boy had eagerly taken up the belt, but a feeling that he was too feckless, inquisitive and at the same time unreasoning, made me refuse. Seeing his resentful look, how could I explain? With the belt as well as the gun I could not be sure he would resist the temptation to experiment – loading the gun or maybe digging open a cartridge with his knife to see what made it go off.

Following an article I had written for a geographical magazine I received requests from three natural history museums in Europe and America for the supply of new specimens and observations on the smaller migrant birds with a special interest in that tiniest of all the waders, the Little Stint. I discussed the subject with Johan van Zyl and his wife Ria one winter night around a comfortable fire after the children had gone off to bed. We accepted that the bird population of the world faced extinction. The threat was critical and it came from man and man alone.

'I know it – whatever I can do is a drop in the ocean,' Johan said. 'In a few generations, as things are going, I can see a time when there may not be a single bird on the earth. Not even chickens or turkeys or ducks. Eggs and poultry protein will be manufactured synthetically.'

I did not go so far as that. 'Look, you'll find worthwhile financial rackets being worked, never fear. The wild birds may be blotted out but any number of species will go on being bred in captivity and sold on a scarcity market. They'll bring out new and strange mutants by radiation or dye embolism on the genes. Maybe some cracked scientist will even reconstitute a living dodo.'

'Or a pterodactyl,' Johan said.

The Nature Conservation people of the Cape were helpful, granted me permits and put their research at my disposal. And now without being asked Johan gave me the freedom of his family land to photograph or film the wild life, collect museum types and make sound-recordings. I promised to be back in the southern Spring. I was interested also in seeing again the northern breeding grounds of these migrant birds beyond the Arctic Circle in Lapland,

North Russia and the island of Novaya Zemlya. Seven or eight thousand miles each way, the super-tourists of the world, some only a few ounces in weight and fitting easily in the palm of one's hand, run the gauntlet, in their yearly flight, of every danger – chiefly the rapacity of their human enemies.

Sounding Kiep out on our trek to the marshlands next morning I wanted to pin him down to my main point of interest – had he actually seen Little Stints back from the North?

'Klein strandlopertjies? Ja, some were back.'

'I mean the smallest of all, Kiep, those I have spoken of.' I tried to give an imitation of the bird's flight call: 'Wit – wit!'

Kiep looked aside shyly, then burst into a snort of half-suppressed laughter. The boy grinned in delight. I had not impressed these two realists. But for my part I was confirmed in my suspicion that Kiep in fact could not distinguish between the minor species, some being so alike, of course, that it takes an expert to classify them, and only on checking closely. Well, let me sort out the problem myself.

We pitched camp on reasonably dry ground at the edge of the bush; Kiep scooped a waterhole in the hollow of a tiny stream and built a fireplace of sods cut with his hunting knife. My small green tent stood square between the bushes and at a little distance Kiep and the boy put together a *skerm* crudely roofed and sheltered on three sides with branches and cut reeds. The ground-covering was of rushes and grass and it looked quite a serviceable little hut though poor protection should it rain.

It was still dark the following morning when we arrived at the lookout. I stowed the camera, the gun and cartridge-belt, settled myself comfortably in an angle and lit up a pipe to wait for the dawn. Mosquitoes were about and the smoke kept them off. Kiep, squatting in the entrance that faced away from the vlei, also lit up. A chip of the old moon rode low in the east and would soon merge with the dawn.

I found my heart beating hard as if in the excitement of a dark dream yet without any undertone of fear. This waking dream – what did it mean? I thought of my many vigils in the living heart of nature, but none compared with what I now experienced. The reeds, the swamp, the countless and unimaginable stirrings all around led back to the very beginnings. The reed cracks, in the lore of Africa, and out of that insignificant but immense event comes the first Man. He is not man originally – he is snake, insect, egg; he is bird, he is a cry to the moon and on the wind. He is greater than all things and still the weakest because he is Man. The wind flies away with his voice and he goes unheard. The first Man is very old and small but his children are tall as shadows cast by the rising sun. These are stories like old memories, only until then I had never experienced them in the way that my thought fused now with every sense in my body. Strangely, I had no expectation of anything about to happen – rather I felt a continuous sense of happening, both within and outside of me. What was Kiep thinking? I listened for the slightest movement, the lightest sound of his breath or heartbeat. He did not seem to be there at all in the darkness. Maybe that was the explanation – it was coming from him. Or was this the merest fantasy?

Then in the glimmer of the still, almost imperceptible day-spring I could make out Kiep's shape, solid and commonplace. His pipe had gone out and so had mine. For quite some minutes I felt shaken by this half-dream and wondered if I had not in fact fallen asleep. No, I had been fully awake, alert even, of this I could not be more sure.

'Kiep,' I said.

'Ja, my …' He left the address word unspoken like a syncopated note.

'Drink coffee?'

'Assamblief …'

I got the screw-top off the vacuum flask and poured two beakers of black sweet coffee.

'Where is the boy?'

'I told him blow up the fire.'

'Ah.'

That day I identified and photographed my first sighting of Little Stint. Only five of them, in full easy view of the shelter. One moment a stretch of empty sand marked by darker ripple lines above the water-level, the surface of the inlet placid as glass. Then they were there, folding quickly their slightly spread wings. A very small group – they had in all likelihood split off from the mainstream of the great exodus or gone on ahead of the exhausted travellers. A small waft of air laid wrinkles on the water and made a rustling sound around us … fluttered the feathers of the birds. My camera quietly whirred. I had caught that light flutter of feathers – a sign, I felt sure, of the extreme emaciation of the Stints. The skin would be loose on their delicate bones from consuming a third part or more of their total weight in the heroic circling of the hemisphere.

I should perhaps have shot at least one or a brace of those forerunners to check their condition. But my finger remained on the trigger-button of the camera. There, in the sight, I watched the pale, lightly mottled little birds turn in a single movement like parts of a mechanism, run to the water's edge and pause with heads up. Then down went their heads and they were all dabbling right and left in the rich mud. They had before them almost eight months of luxurious feeding and sun in the dry Cape summer, the vigour of warm gales scented with the sea, and comparative safety from predators. By the time the inexorable call of the North vibrated in their nerve cells they would have plumped out with stores of energy to carry them back around the earth, their mating plumage already coming on.

As suddenly as they came, they were gone again. It seemed that they simply erased themselves from the circle of my viewfinder. I turned to Kiep but found that he too had gone off on his own affairs, and I guessed he would find himself a dry spot and curl up there in the sun.

So in the drowsy end of the afternoon I went back on my own to the camp site, a little dazed with the richness of that spring day and with nothing under my belt save a few dry sandwiches I had stuffed in my pocket. Once inadvertently I missed the firm track along the sandbank and sank, or rather fell, almost knee-deep in the black ooze below the crust. The gun went flying and my camera and glasses tumbled around me. The boy appeared from among the rushes and came to collect the gun while I scrambled to my feet on firm sand.

'Mud, baas,' he said, shaking his head and holding down his laughter.

'Ja, so it seems.'

'Hai!'

There was a pot of stew at the camp hung on a tripod of sticks and bubbling slowly over the coals. If this was the boy's unaided cooking he had certainly learnt some useful hints in his short life. Flavoured with wild herbs he had collected, it was an unusually good meal itself along with coarse bread and a mug of red wine. Kiep waited until I had done eating and then came himself to collect my mess-tin and spoon. He hesitated before accepting the wine bottle and the stew-pot. I could see that his rules were firm and unchanging – he would take nothing of his own accord and it was against his feelings to ask. To join me at a meal was unthinkable. I was the *stranger*. Though I had been born and spent my boyhood in this country to which he was attached by the weight, perhaps, of thousands of years, I remained outside. I was not 'of him', not seen by the soul of the place, the *anima loci* that infused and united every living and every silent thing; and how to become attuned in his way to this great harmony I can't say.

Kiep carefully scratched my fire together and added a few sticks. On the point of leaving he halted and said as if speaking to someone in the darkness: 'Tomorrow I set a net.'

I heard their voices as they sat and ate at their own fire beyond the *skerm*. The boy laughed once in a stifled way. Small flames flickered from the red core of my fire. With the air so clear the night had turned cold and I could have wished for a stronger blaze. But I accepted what was and did not move.

I suppose from the exposure to a long warm day, the first-rate stew for supper and the wine I must have dozed off, sitting with my back to the stem of a warped and dried-out bush. I was not asleep for more than a few minutes, for the fire when I jerked awake was unchanged. What had woken me? Almost at once I was aware of the form hunched in a shadow so near I could have reached out and touched him: Kiep!

'So — it's you, Kiep. I fell asleep.'

'Ja, so …' his voice trailed off.

'You have something to tell me?'

'This, I bring to show …' He held out something indistinct and shape-less resting in his hand, and when I took it I found it was a small dead bird. I leaned forward to bring it closer to the firelight, opened the eye which appeared totally black and still bright and felt the thin hard breastbone. It could not have been long dead and — what was significant to me — it was without doubt a Little Stint. Kiep had somehow managed to kill it without damaging it, for there was no mark of blood or sign of injury. Then I noticed and sat staring with disbelief at one of the stick-like black legs. Above the foot it was ringed with a minute yellow plastic band. Could Kiep have clipped on the ring himself? After all, he had taken part in ringing birds on the West Coast. I glanced up and saw he was watching me intently.

'This ring — I mean, was it on the bird, Kiep?'

'It was on, sieur.'

'The bird is a klein strandlopertjie, the kind I have spoken about.'

'I know that.'

'Did you recognise it before you killed it?'

'I picked it up. Dead. It lay near the water. I bring it, sieur, like I found it.'

The sincerity in every word and the way he paused to say 'Dead' made me feel my doubts had been absurd. I struck a match and by its light could read the number and serial letters on the ring. After a routine check of the time and place of the ringing, the band could be restored, greatly adding to the interest of the specimen when prepared for display. It was a piece of extraordinary good luck.

Kiep got the gas lantern lit, throwing out a harsh white glare into the night. I recorded the find in my field notebook and treated the bird with formalin for later taxidermy. The small carcass was so emaciated it was difficult to believe the bird could have been capable of flight. Yet it had come in over the last mountains and vineyards and blossoming white orchards using its ultimate milli-gram of strength to reach the marshlands. What brought it there, more than a hundred miles off course to the east, when it had almost certainly been ringed on the West Coast or the Cape Peninsula? Possibly it had mated with a bird from Van Zyl's marshlands and joined the migration with its partner and chicks. One other chance, that it had wintered in the Cape and somehow found its way across country, I ruled out as unlikely. The conclusion was reasonable that this featherweight creature, guided and impelled by what col-lective forces remain beyond conjecture, had at least once flown from the Far North where it was hatched and then made the return journey from its summer feeding grounds over mountains, deserts, seas, jungles – more than twenty thousand miles all told, or nearly the circumference of the earth.

I packed it away in the specimen case. As Kiep turned out the lamp the darkness collapsed over us again. My fire glowed dimly and sent up a dying lick of blue flame. I slumped back against the dry tree, filled and lit my pipe while Kiep carefully built up the coals to a tense small cone of heat. Then he hung over it the coffee pot and drew back into the shadows. I passed the tobacco pouch and he lit up too; he seemed in no hurry to leave.

I knew almost with certainty that he had in his heart something he wanted to tell me, and while he waited for the pot to boil he was also waiting for the moment to speak ... I saw the gauze-like pattern of innumerable wings beating with a slowing agonised rhythm over the iron-dark ribs of the Great Karoo. Then the metronome quickened and the wings lifted up and up to top the grey heights of the range ahead, a single insignificant dot trailing behind, wings going in double-beat like a failing heart.

Kiep said: 'The meat is finished, sieur.'

'Right, I'll send the boy for more supplies, he can take the horse in the morning – with a note for Mrs Slabbert.'

The stars had come in closer when I looked up. There was only the movement of space, time flowing into the horizon.

'Did they tell you the strandlopertjies nest in the lands of the Midnight Sun?' I asked Kiep.

'Ja, they tell me. But I know.'

'Did you know that already?'

'The Sun goes to fetch the year. It turns back and it brings the year, the Summer. The Bird comes with the Sun.'

'What is this Bird?' I asked.

'The Bird is the Wind,' he said.

This was of course the fragment of a legend and I waited for him to go on. But it seemed for him to end there and he did not add anything.

I was in the Far North for some time at the end of the war. A very long time ago it seems now. On a food convoy. Our ship was damaged in the ice and we went ashore on one of the islands. Later, I was given permission to join a scientific party and accompanied them as far as Novaya Zemlya. I had barely begun my studies in zoology and my memory is not all that clear about the island which came to represent in my mind a kind of numbness, a grey patch. Frightening too. I must have somehow shut out my memories of it, but in after years details would strike me quite distinctly. I have, for instance, a visual picture of a stretch of trees – birch and larch and other northern species that grow normally into great forests. Only there on Novaya Zemlya they were only a

410

few inches high. Everything living had to cower against the ground – mosses and lichens too, primitive plants whose life is half a death. The summer was one long gloomy day from mid May to August. The Midnight Sun, except that you don't often see it for the perpetual fog. And into that strange submerged unconscious world flood millions of birds to mate, hatch and nestle their young; and then off before the long congealed night of Arctic death overtakes them. I appreciated little enough of the cycles of life there; on the other hand I plainly witnessed something of the brutal seal and walrus fishing and fur catching. Why 'brutal' though, where every creature is poised anyway on the edge of extinction?

'The Midnight Sun …' Kiep said in a rising voice, and I thought he might have a question to put to me which had long troubled him. Instead, he leaned forward and with a bent stick lifted off the pot lid and dropped into the bubbling water a handful of ground coffee. The brew seethed up and he swung the pot off the fire.

'That sun up at night,' he said after a silence, '– how then do the birds tell when to sleep?'

I had no answer, thinking how he looked at this through the eyes of nature while the greater mystery remained secretly within him. 'If we knew that,' I said, 'we might also know what brings them here so far away in the world.'

'They come back to the yard where they were made in the beginning,' he said. From somewhere under the stars came the sad wrung cry of night plovers calling each other as they flew by, more and more faint until they could not be heard … I saw farther through time a spiral of wildly fluttering wings go up, coil after coil like thin smoke into a pink-red Arctic sky, their whickering merged into a high vibration. Then the topmost wisp of the spiral uncoiled and sped arrowlike into the eye of the sun, flattened out huge and crimson on the skyline. One speck inseparable from the flight, high above earth and freezing sea, beat the air stoutly with its sickle wings now settling to a steady almost tireless ictus, a minute yellow plastic band circling its black leg. Heading for the great South, for warmth and safety – the blank history of millions of years in its unerring bloodstream.

Kiep got to his feet and, looking away, repeated – 'Tomorrow I set a net.'

Among the shadows thrown by the gas lamp in the darkness before morning the boy untethered the horse from its sheltered corner among the bushes. When he tried to lift the bridle over its ears I saw it jerk back and the light made a red reflection in one of its eyes: an old horse and a little blind. The boy tried again, twice, and then he struck the animal across the nose.

'Los!' Kiep said sharply out of the dark. 'Leave off hitting – speak to him.'

A minute after the boy had ridden off Kiep also disappeared. I collected my things and set off for the lookout in the reeds, leaving behind the shotgun, which I reckoned I would not need that day. My camera work was yielding the most promising footage and I made a small prayer in my heart that nothing might go wrong with the film or mechanism. I knew eventually I must use the gun. Even if Kiep had the luck to net the birds I was after, they would then have to be put out with chloroform.

Nothing had more disconcerted me on this expedition than the feeling which had grown almost to a conviction, a moral principle, against taking the life of a single one of the countless birds all around me. Whatever dangers lay in wait for them, let me at least not be numbered as yet another enemy. On the one hand I strongly resisted the thought of being bound by any closed postulate or rule, above all one self-imposed – the quickest way to an obsession. It was easy to argue with myself that there was a scientific necessity to study, collect and preserve specimens; or the shallower approach that the birds were in any case due after a short life to die at the hands of peasants or huntsmen on their long migrations or by natural causes or predators. But to be honest in my heart I should either examine what cause had thrown up this powerful restraint into my conscious thoughts – or else put myself to the immediate test by taking the gun and shooting whatever birds I required. As for killing, this was nothing new to me, but at the worst I had not since my schooldays shot any wild creature for sport or food; nor had I taken part as a combatant in the war. Once on a farm in England I shot dead a horse which had broken its leg because the owner, a young woman, lacked the will to face this act of mercy. And the look she gave me as she thanked me seemed to recognise me as a killer. Here in Van Zyl's marshlands, alone, I had time enough for thought. And perversely I came back to the idea I had the first morning in the lookout, that the presence of Kiep was somehow touching off submerged feelings in me. I tried to dismiss this as illusion and was soon so busy with observations that I thought little more of it.

The boy was back at the camp when I returned and had brought the saddle-bags packed with supplies from Mrs Slabbert, the housekeeper. Kiep came in soon afterwards and produced from his bag four small birds he had trapped and carefully trussed. Two were sand-plovers, one a sandpiper and the last, surprisingly enough, a kingfisher. He held them in his short deft hands, one by one, while I measured and ringed them, and then he took them back to the reeds to be set free. I found a sense of relief in myself that the birds were not species I especially wanted to collect, but this only postponed the decision I must make. He said nothing during our work and only once I noticed his eyes on me while I examined the sandpiper. He looked away and after a moment told me he had seen a large flock of Little Stints, but they kept away from the net.

I was alone in the lookout the next morning early while Kiep and the boy struck southwards along the shoreline to set the net again. As the daylight came in and was greeted with such tokens of rapture by the bird population all around me, seen and unseen, I could not help but share in this age-old feeling of buoyancy, the celebration of life at the passing of darkness. Maybe it is fated after all that bird-life, reflecting nature, will survive to continue into eternity the daily ceremony of renewal long after men have returned into the mud through their own hubris. A more sober strain of thought, dredged up from science, came to my rescue as I brought the scene detail by detail into the lens of the camera viewfinder. Long periods of waiting and inaction for a few seconds of filming; missed chances, sudden gifts of pure luck. A small flock of stilts poised on their long red legs in a delicate frieze, a quadrille of sandpipers combining dance and flight in a pattern of pure ecstasy! And yet there was not the slightest evidence that a bird's song or movements expressed anything beyond a reflex of instinct frozen into aeons of fixed behaviour. Only the presence of man brought these natural creatures to conscious life, lent them beauty and shed around them the aura of emotion.

The boy reached me at midday to tell me where Kiep was trapping. Now there were large flocks of strandlopertjies, many kinds, the smallest ones too, he said. So far none had fallen into the net. I sent him off to the camp to boil up a stew. As he left I called in an afterthought – 'When you come back bring the gun, and the cartridge-belt. Be careful with them … and you can fill my coffee flask.'

'Ja, my baas.'

The sun moved over and began to sink. The boy was taking a long time with his cooking, I thought. It was becoming uncomfortably hot and close in the shelter. This was a time, however, when an unaccountable restlessness seized on the birds. They had fed long hours in the sun and now they began flying up in formations, settling and then away again, turning and flashing against the blue of the sky. Pelicans on an island had their wings raised half open to sun or maybe to dry out after a fishing expedition. A flock of at least a hundred Little Stints alighted as if from nowhere, raced forward, paused with heads up and suddenly were away, evaporated into nothing.

I turned from sighting this graceful little interlude and found Kiep had come, without making a sound, to the entrance of the lookout. He opened his bag to show me his catch and there among the heads of the birds staring at me with resigned unwinking eyes as if death were already upon them, was that of a Little Stint. I could not be mistaken.

'Take them to the camp, Kiep. I'll be along too. I was waiting for the boy to bring the gun, but it's getting late. If you are there first tell him to stay put.'

'Ja, my …' he paused. He was turning to go, and at that moment there was the boom of the shotgun, near and startling. A roll of echoing soundwaves was dying when the air was pierced with an agonised high scream … long-drawn, ending in a sob. And the shrilling of birds lifting off everywhere.

Kiep dropped his bag and net and was gone. I followed, crashing after him through the dense water-plants. We found the boy moaning and rocking his head. He was curled up in a convulsive knot on the ground near the edge of the reeds gripping one ankle with both hands. The gun had gone off and blasted a ragged wound in his bare foot.

We stanched the bloodflow and bandaged the wound with pads and strips of shirting. We carried the boy, still sobbing and moaning, back to the camp. When I went back for my things I found the shotgun had been loaded in both barrels and the safety-catch pushed down into the 'fire' position. Standing or walking with the gun dangled at his side he had accidentally caught the back trigger. I found Kiep's bag and set the trapped birds free.

The sun was sinking beyond the western limits of the marshlands by the time we started on our way to the farmhouse. Kiep led the horse by the reins, his bundle tied across his back, and I walked alongside to keep the boy from falling off. Thousands of birds were homing through the fading light to roost for the night in the marshes, in reed beds and sedges, on islands, rocks, in every conceivable refuge. Flights of white cattle egrets, ibis, cormorants in dark wedge lines, plovers, avocets, gulls, herons – I had hardly the will to glance up at them. The specimen box containing only the one ringed Stint was tied behind the saddle and bobbed on the horse's rump. It was soon pitch dark and by the faint starlight I could barely make out Kiep's small shape going on ahead between crouching bushes.

ALAN PATON

A Drink in the Passage

From: *Debbie Go Home* (1961)

In the year 1960 the Union of South Africa celebrated its Golden Jubilee, and there was a nation-wide sensation when the one-thousand-pound prize for the finest piece of sculpture was won by a black man, Edward Simelane. His work, 'African Mother and Child', not only excited the admiration, but touched the conscience or heart or whatever it is, of white South Africa, and was likely to make him famous in other countries.

It was by an oversight that his work was accepted, for it was the policy of the Government that all the celebrations and competitions should be strictly segregated. The committee of the sculpture section received a private reprimand for having been so careless as to omit the words 'for whites only' from the conditions, but was told, by a very high personage it is said, that if Simelane's work was indisputably the best, it should receive the award. The committee then decided that this prize must be given along with the others, at the public ceremony which would bring this particular part of the celebrations to a close.

For this decision it received a surprising amount of support from the white public, but in certain powerful quarters there was an outcry against any departure from the 'traditional policies' of the country, and a threat that many white prize-winners would renounce their prizes. However, a crisis was averted, because the sculptor was 'unfortunately unable to attend the ceremony'.

'I wasn't feeling up to it,' Simelane said mischievously to me. 'My parents, and my wife's parents, and our priest, decided that I wasn't feeling up to it. And finally I decided so too. Of course Majosi and Sola and the others wanted me to go and get my prize personally, but I said, "Boys, I'm a sculptor, not a demonstrator."'

'This cognac is wonderful,' he said, 'especially in these big glasses. It's the first time I've had such a glass. It's also the first time I've drunk a brandy so slowly. In Orlando you develop a throat of iron, and you just put back your head and pour it down, in case the police should arrive.'

He said to me, 'This is the second cognac I've had in my life. Would you like to hear the story of how I had my first?'

You know the Alabaster Bookshop in Von Brandis Street? Well, after the competition they asked me if they could exhibit my 'African Mother and Child'. They gave a whole window to it, with a white velvet backdrop, if there is anything called white velvet, and some complimentary words, '*Black man conquers white world.*'

Well somehow I could never go and look in that window. On my way from the station to the *Herald* office, I sometimes went past there, and I felt good when I saw all the people standing there, but I would only squint at it out of the corner of my eye.

Then one night I was working late at the *Herald*, and when I came out there was hardly anyone in the streets, so I thought I'd go and see the window, and indulge certain pleasurable human feelings. I must have got a little lost in the contemplation of my own genius, because suddenly there was a young white man standing next to me.

He said to me, 'What do you think of that, mate?' And you know, one doesn't get called 'mate' every day.

'I'm looking at it,' I said.

'I live near here,' he said, 'and I come and look at it nearly every night. You know it's by one of your own boys, don't you? See, Edward Simelane.'

'Yes, I know.'

'It's beautiful,' he said. 'Look at that mother's head. She's loving that child, but she's somehow watching too. Do you see that? Like someone guarding. She knows it won't be an easy life.'

He cocked his head on one side, to see the thing better.

'He got a thousand pounds for it,' he said.

'That's a lot of money for one of your boys. But good luck to him. You don't get much luck, do you?'

Then he said confidentially, 'Mate, would you like a drink?'

Well honestly I didn't feel like a drink at that time of night, with a white stranger and all, and me still with a train to catch to Orlando.

'You know we black people must be out of the city by eleven,' I said.

'It won't take long. My flat's just round the corner. Do you speak Afrikaans?'

'Since I was a child,' I said in Afrikaans.

'We'll speak Afrikaans then. My English isn't too wonderful. I'm Van Rensburg. And you?'

I couldn't have told him my name. I said I was Vakalisa, living in Orlando.

'Vakalisa, eh? I haven't heard that name before.'

By this time he had started off, and I was following, but not willingly. That's my trouble, as you'll soon see. I can't break off an encounter. We didn't exactly walk abreast, but he didn't exactly walk in front of me. He didn't look constrained. He wasn't looking round to see if anyone might be watching.

He said to me, 'Do you know what I wanted to do?'

'No,' I said.

'I wanted a bookshop, like that one there. I always wanted that, ever since I can remember. When I was small, I had a little shop of my own.' He laughed at himself. 'Some were real books, of course, but some of them I wrote myself. But I had bad luck. My parents died before I could finish school.'

Then he said to me, 'Are you educated?'

I said unwillingly, 'Yes.' Then I thought to myself how stupid, for leaving the question open.

And sure enough he asked, 'Far?'

And again unwillingly, I said, 'Far.'

He took a big leap and said, 'Degree?'

'Yes.'

'Literature?'

'Yes.'

He expelled his breath, and gave a long 'Ah'. We had reached his building, Majorca Mansions, not one of those luxurious places. I was glad to see that the entrance lobby was deserted. I wasn't at my ease. I don't feel at my ease in such places, not unless I am protected by friends, and this man was a stranger. The lift was at ground level, marked 'Whites only. Slegs vir Blankes'. Van Rensburg opened the door and waved me in. Was he constrained? To this day I don't know. While I was waiting for him to press the button, so that we could get moving and away from that ground floor, he stood with his finger suspended over it, and looked at me with a kind of honest, unselfish envy.

'You were lucky,' he said. 'Literature, that's what I wanted to do.'

He shook his head and pressed the button, and he didn't speak again until we stopped high up. But before we got out he said suddenly, 'If I had had a bookshop, I'd have given that boy a window too.'

We got out and walked along one of those polished concrete passageways, I suppose you could call it a stoep if it weren't so high up; let's call it a passage. On the one side was a wall, and plenty of fresh air, and far down below, Von Brandis Street. On the other side were the doors, impersonal doors; you could hear radios and people talking, but there wasn't a soul in sight. I wouldn't like living so high; we Africans like being close to the earth. Van Rensburg stopped at one of the doors, and said to me, 'I won't be a minute.' Then he went in, leaving the door open, and inside I could hear voices. I thought to myself, he's telling them who's here. Then after a minute or so, he came back to the door, holding two glasses of red wine. He was warm and smiling.

'Sorry there's no brandy,' he said. 'Only wine. Here's happiness.'

Now I certainly had not expected that I would have my drink in the passage. I wasn't only feeling what you may be thinking. I was thinking that one of the impersonal doors might open at any moment, and someone might see me in a 'white' building, and see me and Van Rensburg breaking the liquor laws of the country. Anger could have saved me from the whole embarrassing situation, but you know I can't easily be angry. Even if I could have been, I might have found it hard to be angry with this particular man. But I wanted to get away from there, and I couldn't. My mother used to say to me, when I had said something anti-white, 'Son, don't talk like that, talk as you are.' She would have understood at once why I took a drink from a man who gave it to me in the passage.

Van Rensburg said to me, 'Don't you know this fellow Simelane?'

'I've heard of him,' I said.

'I'd like to meet him,' he said. 'I'd like to talk to him.' He added in expla-nation, 'You know, talk out my heart to him.'

A woman of about fifty years of age came from the room beyond, bring-ing a plate of biscuits. She smiled and bowed to me. I took one of the biscuits, but not for all the money in the world could I have said to her 'Dankie, my nooi,' or that disgusting 'Dankie, missus,' nor did I want to speak to her in English because her language was Afrikaans, so I took the risk of it and used the word 'mevrou' for the politeness of which some Afrikaners would knock a black man down, and I said, in high Afrikaans, with a smile and a bow too, 'Ek is u dankbaar, mevrou.'

But nobody knocked me down. The woman smiled and bowed, and Van Rensburg, in a strained voice that suddenly came out of nowhere, said, 'Our land is beautiful. But it breaks my heart.'

The woman put her hand on his arm, and said, 'Jannie, Jannie.'

Then another woman and a man, all about the same age, came up and stood behind Van Rensburg.

'He's a BA,' Van Rensburg told them. 'What do you think of that?' The first woman smiled and bowed to me again, and Van Rensburg said, as though it were a matter for grief, 'I wanted to give him brandy, but there's only wine.'

The second woman said, 'I remember, Jannie. Come with me.'

She went back into the room, and he followed her. The first woman said to me, 'Jannie's a good man. Strange, but good.'

And I thought the whole thing was mad, and getting beyond me, with me a black stranger being shown a testimonial for the son of the house, with these white strangers standing and looking at me in the passage, as though they wanted for God's sake to touch me somewhere and didn't know how, but I saw the earnestness of the woman who had smiled and bowed to me, and I said to her, 'I can see that, mevrou.'

'He goes down every night to look at the statue,' she said. 'He says only God could make something so beautiful, therefore God must be in the man who made it, and he wants to meet him and talk out his heart to him.'

She looked back at the room, and then she dropped her voice a little, and said to me, 'Can't you see, it's somehow because it's a black woman and a black child?'

And I said to her, 'I can see that, mevrou.'

She turned to the man and said of me, 'He's a good boy.'

Then the other woman returned with Van Rensburg, and Van Rensburg had a bottle of brandy. He was smiling and pleased, and he said to me, 'This isn't ordinary brandy, it's French.'

He showed me the bottle, and I, wanting to get the hell out of that place, looked at it and saw it was cognac. He turned to the man and said, 'Uncle, you remember? When you were ill? The doctor said you must have good brandy. And the man at the bottle-store said this was the best brandy in the world.'

'I must go,' I said. 'I must catch that train.'

'I'll take you to the station,' he said. 'Don't you worry about that.' He poured me a drink and one for himself.

'Uncle,' he said, 'what about one for yourself?'

The older man said, 'I don't mind if I do,' and he went inside to get himself a glass.

Van Rensburg said, 'Happiness,' and lifted his glass to me. It was good brandy, the best I've ever tasted. But I wanted to get the hell out of there. I stood in the passage and drank Van Rensburg's brandy. Then Uncle came back with his glass, and Van Rensburg poured him a brandy, and Uncle raised his glass to me too. All of us were full of goodwill, but I was waiting for the opening of one of the impersonal doors. Perhaps they were too, I don't know. Perhaps when you want so badly to touch someone you don't care. I was drinking my brandy almost as fast as I would have drunk it in Orlando.

'I must go,' I said.

Van Rensburg said, 'I'll take you to the station.' He finished his brandy, and I finished mine too. We handed the glasses to Uncle, who said to me, 'Good night, my boy.' The first woman said, 'May God bless you,' and the other woman bowed and smiled. Then Van Rensburg and I went down in the lift to the basement, and got into his car.

'I told you I'd take you to the station,' he said. 'I'd take you home, but I'm frightened of Orlando at night.'

We drove up Eloff Street, and he said, 'Did you know what I meant?' I knew that he wanted an answer to something, and I wanted to answer him, but I couldn't, because I didn't know what that something was. He couldn't be talking about being frightened of Orlando at night, because what more could one mean than just that?

'By what?' I asked.

'You know,' he said, 'about our land being beautiful?'

Yes, I knew what he meant, and I knew that for God's sake he wanted to touch me too and he couldn't; for his eyes had been blinded by years in the dark. And I thought it was a pity, for if men never touch each other, they'll hurt each other one day. And it was a pity he was blind, and couldn't touch me, for black men don't touch white men any more; only by accident, when they make something like 'Mother and Child'.

He said to me, 'What are you thinking?'

I said, 'Many things,' and my inarticulateness distressed me, for I knew he wanted something from me. I felt him fall back, angry, hurt, despairing, I didn't know. He stopped at the main entrance to the station, but I didn't tell him I couldn't go in there. I got out and said to him, 'Thank you for the sociable evening.'

'They liked having you,' he said. 'Did you see that they did?'

I said, 'Yes, I saw that they did.'

He sat slumped in his seat, like a man with a burden of incomprehensible, insoluble grief. I wanted to touch him, but I was thinking about the train. He said good night, and I said it too. We each saluted the other. What he was think-ing, God knows, but I was thinking he was like a man trying to run a race in iron shoes, and not understanding why he cannot move.

When I got back to Orlando, I told my wife the story, and she wept.

ALAN PATON

The Quarry

First pubished, 1967

Everywhere the city was driving back nature, to the south and the west and the north. Only the east was safe, for there lay the ocean. Skyscrapers stood on the places where elephants had crashed through the forest. Hippopotamus Pool was a city square full of the smells of buses, Lions' River ran down a straight concrete channel into the Bay.

Only Mitchell's Quarry had resisted the march of the city. It was a stony scar cut out of the side of Pigeon Hill, and though it was ugly it was a piece of nature. The large green pigeons had long since gone, but small birds and animals still clung to it, and lived in the trees and grass that ran down each side of the scar. Frogs and very small fish lived in the pools. Children were attracted there, for it was the only bit of wildness in the city.

It was Johnny Day's favourite place. Sometimes he sat by the pools for hours, watching the fish. Sometimes he climbed up through the trees, and sat on the very edge of the quarry, in the cool exciting wind from the dancing ocean. He more than once wondered whether anyone could climb down, but Tom Hesketh, who was sixteen and very manly, told him it was impossible, and had never been done, and never would be done unless one came down on a rope. One could climb up from the bottom and Tom had done it once with two of his friends.

'Which way did you take, Tom?'

'I'm not telling you,' said Tom, 'it's not for kids. Can't you see the notice?'

The notice said, 'No Climbing, By Order', only whose order it was, no one knew.

'And I'm not doing it again,' said Tom, 'because when I was half-way up, all I wanted to do was to come down again, and I couldn't.'

Sitting by one of the pools, Johnny looked at the quarry face, wondering which way Tom had taken. All he knew was that Tom had begun by the notice-board 'No Climbing, By Order', and that is where he would begin too, on the day after Christmas Day. He would climb in a direction half-right, where it seemed there was a track of footholds made for just such a purpose. Half-way up the quarry face the track seemed to peter out, but another track bearing half-left could be seen some feet higher. All that he must do was to find the way from one to the other.

On the morning of the day after Christmas Day Johnny arrived at the quarry and found nobody there. Confident of success he took off his jacket and cap, and laid them on a stone under the noticeboard. He was wearing sandshoes, because that was what Tom Hesketh had worn. He looked up at the quarry face which was roughly a perpendicular plane. He placed his right foot in a niche that seemed to have been made for it. He drew his left foot up and now stood about a foot above the level floor and the pools. The climb had begun, and the feeling of the climber was not nervousness but pure ambition, strong in one so young, for he was only twelve.

It certainly seemed that the track had been cut deliberately, perhaps to enable the quarry workers to climb the face. There was always a place for the foot, and the rock face inclined away from him a few degrees from the perpendicular, so that he had a feeling of security. There was no need so far for skill or ingenuity, for the method was simple – a hold with the hands, right foot up, left foot up, an inching forward on the same small ledge if possible, a searching for another hold with the hands and another small ledge for the right foot. He was about twenty feet up, and could see that he could return safely, if it was necessary. He looked down, and this gave him a feeling of exhilaration. He looked up, but decided not to do it again, because it seemed to reveal his own insignificance against the vast wall of the quarry, and above that the vast emptiness of the sky. From now on he would confine his attention to the handhold, the foothold and the rock face that so obligingly allowed him to lean against it.

The track continued as before for a short distance and he was at a height of about thirty feet when he reached a place where the rock face became suddenly perpendicular for a length of some three feet, so that he would not be able to lean against it. He wondered if he could take a step direct from safety to safety, but knew that the step would be too big for him. His only hope was a good hold for hands and feet. He was the slightest bit nervous, because he knew something else too, that if he decided to take the next two steps it would be twice as hard to return.

Tom Hesketh had said to him, 'If you're frightened to take the next step, don't take it, just climb down, if you can. If you can't climb down, then you've got to take the next step, that's all. And I can tell you, kid, it's dangerous getting frightened up there.'

Well, he might be a bit nervous but he wasn't climbing down. He could see the trail clearly, and it looked easy except for this one next step. There was a place for the hands and a place for the right foot, just as good as any he had used so far.

Someone shouted at him from below. It was a big Indian man who was shouting with some Indian boys.

'Come down, sonny,' shouted the big Indian man.

Johnny shook his head. Without looking he pointed at the sky. The big Indian man shook his head too.

'No, no,' he shouted. 'It's too dangerous, sonny. Come down.'

Again Johnny shook his head, and pointed up. The Indian man tried warnings.

'Last year,' he shouted, 'an Indian boy was killed here. He was climbing the same way you are climbing now.' This wasn't true. There never had been such an Indian boy, but the Indian man believed that if the end was good, one shouldn't worry too much about the means. When the warnings failed, he invoked Divine aid.

'God sent me here,' he shouted, 'to tell you to come down. He is telling you now to come down. He does not mean for you to be up there. If you don't come down, He will be plenty angry.' He added a clever afterthought. 'Just like He was angry with that Indian boy.'

'Don't let anything take your mind off your hands and feet,' said Tom, 'or off the rock face. Don't think of the height, or of the spectators. Don't look at birds or ships on the sea. Just think of the climb.'

That is what Johnny did. To the despair of the big Indian man, and the admiration of the Indian boys, be addressed himself to the task of finding a place for his right hand and a place for his right foot, and when he had found them, he took the dangerous step. It was done. The ledge was generous, and he brought up his left foot. Tom's instruction was immediately forgotten, and he looked down at the growing crowd of Indian men and women and boys and girls, and African men from the factory near the quarry.

The big Indian man shouted at him again to come down, and it was this very shouting that brought Tom's instruction back to Johnny's mind, so that the louder and more desperate the warnings and the threats, the less he paid attention to them. He took his next step with confidence, and the trail before him was now straightforward and easy for at least seven steps. Then it stopped dead. He braced himself to look up, and there, about ten or twelve feet above him, he could see the second trail that ran half-left, and would take him to the top. He could see almost at once that he could go no further in a half-right direction, that he would have to climb straight up. He could also see toeholds for the first five feet, for that was his own height. It would all depend whether there were handholds also, and that he would have to tell by feeling for them, partly because he was apprehensive about looking up, and partly because the rock face seemed to be nearer the perpendicular when one thought of climbing it perpendicularly.

These thoughts and speculations took him some minutes, so that the crowd below knew that he was facing some kind of crisis. He was nearly fifty feet up, about one-third of the height of the quarry face. There were now a hundred people watching him, talking to each other, but not loudly, because they were subdued by contemplation of the dangers that lay ahead. The boys were filled with admiration and awe, and the women with tender feeling and care. It was a white boy, it is true, but there in the danger and excitement of his journey up the quarry face he had become one of their own. The boys wished him luck and the women shook their heads, unable to be indifferent to either his naughtiness or his plight.

Johnny lifted his right foot to make the first step of the ascent, and this action put the big Indian man into a panic.

'Sonny,' he cried, 'true's God, don't go up any more. You'll die, sonny, and no one here wants you to die. Sonny, I ask you to come down.' He went down on his knees on the quarry floor, and said, 'I pray God to make you come down. I pray God not to be angry with you.' The women there, both Indian and African, seeing him kneeling there, cried out, 'Shame,' but not because they thought his action was shameful, they were merely saying how sad the whole thing was.

The Indian man was now struck by a new idea, and he shouted, 'Sonny, what's your address?' Johnny heard him but he tried to pay no attention, needing it all for the dangerous piece ahead. However, the question disturbed him slightly, and he brought his right foot down again, causing the crowd to give a composite groan, with many meanings. The Indian man took it as a reprieve, and shouted, 'Sonny, I pray to God, give me your address.'

It was now clear to all but his would-be rescuer that the small boy intended to continue the climb. His small exploratory movements showed that he meant to go up, not down. Again he placed his right foot, but this time he pulled himself up, causing the Indian man to rise from his knees and to collapse groaning onto a rock with his hands covering his eyes. So was silenced his vocal opposition to the climb, but the rest were quiet too, speaking in low voices, even whispers, as Johnny placed his hands and his foot, and pulled himself up, two feet now above the safety of the sloping trail. Then again the hands exploring, the right foot testing, the body bracing, the small boy like a fly on a cinema screen, except that he was no intruder, rather the creator of a drama never before witnessed in this city, of a crowd of every colour and class and tongue, bound all of them together for these moments by unbreakable bonds, to a small white boy climbing a quarry face made of a stone that knew nothing of admiration or anxiety or pity. And again a step, and again the low talking, and again the exploring hands and the testing foot, and again the bracing of the body. And down below silence, and silent prayers, and silent apprehension. The Indian man took his hands from his eyes, and watched despairingly; it was clear he was in an agony of care and pity over this child of an alien race, many of whose members had shown neither care nor pity for himself or his people. And up above again the winning of another step, again the murmur from below, from a crowd groaning every moment, swollen by people streaming over the waste ground between the quarry and the tarred road. There they stood, shoulder to shoulder, ruler and ruled, richer and poorer, white and black and yellow and brown, with their eyes fixed on a small piece of whiteness half-way up the quarry face, and those of them who knew a thing or two knew that the boy was in a position of considerable danger.

Fortunately Johnny himself did not know it. He was surprised that his right hand searching above his head had found another generous ledge, at least nine inches wide. Once he had reached it, he would be able to rest, even perhaps to look upward to plan the last piece of climbing that would enable him to reach the half-left trail. Therefore he set out to reach it, alternately terrifying and gratifying the watching crowd below.

The crowd did not realise the achievement when at last Johnny's feet were both planted on the nine-inch ledge. He himself decided not only to rest, but to allow his attention to be diverted from the climb. The ledge was so wide that he could turn himself about for the first time, stand with his back to the quarry face, and look down on the hundreds of people below. Some of them clapped and cheered him, some of them looked at him out of troubled eyes. The big Indian man stood up from the rock onto which he had collapsed, and called out, in a less assured voice than hitherto, for the small boy to come down, but after another man had spoken quietly to him, he desisted and it was generally understood that the second man had told him that the small boy had reached a point of no return, and it were better to leave him alone, and to pray rather for his salvation.

For three minutes, four minutes, it must have been, Johnny stood with his back to the quarry face. After acknowledging the crowd's cheers, he had cut them off from attention, and stood there reassembling his small boy's powers. Everything was silent when again he turned his face to the quarry wall. The foothold was there, the handhold for the left hand was there, but of handhold for the right hand there was no sign whatsoever. At first he could not believe it, but when he tried again he knew there was no doubt of it. Had the hand-hold been perpendicularly above the toehold he might have done it, but it was at least a foot to the left of his body line. No one could pull himself up from such a position.

A growl went up from the crowd, of defeat and frustration, and from the more knowledgeable, of sharpened anxiety. Again the questing hands, again the finding of nothing. The small boy, leaving his two arms in this upstretched position, put his face to the face of the quarry, almost as if he were weeping or praying, which indeed is what some thought he was doing. He brought down his arms and caused the crowd to groan and shudder as his left foot explored the rock below him, trying to find the foothold he had used to reach the ledge.

In complete silence they watched him put his foot on it, but after a moment he withdrew and again laid his face against the face of the quarry. It was then clear that his ambition to climb had gone, and in its place was the frightenedness of a small boy. Again he turned himself round so that he faced the crowd, who could see clearly his loneliness and despair. His movements, so splendidly co-ordinated until now, gave alarming signs of randomness, and for one terrible moment it seemed that he might panic and fall.

This was the signal for a young African man of about twenty to take charge.

'Hi, sonny,' he shouted, waving with outstretched arm to the small boy, 'don't be frightened. Thomas Ndhlovu is coming.'

On his way to the starting-point by the noticeboard, Thomas spoke to a white man who seemed to be senior to the others.

'Get the police, master, or the fire brigade. I go up to stay with the small boy.'

Then he started his climb, amid a new noise of laughs, cheers, approval, and advice. Thomas soon showed himself to be vigorous and unskilled, and his friends below, who had been so anxious about the first climber, made jokes about the second. As for Thomas himself, whenever he had brought off what he thought a piece of good climbing, he would turn to the crowd and raise his clenched fist, to be greeted by cheers and laughter. Every few steps he would shout at the small boy, urging him to be of good heart, because one Thomas Ndhlovu was coming. The small boy himself had recovered from his panic and watched absorbedly the progress of his saviour. What had been a tense and ter-rifying affair had become a kind of festival. Jests and laughter had replaced groans and sighs, and Thomas, with intention somewhat foolish, climbed flam-boyantly and wildly, shouting encouragement in English to the small boy and exchanging banter in Zulu with his friends on the ground. It was only when he reached the end of the first trail, and began to inspect the sharp perpendi-cular ascent that the crowd again fell silent.

Thomas however would not tolerate this new respect. Turning round he shouted something at his friends that caused much laughter. He too made the exploratory motions of hands and it was very clear that he was caricaturing the small boy's motions. Nevertheless the laughter died away as he began the ascent and the atmosphere was tense, without being fearful. When at last he placed his foot on the nine-inch ledge, rulers and ruled, richer and poorer, joined in an ovation of shouting and clapping, which was doubled and redoubled when he too turned to face the crowd. He smiled down at the small white boy and put his hand on his shoulder, as if to assure him that no one fell from a ledge when Thomas Ndhlovu was on it.

'Now be quiet,' he said, 'some time the police come, and the fire brigade, and you go home to your mother.'

The small boy said, 'Thanks a million,' and Thomas said, 'What your mother say?'

'I won't tell my mother,' said Johnny.

Thomas laughed uproariously, and pointed at the crowd below, where newspapermen were taking photographs and interviewing spectators.

426

'Tomorrow,' said Thomas, 'big picture in paper, you and me. Your mother open paper, she say, what you doing there with that native boy?'

He thought this very funny, and for a time occupied himself with it. Then he asked, 'What's your name, sonny?'

'Johnny Day.'

'Johnny Day, eh? Very good name. My name Thomas Ndhlovu.'

'Very good name too,' said Johnny.

'Police coming,' said Thomas pointing. 'When police coming other times, Thomas running. Now police coming, Thomas staying.'

The arrival of the police was greeted with great good humour, for here was an occasion on which their arrival was welcome. Words in Zulu were shouted at them, compliments tinged with satire, for the crowd was feeling happy and free. The policemen grasped the whole situation immediately. Two of them, armed with ropes, set off up through the trees that grew at the side of the quarry and in a few minutes had reached the upper edge, where they took up a position directly above the man and the boy. Instructions were shouted and a rope was lowered to Thomas, who, once he had the cradle-like end in his hand, laughed with uproarious delight. To the end of this rope was attached another which Thomas threw to the policemen below. More instructions were shouted and Thomas soon had the small boy in the cradle. The policemen above lowered the cradle down the quarry wall. The policemen below held it away from the stony face. In one minute Johnny was on the quarry floor, lost to sight in a swirling multicoloured mass, shouting their joy and congratulation. This celebration was still in progress as Thomas Ndhlovu landed on the quarry floor, when it transferred itself to him. Everybody, white, yellow, brown, black, wanted to shake hands with him, to thank him for his splendid act, to ask God to bless him. The Indian man, now fully restored, was one of the most enthusiastic of these participators.

'Come, sonny,' said the senior white man. 'Tell me where you live and I'll take you home.'

'I must thank Thomas first,' said Johnny.

The senior white man looked at the tumultuous scene. 'How are you going to do that?' he said.

'I'll wait,' said Johnny.

But he did not need to wait. The policemen cleared a way through the mob of congratulators, and there, under the eyes of authority, Johnny Day put out his hand and thanked Thomas Ndhlovu again for the act which, for all we know, saved his life. This second evidence of gratitude was extremely pleasurable to Thomas and, moved to great heights by it, he led the small white boy to the noticeboard which said, 'No Climbing, By Order'. What he said, no one heard, for it was lost in an outburst of catcalls, laughter, jeering and cheering.

427

ALEX LA GUMA

A Matter of Taste

From: *A Walk in the Night: Seven Stories from the Streets of Cape Town* (1962)

The sun hung well towards the west now so that the thin clouds above the ragged horizon were rimmed with bright yellow like the spilt yolk of an egg. Chinaboy stood up from having blown the fire under the round tin and said, 'She ought to boil now.' The tin stood precariously balanced on two half-bricks and a smooth stone. We had built the fire carefully in order to brew some coffee and now watched the water in the tin with the interest of women at a childbirth.

'There she is,' Chinaboy said as the surface broke into bubbles. He waited for the water to boil up and then drew a small crushed packet from the side pocket of his shredded windbreaker, untwisted its mouth and carefully tapped raw coffee into the tin.

He was a short man with grey-flecked kinky hair, and a wide, quiet, heavy face that had a look of patience about it, as if he had grown accustomed to doing things slowly and carefully and correctly. But his eyes were dark oriental ovals, restless as a pair of cockroaches. 'We'll let her draw a while,' he advised. He put the packet away and produced an old rag from another pocket, wrapped it around a hand and gingerly lifted the tin from the fire, placing it carefully in the sand near the bricks.

We had just finished a job for the railways and were camped out a few yards from the embankment and some distance from the ruins of a one-time siding. The corrugated iron of the office still stood, gaping in places and covered with rust and cobwebs. Passers had fouled the roofless interior and the platform was crumbled in places and overgrown with weeds. The cement curbing still stood, but cracked and covered with the disintegration like a welcome notice to a ghost town. Chinaboy got out the scoured condensed-milk tins we used for cups and set them up. I sat on an old sleeper and waited for the ceremony of pouring the coffee to commence.

It didn't start right then because Chinaboy was crouching with his rag-wrapped hand poised over the can, about to pick it up, but he wasn't making a move. Just sitting like that and watching something beyond us.

The Port Jackson bush and wattle crackled and rustled behind me and the long shadow of a man fell across the small clearing. I looked back and up. He had come out of the plantation and was thin and short and had a pale white face covered with a fine golden stubble. Dirt lay in dark lines in the creases around his mouth and under his eyes and in his neck, and his hair was ragged and thick and uncut, falling back to his neck and around his temples. He wore an old pair of jeans, faded and dirty and turned up at the bottoms, and a torn leather coat.

He stood on the edge of the clearing, waiting hesitantly, glancing from me to Chinaboy, and then back at me. He ran the back of a grimy hand across his mouth.

Then he said hesitantly: 'I smelled the coffee. Hope you don' min'.'

'Well,' Chinaboy said with that quiet careful smile of his. 'Seeing you's here, I reckon I don' min' either.' He smiled at me, 'You think we can take in a table boarder, pal?'

'Reckon we can spare some of the turkey and green peas.'

Chinaboy nodded at the stranger. 'Sit, pally. We were just going to have supper.'

The white boy grinned a little embarrassedly and came around the sleeper and shoved a rock over with a scarred boot and straddled it. He didn't say anything, but watched as Chinaboy set out another scoured milk tin and lifted the can from the fire and poured the coffee into the cups.

'Help yourself, man. Isn't exactly the mayor's garden party.' The boy took his cup carefully and blew at the steam. Chinaboy sipped noisily and said, 'Should've had some bake bread. Nothing like a piece of bake bread with cawfee.'

'Hot dogs,' the white boy said. 'Huh.'

'Hot dogs. Hot dogs go with coffee.'

'Ooh ja. I heard,' Chinaboy grinned. Then he asked: 'You going somewhere, Whitey?'

'Cape Town. Maybe get a job on a ship an' make the States.'

'Lots of people want to reach the States,' I said.

Whitey drank some coffee and said: 'Yes, I heard of money and plenty to eat.'

'Talking about eating,' Chinaboy said, 'I see a picture in a book, one time. 'Merican book. This picture was about food over there. A whole mess of fried chicken, mealies – what they call corn – with mushrooms an' gravy, chips and new green peas. All done up in colours, too.'

'Pass me the roast lamb,' I said sarcastically.

'Man,' Whitey said warming up to the discussion. 'Just let me get to something like that and I'll eat till I burst wide open.'

Chinaboy swallowed some coffee: 'Worked as a waiter one time when I was a youngster. In one of that big caffies. You should've seen what all them bastards ate. Just sitting there shovelling it down. Some French stuff too, patty grass or something like that.'

I said: 'Remember the time we went for drunk and got ten days? We ate mealies and beans till it came out of our ears!'

Chinaboy said, whimsically: 'I'd like to sit down in a smart caffie one day and eat my way right out of a load of turkey, roast potatoes, beet salad and angel's food trifle. With port and cigars at the end.'

'Hell,' said Whitey, 'it's all a matter of taste. Some people like chicken and others eat sheep's heads and beans!'

'A matter of taste,' Chinaboy scowled. 'Bull, it's a matter of money, pal. I worked six months in that caffie and I never heard nobody order sheep's head and beans!'

'You heard of the fellow who went into one of these big caffies?' Whitey asked, whirling the last of his coffee around in the tin cup. 'He sits down at a table and takes out a packet of sandwiches and puts it down. Then he calls the waiter and orders a glass of water. When the waiter brings the water, this fellow says: "Why ain't the band playing?"'

We chuckled over that and Chinaboy almost choked. He coughed and spluttered a little and then said, 'Another John goes into a caffie and orders sausage and mash. When the waiter bring him the stuff he take a look and say: "My dear man, you've brought me a cracked plate." "Hell," says the waiter, "that's no crack. That's the sausage."'

After we had laughed over that one Chinaboy looked westward at the sky. The sun was almost down and the clouds hung like bloodstained rags along the horizon. There was a breeze stirring the wattle and Port Jackson, and far beyond the railway line a dog barked with high yapping sounds.

Chinaboy said: 'There's a empty goods going through here around about seven. We'll help Whitey, here, onto it, so's he can get to Cape Town. Reckon there's still time for some more pork chops and onions.' He grinned at Whitey. 'Soon's we've had dessert we'll walk down the line a little. There's a bend where it's the best place to jump a train. We'll show you.'

He waved elaborately towards me: 'Serve the duck, John!'

I poured the last of the coffee into the tin cups. The fire had died to a small heap of embers. Whitey dug in the pocket of his leather coat and found a crumpled pack of cigarettes. There were just three left and he passed them round. We each took one and Chinaboy lifted the twig from the fire and we lighted up.

'Good cigar, this,' he said, examining the glowing tip of the cigarette. When the coffee and cigarettes were finished, the sun had gone down altogether, and all over the land was swept with dark shadows of a purple hue. The silhouetted tops of the wattle and Port Jackson looked like massed dragons.

We walked along the embankment in the evening, past the ruined siding, the shell of the station house like a huge desecrated tombstone against the sky. Far off we heard the whistle of a train.

430

'This is the place,' Chinaboy said to Whitey. 'It's a long goods and when she takes the turn the engine driver won't see you, and neither the rooker in the guard's van. You got to jump when the engine's out of sight. She'll take the hill slow likely, so you'll have a good chance. Jus' you wait till I say when. Hell, that sound like pouring a drink!' His teeth flashed in the gloom as he grinned. Then Whitey stuck out a hand and Chinaboy shook it, and then I shook it.

'Thanks for supper, boys,' Whitey said.

'Come again, anytime,' I said, 'we'll see we have a tablecloth.' We waited in the Port Jackson growth at the side of the embankment while the goods train wheezed and puffed up the grade, its headlamp cutting a big yellow hole in the dark. We ducked back out of sight as the locomotive went by, hissing and rumbling. The tender followed, then a couple of box-cars, then some coal-cars and a flat-car, another box-car. The locomotive was out of sight.

'Here it is,' Chinaboy said pushing the boy ahead. We stood near the train, hearing it click-clack past. 'Take this coal box coming up,' Chinaboy instructed. 'She's low and empty. Don't miss the grip, now. She's slow. And good luck, pal!'

The coal-car came up and Whitey moved out, watching the iron grip on the far end of it. Then as it drew slowly level with him, he reached out, grabbed and hung on, then got a foothold, moving away from us slowly.

We watched him hanging there, reaching for the edge of the car and hauling himself up. Watching the train clicking away, we saw him straddling the edge of the truck, his hand raised in a salute. We raised our hands too.

'Why ain't the band playing? Hell!' Chinaboy said.

JAMES MATTHEWS

The Park

First published, 1962
From: *The Park and other Stories* (1974; 1983)

He looked longingly at the children on the other side of the railings; the children sliding down the chute, landing with feet astride on the bouncy lawn; screaming as they almost touched the sky with each upward curve of their swings; their joyful demented shrieks at each dip of the merry-go-round. He looked at them and his body trembled and ached to share their joy; buttocks to fit board, and hands and feet to touch steel. Next to him, on the ground, was a bundle of clothing, washed and ironed, wrapped in a sheet.

Five small boys, pursued by two bigger ones, ran past, ignoring him. One of the bigger boys stopped. 'What are you looking at, you brown ape?' the boy said, stooping to pick up a lump of clay. He recognised him. The boy had been present the day he was put out of the park. The boy pitched the lump, shattering it on the rail above his head, and the fragments fell on his face.

He spat out the particles of clay clinging to the lining of his lips, eyes searching for an object to throw at the boys separated from him by the railing. More boys joined the one in front of him and he was frightened by their number.

Without a word he shook his bundle free of clay, raised it to his head and walked away.

As he walked he recalled his last visit to the park. Without hesitation he had gone through the gates and got onto the nearest swing. Even now he could feel that pleasurable thrill that travelled the length of his body as he rocketed himself higher, higher, until he felt that the swing would up-end him when it reached its peak. Almost leisurely he had allowed it to come to a halt like a pendulum shortening its stroke and then ran towards the see-saw. A white boy, about his own age, was seated opposite him. Accordionlike their legs folded to send the see-saw jerking from the indentation it pounded in the grass. A hand pressed on his shoulder stopping a jerk. He turned around to look into the face of the attendant.

'Get off!'

The skin tightened between his eyes. Why must I get off? What have I done? He held on, hands clamped onto the iron attached to the wooden see-saw. The white boy jumped off from the other end and stood a detached spectator.

'You must get off!' The attendant spoke in a low voice so that it would not carry to the people who were gathering. 'The council say,' he continued, 'that us blacks don't use the same swings as the whites. You must use the swings where you stay,' his voice apologising for the uniform he wore that gave him the right to watch that little white boys and girls were not hurt while playing.

'There no park where I stay.' He waved a hand in the direction of a block of flats. 'Park on the other side of town but I don't know where.' He walked past them. The mothers with their babies, pink and belching, cradled in their arms, the children lolling on the grass, his companion from the see-saw, the nurse girls – their uniforms their badge of indemnity – pushing prams. Beside him walked the attendant.

The attendant pointed an accusing finger at a notice board at the entrance. 'There. You can read for yourself.' Absolving him of all blame.

He struggled with the red letters on the white background. 'Blankes Alleen. Whites Only.' He walked through the gates and behind him the swings screeched, the see-saw rattled, and the merry-go-round rumbled.

He walked past the park each occasion he delivered the washing, eyes wistfully taking in the scene.

He shifted the bundle to a more comfortable position, easing the pain biting into his shoulder muscles. What harm would I be doing if I were to use the swings? Would it stop the swings from swinging? Would the chute collapse? The bundle pressed deeper and the pain became an even line across his shoulders and he had no answer to his reasoning.

The park itself, with its wide lawns and flower beds and rockeries and dwarf trees, meant nothing to him. It was the gaily painted red-and-green tubing, the silver chains and brown boards, transport to never-never land, which gripped him.

Only once, long ago, and then almost as if by mistake, had he been on something to beat it. He had been taken by his father, one of the rare times he was taken anywhere, to a fairground. He had stood captivated by the wooden horses with their gilded reins and scarlet saddles dipping in time to the music as they whirled by.

For a brief moment he was astride one, and he prayed it would last forever, but the moment lasted only the time it took him to whisper the prayer. Then he was standing clutching his father's trousers, watching the others astride the dipping horses.

Another shifting of the bundle and he was at the house where he delivered the clothing his mother had washed in a round tub filled with boiling water, the steam covering her face with a film of sweat. Her voice, when she spoke, was as soft and clinging as the steam enveloping her.

He pushed the gate open and walked around the back watching for the aged lap-dog, which at his entry would rush out to wheeze asthmatically around his feet and nip with blunt teeth at his ankles.

A round-faced African girl, her blackness heightened by the white starched uniform she wore, opened the kitchen door to let him in. She cleared the table and he placed the bundle on it.

'I call madam,' she said, the words spaced and highly pitched as if she had some difficulty in uttering the syllables in English. Her buttocks bounced beneath the tight uniform and the backs of her calves shone with fat.

'Are you sure you've brought everything?' was the greeting he received each time he brought the bundle, and each time she checked every item and as usual nothing was missing. He looked at her and lowered his voice as he said, 'Everything there, merrum.'

What followed had become a routine between the three of them. 'Have you had anything to eat?' she asked him.

He shook his head.

'Well, we can't let you go off like that.' Turning to the African woman in the white, starched uniform. 'What have we got?'

The maid swung open the refrigerator door and took out a plate of food. She placed it on the table and set a glass of milk next to it.

The white woman left the kitchen when he was seated and he was alone with the maid.

His nervousness left him and he could concentrate on what was on the plate.

A handful of peas, a dab of mashed potatoes, a tomato sliced into bleeding circles, a sprinkling of grated carrot, and no rice.

White people are funny, he told himself. How can anyone fill himself with this? It doesn't form a lump like the food my mama makes.

He washed it down with milk.

'Thank you, Annie,' he said as he pushed the glass aside.

Her teeth gleamed porcelain-white as she smiled.

He sat fidgeting, impatient to be outside away from the kitchen with its glossy, tiled floor and steel cupboards ducoed a clinical white to match the food-stacked refrigerator.

'I see you've finished.' The voice startled him. She held out an envelope containing the rand note – payment for his mother's weekly struggle over the washtub. 'This is for you.' A five-cent piece was dropped into his hand, a long fingernail raking his palm.

'Thank you, merrum.' His voice was hardly audible.

'Tell your mother I'm going away on holiday for about a month and I'll let her know when I'm back.'

Then he was dismissed and her high heels tapped out of the kitchen.

He nodded his head at the African maid who took an apple from a bowl bursting with fruit and handed it to him.

He grinned his thanks and her responding smile bathed her face in light. He walked down the path finishing the apple with big bites.

The dog was after him before he reached the gate, its hot breath warming his heels. He turned and poked his toes on its face. It barked hoarsely in protest, a look of outrage on its face.

He laughed delightedly at the expression which changed the dog's features into those of an old man.

'See you do that again.' He waved his feet in front of the pug's nose. The nose retreated and made an about-turn, waddling away with its dignity deflated by his affront.

As he walked, he mentally spent his sixpence.

I'll buy a penny drops, the sour ones that taste like limes, a penny bull's-eyes, a packet of sherbet with the licorice tube at the end of the packet, and a penny star toffees, red ones that turn your spit into blood.

His glands were titillated and his mouth filled with saliva. He stopped at the first shop and walked in.

Trays were filled with expensive chocolates and sweets of a type never seen in the jars on the shelves of the Indian shop on the corner where he stayed. He walked out not buying a thing.

His footsteps lagged as he reached the park.

The nurse girls with their babies and prams were gone, their places occupied by old men, who, with their hands holding up their stomachs, were casting disapproving eyes over the confusion and clatter confronting them.

A ball was kicked perilously close to an old man, and the boy who ran after it stopped short as the old man raised his stick, daring him to come closer.

The rest of them called to the boy to get the ball. He edged closer and made a grab at it as the old man swung his cane. The cane missed the boy by more than a foot and he swaggered back, the ball held under his arm. Their game was resumed.

He watched them from the other side of the railings – the boys kicking the ball, the children cavorting on the grass, even the old men, senile on the seats; but most of all, the children enjoying themselves with what was denied him, and his whole body yearned to be part of them.

'Shit it!' He looked over his shoulder to see if anyone had heard him. 'Shit it!' he said louder. 'Shit on them! Their park, the grass, the swings, the see-saw, everything! Shit it! Shit it!'

His small hands impotently shook the tall railings towering above his head.

It struck him that he would not be seeing the park for a whole month, that there would be no reason for him to pass it.

Despair filled him. He had to do something to ease his anger.

A bag filled with fruit peelings was on top of the rubbish stacked in a waste basket fitted to a pole. He reached for it and frantically threw it over the railings. He ran without waiting to see the result.

Out of breath three streets further, he slowed down, pain stabbing beneath his heart. The act had brought no relief, only intensified the longing.

He was oblivious of the people passing, the hoots of the vehicles whose paths he crossed without thinking. And once, when he was roughly pushed aside, he did not even bother to look and see who had done it.

The familiar shrieks and smells told him that he was home.

The Indian shop could not draw him out of his melancholy mood and he walked past it, his five-cent piece unspent in his pocket.

A group of boys were playing with tyres on the pavement.

Some of them called him but he ignored them and turned into a short side-street.

He mounted the flat stoep of a two-storeyed house with a façade that must once have been painted but had now turned a nondescript grey with the red brick underneath showing.

Beyond the threshold the room was dim. He walked past the scattered furniture with a familiarity that did not need guidance.

His mother was in the kitchen hovering over a pot perched on a pressure stove.

He placed the envelope on the table. She put aside the spoon and stuck a finger under the flap of the envelope, tearing it into half. She placed the rand note in a spoutless teapot on the shelf.

'You hungry?'

He nodded his head.

She poured him a cup of soup and added a thick slice of brown bread. Between bites of bread and sips of soup which scalded his throat, he told his mother that there would not be any washing coming during the week. 'Why? What the matter? What I do?'

'Nothing. Merrum say she go away for month. She let mama know she back.'

'What I do now?' Her voice took on a whine and her eyes strayed to the teapot containing the money. The whine hardened to reproach as she continued. 'Why don't she let me know she going away then I look for another merrum?' She paused. 'I slave away and the pain never leave my back but it too much for her to let me know she go away. The money I get from her keep us nice and steady. How I go cover the hole?'

He wondered how the rand notes he had brought helped to keep them nicely steady. There was no change in their meals. It was, as usual, not enough, and the only time they received new clothes was at Christmas.

'I must pay the burial, and I was going to tell Mr Lemonsky to bring lino for the front room. I'm sick looking at the lino full of holes but I can forget now. With no money you got as much hope as getting wine on Sunday.'

He hurried his eating to get away from the words wafted towards him, before it could soak into him, trapping him in the chair to witness his mother's miseries.

Outside, they were still playing with their tyres. He joined them half-heartedly. As he rolled the tyre his spirit was still in the park on the swings. There was no barrier to his coming and he could do as he pleased. He was away from the narrow streets and squawking children and speeding cars. He was in a place of green grass and red tubing and silver steel. The tyre rolled past him. He made no effort to grab it.

'Get the tyre.' 'You sleep?' 'Don't you want to play anymore?' He walked away ignoring their cries.

Rage boiled up inside him. Rage against the houses with their streaked walls and smashed panes filled by too many people; against the overflowing garbage pails outside doors; the alleys and streets; and against a law he could not understand − a law that shut him out of the park.

He burst into tears. He swept his arms across his cheeks to check his weeping.

He lowered his hands to peer at the boy confronting him.

'I think you cry!'

'Who say I cry? Something in my eye and I rub it.'

He pushed past and continued towards the shop. 'Cry-baby!' the boy's taunt rang after him.

The shop's sole iron-barred window was crowded. Oranges were mixed with writing paper and dried figs were strewn on school slates. Clothing and crockery gathered dust. Across the window a cockroach made its leisurely way, antennae on the alert.

Inside the shop was as crowded as the window. Bags covered the floor leaving a narrow path to the counter.

The shopkeeper, an ancient Indian with a face tanned like cracked leather, leaned across the counter. 'Yes, boy?' He showed teeth scarlet with betel. 'Come'n, boy. What you want? No stand here all day.' His jaws worked at the betel nut held captive by his stained teeth.

He ordered penny portions of his selection.

He transferred the sweets to his pockets and threw the torn containers on the floor and walked out. Behind him the Indian murmured grimly, jaws working faster.

One side of the street was in shadow. He sat with his back against the wall, savouring the last of the sun.

Bull's-eye, peppermint, a piece of licorice − all lumped together in his cheek. For a moment the park was forgotten.

He watched without interest the girl advancing.

'Mama say you must come'n eat.' She stared at his bulging cheek, one hand rubbing the side of her nose. 'Gimme.' He gave her a bull's-eye which she dropped into her mouth between dabs at her nose.

'Wipe your snot!' he ordered her, showing his superiority. He walked past. She followed sucking and sniffing.

Their father was already seated at the table when they entered the kitchen. 'Must I always send somebody after you?' his mother asked.

He slipped into his seat and then hurriedly got up to wash his hands before his mother could find fault with yet another point.

Supper was a silent affair except for the scraping of spoon across a plate and an occasional sniff from his sister.

A thought came to his mind almost at the end of the meal. He sat spoon poised in the air shaken by its magnitude. Why not go to the park after dark? After it had closed its gates on the old men, the children, and nurses with their prams! There would be no one to stop him.

He could think no further. He was lightheaded with the thought of it. His mother's voice, as she related her day to his father, was not the steam that stung, but a soft breeze wafting past him, leaving him undisturbed. Then qualms troubled him. He had never been in that part of town at night. A band of fear tightened across his chest, contracting his insides, making it hard for him to swallow his food. He gripped his spoon tightly, stretching his skin across his knuckles.

I'll do it! I'll go to the park as soon as we're finished eating. He controlled himself with difficulty. He swallowed what was left on his plate and furtively watched to see how the others were faring. Hurry up! Hurry up!

He hastily cleared the table when his father pushed the last plate aside and began washing up.

Each piece of crockery washed was passed to his sister whose sniffing kept pace with their combined operation.

The dishes done, he swept the kitchen and carried out the garbage bin. 'Can I go play, mama?'

'Don't let me have to send for you again.'

His father remained silent, buried behind the newspaper.

'Before you go,' his mother stopped him, 'light the lamp and hang it in the passage.'

He filled the lamp with paraffin, turned up the wick and lit it. The light glimmered weakly through the streaked glass.

The moon, to him, was a fluorescent ball: light without warmth – and the stars, fragments chipped off it. Beneath street lights, card games were in session. He sniffed the nostril-prickling smell of dagga as he walked past. Dim door-ways could not conceal couples clutching at each other.

438

Once clear of the district, he broke into a trot. He did not slacken his pace as he passed through the downtown area with its wonderland shop windows. His elation seeped out as he neared the park and his footsteps dragged.

In front of him was the park with its gate and iron railings. Behind the railings, impaled, the notice board. He could see the swings beyond. The sight strengthened him.

He walked over, his breath coming faster. There was no one in sight. A car turned a corner and came towards him and he started at the sound of its engine. The car swept past, the tyres softly licking the asphalt.

The railings were icy-cold to his touch and the shock sent him into action. He extended his arms and with monkey-like movements pulled himself up to perch on top of the railings then dropped onto the newly turned earth.

The grass was damp with dew and he swept his feet across it. Then he ran and the wet grass bowed beneath his bare feet.

He ran towards the swings, the merry-go-round, see-saw to chute, hands covering the metal.

Up the steps to the top of the chute. He stood outlined against the sky. He was a bird; an eagle. He flung himself down on his stomach, sliding swiftly. Wheeeeeee! He rolled over when he slammed onto the grass. He looked at the moon for an instant then propelled himself to his feet and ran for the steps of the chute to recapture that feeling of flight. Each time he swept down the chute, he wanted the trip never to end, to go on sliding, sliding, sliding.

He walked reluctantly past the see-saw, consoling himself with pushing at one end to send it whacking on the grass.

'Shit it!' he grunted as he strained to set the merry-go-round into action. Thigh tensed, leg stretched, he pushed. The merry-go-round moved. He increased his exertions and jumped on, one leg trailing at the ready to shove if it should slow down. The merry-go-round dipped and swayed. To keep it moving, he had to push more than he rode. Not wanting to spoil his pleasure, he jumped off and raced for the swings.

Feet astride, hands clutching silver chains, he jerked his body to gain momentum. He crouched like a runner then violently straightened. The swing widened its arc. It swept higher, higher, higher. It reached the sky. He could touch the moon. He plucked a star to pin to his breast. The earth was far below. No bird could fly as high as he. Upwards and onwards he went.

A light switched on in the hut at the far side of the park. It was a small patch of yellow on a dark square. The door opened and he saw a figure in the doorway. Then the door was shut and the figure strode towards him. He knew it was the attendant. A torch glinted brightly as it swung at his side.

He continued swinging.

The attendant came to a halt in front of him, out of reach of the swing's arc, and flashed his torch. The light caught him in mid-air.

'God dammit!' the attendant swore. 'I told you before you can't get on the swings.'

The rattle of the chains when the boy shifted his feet was the only answer he received.

'Why you come back?'

'The swings. I come back for the swings.'

The attendant catalogued the things denied them because of their colour. Even his job depended on their goodwill.

'Blerry whites! They get everything!'

All his feelings urged him to leave the boy alone, to let him continue to enjoy himself but the fear that someone might see them hardened him.

'Get off! Go home!' he screamed, his voice harsh, his anger directed at the system that drove him against his own. 'If you don't get off, I go for the police. You know what they do to you.'

The swing raced back and forth.

The attendant turned and hurried towards the gate.

'Mama. Mama.' His lips trembled, wishing himself safe in his mother's kitchen, sitting next to the still-burning stove with a comic spread across his knees. 'Mama. Mama.' His voice mounted, wrenched from this throat, keeping pace with the soaring swing as it climbed the sky. Voice and swing. Swing and voice. Higher. Higher. Higher. Until they were one.

At the entrance of the park the notice board stood tall, its shadow elongated, pointing towards him.

440

CAN THEMBA

Crepuscule

Written c1964

From: *Requiem for Sophiatown* (2006)

The morning township train cruised into Park Station, Johannesburg, and came to a halt in the dark vaults of the subterranean platforms. Already the young of limb, and the lithe and lissom had leapt off and dashed for the gate that would let them out. But the rest of us had to wade ponderously, in our hundreds, along the thickening platforms that gathered the populations disgorged by Naledi, Emdeni, Dube, Orlando, Pimville, Nancefield, Kliptown, Springs, Benoni, Germiston. Great maws that spewed their workership over Johannesburg.

I was in the press that trudged in the crowd on the platform. Slowly, good-humouredly we were forced, like the substance of a toothpaste tube, through the little corridor and up the escalator that hoisted us through the outlet into the little space of breath and the teeth of pass-demanding South African Police.

But it was with a lilt in my step that I crossed the parquet foyer floor and slipped through the police net, because I knew which cop to pass by: the one who drank with me at Sis Julia's shebeen of an afternoon off. It was with a lilt, because it was spring as I walked out of Park Station into a pointillist morning with the sun slanting from somewhere over George Goch, and in spring the young ladies wear colourful frocks, glaring against the sunlight and flaring in the mischievous breezes. I joyed as I passed into Hoek Street, seeing the white girls coming up King George Street, the sunlight striking through their dresses, articulating the silhouettes beneath to show me leg and form; things black men are supposed to know nothing of, and which the law assininely decrees may not even be imagined.

Funny thing this, the law in all its horrificiency prohibits me, and yet in the streets of Johannesburg I feast for free every morning. And, God, if I try hard enough, I may know for real in Hillbrow every night.

There is a law that says (I'm afraid quite a bit of this will seem like *there is a law that says*), well, it says I cannot make love to a white woman. It is a law. But stronger still there is a custom – a tradition, it is called here – that shudders at the sheerest notion that any white man could contemplate, or any black man dare, a love affair across the colour line. They do: white men *do* meet and fall in love with black women; black men do explore 'ivory towers'. But all this is severely 'agin the law'.

There are also African nationalists who profess horror at the thought that any self-respecting black man could desire any white woman. They say that no African could ever debase himself as to love a white woman. This is highly cultivated and pious lying in the teeth of daily slavering in town and in cinema. African girls, who are torturing themselves all the time to gain a whiter complexion, straighter hair and corset-contained posteriors, surely know what their men secretly admire.

As for myself, I do not necessarily want to bed a white woman; I merely insist on my right to want her.

Once, I took a white girl to Sophiatown. She was a girl who liked to go with me and did not have the rumoured South African inhibitions. She did not even want the anthropological knowledge of 'how the other South Africans live'. She just wanted to be with me.

She had a car, an ancient Morris. On the way to Sophiatown of those days, you drove along Bree Street, past the Fordsburg Police Station in the Indian area, past Braamfontein railway station, under a bridge away past the cemetery, past Bridgetown Memorial Hospital (known, strangely, for bringing illegitimate non-European children into the world), up Hurst Hill, past Talitha Home (a place of detention for delinquent non-European girls), past aggressive Westdene (sore at the proximity of so many non-white townships around her), and into Sophiatown.

So that night a black man and a white woman went to Sophiatown. I first took Janet to my auntie's place in Victoria Road, just opposite the bus terminus. It was a sight to glad a cynic's heart to see my aunt shiver before Janet.

'Mama' – in my world all women equivalents of my mother are mother to me – 'Mama, this is my girl. Where is Tata?' This question, not because my uncle might or might not approve, but because I knew he was terribly fond of brandy, and I was just about to organise a little party; he would not forgive me for leaving him out. But he was not there. He had gone to some meeting of *amagosa* – church stewards, of whom he was the chief.

'Mama, how about a doek for Janet.'

The doek! God save our gracious doek. A doek is a colourful piece of cloth that the African woman wears as headgear. It is tied stylistically into various shapes from Accra to Cape Town. I do not know the history of this innocuous piece of cloth. In Afrikaans, the language of those of our white masters who are of Dutch and Huguenot descent, doek meant, variously, a tablecloth, a dirty rag, or a symbol of the slave. Perhaps it was later used by African women in contact with European ideas of beauty who realised that 'they had no hair' and subconsciously hid their heads under the doek. Whatever else, the doek had come to designate the African woman. So that evening when I said, 'Mama, how about a doek for Janet', I was proposing to transform her, despite her colour and her deep blue eyes, into an African girl for the while.

Ma dug into her chest and produced a multi-coloured chiffon doek. We stood before the wardrobe mirror while my sisters helped to tie Janet's doek in the current township style. To my sisters that night I was obviously a hell of a guy.

Then I took Janet to a shebeen in Gibson Street. I was well known in that particular shebeen, could get my liquor 'on tick' and could get VIP treatment even without the asset of Janet. With Janet, I was a sensation. Shebeens are noisy drinking places and as we approached that shebeen we could hear the blast of loud-mouthed conversation. But when we entered a haunted hush fell upon the house. The shebeen queen rushed two men off their chairs to make places for us, and: 'What would you have, Mr Themba?'

There are certain names that do not go with Mister, I don't have a clue why. But, for sure, you cannot imagine a Mr Charlie Chaplin or a Mr William Shakespeare or a Mr Jesus Christ. My name – Can Themba – operates in that sort of class. So you can see the kind of sensation we caused when the shebeen queen addressed me as Mr Themba.

I said, casually as you like, 'A half a jack for a start, and I suppose you'd like a beer, too, my dear?'

The other patrons of the shebeen were coming up for air, one by one, and I could see that they were wondering about Janet. Some thought that she was coloured, a South African mulatto. One said she was white, appending, 'These journalist boys get the best girls.' But it was clear that the doek flummoxed them. Even iron-coloureds, whose stubborn physical appearances veer strongly to the Negroid parent, are proud enough of whatever hair they have to expose it. But this girl wore a doek!

Then Janet spoke to me in that tinkling English voice of hers, and I spoke to her, easily, without inhibition, without madamising her. One chap, who could contain himself no longer, rose to shake my hand. He said, in the argot of the townships, 'Brer Can, you've eaten caustic soda. Look, man, get me fish-meat like this, and s'true's God, I'll buy you a *vung* (a car)!' That sort of thawed the house and everybody broke into raucous laughter.

Later, I collected a bottle of brandy and some ginger ale, and took Janet to my room in Gold Street. There were a few friends and their girls: Kaffertjie (Little Kaffer – he was quite defiantly proud of this name) and Hilda, Jazzboy and Pule, Jimmy, Rockefeller and a coloured girl we called Madame Defarge because day or night she always had clicking knitting needles with her. We drank, joked, conversed, sang and horse-played. It was a night of the Sophia-town of my time, before the government destroyed it.

It was the best of times, it was the worst of times; it was the age of wisdom, it was the age of foolishness; it was the season of Light, it was the season of

Darkness; it was the spring of hope, it was the winter of despair; we had everything before us, we had nothing before us; we were all going direct to Heaven, we were all going direct the other way – in short, the period was so far like the present period that some of its noisiest authorities insisted on its being received, for good or for evil, in the superlative degree of comparison only.

Sometimes I think, for his sense of contrast and his sharp awareness of the pungent flavours of life, only Charles Dickens – or, perhaps, Victor Hugo – could have understood Sophiatown. The government has razed Sophiatown to the ground, rebuilt it, and resettled it with whites. And with appropriate cheek, they have called it Triomf.

That night I went to bed with Janet, chocolate upon cream. I do not know what happened to me in my sleep; the Africans say *amadhlozi* talked to me – the spirits of my forefathers that are supposed to guide my reckless way through this cruel life intervened for once. In the mid of the night I got up, shook Janet and told her we got to go.

'Ah, Can, you're disturbing me, I want to sleep.'

'Come-ahn, get up!'

'Please, Can, I want to sleep.'

I pulled off the blankets and marvelled awhile at the golden hair that billowed over her shoulders. Then she rose and dressed drowsily.

We got into her ancient Morris and drove to town. I think it was the remembrance of a half-bottle of brandy in her room in Hillbrow that woke me and made me rouse her, more than the timely intervention of the *amadhlozi*. We saw a big, green *Kwela-Kwela* wire-netted lorry-van full of be-batonned white cops driving up Gold Street, but we thought little of it, for the cops, like fleas in our blankets, are always with us. So we spluttered up Hurst Hill into town.

Later, I heard what had happened.

I used to have a young Xhosa girl called Baby. She was not really my class, but in those days for what we called love we Sophiatonians took the high, the middle and the low.

Baby was pathologically fond of parties, the type of parties to which tsotsis go. They organise themselves into a club of about half-a-dozen members. On pay-day they each contribute, say £5, and give it to the member whose turn it is. He then throws a party to entertain all the members and their girlfriends. Almost invariably guys trespass on other guys' girls and fights break out. Baby liked this kind of party, but it soon became clear to me that I was risking the swift knife in the dark so long as I associated with her. So I talked it over with her, told her we should call it a day and that I did not want to clash with her tsotsi boyfriends. She readily accepted, saying, 'That-so it is, after all you're a teacher type and you don't suit me.'

So far as I was concerned that had been that.

But that star-crossed night, Baby heard that I was involved with a white girl. She went berserk. I gathered that she went running down Gold Street tearing out her hair and shrieking. At the corner of Gold Street and Victoria Street, she met a group of tsotsis playing street football under the street lamp with a tennis ball. They asked her, 'Baby, whassamatter?' She screamed, 'It's Can, he's with a white woman,' and they replied, 'Report him!'

Africans are not on the side of the cops if they can help it. You do not go to a policeman for help or protection or the which way to go. You eschew them. To report a felon to them, good heavens! It is just not done. So for a tsotsi to say about anyone, 'Report him!' means the matter is serious.

Baby went to Newlands Police Station and shouted, 'Baas, they're there. They're in bed, my boyfriend and a white woman.' The sergeant behind the counter told her to take it easy, to wait until the criminals were so well-asleep that they might be caught *flagrante delicto*. But Baby was dancing with impatience at 'the law's delay'.

Still, that sergeant wanted to make a proper job of it. He organised a lorry-full of white cops, white cops only, with batons and the right sadistic mental orientation. Or, perhaps, too many such excursions had misadventured before where black cops were suspected of having tipped off their brethren.

When we went down Gold Street, it was them we saw in the green lorry-van bent on a date with a kaffir who had the infernal impertinence to reach over the fence at forbidden fruit.

I understood they kicked open the door of my room and stormed in, only to find that the birds had flown. One white cop is reported to have said, wistfully, 'Look, man, there are two dents in the pillow and I can still smell her perfume.' Another actually found a long thread of golden hair.

I met Baby a few days later and asked her resignedly, 'But you said we're no more in love, why the big jealous act?'

She replied, 'Even if we've split, you can't shame me for a white bitch.'

I countered, 'But if you still loved me enough to feel jealous, didn't you consider that you were sending me to six months in jail! Baby, it could be seven years, you know.'

'I don't care,' she said. 'But not with a white bitch, Can. And who says that I still love you? It's just that you can't humiliate me with a white bitch.'

I threw up my hands in despair and thought that one of these days I really must slaughter a spotlessly white goat as a sacrifice to the spirits of my forefathers. I have been neglecting my superstitions too dangerously long.

Funny, one of the things seldom said for superstitious belief is that it is a tremendous psychological peg to hang on to. God knows the vehement attacks made upon the unreason and stark cruelty of superstition and witchcraft practices are warranted. Abler minds than mine have argued this. But I do want to say that those of us who have been detribalised and caught in the characterless world of belonging nowhere, have a bitter sense of loss. The culture that we have shed may not be particularly valuable in a content sense, but it was something that the psyche could attach itself to, and its absence is painfully felt in this white man's world where everything significant is forbidden, or 'Not for thee!' Not only the refusal to let us enter so many fields of human experience, but the sheer negation that our spirits should ever assume to themselves identity. Crushing.

It is a crepuscular, shadow-life in which we wander as spectres seeking meaning for ourselves. And even the local, little legalities we invent are frowned upon. The whole atmosphere is charged with the white man's general disapproval, and where he does not have a law for it, he certainly has a grimace that cows you. This is the burden of the white man's crime against my personality that negatives all the brilliance of intellect and the genuine funds of goodwill so many individuals have. The whole bloody ethos still asphyxiates me. Ingratitude? Exaggeration? Childish, pampered desire for indulgence? Yes – yes, perhaps. But leave us some area in time and experience to be true to ourselves. It is so exhausting to have to be in reaction all the time. My race believes in the quick shaft of anger, or of love, or hate, or laughter: the perpetual emotional commitment is foreign to us. Life has contrived so much, such a variegated woof in its texture, that we feel we can tarry only a poignant moment with a little flare of emotion, if we are ever to savour the whole. Thus they call us fickle and disloyal. They have not yet called us hypocritical.

These things I claim for my race, I claim for all men. A little respite, brother, just a little respite from the huge responsibility of being a nice kaffir.

After that adventure in Sophiatown with Janet, I got a lot of sympathy and advice. I met the boys who had said to Baby, 'Report him!' I was sore because they had singled me out like that and made me the pariah that could he thrown to the wolves. They put their case:

'You see, Brer Can, there's a man here on this corner who plays records of classical music, drinks funny wines and brings white men out here for our black girls. Frankly, we don't like it, because these white boys come out here for our girls, but when we meet them in town they treat us like turds. We don't like the way you guys play it with the whites. We're on Baby's side, Brer Can.'

'Look, boys,' I explained, 'you don't understand, you don't understand me. I agree with you that these whites take advantage of our girls and we don't like the way our girls act as if they are special. But all you've done about it is just to sit and sizzle here at them. No one among you has tried to take revenge. Only I have gone to get a white girl and avenge with her what the whites do to our sisters. I'm not like the guys who procure black girls for their white friends. I seek revenge. I get the white girls – well, it's tough and risky, but you guys, instead of sitting here crying your hearts out, you should get yourselves white girls, too, and hit back.'

I got them, I knew.

One guy said, 'By right, Brer Can's telling the truth.'

Another asked, 'Tell me, Brer Can, how does a white woman taste?' That was going too far. I had too great a respect for Janet, the woman, to discuss that with anybody whether he was white or black.

I said, 'You go find out for yourself.'

The piece of advice I got from the mother of a friend of mine who stayed in the same street, Gold Street, was touching.

She said to me: 'Son, I've heard about your trouble with the white girl. It's you that was foolish. People know that your white girl is around because they recognise the car. If they see it parked flush in front of your house, they say, "Can has got silver-fish." What you should do is to drive the car into my yard here, right to the back of the house so that nobody could see it from the street, and then they wouldn't suspect that you have the white girl in your room down there.'

It seemed to me to be excellent, practical advice.

So the next time I got home with Janet, we drove the car into the yard of my friend's mother, right back behind the house, and walked down in the dead of night to my room.

In the middle of the night, my friend came clattering on the window of my room and shouted, 'Can, get up, the cops!' We got up, got dressed in breath-less time, rushed to the car at his mother's place and zoomed out of Sophia-town on a little-used route past St Joseph's Mission through Auckland Park into Hillbrow, where in the heart of the white man's flat-land we could com-plete breaking the white man's law as, apparently, we could not do in Sophia-town.

Later, I heard the sordid details of what had happened that night. My friend came home late, and overheard his mother and sisters discussing the Morris we had left in their yard. The mother felt that it was not right that I should be messing around with a white woman when she had unmarried daughters of her own and my eligibility rated high. So she sent one of her daughters to go and tell Baby that I was with the white woman again and that I had left the car in their yard. My friend felt that he did not have the time to argue with his family, that his job was to warn us as quickly as he could to get the hell out of there.

As it turned out, I need not have bothered. The darling Afrikaner at the desk told Baby, 'Look here, woman, every time you have a quarrel with your boyfriend, you rush to us with a cock-and-bull story. Clear out!'

CAN THEMBA

The Suit

First published, 1963

From: *Requiem for Sophiatown* (2006)

Five-thirty in the morning, and the candlewick bedspread frowned as the man under it stirred. He did not like to wake his wife lying by his side – as yet – so he crawled up and out by careful peristalsis. But before he tiptoed out of his room with shoes and socks under his arm, he leaned over and peered at the sleeping serenity of his wife: to him a daily matutinal miracle.

He grinned and yawned simultaneously, offering his wordless Te Deum to whatever gods for the goodness of life; for the pure beauty of his wife; for the strength surging through his willing body; for the even, unperturbed rhythms of his passage through days and months and years – it must be – to heaven.

Then he slipped soundlessly into the kitchen. He flipped aside the curtain of the kitchen window, and saw outside a thin drizzle, the type that can soak one to the skin, and that could go on for days and days. He wondered, head aslant, why the rain in Sophiatown always came in the morning when workers had to creep out of their burrows; and then at how blistering heatwaves came during the day when messengers had to run errands all over; and then at how the rain came back when workers knocked off and had to scurry home.

He smiled at the odd caprice of the heavens, and tossed his head at the naughty incongruity, as if, 'Ai, but the gods!'

From behind the kitchen door, he removed an old rain cape, peeling off in places, and swung it over his head. He dashed for the lavatory, nearly slipping in a pool of muddy water, but he reached the door. Aw, blast, someone had made it before him. Well, that is the toll of staying in a yard where twenty ... thirty other people have to share the same lean-to. He was dancing and burning in that climactic moment when trouser-fly will not come wide soon enough. He stepped round the lavatory and watched the streamlets of rainwater quickly wash away the jet of tension that spouted from him. That infinite after-relief. Then he dashed back to his kitchen. He grabbed the old baby-bathtub hanging on a nail under the slight shelter of the gutterless roof-edge. He opened a large wooden box and quickly filled the bathtub with coal. Then he inched his way back to the kitchen door and inside.

He was huh-huh-huhing one of those fugitive tunes that cannot be hidden, but often just occur and linger naggingly in the head. The fire he was making soon licked up cheerfully, in mood with his contentment.

He had a trick for these morning chores. While the fire in the old stove warmed up, the water kettle humming on it, he gathered and laid ready the things he would need for the day: briefcase and the files that go with it; the book that he was reading currently; the letters of his lawyer boss which he usually posted before he reached the office; his wife's and his own dry-cleaning slips for the Sixty-Minutes; his lunch tin solicitously prepared the night before by his attentive wife; and, today, the battered rain cape. By the time the kettle on the stove sang (before it actually boiled), he poured water from it into a washbasin, refilled and replaced it on the stove. Then he washed himself carefully: across the eyes, under, in and out the armpits, down the torso and in between the legs. This ritual was thorough, though no white man a-complaining of the smell of wogs knows anything about it. Then he dressed himself fastidiously. By this time he was ready to prepare breakfast.

Breakfast! How he enjoyed taking in a tray of warm breakfast to his wife, cuddled in bed. To appear there in his supremest immaculacy, tray in hand when his wife comes out of ether to behold him. These things we blacks want to do for our own ... not fawningly for the whites for whom we bloody-well got to do it. He felt, he denied, that he was one of those who believed in putting his wife in her place even if she was a good wife. Not he.

Matilda, too, appreciated her husband's kindness, and only put her foot down when he offered to wash up also.

'Off with you,' she scolded him on his way.

At the bus-stop he was a little sorry to see that jovial old Maphikela was in a queue for a bus ahead of him. He would miss Maphikela's raucous laughter and uninhibited, bawdy conversations in fortissimo. Maphikela hailed him nevertheless. He thought he noticed hesitation in the old man, and a slight clouding of his countenance, but the old man shouted back at him, saying that he would wait for him at the terminus in town.

Philemon considered this morning trip to town with garrulous old Maphikela as his daily bulletin. All the township news was generously reported by loud-mouthed heralds, and spiritedly discussed by the bus at large. Of course, 'news' included views on bosses (scurrilous), the Government (rude), Ghana and Russia (idolatrous), America and the West (sympathetically ridiculing), and boxing (bloodthirsty). But it was always stimulating and surprisingly comprehensive for so short a trip. And there was no law of libel.

Maphikela was standing under one of those token bus-stop shelters that never keep out rain nor wind nor sun-heat. Philemon easily located him by his noisy ribbing of some office boys in their khaki-green uniforms. They walked together into town, but from Maphikela's suddenly subdued manner, Philemon gathered that there was something serious coming up. Maybe a loan.

Eventually, Maphikela came out with it.

'Son,' he said sadly, 'if I could've avoided this, believe you me I would, but my wife is nagging the spice out of my life for not talking to you about it.'

It just did not become blustering old Maphikela to sound so grave and Philemon took compassion upon him.

'Go ahead, dad,' he said generously. 'You know you can talk to me about anything.'

The old man gave a pathetic smile. 'We-e-e-ll, it's not really any of our business ... er ... but my wife felt ... you see. Damn it all! I wish these women would not snoop around so much.' Then he rushed it. 'Anyway, it seems there's a young man who's going to visit your wife every morning ... ah ... for these last bloomin' three months. And that wife of mine swears by her heathen gods you don't know a thing about it.'

It was not quite like the explosion of a devastating bomb. It was more like the critical breakdown in an infinitely delicate piece of mechanism. From outside the machine just seemed to have gone dead. But deep in its innermost recesses, menacing electrical flashes were leaping from coil to coil, and hot, viscous molten metal was creeping upon the fuel tanks ...

Philemon heard gears grinding and screaming in his head ...

'Dad,' he said hoarsely, 'I ... I have to go back home.'

He turned round and did not hear old Maphikela's anxious, 'Steady, son. Steady, son.'

The bus ride home was a torture of numb dread and suffocating despair. Though the bus was now emptier Philemon suffered crushing claustrophobia. There were immense washerwomen whose immense bundles of soiled laundry seemed to baulk and menace him. From those bundles crept miasmata of sweaty intimacies that sent nauseous waves up and down from his viscera. Then the wild swaying of the bus as it negotiated Mayfair Circle hurtled him sickeningly from side to side. Some of the younger women shrieked delightedly to the driver, '*Fuduga!* ... Stir the pot!' as he swung his steering-wheel this way and that. Normally, the crazy tilting of the bus gave him a prickling exhilaration. But now ...

He felt like getting out of there, screamingly, elbowing everything out of his way. He wished this insane trip were over, and then again, he recoiled at the thought of getting home. He made a tremendous resolve to gather in all the torn, tingling threads of his nerves contorting in the raw. By a merciless act of will, he kept them in subjugation as he stepped out of the bus back in the Victoria Road terminus, Sophiatown.

The calm he achieved was tense ... but he could think now ... he could take a decision ...

With almost boyishly innocent urgency, he rushed through his kitchen into his bedroom. In the lightning flash that the eye can whip, he saw it all ... the man beside his wife … the chestnut arm around her neck … the ruffled candle-wick bedspread … the suit across the chair. But he effected not to see.

He opened the wardrobe door, and as he dug into it, he cheerfully spoke to his wife, 'Fancy, Tilly, I forgot to take my pass. I had already reached town, and was going to walk up to the office. If it hadn't been for wonderful old Mr Maphikela.'

A swooshing noise of violent retreat and the clap of his bedroom window stopped him. He came from behind the wardrobe door and looked out from the open window. A man clad only in vest and underpants was running down the street. Slowly, he turned round and contemplated … the suit.

Philemon lifted it gingerly under his arm and looked at the stark horror in Matilda's eyes. She was now sitting up in bed. Her mouth twitched, but her throat raised no words.

'Ha,' he said, 'I see we have a visitor,' indicating the blue suit. 'We really must show some of our hospitality. But first, I must phone my boss that I can't come to work today … mmmm–er, my wife's not well. Be back in a moment, then we can make arrangements.' He took the suit along.

When he returned he found Matilda weeping on the bed. He dropped the suit beside her, pulled up the chair, turned it round so that its back came in front of him, sat down, brought down his chin onto his folded arms before him, and waited for her.

After a while the convulsions of her shoulders ceased. She saw a smug man with an odd smile and meaningless inscrutability in his eyes. He spoke to her with very little noticeable emotion; if anything, with a flutter of humour.

'We have a visitor, Tilly.' His mouth curved ever so slightly. 'I'd like him to be treated with the greatest of consideration. He will eat every meal with us and share all we have. Since we have no spare room, he'd better sleep in here. But the point is, Tilly that you will meticulously look after him. If he vanishes or anything else happens to him …' A shaft of evil shot from his eye … 'Matilda, I'll kill you.'

He rose from the chair and looked with incongruous supplication at her. He told her to put the fellow in the wardrobe for the time being. As she passed him to get the suit, he turned to go. She ducked frantically, and he stopped.

'You don't seem to understand me, Matilda. There's to be no violence in this house if you and I can help it. So, just look after that suit.' He went out.

He went out to the Sophiatown Post Office, which is placed on the exact line between Sophiatown and the white man's surly Westdene. He posted his boss's letters, and walked to the beerhall at the tail end of Western Native Township. He had never been inside it before, but somehow the thunderous din laved his bruised spirit. He stayed there all day.

He returned home for supper … and surprise. His dingy little home had been transformed, and the air of stern masculinity it had hitherto contained had been wiped away, to be replaced by anxious feminine touches here and there. There were even gay, colourful curtains swirling in the kitchen window. The old-fashioned coal stove gleamed in its blackness. A clean, chequered oil cloth on the table. Supper ready.

Then she appeared in the doorway of the bedroom. Heavens! here was the woman he had married; the young, fresh, cocoa-coloured maid who had sent rushes of emotion shuddering through him. And the dress she wore brought out all the girlishness of her, hidden so long beneath German print. But no hint of coquettishness, although she stood in the doorway and slid her arm up the jamb, and shyly slanted her head to the other shoulder. She smiled weakly.

What makes a woman like this experiment with adultery? he wondered.

Philemon closed his eyes and gripped the seat of his chair on both sides as some overwhelming, undisciplined force sought to catapult him towards her. For a moment some essence glowed fiercely within him, then sank back into itself and died …

He sighed and smiled sadly back at her, 'I'm hungry, Tilly.'

The spell snapped, and she was galvanised into action. She prepared his supper with dexterous hands that trembled a little only when they hesitated in mid-air. She took her seat opposite him, regarded him curiously, clasped her hands waiting for his prayer, but in her heart she murmured some other, much more urgent prayer of her own.

'Matilda!' he barked. 'Our visitor!' The sheer savagery with which he cracked at her jerked her up, but only when she saw the brute cruelty in his face did she run out of the room, toppling the chair behind her.

She returned with the suit on a hanger, and stood there quivering like a feather. She looked at him with helpless dismay. The demoniacal rage in his face was evaporating, but his heavy breathing still rocked his thorax above the table, to and fro.

'Put a chair, there.' He indicated with a languid gesture of his arm. She moved like a ghost as she drew a chair to the table.

'Now seat our friend at the table … no, no, not like that. Put him in front of the chair, and place him on the seat so that he becomes indeed the third person.'

Philemon went on relentlessly: 'Dish up for him. Generously. I imagine he hasn't had a morsel all day, the poor devil.'

Now, as consciousness and thought seeped back into her, her movements revolved so that always she faced this man who had changed so spectacularly. She started when he rose to open the window and let in some air.

She served the suit. The act was so ridiculous that she carried it out with a bitter sense of humiliation. He came back to sit down and plunge into his meal. No grace was said for the first time in this house. With his mouth full, he indicated by a toss of his head that she should sit down in her place. She did so. Glancing at her plate, the thought occurred to her that someone, after a long famine, was served a sumptuous supper, but as the food reached her mouth it turned to sawdust. Where had she heard it?

Matilda could not eat. She suddenly broke into tears.

Philemon took no notice of her weeping. After supper, he casually gathered the dishes and started washing up. He flung a dry cloth at her without saying a word. She rose and went to stand by his side drying up. But for their word-lessness, they seemed a very devoted couple.

After washing up, he took the suit and turned to her. 'That's how I want it every meal, every day.' Then he walked into the bedroom.

So it was. After that first breakdown, Matilda began to feel that her punishment was not too severe, considering the heinousness of the crime. She tried to put a joke into it, but by slow, unconscious degrees, the strain nibbled at her. Philemon did not harass her much more, so long as the ritual with the confounded suit was conscientiously followed.

Only once, he got one of his malevolent brainwaves. He got it into his head that 'our visitor' needed an outing. Accordingly the suit was taken to the dry-cleaners during the week, and, come Sunday, they had to take it out for a walk. Both Philemon and Matilda dressed for the occasion. Matilda had to carry the suit on its hanger over her back and the three of them strolled leisurely along Ray Street. They passed the church crowd in front of the famous Anglican Mission of Christ the King. Though the worshippers saw nothing unusual in them, Matilda felt, searing through her, red-hot needles of embarrassment, and every needle-point was a public eye piercing into her degradation.

But Philemon walked casually on. He led her down Ray Street and turned into Main Road. He stopped often to look into shop windows or to greet a friend passing by. They went up Toby Street, turned into Edward Road, and back home. To Philemon the outing was free of incident, but to Matilda it was one long, excruciating incident.

At home, he grabbed a book on abnormal psychology, flung himself into a chair and calmly said to her, 'Give the old chap a rest, will you, Tilly?'

In the bedroom, Matilda said to herself that things could not go on like this. She thought of how she could bring the matter to a head with Philemon; have it out with him once and for all. But the memory of his face, that first day she had forgotten to entertain the suit, stayed her. She thought of running away, but where to? Home? What could she tell her old-fashioned mother had happened between Philemon and her? All right, run away clean then. She thought of many young married girls who were divorcées now, who had won their freedom.

What had happened to Staff Nurse Kakile? The woman drank heavily now, and when she got drunk, the boys of Sophiatown passed her around and called her the Cesspot.

Matilda shuddered.

An idea struck her. There were still decent, married women around Sophia-town. She remembered how after the private schools had been forced to close with the advent of Bantu Education, Father Harringay of the Anglican Mission had organised Cultural Clubs. One, she seemed to remember, was for married women. If only she could lose herself in some cultural activity, find absolution for her conscience in some doing good; that would blur her blasted home life, would restore her self-respect. After all, Philemon had not broadcast her disgrace abroad … nobody knew; not one of Sophiatown's slander-mongers suspected how vulnerable she was. She must go and see Mrs Montjane about joining a Cultural Club. She must ask Philemon now if she might … she must ask him nicely.

She got up and walked into the other room where Philemon was read-ing quietly. She dreaded disturbing him, did not know how to begin talking to him … they had talked so little for so long. She went and stood in front of him, looking silently upon his deep concentration. Presently, he looked up with a frown on his face.

Then she dared, 'Phil, I'd like to join one of those Cultural Clubs for married women. Would you mind?'

He wrinkled his nose and rubbed it between thumb and index finger as he considered the request. But he had caught the note of anxiety in her voice and thought he knew what it meant.

'Mmmm,' he said, nodding. 'I think that's a good idea. You can't be moping around here all day. Yes, you may, Tilly.' Then he returned to his book.

The Cultural Club idea was wonderful. She found women like herself, with time (if not with tragedy) on their hands, engaged in wholesome, refreshing activities. The atmosphere was cheerful and cathartic. They learned things and they did things. They organised fêtes, bazaars, youth activities, sport, music, self-help and community projects. She got involved in committees, meetings, debates, conferences. It was for her a whole new venture into humancraft, and her personality blossomed. Philemon gave her all the rein she wanted.

Now, abiding by that silly ritual at home seemed a little thing … a very little thing …

Then one day she decided to organise a little party for her friends and their husbands. Philemon was very decent about it. He said it was all right. He even gave her extra money for it. Of course, she knew nothing of the strain he him-self suffered from his mode of castigation.

There was a week of the hectic preparation. Philemon stepped out of its cluttering way as best he could. So many things seemed to be taking place simultaneously. New dresses were made. Cakes were baked: three different orders of meat prepared; beef for the uninvited chancers; mutton for the nor-mal guests; turkey and chicken for the inner pith of the club's core. To

Philemon, it looked as if Matilda planned to feed the multitude on the Mount with no aid of miracles.

On the Sunday of the party, Philemon saw Matilda's guests. He was surprised by the handsome grace with which she received them. There was a long table with enticing foods and flowers and serviettes. Matilda placed all her guests round the table, and the party was ready to begin in the mock-formal township fashion. Outside a steady rumble of conversation went on where the human odds and ends of every Sophiatown party had their 'share'.

Matilda caught the curious look on Philemon's face. He tried to disguise his edict when he said, 'Er ... the guest of honour.'

But Matilda took a chance. She begged, 'Just this once, Phil.'

He became livid. 'Matilda!' he shouted. 'Get our visitor!' Then with incisive sarcasm, 'Or are you ashamed of him?'

She went ash-grey; but there was nothing for it but to fetch her albatross. She came back and squeezed a chair into some corner, and placed the suit on it. Then she slowly placed a plate of food before it. For a while the guests were dumbfounded. Then curiosity flooded in. They talked at the same time. 'What's the idea, Philemon?' ... 'Why must she serve a suit?' ... 'What's happening?' Some just giggled in a silly way. Philemon carelessly swung his head towards Matilda. 'You better ask my wife. She knows the fellow best.'

All interest beamed upon poor Matilda. For a moment she could not speak, all enveloped in misery. Then she said, unconvincingly, 'It's just a game that my husband and I play at mealtime.' They roared with laughter. Philemon let her get away with it.

The party went on, and every time Philemon's glare sent Matilda scurrying to serve the suit each course; the guests were no-end amused by the persistent mock-seriousness with which this husband and wife played out their little game. Only, to Matilda, it was no joke; it was a hot poker down her throat. After the party, Philemon went off with one of the guests who had promised to show him a joint 'that sells genuine stuff, boy, genuine stuff'.

Reeling drunk, late that sabbath, he crashed through his kitchen door, onwards to his bedroom. Then he saw her.

They have a way of saying in the argot of Sophiatown, 'Cook out of the head!' signifying that someone was impacted with such violent shock that whatever whiffs of alcohol still wandered through his head were instantaneously evaporated and the man stood sober before stark reality.

There she lay, curled as if just before she died she begged for a little love, implored some implacable lover to cuddle her a little ... just this once ... just this once more.

In screwish anguish, Philemon cried, 'Tilly!'

CAN THEMBA

The Will to Die

Written *c*1974

From: *Requiem for Sophiatown* (2006)

I have heard much, have read much more, of the Will to Live; stories of fantastic retreats from the brink of death at moments when all hope was lost. To the aid of certain personalities in the bleakest crises, spiritual resources seem to come forward from what? Character? Spirit? Soul? Or the Great Reprieve of a Spiritual Clemency – hoisting them back from the muddy slough of the Valley of the Shadow.

But the Will to Die has intrigued me more ...

I have also heard that certain snakes can hypnotise their victim, a rat, a frog or a rabbit, not only so that it cannot flee to safety in the overwhelming urge for survival, but so that it is even attracted towards its destroyer, and appears to enjoy dancing towards its doom. I have often wondered if there is not some mesmeric power that Fate employs to engage some men deliberately, with macabre relishment, to seek their destruction and to plunge into it.

Take Foxy ...

His real name was Philip Matauoane, but for some reason, I think from the excesses of his college days, everybody called him Foxy. He was a teacher in a small school in Barberton, South Africa. He had been to Fort Hare University College in the Cape Province, and had majored in English (with distinction) and Native Administration. Then he took the University Education Diploma (teaching) with Rhodes University, Grahamstown.

He used to say, 'I'm the living exemplar of the modern, educated African's dilemma. I read English and trained to be a teacher – the standard profession for my class those days; but you never know which government department is going to expel you and pitchfork you into which other government department. So I also took Native Administration as a safety device.'

You would think that that labels the cautious, providential kind of human.

Foxy was a short fellow, the type that seems in youth to rush forward towards old age, but somewhere, around the eve of middle-age, stops dead and ages no further almost forever. He had wide, owlish eyes and a trick with his mouth that suggested withering contempt for all creation. He invariably wore clothes that swallowed him: the coat overflowed and drowned his arms, the trousers sat on his chest in front and billowed obscenely behind. He was a runt of a man.

But in that unlikely body resided a live, restless brain.

When Foxy first left college, he went to teach English at Barberton High School. He was twenty-five then, and those were the days when high school pupils were just ripe to provoke or prejudice a young man of indifferent morals. He fell in love with a young girl, Betty Kumalo, his own pupil.

I must explain this spurious phenomenon of 'falling in love'. Neither Foxy nor Betty had the remotest sense of commitment to the irrelevance of marrying some day. The society of the times was such that affairs of this nature occurred easily. Parents did not mind much. Often they would invite a young teacher to the home, and as soon as he arrived, would eclipse themselves, leaving the daughter with stern but unmistakable injunctions to 'be hospitable to the teacher'.

We tried to tell Foxy, we his fellow-teachers, that this arrangement was too nice to be safe, but these things had been written in the stars.

Foxy could not keep away from Betty's home. He could not be discreet. He went there every day, every unblessed day. He took her out during weekends and they vanished into the countryside in his ancient Chevrolet.

On Mondays he would often say to me, 'I don't know what's wrong with me. I know this game is dangerous. I know Betty will destroy me, but that seems to give tang to the adventure. Hopeless. Hopeless,' and he would throw his arms out.

I had it out with him once.

'Foxy,' I said, 'you must stop this nonsense. It'll ruin you.'

There came a glint of pleasure, real ecstasy it seemed to me, into his eyes. It was as if the prospect of ruin was hallelujah.

He said to me, 'My intelligence tells me that it'll ruin me, but there's a magnetic force that draws me to that girl, and another part of me, much stronger than intelligence, just simply exults.'

'Marry her, then, and get done with it.'

'No!' He said it so vehemently that I was quite alarmed. 'Something in me wants that girl pregnant but not a wife.'

I thought it was a hysterical utterance.

You cannot go flinging wild oats all over a fertile field, not even wild weeds. It had to happen.

If you are a school-teacher, you can only get out of a situation like that if you marry the girl, that is if you value your job. Foxy promptly married – another girl! But he was smart enough to give Betty's parents £50. That, in the hideous system of *lobola*, the system of bride-price, made Betty his second wife. And no authority on earth could accuse him of seduction.

But when his wife found out about it, she battered him, as the Americans would say, 'to hell and back'.

Foxy started drinking heavily.

Then another thing began to happen; Foxy got drunk during working hours. Hitherto, he had been meticulous about not cultivating one's iniquities in the teeth of one's job, but now he seemed to be splashing in the gutter with a will.

I will never forget the morning another teacher and I found him stinkingly drunk about half-an-hour before school was to start. We forced him into a shebeen and asked the queen to let him sleep it off. We promised to make the appropriate excuses to the headmaster on his behalf. Imagine our consternation when he came reeling into the assembly hall where we were saying morning prayers with all the staff and pupils. How I prayed that morning!

These things happen. Everybody noticed Foxy's condition, except, for some reason, the headmaster. We hid him in the Biology Laboratory for the better part of the day, but that did not make the whole business any more edifying. Happily, he made his appearance before we could perjure ourselves to the headmaster. Later, however, we learned that he had told the shebeen-queen that he would go to school perforce because we other teachers were trying to get him into trouble for absence from work and that we wished to 'outshine' him. Were we livid?

Every one of his colleagues gave him a dressing down. We told him that no more was he alone in this: it involved the dignity of us all. The whole location was beginning to talk nastily about us. Moreover, there was a violent, alcoholic concoction brewed in the location called Barberton. People just linked 'Barberton', 'High' and 'School' to make puns about us.

Superficially, it hurt him to cause us so much trouble, but something deep down in him did not allow him really to care. He went on drinking hard. His health was beginning to crack under it. Now, he met every problem with the gurgling answer of the bottle.

One night, I heard that he was very ill, so I went to see him at home.

His wife had long since given him up for lost; they no more even shared a bedroom. I found him in his room. The scene was ghastly. He was lying in his underwear in bed linen which was stained with the blotches of murdered bugs. There was a plate of uneaten food that must have come the day before yesterday. He was breathing heavily. Now and then he tried to retch, but nothing came up. His bloodshot eyes rolled this way and that, and whenever some respite graciously came, he reached out for a bottle of gin and gulped at it until the fierce liquid poured over his stubbled chin.

He gibbered so that I thought he was going mad. Then he would retch violently again, that jolting, vomitless quake of a retch.

458

He needed a doctor but he would not have one. His wife carped, 'Leave the pig to perish.'

I went to fetch the doctor, nevertheless. We took quite a while, and when we returned, his wife sneered at us, 'You wouldn't like to see him now.' We went into his room and found him lost in oblivion. A strange girl was lying by his side.

In his own house!

I did not see him for weeks, but I heard enough. They said that he was frequenting dangerous haunts. One drunken night he was beaten up and robbed. Another night he returned home stark naked, without a clue as to who had stripped him.

Liquor should have killed him, but some compulsive urge chose differently. After a binge one night, he wandered hopelessly about the darksome location streets, seeking his home. At last, he decided on a gate, a house, a door. He was sure that that was his home. He banged his way in, ignored the four or five men singing hymns in the sitting-room, and staggered into the bedroom. He flung himself on to the bed and hollered, 'Woman, it's time that I sleep in your bed. I'm sick and tired of being a widower with a live wife.'

The men took up sticks and battered Foxy to a pulp. They got it into their heads that the woman of the house had been in the business all the time; that only now had her lover gone and got drunk enough to let the cat out of the bag. They beat the woman, too, within millimetres of her life. All of them landed in jail for long stretches.

But I keep having a stupid feeling that somehow, Philip 'Foxy' Matauoane would have felt: 'This is as it should be.'

Some folks live the obsession of death.

ABRAHAM H DE VRIES

The Girl with the Bra-pistol

Translated from the Afrikaans by Martin Trump
From: *Vliegoog (1965)*

Seated against the multicoloured cushions on the divan, the girl's face and arms have an olive hue. But where she is not tanned, her skin is as pale as milk under the electric light that reflects off the ceiling and showers on everyone like invisible rain. Her long blonde hair hangs restfully on either side of her oval face.

'Insane!' the woman beside her shrieks as Van Schaikwyk, the art teacher, whispers something in her ear. 'Insane!' and she spills her drink on the floor. The girl smiles and turns her glass slowly so that its curved surface seeks the light. Without anybody noticing it she adjusts her bra with the wrist of her goblet-hand. She drinks slowly.

'It's a problem,' says Cloete, a small little man with a pair of thick-lensed glasses, to the coloured man beside him. 'Their kind of imperialism. They seem to be unable to grasp all the nuances of the problem. Look for generalisations, easy ways out. And you people have been given the short end of the stick.'

The man shrugs and smiles, puzzled. (Why does everyone always have to help him remember?)

'Yes, it's difficult, isn't it?' he replies with nervous caution.

'Are you buggers still talking politics in my house?' Markus asks with a glass of red wine in one hand and his bent stem pipe in the other. Markus is the host, but because he and his wife occupy separate rooms, he is also rather like a guest at her parties. His hypersensitive movements continually incline to moments of confusion.

'I'm on the Church council,' Cloete says. 'And I can assure you the problems are not as simple as you think, Markus.'

'Would you then rather have sat on Jan van Riebeeck's?' Markus lights his pipe, pressing the tobacco down with his thumb.

'Meaning?'

'Everything was so uncomplicated. Simple. Jannie's times knew none of our problems, as you call them. Remember Cloete, you are the person who sees all the problems in every situation. But, problems might just be the stones out of which we build our own Tower of Babel.'

In the corner of the room, the record player reaches the end of the record, the stylus scratches in the last groove. Markus quickly walks over, changes the record, then straightens a row of books on the shelf.

'Markus always makes me think of someone who opens your bedroom door, curses you, and then, gone, away on tiptoes down the passage to the next room,' says Pieterse, the publisher, who has just joined the conversation.

'Insane!' shrieks the same woman on the divan.

'Just bloody hysterical,' comments Pieterse without looking in her direction.

'Out with it, Pieterse,' – it's Markus again – 'Are you going to publish Hein Hansen's latest book now that he is a political exile from his land of birth? No? Cowards!' and he sniggers behind his pipe. 'Don't look so bloody guilty. I'm only teasing you. You are all so damned serious tonight! Why?'

'And he's the one to talk!' Pieterse retorts. 'He who has of late invited women to his home who walk around in his castle with bra-pistols.'

'Who?'

'That girl over there on the divan. Don't you know her?'

'No, I don't. What about her? She's innocent and beautiful.'

'And she's wearing one of these new gadgets. A bra-pistol.' And talking behind his hand: 'Did you imagine in all your naiveté that her tits alone could be so big?'

'Look, Pieterse, I don't know what the hell you're talking about,' Markus says seriously.

'I'll show you. Do you see that piece of string hanging out of her sleeve? There! Now, within that little piece of string there is another one, and that is the pistol's trigger. She simply hooks it round her forefinger, opens her hand, and she spits fire. That, dear Markus, is what I'm talking about.'

'I don't know the girl. Ag, perhaps she's just afraid or something. Where do you find these bullshit stories?'

The coloured man has walked over to the window. He peers out. And he is no longer smiling as he turns back.

'Klaas brought her with him. She's nursing in Paarl. Klaas told me about the pistol. He knows her well. She takes lessons at one of those shooting schools which they now have for women. Bloody good shot with the thing, I hear.'

'It must be fun to coach them when they're wearing those pistols,' Cloete says with his hands in his blazer pockets. 'I made my auntie join a club too. She often returns home quite late from work. It's dangerous.'

'Ag, that girl is completely harmless,' Markus says as if to close the conversation. 'Tell her to take a few pot shots at the telephone pole behind the house if she feels the urge. John, what about another drink?' It's only when Markus speaks to him that the others become aware of the coloured man in their presence. He nods. 'I'll take one for the road when we leave. I have to be at the office again tomorrow.'

'Excuse the others; they're a bunch of boozers!'

* * *

Later as he steps out onto the veranda, the man notices that it's overcast. Behind the Cape-Dutch houses hangs a veil of grey rain. Dark and heavy fir trees bend as if they're trying to drag themselves free. He looks attentively through the glass doors at the people in the room. Then he takes three darts from the hoard against the wall and starts throwing them. His face is taut, expressionless. But his knuckles show up white on the hand with which he clasps the darts.

Markus walks across to the girl on the sofa. Klaas sits next to her, prods her bra with his fingers.

'Shoot the clown!' Markus says to her, and then, extending a hand: 'We've not yet met.'

'She can shoot a coin off the top of a bottle,' says Klaas with hazy pride. 'Just like that, *pienggg* …'

'Give it a miss, Klaas!' the girl says.

'But it's true,' he argues. 'You shoot it, *pienggg*.'

Markus laughs, but his eyes are unnaturally dark beneath his thick eyebrows.

'You have to work late into the evenings, I suppose?' he enquires gently.

'No,' the girl answers.

'It's at me. She fires at me,' Klaas says, and he starts to sing: 'Three blind mice, see how they run … Give us another dop, Markus old chap. Before we're all blasted to hell and gone.'

The girl places her hand over her glass. 'No thanks, no more for me,' she says.

'Strange lady,' Markus jokes somewhat uncomfortably. 'Doesn't drink, but carries naughty firearms!'

'Three blind mice,' Klaas sings. Everyone else in the room has suddenly stopped talking.

'Show us how you shoot with that thing,' Cloete says. 'So my wife can see that it's a good thing …'

The girl looks embarrassedly at Klaas. He says unhelpfully: 'Ja, come on, show them. Show how you can shoot a coin *pienggg* …!'

'Ja, come on …'

'Ja, come on …'

The girl looks out at the veranda. 'I can't shoot inside the room,' she says.

'Outside on the veranda then?' Markus asks uneasily.

'OK.' She stands up, pulls down the string and fastens it around her wrist with a leather thong. She hooks the eye of the inner thread about her fore-finger.

Outside, on the veranda, she poises herself against the wall. The coloured man removes the darts from the board and joins the other guests.

Markus removes the dartboard from the wall, searches in his blazer pocket for a pencil and draws a circle on the worn plywood. 'One shot only,' he says. 'Otherwise somebody's going to get hurt here tonight. Guns are not toys.'

'Boeeeeee!' the others respond in a chorus.

The girl stands at ease with her feet a few inches apart. She holds her right hand stiffly at her side, then turns with a quick movement of her wrist. A dull crack sounds.

'That's it!' Klaas shouts out. 'Bull's-eye!'

'Hooray!' Cloete says and he staggers over to the low wall of the veranda. His wife joins him there.

'Insane!' shrieks the woman with the low-necked dress and she holds her glass out in front of her. 'Let's drink to the security of the Republic!'

Klaas staggers forward, draws another line on the plywood and quickly steps back. He signals with his hand.

With breaks of varying length, four shots crack out. Four little holes appear on the line.

'Insane!'

'Let's call it a day now,' Markus says. 'Somebody is going to get hurt here tonight.'

But Klaas says, 'Don't worry, I'm her instructor. I know what can happen.' The girl nods her head in agreement.

'She'll – you know what – she'll shoot your silhouette out against the wall if you go and stand there,' Klaas says. 'Ja ... And it won't be the first time she's done it either. It's the way we teach them. Best method to get rid of their fears.'

Once again, a silence falls.

'She's had a few drinks, Klaas. Damn it, don't be obstreperous now. Come on chaps, let's go and top up. Hell, miss, but ...' Markus walks towards the door.

But everyone remains standing.

'It's just like the circus trick with the knives,' Klaas explains.

Markus stands in the doorway with his hand against the frame. 'Go and stand there yourself. Loud mouth!'

No one has seen the coloured man stepping forward.

He positions himself against the board. His eyes are dark and big, but his face shows no emotion. He stares straight at the girl in front of him. She shifts her feet.

Then she bends forward and releases two swift shots. On either side of his hips two holes are smashed into the wood.

'Crop his candle!' Klaas chortles.

The man looks down, smiles broadly. As he lifts his gaze, the girl turns away and presses past Markus into the room.

No one follows her.

Everyone gazes at him.

He lifts his glass off the low wall. 'To the security of the Republic,' he says and his mouth is smiling. But his eyes are not.

ABRAHAM H DE VRIES

Ruins

Translated from the Afrikaans by Ina Rousseau
From: *Om tot verhaal te kom* (2003)

It started with the letter. She wrote:

The school about which you often spoke is still there, high up against the Karoo kop-pie, but it's just a skeleton, virtually a ruin, the window panes are shattered, some of the window frames have been removed, the door frames are long gone, the roof tiles clatter in the wind. It's a cold northwesterly wind this time of the year, that makes one imagine that one hears the school bell, the shuffling of feet, the voices of the children drifting from the direction of the playground. But the ring at the top of the netball pole has been rusted off and now the pole itself has been removed and used as firewood.

Regular prayer meetings were held in this school, serving all the farms. But there wasn't a soul who knew the first two lines of any hymn or psalm. The lead singer was old Jan Bekkies and his friend, old Piet Skapie, was his very real help. Jan had a deep, husky voice which sounded wobbly, like a branch dragged over corrugated iron; when he set in the tune it felt as though it echoed in one's stomach. Piet's voice, on the other hand, sang in tune, but it was high pitched, almost a whistle, and when he really wanted to impress (for instance, when the dominee was present), the notes broke up like a musical morse code. Jan would set in the tune of *On a Hill Far Away* at too low a pitch, then Piet would drag it out with the line about the old rugged cross, and the other prayer-goers only joined in singing about the emblem of suf-fering and shame.

Now, prayer meetings on the farms took place in the evening. And this is where the devil himself regularly filled his lungs and joined in the singing. The school had no electricity, there were lamps and candles in the windows, on the table and on the little bookshelf at the back of the classroom. Only the two lead singers had their own candles.

Need I say more? To sing a note, one needs to breathe, but breath extin-guishes candles easily.

At every prayer meeting. The candle in the candlestick would appear between the eyes and the hymnal, the flickering light would reflect brightly in the old reading glasses and on the unsteady white page of the book, then the first note sounded, then there was darkness. That is why no one attending those prayer meetings knew the first two verses of any psalm or hymn.

In previous years quite a few of the farmers were in the habit of milking their cows to the rhythm of *The Storm May Roar without Me* or *Praise the Lord O my Soul*, sung softly. I'm sure they still do it at present, the world doesn't change all that fast. Or one could hear the women kneading loaves of bread. 'Jesus loves me that I know' – the notes drawn out lengthily in a whiny manner. But on returning from the prayer meetings, they didn't sing the words, they only la … la … la … laaaed amongst the cows and over the bread flour.

What makes one remember this kind of triviality more vividly than the sermons? Laughter is – to quote Balzac from memory – a privilege granted to man alone because he has sufficient causes for tears within his reach.

What saddens us so are the dilapidated homesteads in the district. The substantial farmers have bought the land of the lesser ones and on every small farm there used to be a homestead too, as you know. Some of them have been restored, four of them, next to the road as one drives to town; they are now inhabited by professional people who prefer not to live in town, I know of a teacher and an attorney's clerk, that's the type of person. But many of the homesteads have been abandoned to the mercy of the elements and you know what happens: at first a large rust spot appears on the corrugated iron roof, the outlet-pipe between the roof and the tank disappears; where the water runs down the wall, the plaster peels off piecemeal. The termites eat tunnels and holes into the walls, until they crumble and collapse.

A few of the homesteads are maintained by the owners at as little cost as possible. Coloured families of farm labourers have been permitted to go and live there. In fact, two, I can't think of any more now. And I say permitted but that's not quite what happened. Some farmers are quite glad to have people whom they know well living there and more would presumably grab the chance, but some of the houses are haunted, they say. Where this or that family used to live, an old man in a nightshirt with a candle in one hand and a rifle or sjambok in the other walks from room to room. Just their way of saying: we know those families and none of us ever ventured beyond the kitchen. Many bad and ugly things happened there. Let go, let go, let the past be over and done with. Let those houses crumble and fall to dust.

Ghosts past and present still abound here.

So it was. Don't let nostalgia erase from our memory that which those who were separated from us by law remember. I won't name the man in this story, out of shame because he could have so many names. Let's just say that he lived on Sias's farm against the koppie behind the irrigation canal. When his wife was still alive it was a pleasant-looking, neat house overlooking Sias's dam and the finches settling on the willow branches at nightfall.

They always used to say that when his parents were still alive (they also lived there), he already had a foul temper. People blamed his father for not scolding him sufficiently for this. I don't attach overmuch importance to the guilt of the fathers, he got mixed up with the wrong bunch of friends in the school of agriculture, that's where he already hit the coloured servant in the dining hall so hard with his fist that the poor bloke had to go to hospital. The principal suspended him for two months. Only two months and he had already had a warning. No, I never knew his wife, but I attended her funeral because it was during the school holidays and I was at home. He walked beside her coffin, cursing, when they passed me (I was standing underneath the pepper tree) he was cursing her for doing this to him. A week before that he had arrived from town early one afternoon, something he very seldom did – and a scarf which she used to tie around her hair-knot was floating on the dam. He couldn't find her anywhere.

After that he turned the devils in him loose on his labourers. Two or three times he was sentenced for assault (every time with a money fine). Norrie Willemse who worked for him at the time was the first labourer who hit back and spent almost a year in gaol for that. Yes, I am talking about the same Willemse about whom you are probably thinking now.

Then a strange thing happened. The police were there with him on the farm, they had gone there to warn him after a fight with Norrie. But it wasn't necessary and he told them so. He stopped drinking and in what was left of that year a complete change came over him. That is the way people told the story, they say he even attended a prayer meeting one Wednesday. Things were getting better for him.

And at the same time things became worse. The story of the locks I heard from De Necker, who used to work at the Co-op. He told me that man had him guessing, because every week, every blessed week, he walked in there to buy a different kind of lock. Until De Necker's curiosity got the better of him one day and he enquired about it point blank; that's how he came to know. Because the old man no longer drank at that time, he was lying awake at night, and as a result of that wakefulness, I suppose, his conscience started to niggle him. He developed a terrible fear of burglars. De Necker told me there were locks inside and around that house, on the gates, on the screen doors, the windows, whatever could be locked, he closed with a lock. Even the tap of the water tank.

It must have gone on like this for the best part of a year, because Willemse was sentenced in February, the sentence was reduced because of good behaviour, he walked out of prison at the beginning of October. On the very evening that Willemse was released the man who was responsible for his unjust imprisonment once more locked his house from front to back, every outside door, all the windows, all the inside doors. The next morning the police wanted to call in a locksmith from Mossel Bay, they didn't know how to gain entry, because he had the keys with him, they found the keys under the bed.

The old man was lying on the bed, a corpse, he had been strangled. But the windows showed no sign of a break-in, on the contrary, the pane was lying outside in smithereens. Someone must have tried to get out. It didn't take the police long to arrest Willlemse again. He admitted that he had been waiting in a concealed corner of the bedroom until the man for whom he had felt such hatred had both of them locked up in the room.

What can one do about the ruins? It was only here that we heard the expression for the first time; the people say that an old house mourns when uninhabited. It is as though the house is aware of the fact that there is no longer anybody to accommodate, nobody to be sheltered against the onslaught of wind and weather. As though the hollow sounds of the wind in the rooms and the passages become unbearable. Then the tears start streaming down the gutters.

But I don't want to create the impression that everything just collapses into a state of wrack and ruin, even around the old dwellings new farmlands developed. The vineyards are trellissed high because a harvesting machine brings the harvest in more rapidly than hands. They foresee a time in the future when manual labour will become even scarcer. By means of filter irrigation the farmers can now plant vineyards halfway up some of the koppies where previously only elephant's food and Karoo shrubs had grown. This landscape has changed more dramatically in the past few years than in the previous decades.

... But it was also different, oh yes, it was different.

As one drives into town from your farm, just about where the tarred road starts, you'll find on the left side of the road, beside the river, an earlier flat-roofed house which was provided with a stoep and broekie lace and still later a pitched roof of Sandveld thatch. Neels, the owner, was a respected and wealthy man for those days, he didn't buy on credit and he didn't undertake extensions on his farm for which he couldn't pay in cash. His wife, Isa, supported him in everything. But Isa was not very well – one could notice that in her appearance, she was pale and in her eyes she had that strange softness of people who had made their peace with the worst that could happen to them. They were gregarious, Neels and Isa. On Sunday afternoons, parked underneath the pepper trees, there were always cars of townsfolk, of neighbours, of guests from as far as Riversdale and Worcester. On the chairs in the sitting room and on the backs of the benches the antimacassars were spotlessly clean and for coffee or tea drips there was a little round serviette in every saucer. Every Friday Isa baked melkterte and raisin tarts and a few loaves.

In the late afternoon after the cars had all left, Neels would say to Ouma Janie, who worked for them: Janie, come, I will take you home, then I will come and help missus Isa with the dishes, come on, let's go, we can start again tomorrow. And usually Ouma would then reply, the kitchen is my pride, meneer Neels, it is an unknown night we are entering, please wait for me a little longer.

But that afternoon even before Neels had taken Ouma Janie home, he had noticed that Isa was not herself. She had been so quiet while the guests were there. Janie had said: Meneer, I'm sleeping in the outside room tonight, some of my laundry still needs ironing, and also in case meneer and missus need me. And Neels did not stop her.

Neels and Isa went to bed early, when everything in the farmyard was quiet, the cows back in the little field, the milk foaming warm in the big tank where the big lorry of the cheese factory was to come and slurp it up in the morning, the chickens asleep on the lowest branches of the fig tree, the mountain behind the house dark and far away and peaceful.

Towards the small hours of the morning he woke up and reached over to light the candle. But in the light of the moon shining through the slits in the blinds from the side of the fig tree, he saw that Isa was lying still, very still beside him, the one hand on her breast, the other on his arm. That must be the reason why he woke up, he thought.

Her hand was cold. He listened but there was no breathing, no heart beating any longer. Neels then lit the candle, took his Bible and started reading. Then he went to her side of the bed, knelt down and said a prayer for her immortal soul, for the empty place in his home and for everybody on the farm who would miss her so much. After his words dried up, he remained on his knees for a while, then he said amen. And even before he'd finished talking to his God, he resumed in his heart the conversation with her of so many years.

The next morning when Ouma Janie knocked on the door to bring the coffee, he said to her: 'Come in. But, Janie, bring from now on only one cup, please.'

That is also how it was.

Tinus has survived the dark times following in the wake of his dismissal. He no longer at night in his sleep grinds his teeth. And he no longer talks about it. Foreign affairs and the missions in which he served, The Hague, Washington, Oslo, served one purpose only: we came to stay here as though we were sent here, it's also the game which we used to play with each other when we were still on the move from country to country. We'll stay here till we're called back. Let's not get too involved with local matters. Remember it's temporary.

I can hear you laughing. All right, laugh. It's now getting to be more than five years and even I now admit, there is no longer any 'home' to which we want to return, we have been generally adopted. I can cook tripe already, I know how to prepare jam from pieces of *kambro*, we belong to the open tennis club and Tinus has been chosen as a director of the KWS.

Last night Jan (Le Grange; Jan van Zijlsdamme, as he is called) came to visit and was talking about the ever-topical good old days (as though we had experienced them, I suppose it is these folks' way of saying: it feels as though you have been living here all along), Jan said he had thought about you the whole day, I must write to you and ask what could be done about the old buildings and the new problems. Of the latter I haven't written. Things will improve, we do believe that. The Little Karoo gave us back our future.

I started answering you yesterday. Some deterioration we can never stop, I wrote. Dilapidated old farmsteads are ugly, they are not worthy of those who lived in them and of their histories. I said, they gave shelter to ways of life, and I have added, you should take note of the plural, the spirit of the time sometimes wants to make one believe that there was only one kind of relationship in all the houses: that of master and slave. Those also occurred – let us not deny anything. I wanted to add that we dare not ever forget what happened to all of us, no matter how tragic, how repulsive, how silly, we know by now how our stories outlive our judgements.

But then the telephone rang, it was Izak and he told me about the cruel and senseless murders of Hannes and Anna Marais of Bobbejaankrans, a farm twelve miles away from you. Why did I think farm murders are committed elsewhere, in Gauteng, in the Free State, but never in the Little Karoo, never involving people whom I know? (The policeman who was murdered in Lindley last week was a friend of Hannes, we met him on their farm and Anna told me on the telephone just last week how brave his wife was.)

Further than that I didn't write, you'll understand. I walked around in the back garden because I wanted to let at least part of the night pass before telling my family.

Towards the early hours before going to bed I reread your letter. And then more clearly than ever I realised it is not any earlier time we long for, it is not with the crumbling ruins of the past that we know not what to begin.

I long for now, for a present, for the village and the people about whom you write, the vineyards, the lucerne fields, the houses, the Karoo koppies, irrigation, neighbours who talk about the weather and about the country and about problems and about where in the Swartberg mountain the most beautiful *Protea Aristatas* grow this year.

I yearn for all our dreams and for all our illusions of being at home.

JAN RABIE

Maiden Outing to Rondebosch

Translated from the Afrikaans by Wally Smuts
From: *Nooinsrit* (1965)

The day after the *Vogelsang* dropped anchor in the bay the commander gave all the Netherlands women an opportunity of travelling to the *ronde bos* [circular patch of bush]. Never before had any of them gone farther than a mile or two into the interior of the strange, perilous land, but all were only too eager for a chance of getting away from the fort.

At crack of dawn the five matrons and the three young girls, whispering and giggling, settled themselves on the wagon. Amid the laughter and cheers of the escorting soldiers and infantrymen the commander dashingly swung himself onto his horse and raised his hand as a signal. A gun-salute boomed from the walls of the fort, the echo rebounded from the Table Mountain, and the sound died away over the bay which was lightly brushed by a gentle breeze from the west. At once the drivers shouted to their oxen and the creaking wheels began to turn.

The clumsy wagon of Cape wood and the rugged road had the women frequently clutching at each other or hastily disposing their dresses. The stately Mevrou de Stael, especially, seated up in front beside her sister-in-law Maria van Riebeeck, was hard put to hold firmly onto the luncheon basket *and* maintain her dignity. Yet it was a real pleasure excursion. The sallies of Antjie die Boerin who was holding her latest scion of many, the six-week-old Dirkie in one practised arm while indicating the scenery with the other; the excited exclamations of the girls, Cornelia Boom and Christina and Petronella Does; the fresh summer morning smelling of aromatic herbs; the unfamiliar cornet-shaped flowers as large as saucers growing on the slopes of the Windberg; and perhaps, too, a subconscious awareness of the significance of the outing, had made each woman there experience a glad tingling as never before in all their four-and-a-half years at the Cape, the hard, hungry years of struggling to get a foothold on the southern tip of Africa.

More than the others Maria sensed that this was an exceptional day. After so many nights of lying awake and hearkening she knew all about her husband's cherished plan: that now, after the blessing and providence of God, the Dutch settlement should be established even more securely with the aid of free-burghers – the first colonists.

A smile lit up and softened her face every time she noted how her husband would spur impatiently ahead and then ride back again at a gallop to point out something they ought certainly not to miss. His slight, vibrant figure, impeccable in fine broadcloth set off with silver cord above the rich garters and stockings of Napolese silk, reassured her and confirmed her thoughts: he has a right to be proud of what he has achieved so far, and to feel optimistic about what lies ahead.

Beside her Mevrou de Stael spoke: 'If only Jan does not need to spoil his fine clothes again by having to embrace the greasy, sooty Hottentots!'

'Yet I should like to see the commander cutting capers with them,' Antjie quipped irreverently.

Mevrou de Stael's disapproving eye quickly changed the girls' suppressed laughter into hasty speculations about other possible dangers. Such as lions, for instance, or the hyena that was shot as recently as the Saturday before last. With stealthy glances and delicious tremors they observed the armed soldiers before and behind the wagon, and then asked whether they might get down and walk a bit. But their mothers refused curtly, and made them pull their skirts down even more decorously.

For the troops and foot soldiers, mostly young and unmarried, it was also an out-of-the-ordinary day. One of them, Elbert Dirksen, had such goggling calf's eyes for the elder of the two Does maidens, the sixteen-year-old Christina, that his mates began to chaff him, till the corporal sent him ahead to roll rocks out of the road.

Whenever they paused to give the beasts a breather and allow the men a draw at their pipes, Christina was blushing with crimson cheeks. The worst part was the teasing of the mischievous Cornelia who was no older than she and would be marrying the second gardener in four months' time. Even the commander's wife had to lean over and, under the pretext of settling Petronella's headband, chide the girls, yet softly so that the menfolk shouldn't hear.

Noon was still far off when they came to the new lands close to the *ronde bos*. Here the soil was richer and the mountain even more beautiful, romantic and crenellated like a castle wall with deep, craggy battlements. At the little guardhouse everyone got off.

The commander immediately led the ladies off to view the wheat and tobacco fields within a sturdy paling. He drew attention to everything: the clover field where three men were making hay, the young apple and orange trees, the luxuriant Turkish and Roman beans, the full heavy ears of wheat which the harsh south-easter could never blast here in the shelter of the mountain.

'And all this has been accomplished in only six months. Just imagine what a number of industrious farmers could produce here,' he exclaimed enthusiastically and gestured with his Gouda pipe, that had long since gone out, to embrace the whole valley of the Liesbeek River.

'The honourable Company could really not do better than lay out permanent farms here.'

Beside him his wife nodded approvingly, but half distracted like the other women, enchanted by the splendour of the bushy landscape and the luxuriant golden corn below the mountain's flanks.

'Indeed, it is more beautiful even than in the fatherland,' one of them sighed dreamily – Janneke Boddys who had arrived at the Cape only recently.

'For the young children this is already their fatherland,' someone else said.

'Well now, I don't know,' Janneke objected, 'what about all the savage natives that …' But her words were swallowed by the commander's laugh. The roguish and daring Cornelia had come from behind and placed her hands over his eyes as he was trying to relight his pipe, and in a high falsetto voice she now demanded that he should guess who it was otherwise he would remain 'blindman's-buff'. The commander good-naturedly entered into the spirit of the prank.

Wherever they went the corporal and his six men followed at a short distance. Herry [leader Khoi/Hottentot band] and his treacherous minions were still skulking around here somewhere, near the Bush Hill, though, in truth, shivering with fear like a lady's lapdog whenever he saw a Dutchman, but a guilt-ridden Hottentot is also a dangerous one. When the girls kept straying off carelessly the corporal respectfully asked them please to keep close to the party.

It was Maria who finally persuaded her husband to return to the thatched watch-post, where Antjie Boom was expertly arranging the picnic luncheon. The two sentries had betimes gathered green branches and erected a cool shady bower against one of the turf-built walls. While the commander in his restless way was still supervising elsewhere and giving instructions, the women spread cloths, laid out the cutlery, and seated themselves serenely in the shade. Antjie die Boerin detracted somewhat from the genteel scene, by loosening her clothing and beginning to suckle her baby. Mevrou de Stael found it expedient to direct the sentries' attention to their duty of standing somewhat farther off to watch out for advancing hordes of Hottentots.

The portly Antjie looked after the men and sighed: 'The poor things, they do not see a baby every day.'

The women were so convulsed with laughter that quite a few dress fastenings had to be unobtrusively slackened.

The commander arrived at last and smiling at his wife he asked: 'Well, well, and are the ladies enjoying the day out?' Satisfied with the reply, he turned to the soldier who had come to stand ramrod stiff as a sentinel near him: 'No, no, Dirksen,' he said, 'go and relax: for you and the others today is also a holiday.'

'All men are as blind as moles,' the daughter of Janneke Boddys whispered to Christina, and was given a little pinch in reply.

Everything went merrily, except for a troublesome wasp that made Janneke sit rigid with tightly closed eyes while she asked repeatedly in a trembling voice: 'Is it still there?'

After the repast the commander led them higher up to see the mountain stream and the work of woodcutting in the forest.

It was hot: still, balmy warmth like the feel of a sleeper's skin. The young women were constantly running ahead, but the older women were slower, quieter and more sedate, as if the sight of the men's activity all around to tame the new rich earth made them realise more acutely that they were women and mothers of children.

The mountain stream whispered its soft urgency through the languid summer afternoon, and in the bush the doves cooed and the echoes of the axe strokes resounded from the nearby crags. Once some foresters passed close to them with two ponderous, straining oxen hauling a baulk of timber for the pier. Later on and higher up they were able to overlook the glorious landscape, far out to beyond the neck between Bush Hill and the mountain, where they could just descry tiny cattle grazing near the little brown hive-like huts of the Cape-men.

Jan van Riebeeck explained everything: where a mill to grind the wheat could be erected beside the stream, and which of the sturdy yellowwood trees they would try to preserve. His wife listened as attentively as possible but the faint smile hovering about her lips wavered at times to betray some trepidation, especially when the growth of trees began to draw in more densely and the close, dank odour of moss enfolded them.

'We've come far enough now, Jan,' she warned gently. 'See, the others are getting tired.'

But now a search had to be made for two of the girls who had strayed farther ahead, accompanied by one of the soldiers. The commander sent two others to call them back, and the women sat down to rest. Only poor Mevrou de Stael remained standing in order to conceal a torn stocking beneath the stately tent of her dress.

A flower had been the cause of this interruption. The soldier, Elbert Dirksen, had told the girls about a waxen red flower growing just off the narrow track, and of course they had to go and examine it. Awkward and trembling he had plucked one for Christina and she scolded him for his vandalism. And then her younger sister had to run to a great yellowwood tree, after borrowing his knife, to carve out her name.

'This will remain here very, very long,' she said, pouting prettily, and proceeded to add the date: 5 December 1656.

Suddenly Christina gave a little scream. Framed in the wild foliage were two brown faces staring open-mouthed at her.

Elbert immediately reached for his flintlock, but the Hottentots laid down their bundles of spears and with expressions of crafty pleading made signs with their hands.

When the girls backed away the Hottentots emerged from the shrubbery, their mantles of oxhide draped proudly over their shoulders, and their necks and wrists glistening with copper circlets. They did not look at the soldier, only at the young girl. Then there was a thrashing in the bush where the blue tunics of more soldiers appeared, and suddenly one of the Hottentots began to stammer in broken Hollands: 'Why you drive us away?' And in hesitant, apprehensive pride he called again to the girls: 'Why you want to take our land?'

Then the two soldiers came up with levelled muskets, and he and his companion sprang round and vanished into the bush.

'Wh ... what ... why did he ... talk so to me?' the girl stuttered.

'They often plague us like this, ever since we began the fields and the watch-posts here, but we only wish to raise food for ourselves ...' Elbert began to explain.

But his fellow-soldiers laughed: 'Oh, forget the savage heathens. Eh, Christina, you lovely thing?' And boldly they wanted to touch her and Petronella. Giggling and coy, the two sisters warded off their eager hands and ran back to the little path where the others were waiting.

A little while later, after the girls had been thoroughly reprimanded by their mother, and the commander had praised the soldiers for not acting over-hastily, the stroll back to the guardhouse was resumed. No afternoon could possibly be more beautiful, and more soothingly evoke obliviousness to care.

When the shadow of the mountain began to lengthen Maria became restless to return to the fort where her youngest had been left in the sole care of a young slave girl. Antjie's sleeping infant, who had been carried a while by an embarrassed soldier, now also awoke protesting loudly.

Tired yet satisfied they all gathered by the wagon. But before they left, the commander celebrated the memorable day by distributing tobacco and broaching a small vat of Spanish wine. Those of the ladies who wished were given some, as also the male escort, who jubilantly proposed a rousing toast to this maiden journey of the ladies, the founders of the nation.

Finally the commander clapped his hands for silence and called: 'We're leaving now. Think well whether we've forgotten anything!'

Nobody had; only Christina looked perplexed for a moment as if she were trying to think.

Then a box was placed beside the wagon to enable the older women to ascend. The soldiers fell in again, and the procession started off light-heartedly from the *ronde bos*, back to the fort in Table Bay. In front rode Jan van

Riebeeck, dapper and elegant as always on his horse that tomorrow would be drawing heavy loads again.

The trumpeter was among the infantry, and Antjie Boom asked him please to blow the rust from his throat. Which he proceeded to do with good heart. In this changed, contented yet somewhat subdued mood they fell to singing, one by one. Past the golden-crowned corn field and for long stretches of the peaceful road homeward the men and women sang, gay songs and sad ones, also the one they all remembered best: the national anthem, the 'Wilhelmus van Nassauwe'.

KAREL SCHOEMAN

Seed in a New Earth

Translated from the Afrikaans by Wallie Smuts
From: *Die saad in die nuwe aarde* (1967)

It was in 1905 that my grandfather came to Bloemfontein with his wife and children – a Dutch teacher who had accepted a post here and so emigrated to the Orange River Colony. Dominee Postma met them at the station, and for a time they stayed at the parsonage.

My grandfather was soon wholly caught up in the work of the newly-founded school and in various activities of a language-and-politics nature, where he strove with characteristic Dutch energy and intransigence; but his wife stayed at home, and for her there was no escape from each day's reality. They already had two little girls, and soon after their arrival in Bloemfontein a third was born. They had little money, and she toiled alone without the help of servants in one rented house after another – from Blignault Street they moved to Grey Street, from Grey Street to Victoria Road, from Victoria Road to Charles Street, from Charles Street to St John Street, from St John Street to Cromwell Road and back again. That was her life; packing and unpacking, irons heating on the stove, bread being kneaded in the kneading pail; grime in the bath, dishwashing, darning, scrubbing the floors; food to be cooked, and clothes that had to be made, so that the children, when in bed at night, were lulled to sleep by the soothing whirr of her sewing machine.

The baby that came soon after their arrival did not live long, and she sat before the window, pregnant for the fourth time, and watched as her husband left in a hired cab, with the little coffin on his knees, away up the long, straight road, under the summer sun, past the last few scattered houses and bluegum trees to the cemetery in the veld.

When the burial was over he returned alone to the house leaving his child in the strange earth, the soil of the new land. Alone in the silence of the day, scorched by the sun, where a bird called somewhere in distant trees and the veld stretched bleakly away to the horizon, alone with no shadow before him on the dust of the road; and from the top of the little rise he saw again the town with its orange roofs and brick walls among the green pepper trees and karees, cypresses and pines, a tiny oasis in the vastness of the veld. He drove on down the slope, his child left behind in this earth: down to the long shadow of the bluegums, streets with carriages and horses, houses with open front doors, and children playing; over the market square and past the church back home.

It had always been a country town, nothing more, a simple place with long straight streets and rows of unpretentious houses sheltered from the sun by scattered trees. At Nagmaal – the Communion services – the farmers came and pitched camp with their wagons and tents, and market days brought a bustle to the square, but nothing else disturbed the tranquillity, only the wind soughing through the leaves, and a driver calling to his oxen somewhere down the street. And the eddying dust settled again.

The war came; the enemy's soldiery, travel-worn from their long advance through the summer, marched into Bloemfontein, and the English took over. The people of the land stayed on in their little 'church' dwellings, shaded by pepper trees; they came from the country districts in their horse-drawn carts, sun-bonneted women and bearded men. They passed the long days, and went to church on Sundays with Bible and hymn book; they thought of their lost ones, and in the evenings they gathered by lamp or candlelight, their rare utterances dropping into the great silence.

The silence enclosed them and swallowed up their last dismayed words. The land with its distant horizons and lofty sky, the land with its blockhouses and scattered ruins had passed into the power of strangers, and in this town a strange flag waved from the flagpoles and outlandish uniforms moved on the streets.

The rulers were foreigners who possessed the land, though it could never have a claim on them; they governed it, but never had any love for it. They had come to the colony as strangers, and as strangers they left it. Their stay was merely a temporary exile which could wring no concession from them, and their lives in this foreign clime consisted of a series of gestures and conventions that bore no relation to reality, but which was at the same time very gracious, so gracious that the years of the occupation were perhaps also the golden years of the town's history.

It remained a little town, nothing more, with peaceful streets and dogs and children playing; at dusk the cows were brought in from their grazing on the commonage, and each one took her own way home to be milked. The status of capital rested somewhat uneasily on this simple rural community, what with the presence of a Lieutenant-Governor and garrison, government offices, high court of justice and cathedral; but the people who came to sojourn here were little concerned with the harsher facts of their existence.

They have all long since left, or have died, but their memory has lingered like an aroma, and one still unexpectedly comes across faint reminders of their tenure. They dwelt in great brick houses with gables and turrets and wide stoeps; they lived in shaded rooms filled with furniture and ornaments. Behind the dim green of spreading creepers they gathered in the coolness round their

478

tea-tables, under masses of wistaria and pergolas glowing with roses, under acacias where the bees buzzed in the cloying sweetness of the blooms. Scent of flowers and smell of dust in the heat of summer, with men in light suits and women trying to dispel the heat with their fans. The land sweltered in the sun, with shadows dark beneath the trees, and no motion in the leaves. In the distance Bantu women called to each other and then the sound was lost again in the silence; only the woman in the rocking chair moved gently to and fro as she looked out at the green of the garden and the blinding glare of the street beyond.

A vehicle would pass – buggy, spider, cab – with the beat of hoofs muffled in the dust, and then the street was empty again, empty and straight with its rows of houses, and rows of shops, and nothing at all moved until the wind breathed, making the flag before the city hall stir lazily. Dusty streets and brick houses and pepper trees and corrugated iron hoardings; a dog asleep in the shade, a shopkeeper standing in his doorway. Slowly the shadows lengthened, and the civil servants drank their whisky while, from the veranda of the Club, they watched the colour changes wrought by the late afternoon, the dust clouds bright gold in the last declining light. It became cooler, and the man in shirtsleeves, watering his garden, heard the drops from his watering can rustle over the banked flowers.

Periodicals were paged through, meals planned; tables were laid and innumerable bits of bric-a-brac dusted; servants polished stoeps and rubbed the harness bright. Invitations were sent out and accepted, newspapers unfolded, letters written. A woman stepped across the street under her parasol, the hem of her dress slightly raised, and the dust retained the narrow pointed impressions of her shoes. People gathered for races, gymkhanas, and parades, and when the orchestra played in the park they came to saunter over the lawns, and far under the trees, to the measure. of the music; they went to the theatre, and dined with each other, little enclaves in the gentle intimacy of the lamplight, with a toast to the Queen at the end of the meal. They played cards, they listened to music. The nights were oppressive and dark and hot, with little night creatures that called in the silence, and the fragrance of roses lying heavy on the air. On the tables brightly polished crystal caught the light, glittering and translucent.

In the details of old photographs and the finely printed columns of the newspapers you can rediscover their world, their gestures and voices caught and fixed for all time – the bend of an arm, the sweep of a train; the hand raised, the head turned – and from reports of weddings and receptions, the guest-lists, names and colours of dress materials, and all the incidental detail, one can recapture the texture of their lives. The carriages assembled, gentlemen helped the ladies alight for the social gatherings that brought variety to the the long uneventful days ('the bride, who looked charming, was attired in the purest white crepe de Chine'), and they paused to exchange greetings and bows, and chat in bright clear voices, the men in dark suits or morning coats, glossy top hat in hand, and the women brilliant as flowers. ('The bride's mother wore a pretty reseda green gown and white toque, trimmed with pink roses and reseda green velvet.') Everyone knew everyone else, and each one had his place in the hierarchy of this outpost: Lieutenant-Governor, clerics, justiciaries, the military, and the civil service officials – a tightly integrated band, a small garrison for foreign service ('the sergt-majors and others of the regiment formed up outside the porch of the cathedral and formed an arch with their swords, under which the happy bride and bridegroom repaired to their carriage'). No doubt or fear disturbed their self-assurance, and there were no threats to set the security of their little world aquiver. Bolstered by pride, prestige, wealth ('Mr and Mrs Fawkes, silver inkstand; Mr Sennet, card stand') they bowed and took their leave, returned in their equipages to the great, over-furnished houses (Sir Andries and Lady Maasdorp, silver card case'), and carried on ('Mr and Mrs GA Hill, set of bon-bon dishes') day after day, performing the ritual gestures, until the exile finally ended, and freedom returned. Then they departed, and their going held no pain or loss.

Just as they, my grandmother never gave her love to the land, and she too remained a stranger and an uitlander. She was Dutch like her husband: as a child she had come to Rotterdam with her parents, and lived there till she was thirty, near the cattle market where the pigs were dragged squeaking by their tails from the cart, in a city where wagons and carriages clattered over the cobbles and the harbour was full of foreign ships. She had minded children and knitted stockings and scrubbed the doorsteps; from the water channels in the park they had gathered duckweed for their goldfish. She became a teacher, and had met my grandfather during a vacation, one summer in the green rusticity of Oosterbeek.

She had followed her fiancé to South Africa just before the war broke out, and they were married in Pretoria. One Sunday morning they had walked down Church Streeet, and seen the old president sitting on his stoep. They stayed on a farm for a while where my grandfather taught at the school, until the war broke out. He was taken away by the English as a prisoner of war, and she, ill with malaria, had remained behind when everyone else fled. The farm buildings were burnt down, and for days the smoke pall hung in the air.

The war came to an end; children were born; they came to Bloemfontein and settled there. Life went on. The bread rose under the blanket with its lion design, white sheets on the line billowed in the wind; on Sundays they went to church. With the years came acquiescence, but nothing more.

This land does not ask to be loved, neither does it try to command love: it is just there, to be accepted or not, without any dependence on man, its starkness unrelieved by the chance beauty of mountain or forest. It is just there –

480

the flat monotonous land, vast under the sun, with its profound silence and its remote distances, far-away hills hazy in the heat, the wind in the long grass and the dry scent of the afternoon; thorn trees, a rare road, an arching heaven – what else can one say of it? An aloof, detached land that asks no love, but when love has once been given it is given irrevocably, and nothing else matters, nothing else worth loving remains.

Her love she never gave. From the line where she hung her washing, from the kitchen door where she paused with a dishcloth in her hand, she could see the veld stretching beyond the last bluegum trees with the clear horizon etched against the sky. She heard the birds calling in the distance and the wind that stirred the leaves; she saw the clouds gather sparkling white in the sky, and she turned her back on them to go inside. The land remained alien to her, and the people with their flat intonations and long silences were not her people.

Like the English colonials she remained a stranger and an uitlander, and who can blame her? For like them she had her memories: the high-stacked greyness of a city, misty mornings and the tenderness of the light, parks and trams and trains, and voices calling in another, a familiar language; a cool, damp atmosphere, and mud-trampled streets after the thaw set in; Spangen and Kralingen and the Bergsche Plassen; Delfshaven, Waalhaven and Katendrecht. She never succeeded, as her husband had done, in freeing herself of the world into which she had been born, and she never attempted to do so.

Yet, even though, cherishing all these memories, she remained a stranger, she was not like the soldiers and the officials. She never gave her heart to this land, but she did give her life, more than fifty years long; she gave her loneliness, her homesickness and longing for what had been, and which she now yielded up forever; and so this land, after all, became hers too, and not as it was with the English colonials.

Wounds heal with time, but the scars remain. As time passed the sharpness of her longing became dulled – her children married and grandchildren were born – but she retained her memories and the heartache lessened very slowly. She was a silent, withdrawn woman, with little weakness or self-pity, and she did not complain. As a child I often heard her speak of Holland, but the things she told were merely stories to me, and I never realised the actuality all these things held for her. So she bore them around within herself, dwelling solitarily in that past from which she stemmed.

Wounds heal and grief gradually passes, until even their memory is finally erased. In a later war Rotterdam was levelled from the air, street after street destroyed, and house after house razed to the ground, all the familiar landmarks blotted out. Oosterbeek was also ravaged by great fires, and the trees that had shaded and made green the days were all consumed. My grandmother died when she was well in her eighties, and her husband died a few days later. In Bloemfontein, too, old houses have been pulled down and old trees felled: what remains is forlorn, neither town nor city, with the earlier graciousness gone, and only an awkward attempt at modernity to replace it. The dust has not retained the track of the foot; the glass has slipped, fallen, and lies shattered on the ground. The pressed flower has not kept its sweetness, and old paper has become yellow and fragile. She is dead, and the silence has finally enfolded her.

I knew her as a child, but I did not know then how desperately lonely one can be in a strange land, how nostalgia for the things that have been part of you can grow to be a physical pain. Long, long after her death did I get some inkling of what her exile must have cost her, and what never-ceasing longing she must have endured in a strange land for fifty years; and then, in this single facet of her life, I realised how, in an accumulation of individual lives, a new country and people originate, a new nation is born. It is not easy for seed to germinate, to burst its sheath in the darkness of strange soil. Only in the second or third generation does the plant grow to maturity, the roots reaching deep and wide into that new earth.

DUGMORE BOETIE

Three Cons

First published, 1968

My friend Tiny and I were walking through the streets of Johannesburg back to Sophiatown, determined to steal nothing on the way. To ensure this, we rammed our hands in our pockets and kept our eyes glued on to the pavement before us. As we crossed Main Street, someone in a khaki dust coat with a duster rag in his hand paused from cleaning a shoe shop window and greeted Tiny. After walking on for a few yards, Tiny said to me, 'Will you believe it, Duggie, if I tell you that the man we just saw cleaning the window back there doesn't work at that shop?' I nearly stopped in my tracks. Tiny said, 'Don't stop, man, walk on … He works all the blocks in town dressed as he is: dust coat and red duster. His name is Victor. He's what the Americans call a confederate trickster.'

'Confidence trickster,' I corrected.

'When he sees a likely victim admiring what's in a window, he'll move and start cleaning that window. After a few strokes with the duster he'll move in and say, 'If you like that, I can get it for you. You see, I work here. If you want it I can get it for you Back Door at half price.' It never fails, Duggie. Victor goes to the back of the shop. When he comes back, he'll be carrying a neatly-wrapped shoe box. The victim won't open the box for fear of getting Victor into trouble with his employers. Money will exchange hands. His victims are mostly domestic servants. When they reach wherever they're going, they find that they've just bought themselves something like a pair of old useless shoes. I don't care for such a profession, Duggie, it's too slimy for my liking. I prefer the open game. Like the gangster, the shoplifter, the smash-and-grabber. A life with no strings attached, no conscience pricker. Something that needs no brains, you know what I mean, something like jazz that goes in the one ear and out the other. No regrets, no nothing. Like food you ate the previous day.

'But Victor's game, it's too classic. It has to be because it lives with you forever. It sticks to the subconscious mind like meat in pie. A future of "Brother, look over your shoulder!" The danger in this game, Duggie, lies in injured ego. Not the deed, but the principle will get you in the end. What greater provocation is there on earth than when you enter a human being's mind and start misplacing things? No living soul wants to be made a fool of.

483

'The success of every confe … I mean confidence trickster depends upon cleverness. Cleverness that oozes from a brain that gets its stimulants from the vitamins of an empty stomach. It's like a game of snakes and ladders; the victim usually prefers the rungs of the ladders instead of the long and safe way around. Only to be swallowed by the snakes, and emerging from its bowels with nothing to show but grief and misery.

'The seekers of manna from heaven are responsible for the con-man's bulging waistline, Duggie. If they ignore the shortcuts of life, they won't be touched. They should let the perspiration of their brows tighten their purse strings. Be deaf, and he'll never reach you, let alone touch you. Remember, his life depends upon explaining.'

'Tiny,' I said with awe, 'I didn't know you got education!'

After listening to Tiny, I started thinking deeply. I was mauling over what Tiny told me. Like Tiny, I didn't care much for such a game. In spite of that, that confidence trickster gave me an idea. An idea that could be made to work. All it needed was guts and brains. And I think I had them both.

The following day I went to the Indian Market alone. I didn't want to tell Tiny my idea, in case it back-fired. At the Market I bought a second-hand khaki overall. I took it to an Indian tailor shop. I instructed the Indian to sew the letters 'OK' on the shoulder-blades. The letters should be red. This is the uniform of the African staff at the OK Bazaar, a department store.

This Bazaar is big. It boasts three storeys and a basement and about two to three hundred African workers. It's always packed with customers of all races, so it's only natural to see African labourers carrying goods about the place.

I spent one whole week studying the place from the inside. When I was sure of all the angles, I donned my overalls and went to work. I wasn't a registered employee, but that did not worry me because only I knew it.

I took advantage of two facts. One: to all whites, a black man's features don't count. Only his colour does. To them, we are all alike. When you're black, you're just another black man. It's all contempt. They don't even bother about your real name. To them, you're just John, Jim, or Boy. Your daddy spends nine months thumbing through a dictionary for a fancy name to bestow on you and then some white trash comes and calls you what he feels like without even bothering to think or look at you. If that isn't contempt, then what is?

The second fact – and I like it best – is that they have a total disregard for our mental efficiency. That's why they couldn't dream that anyone, especially a black man, could be capable of doing what I did in this big Bazaar.

If I took from the third floor, the staff there thought I was from the second floor. If I looted the basement they thought I was from the ground floor. A white assistant actually said to me in the basement department, 'Boy, leave that and help me here.'

If I carried the goods across town to Black Mischark's shop, the police thought I was a delivery boy. I was the only one who didn't think. It wasn't worth it. Not while everyone else did the thinking for me.

As time went on things became even easier for me. I was getting accustomed to the place. I learned where to take and where not to take. Best of all, the staff, both black and white, took a liking to me. Hell, it looked as if I was going to get promotion. A few white sales ladies would send me out for sandwiches and cigarettes for them. I was a John-do-this and a John-do-that. The only place I kept well away from was the pay-master's office. Hell, I'm not greedy. Fridays, when the boys queued for their pay, I was gone.

Good things never last, and they always seem to stop lasting on a Saturday. 'Stop thief!'

I froze. At last, I thought. When I looked back, I saw one of our European female workers frantically pointing at an African who was hurrying away with four boxes under his armpits.

'Stop thief! Stop him, John!' She was looking directly at me. When I hesitated, she said, 'Hurry, he's getting away!' I cursed the thief under my breath and made after him with every intention of letting him get away. Just as I was about to veer off at one of the entrances, two interfering white men caught him just as he was about to sprint through the street door.

'Here Boy, we got him for you.' I was going to ignore them when I became conscious of someone breathing down my neck. Looking back, I saw the floor manager breathing flames like a dragon. With him were two African workers. There was nothing I could do. So I did the next best thing. I grabbed the thief.

There was fear in the man's eyes; he was shaking badly. I was shaking just as badly, but they must have thought that it was because I was holding him.

As we led the thief back to the manager's office, I sought for a way out of this awkward situation. I felt certain that once I entered that office my doom would be sealed. Desperately I reviewed my position, but everything looked hopeless. I stole a quick glance at the floor manager and saw him angrily grinding his teeth as he led the procession toward his office. Clearly this was no time for me to ask one of the African workers to hold the thief for me. Spectators made way for us and as we moved on our number swelled with officials and curious onlookers. You'd have thought we'd just caught a dangerous maniac. I saw my chances of getting away slip with every step we took. As he opened the office door, the manager looked at me and growled, 'Don't lose him, or you lose your job.' I didn't mind. You can't lose what you haven't got. I pushed the thief roughly in, meaning to retreat, but someone pushed me from behind and heeled the door shut. It was the second white man.

Putting up a bold front, I went to the closed door. My hand was closing around the knob when the floor manager paused, phone in hand and said to the second white man, 'Don't think we didn't know.'

'Oh God!' I groaned. So all the time he knew. Turning to me he said, 'You stay right here and guard this kaffir.' The kettle and the pot are on the same stove, I thought. All sizzling equally. After that I was completely disregarded. It was as if I didn't exist.

There's nothing so gnawing and nerve-wracking as uncertainty, especially if you're guilty. It's like hanging in mid-air with nothing holding you up. You know you're going to fall and break your neck. That's all right, you've half expected it. But what produces mental agony to a point of madness is this unseen thing that's holding you up. I was fast becoming a total nervous wreck.

There was a light tap on the door. Me and the thief both stiffened visibly. Instead of the expected police, the lady who served at the counter where the goods were stolen came in. She gave me a dazzling smile and the thief a dirty look.

'You want me, *mynheer*?' she asked, addressing herself to the floor manager.

'No, Miss Smith, you go back to your counter, I'll send for you when the time comes.' She turned and left the office, but not before flashing me another smile.

I was changing my weight to the other foot when my jaw itched violently. Before I could guess again, they came in. I don't know whether it's imagination, but every time I see a policeman, my jaw begins to itch violently. They didn't even knock, and I didn't have to guess their size. They were there. I felt my skin crawl.

'Boy!' The floor manager had to call me twice before I could swallow my fear.

'Boy, will you go and tell Miss Smith that the police are here.'

'Heh? Yes, *Baas*.'

'Then come back here with her.'

I walked out of that office stiff-legged, as if I was leading a funeral procession. I just couldn't believe such luck.

'Then come back here,' the man had said. What kind of fool did he take me to be? In pirate stories, once they make you walk the plank, you don't walk it twice.

Once through that door, they never saw me again.

* * *

Durban stank of one problem. All the domestic servants were men. In Johannesburg we have women. You can always make love to one of them and live with her in her room at the back of the master's house. No rent, free food and one or two of the master's shirts while he imagines that they are in the wash.

In Durban there was no such thing. Otherwise I wouldn't have bothered with sleeping accommodation. I would have done what I used to do back in Johannesburg. Made love to one of the working girls and lived with her. Even if living in the backyards of white men's houses is not without its ups and downs.

I'm reminded of one night when I went to my girl's room at the back of a white man's house. It was late when I got there and my girl must have long been through with her duties. What I really remember about that night, is that it was so cold that my nose wouldn't stop running. When I got to the room I knocked. But there was no reply. I tried again. Still no result. I made for the spot where she always kept the key for me to find when she was on her day off, but I drew a blank.

Again I repeated the knock and still nothing happened. I was afraid to knock loud for fear of waking up the house. That time of night they have a dangerous tendency to shoot first and ask questions after. After repeated knocks, I gave up. I decided to think.

One thing stood out like the sharp point of a Zulu warrior's spear, and that was if I tried reaching Sophiatown at that time of the night, I would end up in gaol for having no night special. I looked around for a place to spend the night, but could see none. Then I became conscious that I was leaning against one of those giant trees that are so frequently found in white suburbs. Without a moment's hesitation, I climbed the tree, meaning to spend the remainder of the night there. Better a human bird than a gaol bird.

I must have dozed off because something startled me. I would have fallen headfirst to the ground if I hadn't taken the precaution of tying my belt to a branch and then around my arm. I peered into the night hoping to see what it was. Then I heard a noise coming from my girl's room. Someone unfamiliar with the mechanism of the lock was fumbling with it from inside.

Hurriedly I undid my belt from the branch. My fingers were numb with cold and my descent was not without hazards. Finally, I made the ground without much damage except bruised hands and torn pants. I was in time to see a stark naked figure emerging from the door and making his way to the toilet which was situated on the other side of the garden. Like lightning I went into the dark room and locked the door behind me. I groped toward the bed where the bitch was deep in sleep. Undressing quickly, I crawled into bed. As my icy body came into contact with hers, she moaned and said, 'Why so cold dear?'

'Shut up you bitch.' I felt her shiver, and knew it was not from cold.

I waited. Then it came. First softly, then loud, then louder, then frantic. It was the naked bum outside. Unlike him, I raised my voice triumphantly and said, 'Climb the tree, pal, climb the tree.'

As usual, I'm not the brainiest of men. There are people with far more. The bastard pushed the mouth of the garden-hose through the small window, and before I knew what was happening, the water tap was turned on full force, soaking me, bitch, blankets and all …

* * *

'How do you like the town, Duggie, after three whole weeks at home?'

'I don't.'

It was Tiny talking to me. We were walking down Bree Street in the direction of Doornfontein. There was a bitter feeling in me. I don't know whether it was caused by failure to prove myself, or just plain fear. I had just recovered after getting my jaw broken in a mix-up with the police.

Tiny was penniless. I had a shilling piece somewhere in one of my pockets.

He interrupted my troubled thoughts by saying, 'Give me one of your cigarettes, Duggie.' Shaking my head, I said, 'I wish I had some, Tiny.'

The tips of my fingers went into the top small pocket of my jacket where I kept stubs. They came out empty. I went through all my pockets with the same results. Then my fingers met with the shilling piece.

I looked around and spied a tea-room. Holding the shilling exposed in the palm of my hand I said to Tiny, 'What do I get with this? Lotus or Rhodian?'

'Get Lotus, Duggie, I want to smoke, not brag. When one is broke, it's always wise to stick to necessities.' I went into the shop.

In the shop, lined next to the counter, stood five Africans all dressed in blue overalls. In their hands were empty jam tins for tea-buying purposes. Daily customers I thought. Just behind, sat European customers having their lunch.

I took a place next to the first African, I didn't want to waste time. I rapped the shilling piece on the glass counter to draw the owner's attention. If you irritate them that way, they quickly get rid of you by serving you first.

'Packet of ten Lotus please.' He gave me the packet. I handed over the shilling. He was about to give me my four pennies change and there the matter would have ended. But fate took a hand. Just before he gave me my change, he was urgently beckoned by one of his servants. Instead of giving me my change he answered the summons.

Then I saw it. I didn't see it before because his body had been screening it. A roll of pounds as thick as my wrist lay just within arm's reach. It was tied with a rubber band.

I must be a born thief. A real stranger to hesitation with impulses that work overtime. Without thinking or looking around, my hand shot out like the tongue of a deadly cobra. At the same time I sensed rather than saw Tiny inspecting the window display just outside the shop entrance.

It was fast. Too damn fast, especially for the naked eye. One minute the roll was in my hand, the next it was sailing through the air towards Tiny who caught it expertly and without thinking. Then he slowly made his way to the opposite pavement.

I was about to bolt through the door after Tiny, but when I looked at the African next to me, I saw to my amazement that he wasn't a bit concerned with me. Instead, he was grumbling to his fellow worker about the slowness of the shopkeeper. It was unbelievable, yet it happened. NO ONE SAW ME!

I decided to wait for my change.

When the shopkeeper came back, the first thing he noticed was that the money was missing. Next, he looked at me. The look he gave me made me curse myself for still being where I was. What kept me rooted to the spot still disturbs me right up to this day.

Without a word he went around the counter and bolted the door, surprising everyone in the cafe. Then he told the Africans to point out the one who took the money. They all denied having seen the money, let alone having stolen it.

After carefully searching each one of them, he told them to go. Then he turned to me. Before touching me he told me to give back the money. For the first time in my life I became truthful. I told him I didn't have any money. As always, people just never believe.

'Look,' he said as he released a long-held breath. His body bent sideways and he leaned with his elbow on the glass counter. 'I know you have the money even if I didn't see you take it. Now let's be sensible; if you give me the money of your own free will l promise to let you go and there the matter will end. But if I search you and find it on you, I'll make you suffer.'

'Go to hell! I haven't got your money, but you got mine, you got my four penny change.'

'Listen, for the last time, give me the money.' I stood my ground. Then he searched me. He didn't find anything of course. How could he when the money was on the other side of the street?

'Now you give me my change,' I said, full of confidence.

'You stay right there,' he said meaningfully.

He was picking on me because those other Africans were his daily customers, also I was nicely dressed in a way. My clothes alone made me suspect number one, also the fact that it was my first time in his bloody shop. He was bright, but in a dull way.

Again he searched me. This time he was more careful. When he didn't find anything, he went to the phone and rang for the police. While we waited, he kept pestering me about his money, promising to let me go if I showed him where it was.

I told him I didn't know anything about any money. That the only money I know of was my four pennies change. And that still had to come to me.

I was more sure of myself. My only prayer was that they wouldn't send the same policeman who broke my jaws the month before. The shopkeeper could go to hell. He wasn't going to get any money from me even if he borrowed.

There was a sharp rap on the door and in they came. I mean the police. It wasn't the same one as before. This one was even bigger. With him was another one with a young pink face.

'Where is the Kaffir?' he asked. The shopkeeper indicated with his head towards where I stood.

He turned to me and bellowed, 'Where is the money, Kaffir?' I told him I don't know anything about any money except my four pennies change. The child policeman came nearer me and started jabbing me in the ribs with his baton. I kept facing the burly one who kept repeating the question. I was about to repeat that I didn't know anything about any money when they started working on me.

Suddenly, I heard a female voice scream, 'Stop! Stop! Can't you see you're killing him?'

The burly policeman said, 'Keep out of this lady, it's none of your business.'

'Where's the money, Kaffir?'

'No money, Baas, only my change.'

'You'll talk yet, you black bastard.'

My face was so numb, it didn't seem to hurt anymore. It lost all sense of feeling.

He was throttling me with the front of my shirt by screwing it into my Adam's apple. The veins on my forehead stood out like ropes.

His right knee turned my face into putty while his right fist kneaded different images into it.

I heard the lovely voice again, now more furious, 'Of course it's my business. I was sitting right here when this whole filthy business started!'

'Lady, for Godsake,' said the policeman impatiently, 'Will you for Godsake keep out of this?'

Squinting, I saw a white woman glaring at my tormentors with bared teeth, hair drooping over eyelids and arms resting palm-down on the table. She was spitting out words faster than a green snake could spit poison. And the words were just as venomous. The way she went on, it was as if she was suffering more than I was. A lovely bundle of fury.

'The fact that I was sitting right here when this whole thing started makes it my business.'

'Lady, for the last time mind your own business.' I began to wonder if those were the only words he knew.

'To begin with, that boy didn't take the blasted money.'

'How do you know?' scowled the policeman.

'Because it's a logical, if not a physical impossibility for him to have taken the money.'

'Lady, you're not telling me anything.'

'If,' continued my guardian angel, 'God did not use some of your brains to give you extra buttocks, you would have arrived at the same conclusion. Stop behaving like a third-rate bully and start using that machinery in your head! Leaving it to rust won't get the money back!'

'Madam, one more word out of you and I'll run you in for obstructing the police in the course of their duty.'

'Since when does duty mean beating up a man who hasn't been formally charged, and on private premises for that matter? In fact you are so brainless that I believe you would make a fool of yourself in front of your superiors by locking me up for trying to help you!'

As the man straightened up from beating me, I saw that his trouser at the knee was soggy with my blood.

'All right, lady,' he said harshly. 'You tell us what happened to the money.'

'I can give you a hundred reasons why it is absurd to think that this poor boy could have taken the money. But three should be enough for a brain like yours!'

Then she went into detail. It was like a school teacher explaining a simple subject to a sixteen-year-old pupil who had no business in the third grade.

'That boy was searched twice by that insolent shopkeeper, yet the money was not found. If, as you say, he took the money, then where in heaven's name could he have hidden it? Because,' said my lady with great emphasis and spacing every word, 'he never once left the shop, nor did he move from where you found him! Tell me now,' she was almost begging, 'do you for one minute think that if anyone could steal a roll of pounds he would be so stupid as to stand and wait for a measly fourpence change when the door was wide open and he had every chance of running away? I', she spat, 'would give everything I possess, and I can assure you it's considerable,' (Chancer, I thought) 'if that boy is guilty of theft.' I stole a glance at the other customers and saw most of them shaking their heads in agreement.

The burly policeman said, 'Then who the hell has stolen the money?'

'That's the first sensible question you've asked since coming through that door! Now kindly direct that same question to the man who phoned for you. For all we know, he might not have lost a penny, it's just his word against this poor boy's.'

The law turned his eyes from the lady to the shopkeeper and there was fury in them.

The shopkeeper said to the lady, 'Do you think I would have gone to all the trouble of searching the Natives and calling the police all for nothing?'

'There! You have done it!' said my lady triumphantly.

'Did you really lose money?' asked the policeman facing the shopkeeper.

'Of course!' sputtered the man indignantly.

'Show me the spot where the money was.' The man pointed at the spot behind the counter. The policeman released his hold on me for the first time, leaving me to sway with the tide. Examining the spot the policeman asked, 'Was he the only Kaffir that was standing next to the counter at the time?' Worriedly the shopkeeper shook his head.

'There were four or five others,' he added hastily, 'But those were my daily customers. They would not steal from me.'

'What!' barked the policeman, throwing his hands into the air in a hopeless show of disgust. 'Are you standing there telling me that Kaffirs don't steal when they were born for nothing else? Why did you let the rest of them go?'

There was a note of anger in the shopkeeper's voice as he said, 'I tell you those other natives are my daily customers, and this boy, well, you can see for yourself how he's dressed, he's a skellum.'

'Now you're judging the man by his clothes!' came the voice of my guardian angel. 'If I remember right, those boys that were here were in a much better position to have made off with the money! They were all dressed in overalls – right! And in their hands they carried jam tins – right! Jam tins full of tea bought from this shop! It's my guess that the roll of pounds – if he did lose a roll of pounds – is safely reposing at the bottom of a jam tin of tea!'

The big policeman started to say something, when an eager voice from the cradle said, 'Should I lock up this Kaffir?'

'No, better let him go. What will we charge him with? We've already messed up his face.'

Turning to me, the policeman said, 'Scoot, Kaffir.' I slowly shook my head and stood my ground. Glaring at me he said, 'Well, what the hell are you waiting for?' Through bloody, swollen lips I said, 'My four-penny change.'

Turning to the shopkeeper he asked, 'Has he got change coming?'

'Yes, he gave me a shilling for an eight-penny packet of cigarettes.'

From his pocket he selected four pennies and threw them at me. I picked up the pennies and counted them carefully before pocketing them.

CHRIS BARNARD

Bush

Translated from the Afrikaans by Sharon Meyering; revised by André P Brink
From: *Duiwel-in-die-Bos* (1968)

There is a kind of stillness that consists of more than just the absence of sound; a stillness without movement; a stillness that is almost death itself. The air is still, the leaves and grass are still, the birds are unbelievably still. In the afternoon when the women leave the mango pips and disappear amongst the trees, that is when the stillness comes. It is the hour without cicada – the lifeless hour when one begins to suspect that even the sun has become stuck somewhere.

It is in an hour like this that Kirst comes.

The hollow footpaths of the bush bring him here, over a hundred rivers and just as many plains – each river, each plain, each night's hyenas closer to a godforsaken moment. He approaches over the rock ledge where the women dry the mango pips in the morning, over the bright and hard yard; I hear his footsteps over the stones, see him climbing the wooden stairs of my high stoep, into the shadows. Then he stands between the pot plants and I wait for him to cross the threshold.

His face shines, presumably from sweat. He looks at me where I sit at the table, and perhaps I think that he has grown old. But I recognise him despite this. I have already recognised his footsteps.

'Good day, Kirst,' I say.

Or perhaps we don't speak. Kirst says nothing either way. I hear him approaching and wait for him, as I have waited for him all these years. Yes, my heart thumps in my chest, and there is a warm feeling on my tongue; but that is all that has changed. I don't move. I do not try to escape. My eyes are fixed on the door and I wait for him. He appears – his face wet with sweat. That's right: his face shines with sweat. He says nothing and I say nothing.

It's dead simple.

Perhaps even the same revolver; a small black Beretta with a snub nose. He trains it on me and I take my pipe out of my mouth and put it down on the table.

Is he swaying slightly on his feet? Or is it I moving to and fro? Initially, I can't decide. Only later do I realise what is wrong: it is my head; I am shaking my head. Maybe I am trying to say: 'No, Kirst, not after all these years!' Or maybe there is something inside me that merely wants to say how terribly old he's become.

But it's not I who eventually speaks; it's Kirst who says, 'It's you ...'

How well I remember you, Kirst! For almost an entire lifetime, day in and day out, I have been breaking down and building up your face, piece by piece: the broad forehead under windblown hair, brown eyes that probe everything, sharp cheekbones and a full, manly mouth and square chin. But now? What is this, Kirst? What is this wrinkled forehead, thin hair, hollow cheeks with stubble, this toothless raisin mouth? Only the skull is unmistakably you.

You cross the threshold and see me and say, 'It's you ...' as if you believed, until this very moment, that all your searching for me would turn up nothing.

If you are surprised to see me sitting here, Kirst, it is probably because I haven't stayed the same either: for almost a lifetime you searched for a young and inexperienced man, and now that you have caught up with him ...

It would be inappropriate to offer you something to drink. And I dare not ask about your wellbeing.

Talk about myself? What can I say? That I was expecting you? That I am glad you came?

There is, however, something we could speak much about. Loneliness. But then again your loneliness and mine were never the same. Mine was that of someone waiting for his punishment; yours, that of someone who had punishment to inflict. Self-pity and hate. But perhaps they are the same thing.

I think about it, every day. And of all the places in Africa where I noticed you on a street corner, or in a bar, alongside a quay, on a river boat, by a customs house, in a lodge. But every time I was disappointed that it was not really you.

On a godforsaken town square in Zanzibar I see a man with his shoulders. And it is him. After all these years it is him. And he turns and sees me and walks towards me. And I wait for him, wait for his hand to move to his pocket, wait for the small Beretta and the white knuckles. But the man with Kirst's shoulders walks past, bored, and doesn't see me.

In a sultry hotel room in Luanda, a room with cockroaches and cracks in the wall, someone comes slowly up the stairs. I recognise Kirst's footsteps. I wait. Know, at long last, now. But he passes by; his footfalls disappear down the passage.

Somewhere in the Karoo, on a cold station where I wait between the milk cans for the next train, he appears suddenly out of the signal room. He has a flag in his hand, but his flag and tattered uniform do not fool me. I recognise his nose and high forehead. He comes closer in the dusk, very slowly. And I wait. I know: if he stands beside me, the Beretta will appear under the flag and he will lift the barrel and a blue flame will burst out into the dusk. He stands near me, for more than a quarter of an hour; and the train comes and I climb in without him noticing me.

In front of the post office in Mbabane, between the dead fish at the market in Beira, suddenly on an afternoon, some distance behind me between the silver trees near Seinheuwel, on the open deck that night on Lake Victoria en route to Muhutwe, in Swakopmund, Coquilhatville, even in Ibadan the last summer before I came here.

And since I came here, I have been expecting him.

I stand among the banana trees and watch two bantams scratching in the dusty backyard under a small, withered lemon tree. The afternoon sun shivers against the white kitchen wall and the bougainvillea is a feverish purple dance against the steel-grey sky. And suddenly he stands in the footpath that leads up from the river, the sweat silvery in his eyebrows.

It is different from what I expected it to be.

All these years had made me resign myself to the idea of his ultimate coming. I thought I would remain dead still if I saw him; I wouldn't move, wouldn't run.

But the fear is suddenly in me and as terrible as the sun. He stands there, weary and dishevelled, much older than I expected.

His hand moves towards his pocket and I know it is so he can take out the Beretta, but my hand comes up to my face and I want to say: 'Wait, Kirst – wait first!' Yet I say nothing. My throat is bone dry and no sound escapes; nothing. It is he who speaks first; Kirst says, 'It's you …'

You probably already know for yourself: one's memory, when one gets older, loses its sharpness. You have discovered this? And nevertheless, I hesitate to ask – you might think it is a ploy to try and prove my innocence. Like a naïve child who kills a cat and then faces his mother, whistling, with angelic eyes when she comes to punish him.

No, Kirst. I ask for nothing. I might not even try to hide my fear. I must only look at you. And wait.

Yet: it would actually be easier, wouldn't it? If I could just remember?

Strange, and maybe a bit comical, that for some reason or other one starts running, and becomes compelled to keep running, focusing one's whole life on running, abandoning oneself completely and utterly to the chase – so totally that in the process one forgets the cause of it all.

That is not important. I know. What is important is that you came, at last you have finally caught up with me.

It's late afternoon and the reeds stand motionless in the lazy river. I kneel barefoot among the round stones, scoop up the tepid water with cupped hands, rinse the soap from my face and shoulders and chest. The foam dams up around my pale knees, comes free and disappears on either side of my calves. Drops of water cling between my eyelashes and in these drops the sun sets, a thorn tree squats lopsided on the riverbank, a reed stem pricks the green evening sky. And, suddenly, close to the sun, between the trees and reeds, he stands motionless looking at me.

I close my eyes. But his image remains. Through my red eyelids I see him standing, watching, his face expressionless, his arms slack against his body – only one hand slightly more alert than the other.

He looks at my naked body as if looking at a rock. And I suddenly remember what I look like. The chest muscles already limp, the shoulder bones much more prominent these days, the elbows sharper, the thighs whiter and skinnier, the veins on my hands bluer.

You could have spared me this, Kirst! This naked moment.

But even this, I fear, is of less importance now. And I struggle to stand up, step awkwardly between the round and dark stones. I stand erect before you in the water and my hands grope humiliated over my shapeless genitals.

God, was this really necessary? On top of everything *this* moment of complete defencelessness? Since your childhood you have been merciless, Kirst – very thorough and frighteningly precise.

So this is the moment, I take it.

Don't laugh, but all of a sudden I remember a strange finger on a map of Africa. How many different nights did I send it out on safari, bored, a small divining rod searching for water that suddenly stops triumphant over Angola or the Sudan and says: Kirst is here tonight.

And sometimes, less triumphant, more tired, mostly in the tepid and smothering heat of the summer, bent over an increasingly crumpled continent, the embittered prayer: I give up; I don't want to play any more.

In the white lamplight, the night an unspoken word outside, the night sweet about the ferns and bats, I suddenly know it is him at the window. And I look up and see his lonely figure, slightly unsure under his hat.

He comes out of the wet night. While I stand and wait in front of the window for the small gecko to come for his grain of sugar, the lightning flashes quickly, almost invisible behind the rain. But the fleeting moment is enough to recognise him: he stands watching the house, tired, in his dark raincoat.

Where the women dry their brown mango pips in the sun every day between the dark trees, the first light rosy against the bunches of frangipanis, he suddenly appears.

He doesn't know that I see him. Or perhaps he knows. But he stands a long time, looking. He is waiting.

And I watch him while he waits. I don't know if I am afraid. I only know that this is entirely different from what I imagined. Nothing in this moment is out of the ordinary. It is merely daybreak and he is standing in the yard.

Then, much later, he moves, I see his hand disappear into his trouser pocket. And it stays there. And in the backyard, half-heartedly, I hear the bantam crow. And he comes across the yard from the trees.

The morning smells of damp earth, of autumn grass, of plover eggs.

The morning smells of Africa, Kirst.

And I see you coming. I see you approaching slowly over the dry gravel. And the wooden stairs creak as you ascend, at your leisure, without haste, not at all afraid.

I don't look at your trouser pocket, although I want to. No, I look at your eyes; I search for your eyes – because, God, you've grown old, Kirst! Entirely too old.

Entirely too old.

And I say, without meaning to: 'Good day, Kirst.'

And he says, 'It's you …'

AC JORDAN

The Turban

From: *Tales from Southern Africa* … (1973; 2004)

It came about, according to some tale, that there was a man named Nyenge-bule. This man had two wives, and of these two, it was only the head wife who bore him children. But Nyengebule's *ntandanekazi* (favourite wife) was the junior one, because she was younger, livelier and more attractive than the head wife. Nyengebule's in-laws by the junior wife were very fond of him, all of them. He was a warm-hearted and generous man. The women especially – his sisters-in-law including his wife's brothers' wives – used to be delighted when he paid them a visit. They would crowd round him and listen to the amusing stories he had to tell and also to demand the gifts to which they were entitled. These Nyengebule never failed to bring, but because he knew he was the favourite *mkhwenyethu* (brother-in-law), he delighted in teasing the women before producing the gifts, pretending he had not brought them any gifts because he had had to leave home at short notice, or because he had lost the bag that contained them on his way, or because his wife had offended him in one way or another just before he left home, and he had decided to punish her by not bringing her people any gifts. Then he would sit listening and smiling as the women coaxed and cajoled him, calling him by the great praises of his clan and by his personal ones. But in the end the gifts always came out, each one of them accompanied by an appropriate spoken message of flattery to the receiver. Nyengebule was very popular with the friends and neighbours of his in-laws too, because he was a great entertainer, a great leader of song and dance. Whenever there was a *mgidi* (festival) at his in-laws, the whole neigh-bourhood used to look forward to his coming, because things became lively as soon as he arrived.

Nyengebule's in-laws were sad that their daughter could not bear this man children. In the early years of this marriage, they tried everything they could to doctor her, and when they were convinced that she was barren, they sug-gested that one of the younger sisters should be taken in marriage by Nyengebule so that she could bear children for her sister. Nyengebule's own people supported this and urged him, reminding him that, by virtue of the *khazi* (bride-tribute) he had already given for the woman who turned out to be barren, he could marry one of the younger sisters without giving any more cattle. But Nyengebule kept on putting this off. To his own people he stated quite openly that he did not desire to do such a thing, that he did not see the need for it because he had enough children by his head wife, and because he loved his junior wife even though she bore him no children. To his senior in-laws he spoke more tactfully, because he knew that it would hurt them if he stated that it made no difference to him whether or not there were children by his marriage with their daughter. So he asked them to give him time. With his brothers-in-law he treated the matter as a joke.

'Oh, get away, you fellows!' he said on one occasion. 'I know you will be the first to hate me if I do this, because it will deprive you of the opportunity to extort cattle from some other fellow who would have to give some cattle for the girl you offer me.'

Everyone present laughed at this. But one of the senior brothers-in-law pressed him. Then Nyengebule said he wanted time to decide which one of his growing sisters-in-law would get on well with his wife as a co-wife. But when the girls he promised to choose from reached marriageable age, he had some other excuse for his delay. At last there came a time when the in-laws decided never to raise the matter again. Nyengebule was happy with their daughter, and the best thing to do was to leave it to these two to raise the matter, if and when they should desire such an arrangement.

One day, there came an invitation to Nyengebule and his junior wife. There was going to be a great festival at his in-laws, on such and such a day and he was being invited to be present with his wife. With great delight these two made all the necessary preparations. Two days before the day of departure, it occurred to the wife that on her return from these festivities she would be too tired to go gathering firewood, and that it would be wise to gather sufficient wood now, to last her some time after her return. She mentioned this to her co-wife, who decided she might as well go and gather some wood too.

The two women left home early the following morning. When they entered the woods, they separated, each one taking her own direction to find, cut, and pick dry wood and pile it to make her own bundle. But they kept in touch all the time, ever calling to each other to find out if things were going well. The final calls came when each one thought her bundle was big enough, and the two came together to sit and rest before carrying the firewood home. This was early in the afternoon.

While they were sitting there, there was a chirrup! chirrup! The junior wife was the first to hear it and she immediately recognised it as the call of the honeybird. She looked about, and saw this tiny bird fluttering about, now towards her, now away from her, and then towards her and away again.

'The honeybird!' she said and sprang up to follow it.

The honeybird led her on and on, chirruping as it went, until it came to a bees' nest. As soon as she saw this the woman called out to tell her co-wife what she had 'discovered'. The head wife came immediately, and the two gathered the honeycombs and piled them on a patch of green grass while the honeybird fluttered about hopefully. When they had finished, they picked up all the honey, except one comb that they left for the bird, and returned to the place where they had left their bundles of wood, and they sat down and ate together.

As they ate, the head wife took two pieces at a time, ate one and laid the other aside. She did this until they finished. It was only when she saw the head wife packing together what she had been laying aside that the junior wife became aware of what had been happening.

'Oh!' she said. 'I didn't think of that. Why didn't you tell me to put some aside too?'

In reply the head wife said, 'You know why you didn't think of it? It's because you have no children. It's only a woman who has children who re-members that she must lay something aside as she eats.'

The junior wife made no reply to this, and the two picked up their bun-dles and carried them home.

Nyengebule had been busy all day setting things in order. As far as his side of the preparations was concerned, everything that he intended to take with him to this festival was ready. Even the large fat gelded goat he was going to give as a son-in-law's customary contribution to the festival had already been chosen and fastened to the gatepost, so that it should be ready to lead away the following morning. Now he was waiting until his wives returned so that he should announce to his head wife formally that he and the junior wife would leave at cock-crow, and also to give orders to his boys as to what had to be done by this one and by that one while he was away.

As soon as his wives had entered their respective houses and seen to the few things that usually need straightening up when a wife has been away from her house the whole day, Nyengebule went to the house of his head wife and made this announcement and gave the orders to the boys. His head wife lis-tened very carefully as he gave orders to the boys, and when he had finished, she went over them all, taking one boy after the other:

'Have you heard then, So-and-so? Your father wants you to do this and that while he is away. And you, So-and-so, have you heard what your father says? He wants you to do this, and this, and that.'

After this, she brought out the honey. She took some combs and served them up to her husband in a plate made of clay, and the rest she gave to her children.

'So you women discovered bees today!' said Nyengebule as he gratefully received his share.

'Yes,' said his head wife. 'It was *Nobani* (So-and-so) who discovered them. She was drawn by the honeybird.'

'Well done!' said Nyengebule. 'But aren't you going to have any yourself?'

'No, thank you. I had enough in the woods.'

So Nyengebule ate his share and finished it. Then, thanking his head wife for the honey, he said goodbye to them all and went to the junior house. He was looking forward to a much bigger feast of honey. If his head wife had so much to give him, certainly his *ntandanekazi* must have laid aside much more for him, especially as it was she who had 'discovered'. There were no children to share the honey with, and he and his *ntandanekazi* would enjoy the honey together, just the two of them.

He found his junior wife busy with her packing. The evening meal was not yet ready. Nyengebule did not say anything about the honey, because he thought his *ntandanekazi* wanted to give him a pleasant surprise. Maybe she would produce the honey just before the evening meal. But when the food was ready, his wife served it up to him and said nothing about the honey. After the meal, she removed the dishes and washed them and put them away. Now, surely, the honey was coming? But the woman resumed her packing, paying particular attention to each ornament before deciding whether to take it with her or not. She would pick this one up and add it to her luggage, and then replace it by another one. Now and again she would find something wrong with the beads of this or that necklace and pull them out and reset them. She would dig out some ornament that she had not worn for a long time and compare it with one that she had acquired recently, taking long to make up her mind which one was more suitable than the other for this occasion. This went on and on until everyone else had gone to sleep and the whole village was quiet.

When at last she was satisfied that her luggage contained everything she would require for the festivities, the woman yawned and looked at her husband.

'I think we had better sleep now if we mean to leave at cock-crow,' she said.

'Sleep? Isn't there something you've forgotten to give me?'

'Something to give you?'

'Yes! Where's all the honey you brought me?'

'I didn't bring you any honey.'

'You're playing!'

'In truth, I didn't bring you any honey. If you think I'm playing, look for yourself. I forgot really.'

'You forgot? You forgot *me*? What is it that you remember then, if you forget *me*?'

Before she could reply, Nyengebule grabbed a heavy stick and in his anger he struck her hard. The blow landed on her left temple, and she fell to the ground. Terrified at this sight, Nyengebule flung the stick away and ran across the hut and bent over her body, calling her softly by name. Weakly her eyes opened, and then they closed, never to open again.

Nyengebule burst out of the hut, his first impulse being to shout for help, but no sooner had he run out than he retreated into the hut on tiptoe, frightened by the peace and silence of the night. He knelt by his wife's body and touched her here, here, and there. Dead! His *ntandanekazi* dead? Yes, quite dead! What is he going to do? He cannot call anyone in here now. He must bury her before dawn. Yes, he must bury her alone. He is lucky too that everyone knows that he should be away at cock-crow. He must bury her and leave at cock-crow as arranged. Then his head wife and the children and all the neighbours will think she has gone with him.

He took a shovel and a long digging-rod and crept out to dig the grave. When he had finished he returned to the hut and looked around. That luggage! That luggage of his wife's! That must be buried with her. He carried the woman's body and laid it in the grave. Then he brought the luggage and laid it beside her body. He covered the body with earth and removed every trace he could find of this night's happenings. But there was one thing he had not noticed. The turban his wife had been wearing that evening had dropped on the ground between the house and the grave.

Nyengebule returned to his house, but not to sleep. What must he do now? Can he still go to his in-laws? Yes, that he must, because if he and his wife do not turn up, the in-laws will know there's something wrong and send someone to come and see what it is. But he has never gone to such festivities alone. His wife has always gone with him. How is he going to explain her absence this time? It will not sound good to his in-laws to say their daughter is ill, for how could he leave her alone then? What is more, they might do what they have always done when their daughter was reported ill — send one of her younger sisters to come and look after her and her husband. But go he must, for this is the only way he can find time to decide what to do. He will leave at cock-crow as arranged. Then he will try to be as he has always been until the festivities are over. Then what? Then what?

'*Kurukuku-u-u-u-ku*' crowed the cocks. Nyengebule crept out of bed and picked up his bags. He tiptoed out of the hut and fastened the door. He spoke softly to the goat as he approached it, in case it should make a noise and rouse his dogs as well as those of his neighbours. But the goat did not give him the least trouble. It was willing to be unfastened and led away.

Nyengebule travelled fast, like one who was running away from something. The goat did not handicap him because his boys had trained it for purposes of riding. Sometimes he led it by the rope, and sometimes he drove it before him.

Early in the afternoon, he had to leave the straight road by which he had been travelling most of the time and take a turn, walking along a path that led straight to his in-laws. Nyengebule stood for a while at this point, undecided whether to take the turn to his in-laws or continue along the straight road, going he knew not where. At last he took the turn. He had taken only a few paces when a honeybird appeared. It fluttered a little ahead of him and led him the way he was going, but the calls it made were not those that a honeybird makes when it leads a person to a bees' nest:

UNyengebul' uyibulel' intandanekazi,
Ibonisel' iinyosi, yaphakula,
Yatya, yalibal' ukumbekela;
Uyiselele kunye nezivatho zomgidi,
Akasibon' isankwane sisiw' endleleni.

Nyengebule has killed his favourite wife,
She discovered bees and gathered honey,
She ate and forgot to leave him a share;
He buried her together with her festival clothes,
And saw not the turban dropping on the way.

Nyengebule was startled. Did these words really come from that bird? And where had this bird gone to now? It had vanished. He went on. The bird appeared again and repeated its actions and song, but before he could do anything about it, it had vanished. But now he made up his mind what to do if it could come again. He would throw a stick at it and kill it. The honeybird appeared a third time and repeated its actions and song. Nyengebule let fly his stick and hit it, breaking one of its wings. The bird vanished, but the broken wing fluttered a little and then fell at his feet, no longer a honeybird's wing but the turban worn by his wife the time he killed her.

He let it lie there for a while and stood looking at it. His *ntandanekazi's* turban! Can he leave it there? It should have been buried with her. He must keep it until he can find an opportunity to do this. He picked it up and put it into the bag that contained gifts for his in-laws.

As soon as he came in sight of his in-laws, the married women came out to welcome him with the shrills and ululations that announce the arrival of anyone who comes driving an animal for slaughter to such festivals. As soon as Nyengebule reached the *nkundla* (courtyard), his brothers-in-law relieved him of the goat, and their wives continued to sing his people's praises as they led him to the hut set aside for him and his wife. In no time, the sisters-in-law came crowding in this hut.

'But where's our sister?' they asked.

'So she hasn't arrived yet?' asked Nyengebule.

'No, she hasn't arrived. When did she leave home?'

'I left a little earlier than she because of the goat I had to bring with me. But she was almost ready when I left, and I thought she would be here before me because she was going to take a short cut and wasn't handicapped like me. She should be here soon.'

They brought him water so that he could wash, and immediately after, some food and beer to make him the jolly *mkhwenyethu* they knew he could be.

The festival was to open on the following day, and therefore the in-laws and their closest friends were busy with the final preparations. The women were straining those quantities of beer that must be ready for the next day, and the men were chopping wood and slaughtering oxen and goats. All the people working at these assignments were already keyed up for the festival. There was plenty of meat and beer for them, and there were far more people than work to do. Therefore most of them were practising the songs and dances with which they intended to impress the guests expected. Nyengebule's arrival therefore caused a great deal of excitement. Now that he had come, they could be sure that they would more than measure up to the famous expert singers and dancers with whom they would have to compete during these festivities. They were sure that this great singer and dancer had added something to his store since they last met him, and they were eager to learn these new things before 'that great day of tomorrow'. So, even before Nyengebule had finished eating and drinking, there were loud, impatient calls from his brothers-in-law and their friends to the *mkhwe* to 'come to the men'. But his sisters-in-law were not prepared to let him go until they had fed him, and until they knew what gifts he had brought them. For some of these gifts might be dainty ornaments that would just be suitable for the festivities.

At last, two of his brothers-in-law went to him.

'On your feet, *mkhwe!*' they said. 'These wives and sisters of ours can get their gifts later. Get up and come to the men.'

So saying, they lifted him up and carried him away, amid the amused protests of his sisters-in-law, as against the shouts of triumph from the onlookers to whom Nyengebule was being carried. As soon as he arrived, the men greeted him with his praises and with song and dance, and invited him to join them. Many of the less busy women in the courtyard cheered, and in no time the place was crowded with onlookers of all ages.

The sisters-in-law, however, remained in the hut, more curious to know what gifts they were getting than to join the admiring crowds. 'I wonder what gift he has brought me this time, and what naughty things he is going to say when he gives it to me!' thought each one. After all, he was their favourite *mkhwenyethu*, and if he should discover at some time that while he was dancing in the courtyard they opened the bag of gifts just to have a look, of course he would pretend to be offended, but in fact he would be delighted. So thought the sisters-in-law, and they pulled out the bag of gifts and opened it. When a little bird's wing flew out of the bag and fluttered above their heads

504

towards the roof, there were screams of delight, for everyone thought this was just one of the *mkhwenyethu's* endless pranks. But the next moment, the women huddled together, horrifed by the song of the honeybird:

Nyengebule has killed his favourite wife,
She discovered bees and gathered honey,
She ate and forgot to leave him a share;
He buried her together with her festival clothes,
And saw not the turban dropping on the way.

The women watched the wing speechlessly as it came down, down, down, until it landed on the floor and became a turban that they all knew very well.

Shouts and cheers in the courtyard! Shrills and ululations in the courtyard! Hand-clapping, song and drums in the courtyard! Admiration and praises for Nyengebule in the courtyard! Few of the onlookers, and none of the dancers, have noticed that the sons of this house – Nyengebule's brothers-in-law and their cousins – are quietly being called away, one by one, from this rejoicing. To the few who have noticed this, nothing is unusual about *imilowo* (those of the family) occasionally withdrawing quietly to hold council about the running of a big festival of this nature.

Nyengebule was just beginning to teach a new song when two of his in-laws' elderly neighbours came to tell him that he was wanted by his in-laws. Up to this moment, he had not met his parents-in-law, and he assumed that he was being requested to go to the great hut and present himself formally. But when he indicated to the two elders that he would have to go to his hut and change his dress before meeting his parents-in-law, one of them said, 'There's no need for that. It's over there that you are wanted.' The elder was pointing higher up the slope, to an old, high-walled stone building – the most prominent building among the ruins of what used to be the home of the forebears of Nyengebule's in-laws.

The elders walked a few paces alongside him, and then they stopped and once again pointed out the building to which he had to go. Who wanted him? he wondered. Maybe his brothers-in-law needed his help about something or other? Maybe they expected so many guests that they thought they could prepare this old building for the overflow? But when he reached the door, the place was so quiet that he did not expect to find anyone inside.

He pushed the door open without knocking, and he felt cold in the stomach when he entered. Here were all his in-laws – his parents-in-law, his wife's father's brothers and their wives, his wife's father's sisters and their husbands, his wife's mother's brothers and their wives, his wife's mother's sisters and their husbands, his brothers-in-law and their wives, his wife's cousins and their wives or husbands, his sisters-in-law – all of them standing, silent, solemn. In the centre of the building there was a newly dug grave. On the piles of earth that came out of the grave was the bag containing the gifts he had brought his sisters-in-law. Next to this lay the body of the large fat gelded goat he had brought as his contribution to the festival. No one acknowledged his hoarse, half-whispered greetings. Instead, his father-in-law pointed a finger at the bag of gifts.

'Open that,' was all he said.

Nyengebule lifted up the bag and opened it, but he dropped it again, his knees sagging a little. The wing of the honeybird had flown out and was fluttering above the heads of those present, singing its song. When it finished, it dropped at Nyengebule's feet and became his dead wife's turban. Nyengebule gave it one look and then raised his head to look at his father-in-law for the next order. But the father-in-law turned his face away from him and signalled his eldest sister, a married woman. She stepped forward, lifted the bag of gifts, and cast it into the grave. The father-in-law signalled his two eldest sons. They stepped forward, lifted the dead goat, and cast it into the grave. Once more the father-in-law signalled, and this time all his sons and brother's sons stepped forward and closed in on Nyengebule. All the women covered their faces, but the men looked on grimly, noting every little detail of what was happening. They noted with silent admiration that Nyengebule did not shudder when these men laid their hands on him. They noted that he did not struggle or try to resist when they laid him down on the floor, face down. They noted that he did not wince when some of the men bound his feet together and sat on his legs, while others stretched out his arms sideways and sat on them. They noted that he did not groan when his two senior brothers-in-law raised his head and twisted his neck.

Four men jumped into the grave and stood ready to receive his limp body from their kinsmen. Everyone was looking now. As the four men laid him carefully on his back beside his rejected gifts, everyone saw the wing of the honeybird fluttering over the grave. As soon as the four men had done their solemn duty and climbed out of the grave, everyone saw the wing of the honeybird landing on the chest of the dying man and becoming his dead wife's turban. Everyone saw Nyengebule's arms moving weakly and rising slowly, slowly, slowly from his sides to his chest. The women sobbed when they saw his hands closing on the turban and pressing it to his heart.

His brothers-in-law and their cousins brought shovels and took their places round the grave. They lifted their first shovelfuls, but before throwing the earth onto his motionless body, they paused just for one moment and bowed their heads, for they noticed that the turban was still pressed to the heart of the dead man.

BARNEY SIMON

Joburg, Sis!

From: *Joburg, Sis!* (1974)

Sit down, the blond man said, It's nice of you to come up and keep me company like this. I never know what to do when the pub closes. That's Joburg all
right. Joburg. Sis. Honestly you know, you can't walk down a street without
every three seconds somebody biting you. For a start I mean. You know. Ag
please ou china gooi my sommer a five cents please. Sis. They walk around there
with their long hair and their tight jeans and so bladdy filthy dirty man. This
one came up to me just now. He had on this checked shirt and don't ask me
what was its original colour. Ag please ou china he says to me gooi my five
cents. So I said I haven't got no money. So he says ag na please sir what's that
rattling there in your pocket and I said keys and I showed him these keys and I
said if I had all my pockets full of cash you still wouldn't get a single fucken cent.

No you know cleanness is important. I always have my bath and I always
buy nylon shirts and underpants that's easy to keep clean. I wash them myself
there in the basin. Like this flat makes me bladdy sick. I'm going to paint it
white and when I'm finished I'm going to scrape the fucken floors. And that
useless little window there in the corner I'm going to run curtains along the
whole wall there so it'll look like a modern window. Ja. I can get things cheap.
Like Marley tiles for the kitchen and bathroom because I'm in the trade. And
then I think it is worth it. You know, I know this building's going to stand for
at least a year because down there in the bicycle shop they just took a lease.
But Joburg sis. You know, I might just decide to go to Cape Town or East
London. I do that. You know I got engaged in Boksburg and I had three
bladdy bedroom suites – beautiful man, one of them was solid kiaat and then
I said no fuck it and I went down to Phalaborwa. You know. You never know.
Like when Joburg really gets bad I think of just moving in with the old
people at Kempton Park. Shame, the old boy's in bad shape. His stomach's
swollen and all around is just dust. They bought that bladdy plot and it's a
bladdy waste of time man. Not a bladdy drop of water. I wouldn't mind you
know to just take him down to Warmbaths. Ja. I don't feel so good either. I
used to weigh 142. Now I weigh 135. People notice it you know. A few of my
friends said to me you know you look thinner. But now I'm fit I'm picking up
nicely again. They fuck me around too much at the bladdy hospital.

You know I was just walking to work the other morning just by the station and my legs just went like lame. I thought no man I mustn't make a bladdy fool of myself in front of all these people – you know, if a man starts walking funny and holding onto walls they think he's drunk. So I just sat down on a bench and when I could I got up and cut through the park there back to the flat and I got into bed and then I got up and I went to my friend and we had a beer by his room there and my legs went lame again so he said come on man let's go to a pub and I said no wait man I can't move so he said you serious so I said ja I can't move so he said I'm going to get a doctor and I said no wait man I'll be OK. So we sat and I felt a little better so we went down to the pub and we had another beer there and then I went lame again. You know I just couldn't move. You know my legs man they just weren't there. So he said come on you better get back to the flat so I said fuck you – you expect me to go through the street like this hey – from a pub – with you holding me up hey – in the middle of the day hey. You know, people see you walking in the street coming out of a pub holding onto things. No thanks. Anyway so we just sat there until it passed again and then we went to my flat and I got into bed and then the doctor came. Dr Miles. Ja. My friend must of phoned for him from the pub when he said he was going for a piss. Anyway, hell I was pleased my sheets were nice and white and clean. I'm going to put this carpet in the bedroom then the stained part will be under the bed. Hell I scrubbed this bladdy thing. But this friend of mine, this other one was a operator and he used to stand in oil and that and sometimes he used to kip over and I used to say to him no man don't walk all over the carpet with your boots man take them off, I scrubbed it man. Look, you can see, the strings showing there.

I don't know, people you know. Like my nephew. I told my sister what he did and she said did he? did he? She couldn't believe it. He comes with his friend here from army camp in Pretoria and he tells the caretaker to fuck off. You know I said to him listen you can see the floor's bladdy dirty so when you finished with your bath don't walk around bladdy barefoot then you get into bed and you know he dirties the bladdy sheets. I told him, you know, you come and scrub the fucken sheets. So he goes onto the balcony and the caretaker says who you and that and he says I'm visiting my uncle fuck you. So I had to go to apologise to the caretaker and when I came back he says so must I put on my boots after the bath and I said to him no man you don't talk to people like that. If you want to dress like a bladdy ducktail he can ask you what he likes. I pay twenty-five rands for this flat go and find a two-room flat for twenty-five rands so don't go sukkeling around the caretaker like that. You don't sukkel with anybody like that. I'm right hey. My sister. I told her and she didn't believe it. Did he? she said, did he? So I said he could go back to Pretoria. Then and there. Suh. Voetsak. Goodbye. Tot siens. Ja. The bladdy army. You think they teach them something there. Ja. Ja, you know you walk three feet one yard in the bladdy street and there's somebody there gooi us a start asseblief ou China. And there's these kaffir beggars on the pavement – Africans they call them now – shit – you know I went into this pub and there's this police sergeant there. I don't know he's this police sergeant and I say shit no man what a bladdy country – you walk three feet in the bladdy street and there's somebody there next to you saying to you ag gooi us a start a man's hungry man or there's all these bladdy kaffir beggars. And you go and you look hey it's a bladdy dis-grace all those police and those priests fucking kaffir girls. It's always in the papers there. No I said I don't call this a marvellous country. Ja. And I didn't know he was a bladdy policeman. He pissed himself when he told me and he saw my face. No man this Joburg, sis.

I'm going up the stairs there outside and it's dark and there's this kaffir girl standing next to me and I get such a bladdy fright she jumps too and then she sticks her thumb between her fingers in the dark and she says fuck baas fuck five bob and I said I'll fucken kick you down moer and gone that's what I'll do. But these bladdy Portuguese want them here all the time man. The cops are always around. Ja. Actually I haven't seen the Portuguese here lately. Must look out for them in the paper. Ja. Sis man.

At the station the other day this ou comes and chaffs me for a start so I say no, I've got no money. You know here in Joburg I lock my money up when I go out and I just take what I'm going to spend. So this ou chaffs me and I tell him I've got nothing. So he feels my pocket there so my cigarettes fall out so I say OK have them they're coffin nails all the same. You know people man. Why do they have to be like that? They just want to take. They don't want to know each other they just want what they can get. I say leave people man, leave them. This friend of mine in Benoni he always wants to break in, to scale, you know he's always saying what's there, let's look in that window there, and I say leave people man, leave their things, let them try. They worked to get them just like I did. And these dirty bastards with their tight jeans man – OK there's nothing wrong with tight jeans I wear them too man, I'm game for any-thing. I've got these terylene ones, I should've washed them for tomorrow but ag I couldn't give a stuff. Anyway so they just *want* man. Anything. Just so they can bite you just so they can eat you. Not because they want it. Just because it's there and they can take it from you. Anything. You know. They'll take a tie. A ashtray. Anything. As long as they can take something from you. Even if it doesn't get them anything. Ja they rubbish. My fiancée used to say you can always tell a man's character by the music he likes and his friends. So when he took my cigarettes I phoned the cops and said I've got a complaint and they said what's my name and I gave the wrong one. I said Fourie and the cop said you're sure Fourie who Fourie so I said my real name, Bobby. Bobby Fourie instead of Fereira. Then when I get out of the booth these two start sukkeling with me again and they don't believe me that I've phoned the cops and they think they're chaffing me along nicely and I'm chaffing them along all the time. I was quite sorry when the cops did come. You should've seen how quiet they got then. Hell I wanted to laugh. Then the cops ask me what kind of cigarettes they were and I said Lexington and I only smoked one so they look and they're Lexington and there're three missing. But the two of them the bladdy fools are standing there like chimneys and the other one had a gold watch with a name and a date on the back. I don't know what's happened to them. But they all over man. The other day just outside there they shot a battler in the leg. Him and another one jumped an old man in the lavatory and took twenty-five rands and the cops came in and they ran. I heard it, and the bugger screaming like a mad old woman. No man, I'm telling you, I'm going back to Kempton. I'm going to Warmbaths. If somebody knocks on the door you stand still, you know what I mean? You don't expect a friend. You can't just open. Ja. So Dr Miles sent me straight to the hospital and I fought them like mad, man. You know, I felt like a bladdy fool. I was wearing these pale jeans and white shoes. You know you feel like a bladdy fool going to hospital like that. Anyway then these three specialists look at me and they give me a lumber punch. He sticks it in and it hurts man and my leg starts jumping and my balls – tha-WA tha-WA tha-WA I can feel them go. So he says what's the matter so I say it hurts man – it's in my leg. So he pulls the bladdy needle out and then he pushes it in again and I scream like ten bladdy old women. Ja. But that lumber punch helped man. And then a whole lot of other doctors came, even woman doctors and they poked around my balls and even asked me to come. Hell man I felt like a bladdy fool – you know when a man's lying there man. It's a good hospital that whatever anyone tells you. They looked after me all right. They didn't want me to go. They said I must wait till they work out properly what it was that was making my legs like that. But you know. I've got four bladdy suits. I didn't like lying there worrying about somebody breaking into my flat. One of them's tailor-made. And that cable-stitch jersey my mother made. And then I got this headache, tha-wA tha-wA in the back of my head so I didn't tell them anything about it and I just thought no and I went home and got Grandpa's Headache Powders from the chemist and that was that man. I was bladdy lucky, nobody broke in. You know, you just don't know who's going to knock. You just stand there. Like that young ou yesterday he knocks and asks for the caretaker and I'm just out of the bath all wet and my hair dangling and this little hand-towel around me and everything dangling underneath and he looks all funny and asks for the caretaker and I tell him where and he still looks funny and I think hey no, what's this and then I see there's this girl on the other side with a face like a box of bladdy tomatoes. Hey man, I laughed and I laughed.

I always walk kaal here. You know, a man likes to feel free. You look tired man. Then later on there was someone from the hospital. They want me to go back. They didn't even know when I went. So I said I'll come tomorrow. That means I should've gone back today but I forgot all about it. You know, I was doing my washing and listening to the wireless. It's depressing there man. On one side there's a man full of tubes with cancer and on the other side a young ou also with cancer. Hell, three o'clock! No! That wasn't a hint man, don't go yet. This is when a man mos comes alive. I'll just take off my jacket. And loosen my tie. And my old belt. This was a army belt. Hell man, my balls are itchy. I get so bladdy restless a man's game for anything. I must remember about the hospital tomorrow. Ja. I've got this double bed. Have you seen it next door there. None of those buttons in the mattress that stick into you. Hell, my balls! You don't have to go — I mean it, man, really. You can even kip over. I'll set my alarm clock for any time you like. Hey. You mustn't be shy man. Are you sure? You know, I'm not like a formal type. People are welcome. Hell, look at me. I'm a randy old dog hey. Don't go. D'you really have to? OK then. But look, I'll tell you what hey. I mean it was hell of a nice of you to keep me company like this. Really thanks hey. But look hey why don't you try to come back. See, see if you can't. And then, you know, just knock three times so I'll know it's you.

PERSEUS ADAMS

A True Gruesome
First published, 1975

When Dawn Vermaak first asked Eric Featherstone to come out with her he hesitated before accepting the invitation and even after he had given his answer he felt more than a little uneasy about it. For Dawn had just turned thirteen years old and Eric Featherstone – apart from being thirty-two years old – was also her history teacher.

But the difference in ages and the fact that he was the girl's teacher were not the only reasons for his feeling somewhat apprehensive about his acceptance. In spite of his university degree and his eight years' teaching experience, Eric Featherstone had a deeply-rooted conviction that he was one of life's failures, one of those people doomed to misfortune whenever they embark on any act of initiative or enterprise. This conviction had not happened suddenly but had grown from a series of disappointments over the years – partly from his job and partly through his marriage which had ended three years earlier with his wife running away with another man. Recently it was confirmed in his own mind by a conversation he had overheard when members of the staff were discussing him.

'He's too soft,' Mr Beardsley who taught arithmetic and coached rugby had said.

'Too friendly with the kids – no sense of discipline.' That had been the scornful censuring voice of Mr Lindsay who was Dawn's geography teacher.

'Why doesn't he move out – get a less demanding job like a clerk in a bank or an insurance office?' Beardsley had gone on to say.

'Even bad teachers usually manage to put *something* across to the pupils in their classes – they inspire them with some completely private interest or obsession of their own, but one cannot imagine that character inspiring anyone to feel anything except boredom or contempt.'

'At least one cannot say he has not been aptly named,' Lindsay had replied. 'A personality with the effect of a feather and as airtight to real living as a stone. Can't imagine how he ever got married in the first place.'

'Well it didn't take long before she realised her mistake, did it?'

And as usual Miss Gregg, Dawn's pretty blonde English teacher, had stuck up for him.

512

'I think you're both being very cruel – he's really a very sensitive person and the children really love him. He tells them all sorts of interesting stories ...'

'Stories' – Lindsay snorted, irritated by her sympathy. 'No wonder they don't know any history. It's probably the only way he has of keeping them quiet.'

Eric Featherstone had gone away then, not wanting to hear any more.

He stood now at the bus-stop in the suburb where Dawn and he both lived, and waited for her to arrive. He recalled how she had made the invitation and his own mixed feelings upon hearing it. For Dawn was a quiet, reserved child who, as far as he knew, had no close friends. Someone had mentioned her name one day in the staffroom and the comments had been mostly negative. 'She's like a clam – just to get her to speak is an arduous business,' one had said. Beardsley had said he could not remember who she was and Miss Gregg had said she was very introverted but that her compositions were excellent.

It was at the end of the last period of the day that Dawn, strangely confident and with eyes shining, had approached the table and asked the history teacher:

'Have you ever been to Moore's farm?'

'No-o.' He had smiled at her gently, absent-mindedly. 'Where is it?'

'It's in Walmer – not far from where you stay. I would like to show it to you – it's very beautiful – there are hills and streams and one can be all alone and I have a secret place ... Will you come?'

He had been grateful that she had waited until the others had gone before she asked him. After a brief moment of conflict he had given her the answer she sought, remembering his own shyness and loneliness when he was her age and how he, too, had had 'a secret place'. But, as he waited for her to come, the sun shining brightly, the birds singing happily, the people hurrying out to do their Saturday morning shopping, he began to feel uneasy once again. Suppose their meeting and going away together were observed by someone from the school? Walmer was like a small village and, while the people seemed friendly enough, he knew that the Beardsleys and Lindsays would be only too glad to make the most of any unfavourable gossip about him. Well, let them. What he was doing was being done from a heart free of any intentions other than an act of friendship towards a lonely girl. If they did not like it, they could lump it.

It was seven minutes after nine when she came to him. As far as her features went, she was what kind people would call 'homely' – except for her eyes. These were dark and doe-soft and made you think of moss and mulberries. She looked much older than she was, partly because she was tall for her age, but mostly because of a rare poise, a self-possessed dignity. The rhythm of her movements was quieter, deeper than her classmates', who mostly swung in a sharp pendulum between gawkiness and animal grace. Her hair hung down over her shoulders in two brown plaits and she wore a yellow dress that had no sleeves.

'I am sorry I'm late; shall we go?'

They walked together, the girl slightly in front, down a long avenue that bisected the bus-route road and lay at a ninety-degree angle to it. They walked in silence for a few minutes and then she said:

'I told my mother I was going to visit a school-friend. Grown-ups, especially mothers, don't like people of my age to make friends with someone much older.'

'I know,' he said.

'They don't understand about many things – grown-ups, I mean,' she added.

He smiled. 'I agree with you.'

'Of course, you're different,' she said, noticing his smile and sensing the reason for it.

'Am I?'

'Of course, or I wouldn't have asked you.'

The houses began to thin out now and the tarred avenue became a rough corrugated track that seemed to slope abruptly downwards about eighty yards ahead.

'Can anyone go and visit Moore's farm?' he asked her.

'No – I have special permission from the owner.'

'Won't he object to my coming too?'

'No; in any case, he won't be there. He never comes out on a Saturday.'

Soon they reached the point where the track descended. They stood on the brim of a huge, roughly circular hollow in the middle of which a hill, some several hundred feet tall reposed in fiercely green serenity, making the teacher think of psalms and prophets and the ambushes of Zulu impis. On the eastern side was a thickly wooded kloof where, he was told by his young companion, the Baakens River flowed; and on all sides there was evidence of a spacious bird-singing wilderness. Moore's farm began in a valley at their feet and its northern boundary was a fence that cut the crown of the hill in the middle. The air they breathed now was fresh and clean – it seemed to come from an untapped spring and he felt suddenly glad that he had come.

They went down the track that stopped at a rushing stream with a frail-looking suspension bridge over it. The stream was about fifteen feet wide and Dawn went first, the teacher waiting until she had reached the other side before gingerly making his way across. Seeing his caution, she laughed and he was glad that she did; the sound was like pure silver water and it rose up as the voice of a talented soloist sometimes does from the choir in full song surrounding it; an effect that seals rather than detracts from its harmony.

'You're now in Moore's farm.'

Bars of shadow and sunlight alternated as they followed a grassy path past a huddle of sheds; Africans in a blanketed group smoking long-stemmed pipes who gazed at them long and silently as they passed; grazing cows that did the same without stopping their chewing. A dog streaked towards them, a silver arrow in a crescendo of barks, the hail of his indignation changing to a joyful storm of welcome as he recognised Dawn, the furiously wagging tail putting you beyond doubt as to his pleasure as he circled wildly about. Being a faithful watch-dog, he followed them a short distance only and then returned. A mealie-field dropped behind them; several platoons of cabbages, strawberries; and when a beehive that looked like a postbox and made a sound like a dynamo had done the same, they found they had reached the bottom of the hill. Here there were tall trees with thick undergrowth and the dishevelled playfulness of the nearby river. Gaunt lines infiltrated by music.

He was beginning to pant now and asked her, 'Are we going to climb all the way to the top?'

'Not all the way if you don't want to, but my secret place is up here – and you do want to see it, don't you?'

There was a note of anxiety, of an unstated hope that he would not refuse in her voice, and, though he was not looking forward to the climb, he hastened to reassure her.

'Of course I do. I just wanted to know where we were heading.'

About half an hour of trudge, sweat and climb later, he joined her, leaning against a shelf of rock that curved in a half-moon around the entrance to a shallow cave about three-quarters of the way up the hill. Even through the discomfort of heaving lungs, of having to gulp to catch his breath, the sight beneath stirred him with its breadth and height and superb indifference to the schemes and designs of men.

He knew without being told that this was her secret place and thought to himself – she has chosen well – this is a secret place worth having. The two of them stood quite close and looked down without speaking. As their bodies restored their balances, the woodland silences, punctuated agreeably only by chirruping insects and the call of a shrike or sombre bulbul, moved even further within them both, till the wounds of the past became less harsh and the shape of the future not quite so daunting in the shadow it threw.

Eventually he spoke: 'Do you come here often?'

'As often as I can. I think I'm the only one who knows about this place – you can't really see it till you are right on top of it … It's peaceful, isn't it?'

'It's magnificent.'

And then he looked at her and thought about her, and she blushed, feeling him do so. Why am I thirty-two and why is she thirteen? he asked himself and grew sad. They seemed so right for each other – and then he wondered if things would be different if the gap between their birth-dates had been smaller or if they lived in a society where their going together did not have to be kept a secret. I must prize every moment of our togetherness here for it must end soon and the chance of another outing is doubtful, considering the risks involved.

After a while she asked him if he would like to climb the remaining distance to the top. ('You can see my home from there …') and he agreed. They left the cave and climbed slowly, a clump of trees shutting out the view until they reached the long grass that fell like a boy's fringe over the forehead of the hill. On the summit, she pointed out her home, a white matchbox at the very end of a road parallel with the one they had walked down. Then they returned to an open space between some bushes and lay down a few feet apart and looked up at the sky. The girl studied a ladybird as it moved up the stem of a flower and the teacher, watching her, felt himself become part of the insect's world, a world where the skyscrapers were paper-thin and green and trembled in a breeze.

How blue the sky was – and the sun just right – not too warm … If only life could always be like this. The breeze increased slightly and stirred the long grass to restless sighs and sibilant caresses as if the earth was gently, tremulously kissing the throat of the morning. Dawn, half emerging from her dream-laced idleness, began to peel the bud she had plucked from one of the Red Disas. She did not strip it roughly, impatiently, as most children would, he observed, but very delicately, as if it held an uncovered star.

Suddenly she asked him, 'Do you like Mr Lindsay?'

He considered her question in silence for a few moments and then said: 'I don't know him very well. They say he's a good geography teacher – do you like him?'

'No,' she said, cupping her hand around the open bud as if it were a candle that might go out – 'No. He's a Grudging and I don't like Grudgings.'

'A Grudging?'

'I divide people into four main groups: Grudgings, Gleesons, Gruesomes and Eternals.'

'A Grudging –'

'Grudgings are sheep that butt other sheep. They want to be Gruesomes but they can't. Gleesons are people who are content to be sheep and nothing else. They sort of drift along and do what the rams – the leader sheep – say they should do. Gruesomes are the best really. They are people who are truly different. They make their own world inside themselves if they cannot get away to a secret place. They're anti-Gleeson but they don't really bother too much about them. What they have to watch out for are the Grudgings who are jealous of them.'

516

'And Eternals?'

'Serious, rather sinister people without a sense of humour. They preach a lot.'

He smiled as he considered her divisions. Then asked: 'What do you class me as?'

'You're a Gruesome like me but you worry about it.' After a thoughtful pause she added, 'A Gruesome that worries too much about being a Gruesome soon becomes a Gleeson.'

'You're a wonderful girl. Do you know that?'

'No, not really. I'm a Gruesome and we are few, that's all.'

'Why do you choose such a name for a type you think highly of? – You know that gruesome means horrible, don't you?'

'Yes, I know, but the others usually think of us as airy-fairy people and I wanted a word that meant the opposite to this because they don't really know us, do they?'

'No,' he said wonderingly. 'No. I don't suppose they do.' As one o'clock drew near, Dawn jumped up. 'I will have to go now – are you coming?'

They descended hand in hand till they arrived at the farm dwellings when they became aware of the world they were returning to and the narrow views and suspicions it harboured, and let go. But the rapport between them did not die – if anything, it was confirmed by the act. On the town side of the suspension bridge they stopped. A path veered to the left and the rough track to the right.

'This path is a short cut to my home,' she said.

'Will I see you here again?' he asked her.

'Yes, but we had better not go together – we'll be seen and then –'

'Then the Gleesons and Grudgings will close in on us,' he smiled.

'Not to mention the Eternals,' she returned, and smiled too, her eyes big and soft, expressing her thanks to him.

'Come whenever you feel like it and if you see me we can talk and I'll show you other places almost as good as my secret place –'

You already have, he thought as she went away from him. After about fifteen yards she stopped and called down, 'Saturday morning is the best time ...'
He nodded and returned her farewell wave.

On the following Wednesday, at first recess in the staffroom Miss Gregg made the excited announcement that she had just been give a wonderful definition of love by one of the pupils.

'Love!' snorted Mr Lindsay. 'What do they know about love?'

'The person concerned must know about it because it's such a true description in just a few words. I had given them a kind of free association test ... you know, when you say certain words and they have to write down the first thing they think of upon hearing the word.'

'A bit risky, isn't it?' Beardsley asked her, but sounded, Eric Featherstone noticed, more than a little interested.

'Not with standard six.'

'Well, let's hear, what was it?'

'Love is two people alone on a mountain,' Miss Gregg said triumphantly.

'What's wonderful about it?' Lindsay asked her sceptically. A typical Grudging, Eric thought. No doubt he would favour a more horizontal definition.

'But don't you see,' Miss Gregg said, her voice expressing amazement at his lack of comprehension – 'that's exactly what love is. In a few words she's captured so much of the experience, the sense of awe, the feeling of vulnerability ...'

'I think it's a very good definition,' Beardsley said surprisingly. 'Who made it?'

'Dawn Vermaak – you know, that quiet one you didn't even remember was in your class.'

'Dawn Vermaak!' Lindsay exploded. 'She doesn't know a thing about mountains – in the last exam when they had to fill in things on a map, she put the Drakensberg somewhere over the equator ...'

'She may not know about mountains but she knows about love,' Miss Gregg said firmly. 'It's one of the best short definitions of the subject I have ever heard – what do you think, Mr Featherstone?'

'I think,' he said, 'it's really memorable – a definition only a true Gruesome could have made.' And his voice was proud and sinewed with so much fierce tenderness that the others stared and one or two wondered if they would not have to reclassify the previous assessments they had made of him.

SHEILA ROBERTS

For No Reason

From: *Outside Life's Feast* (1975)

The yellow-grey veld and the acres of mealie stubble looked as if they had never known luxuriance or fertility. The sand of the uneven path leading from the house to the yard was also yellow, and the stench from the chicken hoks was awful. Ann stared across the fields and the open veld patterned purple with thorn trees. The farm seemed bewitched into everlasting monotony and dreariness. The backyard in which she stood with her small son was in a state of resigned neglect; the piles of corrugated iron and timber, with which someone was once going to build a shed, were old and settled; bricks, stones and empty tins lay as if immovable and the door on the outside lavatory was buckled and would not shut properly. Over all, the yellow dust blew every time the wind rose.

Ann turned disconsolately to the baby owl in one of the lopsided wire cages which stood wearily in a row. The owl had retreated to the back frame and stood in the mud and filth with ruffled feathers and wide eyes.

'See the birdie,' she said to her small son. She squeezed his soft, lax hand.

Loud noise and laughter came from the empty stables where the others were admiring Karel's motor bike. Denise had probably told another joke.

'Let's go and see the kiepies,' said Ann.

They walked to the farthest cage and stood hand-in-hand looking at the shabby, self-important chickens that milled about gossiping and complaining in a tiny hok. They seemed so uninteresting and so lacking in dignity after the silence and immobility of the frightened owl that Ann felt they deserved to be in a cage. Ann and the child loitered towards the stables.

'Isn't it time we went,' she called to the others.

'We've only just come,' said Denise.

Koen came over to Ann and put his arm across her shoulders.

'We can go now if you want to,' he said.

'We're *not* going now,' said Denise loudly. 'I want to shoot!'

'You *can't* shoot,' said Len.

'Why can't I?'

'Because we have to go to the bottom veld over the river to shoot and there isn't time.'

'Why can't I shoot over there?' asked Denise, pointing to the fallow stretch next to the mealie-field.

'Because there's kaffirs living just beyond the trees,' said Barendjie. 'So? I won't hit them!'

'Denise, you can't shoot now,' said Ann.

'Shut up!' said Denise.

Ann turned away.

'Shall we look at the kiepies again?' she said to the child.

They stood again in front of the fowl-run and the child put his fingers through the wire netting. Ann saw from the dark patch at the seat of his trousers that the child had wet his pants. Next to the fowls was an empty cage that looked as if it had recently had an inmate. There were filaments of straw, thin, withered old carrots, the rags of some green leaves in the dust, and a sand-caked water bowl. She thought of the location that lay beyond the farm like a dull encrustation on the veld, with a film of smoke hovering over it always. She hoped the others had decided against shooting.

Ann craned her neck slightly to see what Koen was doing. He was listening attentively to something Georgie was saying. His eyes were screwed up against the smouldering cigarette in the side of his mouth, and his hands held his narrow hips lightly. He looked cityish in contrast to her brothers who wore old jeans, clumsy jerseys and velskoens. Ann wondered whether he was enjoying himself. She had brought him to meet her family, and while their mother was preparing lunch Len and Georgie had offered to show them the farm, where they often came gamebird hunting. If Koen were enjoying himself, it would be inconsiderate and, perhaps, even a mistake for her to try and coax them to return in time for lunch. She had better keep quiet.

'Get your gun, Len!' ordered Denise.

'No.'

'Ah, don't be so bloody mean.'

'Look, I've only got a few cartridges with me and I need them.'

'Jesus, how snoep can you *get!*'

'Oh dammit … all right then.'

'Wouldn't you like to shoot, Koen?' asked Denise politely.

'I don't mind.'

'Come on, Len!'

'All right, all right.'

Ann and the child settled themselves on a mound which must have been dung at one stage, Ann thought. She lifted her head into the breeze for relief from the stench. The others had started shooting, and each time the gun went off the owl lifted one of its ruffled feet high, like a warrior in a dance, and blinked. The child sat very still.

'I hit it that time!' screamed Denise.

'No you didn't! '

'I did!'

'I tell you, you *didn't!*'

'Well, let Koen try,' said Denise. 'Come Koen.'

'Let me try,' begged Barendjie.

'Oh don't hum and haw, let *Koen* shoot,' said Denise.

'Have you shot before, Koen?' asked Len.

'Yes.'

'Let me try,' said Barendjie.

'Here, go ahead,' said Len.

'He's hit the tin! He's hit it! Good shot!' shouted Denise.

The owl danced slowly as if carrying out an agonised ritual, and the dogs crept to the far side of the stables. Ann sat worriedly with her head resting on her knees, trying to work out the reason for her sister's state of excitement.

'Ah, let me try,' wailed Barendjie.

'All right. Here. Now be careful.'

'It's not fair; he's resting his arm on the fence,' protested Denise.

'So?'

'So, it's not fair.'

'You could've done it.'

'Well I didn't.'

'But you could've.'

'Well let me try again.'

'No. I've no more cartridges,' said Len.

'Oh, you *have!*'

'I haven't. Besides you don't know how to shoot.'

'I'm a very good shot!'

'Mom will be waiting for us,' yelled Ann suddenly, and her son jerked in surprise.

'Sorry, lovey,' she said softly.

'*You* can go,' called back Denise. 'I still want to ride.'

'But the horses are grazing in the field,' said Georgie.

'Well, go and fetch them!'

'Man, it'll take time and then we still have to saddle them. Let's rather go and have lunch. Besides Barendjie must go and have his lunch too.'

'Oh don't be a spoil-sport! It's not every day Ann and her *boyfriend* come to see us.'

'Do you want to ride, Koen?' asked Georgie politely.

'You don't have to treat him as if he's gold just because he's a stranger,' said Denise. She smiled cheekily at Koen.

'I don't mind riding,' said Koen quietly.

'I bet you *can't* ride!' said Denise with coquettish eyes.

'Actually … I grew up on a horse.'

'Fetch the horses!' she demanded.

'There's no time for saddling and all that,' warned Georgie.

'We can ride bareback,' said Denise. She stared rudely at Koen's well-cut, expensive trousers.

'Let's take Karel's bike to round the horses in,' said Len to Georgie. He handed his gun to Barendjie, who, grateful, ran carefully with it indoors. Then he wheeled Karel's bike out of the stables and started it.

Len and Georgie roared slowly and bouncing over the bumps and potholes in the path, and the farm boy ran ahead to open the gate to the enclosed field where the horses were grazing. They herded the three animals together and forced them through the fence with the noise of the bike. The rather dingy horses looked unusually magnificent as they galloped in formation, their manes and tails flying and the dust billowing on either side. The boy let the horses through the gate and waited for Len and Georgie on the bike, then he quickly shut it. The child crept closer to Ann as the animals stamped and whinnied round the yard. Len propped up the bike and went to fetch the bridles. Then he threw himself about the neck of the bay mare and got the bridle over her head.

'Here, Denise, ride her!' he said.

'Where's the saddle?'

'I thought you said …?'

'Well seeing you've gone to all this trouble, you may as well saddle her too.'

'Oh Jesus! Hey, Barendjie … get a saddle from the shed.'

'But she said …'

'Ag man, just get it.'

'You ride that one,' said Denise to Koen and she pointed to the frisky grey horse Georgie was trying to steady.

'All right,' he said.

'*You* don't need a saddle, do you?' she asked mockingly.

'I'll … see,' said Koen.

Georgie led the grey towards them and Koen grabbed the bridle and tried to mount. The horse moved and spun round slightly. Koen managed to hold it, and mounted with difficulty. He headed the horse towards the gate.

'Koen, why don't you put a saddle on that horse?' called Ann unhappily.

He waved in acknowledgement, but kept his eyes frowningly on the horse's head. Ann sank her head onto her knees again. Noisy, persistent, randy bitch, she thought angrily. Denise shot past on the bay. She sat the horse well and her hair streamed out behind her. Ann watched her catch up with Koen and the grey. They trotted side by side across the stretch of long dry whitish grass, and wove in and out of the clumps of ash-coloured trees. The clusters of white thorns on the soetdoringbome looked to Ann like blossoms from a distance. She turned her head.

'Look at the horsie,' she said to the child. They both stared at Barendjie and the untrained, saddleless pony he had mounted. Both rider and mount were still and relaxed. The owl lowered its wings and frowned.

'Ag kom tog binne,' said Barendjie's mother, coming from the kitchen door. Ann twisted round.

'No thank you, Mrs Nel,' she called.

'Man there's Cokes in the fridge and melktert. Come in!'

'No thanks. It's so pleasant outside.'

'It's so seldom man that we see new faces …'

'We're enjoying the sunshine,' lied Ann. 'In any case, we only dropped in to show my little boy the animals.'

Mrs Nel came up to them.

'Ag, I should get out of the house too, it's driving me mad. You know I'm sure that kitchen kaffir is mental; he came in late this morning man, covered in river mud and filth. I had to send him to clean himself and had to maar start the breakfast myself. I said listen here you blikskottel if you do this again you're out …'

She interposed herself, swaying, her scrawny legs in tattered slippers and concertinaed stockings, between Ann and Barendjie, who was controlling the pony by hooking his bare feet round the pony's hind legs from the inside. The old woman's face was grey and lined, and her flesh was withered and sinewy.

'Would you like to share our seat, Mrs Nel?'

'Ag, I may as well. Oh hullo Lennie, hullo Georgie.'

'Hullo Mrs Nel,' said Ann's brothers, coming towards the group on the mound.

'What was in *that* cage, Mrs Nel?' asked Ann.

'Where? Oh there! Man it was an otter.'

'No, it was a mongoose,' said Len.

'Well a mongoose, but the bladdy thing died.'

'When?' asked Ann.

'I think the day before yesterday or the day before that.'

'You *shouldn't* have put the thing in a cage,' said Len.

'Man where must I put it then?'

'Len, I'm sure Mom's food is going to be spoilt if we don't go soon,' said Ann.

'Ja, well we can go now, when the others are finished riding.'

'Yes, we must.'

Denise and Koen were out of sight.

'That's what I call communication,' said Ann, making an effort to be cheerful. She pointed to Barendjie and the pony, who were still standing welded together.

'Hey? Ag ja, but he's ridden since before he could walk. My Karel could ride too, hey? He was good at everything. He ran this farm. I never had to worry about a thing. *Ag, Here* …'

'Tannie, you mustn't start on that now,' warned Len.

Ann could smell the alcohol on the woman's breath. She would probably take to drink herself if she had to live on this farm, she thought. Poor old girl. She looked so tired and colourless, even her eyelashes and eyebrows had no colour, and the whites of her eyes were dull. The way she moved her dentures frequently with her tongue was embarrassing too.

'Are you keeping all right, Mrs Nel?' asked Ann.

'Ag, dit help nie om to kla nie. But you know, this farm is really too much for me.'

'Yes, it must be a lot of work.'

'Yes man, and it's all on my shoulders. You see there … that's Karel's bike and his car. Brand new. Still standing there.'

'Yes … I see.'

'You should sell them, Mrs Nel,' said Georgie.

'Ag I can't bring myself to sell *anything*. Karel used to want me to sell too, and I must say that the other day when I was really finished I said to Barendjie I'm going to sell this bladdy farm and you know what he said? What about the dogs, Ma? Must I keep the farm going for *dogs*? I said. That'll be the bladdy day! Ag man, but I do keep it. What can I do?'

'If you sell,' said Len, 'where'll I go to ride and shoot?'

'Yes the boys love it, don't they?' she said, melting into sentimentality. 'It's lovely for them to be out-of-doors riding and shooting. Man, it's too much city life that turns them into moffies and queers …'

'Yes,' said Ann.

Ann saw the bay horse and Denise emerge from the thorn trees in the distance.

'Your sister's a dare-devil isn't she,' laughed Mrs Nel. 'Lennie says she's a bok for anything.'

'Yes, she is,' said Ann.

Then Koen appeared, but he made no attempt to catch up with Denise. They approached the farmyard separately. Ann watched them worriedly. 'God, that was lovely,' sang out Denise.

'I hope you're satisfied now,' called Len.

'No, I'm *not!*'

'We must go, Denise,' said Ann.

'You should learn to ride, *old* girl.'

'I'll do that, but not now. Mom's food is going to be spoilt.'

'Well she can put mine in the oven. I'm going to ride some more.'

'Koen, I think we should go,' said Ann, as the grey trotted up to the bay mare. She wished her voice did not sound so shrill.

'Yes man, let's go and eat,' said Georgie.

'Righto,' said Koen.

'*I'm* staying,' said Denise.

'You can stay,' said Len.

Koen dismounted and the farm boy ran up to take the bridle from him. Koen's trousers were creased and covered in hairs.

'Riding bareback plays up hell with your nacks,' said Georgie. Koen laughed.

'Ag, the way the kids of today talk,' said Mrs Nel, but she also laughed.

'Man, Tannie, you're used to sons,' said Len.

'*Here*, Len ...' said Mrs Nel.

'Say goodbye to the kiepies,' said Ann to the child.

'Ag, come inside for a bit,' said Mrs Nel.

'No, we must go, but thank you. Are you riding some more, Koen?' asked Ann.

'No, I said I'll be coming with you and the kid for lunch.'

'We're coming too,' said Len.

They walked towards their parked cars, leaving Denise and Barendjie still on horseback.

'That's Karel's ... my late son's bike and car ... there,' said Mrs Nel to Koen. She caught his arm as she stumbled over the uneven path. He steadied her.

'Yes ... Len told me.'

'Did he tell you that ...'

'Yes, yes. I'm very sorry ...'

Mrs Nel started to cry.

'Ag Tannie, don't *cry*,' said Len.

'Lennie, man. I can't help it. But listen here ... you mustn't worry ... I won't sell ... I'll never sell ... you boys can all come inside now ... come ...'

'We *must* go,' said Ann.

'Well next time ... you must really come inside for tea.'

'Thank you, Mrs Nel.'

'Totsiens Tannie.'

'Ag, goodbye my boy ... come again hey!'

Ann and Koen and the child got into their car and Len and Georgie climbed into Georgie's old dented Ford. They waved to Mrs Nel who was swaying unsteadily in the wind, screwing her eyes up against the glare. As Koen reversed the car, Denise came running up to them waving both arms.

'I'm coming with you! I'm coming with you!' she yelled.

Koen braked. Denise scrambled into the car.

'Aren't you going to ride some more?' asked Ann.

'No! I changed my mind!'

Denise ran her hands through her hair and then tucked her blouse into her slacks. Her face was red and her eyes very bright. She sank back into the seat.

'Mrs Nel drunk again?' she asked.

'Not really ... drunk,' said Ann. 'Why? Does she often drink?'

'She's always been a heavy drinker.'

'Is that so? It's odd to think of a farmer's wife being a drinker. Don't you think so, Koen?'

'Yes.'

'Was she crying over Karel again?' asked Denise.

'Yes,' said Ann.

'Koen, did she tell you about her eldest son?'

'Yes, partly. Actually, Lennie told me about it.'

'Did you hear that he gassed himself in his car?' asked Denise.

'Ja, Len told me.'

'And for no reason at all. He was like Len, just twenty.'

'Yes, so I heard.'

'For no reason ... just like that ... five minutes and he was dead.'

'Yes ... I ... let's not talk about it.'

'All right, if you can't face ugly facts!'

Denise suddenly burst out sobbing.

'Denise!' said Ann, shocked, but the girl brushed her sister's offered hand away and continued to cry.

'Oh Lord!' said Ann. She buried her face into her child's downy hair. It was all just awful. Denise had spent the drive to the farm telling dirty jokes. Now she was crying.

'What's the matter?' asked Koen, slowing down the car.

'Go on, go on,' yelled Denise in an intense, harsh voice.

All the way home she sat bent over on the back seat, weeping. Koen and Ann could not bring themselves to talk, over the sound of her sobs.

'Come, let me help you,' said Koen when he had stopped the car behind Georgie's Ford in the driveway.

'Just leave me *alone!*' yelled Denise.

'What did I do?' asked Koen.

Ann shrugged.

Koen and Ann and the child crossed the even lawn together. The wind had dropped, the sky was cloudless, and orderly beds of flowers stood in still, Sunday reverence. At the sight of the well-polished front stoep and the spotless lace curtains in the lounge windows Ann's body relaxed.

'You ride beautifully, Koen,' she said to him softly.

SHEILA ROBERTS

Carlotta's Vinyl Skin

From: *Coming In and other Stories* (1993)

My friend David, a successful lawyer who helped me with my immigration papers for this country, is unhappy in a niggled, half-tortured sort of way because of the unimpressive salary I earn as an English professor. Once a month, regularly, he will phone me to beg me to write a lurid romantic novel that might get on the best-seller list and enable me to buy the house and car he thinks I owe it to myself to own. I have told him over and over again that I *cannot* write such a novel – I would become immobilised with ennui and self-disgust at my very typewriter. I would waste my time trying, and simply be inserting my hands and head into a stock-like writer's block.

'Sheila, can't you just prostitute yourself for once?' he pleads. 'Just once. Then you could keep writing the egghead stuff no one wants to read in comfort, at least.'

Sometimes a little inner voice joins its harangue with his. *If* I have endurance and energy (which perhaps I don't have and am therefore lacking the essentials of a full human being) I could indeed write a money-bringing book, the voice insists. Think up a simple plot, set it in a foreign country during a time of turmoil. Be prepared to write six hundred pages. Create a beautiful heroine who falls in love with a rebel/renegade/revolutionary/freedom fighter/innocent fugitive from justice/political activist/disinherited son later to be re-inherited/wildcat unionist/or even a handsome Dracula-like fellow, eyes heavy-lidded, soul possessed. Or she could be in search of a lost father. Contrive to have the lovers separated and then bring them together in a grand finale. They are both, or all three, hot-blooded. Here's your chance, Sheila, to portray the sex act from the woman's point of view. You could do a service to womankind while making money.

Weaving, weaving, I stick a sheet of paper in the typewriter. A foreign country? The only country I know well, whose landscape forms part of my own mental baggage, is South Africa. My setting will have to be South African – it's foreign enough to most Americans and it's their money I'm after. I couldn't presume to write about America: I know too little about American turmoil and even less about the various historic sites. I have no doubt that I could recreate in words the look of the Cape coast, the Karoo, the Bushveld, the Highveld, the Natal highlands, the Drakensberg. In fact, if I invented a country, calling it something like Sylvanvakia or Prinsenmania or Eendt-sur-Mer, I would only end up describing either the Cape coast, the Karoo, the Bushveld, the Highveld, the Natal highlands, or the Drakensberg. Geography is destiny.

Turmoil? If I want this book to sell, I have to keep all racial discrimination or conflict out of it, except for a bit of jungle-enshrouded sex to the beat of tom-toms, but that could come into the sub-plot. So I could go along with the myth of the 'white man's' war and set my story in South Africa on the eve of Anglo-Boer hostilities. My heroine will be a peaches-and-cream English girl who comes out with her wealthy father to visit the mines and falls in love with … an Afrikaner? No, no. A descendant of the 1820 Settlers? A South African English Gentleman and a Rebel. How about that?

I visualise delicate Victorian blouses, thick blonde hair done up in a chignon, large hats, many petticoats, soft white hands, large blue eyes, a vulnerable but brave mouth. Oh no, I am regurgitating memories of Bo Derek starring in *Tarzan the Ape Man*. Why does schlock always stick? I must start afresh. I *must* start afresh. The image of one of my best-looking writing students comes to mind. She has slightly curly, untidy brown hair, a thin face, and slanting cat-like eyes. She usually wears long peasant skirts or calf-length tight trousers in Hot Pink or Luminous Blue, and soft suede boots with a foldover at the ankle, such as medieval pages must have worn, three earrings in one ear and none in the other, oversized T-shirts or fifties blouses. I try dressing her in a Victorian outfit. She looks okay although her shoulders are a bit broad and she stands rather sardonically and firmly on the ground surveying the desolation of a burnt-down Free State farm. Allie, get those boots off, and for God's sake, wilt a little!

Get her off that farm. I'll send her in a donkey cart with her wealthy but dying father into the interior. They are on their way to Kimberley. But the father dies on the road and she is left a pile of money. I love bumping off fathers in my stories; like other egghead writers, I am haunted by Oedipus, Electra and Jocasta.

So there she is alone, on her way to Kimberley. She will have to have picked up some passengers, though. Poor girl. Look, I'm sorry, but I have to think about these things: how will she wash properly on the road? Wonderful complexions don't stay that way without cleansing. How will she be able to urinate and move her bowels out in the bush with all those skirts on? Just bundle them up? But won't they still get splashed and stained? How much toilet paper does her party have? Did they *have* toilet paper in those days? Did they have toothbrushes? When was the first toothbrush marketed, hey you Popular Culturists? What if she gets her period? Of *course* she'll get her period, unless she's anorexic. But an anorexic girl won't be able to handle the boisterous sex scenes in the book. And what about mosquitoes? I mean, have you *ever* spent a night out of doors in the summer without netting and that new insecticide you rub on hands, face and feet, or whatever parts of the body are exposed? The perspiration! The food going bad!

Let me tell you, I know from experience that when my skin breaks out, I lose all sense of the romantic occasion. I don't feel like going to bed with some guy whose skin is fine and who'll want to leave the light on while we make love. I don't like making love when I'm sweaty or dirty. I don't fancy sweaty or dirty men. Also, I find it excruciating to be 'confined' with a man in bed, or even in a car, when I'm suffering from flatulence. Yes, contrary to masculine belief, women *do* fart. Over the centuries we've worked hard to establish the conviction of our continence. But out in the bush the pretence would have to go. I simply cannot muster up enthusiasm for Romance as I regard Carlotta, my beautiful heroine, waddling like a duck as she squats, searching for a place to hold steady where the tough grass won't prick her bare butt.

In my imagination my student Allie walks into my office. Today she is sporting an old stained braided coat of the kind major-domos of hotels wear, a limp miniskirt and army boots. I know that she (like many other students these days) buys her clothes from a popular second-hand clothing store that sometimes stocks astonishing antique garments, things people have stolen out of their grandparents' attics, or defunct theatre companies have hawked. Allie has on bottle-green tights and a little head-hugging hat from the twenties.

'Why do you want to write that trash?' she asks me.

'To make money.'

'Then you've got to stop thinking about physical discomfort. Your heroine has to have skin of vinyl, teeth of white stainless steel (if that is possible), her polyfibrous hair does not grow damp and scraggly, and her crystalline eyes have the three or four necessary expressions, depending on the light, for your purposes: joy, indignation, love, and sorrow. She doesn't have periods, or perspiration, or pee, or poo!'

'I can't write about a vinyl *dummy*,' I say, my own eyes flashing indignantly.

'What is the least you can write about?'

'Well, to begin with, I need to see real people in my mind's eye, a woman like you, for instance. Say, what does your boyfriend do?' Deep down in me a little hope is born that she will say he is completing training as an officer in the Air Force Academy. A shadowy Richard Gere starts forming. *Would* such a gorgeous thing date Allie the Punk in her tights and boots?

'My boyfriend has a degree in Agriculture, but because of the recession he can't find a job in his field, no pun, so he's working as a male nurse at Hannah Hospital. Oh boy, you wouldn't believe the kinds of things he's learned to do! Give people enemas, stick catheters into them, give them shots in the bee-hind, and hold pans for them when they want to throw up. But it's done him good, especially seeing old people naked and having to wash the shit off them and all that. He's much more sympathetic toward people these days. He never criticises women for their bodies the way most guys do.'

'What does he look like?' I ask, a bit disconsolately, pulling the paper out of the machine.

'He's no Mister Universe. He's okay. He's going to have to go on a bit of a diet because of the tummy he's getting. Twenty-five's too young to get a tummy. Not that I mind. He's got a sweet face, but his skin is very pale. He can't suntan at all: he just goes red, mostly his nose, and he was never good at sports at school because of his flat feet. Would you listen to this: no one realised that he was flat-footed until he was about fourteen? He got out of the swimming pool at school and by chance the coach noticed his wet footprint. As flat as a fish.'

'What will he do? Keep looking for a job in his "field" or settle for nursing?'

'Naa … he's decided to go on to grad school next year. He may as well. He's saved enough to put himself through, and he still wants to get into some branch of agricultural science, maybe at a higher level.'

'And you?'

'I'll keep on with my studio art. Though I wouldn't mind farming. I've always wanted to farm. That's why Percy and I get on so well.' She settles herself on the corner of my desk, running one hand over a pile of books. I see that each fingernail is painted a different colour. She looks at me confidentially. 'You know, Percy my boyfriend had a terrible time as a kid. His mom used to dominate him totally. Even when he was in high school she'd clean his room and go through all his things. She'd even examine the underclothes he'd thrown in the wash. He had no privacy whatsoever. And the one time he came home a little drunk, both his parents created such a scene, even though he was already twenty-one, that now he simply can't, *he can't* drink in front of them. Now his dad offers him beers and beers and beers, but he can't accept them. I've had a lot of trouble getting him to loosen up with me, you know. Do you know he stayed a virgin until he was twenty-four?'

'Allie, you don't have to tell me all this stuff.'

'I know you'll keep it to yourself.'

'Of course.'

'I had to teach him a lot,' she says coolly, getting off the desk and clumping to the door, her boots heavy against the floorboards. 'I hope you can write your Romance and make some big bucks,' she adds, but without much interest. She wiggles her painted nails at me and leaves. I put the paper back into the typewriter.

My story begins to take form. Percy, my male protagonist (I dare not call him a hero, which is not to say he isn't heroic), will be a civilian helper in the military hospital at Bloemfontein where more British soldiers are dying of diarrhoea than are being killed by the Boers. But I won't go into details that will nauseate the reader; I might draw a Daumieresque picture of grey skeletal bodies with sombre young faces in overcrowded wards. But Percy is a short, shy, pink-faced fellow with not too noticeably flat feet and a deep desire to be a farmer. He has never known a woman (in the biblical sense) until he meets Petronella, a farm girl who has had to take on many of the chores at 'Bloustroom' because the men are away fighting in the Transvaal. She wears army boots and hitches up her skirts for ease of movement by means of an old cartridge belt. She ties her hair up in pony tails with string, which causes her cotton sunbonnet to sit oddly on her head. The neighbours think she is eccentric if not mad (The Mad Woman of Africa – cliché alert!) and no young man comes riding up to 'Bloustroom' to court her when the farmer-fighters are on leave. But Percy doesn't notice anything out of the ordinary about Petronella. Besides, he is lonely. His widowed mother, who wielded inflexible control over his life, has herself passed on to the Fathers as a result of a stray shell crashing through Percy's suburban bedroom just as she was about to riffle through the things her son stores in his tin trunk. (Am I killing Mothers off too now?)

Petronella has great trouble with stomach wind, mostly because of the high-starch diet forced on all the population, but Percy is unaware of her sneaky farts – because of his job, his hair and clothes are infused with excremental and medicinal smells. One afternoon in the barn, she shows him how to make love (*this* will be my main sexual scene, putting male readers straight about female arousal once and for all), whereafter he becomes insatiably attracted to her. He nearly gets shot by the British at one point because they suspect that he is consorting with the enemy, but Petronella is not the enemy, nor do any of the enemy come near her. But Percy goes to gaol (SAD scene), and the British burn Petronella's farm (TRAGIC scene, Petronella's unusual silhouette seen against the brilliant orange and blues of the fire). But after the war Percy marries Petronella and takes up farming with her – her father and brother died in prison camps set up by the British for Boer prisoners in the West Indies. This information is conveyed to Petronella in a letter written by General de Wet, a letter which she frames.

My telephone rings. 'Sheila, honey …' (it is David, my lawyer-friend), 'I've just been reading in the Free Press about a housewife in Troy, Michigan, I mean *Troy*, Michigan! And she's making plenty of money writing these novels to a formula. Apparently her publishers supply her with an outline which she merely fleshes out. Now you could do that!'

The strong picture I have of Petronella and Percy clearing away the debris of the burnt-down farmhouse begins to dissipate. Behind them I see beautiful Carlotta, her blonde hair wisping the sides of her lovely vinyl skin, her lacy petticoats caught up against the breeze in one small hand, her lips pursed redly in anticipation. She waves. At a handsome horseman? No, at me. I am surprised. I see that she wants me to bring her to life, rescue her from that vinyl skin, allow her to experience hot tearful afternoons of toothache, days when she can't get a comb through her sweating hair, the bloated feeling of food moving through her digestive system, messy periods at the wrong time, just when she wanted to wear a white gown to the officers' dinner, and she wants me to give her the good sense to guide her lover's hand and penis so that they move in ways she wants, instead of having to submit to one of those writhing, grunting, quick, harsh sex acts always inflicted on Romantic heroines. I hesitate. I do pity her. Mmm … Carlotta could be Petronella's cousin from overseas. Percy introduces her to Captain Coninghame, the Chief Surgeon. Carlotta uses part of her fortune to rebuild Petronella's farm.

'Look, David, I don't think I want some publisher's outline. I can think up my own outline,' I say.

'Don't tell me I've persuaded you to *do* it?'

'I am thinking about … the project … very seriously.'

'I mean, if someone in Troy, Michigan, can do it, so can you.'

'Ja, ja, I'm thinking about it,' I say, beckoning to Carlotta.

PETER WILHELM

Lion

From: *LM and other Stories* (1975)

Towards the end of summer, everything poised for decay, the final bold shapes
tottering under parabolas of hot straining insects, a lion was observed wandering across the rich farmlands to the north-west of Johannesburg: only miles
from the city, a golden shape barred by trees fringing mapped-out regions of
cultivation and order, crossing the thrusting highways in vast lopes that evaded
destruction by the thundering, astonished traffic.

There was no formal record of the lion, so he sprang into the city's awareness fully extant, fused out of the shining air; and the first premonitory
twitches of fear manifested themselves in the dreams of the inhabitants of
Sandown, Bryanston, Houghton, all the green suburbs with women beside
blue swimming pools with drinks at 11 a.m. The pounce, the yellow teeth, the
cavernous dark jaws, the feral rush through the flowering shrubbery – it was
all there, a night-time code.

Posses of police and farmers – guns out and oiled, trusty – walked through
the high grass and weeds, stung by immature maize stalks, looking. They had
dogs with them who cringed and whimpered, showing their own calcium-
charged fangs, white and somehow delectable like the tips of asparagus. They
and the children who ran after them shrieking with terror and breathlessness,
black and white tumbled together in the mordant adventure, were all on a
hampered search; the skills of tracking were forgotten, they could only go by
the obvious. Members of the press went along too, with flushed faces and
cameras.

At an early stage it was decided that, given the high price of lions on the
international zoo market, the animal would not, when found, be killed: anaes-
thetic darts would be used to stun it first, then it would be lifted into a cage
and transported to a convenient central point for the disposition of lions.

They followed a trail of kills, day after day, puffing and lagging. Here they
found a dog contemptuously munched and discarded; there a mournful heifer,
brown licked eyes startled by death, a haunch ripped open – purple and blue
ravines, Grade A waste spoiled for the abattoir and the hungry steakhouses.

The heavy, overripe rains had given a lush feel to the fields, spreading green
paint over growth, and wild flowers and weeds hammered into the air from

uncultivated edges. Fruit fell into mud with sodden plops; irrigation ditches and small streams throbbed, the water corded and waxy. It had been a superb year, a harvest of a year, and the granaries and exchequer were loaded. So the lion penetrated a structure of assent and gratitude with a dark trajectory: his streaming mane, a Tarzan image, cast gaunt shadows on the end of the commercial year.

The boots of the hunters stuck in the mud; they were like soldiers going over the top in 1916, sent into barbed wire and indeterminate sludge by drunken generals; they floundered; the brims of their hats filled with rain; their pants soaked through like those of terrified schoolboys. They made no headway.

Inexorably, champing at the livestock, the lion ate his way towards the northern suburbs of the city, past roadhouses and drive-in cinemas showing documentaries on wild life and the adventures of Captain Caprivi.

The frequency of dreams involving lions and lion-like beings increased significantly among the inhabitants of the green park-like suburbs of the city. The thud of tennis balls against the netting of racquets lost its precision: the shadow was there, in the tennis court, in the cool waves of the swimming pool, in the last bitter juices of the evening cocktail, tasting of aniseed.

The lion came down.

The farmers – who grew plump chickens for the frozen food ranges of the great supermarkets, and poppies for certain anniversaries – were furious at the terroristic incursion. It blighted their reality, shaming them. They woke to fences offensively broken, to minor household animals sardonically slaughtered, not even used for a snack on the road.

The lion behaved precisely like a lion; each animal was decisively killed; there was never any maiming, inadvertent or intentional; his great jaws crunched down on bone and splintered through domesticity.

He took a roving way toward the city: first directly south through well-manured farmlands, then tracing a stream westwards away from the sprawl of concrete and glass – sniffing at it, perhaps, and choosing to skirt.

He seemed to vanish, back into the diminishing lights of early autumn, back into the air, his lithe yellowish body no longer even glimpsed at a distance by the frenzied posses, watched from behind earth walls by large-eyed farmhands, and howled at by dogs with their black testicles in the dust.

The pressure abruptly diminished like that in a garden hose when the tap is turned commandingly to the left.

Something like silence descended, mote-like and uneasy. The lion had gone away; there had never been a lion; the lion had been a hypnagogic hallucination.

Then he killed a man, most savagely tearing out his guts next to a road, and pin-pointed on a map the kill showed that the westward drift had been

534

temporary and that the lion had in reality resumed coming back. He had followed a stream away from the city, now he was coming back on the opposite bank: all he had done was seek out a place to cross.

Until the occurrence of the first human death, the press and other communications media had adopted an editorial stance towards the lion in which a certain light-heartedness had been mandatory. There had been jibes at authority's inability to find the beast, or even trace its origins. Now, as telephones began to ring incessantly with queries from troubled householders as to the lion's progress, and a sermon was preached in which the light of Christianity was set favourably against the unplumbed blackness of the wilderness and its denizens, the newspapers realised that public opinion was turning against the lion, and they adopted a harder editorial approach: the lion must be shot, or at least swiftly captured, before there were more deaths.

The dead man was reported to be a Bantu male called Samuel Buthelezi, a distant relation of the Zulu Royal family.

It emerged that the followers had in fact passed the lion, going west when he was coming east; he had been asleep on a rock, or in a warm bowl of sand, sunning himself invisibly.

And so the feeling arose that the search had to be made by professionals. A former professional game hunter was accordingly brought out of retirement to put the affair on a more scientific or knowing footing. However, it was impossible to search by night, which was too preponderantly blank to make for ease of vision, silence of movement, or comfort of heart; and so the lion continued to get away. His getting away became the present tense of the searchers and they began to feel he was invincible, that he took devious routes with prior awareness of topography and demography; and when a day or so passed without reports of a kill they indulged in grotesque fantasies – remarking that the lion must be dead in a ditch, or whimpering in a cave with a thorn in his foot. Any of a dozen possibilities, and impossibilities, presented themselves according to the number of searchers involved.

The former professional game hunter was an alcoholic; he drank himself into a stupor and issued contradictory orders.

Small units of the army and air force were summoned to help in the search; it was reasoned that the experience would aid them in tracing terrorists in hostile terrain. Platoons of young men in green and khaki camouflage uniform – bayonets ready at the tips of their rifles – moved lumpily over hills and through lower muddy regions looking for the lion, their boots mired indescribably. In the air fighter and reconnaissance jets flashed from one edge of the horizon to the other, ceaselessly photographing. A helicopter, normally used for the control of traffic and the detection of illegally cultivated marijuana, also chopped its way through the search pattern.

The first white person to be killed by the lion was Dr Margaret Brierwood.

535

A graduate in palaeontology, Dr Brierwood had taken her two children to school and was settling down beside the swimming pool of her and her husband's three-acre holding in a wooded area only ten miles from the city centre. In the course of the preceding night the lion had doubled the distance between him and his pursuers, racing along the fringes of a dual highway connecting the cities of Pretoria and Johannesburg. He had failed to make a kill at dawn and was correspondingly nettled at his own inadequacies – a horse had whinnied to freedom because of a misjudged leap – and driven by hunger.

The Brierwoods' estate was surrounded by a low wooden fence, easily hurdled, and the lion sat for some time within the grounds, panting softly, his tail rapidly frisking dust and grass, before moving. He observed the morning activity narrowly, tempted at one point to carry off a black man who swept the floor of the swimming pool with a long vacuum brush. He was deterred by innumerable activities in his immediate environment: a large fly that bit his haunch and made him snap irritably at the air, two birds that made trilling love in overhead leaves, a subtle alteration in the quality of the morning light which stirred inchoate levels of unease in the beast.

The strangeness of the pool – its non-drinking-place aspects – had a dazzling effect on the mind of the lion. It made him indecisive about striking.

Eventually, however, he made his charge – out of the wooded garden, up a grass slope to the pool's verge, then a leap across a tea table – glass shattering, sugar cubes ascending white in the clear air – and a last controlled embrace with Dr Brierwood, his vast paws over her breasts, the talons holding firm, his jaws clamping down on her neck to draw up spouts of blood.

Dr Brierwood had been midway through a paragraph in an article pointing out certain anomalies in a palaeontologist's analysis of recent finds at unexpected levels of the Olduvai Gorge in Kenya. When the intimidating, blood-freezing, total horror of the lion's roar swept over her like a wave of pure death from an opened crypt, she looked up and screamed. The lion dropped down out of the sky to seize her; one finger convulsively jabbed at the place where she had stopped reading; and she felt her bones being crushed with more force than she had ever conceived.

Terrified servants ran for help. Within an hour a cordon of men and weaponry had been set in a ring around the Brierwood estate. For miles in all directions traffic began to slow, to stop, to impact into jarring hooting masses. Thousands of sightseers came from all directions, hampering operations.

At the centre of command was the former professional game hunter, who was half mad from anxiety and gracelessly attempted to defer to anyone in uniform; but orders had been given that he alone was in charge, and as the crisis gained dimension, moving towards a critical moment when something would after all have to be done, he realised that a decision – on something, anything – would have to be taken. He pushed his way through people who shouted into each other's faces and went into a house which instantly transformed into a headquarters. Maps were pinned on walls, markers were moved on boards, grids were established; the military apparatus became dominant, and he realised that a military solution might be inevitable.

To think more clearly the game hunter locked himself in a lavatory and drank.

The lion left the remains of his kill beside the swimming pool and made his way into the woods to sleep. It was a fine autumn morning, holding the last of the summer heat in the bright dappled areas of light under the trees, and soothing and cool in the shade. Drowsiness overcame him and he stretched at his full length to digest Dr Brierwood.

The small, frightened, trigger-happy group which – under the dilatory leadership of the former professional game hunter – finally made its way to the swimming pool and found the dead woman, was incapacitated by the sight. Each registered an atrocity; each felt an impulse to shout, or rescript the terms of the find; inevitably there was a sickly anticipation of retribution and subsequent guilt.

In the judicial inquiry which was later held into the circumstances of the killing, it was considered extraordinary that the grounds of the Brierwood estate were not fully, immediately searched. No search was made; once Dr Brierwood had been removed the servants were questioned on the movements of the lion, and when two agreed that it had been seen wandering along a stretch of country road north of the estate there was a surge in that direction. The testimony of the servants was instantly accepted: it had a satisfactory emotional content, and the searchers were in any case dazed at the fury that had broken out at the edge of the swimming pool.

On a bed of brown fallen leaves at the outer boundary of the Brierwood estate the lion slept peacefully all day; he moaned softly in his sleep like a dreaming cat, his immense male head on his paws.

By midnight the curious had moved away, and the searchers were bunched together indecisively in a small army camp. A violent electric storm had disrupted communications, and the various groups who were out on the roads and in the fields with torches and guns blundered through wet darkness, seeing nothing, knowing nothing, dead at heart. Damage to an underground telephone cable at two a.m. put several thousand receivers out of order in the area; and this contributed to an impression of profound devastation. There was a universal sense of depression, and sleepers were driven down into grey underworlds where faceless statues intoned meaningless arguments.

Shortly after dawn the lion left the woods, through which horizontal light splintered prismatically. He sniffed the wind and plodded south again, through landscaped terraces and sprawling ranch-style homesteads. Down pine-needle matted lanes and across dew-spotted lawns he padded with no more noise than soft rustlings and the snap of small twigs.

Soon the terrain changed, and taking the easiest way he was beguiled towards the exact heart of Johannesburg along the concrete swathes of the M1 motorway. It was a bright, crisp morning; the sky was enormous, blue to violet at the zenith, streaked with high tufts of cirrus, almost invisible. Ahead, the dark autumnal cone of ash and smoke remained to be burned off the city, dense, dirty but giving a solid emphasis to the tower blocks: an appropriate frame.

He went on through the awakening suburbs, stinging smells of coffee and morning toast, the first cars coughing into life. And then the first cars began to pass him, early motorists staring with incredulity, astonishment, in tumults of weirdness at the apparition. They accelerated around the lion, so that there was an aspect of untampered serenity about his passage.

He walked into Johannesburg, quite alone after a time, since once word had reached the authorities of his route the motorway was closed and for the second time in twenty-four hours traffic choked to a standstill. The lion could hear distant clangour and uproar, meaningless. Soon he began to sniff irritably at acrid fumes and the like, but his entry remained inflexible; he took no offramps, and remained on the left of the road within the speed limit.

By mid-morning he was weary, and stopped, and looked around. This was the city: geometrical mountains advanced into themselves, making no horizon, netting together like stone fronds into an impassivity of yellow, grey, gold, black. He had no sense of distance or perspective and could not see into the new environment.

He roared at it.

His roar echoed back.

He stood at the edge of the motorway, where it swept over old buildings and streets and looked down past John Vorster Square to the Magistrates' Courts and the Stock Exchange, and beyond that to the Trust Bank and the Carlton Centre: the shapes impacted up against his sight.

Below him when he looked again, men and women seethed, their clothing briskly making fresh patterns as they moved around, then settling or resettling into something else.

North and south the motorway spread dully; nothing whatsoever moved; a small wind beat miserably at pieces of brown newspaper gusted over the tar.

He roared at everything.

And, tinnily, a kind of echo came back: but buzzing, inconsequential, intermittent. Far above a small black dot came down at him.

The helicopter, the former professional game hunter.

Suddenly the lion was deafened and shaken by fear: a metal thing jabbered at him only yards away, black grit tossed up by mad winds into his nose. Men with strained white faces spilled out into the motorway, pincered him.

And then, of course, the military solution.

PETER WILHELM

Pyro Protram

From: *LM and other Stories* (1975)

The last man in the world, Pyro Protram, came up from the sea, climbing the steep bone-white steps to the ruined hotel. He carried over his shoulder a large American-made automatic rifle and ammunition belt; and, since he had successfully hunted, the carcass of a small rabbit shot in the dune scrub.

He was a prime male: towering, burnt by the sun to an ashy goldenness, his hair hanging in slick black ringlets on naked gleaming shoulders. If you had seen early Tarzan movies, with Johnny Weissmuller, the sight of Pyro would have brought them to mind. His muscles were corded; he wore a loin cloth. His age could have been anything – thirty, forty – but if you were watching from above, only the power and grace would have been apparent. Certainly, he made a better representative for mankind than a funny balding fellow in eye-glasses would have done.

But who was there to see?

Only the crabs.

Pyro watched for crabs, always. He had to. Since certain things occurred to the universe, and he found himself the last man in the world, the crabs had become the greatest menace in his life.

Along with the Janets.

Janet had been his wife, but he found her with another man and shot her. Now, in this new universe, in which he suspected the laws of nature were weakening, she often waited for him on rocks along the shoreline, or in the hotel. Once he found her in his bed, in the big bridal suite he had comman-deered, and had to strangle her because his guns were out of reach against a wall. Now he kept a big refashioned carving knife strapped to his thigh. In case of the Janets.

Pyro stopped halfway up the salt-white steps and looked down at the sea. It smashed the black rocks of the coast. Left and right the beach stretched in unusual Daliesque contours: corroded pipes stuck into the sky, sunken trees shone like dead puffed-up fish. Out in the grey-green sea sharks patrolled in murderous schools.

On a level dark rock exposed by the retreating tide he saw a crab sunning itself, its enormous bulk – as large as a rhinoceros – resonant with evil. Its shell had the familiar greenish stripes like threads in coal, and its eyes protruded upwards, slanting in his direction.

Pyro laid down the bloody rabbit, which bled into the stone. He levelled his rifle, taking aim with blue eyes like steel. 'You bastard,' he said into the air frosty with spray, and fired. The detonation broke into the morning, shocking, disruptive.

And an eye of the crab disintegrated abruptly, The monster clattered metal-lically on the rock, the great claws crushed together and he heard its bizarre cry of pain – something like glass eggs grinding against each other.

The white surf covered the crab and he saw its dark shape flow into the darkness of the deep water around the rock. It was not dead, it would survive, return.

Pyro gloated at the crab's pain. This was his greatest pleasure: the destruc-tion of the monstrous forms of the new reality.

He had been alone for so long he knew nothing else; memories, images of the past, were vague now; the peopled cities of the interior, the woman called Janet, the orderly farms and thrusting economy – once they went, leaking away and leaving him in the fluid landscapes of his eternal present, his mind lost its ability to believe in them.

The rabbit he had shot shuddered and flopped down a few steps. He lifted it again and closed his thick fingers around the neck, twisting. It became finally still.

Suddenly there was a diminution of the light around Pyro. He looked up at the sun, noting the beginning of the daily eclipse. Though the darkness was short-lived and never total, it was best to be in the hotel behind his barricades.

He hastened up the stairs to where giant walls of barbed wire protected the hotel's entrance. Cautiously, he navigated the maze he had created against the crabs and when he reached the deserted tables and chairs of the lounge he bolted the big double doors behind him, feeling safe.

But a Janet sat against a far wall, drinking a gin and tonic. She wore a blue blouse and tight blue jeans, her long attractive legs spread invitingly. As usual, her eyes were unfocused and disturbing in odd ways. It was quite gloomy now, so he took aim carefully and the Janet began to speak before he could kill it.

The Janet said: 'Hello Pyro, you queer. You simpering faggot. You creep. You've been out killing again, I see. Why do you kill so much? Is it because you know, secretly, you're a spineless homosexual? You have to kill to show what a man you are, but all the time you know you're just a mincing queer. When you came to bed I used to laugh and smirk and snigger because I knew what you were. I was never deceived.'

'Shut up, you bitch,' said Pyro and blew her head off, stopping the tirade. Most of her hair and face stuck to the wall behind her and her body crumpled slowly forward over the table. As he watched it began to fade out and the terrible stains of blood and gore vanished, became invisible.

The process of disappearance took several minutes, during which time Pyro poured himself a stiff drink at the bar and downed it without water. He felt the alcohol drop down and warm him. Quite soon he stopped shivering and lit three candles in the gloom.

He cursed God for having left him alone in this place, where elementary truths of the past were flexible and change was arbitrary. Over the past few years he had killed thousands of Janets: but there was no end to them.

During the eclipse another appeared, this time in evening dress with a rose pinned over its breast.

It played the untuned piano with spectral fingers and long after Pyro had garrotted the thing with steel wire he heard the notes echoing in the fortressed hotel.

He skinned the rabbit and marinated it in fine red wine and herbs, following a recipe in a book found long ago in the sumptuous kitchen. He had become a fine cook – he could take time, labour over the smallest details for hours. It was a small satisfaction, but a fulfilling one. At night he spent hours over his meals, bringing in course after course from the wood-fired stove that he never let grow cold, downing the noble wines ransacked from the hotel's lavish stores. There was enough wine there for a hundred years, enough for him.

And he conducted scintillating conversations with himself:

'Well Pyro, we showed up that bitch today. She thinks she can get at me with her lies, but she can't. She never could, not even in the other place. Before all this. She tried to break me down, to show me up to her smart friends. But I showed her. I showed her all right. There's only one way to put a woman right. Kill her. Rape her. Kill her. Over and over; never let up, never let them get an edge, never listen to their whining lies.'

After his banquet Pyro lay in his double bed in his locked suite. Hideous things scuttled on the roof, but he was safe in the night, safe in the warm night, safe to pass out down into the tunnels of wine and food which carried him oblivious to dawn.

Next morning he went fishing. His powerful arms enabled him to cast far out to sea, beyond the rocks and dark vortices of water where the crabs lurked. And, within seconds, he knew he had a shark on the end of his line. His arms wrenched in their shoulder sockets and he shouted in glee. He loved the battle, which he always won.

It took an hour. First the shark dragged the line far out to sea, and he let it run, braking only marginally. Then he braced himself and wound in, slowly, tirelessly, exerting his force with care, vividly sensing each flurry of shark movement in the storming waves.

It lashed its grey body on the rocks and he heaved it into the poisonous air. The shark was not big, but it sprang into the sky above him, vicious, desperate, and it was like war between the sky and sea. When it was near he took his knife and slashed the smooth belly till it spilled blood and viscera everywhere.

It took a long time to die and Pyro watched intently, beyond thought. Then he cut great fishy steaks, his mouth watering at the anticipated taste.

Retreating back to shore over the slick rocks he saw his mistake: while engaged in battle he had left his back unprotected, and six crabs were spread out on the beach waiting for him. Their huge pincers were outstretched; and closest was one with a single baleful eye at the end of a stalk.

This was bad. He had never faced so many before, and even one would have been deadly. Their knobbed eyes were on the same level as his own, glistening with intelligence and cunning.

The tide had come in and between Pyro and the crabs several metres of water sluiced whitely. Normally he would have breasted his way to land. Now he paused, assessing his position.

It seemed impossible. There was no way to reach the steps from the beach to the hotel without going through the crabs.

He unslung his rifle and fired at the one-eyed crab. The bullet chipped fragments of shell, but missed anything vital. The crab scuttled sideways fractionally; it clacked its pincers and he heard it hissing with hostility.

Pyro had a sense of total desolation, and self-pity nagged his guts briefly. Then he straightened his shoulders and stepped down into the water, leaving his rod and the shark steaks behind.

He stood waist deep in the water, the sand sucking at his feet, and advanced on the crabs.

Before reaching the beach he fired again – successfully, between the eyes of a crab deep into its body. It died abominably, its six jointed limbs stretched in agony, battering the sand.

And he ran directly towards it, leaping up and scrambling insanely over its shell, screaming, making for the steps.

Of course the other crabs could move with lightning rapidity, but the dead crab lay between them and their prey and impeded them for the few necessary seconds.

He raced up the stairs, turned, and fired again and again. Vast claws snapped at his feet and he had a crystal vision of exploding shell as he emptied his magazine at the seething, nightmarish cluster of crustacean beings at the base of the stairs.

Somehow, clambering over its fellows, the one-eyed crab reached the barbed wire, there to be held back, its remaining eye tugging monstrously where it became hooked.

In the hotel Pyro dragged a wooden box to the entrance and took from it two Molotov cocktails he had constructed from soap, sand, petrol and whisky bottles. He lit the rag fuses simultaneously and hurled them at the hooked crab. They exploded in panoramas of black smoke and lurid flame and – gratifyingly – the crab shrieked. Burning petrol ran into its shell and cooked it to death; it tumbled backwards and smashed down the steps into the remaining, enraged, wounded crabs.

Pyro locked the hotel door and fell to the dusty carpet, panting like a dog.

'Look at you,' sneered the Janet who was drinking at the bar, her sleek form encased in an orange airline hostess's uniform. 'I've never seen anything look less like a man than you. What happened? Did a bully kick sand in your face, you abysmal queen? You came up those stairs quickly enough; you even forgot to mince and show off.'

'O Jesus and Christ and God,' whimpered Pyro. He dragged himself to his feet and crossed to the Janet, punching her face. Blood spurted from her nose, and her insults bubbled: 'Hitting a woman again, Pyro? Got to show what a man you are? You stupid little homosexual twerp.'

Pyro lifted the Janet and staggered to the doorway. He held her over one shoulder when he unlocked it but then used both arms to hurl her into the barbed wire. She lay on her back, looking down slightly at him, saying:

'What's it going to be this time, you queer? A Molotov cocktail?' Her exposed flesh was bloody from the wire.

'Yes,' he snarled, 'a Molotov cocktail.' He lit one and threw it at her. Lacking anything really solid to break against, the cocktail spattered flaming petrol over her and she sizzled into blackness, still cursing him doggedly until the equipment for cursing was ruined and she was dead and beginning to fade out.

Pyro got drunk on brandy, a full bottle in an hour. But it was not a releasing drunkenness: even as he drank he felt the hangover beginning. When the eclipse began he was delirious and vomiting.

Somehow he got through the day, and drank again at night, opening a can of stewed beef from his dwindling store for his evening meal.

Sleep would not come. It seemed, as he lay in his double bed in his locked room, that the distant crashing of the sea – normally a comforting sound – had about it a scratchy quality, something not natural – almost patterned.

Sweating with fear he sat upright. The scratching sound was not the sea: it was a distinct sound, somewhere in the room. He got up, got his gun, lit a candle.

At first he could see nothing unusual. Then he located the scratching sound. It came from a wall, and when he looked closely he observed the paint powdering down to the floor. Something was attempting to force its way through the wall, to get him.

Little barbed cilia made their appearance over a patch of wall about a metre high and half a metre across. More appeared by the second.

543

He fired into the centre of the ravening cilia and the movement stopped. Then, appalled, he cut at the wall and found it rotten as punk. He dug deeper; the point of his knife found hollowness around the body of the scratching thing, and hard rind-like material elsewhere. Something spurted and his hands were coated with a greyish stinking ooze.

Disgusted, he forced himself to clear the thing's body. He had to see.

It plopped down to the floor finally, a dark grey-yellow cockroach with abnormally large jaws.

Pyro went to the bar and drank, nauseated. Then he stood at the entrance to the hotel and looked out, up at the diamond-like stars. He was seized by an hallucination. The stars went on forever and he experienced infinity directly, a pressure of total anxiety.

The next morning Pyro went hunting again in the dunes. They rose and fell around him like the landscapes of a dream. He was exhausted, stumbling.

He found footprints in the sand; unbelievingly he examined them. They were of a large man, barefoot like himself. In this new universe they filled him with a premonition of disaster.

He followed them, winding through the blazing white dunes. His blood sang in his ears, sounding like ghostly fiddlings of intelligent cockroaches.

The track led towards the hotel, and he moved increasingly cautiously, alert for danger. Whoever it was could well have gone there to search him out, to kill him. Well, he would have to kill the other first: that was the way of the new reality.

He hid in scrub and watched the hotel. Nothing. The other was inside, then, possibly searching the rooms. Was he armed? It was certain. Logic required that the other be armed, deadly.

Pyro would not be seen on the stairs. But he could be seen if he dashed from the scrub to the stairs, and there could be an ambush at the top. But there was nothing else to be done. He would have to go directly, across the sand to the stairs, up the stairs, into the hotel. Let it be face to face: that was his way. What did it matter if he was killed? What was life in this place, anyway?

Pyro Protram went up the stairs.

He went into the hotel.

Nothing. Nobody.

Only a Janet, lounging in a bikini with a tall glass of orange juice and vodka. She laughed raucously when she saw him.

'Oh God, look what's come up again. It's the pansy. Hello Pyro, you unnameable faggot. What have you been doing, creeping around in the dunes? Following yourself again?'

Yes, he realised, that was what he had been doing. He felt unutterably foolish. He laid down his gun and sat in a chair facing the Janet.

'Why do you come after me like this?' he asked, pained, puzzled. 'Every day

544

you're back. I can't kill you. I give up. Look at me now: I didn't sleep last night, my mind's not right. And now you again. Again and again. Will you never leave me alone?'

'Never. Not while this place lasts.'

'But how long will it last? Can you tell me?'

'For you, forever. You will always be here. And I will always be here.'

'Why, why, why?'

'Because.'

'Because? You say that like a woman. That's no answer.'

'Then kill me again. It's all the answer you're going to get, you cringing queer.'

With infinite disdain, infinite weariness, Pyro shot his wife for the 6 789th time.

Curiously, there was no carnage now. She sat brokenly in the chair, but there was no blood, no human wreckage. It all seemed unlikely to Pyro, since he used dumdum bullets of a high calibre.

He examined the Janet closely, peering into the gaping chest wound. What he saw was enormously intricate clockwork, tiny oiled cogs and levers and ratchets.

Pyro Protram went to his room, stepped over the rotting body of the cockroach and sat on his bed. He found himself weeping deliriously.

'That's the last time. No more now. Please.'

But nothing went away and he heard renewed scratching in the walls.

As the eclipse began he put the end of the rifle in his mouth, and operated the trigger with a toe. 'Mother!' he screamed silently as he went all the way out.

'He died last night?' queried the first psychiatrist.

'Yes,' replied the second. 'About time too. He'd been in a coma for years. At least now we'll have another bed available.'

'You know,' said the first psychiatrist, 'until he killed his wife people pointed to him as a great South African. He played Springbok rugby against the Argentinians, and could have had a place in parliament if he had wanted it. God knows what went wrong.'

As the two psychiatrists passed down the corridor a homely nurse wheeled behind them a trolley on which lay the shrouded body of a very old, quite dead man called Pyro Protram.

PETER WILHELM

Jazz

(In memoriam KM)
From: *At the End of a War* (1981)

I had left school and was in my first year at university; eighteen years old, scrabbling around the campus with my bag of books and short-sightedness. Jane was in my English class and we sat near each other. She was very beautiful, a target for the predatory men who stalked women there in those times, in all times. But she held aloof, being an intellectual and, for those times, a radical.

Joseph Conrad, DH Lawrence, Henry James: prompted by mid–century critics and moralists such as FR Leavis, we read their famous books and wrote clever papers on them. I struggled, for my background was impoverished; not simply in the cash valuation you could put on it, though that was scant enough: but in the very aridity of the mental climate. I moved in the remotest suburbs of thought; in the remotest suburbs west of the city. Far away I saw the lights, and was drawn like a moth.

I cannot easily describe Jane. Her hair was blond, she was tanned and 'athletic' (my mother's curious euphemism for big-breasted). Etc. The fact of beauty was there, like a cat in the house: but then I could match that by being handsome in a parodic fashion, and I played all the sports. She would not have been drawn to me through a reciprocation of prettiness. Had that been on, other men would have put her in their pockets with their meaty hands: after all, just ahead is the man who is better than you in every respect.

But because I had a carnal wish for learning, Jane came my way.

We dated regularly. We went to art movies. Now in those days sex had not yet reached our shores, so to speak. One took oneself to extremes of passion in parked cars or bedrooms when parents were out for the night: but the essential was infrequently consummated. Rebuttal was somewhat more in force then than now, but with no certainty of outcome: we drifted in grey sexual nothingness, always afraid. At the end of a fruitful and natural consummation could come a burgeoning foetus. And after that marriage, abortion, God knew what. Alien territory. So one did not transgress easily, and there was an understanding implicit in the gropings that in the end we would go home in sexual agony.

I had worked part-time to buy an electric guitar, and I was a member of a band that played on Friday or Saturday nights at various student parties. We barely got by, musically and financially. There were four of us: lead guitar (myself), electric bass, drums, and a perpetually stoned proto-hippie who played all kinds of instruments very well – piano, saxophone, flute. We had no real musical 'voice'.

We played to order, like robots. There was no improvisation, no complexity, no jazz unless a few rehearsed riffs in the midst of a twelve-bar-blues number can be accounted such.

I had no ambitions musically; I played to earn money to keep up payments on my crotchety old Ford, so essential to getting around, and for spare change to buy Jane hamburgers after we had seen Ingmar Bergman's latest contribution to cosmic pessimism. Jane generally accompanied me to the various dances at which I played, but was mostly bored. 'Why don't you ever play *real* music?' she would ask. She meant jazz.

'It's not that kind of band,' I would reply, hotly on the defence. 'I can play jazz if I want to.' Jazz was the fashion.

She came from a very rich background; her parents had a castle in Houghton, with uniformed servants, a bar, everything. She did not merely have her own room; it had an adjacent study. Her father was the head of an important liberal organisation, and needed a study to concoct his ringing denunciations of apartheid; so, in a kind of dreamy intellectual deliverance, he had provided his sons and daughter with studies. They would need them. Everybody needed them, right?

'Prove to me you can play jazz,' Jane said once. 'Bring your guitar to my house and see if you can play along with Parker or Mingus.' She had all the records. 'See if you play like Coltrane, or only imitate Cliff Richard and The Shadows!' A later generation might have said 'The Pet Shop Boys'.

Damn right I was going to try. So I practised at home, sending my fretful fingers over the frets, learning apparently spontaneous sequences of notes. I went over them, and over them again. Mother threw fits. 'Switch that thing off or I'll break it over your head! You'll have me in the bladdy lunatic asylum if you go on.'

'I make money out of it,' I would reply. 'I pay for my textbooks by playing the guitar.'

'No you don't. Your father pays for your textbooks by repping in the northern Transvaal, leaving me alone here to listen to your crap. You just play to show off to your rich little girlfriend.'

So it went on.

I went to Jane's house and played along with Parker and Mingus, their rich organic sounds coming out of vast hi-fi speakers that cost more than I could make out of my playing in a year. I played along, not very well, but surprisingly well enough to please Jane. Jazz, she explained to me (after all this was the Sixties), was the authentic music of the 'Negro'. It was, therefore, a bold statement about life from men who lived on the raw edge of danger and prejudice.

By implication, even listening to jazz showed not merely one's solidarity with an oppressed people, but was in itself a quasi-revolutionary act. Your heart was in the right area.

However. Jazz – as codified in those giant piles of records she had in racks and on shelves – was an imported subversion; the players were Americans. I put a hard point to Jane: isn't all this a posture? In what way did it relate to the life content of South African blacks, 'our' blacks?

'It's the same thing. They use music in the same way. Look at Dollar Brand and Adam Moletsi.'

Adam Moletsi was invited from time to time to play on campus. The attentive white liberals would listen to him producing tortured notes from his saxophone, veritable cries of anguish and pride on which they would comment favourably.

After I had played along with Jane's records, we lay together on the bed and kissed. I took matters further.

'No, no.'

'Yes, yes.'

'No, stop.

'I'll do anything for you. I want to make love to you.'

'You'd never respect me afterwards.'

'Of course I'd respect you afterwards. I'd respect you even more.'

'No'

I sat upright, hurt and almost angry. 'You talk so much about freedom and all: why can't you be free with me?'

She shook her head. 'I'm not like that. I don't want to be used and thrown away.' Poor Jane: in a decade or so she would find the strong female voices she heard distantly in our future. But when she did, it was too late. 'I'm not that kind of girl,' she murmured sadly.

'Well perhaps you should become that kind of girl. You're nothing but a …' But there I stopped short of using a term very familiar in my background, though alien to hers.

'A what?' she snorted, also sitting up. 'Just what am I? Go ahead and say what you were going to say.'

'A hypocrite,' I mumbled slackly, for that was the most acceptable alternative that occurred to me right then.

She laughed. 'So I'm supposed to go to bed with you because I believe in freedom for the African people? That's the most nonsensical argument I've ever heard.'

'Well,' I said, producing like a magic rabbit an idea, a threat, a strategy.

'Would you go to bed with me if I stood up on stage with Adam Moletsi and played jazz just as well as he can?'

The proposition had coalesced out of the variant threads of our conversation, our relation of bodies, our sense of each other's dimensions of soul.

And: 'Yes,' she said.

It happened that Adam Moletsi was coming to the campus within the next week. He would bring his usual backing band with him and would give a mid-afternoon concert in a medium-sized hall. Several hundred students could be expected to attend; the University Jazz Society (to which Jane and I belonged) would charge admission to non-members; and Adam and his band would be given the money that was taken in. It was an easy arrangement.

I went to the president of the Jazz Society and told him I wanted to play with Adam.

'No, you can't do that,' he said firmly. 'People will be paying to hear Adam, not you. Besides, it would be ridiculous if you, a white, went up and tried to compete with an assured black jazzman.' The president spoke snottily; I had offended some sense of racial propriety.

'Well,' I said, 'I'm going to ask Adam if I can play with him. It's his scene; he can decide.'

'I still say no,' said the president; but he was unsure now. 'Perhaps if Adam says yes it'll be OK. But I don't want trouble.'

'Piss off.'

'Piss off yourself, you arrogant twerp.'

Let me speak about myself briefly, as I then was. I was just a young white boy from a succession of poor suburbs. Blacks were not, so to speak, visible to me. I had been brought up in the proprieties and rectitudes of a normal lower-middle-class family for that time and place – except that an entire section, a nation one might say, had been rendered invisible to me. My parents spoke easily of 'boys', and I seldom met black people who were not servants – not of that amorphous gestation of 'garden boys' and 'kitchen girls' who scurried around and beneath the skirts of white society, cleaning up and being humble. My view of the real world was therefore unbalanced.

Jazz players, for people like Jane, myself, and indeed the president of the Jazz Society, represented far more than a musical ambience: they stood for their people, a symbol in the liberal's mind. Yet, after all, they were simply men and women; they struggled under an additional yoke when the liberals made their play of them, as if they were cards in a bridge game.

No wonder Adam Moletsi drank. He had to stand up there in the face of those white youths and play at being a nigger – for them. Who of us saw him otherwise?

I made my preparations for the afternoon of the concert. Because I, a white, was going to stand up with those said representatives of blackdom, I would take upon myself a quantum of blackness. I knew that (and knew it was why Jane would go to bed with me because of it: in muted rebellion, she really wanted to sleep with a black man). However, because I realised my physical limits when it came to playing the guitar, and knew I would be up front with professionals, I prepared myself psychologically for the encounter: I boosted my pride, lest there be cataclysm.

The hall filled. Adam and his band arrived. He was drunk. He waved to the girls and waggled his hips. There was some laughter in the hall.

Adam. A tall, cadaverous man, his liver mostly gone but giving to his light skin a yellow tinge. His blackness was inside him, not folded over his bones.

I went up. 'I want to play with you.' I pointed to a corner where I had in advance stacked my guitar and amplifier: a mean red Fender and a fine wood and metal amplifier with a great speaker attached.

Adam laughed, swaying over me. 'Hey man, you want to play with us?' He had an adopted American accent, like many black men of his generation. He was perhaps forty-five. An old soul, as they said.

The whole band laughed. The president of the Jazz Society, blushing like a rose, came up and whispered to Adam. I saw Jane sitting in the audience. Then Adam turned to me and said, 'Sure, you can join in on some numbers. Get set up.'

The band went straight into 'Bloomdido', the Bird and Diz number that is scatty and great. Adam played a solo and then turned to me to bring me in. I felt total exposure. 'Bloomdido' was far out of my range. Absurdly, I shook my head and Adam let the drummer go for thirty-two bars, an impressive explosion that diverted attention away from my initial, devastating failure. I sensed Adam's concern not to embarrass me and was swayed by curious emotions. Not merely gratitude, but not least wonder.

The next number was a straightforward twelve-bar-blues: three chords, up and down. A child could do well. Adam, I was certain, had set this up for me and I played a perfect solo when my turn came, being really fancy and over-riding notes so that it sounded like Chet Atkins had come in, but funky, good. You could feel it was good. I was applauded.

So it went. Adam now knew what I could do, so he did not ask me in on numbers beyond my scope. At one point he took a nip of brandy out of his coat pocket, sipped, and offered it to me. I took it, proud in front of all those envious white dudes.

The concert came to an end and the students filed out. I was left standing with Adam and the band, the president, and Jane, who came up and took my arm like Miss Universe. That was the proudest moment of my youth. I felt on fire. Perhaps the brandy helped, but I was at ease with Adam, and the thought of sex with Jane – assured now, on the line – lent me an enormous physical assurance.

'You were very good,' said Jane. She smiled.

The president of the Jazz Society paid the band out and the men split, except Adam who sat back in one of the chairs, just like a student, and thoughtfully drank his brandy. His saxophone was in a case on the bench before him.

Finally, there was just Adam, myself and Jane. We talked desultorily, unsure of each other. Then Adam said: 'Hey, man: you got a car?'

'Sure.'

'Let's go for a ride. Us three.'

This was Life. I was tense and excited. So was Jane. 'Us three.'

So we went driving, packed into my Ford with conversation and brandy. Adam told us a lot about himself, how he lived close to the edge but had good high-class gangster friends who helped him out. He actually sat there, reclining in the back seat and told us stuff like that, nodding off from time to time. He directed me, and soon I found that we were on our way to Alexandra township. A black area: I felt trepidation.

But we were not soon into the township when Adam sat up alertly and told me to park.

'You stay here,' he instructed Jane. Then he took my arm and we walked out together in those bitter streets, frozen in the early winter, to a shop where a Chinese man sat and watched.

We bought from him dagga, the weed, *boom*: that which I had always associated with precipitation into blackness, the revenge of the black man on the white whose consciousness cannot bear alteration.

A secret about drugs: any hell they give is better than the hell of the white man for the black.

We drove out of Alex, through mute, manicured, varnished suburbs, all order and the law incarnate, drove 'us three' with our cargo of hallucination and communication and blazing withheld sex. We smoked the stuff and laughed like crazy as the world twisted and warped, and we twisted and warped and flickered into bizarre, meaningless awareness: that point where just one more toke will be too much, or will reveal all. The Allness waiting there in the next joint, like reality about to serve a summons.

We drove to the top of the Melville Koppies, looking down on the suburbs and the city itself: far from any cop, smoking, smoking, pushing out smoke from our lungs as if we were on fire.

And what did we talk about? God knows.

But I came to clarity when Adam said: 'Listen man, give up playing. You're no good. This afternoon, that was just playing games.'

'But I was ... fluent ... I was OK, wasn't I?'

Jane looked intently at us two.

'You were OK, but you don't understand it. You don't understand jazz.

551

You don't understand the pain, the suffering, the longing, the rocking, the rolling ...' Adam was almost gibbering. He was very stoned. But, of course, I understood him all too well.

'I tried,' I said defensively.

'Sure. But that's not good enough. You'll never get there man: just face it, and you'll be happier.'

'What was wrong with my playing?'

'It was the wrong colour, man, that was all.'

'I don't ...'

'It was the wrong colour! It's not your music and you can't play it and you never will play it. Even if you put out sounds just like Charlie Parker, just the same, there will still be a difference. It's not your music.'

Then he turned to Jane: 'But you're my woman, you're my music.'

'No she's not,' I shouted. 'Take your hands off her.'

We all pummelled each other; it was a farce. At last Adam gave up and simply laughed. 'OK, white boy, she's your woman. Just take me to the station and drop me off. She's all yours.' Then, abruptly, he leaned over to me and kissed me; I could actually feel the essence of love there, a tolerance and an anguish; I smelt him.

I kissed him back.

I gave up my guitar. Jane gave me up. Adam died of cirrhosis of the liver. Jane married and had a child who drowned in her swimming pool, so she committed suicide.

The difference between youth and all that comes afterwards is a simple one, a stage or an event that puts matters into perspective. Real people really die. Real people have real limits.

Jazz is something I have on my record player.

BESSIE HEAD

The Deep River

A story of ancient tribal migration

From: *The Collector of Treasures and other Botswana Village Tales* (1977)

Long ago, when the land was only cattle tracks and footpaths, the people lived together like a deep river. In this deep river which was unruffled by conflict or a movement forward, the people lived without faces, except for their chief, whose face was the face of all the people; that is, if their chief's name was Monemapee, then they were all the people of Monemapee. The Talaote tribe forgot their origins and their original language in their journey southwards — they were to merge and remerge again with many other tribes and the name, Talaote, was all they were to retain in memory of their history. Before a conflict ruffled their deep river, they were all the people of Monemapee, whose kingdom was somewhere in the central part of Africa.

They remember that Monemapee ruled the tribe for many years as the hairs on his head were already saying 'white!' by the time he died. On either side of the deep river, there might be hostile tribes or great dangers, so all the people lived in one great town. The lands where they ploughed their crops were always near the town. That was done by all the tribes for their protection and their day-to-day lives granted them no individual faces either for they ploughed their crops, reared their children and held their festivities according to the laws of the land.

Although the people were given their own ploughing lands, they had no authority to plough them, without the chief's order. When the people left home to go to plough, the chief sent out the proclamation for the beginning of the ploughing season. When harvest time came, the chief perceived that the corn was ripe. He gathered the people together and said:

'Reap now, and come home.'

When the people brought home their crops, the chief called the thanksgiving for the harvest. Then the women of the whole town carried their corn in flat-baskets, to the chief's place. Some of that corn was accepted on its arrival, but the rest was returned that the women may soak it in their own yards. After a few days the chief sent his special messenger to proclaim that the harvest thanksgiving corn was to be pounded. The special messenger went around the whole town and in each place where there was a little hill or mound, he climbed it and shouted:

'Listen, the corn is to be pounded!'

So the people took their sprouting corn and pounded it. After some days the special messenger came back and called out:

'The corn is to be fermented now!'

A few days passed and then he called out: 'The corn is to be cooked now!'

So throughout the whole town the beer was boiled and when it had been strained, the special messenger called out for the last time:

'The beer is to be brought now!'

On the day on which thanksgiving was to be held, the women all followed one another in single file to the chief's place. There were prepared large vessels at the chief's place, so that when the women came, they poured the beer into them. Then there was a gathering of all the people to celebrate thanksgiving for the harvest time. All the people lived this way, like one face, under their chief. They accepted this regimental levelling out of their individual souls but on the day of dispute or when strife and conflict and greed blew stormy winds over their deep river, the people awoke and showed their individual faces.

Now, during his life time Monemapee had had three wives. And of these marriages he had four sons; Sebembele by the senior wife, Ntema and Mosemme by the second junior wife and Kgagodi by the third junior wife. There was a fifth son, Makobi, a small baby who was still suckling at his mother's breast by the time the old chief, Monemapee, died. This mother was the third junior wife, Rankwana. It was about the fifth son, Makobi, that the dispute arose. There was a secret there. Monemapee had married the third junior wife, Rankwana, late in his years. She was young and beautiful and Sebembele, the senior son, also fell in love with her; but in secret. On the death of Monemapee, Sebembele, as senior son, was installed as chief of the tribe and immediately made a blunder. He claimed Rankwana as his wife and exposed the secret that the fifth son, Makobi, was his own and not that of his father.

This news was received with alarm by the people as the first ripples of trouble stirred over the even surface of the river of their lives. If both the young man and the old man were visiting the same hut, they reasoned, perhaps the old man could not have died a normal death. They questioned the councillors who knew all secrets.

'Monemapee died just walking on his own feet,' they said, reassuringly.

That settled, the next challenge came from the two junior brothers, Ntema and Mosemme. If Sebembele were claiming the child, Makobi, as his son, they said, it meant that the young child displaced them in seniority. That they could not allow. The subtle pressure then presented to Sebembele by his junior brothers and the councillors was that he renounce Rankwana and the child and all would be well. A chief lacked nothing and there were many other women more suited as wives. Then Sebembele made the second blunder. In a world where women were of no account, he said truthfully:

'The love between Rankwana and I is great.'

This was received with cold disapproval by the councillors. 'If we were you,' they said, 'we would look for a wife somewhere else. A ruler must not be carried away by his emotions. This matter is going to cause disputes among the people.'

They noted that on being given this advice, Sebembele became very quiet and thoughtful and they left him to his own thoughts thinking that sooner or later he would come to a decision that agreed with theirs.

In the meanwhile the people quietly split into two camps. The one camp said:

'If he loves her, let him keep her. We all know Rankwana. She is a lovely person, deserving to be the wife of a chief.'

The other camp said:

'He must be mad. A man who is influenced by a woman is no ruler. He is like one who listens to the advice of a child. This story is really bad.'

There was at first no direct challenge to the chieftaincy which Sebembele occupied but the nature of the surprising dispute, that of love for a woman and a child, caused it to drag on longer than time would allow. Many evils began to rear their heads like impatient hissing snakes while Sebembele argued with his own heart or engaged in tender dialogues with his love, Rankwana.

'I don't know what I can do,' Sebembele said, torn between the demands of his position and the strain of a love affair that had been conducted in deep secrecy for many many months. The very secrecy of the affair seemed to make it shout all the louder now for public recognition. Now his heart urged him to renounce the woman and child, but each time he saw Rankwana, it abruptly said the opposite. He could come to no decision.

It seemed little enough that he wanted for himself – the companionship of a beautiful woman to whom life had given many other attractive gifts; she was gentle and kind and loving. As soon as Sebembele communicated to her the advice of the councillors, she bowed her head and cried a little.

'If that is what they say, my love,' she said in despair, 'I have no hope left for myself and the child. It were better if we were both dead.'

'Another husband could be chosen for you,' he suggested.

'You doubt my love for you, Sebembele,' she said. 'I would kill myself if I lose you. If you leave me, I would kill myself.'

Her words had meaning for him only because he was trapped in the same kind of anguish. It was a terrible pain which seemed to paralyse his movements and thoughts. It filled his mind so completely that he could think of nothing else, day and night. It was like a sickness, this paralysis and like all ailments it could not be concealed from sight; Sebembele carried it all around with him.

'Our hearts are saying many things about this man,' the councillors said among themselves. They were saying that he was unmanly; that he was unfit to be a ruler; that things were slipping from his hands. Those still sympathetic approached him and said:

'Why are you worrying yourself like this over a woman, Sebembele? There are no limits to the amount of wives a chief may have, but you cannot have that woman and that child.'

And he only replied with a distracted mind: 'I don't know what I can do.'

But things had been set in motion. All the people were astir over the event and if a man couldn't make up his mind, other men made it up for him.

Everything was arranged in secret and on an appointed day Rankwana and the child were forcefully removed back to her father's home. Ever since the controversy had started her father had been harassed day and night by the councillors as an influence that would help to end it. He had been reduced to a state of agitated muttering to himself by the time she was brought before him. The plan was to set her up immediately with a husband and so settle the matter. She was not yet formally married to Sebembele.

'You have put me in great difficulties, my child,' her father said, looking away from her distressed face. 'Women don't ever know their own minds and once this has passed away and you have many children you will wonder what all the fuss was about.'

'Other women may not know their minds ...' she began, but he stopped her with a raised hand, then indicated the husband that had been chosen for her. In all the faces surrounding her there was no sympathy or help and she quietly allowed herself to be led away, to her new home.

When Sebembele arrived in his own yard after a morning of attending to the affairs of the land, he found his brothers, Ntema and Mosemme there.

'Why have you come to visit me?' he asked, with foreboding. 'You never come to visit me. It would seem that we are bitter enemies rather than brothers.'

'You have shaken the whole town with your madness over a woman,' they replied mockingly. 'She's no longer here so you don't have to say anymore I-don't-know-what-I-can-do. But we still request that you renounce the child, Makobi, in a gathering before all the people so that our position is clear. You must say that child Makobi is the younger brother of my brothers, Ntema and Mosemme, and not the son of Sebembele who rules.'

Sebembele looked at them for a long moment. It was not hatred he felt but a peace at last. His brothers were forcing him to leave the tribe.

'Tell the people that they should all gather together,' he said. 'But it is my own affair what I say to them.'

The next morning the people of the whole town saw an amazing sight which stirred their hearts. They saw their ruler walk slowly and unaccompanied through the town. They saw him pause at the yard of Rankwana's father. They saw the two walk to the home where Rankwana had been secreted. They saw Rankwana and Sebembele walk together through the town. Sebembele held the child Makobi in his arms. They saw that they had a ruler who talked with deeds rather than words. They saw that the time had come for them to offer up their individual faces to the face of this ruler. But the people were still in camps. There was a whole section of the people who did not like this face; it was too out-of-the-way and shocking; it made them very uneasy. Theirs was not a tender, compassionate and romantic world. And yet it was. The arguments in the camp that supported Sebembele had flown thick and fast all this time. They said:

'Ntema and Mosemme are at the bottom of all this trouble. What are they after for they have set a difficult problem before us all? We don't trust them. But why not? They have not yet had time to take anything from us. Perhaps we ought to wait until they do something really bad; at present they are only filled with indignation at the behaviour of Sebembele. But no, we don't trust them. We don't like them. It is Sebembele we love, even though he has shown himself up as a man with a weakness ...'

That morning Sebembele won his camp completely with his extravagant, romantic gesture, but he lost everything else and the rulership of the kingdom of Monemapee.

When all the people had gathered at the meeting place of the town, there were not many arguments left. One by one the councillors stood up and condemned the behaviour of Sebembele. So the two brothers, Ntema and Mosemme won the day. Still working together as one voice they then stood up and asked if their senior brother had any words to say before he left with his people.

'Makobi is my child,' he said.

'Talaote,' they then said, meaning – in the language then spoken by the tribe – 'All right, you can go.'

And the name Talaote was all they were to retain of their identity as the people of the kingdom of Monemapee. Sebembele and his people that day packed their belongings on the backs of their cattle and slowly began the journey southwards. They were to leave many ruins behind them and it is said that they lived, on the journey southwards, with many other tribes like the Baphaleng, Bakaa and Batswapong until they finally settled in the land of the Bamangwato. To this day there is a separate Botalaote ward in the capital village of the Bamangwato and the people refer to themselves still as the people of Talaote. The old men there keep on giving confused and contradictory accounts of their origins. But they say they lost their place of birth over a woman. They shake their heads and say that women have always caused a lot of trouble in the world. They say that the child of their chief was named Talaote to commemorate their expulsion from the kingdom of Monemapee.

Author's note
The story is an entirely romanticised and fictionalised version of the history of the Botalaote tribe. Some historical data was given to me by the old men of the tribe but it was unreliable as their memories had tended to fail them. A reconstruction was therefore made in my own imagination and I am also partly indebted to the London Missionary Society's school textbook, *Livingstone Tswana Readers, Padiso 111*, for that graphic paragraph on the harvest thanksgiving ceremony which appears in the story.

BESSIE HEAD

Life

From: *The Collector of Treasures and other Botswana Village Tales* (1977)

In 1963, when the borders were first set up between Botswana and South Africa, pending Botswana's independence in 1966, all Botswana-born citizens had to return home. Everything had been mingled up in the old colonial days, and the traffic of people to and fro between the two countries had been a steady flow for years and years. More often, especially if they were migrant labourers working in the mines, their period of settlement was brief, but many people had settled there in permanent employment. It was these settlers who were disrupted and sent back to village life in a mainly rural country. On their return they brought with them bits and bits of a foreign culture and city habits which they had absorbed. Village people reacted in their own way; what they liked, and was beneficial to them – they absorbed, for instance, the faith-healing cult churches which instantly took hold like wildfire – what was harmful to them, they rejected. The murder of Life had this complicated undertone of rejection.

Life had left the village as a little girl of ten years old with her parents for Johannesburg. They had died in the meanwhile, and on Life's return, seventeen years later, she found, as was village custom, that she still had a home in the village. On mentioning that her name was Life Morapedi, the villagers immediately and obligingly took her to the Morapedi yard in the central part of the village. The family yard had remained intact, just as they had left it, except that it looked pathetic in its desolation. The thatch of the mud huts had patches of soil over them where the ants had made their nests; the wooden poles that supported the rafters of the huts had tilted to an angle as their base had been eaten through by the ants. The rubber hedge had grown to a disproportionate size and enclosed the yard in a gloom of shadows that kept out the sunlight. Weeds and grass of many seasonal rains entangled themselves in the yard.

Life's future neighbours, a group of women, continued to stand near her.

'We can help you to put your yard in order,' they said kindly. 'We are very happy that a child of ours has returned home.'

They were impressed with the smartness of this city girl. They generally wore old clothes and kept their very best things for special occasions like weddings, and even then those best things might just be ordinary cotton prints. The girl wore an expensive cream costume of linen material tailored to fit her tall, full figure. She had a bright, vivacious, friendly manner and laughed freely and loudly. Her speech was rapid and a little hysterical but that was in keeping with her whole personality.

'She is going to bring us a little light,' the women said among themselves, as they went off to fetch their work tools. They were always looking 'for the light' and by that they meant that they were ever alert to receive new ideas that would freshen up the ordinariness and everydayness of village life.

A woman who lived near the Morapedi yard had offered Life hospitality until her own yard was set in order. She picked up the shining new suitcases and preceded Life to her own home, where Life was immediately surrounded with all kinds of endearing attentions – a low stool was placed in a shady place for her to sit on; a little girl came shyly forward with a bowl of water for her to wash her hands; and following on this, a tray with a bowl of meat and por-ridge was set before her so that she could revive herself after her long journey home. The other women briskly entered her yard with hoes to scratch out the weeds and grass, baskets of earth and buckets of water to re-smear the mud walls, and they had found two idle men to rectify the precarious tilt of the wooden poles of the mud hut. These were the sort of gestures people always offered, but they were pleased to note that the newcomer seemed to have an endless stream of money which she flung around generously. The work party in her yard would suggest that the meat of a goat, slowly simmering in a great iron pot, would help the work to move with a swing, and Life would imme-diately produce the money to purchase the goat and also tea, milk, sugar, pots of porridge or anything the workers expressed a preference for, so that those two weeks of making Life's yard beautiful for her seemed like one long wed-ding-feast; people usually only ate that much at weddings.

'How is it you have so much money, our child?' one of the women at last asked, curiously.

'Money flows like water in Johannesburg,' Life replied, with her gay and hysterical laugh. 'You just have to know how to get it.'

The women received this with caution. They said among themselves that their child could not have lived a very good life in Johannesburg. Thrift and honesty were the dominant themes of village life and everyone knew that one could not be honest and rich at the same time; they counted every penny and knew how they had acquired it – with hard work. They never imagined money as a bottomless pit without end; it always had an end and was hard to come by in this dry, semi-desert land. They predicted that she would soon set-tle down – intelligent girls got jobs in the post office sooner or later.

Life had had the sort of varied career that a city like Johannesburg offered a lot of black women. She had been a singer, beauty queen, advertising model, and prostitute. None of these careers were available in the village – for the illiterate women there was farming and housework; for the literate, teaching, nursing, and clerical work. The first wave of women Life attracted to herself were the farmers and housewives. They were the intensely conservative hard-core centre of village life. It did not take them long to shun her completely because men started turning up in an unending stream. What caused a stir of amazement was that Life was the first and the only women in the village to make a business out of selling herself. The men were paying her for her services. People's attitude to sex was broad and generous – it was recognised as a necessary part of human life, that it ought to be available whenever possible like food and water, or else one's life would be extinguished or one would get dreadfully ill. To prevent these catastrophes from happening, men and women generally had quite a lot of sex but on a respectable and human level, with financial considerations coming in as an afterthought. When the news spread around that this had now become a business in Life's yard, she attracted to herself a second wave of women – the beer-brewers of the village.

The beer-brewing women were a gay and lovable crowd who had emancipated themselves some time ago. They were drunk every day and could be seen staggering around the village, usually with a wide-eyed, illegitimate baby hitched on to their hips. They also talked and laughed loudly and slapped each other on the back and had developed a language all their own:

'Boy-friends, yes. Husbands, uh, uh, no. Do this! Do that! We want to rule ourselves.'

But they too were subject to the respectable order of village life. Many men passed through their lives but they were all for a time steady boy-friends. The usual arrangement was:

'Mother, you help me and I'll help you.'

This was just so much eye-wash. The men hung around, lived on the resources of the women, and during all this time they would part with about two rand of their own money. After about three months a tally-up would be made:

'Boy-friend,' the woman would say. 'Love is love and money is money. You owe me money.' And he'd never be seen again, but another scoundrel would take his place. And so the story went on and on. They found their queen in Life and like all queens, they set her activities apart from themselves; they never attempted to extract money from the constant stream of men because they did not know how, but they liked her yard. Very soon the din and riot of a Johannesburg township was duplicated, on a minor scale, in the central part of the village. A transistor radio blared the day long. Men and women reeled around drunk and laughing and food and drink flowed like milk and honey. The people of the surrounding village watched this phenomenon with pursed lips and commented darkly:

'They'll all be destroyed one day like Sodom and Gomorrah.'

Life, like the beer-brewing women, had a language of her own too. When her friends expressed surprise at the huge quantities of steak, eggs, liver, kidneys, and rice they ate in her yard – the sort of food they too could now and then afford but would not dream of purchasing – she replied in a carefree, offhand way: 'I'm used to handling big money.' They did not believe it; they were too solid to trust to this kind of luck which had such shaky foundations, and as though to offset some doom that might be just around the corner they often brought along their own scraggy, village chickens reared in their yards, as offerings for the day's round of meals. And one of Life's philosophies on life, which they were to recall with trembling a few months later, was: 'My motto is: live fast, die young, and have a good-looking corpse.' All this was said with the bold, free joy of a woman who had broken all the social taboos. They never followed her to those dizzy heights.

A few months after Life's arrival in the village, the first hotel with its pub opened. It was initially shunned by all the women and even the beer-brewers considered they hadn't fallen *that* low yet – the pub was also associated with the idea of selling oneself. It became Life's favourite business venue. It simplified the business of making appointments for the following day. None of the men questioned their behaviour, nor how such an unnatural situation had been allowed to develop – they could get all the sex they needed for free in the village, but it seemed to fascinate them that they should pay for it for the first time. They had quickly got to the stage where they communicated with Life in shorthand language:

'When?' And she would reply: 'Ten o'clock.' 'When?' 'Two o'clock.' 'When?' 'Four o'clock,' and so on.

And there would be the roar of cheap small talk and much buttock slapping. It was her element and her feverish, glittering, brilliant black eyes swept around the bar, looking for everything and nothing at the same time.

Then one evening death walked quietly into the bar. It was Lesego, the cattle-man, just come in from his cattle-post, where he had been occupied for a period of three months. Men built up their own, individual reputations in the village and Lesego's was one of the most respected and honoured. People said of him: 'When Lesego has got money and you need it, he will give you what he has got and he won't trouble you about the date of payment ...' He was honoured for another reason also – for the clarity and quiet indifference of his thinking. People often found difficulty in sorting out issues or the truth in any debatable matter. He had a way of keeping his head above water, listening to an argument and always pronouncing the final judgement: 'Well, the truth about this matter is ...' He was also one of the most successful cattle-men with a balance of R7 000 in the bank, and whenever he came into the village he lounged around and gossiped or attended village kgotla meetings, so that people had a saying: 'Well,

I must be getting about my business. I'm not like Lesego with money in the bank.'

As usual, the brilliant radar eyes swept feverishly around the bar. They did the rounds twice that evening in the same manner, each time coming to a dead stop for a full second on the thin, dark, concentrated expression of Lesego's face. There wasn't any other man in the bar with that expression; they all had sheepish, inane-looking faces. He was the nearest thing she had seen for a long time to the Johannesburg gangsters she had associated with – the same small, economical gestures, the same power and control. All the men near him quietened down and began to consult with him in low, earnest voices; they were talking about the news of the day which never reached the remote cattle-posts. Whereas all the other men had to approach her, the third time her radar eyes swept round he stood his ground, turned his head slowly, and then jerked it back slightly in a silent command:

'Come here.'

She moved immediately to his end of the bar.

'Hullo,' he said, in an astonishingly tender voice and a smile flickered across his dark, reserved face. That was the sum total of Lesego, that basically he was a kind and tender man, that he liked women and had been so successful in that sphere that he took his dominance and success for granted. But they looked at each other from their own worlds and came to fatal conclusions – she saw in him the power and maleness of the gangsters; he saw the freshness and surprise of an entirely new kind of woman. He had left all his women after a time because they bored him, and like all people who live an ordinary humdrum life, he was attracted to that undertone of hysteria in her.

Very soon they stood up and walked out together. A shocked silence fell upon the bar. The men exchanged looks with each other and the way these things communicate themselves, they knew that all the other appointments had been cancelled while Lesego was there. And as though speaking their thoughts aloud, Sianana, one of Lesego's friends commented: 'Lesego just wants to try it out like we all did because it is something new. He won't stay there when he finds out that it is rotten to the core.'

But Sianana was to find out that he did not fully understand his friend. Lesego was not seen at his usual lounging-places for a week and when he emerged again it was to announce that he was to marry. The news was received with cold hostility. Everyone talked of nothing else; it was as impossible as if a crime was being committed before their very eyes. Sianana once more made himself the spokesman. He waylaid Lesego on his way to the village kgotla:

'I am much surprised by the rumours about you, Lesego,' he said bluntly. 'You can't marry that woman. She's a terrible fuck-about!'

Lesego stared back at him steadily, then he said in his quiet, indifferent way: 'Who isn't here?'

Sianana shrugged his shoulders. The subtleties were beyond him; but whatever else was going on it wasn't commercial, it was human, but did that make it any better? Lesego liked to bugger up an argument like that with a straightforward point. As they walked along together Sianana shook his head several times to indicate that something important was eluding him, until at last with a smile, Lesego said: 'She has told me all about her bad ways. They are over.'

Sianana merely compressed his lips and remained silent.

Life made the announcement too, after she was married, to all her beer-brewing friends: 'All my old ways are over,' she said. 'I have now become a woman.'

She still looked happy and hysterical. Everything came to her too easily, men, money, and now marriage. The beer-brewers were not slow to point out to her with the same amazement with which they had exclaimed over the steak and eggs, that there were many women in the village who had cried their eyes out over Lesego. She was very flattered.

Their lives, at least Lesego's, did not change much with marriage. He still liked lounging around the village; the rainy season had come and life was easy for the cattle-men at this time because there was enough water and grazing for the animals. He wasn't the kind of man to fuss about the house and during his time he only made three pronouncements about the household. He took control of all the money. She had to ask him for it and state what it was to be used for. Then he didn't like the transistor radio blaring the whole day long.

'Women who keep that thing going the whole day have nothing in their heads,' he said.

Then he looked down at her from a great height and commented finally and quietly: 'If you go with those men again, I'll kill you.'

This was said so indifferently and quietly, as though he never really expected his authority and dominance to encounter any challenge.

She hadn't the mental equipment to analyse what had hit her, but something seemed to strike her a terrible blow behind the head. She instantly succumbed to the blow and rapidly began to fall apart. On the surface, the everyday round of village life was deadly dull in its even, unbroken monotony; one day slipped easily into another, drawing water, stamping corn, cooking food. But within this there were enormous tugs and pulls between people. Custom demanded that people care about each other, and all day long there was this constant traffic of people in and out of each other's lives. Someone had to be buried; sympathy and help were demanded for this event – there were money loans, new-born babies, sorrow, trouble, gifts. Lesego had long been the king of this world; there was, every day, a long string of people, wanting something or wanting to give him something in gratitude for a past favour. It was the basic strength of village life. It created people whose sympathetic and emotional responses were always fully awakened, and it rewarded them by richly filling in a void that was one big, gaping yawn. When the hysteria and cheap rowdiness were taken away, Life fell into the yawn; she had nothing inside herself to cope with this way of life that had finally caught up with her. The beer-brewing women were still there; they still liked her yard because Lesego was casual and easy-going and all that went on in it now – like the old men squatting in corners with gifts: 'Lesego, I had good luck with my hunting today. I caught two rabbits and I want to share one with you …' – was simply the Tswana way of life they too lived. In keeping with their queen's new status, they said:

'We are women and must do something.'

They collected earth and dung and smeared and decorated Life's courtyard. They drew water for her, stamped her corn, and things looked quite ordinary on the surface because Lesego also liked a pot of beer. No one noticed the expression of anguish that had crept into Life's face. The boredom of the daily round was almost throttling her to death and no matter which way she looked, from the beer-brewers to her husband to all the people who called, she found no one with whom she could communicate what had become an actual physical pain. After a month of it, she was near collapse. One morning she mentioned her agony to the beer-brewers: 'I think I have made a mistake. Married life doesn't suit me.'

And they replied sympathetically: 'You are just getting used to it. After all it's a different life in Johannesburg.'

The neighbours went further. They were impressed by a marriage they thought could never succeed. They started saying that one never ought to judge a human being who was both good and bad, and Lesego had turned a bad woman into a good woman which was something they had never seen before. Just as they were saying this and nodding their approval, Sodom and Gomorrah started up all over again. Lesego had received word late in the evening that the newborn calves at his cattle-post were dying, and early the next morning he was off again in his truck.

The old, reckless wild woman awakened from a state near death with a huge sigh of relief. The transistor blared, the food flowed again, the men and women reeled around dead drunk. Simply by their din they beat off all the unwanted guests who nodded their heads grimly. When Lesego came back they were going to tell him this was no wife for him.

Three days later Lesego unexpectedly was back in the village. The calves were all anaemic and they had to be brought in to the vet for an injection. He drove his truck straight through the village to the vet's camp. One of the beer-brewers saw him and hurried in alarm to her friend.

'The husband is back,' she whispered fearfully, pulling Life to one side.

'Agh,' she replied irritably.

She did dispel the noise, the men, and the drink, but a wild anger was driving her to break out of a way of life that was like death to her. She told one of the men she'd see him at six o'clock. At about five o'clock Lesego drove into the yard with the calves. There was no one immediately around to greet him. He jumped out of the truck and walked to one of the huts, pushing open the door. Life was sitting on the bed. She looked up silently and sullenly. He was a little surprised but his mind was still distracted by the calves. He had to settle them in the yard for the night.

'Will you make some tea,' he said. 'I'm very thirsty.'

'There's no sugar in the house,' she said. 'I'll have to get some.'

Something irritated him but he hurried back to the calves and his wife walked out of the yard. Lesego had just settled the calves when a neighbour walked in, he was very angry.

'Lesego,' he said bluntly. 'We told you not to marry that woman. If you go to the yard of Radithobolo now you'll find her in bed with him. Go and see for yourself that you may leave that bad woman!'

Lesego stared quietly at him for a moment, then at his own pace as though there were no haste or chaos in his life, he went to the hut they used as a kitchen. A tin full of sugar stood there. He turned and found a knife in the corner, one of the large ones he used for slaughtering cattle, and slipped it into his shirt. Then at his own pace he walked to the yard of Radithobolo. It looked deserted, except that the door of one of the huts was partially open and one closed. He kicked open the door of the closed hut and the man within shouted out in alarm. On seeing Lesego he sprang cowering into a corner. Lesego jerked his head back indicating that the man should leave the room. But Radithobolo did not run far. He wanted to enjoy himself so he pressed himself into the shadows of the rubber hedge. He expected the usual husband-and-wife scene – the irate husband cursing at the top of his voice; the wife, hysterical in her lies and self-defence. Only Lesego walked out of the yard and he held in his hand a huge, blood-stained knife. On seeing the knife Radithobolo immediately fell to the ground in a dead faint. There were a few people on the footpath and they shrank into the rubber hedge at the sight of that knife.

Very soon a wail arose. People clutched at their heads and began running in all directions crying yo! yo! yo! in their shock. It was some time before any-one thought of calling the police. They were so disordered because murder, outright and violent, was a most uncommon and rare occurrence in village life. It seemed that only Lesego kept cool that evening. He was sitting quietly in his yard when the whole police force came tearing in. They looked at him in horror and began to thoroughly upbraid him for looking so unperturbed.

'You have taken a human life and you are cool like that!' they said angrily. 'You are going to hang by the neck for this. It's a serious crime to take a human life.'

He did not hang by the neck. He kept that cool, head-above-water indifferent look, right up to the day of his trial. Then he looked up at the judge and said calmly: 'Well, the truth about this matter is, I had just returned from the cattle-post. I had had trouble with my calves that day. I came home late and being thirsty, asked my wife to make me tea. She said there was no sugar in the house and left to buy some. My neighbour, Mathata came in after this and said that my wife was not at the shops but in the yard of Radithobolo. He said I ought to go and see what she was doing in the yard of Radit-hobolo. I thought I would check up about the sugar first and in the kitchen I found a tin full of it. I was sorry and surprised to see this. Then a fire seemed to fill my heart. I thought that if she was doing a bad thing with Radithobolo as Mathata said, I'd better kill her because I cannot understand a wife who could be so corrupt …'

Lesego had been doing this for years, passing judgement on all aspects of life in his straightforward, uncomplicated way. The judge, who was a white man, and therefore not involved in Tswana custom and its debates, was as much impressed by Lesego's manner as all the village men had been.

'This is a crime of passion,' he said sympathetically. 'So there are extenuating circumstances. But it is still a serious crime to take a human life so I sentence you to five years imprisonment …'

Lesego's friend, Sianana, who was to take care of his business affairs while he was in jail, came to visit Lesego still shaking his head. Something was eluding him about the whole business, as though it had been planned from the very beginning.

'Lesego,' he said, with deep sorrow. 'Why did you kill that fuck-about? You had legs to walk away. You could have walked away. Are you trying to show us that rivers never cross here? There are good women and good men but they seldom join their lives together. It's always this mess and foolishness …'

A song by Jim Reeves was very popular at that time: *That's What Happens When Two Worlds Collide*. When they were drunk, the beer-brewing women used to sing it and start weeping. Maybe they had the last word on the whole affair.

BESSIE HEAD

The Wind and a Boy

From: *The Collector of Treasures and other Botswana Village Tales* (1977)

Like all the village boys, Friedman had a long wind blowing for him, but perhaps the enchanted wind that blew for him filled the whole world with magic.

Until they became ordinary, dull grown men, who drank beer and made babies, the little village boys were a special set all on their own. They were kings whom no one ruled. They wandered where they willed from dawn to dusk and only condescended to come home at dusk because they were afraid of the horrible things in the dark that might pounce on them. Unlike the little girls who adored household chores and drawing water, it was only now and then that the boys showed themselves as useful attachments to any household. When the first hard rains of summer fell, small dark shapes, quite naked except for their loincloths, sped out of the village into the bush. They knew that the first downpour had drowned all the wild rabbits, moles and porcupines in their burrows in the earth. As they crouched down near the entrances to the burrows, they would see a small drowned nose of an animal peeping out; they knew it had struggled to emerge from its burrow, flooded by the sudden rush of storm water and as they pulled out the animal, they would say, pityingly: 'Birds have more sense than rabbits, moles and porcupines. They build their homes in trees.'

But it was hunting made easy, for no matter how hard a boy and his dog ran, a wild rabbit ran ten times faster; a porcupine hurled his poisonous quills into the body; and a mole stayed where he thought it was safe – deep under the ground. So it was with inordinate pride that the boys carried home armfuls of dead animals for their families to feast on for many days. Apart from that, the boys lived very much as they pleased, with the wind and their own games.

Now and then, the activities of a single family could captivate the imagination and hearts of all the people of their surroundings; for years and years, the combination of the boy, Friedman, and his grandmother, Sejosenye, made the people of Ga-Sefete-Molemo ward smile, laugh, then cry.

They smiled at his first two phases. Friedman came home as a small bundle from the hospital, a bundle his grandmother nursed carefully near her bosom and crooned to day and night with extravagant care and tenderness.

568

'She is like that,' people remarked, 'because he may be the last child she will ever nurse. Sejosenye is old now and will die one of these days; the child is a gift to keep her heart warm.'

Indeed, all Sejosenye's children were grown, married, and had left home. Of all her children, only her last-born daughter was unmarried and Friedman was the result of some casual mating she had indulged in, in a town a hundred miles away where she had a job as a typist. She wanted to return to her job almost immediately, so she handed the child over to her mother and that was that; she could afford to forget him as he had a real mother now. During all the time that Sejosenye haunted the hospital, awaiting her bundle, a friendly foreign doctor named Friedman took a fancy to her maternal, grandmotherly ways. He made a habit of walking out of his path to talk to her. She never forgot it and on receiving her bundle she called the baby Friedman.

They smiled at his second phase, a small dark shadow who toddled silently and gravely beside a very tall grandmother; wherever the grandmother went, there went Friedman. Most women found this phase of the restless, troublesome toddler tedious; they dumped the toddler onto one of their younger girls and were off to weddings and visits on their own.

'Why can't you leave your handbag at home sometimes, granny?' they said.

'Oh, he's no trouble,' Sejosenye would reply.

They began to laugh at his third phase. Almost overnight he turned into a tall spindly-legged, graceful gazelle with large, grave eyes. There was an odd, musical lilt to his speech and when he teased, or was up to mischief, he moved his head on his long thin neck from side to side like a cobra. It was he who became the king of kings of all the boys in his area; he could turn his hand to anything and made the best wire cars with their wheels of shoe-polish tins. All his movements were neat, compact, decisive, and for his age he was a boy who knew his own mind. They laughed at his knowingness and certainty on all things, for he was like the grandmother who had had a flaming youth all her own too. Sejosenye had scandalised the whole village in her days of good morals by leaving her own village ward to live with a married man in Ga-Sefete-Molemo ward. She had won him from his wife and married him and then lived down the scandal in the way only natural queens can. Even in old age, she was still impressive. She sailed through the village, head in the air, with a quiet, almost expressionless face. She had developed large buttocks as time went by and they announced their presence firmly in rhythm with her walk.

Another of Sejosenye's certainties was that she was a woman who could plough, but it was like a special gift. Each season, in drought or hail or sun, she removed herself to her lands. She not only ploughed but nursed and brooded over her crops. She was there all the time till the corn ripened and the birds had to be chased off the land, till harvesting and threshing were done; so that even in drought years with their scanty rain, she came hone with some crops. She was the envy of all the women of the surroundings.

'Sejosenye always eats fine things in her house,' they said. 'She ploughs and then sits down for many months and enjoys the fruits of her labour.'

The women also envied her beautiful grandson. There was something special there, so that even when Friedman moved into his bad phase, they forgave him crimes other boys received a sound thrashing for. The small boys were terrible thieves who harassed people by stealing their food and money. It was all a part of the games they played but one which people did not like. Of them all, Friedman was the worst thief, so that his name was mentioned more and more in any thieving that had been uncovered.

'But Friedman showed us how to open the window with a knife and string,' the sobbing, lashed boys would protest.

'Friedman isn't as bad as you,' the parents would reply, irrationally. They were hypnotised by a beautiful creature. The boy Friedman, who had become a real nuisance by then, also walked around as though he were special. He couldn't possibly be a thief and he added an aloof, offended, disdainful expression to his pretty face. He wasn't just an ordinary sort of boy in Ga-Sefete-Molemo ward. He was …

It happened, quite accidentally, that his grandmother told him all those stories about the hunters, warriors, and emissaries of old. She was normally a quiet, absent-minded woman, given to dreaming by herself but she liked to sing the boy a little song now and then as they sat by the outdoor fire. A lot of them were church songs and rather sad; they more or less passed as her bed-time prayer at night – she was one of the old church-goers. Now and then she added a quaint little song to her repertoire and as the night-time, fire-light flames flickered between them, she never failed to note that this particular song was always well received by the boy. A little light would awaken in his eyes and he would bend forward and listen attentively.

'Welcome, Robinson Crusoe, welcome,' she would sing, in clear, sweet tones. 'How could you stay, so long away, Robinson how could you do so?'

When she was very young, Sejosenye had attended the mission school of the village for about a year; made a slight acquaintance with the ABC and one, two, three, four, five, and the little song about Robinson Crusoe. But girls didn't need an education in those days when ploughing and marriage made up their whole world. Yet Robinson Crusoe lived on as a gay and out-of-context memory of her schooldays.

One evening the boy leaned forward and asked: 'Is that a special praise-poem song for Robinson Crusoe, grandmother?'

'Oh yes,' she replied, smiling.

'What great things did he do?' the boy asked, pointedly.

'They say he was a hunter who went by Gweta side and killed an elephant all by himself,' she said, making up a story on the spot. 'Oh! In those days, no man could kill an elephant by himself. All the regiments had to join together and each man had to thrust his sword into the side of the elephant before it died. Well, Robinson Crusoe was gone many days and people wondered about him: "Perhaps he has been eaten by a lion," they said. "Robinson likes to be a solitary person and do foolish things. We won't ever go out into the bush by ourselves because we know it is dangerous." Well, one day, Robinson suddenly appeared in their midst and people could see that he had a great thing on his mind. They all gathered around him. He said: "I have killed an elephant for all the people." The people were surprised: "Robinson!" they said. "It is impossible! How did you do it? The very thought of an elephant approaching the village makes us shiver!" And Robinson said: "Ah, people, I saw a terrible sight! I was standing at the feet of the elephant. I was just a small ant. I could not see the world any more. Elephant was above me until his very head touched the sky and his ears spread out like great wings. He was angry but I only looked into one eye which was turning round and round in anger. What to do now? I thought it better to put that eye out. I raised my spear and threw it at the angry eye. People! It went right inside. Elephant said not a word and he fell to one side. Come, I will show you what I have done." Then the women cried in joy:"Loo-loo-loo!" They ran to fetch their containers as some wanted the meat of the elephant; some wanted the fat. The men made their knives sharp. They would make shoes and many things from the skin and bones. There was something for all the people in the great work Robinson Crusoe did.'

All this while, as he listened to the story, the boy's eyes had glowed softly. At the end of it, he drew in a long breath.

'Grandmother,' he whispered, adroitly stepping into the role of Robinson Crusoe, the great hunter. 'One day, I'm going to be like that. I'm going to be a hunter like Robinson Crusoe and bring meat to all the people.' He paused for breath and then added tensely: 'And what other great thing did Robinson Crusoe do?'

'Tsaa!' she said, clicking her tongue in exhaustion, 'Am I then going away that I must tell *all* the stories at once?'

Although his image of Robinson Crusoe, the great hunter, was never to grow beyond his everyday boyish activities of pushing wire cars, hunting in the fields for wild rabbits, climbing trees to pull down old birds' nests and yelling out in alarm to find that a small snake now occupied the abandoned abode, or racing against the wind with the spoils of his latest theft, the stories awakened a great tenderness in him. If Robinson Crusoe was not churning up the dust in deadly hand-to-hand combat with an enemy, he was crossing swollen rivers and wild jungles as the great messenger and ambassador of the chief – all his activities were touchingly in aid of or in defence of the people. One day Friedman expressed this awakened compassion for life in a strange way. After a particularly violent storm, people found their huts invaded by many small mice and they were hard-pressed to rid themselves of these pests. Sejosenye ordered Friedman to kill the mice.

'But grandmother,' he protested, 'they have come to us for shelter. They lost all their homes in the storm. It's better that I put them in a box and carry them out into the fields again once the rains are over.'

She had laughed in surprise at this and spread the story around among her women friends, who smiled tenderly, then said to their own offspring: 'Friedman isn't as bad as you.'

Life and its responsibilities began to weigh down heavily on Friedman as he approached his fourteenth year. Less time was spent in boyish activities. He grew more and more devoted to his grandmother and concerned to assist her in every way. He wanted a bicycle so that he might run up and down to the shops for her, deliver messages, or do any other chore she might have in mind. His mother, who worked in a town far away, sent him the money to purchase the bicycle. The gift brought the story of his life abruptly to a close.

Towards the beginning of the rainy season, he accompanied his grandmother to her lands which were some twenty miles outside the village. They sowed seed together after the hired tractor had turned up the land but the boy's main chore was to keep the household pot filled with meat. Sometimes they ate birds Friedman had trapped, sometimes they ate fried tortoise meat or wild rabbit; but there was always something as the bush abounded with animal life. Sejosenye only had to take a bag of mealie meal, packets of sugar, tea and powdered milk as provisions for their stay at the lands; meat was never a problem. Midway through the ploughing season, she began to run out of sugar, tea and milk.

'Friedman,' she said that evening, 'I shall wake you early tomorrow morning. You will have to take the bicycle into the village and purchase some more sugar, tea and milk.'

He was up at dawn with the birds, a solitary figure cycling on a pathway through the empty bush. By nine, he had reached the village and first made his way to Ga-Sefete-Molemo ward and the yard of a friend of his grandmother, who gave him a cup of tea and a plate of porridge. Then he put one foot on the bicycle and turned to smile at the woman with his beautiful gazelle eyes. His smile was to linger vividly before her for many days as a short while later, hard pounding feet came running into her yard to report that Friedman was dead.

He pushed the bicycle through the winding, sandy pathway of the village ward, reached the high embankment of the main road, peddled vigorously up it and out of the corner of his eye, saw a small green truck speeding towards him. In the devil-may-care fashion of all the small boys, he cycled right into its path, turned his head and smiled appealingly at the driver. The truck caught him on the front bumper, squashed the bicycle and dragged the boy along at a crazy speed for another hundred yards, dropped him and careered on another twenty yards before coming to a halt. The boy's pretty face was a smear all along the road and he only had a torso left.

People of Ga-Sefete-Molemo ward never forgot the last coherent words Sejosenye spoke to the police. A number of them climbed into the police truck and accompanied it to her lands. They saw her walk slowly and enquiringly towards the truck, they heard the matter-of-fact voice of the policeman announce the death, then they heard Sejosenye say piteously: 'Can't you return those words back?'

She turned away from them, either to collect her wits or the few possessions she had brought with her. Her feet and buttocks quivered anxiously as she stumbled towards her hut. Then her feet tripped her up and she fell to the ground like a stunned log.

The people of Ga-Sefete-Molemo ward buried the boy Friedman but none of them would go near the hospital where Sejosenye lay. The stories, brought to them by way of the nurses were too terrible for words. They said the old woman sang and laughed and talked to herself all the time. So they merely asked each other: 'Have you been to see Mma-Sejosenye?' 'I'm afraid I cannot. It would kill my heart.' Two weeks later, they buried her.

As was village habit, the incident was discussed thoroughly from all sides till it was understood. In this timeless, sleepy village, the goats stood and suckled their young ones on the main road or lay down and took their afternoon naps there. The motorists either stopped for them or gave way. But it appeared that the driver of the truck had neither brakes on his car nor a driving licence. He belonged to the new, rich, civil-servant class whose salaries had become fantastically high since independence. They had to have cars in keeping with their new status; they had to have any car, as long as it was a car; they were in such a hurry about everything that they couldn't be bothered to take driving lessons. And thus progress, development, and pre-occupation with status and living standards first announced themselves to the village. It looked like being an ugly story with many decapitated bodies on the main road.

MBULELO VIZIKHUNGO MZAMANE

The Party

First published, 1977

I'm the first to admit that the party was a rowdy affair. A delegation of neighbours came, at least three times, to complain about the noise. Each time those who were not persuaded to join the party retired, shaking their heads and making various click sounds to express their disgust. The party had to go on. We'd hitched-hiked from the university to town – more than thirty kilometres. Besides, the country was in a state of emergency. Dispersing to our homes at that time of the night would have been tantamount to suicide. There were trigger-happy police hordes all over town. Toyi couldn't have realised this when she chased us out of her house at that time of the night.

Those who know say the state of emergency was caused by the near-defeat of the ruling People's Party. The results from each constituency were being announced over the radio as they became available. Some claim that when it became clear that the opposition People's Front was winning, the PP decided to stop the elections. The Prime Minister came over the air and declared the elections invalid. He accused the PF of rigging the elections and intimidating the electorate. A state of emergency was declared. There was to be a dusk to dawn curfew in the rural areas. In towns, movement was restricted between midnight and six in the morning. Paradoxically, people in the villages enjoyed a greater degree of freedom than those living in towns.

Just as the remote villages are usually the last to benefit from any developmental project initiated by the government, they're also the last to be affected by any adverse legislation. People in the villages knew, from listening to their radios, what laws had been promulgated, ignored them and behaved as before. The curfew was neither observed nor enforced. In the village adjoining the university, we drank with the police until sunrise. When we drank one shebeen dry, we moved to another and so on, in a spirit of friendly camaraderie. Sometimes in the very early hours of the morning I'd be carrying Trooper Lepholisa's rifle or Corporal Lesenya's, as we staggered into MaMokone's where we knew they never ran out of stock.

The village police always evinced the same degree of humaneness whenever we transgressed the law, a fairly regular Saturday-night occurrence.

574

There were several offences for which we were usually arrested, such as gate-crashing at parties or ringing the bells of the nearby Catholic church in the middle of the night, whenever we were ejected from a party. Sometimes we failed to pay for our drinks so that one of us, usually the tipsiest, had to volunteer to spend the night in the cells, as security, while we returned to the campus to raise money for his ransom. Drunken brawling, always among ourselves, was another. The officer on duty would scribble on the sheet: 'Disturbance to Public Peace' – the offence never varied so that we sometimes filled in the form ourselves – and promptly shut the offender in the cell. On Sunday morning, laden with bacon and eggs from the refectory, we visited the culprit and let the officers on duty have the lot, including the plates, for themselves and their families, and thereby earned the prisoner a respite from the cell. He was then allowed to bask in the sun the whole morning. We returned during lunch with enough chicken and rice to feed a small army, and spent the rest of the afternoon exchanging jokes and sharing drinks with the prisoner and the police. On Sunday evening we had the satisfaction of seeing the officer who had made the arrest the previous night come on duty, crumple the charge sheet, before we left him with the day's leftovers and hurried off with the offender to supper and then to the film. Our relations with the village police were too congenial to permit the intrusion of petty prejudices.

The police in the capital viewed matters differently. For some reason they regarded us with suspicion and treated us with hostility. This emerged from the way they dealt with us whenever we travelled to town in the school bus. During each road-block, they showed such obvious delight in harassing us that I eventually decided to stop using the school bus. I should have carried out my decision sooner, before our near-fatal encounter with one especially sadistic and vengeful unit. That was the day we were ordered out of the bus, at gun point, by a group of police, among them 'Me 'Makhauta's son.

'Me 'Makhauta's son had defied his mother – his father was a contract labourer on the mines – and left school after Form Two. He landed a job as a messenger with the university post-office, but was dismissed when missing stamps and postal orders to the value of seventy-five rands were found in his possession. His mother was in charge of the women who cleaned one of the women's residences. They stayed in a house on the campus. It was not unusual to see him around the women's residence, looking for his mother.

One evening, at supper, Nozipho and Lerato who were room-mates reported thirty rands missing from their rooms. We'd recently been given our personal allowances for the semester, although Phambili, Kali, Scara, Speakit and myself had not been to collect ours. For my part, I'd hoped that one of the others would have had the foresight to withdraw something for the weekend. As it turned out, each of us had entertained similar hopes, with the result that none had drawn out his allowance. It was Friday evening and we'd have to wait until Monday morning for the accounts office to open. We were trying to raise a loan from the girls, when they made their shattering revelation.

As we were discussing the matter in the cafeteria, Keneuoe joined our table.

'Wait a minute,' she said when she'd heard what we were talking about. She then told us that she'd seen 'Me 'Makhauta's son, that very afternoon, loitering around the women's residence. 'In fact, come to think of it, he was sitting just outside Nozipho and Lerato's open window.'

That wasn't unusual, but I suppose the grim prospects of a dry weekend spurred us to desperate action. We'd recover every single cent from him, if that was the last thing we ever did. We were intoxicated with optimistic expectation as we trooped out of the dining hall.

Our ancestors must have been with us. We were waiting for the tuckshop to open — Keneuoe had promised to stand each of us a Coke and a communal packet of Van Rijn — when 'Me 'Makhauta's son sauntered in. We immediately surrounded him and began punching him to see who could send him reeling fastest from one end of the circle to the other.

'You'll return every single cent of the money you stole, sonny,' I said, burying a big one in his ribs.

'I didn't steal any money.'

'Did you think we couldn't see you sneaking in through the window of the women's residence?' Speakit asked as he connected with a fancy punch, which missed.

'I tell you, I've no money.'

We know you've no money of your own,' Phambili said. 'That's not what we're talking about. He landed one on the back which catapulted the boy towards Scara.

'It's the money you stole from the girls' room we want,' Scara said, sinking a hard one into the stomach. The boy ran out of breath and collapsed like an empty sack.

'... You'll ... er ... you'll get the money back, only give ... er ... give me some air.'

We ransacked his pockets and recovered twenty-eight rands and some odd cents.

'You'll pay the rest in full before sunrise,' Kali said and kicked the boy so that he groaned and rolled to one side.

It was hardly a month since we'd clobbered 'Me 'Makhauta's son. Since then he'd joined the police force and now here he was, holding a rifle aimed at us.

As we filed out of the bus I felt my stomach muscles loosen. I tightened them to avoid disgrace spilling out.

The boy wore a grin as wide as a crocodile-infested river. There was obviously a desperate shortage of police if recruits, hardly three weeks in the force, were already parading the streets with guns.

I involuntarily raised my hands although nobody had asked me to. Phambili, Kali, Speakit and Scara, who were behind me, instinctively followed my example, to the great delight of the policemen. We kept our hands well above our heads until they had finished searching our bus for subversive literature, explosives and other dangerous materials. Then they ordered us back into the bus.

I was first to dash for the bus but one policeman, who obviously thought very highly of our act, blocked my way and shouted to the other students to get in first. That also left Phambili, Scara, Speakit and Kali outside.

'*Ntate*,' 'Me 'Makhauta's son shouted. 'Drive on.'

We watched the old bus, which we'd nicknamed 'Jacobo' after somebody's donkey, clamber up and slowly disappear over the hill, towards town.

'What do we do with these?' one policeman asked.

'Send them trotting back the way they came, with their hands raised,' replied the one who had prevented us from getting into the bus.

'You can tell a guilty student by his behaviour,' 'Me 'Makhauta's son said. 'It is inconceivable that these five should have behaved this way unless they feel guilty about something. They obviously know a lot. Probably regular communists,' (only he pronounced it *komanisi*) 'all of them, We'll find out more about that when we get back to headquarters.'

We were neglected for some time while the police stopped a few other cars, peered briefly inside and, recognising the owners, waved them on.

Phambili took out a packet of Van Rijn from the inside pocket of his jacket and withdrew a cigarette. When he raised the cigarette to his mouth the packet dropped to the ground. He fumbled in his pockets for matches. The first match went out, but he was steadier with the second.

'*Skyf*,' Kali and Scara requested.

'There are only three left,' Phambili said, then retrieved the packet and pocketed it.

'Hey, come over here,' said a policeman who was leaning against the police van.

We were herded into the waiting Landrover. All around, guns were pointed at us with the muzzles so close you could feel the hot air from the barrels on your back.

'Who gave you permission to smoke?' the policeman who had called us towards the Landrover asked.

Phambili instantly flung his cigarette away. It went flying and landed on the feet of one absent-minded policeman, who promptly jumped to one side, as though a cigarette were the deadliest bomb ever devised.

'Who did that?' he asked.

His reaction sent the rest into peals of laughter, which drowned his repeated questions and probably saved Phambili from some terrible calamity. Unable to draw any sympathy from his colleagues, the policeman began to feel foolish. When his fear and anger had sufficiently subsided, he picked up the cigarette and inhaled deeply, a process which seemed to restore his sense of humour so that he laughed with the rest.

Somebody shouted: 'Move!'

We all scrambled for the same corner of the Landrover, where we remained cramped like live sardines in an undersized container.

Nor did matters improve when the policemen climbed in after us and demanded we make room. I sat between Speakit's legs who rested his elbows, like a vice, on either side of my neck. Kali, on top of whom somebody else was seated, sat on my head. We drove the eight kilometres to town in these impossible positions.

At the police station we were intimidated for a further three hours. First they wanted to know who of us were studying science. There was Kali and Speakit. Was it true, they asked, that we were being taught to manufacture small firearms and Molotov cocktails under the tutelage of American and British lecturers? Somebody produced a dissecting kit. Were these instruments sometimes used to commit ritual murder? The rest of us, what were we studying? The questions accordingly revolved around political science and literature. The chief inquisitor was leisurely paging through the university calendar and periodically raising his eyes. Wasn't it true that such authors as Tolstoy, Chekhov and Dostoevsky, who were actually prescribed in our syllabus, were Russians? What was political science doing in a university syllabus or didn't we have sense enough to leave politics to the politicians?

After about three hours the group of policemen who'd brought us to the police station knocked off. 'Me 'Makhauta's son who'd been providentially sent out on patrol duty again, during our session at the charge office, came back to take a last look at us. He passed some witty remark about those who live in glass houses – I think he got the proverb wrong or applied it incorrectly, I can't remember which – before taking his leave. Our inquisitors similarly got bored with us and left us to our devices. We were so long by ourselves that several distressed people who came to the charge office with cases to report brought them to us. No doubt we would have remained there longer (perhaps for another viva voce on the Copernican system), if among the officers who came on duty there hadn't been several who played for the police football team. They immediately recognised Phambili and Scara who turned out regularly for the university first team. They congregated around us and started talking about the Champion of Champions competition that was currently on. Our team had reached the semi-finals by eliminating the police team. How did we fancy our chances of winning the trophy?

Everybody knew we could do it if we laid off wine and women – and here a knowing wink came from the policeman who had made the remark and Phambili returned the compliment.

What business had brought us to the police station? Scara explained, in the vaguest terms possible, that we'd come in that morning for routine questioning.

I looked around, to ascertain that none of the police who'd been present during our interrogation was about, before venturing to suggest to our football friends that perhaps they could find somebody to authorise our dismissal, if we were not to miss a crucial game against Capital City United at the university that very afternoon. The school bus would soon be leaving and we needed to test our full strength against Capital City United, in preparation for the semi-finals the following weekend.

One of our friends looked sympathetically around and seeing a police sergeant, who'd just come in, busy at his desk making some entries in his book, went up to him and asked what we were still being held for. The sergeant raised his eyes quizzically and, as the conversation was being carried on in loud whispers, we overheard him ask who we were. Our friend explained. The sergeant paged through his book and announced that he could find nothing on record. Better hold on until he could make absolutely certain, he said. He got on the phone and took up the matter with somebody who must have been his senior, judging from the deferential manner in which he stood at attention and took off his cap as he spoke – a gesture which produced smiles from all who noticed. At length he dropped the receiver and spoke in agitated tones to our friends, stealing nervous glances at us all the time. This time he spoke more softly so that we could catch very little.

Our friend rejoined us and communicated the good news of our release.

'My apologies, gentlemen. Must have been a mistake,' the sergeant said aloud.

We heard his mutter ' … overzealous upstarts, regular trouble-shooters, cost a man, who has many mouths to feed, his job, fit for the firing squad, the whole bang shoot of them' and other such imprecations, as we marched out of the charge office.

We headed for the bus-stop, feeling as thirsty as Kalahari Bushmen. We passed the Capital Hotel and the neighbouring Portuguese-owned cafés with envious sidelong glances. There seemed to be one thought uppermost in our minds and that was to get back to the campus and to get there fast. By our estimation there were still a few minutes before the school bus pulled out.

When we reached the bus-stop we learnt, to our very great dismay, that our bus had left some ten minutes ago.

There are people, I believe, who take misfortune in their stride and can turn it to their advantage, people who'll make faces at adversity and get away with it. Such a person is Phambili: a man of the moment who thrives on any crisis. His enthusiasm and energy can be so infectious that I've seen him, at the height of the state of emergency, lead agitated student members of the ruling People's Party in the singing of anti-government protest songs, 'to ease their tension'.

'We're hitch-hiking back to campus,' I said.

'Who'll ever give all five of us a lift?' Phambili asked.

Damn the fellow! Why doesn't he come out with it, instead of rubbing pepper into a fresh wound?

'What do you suggest we do?' I asked.

'Look, chaps,' Phambili appealed to the others. 'We haven't had a bite all day. If we're going to hitch-hike, anyhow, we might as well blow the fare. Let's go and see what gives at the Capital?'

We filed into the hotel, with Phambili in the lead. Immediately somebody hailed us with a loud hearty, 'Hi, chaps!' and invited us to join his table. It was Neo, the most popular man of means about town.

Neo was the first, and for a very long time, the only man in the country to drive in a Ford Capri. We knew him from his frequent visits to the university. He often came to have a good time and naturally fell into our hands. He was an extremely valuable asset because he let you drink your fill at his expense. All we had to do was to send for a girl of his choice, not a very difficult task considering we suggested the suitable girls for him. Naturally, we only pointed out those who were known never to refuse a date. He was also famous for throwing weekly parties at his place, mammoth affairs at which we were always welcome.

We pulled our seats and arranged ourselves round Neo's table where he was with another gentleman and two ladies.

'*Ke ma-students ko university,*' Neo said, by way of introduction.

We shook hands all round and murmured our names to each of the other three. The gentleman's name escapes me because everybody called him Toyi's husband. Next to him sat Toyi, a lady whose intake of brandy is comparable to the fuel consumption of a Rolls Royce. She had a reputation for standing no nonsense. We'd bumped into the couple before, at Neo's. The other member of the group was Poppy, Neo's latest girlfriend from Johannesburg.

'*Jerrr!* you should have been with us last night. We drank until cock-crow,' Neo said. '*Wat gaan julle drink?*'

We went through the motions of consulting one another, although we knew we'd all decide on Smirnoff.

Speakit complained, to no one in particular, that he was hungry. Neo summoned a boy who'd been idling outside the hotel and sent him for fish and chips, russians and bread rolls.

As Neo made for the counter, Toyi detained him. '*Sheba, e re ba u fe mpand-lane, Oudemeester,*' she said.

'We don't mind,' Phambili said, speaking for us all.

The Capital was the kind of hotel where you could buy in tots, nips, half-jacks or straights. Although officially registered as a private club, it had opened its doors to the public because very few people ever registered. Of the few who were in its books fewer still ever renewed their membership, obviously preferring to drink the money meant for subscriptions. I only knew of two fee-paying members, both of them expatriates of the university staff who had once expressed an eagerness to meet the local people. When they were inevitably referred to us, we suggested the Capital where we drank what we could of their money (including a post-dated cheque) and then saddled them with club membership. The proprietor, Mr Masuku, accordingly rewarded us with two bottles of Paarl Perlé. As a club, the Capital was not subject to any of the laws affecting hotels in general, so that it operated very much like some glorified shebeen. It is the only hotel I know where you can wake up the proprietor in the middle of the night and get a drink on credit.

Neo returned with a bottle of brandy and was followed by a waitress with five glasses.

'What will you mix it with?' Neo asked.

'Plain water will do,' Toyi said. '*Khaitseli,*' she requested the waitress, '*a k' u ntlele le li-ice blocks.*'

So brandy and water on the rocks it had to be. Meanwhile our food had arrived which we wolfed down.

We then settled down to the brandy. Neo was on whisky, Poppy on Baby Cham and Toyi's husband drank beer. That cut out three from our bottle, but we still had to drink like fish to keep pace with Toyi.

'*Le tseba Keneuoe ne?*' Poppy asked. '*Le eena ke student ko university.*'

Of course, we knew Keneuoe.

'*Ke sister oa ka,*' she said.

'*Au!*' several of us exclaimed. We viewed her like a heifer on sale and remarked upon the close resemblance between Keneuoe and herself.

'She should be here any minute,' Poppy said. 'Neo has sent for her in his car.'

I inwardly cursed myself for having missed a sure lift. I should pull Neo aside so that he doesn't forget me when they drive Keneuoe back to school.

'Actually,' Neo said, 'are you, gentlemen, in a hurry to get back? We're throwing party for Poppy at Toyi's place tonight. You see, at my house it would simply attract too many gatecrashers.' He anticipated our objection and added: 'No need to worry about accommodation because it's going to be a whole-night affair.'

Speakit began to whistle a popular mbaqanga tune, '*Akulalwa ngolwesihlanu*'.

We again conferred, although we knew we'd accept the invitation.

One bottle to six hosepipes is simply not enough. Neo bought another. Toyi shouted, '*Mpandlane!*', stood and danced the jitterbug, and then resumed her seat.

Not long after, one of Neo's stool-pigeons, Chicks, drove in from the university. He'd brought Keneuoe who was accompanied by Nozipho and Lerato.

Neo proposed that we adjourn to his house for an early supper. 'Just the select few,' he added. 'We need a good base. There'll simply be too much booze at the party.'

Neo told Chicks he'd collect him later. Some of us got into Toyi's car and the others into Neo's and we left.

I've attended chaotic parties before, but that evening's was in a class by itself. To start off with, Neo decided, at the last moment, to hire Sound Power, a soul group from Vereeniging whose name very accurately describes their most striking attribute.

Members of the band protested that they had an engagement that same evening at the community hall, but Neo, at whose house some of them were being accommodated, persuaded them to come and play, at least for part of the night. The result was that they were fetched away from the party by the police.

I believe what happened was this: as Sound Power were playing at our party, people, who'd bought their tickets well in advance, arrived in large numbers at the hall. Capital City is a small town. A band with the sonic capacity of Sound Power can be heard from one end of town to the other. When the people at the hall heard the music, their restlessness increased – it was long past starting time – and nearly erupted into a riot. The promoters of the show summoned the police just in the nick of time.

Meanwhile, at the party, Sound Power who'd been announcing for at least an hour, 'This is our very, very last number, ladies and gentlemen,' found their way out completely blocked by the audience. It had become impossible to limit the numbers to the invited few and it was the uninvited who had become as menacing as they were impatient with the band.

The first delegation of neighbours who came to complain about the noise withdrew, with the exception of those who were persuaded to stay on for the party. One particularly nasty, pregnant lady member of this delegation apparently decided to carry out her threat to call the police. The same group of policemen who'd been sent to quell the disturbances at the hall were sent. They came and simply transported the intimidated members of the band, at gun point, to the community hall.

Two later delegations which came for the same purpose as the first, even after the band had left, met with no success. Nor did their frantic calls to the police produce any results. We'd taken care of that. Each policeman who'd called at the house upon the first summons – some of them were the members of the police football team we'd been talking to earlier in the day – had left laden with so much liquor that it would have been positively embarrassing and unethical for them to call a second time.

After the band had left, the party resumed, not without some difficulties. Speakit was sprawled on top of the radiogram and snoring rather like an off-key version of the double bass Sound Power had used. We who live with him know the hazards of waking Speakit from drunken slumber, not so the crowd who attempted to shove him off the gram. He rose like a sleepwalker and, with his eyes wide open, shot out his left arm like a piston. It landed on the jaw of the youth immediately before him. Speakit delivered several other punches of a variety unknown to orthodox boxing, all of which fortunately whizzed through the air without finding a target. Kali found a glass, half-filled it with vodka, and, approaching Speakit stealthily from the rear, placed it on his lips. He swallowed, grabbed the glass to his bosom, and retired to a corner to gulp down the rest.

Music boomed from the speakers and dancing began. Speakit jumped up like a spring released – those nearest him quickly worked their way to safer nooks – and began to dance, with all the abandon of a man possessed. He never danced with a partner.

Although Toyi had earlier announced that nobody but herself was to touch the gram, at a certain stage I found myself operating it. It seemed to take a load off her shoulders for she clung to a young man, at waltz tempo, for the greater part of the night. As disc jockey, I wasn't the least inconvenienced because I piled the records very high and only inserted a new pile when the machine stalled from overloading.

I was summoned from a very intimate dance with an extremely curvaceous lady, though rather too heavily corsetted, by Nozipho and Lerato, shouting and pulling frantically at me.

'What's the matter?' I asked.

'Sabelo, please, come and settle this dispute,' Nozipho said. 'They won't listen to us. And they've never even met the lady before.'

'*Wu, batho, Ke embarrassed joang!*'

I dragged my partner with me, for fear I'd be 'overtaken' if I left her all by herself. We wormed our way through the crowd to a corner where Scara and Kali were arguing.

'What's the matter?' I asked.

'*Kyk hier*, Sabelo,' Kali answered, 'I approach the girl first, you see, then when I'm beaten, Scara takes over. That way we lower her every defence.'

'Nix!' Scara said. 'I talk to her alone and you keep your distance.'

It turned out they were talking about Poppy, who seemed content to remain ensconced on the sofa and talk to the various people who came to her. Neo had asked to be excused to sleep off some of the previous evening's fatigue in one of Toyi's bedrooms.

'*Ha ho etsuoe joala,*' Lerato said, trying to appeal to their sense of propriety.

Kali and Scara were bent upon settling their argument their way and I knew that no amount of persuasion would make either change his mind.

Upon the first opening, they took their seats on either side of Poppy and began proposing love to that mystified lady.

Phambili had the key to the fridge and was helping Toyi's husband clear the empties and bring in more drinks from the kitchen.

'Sabelo,' he whispered as he passed me. 'Join us in the kitchen.' He glanced at my girl. 'Alone,' he added.

He retired with Toyi's husband.

After I'd piled on more records, I excused myself from my partner. The kitchen door was locked. I knocked.

'*Ke mang?*' Phambili asked.

'*Ke'na,*' I replied.

He opened the door slightly, so that I had to squeeze in, and then locked it again.

They'd set a whole chicken before them and were tearing at it like a pair of eagles.

'Join us, my friend,' Toyi's husband said.

'Where are the others?' Phambili asked.

'I'll get them.'

Phambili saw me out and promptly locked the door.

I found Kali and Scara still at their pursuit. Kali was on his knees in front of Poppy, and Scara was holding her arm.

'I'm afraid we have some very pressing business to attend to in the kitchen,' I said.

'*Wag!*' Both of them shoved me off.

Not until Poppy urged them to go and return soon did they finally agree to come with me to the kitchen.

I found Speakit sobbing softly to himself, his head resting on the lap of a very skinny girl. I simply dragged him with me, to that alarmed lady's great relief.

Of the chicken, only the bony parts remained and considerable expertise was required to extract any meat from the leftovers.

'*Ha e ea lekana,*' Phambili said as he unlocked the fridge.

Speakit grabbed half a packet of salt and emptied three quarters of its contents on the bones.

'*Hayi, wena!*' Scara admonished, '*u senya lintho tsa batho.*'

'There are some mutton chops in there, just behind those three bottles of KWV to your right,' Toyi's husband said. 'The only problem is, the meat's uncooked.'

'We fry it,' Kali said as he spat the bones into the sink.

584

To get to the meat, Phambili first had to place several bottles of liquor on the floor. He passed Kali a bottle of Smirnoff. The meat followed and Toyi's husband began to fry it.

We were feasting on the meat and drinking when we heard loud knocking on the kitchen door followed by shouts of, 'Who locked here? Who did?'

'Switch off that light,' Toyi's husband whispered. When nobody responded he put out the light himself.

The music also stopped the moment a voice ordered, '*Tema ntho eo.*'

'What fools are these who are trying to lock me out of my own house? Who are they?' Toyi's voice had risen to a crescendo.

'Leave my glass alone, *wena*,' Scara said, slapping somebody's hand. 'Gentlemen, please, dump all the glasses in the sink. Never mind the liquor,' Toyi's husband whispered.

Several people had gathered outside the kitchen door.

'I'm sure, *ke matahoa a ko university.*' I thought the voice belonged to my erstwhile partner. Calling us drunkards! Must be feeling terribly slighted, the bitch! Thought I didn't realise my priorities.

'They said they had some urgent business to attend to in the kitchen,' another voice cut in.

'Damn that *skerberesh!*' Kali said through clenched teeth.

'*Ke mang?*' I asked.

'*Ke Poppy,*' Kali said.

'*Mhh! ho nkha nama*' – my partner again.

'That's right, they're feasting on my meat. Trying to eat me out of my house, are they? We'll see! Get out of my house, you –' and here Toyi followed with an impressive list of invectives, delivered with the speed and fluency of a praise-singer.

'I'm going out through the window,' I said and immediately reached for it, only to be prevented by burglar bars.

'I'm calling the police,' Toyi shouted.

'How long shall we remain locked up in here like low-caste criminals?' Speakit asked. 'This morning it was the police and now … I'm going out. Where's the key?'

'Where's my husband?'

I made sure of the bottle of Smirnoff before Toyi's husband approached the door and unlocked.

Toyi descended upon us like a tornado. Speakit tried to edge past her but she shoved him back.

'We were only clearing up, darly,' Toyi's husband said.

'I don't want to hear anything from you,' she said. 'I'll talk to you later.'

She turned to Speakit. 'Tell me,' she said, 'why did you lock that door and put out the lights?'

'Switching off the lights was his idea,' Speakit said, pointing at Toyi's husband. 'As for me, I was dragged into this kitchen, very much against my will.'

'I'll teach you to go stealing meat in other people's houses. You'll get out of my house, this instant. *Ba buleleng tsela.*'

A woman's house is her last bastion. The futility of arguing against eviction is best appreciated by those who've actually undergone the ordeal before. Sometimes even husbands are not immune from the common lot.

A path was open for us, as Toyi had ordered, all the way to the front door. We filed out of the house, with Toyi's husband bringing up the rear. He'd made the mistake of trying to put in a good word for us. The tigress that had been aroused in Toyi was unleashed on him.

'*Ba latele le uena. U ipona u se u le student, eh?*' she said, motioning to him to follow us.

It was drizzling outside. Somebody asked for the time and Toyi's husband replied, 'Two o'clock.' The house had no veranda so that we stood against the wall and watched the water from the gutter, dripping onto our feet.

I produced the bottle of Smirnoff which I'd tucked between my stomach and my trousers, but even that failed to produce any soothing effect. Toyi's husband flatly refused to drink. He shook his head from side to side, so vigorously you'd have imagined we were trying to persuade him to take poison.

'What do we do?' I asked as the bottle was circulating.

'Work our way back to the house, I suppose,' Kali said.

At such moments when no easy solution is in sight, we usually break into groups and abandon each group to its creative resources. I always pair with Phambili; Kali with Scara. Speakit is the individualist who somehow always comes out best.

Speakit took Toyi's husband aside. We heard him ask whether there wasn't a window, no matter how small, which they could use to get into the house.

Phambili pulled at my jacket in such a way that Kali and Scara would not see. We moved to a corner of the house.

'Remember Sis' Dora?' he asked.

I remembered her very well. She owned a two-roomed house, very neatly kept, in the location. We'd been introduced to her by one of Neo's decoys, I think it was Chicks. She was very fond of talking English and took an immediate liking to us. But what was more important, she stayed alone.

Phambili and the boys had slept at her place on more than one occasion, but I'd only been to her place once and wasn't sure how to get there.

There's actually a good reason why I never went there after the first time. I like all these boys but they can be very embarrassing, especially Speakit. The first time we went there Sis' Dora had said, 'Feel at home.' Before you could say 'Thanks', Speakit had disappeared into the bedroom. After a while we heard him shout to Sis' Dora to hurry. What Speakit had done was to interpret Sis'

Dora literally. It took a few blows to get him dressed and out of Sis' Dora's blankets. Such things have a way of embarrassing me; but tonight I was prepared to put up anywhere rather than catch pneumonia in that rain. So I listened intently.

'She's my girlfriend.' That was news to me. But then anything is possible with Phambili. She was old enough to have been his mother.

'We'll go there. Just the two of us.'

We marched resolutely out of the yard. The others gaped at us and said nothing.

We must have been walking for more than an hour, in a heavy downpour, when I asked Phambili how near Sis' Dora's he thought we were.

'To tell the truth,' he said, 'I don't know where we are.'

Neither did I, except that we were somewhere in Capitalonia.

It also dawned on me, with electrocuting effect, that we were breaking the curfew, right in the capital.

'We'd better seek some shelter from this rain,' I said. 'And wait until we've enough light to see by.'

'Come on, Sabs,' he said. 'We'll soon be there.'

'Nope.'

We spent the night under some trees in the posh suburb of Capitalonia, where all the Ministers and top civil servants stay.

We were lucky in that the rain began to ease and eventually ceased.

Phambili wanted us to leave as soon as light began to cut through the dark. I refused and we only started off when I saw the milkman cycle past on his morning rounds. I knew then that it was after six.

Half an hour later we were at Sis' Dora's. She welcomed us with hot coffee and allowed us to lie on her bed, while our clothes dried outside.

We were woken up, just thirty minutes later, by Kali, Scara and Speakit, the latter wet to the skin. They'd brought two bottles of Smirnoff with them. We sat up and listened while they told us how they'd spent the night.

Kali and Scara had made several attempts to enter the house, but each time Toyi met them at the door and sent them scuttling back. It wasn't until shortly before six, when most of the guests were already preparing to leave, that they eventually got into the house. Toyi was apparently worn out and sleeping on the sofa.

Speakit had had a royal time, almost to the end. He'd managed to fling in Toyi's husband through the bathroom window, which was always left open. The only miracle was how Toyi's husband had succeeded in going in through the small bathroom window – Neo later reported that Toyi's husband had sustained a mysterious bump, the size of a small egg, on his forehead. Anyhow, Toyi's husband brought Speakit in through the back door, and together they crept into the bedroom and made themselves comfortable in their various ways.

Toyi had been sleeping uncomfortably on the sofa. She decided to retire to her bedroom. Her husband was sleeping under the bed, only his feet showing, but on their bed, snoring with all the sonic fury of Sound Power, was Speakit. With little regard for her blankets, she emptied a bucket of cold water on him. He woke up, without his usual fighting, and left.

'And the bottles?' I asked, pointing at the Smirnoff.

'When Speakit was being baptised, that was it,' they said.

After Sis' Dora had served them coffee and when Speakit's clothes had been taken to be hung with ours on the line, we decided to sleep for a while before returning to school.

Kali and Scara joined a number of small mats together and dozed off. Speakit camelled his way onto our bed and we slept.

RICHARD RIVE

The Visits

From: *Selected Writing* (1977)

It was on the evening The Student had gone out that The Woman had first arrived. It wasn't actually a visit, but that was the nearest he could come to it. He remembered it very clearly. First the phonecall for The Student, some girl or other (the ringing sounded brazen and adolescent), then the front door banging. The Student revving his engine and the tortured whine as the Honda gathered speed up the driveway.

He was distinctly annoyed. He went to the front door, opened it, peered out from long habit, then closed the door gently as if to make up to it for The Student's treatment. He returned to his study and sat down at the cluttered desk. Should he read or mark books? He was busy fighting his way through *A Century of South African Verse in English*. What a bore. What a boring bore. Should he mark the Standard Ten compos instead? Mark books?

There was a quietness which settled over the flat. It was like that when-ever The Student went out and he took the phone off the cradle. The silence surging softly ... but first the storm before the calm. The phone, then the revving of that damn engine, then peace. Mark books. Standard Ten com-pos. Remember dearest children the word *can* denotes ability, whereas *may* denotes possibility. Ability and possibility. Can ability. May possibility. Can-ability, may-possibility. He repeated it mentally until a rhythm formed. May-possibility sounded clumsy, so he changed it to canability, mayability. But that was wrong. Sacrificing rhythm for meaning. Maybe he could use it on his seniors. His students. The Student?

He got up, uncomfortable at the triviality of his ideas. Must be getting old. Mr Chips. Old at forty-five. Young at forty-five. He walked to the kitchen to make some tea and turned on the tap for hot water. The gurgle echoed through the flat. How vacant the place sounded without The Student.

How empty when he wasn't there. How empty when he was there. A different kind of emptiness.

Impossible to speak to him any longer. He was too ... too physical. Throwing his weight and looks around. Girls, the telephone and the Honda. Looks and muscle. A student of rags and tatters. He switched on the stove reflectively, and put on the water. Mayability, canability. Canability, mayability.

It was then that he heard the knocking at the door. Not loudly but it could be heard throughout the flat. Who could it be? He was curious but didn't answer the door at once. He fussed loudly in the kitchen to show that he was in (he knew he could be heard at the entrance), until the knocking was repeated. He coughed and said, 'Coming.'

When he opened the door he was surprised and disappointed to see the African woman standing there.

'Yes?' he asked, somewhat annoyed.

She said nothing, just stood there, her eyes downcast. He took in her appearance. She was extremely unattractive, seemed all of a heap from her doughy bosom to her thick ankles hanging over her shoes.

'Yes?' he repeated, showing his impatience.

She looked at him for the first time and he noticed a mixture of shyness and aggression. He felt like shutting the door on her, but was incapable of such behaviour. He braced himself and became the teacher. (For God's sake boy, open your mouth when you recite. Can denotes ability. May possibility.)

Then she said in a half-whisper, 'I want food.' And as an afterthought, 'Please.'

It was the way she said it that made him look at her more closely. Although she whispered, her tone was not servile or pleading. She spoke almost as if the asking for food was hers by right. Not quite a demand, more a taking for granted. He wanted her to go, but there was something about her he didn't quite understand. He couldn't see her eyes very clearly but sensed they were laughing and mocking him. When he tried to see she cast them down.

'Food?' he repeated, and knew he sounded foolish. She maintained her silence, not looking him in the face.

'Wait here, I'll see.' He realised that this was a sign of defeat. But why should he be defeated? There was no contest, or was there? What he knew was that he had to get away from her. He wished The Student was there. He could deal physically with the situation. But this was so different. He went back to the kitchen and stood for some time staring at the water boiling over on the stove and hissing on the plate. Then he opened the provisions cupboard and started filling an empty carrier bag. Sugar, rice, a tin of mushrooms. There was some apricot jam left over, a bottle of pickles, stuffed olives. What the hell could she do with stuffed olives? He opened the fridge and removed cheese, butter and two pints of milk. Then he opened the bread bin. He stared at the bulging carrier on the kitchen table.

He seemed afraid to face her and hoped she would be gone by the time he returned to the door. He decided to have a cup of tea while playing for time. Should he invite her in? He smiled and decided against the tea. Then resolutely he took the paper carrier. Give her the food and tell her to get the hell away.

When he handed over the provisions she made a slight, old-fashioned bow. It seemed comical because he estimated she could not be more than forty. Still, one could never tell with these people. Or could one?

'Thank you,' she said in the same whisper. Then she was gone. He returned to the kitchen and felt relieved, and for no reason at all, he felt completely exhausted.

The second time The Woman came it was almost like her first visit. Had she visited him? One did not visit and ask for food. The Student was out again (flexing his muscles at some giddy fresher in a coffee bar). He had been in his study for some time reading the book on South African verse. It wasn't quite as boring as he had thought at first.

Roy Campbell. *Upon a dark and gloomy night.* Yes it was a dark and gloomy night. Outside it was dark with squalls of northwester. *Upon a gloomy night with nobody in sight, I went abroad when all my house was hushed.* To waste the poetry of that great Spanish mystic St John of the Cross upon the snot-nosed brats in his matriculation class. (For goodness' sake, try to feel what the poet is trying to get at. Feel the *brio*.) They lived for Hondas and girls and pop. Telephones and screaming singers. The Animals. The Insecticides.

He settled down for more Roy Campbell. *In safety, in disguise, in darkness up the secret stair I crept* ... he recognised the knock at once when it came and was afraid to answer.

She stood half-way in the shadow of the entrance but he had no difficulty recognising the dumpy figure, the heavy legs and the downcast eyes. This time he was determined that she should speak first. She had the empty carrier bag with her. He didn't want to break the silence. Somehow he seemed afraid of his own voice. She held out the bag without saying anything.

'What is it this time?' he said in his schoolmaster voice. Then he regretted his tone and felt his attitude was wrong, far too aggressive. There was certainly no cause for aggression.

'More food?' he asked, hoping he sounded friendly.

'Yes, please,' she said at last.

He went into the kitchen and half-filled the bag with all the leftovers he could find. By the time he returned he felt more at ease, more in control of himself, and was determined to speak.

'Tell me,' he said without handing over the bag, 'what is your name? Who are you?'

She mumbled something which sounded like 'Edith'. The surname was inaudible. He didn't bother to ask her to repeat it.

'Now look here, Edith or whoever you are.' He spoke faster than usual, his voice a trifle raspy. 'Now look here. You're a grown woman. You should be working instead of begging like this. Take the carrier but don't come back again. Do you understand?'

She nodded slightly and took the food with the same old-fashioned bow. Then, like the first time, she was gone.

He went back to his study and slumped down in the chair. He took up his book but had no further interest in Roy Campbell. Edith something or other. For God's sake why must she come to him? What had he done to her? What had he done for her? He felt guilty but there was nothing he could think of to feel guilty about. He had given her food. He had done his duty. What was his duty and why should he do it? Again the nagging feeling of guilt. Well he had to tell her not to come again. Couldn't keep giving food away. Not a charitable institution. He wished The Student would come home earlier so that they could talk. No, not about The Woman necessarily. Only just talk.

He sat in the dark until well after eleven o'clock when he heard The Student's Honda whining up the driveway. Then he went to bed.

Even after her third visit he said nothing to The Student about it. They seldom spoke and communicated only when it was necessary. (The Student was in sometimes now because examinations were pressing.) The night of her third visit, however, The Student was out, and he was alone in the flat, although himself on the verge of going out. He was going out more frequently now. He sometimes visited two members of his staff with whom he was quite intimate, and his one married sister. Most times he sat in the public library reading until closing time. He even went to cinemas although he detested them. What he seemed afraid of was being alone in the flat. The loneliness got him down. Or was it the aloneness? He used to enjoy it before. The silence, his books, his pipe. A cup of tea and a small brandy with water before turning in for the night. He couldn't stand the sameness any longer. And the loneliness. One tired of too much routine.

He had put on his overcoat and prepared himself mentally for the brisk walk to the library. The dark shadows of the trees lining the avenue, the smell of rain. He was about to pick up his books when the knock came. He looked around for possible escape routes but there was only the bathroom window and he realised how absurd it was for him to climb through that.

She stood in the doorway holding the same empty carrier.

'But I told you not to come back!' He tried to control himself. 'I told you not to come again.'

She maintained her silence, her eyes as usual, downcast. He clenched the library books till he could feel the edges cutting into his palm.

'Do you understand me?'

She nodded slightly.

'I told you to stay away! Do you understand? Stay away!' She stood dumbly, not looking at him.

'If you come again I'll be forced to call the police. Police!' he repeated. She started slightly and cast a quick glance at him. He felt it was hostile. 'Police!' he repeated. 'Police!'

There was a pause that lasted longer than it should have done.

'Hell,' he said, dropping the books on the table. 'Hell, what do I do now?' He decided to try to be reasonable and sat down wearily. 'Where you from?'

She kept her eyes down, not replying.

'Look,' he said frustratedly, 'I'll give you food for the last time. For the last time. You understand? You must never come again. If you do come I'll call the police. Then you'll go to jail! Understand?'

She stared at him, her eyes no longer downcast.

'Jail! Police! Jail!'

Then he noticed, almost with a start that she was crying. Two tears rolled down her cheeks but her face remained immobile. The tears did not seem part of her. He felt the sense of guilt again, felt like assuring her that he would not call the police. That he was only pretending. But she must not come again.

He went into the kitchen, and when he returned she took the carrier with the same quaint bow. He watched her walking down the driveway. Then he saw another dark figure joining her. They seemed to speak for a short time, but it was too far for him to hear what they were saying. She pointed at him still standing in the open doorway. The other figure (he could not make out the sex) also turned. He heard their loud laughter. He shut the door and felt sick to the stomach.

She came again the following week, and the week after that, and every week after that. Now he merely went to the door, took her empty carrier and then filled it. No words passed between them, only the ritual. The quaint bow and she was gone. He bought extra groceries which he set aside for her. She did not always come on the same evening, but she never came more than once a week. She seemed to time it so that The Student was out and he was in.

Although he watched her when she left, he never saw her companion again. He started suffering from lack of sleep, was short-tempered with his pupils at school and was seriously thinking of giving The Student notice and then himself moving from the flat. There was no one to whom he could speak seriously about the visits.

He told The Student about it one evening but he turned it into a joke and they both laughed. He seemed to welcome and dread her visits at the same time. He wanted to find out more about her, follow her and see where she lived. Was she married? Did she have children? Why did she have to beg? Was it only to him she came? But somehow he was afraid, afraid he might find out. He could ask her in, give her some tea and then ask questions. He was afraid of her answers.

Then one week she did not appear. Her groceries remained in the closet. The following week she did not come either. He kept her groceries in case.

After she had not appeared for a month he decided to use the provisions he had bought for her. With a strange sense of fear he opened the bags and was relieved when nothing happened. He felt as if an enormous burden had dropped from his shoulders and wanted to speak to someone about it. Anyone. The Student was in his room trying in vain to study. He made some coffee and took it to The Student standing in the doorway attempting to keep the conversation alive.

'By the way,' The Student said, not annoyed at being disturbed, 'your girl friend turned up last week but you were out.'

'I was out?' he said bewildered. He was eager to know more.

'I answered the door and there she was. What an ugly bitch.'

'Yes?' He hoped he didn't sound over-anxious.

'I told her to get away, clear off, hamba!' He waved his arms to indicate the action. 'She wouldn't.'

'What did you do?' His lips were trembling.

'What you should have done the first time.'

'What I should have done?'

'Yes. I took her by her black neck and frog-marched her down the driveway. Then threw her out.'

He felt a tightening across his chest. His fists balled and he felt like hitting The Student. He was shivering all over.

'She won't come again,' The Student assured him.

'You shouldn't have done that.' He tried to control his voice.

'Why the hell not?' The Student looked at him puzzled.

'You shouldn't have done that,' he repeated lamely.

'Are you sick or something?' The Student asked.

'I'm all right. Only have to get back to my books. Marking to be done.'

The Student looked at him in a strange way. Then the phone rang.

He went into his study and slumped down at the desk. He felt like crying but couldn't. He heard The Student banging the front door then the revving of the Honda engine. Long after the whine had faded away he sat at his desk just staring in the dark.

AHMED ESSOP

The Hajji

From: *The Hajji and other Stories* (1978)

When the telephone rang several times one evening and his wife did not attend to it as she usually did, Hajji Hassen, seated on a settee in the lounge, cross-legged and sipping tea, shouted: 'Salima, are you deaf?' And when he received no response from his wife and the jarring bell went on ringing, he shouted again: 'Salima, what's happened to you?'

The telephone stopped ringing abruptly. Hajji Hassen went on sipping tea in a contemplative manner, wondering where his wife had disappeared. Since his return from Mecca after the pilgrimage, he had discovered novel inadequacies in her, or perhaps saw the old ones in a more revealing light. One of her salient inadequacies was never to be around when he wanted her. She was either across the road confabulating with her sister, or gossiping with the neighbours, or away on a shopping spree. And now, when the telephone had gone on assaulting his ears, she was not in the house. He took another sip of the strongly spiced tea to stifle the irritation within him.

When he heard the kitchen door open he knew that Salima had entered. The telephone burst out again in a metallic shrill and the Hajji shouted for his wife. She hurried to the phone.

'Hullo ... Yes ... Hassen ... Speak to him? ... Who speaking? ... Caterine? ... Who Caterine? ... Au-right ... I call him.'

She placed the receiver down gingerly and informed her husband in Gujarati that a woman named 'Caterine' wanted to speak to him. The name evoked no immediate association in his memory. He descended from the settee and squeezing his feet into a pair of crimson sandals, went to the telephone.

'Hullo ... Who? ... Catherine? ... No, I don't know you ... Yes ... Yes ... Oh ... now I remember ... Yes ...'

He listened intently to the voice, urgent, supplicating. Then he gave his answer:

'I am afraid I can't help him. Let the Christians bury him. His last wish means nothing to me ... Madam, it's impossible ... No ... Let him die ... Brother? Pig! Pig! Bastard!' He banged the receiver onto the telephone in explosive annoyance.

'O Allah!' Salima exclaimed. 'What words! What is this all about?'

He did not answer but returned to the settee, and she quietly went to the bedroom.

Salima went to bed and it was almost midnight when her husband came into the room. His earlier vexation had now given place to gloom. He told her of his brother Karim who lay dying in Hillbrow. Karim had cut himself off from his family and friends ten years ago; he had crossed the colour line (his fair complexion and grey eyes serving as passports) and gone to cohabit with a white woman. And now that he was on the verge of death he wished to return to the world he had forsaken and to be buried under Muslim funeral rites and in a Muslim cemetery.

Hajji Hassen had of course rejected the plea, for a good reason. When his brother had crossed the colour line, he had severed his family ties. The Hajji at that time had felt excoriating humiliation. By going over to the white herrenvolk, his brother trampled on something that was vitally part of him, his dignity and self-respect. But the rejection of his brother's plea involved a straining of the heartstrings and the Hajji did not feel happy. He had recently sought God's pardon for his sins in Mecca, and now this business of his brother's final earthly wish and his own intransigence was in some way staining his spirit.

The next day Hassen rose at five to go to the mosque. When he stepped out of his house in Newtown the street lights were beginning to pale and clusters of houses to assume definition. The atmosphere was fresh and heady, and he took a few deep breaths. The first trams were beginning to pass through Bree Street and were clanging along like decrepit but yet burning spectres towards the Johannesburg City Hall. Here and there a figure moved along hurriedly. The Hindu fruit and vegetable hawkers were starting up their old trucks in the yards, preparing to go out for the day to sell to suburban housewives.

When he reached the mosque the Somali muezzin in the ivory-domed minaret began to intone the call for prayers. After prayers he remained behind to read the Koran in the company of two other men. When he had done the sun was shining brilliantly in the courtyard among the flowers and the fountain with its goldfish.

Outside his house he saw a car. Salima opened the door and whispered, 'Caterine'. For a moment he felt irritated, but realising that he might as well face her he stepped boldly into the lounge.

Catherine was a small woman with firm fleshy legs. She was seated cross-legged on the settee, smoking a cigarette. Her face was almost boyish, a look that partly originated in her auburn hair which was cut very short, and partly in the smallness of her head. Her eyebrows, firmly pencilled with secular emphasis, accentuated the grey-green glitter of her eyes. She was dressed in a dark grey costume.

He nodded his head at her to signify that he knew who she was. Over the telephone he had spoken with aggressive authority. Now, in the presence of the woman herself, he felt a weakening of his masculine fibre.

'You must, Mr Hassen, come to see your brother.'

'I am afraid I'm unable to help,' he said in a tentative tone. He felt uncomfortable; there was something so positive and intrepid about her appearance.

'He wants to see you. It's his final wish.'

'I have not seen him for ten years.'

'Time can't wipe out the fact that he's your brother.'

'He is a white. We live in different worlds.'

'But you must see him.'

There was a moment of strained silence.

'Please understand that he's not to blame for having broken with you. I am to blame. I got him to break with you. Really you must blame me, not Karim.'

Hassen found himself unable to say anything. The thought that she could in some way have been responsible for his brother's rejection of him had never occurred to him. He looked at his feet in awkward silence. He could only state in a lazily recalcitrant tone:

'It is not easy for me to see him.'

'Please come, Mr Hassen, for my sake, please. I'll never be able to bear it if Karim dies unhappily. Can't you find it in your heart to forgive him, and to forgive me?'

He could not look at her. A sob escaped from her, and he heard her opening her handbag for a handkerchief.

'He's dying. He wants to see you for the last time.'

Hassen softened. He was overcome by the argument that she had been responsible for taking Karim away. He could hardly look on her responsibility as being in any way culpable. She was a woman.

'If you remember the days of your youth, the time you spent together with Karim before I came to separate him from you, it will be easier for you to pardon him.'

Hassen was silent.

'Please understand that I'm not a racialist. You know the conditions in this country.'

He yielded. He excused himself and went to his room to change. After a while he set off for Hillbrow in her car.

He sat beside her. The closeness of her presence, the perfume she exuded stirred currents of feeling within him. He glanced at her several times, watched the deft movements of her hands and legs as she controlled the car. Her powdered profile, the outline taut with a resolute quality, aroused his imagination. There was something so businesslike in her attitude and bearing, so involved in reality (at the back of his mind there was Salima, flaccid, cowlike and inadequate) that he could hardly refrain from expressing his admiration.

'You must understand that I'm only going to see my brother because you have come to me. For no one else would I have changed my mind.'

'Yes, I understand. I'm very grateful.'

'My friends and relatives are going to accuse me of softness, of weakness.'

'Don't think of them now. You have decided to be kind to me.'

The realism and commonsense of the woman's words! He was overwhelmed by her.

The car stopped at the entrance of a building in Hillbrow. They took the lift. On the second floor three white youths entered and were surprised at seeing Hassen. There was a separate lift for non-whites. They squeezed themselves into a corner, one actually turning his head away with a grunt of disgust. The lift reached the fifth floor too soon for Hassen to give a thought to the attitude of the three white boys. Catherine led him to apartment 65.

He stepped into the lounge. Everything seemed to be carefully arranged. There was her personal touch about the furniture, the ornaments, the paintings. Catherine went to the bedroom, then returned soon and asked him in.

Karim lay in bed, pale, emaciated, his eyes closed. For a moment Hassen failed to recognise him: ten years divided them. She placed a chair next to the bed for him. He looked at his brother and again saw, through ravages of illness, the familiar features. Catherine sat on the bed and rubbed Karim's hand to wake him. After a while he began to show signs of consciousness. She called him tenderly by his name. When he opened his eyes he did not recognise the man beside him, but by degrees, after she had repeated Hassen's name several times, he seemed to understand. He stretched out a hand and Hassen took it, moist and repellent. A sense of nausea swept over him, but he could not withdraw his hand as his brother clutched it firmly.

'Brother Hassen, please take me away from here.'

Hassen's affirmative answer brought a smile to his lips.

Catherine suggested that she drive Hassen back to Newtown where he could make preparations to transfer Karim to his home.

'No, you stay here. I will take a taxi.' And he left the apartment.

In the corridor he pressed the button for the lift. He watched the indicator numbers succeeding each other rapidly, then stop at five. The doors opened – and there they were again, the three white youths. He hestitated. The boys looked at him tauntingly, their eyes aglitter with cynical humour. Then suddenly they burst into laughter, coarse, raw, deliberately brutish.

'Come into the parlour,' one of them said in a satirically ingratiating tone.

'Come into the Indian parlour,' another said in a cloyingly mocking voice.

Hassen looked at them, annoyed, hurt. Then something snapped within him and he stood there, transfixed. They laughed at him in a raucous chorus as the lift doors shut.

He remained immobile, his dignity clawed. Was there anything so vile in him that the youths found it necessary to maul that recess of self-respect within him? 'They are whites,' he said to himself in bitter justification of their attitude.

He would take the stairs and walk down the five floors. As he descended he thought of Karim. Because of him he had come here and because of him he had been insulted. The enormity of the insult bridged the gap of ten years when Karim had spurned him, and diminished his being. Now he was diminished again!

He was hardly aware that he had gone down five floors when he reached ground level. He stood still, expecting to see the three youths again. But the foyer was empty and he could see the reassuring activity of street life through the glass panels. He quickly walked out as though he would regain in the hubbub of the street something of his assaulted dignity.

He walked on, structures of concrete and glass on either side of him, and it did not even occur to him to take a taxi. It was in Hillbrow that Karim had lived with the white woman and forgotten the existence of his brother; and now that he was dying he had sent for him. For ten years Karim had lived without him. O Karim! The thought of the youth he had loved so much during the days they had been together at the Islamic Institute, a religious seminary governed by ascetics and bearded fanatics, brought the tears to his eyes and he stopped against a shop-window and wept. A few pedestrians looked at him. When the shopkeeper came outside to see the weeping man, Hassen, ashamed of himself, wiped his eyes and walked on.

He regretted his pliability in the presence of the white woman. She had come unexpectedly and had disarmed him with her presence and subtle talk. A painful lump rose in his throat as he set his heart against forgiving Karim. If his brother had had no personal dignity in sheltering behind his white skin, trying to be what he was not, he was not going to allow his moral worth to be depreciated in any way.

When he reached central Johannesburg he went to the station and took the train. In the coach with the non-whites he felt at ease and regained his self-possession. He was among familiar faces, among people who respected him. He felt as though he had been spirited away by a perfumed well-made wax doll, but had managed with a prodigious effort to shake her off.

When he reached home Salima asked him what had been decided and he answered curtly, 'Nothing.' But feeling elated after his escape from Hillbrow he added condescendingly, 'Karim left on his own accord. We should have nothing to do with him.'

Salima was puzzled, but she went on preparing supper.

Catherine received no word from Hassen and she phoned him. She was stunned when he said:

'I'm sorry but I am unable to offer any help.'

'But …'

'I regret it. I made a mistake. Please make some other arrangements. Goodbye.'

With an effort of will he banished Karim from his mind. Finding his composure again he enjoyed his evening meal, read the paper and then retired to bed. Next morning he went to mosque as usual, but when he returned home he found Catherine there again. Angry that she should have come, he blurted out:

'Listen to me, Catherine. I can't forgive him. For ten years he didn't care about me, whether I was alive or dead. Karim means nothing to me now.'

'Do you find it so difficult to forgive him?'

'Don't talk to me of forgiveness. What forgiveness when he threw me aside and chose to go with you? Let his white friends see to him, let Hillbrow see to him.'

'Please, please, Mr Hassen, I beg you …'

'No, don't come here with your begging. Please go away.'

He opened the door and went out. Catherine burst into tears. Salima comforted her as best she could.

'Don't cry Caterine. All men hard. Dey don't understand.'

'What shall I do now?' Catherine said in a defeatist tone. She was an alien in the world of the non-whites. 'Is there no one who could help me?'

'Yes, Mr Mia help you,' replied Salima.

In her eagerness to clutch at any straw, she hastily moved to the door. Salima followed her and from the porch of her home directed her to Mr Mia's. He lived in a flat on the first floor of an old building. She knocked and waited in trepidation.

Mr Mia opened the door, smiled affably and asked her in.

'Come inside, lady; sit down … Fatima,' he called to his daughter, 'bring some tea.'

Mr Mia was a man in his fifties, his bronze complexion partly covered by a neatly trimmed beard. He was a well-known figure in the Indian community. Catherine told him of Karim and her abortive appeal to his brother. Mr Mia asked one or two questions, pondered for a while and then said:

'Don't worry, my good woman. I'll speak to Hassen. I'll never allow a Muslim brother to be abandoned.'

Catherine began to weep.

'Here, drink some tea and you'll feel better.' He poured tea. Before Catherine left he promised that he would phone her that evening and told her to get in touch with him immediately should Karim's condition deteriorate.

Mr Mia, in the company of the priest of the Newtown mosque, went to

Hassen's house that evening. They found several relatives of Hassen's seated in the lounge (Salima had spread the word of Karim's illness). But Hassen refused to listen to their pleas that Karim should be brought to Newtown.

'Listen to me, Hajji,' Mr Mia said. 'Your brother can't be allowed to die among the Christians.'

'For ten years he has been among them.'

'That means nothing. He's still a Muslim.'

The priest now gave his opinion. Although Karim had left the community, he was still a Muslim. He had never rejected the religion and espoused Christianity, and in the absence of any evidence to the contrary it had to be accepted that he was a Muslim brother.

'But for ten years he has lived in sin in Hillbrow.'

'If he has lived in sin that is not for us to judge.'

'Hajji, what sort of a man are you? Have you no feeling for your brother?' Mr Mia asked.

'Don't talk to me about feeling. What feeling had he for me when he went to live among the whites, when he turned his back on me?'

'Hajji, can't you forgive him? You were recently in Mecca.'

This hurt him and he winced. Salima came to his rescue with refreshments for the guests.

The ritual of tea-drinking established a mood of conviviality and Karim was forgotten for a while. After tea they again tried to press Hassen into forgiving his brother, but he remained adamant. He could not now face Catherine without looking ridiculous. Besides he felt integrated now; he would resist anything that negated him.

Mr Mia and the priest departed. They decided to raise the matter with the congregation in the mosque. But they failed to move Hassen. Actually his resistance grew in inverse ratio as more people came to learn of the dying Karim and Hassen's refusal to forgive him. By giving in he would be displaying mental dithering of the worst kind, a man without an inner fibre, decision and firmness of will.

Mr Mia then summoned a meeting of various religious dignitaries and received the mandate to transfer Karim to Newtown without his brother's consent. Karim's relatives would be asked to care for him, but if they refused Mr Mia would take charge.

Karim's relatives refused to accept him. They did not want to offend Hassen, and they also felt that he was not their responsibility.

Mr Mia phoned Catherine and informed her of what had been decided. She agreed that it was best for Karim to be amongst his people during his last days. So Karim was brought to Newtown in an ambulance hired from a private nursing home and housed in a neat little room in a quiet yard behind the mosque.

The arrival of Karim placed Hassen in a difficult situation and he bitterly regretted his decision not to accept him into his own house. He first heard of his brother's arrival during the morning prayers when the priest offered a special prayer for the recovery of the sick man. Hassen found himself in the curious position of being forced to pray for his brother. After prayers several people went to see the sick man, others offered help. He felt an alien and as soon as the opportunity presented itself he slipped out of the mosque.

In a mood of intense bitterness, scorn for himself, hatred of those who had decided to become his brother's keepers, infinite hatred for Karim, Hassen went home. Salima sensed her husband's mood and did not say a word to him.

In his room he debated with himself. In what way should he conduct himself so that his dignity remained intact? How was he to face the congregation, the people in the streets, his neighbours? Everyone would soon know of Karim and smile at him half-sadly, half-ironically, for having placed himself in such a ridiculous position. Should he now forgive the dying man and transfer him to his home? People would laugh at him, snigger at his cowardice, and Mr Mia perhaps even deny him the privilege; Karim was now his responsibility. And what would Catherine think of him? Should he go away somewhere (on the pretext of a holiday) to Cape Town, to Durban? Besides the stigma of being called a renegade, Karim might take months to die, he might not die at all.

'O Karim, why did you have to do this to me?' he said, moving towards the window and drumming at the pane nervously. It galled him that a weak, dying man could bring such pain to him. An adversary could be faced, one could either vanquish him or be vanquished, with one's dignity unravished, but with Karim what could he do?

The hours passed by. He paced his room. He looked at his watch; the time for afternoon prayers was fast approaching. Should he expose himself to the congregation? 'O Karim! Karim!' he cried, holding on to the burglar-proof bar of his bedroom window. Was it for this that he had made the pilgrimage – to cleanse his soul in order to return into the penumbra of sin? If only Karim would die he would be relieved of his agony. But what if he lingered on? What if he recovered? Were not prayers being said for him? He went to the door and shouted in a raucous voice: 'Salima!'

But Salima was not in the house. He shouted again and again, and his voice echoed hollowly in the rooms. He rushed into the lounge, into the kitchen, he flung the door open and looked into the yard.

Several hours passed. He drew the curtains and lay on his bed in the dark. Then he heard the patter of feet in the house. He jumped up and shouted for his wife. She came hurriedly.

'Salima, Salima, go to Karim, he is in a room in the mosque yard. See how he is, see if he is getting better. Quickly!'

Salima went out. But instead of going to the mosque, she entered her neighbour's house. She had already spent several hours sitting beside Karim. Mr Mia had been there as well as Catherine. She had wept.

After a while she returned from her neighbour. When she opened the door her husband ran to her. 'How is he? Is he very ill? Tell me quickly?'

'He is very ill. Why don't you go and see him?'

Suddenly, involuntarily, Hassen struck his wife in the face.

'Tell me, is he dead? Is he dead?' he screamed.

Salima cowered in fear. She had never seen her husband in this raging temper. What had taken possession of the man? She retired quickly to the kitchen. Hassen locked himself in the bedroom.

During the evening he heard voices. Salima came to tell him that several people, led by Mr Mia, wanted to speak to him urgently. His first impulse was to tell them to leave immediately; he was not prepared to meet them. But he had been wrestling with himself for so many hours that he welcomed a moment when he could be in the company of others. He stepped boldly into the lounge.

'Hajji Hassen,' Mr Mia began, 'please listen to us. Your brother has not long to live. The doctor has seen him. He may not outlive the night.'

'I can do nothing about that,' Hassen replied, in an audacious, matter-of-fact tone that surprised him and shocked the group of people.

'That is in Allah's hand,' said the merchant Gardee. 'In our hands lie forgiveness and love. Come with us now and see him for the last time.'

'I cannot see him.'

'And what will it cost you?' asked the priest who wore a long black cloak that fell about his sandalled feet.

'It will cost me my dignity and my manhood.'

'My dear Hajji, what dignity and what manhood? What can you lose by speaking a few kind words to him on his deathbed? He was only a young man when he left.'

'I will do anything, but going to Karim is impossible.'

'But Allah is pleased by forgiveness,' said the merchant.

'I am sorry, but in my case the circumstances are different. I am indifferent to him and therefore there is no necessity for me to forgive him.'

'Hajji,' said Mr Mia, 'you are only indulging in glib talk and you know it. Karim is your responsibility, whatever his crime.'

'Gentlemen, please leave me alone.'

And they left. Hassen locked himself in his bedroom and began to pace the narrow space between bed, cupboard and wall. Suddenly, uncontrollably, a surge of grief for his dying brother welled up within him.

'Brother, brother!' he cried, kneeling on the carpet beside his bed and smothering his face in the quilt. His memory unfolded a time when Karim had been ill at the Islamic Institute and he had cared for him and nursed him back to health. How much he had loved the handsome youth!

At about four in the morning he heard an urgent rapping. He left his room to open the front door.

'Brother Karim dead,' said Mustapha, the Somali muezzin of the mosque, and he cupped his hands and said a prayer in Arabic. He wore a black cloak and a white skull-cap. When he had done he turned and walked away.

Hassen closed the door and went out into the street. For a moment his release into the street gave him a feeling of sinister jubilation, and he laughed hysterically as he turned the corner and stood next to Jamal's fruit-shop. Then he walked on. He wanted to get away as far as he could from Mr Mia and the priest who would be calling upon him to prepare for the funeral. That was no business of his. They had brought Karim to Newtown and they should see to him.

He went up Lovers' Walk and at the entrance of Orient House he saw the nightwatchman sitting beside a brazier. He hastened up to him, warmed his hands by the fire, but he did this more as a gesture of fraternisation as it was not cold, and he said a few words facetiously. Then he walked on.

His morbid joy was ephemeral, for the problem of facing the congregation at the mosque began to trouble him. What opinion would they have of him when he returned? Would they not say: He hated his brother so much that he forsook his prayers, but now that his brother is no longer alive he returns. What a man! What a Muslim!

When he reached Vinod's Photographic Studio he pressed his forehead against the neon-lit glass showcase and began to weep.

A car passed by filling the air with nauseous gas. He wiped his eyes, and looked for a moment at the photographs in the showcase; the relaxed, happy, anonymous faces stared at him, faces whose momentary expressions were trapped in celluloid. Then he walked on. He passed a few shops and then reached Broadway Cinema where he stopped to look at the lurid posters. There were heroes, lusty, intrepid, blasting it out with guns; women in various stages of undress; horrid monsters from another planet plundering a city; Dracula.

Then he was among the quiet houses and an avenue of trees rustled softly. He stopped under a tree and leaned against the trunk. He envied the slumbering people in the houses around him, their freedom from the emotions that jarred him. He would not return home until the funeral of his brother was over.

When he reached the Main Reef Road the east was brightening up. The lights along the road seemed to him to be part of the general haze. The buildings on either side of him were beginning to thin and on his left he saw the ghostly mountains of mine sand. Dawn broke over the city and when he looked back he saw the silhouettes of tall buildings bruising the sky. Cars and trucks were now rushing past him.

He walked for several miles and then branched off onto a gravel road and continued for a mile. When he reached a clump of bluegum trees he sat down on a rock in the shade of the trees. From where he sat he could see a constant stream of traffic flowing along the highway. He had a stick in his hand which he had picked up along the road, and with it he prodded a crevice in the rock. The action, subtly, touched a chord in his memory and he was sitting on a rock with Karim beside him. The rock was near a river that flowed a mile away from the Islamic Institute. It was a Sunday. He had a stick in his hand and he prodded at a crevice and the weather-worn rock flaked off and Karim was gathering the flakes.

'Karim! Karim!' he cried, prostrating himself on the rock, pushing his fingers into the hard roughness, unable to bear the death of that beautiful youth.

He jumped off the rock and began to run. He would return to Karim. A fervent longing to embrace his brother came over him, to touch that dear form before the soil claimed him. He ran until he was tired, then walked at a rapid pace. His whole existence precipitated itself into one motive, one desire, to embrace his brother in a final act of love.

He reached the highway and walked as fast as he could, his heart beating wildly, his hair dishevelled. He longed to ask for a lift from a passing motorist but could not find the courage to look back and signal. Cars flashed past him, trucks roared in pain.

When he reached the outskirts of Johannesburg it was nearing ten o'clock. He hurried along, now and then breaking into a run. Once he tripped over a cable and fell. He tore his trousers in the fall and found his hands were bleeding. But he was hardly conscious of himself, wrapped up in his one purpose.

He reached Lovers' Walk, cars growling at him angrily; he passed Broadway Cinema, rushed towards Orient House, turned the corner at Jamal's fruit-shop. And stopped.

The green hearse, with the crescent moon and stars emblem, passed by; then several cars with mourners followed, bearded men, men with white skull-caps on their heads, looking rigidly ahead like a procession of puppets, indifferent to his fate. No one saw him.

AHMED ESSOP

Hajji Musa and the Hindu Fire-walker

From: *The Hajji and other Stories* (1978)

'Allah has sent me to you, Bibi Fatima.'

'Allah, Hajji Musa?'

'I assure you, Allah, my good lady. Listen to me carefully. There is something wrong with you. Either you have a sickness or there is an evil spell cast over your home. Can you claim that there is nothing wrong in your home, that your family is perfectly healthy and happy?'

'Well, Hajji Musa, you know my little Amir has a nasty cough that even Dr Kamal cannot cure and Soraya seems to have lost her appetite.'

'My good woman, you believe me now when I say Allah has sent me to you?'

Bibi Fatima's husband, Jogee, entered the room. Hajji Musa took no notice of him and began to recite (in Arabic) an extract from the Qur'an. When he had done he shook hands with Jogee.

'Listen to me, Bibi Fatima and brother Jogee. Sickness is not part of our nature, neither is it the work of our good Allah. It is the work of that great evildoer Iblis, some people call him Satan. Well, I, by the grace of Allah' (he recited another extract from the Qur'an) 'have been given the power to heal the sick and destroy evil. That is my work in life, even if I get no reward.'

'But Hajji Musa, you must live.'

'Bibi Fatima, Allah looks after me and my family. Now bring me two glasses of water and a candle.'

She hurried to the kitchen and brought the articles.

'Now bring me the children.'

'Jogee, please go and find Amir in the yard while I look for Soraya.'

Husband and wife went out. Meanwhile Hajji Musa drew the curtains in the room, lit the candle and placed the two glasses of water on either side of the candle. He took incense out of his pocket, put it in an ashtray and lit it.

When husband and wife returned with the children they were awed. There was an atmosphere of strangeness, of mystery, in the room. Hajji Musa looked solemn. He took the candle, held it about face level and said: 'Look, there is a halo around the flame.'

They looked and saw a faint halo.

He placed the candle on the table, took the glasses of water, held them above the flame and recited a verse from the Qur'an. When he had done he gave one glass to the boy and one to the girl.

'Drink, my children,' he said. They hesitated for a moment, but Bibi Fatima commanded them to drink the water.

'They will be well,' he said authoritatively. 'They can now go and play.' He extinguished the candle, drew the curtains, and sat down on the settee. And he laughed, a full-throated, uproarious, felicitous laugh.

'Don't worry about the children. Allah has performed miracles on what are coughs and loss of appetites.' And he laughed again.

Bibi Fatima went to the kitchen to make tea and Jogee and I kept him company. She returned shortly with tea and cake.

'Jogee,' she said, 'I think Hajji Musa is greater than Dr Kamal. You remember last year Dr Kamal gave me medicines and ointments for my aching back and nothing came of it?'

'Hajji Musa is not an ordinary doctor.'

'What are doctors of today,' Hajji Musa said, biting into a large slice of cake, 'but chancers and frauds? What knowledge have they of religion and the spiritual mysteries?'

'Since when have you this power to heal, Hajji Musa?'

'Who can tell the ways of Allah, Bibi Fatima. Sometimes his gifts are given when we are born and sometimes when we are much older.'

'More tea?'

She filled the cup. He took another slice of cake.

'Last month I went to Durban and there was this woman, Jasuben, whom the doctors had declared insane. Even her own yogis and swamis had given her up. I took this woman in hand and today she is as sane as anyone else.'

'Hajji Musa, you know my back still gives me trouble. Dr Kamal's medicine gave me no relief. I have even stopped making roti and Jogee is very fond of roti.'

'You should let me examine your back some day,' the healer said, finishing his tea.

'Why not now?'

'Not today,' he answered protestingly. 'I have some business to attend to.'

'But Hajji Musa, it will only take a minute or two.'

'Well that's true, that's true.'

'Will you need the candle and water?'

'Yes.'

She hurriedly went to refill the glass with water.

'Please, Jogee and Ahmed, go into the kitchen for a while,' she said, returning.

We left the room, Jogee rather reluctantly. She shut the door. I sat down on a chair and looked at a magazine lying on the table. Jogee told me he was going to buy cigarettes and left. He was feeling nervous.

I was sitting close to the door and could hear Hajji Musa's voice and the rustle of clothing as he went on with the examination.

'I think it best if you lie down on the settee so that I can make a thorough examination ... Yes, that is better ... Is the pain here ... ? Bibi Fatima, you know the pain often has its origin lower down in the lumbar region. Could you ease your ijar a little ... ? The seat of the pain is often here ... Don't be afraid.'

'I can feel it getting better already, Hajji Musa.'

'That is good. You are responding very well.'

There was a silence for some time. When Jogee returned Hajji Musa was reciting a prayer in Arabic. Jogee puffed at his cigarette. When Bibi Fatima opened the door she was smiling and looked flushed.

'Your wife will be well in a few days,' Hajji Musa assured the anxious man. 'And you will be having your daily roti again. Now I must go.'

'Hajji Musa, but we must give you something for your trouble.'

'No nothing, Bibi Fatima. I forbid you.'

She was insistent. She told Jogee in pantomime (she showed him five fingers) how much money he should give. Jogee produced the money from his pocket, though inwardly protesting at his wife's willingness to pay a man who asked no fees. Bibi Fatima put the money into Hajji Musa's pocket.

* * *

In appearance Hajji Musa was a fat, pot-bellied, short, dark man, with glossy black wavy hair combed backwards with fastidious care. His face was always clean-shaven. For some reason he never shaved in the bathroom, and every morning one saw him in the yard, in vest and pyjama trousers, arranging (rather precariously) his mirror and shaving equipment on the window sill outside the kitchen and going through the ritual of cleaning his face with the precision of a surgeon. His great passion was talking and while shaving he would be conducting conversations with various people in the yard: with the hawker packing his fruit and vegetables in the cart; with the two wives of the motor mechanic Soni; with the servants coming to work.

Hajji Musa was a well-known man. At various times he had been a commercial traveller, insurance salesman, taxi driver, companion to dignitaries from India and Pakistan, Islamic missionary, teacher at a seminary, shopkeeper, matchmaker and hawker of ladies' underwear.

His career as a go-between in marriage transactions was a brief, inglorious one that almost ended his life. One night there was fierce knocking at his door. As soon as he opened it an angry voice exploded: 'You liar! You come and tell me of dat good-for-nutting Dendar boy, dat he good, dat he ejucated,

608

dat he good prospect. My foot and boot he ejucated. He sleep most time wit bitches, he drink and beat my daughter. When you go Haj? You nutting but liar. You baster! You baster!' And suddenly two shots from a gun rang out in quick succession. The whole incident took place so quickly that no one had any time to look at the man as he ran through the yard and escaped. When people reached Hajji Musa's door they found him prostrate, breathing hard and wondering why he was still alive (the bullets had passed between his legs). His wife and eight children were in a state of shock. They were revived with sugared water.

Hajji Musa's life never followed an even course: on some days one saw him riding importantly in the chauffeur-driven Mercedes of some wealthy merchant in need of his services; on others, one saw him in the yard, pacing meditatively from one end to the other, reciting verses from the Qur'an. Sometimes he would visit a friend, tell an amusing anecdote, laugh, and suddenly ask: 'Can you give me a few rands till tomorrow?' The friend would give him the money without expecting anything of tomorrow, for it was well known that Hajji Musa, liberal with his own money, never bothered to return anyone else's.

Hajji Musa considered himself a specialist in the exorcism of evil jinn. He deprecated modern terms such as neurosis, schizophrenia, psychosis. 'What do doctors know about the power of satanic jinn? Only God can save people who are no longer themselves. I have proved this time and again. You don't believe me? Then come on Sunday night to my house and you will see.'

On Sunday night we were clustered around Hajji Musa in the yard. As his patient had not yet arrived, he regaled us with her history.

'She is sixteen. She is the daughter of Mia Mohammed the Market Street merchant. She married her cousin a few years ago. But things went wrong. Her mother-in-law disliked her. For months she has been carted from doctor to doctor, and from one psychiatrist to another, those fools. Tonight you will see me bring about a permanent cure.'

After a while a car drove into the yard, followed by two others. Several men – two of them tall, bearded brothers – emerged from the car, approached Hajji Musa and shook hands with him. They pointed to the second car.

'She is in that car, Hajji Musa.'

'Good, bring her into the house.' And he went inside.

There were several women in the second car. All alighted but one, who refused to come out. She shook her face and hands and cried, 'No! No! Don't take me in there, please! By Allah, I am a good girl.'

The two brothers and several women stood beside the opened doors of the car and coaxed the young lady to come out.

'Sister, come, we are only visiting.'

'No, no, they are going to hit me.'

'No one is going to hit you,' one of the women said, getting into the car and sitting beside her. 'They only want to see you.'

'They can see me in the car. I am so pretty.'

Everyone living in the yard was present to witness the spectacle, and several children had clambered onto the bonnet of the car and were shouting: 'There she is! There she is! She is mad! She is mad!'

'Come now, Jamilla, come. The people are laughing at you,' one of the brothers said sternly.

Hajji Musa now appeared wearing a black cloak emblazoned with sequin-studded crescent moons and stars, and inscribed with Cufic writing in white silk. His sandals were red and his trousers white. His turban was of green satin and it had a large round ruby (artificial) pinned to it above his forehead.

He proceeded towards the car, looked at Jamilla, and then said to the bearded brothers, 'I will take care of her.' He put his head into the interior of the car. Jamilla recoiled in terror. The lady next to her held her and said, 'Don't be frightened. Hajji Musa intends no harm.'

'Listen, sister, come into the house. I have been expecting you.'

'No! No! I want to go home.' Jamilla began to cry.

'I won't let anyone hurt you.'

Hajji Musa tried to grab her hand, but she pushed herself backwards against the woman next to her and screamed so loudly that for a moment the healer seemed to lose his nerve. He turned to the brothers. 'The evil jinn is in her. Whatever I do now, please forgive me.'

He put his foot into the interior of the car, gripped one arm of the terrified Jamilla and smacked her twice with vehemence.

'Come out, jinn! Come out, jinn!' he shouted and dragged her towards the door of the car. The woman beside Jamilla pushed her and punched her on the back.

'Please help,' Hajji Musa said, and the two brothers pulled the screaming Jamilla out of the car.

'Drive the jinn into the house!' And they punched and pushed Jamilla towards the house. She pleaded with several spectators for help and then in desperation clung to them. But they shook her off and one or two even took the liberty of punching her and pulling her hair.

Jamilla was pushed into the house and the door closed on her and several of the privileged who were permitted to witness the exorcism ceremony. As soon as she passed through a narrow passage and entered a room she quietened.

The room was brilliantly lit and a fire was burning in the grate. A red carpet stretched from wall to wall and on the window sill incense was burning in brass bowls. In front of the grate were two brass plates containing sun-dried red chillies.

We removed our shoes and sat down on the carpet. Jamilla was made to sit in front of the grate. She was awed and looked about at the room and the people. Several women seated themselves near her. Hajji Musa then began to recite the chapter 'The Jinn' from the Qur'an. We sat with bowed heads. When he had done he moved towards the grate. His wife came into the room with a steel tray and a pair of tongs. Hajji Musa took some burning pieces of coal and heaped them on the tray. Then he scattered the red chillies over the coals. Smoke rose from the tray and filled the room with an acrid, suffocating smell. He seated himself beside Jamilla and asked the two brothers to sit near her as well. He pressed Jamilla's head over the tray and at the same time recited a verse from the Qur'an in a loud voice. Jamilla choked, seemed to scream mutely and tried to lift her head, but Hajji Musa held her.

As the smell of burning chillies was unbearable, some of us went outside for a breath of fresh air. Aziz Khan said to us: 'That primitive ape is prostituting our religion with his hocus-pocus. He should be arrested for assault.'

We heard Jamilla screaming and we returned quickly to the room. We saw Hajji Musa and the two brothers beating her with their sandals and holding her face over the coals.

'Out Iblis! Out Jinn!' Hajji Musa shouted and belaboured her.

At last Jamilla fell into a swoon.

'Hold her, Ismail and Hafiz.' Hajji Musa sprinkled her face with water and read a prayer. Then he asked the two brothers to pick her up and take her into an adjoining room. They laid her on a bed.

'When she wakes up the jinn will be gone,' Hajji Musa predicted confidently.

We went outside for a while. Aziz Khan asked a few of us to go with him in his car to the police station. But on the way he surprised us by changing his mind.

'It's not our business,' he said, and drove back to the yard.

When we returned Jamilla had opened her eyes and was sobbing quietly.

'Anyone can ask Jamilla if she remembers what happened to her.'

Someone asked her and she shook her head.

'See,' said the victorious man, 'it was the evil jinn that was thrashed out of her body. He is gone!'

★ ★ ★

There had been the singing of hymns, chanting and the jingling of bells since the late afternoon, and as evening approached there was great excitement in the yard. Everyone knew of the great event that was to take place that evening: the Hindu fire-walker was going to give a demonstration.

'There is nothing wonderful about walking on fire,' Hajji Musa declared in a scornful tone. 'The Hindus think they are performing miracles. Bah! Miracles!' And he exploded in laughter. 'What miracles can their many gods perform, I ask you? Let them extract a jinn or heal the sick and then talk of miracles.'

'But can you walk on fire or only cook on fire?' Dolly asked sardonically. There was laughter and merriment.

'Both, my dear man, both. Anyone who cooks on fire can walk on fire.'

'If anyone can, let him try,' said the law student Soma. 'In law, words are not enough; evidence has to be produced.'

'Funny, you lawyers never get done with words. After gossiping for days you ask for a postponement.'

Everyone laughed boisterously.

'Hajji Musa,' Dolly tried again, 'can you walk on fire?'

'Are you joking, Dolly? When I can remove a jinn, what is walking on fire? Have you seen a jinn?'

'No.'

'See one and then talk. Evil jinn live in hell. What is walking on fire to holding one of hell's masters in your hands?'

'I say let him walk on fire and then talk of jinn,' said Raffia, the dwarfish Hindu watchmaker, but he walked away fearing to confront Hajji Musa.

'That stupid Hindu thinks I waste my time in performing tricks. I am not a magician.'

A fire was now lit in the yard. Wood had been scattered over an area of about twenty feet by six feet. An attendant was shovelling coal and another using the rake to spread it evenly.

Meanwhile, in a room in the yard, the voices of the chanters were rising and the bells were beginning to jingle madly. Every now and then a deeper, more resonant chime would ring out, and a voice would lead the chanters to a higher pitch. In the midst of the chanters, facing a small altar on which were placed a tiny earthenware bowl containing a burning wick, a picture of the god Shiva surrounded by votive offerings of marigold flowers, rice and coconut, sat the fire-walker in a cross-legged posture.

The yard was crowded. Chairs were provided but these were soon occupied. The balconies were packed and several agile children climbed onto rooftops and seated themselves on the creaking zinc. A few dignitaries were also present.

The chanters emerged from the doorway. In their midst was the fire-walker, his eyes focused on the ground. He was like a man eroded of his own will, captured by the hand of chanters. They walked towards the fire which was now glowing flames leaping here and there.

The chanters grouped themselves near the fire and went on with their singing and bell-ringing, shouting refrains energetically. Then, as though life had suddenly flowed into him, the fire-walker detached himself from the group and went towards the fire. It was a tense moment. The chanters were gripped by frenzy. The coal-bed glowed. He placed his right foot on the fire gently, tentatively, as though measuring its intensity, and then walked swiftly over from end to end. He was applauded. Two boys now offered him coconuts in trays. He selected two, and then walked over the inferno again, rather slowly this time, and as he walked he banged the coconuts against his head several times until they cracked and one saw the snowy insides. His movement now became more like a dance than a walk, as though his feet gloried in their triumph over the fire. The boys offered him more coconuts and he went on breaking them against his head.

While the fire-walker was demonstrating his salamander-like powers, an argument developed between Aziz Khan and Hajji Musa.

'He is not walking over the fire,' Hajji Musa said. 'Our eyes are being deceived.'

'Maybe your eyes are being deceived, but not mine,' Aziz answered.

'If you know anything about yogis then you will know how they can pass off the unreal for the real.'

'What do you mean by saying if I know anything about yogis?'

'He thinks he knows about everything under the sun,' Hajji Musa said jeeringly to a friend. He turned to Aziz.

'Have you been to India to see the fakirs and yogis?'

'No, and I don't intend to.'

'Well, I have been to India and know more than you do.'

'I have not been to India, but what I do know is that you are a fraud.'

'Fraud! Huh!'

'Charlatan! Humbug!'

'I say, Aziz!' With a swift movement Hajji Musa clutched Aziz Khan's wrist. 'You are just a big-talker and one day I shall shut your mouth for you.'

'Fraud! Crook! You are a disgrace to Islam. You with your chillies and jinn!'

'Sister …!' This remark Hajji Musa uttered in Gujarati.

'Why don't you walk over the fire? It's an unreal fire.' And Aziz laughed sardonically.

'Yes, let him walk,' said the watchmaker. 'Hajji Musa big-talker.'

'The fire is not as hot as any of your jinn, Hajji Musa,' Dolly said slyly, with an ironic chuckle.

'Dolly, anyone can walk on fire if he knows the trick.'

'I suppose you know,' Aziz said tauntingly.

'Of course I do.'

'Then why don't you walk over the fire?'

'Jinn are hotter!' Dolly exclaimed.

'Fraud! Hypocrite! Degraded infidel, you will never walk. I dare you!'

'I will show you, you fool. I will show you what I can do.'

'What can you show but your lying tongue, and beat up little girls!'

'You sister …! I will walk.'

While the argument had been raging, many people had gathered around them and ceased to look at the Hindu fire-walker. Now, when Hajji Musa accepted the challenge, he was applauded.

Hajji Musa removed his shoes and socks and rolled up his trousers. All eyes in the yard were now focused on him. Some shouted words of encouragement and others clapped their hands. Mr Darsot, though, tried to dissuade him.

'Hajji Musa, I don't think you should attempt walking on fire.'

But Dolly shouted in his raucous voice: 'Hajji Musa, show them what you are made of!'

Hajji Musa, determined and intrepid, went towards the fire. The Hindu fire-walker was now resting for a while, his body and clothes wet with sweat and juice from broken coconuts, and the chanters' voices were low. When Hajji Musa reached the fire he faltered. His body tensed with fear. Cautiously he lifted his right foot over the glowing mass. But any thought he might have had of retreat, of giving up Aziz Khan's challenge and declaring himself defeated, was dispelled by the applause he received.

Crying out in a voice that was an invocation to God to save him, he stepped on the inferno: 'Allah is great!'

★ ★ ★

What happened to Hajji Musa was spoken of long afterwards. Badly burnt, he was dragged out of the fire, drenched with water and smothered with rags, and taken to hospital.

We went to visit him. We expected to find a man humiliated, broken. We found him sitting up in bed, swathed in bandages, but as ebullient and resilient as always, with a bevy of young nurses eagerly attending to him.

'Boys, I must say fire-walking is not for me. Showmanship … that's for magicians and crowd-pleasers …those seeking cheap publicity.'

And he laughed in his usual way until the hospital corridors resounded.

CHRISTOPHER HOPE

The Fall of the British Empire

From: *Private Parts and other Stories* (1980)

Having been introduced to the boys by the headmaster, Mr Sessi stands silent
for a moment with a look both bright and pleasant on his face. He is the first
Sierra Leonian we have seen, certainly the first to whom we can put a name,
and we gaze back with interest. To the students slouched in their uncomfortable chairs, Mr Sessi is familiar only by the colour of his skin, the prevalence
of which, in all its shades, is deplored across the Midlands even if seldom seen
in such blackness, a special item of interest in Mr Sessi's case. So many people
have said to me: 'We used to have very good relations with the coloured
people but, of late, we've been feeling rather overwhelmed.' On such occasions,
I never know what to answer, so I nod and look away, which is often taken as
an expression of sympathy. Since I am known as a South African, I don't suppose it could be taken any other way.

To the boys who comprise his audience, Mr Sessi could not be more
remote in his origins, in the cast of his mind and the exoticism of his perspiration, had he come from the dark side of the moon. These boys are fourteen
years old, the Easter School-Leavers the staff call them; to the school they are
known as the dum-dums. Their clothes are carefully chosen to show that they
regard themselves as pretty tough, showing a lot of denim, carefully faded and
raggy in the right places, and heavy boots, studded at heel and toe. In the
matter of his foreignness, I have the advantage over them because Mr Sessi
comes from black Africa which is geographically close to South Africa, and
geography is my subject. That is to say, I'm paid to teach it. In actual fact, I
spend lesson times fending off diversionary questions about Zulu chiefs and
witchdoctors, but no matter.

Sierra Leone, named by the Portuguese (England's oldest ally), was firstly
famous for its slaves, and secondly for its role as a settlement for destitute
Negroes, native chiefs having ceded the peninsula to Britain in 1787 for this
purpose – features of his country which Mr Sessi is too obliging to mention.
Patently he is not a slave, although his great-grandfather may well have been.
Mr Sessi is from the Mende tribe, in the south of the country, and this tribe,
now that the Creole influence is finally broken for ever, is growing in prestige
and breeding fine administrators. Perhaps he will be one of them. You can be

615

sure that they think so at the University, and at the Embassy, which he mentions so happily, so often. No doubt the government of Sierra Leone think the money that they're paying out on Mr Sessi's education at Birmingham University, where he is probably reading sociology or social anthropology, well spent. In South Africa, Mr Sessi would be called a clever kaffir, and he would probably be doing much the same thing that he is doing in England; reading sociology or anthropology at one of the new tribal universities.

'I'm not going to talk to you for very long,' Mr Sessi explains kindly, 'and when I finish we will take a look at a film of my country, Sierra Leone, which I have had sent to the school from my embassy in London. I'd be glad if you would keep any questions that you may have until then.' He smiles charmingly. 'Your headmaster tells me that at these sessions, usually after the film show, you break up into groups to originate the questions you wish to put to me. I'm sure that some of them will be real stinkers! I only hope that I can oblige you with the answers when the time comes.'

His audience, though no less stony-eyed, leans forward, shoulders hunched; their sign that they are prepared to suspend judgement on Mr Sessi, in the face of such pleasantries. They have no hope that his lecture will interest them – but it just might be diverting.

Mr Sessi turns and traces the portable cinema screen that has been erected on a table at the head of the class, contemplating it with a cock of his head, this way and that, then he turns back to the waiting audience: 'Perhaps someone has a piece of chalk?' he asks diffidently, with an upward shift of the eyebrows, a flick of the head, including in his enquiry the boys and teachers who stand beside and behind them.

The Deputy Head, flustered by the request, hurries from the hall. He has no sooner disappeared through the big double doors in search of a box of chalk than a boy stands up in the first row and produces from his blazer pocket a piece of chalk which he offers to Mr Sessi who beams his thanks. A murmur, of approbation I think it is, rises from his classmates who doubtless approve of this brutally swift response; natural dramatists, they appreciate any device that safeguards the smooth development of the action. Although it is impossible, it seems that Mr Sessi has mistaken the cinema screen for a blackboard.

He stands gazing at it, chalk in hand. His back is turned for a few seconds only before he faces us again. His smile continues but he makes no secret of his perplexity. His chalk hand, the right, is thrown out behind him, gesturing, as it were, towards the white screen. The murmur grows louder amongst the rows of intent boys. I won't swear to this, but it seems as if Mr Sessi is about to lose his air of good-humoured, honest confusion, and become rather quizzical. He is certainly sensitive to the unmarked silvery white screen at his back and the silent boys before him. He scrutinises the piece of chalk he holds: 'Please,' he says rather diffidently, as if he were sparing us embarrassment, 'do you write on a white board with white chalk?'

The class groans and snuffles to itself. All this, their frantic wrigglings clearly say, is too much to be borne. 'We've gorra right 'un here, all right.' It's one thing for the stupid black bugger to take a cinema screen for a blackboard, but to go so far as to offer to write on it with a piece of chalk, in good faith, is simply too good to be true. The class casts around desperately, looking for the Head, wanting to gauge his reaction to their reaction to these extraordinary goings-on. It would be unreasonable for him, their contorted expressions say, to expect from them the usual decorum he demands during these lectures. It is enough to have to stop themselves from laughing out loud.

Fighting his face muscles into a disarming, apologetic, unembarrassed smile, but reddening to the roots of his hair, the Head shuffles his slack-kneed way down the aisle and lifts up the heavy linen flap of a large Phillips map of Africa, obviously an old one, still patched in Imperial pink, which is displayed beside the cinema screen, to reveal beneath it a portable blackboard pegged on a tripod. The Deputy Head returns and hands a fistful of chalk to Mr Sessi.

'In the University,' says Mr Sessi, graciously accepting the chalks and the discovery of an orthodox blackboard with an unwavering smile and not the slightest hint of irony, 'we usually write with coloured chalks on a white board.'

We are unprepared for the novelty of this suggestion and it gives us that faintly uncomfortable feeling we have when we catch someone out in a clumsy evasion and yet feel at the same time that to point it out to him would be more embarrassing still. So we flush, as the Head is doing, and look the other way. Yet it is a little tiresome to observe how blandly Mr Sessi ignores our scruples. I put this down to an iron nerve. God knows what the boys think of it. Probably that Mr Sessi is making a swift but silly effort to slip out of a tricky situation, choosing to make up this unlikely explanation rather than risk our scorn by admitting that he has never been face to face with a blackboard in his life. Who knows, perhaps he has never seen the inside of Birmingham University either. Certainly he has a very thick skin if he thinks he can brazen it out like this.

At the same time I can't help wondering whether any of the boys envy Mr Sessi his black face at this moment. Surely, in one or two minds, there is the thought that the guilty blush, which to their irritation they know may spread across a face with treacherous suddenness regardless of innocence, does not show on a black face. With sidelong glances I see them searching his face for the tell-tale flush. It is a waste of time, unless you know what you are looking for. Of course, black faces do blush, as any South African will tell you, and it is becoming plain to me that Mr Sessi doesn't share our embarrassment.

Some weeks later, when Mr Sessi's visit was barely remembered, I was to discover in a trade magazine an advertisement for a piece of classroom equipment described as a magnetic white marker board, the 'Twinlock Saxo Wyte Bord'. Writing and drawing are accomplished with coloured marker pens. The 'Wyte Bord' has an additional advantage; it can double as a cinema screen, so the advertisement claimed, and it is often used in the universities.

At the time of Mr Sessi's lecture on Sierra Leone, I will admit that I was more interested in Worcestershire than in Africa. I was living and working there, so it was the part of England most open to study. Some people associate Worcestershire with countryside, with the Vale of Evesham, with apple orchards, cherries and whatnot. As a geographer I find this curious. Worcestershire, the closer one gets to Birmingham, seems to be far more factory than farm to the visitor from a less industrially developed, emptier, larger country. An area of 716 square miles with a population of some 700 000, Worcestershire melds in the north into the indistinguishability of Birmingham's environs. Villages, dispossessed by characteristic housing estates of their surrounding countryside, seem to run one into another, village into suburb, into town, into city: unsettled places floating aimlessly around and about the blast furnaces of Birmingham. This displacing instils a feeling of edginess in the inhabitants, most now drawn from the farms into the manufacturing industries, or those industries that service the manufacturing industries.

This is Worcestershire for me, perhaps for Mr Sessi too. But for both of us, this is also Africa. Simply by being here, we affect the geography of the place, we Africanise it a little. Only for a moment perhaps, but that is as long as anything lasts. This has been proved to me, as it will be to Mr Sessi, and as painfully. We are strangers to this place, quickly recognised by the natives as fearsome Captain Cooks. Since we are apparently peaceful, and come bearing gifts of novelties and wonders, they are prepared to wait before deciding what to do with us. Yet they are wary nonetheless, and hostile, in a dull, taciturn way. Men may very well be islands, as the geographer suspects, as Captain Cook learnt to his dreadful cost. And where is this more likely to prove true than on this most insular of islands?

But Mr Sessi of the Mende tribe of Sierra Leone, now of Birmingham and the University, sooner than later to be of the Civil Service, earnest and willing ambassador to the English Secondary Schools, incipient administrator, smiles on the sons of men who brush shoulders with too many of his colour in a working day to bear it without protesting: 'I'm no racialist, mind, but there's too many of them coloureds around these parts now.'

He speaks plainly and very slowly, determined to be understood. Whether he does this from long experience in a hundred school halls built to the Department of Education's uniplan, I couldn't say. His bland, unreasonable composure offers no clue. The chances are that he has never faced an audience like this: boys of fourteen, who failed to get into grammar school and failed thereby to qualify for any jobs but those only slightly better than black immigrants take on nowadays.

Then again, perhaps I romanticise, and all he feels up there on the rostrum is uncertainty in his new role of lecturer, and in the faces of boys who have inherited sevenfold their fathers' frustrations and fears, he sees nothing but young white students eager for a glimpse of how the other half of the world lives; and perhaps, too, his smile is really benign and falls on each equally. It is not possible for a South African to know.

'Sierra Leone is not a very big country. Now, when I say big, I don't know what picture comes into your heads. Perhaps it will help to give you an idea of the size of Sierra Leone if I tell you that my country is not much more than half the size of England. Who knows the size of England?'

No one answers. It is unlikely that many of the class even hear the question. Resistant to language, they are still undergoing a process of adjustment to the strange presence of the speaker. It is not simply that Mr Sessi is so shiningly black and speaks a queer sort of English in a peculiar accent. No, the extraordinary thing about Mr Sessi is that he somehow manages to suggest that he is a person of some importance – to somebody. Despite his not very firm control of the language, he has an air of assurance. He doesn't speak with a Birmingham accent. It is unlikely that he comes from Bradford. He is in the country, the Head has reassured them in comforting tones before the lecture, to study. He is not an immigrant, then, and he does not speak like a coloured. They are puzzled.

Who can blame them? I know something of their incomprehension. In South Africa we would call Mr Sessi an educated kaffir. He speaks English like every blackface parody from Cape Town to Baton Rouge. He is Uncle Tom, Malcolm X and Shaka, King of the Zulus, rolled up into one. And yet – he is *real*.

'Sierra Leone, you might be interested to know, has an area of 27 925 square miles. But I think that I will leave you the problem of working out from that figure how big England is by comparison,' Mr Sessi says, and his smile does not falter. 'I'm sure that you will discover that my country is a small country, relatively, but then, with only two and a half million of us, we do not face the problem of over-population.'

I see the Head smiling sheepishly and he looks almost longingly at the speaker, trying to communicate his extreme sadness at the thoroughly unsuitable mode of address which Mr Sessi has chosen to adopt. To ask specific questions of these boys on any subject other than football is so novel that it might actually have succeeded in diverting the now increasingly restless class. But to expect answers from them looks like madness.

'Our climate is rather different to yours. I wonder if one of you can tell me what kind of climate you have here in Britain?'

The silence which follows this question pains me, as it will pain all geographers. More so one who has talked for weeks to these same boys in cunningly colloquial fashion, in no way resembling a geography lesson, of the vagaries of the English weather. It is specially galling to a South African to observe such ignorance in the face of black assurance, made worse because the boys are exchanging contemptuous and knowing smiles between themselves, confidently imputing the ignorance of procedure to Mr Sessi.

Yet he waits good-naturedly for an answer, and astonishingly, it comes:

'Rainy?' someone enquires tentatively.

I control an impulse to laugh. Luckily I succeed, because the boys do not laugh. In fact, from the anxious looks on their faces it appears that they are actually considering the answer, hoping that it will somehow do as a gesture of their good faith and Mr Sessi will now stop asking questions.

But Mr Sessi is unaffected. He simply replies, 'No, no – temperate, I would say.'

Merely by extracting an answer, Mr Sessi has scored, and it rankles. To prolong my chagrin, I go over in my mind all that I know of Sierra Leone, the last of the English monarchical possessions in Africa. It is no longer a country which holds significance for Britain and thus for the world at large. The industrious slavers who worked their monopolies so successfully are dead, gone and forgotten. When slaving was found to be no longer viable as an industry, those patriarchs, that is to say, their Imperial bookkeepers, allowed the trade to be written off and did not object when the Imperial abolitionists turned it to their credit. Sierra Leone, with its apt capital of Freetown, became the settling place of freed slaves from America, Europe and the surrounding colonies in Africa. They put their freedom to the test by cohabiting with the white settlers of Sierra Leone. The Creoles, born of this union, learned the craft of government from their British masters. When the British began to leave, it was the Creoles who took over the job of administering the indigenous tribes, from Freetown with its excellent harbour, once a Second-Class Imperial Coaling Station. Now the Creoles are in decline. It is Mr Sessi of the Mende tribe who is being groomed for the business of administration. For the tribes of Sierra Leone are a little fractious, and need proper government.

'You must understand that I come from what is known as a developing country, in the Third World. Please realise that as you in Britain have had your industrial revolution, we are just beginning now to have ours. We are learning to stand on our own two feet. And if Sierra Leone is to progress and to take her rightful place among the free nations, people in faraway countries must get out of their minds the notion that we are a small, uninteresting country offering no more than a good harbour and exportable crops of kernels, nuts and palm oil.'

Mr Sessi's longest speech: I find myself nodding in agreement or sympathy,

I'm not sure which. It is plain that Mr Sessi is sentimentally attached to his former colonial masters. He pays them the compliment of studying at one of their newer universities, aping their manners and dress, and continually comparing with just the right amount of patriotic pride and fervour his homeland with the Old Country. By the standards of diplomacy, he is inarticulate, but then he is young, and will soon improve out of all recognition. This lecture to this speechless class in a secondary modern school in semi-rural Worcestershire is good practice for a man who will one day have charge of an area the size of this county and who will have to deal there with tribes no less sullen, inarticulate and suspicious than the young men he now faces.

Does it occur to him, I ask myself, that the British have no one left to administer but themselves, nowhere left to direct their energies? Mr Sessi from post-Imperial black Africa stands lecturing this bored, uncomprehending audience of resentful, truculent and occasionally dangerous young men who chafe at school discipline – so like colonial paternalism – on the complexities of familial and tribal structures, and the difficulties of administering mutually antagonistic tribes in a huge country.

'In Sierra Leone we have only two seasons in the year. Can one of you tell me how many seasons you have here in Britain? You have four, right? Who knows what they are called? No one? Well, for a start there is spring – now, which are the others? Summer, that's right, well done, and …? Come on, now. What about autumn? Right! And the last one …'

Obviously the spell which Mr Sessi's performance before the cinema screen cast upon the audience has worn off. No one answers him. But he is undeterred.

'You see, where you in Britain have four seasons a year, we in Sierra Leone have only two – the rainy season and the dry season. Now, is there anyone here who knew that? Hands up!' He delivers the injunction like an actor in a gangster film.

Obviously the Head finds the breathy silence that follows this remark more than he can bear. He stands. 'It's very unlikely that we could accustom ourselves to the extreme climate which you experience in Sierra Leone. Luckily your people are bred to withstand it.'

I have the feeling that he means this as a compliment, and a salutary reflection for the boys to ponder on in case they feel too cocky about their own toughness. He considers strength of character to be the best of virtues.

Mr Sessi says nothing, but waits politely for the Head to finish talking. The Head continues: 'We don't always realise, enjoying as we do a temperate climate, what rigours of weather must be faced by people living in the wilder parts of the globe. How harsh the conditions must be for a white man unused to great heat, dust or tropical rainstorms. The very worst that we in Britain have to worry about is a cold winter.'

621

He has given up the meagre pretence of including Mr Sessi in his remarks and is now talking directly to the boys. He is talking with that tone of voice, cock of his head, hunch of his shoulders, very pose of a none too bright but nonetheless articulate, properly English, uncle, which he affects on occasions when his students are baffled by something outside their range of experience. He manages to soothe without subjecting them to the stress of having to digest new information, while at the same time appearing to be teaching them something. To those who know him, his demeanour also suggests a rebuke to the speaker for his handling of the lecture and manages to imply that by smoothing over the unsightly gulf yawning between Mr Sessi and his audience he has earned our gratitude. The effect of his intervention is to reassure the boys that all is well, despite this black man's strange behaviour; that England, in the guise of this northern corner of Worcestershire near Birmingham, still stands. Mr Sessi has only made a temporary incursion upon this stable place. Soon he will be gone and by tomorrow or the next day, the Head's tone promises them, they will have forgotten all about him. But in the meantime, it is surely not too much to ask that they put up with his strange manners. He will be quick to step in and iron out any misunderstandings, they can feel sure of that. Besides, his look says, we must know, just as he does, that the black man is not really odd, but only appears so to us.

The Head's demeanour leaves none of this unsaid. The class is calm again, for a while. While he speaks, we all, boys and teachers, gaze at the floor, sneaking glances at him. When he finishes, we can look Mr Sessi in the eye again. No one in the hall has listened to what he has said, except perhaps Mr Sessi, but the fact that he has spoken brings comfort.

I am uneasily aware how my identity as a white South African, were it known to Mr Sessi, will alter his conception of his audience. As it is, I felt uneasy when the Head talked of the difficulties white settlers have with lousy weather. Remarks like this often have the boys in assembly turning round to gawp at me. They do so whenever anything is mentioned which is associated in their minds with the other side of the world, however oblique the reference, whether to missionaries, David Livingstone, the Dark Continent, Zulu chiefs or witchdoctors. When their attention is too pointedly drawn to their own country, it has much the same effect. Goggling heads on craning necks stare at me as if my foreignness reassures them that universes other than their own really do exist, for I stand as living proof of them. Perhaps they are grateful for this because it means that they do not have to take on trust everything they see on television.

Mr Sessi shows no resentment at the Head's interruption. He seems anxious to get on with his lecture. But I notice that he has stopped smiling. I am beginning to feel something for Mr Sessi. His English is no more than makeshift, his assurance is irritating, his knowledge of the geography of his own country is limited. But in this depressing school hall, he is someone with whom I feel a kinship. I would like to reach out and touch him. However, he might not like that. Certainly such behaviour would be novel and unwelcome. I am the geography master. I might seem eccentric because I am from Africa and the boys confuse my foreignness with eccentricity, and in their un-plumbable ignorance are moved to play superstitious, rather giggly aborigines to my Captain Cook. My trinkets are welcome diversions in the monotony of their prison island. But if I dared to express my sense of closeness with Mr Sessi, I'd immediately be damned as a lunatic. I am expected to show myself in every important respect to be British. So too, of course, is Mr Sessi.

At times like this I am always grateful for my training which has taught me to stick to the facts. I am most at home with geographical facts. The Republic of South Africa lies at the southern tip of the African continent. It was once a refreshment station of the Dutch East India Company; later the gold mine of the British Empire. In an area some five times that of Great Britain there are 21 448 169 people of varying colours of skin – not only black and white, but the varying intermediate colours of Bushmen, Hottentots, Chinese, Japanese, Malays and Englishmen.

These are the facts. I verify them in my books. I am sure of them. I have many more at my fingertips.

Mr Sessi is still talking, but more incoherently now. If only his sense of geography were better and he knew where he was. He is explaining the role of the chief in the tribes of Sierra Leone, quite oblivious to the fact that he has lost his audience. He talks to us as equals; working on the assumption, no doubt encouraged at his university, and his embassy for that matter, that in academic matters at least skin colour plays no part. It's not going to help him with these boys. They are pragmatists. They admit only the evidence of their senses. They accept only those illusions that entertain them.

But the good-humoured interrogation does not stop, or even wind down. Mr Sessi is deaf to the widespread, almost frantic fidgeting of the boys and the soft shrieks of the rubber-tipped chair legs on the floorboards. But we hear it.

The Head intervenes again. He senses that the boys are on the point of mutiny. He is on his feet and talking before anyone is aware of it. We turn inter-estedly to see him newly risen from his chair, right foot flung forward giving the impression of leaning into a stride while standing still, his right hand raised with two fingers erect in a gesture recalling papal benediction, or absolution, his face pink and earnest beneath its cap of silver-grey hair.

'I think perhaps we could have the film now,' he is saying, 'and after that we will divide the class up into their groups for a question-and-answer session.'

Mr Sessi stops in mid-sentence as the Head's voice reaches him. 'Oh, yes …' he says, 'but of course, the film, of course.' He casts around desperately behind him, fluttering his eyelashes at the blackboard, then at the cinema screen.

'Would you care to sit here, perhaps?' The Head indicates a seat beside him. Mr Sessi makes his way down the aisle between the rows of boys, smiling and nodding from side to side. The Head signals to the boy operating the projector, and gives me a meaningful glance. I walk to the back of the hall and switch off the lights. A greenish twilight settles on the hall. Things darken to a blur.

The film is barely on the screen before we realise that it is not what we had hoped. However hard we may have longed for the kindness of darkness to allow us to relax into the pleasant distractions of faraway Sierra Leone, after the assaults of the indefatigable Mr Sessi, there is to be no rest for us in the flickering images on the screen. This is not what we expected: the public relations creation of colourful native life, the import of industrial plant and motor cars, the export of palm oil, nuts and kernels for which the country is famed, together with unusual views of derricks and cranes in Freetown harbour, and ships with recognisable Union Jacks on their funnels being loaded with the country's fruits by singing stevedores, and everywhere the smiling black faces of happy Sierra Leonians. Instead I am staring at the broad back of a white man sitting across a table from an earnest, bespectacled black man. Both are talking at once. It seems that we are being exposed to another interrogation. The sound track is muddy and very noisy. Yet it approximates to the sound of human voices in conversation, and instinctively I try to make out what is being said. The black man is doing most of the talking. His lips move rapidly, he shifts in his chair, giving the other's questions serious consideration before replying lengthily. The film is in black and white and the print is grainy. After five long minutes of this I am suddenly certain that the scene will not alter while the projector continues to run. The boys slump miserably in the darkness. Rubber chair legs begin their cries again. Blurred white faces turn to the back of the hall where the Head and Mr Sessi sit side by side in the darkness. I can see him conferring with Mr Sessi who is nodding a great deal. The Head whispers to the projectionist and the conversationalists fade from the screen. I walk to the back of the hall and switch on the light. Everyone blinks furiously, rubbing their eyes, hiding their embarrassment so painfully renewed. The Head is on his feet again, his head bobbing about the way a hen's does, vigilant for any sign of trouble. Mr Sessi remains seated. His head hangs low. The Head calls for silence.

'We're going to stop the film there. Hmm, yes, we have to end it, I'm afraid. Mr Sessi tells me that there appears to have been a misunderstanding. Got the film at the last moment, you see, and didn't have time to check it. Took it for granted, hmm, that the people at his embassy in London knew what they were doing. As you'll have noticed, seems somebody has slipped up. This was, hmm, a political film, dealing with the trade union movement in Sierra Leone and, er, its relationship with the International Labour Organisation. Not really your cup of tea, ha, as Mr Sessi himself was quick to point out. I'm sorry, of course, you'll have no glimpse of Sierra Leone after the valuable insights of Mr Sessi's lecture. But these things happen.'

Mr Sessi rises slowly to his feet. Giving the Head a little bow he walks up to the head of the class and takes up a position in front of the cinema screen, with his hands behind his back. Clearly he is unhappy. He has a hangdog look to him now. He clears his throat. He appears to be having trouble with his eyes, passing his hand across them – when he speaks, his voice is soft: 'In view of what has happened, for which I cannot apologise too much, I think you can dispense with your usual discussion groups. In the time remaining, I will simply invite questions from the floor.' There is no response. For a moment he stands silently, with his head drooping almost to his breast; then he straightens and it looks as if he has regained some of his old cheerfulness. At any rate, he faces all of us unflinchingly.

'All right,' he says, 'fire away.'

CHRISTOPHER HOPE

Learning to Fly

From: *Private Parts and other Stories* (1980)

Long ago, in the final days of the old regime, there lived a colonel who held an important job in the State Security Police and his name was Rocco du Preez. Colonel du Preez was in charge of the interrogation of political suspects and because of his effect on the prisoners of the old regime he became widely known in the country as 'Window jumpin' du Preez. After mentioning his name it was customary to add 'thank God', because he was a strong man and in the dying days of the old regime everyone agreed that we needed a strong man. Now Colonel du Preez acquired his rather strange nickname not because he did any window jumping himself but rather because he had been the first to draw attention to this phenomenon which affected so many of the prisoners who were brought before him.

The offices of State Security were situated on the thirteenth floor of a handsome and tall modern block in the centre of town. Their high windows looked down on to a little dead-end street far below. Once this street had been choked with traffic and bustling with thriving shops. Then one day the first jumper landed on the roof of a car parked in the street and after that it was shut to traffic and turned into a pedestrian shopping mall. The street was filled in and covered over with crazy paving and one or two benches set up for weary shoppers. However, the jumpings increased. There were sometimes one or two a week and several nasty accidents on the ground began to frighten off the shoppers.

Whenever a jump had taken place the little street was cordoned off to allow in the emergency services: the police, the undertaker's men, the municipal workers brought in to hose down the area of impact which was often surprisingly large. The jumpings were bad for business and the shopkeepers grew desperate. The authorities were sympathetic and erected covered walk-ways running the length of the street leaving only the central area of crazy pavings and the benches, on which no one had ever been known to sit, exposed to the heavens; the walk-ways protected by their overhead concrete parapets were guaranteed safe against any and all flying objects. But still trade dwindled as one by one the shops closed, and the street slowly died and came to be known by the locals, who gave it a wide berth, as the 'landing field'.

As everyone knows, window jumpings increased apace over the years and being well placed to study them probably led Colonel Rocco du Preez to his celebrated thesis afterwards included in the manual of psychology used by recruits at the Police College and known as Du Preez's Law. It states that all men who, brought to the brink, will contrive to find a way out if the least chance is afforded them and the choice of the means is always directly related to the racial characteristics of the individual in question. Some of Du Preez's remarks on the subject have come down to us, though these are almost certainly apocryphal, as are so many tales of the final days of the old regime. 'Considering your average white man,' Du Preez is supposed to have said, 'my experience is that he prefers hanging – whether by pyjama cord, belt, strips of blanket; providing he finds the handy protuberance, the cell bars, say, or up-ended bedstead, you'll barely have turned your back and he'll be up there swinging from the light cord or some other chosen noose. Your white man in his last throes has a wonderful sense of rhythm – believe me, whatever you may have heard to the contrary – I've seen several Whites about to cough it and all of them have been wonderful dancers. Your Indian, now, he's something else, a slippery customer who prefers smooth surfaces. I've known Asians to slip and crack their skulls in a shower cubicle so narrow you'd have sworn a man couldn't turn in it. This innate slitheriness is probably what makes them good businessmen. Now, your Coloured, per contra, is more clumsy a character altogether. His hidden talent lies in his amazing lack of co-ordination. Even the most sober rogue can appear hopelessly drunk to the untrained eye. On the surface of things it might seem that you can do nothing with him; he has no taste for the knotted strip of blanket or the convenient bootlace; a soapy bathroom floor leaves him unmoved – yet show him a short, steep flight of steps and he instinctively knows what to do. When it comes to Africans I have found that they, perverse as always, choose another way out. They are given to window jumping. This phenomenon has been very widespread in the past few years. Personally, I suspect its roots go back a long way, back to their superstitions – i.e. to their regard for black magic and witchcraft. Everyone knows that in extreme instances your average blackie will believe anything; that his witch-doctors will turn the white man's bullets to water; or, if he jumps out of a window thirteen stories above terra firma he will miraculously find himself able to fly. Nothing will stop him once his mind's made up. I've seen up to six Bantu jump from a high window on one day. Though the first landed on his head and the others saw the result they were not deterred. It's as if despite the evidence of their senses they believed that if only they could practise enough they would one day manage to take off.'

'Window jumpin' du Preez worked in an office sparsely furnished with an old desk, a chair, a strip of green, government-issue carpet, a very large steel cabinet marked 'Secret' and a bare, fluorescent light in the ceiling. Poor though the furnishings were, the room was made light and cheerful by the large windows behind his desk and nobody remembers being aware of the meanness of the furnishings when Colonel du Preez was present in the room. When he sat down in his leather swivel chair behind his desk, witnesses reported that he seemed to fill up the room, to make it habitable, even genial. His reddish hair and green eyes were somehow enough to colour the room and make it complete. The eyes had a peculiar, steady glint to them. This was his one peculiarity. When thinking hard about something he had the nervous habit of twirling a lock of the reddish hair, a copper colour with gingery lights, in the words of a witness, around a finger. It was his only nervous habit. Since these were often the last words ever spoken by very brave men, we have to wonder at their ability to register details so sharply under terrible conditions; it is these details that provide us with our only glimpse of the man, as no photographs have come down to us.

It was to this office that three plainclothes men one day brought a new prisoner. The charge-sheet was singularly bare: it read simply, 'Mphahlele ... Jake. Possession of explosives'. Obviously they had got very little out of him. The men left closing the door softly, almost reverently, behind them.

The prisoner wore an old black coat, ragged grey flannels and a black beret tilted at an angle which gave him an odd, jaunty, rather continental look, made all the more incongruous by the fact that his hands were manacled behind him. Du Preez reached up with his desk ruler and knocked off the beret revealing a bald head gleaming in the overhead fluorescent light. It would have been shaved and polished, Du Preez guessed, by one of the wandering barbers who traditionally gathered on Sundays down by the municipal lake, setting up three-legged stools and basins of water and hanging towels and leather strops for their cutthroat razors from the lower branches of a convenient tree and draping their customers in large red and white check clothes, giving them little hand mirrors so that they could look on while the barbers scraped, snipped, polished and gossiped away the sunny afternoon by the water's edge beneath the tall bluegums. Clearly Mphahlele belonged to the old school of whom there were fewer each year as the fashion for Afro-wigs and strange woollen bangs took increasing hold among younger Blacks. Du Preez couldn't help warming to this just a little. After all, he was one of the old school himself in the new age of trimmers and ameliorists. Mphahlele was tall, as tall as Du Preez and, he reckoned, about the same age – though it was always difficult to tell with Africans. A knife scar ran from his right eye down to his collar, the flesh fused in a livid welt as if a tiny mole had burrowed under the black skin pushing up a furrow behind it. His nose had been broken too, probably as the result of the same township fracas, and had mended badly turning to the left and then sharply to the right as if unable to make up its mind. The man was obviously a brawler. Mphahlele's dark brown eyes were remarkably calm – almost to the point of arrogance, Du Preez thought for an instant, before dismissing the absurd notion with a tiny smile. It shocked him to see an answering smile on the prisoner's lips. However he was too old a hand to let this show.

'Where are the explosives?'

'I have no explosives,' Mphahlele answered.

He spoke quietly but du Preez thought he detected a most unjustifiable calm amounting to confidence, or worse, to insolence, and he noted how he talked with special care. It was another insight. On his pad he wrote the letters MK. The prisoner's diction and accent betrayed him: Mission Kaffir. Raised at one of the stations by foolish clergy as though he was one day going to be a white man. Of course, the word 'kaffir' was not a word in official use any longer. Like other names at that time growing less acceptable as descriptions of Africans: 'native', 'coon' and even 'Bantu', the word had given way to softer names in an attempt to respond to the disaffection springing up among black people. But Du Preez, as he told himself, was too old a dog to learn new tricks. Besides, he was not interested in learning to be more 'responsive'. He did not belong to the ameliorists. His job was to control disaffection and where necessary to put it down with proper force. And anyway, his notes were strictly for his own reference, private reminders of his first impressions of a prisoner, useful when, and if, a second interview took place. The number of people he saw was growing daily and he could not expect to keep track of them all in his head.

Du Preez left his desk and slowly circled the prisoner. 'Your comrade who placed the bomb in the shopping centre was a bungler. There was great damage. Many people were killed. Women and children among them. But he wasn't quick enough, your friend. The blast caught him too. Before he died he gave us your name. The paraffin tests show you handled explosives recently. I want the location of the cache. I want the make-up of your cell with names and addresses as well as anything else you might want to tell me.'

'If the bomb did its business then the man was no bungler,' Mphahlele said.

'The murder of women and children – no bungle?'

Mphahlele shrugged. 'Casualties of war.'

Du Preez circled him and stopped beside his right ear. 'I don't call the death of children war. I call it barbarism.'

'Our children have been dying for years but we have never called it barbarism. Now we are learning. You and I know what we mean. I'm your prisoner of war. You will do whatever you can to get me to tell you things you want to know. Then you will get rid of me. But I will tell you nothing. So why don't you finish with me now? Save time.' His brown eyes rested briefly and calmly on Du Preez's empty chair, and then swept the room as if the man had said all he had to say and was now more interested in getting to know that notorious office.

A muscle in Du Preez's cheek rippled and it took him a moment longer than he would have liked to bring his face back to a decent composure. Then he crossed to the big steel cabinet and opened it. Inside was the terrible, tangled paraphernalia of persuasion, the electric generator, the leads and electrodes, the salt water for sharpening contact and the thick leather straps necessary for restraining the shocked and writhing victim. At the sight of this he scored a point; he thought he detected a momentary pause, a faltering in the steady brown eyes taking stock of his office, and he pressed home the advantage. 'It's very seldom that people fail to talk to me after this treatment.' He held up the electrodes. 'The pain is intense.'

In fact, as we know now, the apparatus in the cabinet was not that actually used on prisoners – indeed, one can see the same equipment on permanent exhibition in the National Museum of the Revolution. Du Preez, in fact, kept it for effect. The real thing was administered by a special team in a soundproof room on one of the lower floors. But the mere sight of the equipment, whose reputation was huge among the townships and shanty towns, was often enough to have the effect of loosening stubborn tongues. However, Mphahlele looked at the tangle of wires and straps as if he wanted to include them in his inventory of the room and his expression suggested not fear but rather – and this Du Preez found positively alarming – a hint of approval. There was nothing more to be said. He went back to his desk, pressed the buzzer and the plainclothes men came in and took Mphahlele downstairs.

Over the next twenty-four hours 'Window jumpin' du Preez puzzled over his new prisoner. It was a long time before he put his finger on some of the qualities distinguishing this man from others he'd worked with under similar circumstances. Clearly, Mphahlele was not frightened. But then other men had been brave too – for a while. It was not only bravery, one had to add to it the strange fact that this man quite clearly did not hate him. That was quite alarming: Mphahlele had treated him as if they were truly equals. There was an effrontery about this he found maddening and the more he thought about it, the more he raged inside. He walked over to the windows behind his desk and gazed down to the dead little square with its empty benches and its crazy paving which, with its haphazard joins where the stones were cemented one to the next into nonsensical, snaking patterns, looked from the height of the thirteenth story as if a giant had brought his foot down hard and the earth had shivered into a thousand pieces. He was getting angry. Worse, he was letting his anger cloud his judgement. Worse still, he didn't care.

Mphahlele was in a bad way when they brought him back to Du Preez. His face was so bruised that the old knife scar was barely visible, his lower lip was bleeding copiously and he swayed when the policemen let him go and might have fallen had he not grabbed the edge of the desk and hung there swaying. In answer to Du Preez's silent question the interrogators shook their heads. 'Nothing. He never said *nothing*.'

Mphahlele had travelled far in the regions of pain and it had changed him greatly. It might have been another man who clung to Du Preez's desk with his breath coming in rusty pants; his throat was choked with phlegm or blood he did not have the strength to cough away. He was bent and old and clearly on his last legs. One eye was puffed up in a great swelling shot with green and purple bruises, but the other, he noticed with a renewed spurt of anger, though it had trouble focusing, showed the same old haughty gleam when he spoke to the man.

'Have you any more to tell me about your war?'

Mphahlele gathered himself with great effort, his one good eye flickering wildly with the strain. He licked the blood off his lips and wiped it from his chin. 'We will win,' he said, 'soon.'

Du Preez dismissed the interrogators with a sharp nod and they left his presence by backing away to the door, full of awe at his control. When the door closed behind them he stood up and regarded the swaying figure with its flickering eye. 'You are like children,' he said bitterly, 'and there is nothing we can do for you.'

'Yes,' said Mphahlele, 'we are your children. We owe you everything.'

Du Preez stared at him. But there was not a trace of irony to be detected. The madman was quite plainly sincere in what he said and Du Preez found that insufferable. He moved to the windows and opened them. It was now that, so the stories go, he made his fateful remark. 'Well, if you won't talk, then I suppose you had better learn to fly.'

What happened next is not clear except in broad outline even today, the records of the old regime which were to have been made public have unaccountably been reclassified as secret, but we can make an informed guess. Legend then says that Du Preez recounted for his prisoner his 'theory of desperate solutions' and that, exhausted though he was, Mphahlele showed quickening interest in the way out chosen by white men – that is to say, dancing. We know this is true because Du Preez told the policemen waiting outside the door when he joined them in order to allow Mphahlele to do what he had to do. After waiting a full minute, Du Preez entered his office again closing the door behind him, alone, as had become customary in such cases, his colleagues respecting his need for a few moments of privacy before moving on to the next case. Seconds later these colleagues heard a most terrible cry. When they rushed into the room they found it was empty.

Now we are out on a limb. We have no more facts to go on. All is buried in obscurity or say, rather, it is buried with Du Preez who plunged from his window down to the landing field at the most horrible speed, landing on his head. Jake Mphahlele has never spoken of his escape from Colonel 'Window jumpin' du Preez. All we have are the stories. Some firmly believe to this day that it was done by a special magic and Mphahlele had actually learnt to fly and that the colonel on looking out of his window was so jealous at seeing a black man swooping in the heavens that he had plunged after him on the supposition, regarded as axiomatic in the days of the old regime, that anything a black man can do, a white man could do ten times better. Others, more sceptical, said that the prisoner had hidden himself in the steel cabinet with the torture equipment and emerged to push Du Preez to hell and then escaped in the confusion you will get in a hive if you kill the queen bee. All that is known for sure is that Du Preez lay on the landing field like wet clothes fallen from a washing line, terribly twisted and leaking everywhere. And that in the early days of the new regime Jake Mphahlele was appointed chief investigating officer in charge of the interrogation of suspects and that his work with political prisoners, especially white prisoners, was soon so widely respected that he won rapid promotion to the rank of colonel and became known throughout the country as Colonel Jake 'Dancin' Mphahlele, and after his name it was customary to add 'thank God', because he was a strong man and in the early days of the new regime everyone agreed we needed a strong man.

PJ HAASBROEK

Departure

Translated from the Afrikaans by Lynette Paterson
From: *Verby die vlakte* (1982)

The train was to depart at 22h00. You all arrived a little early with your families, your girls and a few friends, with your kitbags and rifles, and stood about
on the platform, self-conscious because the train was not there and the wind
was blowing so; uncomfortable in brown uniforms amidst the colourful, soft
people who have come to see you off. Fortunately you are all spruce again,
even those who have come out of the plastic bags. The authorities have at least
arranged that properly.

'This will take some getting used to,' you hear Petrus Bosman's father say.
'We had so many plans.' You glance in his direction, because you remember
what Petrus had said about his father's plans, and you see how his mother
clutches the man's arm in both her hands. 'I'm going to miss him so,' she says.
'I can tell what Christmas is going to be like without him. Everyone will
come for a swim and a braaivleis again. Carol-Anne will probably arrive early
to help with the salads. Now I won't even be able to send him a little something any more,' and she begins to sob. 'We'll just have to vasbyt,' says his
father.

You feel you could laugh. 'Vasbyt!' Easily said. Easy army talk. Like 'min
dae'. No, certainly not that. 'Vasbyt', yes but not 'min dae'. You keep a casual
eye on the other men, a little surprised at the civilised geniality, the playful
bravado at how different your companions are amongst their families. It is
clear that they want to caress their girls, that they are anxious to comfort and
to keep sentimentality at bay, but every now and then they glance at the signal in the distance which has been an unwavering green for the past quarter
of an hour.

Even though you are alone, you also wish that the train would come. The
station is a no-man's-land, a place one comes to only to depart for somewhere else. It was not designed or built for people who wish to be together,
but for separation. Domestic chats do not belong in these stark, rectangular,
open spaces. The dirty concrete and tar, red brick and steel are unfriendly,
intentionally unfriendly like the massive pillars and the cold gleam of the
tracks in the dark under the electric light. The station is open so that the
wind can blow in and snatch at people's clothing to separate them from each

other. You tap your pipe against the side of the platform and watch the coals spill out in the dark and die. Why can't departure be just as easy?

You pick up your bag when you see the train light, a sudden star growing, brightening and blinding as it approaches. The pitch-black locomotive passes you with a gnashing of steel wheels on steel. For a moment you see red fire and the white, curious face of the engine driver in his window, and then come the third-class passenger cars. The pale yellow light is like thin oil washing over the crowded commuters. 'Are they actually going to send the blacks with them?' a man behind you enquires angrily.

You all walk down the length of the train in search of your compartments. The last two carriages are yours. You throw your kitbags onto the luggage racks and hang your rifles on the clothes hooks. Many get off the train again, but others remain in the passage, leaning out through the window to say goodbye. You sit in the compartment and gaze through the window at the deserted, windy platform on your side of the train, relieved not to have any part in the farewell. The train jerks, and you hear the wails of the people and comforting words of the soldiers. The station glides slowly by.

They were only shunting. Your carriages now stand alongside another platform, number 6, without a locomotive. The devil alone knows where in the dark night it has been moved to with the blacks' cars in tow. Fortunately all the people left before you were returned here, and you all are alone; there is not even a railway worker in sight.

Slowly, cautiously, the men begin to question one another. How it had happened, where, on what day and at what time, and are surprised at the degree of similarity, often the exact concurrence, but you keep quiet. Your story is none of their business. Your honour is your own.

In their conversations they return to the border camps surrounded by trenches, and machine-gun installations protected by sandbags, to the sand-tracks reaching in endless straight lines to the flat horizons, and the bush where all memories have become indistinct like the haze in the afternoon sky. Whatever may have happened before is no longer relevant. Only that which caused you all to end up on this train. Nothing else.

You have taken the hidden bottles of alcohol from your bags and drink large mugs of brandy and coke, cane spirits, vodka and beer with great gulps straight from the bottles. Each one has a story to tell, each one knows a joke, and there is much boisterous laughter and comradely backslapping. No longer accustomed to the raw, strong spirits, you are all soon drunk.

Men fall about, cursing. Some pick quarrels and fist fights break out. Petrus laughingly holds a quarrelsome soldier by the wrists, but when he tries to butt Petrus with his head, Petrus flings him off. The soldier staggers into someone else, and begins to swipe wildly at the broad, dense face which confronts him.

His fists strike bone, eye socket, nose and chin, but the sweaty, shiny skin shows no damage; no bruising, no blood, the eyes expressionless, uncomprehending. The soldier abruptly stops his blows, turns and walks out of the compartment, his anger quenched.

You can hear the noise of fighting in the passage and the other compartments too, but you ignore the hubbub. That is just your way of keeping to yourself, and here it is each to his own. You sit with your head in your hands, as you always do, and feel your companions' shoulders against you, their breath warm as blood. Their hands grab at you when they stumble but you do not look up. Nor do you answer their questions, trying only to concentrate on the hissing and heaving of the train, the rocking, rolling and upward rearing. The loud, shrill voices recede to a soft continuous sigh.

It occurs to you that the authorities have left you here with a purpose. Were you meant to get drunk and start brawling before the journey could begin? Were you meant to confront each other with the meaninglessness of your short lives and your deaths, or are they allowing you first to reconcile yourselves to the journey? You stand up, suddenly suspicious, and put your head out of the window.

There is a man crossing the platform. He is carrying a zinc basin and is elderly; he looks about fifty to you, with his thin hair and his bent-over, plodding walk. Judging by his khaki trousers, open-neck shirt and dirty, crumpled jacket, you presume that he is a labourer. He has either been misdirected or he has misunderstood, but this cannot be the train he intends to catch. He pays no attention to the lists of passengers' names, slogs unsuspectingly by to the door at the end of the carriage, and climbs in.

You feel you should warn him.

'Oom,' you say, 'you're on the wrong train.'

He looks blankly at you and lowers his little bathtub onto the floor of the passage. 'No,' he says, 'I'm going with you.'

'This is a troop train,' you say, afraid of alarming him. 'You are not a soldier, Oom.'

'I do not mind with whom I travel,' he says. 'This is my last journey. Don't spoil everything now. Where can I find a seat?'

You wanted to tell him that the train is full, but then it occurred to you to play a trick on the old man. He would not know that this train does not stop anywhere. He would have to make the entire journey.

'Let's put the tub in the toilet,' you say. Maybe he'll still realise his mistake.

'No, I'd rather keep it with me,' he says.

The tub is bulging, covered with a towel and tied with a string. You carry it ahead of him to your compartment.

The others are surprised. 'Jesus, Oom,' says one, 'where do you think you're going?'

'At least I know where I come from,' the old man says and sits down next to Petrus. 'And that's enough for me.'

You nod at the soldier. 'The Oom knows,' you say.

Someone else asks about the bathtub, and the old man begins to undo the string. No one stops him. He removes the towel. In the tub is a framed wedding picture, a sheaf of papers, a toolbox and a few articles of children's clothing neatly folded. He unpacks the contents onto his lap so that he can dig deeper. He uncovers a worn blue overall and a white tie. He hesitates. 'They said I must bring this all with me,' he says. 'It must show who I am. It's easy. Apprentice, carpenter, married, had two little girls. And I was church warden in my day.' His hands fold lovingly around the bundle of possessions. 'My whole life,' he says.

'That's more than we've had,' says Petrus. 'I've not even had a job.' He takes the overall from the basin and holds it up to his chest as though to measure it for size, but you are no longer watching him.

Right at the bottom of the bathtub are two dolls. A pink rubber doll like the ones children play with in the bath, and a grinning black golliwog with white eyes and checkered pants. Suddenly you remember, you see them, and the blood roars in your ears like an approaching storm. You feel your guts contracting beneath your chest, a miserable nausea rises thickly in your throat, and your body begins to convulse as it did on that day. You vaguely hear someone say: 'Look what we have here. A terrorist!' and someone else adds: 'And sharing a bath with the white baby.'

You see them standing around you in their tattered bush wear, see them dragging you from the hut where you were hiding. You hear them laughing as they shove you with their rifle butts. You had no idea what they were planning to do. The sun pierced your eyes and you found yourself at the split-pole fence, at the high, sharpened corner stake, and you felt their hands. They lifted you. You screamed, but no sound came from between your clenched teeth.

You lift your rifle from the hook and fix the bayonet.

The old man looks in amazement at the golliwog. 'It's just a doll,' he says.

The blade impales it and you lift it high, higher than the old man's snatching hands. Right up to the light where it hangs like a flopping dead bird against the sun on the point of the bayonet.

The old man shakes his head. 'We are on the point of departure,' he says. 'And you have still not made your peace.'

Then you realise that the old man knows where you are headed. Your destination is also his.

The black locomotive barks abruptly a few times into the wide mouth of the dark, and your journey begins.

MARGUERITE POLAND

The Wood-ash Stars*

From: *The Wood-ash Stars* (1983)

Once, long ago, a small band of San (also called Bushman) hunters lived near a water hole far off in the desert wastes. There, each family built its fire and its low shelter of branches and grass.

Early in the day the men would prepare their delicate small arrows, poisoning the shafts, and go off hunting. While they were gone the women and young girls would take their digging-sticks, tie their karosses around them and walk out together to look for tsama melons, mongongo nuts, tsin beans, and all the other roots and fruits they gathered for their food.

When they returned in the afternoon to cook what they had gathered, the children and young girls would play games, using a hard round tsama melon as a ball. Then they would sing and stamp as they threw the melon to each other.

They could sing many different songs as they played: the song of the grey loerie bird that calls '*kuri mama, kuri mama*', and the song of the wasp and the slow puffadder. But Xama, who was young and whose hair was decorated with loops of ostrich-eggshell beads, would sing her own lament: that she, of all the young girls, wore an old and ragged kaross. What she wanted most was a kaross that was sleek and new, made of soft gemsbok skin. Her old one had holes in it through which the small, cold fingers of the wind crept. Wearing it, she felt as shaggy as a brown hyena.

As she sang she hoped that Gau was listening. If Gau could kill an eland or a gemsbok or a hartebeest with his small poisoned arrows, and make her a kaross, she would surely be the most contented girl in camp.

Gau heard her songs as she stood in the line with the others, tossing the tsama melon back and forth. And though it was the driest time of the year and the herds of buck were scattered so widely across the plains that they were hard to find, he gathered up his bow and arrows and his hunting-bag and went to his brothers and companions asking if they would go with him to hunt.

But this they refused to do, for the hottest winds of summer were blowing that day. The sky was grey with dust. Where, they asked, would Gau find a gemsbok in all that waste, when only the desert scorpions and lizards would be out? So Gau set off alone.

'Where is Gau?' asked the girls.

'Gau has gone to hunt a gemsbok to make a fine kaross for Xama.'

'Ah, ah, ah, ah, ah!' cried Xama, her hands fluttering to her face. 'At such a time!' She looked at the fierce midday sun, afraid of what she'd sung.

All day Gau hunted, finding nothing. Night came. The moon rose up above the hills. He stared at it, thinking that its face was round and light and shining as the face of Xama. Then he took his firesticks from his bag, made a small fire, and lay down to sleep.

The next day he travelled on and, at last, he found the prints of many hooves. A herd of gemsbok had passed that way some time before. He followed, trotting now – trotting as a jackal does, intent upon a trail.

At midday, when the sun is fiercest and highest in the sky, he found some gemsbok resting in the shade of thorn trees. Gau laid down his quiver and his bag, stuck a number of arrows in his belt and crept forward, moving slowly towards the herd.

The buck watched him, stamping their hooves every now and then. Closer and closer crept Gau. Then he drew back his bowstring, tight in the notch of the arrow, and fired. And though he knew his arrow had found its mark somewhere in the herd, the buck all turned and stampeded away through the bush.

Back at the encampment Xama waited.

'Xama, come and play the melon game with us,' cried the others.

She shook her head and sat to one side. A day passed. A night. Another day. Already the crickets were singing loudly in the shadows and still Gau had not returned. Xama wept for having sung the song of the old kaross that had sent Gau out into the desert all alone to hunt.

Out on the plains, the hunter Gau followed the tracks of the wounded gemsbok for many, many hours. Then he saw – far over the Aha hills – the vultures gathering in the sky. He set out, jogging fast, his arrows rattling in the quiver. When at last he saw the big buck lying dead in the sand, he squatted by it and stroked its smooth skin. He thought of Xama's joy and how she would clap her hands and sing a song of praise. Then he would bray the hide so Xama could fold it softly round her. And she would smile.

Gau could not carry the dead gemsbok away by himself and so he skinned it and cut the meat into strips. These he placed in the skin, which he tied to his carrying-stick. When the sun rose the next morning he set out for home.

But in the time that he'd been gone, the winds had blown up and down the plains smoothing away his tracks in the sand. Gau was young and he could not read the signs of the bush as well as the older hunters. So on he went uncertainly – this way, that way. But no matter which direction he took he saw no sign of his passing – no tree, no stone, no bush that was familiar. The sun came up. The sun went down. It rose again and Gau the hunter, whose thirst was as sharp as the sting of a scorpion in his throat, knew he was lost.

All day he walked. Then towards evening he found a small water hole. He drank and drank until he could drink no more. But when he picked up his carrying-stick with the gemsbok skin tied to it, and turned away, he knew that not very far behind, something followed silently. Something followed … followed on his tracks.

If he walked, so the bush behind him moved a little in his wake. If he stopped to listen, so he knew that something listened too, as if the wind had held its breath. Gau went faster, keeping just ahead of the footfalls in the sand. When night came there was no moon, but from the bush nearby a pair of eyes gleamed in the dark.

Hastily Gau hung his hunting-bag in a thicket, took his firesticks, dragged together twigs and grass and brush and made a flame. Suddenly, into the clearing stepped a huge hyena. It was bigger than any Gau had seen before. It put back its head and howled. Then it stood and watched Gau, whuffling to itself. It shuffled nearer, nose quivering to catch the scent of gemshok meat. Gau dragged the meat-filled skin closer and stretched out his hand for his bow and quiver. He would drive the hyena away with an arrow.

Then Gau saw, with alarm, that he had left his hunting-bag slung in a bush. He could see it hanging there – out of reach – at the other side of the fire. He shouted at the hyena. But it only stared at him and growled deep in its throat, backing off a little. And as it did, it caught the scent of Gau's hunting-bag. It jumped up on its hindlegs and pulled at the bag with its strong teeth.

It fell with a clatter. The hyena licked at the prints of Gau's meat-smeared fingers on the strap. It scratched at it with a paw and then looked once more towards the gemsbok skin over which Gau sat huddled. It approached, its long shadow creeping towards him in the firelight.

Xama sat outside her mother's shelter and listened to the calls of the night birds. No moon rose. The stars were dim. The wind was fierce and cold. Far off she heard – again and again – the whooping of a lone hyena. Somewhere in the darkness of the plains was Gau the hunter, who had gone to shoot a gemsbok so that he could make a soft, warm, grey kaross for her.

Gau poked the fire and made it blaze. He was afraid. Never had he seen a beast so bold and powerful and unafraid of man. He shifted round the fire, keeping it between the hyena and himself. His arms and legs ached with tiredness but he dared not close his eyes and sleep.

The embers of Xama's cooking-fire glowed softly, for it was late.

'It is the darkness,' she cried. 'There is no light for Gau to guide him home. Oh foolish Gau for going out alone! Oh foolish Xama for wishing for a fine kaross!'

In despair Xama plunged her hands among the coals of the fire. She flung the embers high – as high as she could reach. Again she thrust her fingers in the fire and tossed the fine red ash up into the night.

'Light the way for Gau the hunter!' she cried.

She held her small, burnt hands before her face and wept. The tears stung her eyes and slid painfully between her blistered fingers, cooling them. Then she stared in disbelief as the embers of the cooking-fire she'd thrown in her despair were driven forward by the wind. They glowed in the darkness, stretching out into the desert sky.

The hyena crept closer. Gau peered into the dark, looking for a tree into which he might climb with the gemsbok skin. But there was none. The hyena licked its jowls and Gau, not knowing what else to do, threw it a piece of meat – and another, and another, until his store was almost finished. Still the hyena, growing bolder all the time, came nearer.

Desperately Gau threw the last strip of meat. As he did, the sky flared as embers do when blown suddenly to send sparks scattering. Then, across the sky there blazed a strange soft light. Thousands of little stars burned like wood-ash strewn in the sky. The path of stars arched low – from the far horizon to just above where Gau stood.

The hyena howled and whooped. It cowered low on the sand and stared at the sky, cringing, its lip drawn up above its yellow teeth. Shaking its shaggy head from side to side, it backed away and slunk into the gloom, moaning to itself.'

'It is a sign for me!' cried Gau. He leapt up and took his hunter's bag, bow, quiver and carrying-stick and ran, unafraid, following the pathway in the sky.

Xama nursed her burnt and blistered hands. She sang sadly to herself and gazed every now and then at the wood-ash stars she had made. Only in the dawn, when she heard the loud cries of the people, did she leave her brooding and turn and run to where they stood together, pointing excitedly.

There, walking down across the plain, swaggering as if he'd been no further than the waterhole, came Gau. And tied to his carrying-stick hung a gemsbok skin, soft and mauve and grey as a rainy summer sky.

So it was that Gau, the youngest hunter in the band, shot his first big buck and made a warm kaross for Xama, the keeper of his heart.

And so it is – the old ones say – that the thousands of little stars that form the Milky Way are really a handful of wood-ash glowing in the dark. For once a young San girl named Xama threw the embers of her fire into the sky to light the way for Gau the hunter, lost out in the desert wastes in the darkness of the night.

★See the San tale 'The Girl who Made Stars' [ed.]

ERNST HAVEMANN

A Farm at Raraba

From: *Bloodsong and other Stories of South Africa* (1987)

My late dad was a magnificent shot. One time when we were hunting in the Low Veld and had paused for a smoke, there was the yelp of a wild dog, and a troop of impala came bounding over the tall grass. Opposite us, three hundred yards off, was a stony ridge like a wall, six feet high. You would think those buck would avoid it, but no, they went straight at it. One after the other, without pausing or swerving, they leapt over it. They cleared it by three or four feet. I tell you, friend, it was a beautiful sight. You can't beat Nature for beauty, eh.

By the time the first two impala were over the ridge, late Dad was ready, and as the next one leapt, Dad got him. In mid-air. Same with the next one, and the next, and the next. And the next. And the next. That was six buck, one after the other.

Do you know, the wild dogs chasing those buck didn't pause for the impala that late Dad had killed. They didn't even react to the shots. They just followed one particular buck that they had marked, and we saw them pull it down a couple of minutes later. You've got to hand it to Nature; she knows what she's doing.

But the most wonderful thing was when we got to the dead impala. Four of them were piled one on top of the other, neatly, like sacks in a store. Late Dad had shot each of them through the heart, at exactly the same point in its leap. The other two had been a bit slow. Late Dad had got each of them in the shoulder. If you can't get a head or a heart shot, the next best is the shoulder, because there's a lot of bone there, and if you hit bone it brings a creature down. It can't run, you see. The worst place is behind the heart, because then your bullet goes through a lot of soft entrails, eh. A gut-shot animal will sometimes run a couple of miles before it drops and you may never find it. When I hear of fellows shooting like that, it makes me want to put a slug into their guts and see how they would like to die that way.

Those impala were a bit of a problem. We only had a licence for two and we only had the two mules we were riding. But God sent the ravens to Elijah, eh, so he sent us this Hottentot, Khamatjie. He worked crops on a share on the same farm as late Dad, but he was luckier with his farming – they lived on the smell of an oil rag, those bastards. I don't mean 'bastard' in a nasty way. I just mean there was a white father or grandfather, you understand. Well, thank God, this Khamatjie pitches up with his Ford pick-up and a mincing machine, because he thought he would shoot a zebra. Nobody wants to eat zebra, but when it's sausage it's lovely; you call it beef or koodoo or eland. Late Dad and Khamatjie and I made impala sausages for two days.

In front of other white people Dad always treated Khamatjie like dirt, but otherwise he was very respectful, because he was always borrowing money from Khamatjie and getting drunk with him. He said Khamatjie didn't mind supplying the brandy so long as he could say he drank with a white man.

The training late Dad gave me in bushcraft and using a rifle came in pretty handy when I was on the border of South-West, doing my army service. The call-up interrupts a man's career, if he's got a career, but a fellow that hasn't had army has missed an experience – the outdoor life, learning about musketry and map reading and section leading, and who's what in these little frontline states, and the tribes and the various movements in Angola and Caprivi and Botswana. The big thing, though, is the companion-ship. Until you've marched with four hundred other chaps, all in step, all singing 'Sarie Marais' or 'Lili Marlene' or 'You can do with your loo loo what you will' – until you've sat with five or six buddies in an ambush, not daring to take a breath in a case a guerrilla gets you – until you've done things like that, you don't know what loving your land and your folk is.

Out there, in the bundu, the action is sort of clean, like they say it was in North Africa when we were fighting Rommel in late Dad's war. Not like shooting little black schoolgirls in the bum from inside an armoured car. How brave does a fellow have to be for that? I wonder what these township heroes would do if they were faced with Swapo guerrillas like my lot were.

Because I was keen and liked the bush, eh, I got to be a sergeant, and they gave me six munts they had scratched up in Damaraland, and sent us off across the border into Angola. An intelligence probe, they said. Just these six munts, and me, and an intelligence corporal named Johan. He had had a course of interrogation training and his main job was to train these munts to get infor-mation out of prisoners. Scary stuff, man. You've got to hate a person to do it properly, or just hate people, eh.

Our first ten days on patrol yielded nothing. Then on the eleventh day, I had left Johan and the munts to fix our bivvie for the night while I went ahead for a looksee, at a big granite outcrop about two miles ahead. Just before I got to it there were shots from our camp, then some answering shots, then silence. I hid and waited quietly. After five minutes I saw four Swapies, running for all they were worth, along the side of a kopje half a mile away. They disappeared behind a dune, then bunched up on the big granite out-crop before the first Swapie launched himself off it to cross a crevasse. By that time I was ready, and I got him as he jumped. The next one was too close behind to stop, and I dropped him and number three as fast as it takes to press the trigger. The last one in the bunch pulled back, but I was quick and ready. I hit him, too. I heard the bullet ricochet off the rock, so I reckoned he was probably only wounded.

I was sure the first three would be dead, and I thought, Late Dad, look at that! Three in mid-air! And they're not impala, Dad. They're Royal Game.

Do you know about Royal Game? Late Dad told me, in the old days, before we became the Republic, anything that you were not allowed to shoot, because it was rare or useful, like tickbirds or ibises or oribi, was called Royal Game. Kids in those days believed it was because these birds or animals were reserved for the Royal Family to shoot. Fancy Prince Charles potting away at a flock of egrets or an iguana, eh! So Dad and his friends called desert natives Royal Game, because they are wild but you're not allowed to shoot them, see?

Like I told you, man, I can't bear to think of a gutshot animal, lying in pain for hours. I felt the same way about this guerrilla, but I was on edge too. They say a wounded lion or buffalo is the most dangerous game in the wild, because he stalks the hunter. A wounded munt guerrilla must be worse, because he's got more IQ, eh, so I circled very cautiously round the granite rock. When I got opposite the crevasse I could see three bodies, one on top of the other, quite still. At eight hundred yards, three in three shots, it's a satisfaction, man.

And there, thank God, was guerrilla number four, just round the corner. He was standing upright in a narrow cleft in the rock, with one foot apparently stuck, and he was gripping his left bicep. A pressure point, I supposed. Through my field glasses I could see his left sleeve was a thick mat of blood. So all I had got was his arm. I found myself making excuses, thinking I had been slow because I used a peepsight. Late Dad always shot over open sights; he reckoned a sniper's eye aimed his hand, like a cowboy with a pistol, or a kid with a catapult.

The guerrilla's rifle was wedged above his head. For safety's sake I put a bullet into it. That left him unlikely to do much damage. When I edged my way closer I saw his leg was held fast in a crack, so he really was stuck and helpless. He was one of those yellow Hottentot types, with spaces between his peppercorns of hair, about my age but as wrinkled as a prune. These Kalahari natives go like that by the time they're twenty: it's the sun or glands, I don't know. He was wearing a cast-off Cuban tunic.

I climbed up the rock and looked down on him, trying to remember the few words of local lingo I had picked up from my men, but when he heard me he said in Afrikaans, 'Good day, my baas.'

I was pleased, I can tell you. It meant I could interrogate him myself and, as he was our first prisoner, it would show Johan and my black soldiers that I was one step ahead of them, and it wasn't for nothing I was a sergeant.

The guerrilla bowed his head and pointed with his good hand. 'If you are going to shoot, make it two shots, please, so that I will be properly dead.'

'I don't shoot tethered goats,' I said.

After a moment or two he looked up. 'Can the goat have some water?'

'First, talk.'

'Yes, I talk, baas. What would baas like to talk about?'

I interrogated him, in the way we had been instructed, using trick questions and repetitions. In case he was lying or hiding anything I prodded his wounded arm once or twice. He bore it as if he had it coming to him, but he didn't appear to keep information back, and when his voice cracked I passed down my water bottle.

His name was Adoons, which is a jokey way of saying Adonis. It is what one calls a pet baboon. The farmer his family had worked for called him that. Eventually his own family stopped using the native name his father gave him and almost forgot it. It seemed to belong to someone else, Adoons said.

He had been a hunters' guide and a shepherd. When his family was pushed off the farm – for sheep stealing, it seemed – he joined the guerrillas who were fighting for Namibian independence. He had only the vaguest idea what the fighting was about. He knew it was against whites, but he had never heard of Namibia. Not surprising, when you think that there is no such place. He called it 'South-West', just like we do. He moved from one guerrilla band to another, depending on how he liked the band's leader, and how much food or loot was available. His present band was under an Ndebele refugee from Zimbabwe. They were supposed to report to a General Kareo, but they had never seen him. I carefully recorded it all in my field notebook.

When I had done with questions, I sat back and lighted a cigarette. At the sound of the match he looked up. Smoking alone or drinking alone is not something a decent man wants to do; it's like making love alone, late Dad used to say. I gave Adoons the cigarette and lighted another one for myself.

He exhaled till his chest was flat, and then inhaled the smoke to fill his lungs. He held it for a long time before letting it out and saying, 'Thank you, baas. Baas is a good man.'

He smoked in deep gulps, keeping his head down. When he finished the cigarette he looked up. 'Why didn't baas shoot when I was full of smoke?'

'I told you I don't shoot jackal bait,' I said.

'I can see baas is a good man, but if baas's men find me here, they will do bad things to me. Perhaps it will take three days.'

'I will tell them you have already talked.'

'They will not care. They will torture me to make a game. My people will do it, too, if they catch one of your black soldiers. This is not Sunday school, my baas.'

'We don't torture prisoners,' I replied angrily. I knew he would not believe me.

'What will baas do with me?'

The fact was I didn't know what the hell I could do with Adoons. Once he has been interrogated, a native prisoner is worthless – worse, he would be a danger. He would have to be fed and guarded, and if he escaped he could give the enemy all sorts of valuable information. We didn't keep prisoners, except white men and Cubans: you can exchange or use them for propaganda.

As if sharing my problem, he said, 'Has baas perhaps room for another shepherd on baas's farm?'

'I haven't got a farm and if I wanted a shepherd I would not employ a bloody Hottentot rebel.'

'It is near sunset. Baas will go soon, before it gets dark. And when baas goes the hyenas will come. A hyena can bite right through a man's leg. A living man's leg.'

I looked down at his skinny leg disappearing into the rock cleft, then climbed down and looked at his imprisoned foot. All I had to do was untie the laces and manipulate his ankle to get his foot out, leaving the boot behind. Then I gave the empty boot a kick and it came loose, too. Adoons wriggled till he found a purchase for his toes and raised himself a few inches.

'Give me your hand, Hottentot,' I said. 'I'll pull you out.'

He put up his hand. I took him by the wrist and he clasped my wrist. With unexpected agility he braced his feet against the side of the cleft and scrambled up. I threw him his boot. When he stood up to catch it, his tunic opened to reveal a pistol loose in a leather holster on a broad, stylish belt round his waist.

He smiled shamefacedly. 'I took it from the policeman who arrest me for stealing sheep.'

'Is it loaded?'

'Oh, yes. Five bullets. I used one to learn to shoot it, but I've never fired it since. One has to be close to a man.'

'You could have shot me.'

'Yes, my baas. The pistol was stuck fast, like me, but when you were asking all those questions and leaning down to hear what I was saying, the barrel was pointing straight at you.'

'Why didn't you shoot?'

'If baas was dead I would still be stuck in that rock with no one to help me before the soldiers or the hyenas came.'

His wounded arm had been banged as he made his way up. It now began to bleed through the clot, not actively but *clthip, clthip, clthip*. Since I carried three field dressings, I could spare one. I dusted the antiseptic powder that came with it on Adoons's wound, bandaged it, and gave him one of the painkiller pills we were issued with.

'I would be a good shepherd for you. It is easy to work well for a kind master. Anyone can see baas will give good food, and a hut with a proper roof, and no sjambok whippings. Except for cheeky young men who have been to school.'

'Come on, we must find a shelter for the night,' I said. I didn't like the thought of the hyenas he had talked about.

'These pills are good. The pain is quiet. Baas is like a doctor, eh? A sheep farmer has to be a doctor. I am very good with karakul ewes at lambing time. Baas knows, for the best fur you must kill the lambs as soon as they are born. Stillborn lambs are better. Their skins shine like black nylon with water spilled on it. It's messy, clubbing and skinning the little things without damaging the pelts. It's sad to hear all those ewes baa-ing. The meat is only fit for cows and vultures. But the rich ladies want the pelts before they get woolly.'

He pointed out an overhanging rock twenty yards away. 'Shall we spend the night there? Out of the dew, and it's open only on one side.'

As we moved, I picked up dry sticks for kindling, but he put his hand on my arm. 'If the soldiers see me in the firelight, or my people see baas, they will shoot.'

I felt foolish and amateur.

'The dead men have clothes. Shall I fetch some?'

'We'll go together,' I said. I wasn't going to get myself ambushed.

We went round the rock to the little cliff where the bodies lay. He whistled in admiration. 'Baas shoots like a machine. These dead Ovambos look as if they've been arranged with a forklift truck.' He added proudly, 'I can drive a forklift. I learned on the sheep ranch.'

We collected a couple of goatskins, a bush shirt with only a small blood patch, a water bottle, and a haversack of boiled ears of corn. There were three rifles. I grabbed two and took the bolts out of them. Adoons had already taken possession of the third. He grinned mischievously as he worked the bolt and demonstrated how he could use the rifle by tucking its butt under his sound arm.

'Now we can help each other, eh, baas. Like that bird that sits in a crocodile's mouth and cleans bits of meat out from between the crocodile's teeth. The crocodile does not eat him.'

We settled down close together under the overhang and had an ear of corn each, and a pull from my hip flask. My dear old ma gave it to me when I was leaving for the border. 'When you put it to your lips, it is your old momma kissing you,' she said. I wondered what she would say if she knew she was kissing a Swapie Hottentot, too.

'Angora goats pay better than karakul sheep in the Dry Veld,' Adoons said.

'When I am the head shepherd, baas will give me a few sheep of my own. I will have a woman with buttocks that stick out so much you can use them for a step-ladder. Ai! What fat yellow legs that woman has!' He sucked his breath in lasciviously. 'Baas will have white girls in town but on the farm now and then a Bushman girl. Ai, what a surprise he gets when he finds that the girl has an apron!' He described in detail the strip of skin some Bushman women have hanging down from their gashes, and how some Bushmen have an erection all the time, just like in the rock paintings.

I got sleepy and he shook me. 'No sleep tonight,' he said. 'Listen.' There were sounds of animals round the bodies. 'Better we talk. Also it is good for a man and his mate to chat, isn't it?'

'I thought you fellows didn't want white men to have farms,' I said. 'You want all the land for yourselves.'

'Oh, yes. Yes, that's right. General Kareo says I will have a farm of my own. And a hundred sheep.'

'Why stop at a hundred? Why not a thousand? Be a big boss. Make people call you "*Mr* Adoons".'

'How will I look after a thousand animals? I can't even count past twenty sheep without taking stones out of one pocket and putting them in the other. No, not a thousand. Unless – unless bass was my foreman.' He laughed like a drunkard. 'If my people win the war, will baas be my foreman? Please. Baas could have the big farmhouse and a motor car. Baas need not call me "baas", just "Mr Adoons". Everything my foreman wants to do, he can do. Will my foreman be angry if some of the shepherds hide away when the police visit?'

'If your lot were the government, they would be your policemen.'

'Policemen are policemen. Dogs' turds. Always after passes.'

'Your lot say there won't be passes anymore.'

'No passes! If people don't have passes, how can you trace a stock thief? What will we do if bad Ovambo kaffirs steal my karakuls?'

'That's your problem. Perhaps you'll have to get fierce German guard dogs.'

'Oh, yes. That's a clever idea. My foreman will always find a way. Now, let's talk of nice things, not problems. What is baas's name?'

'Martinus.'

'That is a friendly name for a foreman. In the evenings, after the shepherds have done their work and the sheep and goats are in their thorn kraals, Mr Adoons and foreman Martinus will sit together and talk and look at the veld. Ai, it's pretty country, between Platberg and the Boa River. Short sweet grass and big flat-crown thorn trees for shade. Animals eat the pods in the winter. There are eland and kudu and impala and bushpigs, but enough grass for karakul sheep too.'

'Sounds all right,' I said.

'In the kloof there are wild bees and baboons. Ai, those baboons! When a baboon finds a marula tree where the plums have fermented, he gets as drunk as a man. Ai, those drunk baboons! The leopards eat only baboons, never sheep.'

'Any water?'

'Water! There is the Boa River and big freshwater pans full of barbel and eels and ducks, and widow birds with long black tails like church deacons, and spur-wing geese on the mud flats. The place is called Raraba. We shall sit and drink buchu brandy and talk. Or just sit silent, like old friends do.'

'What the hell would you and I find to talk about?'

'Ai, pals' talk. About the grazing and the government and women and hunting and what happens after you die. I suppose baas knows lots of Jesus stories.'

'I don't like buchu,' I said.

'Do you like the kind of brandy called Commando? They say it is good.'

'Klipdrif is the best kind.'

'Then we will have Klipdrif, Martinus.'

'If it's hot and dry, one could irrigate a few acres for a vineyard,' I said.

'Does Martinus know about wine?'

'My grandfather used to make wine with grapes from his backyard.'

'Ai, but this is lucky! So Foreman Martinus would grow grapes and make sweet wine. They say if you give a girl a bottle of that red Cape wine, her legs open before the bottle is finished. But I like brandy better.'

'Me too,' I said.

'Sometimes we will give a bottle of wine to the old people, too. On Mr Adoons's farm the labourers can stay even when they are too old to work. And when the rations are given out, the old people get meat and mealie-meal, too, just like the others. Is that right, Martinus?'

'If the baas says so,' I said.

At first light we stretched and scouted. There was no activity. Adoons tore a sleeve out of a dead guerrilla's shirt; I made a sling and tied his wounded arm against his chest. He kept a grip on the rifle all the time.

I offered him my flask, and we each took a swallow. He handed me one of the two ears of corn left in the haversack, and pointed south. 'Foreman Martinus must walk that way. I will go north.'

'Good luck, Mr Adoons. I'll come and visit you at your farm at Raraba after the war, and see if you still need a foreman.'

'Ai, Martinus,' he said, 'we will drink and talk, eh. Ai, how we will talk!' He knocked his rifle barrel against mine, like clinking a glass, and set off.

I slid behind the rock where I could watch him without exposing myself. Late Dad used to say if you trust a Hottentot you might as well wear a cobra for a necklace; so I kept my crossed hairs on him, expecting him to whirl round any moment and loose off, or to disappear behind a boulder or thick shrub and perhaps circle round to take me in the rear. However, he walked very deliberately up the hill, and did not dodge behind trees or rocks like an experienced veld man would, nor did he look back to see what I was doing.

When he reached the top of the kopje he stood for some moments silhouetted against the sky and waved his gun. Challenging me to shoot? When he disappeared over the top, I quickly shifted to another position a couple of hundred yards away so that if he crawled round to the side of the kopje I would be ready for him. By sun-up nothing had happened, so I decided he was on his way to find his band. He would probably keep the field dressing I put on his arm and pretend that he had shot a South African soldier.

I found my chaps easily enough – I told them I could have shot three or four of them if I had been a guerrilla – and sent them to see what they could find on the Swapies I had shot; even those fellows sometimes have letters or helpful papers.

You would think a man's second-in-command would want to say a warm word about the marksmanship. The blackies were impressed, but Johan said, 'You shouldn't have shot to kill, Sarge. We're not in the humane hunting business, you know. A dead Swapie is nafi, isn't he?' He liked showing off his intelligence jargon, like using 'nafi' to mean 'not available for interrogation'.

I shut up about Adoons. My blackies might have been able to pick up his trail and perhaps find him before he rejoined his lot, especially if his wound started bleeding again. Then, if they roughed him up a bit, he could hardly avoid giving the whole story away, and that would mean a court martial for me, wouldn't it?

We eventually caught a few Swapies. I did not like Johan's attitude, but he was right – a dead prisoner is nafi – so I shot for the leg and told the men to do the same. I stood by with a sub-machine-gun at the ready during the interrogations in case any of the prisoners knew about me and Adoons. Fortunately, none did.

When I finished my army I took my discharge there in South-West and went to have a look at the Platberg area and especially Raraba.

It is nice country, if you like desert, and a man could pick up a thousand hectares cheap from fellows who are getting cold feet about the UN. Also the market for Persian lamb – that's karakul – is looking up again, now that Greenpeace has stopped women from buying baby seal. Some sheep ranchers say they would send Greenpeace a donation if it wasn't for the currency restrictions.

I followed the Boa River up to Platberg. The river runs against the mountain cliffs, so there is no space in between for a farm. I thought I must have misunderstood Adoons.

That evening there was a drunk lying asleep in the gutter outside the hotel. The doorman laughed when I bent down to shake the man. 'Leave him, mister,' he said. 'He's happier in Raraba.'

It turns out that is what the Hottentots around there call a lullaby, a dream-land that is too nice to be real. At first I was disappointed. Then I thought, Just as well. Suppose a man had a nice sheep ranch, and then one day a bloody old yellow Hottentot pitched up and said, 'Martinus, old friend, do you remember your baas, Mr Adoons? I've brought a bottle of Klipdrif brandy. That's the kind you like, isn't it? Let us sit and drink and talk pals' talk.'

It would be embarrassing, eh.

GCINA MHLOPHE

The Toilet

First published, 1987
From: *Love Child* (2000)

Sometimes I wanted to give up and be a good girl who listened to her elders. Maybe I should have done something like teaching or nursing as my mother wished. People thought these professions were respectable, but I knew I wanted to do something different, though I was not sure what. I thought a lot about acting ... My mother said that it had been a waste of good money educating me because I did not know what to do with the knowledge I had acquired. I'd come to Johannesburg for the December holidays after writing my matric exams, and then stayed on, hoping to find something to do.

My elder sister worked in Orange Grove as a domestic worker, and I stayed with her in her back room. I didn't know anybody in Jo'burg except my sister's friends whom we went to church with. The Methodist church up Fourteenth Avenue was about the only outing we had together. I was very bored and lonely.

On weekdays, I was locked in my sister's room so that the Madam wouldn't see me. She was at home most of the time: painting her nails, having tea with her friends, or lying in the sun by the swimming pool. The swimming pool was very close to the room, which is why I had to keep very quiet. My sister felt bad about locking me in there, but she had no alternative. I couldn't even play the radio, so she brought me books, old magazines, and newspapers from the white people. I just read every single thing I came across: *Fair Lady*, *Woman's Weekly*, anything. But then my sister thought I was reading too much.

'What kind of wife will you make if you can't even make baby clothes, or knit yourself a jersey? I suppose you will marry an educated man like yourself, who won't mind going to bed with a book and an empty stomach.'

We would play cards at night when she knocked off, and listen to the radio, singing along softly with the songs we liked.

Then I got this temporary job in a clothing factory in town. I looked forward to meeting new people, and liked the idea of being out of that room for a change. The factory made clothes for ladies' boutiques.

The whole place was full of machines of all kinds. Some people were sewing, others were ironing with big heavy irons that pressed with a lot of steam. I had to cut all the loose threads that hang after a dress or a jacket is

651

finished. As soon as a number of dresses in a certain style were finished, they would be sent to me and I had to count them, write the number down, and then start with the cutting of the threads. I was fascinated to discover that one person made only sleeves, another the collars, and so on until the last lady put all the pieces together, sewed on buttons, or whatever was necessary to finish.

Most people at the factory spoke Sotho, but they were nice to me – they tried to speak to me in Zulu or Xhosa, and they gave me all kinds of advice on things I didn't know. There was this girl, Gwendolene – she thought I was very stupid – she called me a 'bari' because I always sat inside the changing room with something to read when it was time to eat my lunch, instead of going outside to meet guys. She told me it was cheaper to get myself a 'lunch boy' – somebody to buy me lunch. She told me it was wise not to sleep with him, because then I could dump him anytime I wanted to. I was very nervous about such things. I thought it was better to be a 'bari' than to be stabbed by a city boy for his money.

The factory knocked off at four-thirty, and then I went to a park near where my sister worked. I waited there till half-past six, when I could sneak into the house again without the white people seeing me. I had to leave the house before half-past five in the mornings as well. That meant I had to find something to do with the time I had before I could catch the seven-thirty bus to work – about two hours. I would go to a public toilet in the park. For some reason it was never locked, so I would go in and sit on the toilet seat to read some magazine or other until the right time to catch the bus.

The first time I went into this toilet, I was on my way to the bus stop. Usually I went straight to the bus stop outside the OK Bazaars where it was well lit, and I could see. I would wait there, reading, or just looking at the growing number of cars and buses on their way to town. On this day it was raining quite hard, so I thought I would shelter in the toilet until the rain had passed. I knocked first to see if there was anyone inside. As there was no reply, I pushed the door open and went in. It smelled a little – a dryish kind of smell, as if the toilet was not used all that often, but it was quite clean compared to many 'Non-European' toilets I knew. The floor was painted red and the walls were cream white. It did not look like it had been painted for a few years. I stood looking around, with the rain coming very hard on the zinc roof. The noise was comforting – to know I had escaped the wet – only a few of the heavy drops had got me. The plastic bag in which I carried my book and purse and neatly folded pink handkerchief was a little damp, but that was because I had used it to cover my head when I ran to the toilet. I pulled my dress down a little so that it would not get creased when I sat down. The closed lid of the toilet was going to be my seat for many mornings after that.

I was really lucky to have found that toilet because the winter was very cold. Not that it was any warmer in there, but once I'd closed the door it used to be a little less windy. Also the toilet was very small — the walls were wonderfully close to me — if felt like it was made to fit me alone. I enjoyed that kind of privacy. I did a lot of thinking while I sat on that toilet seat. I did a lot of day-dreaming too — many times imagining myself in some big hall doing a really popular play with other young actors. At school, we took set books like *Buzani KuBawo* or *A Man for All Seasons* and made school plays which we toured to the other schools on weekends. I loved it very much. When I was even younger I had done little sketches taken from the Bible and on big days like Good Friday, we acted and sang happily.

I would sit there dreaming ...

I was getting bored with the books I was reading — the love stories all sounded the same, and besides that I just lost interest. I started asking myself why I had not written anything since I left school. At least at school I had written some poems, or stories for the school magazine, school competitions and other magazines like *Bona* and *Inkqubela*. Our English teacher was always so encouraging; I remembered the day I showed him my first poem — I was so excited I couldn't concentrate in class for the whole day. I didn't know anything about publishing then, and I didn't ask myself if my stories were good enough. I just enjoyed writing things down when I had the time. So one Friday, after I'd started being that toilet's best customer, I bought myself a notebook in which I was hoping to write something. I didn't use it for quite a while, until one evening.

My sister had taken her usual Thursday afternoon off, and she had delayed somewhere. I came back from work, then waited in the park for the right time to go back into the yard. The white people always had their supper at six-thirty and that was the time I used to steal my way in without disturbing them or being seen. My comings and goings had to be secret because they still didn't know I stayed there.

Then I realised that she hadn't come back, and I was scared to go out again, in case something went wrong this time. I decided to sit down in front of my sister's room, where I thought I wouldn't be noticed. I was reading a copy of *Drum* magazine and hoping that she would come back soon — before the dogs sniffed me out. For the first time I realised how stupid it was of me not to have cut myself a spare key long ago. I kept on hearing noises that sounded like the gate opening. A few times I was sure I had heard her footsteps on the concrete steps leading to the servant's quarters, but it turned out to be something or someone else.

I was trying hard to concentrate on my reading again, when I heard the two dogs playing, chasing each other nearer and nearer to where I was sitting. And then, there they were in front of me, looking as surprised as I was. For a brief moment we stared at each other, then they started to bark at me. I was sure they would tear me to pieces if I moved just one finger, so I sat very still, trying not to look at them, while my heart pounded and my mouth went dry as paper.

They barked even louder when the dogs from next door joined in, glared at me through the openings in the hedge. Then the Madam's high-pitched voice rang out above the dogs' barking.

'Ireeeeeene!' That's my sister's English name, which we never use. I couldn't move or answer the call – the dogs were standing right in front of me, their teeth so threateningly long. When there was no reply, she came to see what was going on.

'Oh, it's you? Hello.' She was smiling at me, chewing that gum which never left her mouth, instead of calling the dogs away from me. They had stopped barking, but they hadn't moved – they were still growling at me, waiting for her to tell them what to do.

'Please Madam, the dogs will bite me,' I pleaded, not moving my eyes from them.

'No, they won't bite you.' Then she spoke to them nicely, 'Get away now – go on,' and they went off. She was like a doll, her hair almost orange in colour, all curls round her made-up face. Her eyelashes fluttered like a doll's. Her thin lips were bright red like her long nails, and she wore very high-heeled shoes. She was still smiling; I wondered if it didn't hurt after a while. When her friends came for a swim, I could always hear her forever laughing at something or other.

She scared me – I couldn't understand how she could smile like that but not want me to stay in her house.

'When did you come in? We didn't see you.'

'I've been here for some time now – my sister isn't here. I'm waiting to talk to her.'

'Oh – she's not here?' She was laughing, for no reason that I could see. 'I can give her a message – you go on home – I'll tell her that you want to see her.'

Once I was outside the gate, I didn't know what to do or where to go. I walked slowly, kicking my heels. The street lights were so very bright! Like big eyes staring at me. I wondered what the people who saw me thought I was doing, walking around at that time of the night. But then I didn't really care, because there wasn't much I could do about the situation right then. I was just thinking how things had to go wrong on that day particularly, because my sister and I were not on such good terms. Early that morning, when the alarm had gone for me to wake up, I did not jump to turn it off, so my sister got really angry with me. She had gone on about me always leaving it to ring for too long, as if it was set for her, and not for me. And when I went out to wash, I had left the door open a second too long, and that was enough to earn me another scolding.

654

Every morning I had to wake up straight away, roll my bedding and put it all under the bed where my sister was sleeping. I was not supposed to put on the light although it was still dark. I'd light a candle, and tiptoe my way out with a soap dish and a toothbrush. My clothes were on a hanger on a nail at the back of the door. I'd take the hanger and close the door as quietly as I could. Everything had to be ready set the night before. A washing basin full of cold water was also ready outside the door, put there because the sound of running water and the loud screech the taps made in the morning could wake the white people and they would wonder what my sister was doing up so early. I'd do my everything and be off the premises by five-thirty with my shoes in my bag – I only put them on once I was safely out of the gate. And that gate made such a noise too. Many time I wished I could jump over it and save myself all that sickening careful-careful business!

Thinking about all these things took my mind away from the biting cold of the night and my wet nose, until I saw my sister walking towards me.

'Mholo, what are you doing outside in the street?' she greeted me. I quickly briefed her on what had happened.

'Oh Yehovah! You can be so dumb sometimes! What were you doing inside in the first place? You know you should have waited for me so we could walk in together. Then I could say you were visiting or something. Now, you tell me, what am I supposed to say to them if they see you come in again? Hayi!'

She walked angrily towards the gate, she turned to me with an impatient whisper.

'And now why don't you come in, stupid?'

I mumbled my apologies, and followed her in. By some miracle no one seemed to have noticed us, and we quickly munched a snack of cold chicken and boiled potatoes and drank our tea, hardly on speaking terms. I just wanted to howl like a dog. I wished somebody would come and be my friend, and tell me that I was not useless, and that my sister did not hate me, and tell me that one day I would have a nice place to live … anything. It would have been really great to have someone my own age to talk to.

But also I knew that my sister was worried for me, she was scared of her employers. If they were to find out that I lived with her, they would fire her, and then we would both be walking up and down the streets. My eleven rand wages wasn't going to help us at all. I don't know how long I lay like that, unable to fall asleep, just wishing and wishing with tears running into my ears.

The next morning I woke up long before the alarm went off, but I just lay there feeling tired and depressed. If there was a way out, I would not have gone to work, but there was this other strong feeling or longing inside me. It was some kind of pain that pushed me to do everything at double speed and run to my toilet. I call it my toilet because that is exactly how I felt about it. It was very rare that I ever saw anybody else go in there in the mornings. It was like they all knew I was using it, and they had to lay off or something. When I went there, I didn't really expect to find it occupied.

I felt my spirits really lifting as I put on my shoes outside the gate. I made sure that my notebook was in my bag. In my haste I even forgot my lunchbox, but it didn't matter. I was walking faster and my feet were feeling lighter all the time. Then I noticed that the door had been painted, and that a new window pane had replaced the old broken one. I smiled to myself as I reached the door. Before long I was sitting on that toilet seat, writing a poem.

Many more mornings saw me sitting there writing. Sometimes it did not need to be a poem; I wrote anything that came into my head – in the same way I would have done if I'd had a friend to talk to. I remember some days when I felt like I was hiding something from my sister. She did not know about my toilet in the park, and she was not in the least interested in my notebook.

Then one morning I wanted to write a story about what had happened at work the day before; the supervisor screaming at me for not calling her when I'd seen the people who stole two dresses at lunch time. I had found it really funny. I had to write about it and I just hoped there were enough pages left in my notebook. It all came back to me, and I was smiling when I reached for the door, but it wouldn't open – it was locked!

I think for the first time I accepted that the toilet was not mine after all … Slowly I walked over to a bench nearby, watched the early spring sun come up, and wrote my story anyway.

MAUD MOTANYANE

Two Minutes

First published, 1987

Tosh and I were an odd pair; she was tall and thin, and I was short and plump. People called us the big and small twins, or B & S for short. In very many ways we were different, and yet there was something strong that bound us together. We stood out like sore thumbs from the rest of the girls, who were adventurous and full of pranks. They were wild, while Tosh and I tried to lead a life as pure as possible.

It is twenty years since I last saw Tosh, and I feel guilty that I have not been back to see her. I am sure she is plagued by the same guilt. We made a vow many years ago, and we promised to keep it whatever happened. We crossed each other's hearts and spat on the ground as we promised.

'Strue's God, my friend, if I ever do it I will come back and tell you.' There was only one 'it' that little girls in a convent school could promise not to get themselves involved in. According to Sister Marietta, the matron of the convent, boys came second after witches and ghosts as the deadliest poison for little girls. It could take less than two minutes for a boy to ruin a girl's entire life, she said.

The Little Flower Girls' Hostel formed part of a huge mission station founded by Catholic missionaries at the turn of the century. Most of them were of European origin, but over the years the mission, set in the village of Asazi in Natal, had become a fully fledged community, producing its own breed of African nuns and priests from the surrounding villages.

Sister Marietta was a mouse-like creature of German origin. Armed with a Bible and a strict Catholic upbringing, she was determined to save the whole African continent from death and destruction. Her biggest challenge while at The Little Flower was to keep the girls away from the evil clutches of men. Old Marie, as the girls referred to her, made it her business to slot in her anti-male propaganda whenever she could. Her best performances were a day or two before we broke up for the school holidays. She seemed to think that a good dose of lecturing would protect us from the menacing world outside.

She marvelled at the story of a boy who once cast a spell on a girl by simply looking at her. The girl, she said, had trusted her own worldly strength instead of asking for protection from the Virgin Mary. The boy had looked at the girl, the story went, and without him saying a word the girl had felt weak. So weak was she that, of her own accord, without the boy even propositioning her, she asked him to 'please kiss me and carry me to the bush'.

'I need not tell you what happened in the bush,' the nun would conclude.

As a rule, anyone who was caught eyeing the boys, whether in church, in class, or in the street, was punished severely. Ten bad marks in Sister Marietta's black book was the highest number one could get at a go, and they indicated the seriousness of the crime. As a result, trying to avoid boys and not being seen with them in a lonely place became our biggest challenge at The Little Flower.

'They will take you and use you, leaving you an empty shell,' Sister Marietta would say, indicating with her hand how a girl would be tossed away as something useless. So ominous was the prospect of being thrown away as a useless shell that Tosh and I would spend long nights discussing ways and means to avoid being subjected to that kind of treatment. Although we did not admire Sister Marietta personally, the idea of being sinless and celibate appealed to us a great deal. Often our night sessions would end with us saying the rosary together, asking for forgiveness for sins we had never committed.

Anastasia, Tasi to her friends, was the most popular girl at The Little Flower. While the rest of the girls loved and admired her, Tosh and I despised her. She dressed in the best fashion clothes, and had all the answers to life's problems. A dark person by nature, Tasi relied on skin lightening cream to make her skin look lighter. So light was her face at one stage that her ebony hands looked borrowed next to it. Somehow her ears never got lighter, no matter how much cream she used on them. They stuck out like little appendages above her oval face. Tosh and I laughed about her ears behind her back. We did not dare do so in her presence. Tasi's tongue was much too scathing.

'I wonder how Old Marie can be so knowledgeable about matters of the flesh when she has never been involved in them,' Tasi would say mockingly. 'She must be displacing her own fears and using us to fight her own inward physical desire. Celibacy … what nonsense. Old Marie must be jealous of our freedom. After all, we never sent her to tie herself to a life devoid of male pleasure.'

Tasi had quite a following, and her bed, which was at the corner of the hundred-bed dormitory, became the girls' rendezvous. This was where all subjects ranging from politics to sex were discussed. Tasi owned a small transistor radio, and often her gang would convene at her bed to listen to the Hit Parade. This had to happen behind Sister Marietta's back because to her, love and rock 'n roll constituted mortal sins. Often the music-listening session would end in a row, with the participants arguing about the lyrics of a song, or which song had been number one on the Hit Parade the previous week.

It was at the rendezvous that the anti-missionary politics were discussed. As far as Tasi was concerned, the missionaries, and that included Sister Marietta, had left Europe because of frustration, hunger and poverty. 'Under the guise of Christianity, they came to save us. Save us from what? When they themselves are guilty of racism and bigotry?' Tasi would ask, pointing at the stone building in which the black nuns were housed.

The Little Flower was not immune from the country's racial laws, which decreed that blacks and whites live separately. The white missionaries were clearly a privileged class. They lived in a glass building at the top of the hill, while their black counterparts were housed in a stone-and-brick building at the bottom of the hill. It looked more like a cave than a hut and, because of the density of the trees around it, it was cold and dark in winter.

Politics was a sacred subject at The Little Flower, and Tasi was the only one who openly challenged the racism of the convent. 'If they were like Jesus, they would be defying the laws of the country,' Tasi would say angrily. When Tasi questioned the school principal at assembly one day, we feared that she would be expelled from school. She was not. Instead she was fobbed off with an 'it was not the policy of the church to get involved in politics' statement, and asked never to bring up the subject again. That did not deter Tasi. She continued to question and attack what she termed inexcusable behaviour from the people of God.

It was at the rendezvous that a perfect plan for smuggling letters was hatched. As a rule, letters sent in and out of the convent were read and censored by Sister Marietta. Incoming parcels were opened too, and every little gift considered to be too fancy for life in a convent school was kept, and not given to the owner until we broke up for the school holidays.

Love-story books were banned from the library, and any pages with kissing couples, or people holding hands were either cut out or blocked with paper. The same applied to movies. Scenes which were remotely sexual were edited out of the movie. We were allowed to watch *The Sound of Music* in my matric class. The movie was so butchered that when I saw it again a couple of years later, it looked completely new.

The smuggling of letters to and from the boys' side took place during morning mass. As the heads bowed down in silent prayer after holy communion, letters would be thrown across the aisle dividing the boys' from the girls' pews. The little pieces of paper, which for some reason were called schemes, would fly like missiles right above the nuns' heads.

One day a scheme which was thrown from the girls' to the boys' side landed right in the lap of Sister Marietta. Her face lit up with glee as she pocketed the letter, waiting for the perfect moment to pounce on the culprit. By the time she did, the school was buzzing with the news of the person who had been found with a scheme. Most of us were not sure who it was, but we were sympathetic because we knew what this would mean.

I had always suspected Sister Marietta to have a mean streak, but never thought her capable of doing what she did with Thoko's letter. Of course Thoko's boyfriend denied any association between them, so she had to face the music alone.

Not only was the letter read to the whole school, it was sent home to her parents, with a letter instructing them to arrive at the school to reprimand Thoko 'or else she will he asked to pack her things and go'.

I could not understand how a private thing such as a letter could be read to the whole school. That convinced me that Sister Marietta was downright malicious, doing that kind of thing to a nice girl like Thoko. Though remote, the thought of becoming a nun had often crossed my mind. What made me hesitate, however, was my mother's deep and sincere wish that I become a nurse. She would have been disappointed if I had gone the way of celibacy. Old Marie made the decision for me. Her reaction to Thoko's letter dashed my wish of ever becoming a nun. I was disgusted.

Tasi teased Thoko for having allowed herself to be caught with the letter. To her it was a big joke, and her friends laughed heartily when she described how foolish Thoko had been.

'There are only two rules,' Tasi said jokingly, 'it is either you keep away from trouble, or get involved, but be smart enough not to get caught.'

Tasi always boasted about how she and her boyfriend Michael smooched right under the nose of the Virgin Mary. She was referring to the statue of Mary on the lawn outside the school's courtyard. For those who had guts like Tasi, the grotto was a perfect lovers' nook.

More than once I heard Tasi tell the story of how she and Michael had climbed into one of the church towers. 'We stood there kissing to the chime of the bells next to us, while the priests heard confessions in the church below. Old Marie herself was playing the organ!' Tasi boasted. 'We did not get caught. What fool has any business to be caught?'

The stigma of being a boy's love followed Thoko until she left The Little Flower. She was banned from going to the movies on Fridays, and all the new-comers were warned that she was a bad influence. With the interesting parts censored out of all movies, Thoko didn't miss much, but it was the boring evenings that drove her nuts.

Thoko's every mistake became a big issue. She was ostracised by the rest of the girls who feared reprisals from Old Marie. As punishment for an offence Thoko was made to clean the local graveyard. It was not so much the hard work which caused grave-cleaning to be regarded as the most severe form of punishment. According to African culture graves are sacred ground where children are not allowed unless they are there to bury a very close relative such as a brother, a sister, or a parent. When Old Marie sent Thoko to dig round the graves for the second time, Tasi suggested we send a delegation to her to protest, and to make it clear what our tradition was regarding being in the cemetery.

'It is a bad omen, and shows no regard for our culture,' Tasi had protested. Although the delegation was given a hearing, their arguments were dismissed as primitive and unChristian, and Thoko was sent to clean up the graves a third and a fourth time. Such punishment was meted out to various other people, but Tasi vowed she would rather pack her bags and leave The Little Flower than dig round the graves. As if to avoid a confrontation, Old Marie never gave her the grave-digging punishment, robbing the girls of a chance to witness a showdown.

Once Sister Marietta embarrassed Thoko by pulling out the hem of her dress, saying that her dress was too short. As a rule, dresses had to be an inch above the knee. Thoko's must have been slightly more than an inch. The poor girl had to walk around with a funny dress the whole day because Sister would not let her change into another. It was her way of punishing her for, according to her mind, trying to be attractive to the opposite sex. But trying to make Thoko unattractive was an impossible task. Besides her God-given beauty, Thoko had natural style which made her look good with or without a torn hem. She looked elegant even in her gymslip, and Sister Marietta hated her for that. So intense was her hatred that she was forever looking for a reason for her to be expelled from school. 'You will dig the graves for a week, or pack your things and leave The Little Flower,' became the nun's familiar cry whenever Thoko did something wrong.

Tosh and I were both eighteen when we left The Little Flower. As we hugged and said goodbye, we renewed the vow we had made so many times before. If we ever slept with a boy, we would write or telephone to say we had finally fallen. I do not know exactly what motivated Tosh to make that vow. But for me, it was Thoko's experience that pushed me and forced me to make that decision. If a love letter could elicit so much hatred and anger, I thought to myself, then surely boys must be a real threat to girls. I sincerely believed that there would be no place for me in the world if I ever fell into the trap which every man around had set to catch me. As Old Marie said, 'The world will spit at you.'

Twenty years have passed since I last saw Tosh. I did not try to find her after my first encounter with a man. I did not feel the urge to write to her that I had finally fallen. To my mind, it had not happened. I remember the incident very clearly. It was on the couch in my mother's own lounge, not even in the bush as Sister Marietta had warned. Because he was Catholic like me, I trusted Sipho more than I would have trusted an ordinary boy. Somehow, I thought he knew the same rules that I knew.

He pleaded with me and told me it would not take long. He fondled my breasts and kissed me all over. I still cannot say whether the feeling was pleasurable. It was as though a cold and a warm shiver went through my body at the same time. I heard two voices, that of Sipho in one ear pleading with me that 'it won't be long', and Sister Marietta in another, warning 'it will take two minutes'. I saw myself being discarded like an empty shell and the whole world spitting at me.

Suddenly I fought like a little monster to push Sipho away. It was too late. I heard him take one deep breath and the act was over. It was exactly two minutes. I pulled myself together and walked out of the door, leaving Sipho sitting on the couch. When I walked away from him, I also walked away from the fact that he had made love to me. As far as I was concerned the incident had not happened. How could I admit that I had been used?

I have had a lot of sexual encounters since that day on my mother's couch. I am married now with two children; still I have not made love to a man. Sister Marietta never told me that there would come a time when being in a lonely place with a boy would be a right and a safe thing to do. So every private moment I have spent with a man has been wrong, and something I have to be ashamed of. Even as I go to bed with my husband every night, Sister Marietta's voice rings in my mind. 'He will take you and use you and throw you away like an empty shell.' When she drummed those words into my innocent mind, she tied a knot that I am unable to undo.

How can I give myself on a platter to a person – a man – who will con me and leave me spent and useless? As I pull myself away from each sexual act, I feel used and unclean. A sense of guilt and emptiness comes over me. Often I have felt the urge to go back to The Little Flower, lock myself into a confessional with my priest, and say, 'Father, I have sinned. I have slept with a boy.'

I have not gone back to Tosh to tell her that I have broken the vow we made so many years ago. I have slept with none of the men I have made love to, none of the men I have met over the past twenty years. Maybe one day I will be able to untangle the knot in my heart and mind. I will be able to say to a man, 'Let us eat together from the sexual pot, let us share the pleasure equally.' I will not write to Tosh. No, not until I reach equality with my men. Tosh has not written either. Could it be that she is plagued by the same anguish, or is she still pure?

JAYAPRAGA REDDY

The Spirit of Two Worlds

From: *On the Fringe of Dreamtime and other Stories* (1987)

The old woman pounded the spices in a wooden mortar. She sat on a grass mat in the sartorial position adopted by generations of women before her. It was cool under the mango tree and the gentle susurration of the breeze among the leaves was like the voice of God murmuring His comfort. Out there it was quiet and she could think her thoughts in peace as she prepared the mangoes for pickling. But today her thoughts were not very pleasant. They were troubled and she was forced to acknowledge the disturbing fact that there was rebellion in her household. Ever since Veeran, her youngest son, had married, there was dissension in her home. He hadn't heeded her advice and had obstinately followed his own desires. So now he reaped the consequences. But a shadow hung over her normally peaceful household. Nothing pleased her new daughter-in-law. Nothing was good enough for her. She complained that the semi-detached house in the Indian township was too cramped and that there was not much diversion in the district. Her discontent and aloofness did not invite intimacy and she remained isolated. She kept to herself, joining the family only when necessary. The other daughters-in-law were tolerant at first but now there was an open resentment. It was time, they maintained, that she took interest in the family and did her share of the housework. She couldn't deny the truth of it. Sharda was headstrong and wilful. By bringing in her new ideas and an alien lifestyle, she had upset the smooth running of her home. In her days, oh in her days, none of this would have been permitted, she lamented inwardly.

Radha, her eldest daughter-in-law, came out to her. 'You like some tea, Ma?' she asked, speaking in Tamil.

The old woman nodded and as she watched her go again, she thought how good and obedient a daughter-in-law she had been. She always wore a sari and her hair was still long and worn in a simple plait. No task was too much for her. Not when it came to doing things for her.

Radha returned with the tea that frothed like beer in an enamel mug. Just the way she liked it, she thought sipping it slowly. The hot, fragrant brew dispelled some of her depression. She wished Radha would go away and leave her to her thoughts. But Radha lingered.

'There is trouble,' Radha informed her.'Now she wants to go to work. He said she cannot go to work. She was very angry.'

The old woman sighed but refrained from comment. She did not ask how she came by such knowledge. In the rather cramped living conditions of the council house, nothing was very private. Quarrels became public and one's tears, unless one cried quietly, were heard by all. Radha went on, giving her all the details, but the old woman stopped her with a gruelling gesture. She rose and went indoors.

Veeran stood at the window looking out vacantly. Sundays were usually so peaceful, the old woman thought as she studied him. Sundays were meant for outings, attending weddings and functions and visits to relatives. Now Sundays were torn by strife and tension.

'What is wrong, my son?' she asked quietly.

He did not turn around. She sensed his humiliation and hurt. 'She wants to ... work,' he said reluctantly.

'Then let her work, my son,' she said.

He turned and regarded her with disbelief.

'You ... want her ... to work!' he exclaimed.

She shook her head sadly. 'No, I don't want her to work. But if that is what she wants and if it will make her happy, then let her work.' He turned away, his jaw setting in a grim, obstinate line.

'She doesn't have to work,' he pointed out.

'All women are not the same,' she reminded him.

'She says she is dying of boredom,' he told her.

Boredom. She left him then and went back to sit under the tree where she reflected upon this new and alien plague which afflicted the young. Her mind went back over the years searching for something that remotely resembled this malady, but there was nothing. There had been hardships, countless sacrifices which had been made willingly, much pain and heartbreak and some rare and memorable moments of joy and happiness, but never boredom. She had married at thirteen, a child bride in an arranged marriage. In those days one did not question these things, merely complied with one's parents' wishes and submitted silently to whatever was arranged. She had nine children, six of whom had survived. An early marriage was followed by early widowhood and at forty she found herself alone at the helm. She hired a stall in the Indian market and managed to keep the family together. Over the years her struggle eased a little when her children were educated and settled in comfortable jobs. Soon she was able to give up the stall and retire, and so come to a quiet port. But there were so many lessons in one's life that one could not pass on to the young.

Sharda went to work as a hairdresser in an elegant new salon in Durban. The old woman wondered whether her new-found financial independence brought her any happiness. She bought a whole lot of new clothes, all modern and fashionable. Her short hair was styled often and in different ways. There were murmurs of jealousy and resentment among the other daughters-in-law. Even Radha fell prey to this.

'What does she work for? Only her clothes and her perfumes! While we stay at home like slaves, she lives like a queen!' Radha observed acidly. But that was only the beginning. Having got her way once, Sharda demanded other things. Her heart heavy with grief, the old woman looked on while Veeran weakly surrendered to her whims. Sharda learned to drive and demanded a car of her own. Bus journeys were long and tedious, she maintained. With a car of her own, she could get home earlier and have more time. More time for what? the old woman wondered. He was as malleable as clay in her hands. It was not right. No woman ought to have that much power over any man.

The car was small and sleek. The day she brought it home, the other daughters-in-law stood at their windows and watched her furtively. She drove with an enviable ease, and they could sense her irrepressible excitement as she sprang out of the car. But her pleasure was short-lived.

At supper that night the family sat around the table in a grim silence, united in their resentment and disapproval. For once, Sharda was not immune to their feelings. At first she ate in quiet defiance. A small knot of anger began to form at the pit of her stomach. It was unfair! What had she done that was wrong? Was it her fault if she could not fit in with their narrow conformity? Surely not! She rose abruptly and left the room. The silence around the table intensified. The old woman watched her go with a heavy heart.

In the weeks that followed, the old woman tried to hold her disintegrating family together. But the task was too much for her. There were lessons in this for her too. She was discovering that her matriarchal authority had its limits and had to give way to a way of life that was rapidly becoming the norm. The things her generation had cherished and valued were being replaced by an alien culture which sacrificed love and caring on the altar of Mammon and whose devotees foolishly pursued the things of the flesh. The old woman took her troubles to her gods in prayer. But there were no answers. Her heart heavy with grief, she saw the rift between her and Sharda widen and was powerless to halt the inevitable. And the inevitable came one afternoon when Veeran announced that he was moving out on his own. The old woman received the news in chill silence. Her initial reaction was one of grief and then anger. Anger because he was allowing it to happen. He didn't want it to happen but he was giving in to his wife once too often. She studied him for a long moment, undeceived by his outward composure. He did not meet her eyes directly for he feared the betrayal of his true emotions.

'Are you sure you want to do this, my son?' she asked quietly.

It took him a long while to answer, and when he did it was with an effort. 'It ... is ... for the best.'

Surely he did not believe that! She rose and left the room and he did not see the naked pain in her eyes.

She sat in her room for a long while, her hands resting in her lap, numb with pain. He had been her youngest son and her best loved. Perhaps that had been a mistake. Sons were not yours to hold. They were arrows to be released into the world.

The old woman read the surprise in her daughter-in-law's eyes. For the first time they were confronting each other directly. For a long moment their glance met and held. It was the younger woman who looked away first. The old woman recalled the day Veeran told her of his wedding plans. He had met her at a party, he said. She was very pretty and so full of fun. She hadn't objected to his choice but had merely advised him to wait. But he hadn't waited. Alas, the young wanted everything quickly and easily.

'So you are splitting my home,' the old woman commented.

The younger woman's glance wavered. Then she straightened and her glance sturdied.

'No, that's not true. All I want is to live on my own. Is that wrong?' said Sharda.

The old woman did not reply for a long moment. 'Have you slipped so far from our teachings that you've forgotten a son's first duty is to his mother?' she reminded grimly.

Sharda looked up and met the old woman's eyes. There was none of the old defiance or antagonism. But in the wordless silence the old woman studied her for a long while. There was strength in silence. She would not give her the satisfaction of having the last word. 'You came to this house in peace, so leave in peace. You are leaving this house on your free will. All I ask is that you look after my son. You have my blessing and I hope you will be happy. If this is your wish, then let it be. But know this, you too will have children. And you too will need them in your old age. I hope when you do, they will be there.'

Sharp words sprang to Sharda's mind then. She wanted to remind the old woman that her son's duty was now to his wife. That times had changed. That she had tried to fit in with her family but had failed. But something within her checked her. Something of her mother's teachings came to her mind. She looked away. The old woman's words touched a chord in her mind and, dimly, she recalled something about respect for the elderly and submission to one's husband. Did these things really matter in these times? Perhaps they did. Who was she to question these things? Her world, her generation had all the questions but no answers.

Sharda and Veeran moved into a flat in Durban. Occasionally they came to visit the family. With time, the old woman came to accept the change. Some of the hurt was gone. But although she treated Sharda with the fairest consideration, she could not easily forgive her. Pride would not allow her to acknowledge defeat. There were some things she would not give in to. Like visiting Sharda. On special occasions, Sharda would try to get her to visit her, but the old woman always declined. When pressed for reasons, she maintained a tight-lipped silence. She was determined that nothing would make her yield to that. On one occasion, Sharda left in tears, chagrined by the old woman's obstinacy. The old woman watched her go and savoured the lone power of triumph. Let that be a lesson to them, she thought. She was not putty in their hands, to be moulded according to their will. Age did not mean easy capitulation to the whims of the young. She would not bend to their will! The winds of change were blowing down all the old pillars, but there were some things she would not easily give in to. There were times when the thought came to her mind unbidden, that perhaps she ought to bow to change gracefully, while time and strength were on her side. But she harboured the thought only fleetingly. The old, unyielding core of obstinacy would come to the fore, she would be strengthened in her resolve to remain adamant.

One morning Veeran came to see her. She wondered why he should call so early. She sensed his excitement and knew it meant good news.

'Ma, Sharda has a son,' he announced. 'You must come and see him.'

She received the news with mixed feelings. Her grandson. A new life, a new beginning. This was a moment for rejoicing, for thanksgiving. For a long moment, she struggled with herself, longing for the release of surrender. Her spirit was tired and she was strongly tempted to call a truce. Wordlessly, she followed Veeran to the car.

Later, as she held the child in her arms, she recalled another birth in the distant past, when she cradled her last born who looked so very much like this child. She looked at Veeran and smiled.

'He's a beautiful child and he looks just like you did,' she said.

'Sharda will have to give up work now,' he pointed out.

The old woman turned to Sharda. When their eyes met, there was a new gentleness, a new peace in the old woman's eyes.

'No, she doesn't have to. I will look after the child,' she stated serenely. She put the child down and rose. The spirit of two worlds had emerged in a new beginning.

NJABULO S NDEBELE

Death of a Son
First published, 1987

At last we got the body. Wednesday. Just enough time for a Saturday funeral. We were exhausted. Empty. The funeral still ahead of us. We had to find the strength to grieve. There had been no time for grief, really. Only much bewilderment and confusion. Now grief. For isn't grief the awareness of loss?

That is why when we finally got the body, Buntu said: 'Do you realise our son is dead?' I realised. Our awareness of the death of our first and only child had been displaced completely by the effort to get his body. Even the horrible events that caused the death: we did not think of them, as such. Instead, the numbing drift of things took over our minds: the pleas, letters to be written, telephone calls to be made, telegrams to be dispatched, lawyers to consult, 'influential' people to 'get in touch with', undertakers to be contacted, so much walking and driving. That is what suddenly mattered: the irksome details that blur the goal (no matter how terrible it is), each detail becoming a door which, once unlocked, revealed yet another door. Without being aware of it, we were distracted by the smell of the skunk and not by what the skunk had done.

We realised something too, Buntu and I, that during the two-week effort to get our son's body, we had drifted apart. For the first time in our marriage, our presence to each other had become a matter of habit. He was there. He'll be there. And I'll be there. But when Buntu said: 'Do you realise our son is dead?' he uttered a thought that suddenly brought us together again. It was as if the return of the body of our son were also our coming together. For it was only at that moment that we really began to grieve; as if our lungs had suddenly begun to take in air, when just before we were beginning to suffocate. Something with meaning began to emerge.

We realised. We realised that something else had been happening to us, adding to the terrible events. Yes, we had drifted apart. Yet, our estrangement, just at that moment when we should have been together, seemed disturbingly comforting to me. I was comforted in a manner I did not quite understand.

The problem was that I had known all along that we would have to buy the body anyway. I had known all along. Things would end that way. And when things turned out that way, Buntu could not look me in the eye. For he had said: 'Over my dead body! Over my dead body!' as soon as we knew we would be required to pay the police or the government for the release of the body of our child.

'Over my dead body! Over my dead body!' Buntu kept on saying.

Finally, we bought the body. We have the receipt. The police insisted we take it. That way, they would be 'protected'. It's the law, they said.

I suppose we could have got the body earlier. At first I was confused, for one is supposed to take comfort in the heroism of one's man. Yet, inwardly, I could draw no comfort from his outburst. It seemed hasty. What sense was there to it when all I wanted was the body of my child? What would happen if, as events unfolded, it became clear that Buntu would not give up his life? What would happen? What would happen to him? To me?

For the greater part of two weeks, all of Buntu's efforts, together with friends, relatives, lawyers and the newspapers, were to secure the release of the child's body without the humiliation of having to pay for it. A 'fundamental principle'.

Why was it difficult for me to see the wisdom of the principle? The worst thing, I suppose, was worrying about what the police may have been doing to the body of my child. How they may have been busy prying it open 'to determine the cause of death'.

Would I want to look at the body when we finally got it? To see further mutilations in addition to the 'cause of death'? What kind of mother would not want to look at the body of her child? people will ask. Some will say: It's grief. She is too grief-stricken.'

'But still ...' they will say. And the elderly among them may say: 'Young people are strange.'

But how can they know? It was not that I would not want to see the body of my child, but that I was too afraid to confront the horrors of my own imagination. I was haunted by the thought of how useless it had been to have created something. What had been the point of it all? This body filling up with a child. The child steadily growing into something that could be seen and felt. Moving, as it always did, at that time of day when I was all alone at home waiting for it. What had been the point of it all?

How can they know that the mutilation to determine 'the cause of death' ripped my own body. Can they think of a womb feeling hunted? Disgorged?

And the milk that I still carried. What about it? What had been the point of it all?

Even Buntu did not seem to sense that that principle, the 'fundamental principle', was something too intangible for me at that moment, something that I desperately wanted should assume the form of my child's body. He still seemed far from ever knowing.

I remember one Saturday morning early in our courtship, as Buntu and I walked hand-in-hand through town, window-shopping. We cannot even be said to have been window-shopping, for we were aware of very little that was not ourselves. Everything in those windows was merely an excuse for words to pass between us.

We came across three girls sitting on the pavement, sharing a packet of fish and chips after they had just bought it from a nearby Portuguese cafe. Buntu said: 'I want fish and chips too.' I said: 'So seeing is desire.' I said: 'My man is greedy!' We laughed. I still remember how he tightened his grip on my hand. The strength of it!

Just then, two white boys coming in the opposite direction suddenly rushed at the girls, and, without warning, one of them kicked the packet of fish and chips out of the hands of the girl who was holding it. The second boy kicked away the rest of what remained in the packet. The girl stood up, shaking her hand as if to throw off the pain in it. Then she pressed it under her armpit as if to squeeze the pain out of it. Meanwhile, the two boys went on their way laughing. The fish and chips lay scattered on the pavement and on the street like stranded boats on a river that had gone dry.

'Just let them do that to you!' said Buntu, tightening once more his grip on my hand as we passed on like sheep that had seen many of their own in the flock picked out for slaughter. We would note the event and wait for our turn. I remember I looked at Buntu, and saw his face was somewhat glum. There seemed no connection between that face and the words of reassurance just uttered. For a while, we went on quietly. It was then that I noticed his grip had grown somewhat limp. Somewhat reluctant. Having lost its self-assurance, it seemed to have been holding on because it had to, not because of a confident sense of possession.

It was not to be long before his words were tested. How could fate work this way, giving to words meanings and intentions they did not carry when they were uttered? I saw that day how the language of love could so easily be trampled underfoot, or scattered like fish and chips on the pavement, and left stranded and abandoned like boats in a river that suddenly went dry. Never again was love to be confirmed with words. The world around us was too hostile for vows of love. At any moment, the vows could be subjected to the stress of proof. And love died. For words of love need not be tested.

On that day, Buntu and I began our silence. We talked and laughed, of course, but we stopped short of words that would demand proof of action. Buntu knew. He knew the vulnerability of words. And so he sought to obliterate words with acts that seemed to promise redemption.

On that day, as we continued with our walk in town, that Saturday morning, coming up towards us from the opposite direction, was a burly Boer walking with his wife and two children. They approached Buntu and me with an ominously determined advance. Buntu attempted to pull me out of the way, but I never had a chance. The Boer shoved me out of the way, as if clearing a path for his family. I remember, I almost crashed into a nearby fashion display window. I remember, I glanced at the family walking away, the mother and the father each dragging a child. It was for one of those children that I had been cleared away. I remember, also, that as my tears came out, blurring the Boer family and everything else, I saw and felt deeply what was inside of me: a desire to be avenged.

But nothing happened. All I heard was Buntu say: 'The dog!' At that very moment, I felt my own hurt vanish like a wisp of smoke. And as my hurt vanished, it was replaced, instead, by a tormenting desire to sacrifice myself for Buntu. Was it something about the powerlessness of the curse and the desperation with which it had been made? The filling of stunned silence with an utterance? Surely it ate into him, revealing how incapable he was of meeting the call of his words.

And so it was that that afternoon, back in the township, left to ourselves at Buntu's home, I gave in to him for the first time. Or should I say I offered myself to him? Perhaps from some vague sense of wanting to heal something in him? Anyway, we were never to talk about that event. Never. We buried it alive deep inside of me that afternoon. Would it ever be exhumed? All I vaguely felt and knew was that I had the keys to the vault. That was three years ago, a year before we married.

The cause of death? One evening I returned home from work, particularly tired after I had been covering more shootings by the police on the East Rand. Then I had hurried back to the office in Johannesburg to piece together on my typewriter the violent scenes of the day, and then to file my report to meet the deadline. It was late when I returned home, and when I got there I found a crowd of people in the yard. They were those who could not get inside. I panicked. What had happened? I did not ask those who were outside, being desperate to get into the house. They gave way easily when they recognised me.

Then I heard my mother's voice. Her cry rose well above the noise. It turned into a scream when she saw me. 'What is it, mother?' I asked, embracing her out of a vaguely despairing sense of terror. But she pushed me away with an hysterical violence that astounded me.

'What misery have I brought you, my child?' she cried. At that point, many women in the room began to cry too. Soon, there was much wailing in the room, and then all over the house. The sound of it! The anguish! Understanding, yet eager for knowledge, I became desperate. I had to hold onto something. The desire to embrace my mother no longer had anything to do with comforting her; for whatever she had done, whatever its magnitude, had become inconsequential. I needed to embrace her for all the anguish that tied everyone in the house into a knot. I wanted to be part of that knot, yet I wanted to know what had brought it about.

Eventually, we found each other, my mother and I, and clasped each other tightly. When I finally released her, I looked around at the neighbours and suddenly had a vision of how that anguish had to be turned into a simmering kind of indignation. The kind of indignation that had to be kept at bay only because there was a higher purpose at that moment: the sharing of concern.

Slowly and with a calmness that surprised me, I began to gather the details of what had happened. Instinctively, I seemed to have been gathering notes for a news report.

It happened during the day, when the soldiers and the police who had been patrolling the township in their Casspirs began to shoot in the streets at random. Need I describe what I did not see? How did the child come to die just at that moment when the police and the soldiers began to shoot at random, at any house, at any moving thing? That was how one of our windows was shattered by a bullet. And that was when my mother, who looked after her grandchild when we were away at work, panicked. She picked up the child and ran to the neighbours. It was only when she entered the neighbour's house that she noticed the wetness of the blanket that covered the child she held to her chest as she ran for the sanctuary of neighbours. She had looked at her unaccountably bloody hand, then she noted the still bundle in her arms, and began at that moment to blame herself for the death of her grandchild ...

Later, the police, on yet another round of shooting, found people gathered at our house. They stormed in, saw what had happened. At first, they dragged my mother out, threatening to take her away unless she agreed not to say what had happened. But then they returned and, instead, took the body of the child away. By what freak of logic did they hope that by this act their carnage would never be discovered?

That evening, I looked at Buntu closely. He appeared suddenly to have grown older. We stood alone in an embrace in our bedroom. I noticed, when I kissed his face, how his once lean face had grown suddenly puffy.

At that moment, I felt the familiar impulse come upon me once more, the impulse I always felt when I sensed that Buntu was in some kind of danger, the impulse to yield something of myself to him. He wore the look of someone struggling to gain control of something. Yet, it was clear he was far from controlling anything. I knew that look. Had seen it many times. It came at those times when I sensed that he faced a wave that was infinitely stronger than he, that it would certainly sweep him away, but that he had to seem to be struggling. I pressed myself tightly to him as if to vanish into him; as if only the two of us could stand up to the wave.

'Don't worry,' he said. 'Don't worry. I'll do everything in my power to right this wrong. Everything. Even if it means suing the police!' We went silent.

I knew that silence. But I knew something else at that moment: that I had to find a way of disengaging myself from the embrace.

Suing the police? I listened to Buntu outlining his plans. 'Legal counsel. That's what we need,' he said. 'I know some people in Pretoria,' he said. As he spoke, I felt the warmth of intimacy between us cooling. When he finished, it was cold. I disengaged from his embrace slowly, yet purposefully. Why had Buntu spoken?

Later, he was to speak again, when all his plans had failed to work: 'Over my dead body! Over my dead body!'

He sealed my lips. I would wait for him to feel and yield one day to all the realities of misfortune.

Ours was a home, it could be said. It seemed a perfect life for a young couple: I, a reporter; Buntu, a personnel officer at an American factory manufacturing farming implements. He had travelled to the United States and returned with a mind fired with dreams. We dreamed together. Much time we spent, Buntu and I, trying to make a perfect home. The occasions are numerous on which we paged through *Femina, Fair Lady, Cosmopolitan, Home & Garden, Car*, as if somehow we were going to surround our lives with the glossiness in the magazines. Indeed, much of our time was spent window-shopping through the magazines. This time, it was different from the window-shopping we did that Saturday when we courted. This time our minds were consumed by the things we saw and dreamed of owning: the furniture, the fridge, TV, video cassette recorders, washing machines, even a vacuum cleaner and every other imaginable thing that would ensure a comfortable modern life.

Especially when I was pregnant. What is it that Buntu did not buy, then? And when the boy was born, Buntu changed the car. A family, he would say, must travel comfortably.

The boy became the centre of Buntu's life. Even before he was born, Buntu had already started making inquiries at white private schools. That was where he would send his son, the bearer of his name.

Dreams! It is amazing how the horrible findings of my newspaper reports often vanished before the glossy magazines of our dreams, how I easily forgot that the glossy images were concocted out of the keys of typewriters, made by writers whose business was to sell dreams at the very moment that death pervaded the land. So powerful are words and pictures that even their makers often believe in them.

Buntu's ordeal was long. So it seemed. He would get up early every morning to follow up the previous day's leads regarding the body of our son. I wanted to go with him, but each time I prepared to go he would shake his head.

'It's my task,' he would say. But every evening he returned, empty-handed, while with each day that passed and we did not know where the body of my child was, I grew restive and hostile in a manner that gave me much pain. Yet

Buntu always felt compelled to give a report on each day's events. I never asked for it. I suppose it was his way of dealing with my silence.

One day he would say: 'The lawyers have issued a court order that the body be produced. The writ of *habeas corpus*.'

On another day he would say: 'We have petitioned the Minister of Justice.'

On yet another he would say: 'I was supposed to meet the Chief Security Officer. Waited the whole day. At the end of the day they said I would see him tomorrow if he was not going to be too busy. They are stalling.'

Then he would say: 'The newspapers, especially yours, are raising a hue and cry. The government is bound to be embarrassed. It's a matter of time.'

And so it went on. Every morning he got up and left. Sometimes alone, sometimes with friends. He always left to bear the failure alone.

How much did I care about lawyers, petitions and Chief Security Officers? A lot. The problem was that whenever Buntu spoke about his efforts, I heard only his words. I felt in him the disguised hesitancy of someone who wanted reassurance without asking for it. I saw someone who got up every morning and left not to look for results, but to search for something he could only have found with me.

And each time he returned, I gave my speech to my eyes. And he answered without my having parted my lips. As a result, I sensed, for the first time in my life, a terrible power in me that could make him do anything. And he would never ever be able to deal with that power as long as he did not silence my eyes and call for my voice.

And so, he had to prove himself. And while he left each morning, I learned to be brutally silent. Could he prove himself without me? Could he? Then I got to know, those days, what I'd always wanted from him. I got to know why I have always drawn him into me whenever I sensed his vulnerability.

I wanted him to be free to fear. Wasn't there greater strength that way? Had he ever lived with his own feelings? And the stress of life in this land: didn't it call out for men to be heroes? And should they live up to it even though the details of the war to be fought may often be blurred? They should.

Yet it is precisely for that reason that I often found Buntu's thoughts lacking in strength. They lacked the experience of strife that could only come from a humbling acceptance of fear and then, only then, the need to fight it.

Me? In a way, I have always been free to fear. The prerogative of being a girl. It was always expected of me to scream when a spider crawled across the ceiling. It was known I would jump onto a chair whenever a mouse blundered into the room.

Then, once more, the Casspirs came. A few days before we got the body back, I was at home with my mother when we heard the great roar of truck engines. There was much running and shouting in the streets. I saw them, as I've always seen them on my assignments: the Casspirs. On five occasions they ran down our street at great speed, hurling tear-gas canisters at random. On the fourth occasion, they got our house. The canister shattered another window and filled the house with the terrible pungent choking smoke that I had got to know so well. We ran out of the house gasping for fresh air.

So, this was how my child was killed? Could they have been the same soldiers? Now hardened to their tasks? Or were they new ones being hardened to their tasks? Did they drive away laughing? Clearing paths for their families? What paths?

And was this our home? It couldn't be. It had to be a little bird's nest waiting to be plundered by a predator bird. There seemed no sense to the wedding pictures on the walls, the graduation pictures, birthday pictures, pictures of relatives, and paintings of lush landscapes. There seemed no sense anymore to what seemed recognisably human in our house. It took only a random swoop to obliterate personal worth, to blot out any value there may have been to the past. In desperation, we began to live only for the moment. I do feel hunted.

It was on the night of the tear gas that Buntu came home, saw what had happened, and broke down in tears. They had long been in the coming …

My own tears welled out too. How much did we have to cry to refloat stranded boats? I was sure they would float again.

A few nights later, on the night of the funeral, exhausted, I lay on my bed, listening to the last of the mourners leaving. Slowly, I became conscious of returning to the world. Something came back after it seemed not to have been there for ages. It came as a surprise, as a reminder that we will always live around what will happen. The sun will rise and set, and the ants will do their endless work, until one day the clouds turn grey and rain falls, and even in the township, the ants will fly out into the sky. Come what may.

My moon came, in a heavy surge of blood. And, after such a long time, I remembered the thing Buntu and I had buried in me. I felt it as if it had just entered. I felt it again as it floated away on the surge. I would be ready for another month. Ready as always, each and every month, for new beginnings.

And Buntu? I'll be with him, now. Always. Without our knowing, all the trying events had prepared for us new beginnings. Shall we not prevail?

KEN BARRIS

The Questioning

From: *Small Change* (1988)

Martin Bennet was a large, greasy poet of uncertain stability. He had a gentle mild face and an unsteady eye. It blinked at you, or twitched at the worst possible times. There was something independent about the left one. It was slightly smaller than the right, drooped, roved more restlessly than its neighbour. His irrational eye. In fact, it was dyslexic, being unable to order perceptual sequences correctly.

He wrote poems about mournful gnats, the defunct river mill of his childhood, and faded hydrangeas.

He was unemployable in other respects. He had a pathological fear of structures and was prone to serious depressions. Like Joyce, he disliked water, and the consequences were obvious. Not that he was overtly dirty; he was simply stale in appearance and smell, he had the impact of a mildewed cabbage on an unexpectant world.

He lived off a hedge of capital that his mother had left him. Over the last seven years, it had grown smaller. He was often desperately worried about where he would get more money when inflation made that lot completely worthless.

Despite the fact that he was thirty-seven years old, he lived in Rondebosch in a student boarding house occupied by youngsters suffering from pimples or excessive religion or no friends. It had avacado-green high-gloss enamel corridors with echoing wooden floors. Their portable TVs and Philips record players bounced tinny sounds along this space, making the claustrophobia worse.

Not that he was unhappy: when he was insomniac he could take out his pad of yellow paper, and his black fountain pen, and scribble lengthy rhyming odes. On Saturday nights he could walk along Rondebosch Main Road, around the Pig, or look into the Hard Rock and smell the steak fumes, or go round the corner and watch the water of the Liesbeeck Canal flow under the Belmont Road bridge. On Sunday mornings he could eat at the Wimpy Bar, where he liked to treat himself to a *Sunday Times*, a Bender Brunch, and a glass of Horlicks.

He was called to the phone one morning. It was a wistful winter morning, with the sun attempting to shine through a drizzle. When he was a child, that was called a monkey's wedding. He picked it up, and the line went dead. It happened again that morning, and twice more the next week.

He didn't know what to make of it, but the mystery upset him. He found himself confined to the toilet with diarrhoea. To make matters worse, he had no one to confide in. He had nothing to confide in anybody about. Then the incidents receded glibly into the past.

He began to feel that he was being followed. Once he imagined that the occupants of a large white Japanese car, which was idling along behind him, were scrutinising him. As soon as he looked squarely at it, it accelerated away with a smooth whine. The glass was polarised, so he couldn't see who was in it. While sitting in a restaurant having anchovy toast and tea, he thought he saw a man standing outside training a video camera on him. But that proved nothing.

He was quite put off his food. Although there were no repetitions of the telephone incident, he found it difficult to sleep. The net result was that he wrote more poetry than usual, under greater pressure. The poetry showed no improvement.

★ ★ ★

The security police came for him in the early hours of the morning. He heard the bell ringing, footsteps echoing down the passage – heavy footsteps, many people – then his door burst open and the light was snapped on. He shrieked and sat up in bed, with the covers up to his chin. He felt intensely foolish.

There were five men crowding his small bedroom, looking at him. Their expressions were serious and unreadable. They wore loud sports jackets and open-necked shirts.

'Martin Bennet,' pronounced one of them. 'You are Martin Bennet.'

'I am,' said Martin. His voice shook. 'Who are you?'

'Lieutenant Strimling, Security Branch.' He stepped forward and showed Martin a green plastic card. It had his name, rank and number, and identified him as a member of the South African Police. 'I have bad news for you. You are now under arrest, in terms of Section 29 of the Internal Security Act.' He leaned forward and showed Martin a form on a clipboard. It had a state letter-head, and was stamped and signed by a magistrate. Martin felt too sick and guilty to see, let alone read it.

'Get up, please,' said Lieutenant Striniling, 'and get dressed. It will be in your interests to do so as quickly as possible. We are going to search your room, and we must do so in your presence.'

Martin looked around. There was no way his presence could be avoided in his room. It was the only one he had, and it was virtually impossible to move in. He got out of bed, and shifted carefully past the nearest of the five police-men and walked to his cupboard. He looked at them. They stood there wait-ing for him. He took out the clothes he needed and put them on as quickly as possible. They watched him in silence. He could feel them watching his white, plump flesh. He was shivering.

The search did not take long. There was very little in his room to find. One of the policemen found a file of his poetry and showed it to him. 'What's this?' he asked.

'Poetry,' said Martin.

'Pro-ANC,' suggested the policeman.

Martin said nothing for a whole minute. Then: 'I don't know why you are doing this. Are you sure you have the right person? I'm not a political person at all. I know nothing about politics.'

The official holding his file of yellow pages shook it at him and grinned.

There was a small crowd of sleepy, puzzled, worried lodgers standing in the passage when they came out. Martin looked at them, trying desperately to make some kind of contact with the people with whom he lived, but his left eye went into its tic. He was horribly worried that they would think he was guilty. The Security Police only detain people who are involved in something. The onlookers blurred. He wanted to tell one of them something, leave a message, arrange for his rent. Lieutenant Strimling stopped, and gave him an opportunity. Then he realised there was no one to give a message to, and he felt too helpless about the rent to do anything about it. The four policemen hurried him on.

He was bundled into a white Ford with Lieutenant Strimling and two others. The remaining two climbed into another car, and they all sped off down Main Road in the direction of Muizenberg. 'Where are you taking me?' he asked. He could hear his tongue sticking against the roof of his mouth. He needed to brush his teeth.

They ignored him. They chatted to each other about people he didn't know. It was as if they were on their way to meet some friends, or to a movie.

They turned right into Lansdowne Road and took him to the Claremont Police Station. The cars squealed in through the side gate in First Avenue, and jerked to a halt. He was taken into a dimly lit room and told to wait. All the policemen disappeared. There were five dustbins in the room. He counted them. The floor was dirty anyway.

A young constable came in. He was stooped and had a hooked nose. He was very ugly, and obviously stupid. Martin felt sorry for him. He had a clip-board in his hand with some forms on it, and there was a government-issue ballpoint pen tied to it with a string. He started to take down Martin's particu-lars. Martin had to help him with his spelling, and then gave up. The man was obviously dyslexic. He completed his form.

'I must just check this out with Staff,' he said. He disappeared. Martin waited in complete terror. He was sure that if a more senior officer came along, he could explain that it was a mistake, and then they would release him.

The constable cane back. 'Staff says this are the wrong forms. I must fill in this other lot.' Martin wondered who Staff was. He thought Staff was some mysterious form of control. Like Weather. I must check with Weather, or with Meteorology. They filled the new forms in, and the constable disappeared.

Martin wanted to pass water badly.

A new person came back. He was very fat and had a gravel voice. He was holding the clipboard. There were new forms in it.

'Name?' he asked.

Martin wanted to cry. 'I've told him that,' he said.

'Told who?'

'I told this other man who was here.'

'Told him what?'

'I told him ...' Tears spurted into his eyes. He started again. 'I told him all that.'

The staff-sergeant looked uncomfortable. He didn't like to see men cry. 'He filled in the wrong forms,' he explained.

'I know that. He filled in another set.'

'Ja,' said the policeman. 'That's the problem. You see, he signed those. He's not supposed to fill in those other forms. I am.'

They filled in the new forms.

Martin was taken upstairs by the first policeman to have his fingerprints taken. But first he was taken into a washroom — where at last he had a chance to relieve himself — to wash his hands. 'You must dry them,' said the constable. Martin looked around at the empty towel rack, then under the basin. He couldn't see a towel. He looked around again, because he was sure he must be wrong. 'There are no towels,' he said.

'Dry your hands!' shouted the policeman.

Martin could feel the blood draining from his face. 'What with?'

The policeman looked round. 'Fuck it, man,' he said, 'just dry your hands on any fucking thing.' Martin wiped his hands on his pants.

They walked across the passage to the room where fingerprints were taken. 'Are your hands dry?' asked the corporal in charge. The corporal pressed each of his fingers and thumbs hard onto the appropriate blocks, and rolled them round so that the whole profile would show. They rolled off the paper stickily.

His first night in the cell was too distressing to bear. The only problem was that he had to bear it. Down the road was Checkers. Just up the road was Tonneson's Garage. It was so normal out there. He just had to raise his voice and shout, or reach out his hand, and normality would see and hear him. But there was no way that he could reach normality. There was no reason for its absence either. He was simply locked up.

He was in a single cell with its own toilet and washbasin. It was a very little toilet, the kind they have in nursery schools. Although the enamel was deeply stained, it was reasonably clean. There were no other people in his cell; there were a couple of drunks in the cell next door who spent the night moaning and vomiting. By the time morning announced itself and he could hear the traffic in Lansdowne Road, he was distraught.

The day passed like the next three: no one would answer his questions. He remained alone in his cell, although from the sounds and the people passing in the passage it was a busy police station filled with criminal or merely vagrant traffic. A breakfast of grey porridge in an aluminium bowl was slid under his door before it was light outside; he was given seven slices of bread at eleven, with a square of margarine, a square of jam, and a spoon with which to spread them. At half past three he was given supper: stywe pap, mashed potatoes, boiled cabbage, and a sprinkling of shredded chicken.

He couldn't believe how hungry he grew by midnight. On the third day he held back three slices of his lunchtime bread and waited till sunset. Then he nibbled one after the other, as slowly as he could, drinking mugs of water in between and walking around his cell until he judged it was time to start on the next slice. He finished the bread before it was completely dark.

He still had no idea what the police intended to do with him, or why he was there. No one found it necessary to inform him.

* * *

Martin Bennet was placed in the back of a yellow police van and driven to a huge police station in the centre of Cape Town that he didn't know. It was like a fort of naked red brick. He was taken into a cell that faced inwards into an open courtyard. The coir mattress on the steel bed stank, and there were obscene, lonely graffiti scratched on the enamel green walls. There were no washing or toilet facilities. Every few hours a warder came round and took him to the toilet. He was allowed out to shower once a day, and had to stand in a queue with the other prisoners. They terrified him.

The food was worse than at the Claremont police station. He became extremely depressed. In the afternoon of his fourth day in the new prison – possibly his fifth – a policeman came round and poked an orange through the bars at him, grinning in pleasure and gesturing invitingly. He approached, and the policeman thrust the orange through the bars. Martin took it. The act of kindness was too much for him. This time he did cry.

There was a high window in his cell. By standing on his cot and pulling himself up by the bars, he could catch a brief glimpse of Table Mountain. Then he would fall back again.

The nights were extremely cold, but he had been given enough blankets. It was almost like camping outside, because air moved freely through the bars, and he could see the cells opposite his across an outdoors space. In the stillness of the early hours, he could hear the sounds of many people dreaming or snoring, turning in their cells restlessly, the distant nightmarish clanking of gates. Occasionally a police van would come in or go out through the large central entrance. It was as if he had been swallowed by a gargantuan animal that moved with difficulty, and wheezed rather than breathed. Only something like the vital roar of a motor bike outside could break its lassitude.

The whole jail stank.

The day he was fetched for his first interrogation, it was pouring with rain, and the smells closed on him more heavily. Two warders came to fetch him from his cell. One was the benevolent policeman who had given him the orange. He didn't know the other one. He was taken upstairs to a dusty grey office and left to wait. There were two metal tables with telephones, and a filing cabinet. He noticed a dark stain on the floor and his bowels turned to jelly. He had trouble not disgracing himself.

Thick-limbed, absent-minded people wandered in and out of the office — it adjoined another one, which seemed to be more the centre of activity. He couldn't see what was in it, although he timidly craned his head towards the door.

He was getting tired of standing when an important-looking policeman or official of some kind came in. He was in his forties, and he had large, definite hands. Each feature was terribly definite: his lips and nose might have been carved crudely out of wood, his eyes were bulbous but clear. He looked Martin up and down.

Martin's intestines contracted. The official sighed, and pressed down his intercom button with his thumb. A crude male voice answered. Then a young uniformed policeman came in. 'Take him out and get him cleaned up. I can't speak to someone in such a distasteful condition.' The constable shook his head sadly at Martin. 'Didn't your mother teach you what to do?' he asked.

They left him alone until the next day. This time the one who had given him an orange came on his own. 'You mustn't worry so much,' he told Martin. 'Fuck it, man, they're not going to kill you.' Martin couldn't say anything in reply. His voice wasn't working, but he was determined he would stand up to anything they did to him. He was not going to degrade himself again.

At that point his left eye went into its spasm and started blurring. This almost gave him courage: it was the one condition he was used to. The trouble was that his right eye was astigmatic, and he had difficulty seeing an undistorted world at all.

He was taken to the same office. There was no waiting this time. There were three officers behind the desk, including the one who had frightened him so much.

The man lit a cigarette and smiled at Martin. 'I haven't introduced myself. I'm Captain van Wyk. Pieter van Wyk.'

Martin stared at him like a trapped rabbit.

'Look, Martin,' he said, 'we are reasonable people. We just want to talk to you, really. Just think of this as a friendly chat.'

Martin looked around at him in confusion. They waited for him to speak. 'Why am I here?' he asked.

The captain looked a little embarrassed. He even had to clear his throat. 'We were hoping you could tell us that,' he asked. 'You see, we don't seem to have a file on you.'

Martin stared at him. Van Wyk turned to the man next to him, who scraped back his chair, got up and left the room. He returned with a chair, placed it behind Martin, and disappeared.

'Ja,' said Captain van Wyk. He didn't seem to know what to say. He picked up a pencil and fiddled with it. 'You don't seem to be terribly involved in much. I mean, not much that we consider important. In the sense of subversive, that is. In fact, you don't seem to be involved in terribly much at all.'

Martin was still standing. Van Wyk gestured. 'Please take a seat,' he said. Martin sank into the chair. His heart was thudding so hard he thought it would fail, and the face across the table was blurring into a kind of stewy mist. He didn't dare look at the other face next to it.

'Jesus,' said Martin.

'We're only human,' said the captain. 'If you had to do our job, you could also make mistakes. Not that that proves anything,' he added warningly. 'Remember, we don't actually know that you're innocent.'

Martin could feel time sucking away at him, with suffocating brightness. He was shaking violently.

'Can I go?' he asked. 'I mean, is there any reason why I am still here?'

'Well, yes. We'd like to offer you a cup of tea. I'm sure it's on its way.'

It's a trap, he thought. They let you go and then they shoot you in the back. He looked around wildly. There was a terrible crash from the room next door. The policeman bringing the tea had tripped.

★ ★ ★

Martin celebrated his release by dining at a restaurant that he couldn't afford. He chose the Hard Rock Café in Rondebosch. There were large photographs on the wall of Marilyn Monroe, John Wayne, and other icons of Western culture. There was a dais at the far end, on which sat a pianist inaudibly playing songs like *Moon River* and *Tennessee Waltz*. The waitresses were all attractive women wearing white dresses that weren't quite virginal and hairstyles that weren't quite androgynous. He ordered a steak Rossini rare, understanding that that was how things should be done.

He sat on his own, bemused and lonely – drowning in the bright noise and conversation of others. Everyone seemed to have so much energy with which to celebrate their mouths, one way or another. All around him sat people wading through enormous platters piled with red juicy meat and steaming salted chips, or prime seafood and wondrous salads. Everyone was drinking wine, gesturing animatedly, telling jokes and roaring with laughter, or leaning forward and gazing intimately into each other's eyes.

When Martin's steak came, saliva spurted into his mouth. He scraped the rich red sauce off and cut into his meat. It was far bloodier than he thought it would be. In fact, blood leaked effortlessly from the pink flesh and collected in a shallow pool. He cut off a piece, put it into his mouth and chewed it slowly.

He couldn't swallow. It was an excellent piece of beef but something made it grow larger and more rubbery the more he chewed. He had to spit it into his serviette. Then he folded it out of sight, cleared his throat, and stood up. He tried to say something, but no one was interested in listening to him. Besides, even if they were, he had a very small voice.

He cleared his throat more loudly, but it didn't help at all. 'It's not normal,' he shouted out. No one heard him. Glancing wildly about to see the effects of this pronouncement, his eye fell on the pianist, who was still morosely doing his duty. There was a microphone standing nearby.

Martin started towards it. The conversations around him grew louder and louder as he waded through chairs and ankles towards his destination. One particularly vital gust of laughter from a large table almost extinguished him. But a strange singleness had taken hold of his movement. He tapped on the microphone. It was on. The pianist looked up at him, but carried on playing *Blueberry Hill*. 'It's not normal,' he shouted into the microphone. He recoiled at the volume of his own voice. 'All this,' he explained to the microphone. 'You think they only take the guilty, but it's not like that. Not only them!'

The voices were gradually dying down, and people were swivelling their faces towards him. The pianist gave up. The manageress was struggling through the crowded room towards the dais, a competent, attractive hostess in her thirties. Martin leaned forward again, speaking as quickly as he could. 'Where there's smoke there's fire – that's what they say, but it's not like that. Not only commies or whatever. They're controlling you, right now. Just because they're there. You think you're free!'

There were a few ripples of laughter. Someone pointed his finger at his head and whirled it round and round. By now the manageress had almost reached Martin. 'The rule of law, I mean,' he shouted lamely, realising that he hadn't mentioned what he was talking about. The manageress switched the microphone off. Martin stared at her.

Her face was a terrible mixture of emotions: outrage, bewilderment, amusement. Beneath the set of her make-up. All of them were pointed at Martin. 'Do you have a problem, sir?' she asked, very firmly. 'Can you please come down from there.'

'I'll go quietly,' he said. 'No fuss, no bother. I'm going.' He raised his hands in surrender and stepped down. Tears started streaming down his face, effortlessly. She couldn't look at him. He couldn't see.

'Would you mind leaving,' she asked. Around them the voices started rising again as people realised the show was over, although many had stopped eating to stare at Martin.

'I haven't paid for my meal yet.'

'Don't worry,' she said, competently and inarguably, 'it's on the house.'

She took his arm and hurried him on towards the entrance. She could feel his helplessness: she led him out.

★ ★ ★

It was cold outside the restaurant. Green and mauve neon lights robbed flesh of colour, and streams of headlights went by, blinding and indifferent to Martin's anguish. He turned around a few times, stared into the restaurant, sighed, shrugged his shoulders, stared up at the sky. The low clouds overhead reflected back the sodium vapour light of the city. He felt like a vast sac filled with clear fluid, close to tearing.

A brightly dressed couple passed Martin and turned into the Hard Rock. As they opened the door, warm air and laughter gusted out. Martin turned and walked wearily away. Perhaps he would go and stand on the Belmont Road bridge, and watch the shallow black water scurry under it in the Liesbeeck Canal.

Zoë Wicomb

Ash on my Sleeve

From: *You Can't Get Lost in Cape Town* (1987)

Desmond is a man who relies on the communicative powers of the handshake. Which renders my hand, a cluster of crushed bones, inert as he takes a step back and nods approvingly while still applying the pressure. He attempts what proves impossible in spite of my decision to co-operate. That is to stand back even further in order to inspect me more thoroughly without releasing my hand. The distance between us cannot be lengthened and I am about to point out this unalterable fact when his smile relaxes into speech.

'Well, what a surprise!'

'Yes, what a surprise,' I contribute.

It is of course no longer a surprise. I arranged the meeting two months ago when I wrote to Moira after years of silence between us, and yesterday I telephoned to confirm the visit. And I had met Desmond before, in fact at the same party at which Moira had been struck by the eloquence of his handshake. Then we discussed the role of the Student Representative Council, he, a final-year Commerce student, confidently, his voice remaining even as he bent down to tie a shoelace. And while I floundered, lost in subordinate clauses, he excused himself with a hurried, 'Back in a moment.' We have not spoken since.

'You're looking wonderful, so youthful. Turning into something of a swan in your middle age, hey!'

I had thought it prudent to arrange a one-night stay which would leave me the option of another if things went well. I am a guest in their house; I must not be rude. So I content myself with staring at his jaw where my eyes fortuitously alight on the tell-tale red of an incipient pimple. He releases my hand. He rubs index finger and thumb together, testing an imagined protuberance, and as he gestures me to sit down the left hand briefly brushes the jaw.

It always feels worse than it looks, he will comfort himself, feeling its enormity; say to himself, the tactual never corresponds with the appearance of such a blemish, and dismiss it. I shall allow my eyes at strategic moments to explore his face then settle to revive the gnathic discomfort.

Somewhere at the back of the house Moira's voice has been rising and falling, flashing familiar stills from the past. Will she be as nervous as I am? A

685

door clicks and a voice starts up again, closer, already addressing me, so that the figure develops slowly, fuzzily assumes form before she appears: '... to deal with these people and I just had to be rude and say my friend's here, all the way from England, she's waiting ...'

Standing in the doorway, she shakes her head. 'My God Frieda Shenton, you plaasjapie, is it really you?'

I grin. Will we embrace? Shake hands? My arm hangs foolishly. Then she puts her hands on my shoulders and says, 'It's all my fault. I'm hopeless at writing letters and we moved around so much and what with my hands full with children I lost touch with everyone. But I've thought of you, many a day have I thought of you.'

'Oh nonsense,' I say awkwardly. 'I'm no good at writing letters either. We've both been very bad.'

Her laughter deals swiftly with the layer of dust on that old intimacy but our speech, like the short letters we exchanged, is awkward. We cannot tumble into the present while a decade gapes between us.

Sitting before her I realise what had bothered me yesterday on the telephone when she said, 'Good heavens man, I can't believe it ... Yes of course I've remembered ... OK, let me pick you up at the station.'

Unease at what I now know to be the voice made me decline. 'No,' I said. 'I'd like to walk, get to see the place. I can't get enough of Cape Town,' I gushed. For her voice is deeper, slowed down eerily like the distortion of a faulty record player. Some would say the voice of a woman speaking evenly, avoiding inflection.

'I bet,' she says, 'you regretted having to walk all that way.'

She is right. The even-numbered houses on the left side of this interminable street are L-shaped with grey asbestos roofs. Their stoeps alternate green, red and black, making spurious claims to individuality. The macadamised street is very black and sticky under the soles, its concrete edge of raised pavement a virgin grey that invites you to scribble something rude, or just anything at all. For all its neat edges, the garden sand spills on to the pavement as if the earth were wriggling in discomfort. It is the pale porous sand of the Cape Flats pushed out over centuries by the Indian Ocean. It does not portend well for the cultivation of prize-winning dahlias.

I was so sure that it was Moira's house. There it was, a black stoep inevitably after the green, the house inadequately fenced off so that the garden sand had been swept along the pavement in delicately waved watermark by the previous afternoon's wind. A child's bucket and spade had been left in the garden and on a mound of sand a jaunty strip of astroturf testified to the untameable. I knocked without checking the number again and felt foolish as the occupier with hands on her hips directed me to the fourth house along.

Moira's is a house like all the others except for the determined effort in the garden. Young trees grow in bonsai uniformity, promising a dense hedge all around for those who are prepared to wait. The fence is efficient. The sand does not escape; it is held by the roots of a brave lawn visibly knitting beneath its coarse blades of grass. Number 288 is swathed in lace curtains. Even the glass-panelled front door has generously ruched lengths of lace between the wooden strips. Dense, so that you could not begin to guess at the outline approaching the door. It was Desmond.

'Goodness me, ten, no twelve years haven't done much to damage you,' Moira says generously.

'Think so, Moi,' Desmond adds. 'I think Frieda has a contract with time. Look, she's even developed a waistline,' and his hands hover as if to describe the chimerical curve. There is the possibility that I may be doing him an injustice.

'I suppose it's marriage that's done it for us. Very ageing, and of course the children don't help,' he says.

'It's not a week since I sewed up this cushion. What do the children do with them.' Moira tugs at the loose threads then picks up another cushion to check the stitching.

'See,' Desmond persists, 'a good figure in your youth is no guarantee against childbearing. There are veins and sagging breasts and of course some women get horribly fat; that is if they don't grow thin and haggard.' He looks sympathetically at Moira. Why does she not spit in his eye? I fix my eye on his jaw so that he says, 'Count yourself lucky that you've missed the boat.'

Silence. And then we laugh. Under Desmond's stern eye we lean back in simultaneous laughter that cleaves through the years to where we sat on our twin beds recounting the events of our nights out. Stomach-clutching laughter as we whispered our adventures and decoded for each other the words grunted by boys through the smoke of the braaivleis. Or the tears, the stifled sobs of bruised love, quietly, in order not to disturb her parents. She slept lightly, Moira's mother, who said that a girl cannot keep the loss of her virginity a secret, that her very gait proclaims it to the world and especially to men who will expect favours from her.

When our laughter subsides Desmond gets a bottle of whisky from the cabinet of the same oppressively carved dark wood as the rest of the sitting-room suite.

'Tell Susie to make some tea,' he says.

'It's her afternoon off. Eh …' Moira's silence asserts itself as her own so that we wait and wait until she explains, 'We have a servant. People don't have servants in England, do they? Not ordinary people, I mean.'

'It's a matter of nomenclature I think. The middle classes have cleaning ladies, a Mrs Thing, usually quite a character, whom we pretend to be in awe of. She does for those of us who are too sensitive or too important or intelligent to clean up our own mess. We pay a decent wage, that is for a cleaner, of course, and not to be compared with our own salaries.'

Moira bends closely over a cushion, then looks up at me and I recall a photograph of her in an op-art mini-skirt, dangling very large black and white earrings from delicate lobes. The face is lifted quizzically at the photographer, almost in disbelief, and her cupped hand is caught in movement perhaps on the way to check the jaunty flick-ups. I cannot remember who took the photograph but at the bottom of the picture I recognise the intrusion of my right foot, a thick ankle growing out of an absurdly delicate high-heeled shoe.

I wish I could fill the ensuing silence with something conciliatory, no something that will erase what I have said, but my trapped thoughts blunder insect-like against a glazed window. I who in this strange house in a new Coloured suburb have just accused and criticised my hostess. She will have seen through the deception of the first-person usage; she will shrink from the self-righteousness of my words and lift her face quizzically at my contempt. I feel the dampness crawl along my hairline. But Moira looks at me serenely while Desmond frowns. Then she moves as if to rise.

'Don't bother with tea on my account,' I say with my eye longingly on the whisky, and carry on in the same breath, 'Are you still in touch with Martin? I wouldn't mind seeing him after all these years.'

Moira's admirers were plentiful and she generously shared with me the benefits of her beauty. At parties young men straightened their jackets and stepped over to ask me to dance. Their cool hands fell on my shoulders, bare and damp with sweat. I glided past the rows of girls waiting to be chosen. So they tested their charm – 'Can I get you a lemonade? Shall we dance again?' – on me the intermediary. In the airless room my limbs obeyed the inexorable sweep of the ballroom dances. But with the wilder Twist or Shake my broad shoulders buckled under a young man's gaze and my feet grew leaden as I waited for the casual enquiry after Moira. Then we would sit out a dance chatting about Moira and the gardenia on my bosom meshed in maddening fragrance our common interest. My hand squeezed in gratitude with a quick goodnight, for there was no question about it: my friendship had to be secured in order to be considered by Moira. Then in the early hours, sitting cross-legged on her bed, we sifted his words and Moira unpinned for me the gardenia, crushed by his fervour, when his cool hand on my shoulder drew me closer, closer in that first held dance.

Young men in Sunday ties and borrowed cars agreed to take me with them on scenic drives along the foot of Table Mountain, or Chapman's Peak where we looked down dizzily at the sea. And I tactfully wandered off licking at a jumbo ice-cream while they practised their kissing, Moira's virginity unassailable. Below, the adult baboons scrambled over the sand dunes and smacked the bald bottoms of their young and the sun-licked waves beckoned at the mermaids on the rocks.

Desmond replies, 'Martin's fallen in love with an AZAPO woman, married her and stopped coming round. Shall we say that he finally lost interest in Moi?'

The whisky in his glass lurches amber as he rolls the stem between his fingers.

'Would you like a coke?' he asks.

I decline but I long to violate the alcohol taboo for women. 'A girl who drinks is nothing other than a prostitute,' Father said. And there's no such thing as just a little tot because girls get drunk instantly. Then they hitch up their skirts like the servant girls on their days off, caps scrunched into shopping bags, waving their Vaaljapie bottles defiantly. A nice girl's reputation would shatter with a single mouthful of liquor.

'The children are back from their party,' Moira says. There is a shuffling outside and then they burst in blowing penny whistles and rattling their plastic spoils. Simultaneously they reel off the events of the party and correct each other's versions while the youngest scrambles onto his mother's lap. Moira listens, amused. She interrupts them, 'Look who's here. Say hallo to the auntie. Auntie Frieda's come all the way from England to see you.' They compose their stained faces and shake hands solemnly. Then the youngest bursts into tears and the other two discuss in undertones the legitimacy of his grievance.

'He's tired,' Desmond offers from the depths of his whisky reverie, 'probably eaten too much as well.'

This statement has a history, for Moira throws her head back and laughs and the little boy charges at his father and butts him in the stomach.

'Freddie, we've got a visitor, behave yourself hey,' the eldest admonishes.

I smile at her and get up to answer the persistent knock at the back door which the family seem not to hear. A man in overalls waiting on the doorstep looks at me bewildered but then says soberly, 'For the Missus,' and hands over a bunch of arum lilies which I stick in a pot by the sink. When I turn round Moira stands in the doorway watching me. She interrupts as I start explaining about the man.

'Yes, I'll put it in the children's room.'

I want to say that the pot is not tall enough for the lilies but she takes them off hurriedly, the erect spadices dusting yellow onto the funnelled white leaves. Soon they will droop; I did not have a chance to put water in the pot.

I wait awkwardly in the kitchen and watch a woman walk past the window. No doubt there is a servant's room at the far end of the garden. The man must be the gardener but from the window it is clear that there are no flowers in the garden except for a rampant morning glory that covers the fence. When Moira comes back she prepares grenadilla juice and soda with which we settle around the table. I think of alcohol and say, 'It's a nice kitchen.' It is true that sunlight sifted through the lace curtains softens the electric blue of the melamine worksurfaces. But after the formality of the sitting room the clutter of the kitchen comes as a surprise. The sink is grimy and harbours dishes of surely the previous day. The grooved steel band around the table top holds a neat line of grease and dust compound.

'Yes,' she says, 'I like it. The living room is Desmond's. He has no interest in the kitchen.'

And all the while she chops at the parsley, slowly chops it to a pulp. Then beneath the peelings and the spilled contents of brown paperbags she ferrets about until she drags out a comb.

'Where the hell are the bay leaves?' she laughs, and throws the comb across the worksurface. I rise to inspect a curious object on the windowsill from which the light bounces frantically. It is a baby's shoe dipped into a molten alloy, an instant sculpture of brassy brown that records the first wayward steps of a new biped. I tease it in the sunlight, turning it this way and that.

'Strange object,' I say, 'whose is it?'

'Ridiculous hey,' and we laugh in agreement. 'Desmond's idea,' she explains, 'but funnily enough I'm quite attached to that shoe now. It's Carol's, the eldest; you feel so proud of the things your child does. Obvious things, you know, like walking and talking you await anxiously as if they were man's first steps on the moon and you're so absurdly pleased at the child's achievement. And so we ought to be, not proud I suppose, but grateful. I'm back at work, mornings only, at Manenberg, and you should see the township children. Things haven't changed much, don't you believe that.'

She picks up the shoe.

'Carol's right foot always leaned too far to the right and Desmond felt that that was the shoe to preserve. More character, he said. Ja,' she sighs, 'things were better in those early days. And anyway I didn't mind his kak so much then. But I'd better get on otherwise dinner'll be late.'

I lift the lace curtain and spread out the gathers to reveal a pattern of scallops with their sprays of stylised leaves. The flower man is walking in the shadow of the fence carrying a carrier-bag full of books. He does not look at me holding up the nylon lace. I turn to Moira bent over a cheese grater, and with the sepia light of evening streaming in, her face lifts its sadness to me, the nut-brown skin, as if under a magnifying glass, singed translucent and taut across the high cheekbones.

'Moira,' I say, but at that moment she beats the tin grater against the bowl.

So I tug at things, peep, rummage through her kitchen, pick at this and that as if they were buttons to trigger off the mechanism of software that will gush out a neatly printed account of her life. I drop the curtain still held in my limp hand.

690

'What happened to Michael?' she asks.

'Dunno. There was no point in keeping in touch, not after all that. And there is in any case no such thing as friendship with men.' I surprise myself by adding, 'Mind you, I think quite neutrally about him, even positively at times. The horror of Michael must've been absorbed by the subsequent horror of others. But I don't, thank God, remember their names.'

Moira laughs. 'You must be kinder to men. We have to get on with them.'

'Yes,' I retort, 'but surely not behind their backs.'

'Heavens,' she says, 'we were so blarry stupid and dishonest really. Obsessed with virginity, we imagined we weren't messing about with sex. Suppose that's what we thought sex was all about: breaking a membrane. I expect Michael was as stupid as you. Catholic, wasn't he?'

I do not want to talk about Michael. I am much more curious about Desmond. How did he slip through the net? Desmond scorned the methods of her other suitors and refused to ingratiate himself with me. On her first date Moira came back with a headache, bristling with secrecy no doubt sworn beneath his parted lips. We did not laugh at the way he pontificated, his hands held gravely together as in prayer to prevent interruptions. Desmond left Cape Town at the end of that year and I had in the meantime met Michael.

There was the night on the bench under the loquat tree when we ate the tasteless little fruits and spat glossy pips over the fence. Moira's fingers drummed the folder on her lap.

'Here,' she said in a strange voice, 'are the letters. You should just read this, today's.'

I tugged at the branch just above my head so that it rustled in the dark and overripe loquats fell plop to the ground.

'No, not his letters, that wouldn't be right,' I said. And my memory skimmed the pages of Michael's letters. Love, holy love that made the remembered words dance on that lined foolscap infused with his smell. I could not, would not, share the first man to love me.

'Is he getting on OK in Durban?' I asked

'Yes, I expect he still has many friends there. I'm going up just after the finals and then perhaps he'll come back to Cape Town. Let's see if we can spit two pips together and hit the fence at the same time.'

So we sat in the dark, between swotting sessions, under the tree with yellow loquats lustrous in the black leaves. Perhaps she mimicked his Durban voice, waiting for me to take up the routine of friendly mockery. I try in vain to summon it all. I cannot separate the tangled strands of conversation or remembered letters. Was it then, in my Durban accent, that I replied with Michael's views about the permanence and sanctity of marriage?

'Ja–ja–ja,' Moira sighs, pulling out a chair. And turning again to check a pot on the stove, her neck is unbecomingly twisted, the sinews thrown into relief.

How old we have grown since that night under the loquat tree, and I know that there is no point in enquiring after Desmond.

'Do you like living here?' I ask instead.

'It's OK, as good as anything.'

'I was thinking of your parents' home, the house where I stayed. How lovely it was. Everything's so new here. Don't you find it strange?'

'Ag, Frieda, but we're so new, don't we belong in estates like this? Coloureds haven't been around for that long, perhaps that's why we stray. Just think, in our teens we wanted to be white, now we want to be full-blooded Africans. We've never wanted to be ourselves and that's why we stray … across the continent, across the oceans and even here, right into the Tricameral Parliament, playing into their hands. Actually,' and she looks me straight in the eye, 'it suits me very well to live here.'

Chastened by her reply I drum my fingertips on the table so that she says gently, 'I don't mean to accuse you. At the time I would have done exactly the same. There was little else to do. Still, it's really nice to see you. I hope you'll be able to stay tomorrow.' Her hand burns for a moment on my shoulder.

It is time for dinner. Moira makes a perfunctory attempt at clearing the table then, defeated by the chaos, she throws a cloth at me.

'Oh God, I'll never be ready by seven.'

I am drawn into the revolving circle of panic, washing down, screwing lids back on to jars, shutting doors on food that will rot long before discovery. Moira has always been hopeless in a kitchen so that there is really no point in my holding up the bag of potatoes enquiringly.

'Oh, stick it in there,' and with her foot she deftly kicks open a dank cupboard where moisture tries in vain to escape from foul-smelling cloths. In here the potatoes will grow eyes and long pale etiolated limbs that will push open the creaking door next spring.

Her slow voice does not speed up with the frantic movements; instead, like a tape mangled in a machine, it trips and buzzes, dislocated from the darting sinewy body.

The children watch television. They do not want to eat, except for the youngest who rubs his distended tummy against the table. We stand in silence and listen to the child, 'I'm hungry, really hungry. I could eat and eat.' His black eyes glint with the success of subterfuge and in his pride he tugs at Moira's skirt, 'Can I sit on your knee?' and offers as reward, 'I'll be hungry on your knee, I really will.'

Something explodes in my mouth when Desmond produces a bottle of wine, and I resolve not to look at his chin, not even once.

'I've got something for you girls to celebrate with; you are staying in tonight, aren't you? Frieda, I promise you this is the first Wednesday night in years that Moira's been in. Nothing, not riots nor disease will keep her away from her Wednesday meetings. Now that women's lib's crept over the equator it would be most unbecoming of me to suspect my wife's commitment to her Black culture group. A worthy affair, affiliated to the UDF you know.' The wine which I drink too fast tingles in my toes and fingertips.

'So how has feminism been received here?' I ask.

'Oh,' he smiles, 'you have to adapt in order to survive. No point in resisting for the sake of it, you have to move with the times ... but there are some worrying half-baked ideas about ... muddled women's talk.'

'Actually,' Moira interjects, 'our group has far more pressing matters to deal with.'

'Like?' he barks.

'Like community issues, consciousness raising,' but Desmond snorts and she changes direction. 'Anyway, I doubt whether women's oppression arises as an issue among whites. One of the functions of having servants is to obscure it.'

'Hm,' I say, and narrow my eyes thoughtfully, a stalling trick I've used with varying success. Then I look directly at Desmond so that he refills my glass and takes the opportunity to propose a toast to our reunion. This is hardly less embarrassing than the topic of servants. The wine on my tongue turns musty and mingles with the smell of incense, of weddings and christenings that his empty words resurrect.

Desmond is in a co-operative mood, intent on evoking the halcyon days of the sixties when students sat on the cafeteria steps soaking up the sun. Days of calm and stability, he sighs. He reels off the names of contemporaries. Faces struggle in formation through the fog of the past, rise and recede. Rita Jantjes detained under the Terrorism Act. 'The Jantjes of Lansdowne?' I ask.

'It's ridiculous of them to keep Rita. She knows nothing; she's far too emotional, an obvious security risk,' Moira interjects.

'No,' Desmond explains, 'not the Lansdowne Jantjes but the Port Elizabeth branch of the family. The eldest, Sammy, graduated in Science the year before me.'

I am unable to contribute anything else, but he is the perfect host. There are no silent moments. He explains his plans for the garden and defers to my knowledge of succulents. There will be an enormous rockery in the front with the widest possible variety of cacti. A pity, he says, that Moira has planted those horrible trees but he would take over responsibility for the garden, give her a bit more free time, perhaps I didn't know that she has started working again?

Moira makes no effort to contribute to the conversation so diligently made. She murmurs to the little one on her knee whose fat fingers she prevents from exploring her nostrils. They giggle and shh–ssht each other, marking out their orbit of intimacy. Which make it easier for me to conduct this conversation. Only once does he falter and rub his chin but I avert my eyes and he embarks smoothly on the topic of red wine. I am the perfect guest, a deferential listener. I do not have the faintest interest in the production of wine.

When we finish dinner Desmond gets up briskly. He returns to the living room and the children protest loudly as he switches off the television and puts on music. Something classical and rousing, as if he too is in need of revival.

'Moi,' he shouts above the trombones, 'Moi, the children are tired, they must go to bed. Remember it's school tomorrow.'

'OK,' she shouts back. Then quietly, 'Thursdays are always schooldays. But then Desmond isn't always as sober as I'd like him to be.'

She lifts the sleeping child from her lap on to the bench. We rest our elbows on the table amongst the dirty dishes.

'He gets his drink too cheaply; has shares in an hotel.' Moira explains how the liquor business goes on expanding, how many professional people give up their jobs to become liquor moguls.

'Why are the booze shops called hotels? Who stays in them? Surely there's no call for hotels in a Coloured area?'

'Search me, as we used to say. Nobody stays in them, I'm sure. I imagine they need euphemisms when they know that they grow rich out of other people's misery. Cheap wine means everyone can drown his sorrows at the weekends, and people say that men go into teaching so that they have the afternoons to drink in as well. I swear the only sober man to be found on a Saturday afternoon is the liquor boss. The rest are dronkies, whether they loaf about on street corners in hang-gat trousers or whether they slouch in upholstered chairs in front of television sets. And we all know a man of position is not a man unless he can guzzle a bottle or two of spirits. It's not surprising that the Soweto kids of '76 stormed the liquor stores and the shebeens. Not that I'd like to compare the shebeen queen making a miserable cent with the Coloured "elite" as they call themselves who build big houses and drive Mercedes and send their daughters to Europe to find husbands. And those who allow themselves to be bought by the government to sit in Parliament ...'

She holds her head. 'Jesus, I don't know. Sometimes I'm optimistic and then it's worth fighting, but other times, here in this house, everything seems pointless. Actually that wine's given me a headache.'

I stare into the dirty plate so hard that surely my eyes will drop out and stare back at me. Like two fried eggs, sunny-side-up. Then I take her hand.

'Listen, I know a trick that takes headaches away instantly.' And I squeeze with my thumb and index finger deep into the webbed V formed by the thumb of her outstretched hand. 'See? Give me the other hand. See how it lifts?' Like a child she stares in wonderment at the hand still resting in mine.

The back door bursts open and Tillie rushes in balancing on her palm a curious object, a priapic confection.

'Look,' she shouts, 'look, isn't it lovely? It's the stale loaf I put out for the birds and they've pecked it really pretty.'

The perfectly shaped phallus with the crust as pedestal has been sculpted by a bird's beak. Delicately pecked so that the surface is as smooth as white bread cut with a finely serrated knife. We stare wanly at the child and her find, then we laugh. Tears run down Moira's face as she laughs. When she recovers her voice is stern. 'What are you doing outside at this hour? Don't you know it's ten o'clock? Where's Carol?'

Carol bursts in shouting. 'Do you know what? There are two African men in the playhouse, in our playhouse, and they've got sleeping bags. Two grown-ups can't sleep in there! And I went to tell Susie but she won't open the door. She spoke to me through the window and she said it's time to go to bed. But there's other people in her room. I heard them. And Susie shouldn't give people my sleeping bag.'

Moira waves her arm at Carol throughout this excited account, her finger across her lips in an attempt to quieten the child.

'Ssht, ssht, for God's sake, ssht,' she hisses. 'Now you are not to prowl around outside at night and you are not to interfere in Susie's affairs. You know people have problems with passes and it's silly to talk about such things. Daddy'll be very cross if he knew that you're still up and messing about out-side. I suggest you say nothing to him, nothing at all, and creep to bed as quietly as you can.'

She takes the children by the hands and leads them out of the room. Moments later she returns to carry off the little one sleeping on the bench. I start to clear the table and when she joins me she smiles.

'Aren't children dreadful? They can't be trusted an inch. I clean forgot about them, and they'll do anything not to go to bed. When adults long to get to bed at a reasonable hour which is always earlier than we can manage … Of course sleep really becomes a precious commodity when you have children. Broken nights and all that. No,' she laughs, looking me straight in the eye, 'I can't see you ever coping with children.'

The dishes are done. There is a semblance of order which clearly pleases Moira. She looks around the kitchen appreciatively then yawns. 'We must go to bed. Go ahead, use the bathroom first. I'll get the windows and doors shut. Sleep well.'

I have one of the children's bedrooms. For a while I sit on the floor; the little painted chair will not accommodate me, grotesque in the Lilliputian world of the child. Gingerly I lay my clothes across the chair. It is not espe-cially hot, but I open the window. For a while. I lie in my night-dress on the chaste little bed and try to read. The words dance and my eyes sting under heavy lids. But I wait. I stretch my eyes wide open and follow a mad moth circling the rabbit-shaped lamp by the side of the bed. I start to the mes-merising scent of crushed gardenia when the book slips and slips from under my fingers. In this diminutive world it does not fall with a thud. But I am awake once more. I wait.

ZOË WICOMB

Another Story
First published, 1990

Approaching DF Malan airport. The view from the window on the right, that is, as you enter the aircraft: it falls out of the blue, suddenly, even with your eyes fixed on the ground rising towards you – a perfect miniature plane, a razor-edged shadow in the last of the sunlight, earthborne, yet flying alongside where before there had been nothing. And then it grows. Because the sun is low and because nothing, no nothing will remain a little toy-thing. (A darling little toy-thing, but that sort of word has no place here and must be excised.) Yes, flying across the earth, it gradually grows larger. Still wonderful while its outline remains sharp, until an ungainly leap in size when overblown, with edges grown soft and arrowed wings blunted, the once-lovely little thing spreads and is swallowed. A simple multiplication and division sum, a working out of velocity, height, angle of the sun etc could have foreseen that moment. But she didn't. Or perhaps couldn't. So that was that. And the plane landed with the usual bump and the ping of the pilot's intercom.

To tell the truth, Miss Kleinhans was scared. And Dollie's voice as she leaned over the wild-with-morning-glory fence, rang in her ears.

'If you asking my advice, Deborah Kleinhans, I say stay right here where you belong. You not young, man, and there's no need to go gallivanting after family you don't know from Adam. I mean, family is now family, but the whole point is that family is family because you know them. It's not a stranger who gets to know you through ink and how-do-you-do on paper. And remember Cape Town is full of troubles with people throwing stones and getting shot. And what with you being a stranger in town. Have you listened to the wireless today?'

Deborah's head spun in an attempt to work out how knowing or not knowing blood relations affected the claims that such people could legitimately make on her, for she had come to see the visit as a duty. Also, the morning-glory trumpets had started yawning and she watched the first fold up neatly, spiralling into a tight spear that betrayed nothing of its fulsome blue.

'Dollie, this thing will take some thinking about. But it's too cold out here for me.' She had not asked for Dollie's advice; she had merely spoken of her inde-cision. But if only she had listened to Doll who was after all a sensible person, a neighbour she could rely on, even if that husband of hers was a good-for-nothing dronklap. I should have been a spinster like you, hey, Dollie sometimes said in exasperation, but Deborah could tell how the word spinster cut into her heart, for Doll would swirl the remains of her coffee and gulp down the lot as she rose with just that hint of hoarseness in her voice, I'll have to go and get ready the old man's bredie. Or his socks, or boots, or ironing, and even she, the spinster, knew that that was not the worst a woman had to do. She who had worked for years in white households knew more about things than people thought.

There had been two letters. The first simply a matter of introduction. A certain Miss Sarah Lindse from a wayward branch had traced her, a great-aunt, wishing to check the family connection and with Old Testament precision had untangled the lines of begetting into a neat tree which Deborah found hard to follow. Coloured people didn't have much schooling in her day but she knew her Bible and there was no better education in the world than knowing the Bible from cover to cover. Still, enough names on those heavy branches looked familiar, although so many children, dear Lord, why ever did her people have so many children. Family tree! It was a thicket, a blooming forest in which the grandest of persons would get lost. And she pursed her mouth fastidiously; she had a lot to be thankful for.

There were times when you had to face the truth; times like this when you'd made a wrong decision and the good Lord allowed you the opportunity to say, I have been guided by vanity. And in the same breath she found her vindication: for a woman who had worked as a respectable housekeeper all her life, but in service all the same, the connection with this grand young woman was only what she deserved. A history teacher at the university in Cape Town. The drop of white blood, no doubt, and she sighed as she thought of that blood, pink and thin and pure trouble. Ag, that was a long time ago and now she had a niece, a lovely girl who was educated and rich and who wrote in the second letter, I'll send you a plane ticket. Come and have a holiday in Cape Town. To her, an old woman whom the child had never even met. And Deborah, who had been timid all her life, who had kept her feet firmly on the ground and kept her eyes modestly fixed on those feet, for once looked up to see the serpent of adventure wink through the foliage of the family tree. And she was undone. And at her age too, but she replied, keeping to the lines of her Croxley pad with a steady hand, although these modern pens behaved as if light upward strokes and bold downward strokes were the last thing they hoped to achieve: I have always wanted to fly and would like to look around Cape Town. But I don't need a holiday so you can save up the darning and mending and of course I could do the cooking while you get on with bookwork. Thank you for the offer.

It was also that nonsense of Dollie's. She had managed to think it through and it simply did not make sense. Family is family and the whole point of such an unnecessary statement was that you didn't have to know the person. Vanity again: she had proven her ability to reason things out for herself and in show-ing off to Dollie had brought upon herself this business – this anxiety.

If only she had someone to talk to on the flight. Silence was something still when you were on your own but here with a flesh and blood person sitting right by your side, the silence fidgets between you, monitors your breathing, stiffens the body and makes you fearful of moving. So many new things cannot become part of you unless you could say to the person sitting right there, My, what a business this is, without of course letting on that you've never flown before. But the red-faced woman next to her had swung round to the aisle as if she, Deborah Kleinhans, freshly bathed and in her best crimplene two-piece, as if she had BO. Ag, it's the way of the world, she consoled herself, these whites don't know how to work things out, can't even run their own blooming homes. If she were in charge she'd have apartheid to serve the decent and god-fearing – that was a more sensible basis for separating the sheep from the goats, but she sighed, for how would one know, how could one tell the virtuous from the hypocrites, the pharisees. These days people grew more and more like jackals and the education business only helped to cover up sorcery and fornication.

And here Miss Kleinhans felt once more a twinge of regret, a tugging at her intestines that happily could be diverted from the new niece to the won-derful South African Airways lunch. All nicely separated in little compartments that Dollie could well be alerted to, her with the eternal bredies, day after day everything mixed together, meat, potatoes, tinned peas and veg and then, on the plate, that man of hers would stir in the rice, pounding, as if it were mor-tar to be shovelled into the cracks of his soul. But it would've been nice just to say to the red-faced woman, Isn't it oulik these little brown dishes like housie-housie things. Last time I flew they were orange you know. Just in case. And she lifted her head high; no one could accuse her of being ignorant, green and verskrik as a young farm-girl. The Goodlord she felt sure would forgive her. Especially after the temptation, the terrible desire to put one in her bag, only the little SAA pudding dish of cream and brown plastic and with the white woman's back virtually turned to her, nothing could be easier. But she didn't. And she praised Dearjesus who resisted forty days in the Wilderness and felt sure that He would not expect her to fast just because He had, not on this her first flight with food so prettily packed.

That was before she thought of the order of eating. She knew that one did not just start any old where you liked. Her De Villiers household always had fish or soup to begin with but how was she to determine the order of things that in fact were the same? A test that would have made the woman, if her back had not mercifully been turned, giggle at her ignorance, for there in the little compartments was tomato and lettuce alone and again tomato and lettuce with meat, and how was she to decide which came first? More than likely the two halves of the same tomato turned into different names on different plates, which only went to show how silly all this blinking business was, but she was grateful all the same for the disdain of the woman who had swung round into the aisle. At what point was she to eat the round bread? Only poor people, her father had always said, ate bread with their dinner, so she would look upon it as a test, like in the fairy tale of a round red apple or something to tempt and catch the heroine out. Why else would the two large black berries have been hidden under the lettuce? She would have arranged it on top to set off the green and red; she had always paid attention to presenting food attractively and Mrs de Villiers never had anything but praise for her dishes.

The pip of the foul-tasting berry proved yet another trap. How was she to get the damned thing out of her mouth and back onto the plate? Would she have to pretend that she was not hungry, that she could only just pick at her food? What nonsense, she admonished herself. This was no boiled sweet destined to dissolve; she could not very well keep a pip hidden in her cheek until god knows when, so she spat it into a paper napkin under cover of wiping her mouth, and niftily tucked it into her sleeve. There was no one watching her; she would tuck in and not waste the poor girl's money; this food – never mind if it didn't live up to the cute containers – was expensive and, what's more, paid for. How could she, a grown person, be so silly and she chuckled audibly so that the red-faced woman took the opportunity to adjust her discomfort, to straighten her spine and allow herself ten degrees that would bring Miss Kleinhans's fork just within her line of vision.

The girl must have been relying on a family resemblance; why else had she not suggested ways of identifying herself? Perhaps she should wave a white handkerchief or something. That was what people did in *Rooi Rose*, which only went to show that *Rooi Rose* then was not for people like her. She could never do such a thing, make a spectacle of herself. It must have been the flight through high air that made her think such unusual thoughts. As if she had taken a feather duster to her head so that those stories, she now clearly saw, were for white people. Which did not mean that she couldn't read them: she was used to wearing white people's clothes and eating their leftovers, so what difference did it make reading their stories. As long as she knew and did not expect to behave like a *Rooi Rose* woman. It was difficult enough just sitting there, waiting, with so many idle eyes roving about. She lifted her head to concentrate on the lights flashing their instructions about smoking and seatbelts until they finally clicked off, the messages exhausted, and felt herself adrift midst empty seats and the purposeful shuffling of people anxious to go.

Deborah looked about and caught sight of the red-faced woman who flashed her a warm smile. What on earth could the person mean? She was not to be lured by a smile of falsehood, here where there was no danger of striking up a conversation. As far as she was concerned it just was too bladdy late. Haai, what a cheek, but then, not keeping track of things, a smile leaked from her lips all the same and she had no choice but to incline her head to nod a greeting.

The usual Cape Town wind awaited her, just as Dollie had said, and Deborah smoothed her skirt and patted her head to check that the doekie was still in place. Crossing that space was not simply a question of putting one foot before another. The tarmac felt sticky underfoot; the wind snapped like a mongrel; and her ankles wobbled unreliably above the Sunday shoes. Ahead, through the glass, a tinted crowd waited, waved, and what would she do if the girl was not there? That she could not allow herself to think about. The Goodlord would provide. Although the Goodlord so often got His messages mixed up, like telephone party lines, so that good fortune would rain into the unsuspecting lap of that heathenish husband of Dollie's, when it was she, Deborah Kleinhans, who had spent the holy hours on arthritic knees, praying. If red-face walking purposefully just ahead of her was expecting no one, you could be sure that some thoughtful niece on the spur of the moment had decided to meet her after all, while she, a stranger in this town … But this time, and Deborah was careful to smile inwardly, this time, He got it just right.

* * *

Sarah was confident that she would recognise her great-aunt by the family resemblance and indeed the woman walking unsteadily across the tarmac could be no other than Deborah Kleinhans. Who, incidentally, was the only elderly coloured woman on the flight. Sarah corrected herself: so-called coloured, for she did not think that the qualifier should be reserved for speech. It grieved her that she so often had to haul up the 'so-called' from some distant recess where it slunk around with foul terms like half-caste and half-breed and she stamped her foot (which had gone to sleep in the long wait) as if to shake down the unsummoned words. Lexical vigilance was a matter of mental hygiene: a regular rethinking of words in common use, like cleaning out rotten food from the back of a refrigerator where no one expects food to rot and poison the rest.

The old woman was stronger, sturdier than she imagined, with the posture of someone much younger. But she was tugging at the navy-blue suit which had got nipped, or so it seemed, by her roll-on, so that her hemline dipped severely to the right. Also, threatening to slip off, was the doekie that had to be hauled back over the grey head as she struggled with a carrier bag in the wind. But they met without difficulty.

'So we found each other. Something to be grateful for these days when you lose and search for things that disappear under your very nose …'

'And people going missing by the dozens,' Sarah interjected. Deborah looked alarmed. Whatever was the child talking about; not her, she had to get back home; Dollie would be expecting her in precisely one week.

'Ag, they say big cities swallow you up but we're old enough to look after ourselves. Dollie's people,' she added, 'even in Kimberley, you know, after the riots. Clean disappeared. But one never knows with these children. Dollie is now Mrs Lategan who's been my neighbour for twenty years.' Then she chuckled, 'But what if we are not the people we think we are, or no, that's not what I mean. Let's sit down, child, I get so deurmekaar and I need to take a good look at you.'

They sat down and looked at each other, surrounded by squeals and hugs and arm-waving reunions. In the two pairs of eyes, the flecked hazel eyes derived from the same sockets of a long-dead European missionary, there was nothing to report. The improbable eyes, set generations ago into brown faces, betrayed nothing, as eyes rarely do, but both claimed to read in the other signs and traces so that they held each other as firmly as the rough and wrinkled hand gripped the young and smooth. Deborah wondered for the first time why the girl had brought her all that way. Sarah thought of her father who in his last years had kept a miscellany of rare physical complaints. A man who knew his viscera like the back of his hand and could identify a feeling of discomfort with self-claimed accuracy – his liver, or pancreas, or lower section of the colon – an unnecessary refinement since the remedy of Buchu Essence served them all. She hoped that her great-aunt would not get ill; those were surely the eyes of a hypochondriac.

The girl was rather disappointing: untidily dressed in denim without a dash of lipstick to brighten her up. There was something impenetrable about her face, a density of the flesh that thwarted Deborah who prided herself on looking right into the souls of strangers. Also, her car was not at all what Deborah had expected but then she did not think any car smart except for a black one. The house that they pulled up at was very nice, but modest, she thought, for a learned person. With so much rain here in Cape Town it seemed a pity not to have a proper garden. Just a little patch of untrimmed grass and a line of flowers sagging against the wall. Yellow and orange marigolds, their heads like torches, so that she turned to look back at the dark mountain and saw the last light gathered in the flaming peak of a cloud.

The medicinal scent of marigolds followed them into the house. Through the passage lined with old photographs. So many people with nothing better to do than stand around and wait for the click of a camera. And right into the kitchen until the marigolds submitted to the smell of coffee. From a blue enamel pot like her very own the girl poured large cupfuls and her heart leapt, for city people, she thought, only drank instant coffee, didn't have time, Dollie said, for Koffiehuis. Washed in a caffeine-induced wellbeing she felt her feet throb all the more painfully so that she eased off her shoes to find two risen loaves straining under the nylon stockings. Why feeling good should have reminded her of feeling bad she did not know, but oh, she felt like a queen being led to her room with a bowl of hot water in which to soak those feet. But queens get their heads chopped off, so it was not too surprising that in that dream-wake state as she rested before dinner, Deborah orbited wildly in a marigold-round, her eyes chasing the pinpoints of light where orange turned to fire, and her head threatening to fly off. She rose clutching her throat.

At table Sarah talked too much. Deborah, used to turning her own thoughts slowly round, this way and that, and then putting them away safely for another inspection day, found the girl's insistent ways too exhausting. Like Mr de Villiers's office with rows and rows of narrow drawers packed with papers – the girl's head was like that. And she spoke fast, whirring like a treadle-machine that made her own head, still delicate from dreaming, spin once again. And all these things from the past, the bad old days that Sarah wanted to talk about. Stories folded and packed in mothballs right at the bottom of Deborah's head. To disturb those was just plain foolish, just asking for things to come toppling down.

'Perhaps later this year I'll come to Kimberley. To look around all those places. The old farm, Brakvlei, all those places where the Kleinhanse lived,' Sarah said.

But the old woman would not be roused. Nothing there to see. Not a coloured person left in those parts. You won't find a riempie or a rusty nail. No, it's years since I left and soon after that the others trekked. The drought, you know. Girlie, this is a lovely bobotie. I haven't had any for so long; being on your own you can't really make such elaborate food.'

The girl was not a bad cook. And the bobotie was good although Deborah liked it just a little bit sweeter. Just a spoonful of apricot jam to set off the sharpness of the dried apricots. That's what she liked about bobotie – the layers, different things packed on top of one another. She always did it in a pyrex dish so that you could see the separate layers of curried mince, apricots and then the thick custard just trying to trickle down to the dried fruit. Almost a pity to eat it.

'No really,' she said through slipping dentures, 'there's nothing like a good bobotie. Bananas are also good you know, but to contrast with the custard, apricot is best.'

In the tall, frosted glass of Fanta, the orange bubbles broke merrily at the brim, almost too pretty to drink. On the same principle Deborah's good clothes remained unworn at the back of the cupboard, but today, in her Sunday wear, eating and drinking the beauty of it all, her old heart was content and this Sarah was a girl to be proud of. She would bring Dollie along next time; my, what a time they could have.

Then Sarah said in a preacher's voice, '… nothing but an untidiness on God's earth – a mixture of degenerate brown peoples, rotten with sickness, an affront against Nature … So that was the farm.'

702

They had slipped into comfortable Afrikaans, a relief to Deborah whose English pinched like the Lycra roll-on that Dollie insisted had to be worn for the visit. And now the girl had switched to English once again so that she groped and grunted, for syllables from the two languages flew to each other to make wild words; because she did not understand about the sickness and death and because she felt a great weariness, a cloud settling around her head. The girl was surely mad. Everybody gets sick and dies, but Brakvlei was never rotten. Oh no, theirs was the cleanest of farmyards, the stony veld swept for hundreds of yards and even the fowls knew not to shit near the house. In that swept yard a young man rested his brown arms on the latched lower door, leant well into the dark but spotless kitchen with the sun behind him lighting the outline of his tightly curled hair. And Deborah, sick with shyness, packed more wood into the full stove and felt her hem a hot hoop below her knees, for she had outgrown that dress, and she had never been looked at in that way. Even when he offered to cleave a log that refused to go into the stove, his eyes burned and then her Pa came, to see his favourite daughter, his miracle late-lamb, younger than the grandchild, tug at her skirt and he ordered Andries away. That day she tore the dress into rags and braved a beating for she knew that a strip of plain cotton could simply have been sewn on to lengthen the skirt. But a beating has never done anyone any harm and she could thank her Pa now for sitting here where the girl's strong hands came to rest on her shoulders.

'Auntie feeling alright? Perhaps a drop of Buchu Essence?' she inquired, once again in Afrikaans.

'No, I'm alright. Just put a little bit of bobotie on my plate.' Then Deborah remembered the libel. 'Cleanliness is next to godliness. That's what my mother always said. And it was my job every morning to sweep all around the house. Really, it was just rearranging the veld, making our own patterns of earth and stone with the grass broom, but Ma said, The veld will swallow us up if we don't sweep. No, you can ask anyone; Brakvlei was the tidiest little place you've ever seen. If your people thought otherwise, well, then they just don't know what tidy means. All my life I have kept that motto: Tidiness is next to godliness.' And then her anger subsided: her mother would not have quoted the adage in English as she just had, not at home. What had she in fact said? How unreliable words were, lodging themselves comfortably in the memory where they pretended to have a rightful place. Deborah did not hold her memory responsible.

'No, no,' Sarah soothed, 'I'm sure you're right. I have no doubt that Brakvlei was well kept. But I wasn't really talking of Brakvlei; it was just something I remembered. From a story.' But the young woman's eyes burned so brightly, so busy-bodily, oh Deborah just knew that passion for probing deep into other people's affairs. Who did this child think she was, wanting to pry into her life and she who had never said a word to anyone about Andries, the tall young man whom she saw just once more before her father waving the old shotgun told him not to set foot in that swept yard again.

'People come and go and in the end it's no bad thing. No point in brooding over things that happened a long time ago. I haven't got time for those old stories,' she said firmly.

'A pity really; it's an interesting story that needs to be told by …'

'And what would you know about it?' Deborah interrupted. 'It's never been interesting. Dreary as dung it was, sitting day after day waiting for something to happen; listening for hooves or the roll of cartwheels.' But she checked herself. Hearing only the wind howl through the bushes and the ewes bleat, she had made up stories. Of driving through streets lined with whitewashed houses; of friends, girls in frilled print frocks who whispered secrets under the breath of the wind; and of Andries on horseback galloping across the swept yard right up to the kitchen door. But she said, 'You know I have my books – *Rooi Rose* every fortnight, I haven't missed a book since I started working for the De Villierses and when I retired I kept it up. Every fortnight. Good stories that seem to be about real life, but well, when you think about it, you won't recognise anyone you know. They'll give you no useful tips. They're no better than the nonsense I used to make up in my own head to kill the time. My advice, child, is to stick to your business and forget about stories of old times.'

'It depends surely on who tells the story. Auntie Deborah, that's what I must ask you about. Do you know if someone has written the story of our family, from the beginning, right from the European missionary? Do you by any chance remember a woman, a white woman speaking to your mother or brothers or yourself about those days? A woman who then wrote a book? Have you ever heard of the book, of …'

'No, I don't believe it. What nonsense, of course there was no such woman. A book for all to read with our dirty washing spread out on snow-white pages! Ag, man, don't worry; it wouldn't be our story; it's everyone's story. All coloured people have the same old story.' And then Deborah slumped in her chair.

Sarah knew it, just her luck, the old woman travelling all this way to put down her head and die at her table. She held a bottle of brandy to the lifeless lips. The eyelids fluttered and Deborah sat up with remarkable agility as if the laying of her head on the table had been a deliberate gesture of exasperation.

'Just tired child. Don't worry, I'm not going to die here; I'll die respectably in my own house and that not for some time yet.'

Sarah helped her to bed. 'Tomorrow evening,' she said, as she tucked her in, 'I have to go to a meeting. But in the morning we'll go out. Somewhere exciting, but let's talk about that tomorrow.'

'To the Gardens, girlie; that's where one should go first. I've heard so much about the Gardens in Cape Town. Where the fine ladies parade.' And she gig-gled for she knew it could not be as her mother had described so many years ago. And even then it was a second-hand account, told by her grown-up sister Elmira whom she had never known.

* * *

Deborah was not surprised by the knock. Her heart had swollen, filling her chest with a thunderous beat and rocking her entire body as she heard the footsteps steal past her window, round to the back of the house. Skollies with armfuls of stones, just as Dollie had warned her. Then a low, barking voice – Quick. Here. Slowly, she twisted her head to look at the clock. Then Deborah leapt out of bed. She would not await death lying prone in her bed. Oh no, if skollies planned to kill her, well, they would meet her standing up straight, ready to meet her Maker. Her hands groped for the dressing gown but the old arms shook too violently to guide them through the sleeves. She crept out to the hall; she could at least telephone the police. But they were already at the door. What kind of cheeky skollies were these who thought she would open the door to her own death? Why did the girl not wake up? She pulled on the dressing gown. The knock grew louder and someone shouted, 'Open up; it's the police.' They had come for Sarah.

* * *

Deborah waited for Dollie in the Lategans' kitchen. Mr Lategan put the kettle on for coffee, making an elaborate display of not knowing where to find things, so that she suggested that he put on his shoes while she made the cof-fee. That the man should be told to make himself decent, as if she would divulge a word to someone sitting in his socks. And she thought of the folly of having expectations, of how she had imagined sitting at that table with Dollie, telling her story.

But there they sat drinking the coffee she made and Mr Lategan knew exactly where to find Dollie's buttermilk rusks which they dunked. And so she told him, for she could not expect the man to ask again. About the police who came for Sarah at 5.30 in the morning, pointing their guns as if they were in a play on the TV. And how they turned the house upside down and even looked in her suitcase. But they were very polite, especially the big one in command who apologised nicely and said to her, 'You should have kept an eye on the girl,' so that she turned to him triumphantly and said, 'So you don't know everything like you said you did. I've known this girl for less than a day.' Mr Lategan interrupted to say that if they didn't know that, they could so easily have got the whole thing wrong, the wrong house, the wrong woman, everything. Which was exactly what Deborah was about to say, but it was so nice to be back and because she could have added, also the wrong Deborah Kleinhans, for she felt as if the story had been playing on the TV, she allowed him to be the author of the observation.

There was also Cape Town to tell about even though she knew that he had been twice. But the city was so big that he could not possibly have been to the same places and he certainly listened with great interest. Sarah had written a letter to her neighbours, the Arendses, and even then Deborah marvelled at the girl's skill, how she wrote like lightning, her hand flying across the paper in such straight lines, even though the big policeman leant over her, checking every word. Busybodies, that's what they were, going through people's things and reading their letters. Mrs Arendse took her to the Gardens but her heart was not in it.

Someone else, a young woman whose name she could not recall, took her to a museum to see what the girl called her ancestors. Hottentots in a big glass box, squatting around an unlit fire of all things, so that she left in disgust. But she said nothing to him of the large protruding buttocks and the shameful loincloths of animal skin. No, her heart was not in it and Mrs Arendse arranged an early return flight for there was no point in waiting to see Sarah again. They telephoned many times but there was no point, everyone said.

When Dollie came she told it all again and she did not mind Mr Lategan sitting there until he tried to correct her. If things were slightly different the second time round, well, she was telling it to someone different and he should have had the decency to keep quiet. So she went, taking her bag, for she had not yet been home and Dollie shouted after her, 'I'll come with,' just as she unlocked her door.

Dollie lay across her bed while she unpacked. The frock for parading in the Gardens, a bold print of yellow daisies on white, she folded away into a bottom drawer for the nights were drawing in and really it was perhaps too bright for someone of her age. And then she told Dollie. Of how she had offered to make a nice pot of coffee because it was so early and that's just what you needed in order to think clearly. If the policemen burst rudely into the house, well, she was brought up decently. Sarah shouted at her but she knew how a civilised person should behave. And she paused in an attempt to trace the moment when things became muddled but all she recalled was an unmistakable smell of marigold, a weariness and the precise timbre of the sergeant's voice as she finished pouring the coffee: 'Milk and sugar for the other two but just black and bitter for me.' Then without thinking, without anticipating the violence of the act, Deborah Kleinhans took each cup in turn and before his very eyes poured the coffee into the sink. Together they watched the liquid splash, a curiously transparent brown against the stainless steel.

IVAN VLADISLAVIĆ

Journal of a Wall

From: *Missing Persons* (1989)

31 May

I have a feeling that I am starting this too late.

It is hardly three weeks since he started the wall – but already he has laid the foundations. That is not too much to catch up, perhaps. But it would have been pleasantly symmetrical to have begun on the same day, to have taken up my pen as he took up his trowel.

I should have foreseen it all. I had a sense, when they delivered the bricks, that something in which I would have a part was beginning. If I had not been watching from behind the curtains in my lounge, like a spy, perhaps it would have been clear to me that I was meant to be more than an observer.

They brought the bricks almost three weeks ago. Saturday 11 May, as I look at my calendar. I was watching the cricket on television when I heard the truck stop across the road. The engine revved for several minutes – I suppose the driver had gone in to check whether he was at the right address -- and that's why I went to investigate.

When I looked out through the curtains he was crossing the lawn with a man wearing blue overalls. His wife was watching from the veranda.

The bricks were packed incongruously in huge plastic bags, very strong plastic, I suppose. He went straight up to the truck, put one foot on the rear wheel and hoisted himself up. He took out a pocket-knife and cut a slit in the plastic, put his finger in to touch the bricks. He held his hand there for a minute, as if he was taking a pulse. Then he put his eye to the slit. It took a long time before he was satisfied. I had an inkling then that something important was beginning. I should have fetched a pen and started recording immediately. I would have had the details now, those all-important beginning moments. Already the memories are fading: I can't remember when she went back inside, for instance, but I don't think that she watched the unloading.

He supervised that task himself. It didn't take long. I wished that the bricks weren't wrapped in plastic; then they could have been passed along a chain of sure hands from the back of the truck to a corner of the garden. Instead the driver of the truck operated a small crane mounted just behind the cab, and the man directed him to pile the bags of bricks one on top of the other on the pavement. I remember at least that there were nine bags. When that was over he went inside – it was probably then that I noticed she was gone – and returned with a pen to sign the delivery papers.

After the truck had gone he went straight back into the house. I was surprised. I expected him to examine the bricks again. But apparently he was satisfied.

I returned to the television set. The game was over. I watched for a while, hoping to get the final score. But I was restless. The news came on. It was Michael de Morgan. He told us there was unrest in the townships again. He showed us a funeral crowd being dispersed with tear-gas. A bus burned in the background. Then a camera in a moving car tracking along the naked faces of houses, and children peeling away from the vehicle like buck in the game reserve. A cloud of black smoke from a supermarket. Soldiers. Some people hurling bricks into the burning bus.

The following scenes may upset some viewers, Michael de Morgan said gently.

I switched off the set. I was upset enough.

I went back to the window. It was almost dark outside, the house across the road a blue shadow. But the front door was open, and in the glow from the lounge I could see him reclining in an easy chair on the veranda, with his feet up on a table, drinking a beer.

The pile of bricks was another dark shape in the twilight. From the way in which he was sitting, with his legs swung to one side, I would say that he was watching over them. He looked as if he was going to stay there all night. Or perhaps he was trying to decide what to build. Or had already decided and could see the final product, with each brick in place.

I was restless that evening, and upset and depressed. I drank too much. The room wanted to spin. That impulse came to me through the bedsprings, just a gentle tremor at first, but the walls of the house held fast. I put one foot on the floor, trying to weigh it down. Then it came again, the room trying to twist itself free from the rest of the house, rip up its tap-root and ascend into the sky. Plaster powder rained down on me as cracks chased through the walls and ran themselves into corners. Then the rafters cracked like ribs and the room began to turn. The whole place rattled and groaned, spun faster and faster, and then rose slowly like an ancient flying-machine, ripping roof tiles like fingernails, tearing the sinew of electrical wiring, bursting the veins of waterpipes, up into the night sky.

I went to look through the bedroom window. The city was spread out below me like a map, but I couldn't get my bearings. There was my house, with its gaping wound. I felt a wind on my neck, and when I looked up I saw the ceiling drift away. The night, effervescent with stars, poured in.

I sat down on the end of my bed. The bricks began to peel away from the walls in squadrons and they flew down to my neighbour's house and assembled themselves into barbecues and watchtowers and gazebos and rondawels and bomb shelters. When all the walls had unravelled completely I was left floating on the raft of the floor, dragged by the currents of the sky this way and that, until the boards all rotted away below me and I sank down into my bathroom and got sick.

I woke up very late on Sunday morning, feeling terrible. It was several hours before I could bring myself to get up and take a shower. The room had fitted itself back into the house imperfectly, with the doors and windows in the wrong places, and the floors were awash with books, broken glass, clockwork, clothing, kindling. I decided to put off tidying up until after breakfast – which was lunch, actually.

While I was eating I suddenly remembered my neighbour's bricks, and rushed to the lounge window. I was surprised and hurt to discover that he had already started work without me. He was digging a trench along the boundary of his property, where the fence used to be. The fence posts were still there, but the wire itself lay in a huge buckled roll on the front lawn. A wall! Of course.

After some minutes of watching him I hit on a plan for getting a closer view of the building operations. I strolled to the shop, bought the Sunday paper, and then took a slightly longer route which would take me past his house on my way home. It worked perfectly. I stopped to tie my shoe-laces, which I had cunningly loosened before I rounded the corner, so that I could get a good look at the trench and, indeed, at him. Fortunately, he was working with his back to me.

The trench seemed to me inordinately deep – although I must say that I have never actually built a wall myself – eighteen inches or more. And at least two foot across. It was possible that he was planning to build an extremely thick, high wall of the kind that is fairly common in our suburb, in which case the foundations would have to be secure. But I was more inclined to think that he was simply an amateur. He didn't look as if he had built a wall before either.

Frankly, he was a disappointment to me. It was the first time I had really seen him from close range. Indeed, until the day before it would be true to say that I had never seen him. He was simply the driver of a car or the pusher of a lawnmower. My first real glimpse of him, swinging up onto the truck, had convinced me that he was strong, seasoned, capable. Now I saw how wrong I was. He had taken off his shirt (it hung limply on one of the fence posts) and his back was pale and flabby. His neck was burnt slightly red. He was wearing long pants, which looked clean and ironed, not at all like work pants. What bothered me most was the way in which he swung the pick; there was no conviction in it at all. I wished that I could get a look at his hands.

Of course, I probably didn't think all this in the time it takes to tie a shoelace: it is more likely that I simply observed and then thought about it all later, as I read my newspaper and in a deckchair in the front garden.

I spent the better part of the afternoon watching him from behind the paper. He never looked my way once. He worked very slowly, but steadily, and by five o'clock, when it had become quite cool and almost time for me to go in, he had finished the trench. He put on his shirt and fetched her out of the house to review the day's achievements. He seemed very pleased with himself: he even sprang into the hole and did a little jig for her, and that made me like him more. And she put her arm around his shoulders when they went back in, and that made me proud of her too.

I waited for a few minutes, thinking that they would perhaps come out onto the veranda for sundowners, but the door remained closed, and eventually I also had to go in. Nothing happened for a week. I had hoped that he would not do any more building while I was away at work. I noted with relief that he was waiting for the following weekend. The week dragged.

Once or twice during the week I saw him inspecting the trench after work, probably checking for subsidence; and once or twice when my evening strolls took me past the trench I too was able to make a quick examination. It seemed to be holding up well. On those occasions I also managed to get a closer look at the bricks. He seemed to have forgotten about them. I admired that in him – his patience, his faith. It is possible, of course, that he inspected the bricks late at night after I had gone to sleep, but I doubt it.

Their habits seemed to be fairly steady. He usually came in at about five-thirty and put the car straight in the garage. They didn't go out much. They would watch television every night until about ten-thirty and then retire to bed. The television was on from about six, and so I presumed that either they ate as soon as he came in from work or they took their meals in front of the set.

I speculated about the programmes they watched. Did the news upset them? I for one was finding the news depressing – full of death and destruction. Who would build amid these ruins? I used to stand behind my curtain and look across at their lounge window, flickering blue as a screen. What on earth were they shoring up?

On the following Saturday (this would have been the 18th of May) I was up early, early enough to see the building sand delivered. Would that I had been ready with pen and paper to describe how the mountain of fine white sand slid from the back of the tip-truck, and the great cloud of dust that boiled up and hung over the houses.

710

I knew when I saw that perfect dune, white as flour, spilling over the kerb and the pavement, that the foundations would be laid that day. He materialised out of the dust-storm, wearing a blue T-shirt this time but the same pants (fortunately starting to look a little grubby and crumpled) and carrying a spade and a bucket of water. He stood for a while staring into the dust as if waiting for instructions. Then he set to, separating a pile of the sand and shovelling it onto a sheet of corrugated iron. He seemed a little more lively this morning. I was pleased. There was quite a spring in his step as he went off to the garage.

The combined haze of the dust-cloud and the net curtain behind which I was standing was making it very difficult for me to see what was going on. By this time a sense was growing in me that it was very important to catch every detail, although I was still blind to the fact that I should have been writing it all down as it happened.

There he was returning with a bag of cement on his shoulder. I could see him quite clearly for a while but then he was back in the haze.

I paced my lounge, searching for an excuse to get closer to him. The one I finally found was a little obvious perhaps, but he generally seemed to take no notice of me, so I decided to chance it. I pulled my car out of the garage, fetched a bucket of water, and started to wash the windscreen. By now the dust had settled somewhat, and I was surprised to see her coming into view. She was sitting on a kitchen chair, and wearing a pale-pink dressing-gown. She was holding a book, and at first I thought she was reading. Then it seemed to me that she was reading out instructions. As I watched he measured out a quantity of cement in a tin and sprinkled it over the sand. He looked at her. She spoke again. He mixed the sand and the cement with the spade and shaped it into a dam.

Jesus! I said to myself, they're following a recipe.

Then I realised with a start that I was staring. I quickly dipped my sponge in the water and sloshed it over the roof of the car. Schooled my arm to keep rubbing as I watched.

When he had finished the mixing he put the cement in a wheelbarrow and carried it to the beginning of the trench. She walked with him, reading all the way, and watched over him as he tipped the cement into the trench and smoothed it with a length of wood.

And so it went. After the third trip she went inside – presumably he had memorised the procedure – and I did not see her again that day. When he broke for lunch so did I. When I heard the spade clattering on the corrugated iron again a half-hour later I went back to washing the car.

He worked as doggedly laying the foundations as he had done digging the trench, and I found my admiration for him growing. After a whole day of washing my car I was exhausted; he neither slackened nor speeded up as he approached the end of the trench, just worked on at the same relentlessly steady pace. He seemed to me to be a remarkable example of soldiering on. I needed to take a leaf out of his book. I thanked him silently as he set to cleaning the wheelbarrow and the spade with meticulous care.

I resolved to try and follow his example in the week ahead. It would be at least a week before the building proper could begin; the foundations would have to settle. He would be patient, and so would I.

On the Monday evening after he had laid the foundations I saw him come home from work. After he had put the car in the garage and closed the door I expected him to walk down to the building-site for some kind of inspection. But he went straight inside. It made me feel a little foolish, as if I was letting the side down. I put the whole thing out of my mind. Yet I was waiting for the weekend with a growing sense of anticipation.

So I was immediately uneasy when he parked the car in the driveway on Friday evening, instead of putting it in the garage as usual. He hurried inside. Surely they weren't planning to go out? I had specifically decided to get an early night so that I would be fresh for the next day's building, and I expected him to do the same.

I was alarmed when he came out just a few minutes later carrying a suitcase. He put it in the boot and went back inside. Could it be true? Would they go away on such an important weekend? It was inconceivable. I brought a bottle over to the window and poured myself a large Scotch. There he was, coming out again. He went to the car and started cleaning the windscreen. Then I knew it was true. I finished the drink, poured another one. Perhaps they were going to the drive-in? With a suitcase? No … He went back inside. The lights in the house went out one by one. Then they both came out of the front door. She was wearing a nightie and large pink slippers and carrying a suitcase, a smaller version of the one he had put in the boot. They left the hallway light burning. He took the case from her and they walked to the car. How could they do this to me!

I quickly opened the curtains, switched the light on, and stood in the centre of the window, one hand holding the bottle of Scotch and the other pressed against the glass. I stared hard at them, took a long swig from the bottle. The car still hadn't moved. Then she got out and went back inside. Going to check that the taps are off, I thought. The swines. She was back very quickly, carrying a book and something in a brown paper bag. She got in and he switched the interior light on. They both looked at the book. Now the car started, the tail-lights glowed red in the dusk, the car was reversing, they were driving away.

The inside of the car was a warm, light bubble. I saw his profile, and beyond it her face, as soft and ripe as a fruit. She was looking at him, or perhaps at me, and I wondered what she thought of me, weeping at my post, holding my pickled tongue in one cupped palm and the bloodied bayonet in the other.

I finished the Scotch and went for a walk. Oh, I walked all over the place, staring into the blank faces of walls, peering into the blind eyes of windows, shouting obscenities into the leafy ears of hedges. I made the dogs bark. I rattled gates and banged on doors. I put the fear of the devil into the whole suburb. Those sleeping houses, their gigantic gasping and snoring, their tossing and turning. I waded through drifts of dry leaves in the culverts. I left my footprints in flowerbeds. I beat their welcome mats against their front doors until their gardens choked on the dust of ten thousand five o'clock feet. The breeze smelt of formalin. Everything was covered in wax and powdered and pinned. I brought back a newspaper billboard that said THREE MORE DIE IN UNREST and it was easy to believe in unrest and death with the rattle of leaves in the throats of the drains, the letterboxes choked with pamphlets, the bottles of milk souring on the doorsteps.

I forgave them.

I went over just after midnight, in an overcoat, in a balaclava. I shone my torch along the length of the trench: it was looking good. In a few places the earth had subsided, and I cleared it with my hands, and swept up a few dry leaves.

I brought back with me a brick.

I put it on my desk, on an embroidered cloth, and turned the fluorescent lamp on it. It was an extraordinary brick. It looked so heavy, as if it had been hewn from solid rock in the quarries of some not yet discovered planet. It was reddish brown, with a cracked, cratered surface, and it was still warm to the touch. It looked as if it would plummet through the desk, the floor, sink down into the earth as if it were water.

Yet the more I looked at it, the more it looked like a familiar object. After a long time of watching it, it began to look like a loaf of bread, hot from the oven, steaming, fermenting inside.

I could hardly sleep that night with its hard presence in the house, its bubbling and hissing. But I eventually sank into the mottled depths of a dreamless sleep.

In the morning the brick had cooled. Its surface had hardened to a stiff crust.

I was tempted to keep it as some sort of memento. But by late afternoon I had begun to resent its stony silence, its impenetrable skin, and I resolved to return it to the pile as soon as it grew dark. I wanted to maintain some connection with it, however, so I marked each of its impassive faces with a small dot of white paint, and put it in the oven to dry.

When it was dark I took the brick over concealed in a folded newspaper which I carried under my arm. On the pavement I was suddenly tempted to explore the house and the back garden. The front lawn lay spread like a huge welcome mat, inviting me into the nooks and crannies of their private spaces. But I was afraid: someone could see me and mistake me for a burglar. So I returned the brick to its pile and carefully folded the plastic wrapper over it.

I was just turning back towards my own house when I spotted the letters, jutting like a tongue from the letterbox. I looked around quickly. There was no one in sight. I was bold enough to take the letters onto their veranda and skim through them in the light from behind the frosted panes of the front door. There were three letters. One was addressed to The Householder. The other two were addressed to Mr GB Groenewald. I returned the letters to the box and scurried home with my discovery.

Mr and Mrs Groenewald returned from their outing on Sunday evening. I was overjoyed to see them. I wanted them to know that I had taken good care of everything in their absence, so I flashed my lounge light in a cryptic morse of welcome and affection. No answering signal came. I suspect that they were tired from their journey and went straight to bed.

The week that followed was uneventful: we were all waiting for the weekend. Then today – yes, it is the 31st of May today – I finally realised what I had to do: I had to write it all down. I have laid my own foundations, and from now on it will be brick for word, word for brick. Tomorrow the building begins. I must have a good night's sleep.

1 June

7.15 a.m.
I have made my arrangements; I have pen and paper, I have a chair in front of the window. I set it all up last night. This morning I was up at six. Showered, shaved, put on my work clothes. Now I am waiting for us to begin.

8.30 a.m.
Here he comes. He is wearing the blue check and the trousers. He pauses on the top step of the veranda, looks out over his kingdom. Ah, if he knew that I was watching he wouldn't stretch in that bone-cracking way. He goes to the garage. He looks quite energetic, although a shadow of sleep drags across the lawn behind him. He opens the garage door, goes into the twilight. Comes out pushing the wheelbarrow loaded with a bag of cement, a spade, a box of tools. Goes to the beginning of the trench. Drags the piece of corrugated iron over, shovels sand onto it.

Let me leave him to mix while I describe briefly the sky behind him: It is a flat sky, like faded blue canvas. It could be dangling from the top of my window frame. At the bottom the canvas is notched raggedly by the roofs of the houses. A slight breeze comes up and the canvas sways: a black edge opens up between it and the houses, closes again as the breeze drops.

He has mixed the cement. He leaves it to set, pushes the barrow to the pile of bricks. He slits the plastic with one long, sure pass of the pocket-knife. There are beads of moisture on the plastic and they run to rivers as he peels it back from the wound. His hand goes in. Comes out with a brick. He weights it in his hand, turns it to look at it from all angles, puts it in the wheelbarrow. Reaches for another. If I had binoculars perhaps I would be able to tell, even at this distance, which brick is mine.

The wheelbarrow is full. He pushes it to the beginning of the trench. He takes a ball of string from the tool-box, stretches a length between the first fence post and the second, checks it with a spirit level. When he stands the string cuts him just below the knee. Surely that is too low? He kneads the cement with the back of the spade. He takes up his trowel. He goes down on his knees in the trench. He reaches for a brick. Weighs it. His hands go down into the earth. Damn! I can't see what he's doing. I've missed the laying of the first brick!

10.30 a.m.
He works incredibly slowly. As if there were only one place in the whole bloody wall where any particular brick will fit.

He has laid three courses so far, and has just started the fourth. This is the first course I can see clearly. He weighs each brick in his hand. Then he settles it on its dollop of cement, shuffles it in, taps it with the handle of the trowel, slices off the oozing cement, taps it again. Sometimes he starts over, scraping the surface clean, putting the brick aside and choosing another. I cannot see why. They look the same to me.

I wonder where she is? I expected her to be there for the first brick.

I should go over and speak to him. It would be simple. Perhaps he would welcome some discussion. I would suggest, for example, that he make the wall slightly higher: what good is a wall if one can see over it? I would also advise him to wear a hat – I could offer to lend him one of mine. He's not used to the sun.

I could tell him how interested I am in his project. That would surprise him. If I told him about my own plan to document the whole process and showed him the work I had done so far, perhaps he would let me bring a chair over and sit right there, where I could record smells, noises; perhaps he would answer a few questions about his motivations, and even listen to some constructive criticism.

On the other hand my interest could affect him badly. Perhaps I should let him carry on unhindered for a while, until we have a clearer picture of the road ahead.

12.30 p.m.

I am pleased to note that he has moved the string to shoulder height. But now he is going inside, probably for lunch.

2.45 p.m.

I don't know whether I will be able to keep this up. He loves this wall, every brick of it, but he loves it so passionlessly, with a love so methodical and disciplined, that it might as well be loathing.

He has loved his wall up to shoulder height, brick by careful brick, and now he fetches a step-ladder and the wall goes higher. He checks each course with the spirit-level, and then stands back to look at his work. It is very boring to watch.

5.00 p.m.

He has finished work for the day. The wall is about two metres high. He has filled in the panel between the first two fence posts. Unless he speeds up considerably, I estimate that it will be several months before the wall is completed.

They are sitting now on the veranda. She came out a few minutes ago and put two beers on the table. Came down to inspect the wall. I couldn't see her response, because she looked at it from the inside, as if that was the more important side. But she seemed to say something to him, because he spoke and listened and then smiled. Then she went back to the veranda and sat in the other chair. They raised their glasses to one another and I raised mine too and clinked it against the window-pane.

2 June

It is Sunday evening. He has finished another panel. This morning he uprooted the second fence post and strung the marker between the wall and the third post.

I think that I have caught up with him only to become bored.

He is a machine. His hands repeat themselves – brick after brick after brick they open and shut like pliers. His flabby muscles contract and relax in a predictable rhythm.

I think I dislike him. Why must he weigh each brick and toss it over in his hand? Why must he tap each brick with the handle of the trowel, twice on one side, three times on the other, and once solidly in the middle, before he is satisfied? The man has no imagination. I can see already that his wall will be just

716

another wall. An ordinary coincidence of bricks and mortar, presentably imperfect. It won't fall down, but then it won't fly either. He'll probably put plaster over his careful bricks and paint it green and people will think it was bought in a shop.

29 June

Today the wall finally passed the half-way mark. For the first time I can no longer see them as they drink their customary beer. I have resolved to speak to them before they disappear entirely.

30 June

I am writing this from the Café Zurich. I simply had to get out. I had to get away from them. I have delayed recording the events of yesterday evening because I needed time to calm down. I was so angry – and it will become clear that I had every reason to be – that I was sure my observations would seem spiteful and unfair.

But I think that I now have sufficient emotional distance from the incident to put it down objectively, as it happened.

During the course of yesterday afternoon, watching another panel of bricks edging up into the air, obscuring the house, I had become worried about the Groenewalds. More specifically, I had become worried about our relationship. There they were, celebrating the crossing of the half-way line, but hidden behind their wall. Here I was, celebrating the same occasion, but hidden behind my curtain. And just fifty metres or so separating us.

I began to regret my reticence. They were nice people, I knew. He was solid and reliable and purposeful. She was quiet and sweet and sensitive. They were my kind of people. If only I had broken the ice earlier. Now there was so much ground to be made up. Yet, at the same time, even though they were unaware of it, we had so much in common. The wall. They knew it from one side, I knew it from the other. I began to see it not so much as a barrier between us, but as a meeting-point. It was the thin line between pieces in a puzzle, the frontier on which both pieces become intelligible. Or perhaps it was like those optical puzzles in which you see the profile of a beautiful young woman or an old hag, but never both at the same time. I tossed these analogies around in my head, hoping to arrive at one I could share with them, an opening line I could call to them as I emerged from around the wall and took my first real steps into their lives. Eventually I decided to take a cup instead and ask for some sugar.

They were on the veranda, as I thought, drinking beer. They looked up as I crossed the lawn, suspiciously perhaps, although I couldn't see their expressions clearly in the blue gleam that the TV set in the lounge threw on them.

717

'Good evening Mr Groenewald, Mrs Groenewald,' I called, approaching them at a pace I thought they would appreciate, neither too fast nor too slow. 'I wonder if you could help me?'

He rose from his chair, put the beer on the table, and took one step to the edge of the veranda. She sat back in her chair and crossed her legs.

I stopped just below him but I spoke to her. 'I'm making a trifle and, you know how it is, I've run out of sugar for the custard. Could you spare me a bit, just until tomorrow?'

She rose quickly, took the cup from my hand, and went into the house. I took a few steps after her, drawn by the flickering blue of her retreating back, but he stepped towards the door, as if to block my path.

I was disappointed. I had hoped to gain access to the house, to measure their space against my imaginings. I heard the familiar fanfare announcing the six o'clock news. If only he would invite me in to watch the news with them: that would give us many opportunities to discuss the state of the country, the newest trouble spots, local and abroad, and get to know one another.

But he made no move. I realised quickly that the more important opportunity was right in my hands – to discuss the wall with its maker. She, after all, had as little to do with the wall as a trowel or a piece of string. It was just as well she had left us alone.

I turned slightly, so that my pose suggested that I was watching the wall.

'I've been following your progress with interest,' I said. 'Perhaps you have seen me? I live right across from you.'

'No,' he said.

'It's a fine wall,' I went on undaunted. After all, hadn't they been invisible to me for months, even years (I couldn't remember whether they had moved in before or after me). 'A very fine wall indeed. A little high perhaps. A little forbidding.'

'I would make it higher,' he said, 'but there are municipal regulations.' I began to feel uneasy. He hadn't invited me to sit, so I perched on the edge of the veranda.

'Have you built a wall before?' I asked

'Many times,' he said. 'More times than I care to remember.'

That threw me. I was going to say that he was doing a good job, for a first attempt. But perhaps I would never have reached that line anyway, for it struck me then, with a sense of loss, that I couldn't see my house at all from this side. It had vanished completely. The sky above the wall was a blank, moronic space, as high as the stars. There was nothing in it that would provide comfort to a human heart, that would fill a human eye. The world beyond the wall was empty: there was not even a world there. Perhaps my house would be visible from the veranda? I stood, hoping to find a way up. But he had moved, while I was musing, to the top of the steps, and was looking back over his shoulder through the open window at the flickering television screen. The curtains were open. You could see right in. I moved towards the steps.

Just then she came out with the cup of sugar. She handed it down to me. It was very full and a few grains spilled onto my fingers.

'I'll replace it tomorrow. Thank you,' I said.

'Please don't bother,' she replied.

I had to leave. The lawn seemed vast. I crossed towards the hard edge of the wall, behind which the world was slowly materialising again. I had an extraordinary sense as I walked, somewhat stiffly, with the sugar trickling onto my fingers, that no eyes were on me. No one was watching me. I wanted to look back, but I couldn't. I couldn't confirm such an obvious insult.

I was mad as hell. I was in my lounge, where everything was still the same. I was mad as could be. I smashed up a chair. Still the rage wouldn't leave me. I smashed up a table. Then I started to feel better, pacing around among the splinters with a bottle of Scotch in my hand. Who the hell did they think they were, treating me like a dog? Who the fuck were they anyway? Lunatics, blind people, fat slobs, smug shit-houses.

I should have gone right into their house and smashed up a few things. That would have been perfect, with the news in the background. I would have shown them unrest and rioting and burning, in three dimensions. I would have given them wanton destruction of private property. I would have given them hell in the eye-level oven, and stonings with the bric-a-brac from the room divider. And then I would have left them uneasy calm after yesterday's violence.

But was it all worth it?

I sat down in the surviving chair and thought about it more carefully. They were such perverse people. What were they planning to do behind that ridiculous wall? Volkspele? Nude braaivleises? Secret nocturnal rituals accessible only to people in helicopters?

Fuck them. I had to tidy up.

17 August

The wall is almost finished.

I have not been thinking about it much. Of course, since the unfortunate incident with the sugar I've had to avoid them, to spare us all embarrassment. I have been going to work early and coming in late – and always careful to avert my gaze. Yet, out of the corner of my eye, as it were, I've watched the wall edge malevolently towards the end of the trench. There is not much space left for it to cross: scarcely a metre. That will be done next weekend and the betrayal will be complete.

I am no longer interested in them. They have blurred into the background out of which they came. But, for the sake of symmetry, I have decided to record the end of it all, the laying of the final brick. It seems necessary. Then I can be done with this journal.

24 August

He is almost finished. He is building the last panel from the garden side.

I have watched him slowly obliterated by his wall. Now all I can see is a pair of hands reaching up.

I imagine that she is there with him, holding a bottle of champagne. No doubt I will see the cork flying up to the stars.

But is there cause for celebration? No. Is there reason for building when things are falling down? No. Is there reason for drinking beer when people are starving? Probably not. Do two people and a bottle of champagne make sense when citizens are pitched against soldiers, when stones are thrown at tanks? Does private joy make sense in the face of public suffering?

There he begins the last course of bricks. How bored I am with the tired repetition of gesture. How bored I am with the familiar shapes of words. How bored I am with this journal. It's just a wall. That must be clear by now. Even a child could see it. And the words that go into it like bricks are as bland and heavy and worn as the metaphor itself.

He lays the last brick. But I have the last word.

THE END

Later that same evening:

I am writing simply because I cannot sleep. And the reason I cannot sleep is that those bastards across the road are having a party. A wall-warming, I suppose. The music is too loud. And the buzzing of voices! They have strung coloured lights in the trees. Candles are burning in paper bags on top of the wall. I would phone the police, but I have already smashed the telephone.

I would gather to me, if I could, the homeless and the hungry, the persecuted, the pursued, the forgotten, those without friends and neighbours, to march around the wall. We would be blowing paper trumpets left over from office parties, and banging on cake tins, and raising up a noise to wake the dead and bring the wall tumbling down.

8 September

Today there was something new attached to the wall: a FOR SALE notice.

17 September

Today a SOLD notice.

2 November

Today they left.

I went across and stood on the pavement to watch their household effects being put into the truck. It is all as I expected: the knotty pine, the wicker, the velveteen, the china, the cotton print, the plastic, the glass, the stainless-steel, the beaten copper.

I stood right next to the truck with my hands on my hips. I dared them to meet my eye but they seemed not to notice me, or not to care. They put a few boxes on the back seat of the car and they followed the pantechnicon. I watched until they disappeared.

The wall looked ashamed of itself.

9 November

The new people have moved in. They are simply people carrying boxes and banging doors. Good.

Today the municipality pruned all the trees in our suburb. The sky has opened up. The wall turns its back on the street. It is a beautiful sunny day. I must get out.

And I must remember to take a stroll past the wall some time and see if I can spot my brick.

IVAN VLADISLAVIĆ

The WHITES ONLY Bench

From: *Propaganda by Monuments and other Stories* (1996)

Yesterday our visitors' book, which Portia has covered in zebra-skin wrapping-paper and shiny plastic, recorded the name of another important person: Coretta King. When Mrs King had finished her tour, with Strickland herself playing the guide, she was treated to tea and cakes in the cafeteria. The photographers, who had been trailing around after her trying to sniff out interesting angles and ironic juxtapositions against the exhibits, tucked in as well, I'm told, and made pigs of themselves.

After the snacks Mrs King popped into the gift shop for a few mementoes, and bought generously – soapstone hippopotami with sly expressions, coffee-table catalogues, little wire bicycles and riot-control vehicles, garish place mats and beaded fly-whisks, among other things. Her aide had to chip in to make up the cost of a set of mugs in the popular 'Leaders Past and Present' range.

The honoured guests were making their way back to the bus when Mrs King spotted the bench in the courtyard and suggested that she pose there for a few shots. I happened to be watching from the workshop window, and I had a feeling the photographs would be exceptional. A spring shower had just fallen, out of the blue, and the courtyard was a well of clear light. Tendrils of fragrant steam coiled up evocatively from a windfall of blossoms on the flagstones. The scene had been set by chance. Perhaps the photographers had something to prove, too, having failed to notice a photo opportunity so steeped in ironic significance.

The *Star* carried one of the pictures on its front page this morning. Charmaine picked up a copy on her way to work and she couldn't wait to show it to me.

The interest of the composition derives – if I may make the obvious analysis – from a lively dispute of horizontals and verticals. The bench is a syllogism of horizontal lines, flatly contradicted by the vertical bars of the legs at either end (these legs are shaped like h's, actually, but from the front they look like l's). Three other verticals assert their position: on the left – our left, that is – the concrete stalk of the Black Sash drinking fountain; in the middle, thrusting up behind the bench, the trunk of the controversial kaffirboom; and on the right, perched on the very end of her seat, our subject: Mrs King.

Mrs King has her left thigh crossed over her right, her left foot crooked around her right ankle, her left arm coiled to clutch one of our glossy brochures to her breast. The wooden slats are slickly varnished with sunlight, and she sits upon them gingerly, as if the last slat's not quite dry. Yet her right arm reposes along the backrest with the careless grace of a stem. There's an odd ambiguity in her body, and it's reflected in her face too, in an expression which superimposes the past upon the present: she looks both timorous and audacious. The WHITES ONLY sign under her dangling thumb in the very middle of the picture might be taken up the wrong way as an irreverent reference to her eyes, which she opens wide in an expression of mock alarm – or is it outrage? The rest of her features are more prudently composed, the lips quilted with bitterness, but tucked in mockingly at one corner.

The photographer was wise to choose black and white. These stark contrasts, coupled with Mrs King's old-fashioned suit and hairdo, confound the period entirely. The photograph might have been taken thirty years ago, or yesterday.

Charmaine was tickled pink. She says her bench is finally avenged for being upstaged by that impostor from the Municipal Bus Drivers' Association. I doubt that Strickland has even noticed.

There seems to be a tacit agreement around here that Mrs King is an acceptable form, although it won't do for anyone else. When I pointed this out, Charmaine said it's a special case because Mr King, rest his soul, is no more. I fail to see what difference that makes, and I said so. Then Reddy, whose ears were flapping, said that 'Mrs King' is tolerated precisely because it preserves the memory of the absent Mr King, like it or not. He said it's like a dead metaphor.

I can't make up my mind. Aren't we reading too much into it?

* * *

Charmaine has sliced the photograph out of the unread newspaper with a Stanley knife and pinned the cutting up on the notice board in Reception. She says her bench has been immortalised. 'Immortality' is easy to bandy about, but for a while it was touch and go whether Charmaine's bench would make it to the end of the week.

We were working late one evening, as usual, when the little drama began. The Museum was due to open in six weeks' time but the whole place was still upside down. It wasn't clear yet who was in charge, if anyone, and we were all in a state.

Charmaine was putting the finishing touches to her bench, I was knocking together a couple of rostra for the Congress of the People, when Strickland came in. She had been with us for less than a week and it was the first time she had set foot in the workshop. We weren't sure at all then what to make of our new director, and so we both greeted her politely and went on with our work.

She waved a right hand as limp as a kid glove to show that we shouldn't mind her, and then clasped it behind her back. She began to wander around on tiptoe, even though I was hammering in nails, swivelling her head from side to side, peering into boxes, scanning the photographs and diagrams pinned to chipboard display stands, taking stock of the contents of tables and desks. She never touched a thing, but there was something grossly intrusive about the inspection. Strickland wears large, rimless spectacles, double glazed and tinted pink, and they sometimes make her look like a pair of television monitors.

After a soundless, interrogative circuit of the room she stopped behind Charmaine and looked over her shoulder. Charmaine had just finished the 'I', and now she laid her brush across the top of the paint tin, peeled off the stencil and flourished it in the air to dry the excess paint.

I put down my hammer – the racket had become unbearable – and took up some sandpaper instead. The people here will tell you that I don't miss a thing.

Strickland looked at the half-formed word. Then she unclasped her hands and slid them smoothly into the pockets of her linen suit. The cloth was fresh cream with a dab of butter in it, richly textured, the pockets cool as arum lilies.

'What are you doing?' Strickland asked, in a tone that bristled like a new broom.

Charmaine stood back with the stencil in her hand and Strickland had to step hastily aside to preserve a decent distance between her suit and the grubby overall. Unnoticed by anyone but myself, a drop of white paint fell from the end of the brush resting across the tin onto the shapely beige toe of Strickland's shoe.

The answer to Strickland's question was so plain to see that it hardly needed voicing, but she blinked her enlarged eyes expectantly, and so Charmaine said, 'It's the WHITES ONLY bench.' When Strickland showed no sign of recognition, Charmaine added, 'You remember the benches. For whites only?'

Silence. What on earth did she want? My sandpaper was doing nothing to smooth the ragged edges of our nerves, and so I put it down. We all looked at the bench.

It was a beautiful bench – as a useful object, I mean, rather than a symbol of injustice. The wooden slats were tomato-sauce red. The arms and legs were made of iron, but cleverly moulded to resemble branches, and painted brown to enhance a rustic illusion. The bench looked well used, which is often a sign that a thing has been loved. But when you looked closer, as Strickland was doing now, you saw that all these signs of wear and tear were no more than skin-deep. Charmaine had applied all of them in the workshop. The bruised hollows on the seat, where the surface had been abraded by decades of white thighs and buttocks, were really patches of brown and purple paint. The flashes of raw metal on the armrests, where the paint had been worn away by countless white palms and elbows, turned out to be mere discs of silver paint themselves. Charmaine had even smeared the city's grimy shadows into the grain.

Strickland pored over these special effects with an expression of amazed distaste, and then stared for a minute on end at the letters WHI on the upper-most slat of the backrest. The silence congealed around us, slowing us down, making us slur our movements, until the absence of sound was as tangible as a crinkly skin on the surface of the air. 'Forgive me,' she said at last, with an awakening toss of her head. 'You're manufacturing a WHITES ONLY bench?'

'Ja. For Room 27.'

Strickland went to the floor plan taped to one of the walls and looked for Room 27: Petty Apartheid. Then she gazed at the calendar next to the plan, but whether she was mulling over the dates, or studying the photograph — children with stones in their hands, riot policemen with rifles, between the lines a misplaced reporter with a camera — or simply lost in thought, I couldn't tell. Did she realise that the calendar was ten years old?

Charmaine and I exchanged glances behind her back.

'Surely we should have the real thing,' Strickland said, turning.

'Of course — if only we could find it.'

'You can't find a genuine WHITES ONLY bench?'

'No.'

'That's very hard to believe.'

'We've looked everywhere. It's not as easy as you'd think. This kind of thing was frowned upon, you know, in the end. Discrimination I mean. The municipalities were given instructions to paint them over. There wasn't much point in hunting for something that doesn't exist, so we decided at our last meeting — this was before your time, I'm afraid — that it would be better if I recreated one.'

'Recreated one,' Strickland echoed.

'Faithfully. I researched it and everything. I've got the sources here some-where.' Charmaine scratched together some photocopies splattered with paint and dusted with fingerprints and tread-marks from her running shoes. 'The bench itself is a genuine 1960s one, I'm glad to say, from the darkest decade of repression. Donated by Reddy's father-in-law, who stole it from a bus stop for use in the garden. It was a long time ago, mind you, the family is very respectable. From a black bus stop — for Indians. Interestingly, the Indian benches didn't have INDIANS ONLY on them — not in Natal anyway, according to Mr Mookadam. Or even ASIATICS. Not that it matters.'

'It matters to me,' Strickland said curtly — Charmaine does go on sometimes – and pushed her glasses up on her nose so that her eyes were doubly magnified. 'This is a museum, not some high-school operetta. It is our historical duty to be authentic.'

I must say that made me feel bad, when I thought about all the effort Charmaine and I had put into everything from the Sharpeville Massacre to the Soweto Uprising, trying to get the details right, every abandoned shoe, every spent cartridge, every bloodied stitch of clothing, only to have this jenny-come-lately (as Charmaine puts it) give us a lecture about authenticity. What about our professional duty? (Charmaine again.)

'Have we advertised?' Strickland asked, and I could tell by her voice that she meant to argue the issue out. But at that moment she glanced down and saw the blob of paint on the toe of her shoe.

I had the fantastic notion to venture an excuse on Charmaine's behalf: to tell Strickland that she had dripped ice cream on her shoe. Vanilla ice cream! I actually saw her hand grasping the cone, her sharp tongue curling around the white cupola, the droplet plummeting. Fortunately I came to my senses before I opened my big mouth.

* * *

It was the first proper meeting of the Steering Committee with the new director. We hadn't had a meeting for a month. When Charlie Sibeko left in a huff after the fiasco with the wooden AK47s, we all heaved a sigh of relief. We were sick to death of meetings: the man's appetite for circular discussion was insatiable.

Strickland sat down at the head of the table, and having captured that coveted chair laid claim to another by declaring the meeting open. She seemed to assume that this was her prerogative as director, and no one had the nerve to challenge her.

The report-backs were straightforward: we were all behind schedule and over budget. I might add that we were almost past caring. It seemed impossible that we'd be finished in time for the official opening. The builders were still knocking down walls left, right and centre, and establishing piles of rubble in every room. Pincus joked that the only exhibit sure to be ready on time was the row of concrete bunks – they were part of the original compound in which the Museum is housed and we had decided to leave them exactly as we found them. He suggested that we think seriously about delaying the opening, which was Portia's cue to produce the invitations, just back from the printers. Everyone groaned (excluding Strickland and me) and breathed in the chastening scent of fresh ink.

'As far as we're concerned, this date is written in stone,' Strickland said, snapping one of the copperplate cards shut. 'We will be ready on time. People will have to learn to take their deadlines seriously.' At that point Charmaine began to doodle on her agenda – a hand with a stiff index finger, emerging from a lacy cuff, pointing at Item 4: Bench.

Item 2: Posters, which followed the reports, was an interesting one. Pincus had had a letter from a man in Bethlehem, a former town clerk and electoral officer, who had collected copies of every election poster displayed in the town since it was founded. He was prepared to entrust the collection to us if it was kept intact. Barbara said she could probably use a couple in the Birth of Apartheid exhibit. We agreed that Pincus would write to the donor, care of the Bethlehem Old Age Home, offering to house the entire collection and display selected items on a rotating basis.

Item 3: Poetry, was Portia's. Ernest Dladla, she informed us, had declined our invitation to read a poem at the opening ceremony, on the perfectly reasonable grounds that he was not a poet. 'I have poetic impulses,' he said in his charming note, 'but I do not act upon them.' Should she go ahead, Portia wanted to know, and approach Alfred Qabula instead, as Ernie suggested?

Then Strickland asked in an acerbic tone whether an issue this trivial needed to be tabled at an important meeting. But Portia responded magnificently, pointing out that she knew nothing about poetry, not having had the benefit of a decent education, had embarrassed herself once in the performance of her duties and did not wish to do so again. All she wanted was an answer to a simple question: Is Alfred Qabula a poet? Yes or no?

No sooner was that settled, than Strickland announced Item 4: Bench, and stood up. Perhaps this was a technique she had read about in the business pages somewhere, calculated to intimidate the opposition. 'It has come to my attention,' she said, 'that our workshop personnel are busily recreating beautiful replicas of apartheid memorabilia, when the ugly originals could be ours for the asking. I do not know what Mr Sibeko's policy on this question was, although the saga of the wooden AK47s is full of suggestion, but as far as I'm concerned it's an appalling waste of time and money. It's also dishonest. This is a museum, not an amusement arcade.

'My immediate concern is the WHITES ONLY bench, which is taking up so much of Charmaine's time and talent. I find it hard to believe that there is not a genuine example of a bench of this nature somewhere in the country.'

'Petty apartheid went out ages ago,' said Charmaine, 'even in the Free State.'

'The first Indian townships in the Orange Free State were established way back in October 1986,' said Reddy, who had been unusually quiet so far, 'in Harrismith, Virginia and Odendaalsrus. Not many people know that. I remember hearing the glad tidings from my father-in-law, Mr Mookadam, who confessed that ever since he was a boy it had been a dream of his to visit that forbidden province.'

'I'll wager that there are at least a dozen real WHITES ONLY benches in this city alone, in private collections,' Strickland insisted, erasing Reddy's tangent with the back of her hand. 'People are fascinated by the bizarre.'

'We asked everyone we know,' said Charmaine. 'And we asked them to ask everyone they know, and so on. Like a chain letter – except that we didn't say they would have a terrible accident if they broke the chain. And we couldn't find a single bench. Not one.'

'Have we advertised?'

'No commercials,' said Reddy, and there was a murmur of assenting voices.

'Why ever not?'

'It just causes more headache.'

'Oh nonsense!'

Reddy held up his right hand, with the palm out, and batted the air with it, as if he was bouncing a ball off Strickland's forehead. This gesture had a peculiarly mollifying effect on her, and she put her hand over her eyes and sat down. Reddy stood up in his ponderous way and padded out of the room.

Pincus, who has a very low tolerance for silence, said, 'Wouldn't it be funny if Charmaine's bench turned out to be the whites' only bench?'

No one laughed, so he said 'whites' only' again, and drew the apostrophe in the air with his forefinger.

Reddy came back, carrying a photograph, a Tupperware lunch-box and a paperknife. He put the photograph in the middle of the table, facing Strickland. She had to lean forward in her chair to see what it was. I wondered whether she fully appreciated the havoc her outsize spectacles wreaked on her face, how they disjointed her features. She looked like a composite portrait in a magazine competition, in which some cartoon character's eyes had been mismatched with the jaw of a real-life heroine.

Everyone at the table, with the exception of our director, had seen this routine before. Some of us had sat through it half a dozen times, with a range of donors, do-gooders, interest groups. For some reason, it never failed to involve me. I also leant forward to view the eight-by-ten. No one else moved.

I looked first at the pinprick stigmata in the four corners. Then I looked, as I always did, at the girl's outflung hand.

Her hand is a jagged speech-bubble filled with disbelief. It casts a shadow shaped like a howling mouth on her body, and that mouth takes up the cry of outrage. The palm Reddy had waved in Strickland's face was a much more distant echo.

I looked next at the right hand of the boy who is carrying Hector Peterson. His fingers press into the flesh of a thigh that is still warm, willing it to live, prompting the muscle, animating it. Hector Peterson's right hand, by contrast, lolling numbly on his belly, knows that it is dead, and it expresses that certainty in dark tones of shadow and blood.

These hands are still moving, they still speak to me.

Reddy jabbed the photograph with the point of his paperknife. 'This is a photograph of Hector Peterson, in the hour of his death,' he said. Strickland nodded her head impatiently. 'The day was 16 June 1976.' She nodded again, urging him to skip the common knowledge and come to the point. 'A Wednesday. As it happened, it was fine and mild. The sun rose that morning at 6.53 and set that evening at 5.25. The shot was taken at 10.15 on the dot. It was the third in a series of six. Hector Peterson was the first fatality of what we would come to call the Soweto Riots – the first in a series of seven hundred odd. The photographer was Sam Nzima, then in the employ of the *World*. The subject, according to the tombstone that now marks his grave, was Zolile Hector Pietersen, P-I-E-T-E-R-S-E-N, but the newspapers called him Hector Peterson and it stuck. We struck out the "I", we put it to rout in the alphabet of the oppressor. We bore the hero's body from the uneven field of battle and anointed it with English. According to the tombstone he was thirteen years old, but as you can see he looked no more than half that age ... Or is it just the angle? If only we had some other pictures of the subject to compare this one with, we might feel able to speak with more authority.'

This welter of detail, and the offhand tone of the delivery, produced in Strickland the usual baffled silence.

'Not many people know these things.' Reddy slid the point of the knife onto the girl. 'This is Hector's sister Margot, a.k.a. Tiny, now living in Soweto.' The knife slid again. 'And this is Mbuyisa Makhubu, whereabouts your guess is as good as mine. Not many people know them either. We have come to the conclusion, here at the Museum, that the living are seldom as famous as the dead.'

The knife moved again. It creased Mbuyisa Makhubu's lips, which are bent into a bow of pain, like the grimace of a tragic mask, it rasped the brick wall of the matchbox house which we see over his shoulder, skipped along the top of a wire gate, and came to rest on the small figure of a woman in the background. 'And who on earth do you suppose this is?'

Strickland gazed at the little figure as if it was someone famous she should be able to recognise in an instant, some household name. In fact, the features of this woman – she is wearing a skirt and doek – are no more than a grey smudge, continuous with the shadowed wall behind her.

I looked at Hector Peterson's left arm, floating on air, and the shadow of his hand on Mbuyisa Makhubu's knee, a shadow so hard-edged and muscular it could trip the bearer up.

The child is dead. With his rumpled sock around his ankle, his grazed knee, his jersey stuck with dry grass, you would think he had taken a tumble in the playground, if it were not for the gout of blood from his mouth. The jersey is a bit too big for him: it was meant to last another year at least. Or is it just that

729

he was small for his age? Or is it the angle? In his hair is a stalk of grass shaped like a praying mantis.

'Nobody knows.'

Strickland sat back with a sigh, but Reddy went on relentlessly.

'Nevertheless, theories were advanced: some people said that this woman, this apparent bystander, was holding Hector Peterson in her arms when he died. She was a mother herself. She cradled him in her lap – you can see the bloodstains here – and when Makhubu took the body from her and carried it away, she found a bullet caught in the folds of her skirt. She is holding that fatal bullet in her right hand, here.

'Other people said that it didn't happen like that at all. Lies and fantasies. When Nzima took this photograph, Hector Peterson was still alive! What you see here, according to one reliable caption, is a critically wounded youth. The police open fire, Hector falls at Mbuyisa's feet. The boy picks him up and runs towards the nearest car, which happens to belong to Sam Nzima and Sophie Tema, a journalist on the *World*, Nzima's partner that day. Sam takes his photographs. Then Mbuyisa and Tiny pile into the back of the Volkswagen – did I mention that it was a Volkswagen? – they pile into the back with Hector; Sam and Sophie pile into the front with their driver, Thomas Khoza. They rush to the Orlando Clinic, but Hector Peterson is certified dead on arrival. And that's the real story. You can look it up for yourself.

'But the theories persisted. So we thought we would try to lay the ghost – we have a duty after all to tell the truth. This is a museum, not a paperback novel. We advertised. We called on this woman to come forward and tell her story. We said it would be nice – although it wasn't essential – if she brought the bullet with her.'

'Anyone respond?'

'I'll say.'

Reddy opened his lunch-box and pushed it over to Strickland with the edge of his palm, like a croupier. She looked at the contents: there were .38 Magnum slugs, 9 mm and AK cartridges, shiny .22 bullets, a .357 hollow-point that had blossomed on impact into a perfect corolla. There were even a couple of doppies and a misshapen ball from an old voorlaaier. Strickland zoomed in for a close-up. She still didn't get it.

'If you'll allow me a poetic licence,' Reddy said, as if poetic licence was a certificate you could stick on a page in your Book of Life, 'this is the bullet that killed Hector Peterson.'

* * *

So we didn't advertise. But Strickland stuck to her guns about the WHITES ONLY bench: we would have the real thing or nothing at all. She made a few

730

inquiries of her own, and wouldn't you know it, before the week was out she turned up the genuine article.

The chosen bench belonged to the Municipal Bus Drivers' Association, and in exchange for a small contribution to their coffers – the replacement costs plus ten per cent – they were happy to part with it. The honour of fetching the trophy from their clubhouse in Marshall Street fell to Pincus. Unbeknown to us, the treasurer of the MBDA had decided that there was a bit of publicity to be gained from his association's public-spirited gesture, and when our representative arrived he found a photographer ready to record the event for posterity. Pincus was never the most politic member of our committee. With his enthusiastic cooperation the photographer was able to produce an entire essay, which subsequently appeared, without a by-line, in the *Saturday Star*. It showed the bench in its original quarters (weighed down by a squad of bus drivers of all races, pin-up girls – whites only – looking over the drivers' shoulders, all of them, whether flesh and blood or paper, saying cheese); the bench on its way out of the door (Pincus steering, the treasurer pushing); being loaded onto the back of our bakkie (Pincus and the treasurer shaking hands and stretching the cheque between them like a Christmas cracker); and finally driven away (Pincus hanging out of the window to give us a thumbs-up, the treasurer waving goodbye, the treasurer waving back at himself from the rear-view mirror). These pictures caused exactly the kind of headache Reddy had tried so hard to avoid. Offers of benches poured in from far and wide. Pincus was made to write the polite letters of thanks but no thanks. For our purposes, one bench is quite enough, thank you.

You can see the WHITES ONLY bench now, if you like, in Room 27. Just follow the arrows. I may as well warn you that it says EUROPEANS ONLY, to be precise. There's a second prohibition too, an entirely non-racial one, strung on a chain between the armrests: PLEASE DO NOT SIT ON THIS BENCH. That little sign is Charmaine's work, and making her paint it was Strickland's way of rubbing turpentine in her wounds.

When the genuine bench came to light, Charmaine received instructions to get rid of 'the fake'. But she refused to part with it. I was persuaded to help her carry it into the storeroom, where it remained for a month or so. As the deadline for the opening neared, Charmaine would take refuge in there from time to time, whenever things got too much for her, and put the finishing touches to her creation. At first, she was furious about all the publicity given to the impostor. But once the offers began to roll in, and it became apparent that WHITES ONLY benches were not nearly as scarce as we'd thought, she saw an opportunity to bring her own bench out of the closet. The night before the grand opening, in the early hours, when the sky was already going grey behind the mine-dump on the far side of the parking lot, we carried her bench outside and put it in the arbour under the controversial kaffirboom.

'When Strickland asks about it,' said Charmaine, 'you can tell her it was a foundling, left on our doorstep, and we just had to take it in.' Funny thing is, Strickland never made a peep.

I can see Charmaine's WHITES ONLY bench now, from my window. The kaffirboom, relocated here fully grown from a Nelspruit nursery, has acclimatised wonderfully well. '*Erythrina caffra*, a sensible choice,' said Reddy, 'deciduous, patulous, and umbrageous.' And he was quite right, it casts a welcome shade. Charmaine's faithful copy reclines in the dapple below, and its ability to attract and repel our visitors never ceases to impress me.

Take Mrs King. And talking about Mrs King, *Mr* King is a total misnomer, of course. I must point it out to Reddy. The Revd King, yes, and Dr King, yes, and possibly even the Revd Dr King. But Mr King? No ways.

It seems unfair, but Charmaine's bench has the edge on that old museum piece in Room 27. Occasionally I look up from my workbench, and see a white man sitting there, a history teacher say. While the schoolchildren he has brought here on an outing hunt in the grass for lucky beans, he sits down on our bench to rest his back. And after a while he pulls up his long socks, crosses one pink leg over the other, laces his fingers behind his head and closes his eyes.

Then again, I'll look up to see a black woman shuffling resolutely past, casting a resentful eye on the bench and muttering a protest under her breath, while the flame-red blossoms of the kaffirboom detonate beneath her aching feet.

DAVID MEDALIE

The Shooting of the Christmas Cows

From: *The Shooting of the Christmas Cows* (1990)

A good Impressionist painting is a memory as well as a vision. The painter is simultaneously the begetter of impressions and the recorder of their afterglow. That is what softens the mists, blurs the vineyards and canals, and makes tremulous the sunrises. To efface without excluding is the aim of the Impressionist painter. Most acts of memory do not accomplish that very fine balance; that is why they are inartistic.

This probably seems like some sort of preamble, but it is not meant to be. I am trying to recall what I can of the shooting of the Christmas cows.

I remember that I awoke even earlier than necessary that morning, and that great feelings of excitement coincided with my waking moments. The excitement was like a squirming ball of kittens that I hugged to my chest and squeezed, if only to make them wriggle the more. My bedroom had been redecorated yet again, several weeks previously, this time in apricot and white, and the sunlight sidled in through the white lace curtains. This was a sun in immediate post-solstice prime, heady and lingering-long with the unleashed length of its African December days. The dressing-table and the headboard of the bed, which had been painted a fresh apricot colour, glowed now as if sunlight were not light but syrup. My rag dolls were arranged, as always, at the foot of the bed. On the dressing-table was a tiny porcelain figurine which Mother had given me for Christmas the year before. It was a milk-maid walking with her pail: her long skirt lay unruffled about her stockings, and her little feet seemed poised for skipping or effortless movement.

That bedroom was more important to Mother than it was to me. She loved it, even though she changed it so frequently, and even now I can see her, tall and brusque, arranging everything in it with deft movements of her hands, creating with undeniable craftmanship a sanctuary pristine. That bedroom was a dove egg lying in the heart of a flower. I would as soon have untidied anything in it as I would have sworn at the teacher at school, or thrown something at her. I maintained that room with dutiful reverence.

After the last redecoration, Mother surveyed the refurbished sanctum with evident satisfaction. She said, 'There, it's perfect. I have made it beautiful for my little girl, haven't I?'

That morning I dressed swiftly and carefully, putting on one of my newest summer dresses and, brushing my hair with swift strokes, I put it back with what we used to call an Alice band. I ran into Mother's room and woke her, gently but insistently. When she opened her eyes, I said, 'Let's go now, it's late.'

She glanced swiftly at her wristwatch with her slightly narrowed blue eyes, and then shook her head. Mother always moved from sleep to full alertness without any intermediate period of sleepiness or languor. When she spoke, her voice was characteristically decisive: 'It's not late, it's far too early. They'll still be eating breakfast. It's not polite to arrive too early.'

I told her that Annemarie had said that I should come as early as possible, for we could spend only the morning together. I did not add that Annemarie had said that if I did not arrive early in the morning, I would miss the shooting of the Christmas cows. This I deliberately suppressed, for I did not want Mother to ask, with her peremptory voice, 'What do you mean? What is she talking about? The shooting of *what?*'

I would simply not have been able to answer. I had not the faintest notion what Christmas cows were, and why or how one shot at them. I had not been able to bring myself to ask this of the blissfully and energetically self-confident Annemarie. I merely knew that it was something I could not bear to miss.

While Mother dressed, I sat on the edge of her bed and waited. The sight of her, her sleek dark hair, her capable, faintly sallow hands, and her precise movements, aroused in me – as always – an emotion verging on awe. There was something so wordlessly hat-lifting about her, about her beige or cream skirts, her long leather boots, and her crocodile-skin handbags.

We ate a rather hurried breakfast and, before long, we were seated in the car, heading out of town to the farm where Annemarie and her family lived. Mother drove a steel-grey Jaguar. With its curious, elongated shape, and its unusual head-lamps, it looked like a gigantic bullet wearing pince-nez. Inside there were sheepskin seat-covers, and the dashboard gleamed with mysterious knobs and dials. The engine always seemed to hum dutifully, but Mother worked the gears as if she were scolding it for tardiness.

Within minutes we passed out of town, and sped along the open road. On either side of us were tall maize plants on the verge of coming into seed. Here and there one or two early plants had already done so, and they held their lone golden sprigs aloft. They were gawky green summer princesses, and the boldest amongst them waved the banners of fertility. There was an almost tactile sense of growth and dampness and process. It was a day bound by that process to the preceding day, and to the day that would come afterwards. The next day was the Day of Nativity itself, but a maize field in late December is too preoccupied with growth to pay much attention to birth and rebirth.

My impatience notwithstanding, we soon reached the turnoff to the farm. A large sign with the letters R.B. JOOSTE – WELGEVONDEN stood at the

734

point where the tarred road and the gravel road met. There were rows of bluegum trees on either side of the gravel road, which lay between them like a long trail of scrambled eggs. Even in the still morning air, the blue-green leaves of the trees moved faintly. Bluegum trees seem always to have devoted their lives to eradicating stasis and symmetry. When they are still, they never seem wholly motionless, and when they are straight, they are never wholly perpendicular. They grow in uneven spurts, and they even die erratically, with a slow, gangrenous browning of each waving arm.

As we neared the house, I felt again the sensation of barely controlled excitement. Characteristically, my bladder stirred: like a well on a dark night, it could not fail to reflect the dangling of the stars.

Annemarie had unaccountably befriended me towards the end of that year, after ignoring me entirely for about ten months. Her company was sought after by the other children in the class; mine was not. Consequently, her befriending of me had the quality of a rich man's bestowing charity on one less fortunate than himself: the riches of the former are brought more sharply into focus because of what they mean to the latter. Nevertheless, I was elated when Annemarie accepted me as her friend. Then she said, 'Come and spend the day before Christmas with us on the farm. Come early, so that you can be there for the shooting of the Christmas cows. Ask your mother today.'

I obtained Mother's consent, omitting all mention of Christmas cows. We had been invited elsewhere for lunch, so it was agreed that Mother would fetch me towards noon.

Mother said, 'Annemarie? You never mentioned her before.'

I said, 'She's a new friend. She lives on a farm, on the Morgenzon road. We've passed it often — she says it's by those bluegums. It's not far.'

Mother said, 'All right. If it's convenient for her parents.'

Apparently it was, and so now the car swept along the gravel driveway to the farmhouse, with a sound as of steel teeth chewing something. The phrase murmured persistently amongst my thoughts: The Shooting of the Christmas Cows. The Shooting of the Christmas Cows. The rhythmical quality itself was suggestive. Perhaps it was all an esoteric pre-Christmas family ritual in which the Jooste family participated. Perhaps it was something peculiar to Afrikaans-speaking families. Perhaps they all shot Christmas cows today, just as they would eat delectable Christmas dishes tomorrow.

Annemarie was waiting impatiently for me outside the house, dancing excitedly from one foot to another, her pigtails whipping animatedly about her head. 'At last,' she muttered to me, but she greeted Mother with the meticulous politeness of rural Afrikaner children. Her father appeared at the back door. He walked slowly towards us, throwing me into a state of alarm. I had met him only once before and, although he seemed kind, he made me nervous. He greeted Mother with slow courtesy, shaking her slender hand with his own large, reddish one. He shook my hand too, and patted me on the head in an avuncular way. 'So, Estelle,' he said, 'you've come to spend the morning with us on the farm?'

I muttered, 'Yes, Oom. Thank you, Oom.'

Shyness lay upon my tongue like aphasia, and I studied my feet, not as if I'd never seen them before, but as if I never expected to see them again. The shyness from which I suffered was too raw to be called self-consciousness. It consisted of an unremitting desire to eradicate, somehow, the attention of all adults except Mother – and attention which not even benevolence could soften.

Mr Jooste invited Mother in for a cup of coffee. She declined, saying that she was pressed for time. She would call for me in a few hours, she said, and Annemarie's father inclined his head, simultaneously managing to suggest that he wished that she could stay longer, but that to demur would be impolite. Then Mother bent to kiss me, reminded me redundantly to behave myself, replaced the sunglasses on her nose, and was gone almost before the scent of her perfume had faded.

As soon as the car swept out of the driveway, Annemarie said, 'You're just in time. The boys are waiting down there. Come, quickly!'

Tugging at my hand, she led me to a small paddock a short distance from the farmhouse, where at least forty black men and youths were gathered. Some were lounging about, and others stood laughing and talking animatedly. Several very small children were there too, and they chased one another with cries of delight, while some older boys stood on the outskirts of the crowd, each holding a large plastic bag or hessian sack. The paddock was bounded by a tall wooden fence, and we clambered onto it – Annemarie with agility, myself with slow doggedness – and sat on top of it, with our legs dangling over the side. I felt the splintery texture of the wood through my thin summer dress, and I smelt the pitch with which the wood had been treated. It was dirtying my dress, I felt certain, and Mother's disapproval sounded in my ears, but there seemed little that could be done without imperilling Annemarie's good opinion of me, and so I ignored it as best I could.

One or two of the men greeted Annemarie, '*Sawubona, Nonna.*'

She responded to each greeting with nonchalant familiarity, '*Yebo*, Petrus. *Yebo*, Timothy. *Kunjani?*'

One man greeted me too, but I averted my face and pretended not to hear, for I didn't know the correct responses, those assured phrases which Annemarie produced so effortlessly.

There was a young man with a huge grin, which divided his face into mouth and eyes as the peeling of an orange divides the fruit into orange rind and orange proper. Throwing his shapeless hat into the air, he shouted suddenly, 'Heppie Krismass! Heppie Krismass!'

Laughing good-humouredly, the others took up the cry: 'Heppie Krismass! Heppie Krismass!'

Annemarie's jaws worked as she chewed on several long blades of grass. Her legs were brown and wiry, and covered with scratches and little scabs. She drummed with her bare heels against the wooden fence. I asked, 'Is this where the Christmas cows are shot?'

She said, 'Oh, yes. Pa deals it out here too. I've seen it every year since I was five. It's very exciting. You'll see.'

At this point, two cows were driven into the paddock by a young boy. Unperturbed by the large crowd, they immediately began cropping the grass, wrapping their tongues around the desired clump, and then pulling at it with ripping sounds. They were angular as only aged cows in poor condition can be. Their bodies were a mass of ridges and hollows and balloonings, like a landscape distorted by floods and droughts. Annemarie explained that they were both — or rather had been — dairy cows. The large one was a Friesland cow, with distinctive black-and-white markings. Her udder was grossly misshapen, one half strangely distended and considerably longer than the other half. Lopsided and flaccid, it swung between her legs as she walked. The other cow was a Jersey. She was a great deal smaller than the Friesland, and golden-dappled in colour, with huge protruding eyes like luminously convex pools.

Not long after the two cows had made their appearance, Mr Jooste and his son Hendrik — Annemarie's elder brother — were seen approaching the paddock. A large rifle was strapped to Mr Jooste's shoulder. The crowd renewed their cry with gusto, 'Heppie Krismass! Heppie Krismass!'

Mr Jooste responded by letting off a shot into the air which produced hoots of laughter. Everything that occurred or was said seemed to enhance the general feeling of merriment and festivity. Annemarie laughed too, thumping energetically with her heels against the fence. Mr Jooste said something, and everyone laughed again. I asked Annemarie what he had said, and she replied, 'Oh, he says they've been drinking already, although it's not Christmas yet.'

I turned to look at Annemarie's brother. Hendrik Jooste was about sixteen years old, a lanky youth with short-cropped hair. He was twisting the lapels of his shirt. Whereas his sister was incorrigibly voluble, Hendrik always seemed to be reluctant to speak at all. When he did, it was as if he had first to rearrange pebbles in his cheeks, or as if his taciturnity was caused by his Adam's apple interfering, in some way, with the progress of sound.

Mr Jooste called Annemarie to him, and a long, vehement conversation ensued, which I was too far away to follow. Annemarie protested about something, gesticulated, pointed towards me, threw up her hands, and threatened with her expressive lower lip to set one of her tearful tantrums in motion. Finally, it seemed that her father relented, for she nodded vigorously, leaped into the air, and came skipping back to me. She greeted me with a broad grin somewhat lacking in teeth – Annemarie had been bankrupting the tooth fairy of late – and took me to a point a short distance away from the paddock, where, by standing on a mound of earth, we had a good view of the proceedings. She said, 'Pa says we can stay. We have to watch from here and not go any nearer. Pa says it's on condition that if you get scared and want to go to the house, you have to say so at once, and I have to take you without any argument and stay with you. He says I must remember that you're not used to all this. But you won't get scared, will you? There's nothing to be scared of. You don't want to go to the house, do you? We'll miss everything.'

I said, 'No.'

Annemarie thereupon ran about in circles, no doubt to express her approbation, as well as her general excitement. She hummed 'Silent Night, Holy Night' as she ran.

A young black man, standing a little apart from the others, was gazing at us. He did not avert his eyes when I looked at him, nor did he offer a greeting. His head was closely shaven, and he wore a dirty-looking green jacket and faded checked trousers. His gaze was neither curious nor hostile – merely direct and impassive. When Annemarie danced about, he smiled faintly, but not in a complicit or indulgent way. I asked Annemarie who he was. She said – loudly enough for him to hear that we were talking about him – 'Simon Mhlangu. He's only been here a few months. He works at the dairy. Pa says he works hard and doesn't shirk like most of the young men, or come to milk drunk on the weekends, but Pa says he's too sour and unfriendly, and not respectful enough.'

Mr Jooste could now be heard ordering everyone to stand well back, and yelling at some young boys who were wrestling on the grass, and who did not hear him at first. We could see everything that went on without having to crane our necks very much. We were almost in the middle of the crowd. A man standing next to me began to rummage in his pocket, and took out a large pocket-knife, the blade of which he wiped ceremoniously on a tuft of grass. I watched as Annemarie's father raised the rifle to his shoulder and aimed it at the large Friesland cow. A strange quiet descended: the uproarious children stood silently, the scuffling of the bags and sacks against the ground ceased, and even Mr Jooste's sheep-dog lay down and was motionless except for the flickering of its ears. The only sound was the distant stirring of the leaves of the bluegum trees, sighing– not *with* the wind, as is usual – but *at* the wind.

Then we heard a crack which sounded different from the shot which Mr Jooste had let off earlier in jest. It was like the sound a whip makes when a ringmaster cracks it.

The cow simply dropped. She fell suddenly and heavily, and emitted a loud grunt of apparent discomfort as she hit the ground. Her legs were folded under her in a splayed sort of way, and blades of grass still dangled from her mouth.

The instant after she fell, several of the men leapt forward, with knives brandished, and the company at large stirred, like a leg shaking and stretching to free itself of a 'pins and needles' sensation. The men who had come forward pushed the jerking body of the cow onto its side, and one seized the head by the horns and bent it backwards, while another began to saw at the throat with a pocket-knife. There was a gurgling sound – clearly audible from where we stood – and then I saw a thick red stream that gushed onto the kikuyu grass and sprayed the faces and clothes of those men who didn't jump away in time, and there was a sound as of the sudden emptying of subterranean drains. The legs continued to kick furiously all the while, with a regular rather than a spasmodic movement, as if desperately trying to rid the body of an ever-tightening net. Annemarie had stood transfixed with rapt attention, and now turned to me with a shining face, and said, 'Pa says it's dead before it hits the ground, because it's been shot through the brain. It's just the nerves that make it kick like that. They cut the throat so that the blood can run out, and then the meat tastes better. Did you see how well Pa shoots?'

I nodded, but did not speak. Fixing me with a baleful look, she asked. 'You don't want to go back to the house, do you?'

I replied that I didn't. She turned back to the spectacle below us with evident relief.

The contortions of the curiously animate dead cow – so much like the twitching of a lizard's discarded tail – finally ceased. The gushing of blood from the hole in the throat slowed down to a slow dripping. The men drew back, and waited for the other cow to be shot. Mr Jooste now did something which surprised everyone. With deliberate and rather grand ceremoniousness, he turned to Hendrik, who stood beside him, and handed the gun over to him. Then he stepped back himself. As his son took the gun from him – his face pale and drawn – cheers and cries of encouragement rose up from the crowd, 'Yebo, Kleinbaas. Nguwe, Kleinbaas. Yebo.'

Annemarie danced on the spot with renewed excitement. She said, 'Oh, look. Hendrik is going to shoot. It'll be the first time. Hendrik is going to shoot.'

The second cow had paid little attention to the death of the first. Hendrik studied her for some moments before he raised the gun to take aim. When he did so, the near-palpable silence returned. It contrasted profoundly with the raucous cries of a minute or two earlier: death imminent, it seemed, was anticipated with silence; death achieved was greeted with noisy jubilation.

This time, when the sharp crack of the rifle was heard, a hoarse, bellowing sound rose, which ceased momentarily, and then began again. No one moved. The sound grew steadily louder. The Jersey cow was running in crazed and flailing circles around the paddock. She shook her head from side to side, and her tongue hung from her mouth as she emitted that great cry. Hendrik reloaded frantically, and fired again. This time he missed completely. The cow was still reeling, and long streams of saliva were dripping from her mouth and tongue. The blind sound of her cry continued throughout. Still the crowd of men and youths remained motionless, as if attempting to ignore politely the unwitting nakedness of someone.

Hendrik now seemed to be pleading with his father to take the gun from him. Mr Jooste – if my reading of the dumbshow was correct – refused and pointed towards the cow. Hendrik's face was very white as he raised the gun to take aim once more. Even Annemarie's tawny little body had not moved an inch. Annemarie's brother fired again, and this time the cow dropped to the ground. This was greeted by a loud cheer, and even more men than previously ran forward to help with the throat-cutting. Mr Jooste and his son both turned away, and, without any further exchange of words, returned to the house. Annemarie pulled me towards the paddock, saying, 'Come, now we must watch the skinning and cutting up.'

The adult men had spontaneously divided themselves into two groups, and were gathered now about the two carcasses. The young man who had beamed and grinned at us so impressively when we arrived, was now performing an energetic dance, slapping his hands against his gumboots, and accepting good-naturedly the railing of the others. Simon Mhlangu, the dour young man, had betrayed no emotion whatsoever during the shooting of the cows. Now he was the first to begin skinning one of the carcasses, his head bowed with concentration, and transluscent droplets of sweat glistening on his forehead.

First, a long cut was made in the skin, all the way along the cow's underside. Then, with much laboured exertion, the men peeled off the skin by pressing with their fists at the place where the skin and the shiny grey-pink flesh were joined. Finally the cow's skin remained joined only to her backbone and her head, and she lay on her own skin, with her feet in the air. Even the huge udder of the Friesland cow was stripped of its skin, revealing a fatty, yellowish mass. The heads of the cows lay, blood-bespattered, and attached only tenuously to the rest of the carcass. The bulging eyes of the Jersey cow were dull now, like dusty black leather. Annemarie lifted the bottom lip away with her finger, and showed how the cow's teeth were worn to the gums and, in several places, missing entirely. That was how one knew, she explained, that the cow was very old. 'Her teeth are a mess. Did you ever see such a mess?' she asked and looked at me to see how well I was responding to all this. I merely shook my head. She evidently wanted to find some way of thanking me for not making her go back to the house, for she giggled in a conspiratorial way, and said, 'Maybe she didn't brush her teeth in the right way, like Miss Fourie said we must.' It was a circuitous way of reaffirming our friendship, which was, after all, a thing of the classroom, but I did not respond to that either.

740

They were using an axe to split the breastbone of the other cow, and splinters of bone flew about in the air for some moments. Numerous pairs of bloodied hands, unhurried but purposeful, busied themselves about the carcasses. From time to time, someone would get up to wipe off the worst of the blood against the long kikuyu grass. Some of the men began to sing, a repetitive song of choruses without verses, which moved amongst them with a slow, regular movement, like someone on a garden swing.

It was hot, and there were swarms of flies. They settled on the carcasses and, in particular, on the voluminous stomachs as they were lifted out onto the grass, leaving exposed a great cavern, dark red and ribbed with white bone. The huge stomachs were glossy-grey in colour, and the seemingly endless intestinal coils lay spread out on the grass with them. They split the stomachs open, and emptied them of their contents, which were mounds of wet green matter, overwhelmingly pungent. I took a few steps backwards at this point, but Annemarie remained unperturbed.

Pieces of meat were rapidly being detached from the carcasses and borne off to the far end of the paddock, where they were laid in a neat row. Haunches lay with the hoof still attached, and there were pieces of the rib-cage, where the long white bones showed through like a section of corrugated-iron roofing. The skins were folded up, the heads were put to one side, and someone was sent to the house to tell Mr Jooste that the meat was ready for distribution.

He soon arrived with Hendrik, as before, in tow. Hendrik looked less pale, but not very much more at ease. Together they inspected the rows of meat. Once or twice, Mr Jooste ordered a regrouping of the pieces, or the cutting into two of a piece that he considered too large. Then he opened a large black book which he carried under his arm, and began to call out the names of the men, putting a tick next to their names after they had come forward and made their selection. Each man, after choosing the chunk of meat he wanted, called forward one of the youths or little boys, who would put it into his plastic bag or hessian sack. Some chose silently, and returned wordlessly to the assembled crowd. Others said, 'Dankie, my baas. Baie dankie.'

The names of the older men were called first. When the younger men were called, several pieces of meat that were appreciably larger than the rest still remained. Mr Jooste now intervened when the men made their selections, directing them to take this piece or that. Simon Mhlangu's name was called, and he moved purposefully towards a large haunch, and lifted it up by the hoof. Mr Jooste said, 'No, no. Not that one. Here, take one of these.'

Simon Mhlangu did not answer. He remained clutching the meat by the hoof, and stared unblinkingly ahead of him. Annemarie's father said, 'What's the matter with you? I said take this one.'

Still the black man made no movement. Speaking slowly and thickly, he said, 'I want this one.'

In a voice of rising irritation, Mr Jooste said, 'Have you got a wife? *Unomfazi wena?*' Simon Mhlangu shook his head. The farmer replied, 'then you must take a small piece. The big pieces are for the men with families.'

Still clutching the meat, Simon Mhlangu said, 'I work hard. I take this one.'

'I'm not going to stand here all day and argue with you,' the farmer said. 'You take a small piece or you get nothing.'

Several of the other men uttered what seemed like warnings or remarks intended to dissuade the dour young man, but he lifted the haunch even higher, and said something in Zulu. It was almost unbearably hot now. The sun stood high, like a golden monocle on the limitless blue eye of the sky. Flies settled on the piece of meat, even as he held it up into the air. 'You take a small piece,' Mr Jooste repeated, 'or you get no meat for Christmas. That's the end of the story.'

Simon Mhlangu hurled the haunch of meat at Mr Jooste. It landed, with a slurpy sort of thud, on the grass in front of the farmer's feet.

In a low voice, Mr Jooste said, 'Get off this farm. You get off this farm. Tomorrow, if you're still on the farm, I call the police. Do you understand me? Now go.'

Turning to go, Simon Mhlangu spat on the ground in front of him. He said, 'I go. I go. I work hard for you all year, you must not tell me what to take. I must take the piece I want.' He strode away, fixing his gaze on Annemarie and me as he left. His eyes were baleful and red-flecked, and he made me want to look away, although I didn't.

Mr Jooste turned to Hendrik and, in a clearly audible voice, said, 'That's the trouble with them. You give them something and they behave as if it's their right.'

The handing-out of the meat continued without further incident. At the end, there were a few small pieces of meat left over, and Mr Jooste gave them to those whom he felt had perhaps not received a sufficiently large share, or who had distinguished themselves in some way during the course of the year. The young boys ran a race, which provoked much interest, and the winner and runner-up were each given one of the heads. Then Mr Jooste fired the rifle into the air, and said, 'Happy Christmas. All right, that's it. Happy Christmas. You must all be back at work on Thursday.'

We turned to go back to the house, and at that point I saw Mother's car pulling up in the driveway in a skein of whitish dust. As soon as we were close enough to catch a glimpse of her, I broke away from Annemarie and her father and brother, and ran towards Mother. I flung myself against her with some force, and cried harsh sobs into the folds of her skirt. When Mother asked me what the matter was, I didn't answer. 'Tell me what it is,' she said, but I merely continued to cry. Mother said, 'Mr Jooste, may I know what is going on?'

Mr Jooste addressed a few low words to Annemarie. A part of her indignant response was audible: 'But she didn't! She never said she wanted to go back to the house. I asked her. She never said a word.' Her father then turned to us and said, 'I am afraid we have succeeded in upsetting your daughter, but without intending to in any way. We allowed her to watch the shooting of the cows, and perhaps we should not have done so. But she showed no sign of being upset until she saw you. I am truly sorry about it.'

There was silence for a few moments, and then Mother said, 'The *what?*' The *shooting of cows?* You made her watch the shooting of cows. How *dare* you subject her to that? I've never heard of such a thing in my life. Is that how you look after children that have been placed in your care?'

Mr Jooste answered, 'I do look after children who have been placed in my care, as you put it. I cannot guess what they are thinking or feeling if they don't say anything. I have apologised for allowing her to become upset. That is all I can say about it.'

My sobs had diluted themselves to a steady sniffle by now. I still held Mother's dress, but no longer buried my face in it. She looked down at me and said, 'Get in the car.'

She too got in, with a great slamming of the door. She started the car up with a toss of her head, and again I heard the wheels crushing the gravel beneath them, as we hurtled away from the farmhouse. I continued to sniffle all the way back to town.

On the way home, I had a mental picture, secret and organic like a flower growing in a cave. It was of Mother's car, entirely dismantled and broken up into little pieces. The pieces were laid out in a row on the grass. First I thought, 'They can't put it together again.' And then I thought, 'But nobody can eat it. Nobody can eat any of it.'

PT MTUZE

The Way to Madam

Translated from isiXhosa by N Saule
From: *Ungakhe uxelele mntu* (1990)

The year was 1933. There was a severe drought throughout the country. Farmers had sleepless nights because their cattle and sheep were dying like flies. The state of the economy had caused prices to skyrocket and South Africa, once regarded as the land of milk and honey, was in the grip of a severe depression, with all its misery.

Most farmers had sold their farms and gone in search of jobs in town, at road construction companies or with the railways, leaving their farm labourers to fend for themselves. As a result the labourers were found wandering all over the country, although they avoided the towns as they feared the corruption of these places.

There was, however, one particular farmer who refused to leave his farm. He was Rooi Willem Poggenpoel, a man known for his strict discipline. He was notorious and even the police would not take chances with him. He was a man of few words but was quick to jump heavily on anyone who opposed him.

Poggenpoel was short and stout. His character was accurately described by the nickname Madangatye (one who spits fire) given to him by his workers, who did not stay long in his employment. At four o'clock each morning he would ring a bell to start the day's work. Any latecomer would be punished, then paid off, and would have to leave the farm by eleven o'clock that very morning. If any worker took the matter to court, Madangatye would lay counter-charges of lost property and the case would simply end.

Among the labourers who worked for him, there was only one who stayed with him for more than ten years. This was Jackson, who had started working for his master at a very young age, had grown up on the farm, and never married.

He was not liked by the other workers because they believed that he was an informer. They believed that was the reason he had stayed for so long. Jackson, on the other hand, knew that it was because he was a hard worker. He felt those who accused him were just jealous.

'Once your employer shows some favour towards you, the others will always accuse you of something. That is a well-known fact, especially amongst the Xhosas,' Jackson used to murmur angrily.

Only once did a black worker show no fear of Madangatye. That was Ngxamfinya, a very muscular Mpondo man who had strong arms and a broad chest. After an argument, he laid Madangatye on the ground with one hand and told him he did not want to hurt him, but was only teaching him a lesson. Madangatye did not argue but paid him his wages and told him to leave the farm lest the other workers should learn from him not to respect white people. The Mpondo man took his time in leaving, while Poggenpoel, obviously shaken, took no chances and kept his distance.

After that Madangatye tried to convince his workers that he was not really a cruel man, but soon he simply went back to his old cruel ways.

One day Madangatye called Jackson to him, the only servant who never gave him any problems. He was not afraid to say that if all the Xhosa people were like Jackson, this whole world would he a wonderful place to live in. Jackson used to appreciate being called 'good kaffir'. To him there was absolutely nothing wrong with that, because it showed that he was unlike the other 'kaffirs'.

'Jackson, I am very grateful for all you have done for this place all these years. I say again that you are the best of all the people I have ever employed, including the ones I now have on this farm. Maybe it is because your grand-mother was a coloured person.' This beginning to the conversation obviously pleased Jackson.

'Therefore I have decided to make you an offer,' Madangatye continued. 'Ask for anything your heart desires and I will give it to you. Don't be wor-ried, just say what you want. I am doing this in appreciation of your support, especially during this time of drought. You have always been on my side. If you had left me, like those fools Ngxamfinya and the others who left, I would have been made a laughing stock. They wanted to see my farm perish just like that of Baas Koos Lategan. Baas Koos Lategan is not a cruel person, isn't that so, Jackson?' he asked with a grin on his face. Jackson made little noises of compliance, and rubbing his hands he said, 'I agree with you, Baas Rooi.'

'What I do not want is a loafer on my farm,' said Madangatye, and again insisted that Jackson should ask for anything he wanted.

Jackson did not know what to say. There were many things on his mind. He would love a car, but he could not drive, and he once saw a man killed because he could not drive. Then something else he badly wanted came to mind: a wife – a white girl who would help him get his own farm. He bright-ened, and again asked if he could really request anything. Madangatye once again assured him that he could have anything he wanted. Madangatye had a grown daughter who was attending school, and during her holidays she had taught Jackson how to write.

'Say something, Jackson. What would you like me to do for you?' insisted the white man, becoming impatient at Jackson's delay.

'Baas, I am not sure whether my request will be acceptable. I want to ask you to give me your little daughter Emmarentia to be my wife,' said Jackson, surprised at how the white man's face instantly reddened. He had hardly finished speaking before he found himself lying flat on the ground with his master on top of him.

'You ungrateful servant! What a disgraceful thing to say! You have shown your true self today. I have always suspected that you wanted to be the master on this farm,' said Madangatye, shaking him like a cat playing with a mouse. He was so tightly gripped that he could only move his legs.

The other workers, now aware that the friendly conversation had turned violent, looked on, amused at the spectacle. Some incited the boss by saying, 'He's got what he deserves!' There were a few who sympathised with Jackson but could do nothing to save the situation.

Rooi's next move shocked all of them. He shouted: 'Throw him into the oven! I am going to watch from the top of that hill. If he escapes, I'll fix him!' The servants went for Jackson without giving him a chance. In the meantime, the white man went to fetch his rifle. It was the rifle with which he hunted game. Then he walked slowly to the hilltop.

Jackson pleaded in vain. He was tied very securely. The white woman, Madangatye's wife, could not bear to see such punishment. She cried hysterically and fainted.

This gave the servants an opportunity to save Jackson. They grabbed a dog and threw it into the oven instead of the man. They told Jackson to run away as fast as he could. The smoke from the oven rose slowly into the sky and convinced the servants that they had got the better of Madangatye who was lying watching from the hill.

After many years the event became a legend. In time, Madangatye's daughter died and so did her mother, while Madangatye remained a lonely old man on the farm.

One day Madangatye heard a knock on the door. To his surprise it was Jackson. He had a broad smile on his face as he entered.

'Jackson, didn't you die a long time ago? Where have you been?' asked the astonished old man.

'I am from heaven, Baas. I am very happy there, together with Madam. Little daughter Emmarentia is also very happy. Madam has sent me to ask if you could make her a special dinner. You must prepare the dinner yourself ...' said Jackson, very politely as usual.

'Jackson, how did you come back?' asked the master again. 'I thought you were dead.'

'Baas, that does not matter, forget it. It's a very long story. All you have to do is to carry out Madam's wish so that I can go back,' Jackson answered.

'Jackson, how can you take food to my wife when you are so untrustworthy? You are just not the right person. Just tell me how I can get there. Which is the right way to Madam? I'll go there myself. I won't mind not coming back. After all, I haven't long to live anyway,' said the master, looking very sad.

Madangatye continued begging to be told how he could be reunited with his wife, and eventually Jackson decided to show him.

He looked at him with great sympathy and said, 'Well, Baas, come with me. The way to heaven is very easy, if you are honest and sincere. The way to heaven is through the oven.'

STEPHEN GRAY

The Building-site

First published, 1991

A lot has changed in my life since the builders arrived, especially as regards Dan. At the beginning of the year I paid no attention, but by Easter their activities on the building-site next door had so intruded into my routine that I'm not surprised we became acquainted.

Omar, my new neighbour, had acquired the modest mining cottage with such difficulty against the Group Areas Act and was converting it into – let's call it – a Muslim pleasure-palace. He was using the unregistered labour of Husein, the foreman who packed all eight of them in on his pick-up from the East Rand. This all takes place in my inner city suburb of Johannesburg, which is integrating faster than the government can do anything about it. During the time I have known Dan I've also become the last white householder within these four blocks.

Husein was to build at Omar's instructions a common wall between our properties to be in line with his general fortifications. To this I had to con-tribute on a fifty-fifty basis – about eighty per cent of the cost, as it turns out. I wasn't used to their methods of dealing. Husein had me lined up for a sucker, and conned me as well into having a security gate built alongside the wall in his own time, on Sundays which were not a holiday for him. He laid the bricks himself to make a bit extra. Dan brought them round on a wheelbarrow. Dan was the show-off type who enjoyed negotiating planks and trenches and muck-heaps of torn-down creeper. He'd jerk up his wrists and pile out the stolen goods.

Husein gave me no choice, really, about tightening up on security. I felt threatened because his ragged labourers were so poorly paid on the Friday, when the building-site whore and her pimp had been around and cleaned them out by the Saturday they were broke again. The petty robberies began on Sundays: washing from the line, the iron in the laundry at the back, spades and secateurs and, once when I was having a bath with the back door open, they tiptoed into the kitchen and filched the clock. I stood on the veranda, dripping, watching my kitchen clock go down the road to be pawned at the dagga-dealers. With the corrugated-iron fence down and no wall up yet, the security gate seemed pointless, but Husein persuaded me I must think of the

748

future; crime was always on the increase. I knew that once his gang moved on the thefts would abate. They slept eight in the one room at the back of Omar's, four yards from my office – each with their patch marked out on the concrete floor and a skimpy blanket … and me all alone in my seven-room mansion, guarding my privacy and possessions.

Husein was outrageous in his small talk. While his capacious wife sat in her smock in the truck hooting for him, he'd tell me of the luscious mistress he'd found in neighbouring Fordsburg: 'A man's got to have some sex life, you know; hell, I'm not over the top yet.' He looked forward to talking dirty with me, patting a few more bricks into cement.

He had me sorted out for what I was, so worked around to his early experiences. These took place in prison in the Cape, before his conversion and reform. During a long term he rose from ripped-apart catamite to gang-boss himself – see his tattoos – protecting his favourite slaves. For ever in his mind homosexuality meant the degradation of prison. Some grew so used to it and unable to adapt to the outside world they'd do anything stupid to be sentenced again – insult a policeman, shit on the mayor's doorstep – just to be back inside with their buddies. 'And some of them got big cocks, hey – *so* big. They not moffies, hey, they really men. But that's all they know, you understand.'

What was he behind bars for? Husein, who was now making my house impregnable, was in for armed robbery with assault.

'Dan, maak gou,' he'd complain, and Dan would trundle off for another load of larceny.

I more or less said that if ever Husein wished to come around for a service (his expression) – no charge – he was welcome, but he really preferred dressing up in his embroidered robes, skullcap on his curly locks, and squandering a fortune in the Fordsburg harem.

One day taking advantage of the quiet (Husein was also building a mosque out his way, so there were weeks without action – but that only protracted the ordeal), I was contemplating what to get on with in my office at the back. I suppose I was aware of a dull chopping sound and that they'd left Dan behind to guard their side of the property. In fact, when I opened my lounge curtains I'd seen the big-shouldered form of Dan and ignored looking at him, as we all agreed to ignore one another despite the enforced proximity. I knew perfectly well they knew every detail of my daily existence, as I knew theirs. With a whipping and twisting and thundering smash, the apricot tree in Omar's yard came down in my direction, the uppermost branches scraping onto my roof. This I could not ignore – it was yet another day wiped off my schedule, without any prior consultation or my consent. I was furious actually, as it was one of the oldest trees in the suburb; it produced enough fruit to fill thousands of jars of that poor African staple – apricot jam – that had always gone to waste and now was weighing down my retreat in its fruity death-throes.

I could not be angry with Dan; Omar was to blame. Nevertheless, I had to go out and help clear the branches off my property, if only to hurry the sad process. Dan had few verbal skills, but he did have the buzz saw, so without any preplanning he sawed off the branches with an excruciating noise and smell of petrol while I dragged them over to Omar's dump. He had dismembered the venerable trunk before I was finished, so we jointly hauled for a while in the blazing sun. Then I gave him a rake to tidy up my garden and went inside.

When I heard he was done, I went out with two glasses of Coke, and we sat on the rockery, sweating and exhausted, and drank them. He didn't look me in the eye and I studied him obliquely. About all we said was, 'Cooldrink,' 'Koeldrank, ja …' 'Ja.' Country-boy, spoke only Afrikaans. Then in the evening he guarded Omar's, playing the local black music station on the radio.

Omar and Husein fell out, which inevitably had implications for my half of the wall – still with only the foundations laid, although all the rendering and extensions Omar wanted on the walls of his house had been done. They went at each other fanatically; money grievances, I suppose, not religious ones, for they were brothers in faith. Husein shouted for his men to lay down tools; Omar that they must continue or no pay (instant hammering). The two of them whaled into one another, grabbing up demolition hammers and taking positions in the street. Logically I was the one positioned to intervene. I wanted the whole business not to stretch over another six months. I stepped reluctantly forth to where all my new neighbours were keyed up, egging them on. They had both lost their tempers – were dangerous, hammers smashing at the glazed tiles and panes of glass. I moved forward, arms held out to separate them. As I jumped towards the breach, I felt hands clutching my belt behind. Dan advised against this intervention and had stopped me. I glanced at his really worried face, and got out of there in disgust. Saved from a broken skull by Dan! He knew I had miscalculated, would only have lost out yet again. It took a lot of guts to get a white man to change his course.

They settled their disagreement only with Husein expelled from Omar's domain and Omar taking over the men personally (since it was all illegal anyway), and good progress was made. Husein crept in at night to work on his subcontract with me for the gate, but only because I had not yet paid him for that part. When I did, he absconded, leaving the gate insecure and incompletely attached. He took the cash and tore off in his truck, which he'd had to hide blocks away. Later I learned from Dan he had gone without giving them their pay for over a month.

Now Friday was the only day I could count on for some peace because Omar was more rigorous and decreed prayer day. So off he went to pray and the rest smoked grass, and I could actually do some work. From my clean-living, occasional domestic servant I found out how bad things were if I went out on a Friday. She did her job with all the windows tightly closed against the fumes and the doors locked for fear that she would be gang-raped by the men on their highs next door. So I stayed home whenever I possibly could, now to protect my maid. The wall, when they finally got it up to ten feet, was no reassurance; they may have built it well, but not well enough to stop themselves climbing over.

On a Friday when I came back from an unavoidable meeting with an editor, I found Dan in my yard, doing his washing and in long conversation with my maid, who explained Omar had cut the water off for them. I said 'Good afternoon,' leaving them to it, knowing she knew best. She had sons of her own whom she kept strictly in Christian marching order. But there in my yard was the incredibly well-built young labourer with admirable shoulders and biceps and the skinny legs of undernourishment wearing an old towel of mine, while his rags dried on the line. Evidently he did not smoke grass, but he had a cigarette and flicked ash into the pots. I knew enough of my maid's interests to understand that in emphatic and school-sounding Xhosa they were discussing their favourite passages of the Bible. They belonged to similar sects. All this was a great relief.

One freezing winter night with a wind howling straight over the veld from the Antarctic and, if you weren't used to it, the tin roof clanking would drive your hair on end, I was trying to finish up when the front doorbell went. I thought to ignore it, but this was obviously an emergency. I was afraid to respond, frankly. But I opened the door and turned on the dim light, and nearly puked at what I saw. A black shape had been stabbed all over, blood pouring like oil down his face and it was squelching out of his boots, leaving ghastly footprints. I'm afraid I said he should go next door to the building-site where they would know how to help him. My fear accounts for my lack of charity.

In due course the bell went again and obviously next door they had elected Dan to soften me up, because they knew I was sweet on Dan. I had misjudged everything: the walking wounded *was* from there in the first place; he had gone to the last café open where they wouldn't let him use the phone – the ambulance would not come for any inarticulate black request, anyway. He had been stabbed ten blocks away by their old dagga-dealers for deserting them for closer and cheaper ones, and now Dan had come to me as a last resort. The victim was one of *them*; in fact, he was the very monster who had whipped my clock!

In the rush of desperation Dan and I were communicating perfectly. I told him to wash the man down and keep him warm; I would phone.

I phoned and the ambulance said they would come and – I'll give them that – they didn't ask if I was white or black, as in the old days. They were next door with sirens going within twenty minutes. Feeling bad about my initial hesitation, I swathed myself in gowns and scarves, and waited in the howling gale with Dan and the towering bloody wreck. He was in pain past communication. I coaxed him to sit out of the wind, as Dan did on one side of the rubble and I did on the other. Such an automaton was he that he built himself a stool out of bricks first, then squatted on it.

When the ambulance made its spectacular arrival, he could let go, and passed out in the drive. All stretcher-bearers are ready for that kind of thing. The commotion brought out the other neighbours. From the few houses of my once tranquil all-white suburb came no less than eighty-nine illegals, wrenched out of sleep in their bedspreads. When the ambulance went round the block they all streamed up to the traffic light to get one last glimpse of the vehicle flying through. He was back at work on the Monday with many stitches.

With the Berlin wall up between us I had little further sight of Dan. Occasionally if I got my car out of an evening, he'd be sitting on the pile on the sidewalk, smoking. And the regular prostitute would be on Omar's veranda, suckling her baby as if she owned the place, waiting for her man to fetch her. God knows what really went on in the back of Omar's place; I no longer wished to know. Eight months had gone by and *still* they were not finished. I'd nod or wink at Dan, and he'd give me a smile, and I'd carry on with my life. Somehow in the back of my mind was the thought that if I left my house empty while he was there, things would be all right.

Then I'd regale my white friends with the Frankenstein episode and how the snitching had become so commonplace I even put out old clothes so that they'd take them in preference to anything else. The finer points of the social mix I was experiencing were not really discussable in bourgeois South Africa, so we settled for decrying the inconveniences of neighbouring building-sites.

Omar came to having his corrugated-iron roof pulled out by the roots. The crashing of tin sheets and rotten roof timbers now really became unbearable. What use was it to explain yet again that as a writer I work at home and need my sanctuary? I had arranged the previous week with Omar that I would be away for their re-roofing, but no, they could never make any convenient accommodation. Try corrugated-iron for a din with African enthusiasm for demolition, all a few feet from your writerly calm. With wax in my ears and a towel round my head, I tried to get my so many words a day done, the chair quivering each time a piece of architectonic plate was smashed free. I was turning into a shuddering wreck.

All of a sudden, the destruction halfway, the shift ended. To soothe myself I went out into my walled garden, to tidy up the new debris and maybe encourage a plant or two with the hose. The soil was warming with spring. I pulled out some runners of grass and clipped at the hydrangea, which was going to bud beautifully. I knew I was being studied at my old-womanish tasks, inexplicably finicky. Dan on the rooftree, up in the clouds in his rags, surveying the neighbourhood.

I gazed at him, shaking with relief from the quiet. I said: 'Do you want a beer?'

He said edgily, no … no way, he didn't drink beer.

Wine, a glass of?

He didn't drink.

Coffee?

He drank coffee.

I said later on he could come round if he wanted for coffee, but he must have misunderstood for within seconds the doorbell was going. I made him coffee with lots of milk and lots of sugar.

We settled at opposite ends of the kitchen table. He was hunched in terror, never having shared a social occasion with a white before. Where he came from if he ordered and paid for coffee at a white establishment, a plastic throwaway cup came out and the hatch slammed down. I emptied six biscuits on a plate and shoved it across to him. When I eventually thought to have one myself, the whole lot had gone. No pay again; he was actually starving.

I offered him a cigarette, but he declined, although I knew he smoked and the sight of me exhaling must have made him desperate. So on an impulse I grabbed a plastic bag and opened the fridge. I emptied into the bag the half-eaten steak and other delectables I was saving for myself, and handed it to him. He took it respectfully. As I wished to continue gardening while the quiet endured, I showed him out. At the front door the TV very obviously came into view and, before I closed the door on him, I said he was welcome to watch it in the evenings if he had nothing better to do. I went back to my budding plants and he to eat his spoils across the wall.

That evening when I had the news on he came to watch with me. He perched on a corner of the bed as if he didn't mean to dirty anything. I tried to gauge how much he took in, because language was a great problem between us. Gorbachev swooping into Malta and Bush braving the swell for a summit important to us all, even to backwater South Africa, I thought might be proving inexplicable to Dan. Anyway, I showed him how to use the remote control and once it had got to the soccer which he loved, went off to have a bath. I was no longer interested, so he could choose what he liked.

Once I'd bathed and, instead of getting into night garb, re-dressed in honour of my guest, I saw he had lost interest in the box and smoked out the end of his pack. I offered him a cigarette and this time he took it. His monosyllables of deference were giving way to more confident sentences of ordinary chat. My pink, waterlogged hands closed over his damaged workman's ones to shield the flame.

After a thoughtful smoke he clearly wasn't ready to go, and had fixed up a way of explaining his absence next door. So I dared to ask the usual give-away question – wouldn't *he* now like to have a bath? He would, so I stacked up all the bath oils and towels I could find and turned on the gushing hot and left him to it. All that prevented me from going any further (rubbing his back, insisting he try on new clothes for old, etc) was the thought of some unforeseeable reaction at the building-site. If he returned there in new garb, sweet-smelling, they would know. Their revenge would be against him, not me. Besides, I was not sure I was ready to admit an illiterate black worker into my life just then, no matter how great the temptation. The gap was too great, or so I thought.

But Dan thought differently. When he was not at work next door he never had anything better to do than take a bath and watch TV with me. These were his special privileges in the neighbourhood. Omar's gang were finishing up and the place was transformed: inlaid brick yard with not a piece of greenery to make a mess, sunken walk-in bath, venetian blinds, wrought-iron burglar bars, Italian tiles. But it was still not too late for Dan to get a screwdriver through him out of sheer jealousy for being someone's pet. I could hear complaints over their pot of stewing chicken gizzards that someone among them was getting the whole mixed grill with the moffie white boss next door.

It also occurred to me that they might have set me up with Dan. I'd come back one night to find everything of value in the house, that he had marked, gone. This was a mean thought on my part, but since Omar was never likely to pay them any more than Husein had, and they had all run up debts at hire-purchase stores on what anywhere else in the world would be considered workmen's basic essentials, provided by the employer (overalls, tools, footwear), and they had now stripped my outside of everything movable, what else could I think?

I was going out one evening to post off an article at the quickest box in the city and I had forgotten Dan was in the bathroom, performing his toilette. The thought did occur: can I leave him alone inside? I mumbled that I would be back soon and left him to it. I posted the article and did a few things I had to do at a late-night bookshop, and returned. The TV was going, but Dan was not before it. Instead, he was before the mirror in the bathroom – door now open – studying the spectacle of himself – stark naked – wiping his skin to a gloss with Vaseline. Obviously I could trust him with all my valuables, and probably with everything else, including my life.

There was a dull strip on his back his fingers had not rubbed over, so I obliged, working the jelly in until he looked polished, agleam. Let me inspect him; I pronounced him stunningly, dazzlingly skin-preserved from scalp to toe. That we both obviously had erections by then, which he could do little to hide, was probably the decisive factor.

I asked Dan what he was going to do once the house next door was finished and he said he didn't wish to continue with Omar-Husein, as they either didn't pay or not enough. I muttered something about I'd need someone to finish the security gate. Then I lavished his shining body in what clothes I had left for him to try on – we were much the same height. When the TV reached its end, the sort of fiddling, stroking, childish glee with which we had gone about this (his incredible narcissism and my only too eager puckering and adjusting) came to an end as well. We reluctantly agreed he'd better return to the site – for now – in his wretched rags with their built-in reek of grime, decay and sweat. For now, because we were both determined to sit this one through.

One evening Dan did not come and I was working to beat an old deadline, anyway. The crazy thought that I'd better pull in more cheques drove me on, now that the racket next door permitted, to afford Dan a new wardrobe, to prepare for a spending spree ... But an unbelievably violent uproar over there interrupted. Clearly it was reckoning-up time, as the next morning Husein would collect them at the corner, not daring to come any closer to Omar (or to me, for that matter). Their building-site whore was the cause of it, she who'd been hired out to all of them for far more than sexual favours – darning their shredded socks and treating their sores and nursing them through bouts of hangover and dagga-depression. To drive her out they threatened her baby – even that, the baby who had learned to walk holding their knees, now that it was reckoning time. She shoved the baby onto her pimp and ordered them both out while she screamingly handled this matter of eight dishonest, exploitative black brutes.

She had to disunify them, pick on a vulnerable target – Dan. She had to stir up their resentments.

'Who done *your* washing for you?' she launched into him.

'It was not you, sisi,' he pleaded, 'for the others, yes.'

'*Where* you have your finger fixed when it was sore?'

'It was not you, sisi, who fix it.' He could not say it was the white man next door who plastered it over.

'Where you get *clean* when you only got *shit*?'

'Please, sisi, I was cleaning my T-shirt all by myself.'

'And where you got your stomach full when you never get pay?'

'No, sisi, no ...

'Where you get money when no one else has? Hey? From the moffie over there!'

'Hai, sisi,' from Dan.

Judging by the rumpus, the tactic didn't work. She could only stride into their circle and shove the contents of their three-legged pot out on the ground. That was her last protest, apart from stomping out and slamming Omar's front door.

Now their final meal together was ruined and Dan was to blame. One of them cracked him a shot, I think the sewn-up oaf, and from over the wall I heard Dan yelp. I was all for getting the ladder and climbing over to extricate him. But Dan had already shown me what little power I had to regulate the affairs of the building-site. I could not stand the thought of his delicate body becoming as smashed and dented as theirs – the scars they bore, the terrible damage they had brought only on themselves; the way they had let themselves be brutalised.

I went into my office. I put my hands over my ears and clenched my eyes and was too deeply shocked even to think if it was that wrong to offer him a glimpse of an alternative way of life. They had no one else to take their frustrations out on other than moffies, those men.

Early the next morning they all stomped out with their toolbags and enamel mugs and scraggy blankets. Back to work on somebody else's mosque on the East Rand. I was not sorry, after close to eleven months, to see the very last of them. Omar came round with his wife, warmly inviting me over to dine – any night, every night, six o'clock – that's when they always eat, curry and special stuff I would like; always they catered for at least six people, in case anyone dropped around, they would always be honoured to have a neighbour; oh and sorry, said Omar, for all the noise.

Just for a while, I replied, I had a lot of work to catch up on and wanted to be left in peace. The very thought of their hospitality and its human cost physically repulsed me. What I really wanted was Dan – nothing else would compensate for what they'd caused: a year of my life lost. And of course Dan had been gone for over a week.

And then a fortnight. I had done nothing to stop him being beaten to a pulp.

'Why don't you come over for dinner?' said Omar, his hairy elbows over the wall, as I was mowing the lawn.

'It's just because I've got a lot of backlog to cope with,' I said.

'You don't like Indian neighbours, that's what it is,' he said.

'I don't like Husein – look how he left that gate. Next thing the wind'll blow it out into the street,' I said.

'That Husein,' he replied. 'He's a real bastard crook. Imagine how my house'd be if I let him carry on like that! Just get yourself a boy, man – he'll fix it up if you supervise him properly.'

I switched on the mower so that I didn't have to hear more neighbourly advice.

I was mowing the lawn down to the toppling gate a month later and there, on the other side of it, behind the bars, was Dan. He had his mug and blanket with him. I could see from the way his eyebrow drooped the physical wounds were not yet healed.

'Come in, come in,' I hauled the gate open. 'How are you, where have you been?'

He was very afraid I would turn him away. He stepped in and put his possessions on the cut grass.

'See, it needs bricks up to here, and a firm socket – and lots of broken glass on top and plaster.'

Dan nodded. He was able to do all that.

'Go inside and put the kettle on, please. I just want to finish off. Honestly, now with summer rains it grows so fast …'

When I had done and put the mower away, Dan had two mugs of coffee made in the kitchen. He had placed them so that we would sit opposite each other, not far apart.

I washed my hands and poured out the obligatory biscuits. He took one and I took one.

We sat facing each other. He looked so emaciated.

'Can I getta job?' he said.

'Yes,' I said.

BHEKI MASEKO

Mamlambo

From: *Mamlambo* (1991)

Mamlambo is a kind of snake that brings fortune to anyone who accommodates it. One's money or livestock multiplies incredibly.

This snake is available from traditional doctors who provide instructions regarding its exploitation. Certain necessities are to be sacrificed in order to maintain it. Sometimes you may have to sacrifice your own children, or go without a car or clothes. It all depends on the instructions of the doctor concerned.

The duties involved are so numerous that some people tend to forget some of them. A beast must be slaughtered from time to time, and failing to comply with the instructions results in disaster. It is said that this monster can kill an entire family, always starting with the children and leaving its owner for last.

Getting rid of this fortune snake is not an easy task when one has had enough of luck and sacrificing. Some say a beast must be slaughtered, then the entire carcass must be enfolded with the skin and thrown away. This is done in the presence of an indigenous doctor who performs the necessary ritual to the end.

Someone will come along, pick up a shiny object, and Mamlambo is his. There are many things about this monster.

Here is an account of how Sophie acquired Mamlambo and what happened to her:

Sophie Zikode was a young, pretty, ebony-faced woman with a plump and intact, moderate body. Ever since she came to stay in the Golden City to work as a domestic servant, she never had a steady boyfriend. The man who lasted longer than any other was Elias Malinga, who was from Ermelo. He was the first man she met when she came to Johannesburg and he was the only man she truly loved.

She was so obsessed with love that she readily abandoned any possessions or habits that Elias disliked. In spite of the priority his children and wife in Ermelo enjoyed, she was still prepared to marry Elias Malinga without the slightest intention of disrupting his marriage during their love affair.

One day, after a quarrel, Elias went away and never came back again. She phoned his place of employment to be told by a friend of Elias that he (Elias) had had enough of her. She never heard from him ever again.

After Elias, Sophie never again had a steady boyfriend. They all deserted her after two or three months. But it no longer hurt. The only name that haunted her day and night was Elias.

Ever since Elias left her she had never loved anybody else. All she wanted now was a husband she could be loyal to. But she just could not find one. Then along came Jonas, a tall, well-built Malawian who was much more considerate than any of the other men.

For the first time in her young life a thought came into her mind: She must consult a traditional doctor for help. She wanted to keep Jonas forever. She must see Baba Majola first thing in the morning.

The following morning Sophie visited Baba Majola, who was a street cleaner. The old man listened sympathetically to her problem while he swept rubbish out of a gutter. He told her to return at four in the afternoon. Sophie was there on time.

Baba Majola gave her some smelly, sticky stuff in a bottle. He told her to rub her whole body with it before the boyfriend came, and to put it under the pillow when they sleep. The poor girl agreed amicably.

She did exactly as she had been told to do. She felt guilty as the atmosphere became tense in the little room.

They ate in silence as the clock on the small table ticked away, disturbing the deep silence. Jonas was not his usual self today. He was quiet in a strange manner.

They were sleeping for some minutes when Jonas felt something peculiar under the pillow. It felt cold and smooth.

'Sophie, Sophie,' he called, shaking her gently. 'What is this under the pillow?'

Sophie had felt the strange object soon after they had climbed into bed. But she had been scared to ask Jonas what it was.

'I don't know,' she replied, pretending to be sleepy. 'Switch on the light, let's have a look.'

With a trembling hand Jonas fumbled for the switch. 'Gosh, what a big snake!'

Jonas was the first to jump out of bed. Sophie followed. They fiddled with the door until it was open and ran into the brightly-lit street.

Semi-naked, they knocked at the servant's door of a house in the neighbourhood to wake up a friend of Sophie's. Sophie's friend was very stunned to find them in that manner.

Quickly they explained the situation and together they went back to Sophie's room. Through the window they could see the snake, lying across the bed. Sophie was very scared, but Jonas – Christ! – Jonas, he could hardly speak.

Realising that things were bad, Sophie decided to tell the whole truth. She told Jonas she did it 'because I wanted to keep you forever'. They decided to go to a traditional doctor who stayed a few streets away.

They knocked and, after waiting awhile, the doctor answered. He opened the door but quickly closed it again. They heard him say: 'Wait outside there. I can sense something melancholy.'

They could hear the indigenous doctor saying something in a strange language, and the smell of burning muti came to them in full force.

He began to moan, as if speaking to gods in a faraway land. He then opened the door and enquired what their problem was. Sophie retold her story.

'Oh, my girl. What you have in your room is Mamlambo,' he shuddered.

'What? Mamlambo!' cried Sophie. 'Oh God, what have I done to deserve such punishment? What big sin have I committed to be punished in this manner?' Tears streamed continuously down her cheeks.

'Crying won't solve the problem, my dear girl,' intervened the doctor in broken Zulu. 'The only solution is to get rid of the snake, and I need your co-operation to do that. I'll give you a suitcase to take to your room, and the snake ...'

'What!' cried Sophie. 'Must I go back to that room again? Oh, no, not me, I'm sorry.'

'The choice is yours, my girl. You either keep it or get rid of it. The sooner the better, because if you don't it will be with you wherever you go. It is your snake. The witch-doctor was tired of it, so he transferred it to you. So you are duty bound to transfer it to someone else or keep it.'

'Transfer it to someone else! Oh no! Why don't we throw it into the river or somewhere?' Sophie grumbled.

'You can't. Either you transfer it, or you keep it. Do you want my help or what?' asked the doctor in a businesslike manner.

'Yes,' Sophie agreed, in a tired voice, eyeing her friend, Sheila, and the timid Jonas, with the 'I hate to do it' look.

The traditional doctor took a large suitcase from the top of the wardrobe, put some muti inside and burnt it. He moaned again, as if speaking to gods they could not see. He chanted on in this manner for what seemed like ages.

'You'll take this suitcase to your room and put it next to your bed. The snake will roll itself into the suitcase.' He saw that Sophie was doubtful so he added: 'It's your snake. It won't harm you.' He continued: 'You will then go to a busy place and give it to someone. That you will figure out for yourself.'

They all went back to Sophie's room. The big snake was still there. Having told herself to 'come what may', Sophie tiptoed into the room and put the suitcase next to the bed.

Slowly, as if it were smelling something, the snake lifted its head, slid into the suitcase and gathered itself into a neat coil.

Her mind was obsessed with Johannesburg Station, where she would give Mamlambo to someone for good. She walked quickly towards the taxi rank, impervious to the weight of the suitcase.

She did not want to do this to anyone, but she had no option.

Remembering that taxis were scarce after eight, she quickened her pace. She saw a few police cars patrolling the area, probably because of the high rate of housebreaking, she thought.

It was while she was day-dreaming at the bus-stop that she realised the car at the traffic lights was a patrol car headed in her direction. Should she drop the suitcase and run? But they had already seen her and she would not get far. How will she explain the whole thing to the police? Will they believe her story? The news will spread like wildfire that she's a witch! What would Elias think of her?

'What are you doing here at this time?' asked the passenger policeman.

'I'm waiting for a taxi, I'm going to the station,' answered Sophie, surprised that her voice was steady.

'We don't want to find you here when we come back,' commanded the policeman, eyeing the suitcase. The car screeched away.

She was relieved when the taxi appeared. The driver loaded the suitcase in the boot asking what was so heavy. She simply told him it was groceries.

There were two other passengers in the taxi who both got off before the taxi reached the city.

'Are you going to the station?' enquired the driver inquisitively. 'No, I'm going to the bus terminus,' Sophie replied indifferently.

'I know you are going to the station and I'm taking you there,' insisted the man.

'You can't take me to the station,' said Sophie, indignant. 'I'm going to Main Street, next to the bus terminus.'

Ignoring her, he drove straight to the station, smiling all the way. When they reached the station he got out of the car and took the suitcase from the boot.

Sophie paid him and gestured that she wanted her suitcase. But the man ignored her.

'To which platform are you going? I want to take you there.'

'I don't want your help at all. Give me my suitcase and leave me alone,' she urged, beginning to feel really hot under the collar.

'Or are you going to the luggage office?' mocked the man, going towards the brightly-lit office.

Sophie was undecided. Should she leave the suitcase with this man and vanish from the scene? Or should she just wait and see what happened? What was this man up to? Did he know what was in the suitcase, or was he simply inquisitive? Even if she bolted, he would find her easily. If only she had brought someone with her!

Suddenly she was overwhelmed by anger. Something told her to take her suitcase from the man by force. He had no business to interfere in her affairs. She went straight into the office, pulled the suitcase from between the man's legs and stormed out.

Stiff-legged, she walked towards the station platform, feeling eyes following her. She zigzagged through the crowds, deaf to the pandemonium of voices and music blaring from various radios. She hoped the taxi driver wasn't following her but wouldn't dare look back to see.

'Hey you, girl! Where do you think you're going?' It was the voice of the taxi driver.

She stopped dead in her tracks, without turning. She felt a lump in her throat and tears began to fall down her cheeks. She was really annoyed. Without thinking, she turned and screamed at the man.

'What do you want from me? What on earth do you want?'

With his worn-out cap tipped to the right and his hands deep in his khaki dustcoat pockets, the smiling man was as cool as ever. This angered Sophie even more.

'You are running away and you are trying to erase traces,' challenged the taxi driver indifferently, fingering his cap time and again.

'What's the matter?' asked a policeman, who had been watching from a distance.

'This man has been following me from the bus rank and is still following me. I don't know what he wants from me,' cried Sophie.

'This woman is a liar. She boarded my taxi and she's been nervous all the way from Kensington. I suspect she's running away from something. She's a crook,' emphasised the taxi driver looking for approval at the crowd that had gathered around them.

'You are a liar! I never boarded your taxi and I don't know you. You followed me when I left the bus rank.' Sophie wept, tears running freely down her cheeks.

'Let her open the suitcase – let's see what's inside.' Sheepish Smile went for the suitcase.

'All right. All right.' The policeman intervened. 'Quiet, everybody. I do the talking now. Young man,' he said, 'do you know this woman?'

'I picked her up at Kens ...'

'I say, do you know her?'

'Yes, she was in my taxi ...'

'Listen, young man,' said the policeman, beginning to get angry. 'I'm asking you a straightforward question and I want a straightforward answer. I'm asking you for the last time now. I-say-do-you-know-this-woman?' He pointed emphatically at Sophie.

'No, I don't know her,' replied Sheepish Smile reluctantly, adjusting his cap once again.

'Did she offend you in any manner?'

'No,' he replied, shamefaced.

'Off you go, then. Before I arrest you for public disturbance,' barked the policeman, pointing in the direction from which the man had come. Then he turned to Sophie.

'My child, go where you are going. This rascal has no business to interfere in your affairs.'

Relieved, she picked up her suitcase, thanked the policeman and walked towards platform fourteen, as the policeman dispersed the people and told them to mind their own business.

★ ★ ★

Platform fourteen. The old lady grew impatient. What's holding him? she thought. She came bi-monthly for her pension pay and each time the taxi dropped them on the platform, her son would go to the shop to buy food for the train journey home. But today he was unusually long in coming back.

These were the thoughts going through her mind when a young, dark, pretty woman approached her.

'Greetings, Gogo,' said the young woman, her cheeks producing dimples.

'Greetings, my child,' answered the old lady, looking carefully at this young pretty woman who was a symbol of a respectable makoti.

'When is the train to Durban departing?' asked Sophie, consulting her watch.

'At ten o'clock.'

The conversation was very easy with the loquacious old lady. The cars and people on the platform increased.

'Excuse me, Gogo, can you look after my luggage while I go to the shop? I won't be long.'

'OK, OK, my child,' agreed the old lady, pulling the suitcase nearer.

She quickly ascended the steps. By the time she reached the top she was panting. To her surprise and dismay, here was Elias shaking hands with another man. They chatted like old friends who hadn't seen each other for a long time.

Sophie stood there confused. Fortunately Elias's back was turned on her and the place was teeming with people. She quickly recovered and mingled with the crowd. Without looking back she zigzagged through the crowded arcade.

She was relieved when she alighted from the bus in Kensington. She had nearly come face-to-face with Elias Malinga. Fortunately he was cheerfully obsessed with meeting his friend. She was scared all the way to the bus terminus, but more so for the taxi driver. Now something else bothered her. The old lady? Who was she? Sophie felt as if she knew, or had at least seen the woman somewhere. She searched into the past, but couldn't locate it.

What will happen to the suitcase? Will the old lady take it?

And Elias? What was he doing there? She suddenly felt hatred for Elias. He had never pitied her, and it was worse when she phoned his place of employment, to be a laughing-stock to his friends. She became angry with herself to have allowed her life to be dominated by love that brought no peace or happiness, while Jonas was there giving all the love and kindness he possessed. For the first time she fell in love with Jonas. But will he still accept her? If only he could ask her to marry him. She would not do it for the sake of getting married. She would be marrying a man she truly loved.

Jonas and the Nyasa doctor were seated on the bed when Sophie came in. Sophie was surprised to see all Jonas's belongings packed up.

'Are you leaving me, Jonas?' Sophie whispered in a shaky voice.

'No, darling. My father wants me back in Malawi because he can no longer handle the farm by himself. And I would be very happy to take you along with me.'

'But I don't have a passport. How can I go to Malawi without one? And besides, my parents won't know where I am.'

'We are in fact not going today. We will negotiate with your parents next Saturday,' said Jonas, pointing at the doctor who sat quietly on the bed, nodding time and again.

* * *

It was a cool, sunny Saturday when the doctor took Sophie and Jonas to Jan Smuts Airport in his small car. Sophie was going to board a plane for the first time in her life. Jonas had made many trips to see his ailing father, who wanted him to take over the farm. For a long time Jonas had ignored his father's pleas for him to take over the running of the farm. But now he had finally relented.

Through the car window Sophie watched the people moving leisurely in and out of shops. The trees lining Bezuidenhout Valley Avenue and the flowers in the Europeans' gardens looked beautiful and peaceful as they fluttered in the cool morning air. It was as if she were seeing this part of Johannesburg for the first time.

They couldn't identify Baba Banda (the doctor) among the crowd that stood attentively on the balcony, as they stared through the plane window.

The flying machine took off and the crowd waved cheerfully. Sophie felt that it was taking her away from the monster that had terrified her a few days ago.

The buildings below became smaller as the airplane went higher, until the undersurface turned into a vast blue sky.

She wondered where, in one of those houses, was Mamlambo. But could never guess that it had become the property of Elias. Yes, after Elias had chatted to his friend, he went back to his mother.

'Whose case is this, Mama?'

'A young girl's. She asked me to look after it for her until she returned. But I don't know what's happened to her.'

'Well, if she doesn't come back, I'll take it.'

JOEL MATLOU

Man Against Himself

From: *Life at Home and other Stories* (1991)

We must work before the sun goes down. The life of a man is very heavy in his bones and his future is a deep unknown grave.

One day when I was alone, struggling to get money, and far away from my home where no one lives or grows, I met a man from Zululand called Dlongolo. He told me to try for work at the offices of Rustenburg Platinum Mine (RPM) in Bleskop, eight kilometres from where I was living.

The following day I went to the offices of RPM. I found work. The man who hires labourers was a black man with three missing upper teeth. I was told to come on Monday. Before I left the premises I saw the sportsground, the mine hospital, a bar, a café, trucks, vans, buses and a compound with many rooms and toilets. But I left because I was sleeping at the hostel in Rustenburg and my home was in Mabopane, Odi.

On Monday morning I returned to the offices with others. At about 9.30 a.m. our passes were taken and looked into. They told me to fill in the forms they gave me in Ga-Rankuwa. So, with the little money that I had, I arrived in Ga-Rankuwa and my forms were filled in, but I was surprised when they told me to pay R1 for the forms. I paid it and left. So I was short of money for the train back to Rustenburg. I had only 85 cents in my pocket, and the journey would cost R1.10. It was 9.30 a.m. and the train left Ga-Rankuwa at 10.00 a.m. I was far from the station and I lost hope of catching the train. I thought of begging for money, but decided I was too young to beg.

My second plan was that I should sleep somewhere in Ga-Rankuwa and at about 4 a.m. I would walk to the station of Wolhuterskop where my 85 cents would be enough for the train. At about 8 p.m. I chose myself a toilet to sleep in at a certain school in Ga-Rankuwa, Zone 4. I went into the toilet at night but it was very dark inside. There were lights all over Ga-Rankuwa roads. I walked slowly to the back of the toilets where I found a big stone. I sat on it trying not to think of dangerous snakes under the stone. At midnight I heard barking dogs. All the people in Ga-Rankuwa were asleep. At about 3 a.m. I heard cars hooting all over Ga-Rankuwa. I thought I was in danger. But those cars belonged to newspapers and were calling for their employees. And there were two buses hooting. I thought they were staff buses for drivers. People started to walk on the roads then, to catch trains and buses to Pretoria and Rosslyn. At about 5.15 a.m. I felt cold. I was wearing a shirt, a jersey, trousers, and shoes without socks. The sun rose and I left Ga-Rankuwa early so that I could catch the 11.30 a.m. train at Wolhuterskop. I ran until De Wild where I started to walk and beg a lift to Brits or Rustenburg.

On the road to Brits I saw a black man sitting on the white government stone indicating bridges. I greeted him and he greeted me. As I passed he called, and stood up. He begged 20 cents from me. With shame I told him my story and showed him the forms I'd filled out in Ga-Rankuwa. He was wearing sandals, black trousers, a red 'hemp',[1] a black jersey and a scarf. He had a camera in his hand. I continued to tell him my story. I told him to beg a lift to Brits, where he was going. A truck carrying sand arrived and we stopped it for a lift. The driver took us to Brits. We got off at the bus rank. He asked me to accompany him to the pass office for a reference book. At the pass office we saw convicts cutting grass and sweeping the pass office floors. He was given a duplicate and we departed.

I started to run through the town until I was outside Brits. The station of Wolhuterskop was very far and there were no short cuts so I used the main roads, like a car. I was tired and felt like a convict on the run. I could not imagine what was going to happen. My stomach was empty. As I was walking on the tar road I met two beautiful girls aged about eighteen to twenty. I am twenty-three. They were carrying boxes with dirty dust coats inside. I greeted them and asked for the Wolhuterskop station. One of the girls, speaking Pedi, told me that it was not so far away. The second girl asked where I was from. I told her that our factory van broke down near Brits, and I was reporting back to work. She asked where I worked and I told her at the United Tobacco Company in Rustenburg, about which I knew nothing really. We parted. Not far from the station I met a traffic inspector resting under the plantation trees. He greeted me nicely and I also accepted his greetings. I thought to myself that my road was now open because I had got a greeting from a white traffic inspector.

That was nearly true and nearly false beause I could never have imagined what was going to happen after my struggles. At the station there was a queue for tickets. My ticket cost 75 cents to Bleskop where Rustenburg Platinum Mine offices are, so I had 10 cents left. I bought myself a half brown bread costing 7 cents at the nearest café, and sat under the trees on the grass where I ate the bread alone. I drank some water and my stomach was full like a strong man. The train arrived, so I boarded it but my mind and future were still missing without hopes. My heart was very heavy as I got on to the train so I thought of my motto: 'If the Lord gives you a burden, he will also provide help to carry it, and in the whole world there are so many people who pray for a new life.'

When I arrived at Bleskop I wondered where I would sleep that night. I just took a stroll until 7.30 p.m., back to Bleskop station. There were a few people going home from the mines. And I started to breathe softly without fearing. There was a big waiting-room in which many people were asleep and I too slept there. People from the mines were playing records with their gumba-gumba.[2] Bleskop was very quiet but gumba-gumba men were blasting records the whole night until 2.30 in the morning, when they boarded the Pretoria train. I was left with the others who were going to the mines the next day.

After the gumba-gumba men left, Bleskop station became quiet. When the sun rose over the mountains of Pretoria, we set off for the Rustenburg Platinum Mine, some wearing blankets. The mine was where we were going to buy our lives with blasted rocks.

We arrived at the offices which were still closed, and sat on the grass. Mine people were training on the sportsground. Some were jumping and singing in the mine hall in the mine language, 'sefanagalo'.[3] At 7.30 a.m. the ambulance arrived at high speed, its top lamp flashing. It stopped near the door of the mine hospital. Two people and the driver got out without speaking. Their faces were in sorrow. From the back came six people in mine clothes, with their head lamps still on. They off-loaded two coffins and carried them into the mine hospital. I shivered like the branches of a tree. My motto was still in my mind but I thought that I had seen Mabopane for the last time, and my parents, relatives and friends too.

At 8 a.m. the offices opened. We were called and our passes were taken from us. At 9 a.m. we collected our passes and the black officer told us that there was work at Swartklip. They gave us tickets to Swartklip which cost R1.35, single.

When we arrived at Swartklip we were shown to empty rooms and given plates for food. Then we saw a film which ended at 10 p.m. Back in our rooms we slept well, with police guarding us with kieries.

On Friday morning the man known as Induna woke us at 5 a.m. He told us to report at the labour office as soon as possible. We did so. At the labour office our passes were taken. At about 9.30 a.m. a black man in white clothes told us to follow him. We were led to a big house with many rooms and beds, which looked like a hospital. We were taken to a room where there was a chair, a desk and a scale ending in 200 kg. There we met another man, all in white, who had many files in his hands, where our names were already written. They told us to undress. We were checked from toes to head for wounds, then weighed. When the doctor produced a big needle and injected us near the heart to kill shocks when we went underground, I felt I was fighting for my dear beautiful life. Late on Friday we returned to the labour offices. We were given three days' tickets for food at the compound and shown a film.

On Sunday at about 7.30 p.m., after my meal, I tried to find an empty tin and get a little chaechae, which is what mageu[4] is called on the mines. Joel! Joel Matlou! someone called out to me. I looked at the people sleeping on the grass, and saw a man with a tape recorder. 'Come here, come here,' he said. I moved slowly towards him. He stood up and said, 'Joel, what do you want here?' When I recognised him I was so happy that I kissed him. It was Joseph Masilo of Mabopane who was now living in Moruleng, Rustenburg. We were at school together at Ratshetlho Higher Primary in Mabopane seven years ago. We started questioning one another about our reasons for being on the mine. I told him I had taken the job because I needed money fast, to pay off a big instalment.

'How do you come here?' I asked him.

'Suffering brought me,' he said. 'In two weeks' time I complete my ticket and get paid.'

'Couldn't your people or relatives and friends help you settle your accounts?' I asked.

'It is difficult to reach relatives and friends. Are you married?'

'No,' I replied. 'I will think first before I marry. Mines do not have girls. Where and how often do you get to have a girl near you here at mines?'

'This place is a jail,' said Joseph. 'No girls around here and you must have respect for yourself until your sentence is finished. Stop asking me silly questions. All the people here have troubles.'

We parted and arranged to meet the following day.

I was so very happy to meet my best friend after seven years. My heart was open and all things were going well.

On Monday morning we went to the labour offices. There were three compounds, A, B and C. A compound is called Union Section. B is called Entabeni and C is called Hlatini. They are far away from each other. The officer told us we would be transferred to C compound, Hlatini. We fetched all our belongings and the mine bus took us to Hlatini compound. There were many people in Hlatini. Some were drinking beers, playing ball, running and playing tape recorders. A big man with a bald head took us to a room called 'School Mine'. In that room we found chairs and a big white board. We were told to sit down quietly and listen. Then all the windows and doors of the room were closed. We were shown a television film of a man teaching new labourers how to build and pack wood and another film on First Aid.

Then a black man wearing a black dust coat, with a missing left eye, called us to the office. He gave us cards, then called us one by one to take boots, belts and iron (copper) hats. Then we were given numbers. A young man came running with a plastic bag containing small numbers. The numbers were on small pieces of iron 200 mm long and 100 mm wide. My number was 3281. That was on Tuesday.

There were twenty little windows, like those at which people buy tickets for buses or trains. There you got your lamp and battery for work when you produced your number. My number was 3281, and my window number was eight. We were told to report at the windows at 6 a.m. for work.

Back at the compound we enjoyed our mine meal, saw a film and went to sleep. At 5 a.m. we were woken by a loudspeaker. We got our lamp and battery and were taken to a big office where we were ordered to sit down on the floor. We were still to see and learn more.

A white man introduced himself as Mr Alfred Whitefield from Northam, Rustenburg. He spoke English, Tswana and Sefanagalo but not Afrikaans. He said: '*Umtheto wase* mine *uthi, aikhona wena sebenzisa umlilo lapha kalo* mine. *Aikhona wena hlala phanzi banye ba sebenza. Vuka umtheto wa* boss boy. *Sebenzisa a ma* toilets *a se* mine. *Aikona choncha. Sebenzisa u*mine Bank *ku beka imali yakho.*' [The law of the mine says: Do not make fire here in the mine. Do not sit down while others are working. 'Wake up!' is the law of the boss boy. Use the mine toilets. Do not steal. Use the mine bank to save your money.] Those were the words which I still remember from Mr A Whitefield.

Before we went to work under the soil of Africa, we were given a hand belt with a number on it. It was a blue belt. My number was 2256731.

At 7.15 a.m. the boss boy took us to the lift. As it went down my ears went dead and I saw dark and light as we passed other levels. The levels go from 6 to 31. The lift stopped at 28 level. There I saw lights, small trains (*makalanyane*), a tool room, a workshop, toilets, a power station, big pipes, drinking water, a telephone and so on.

The boss boy gave us a small book which had twenty-four pages. Every day he tore out one page from it. When it was empty you get your pay and a new book.

We gave our tickets to the boss boy then walked for one hour to the end of the shaft. The mine shaft was very hot. I was wearing a shirt and trousers. The sweat ran off me like water. There were three tunnels. The small trains, the *makalanyana*, had red lights on the back and front indicating danger. Before the blasting, small holes were drilled in the walls and a man referred to as a chessa-boy put explosives into them. After the blasting we found broken pipes, the ventilator on the ground, bent rails, a cracked wall and other damage. The blast gave us heavy work. The *makalanyane* and its trucks were called to collect all stones. You can find a stone weighing 200 kg far from the blast.

A Zulu from King Williamstown was digging *mosele* (water concrete) when part of the ventilator fell on him and his left leg was trapped under it. The boss called us and we lifted the ventilator to take out the trapped man. His leg was broken and bloody. Four men carried him to the lift and an ambulance was called.

Water leaked from the top of the walls. Sometimes small stones fell on us. In another section of the tunnel were people called Loaders (*Malaisha*). My boots were full of water. The time for clocking out started to roll round, so we followed our boss boy to the station. We switched off our lamps while we waited in the queue because at the station there were electric lights. We were wet like fishes and ugly like hippos. Some were sitting and resting with empty stomachs. There were two lifts running up and down, taking people out of the shaft. When one was underground, the other was on the surface, off-loading. After twenty minutes, the lift arrived. The guard opened the door and we flowed in. The notice on the door said the lift took only twenty people. But we were packed like fishes in a small can. At level 6 the guard opened the door and we came out, one by one, as the door is very small. We gave our officer the lamps and he gave us back our numbers.

There was no time or chance to prove yourself: who you are and what you want. I did not wash my clothes or bath because I did not have soap and other clothes to put on. All I did was eat and sleep on the grass and listen to the music from the loudspeaker at the office of Hlatini compound (C).

I had already lost hope of going back to Pretoria where I belonged. I could not even imagine that my girlfriend was thinking about me. Life was so bad; for me life was a little piece of stone. Washing, bathing, cutting nails, dressing in clean clothes and reading newspapers was far from me. It could be about 640 000 miles far from me.

The mine injection makes you forget about your parents, relatives and friends, even your girlfriend. The injection makes you think only about work underground. After three weeks underground I was part of that world.

In the yard of Hlatini compound there was coal and wood and in the rooms was only one stove. If it was cold you could make a fire or cook your own favourite food. The bar and shop were in the yard.

The days went on and on until my ticket said twenty-three days. One month ends on day twenty-four. Then we'd get our money. When my ticket said twenty-four days, I was working underground for the last time. My last day underground went so fast. On the twenty-fifth day I went to the pay-master to get my money. I was told to come back after six days. This was bad news. Waiting for my six days to end, I slept in the bush every night because I did not want to go underground. My main wish was to escape. During my last six days in the lonely bush I came across many dead cattle killed by Pondos and Basotho because these nations like meat. I also saw old shafts and old machines, so I used to enjoy myself going underground using ropes and chains. The shafts were very dark. During my wanderings I saw people ploughing their lands and growing crops. I also came across a slum known as Mantserre near the big mountain, far from the Hlatini compound, where there were schools, shops and churches. In the bush I met some wild animals like springboks, hares and impalas, as well as partridges. I even met people riding bicycles from the mines to Mantserre slum on the narrow paths.

I wore my mine clothes during this time as I didn't want to show people that I wasn't working. When I returned to the mine I took off my mine clothes and wore my own dirty ones. I was so happy to know that tomorrow was pay day. I met young men at Hlatini playing records and singing. I joined in though

I didn't know them. My meal was so good that I ate like a pig and drank chaechae like a drunkard. What I did not know was that I was on the verge of a complete mental breakdown. My last night at Hlatini was very long and terrible. It harboured demons, but it also symbolised escape from dangerous falling rocks to the gentle air of Pretoria City.

At 3.30 a.m. a loudspeaker woke up the people as usual. I was left alone in the room, waiting for 9 a.m., for my pay. I decided to steal clothes, tape recorders and radios but God refused to allow it. Music was playing on the loudspeakers. To me things seemed to be changing; even the birds were singing a chorus which I didn't understand. The hours went by and at 8.30 a.m. people started to queue for pay. I joined them. After an hour the paymaster arrived, police guarding him with revolvers. Each of us was asked for a number, and fingerprints were taken. They gave me a pay slip which had two parts. At a second window they took one part and I was left with the pay slip with my thumb print on it. At the third window they took my pay slip and gave me the money which a policeman counted so that they would not rob me. The money was ninety-six rand. It was for my own work. I risked my life and reason for it.

I went out of the main gates at Hlatini to escape to Northam station. I pretended to be counting my money at the gate so that the police guards would not realise that I was running away. I did not finish counting: I just thrust it into my empty pocket and walked out of the main gate towards the bush to free myself. That time life was not endless but everlasting. The earth was once supposed to be flat. Well, so it is, from Hlatini to Northam. That fact does not prevent science from proving that the earth as a whole is spherical. We are still at the stage that life itself is flat – the distance from birth to death. Yet the probability is that life, too, is spherical and much more extensive and capacious than the hemisphere we know.

The black dots in my eyes turned brown, like a dagga[5] smoker or a dreamer. I felt like a political asylum-seeker, running to Tanzania. To get to Northam I had to cross two compounds. I ran like hell until I crossed A and B compounds. Then I ran to catch the 10.30 train from Northam to Rustenburg. Two black men, and a white man on a tractor, looked at me, surprised. Far from the ploughing men I crossed a ditch in which a half-eaten impala lay. Birds were singing, animals roaring. At 8 p.m. cars passed me, one after another and I started to fear for my life. I hid under small bridges or in the long grass. At 9 p.m. I saw small yellow lights and I realised that it must be the station. My feet were aching and swollen and bloody.

At the station there was a café where I bought chips and a half brown and sat on the grass to eat it. After buying a ticket to Rustenburg, I found a small piece of paper on the grass. I took it to the toilets, wet it and washed my face with it. I even bought Vaseline to smear on my dirty face. My face looked like that of a real man, but not my clothes.

The train arrived at 10.30 p.m. People looked at me. Some of them were laughing instead of crying blood. After I arrived in Rustenburg I went to the shops. People were laughing at my dirty clothes, even white people. The shopkeeper thought I was a robber, so I showed him my pay slip. I bought a three-piece suit, a blue shirt, black and red socks and a Scotch tie. It cost me seventy-one rand and I was left with only twenty-two rand. I couldn't arrive home with dirty clothes, so I decided to buy my pride with my suffering.

I changed my clothes at the Rustenburg station toilets and put the old ones in a paper bag. I was really a gentleman. People, mostly girls, asked for the time when they saw me, just for pleasure. I had a *Rand Daily Mail* newspaper in my right hand, and walked like a president. I was smelling of new clothes.

Suffering taught me many things.

I recall a poem which is a plea for me:

I don't like being told
This is in my heart, thinking
That I shall be me
If I were you
I but not you
But you will not give me a chance
1 am not you
Yet you will not let me be
You meddle, interfere in my affairs as if they were yours
And you were not me
You are unfair, unwise
That I can be you, talk, act and think like you
God made me
For God's sake, let me be me
I see your eyes but you don't see your eyes
I cannot count your fingers because you see them all
Act yourself and I will act myself, not being told but doing it oneself.

Suffering takes a man from known places to unknown places. Without suffering you are not a man. You will never suffer for the second time because you have learned to suffer.

I am grateful to Mr Dlongolo who told me about mine work and that it was a fast way of making money.

It was Friday and most of the people on the train were students and mine workers going home to Pretoria and the Transkei. Everyone was happy. Even I was happy. If suffering means happiness I am happy. The 1.35 p.m. train pulled out and I sat reading the *Rand Daily Mail*. The train stopped at all stations: Colombia, Turfground, Maroelakop, Bleskop, Marikana, Wolhuterskop, Brits

West, Beestekraal, Norite, Stephanus and Taljaardshoop, when it left the Republic of Bophuthatswana and crossed into South Africa. On the train people sold watches, apples, socks, liquor, shoe laces, lip ice and so on. When I saw the beautiful girls I thought of my own beautiful sweetheart, my bird of Africa, sea water, razor: green-coloured eyes like a snake, high wooden shoes like a cripple; with soft and beautiful skin, smelling of powder under her armpits like a small child, with black boots for winter like a soldier, and a beautiful figure like she does not eat, sleep, speak or become hungry. And she looks like an artificial girl or electric girl. But she was born of her parents, as I was. She is Miss Johanna Mapula Modise of Mabopane who was born during a rainy day. As I am Mr Joel Medupe Matlou of Mabopane and I was also born during a rainy day. Mapula and Medupe is our gift from God. So, we accepted these names by living together.

The train arrived in Ga-Rankuwa on time. I bought some groceries and took a taxi to Mabopane. From there I went straight home where I met my mother and young brothers. They were happy and I was happy with them. The following morning I visited my girlfriend.

She cried when she saw me, silently looking down on the soil of Africa. I did not tell her I had worked on the mine. I said I had got a job in Johannesburg.

'Why didn't you tell me that you were going to work in Johannesburg? You didn't even write to me. You just sat there and forgot me,' she said.

'One of my friends took me to Johannesburg where he found me work. So there was no chance, I just left,' I lied to her.

Back on Mabopane's dusty roads again I looked like a real gentleman. Many people were happy to visit me as they knew I was a peace lover and didn't drink or smoke. There was nothing which worried me. I had thought that getting back to Mabopane's dusty roads would lead me to suffer, but eating alone was almost more than I could bear. I learned to forget yesterdays and to think of tomorrows. Each morning in the township, I said to myself: 'Today is a new life.' I overcame my fear of loneliness and my fear of want. I am happy and fairly successful now and have a lot of enthusiasm and love for life. I know now that I shall never again be afraid of sleeping under a tree alone, regardless of what life hands me. I don't have to fear blasting. I know now that I can live one day at a time and that every day is a time for a wise man.

Notes
[1] *hemp*: shirt
[2] *gumba-gumba*: record-player
[3] *sefanagalo*: pidgin
[4] *mageu*: (non-alcoholic) drink
[5] *dagga*: marijuana

EM MACPHAIL

Annual Migration

First published, 1991

Esther likes to leave at the end of summer, well before the first cold nights of the highveld winters. She returns after the early thunderstorms have begun and the jacaranda trees no longer stand in mauve pools of their own making. She stopped going to Europe when her children went to live in the States. But no matter what others may have to say she had met quite a few interesting, as well as friendly, people.

Esther is quite short. Although she isn't fat there is a roundness to her. When she accepts a second slice of cake, she always says with a conspiratorial smile: 'I eat too much. I must go on a diet.' She has neat hands which she uses prettily. They are smooth and white and surprisingly free of the brown smudges which litter her face. She speaks with a strong accent and can talk Russian, French, Italian and Yiddish.

Esther's daughter lives in Houston and her son in New York. After she'd stayed with him the first time her son gave her a book called *How to be a Jewish Mother* and told her to read it carefully. Later on she gave the book to Mrs Ginsberg who, Esther thought, could make better use of it than she could.

It had been a mistake to greet Mrs Ginsberg that first time. Esther, about to walk over to the shops, had stood in the entrance while the chauffeur held open the rear door of the big black car and the maid carried the handbag. She waited while Mrs Ginsberg moved slowly out through the heavy glass security doors on which is etched the name of the building. The hall porter made sure the double doors were firmly closed after they had passed through. All she had said, as she came alongside Mrs Ginsberg, was, 'Have a good day.' She hadn't meant anything by it. You heard it all the time in the States. Mrs Ginsberg turned around. 'What did you say?' she asked. So Esther repeated, 'Have a good day,' and she smiled the second time. But Mrs Ginsberg wanted to know why she must have a good day that day. Which is what happens when you only mean to be friendly. It didn't mean you wanted to be friends for the rest of your life. Mrs Ginsberg had told her to sit in the back with her even though Esther said she wanted the exercise. But Mrs Ginsberg said, 'It is too hot for walking. The wind will blow your hair.

Also they are snatching handbags.' When she asked, 'Are you shy because you haven't got a car?' Esther gave in and sat beside her. By the time the chauffeur parked as near to Woolworths as he could, they each knew that the other's children had left the country.

Esther said she went to visit her family at the beginning of May and, although they would like her to stay longer, she always returned home in the spring.

Every year Mrs Ginsberg's daughter brought her three children from Australia and her son-in-law would come when he wasn't so busy. At first when he was both working and studying at the university he couldn't make it but it would be easier when he had his own business. He was a lawyer. He had a very good brain.

'... and in Manhattan my son has his own apartment. New York is called the Big Apple and it is very stimulating intellectually,' Esther said, and added, 'It is good for the mind.'

Esther always stops off in New York first. Her unmarried son settled there after his sister had written telling him about the opportunities for dentists. She told him a guy could make a stack if he was prepared to work hard, like after hours and especially at the weekends. New Yorkers never seemed to go to bed. The movies even started at midnight and all night long there were people in the streets. So why shouldn't they have their teeth fixed at night? But how was Esther to know that his apartment was also the rooms and the nurse his girl-friend? And there is a new nurse every year. Who would want to stay for more than three days if you have to wait until the last patient leaves before you can go to bed on the convertible couch in the waiting room? And even with the police sirens, the honking of fire engines and helicopters buzzing you heard everything as well as that year's nurse telling her son to choose between herself and that goddam *yenta*.

'My three grandchildren have more intellectuality than any other children I know. When they were born I could tell they were special because their toes were curled up or not curled up – I can't remember which – two hours after birth yet.' Mrs Ginsberg paused to take breath. '... and now they must go to the school for children with special gifts.'

'... New York has so much to give: the theatre, the latest foreign films, the restaurants ... out of this world. And the shops ... fantastic.' Esther rolled her eyeballs back and lifted both hands, palms outward with spread fingers.

There was so much to remember about that first visit. There had been the suitcase which friends advised Esther to take empty because the shopping in the States – especially New York – was outstanding. But she had been a whole month in Houston and her daughter still hadn't found the time to take her to the shops. When the summer school holidays started there was even less time. Her daughter never seemed to sit down.

'And all of my grandchildren are fantastic artistic. And the little one plays the violin yet. And, shame, it's nearly as big as her. And can you believe it also, they are very good at netball,' Mrs Ginsberg said.

'After the New York crowds and the theatre and everything it is good to settle down in Houston and take things easy. Even if my unmarried son wants me to stay longer. But I can't wait to see my grandchildren. They scream with excitement when I arrive and they unpack all the presents.'

It is going on for three years since Esther and Mrs Ginsberg became friends.

After the long flight home Esther always hopes she will have a few days to rest. But the servants talk and Mrs Ginsberg phones at once to say it only seems the other day that she left. And is her son in New York married yet.

On her last trip to the States, Esther found out about telephone recorders and as soon as she returned she had one installed. Now it saves her having to think up on-the-spot excuses for not going to the shops or having coffee or listening to Mrs Ginsberg's youngest granddaughter play the violin.

How Esther had longed for the first letter after the family left. When all the farewell parties were over and they were packed up at last and ready to go, her daughter vowed she would write as soon as they arrived. At the airport she comforted Esther and made her promise she would visit them within a year. She told Esther's maid, who had also come to say goodbye, to take care of her mother. Almost exactly a year after they had gone, Esther herself was at Jan Smuts, leaving to visit the States for the first time. She had wondered if her daughter's husband would be more friendly than he used to be. Perhaps the thousands of kilometres between them would have made a difference.

Right from the beginning Esther insisted on helping.

'Of course I know how to use a vacuum cleaner.'

'I never saw you use one when I lived at home.'

'So I can read the instructions,' Esther had answered.

She told her daughter not to rush back after taking the children to school. But rather to have coffee with her friends like she used to. But how was she to know that liquid detergent was not meant for dishwashers? Still, it hadn't taken the two of them long to mop up the foam before it reached the new rugs.

'... and it will save having to wash the floor,' Esther said.

'I never bloody wash the floor unless I bloody have to.'

There had been only one morning that Esther remembered being able to persuade her daughter to have a cup of tea. She had patted the seat next to her and they sat together on the settee.

'I would have taken the little ones to Bible studies if I wasn't nervous about driving on the wrong side of the road.' Esther sipped her tea and added, 'You must rest more. You're looking much older than when you left. You musn't neglect yourself.'

'What do you mean?'

'You know men are very quick to notice when their wives don't take care of themselves. You used to have your hair done every week at home.'

Her daughter hadn't answered. But Esther knew it was best for her to hear certain things from her mother.

She sighed. 'You know that girl of mine is getting lazier and lazier.'

'How?' her daughter asked.

'Well, she doesn't make pudding as often as she used to. She thinks she can get away with just putting some fruit on the table.'

Accepting another slice of cake, Esther said, as she always does, 'I eat too much. I must go on a diet.'

She smiled as if making a joke.

All of a sudden her daughter had jumped up on the Chesterfield and let loose a long drawn-out scream.

'What is the matter? What is it?' Esther shouted. She had wondered if it was one of those goggas that used to upset her so.

'Is it a Parkview prawn?'

'Don't you know that life isn't just diets and hair and servants?' her daughter had shrieked.

Then, in the sudden silence, Esther asked if it was that time of the month. But the bellowing started again and, like a cow's, it was broken up by moments of quiet which had made Esther wonder if her daughter was beginning to pull herself together. But each time she stood up to help her down from the settee, she screamed, 'Leave me alone, leave me. *Voetsak.*'

Mrs Ginsberg's daughter still lives in Sydney and still brings her children to visit their granny every year. And her daughter's husband is making so much he can come for a month. First class. So there is plenty of time for him and her daughter to go to Botswana, the Kruger Park and the ones in Natal and Namibia. But the kids would only get restless so they must stay with their old granny. And if the weather is good at the Cape, their parents can fit in a few days there as well. Esther agrees that children can't be cooped up all day in a flat, even a penthouse yet. And, of course, they would get fed up being driven around by the chauffeur. She asks why she doesn't send them to the public library. But Mrs Ginsberg says they are never allowed to go anywhere on their own. They might get into trouble. One hears all the time what can happen. Esther says that the librarian will look after them. She has seen this already the first time she was in Houston.

Esther had found the library by accident. When she wasn't able to calm her daughter, she ran outside to find someone who might know what to do. She had seen a car backing into a parking bay just up the street, and she ran towards it, calling, 'Help. Please help me.' But as she came level, the driver changed his mind and drove off quickly. She pressed the bells on two different gates and, although she thought she saw a curtain move in one window, nobody answered. She ran through the little park in the middle of the next block, which was a mistake, because not only was there nobody in it, but she must have taken the wrong exit out of it. Suddenly, there had been so many people in a street which she didn't recognise. Each time she had tried to stop somebody, the person would look at her as if she was speaking a foreign language. If they were old, they shook their heads. If they were young, they looked her up and down and turned away. Perhaps it was her slippers. As she had stood wondering how to find her way back, she noticed an arrow above the words LENDING, READING and REFERENCE LIBRARY. Inside the building, with its high domed ceiling, the sudden shutting out of the traffic noises, as well as the SILENCE notice, made Esther pause. Instead of rushing, she had tiptoed over to the desk labelled INFORMATION.

The librarian had shown her how to find her way back on the street directory. Coming into the house quietly, she was relieved to find that the bellowing had stopped. She sat in her bedroom and listened to what the calm and very controlled voice said on the kitchen telephone. Americans don't use 'bloody' as a swear word and when Esther returns home it always surprises her to hear it so often. The voice had said, 'My mother must not stay in this bloody house any bloody longer. She must bloody fuckoff.' The voice had paused for a moment and then said, 'She talks about home all the time. She insists on helping and she just makes one bloody fuckup after another.' Again there was a pause. 'No, of course she's not here.' Esther's shoulders relaxed and when the back door had banged, she had known that her grandchildren would be picked up from Bible studies in good time.

Once Esther has recovered from the long flight home – this last time she had hardly more than three hours' sleep – she phones Mrs Ginsberg and they arrange to have tea together. She always brings her something from the States. Once it was the book that Esther's son gave her about the irritating ways of Jewish mothers. This time it is a small Statue of Liberty with a black face.

The librarian in Houston had given Esther several brochures. One was about the Salvation Army, which claimed they never turned anyone away. She recalled seeing at home, at Christmas time, a woman in a bonnet, standing at the corner, shaking a tambourine, while a uniformed man played the bugle. Another pamphlet interested her more. The organisation described one of its activities as providing accommodation suitable for women, on their own, in strange towns. She had read on: 'The YWCA operates hotels and residences – one of its first objects is to provide safe, inexpensive and decent places for women to live – summer camps, programs of education and recreation, all without regard to the economic, racial or religious conditions of participants.'

Mrs Ginsberg has such a lot to tell Esther whenever she returns from the States. The Australian family will be arriving shortly and Mrs Ginsberg is glad their stay always coincides with Esther's return. She adds, 'And it looks as if they will be lucky with the weather. It is always perfect when they come. I don't know how they arrange it.'

'When I leave my grandchildren in Houston they ask every year why I don't stay with them for ever and ever.'

Mrs Ginsberg is very keen to hear if there are any signs of Esther's son getting married.

'Will you have your grandchildren to stay all the time?' Esther asks.

Mrs Ginsberg says, but of course they will stay with their granny who loves them so much. And this time she will tell the chauffeur to bring his children to play often.

The Houston librarian and Esther have become great friends. He says her grandchildren are the best behaved children he has ever had in his library. She keeps an eye on them in the afternoons while he tells her about his difficulties. How, in the school holidays, the mothers drop their children off with him. But even though he hires extra help in the summer, they can't stop them from fighting. Once he locked the doors and wouldn't allow them in. This was during the mayoral election and his action was called discriminatory by one of the political parties. Since then, he has never shut anyone out of his library. Esther doesn't mind listening. She feels she owes it to him. As soon as she sees her grandson starting to fidget, she sits down and reads the books they have chosen. And not just once. They only leave when neither of the children can think of another question to ask.

During the rest of that first time with her Houston family, Esther hadn't been able to help because of her back. It was for this reason, too, that when their annual holiday came up, she had asked if they would excuse her. And her son-in-law said, before they left, to be sure not to answer the front door and not on any account to go to the little park on the next block.

It had seemed a pity not to visit Boston while she had the opportunity. Also, it was a good chance to find out more about the YWCA, and Esther decided to go by Amtrak rather than fly. One could see more from a train. She remembers she had no trouble finding the place. It always surprises her how easy it is to get a cab in the States, while at home she has to book a taxi in advance. Right from stepping into the entrance – one could hardly have called it a foyer – she knew it was the right place to stay while deciding where to spend the winter months away from home in future. Esther can't remember exactly when her son and daughter first started telling her what was best for her. But now that she herself knows, she spends three nights in New York and two weeks in Houston. By moving from one Y to another she has found what suits her best. And it is Canada where, in Victoria, British Columbia, she rents a room and bath for four months every year. Her foreign travel allowance is enough and she meets others, like herself, who enjoy the concerts in the summer. She attends lectures, meets people from all over the place, sometimes even makes new friends. When they ask her where she learned to speak so many languages, she tells them she is a real wandering Jewess.

HENNIE AUCAMP

The Coat without End

(For Percy and Clara Gersholowitz)
Translated from the Afrikaans by Ian Ferguson
From: *Dalk gaan niks verlore nie en ander tekste* (1992)

I must say at once, the source of my story is not *The Overcoat* although all stories about clothing have been, ever since Gogol wrote that one, automatically related to his masterly story. Some variations are, like Wolf Mankowitz's *The Bespoke Overcoat*, close family to Gogol's tale.

What makes my assurances suspect is that my story has a Jewish flavour with a pinch of Russian mysticism if you take into account Miriam's eventful youth in Russia. But truly, as I tell it to you so it happened, here in Cape Town and, to be specific, in Vredehoek where the wind always roars down.

Actually, my story really begins in Ireland.

Jacob Lipschitz of Cape Town went there to further his studies in medicine even though he was an established family man. In Ireland, note, where it can get terribly cold. He and his wife, Miriam, consulted each other, concluding that a custom-made tweed coat would be a good investment since they would have to survive three Irish winters.

Now to the appearance of the coat: it is a short coat, one could say, more of a jacket or, rather, a three-quarter coat. In any case, it is made of heavy herringbone tweed, fully lined with black satin. It has a collar that can be pulled up against the wind, deep pockets and a broad belt made of the same tweed. At that time it cost an arm and a leg to have that sort of coat tailored; today only the very rich can consider having such a coat custom made.

That coat saw its owner through three cruel Irish winters; heavy enough to keep out arctic winds. But for Cape Town it was, alas, too heavy.

Even in Vredehoek where the wind slices down from Devil's Peak was it seldom cold enough to wear the Irish tweed coat and Jacob stored it in a wardrobe in the spare room. Miriam, always provident, put soap in the cupboard and mothballs in the pockets of Jacob's Irish coat.

Miriam had a domestic called Maria Mbekushe: she was a quiet, dedicated worker who took in sewing for extra income. Until late into the night Maria would sit in her room at her sewing machine. At weekends she went to her husband who cared for a congregation somewhere on the Cape Flats.

Occasionally her husband would visit her, a courteous, slightly stocky man who liked to discuss the Bible with Miriam since she was a formidable authority on the Old Testament.

It was Maria's husband, Alfred Mbekushe, who made Miriam think of the coat. Within a few weeks Alfred was to leave for the Transkei on parish business and, according to the radio reports, it was freezing in the Eastern Province as well as the surrounding areas. Miriam discussed it with Jacob who had no objections; if it was indeed as cold in the Transkei as the radio reported Alfred was a worthy beneficiary of the coat.

Now even later into the night the sewing machine sang, or whatever sound a sewing machine makes, since Maria had to work hastily to alter the coat in time for Alfred's departure. It had to be opened up and gussets inserted. For these she used material from the belt: Alfred could use an ordinary leather belt, a black one would go nicely with the herringbone.

On the day of his departure Alfred, wearing a neat felt hat and with an umbrella over his arm, came to show off the coat. At Maria's request, Jacob took a photograph of her with Alfred, and Miriam said, 'Now we also have a portrait of the coat as well for the family archives.'

That snapshot of Maria and Alfred led to many tears and sorrows for, on the way back from the Transkei, Alfred was murdered on the train. Possibly he was killed for his coat since his body was discovered without it. Maria resigned from domestic service and went out to continue her husband's work on the Cape Flats.

Meanwhile Jacob and Miriam's daughter, Sarah, reached a marriageable age. She was going out with a fellow student, Max, who was also from a good Jewish family but somewhat leftwing in his political beliefs. He accepted as little as possible from his parents and out of sympathy for the underprivileged he bought his clothes from street markets in the black residential areas. His trousers and jerseys, all, were second hand. He bought a tweed coat, one with a herringbone pattern.

When, one windy night, Max visited his future in-laws it was a good excuse to show off his great bargain. 'Oh,' he said, 'not that I cheated the seller, I gave him double what he asked for this coat.'

Miriam and Jacob looked as if they had seen a ghost. 'The coat!' Miriam shouted and Jacob cried out at the same time, 'My coat! You have my coat on!'

Jacob embraced his future son-in-law while he tried to define the smells in the coat; whether it smelled of him, or of Alfred or Max or of a dry-cleaners. The only smell that he could discover, and it could have been his imagination, was of smoke from a dung fire.

Max and Sarah's astonishment grew by the minute. Sarah knew nothing of the history of the coat that had been given to Alfred Mbekushe since she had been at boarding school when it happened and, in any case, she had long since forgotten about the coat.

Jacob and Miriam from years of living together thought like one person. They looked conspiratorially at each other, then Miriam said, 'Please take off the coat, we will explain in a minute.' She spread the coat across the dining-room table and she and Jacob bent low over it as if they were both myopic. They turned the coat over, turned it satin side out, then they turned it back and fingered it. No, thank the Lord, there were no knife cuts, no dried blood. The coat was still of a piece.

Then they told the story of the coat that had, since Ireland, experienced so much. Sarah listened open-mouthed and Max grew pale. 'No, no, no,' sighed the future son-in-law, 'how could I wear the coat now? It can only bring misfortune.'

'Especially now,' said sensible Miriam, 'especially now. Do you not see this is a coat without end? Chagall could have made a painting of it.' Miriam pointed to an etching on the wall.

'And Malamud could have written a big novel about it,' Jacob added.

Max found the mythologising of his street-market coat somewhat naïve, but to please his future in-laws he wore the coat to an intimate family festival. Miriam lit the candles and their flames were reflected in the copper pans that hung on the walls. Jacob carried in a cast-iron casserole of chicken pieces to the table and much later Miriam brought a glass dish of stewed quinces, red as cherries, to the table.

After the meal Max asked permission to take off his coat. His shirt was soaked through and Miriam loaned him one of Jacob's although it was rather too tight for him.

That was probably the last time that Max wore the tweed coat. Spring was early that year and it was a summery sort of spring.

A few months later, when they were married, Max and Sarah decided to give the coat away as soon as a worthy candidate presented himself. Their flat was far too cramped to keep unnecessary things and, in any event, the coat had become a sullen presence and a constant reproach. Providence, or a happy accident, brought – as it usually does – a solution. Sarah fell pregnant and Max was obliged to hire domestic help since Sarah had much trouble with her back and had to lie flat for long periods.

Ruby Fubesi was lively and cheerful by nature; she became Sarah's friend and companion, and Max could leave Sarah with confidence in Ruby's care.

When the first winter rains fell, Max fetched the Irish coat from the wardrobe where it pressed against Sarah's dresses and fur coat. He held it against himself asking Ruby selfconsciously, 'Can you at least use it?'

Ruby clasped her hands together as if in prayer. It was just the thing for her husband, Jonathan, for when he conducted church services.

Naturally I will have to alter the coat, thought Ruby, my husband is much thinner than Max. But yes, it wouldn't present any difficulties. I'll take the coat in, remove the gussets and turn them into a belt. Look, it already has loops.

But I will need to hurry up, Ruby anxiously concluded, for in less than a month, Jonathan would be leaving for the Transkei.

LIZ GUNNER

The Mandela Days

First published, 1992

So we took him at dead of night and wrapped him in the skin of the beast we had slaughtered for him. We left our place, quietly, so that the dogs of our neighbours wouldn't bark, and we went a distance with him, putting the body in the open truck and driving with no headlights to the forest, the gum-trees at Stamford, not so far from the sea where the old king had crossed the water into exile after the war with the English.

Sipho had brought a spade. We didn't want to throw him into the forest like a dog. He was our son, our kinsman, my child. So we took spades and dug him a grave, not deep because it would attract suspicion even in this time of killing and dying, and it would take time.

We gave him a shallow grave, our Njomane, our young son who had followed the wrong path and gone with the enemy. Brave, like the old Njomane –

You who went away for years
But in the fourth year we saw you again!

Our young one, following where we told him not to go. The skin of the beast was stiff, like his young body and they fitted awkwardly into the hole, deep enough for dogs not to sniff and for the stench of decay to be lost. So we threw earth over him and his wrong ways, asking in our hearts, *How could you follow a stranger from another nation, go with people who burnt and killed and looted and turned children against their elders and make them dance mad dances learnt in the countries to the north?*

Follow a stranger who had spent long years in jail far away in the south, a man who knew nothing of our lives here, our ways.

Singing their mad songs which made you wild with reckless joy – Tambo, Mandela, Sisulu, Slovo, we have never seen them.

Our son, why did you do this?

But this is not the end of it. People will know that we lost a son. Women will tell his story and the fearfulness of it. That out of shame or scorn or anger, or was it fear they took his body and threw it to the dogs far away from the homestead, far from the ancestors, and they will never sing his song with the others. They will talk about us in quiet huts at funerals when the women sit alone guarding the body of the mourned one and what we have done will be a sign of the country dying.

Why did he ask so many questions?

Baba, who is Mandela? Why do we sit with so little and the long cars speed up and down the black road? What is the history of our part, before the sugar came? before the whites came?

Better to have had him dull and quiet but still with a smile and the laughter.

Baba, is it true that the old people called it Ematafeni, because it was like a great green plain scattered with cattle and homesteads stretching out as far as the eye could see, when you came down from the hills to the north, from Hlabisa? And they say it was rich with people and cattle and it was Dube territory, and Mjadu territory. Father tell me, is this true? And ourselves, the Mhlongos, the People of the Sun, we have been here for long years? Isn't it so?

And you who rush along the black tarred road with the speed of meteors and see only the tattered huts and thin cattle and the limping men, know that you see nothing.

LIZ GUNNER

Cattle Passsing

First published, 2004

Aunt Alex, this is for you. It's the story you never told. It's the story your father told me once – half told me – in a tossed-aside sentence that took on a life of its own and wouldn't die down, so that in the sunlight of another afternoon, when I asked to hear it again, he denied its existence, trying to pretend it had never been born. You can't do that to stories.

Look, reader, whoever you are, I'm leading you on, don't expect too much from this. It's about something that never happened – that's the story. But you know, maybe the most important things in the world are the things that never happened? Don't get impatient and turn away; this won't take long. You see, it is this deep, nagging question – 'Why?' I ask myself, 'why all those years after the story and its half-telling, so many, many years after the little event, why disown it? Why disown a non-event?'

'Tell me about the droughts? The really bad ones. Tell me how people coped?' I was sitting close to him, on the cane chairs, stone floor beneath us and the sky ahead. He was chewing his pipe, puffing at it with short spurts and stabs, corroding his one remaining lung, holding the bowl in one powerful, sunburnt hand.

oh hands! They tell you so much, think of Dürer's Praying Hands, knotted supplicant fingers, the hands of the Queen of England in the new portrait, mottled, blunt, ugly, the hands of an old woman, tired, capable hands, then the hands in the taxi – the art man, so quiet, self-effacing, holding all his power inwards, keeping it all to himself, and then I saw his hands, square, large, lying still and watchful, carrying the ancestral memory of coal, wood and iron, at ease with the clamped distant vowels of Sheffield sliding on London polish. The taxi emptying us out on the cobbles at cruel King's Cross. 'Here,' said I, wanderer and dreamer, 'I'll pay, here's my share.'

So I remember his hand on the pipe and the hawk's gaze fixed on the north-west horizon, the land rising to the thick fringe of pines he had planted and the hills girdling the eye to the north and the east. 'Please, tell me about droughts, the real droughts?' He seemed to unfold his mind, peeling back the pages like the notebooks he kept to record, meticulously, the rainfall – usually twenty-nine inches a year – the bags of wheat from each land, the sacks of maize, the milk, the rations, the pay, the loans, the prices, the comings and the goings, the hail. The notebooks were large with dark-blue mottled marble covers and he filled them with his sloping cramped writing – year after year, day upon day. They stayed piled unobtrusively in the cool shade of his office.

'The real droughts? These', he says, 'are not real droughts. This is just very, very dry.' And yet we sit sometimes day after day, looking at the sky. He peers into the distance and claims to see a cloud, 'the size of a man's hand'. He spends a lot of time sitting, watching, he stays quite still, he is almost a tree, a shape in air that remains. We watch 'the man's hand', we watch it drift imperceptibly in the blue. It wisps out a little. We sigh. We drink tea, our feet on stone. We look again – the hand is a string of beads on the far horizon. It will not rain today.

When he does speak, it seems after so long that I have almost forgotten the question. 'Yes, there have been droughts, terrible ones, not like this one. There was the drought of 1931 and then there were the two others, 1924, and 1907. 1924 – that was the time the cattle moved. The whole country quivered under the sun that year, like whiplashes, a punishment. Children died, the old died, cattle, sheep. People were desperate to live, to keep what stock they could, and you know how very much cattle mean to the native. So they moved whole herds – took them across the whole country, or that's what it seemed like to us as we sat here and they came through, passing along the top there, near the pines, which were still growing then and not as tall as you see them now.' He points, jabs his hand ahead and I notice, remember, that his third finger is missing, and he's never told me how that happened and I've never asked.

'Huge herds of cattle came this way, a few men with them, sometimes just young boys but they loved their cattle, you could see that and they knew how to handle them and they grieved for them and wanted to save them. Oh yes, you could see that. They had heard there was food left down in the Natal grasslands so they came this way, close to the mountains, coming up from the south. Word must have gone round that I had water that was holding out in the north dam so they would come and ask if the herds could drink.

'We would sit here, where you and I are sitting now, just the same place, and from a distance they would look like vast herds of game, tawny colours, black, some the colours of mud. You've never seen drought animals drink? The dry muzzles, the long, groaning slurps, kneeling, butting and then they raise the head, the muzzles are damp and soft, the muddy water drips down, the dewlaps quiver. And their eyes, huge, soft brown eyes, holding all the pain. Sometimes I would go down and look at the cattle, thin with their haunches like planks, their sharp bones, and at times they would come up to the house to thank me and we'd talk. After all, we were all cattle men.

'One of them – I heard the women talking – they said he was a chief. He was quite a tall man and very – how can I put it – very well spoken, courteous like one of those old–style English gentlemen only of course he wasn't talking English. He thanked me for helping them and I asked the maids to give them some miealie meal, just to give them food for the road. He took it gravely and said and I remember these were his exact words because somehow they surprised me. He said, "Father of Kindness we thank you, God has blessed you with beautiful daughters. It is as it should be."

'The next morning, the cattle were still there spilling over into the pines. It was still early but very hot even then. I saw two figures coming back towards us from the cattle. I wondered what delayed them, they had so far to go and no promise of anything when they arrived. We exchanged greetings and then I waited. When the man they said was a chief spoke again it was slowly and carefully, "I would like to ask for your daughter, to be my wife. Your beautiful daughter with hair like golden rope. I would not ask her to come now. These are terrible times. I will send my people back for her with cattle and gifts when times are better and when God …" – he used the word 'Modimo', you know, their word for God – "when God blesses us again. You should not worry. We will look after her well. She will be a –" I stopped him. I look at his hand, his arm hangs loosely at his side like a broken branch. He is clasping nothing.

'"My friend. You ask the impossible. You anger me. I let your cattle drink, I give you food for your long journey and you ask for my daughter! Do not anger me. Go! My daughter is not for you." And then, I remember, this man they said was a chief stepped back as if he had seen a snake on the path in front of him and they turned and went. I didn't look at his face but when they walked away, they walked slowly, talking softly and the one who was with him laughed. The laugh I remember very well.

'When I told her – perhaps it was a mistake, but I did – she was quite silent. It is true she was very beautiful then. Her thick hair in its braids, the pale skin and her quick and gentle movements and blue eyes.

'The next morning early they were gone. They must have moved before dawn, travelling before the heat of the day, heading east towards the mountain passes and Natal.'

He did tell me. It is not a dream of the apartheid imagination. The story shocked me and of course fascinated me. I remembered the song of 'The raggle taggle gypsies' – 'She's off with the raggle taggle gypsies oh!' and I wondered if, if … if she had gone? If she had run away, if she had really loved him? What would have become of her? How would it have been? How would they have spoken? And would he have spat her out like a plumstone and taken other wives? Concubines? Kept her as the senior wife? Honoured? Lonely? And if she came back? And if she were happy?

She. Her. You. Of the hair like golden rope seen like that only through words and the portrait in the dining room. You married and led an exemplary life, you worshipped in our small, white church. Your husband was handsome and sturdy, he laughed a lot and he kept you well. You were happy and you bore him beautiful children, your garden was a jewel and your pantry was always full. You had tall grace, but a cutting edge. People loved you, but not too much.

'Tell me again,' I ask him, 'the story about the drought, and the chief who wanted to marry Aunt Alex?'

He puts down his pipe.

MAUREEN ISAACSON

I Could Have Loved Gold

From: *Holding Back Midnight and other Stories* (1992)

Dad talked about gold all the time. Gold standard and shares and world markets and creating work for the masses. The intonation of his voice acted as a soporific on mother and her already pale countenance and air of absence further dissolved. My little brother Jonathan would dip his middle finger into the butter and my aunt would yawn. But sometimes she'd say something and the two would hiss like prize bantams in a sparring match.

Into the spotless order of our Houghton mansion, Aunt Sal would bring the smoke and jazz of the streets of Sophiatown. It was in her walk and in her talk and in her eyes. She vibrated with the sax of Kippie Moeketsi and the huskiness of Dolly Rathebe and all the musos she heard there. As soon as Dad got going, she'd lose that bluesy cool; she'd talk and move fast, like a train chasing its own steam.

'Do you know what happens in the gold mines? About the hostels where there's no place for loving and precious little money to show for it when the miners do get back to their families?'

Dad would swell up with argument and a watery silence would envelop mother. It seemed that this dissension was irrelevant in the face of having an Anglo magnate husband who swathed her in nine carat this and twenty-two that.

She wore it burnished in her ears and round her neck, her wrists and waist and in her teeth. Her eyes were dull with it, with easy living and the loneliness of Dad being away so often.

Aunt Sal adored Jonathan and me. Whenever one of us felt sad she'd say that nothing stays the same and she'd sit with us until it went over. She'd tell us stories; it was only through her that we ever got to hear of cottages in woods and baskets to be taken to grandmothers and people like Rapunzel letting down their hair. She told her own version; with syncopated rhythm and high drama.

Dad believed in facts. When he did tell us stories they would invariably be about gold.

'The Incas of Peru,' he said, 'believed that the tears of the Sun fell in golden drops. They wore huge golden circles in their ears, just like the wooden ones the Nguni natives wear in South Africa.

792

'If you're going to tell kids something, make sure it's useful,' he said. He told us tales of ancient Roman gold mines. He talked about gold leaf death masks, thin as gossamer, used by the early Greeks and said that gold was civilised; it was something to believe in. It had changed his life. 'I didn't make it big through fairy stories. Nor jazz for that matter,' he said.

Aunt Sal laughed at the way my parents listened to the sounds of Elvis Presley and the Everly Brothers, when there was all that going on just around the corner. My parents weren't interested in what was going on round the corner, and told friends that Aunt Sal had a basic problem that made it necessary for her to go into the world of the 'Natives'.

She brought us Glen Miller records and blues and *marabi*, the sounds of the shebeens, and we'd dance until we dropped. It gave mother a headache, she would say, then she'd go and lie down.

Once I heard Aunt Sal say to mother, 'You weren't like this before, Sarah.'

'Well now I am,' mother said.

I was at primary school at the time, and my experience of the world was limited to our Houghton mansion, our many servants and mother's golden unhappiness. She remained passive and inert, it was as if she'd been alchemised into some mystical substance, and was no longer with us. She looked into mirrors for a long time and I wondered what she was thinking; if she was thinking. She was always around, but I missed her.

We waited for Aunt Sal's jazz; she brought us records of Miriam Makeba, the Harlem Swingsters and Zig Zag Zakes. 'I bring you the Bantu Men's Social Centre special,' she'd say. Then she'd roll up her red trousers and she'd ramba and samba and talk about the way people lived in the townships.

'Eight people live in a house the size of this kitchen, minus the breakfast nook, no kidding.'

I couldn't really see how they did it. It all seemed so strange to me, like some foreign country somewhere.

I spent hours playing with mother's jewellery and holding it up to the sun to see what Dad meant when he talked about the purity of gold, the essence of it. I studied the gold plates and vases he brought back from his travels and encased in glass, the gold-bound books, and thought about being as good as gold and silence being golden. I would have loved gold if it wasn't for Aunt Sal.

When I think about the mansion now, maid-polished and ordered, it echoes with a drab silence. Into the odourless shine, Aunt Sal sped; alive with the fumes and stains and conversation of nights in shebeens. Crazy with tales of dark side-streets where gangs of men with American clothes and accents flicked knives and tongues. Talking about the way these guys would ruin concerts and break up cosy evenings in shebeens.

'Aren't you scared?' I asked.

Then the corners of her mouth lifted slightly and turned, and the green of her eyes deepened and she took a draw of her cigarette. She said nothing, but I often saw that expression again.

It was the expression she got when she talked about music and about a friend of hers called Albie. Although I never met him I knew exactly how he walked, hand in one pocket, cigarette dangling; hat cocked, because Aunt Sal would show us. Albie played piano and sang in one of the shebeens where Aunt Sal had her heart torn apart by the blues of Snowy Radebe and the late-night throb and *bebababerop* she came home singing. It was where she drank the home-brewed spirit *skokiaan*, a bout of which Aunt Sal said could knock your head right across the nation.

'Hardly suburbanite stuff,' she said.

My parents' friends were other mining magnates and their wives, and sometimes Jonathan and I would be allowed to join them for dinner. It was the only time mother would come alive. On such occasions Joseph, who cleaned the floors and served at table, would wear a white jacket with a diagonal sash, red as a wound.

The wives would ask us how we were enjoying school and if we liked our teachers and what our friends' names were, then they'd talk to each other about clothes and hair and Italian gold collars with streams of half-point diamonds and say things in very hushed tones. The men would talk loudly and clearly about gold exports and foreign exchange and balance of payments and South Africa's economic role in the world.

Mother said that our cook, Sanna, was a genius at whatever she turned her hand. She cooked Fish Soup Basquaise and Lamb Charlotte to perfection. Mother loved to surprise the guests with treats like black truffles in Italian rice, fresh foie gras or watermelon in glazed wine. Imported white wines were a favourite; their chill glistened from generous crystal glasses.

One such evening, just as mother was saying, 'Children, don't you two think you should be getting to bed now?' Aunt Sal burst in.

'No thanks, I've eaten,' she said. 'How do you do? How do you do?' she greeted everyone, and kissed Jonathan and me. The wives touched their half-moon gold earrings and chunky bracelets and stared at Aunt Sal.

Suddenly, without warning, she shouted, 'Yaabo! Yaabo!' Everybody stopped talking and father said, 'C'mon Sal, not now.'

Then she smiled and said, 'That's what the small boys shout when the police come near the home-brewed beer in the townships.'

'Sal ...' said Dad.

'They keep it in tins underground and cover them with sand and wet sacks — it's illegal to brew beer because of the liquor prohibition for blacks, you know. When the police come they pierce the tins and everyone runs away before they can be arrested.'

'Have some wine, Sal,' Dad said.

'Thanks. Very nice, what vintage?'

'Forty-nine.' Dad looked relieved and everyone relaxed and started talking again. Jonathan pinched me and giggled.

'Mm, very nice wine,' Aunt Sal said again. 'Nothing like *Tswala*.'

'*Tswala*?' asked a magnate's wife.

'Yes, *Tswala*. It's the stuff they give black mineworkers. A kind of non-alcoholic beer, rich in vitamin B.'

Mother wiped the corners of her mouth with her serviette. Father breathed audibly. Then that steam-train speed got hold of Aunt Sal and there was no stopping her.

'*Tswala*, loudspeakers, heat and unbearable noise – that's what you get when you work on the mines.'

One of the magnates said: 'Do you know what you're talking about? To what do you think the country owes its wealth? Has it ever occurred to you that the industry provides work for people? The Natives love the mines. They even call Johannesburg "Egoli", which means "City of Gold". South Africans have a damn lot to thank the people who discovered gold and the mining corporations for.'

'Egoli safoot!' said Aunt Sal. 'A city built on cheap mineworker-sweat, what do you know about their lives?'

'The mines provide employment.' He was rigid.

'Okay, so what about the danger they work with, poison fumes, fires, accidents, rockbursts, and all the people that get killed?'

'Safety measures ...' started the magnate. He was red-cheeked and everyone seemed to have forgotten their food.

'Don't tell me about safety and about us having the deepest mines and not being able to compare with the rest of the world, I know that argument. I'm talking about people's lives!' Aunt Sal's voice quavered.

'Well so are we. We're providing people with an opportunity to eat, people who would otherwise starve.' The magnate was redder.

'What do you know? Have you been there? Have you ever heard of faction fights? Have you ever seen the way they fight amongst themselves? Everyone knows they'd kill each other if we didn't put a stop to it!'

Aunt Sal said nothing. Mother called Joseph to clear the plates and bring in the chestnuts and poached pears.

'It's way past your bedtime, you two,' she said to Jonathan and me. So we left the table and hid in the passage to see if anything more would happen. It didn't.

My parents didn't refer to that evening again and neither did Aunt Sal, but Jonathan and I went over and over the way the red-cheeked magnate who'd shouted at Aunt Sal had never known that there was a piece of lamb lodged in his beard all the while. And how his wife, the one who asked us how school was, had cut up three tomatoes into a million tiny pieces throughout the conversation.

After that Dad and Aunt Sal didn't talk to each other for a while. She visited when he was away. The ice thawed slowly and things returned to normal for a while.

One day she came in, eyes heavy as clay. She wouldn't say what was the matter but I knew it had something to do with Albie.

'Has he gone away?' I asked her.

'Don't talk about it,' she said.

'The shebeens and the bioscopes and the dancehalls were empty,' she said. 'The jazz don't sound and the blues make me cold inside instead of warm and I want to be at home, waiting, in my little tower, to let down my hair.'

But as she believed that things never stay the same, she smoked and drank into shebeeny nights, waiting, becoming thin and ashen, a shadow of her silent older sister.

Time edged along slowly. Aunt Sal's misery encircled her, etching a darkness around her eyes. It weighed down the air. She smoked fifty cigarettes a day, and another twenty at night. She coughed all the time.

Then she decided to go and live in London. She promised to send for us when we were old enough. She left us in the mansion with a distant father who stored gold rings and earrings and promises in a safe for my coming of age.

He left us, finally, with a weight as heavy as a gold bar, and the price we had to pay for his contribution to world economy. He left us with a mother whose sheen was fast fading. She said less than ever, now that Aunt Sal had gone.

MAUREEN ISAACSON

Holding Back Midnight

From: *Holding Back Midnight and Other Stories* (1992)

The night is shooting past. It is bright jet and hot. The air is as smooth as the whisky we sip on the veranda of the old hotel that has become my parents' home. We are safe from the faded neon and slow-moving traffic lights outside. The bubbles of fifty chilled bottles of champagne are waiting to spill as we touch down on the new century. In our own way, we each believe that from that moment on nothing will ever be the same.

Anything could happen at midnight. President Manzwe has said that he has a surprise for us. What can it be?

'Cheers!' shouts my mother. Old opals shine dully against her sagging lobes, her webbed neck. She is flushed, like a dead person who has been painted to receive her final respects.

'Cheers!' echoes her friend Ethel.

Smoke and disillusion have ravaged their voices. Their tongues are too slack to roll an olive pip. They walk slowly among the guests, in silver dresses that were fashionable once. They teeter on sling-back stilettos. They offer salmon and bits of fish afloat on shells of lettuce leaves.

Don't the people at this party ever think about AIDS? Out there in the real world, they give you cling paper gloves in restaurants lest you should bleed from an unnoticed cut. Waiters wear them. Doctors. Environmentalists, like my husband Leon and me. The lack of sterility makes me queasy tonight.

'What is the time, Dad?' I ask.

'Be patient,' he says.

Hopefully the moment we are waiting for will release him from the grip of history. History is ever-present in my father, like the patterns that shimmer from the chandeliers over the cracked walls. It is trapped in the broken paving outside this hotel where angels of delight once fluttered eyelashes as if they were wings at white men. History hovers, with the ghosts of the illicit coup-lings that once heated the hotel's shadowy rooms. It is funnelled through my memory.

Here comes my Uncle Otto, ex-Minister of Home Affairs, glass in hand. Looking at his ginger moustache, I am seven years old again. I am sitting on his lap at the bar. Don't tell your mother, he is saying. His hand is on my knee.

797

I feel the closeness of flesh. Angels are rubbing themselves against the men. Men against angels.

'Why angels?' I want to know.

'Because they take the white men to heaven,' says Uncle Otto.

Like the street names that have been removed for their Eurocentricity, my parents and their friends are displaced. They do not understand the new signs. Their silhouettes glide across the garden, outlining their nostalgia. Through the shrill chirp of the crickets, I catch the desolation in the voices. The talk of lifts that no longer work, of the rubbish that piles up. There goes our old dentist Louis Dutoit and his wife Joyce, speaking of 'Old Johannesburg'. For all the world we are still there. Except for Leon and me of course. We could not have married in the old days, him being coloured and all. Doctor Dutoit would not even have filled Leon's teeth.

How graciously they tolerate us now. We have breezed in from our communal plot in the outer limits of the mega-city these people are too afraid to visit.

'Not without an AK-4777 rifle,' my father has said.

Instead they ruminate in this, the last of the shrunken ghettos that began to decline when cheap labour went out. Not for them the spread of shebeens and malls that splash jazz from what used to be poverty-stricken township to the City Hall. The place we now call Soweto City. Connected by skyway and flyway, over the underground, as steady as the steel and the foreign funding on which it runs. Talk about one door closing. The Old Order was not yet cold in its grave and the place was gyrating, like a woman in love.

And the people out there? There are millions of us — living the good life advertised by laser-honed graphics that dazzle the streets. We are fast-living. Street-wise. Natural. We till the land. Our food is organic. See this party dress? It's made of paper. Tomorrow I'll shred it. Recycle later.

I thank heavens for Leon. I envy him his equilibrium. Forgive and forget. That's what he said before we came here tonight. His kind of thinking has helped me cope with the effect my parents have on me.

'Thank the Lord Leon's surname is also Laubscher. Some people will never know,' is all they said when I told them about our marriage.

Dad is the perfect host. But earlier this evening his sentimentality got the better of him when Uncle Otto reminded him of the New Year's Eve parties, five times the size of this one, held at our old house. Foreign diplomats, caviar, black truffles in Italian rice. Now he embraces Ethel. One-two. One-two. He dances a little jig with her on the veranda, cooled by the breeze that fans the palm tree. I squirm, reminded of the way he used to cavort when the hotel was in its prime.

'I'm a miner at heart,' he used to say, insisting that the place was a private sideline of no consequence.

Was anyone fooled into believing it was anything but a thriving business? We had more maids than rooms that needed polishing in our double-storey house. My parents had owned three game farms and four cars. A relic of the Old Regime, my father will never forgive the New Order for destroying his life-style. I am sure that in his dreams he still sells the kisses of angels to those who would cross the forbidden colour line by night, endorse it by day.

'Would you like to dance?' asks Paul Schoeman, once the minister of Law and Order. 'Mona Lisa ...,' sings Nat King Cole. I shuffle. Our feet collide. He holds me close, looks into my eyes and says, 'How can you live in the native township?'

I am unable to persuade old Schoeman that the change has brought with it a downswing in crime. I say all the things my father will not hear. But like Dad he does not grasp a word about redistribution. About progress. How can they when they insist without blinking that English and Afrikaans are still the official languages?

'You talk too much,' he says and pulls me towards him, gripping me so tightly that my left nipple sets off his security panic button, the kind my parents pay a fortune to wear round their necks. A siren wails. Up here on the veranda, men remove the fleshy fingers they have been rolling over their wives' naked, sagging backs. The whites of the wives' eyes show. Paul Schoeman grabs my breast. I scream. I put my hands to my ears. I want to block out the wailing. The barking of the Rottweilers. The jibbering of the guests. Four armed response security guards appear. Their sobriety creates a striking contrast.

They are not amused when my father says, 'False alarm. Who let the dogs out?' Leon is nowhere to be seen.

'Have a snack,' mother offers. It is anchovy, tart and salty.

'Is it nearly time for champagne?' I want to know.

'It won't be long now,' says Dad, as if he were meting out a punishment.

'What is the time?' shouts someone. One minute to midnight, says my watch. My father pours me another whisky.

'Be patient,' he commands. Any minute now, I tell myself.

'To the year two thousand!' I shout. 'To the future!'

'There is nothing to look forward to.' Dad's voice is weighed down. Now two of him are saying, 'This is the future.' The thick curl of his cigar smoke throws me back into a time when I believed that he had power over the planets. Now I am starting to believe that my father is actually capable of holding back midnight. I want to call the security guards with their military boots and pistols to return.

'Do you want to see the real danger we face here tonight?' I will ask. Then I will see what they can do about the fear that washes this party like a backward-moving current.

I am standing alone when it happens. The blackness of the sky is spoilt as fire crackers explode brightly into two million broken stars. An ethereal chorus resounds above the voice of Nat King Cole, above the marabi jazz that plays on Station Nnwe in the background. As the heavens shift, time dissolves and my rapture rises.

Down below, the profusion of papyrus plants, the beds of lobelia, chrysanthemum and wild hydrangea, the lawn that is overrun with weeds are illuminated by an unearthly light. 'Happy New Year!' Leon embraces me from behind. 'Did you hear what Manzwe said?' he asks.

From a great distance, I hear my father saying that there is still one minute to go.

DEENA PADAYACHEE

The Finishing Touch

From: *The Finishing Touch* (1992)

The shebeen was full of raucous people having a great old time. But Satha noticed that his friend Muthu didn't look too happy. The old man had come into the shebeen a few minutes before and simply plopped down into a chair. He had taken his first drink in one gulp and was now staring at his empty glass like a zombie. That wasn't like Muthu, ruminated Satha, not like Muthu at all. Satha went over to Muthu and focused bleary eyes glassily on his friend. He asked him why he was looking so depressed.

'That Trishen's robbing me blind, man.'

'He's running your Shakas hardware shop for you, eh, Muthu?'

'Ja, and the money he's bringing in isn't 'nough to pay the bleddy rent!'

'But why for you renting that small shop when you own a nice, big hard-ware store next to your house?'

'It's for the licence – I run my big business on that small business's licence.'

'Ja,' Satha nodded sympathetically, 'I suppose it's difficult for our people to get a licence for a business?'

'Ja, man. Where a coolie like me's gonna get a licence from the Wurropean man?'

'Ja, that's true ... white people don't like giving us business licences, pity, man.'

'Ja,' commented Muthu, 'Europeans don't like competition from us Indians.'

Satha contemplated Muthu's morose face for a while. Then he said, 'Why you don't change your name? You know, to white people's name?'

'What! Can't do dat!'

'But can, man. Look my cousin-brother, his name's Jaybalan ... white people call him Jesse. He change his surname from Appadu to Appolos. That's a Greek name. When he write letter now to white man, the white man think him foreign-white man. He now getting top-class foreign-white treatment! You know foreign-whites getting best treatment in our country?'

'But he can only do this when he's writing to somebody?'

'Ja, but man, he getting lot privileges with letters ... because they thinking him one *witou*, not a bloody coolie!'

'But that must have been long ago?'

'No man, it's happening now. Yay! You go, change name from Coopoosamy to something important sounding. Now what I heard that Major Tate calling you? What was it, let me see … Cooper, that's it, COOPER!'

'Go 'way man, you mad!'

'How then you gonna get licence? That Trishen's getting fat. You wasting time, money on that Shakas shop. You can't be two places one time. You got to look after one shop, man.'

'Ja, but the white man will never let me get a white man's name. Besides I'm not Christian.'

'Look, you Tamil, you always Tamil. This white name's just to bluff the *witous*. White name don't make you Christian. My cousin Jaybalan, he not Christian just because white people call him Jesse.'

'Ja, but I don't know, my family always had Indian name. What are my relatives gonna think?'

'Your relatives, they not clever like you. If they had half your brains they'd make money like you, and they too would have English names. What use our Indian names? Only get us into trouble.'

Muthu suddenly looked serious and sober, 'Ja, but it's like spitting on our ancestors, our culture; our names are symbolic of everything that gives us a rich heritage, our identity …'

'Addah, man, what you talking? What's in a name? One name's as good as another. And you know for the white man we're nothing. We just non–whites. He know nutting 'bout our culture, 'bout us. We nothing for him. At least when we use his name we might get somewhere … you not cross when the white customers call you Michael or Cooper?'

'No, I'm not cross. But I donno, Satha, fifty years I been Muthusamy Coopoosamy, now suddenly you want me to be become Michael Cooper … I don't know whether I can adjust to it.'

'For more than twenty years the white people kept name Michael for you. All you doing is making the thing legal, that's all.'

'Hell, I don't know …'

'You'll adjust, man, we Indians know lot 'bout 'dapting. We good at it. The white man, he always closing the front door and we always finding the back door, the side door …'

'Heck, Satha, I feel lousy 'bout this; these damn white people …they name us like they name their cats and dogs and now we add insult to injury by going one step farther and making their 'pet-names' legal …'

Satha was not to be put off, 'Well, you might feel bad about it, but man, it serves a higher purpose. It's gonna help your upliftment.'

Muthu looked away from Satha. For a few moments he became oblivious to the noise around him. He stared into space, much as he did when he played chess, and pondered what Satha had said. In a crazy way it made sense. It was not the first time he had been forced to eat humble pie in order to get ahead. And it was the kind of tactic that had helped people like him to survive.

'We make it by using the opportunity, seizing the initiative, not by sitting on our backsides and letting events overwhelm us! Sometimes it paid to sacrifice the Bishop and gain the Queen,' he reflected to himself. A gleam came into his eyes.

Satha noticed the change in Muthu's face. 'Look,' he said, 'I got one lawyer friend. He tell you.'

The lawyer confirmed Satha's story. Muthu thought about the matter for a few more weeks but there was no hope of getting his hardware licence through a normal application. It was a big thing changing his name, yet he had got used to being called Michael and Cooper. Even his friends and most of the Africans and Indians were calling him by these names. His wife didn't object and he had no children. He thought she actually liked the white name and often called him Michael. It was becoming the vogue for Indians to have shortened English names like Pat for Pathmanandan or Terence for Thenageran. Muthu felt very afraid and nervous, but he decided to put his faith in God and do what was necessary. He had very little land – certainly not enough to farm and survive on. So he had set up a hardware store in a *bundu* when other people thought that he was mad to do so. But he had stocked what the farmers had wanted and his prices were keen. He had behaved with humility and the white farmers had not felt threatened. It was to their advantage to buy from him rather than go to the distant white town and buy hardware.

So Muthu made the long journey to the Department of Indian Affairs in Tegwhite to change his name. He was directed through a maze of offices (and was often given wrong directions by irritable clerks) till he finally arrived at the section that handled many things, including name-changes. The waiting area was empty. The only person in the front office was an Indian clerk who was busy writing at his desk. The man noticed the sheepish-looking, badly dressed Indian come into the office but he continued writing. There were no seats in the reception area and there was just the one solitary desk behind the counter. A plastic name-plate on the desk proclaimed, 'Ahmed Mayet'. Muthu could see a closed door at the back of Ahmed's open office. The fancy brass name-plate had emblazoned on it: SENIOR SUPER-VISOR and below it in elegant capitals: MR BALLARD. Muthu stood respectfully for a minute thinking that the important-looking clerk had noticed him. After another minute Muthu gave a discreet cough. Ahmed ignored the lone, dark man. Then a white man entered the office. Ahmed put on a warm, welcoming, obsequious smile and said, as he stood up: 'Good afternoon, Mr Nicholson, sir! Can I help you, sir?'

'Hello, Ahmed! Yes, I'm just going to see Mr Ballard.' The white man was already entering Ahmed's office through the swing-door. Ahmed's smile widened and Mr Nicholson urbanely breezed through into Mr Ballard's office after barely a knock and calling out of his name.

'Eh, excuse me, sir,' Muthu asked.

But Ahmed acted as if Muthu was not there. The old man didn't know what to do. He needed help from the clerk, and he couldn't afford to get upset, so he waited meekly. Finally, after a further two minutes Ahmed stopped writing and deigned to cast an imperial glance at what looked at him to be a country bumpkin.

'Ja?' he barked, his hand still holding his pen.

'Please, sir,' said Muthu in a plaintive tone as if he was back at school, 'I want to change … to change my name.' Muthu was hunched forward in his shabby clothes clenching his hat in his hands.

He looked thoroughly servile. Ahmed grinned to himself. This was going to be an amusing day after all!

'Ja, well, what is your name now?'

'Muthu, sir, Muthusamy Coopoosamy.'

'So, what are you going to change your name to? Poo-poo or Coopoo?' Ahmed grinned.

'No, sir.' Years of bureaucratic rudeness and insults had largely inured Muthu to any minor attacks launched by second-rate front-office clerks. With great dignity, as if he was already a white man, Muthu said, 'I want to become, eh … I want to be called … I mean …'

'Yes man, out with it. What's going to be your new name?'

'Michael, sir. Michael Cooper!' Even Muthu couldn't believe he had so much effrontery.

'What?' Ahmed said, his eyes bulging. His pale face turned a shade of pink and he pushed his glasses back. This coal-black coolie wanted a white man's name. Everybody knew that lots of coolies were crazy but this …!

Ahmed had some white blood in him and he felt that he was more entitled to take on a white man's name than this, this … But he had stuck to his own name. Now here was a coolie with the gall …

He struggled to maintain his composure and asked, 'Why do you want a white man's name?'

'Oh no, sir, it's not that, it's not that at all; it's just that I got a business and my European customers, they always call me Mike or Michael. My name Muthusamy … well, it's difficult for white people to say. Then, all the white people they calling me Cooper instead of Coopoosamy. Me, I'm thinking, Michael Cooper is a nice-sounding name … and it's not wrong, because the clever white people … they're already calling me like that. So I thought nice to make it legal on the passbook.' Muthu had spoken earnestly and respectfully and Ahmed had listened attentively.

'Really? Well, I don't know about this. Why aren't you proud to be an Indian and have a nice Indian name? You can change your name if you want, but change it to an Indian name. Otherwise the white people, they might get suspicious.'

'Begging pardon, sir, but this way I make things easy for the white man … and this is the white man's country.' Ahmed shook his head … the tricks the coolies got up to: they were too much. He had heard the Europeans say that you couldn't keep them down no matter what you did. They were too cunning, that was the trouble, said the Europeans.

And he knew that the new laws allowed people to change their names to just about anything. That was bad. Soon you'd have a whole lot of subversives changing their names to that of seditious people like Mandela or Gandhi. This reform business was really getting out of hand. The non-whites really didn't seem to know their place anymore and 'elevated' non-whites like himself who were so indispensable to the white baas were coming increasingly under pressure.

Reluctantly he pushed the necessary forms across to Muthu and told him to advertise the name change in the white daily newspaper three times in three weeks.

Muthu felt as if he was walking on air when he left the office. 1969 might be a lucky year after all.

Two months after the advertisements appeared in the paper and after he had personally handed the application forms to Ahmed, Muthu had still not been given official notification of the name change. He went in to see Ahmed. Ahmed found it difficult to ignore the bumbling old man completely and after only two minutes he spoke to him.

'Yes?'

'Please, sir, when will I be informed of my name change? It's gone more than two months now. There haven't been any objections to my name change, have there, sir?'

'No, there haven't been any objections but you must be patient, Coo-poo-sammy, these things take time. Many important Government Departments must be notified of this thing you want to do. My supervisor, Mr Ballard, is a very busy man. The government can't be hurried, you know. You must be very grateful that we allowed you to do all these things.' Ahmed didn't think it was right that a grand thing like a white man's name should come easily to a coolie.

But Muthu was getting a bit irritated now. (Almost like a white man, he reflected to himself with mild surprise.)

'But sir,' he remonstrated, 'I have filled in all the forms and I have advertised as you instructed at great personal expense and nothing's happened.'

Ahmed looked at the Indian with astonishment. Was the fellow completely barmy? Did he think that a white man's name made him even slightly into a white man? The old man was even speaking with a degree of confidence that was not there before and he stood a lot straighter. He was actually looking Ahmed in the eye. This was a coolie who needed to be kept in his place! He had not passed the Cooper file across to Mr Ballard. Now he wondered idly whether he ever should?

'You must go home and wait, Mr Coo-poo-sammy,' he said sternly. 'Patience. Patience is a virtue that certain races will do well to imbibe,' he added in the same tone of voice that he had heard the Europeans use when they said that sort of thing. The blank bureaucratic wall was impenetrable. Muthu left.

However three weeks later, Muthu was finally summoned to appear before Supervisor Ballard. Dressed impeccably (after all, he was going to see a white man this time) by Satha in a new three-piece suit and tie, old man Muthu presented himself at the Indian Affairs office. Nowadays he brought a book along that he was studying, so that he could keep himself busy while Ahmed made him wait. The book was *Learn To Speak English Properly*.

He arrived ten minutes early for his appointment but Ahmed only allowed him to see the European half an hour later.

Trying to look as harmless as possible, Muthu entered the office and stood respectfully at attention till the white man decided to look at him. It was a very large, very untidy office full of files and books all thrown higgledy-piggledy all over the place. After about a minute the official cast a scalding look at Muthu as if he was a horrible filthy mess and curtly addressed him from his sitting position.

'Now what's all this about you wanting to change your name to a ...?' Ballard couldn't bring himself to say it.

He was a big, hairy, fat man with a huge beer belly that made him look many months pregnant. His brown safari suit bulged in an unseemly manner over his abdomen. His hair was an unruly brown thatch. Ballard was not yet fifty and had lived the good life in what had been a model colony. But now things were changing ... as was personified by this ebony, cringing little toad. The awful expression on the pink man's face was thoroughly intimidating. This was a cold, hostile wall that Muthu was facing, somehow worse than Ahmed outside. At least with Ahmed you felt that beyond all the crude harassment was a fellow-being with at least some feeling, that the silly superciliousness was in a sense childish playfulness. But this ... this was a cruel monster. Muthu thought that the official could quite easily issue a decree for him to lose his business or be kicked out of his home without so much as a twinge of his Christian conscience.

He waited for the supervisor to complete the sentence, but then he finally said, 'Sir, I'm not trying to be difficult. I serve the white people, sir. They call me Cooper. Mr Tate is a rich farmer, sir, he told me Cooper is a nice name for me, sir. With respect, sir, I'm not trying to be a cheeky coolie, sir.' Muthu had rehearsed his defence many times at home and he felt quite pleased with his delivery. Even Mr Stevenson, the author of the English book, might have been satisfied, reflected Muthu.

'Well, I don't know about that ...' Ballard glared at the uncomfortable-looking coolie and remembered that he had named his dog, Caesar. Well, what was wrong with the name Cooper for a coolie? It was a good Anglo-Saxon name and perhaps it was all part of the march of Western culture. The Amercian Negroes had lost all their own names and languages. Perhaps that was the destiny of the Indians too. Besides, whatever name the coolies used, they were still coolies. Muthu had known that he would be treated provocatively, but as he had planned, he kept cool.

With a great deal of effort he suppressed the anger welling up within him and continued in an even voice, 'I beg your pardon, sir, but I have a letter from Major Tate, sir.'

'Really?' Ballard was surprised. The Indian handed the Supervisor the letter. Ballard opened the sealed envelope. It was neatly typed and stated:

TO WHOM IT MAY CONCERN

I have known Muthusamy Coopoosamy for the last thirty years. During that time he has rendered valuable service to the local European farming community through his hardware and poultry businesses. He has often served us even on Sundays. During that time he has become known to the local farmers as Michael and at times has been referred to as Michael Cooper. He has always been of a co-operative disposition and I am sure that a name change will merely legalise what has become a statement of fact.

It was signed with a large flourish by the Major. Ballard was impressed. This was the right sort of coolie, then; not one of your agitators. And is seemed the ape was serious about this name-change thing. Ballard played with his little beard, enjoying the feeling of the fur and the sense of sexual power he always revelled in when he tormented a non-white, much like a cat playing with a cockroach. Suddenly he transfixed the Indian with his cold 'white man' look and said imperiously, 'You may go.'

Muthu slid out of the office feeling very inferior, very stupid and a real nuisance. Why had he let Satha talk him into this crazy thing?

After another month, Muthu came into Ahmed's waiting room. This time after only a minute, Ahmed said, with just a touch of irritation, 'Yes?' Muthu was tired of everything: coming here, being treated like a pest, everything. But he had spent good money on this thing and it was only right that he got what he had paid for. After all, what he was doing was not against the white man's law. Muthu didn't say anything. He just looked with a haggard expression on his face at the clerk.

Ahmed stood up, threw his pen down on his desk and said, 'Ah, Mr Coo-poo-samy! We've got to know you well!' He grinned at the old man and came over to the counter. He leaned over and said in a confidential, conspiratorial tone, 'You know, old man, the trouble with us Indians (Ahmed's heart almost gave a lurch when he said this. He didn't really think of himself as an Indian, well, not the ordinary kind of Indian anyway) is that we tend to work very hard on doing something like building a fine temple, but we lack the finishing touch. What the white people call *finesse*. You know, an Indian will sweat blood to build a house, but he won't spend a rand on getting his grass verge cut … Indians will build a magnificent Temple but they'll pay the priest peanuts. An Indian will study hard and qualify as a doctor but he'll talk like a motor-mechanic. Now people like us, you know what I mean,' Ahmed winked a few times at the old man and gave a conspiratorial grin, 'who try for something better with our lives …' Muthu's face feigned ignorance. Ahmed continued, 'Oh, come on now, you know what I mean. We are birds of a feather, you and I. You trying to take on a white man's name like Cooper of all things, and me here …well if you want a white man's name, you better learn to be a little like him …'

'You mean this *finesse* thing?'

'Precisely, old man, precisely!' Who said you couldn't teach an old dog new tricks, thought Ahmed. 'Look here, Muthu,' he growled, 'you don't look stupid to me. (Well not completely stupid, cogitated Ahmed.) But things haven't come right for you, because you haven't put the "finishing touch" to this thing!'

'Finishing touch, sir?'

'Yes, man; the "finishing touch" – a bit of gravy; you know what I mean, some butter on the toast, a bit of grease on the …'

Ahmed looked knowingly at the Indian. For a few moments Muthu was puzzled but then suddenly the devious expression on the clerk's face made sense. 'Have to learn to be a little like the white man,' thought Muthu. 'Is there anything in particular you would like, sir, I mean in the way of gravy?'

'Well, I happen to know that Mr Ballard likes chicken *biryani* … and his mouth absolutely waters for *dhall-roti* … Now if you could see your way clear to …'

'Oh, certainly sir, most stupid of me, sir! I have a little poultry farm I run on the side, sir. Do you think Mr Ballard, and you, would like some eggs too, sir?' Ahmed's face was one big wolfish grin.

Satha and his friend were drinking, and why not? This time they had good reason: they had something to celebrate!

'Mr Cooper, sir, now that you have Trishen in your big shop and under your thumb, are you going to squeeze?'

'Like a white man, Satha, like a white man! With *finesse*, Satha, with loads of ice-cold, decorous *finesse*!'

'Ice-cold *what*?'

'Decorous finesse, Satha, decorous finesse. It means to handle something carefully … with a fine, delicate touch. I'm reading all the books the white people read, Satha. They can't stop us doing that.'

'Really, Mu, I mean Michael.' Satha's eyes were bloodshot and bulging. He was really impressed. He gripped his drink tightly in his left hand and stared at Mr Cooper.

'Yes, man, and I listen to them very carefully when they talk, the white people. Don't you think that I am beginning to sound like them now?'

'Mr Cooper, sir, I think you are.'

'And I've enrolled in a Speech and Drama class … you just wait and see; soon, when I talk to you on the phone you won't be able to make out that Mr Cooper is anything but a dyed-in-the-wool Englishman.'

'Died in the *what*?'

Michael grinned. 'A pukka Englishman, Satha. A real, honest-to-goodness English bulldog!'

'Ja man, that's true; that's how you sound.' Michael gave his friend a benign look of self-assured superiority much like that he had so often seen the whites give the non-whites.

'Well, let's celebrate now, eh, Mike. These days you even drinking like a *witou*!' He held up his drink with a flourish. 'Here's to your new name, Michael, here's to your hardware licence, to the Licensing Bureau, to Capitalism, here's to …'

Michael clicked glasses with Satha: 'To the Indian Affairs bums … to Western Civilisation, to Free Enterprise, and Satha …?'

'Yes, my friend?'

'Here's to the Finishing Touch!'

SINDIWE MAGONA

The Sacrificial Lamb

From: *Push-Push! and other Stories* (1996)

Before Siziwe was fully awake, the receiver – cold, hard and decidedly un-friendly – jabbed at the not-fully-awake flesh in the hollow between her shoulder, the pillow, and her ear. She did not remember how it had got there. There was a vague memory of the phone ringing; but even as she had strug-gled to hold it, sleep had left her in frustrating confusion with a tantalising overlap between reality and dream. But, of course, the phone must have rung, otherwise why had she picked up the receiver? And now, to the remote peep-peep announcing an overseas call she mumbled, 'Hello?' – relief washing through her. It was not the police, calling about her daughter, Fezi. She glanced at the bedside clock-radio thinking, *where, on earth, is that child?* Just then, a voice came through the line.

'Hello? Is that you, Sisi?'

'Yes, it's me. Who is this?' She no longer recognised the voices, her nieces sounded so grown to her whether on the phone or in their infrequent letters. No doubt, Siziwe was sure, distance and nostalgia accelerated and augmented the changes she perceived: with them … with her.

'Is everything all right?' she asked; a new anxiousness replacing the earlier worry. What if her mother were ill? What would she do then? Go home? Or sweat it out here till …? What would be the point of going then? But even as she argued with herself in her mind, she knew: of course, she would go.

'Sisi, it's me, Nozipho. Everything is fine; after a manner of speaking, that is. What else can we say?'

'What has happened? Is Ma okay?'

'Mama is okay. She says can you call her back?' And before she could say yea or nay, there was a clang and the line went dead.

She leapt out of bed and went to make herself a cup of coffee. Might as well make myself comfortable, she thought. Calling Gala was never a simple operation. The call had to go via the telephone exchange … and the Gala Telephone Exchange was slack and inept, and often the lines were down.

The coffee burned her throat the way she liked it. Her mind went back to that long-ago day, the day she had not known would be her last for her to see her father. One would have thought there was a way of feeling, of sensing, of somehow presaging such an event; a kind of body seismograph, reading her the foreshadowing symptoms. But no, despite her great love for him, she had looked at her father, talked to him and then walked away from him with a casual goodbye. Next thing she knew, the sturdy tree that had given her shade from scorching sun and shelter from the storms of life had fallen.

On the second attempt, much to her amazement, she got through.

'Hello, Sisi? It's still me, Nozipho. There's something I forgot to tell you.'

'Yes, Zips? What is it?' She tried not to think of the money she was paying, listening to idle chatter. Sheer waste.

'I have written you a letter and given it to Bhuti Wallace. He is coming there and we gave him your address and telephone number. Please, Sisi, do respond positively to my request. Do not disappoint me, you know I have no one else I can depend on.'

'What is it?'

'No, I can't say it now. Wait till you get the letter.'

'That bad, is it?'

'No, it's not!' A burst of thrilling laughter fractured her speech. 'Sisi, I must get off this phone.' Siziwe knew what was coming. She could hear her mother grumbling in the background. 'Ma is giving me her wicked look. You know her. Bye, Sis'.'

'Bye!' Had she heard? wondered Siziwe for her 'bye' collided with her mother's 'Hello, Siziwe!' as belaboured breathing replaced Nozipho's breezy prattle on the line.

'Hello, Ma! Are you all right?'

'Siziwe, my child, the Lord keeps on minding us. But the devil is also busy, derailing us every which way we turn.'

'What is the matter?' And she had the presence of mind to stop short of adding the 'now' burning the tip of her tongue. But the irritation seared her brain. Can they never call just to see how I am doing? Is each telephone call always only going to be about some catastrophe?

'Ma Tolo is in hospital.' There was a slight pause, no doubt her mother waiting to hear her reaction to this piece of news. But Siziwe waited too ... Whatever she said would end up upsetting her mother; she did not seem ever to come up with anything kind to say about her eldest brother; a complete wash-out of a man.

'Our kind neighbour, Majola, took him to Gunguluza Hospital in his car.'

'What is the matter with him?' This time she was forced to say something since her mother had gone silent on her.

'We really don't know what happened to him. Saturday, early evening, some people come and told us that he was lying, face down, at the corner of NY 1 and NY 3. When we got there, we couldn't even recognise him. Half his face had caved in, probably hit with a brick – what they call the Wonder Loaf here.

He was completely covered in blood that had already caked. As yet, no witnesses have come forward to say who did what to him.'

'But what about him? What does he say happened?'

'He can't even say one word, my child. All he does is groan. He does not even recognise those who have been to see him. I, myself, have not been to see him; could not bring myself to go … no, I just couldn't go and see him looking like that … like a corpse.'

'I am sorry, Ma. I'm really sorry.' And, to her surprise, she realised that she meant what she said. Of course, she was only sorry for the worry MaTolo's troubles always caused her mother. Her sisters and brothers were slowly killing the poor woman; ageing her and wearing her down fast with all the troubles they visited on her: drunken brawls, job loss caused by bad work habits, unemployment due to lack of qualifications, and a host of other causes besides. The same problems that plagued everybody else in the black townships … why did she allow these things to disarrange her? Why would her family be any different from all the others?

Once more, her father's words of farewell led her to a decision. Often had she wondered whether they were a blessing or a curse. '*Mna, kuphela eyam intlungu yeyenyama*. My pain is only that of the flesh.' Thus had he thanked her … or, perhaps ordered is more like it … for those words had forever after directed her actions … especially towards her mother.

Even so far away, in this strange land, among people whose ways were stranger still, she still heard those words. *While other men in this ward cry, not because of physical pain but because they do not know what their children will eat that very day or a man's family is being thrown out of the house because they owe rent money, I am at peace because you, my daughter, see to the needs of the family.*

'So, we thought we should ask for some help from you, my child.' Her mother's voice broke into Siziwe's reflections. 'I know we are forever bothering you with all these stupid problems these children are always getting themselves into. But, what else can we do? Who else can we turn to?'

There was a moment's awkward silence. The unspoken words … '*Now that your father is no longer here*' … heavy between them.

Had her father, in thanking her for giving the family financial support, in fact appointed her his surrogate?

'You must help us, my child.'

'Of course, Ma.' She was embarrassed. 'What did you think I should do?' Of course, that too was just formality. She knew exactly why they had called her … why they always and invariably called her: Money.

'Whatever little money you can send us, will help. We have to go to the hospital to see him. What would people think and how would he feel? We can't abandon him there all on his own … and at a time like this.'

The next morning, a Monday, she got up half an hour earlier than she usually did. She liked to start her workday punctually and purposefully; more so Mondays. She was dressed and getting ready to leave when a groggy voice asked her, 'Want a cup of coffee, Mother, dearest?' Siziwe did not trust herself to say a word in reply. But the look she gave Fezi was more eloquent than anything she could have come up with.

By nine, she had made the transfer from Chemical Bank to her mother's account with Volkskas Bank in Elliot, the nearest town to Cala that boasted such facilities as banks. Over a cup of coffee, she thought about Fezi. *Hope she makes it to class.* When the girl had eventually found her way home the previous night, Siziwe had no idea. Mama's call had come well after two; nearer three than two in fact. And after the call she had gone to see whether Fezi was in her room. Not getting a reply to her knock, she'd gently pushed the door open. And the serene bed so incensed her, blind tears rolled down her cheeks before she even knew she was crying. How many times had she told the girl, 'All I ask is that when you are busy having fun, I should not be lying awake in bed, wondering if the next telephone call will be the police, telling me you've been shot or strangled; raped, robbed or pushed in front of a moving train.'

But her daughter behaved as though the mother were a big fusspot. As if these horrendous things were not happening, every day, in the city where they made their home. As if they were something Siziwe just conjured up to frighten herself and use to chain her daughter to the house. But then, that is the privilege of the young, the singular lack of fear of death; completely believing in their own immortality.

After work, she stopped for Happy Hour at The Ritz, a cosy little restaurant patronised by the foreigners because of its international cuisine. She was meeting Nomsa, a fellow South African who had lived in New York for almost thirty years. As usual, before long their talk was about home, the country, its people and, more particularly, their families.

'Hey, Siziwe, do you want to hear the latest about my crazy family?' When she nodded her head, knowing full well that whether she wanted to hear Nomsa's news or not, hear it she would, Nomsa told her, 'My sister is unbelievable! Do you remember her?' There was a pause but not for long. Nomsa answered herself, 'I've told you so much about her, you must. This is a woman, over forty, who dropped out of university. She is so bright, she had a first-class matric pass, passed the first two years in college with flying colours, but then, despite our advice, despite our protestations, decided she wanted to get married.

'Well, of course, that didn't last. Two children. No profession. Too proud of "My University Education" to do any job unless it is not beneath madam's status.

'Doesn't she call me, collect? Do you know how many times I have told her not to do that? Unless, of course, it is absolutely necessary: a death or grave illness, something of that nature.

'But no, each time she goes on a binge, she remembers she has this rich sister in America and calls me, but I have to pay for those calls. She is not that drunk she forgets that an overseas telephone call costs a lot of money.'

'I also had a call from home yesterday … or, early this morning, I should say.' Siziwe interrupted, still smarting from the hole the morning's withdrawal had made in her savings.

'Ah, but your family, listen to me, your family is reasonable. Mine? Mine, is something else, believe me!'

Siziwe started to tell her about her mother's call. Then, somehow, Fezi's staying out the whole night, '… for she must have come in well after four' – came in and took centre stage.

'I miss having my family help me with the children. You know, at home, this wouldn't be just my problem alone. Her uncles, my brothers, would help. So would Mama. She would talk to her, show her how to behave herself.'

'Yes, that's true,' replied Nomsa. 'Our extended family is truly a blessing. One is never alone, whatever travails one is facing.'

Siziwe nodded her head, thinking of her mother and the strength she drew from her, just knowing she was there. Whatever would she do if anything happened to her mother? She told Nomsa, 'You know something? Often, when I'm troubled, I will pick up the phone and call Mama. But, when I hear her voice, realise how far she is, I ask myself: Why should I bother her with my little troubles? She would only worry. And the Lord knows, she needs that like she needs a second head on her shoulders. And, do you know what? Just hearing her voice; just knowing she is there, I already feel better.'

'Remember what you said, some time ago?' Nomsa was looking at her expectantly.

'No. What?' Which of the numerous things she had said to Nomsa over the years was the other referring to? Well, Nomsa would just have to remind her. Siziwe waited, eyebrows raised in question.

'You said, "Those of us who are supposed to have 'made it' are the ones whom, for whatever reason, the ancestors have chosen as sacrificial lambs for the family!"'

'Oh that? Sure,' said Siziwe, 'but this is slaughter! And when will I save for old age? Things are changing and I would be a big fool if I expected my children to look after me when I am retired.'

'Very true, my friend. But, as you yourself have said, we are helped to be successful, so that the family may endure. How else would so many of us have survived apartheid … were it not for those who, despite overwhelming odds, "made it" to where they could support us?'

814

LEKOTSE'S TESTIMONY AT THE TRC

[retold by Antjie Krog]

The Sheep-herder's Tale

From: *Country of my Skull* (1998)

Krog: The next morning on my way to town I take a detour through the countryside. As far as the eye can reach there is rooigras. I stop. I once wrote: 'I adore *Themeda Triandra* the way other people adore God.' I want to lie down. I want to embrace. I want to sing the shiny silk stems upwards. I want to ride the rust-brown seeds, the rustling frost-white growth around ankles. Grass, red grass bareback against the flanks. This is my landscape. The marrow of my bones. The plains. The sweeping veld. The honey-blonde sandstone stone. This I love. This is what I'm made of. And so I remain in the unexplainable wondrous ambuscade of grass and light, cloud and warm stone. As I stand half-immersed in the grass crackling with grasshoppers and sand, the voices from the town hall come drifting on the first winds blowing from the Malutis – the voices, all the voices of the land. The land belongs to the voices of those who live in it. My own bleak voice among them. The Free State landscape lies at the feet at last of the stones of saffron and amber, angel hair and barbs, dew and hay and hurt.

★ ★ ★

Lekotse: My family was affected since that day. The woman who has testified before me is a picture of my wife. She cannot walk. She goes for treatment. I also go for treatment at Botshabelo Hospital. I took my *last* tablet this morning. Now my life was affected since that day. It was at night …

[Testimony in seSotho; interpreted by Lebohang Matibela]

Ilan Lax: I want to know about your children first.

Lekotse: I have ten children, two have passed away … now – on the day of this assault I was with three children at home and the grandchildren – five

815

in number and they go to school – some of my grandchildren belong to my son who is mentally disturbed. The last-born has a pair of twins. Their father is also mentally disturbed …

Lax: Just try not to speak directly into the microphones … they are very sensitive and will pick up your voice very nicely. Which of these children are still living with you and your wife?

Lekotse: I am staying with Thomas Lekotse, my son, he is now the bread-winner and he is also taking care of the one that I just said is mentally disturbed.

Lax: Can you tell us about the incident that happened. Was it in May 1993?

Lekotse: Maybe you're right – you know my problem is, I was a shepherd. I cannot write and I forget all these days, but I still … Can I repeat what I said earlier on about the harassment? Now listen very carefully, because I'm telling you the story now.

On that day it was at night, a person arrived and he knocked. When I answered, the door just opened and I said, 'Who's knocking so terribly?' He answered, he said: 'Police.' And I said, 'What police are knocking on my door this way?' He forced his way through with many policemen. The door was already down. Three policemen were black and the rest were white and they referred to us as kaffirs. Many of them were white. They were together with big dogs – two in number. They said every door of the house should be opened. They pulled clothes from the wardrobes. I said, 'When a jackal gets into the sheep it does not do this – please unpack neatly and pack them back neatly.' They did not provide an answer. They pushed us outside. I felt on my shoulder: *kaboem!* I asked them, 'What do you want?' but they never provided an answer. They pushed us outside.

It was terribly cold on that day. The children were woken up. I said to them, 'Will you provide me with the money to take these children to the doctor?' They did not answer. I said to them, 'Please, the policemen are not supposed to behave this way.' I said, 'When a policeman goes to a farm he stops first at the farmer's house. If the farmer doesn't allow them entry they leave. Now where do you get the permission from to come into my house and break the doors – is this the way you conduct your affairs?' When I looked thoroughly the door was not just kicked, it was even broken down with their gun butts. Even to this day the doors are still broken. My children took pity on me this year, they bought a new door and a new frame and we had to get another person to come and fix the door. At sunrise life began to be easier. They wanted to cut open the wardrobes that were locked. And I said to them, 'How dare you cut open these doors?' I said to my children, 'Prepare tea, prepare coffee for these people, they are hungry.' I asked them, 'Can I offer you beer, can I offer you drink, can I offer you boerewors? Are you hungry?' I said, 'These people are hungry. I have to provide them with food.' I said to them, 'You are not policemen, you are just boers.' One of them pushed me outside – that is where I fell on my shoulder and hurt myself. I was not supposed to speak that way, I admit but because I was hurt and disturbed that day I spoke wrong words. I said, 'I know you policemen are thieves. You want to take us all outside so that you can implicate us. I know. You're going to leave behind diamonds and dagga and you're going to drop them behind and implicate us.' I said, 'You bloody policemen.' That's what I said on that day, because I was hurt.

(audience laughs)

Lax: Please …

Lekotse: I ended up saying to them: 'Look here, my whole family is standing outside. It's cold. I want you to kill all of us now. I'll be very glad if you kill us all. They were … you know, it's a pity I don't have a stepladder. I will take you to my home to investigate …' I asked the policemen, 'What do you want?' They did not provide an answer. I told them: 'I don't have diamonds. I don't have dagga. What do you want?' No answer was given. I said to them, 'You want to leave after breaking my doors? When are you going to come back and fix them?' They said, 'APLA will fix them up.' I asked them: 'What is APLA?' No answer was given. I don't even know what APLA is, I am expecting APLA even today to come and fix my door.

Now it was just about sunrise. My son Thomas said, 'No, go and search in my garage.' They said, 'Where is the garage?' He said, 'Wait, I have to get a key.' And he said, 'You must be very careful – don't scratch my car.' They went into the garage with their dogs – these were fierce-looking dogs. After searching the garage, he said, 'You are not yet finished. I've got another place where you can search. I have a four-roomed house. Go and search. I also have a supermarket. Go and search it too because you don't seem to get what you want.' And they left with him. Now at sunrise they were still at home. They arrested him for the whole month … There were three kaffirs just like myself, the rest were white. They had many vans. The vans were lining the whole road …

Lax: Was your son Thomas connected to APLA or the PAC?

Lekotse: Yes, sir.

Lax: Was he charged with anything?

Lekotse: I do not know whether they attended a court case. You know – an uneducated person is just down. You cannot follow anything. Just like the whites referred to us as dull donkeys. I do not know many things.

Lax: He would have told you if he went to court, wouldn't he?

Lekotse: Can I give you an answer on that?

(long pause)

I taught these children, but because I provided them with education, the whites used to say we have short hair and our brains and minds are just as short. Now these children do not tell us anything. They just go on their own, you just see things happening – they don't provide you with any information.

(audience laughs)

Lax: You indicate that you injured your shoulder. Did you sustain any other injuries?

Lekotse: I was not injured anywhere else – since that day that the jackals came into my house to bite us, I cannot even carry a spade to do gardening. Otherwise I'm not sick, it's just the usual sickness of old age.

Lax: In your statement you mentioned you were injured in your ribs? I'm just helping you to remember.

Lekotse: Are you not aware that the shoulder is related to the *ribs*, sir?

Lax: Did you or your son ever make a case against the police?

Lekotse: We never took any initiative to report this matter to the police, because how can you report policemen to policemen? They were going to attack us. That is why I said to them, 'Kill us all so that there is no trouble thereafter. It is much better to die – all of us.' It was even going to be easy for the government to bury us – they were going to bury us in just one grave. It could have been much better. If one of these policemen is around here, I'll be happy if one of them comes to the stage and kills me immediately …

★ ★ ★

Krog: During the lunch break I walk over to the Co-op with my tape recorder and approach a farmer getting out of his four-wheel drive. 'Sir, how do you feel about the Truth Commission's visit to Ladybrand?' He stops in his tracks. He looks me up and down, while his lip curls in disgust. 'The SABC and the Truth Commission. *Fôkôf!*' he explodes with such venom that passers-by look in our direction. '*Fôkôf! Fôkôf!*' he screams as he storms into the Co-op. I find myself on the pavement, my blood thick with humiliation. God, has nothing – nothing! – changed?

ROSEMARY H MOEKETSI

Guilty as Charged

First published, 1998

I took the witness stand that morning. I was more confident than I had been on Monday. I knew that the white man in black robes, sitting in a commodious chair behind a long desk on an elevated platform, was the magistrate. I knew that he came into the courtroom when everybody else was already there. I knew that everybody had to rise when he entered and left the courtroom. I knew that he addressed the court seated, while everybody else had to stand when they talked to the court. I remembered, also, that he had said very little on that Monday. He had been writing most of the time.

MmaNtlhane had dropped me off earlier because her husband preferred her to be helpful at home, rather than waste time listening to lies in court. Morongwe could not accompany me; she had to take Mama to the Chris Hani hospital for her check-up. Thabiso could not stay away from work and forfeit a day's wages. I was a big girl. I was strong. 1 would manage just fine.

★ ★ ★

'Do you swear that the evidence you will give this court will be the truth, nothing but the truth? Raise your right hand and say: "So help me God."'

The court interpreter explained to me in seSotho that I had to respond to the defence lawyer's questions truthfully. He could have saved his energy because I had been taught the virtues of honesty from childhood.

'Why did you go to the police only three days later?' Mr van Vuuren asked suspiciously.

I had picked up his name on Monday, when the magistrate had repeatedly requested him to allow the court interpreter to complete what he was saying.

'I did not go to the police three days later. I went immediately. I was lucky to find MmaNtlhane home, and she took me there as soon as she heard what had happened to me.'

I was composed. I was no longer scared of this man because I knew that his intentions were to confuse and confound me, to trick me into saying things I might not be able to retract.

'But according to the statement you gave the police on 12 May, you were assaulted on the 9th,' he said contemptuously.

* * *

My father was a humorous person, and I have missed him ever since that treacherous train accident that bereft us of him. He used to say that it was a waste of time to respond to people who made unfounded statements; he would rather allow them to make fools of themselves.

'Is it not true?'

'I was assaulted two Wednesdays ago, sir, when the bus drivers were on strike, and MmaNtlhane took me to the police the same morning.' The court interpreter conveyed my message accurately, in such impeccable English that I suspected it had been specially polished for that occasion. Mr van Vuuren tried to interrupt him by demanding that I answer 'Yes' or 'No', but the interpreter ignored him and continued until he had completed his say. Thus the two engaged in simultaneous talk, like opponents vying for power.

'Please stop interrupting the court interpreter, Mr van Vuuren. I want to hear everything he has to say,' said the magistrate calmly.

He then turned to the court interpreter and requested: 'Could you repeat the witness' evidence?'

I could sense a tinge of victory in the court interpreter's voice as he repeated my answer emphatically, though quietly.

'Why did MmaNtlhane accompany you?' asked the lawyer.

How did he expect me to know? These lawyers spend years at school only to come out and ask stupid questions. Or is this the so-called art of advocacy?

My thoughts were rudely interrupted by Mr van Vuuren's reminder that he had asked me a question and was, therefore, expecting an answer. I looked at the court interpreter with uncertainty and said innocently, 'I have never really asked her.'

This must have enraged the lawyer because he suddenly changed his line of questioning, and bombarded me with a real barrage of short, direct missiles that gave me very little time to breathe. 'What were you doing in Mr Bongani's car?'

'He gave me a lift.'

'Where to?'

'To school, sir.'

'At a quarter to nine?' he asked in feigned and exaggerated disbelief. 'In fact, it was a quarter past nine, sir,' I said, putting stress on 'past'. After all, we had gone over this on Monday.

'What time does school begin?'

He was deliberate in asking this question. I could hear some uneasy shuffling in the audience behind me, and this gave me the confidence that someone was holding thumbs for me. 'School begins at ten to eight, sir.'

'And, at a quarter past nine you were still in the streets?' Instead of thinking that the defence attorney was casting aspersions on me, I could hear my late father laugh at people who make fools of themselves by making unfounded assertions.

'I was at the bus stop, sir, with about seven other children who attend the same school.' He abruptly changed the topic: 'What car did Mr Bongani drive?'

'A white van.'

'What model?'

'I don't know, but it was a very small one, sir. He normally drives it.'

'Did you say you were with seven other schoolchildren?' He made a precipitous return to information already provided, and the magistrate did not take kindly to this.

'Mr van Vuuren …' The magistrate tried to reprimand him, but I had already answered with:

'Yes, sir, that number, roughly.'

'And you got into Mr Bongani's car?' He emphasised the word 'you'. I was not sure whether this was a question. He repeated his question with 'car' lengthened and raised very high. Was he trying to tell the magistrate that I was not responding properly to crucial questions? Did he think that I would deny getting into Mr Bongani's van?

Mr Bongani had called me by my name: 'Mpule, come let me take you to school, my child, you are going to be late. *Azikhwelwa namhlanje.*'

Indeed, no one could board a bus on that Wednesday because the drivers had disputes to resolve with their employers.

Mr Bongani usually visits Ntate Ntlhane. They often sit under the peach tree next to the fence between our house and Ntate Ntlhane's, and drink a beer or two. On several occasions MmaNtlhane has sent me to MaZola's shebeen to buy them their beer, and the men would often give me the small change to spend at school. Mr Bongani has often said that he liked me very much because I hurried with the beer and brought it still ice-cold to them.

'Yes I did.' Was I not expected to seize the opportunity of ultimately arriving at school?

'Yes I did, sir,' I repeated, emphatically.

'What about your friends?'

What friends? What about them?

'What about the other seven children? Why did they not hitch along with you?'

'I don't know, sir.'

I was already used to these questions that expected me to know exactly what was in other people's minds. On the other hand, the magistrate seemed

822

to be running out of patience with Mr van Vuuren's line of questioning. The court interpreter leaned closer to me as though to protect me from anything sinister. I was brave. I was not scared of Mr van Vuuren and his incisive questions. I had already undergone the worst a child of my age could ever imagine.

'Did you tell this court that you alighted from the car and went into Mr Bongani's house?'

'Yes, sir, I did.'

'So you were no longer interested in going to school. Isn't that so?'

'Mr Bongani had left his driver's licence on his dining-room table, sir, and could not drive without it.'

That is what Mr Bongani had said when he turned left into Mokwena Street and stopped at his house. He had asked me to jump out quickly and get the licence from the dining-room table. The front door was not locked, so I just opened it and walked into a room that had no table. This could, therefore, not be the dining room. I went through to the next room and saw a big wooden table with about six chairs around it. This could be the dining room, I thought, but there was nothing that resembled a driver's licence on the neat and shining table. I wondered whether I had to go deeper into the house.

'Is it not there, Mpule?' Mr Bongani, who was already at the door between the first room and the dining room, frightened me because I thought he had remained in the car.

'It must be in the pocket of the trousers I had on yesterday,' he had said, walking through to where those pants apparently were. 'You will also grow old one day and forget where you put your things,' he had continued from somewhere in the house where I could not see him. 'Just look where I put it; even MaBongani would not have found it. Come and see where it is.'

I had obliged.

'Did you follow Mr Bongani to his bedroom?' Mr van Vuuren asked this question with such contempt that I am sure he thought I would be intimidated and humiliated.

'But I did not follow Mr Bongani to his bedroom; I just went to see where he said he had found his driver's licence,' I answered, with an obstinacy that was not characteristic of me.

'Did you, or did you not follow Mr Bongani to his bedroom?' Mr van Vuuren was generous. He gave me two options, and I boldly took the first.

'Now, when you got there, you admired Mr Bongani's luxurious furniture.'

This was, of course, a statement that assumed that I was susceptible to suggestion. How could I admire Mr Bongani's furniture? My mother also has her double bed, a dressing table, chest of drawers and built-in cupboards to hang her clothes in. What was there to admire in Mr Bongani's bedroom? 'You'll grow up and marry one day and have a bed as big and beautiful as this one. MaBongani likes to sleep on a big bed,' Mr Bongani had said, and emphasised that there was nothing wrong with that.

'And you threw yourself on Mr Bongani's bed.' Mr van Vuuren uttered these words slowly and deliberately, looking me squarely in the eyes. He made me so angry I could have skinned him alive with my fingernails.

'I did not ... throw ... my ...' I tried to resist, but choked on my tears.

★ ★ ★

Mr Bongani had pushed me onto the bed, muttering that I should try it and enjoy the pleasures that MaBongani experienced every night. That was completely unexpected. I had resisted. I had fought and kicked and scratched and screamed. He was stronger and heavier, but I was determined to fight him.

I had grabbed something weighty from somewhere and hit him very hard on his forehead. He had stumbled a bit and loosened his grip on me. Our eyes met. Mr Bongani had changed: his eyes were blood red, his hands were trembling, the front of his pants bulged strangely. He was raving mad and made groaning sounds I could not comprehend. I was scared. I crouched. I whined long and loud. Mr Bongani was not moved by my plaintive cry. I hid my face in my hands and whimpered like an exhausted baby left in the cold. I missed my father. He would have had the strength to match Mr Bongani's. I was only twelve.

My mother had warned us against strangers. But Mr Bongani was no stranger. He was Ntate Ntlhane's friend. They had sent me many a time to buy them this or that. He had greeted and chatted with my mother. He had remembered the days when my father was not too busy to join them with Ntate Ntlhane under the peach tree. Mr Bongani was not a stranger.

★ ★ ★

'I did not throw myself onto Mr Bongani's bed. He pushed me,' I gave Mr van Vuuren an exhausted response.

'And you took your clothes off?' Mr van Vuuren continued, as though he had not heard my answer. All the while I was thinking that one normally takes one's clothes off before one 'throws' oneself on the bed.

'I did not, sir. Mr Bongani ripped them off. He tore them to many, many pieces,' I reported accurately.

★ ★ ★

Mr Bongani had behaved like a wild animal. He had groaned and sweated and scared me and I had hid my face in my hands. I was cold and shivering. He had picked me up and thrown me on the bed, and I had crouched and tried to hide behind my hands. I had sobbed and sobbed and sobbed, and he hurt me like I had never been hurt before.

I must have passed out because, all of a sudden, I came to find myself in a small, dark room. Through the cracks in the door I saw that I was in an outside toilet. I opened the door slightly. I was in tatters – inside and out. I was weak and could hardly stand. I was aching all over. I was filthy and smelly, but not dazed. I knew exactly what had happened to me. Mr Bongani had raped me. He had violated me.

I stood up, opened the door and walked out. I found my bearings. This was Moleboheng's home. My home was eight houses away. I walked home, slowly, but determined to get there. Ndlela's dog barked, and I knew this was not a dream. I suddenly remembered that there was nobody at my home, and I therefore went to MmaNtlhane. Luckily, she was there.

I told her. I was not sobbing anymore. I told her everything. She looked at me sadly, put her warm hand on my shoulder, and said: 'Come, my child. Let us go and report this pig to the police.'

★ ★ ★

For the first time I looked around in the courtroom. I saw Mistress Vilakazi; she smiled and I smiled back. I saw Moleboheng and Thato, Morongwe's friends, and knew I was not alone. Then I saw Mr Bongani, and, indeed, he looked like a pig, plodding in a messy pigsty.

'I did not throw myself onto Mr Bongani's bed, sir, neither did I take off my clothes. Mr Bongani ripped them off, sir; he tore them to pieces. He raped me, sir. He violated me, sir.'

I uttered these words softly but boldly, pointing at Mr Bongani. I was not afraid of him. I was not afraid of Mr van Vuuren. They did not scare me. I hated Mr Bongani, and I despised Mr van Vuuren. I respected the court interpreter and I knew he was proud of me.

I looked at the magistrate, and he looked away.

I learned later that my case ought to have been heard privately.

RIANA SCHEEPERS

Book*

Translated from the Afrikaans by Sharon Meyering
From: *Feeks* (1999)

It was in the third year of the lecturer's academic career when it happened. She discovered in herself something unmentionably evil and malicious; a suspicion because of another person, a pool of anger, an emotion so new and overwhelming that she couldn't name it. She – who for three years had remained unaffected in the midst of rioting, student uprisings and striking, bad marks and toyi-toyiing in the lecture theatres; she who unemotionally rejected impertinent students' sexual advances and mercilessly refused the bribes of the desperate; she who had real compassion for the work-fatigued students who bunked evening classes, pregnant students who stayed away for months and on their return demanded that their lost classes be given to them – was enraged with unreasonable anger over a seemingly insignificant incident.

It happened when she saw a student who had just left her office throw her prescribed book in the bin, and guilelessly walk away.

The lecturer saw it by chance. She remembered that she still had to make arrangements for a tutorial and, seconds after the student left her office, walked out after her. And that was when she saw it happen.

Without hesitation, the student tossed the hardcover book in between papers, banana peels, crushed cold-drink cans and cigarette butts. And she walked on, without looking back, as if she had just rid herself of something of absolutely no importance.

The lecturer stood, looking in stunned silence, unwilling to believe what she had just seen. She could feel her colour drain. And then she became angry. With flames that crept up her throat and spread across her face, she wanted to run after the student and grab her by the arm, by her hair, by her clothes and wrench her to a standstill: How dare you! she wanted to shout across campus.

*Reference is to Adam Small's play, *Kanna hy kô hystoe* (1965) [Kanna's coming home], which in an achronological succession of scenes sets the hardships of a Cape coloured family against the ambivalent return of one of their own, Kanna, who having studied abroad (in Canada) is less than able to adjudge his commitment to the desperation at home over and above his sense of safety at the distance of a foreign (first-world) country. [ed.]

That was a book that I spent an entire morning looking for, that I paid for, that I gave to you, that you threw away as if it was rubbish! Why?

She leaned back against the wall where she stood and watched as the student disappeared into the crowd on campus. Then she walked slowly towards the blue bin clamped to a pole. The book lay with its flyleaf pages spread and open, facing the bottom of the bin. She picked it up, shook the pages loose as if there were sand or crumbs in them, and walked back to her office. It was her consultation hour, she was supposed to be available, but she locked her office door and wearily went to sit at her desk. In front of her lay the book. A drama for which the author should have received the Hertzog Prize, years ago already.

With her hands tightly clasped in her lap she let her head drop forward until it rested on top of the book. She stayed like that for a long time.

'Dear Lord,' whispered the lecturer in the silence of her empty office, 'I am not the right person for this kind of work. How can I possibly teach that girl again? How can I mark her answer papers, give her the marks she needs to pass the course? After she throws a book away, moments after I gave it to her as a gift?'

The lecturer, who walked through the lecture hall, stopping at each row to hand out a number of papers, had survived her first two years at the university. With the experience that comes with time, her self-confidence increased, she felt more at home and more involved with the university and her students. It is the new year's prescribed book list that she is handing out to the students. She knows in advance that they will soon complain about all kinds of things, that they can't get hold of the books on the list, that they are too expensive, that the books in the library are damaged. But she also knows in advance that they are poor, and stingy, that they would rather buy clothes and jewellery than books for a course that will only last a year. If they can't find it second hand, then the book won't be bought. Or it will be illegally photocopied. But for the lecturer it is serious, she insists that all students have their own books. As compensation she allows her students to use their books during the exams, as long as there are not notes written in them. She knows it is usually enough encouragement to buy the books.

It is just as she expected. One of the first students who knocked on her door during her consultation hour was Duduzile Nkulu.

'Yes, Ms Nkulu?'

The girl looked at her seriously. 'I can't get the books.'

'Which books?'

The girl named a few titles of the books she had to acquire. The lecturer, who that morning had dropped into the second-hand bookshop on campus, could hardly believe what she heard. 'Are you sure, Ms Nkulu? This morning I saw that there are second-hand books available of all the titles you are look- ing for!'

The girl looked at her without an excuse, sure of her case. 'There are no books.'

Without meaning to, the lecturer looked at the girl's clothes, her shoes, at the bag over her shoulder in which she carried her books. She saw they were clothes and accessories bought in a factory shop.

Everything new, but not expensive or durable. In a few months they will be past their prime and within a year they will be threadbare. Duduzile was not a student with a lot of money.

'Do you want to buy your books new, Ms Nkulu?' she asked.

'Yes,' answered the student.

'I will find out from the manager of the bookshop if the complete stock of books has come in yet,' she promised. 'Normally it takes a bit of time before everything is available. Luckily you don't need all the books right away. OK?'

'Yes,' said the student.

Once she had left, the lecturer looked at the student's information card. Something about the student's reserved, almost unfriendly attitude pricked her interest. Barely eighteen, and from KwaZulu-Natal. Her school results weren't too impressive, but satisfactory. She was studying on a bursary. The name of the town she comes from was completely unknown to the lecturer. Later she would see it was a hamlet on a map.

It was, in fact, as the student said. The books that she named were not available. The manager let her know that they were still waiting for stock. But as the semester progressed, the lecturer noticed that Ms Nkulu bought all her books. New. She was a thorough student, she soon discovered. In class she would never express her own opinion, but she never missed a lecture and her assignments were promptly handed in. At the beginning of the year she just-just scraped through her tests, but with time her marks improved considerably. Ms Nkulu became *the* achiever of the class without much effort.

When the module for the drama course started, Ms Nkulu sat without a book in front of her for the first time.

'Don't you have the book?' the lecturer asked her in class.

The student looked at her with big eyes that gave nothing away, remaining silent.

The lecturer went on with the reading, but right after the class she stopped in at the bookshop.

'*Kanna* by Adam Small, is it available?' she asked the assistant.

'No, sorry, it's completely out of stock. And it doesn't look like the publisher will make a reprint soon.'

The lecturer walked the length of the campus to the second-hand bookshop. As always there was a hum and throng of students in the place where the books are displayed in reasonable disarray. A smell of old books, some mouldy and ruined, rose out of the area. As she suspected, there wasn't a single copy of the book left. Those that were available had been snapped up long ago. The only copy in the library was also already out, and there was a waiting list of students who had reserved the book.

At the next lecture the lecturer asked to see Ms Nkulu after class. They walked together to her office.

'I'm going to Cape Town this weekend,' she told the student standing uncomfortably near the door, her bookbag tightly folded in her arms. 'Shall I see if I can get hold of a second-hand copy of *Kanna* for you?'

'I don't have money,' said the student. She said it without emotion, but her eyes glowed with a strange shine.

'Come, we'll see if I can get it first, then we can talk about the price.' The student nodded her head, turned and left.

The lecturer's search for the book took her to all the bookshops in Long Street. She spent the whole morning nosing through old, dusty bookshelves in old dusty shops. She discovered a bibliophile first edition of Eugène Marais' poetry collection, a small book, bound in leather for sale at R300; she found Johannes Meintjes's journals, Petronella van Heerden's autobiography – loved, familiar books from her childhood – but couldn't find Small's drama anywhere. At eleven o'clock she drank coffee in a chic restaurant that was once the most famous anti-quarian bookshop in the Cape. A shop with an owner who was so attached to his half-a-million books, that he couldn't find it in his heart to sell them. 'Not for sale!' he shouted, maliciously, on more than one occasion as someone took a rare and expensive edition off the shelf and carried it to the counter. Or he made the prices so excessively expensive that no one could afford to buy them. Eventually the bookshop came tumbling down around him; he couldn't afford the rent any-more. The books were sold per kilo and in the last weeks of the sale, they were taken in truckloads to be pulped. Shortly before closing time the lecturer rode to the last second-hand bookshop she knew of, a charity organisation that received books as donations. It was in this suffocating space, a shop crammed with books, magazines, maps and people, that she found it. For R10. She bought it immediately, relieved that her search was finally successful.

At home the lecturer carefully erased all the hasty pencil scratchings on the pages and covered the book neatly with plastic. It was practically a new book, she realised, one that was well looked after by its previous owner. She would give it to Duduzile Nkulu as a present, decided the lecturer; she had already decided before she went to all the trouble. Monday, right after class, she would call the girl and give her the book. She bought all her books; this one would be a gift.

She put the book in her briefcase, with strange excitement and pleasure at the prospect of giving a gift to someone who needed it.

* * *

The woman emigrating to Canada packs her suitcases with meagre earthly possessions. There is not much that will go with her. Not much has remained to take with her after the raid on her house.

If she could, she wouldn't take a single thing with her out of South Africa, thought the woman while she wrapped a pair of walking boots in newspaper, and if she could, she would prefer to leave without a single reminder. She would especially like to erase the last three months of her life, she thinks exhausted. Involuntarily she touches the injury above her eyebrow, a raised scar that is still painful to touch. I will carry this with me, knew the woman, luggage for a lifetime.

Like the frightening image of the nightmare night that made her finally decide to go for good. Go.

What about my books? thinks the woman. Where will I hear Afrikaans again?

Undecided she stands in front of her bookshelf, caressing the spines of the titles in thought.

Five books, she decides, only five.

Her choice is easier than she thought. Poetry, two collections for times when the language must be more than just words; a dictionary; a book with children's rhymes for the day when she perhaps, who knows … Her hands glide across the alphabet. They come to a standstill at *Die Uur van die Engel*. 'Karel Schoeman,' she says softly, 'I need to see an angel, you come too …' She takes the book out, places it on top of the others. Her hands pause at the gap in the bookshelf, by Adam Small. Her heart aches inside her. How can a person visualise the Afrikaans language without *Kanna hy kô hystoe*?

She flaps the book open. 'Kanna, I am going away,' she whispers in the empty house, 'and I am not coming back.' Her eyes follow the lines on the open page. Little Kytie. The woman sits on the floor.

She remains like this for a long time, reliving the trauma of her night of terror three months ago, hers and Kytie's.

'Kytie, little Kytie,' she whispers, the open book pressed against her chest, 'you couldn't get away, but I can. I'm going to speak a new language, I'm going to start over … and I can't take you with me to remind me of all this pain …'

The following day the woman drove to the shop of a charity organisation in Claremont with four wine boxes full of books. She unceremoniously handed them all over at the counter.

'What kinda books are these?' asked the assistant.

'Afrikaans literature,' she answered over her shoulder, already on her way out.

★ ★ ★

The school child in the small zinc building at Nqutu sits tightly packed between the forty-five other children in the class. They sit on planks that are supported by drums filled with sand at the ends and in the middle. There are no desks. If they must write, their books are pressed against their laps, the blunt pencil is sent skew over their uneven knobbly knees. But at the moment the children aren't writing, they sit with big eyes and watch the teacher in front of the class. He is busy hitting a child with a thin willow cane. The blows rain down at regular intervals on the child's shoulders and back. A naughty child, a stupid child that is worthless in class, will never get anything in his head, after a few years of school still can't write or read. The child wails, tries to block with his thin arms, but the blows strike him regardless on unprotected parts of his squirming body.

The children sit dead still, knowing that no word or sound may come out of their mouths now.

Eventually the teacher has beaten his anger out.

'Bring your books here, all of them!' he commands the moaning child who still stands with his arms over his head, as if he expects more blows.

The child sits on his haunches, takes the three books under the plank to the teacher. Two writing books and a textbook with dog-eared pages.

'Now go home,' commands the teacher, 'and don't come back! There isn't place here for a child without a brain!'

The child flees the classroom. Those who sat next to him on the plank spread out a bit wider, filling the extra space.

The teacher still isn't finished. He holds the three books up for all the other children to see.

'If someone thinks that he can have these books I want to warn you: read the books of an idiot and his stupid soul will transfer into you!'

The school child closes her eyes for a moment. She knows the books cost more than R10. Money her parents don't have.

In front of their eyes he begins to tear out pages. First the exercise books with the uneven pencil writing, then the textbook. The dog-eared pages flutter to the ground, collecting at his feet.

* * *

The lecturer lifts her weary head. It feels as if her head is filled with voices, as if the voices of Kanna and his people – voices that speak of judgement and injustice and a futile return – become part of her thoughts. She has a headache.

I am also a Kanna, she thinks. I can't help these people. And I can't teach with this anger in me; I will fail Duduzile Nkulu immediately if I have to mark anything of hers again. Let me forget that I ever searched for and bought this book!

She picks up the book and drops it in the waste-paper basket under her desk. She pauses for a moment, then bends and removes it again. She stands up, walks out of her office, down the passage to outside. She walks the few steps to the blue bin clamped to the pole – a bin full of papers, banana peels, crushed cool-drink cans, cigarette butts – and lets it fall.

JOHN MATSHIKIZA

Of Renaissance and Rhino Stew

From: *With the Lid Off: South African Insights from Home and Abroad, 1959-2000* (2000)

So what is the 'African renaissance', and where is it going? Cut to a new and kitsch clip joint called Caesar's Palace, Gauteng, perched just off the unfashionable side of Johannesburg International Airport's runway number two (no relation) and close to the historically derided suburb of Benoni.

Why Caesar's Palace? I have no idea. But while the underprivileged of all conceivable races were hunched over blackjack tables and throwing their pensions into slot machines in the horrendously tasteless casino down below, in a conference room on the upper floor the minds of the African nation were gathered.

The Department of Arts, Culture, Science and Technology had invited a select few hundred of us to deliberate on the meaning of that very idea of an 'African renaissance', and come up with some ideas about how to put it into practice.

It was one of those gatherings where everyone showed up, dressed for a party, and then sat there looking at one another, wondering who was going to break the ice and tell us what was what. We all understood the question, but, from the urbane and charming Minister Ben Ngubane down, none of us knew the answers.

Fortunately there were some experts on board who took it upon themselves to give us some clues. Foremost among these, of course, was that celebrated 'Renaissance Man', Thami Mazwai.

Mazwai has many well-known opinions about how to make the 'African renaissance' happen, and is not afraid to regurgitate them, time and time again, in public. One of his recurring themes is that, in order to give Africa its pride back, everything in Africa should be Africanised, renamed and given its proper African place.

'We are still worshipping our former masters in everything we do,' he said, referring to the fact that we tend to dress, eat and think like the people who colonised us.

Notwithstanding the fact that he himself had driven to this most unAfrican of venues in an extremely unAfrican automobile, and was now standing before us in a shamefully unAfrican suit and tie, and addressing us in one of those

833

oppressive ex-colonial languages we are all in the habit of using at functions like these (although he did point out that he should not be expected to get every nuance of this offensive and difficult language right – 'you can take me out of the Transkei, but you can't take the Transkei out of me!') he seemed to have a point.

Following his reasoning as he meandered through his theme proved to be a little difficult, though. He was indignant about the fact that you couldn't get African food on African airlines, including our own remarkably African national carrier.

'Why can't I eat *sadza* (pap) on Air Zimbabwe?' he asked. He didn't stop to ask himself how one would keep that notoriously difficult-to-handle staple fresh, hot and tasty at 30 000 feet, or how those dainty air hostesses would manage to stir the mealie meal to the right consistency in those huge cannibal-sized iron pots within the confines of the tiny airborne cabooses that the foreign devils have bequeathed us. Airline food, it seems to me, is about minimalist practicality, rather than national identity. But I'm no expert.

Food was definitely on Mazwai's mind, even when he expounded on environmental issues. 'No edict from Pretoria will make people feel inclined to protect the African rhino when they are hungry,' he said, referring subtly to the inherent contradiction between true Africans and the various bunny-hugging liberals with whom they are forced to share the continent.

Then, mysteriously, he corrected his reference to the 'African rhino' to the 'black rhino', to demonstrate his mastery of ecological themes. He did not pause to explain why true Africans preferred to eat the black rhino rather than the white rhino. It was one of many intriguing perceptions that were left unchallenged as the debate drifted onwards.

We were fortunate that at least three notable professors were on hand to bring some focus to the debate. Professor Lawrence Schlemmer reminded us that identifying what our true cultural reference points were was essential. The problem we face is that the political leaders who could guide us towards those references have generally withdrawn into a new kind of technocratic laager, where they become increasingly remote from the constituencies they should be representing.

Professor Herbert Vilakazi urged us to look at global models to identify our path. Africa, he said, had tottered into the early stages of an industrial revolution before meeting that essential precondition: an agricultural revolution.

And Professor Kwesi Prah gave a rousing intervention in which he pointed out that the key thing was language – not the simplistic idea that all African languages should be elevated to the same footing, but the more sophisticated idea that there is greater commonality than difference among many African languages, and that therefore unifying elements should be distilled to make up communication tools that could transcend our false colonial boundaries, mental and physical. Liberating the capacity of ordinary Africans to express themselves and communicate with each other was the only way forward towards the desired revolution.

Between the confused bluster and the elevated eloquence, there was consensus that the 'African renaissance' was not pie-in-the-sky (or *sadza*-in-the-sky, for that matter) but an inspiring and potentially liberating concept for Africa's long-awaited upliftment – spiritual, technological, cultural, political and otherwise. As Africans, we have a terrific talent for talking. Whether or not we have an equal talent for doing still remains to be seen.

JOHN MATSHIKIZA

The Purple Man in my Bantustan

First published, 2003

I met a purple man on the hills above the sea on the Transkei coast over Christmas. Now what does this mean?

Well, it was Christmas (whatever that means). And these were the hills of the Transkei – some of the most beautiful we have in this undiscovered country. And it was the Wild Coast sea that was breaking over this haunting part of our shores.

And I say it was the Transkei because that piece of our country remains a remote and seemingly forgotten 'homeland' within our complex territorial space, in spite of all the changes that we have lived through. Just look at the roads, and the way the people continue to live, to see what I mean.

The Transkei seems to have defied the elimination of boundaries established by a previous order and remained the same – treacherously narrow roads slicing through rolling hills whose green slopes give way to endless scars of soil erosion, the legacy of desperation and overpopulation. Cows, sheep, dogs, donkeys and mules roaming across the roads with mute abandon, blissfully unadapted to the perils of the mechanised age.

So it was in a remote part of this beautiful, stunted wilderness that I came across the purple man.

It became evident to me that the man himself was not purple. His face was purple. The man had been born with a birthmark that had covered the whole of his head with a purple cowl.

It could have happened to any of us. But if he had been born into a black family, of course, the birthmark would not have showed up in such a vivid shade of purple. To all other intents and purposes, therefore, in spite of the remarkable purple mask that covered his face, he was a white man.

Well, I was coming up the hill to look at the house the purple man had been staying in with his family over the Christmas holidays, with a vague view to buying it – well, you know, black people like you and me don't tend to own holiday homes on a timeshare basis, or any other basis, for that matter, anywhere in this country despite years of talking about liberation and reclaiming our grandparents' heritage. So I was taking up a local (white) man's challenge to consider this possibility.

So, anyway, here was this purple man standing in his faded blue shorts and naked yellow torso on the crest of the hill in the green Transkei, yelling at his whitish-yellow children outside a brown wooden house with an incredible view over the ocean, which I did not necessarily intend to buy. The purple man was somewhat taken aback when I hove into view.

That was the thing. The thing was, the purple man refused to see me. He could see the white man who was climbing up the hill with me, and who was bringing me to see the brown wooden house, with serious interest in having me buy the place.

But the purple man refused to acknowledge my presence (potentially the man with the interesting money) and would only acknowledge that he was seeing the white man at my side, to whom he was prepared to offer a civil and exclusive greeting in these wildly beautiful surroundings.

Now, we have all sorts of problems in this country and most of the time we would prefer to ignore them, considering how far we have already come. But when a purple man who is really a white man has a reality problem with a black man in what was formerly a black Bantustan, we have to stand back and look at what kind of situation we are actually sitting on.

But I have another question: do I blame the purple man and his people for hogging the country on their own behalf, or do I blame myself and the rest of the black bourgeoisie for failing to turn the country (and indeed the century) back over to the black people who still live here but have no stake in it?

Let's look at it again.

I met a purple man on the top of a hill overlooking some of the most dramatic land and seascapes in the country. We had nothing in common. We Christmassed with our separate families in our own separate worlds, in the same native space. We pretended that we couldn't give a damn about each other.

He couldn't chase me away, as he might have done in the old days, and I couldn't chase him away, much as I might have wanted to in these new times. We were locked together in an unresolved space.

But that nagging question arises once again: to whom does this space belong?

We have easy solutions. Land and property are going begging out there. White people are building and buying into the hinterland like there's no tomorrow, quietly extending the frontiers of the laager.

The black bourgeoisie, on the other hand, prefers to ignore our rural splendours and spend their Christmas holidays on crowded beaches in Cape Town, along with the rest of affluent Johannesburg. Something has to be done if we are to turn our political transformation into something more meaningful. It is not enough just to take your cow with you when you move from Zondi to Bryanston and think you are making a powerful Africanist statement when you decide to slaughter in a white suburb. And it is not enough to drive around in a luxury four-by-four (one you know you cannot possibly afford) with a bumper sticker that says 'Thanx God I'm a Blackman, amen'.

So next time you meet a purple man with an unreconstructed white brain in an unexpected place, remind yourself of this: taking back the country demands engagement of a higher order. Nobody's going to offer you those spectacular timeshares, or anything else, on a plate. The country is being painted overseas as a spectacular land of opportunity. And spectacular it certainly is; when you get out there and look at it.

Nov we have to be prepared to go out and get it, before the whole thing gets taken away again under our noses.

I rest my case.

EBEN VENTER

Tinktinkie

Translated from the Afrikaans by Mariëtte Postma
From: *Twaalf* (2000)

Rose at the crack of dawn on the Sabbath Day to prevent Ouma from nagging him for going out to potter about with his pigs. Shorts, Adidas, same shirt from last night. His keys. He did not use the toilet. Ouma would be lying awake already. Lying there, closed eyes, thinking of the end awaiting her around the corner.

In the kitchen Patience and Kasi were busily at work. They were watching the mealie porridge and peeling the apples to be stewed for the afternoon. The peels fell neatly into a small basin. Always keeping everything neat as a pin. He greeted them and they greeted him back. Tinktinkie noticed a pudding bowl with prunes below a net and nicked one for hiniself. Took care that the screen door did not slam shut behind him.

The women in the kitchen liked the little man. He never got in their way. He just followed his own path. He was different. Once he grew up, he would get the farm back into shape, they were saying.

The morning was cold against his bare legs. He started to run. The dog didn't understand why she had to stay behind in the yard the last few weeks when he went to the pigs. But Tinktinkie didn't want him sniffing and yapping close to his two young sows, they were both almost in farrow. Besides, the Landrace pig was already carrying the stress gene.

He heard Oom Dries saying that. Oom Dries allowed him to bring his two sows to his Chester White boar. Oom Dries said this cross-breeding would stand the heat better.

'You can start fattening up a little sucking-pig for your Tante Rebecca, ready for this Christmas.' And then Oom Dries touched him softly behind his neck. He only reached Oom Dries's belt as yet.

This was all Oom Dries wanted in return for the favour. Tinktinkie knew people cared for him a little bit more because he had lost his dad. He was only little and he already had his own farm going. He had five pigs altogether. He knew too what power this gave him. He could get what an ordinary farmer would have to dish out lots and lots of money for. Oom Dries imported the Chester White seed from America. Tinktinkie wondered if what he was doing could perhaps be sinful.

He kept all along the water furrow below the willows that were just starting to bud. It was not really quite summer yet. Over the bare patch between the house and the pig sties a little wind was scattering past. A tattered rag, broken brick, pebbles and glass splinters. Some wire. He never managed walking across the bareness; it made him feel too poor.

The water furrow was barely going. No longer overflowing, day and night, down to the lucerne fields, the way he could remember from the time when he was still very young. Ouma said they should all pray for the fountain to last, for when it dried up, they could just as well start packing their bags and leave Koppiesfontein. At night Ouma sometimes smelled a little sour.

The pigs heard him coming. Three in a paddock close to the lucerne fields, each of the sows in her own farrow-pen. Aaida and Lolla were their names. When Oom Dries drove up there yesterday, taking stock of the two sows' condition he said: 'Upon my word, 'Tinkie, you can count on farrows of twelve or more.' His eyes started twinkling. 'There are young farmers in our district who should actually come and learn from you.'

Oom Dries pressed against the wall of the pigsty, supported himself with his huge male hands. He was a heavy man, this Oom Dries. One could hear it from his breathing.

'Have you heard about the pigs in Malaysia, 'Tinkie?' he asked while he was watching the sows.

'Nee, Oom Dries.'

'They had to kill off the whole country's pig population. Encephalitis. Transmitted to humans by the culex mosquito. It must have been a terrible massacre. Well yes, 'Tinkie, I should be going now. Fresh air, clean water and a balanced diet. But you know that already. Otherwise your pigs would not be looking the way they do.'

Tinktinkie scraped all the remaining bits from Aaida's feeding-trough, scrubbed the sides clean and watered it down with a hose. Then he washed the water trough and filled it up. He came to his feet when he heard people passing by along the road. They came to visit Patience and Kasi on foot and on bicycles. Dressed up in their Sunday best. Should he shove off? He didn't want to draw any attention to the pigs. He'd rather scram himself. The pig's snout was all around him. They knew him very well.

The sky was a dirty blue. It wasn't going to be hot today. 'My little children,' he said when he touched Aaida's swollen teats. She started eating the mealies and bone meal greedily. They should never be unnecessarily fat when with young; it could cause problems when birthing.

The corners of his eyes were still foggily covered in sleep. When he walked away he took a last look at the pigsty behind him: 'My little children,' he said once more. He quickly went to the tap outside to wash before he entered. Even though he knew it wasn't quite possible to rinse off everything that was clinging to him after having been with the pigs, that didn't put him off.

840

His mother was standing inside in her dressing gown with a Stuyvesant, looking out onto the flower garden. Would she have seen him at the tap?

'Morning, Mummy.'

'Morning,' she replied.

He waited for her to go on talking, but she'd turned back to the window. He went to sit at the table and reached for the toast with his hand. The kitchen door opened and swung shut behind Patience's buttocks and she placed his bowl of mealie porridge in front of him. Her hand touched his on the plastic table cloth. He looked her in the eye and gave her a smile. A lump of butter, sugar, milk. The radio was playing morning hymns. The culex mosquito. There were always mosquitoes around the farrow-pens once sunmer had started. What kept mosquitoes at bay?

Ouma came in, wearing her outfit for church. A mauve dress with mauve lace at the seam and high up against her bosom. With her she had her hymn book, Bible, mauve gloves and handbag with the peppermints and stuff. She placed her precious little bundle on the sideboard. Came and kissed him on the forehead. Scent and smell of bread dough.

'Did you ask the Lord for His grace on your porridge before you started to eat, Sonnie?'

'Yes, Ouma,' he lied. No need to pray on Sundays when you were going to church anyway.

'Aren't you sitting down to eat, Hendrien?' she asked in his mother's direction.

'I'll have something later, Mummy. I won't be going to church with you today.'

'You must let Kris be, Hendrien. He won't get up out of his grave. It was the Lord's will.'

'It's not that, Mummy,' she bit back. Tinktinkie sat there without touching the spoon of porridge at his mouth.

'You won't fool me, Hendrien. You are not leaving Kris alone there where he is now. You are being unfair to him. The Word says, leave the dead to the dead.'

'Ma, you are not going to tell me what to do in my own house.' Her hand fluttered. She wouldn't say anything else, Tinktinkie knew that already.

'I'm only trying to help,' Ouma said very softly and slowly buttered half a slice of toast.

His mom became funny after Daddy had been taken away. Chin on her chest. Two empty packets of Stuyvesant on the small table in front of the television, mornings when he came in. She never asked a thing about his pigs anymore.

With the two litters he should be able to buy himself a computer.

* * *

Remarkable, was the word that came to the Revd Tertius when he thought about this morning's sermon while sitting down at the table for breakfast. Words given unto him by the Higher Hand. But there was also a touch of nerves that he couldn't hide.

'What's wrong with you now, Tertius?' asked his wife when she put the bacon and eggs, mushrooms fried in garlic and scones down in front of him. Bes read him like a book.

'You must stick to the biblical text, Tertius. That's why the Lord has given you good brains. Don't drag politics into your sermon.'

Bes was irritated. In the living room the children, dressed in their Sunday best, were fighting over the new Nintendo. She felt that Tertius did not assert himself properly in this house.

Bes was a charming woman. She had grown up in Oranjezicht. 'You are cut out for modelling,' she had always been told in the Cape. Because of her slender waist. Legs up to her chin. Then she fell in love with the student minister. Must have been his legs that turned her head those days. His total unawareness of his own body. Now she was stuck here in the bloody sticks. And Tertius, who never said a thing about politics, was now off on a dangerous tangent.

Once, when he was balancing on the windowsill to cut his toenails, he turned to her in bed: 'They are going to kill off the last one of us. Nothing has changed. We're back to the days of the border wars. And these days the church is absolutely useless. Even here, Bes, you have to admit to it, the members of the congregation are bolting one after the other. Antjie Krog was spot-on with her remark: the Afrikaners have become totally irrelevant, politically and culturally.'

Head on her arm she lay there, looking at him. Shifted her bosom, grimaced. The tyre hanging over his underpants. Black body-hair creeping from his buttocks up his back. Never used to be there before. And what happened to his faith? His lovely smile?

'Small wonder they're bolting if their minister carries on like this.' She jumped up from the bed and opened the shower taps. She no longer wanted to hear him around her.

The church was not too empty. The weather offered no excuses for not attending.

Bes bent down to her children just before they started filing into the minister's pew: 'Behave yourselves now, or you can forget about your ice-cream today.'

Tinktinkie and Ouma sat in their usual spot in the western wing. Ouma's mauve glove rested lightly on his leg. He sucked a peppermint without anybody seeing or hearing him. If only the long prayer he had to stand for were over.

Since the carnage in the Kenilworth church a few years ago, they started locking the doors. Nobody even mentioned it anymore. Ouma always used to nudge him on the leg and wink when Oom Dries went out in the middle of the sermon for some fresh air under the privets. Now he was caged in. Behind them Tinktinkie could hear him having trouble breathing properly.

Matthew 8 verses 28 to 34 was the biblical passage that was read out from the old translation, from the pulpit. Where Jesus came upon the devil-possessed in Gergesa.

'And suddenly they shouted and said: what do we have to do with you, Jesus, Son of God?' And then followed the passage of the big herd of swine grazing close by. Tinktinkie listened. He heard how the devils had begged the Lord if He could please allow them to possess the swinery when He drove them out. And then the whole swinery stormed off the cliff – into the sea – and drowned.

'This is where the reading ends, brothers and sisters. Let us pray.'

Tinktinkie planted his little legs. The heat was fortunately not too bad yet. During the long prayer in summer spots and curls started swimming behind his eyelids because of having to stand so long. He tried to see them: they looked like the sea-horses at East London's aquarium.

'And Lord, we entrust our children to you, those who are working, but especially those who are struggling to find work ...'

His pigs. He trusted the Koppiesfontein people, but he didn't really know about the visitors who came to see Patience and Kasi. They could break open his tiny little locks like nothing. That was what frightened him the most when he had to attend church: that one of his pigs would be missing when he came home. Please just let them spare Aaida, and Lolla's lives, he prayed silently during the prayer of the Revd Tertius.

'As Bible text, brothers and sisters, verse 29 was imprinted onto my heart: "and suddenly they shouted and said ..." "Suddenly" is expressed here by the Greek word *idoù*. A strong word in the original text, a word demanding an exclamation mark. These people, these devil-possessed people, were therefore terribly frightened when they were confronted by Jesus.

'The Greek here refers to *légontes* which means a great number, rather like a sea of people. We can surely conclude that although only two devil-possessed are mentioned in Matthew, and only one in Mark and Luke, there were a multitude of devils present in these human beings or being. *Légontes!*' The Revd Tertius made his voice fly high. He reached the essence of his sermon. Beneath his jacket and waistcoat and shirt and vest he was wet through. He had anticipated this and used extra deodorant.

'And this great crowd of people shouted against Jesus. It has been written that they had shouted so loudly that it sounded like a croaking. This devilish sound came from the crowd, so that we can assume that the under-worldly croaking sound straight from hell echoed over the beautiful meadow right next to the sea.'

Then the Revd Tertius came to the Greek sentence which he had understood as having special significance. He made a fist above the pulpit. 'What do we have to do with you, Jesus, Son of God?' And then, once more: 'What do we have to do with you, Son of God?'

Tinktinkie started fidgeting. And Ouma pressed another peppermint into his sweaty little palm.

'Brothers and sisters, we are here confronted with the powerful clash between the children of the devil and Jesus himself. Terrifying for the devils, this day, this moment when, despite their own devilish power, they face their own downfall.

'There is today in southern Africa – and more specifically in this beautiful and afflicted country of ours – an equally powerful manifestation of the devil himself. Brothers and sisters, I am talking here about AIDS. It is a virus that is decimating thousands, no, thousands upon thousands.'

Bes blushed and touched her cheeks, hoping that nobody noticed her reddening. Tertius was totally losing it. She knew where he was heading with this. He was going to distort the biblical text with his interpretation. And these fools were going to swallow every word of it. Dammit, the day would come, and that day was just around the corner, when she was going to pack her bags. Back to the Cape. Turn Ennio Morricone's music up just as loud as she wanted to. Tertius should be subjected to the process of censure by the Theological Council or whatever that lot of old fossils in Potchefstroom called themselves.

'The *Afrikaner* of 23 July 1999 reports that, according to the latest survey of UNAIDS, 8,9% of Swaziland's population have been contaminated with the HI-virus; 3,9% of Lesotho's just over two million people have been infected; and 6,5% of our country's population have been affected by the HI-virus. One hundred and forty thousand casualties caused by this virus have been reported in South Africa.

'Brothers and sisters, God does not sit still. We know today which population group here at the Southern Point of Africa is hit the hardest by this virus. God does not slumber or sleep, brothers and sisters.' The Revd Tertius's voice broke as he strove for an even higher tone of voice.

'This devilish virus shouted it out when it came into contact with the Almighty. "Go!" Jesus commanded the enormous number of devils. We know which part of South African society is affected most severely, brothers and sisters. The battle is not in vain, even though that is how it may seem. The end is near. Look out over the meadow and see who are spilling over the cliff into the sea. By the thousands.

'"Go!" Jesus ordered the devils. And the devils took possession of the

844

swinery, the Greek refers here to *boskoméné*, pigs that have been fattened to the point of revulsion. And by the thousands these devilish swines are storming into the depths of the sea.'

Tinktinkie sat up straight as a ramrod. Kicked with his feet against the floor. His heart inside his shirt was going crazy, crazy with these things. He jumped off the pew and raised his hand high as if at school.

'Heavens, child,' hissed Ouma and pulled him down.

But Tinktinkie flared up again, threw his hand high into the air and yelled before anyone could stop him: 'But what about the little ones, Reverend, what about the little children?'

ASHRAF JAMAL

The Beggar-guest

From: *The Shades* (2002)

She is a research psychologist. It is the phrase she uses during dinner conversations. The phrase implies, she hopes, that she does fieldwork; that she is in the field. She pictures herself there, in a field; a handkerchief tied to her head, seated on a foldout campstool, notepad in hand, Tabard on her legs and shoulders. Intrepid, she thinks. The illusion satisfies her, but only briefly. Why not home work? After all, it is there, in homes not in the fields, where the stories unfold. She uses a dictaphone. The notepad she uses for those compelling moments which, she believes, are the clues to the rest of the story. The conversation, more a pointed series of questions and answers, is invariably arduous to unravel. The children, young girls and boys, are not gifted speakers. Then again, neither is she. She has never been one to beat her breast. Over dinner she is usually the silent one. The mistake of others is that they believe that her silence implies she is a good listener. She is not.

She believes she has no gift. At no point does she dress up this lack as a kind of modesty. A drudge, she thinks, though those about the table who claim to be her friends protest. She supposes that they have a vested interest in making her more interesting than she is. She resolves, then, never to reveal what she thinks herself to be. The resolve is destined to fail her. No one cares for silence that means nothing. A *research psychologist* then. A *field-worker*. She must satisfy. All the more so about a dinner table where illusion is more piquant than either wine or food.

A writer is there at the table, a recent arriviste on the campus. Bombastic, she thinks. However she cares enough for what he says. To value him she must disinter the words, fold them one by one, neaten the sense, remove them from the foul cavity that no wine will clean away. It is he who forces her to account for herself. Does he too disinter the words? Does he inwardly ask what a research psychologist might he? Does he dwell upon the unfortunate phrase – fieldwork – and say to himself: A white woman in a field, what is she doing there? Who could possibly tell her the truth? Before a woman like her – pale, fish-eyed – who could possibly reveal anything of value?

The writer's eyes are glazed, the mandible chugs. Food and wine disappear in equal measure. She cannot disavow his relish. His gluttony chastens her.

846

While the others about the table demurely peck, he reveals the hunger that gnaws in all of them. Is it his words that ruin the general appetite? Is it because when he speaks he plunges the heart, draws the heart's conscience up so that it lodges there in the mouth? She watches her guests dab their lips with napkins. They are readying themselves. They expect — each and every one of them — that they will be forced to answer for themselves. It is because of the writer that they peck. Food intercedes. Food stops the heart's expression. It is the taste of conscience that lodges in each and every mouth. The writer has provoked unease. That is why she values his words.

It is to her he turns. She is waiting. He is speaking of *Disgrace*, a book she well knows and does not care for. The author of the book is his passion. She cannot understand why. When told one day in the corridor of the Social Sciences Building that the author of *Disgrace* has been short-listed for the Nobel Prize, she does not say that were he to receive the coveted award it would mean that the very earth on which we stand has been condemned. Now the writer at the table — who has received no award, no short-listing either — talks of disgrace. We are all disgraced, he says. Each and every one of us, he insists. He is given to declamation, hyperbole. He leaves it up to the rest to disinter, neaten, edit. It is a job, she imagines, which he believes to be the province of gifted men and every woman. She marvels at his complacency. She watches her guests as they pat their mouths.

En route to work in another city — he insists that it does not in fact matter where the incident takes place — he drives past a man exercising himself upon the body of a woman. She is struck by the relish with which he yields the telling phrase — *exercising himself upon*. She does not know that the phrase belongs to the author so highly prized by the Nobel committee.

Returning to Cape Town on a Monday morning, cars hurtling through fraught space, I looked to the Block River on my right, then, shifting to the left, my gaze mounting upward along a raised embankment of uncut green, I saw a man clothed from the waist up, his arse hollowed at the sides, taut, the legs sinuous, the trousers like a discarded sweet-wrapper about his legs. He was copulating; with whom was unclear. The man may have been exercising his strength upon a ghost, so insubstantial the figure seemed. Cars hurtled past, no one stopped. Did no one see what I saw? My fellow occupant certainly did not. I thought sex; she thought rape. Since then I've thought of how many cars passed before the man ejaculated. The man ... bald, white, powerful, brazen. What I couldn't imagine was the woman, a ghost, fully clothed, prone, but for a flailing hand, brown.

SA Wildlife. I know the statistics. I read the paper. Rape is a fact I can imagine, simulate, arraign within my interactive cortex. Otherwise, the brutal integrity of rape escapes me.

There was a deliberateness to the bald man; a thoroughness. Shocking though it may sound there was in that one-sided act an impressiveness, a fearlessness, a wild rigour. Is there a difference to watching human beings copulate than, say, dogs? To me, at that moment, there was none. The flannel ghost was not exempt. She had too little shape to muster concern. And he? He was monstrous, fearless, driven, a figure from a Genet novel, in chains, yet free. As for her? There was no reprieve. And so it is in South Africa today. I struggle to be outraged, but my heart fails me; my mouth, aghast, merely sighs.

He proceeds to draw a link between this occurrence which, she is sure, he has reprised before to similar effect, with the novel *Disgrace*. It is a work intimately aware of the unnatural order of life in South Africa, he says. The novel does not dignify or apologise for the existence of the ugly. Disgrace simply is. It is our inheritance, our character, the state of our minds, the sum of our actions. Pleasurable. Revolting. Banal.

Here the writer stops. Throughout he has gazed at her, no one else. Nothing in the conversation has led to the writer's monologue. She suspects he never follows, always leads. A pity. While she acknowledges his ability to hold an audience she believes he would benefit greatly if his ear were not so general, his mouth too. His claims are too large, the illustration does not suffice. Because no one has anything to add, she neither, he casually proceeds. Would that he would listen. Would that he would stop. He shovels food, drinks.

The book deals with rape, the transfer of power, anarchy, the coupling of youth and age, death, the question of whether or not we own our selves, our bodies. It pivots on a charge of sexual harassment and, later, a gang rape. Sex is the seam, an act unlovely, loveless. Of the blurred moment between fucking and rape we read:

'Not rape, not quite that, but undesired nevertheless, undesired to the core. As though she had decided to go slack, die within herself for the duration, like a rabbit when the jaws of the fox close on its neck. So that everything done to her might be done, as it were, far away.'

His memory appears unimpaired. He well knows the power of quotation. No one eats or drinks. It is the writer they consume. Do they imagine themselves in the salon of a nineteenth-century novel? Is he the beggar-guest, she the host? And they, the others, who are they? Children, she thinks.

The dinner is proving a success. It is he who makes it so; he with his bile so eloquently wrapped. They will have something to talk about. No doubt she will increase in their estimation. What do they care that she utterly disagrees? What do they care that she sees hope where he, the writer, sees none? Are they such children, without guile, so easily won over by fluency that they cannot see that fluency will not do? Fluency has no place here. No words will contain this earth. No drunken sot. No glutton.

She sees that now their appetites have grown large too. They no longer

848

peck and dab their mouths. He has restored a zest, an urgency, to the proceedings. The roast lamb is picked clean. When they are done with eating and drinking there is nothing left, nothing to do but nod before their effusive appreciation of the spread. One thing is certain, this is the first time she does not have to freeze the leftovers. There is nothing for the dog. The marrow is sucked dry. Not a single sprout is left in the salad bowl. The bareness of the table horrifies her though she feigns satisfaction. Better dissembled gratitude than such effusive pleasure. Better a stunted repartee about nothing than this twittering of birds, this laughter louder than she has ever heard. Obscene. All of this, obscene. Somewhere, in the midst of her disgust, she finds a lingering sympathy for the author of *Disgrace*.

The cigarettes run out. Those who smoke pat their breast pockets, riffle through their overcoats. The writer lights a butt-end. Those who do not smoke do the same and laugh. A plastic sachet containing dagga appears. This too is consumed. The guests, children all, quit the table. In groups they leave the room. The writer remains before her. His dull eyes see everything. He is thin. What does he do with the food he devours? What is he doing here, before her? A mistake, she knows, inviting him. A misplaced sympathy on her part. She searches for the reason she invited him. She realises it is he who invited himself. A chance remark in the common room. He overhears, draws himself into the fold. She mistakes his inclusion of himself as a sign of vulnerability. There is nothing vulnerable about him at all, though he knows all too well how to affect vulnerability. He is a Namibian, taut, jaundiced. Born in the desert he has regaled many about a dinner table in Oxford, Paris, Accra. He is a visiting lecturer in the School of Psychology. If she deems him a writer it is because this is what matters most to him. He publishes the occasional story, he has a novel in the pipeline. He has little patience for drudges such as her. Why, then, does he stay? Why won't he join the party by the pool? Does he wonder why she remains? Does he imagine her as a kind of prey, something else to devour now that the table is bare? She cannot decipher his eyes. A lion's eyes. Gold. There is nothing attractive about him. Nothing attractive about her either. Does this qualify them as mates? Is she one of an unfortunate couple with her bulbous eyes, her heavy hips, her breasts heavy too?

He thanks her for the dinner and heads for the pool. There, at least, he will have an audience. When he leaves — a seraph, an exclamation mark — she is appeased. She realises that more than the words she has disinterred, she values the simplicity of these final moments because, yes, they are final. She does not care for inference. She does not care for dull all-seeing eyes. She wants no man in her bed, no man in her heart. What then does she want? Peace, she thinks. But when there is none? What then? What does she want? She certainly wants this dinner over and done with. But what of the ricochet? What of the phone calls that will surely follow? Who is he? How do you know him? What is he doing here? Provincial questions; questions which, no doubt, will grow into gossip. She is single after all. She is the subject – the victim – of kindness. If she can disinter him from his words, then why not the rest? Is she not done with him, with the lot of them? She concludes that she is. She will have no more dinner parties. She will reprove herself from the clutches of children. She wonders, for the last time, why she even allowed herself this disgrace.

Some time passes before she finally shuts the door. She adjusts the latch, draws the curtains. She moves from room to room securing each and every cavity. She has no desire to feed the dog. In her study, which opens onto her bedroom, she triggers the alarm. Alone at last. Shut off, shut up, she returns to her desk. She has drunk little. Her mind is clear. A glass of apple juice in hand, she switches on the desk lamp. She is annotating a series of interviews with young boys and girls. She refuses to think of them as teenagers. She does not believe in this awkward and damning middle sphere. After the dinner she wonders if there is such a thing as an adult. Children, she utters, we are all children. She a drudge amongst children.

She reads the handwritten gloss to an interview with an eighteen-year-old girl from Emzamweni. She is not pleased with the notes neatly inscribed in the margins. *Barrier: experience. Barrier: trust. Solution: keep quiet.* The notes refer to an isolation she feels. She has enough detachment to know that her isolation is not the girl's. What then are the barriers she separates with a colon then counterpoints with experience, trust, silence? What would he, the writer, think?

She pictures his dull knowing eyes; eyes, she thinks now, that know too little. Could he feel the plight of a girl from Emzamweni? Does she? What she knows – the little that she knows – is that no dinner-table talk of *Disgrace* would ever move her. How speak of disgrace to someone who knows all too well the meaning? She sees the girl before her. The knees scuffed and bruised. The hands gently folded on a skirt of plaid. Behind her – before her? – a dead mother, dead father, dead stepmother too. In her arms a three-year-old stepsister soon to be dead too. What would he, the writer, make of this? How would he explain the ignominy the girl feels? Outcast. A girl made of death because they, the ones who judge, make her so. In every transcribed interview she reads there is this silence. No one talks of the death that stalks them. Enfolds them. Death, she sees now, is a girl with arms enfolded on a skirt of plaid. She is not dying, the girl. For now she is exempt. It is the little one in her arms, the one the girl cannot save, that wounds. What would he, the writer, make of this? Is this our inheritance, this our character?

Better to have screamed and said enough! Enough of your generalisation! Better to have torn the food from his mouth, broken each and every wine bottle and said: Enough of your pleasure! Enough of your writer's callous fluency. And you, the children who listen and gorge, what of you? What do you know of disgrace? What do you care? And she? What does she make of the barriers that separate lives from hope? How does she vault the chasm that draws all into silence? What is the good of fieldwork? What is the good of listening when the disgraced die by the second; die because no one will heed, no one break the silence? No one, not even the writer, breaks the silence. No eloquence will fill the emptiness of a girl's hands. Without reprieve she sees the baby that no one but the girl will care for. And she with all her rooms, her dog, her salary, what will she do? Perhaps she needs the writer's eloquence. Perhaps she needs his complacency. What is left?

Before her desk, where the glass of apple juice topples, she weeps. She has grown tired with confusion. Grown tired with hope. She wishes she were never born. She cannot change the world. She can only listen. And what good is listening? For years she has believed that listening was enough. She has seated herself before the wounded, recorded their stories. And then? What then? Does she need a writer's skill to make something of their words? If she were capable of doing so — which she is not — what then? What is the good of words?

MARLENE VAN NIEKERK

Labour

Translated from the Afrikaans by Michiel Heyns
First published, 2004

My sister who knows about gardening is standing with her hands on her hips surveying the wilderness surrounding my new house, 'a nifty little piece of property', according to my father.

She clearly finds nothing nifty about it. Inside the house itself she has already thrown up her normally all-capable hands in despair.

'Look,' she says, 'your single greatest problem here is going to be labour. It's expensive and it's complicated. That is to say if you can find it. Because on Saturdays they're drunk, and during the week you can't leave them here on their own, they'll rob you blind. Whatever you do, don't get people off the street, get a gardening service. And for inside you get a cleaning service. Avoid private employment, it's looking for trouble.'

'Yes,' says my brother, 'Cape coloureds, you can't trust them. One day they're all sweetness and light and the next day they switch just like that.' He swivels his hand in the air like an oar to show how they switch.

'You know I was building at my place and then out of the blue one day eight of them pinned me against the wall, in broad daylight. Because their contractor didn't pay them out of the money he got from me. And he just shrugs, the scumbag. So you'd better beware of contractors as well. It's a no-win situation with labour in this country.'

I discuss my plans for home and garden with my parents.

'Just be careful about who you employ, my child,' says my father.

'And keep the doors locked at all times,' says my mother. 'Remember, you're a woman alone.'

Woman alone rummages in her not yet unpacked crates and boxes looking for the warning sign that protected her for ten years against thieves, murderers and rapists. She sticks it in a prominent place against the sitting-room window, with the message to the outside. 'This property is protected by snakes.'

Under the English, the text is rendered also in some or other African language, she doesn't know which one. She grimaces at her own complicity in the ethnographic slandering of the lower orders: that's how they spit, that's how they mourn, that's how scared they are of frogs and snakes.

Well, at least she can say she doesn't own a firearm. And she'll never acquire one either. She can't kill. She can only bluff with pictures of flat-head cobras.

In her mother tongue there is no end to the snake. He goes on his belly in the dust. From him are descended all the laws and commandments of labour. In the sweat of your brow you shall toil all the days of your life.

She used to do all her own gardening. But now she is forty-six. She has tennis elbow and a bad back. And she can no longer give it everything she's got. She is dependent on labour. But she's not scared.

She'll be cautious and correct. Firm and friendly, with distance. She'll make firm arrangements about time, about money, about the use of the toilet. She'll give good food and regular refreshments, a bonus for commendable work. She won't let herself be caught with clever talk, loafing or cheeky behaviour. With her work is work, period.

'Look,' says the estate agent who sold me my house, 'you're welcome to use my gardener. I have first call on him on Saturdays, he knows that, but if you arrange it with me, you can have him. Or otherwise during the week. He's very reliable, and experienced, has been working in florists' gardens for years. And main thing, he's dry. But you're not allowed to pay him more than R45 a day, and he may not work more than three days a week and you may not fetch him from the farm. On Koelenhof station. It's sensitive, you see. He lives and does odd jobs on the farm, and then he gets a disability on top of that, because of his back so-called, and he may not earn too much, else he'll lose it. And then the farm owner's wife is my best friend, she does the flowers for all my clients, so I really don't want any trouble.'

The agent smiles sweetly. She told me once that they are the only agency in town that opens every morning with scripture and prayer. And it works, she assures me, they make a profit.

Because it's the first time, I collect Piet from the farm. The farm has a whitewashed gateway and flags and an estate logo. Cheep cheep cheep, go the sprinklers as far as the eye can see over the vineyards. Next to the gateway another entrance leads to the labourers' cottages. Piet is waiting for me at his garden gate. We shake hands.

'Piet, how is your back?' I ask, 'I don't want you to damage it any further.'

Piet laughs. 'No what, madam,' he says, 'if I stand with my legs nice and apart and I warm it up slowly then it lasts well. It's just when he gets cold, then things get bothersome around here.' He puts his hand on his coccyx.

'That's your sacrum,' I say, 'I have it too, but I'm not taking chances any more. Are you up to digging ditches, Piet? I have to install irrigation.'

Piet gets into the car before replying. 'Depends,' he says.

'On what?'

'Depends on what the madam is going to pay me.' Piet looks at me with an unabashedly calculating smile.

'Well,' I say, and put my cards on the table. I tell him the agent's whole story. Around me I can feel the labour situation congealing.

His reaction is direct. 'That's a bloody stingy woman, that one, madam knows. She'll tell you anything just not to spend money.'

Piet has a scar next to his mouth and tattoos on his arms. 'Friends are few,' I read aloud. 'Where did you get that?' I ask.

'In jail,' he says, 'but I'm on the straight and narrow now. Twelve years since I've had a drop over my lips.'

'Yes,' I say, 'so I've been told.'

Piet laughs. The negotiations are in full swing, that we both know. I push the Volkswagen hard in order to stay ahead.

'Fasten your safety belt, Piet,' I say, 'you never can tell.'

'Nice little car the madam drives,' Piet grins, 'madam doesn't perhaps want to sell it to me?'

At home we reach an agreement. R80 from nine to five. Because it's not routine work, because it's basic installation.

'It's the whole infrastructure,' I hear myself say, 'ditches, holes, carting around wheelbarrowsful of soil, sawing off branches, digging out rocks, it's hard work and hard work must be rewarded accordingly. But it stays between the two of us, not so, Piet? I don't want trouble. And the madam agent has first call on your Saturdays, you understand? It's thanks to her that you're here in the first place, okay?'

'That's fine, madam,' he says. 'We do that.'

He looks at the snake warning in the window. 'Hmmm,' he says, 'clever that, does it work?'

'What do you want for lunch, Piet?' I ask at one o'clock.

He leans on his spade, his whole face one great wrinkle of enjoyment, I don't even want to guess at all the possible reasons.

'Fancy, madam will probably think it's funny, but I don't really eat meat, I'm actually a salad man. Especially in the afternoon, it keeps me nice and light and lively, madam follows?'

Madam follows quite well and she goes off to make, with a dedication that she doesn't understand herself, a delicate and well-dressed little salad, and arranges it on the garden table with a bottle of balsamic vinegar and a bottle of olive oil and a big jug of fruit juice with ice.

All of the first day and the days following Piet works without a break. She sees no sign of a bothersome back. He's quick and he's accurate and he gives excellent advice on all sorts of matters. He gets the compost heap going in a few days and he prunes back the fig tree to manageable proportions. Every evening she gives him a Voltaren tablet from her own supply to drink after his supper for his back that will be cold and aching by then. And his eight new ten-rand notes and more food and fruit to eat at home. They enjoy each other, the woman and the labourer. He is a genuine gardener, she discovers, with a well-developed aesthetic sense. She is touched by the fact that he brings her cuttings and roses from his own garden.

'For a bit of colour,' he says, 'it's still so bare there in the madam's garden, but we'll get there, just give us a break.'

Piet works three days a week and also every other Saturday. And he rubs his hands over the alluring salads she concocts for him. He tells her that the agent is working overtime over weekends and is not at home to issue orders and doesn't need him for the time being. She finds it unnecessary to check these details with the agent.

One fine day she phones.

'I must have a serious talk to you about Piet,' she says. 'You're paying him too much. He now wants R10 an hour from me as well. And he says he's working for your sister in Paarl as well on some Saturdays, also for R10 an hour. So what is this? I thought we had an understanding? And for the rest I hear you go and fetch him from the farm every day. The other workers are grumbling, they know he gets an allowance and they won't think twice about reporting him. You don't understand, there's a lot of jealousy amongst these people. You're obviously not clued up on the situation here in the Boland. And furthermore, I know he likes lettuce, but now he's asking me where's the cheese and the olives and the dark brown vinegar. You're setting a dangerous precedent here. You don't know what it can unleash. You have to play according to the rules here, or you get taken for a ride, more often than not by the workers themselves. They have no loyalty and no respect. Just remember that in future.'

The setter of precedents is left with her head in her hands. She has a sudden backache. She takes a pill and decides not to say anything, to stop the train there and then. How could the man go and do such a thing? He's never worked for her sister in Paarl, and the olives, well olives in salad are a vanity and an acquired taste, she herself was surprised that they weren't left in the bowl. It was meant as a gesture, a kind of joke really, one that she thought he could appreciate because he's certainly not backward. It was a salad in quotation marks, one might say. In exchange for the cuttings, for the expert gardening advice, for the steaming compost heap, for the roses. You can't pay for things like that, can you? He did them from the goodness of his heart, she felt, and they asked for some kind of recompense. A thought rises to surface in her head, but she can't altogether get hold of it. Perhaps the roses were also in quotation marks – triple, quadruple ones.

She decides to leave them both just there without any explanations, the labourer and the estate agent, because she did murmur something about tea and cake, a literary afternoon. Scripture reading with client relations, she thinks now. The angels are posted with burning brands at the gates of her garden, she thinks. And it's high summer, perhaps in any case too hot to try and get the garden going now. She decides to concentrate on the interior for the time being. She phones a cleaning service.

'Hello, Northwest Breeze here,' says a long-suffering woman's voice.

'I'll bring my girls right over to you, I've taught them myself and I supervise them myself, every moment of the day. You never know with these people, we clean where you can never reach yourself: windows, cellars, gutters, garages. And we're used to everything, you'll never believe what my two eyes have seen in my day, you wouldn't say it's white people, sometimes I get quite ashamed before the girls and, you know, they notice everything, every single thing. How many people in your household, if I may enquire, Mrs …?'

'I live on my own,' I say, 'I don't have a lot of stuff.'

'Oh, I beg your pardon, miss, then, in that case, it's R90 for the first time and R80 if it's regular.'

Within the hour they're there, piling rowdily out of a light-blue Cortina. There they are on her front stoep, with their vacuum cleaners and brooms and crates full of cloths and brushes.

'This is Gladys and Sophie and Dolla and Florence, all my little breezes together,' says Mrs Uys. 'Where they've blown it's clean as a whistle. What do you say, Dolla, you're my mainstay, not so? Come on, don't you greet the madam? Come, nicely now, "Good afternoon, Miss!"'

Dolla fixes her stare on the ground with a fuck-you expression on her face. 'Nnmiss-h' she mumbles under her breath.

'Mainstay, noway!' says Sophie, and sends a rich wad of phlegm arching over her shoulder splat on the garden path.

'Keep that trap of yours shut,' mumbles Dolla, 'and watch where you spit.'

'Hey, good heavens, what kind of ugly talk is this in front of the miss?' says Mrs Uys. 'You'll make her send us away before we've even started!'

The women stink of sweat and old cigarettes. Their clothes are in tatters underneath the pink dustcoats they're wearing. I see swollen eyes, a lip bruised blue and black. To a woman they are sullen and jibbing. One complains of a headache. Mrs Uys distributes Panados. 'For everybody, while we're about it,' she says and winks at me.

Another one displays a bloody cut on her finger, sustained at the previous house. The madam takes out the Band Aid. She casts glances at me implying comprehension, confidential, conspiratorial.

'Just like children they are,' she talks at me in a low voice. 'This is just their way of showing off in front of new people, it's just shyness, it will be all over just now.'

I pretend not to hear. I don't want to hear. How can she say such things in front of them?

'So where are the snakes?' Gladys asks me, with a face that says, 'Right on, ignore her, the old cunt.'

'What snakes?' I ask.

'Them!' Sophie jabs a quick index finger at the warning.

Mrs Uys is wide awake, it seems. She winks advice at me. I follow it without quite knowing why. I'm ashamed of my doubleness of heart, but my tongue is even more forked.

'Oh,' I say, 'them. Locked up in the study. You needn't clean in there.' Nobody is going in there, I've decided in advance. Better not cast my chaos of scribblings and scraps to the winds. Just in case I locked my hand-bag with cell phone and wallet in there as well. What the eye does not see, as my mother would say, the heart cannot desire.

You can't even trust the idioms, I think, removing Jackson Hlongwane's three-footed angel from Gladys's hurricane-like progress through my sitting room.

'Rainbow Warrior' the vacuum machines are called. The women poke the black trunks fiercely into every corner and behind every bed and wardrobe. When they see me watching, they mockingly mimic an exaggerated fear of snakes. When the vacuum cleaners now and again cease their noise I hear them name the things in my house. From the various rooms the voices sound.

'Second bedroom,' I hear.

And, from my bedroom, giggling, 'Co'look, the miss has a queensize. Cloud Nine, I say.' I hear my new mattress being whacked with the flat of a hand. The old one is stored in the garage. But to which of the four does one give it? Solomon himself couldn't solve this one.

'Eight-seater,' says one from the dining room. I smell Woodoc.

'Wall to wall,' shrieks another one.

'Chest freezer.' That's Dolla in the kitchen. I hear her slam the lid with gusto. Why would she have opened it? I wonder. And then again, why not? It wasn't locked.

Then, suddenly, from the bathroom, from the toilet, a harmony in two voices, as if they'd rehearsed it: 'Light the lights, close the doors, we're staying home tonight.'

We're of the same generation, I think. Beyond that I don't want to think too much about the implications of the song. They have me taped, that's all I know, my whole story is as clear as daylight to them.

It's half-time. I spread thick slices of bread with the syrup and peanut butter I acquired with a view to Piet's coming. I make big mugs of tea with lots of sugar.

'What do they eat?' Sophie asks with a mouth full of bread and a bold stare.

'What does who eat?'

'The snakes!' they yell in unison. They bend double in glee, heads to one side, buttocks in the air. They screech with open mouths full of bread. 'Oh,' I say, 'white mice, tame ones, from the pet shop.'

'Mouse, mouse, pudding and pie!' They grab at each other's crotches.

'Shame on you, behave yourselves!' the madam scolds. She looks apologetically at me. I ignore her. I improvise with a straight face and an ironic tone. Perhaps in this way I can find favour in their eyes. I shall make my lies visible. Then I will be safe.

'How many?' asks Gladys.

'Two. Michael and Raphael. They're brothers.'

'How big?'

I measure out four long paces on the Novilon in the kitchen.

'Hot stuff!' I hear behind my back.

'How thick?'

'Like that,' I say, and show with my two hands.

'Lord, have mercy!' they scream. 'So thick!' They use their hands. They stroke the snakes.

'He's coming, he's coming!'

'He's going to spit!'

'Every two weeks,' I say, 'I let them loose in the garden at the back so that they can catch squirrels. They have a bit more meat to them than the mice. And they wriggle. The snakes like that, a bit of resistance, otherwise they get depressed.'

'Yow,' says Dolla, 'what's the miss saying?'

'The miss is saying everything,' I say, 'fucking everything.'

Nobody takes any notice of my confession. It looks as if nobody has even heard it.

They yell with laughter, wriggle their bodies out of the back door onto the stoep. The wriggle borders on a ribald dance step. The power of the humiliated, I think.

'Do they bite people as well?' asks one, all sham innocence.

'Yes,' I say, 'of course, otherwise what's the point? Here, this is where they bite, here, on the heel, right there.' I crook my fingers around my heel to demonstrate snake fangs. I don't care any more, I have abandoned myself to insinuation, to try to save myself, to my fate, to embrace it.

I give them a bag of figs from my own tree to take along, counting the fruit carefully so that nobody should have more than her share.

'You're getting very spoiled here, aren't you?' says the Breeze. 'Have you all said thank you nicely?'

'Thank you, miss!' they shout in a little mocking chorus over their shoulders. With a deft foot one rubs the spit on the garden path into an unrecognisable blotch.

858

The work provider winks at me when she takes her cheque. I see how intently the women follow the cheque's progress into her handbag.

'Where in god's name do you find these people?' I ask her softly behind their backs.

'I collect them from the squatter camp, just the other side of Kuils River. And let me tell you something today, Miss, they're only too grateful, believe you me, only too glad and grateful, that somebody wants to come and collect them for work. They have strings of children, all of them, but the fathers you'll never clap eyes on.'

Sincerely, meaningfully, matter-of-factly, she smiles. A businesswoman with a heart. I shut the door quickly. It's just too many expressions on a single face. It's a mixture that could cause a revolution in Kuils River. Why doesn't it happen? I think. Why not?

Suddenly a brilliantly bloodthirsty fantasy blossoms in my mind. A quick grip, strong hands throttling and wrenching, blood against the windscreen of the Cortina, handbag eviscerated, Rainbow Warriors gone with the wind scouring the shacks, no word breathed about it. I think of Pirate Jenny in Nina Simone's version.

Winter comes. The branches and rocks that Piet piled up in front of the house must be carted away. I want to keep it anonymous. I phone the municipality.

'We no longer do that, lady, we contract out,' says a stolid man at the other end.

'Too many contractors,' I say. 'Don't you know a private person who can do it for me quickly?' 'Painlessly,' I want to add, but I don't. The mouth is too secret not to feel pain.

'There's a woman in Vryburger Street,' he says. 'She's cheap. She has her own truck. Take down the number.'

And so I get to phone Beauty du Toit.

Somebody with a clumsy tongue answers the phone. Can Beauty be drunk? I wonder, and for a moment consider putting down the receiver. That would be too much. After the picture-of-piety Breeze, the inebriated Beauty.

'Is that Beauty?'

'No, this is Beauty's mother speaking. Beauty is not here at the moment. Can I perhaps take a message for Beauty?'

The sentences take a long time coming. Not only because the tongue is heavy. The voice dips and flounders with subservience, perhaps from a stroke, from strickenness. Poor whites in Vryburger Street. My curiosity carries the day. I want to see Beauty. I leave a message. Beauty must please come, here is the address. She must come and cart away my rubbish, it's a mess in front of my house, has been for months now. My neighbours look down their noses. This is a tidy neighbourhood.

A few hours later she turns up, corpulently brave and lightly moustached, with a heart of gold. She drives a rickety truck with a rickety trailer. In the back of the truck are three old men with puffy eyes. Baggy pants, liquor breaths. God help us.

Slowly, as if they are afraid their arms will break, they load my branches. They grope carefully like chameleons amongst the thorns. For a long time they ponder the heavy rocks. What would be their considerations? I wonder.

'I'm urgently looking for people to work in my garden,' I say. I sound to myself as if I am pleading. It sounds like a confession. 'I want to prepare it for spring, you see.' That sounds totally inappropriate. You can no longer say even the most ordinary things with a clear conscience in this country. It's almost as if you can only quote. I had a garden in Africa. I wanted a garden in Africa. We used to have a garden in Africa. Roses, foxgloves, snowdrops, blue forget-me-nots. Richman poorman beggarman thief. 'I'm looking for reliable labour,' I say.

'I have that,' says Beauty, 'but not these, these you have to watch all the time or nothing happens, as you can see for yourself. Is your husband around?'

She speaks loudly. They can hear everything. What in god's name must they think of it? I also speak loudly.

'No, he's not here at the moment,' I say. 'He gets home from work quite late in the evenings.'

'Never mind,' she says, 'I don't even have one any more. That's why I have to make a go of it on my own. I have my mother as well, you understand. But what's the use of complaining? And there are many who are even worse off. That's what I tell myself all the time. You have to count your blessings. Do you want to come along to the dumps? Then you can see all the places I get to.'

Friendly. Gullible. Unsuspecting. Am I the only one with agendas? I go along on the spur of the moment. Perhaps there will be old bricks that I can use as a border for my flowerbeds. In the front of the truck is a little boy with a grater of a voice and sores around his mouth.

'My grandson,' says Beauty. 'I get to look after him as well, never a dull moment.' Beauty slaps the outside of the truck with the flat of her hand. 'Hold on!' she shouts backwards to the chameleons.

'The other day one fell off, broke his leg. You won't believe me, the trouble I have with the people, and you see what they look like, just about broken with hardship. But perhaps it's all for the best. With me they earn enough to stay alive and I don't have to be scared of them. People often ask me, "Now Beauty, aren't you scared to be on the road day after day with this class of people?" But I believe the Lord has me in his keeping. And it's not as if I'm just going to lie down and give in. They've never tried anything with me. Or with my mother. But I'm a bit worried about her because they come and ask her for bread when I'm out during the day, and you know she can't say no.'

I look back. The old men like bundles of rags amongst the branches. Only the rough hands and the dull gleam of eye slits betray the presence of bodies.

'Do you hear that?' asks Beauty as we turn into the worn-out dirt road of the dump.

'I don't hear anything,' I say. 'What should I listen for?'

She points with her head towards a bunker-like concrete structure half-hidden in the reeds and Port Jackson trees. 'The dog pound,' she says, 'now there's something that keeps me awake at night. For a fortnight they bark away there in the kennels and if they still haven't found homes then, they get put down, too terrible, I tell you, I drive past here every day and then I hear it and then sometimes I can't stand it anymore and then I go and fetch another one. Dear little things, terribly neglected but just a few days' love and mealie meal then they're cock of the walk again. Then people even want to buy them from me. I find it hard to part from them.'

We drive along picturesque heaps of refuse. Everywhere there are black men and women in ragged clothes chipping away at bricks to clean them. Beauty greets a tanned white man stripping old TV sets. His black T-shirt is dusty and patched with sweat.

'I'm just going to dump the branches a bit further up,' says Beauty. 'It gets a bit grungy further along. Why don't you wait here so long with Gerrie, I won't be long.'

Suddenly I'm standing in the dust under a poisonously hot sun. It's about ten degrees too hot for the time of year. Around us hovers a stench that varies its nature from moment to moment, smelling of fish, of meat, of peels still fermenting, of a more general older smell of the already rotten almost returned to dust, the sweet rich smell of first-world compost.

It's an upside-down world, I think, as Gerrie extends his hand to me and shakes mine firmly. Here, for some or other reason, I am formally welcomed by an upside-down Hephaistos. Not a smithy of the underworld but a gatherer in a throw-away zone. He looks tough and strong. It's just his voice that is wheedling.

'I do it for my son, you see, madam, and it was plain luck that I got the tender. This town's municipality is too broke to work their own dumps. So now I get this little lot that you see here to work for half-shares. They take home some of what they clear and I keep enough to help my son.'

I look where he points. Some distance away I see a man loading old crates onto the back of a truck. 'Yes, that's him, just get a look at that pair of shoulders! You see, madam, he's a champion wrestler just like me in my day. But to get into the Olympic Games he has to go and wrestle his qualifying rounds in a tournament in Tunisia and so now I'm helping him get together the money for it. He works for the police and you know they get paid peanuts.'

The man is tying the crates to the truck with ropes. I see his muscles bulge.

One, two big steps and he's on top of the crates. With the tremendous levers of his thighs he tramples a few underfoot to make space for more. The chunks of plastic crack and splinter under his feet. He looks huge against the sky. Behind him rise the blue blue mountains of the Boland. I look at his firm buttocks, the athletic dents in his hips, as he works. He's wearing old tracksuit pants with holes in them and a bedraggled T-shirt. The prime condition of the body in the old clothes looks comical. Like a circus or a Beckett play. But his face is too unambiguous for any play.

'So how much do you make out of this?' I ask.

'About R500 if we pack it well, they weight it at the other end.' He is friendly and helpful and answers my questions without a trace of suspicion or cynicism, as befits an Olympic hero.

'I manage to get together about three loads a week, I have to dig it out of the rubbish, it takes time and then I work shifts at the station and weekends I bounce a bit.'

'Bounce?'

'Yes, at the coloured clubs where things get rough. But I don't take nonsense. If there's trouble I bounce whole bunches of them. With the women you have to be a bit more careful, but often it's they who start it all. My orders are not to say a word and I bounce only on command.'

'And how much do you get for that?'

'I manage to clear about two fifty a night and at the clubs where the gangs go a bit extra danger pay.'

I hear a hooting. It's Beauty come to collect me.

'Shame,' she says, 'the poor guy, his wife dropped him three months ago because he was never at home. But all he wanted to do was work so that they could get ahead in the world. And all she wanted to do was sit at home with folded hands, lady at large waiting for her prince on a white horse to come home. She didn't even want to cook the pasta and steak he had to eat for his wrestling. She just wanted the limelight if he won. His dream is to open a school of wrestling in town. Proper wrestling, you know, not freestyle, he insists on that point. He lives for his wrestling, that young man.'

The next day I go to fetch the labourers that Beauty has organised for me.

'Jan and Simon from the night shelter,' she introduces me to the two on the pavement of Vryburger Street. 'You'd be surprised at what good people you find in the shelter. Many come from the farms where the farmers can't pay them under the new laws any more. So they know about work and they'll do anything now, won't they, because you can't fill your stomach with laws, not so, you two?'

The tone is friendly and patronising and directed half at them and half at me. Jan and Simon nod in feigned meekness. I feel Jan searching my face for signs of an understanding. Beauty clearly has the power of the mediator here.

Without her presence, today would have been only another empty hungry day. I can see them assessing me. Will I overrule the mediator? Is there a possibility of more permanent work here and more money? What will the language sound like in which they summarise me? In which they discuss me?

I look at them. Jan is light of colour, with curly hair. He looks like me. He feels like family in a way. There is something mocking in his glance, but it's no longer sharp. It's misted over with equanimity and interest. Simon is dark and quiet. He says nothing, but he's thinking something, I can see that.

'But the madam drives half-and-half fast with the little beetle!' says Jan.

'So you're from Caledon?' I ask, pleased to find something concrete to interrupt my directionless reflections.

'Hey, how does the madam know that?' His voice is all affectation, he mimics the tone in which his betters make insincere small talk. The power of the mimes, I think.

'Because you say "half-and-half fast". It's an expression of the region. I grew up there.'

'I see,' he says as we draw up in front of the house, 'and now the madam lives here all alone or are the madam's people here as well?'

I see him register the size of the house.

'My people live around here,' I say, and then add, because I feel that more details are expected and because I feel it is time for bluffing, 'but my friend is coming tonight, he works late, and he has to feed the snakes.'

I point at the sign. Jan ignores the information with a light snort. I shouldn't try to bluff him, I realise. He doesn't find it funny. And he clearly is not satisfied yet. And why should he be? Aren't we from the same area, and haven't I confided our affinity to him? Half-and-half-quick, half-and-half clever.

'Husband or friend?' he asks in a meaningful way.

Simon looks up quickly and then down again.

I pretend not to hear, explain the work, show where the tools are stored and go inside, bolt the door, draw the sitting-room curtains.

Husband or friend, I think, what business is it of his? I feel mildly upset. I phone my lover.

'Mrs Robinson,' I say, 'why don't you come and visit me today at some point, the people working in the garden make me nervous. Bring your son along.'

'You're paranoid,' she says, 'but I'll come, I've made a photo of figs for you, blown up, I thought it would amuse you, it's quite sexy.'

Mrs Robinson has no problems with labour. She is a practical woman. She drives a combi and issues orders in accordance with the prevailing rules. She leaves the house when the Northwest Breezes come to work for her because she doesn't like to see them, she says. The poor, she says, we'll always have with us. Then we almost quarrel. Then I say: 'They turn me into a liar and hypocrite, they make me feel guilty and alone. They immediately know everything about me without asking a single question. They ask if I have old clothes, an old mattress, a few sheets of corrugated iron. The flowers that I throw out they take home in newspaper, and the next time they come they're wearing the shoes that I put into the black bag, with their heels peering out like the mortal remains of my conscience.'

Then she says, 'Heavens, but do you ever sound like a writer again today. Have you taken your St John's Wort yet?'

Through a chink in the curtain I peep at them working. It's hard work. They sweat copiously. I look at my watch, eleven o' clock, time for a break. I take out large beer mugs of Oros and ice.

'Just hang on, madam,' says Jan and removes his shirt ostentatiously.

'There we are,' he says and takes the mug from my hand, drinks with thirsty gulps so that the syrup runs down his chin. It's a spectacle put on just for my sake, I feel. I look at his body. On the soft part of his belly, just above his navel is tattooed: 'Fear not for the Angel of the Lord is with thee'. I know I shouldn't say anything, but I nevertheless say: 'Geez, didn't that hurt?'

'Madam,' he says, 'what could I do? I had it written so that I could feel I was still alive.'

I refrain from comment, go into the house again, peer through the curtain. Simon also takes off his shirt. They say something I can't make out and laugh salaciously. I'm convinced it's about me. Perhaps they suspect that I'm standing here behind the ostentatiously drawn curtain. And why am I peeping? I think, if I really want to see anything I can just go and look. What is it that I don't want to meet face to face?

There where I'm having the devil's grass taken out to construct a gravel garden to save water, they're loading the sods onto the wheelbarrow. They take turns to pack and cart away. The wheelbarrow is heavy. Hup! Jan strains over the furrow, hup! One more time to negotiate the edge of the garden path. The wheel blocks. I watch them devise a ramp up and a ramp down with bricks. Old hands with a blocked wheel. Tricks of the trade.

One o'clock. They dig a trench for the picket fence for the herbaceous border. Their muscles wrench with the effort of the pickaxe in the clay soil. The skin over the ribs ripples and tenses. The gullets jump up and down with the effort and with the swallowing down and scraping away of old slimes, of years of smoking cheap tobacco in newspaper, of TB probably. Of harsh whooping coughs as a child. Five-days-a-week bodies. Now and again resting on the spade, on the pickaxe, they survey their progress. Fifty rand's worth of progress, a week's supply of wine and cigarettes. Spit, spit in the trench. Only this liquid curse has remained. They grab, grasp the spade again, the spade by its handle, the pickaxe by its shaft, and fling their bodies at the herbaceous border trench. Both work up a disconcerting cough. The progress slows down as the afternoon moves on. I bring strong coffee with lots of sugar.

'You mustn't over-exert yourselves,' I say, and hear my own voice sounding in my ears. 'You must say if you want to knock off,' I try to correct myself.

'No, we're holding out, madam, we're holding out, we're going to beat it, this little ditch.'

My friend comes to visit with her still life of figs in a cellophane wrapping.

'My, but you're energetic, aren't you!' she says as she walks up the garden path.

I get a hug and a kiss and have to inspect the figs before we go through the front door.

'Don't be like that with me in front of these people,' I say. 'I don't want them to know my whole story.'

'Oh nonsense, what do they know?' she says.

'They know everything. They look right through you.'

'You're imagining things again.' She looks at me. 'That's why I like you so much, because you have such an active imagination.'

She has taken a photo of me with a chameleon on my shoulder. She tends to think we are in paradise. She persists in thinking this even though a saucepan of stewed quinces is stolen from her stove while she is hanging out the washing. Now she has made photocopies of my snake warnings and put them up all over her house. 'So, is that the madam's sister, then?' asks Jan when she has left.

'Yes,' I say, 'that is my sister.'

'No, I'm asking because it feels half-and-half like family but it doesn't look like family. Me too, I just feel like family, the madam knows, there where I come from I wasn't my mother's child or my father's child, I was a throw-away. So they took me in. Didn't treat me nice, my father. So when I was sixteen I took him by the chest and thrashed him good and proper and from then on it was downhill all the way with me. But now I'm in the shelter and that helps. We support each other a bit there.'

I pack food for Jan and Simon to take with them – cooked sausage, a tin of beans each, fruit, bread. I praise them for their labour. I'm very satisfied, I say. I ask if they're satisfied. They nod politely.

The next day I collect Jan in Vryburger Street again. Simon can't come because Beauty needs him for a removal in town. With him Jan has a small toothless yellow woman wearing a scarf. I have seen her before with him in the neighbourhood, and now, like then, she waves at me exuberantly as if she knows me well. I try to remember, but I don't know her. It's impossible, I've only been back for a few months in the town where I spent my youth. Perhaps she remembers me from way back, I think. It happens to me all the time, that people greet me whose faces I recognise but whose names I've forgotten. Just before Jan bends down to get into the Volkswagen, she taps him on the shoulder from behind and pouts her little mouth at him, her eyes shut tight. I can't believe what I see. Jan from the night shelter with the angel of the Lord carved on his stomach turns to her, takes her face between his hands, and plants a tender kiss on her mouth.

'So who's that, Jan?' I ask when I can no longer contain myself.

'No, how shall I say to madam, she's also from the shelter, I'm half-and-half very fond of that one but how shall I say, actually I'm sorry for her because you know she's been deaf and dumb from birth.'

Jan speaks freely, it doesn't seem to bother him that I interrogate him.

'And it's a nuisance because everybody uses her as they like, she can't scream, you know. Just the other day I had to shovel someone off her with a garden fork. But then it's her own fault too, because let me tell madam this, now there's a girl who can knock it back. I've told her I'm going to leave her if she carries on like that.'

'Heavens, Jan, what are you telling me now?'

'No, madam knows, I give her just one look like this then she knows which way the wind's blowing, but I understand her when she shows me like this.' He shows me how she shows him.

'I think I have, how shall I say? I think I have a how do they say? A talent for that girl.'

He tells me of his own accord how they found each other. There were three of them at first. Her husband was dying of TB and then he died. And because she couldn't talk he took mercy on her, interpreted for her to the doctor and the priest and the undertaker. And spoke the words at the grave as he understood them from her. Since then they've been together.

The work on the new garden is halfway when the first winter rains fall. The pergola is halfway up, the furrow for the picket hedge is full of rain water.

My sister calls to have a look.

'Lord, it looks as if you're building a sheep pen here,' she says.

My brother calls to have a look. 'Yes, well,' he says, 'you and your sister can never let well enough alone, always have to dig everything up and change it.'

My father phones. 'How is your gardening coming along, my child? Are you healthy? Just look well after your safety.'

July. It is snowing in Jonkershoek. I drive into the kloof to go and look at the snowfall from close by, come upon a little steenbok standing with a wet snout trembling against the wall of the pump station. She leaps away in confusion as I come around the corner. In her wake the silver-speckled fynbos branches swing back in a spray of drops. Away, away on delicate hooves. Why do I have such a need for a garden? I think. Here, here in front of me, scarcely ten minutes from my house, is the whole mountain in which I can walk to my heart's content. And what lives and grows there hasn't been collected, hasn't been woven, cultivated or irrigated. It is what it is, the ten thousand joys and sorrows, and it is good.

Back at home I find Simon standing in front of my door. I say but we didn't have an appointment I say I don't have work it's raining I say he mustn't come when we don't have an appointment and I only work through Beauty I say he knows she will say if 1 need someone that's the only way how it works I don't want people standing on my stoep at all times and any time.

He lets me have my say. He listens and looks at his shoes. Am I imagining it, or does he rock gently on his feet, forwards and back, like somebody in a high position listening to a long story from a subordinate?

Suddenly he looks at me straight on. His voice is also straightforward. 'I'm hungry,' he says. 'It's cold and I haven't eaten anything for three days.'

I smell the alcohol on his breath.

'Sorry,' I say. 'Sorry, there's nothing I can do about that. Where do you find money to drink?' He grins. I realise I've made a mistake. Pronounced the greatest cliché in the Boland. He gets his own back on me, changes his tone to the obsequious, pleading vernacular. He advances with the leverage of three centuries.

'Ag Lord, madam,' he says, 'it's cold. Just give me a little piece of bread then please. Does the madam think I'll walk all the way from the shelter just to make a joke? They say it's going to rain for weeks, and then we garden boys can't find jobs. What am I supposed to eat?'

'I'm not your madam,' I say. 'My name is Marlene and if you want to be a boy that's your business.'

Why do you pick on me? I want to say. Why the fuck do you think I'm your customer? What exactly makes me look like a soft target to you? Why don't you go and ask Beauty?

But I don't say anything. Beauty is but skin deep, Beauty is as Beauty does. Or something like that.

I give him bread, I give him R30, I enforce parity, I want to make it into a formal arrangement, an agreement between equals.

'This is an advance,' I say. 'You owe me a few hours of work. Is that clear? Do we have a deal?'

'We have a deal,' he says.

I shake his hand. How else do you make a deal as woman alone? I see his shoes. The toes gape open. How does one make a deal with a shoeless person? What is the meaning of a handshake between somebody with an empty stomach and somebody who gets off on snow-covered peaks?

'Do you want a lift back to the shelter?' I ask. My voice sounds hollow.

He only nods. 'Fasten your safety belt,' I tell him as he gets into the car.

Then I have to laugh. Safety belt. I ask you. I laugh and I laugh. He grins.

I say nothing. I laugh like a clockwork gadget that's running down, less and less, till I've run down.

'If Jan had been here,' says Simon, 'Marlene knows what he would've said? He'd have said: "Now what is now so half-and-half funny, madam?"'